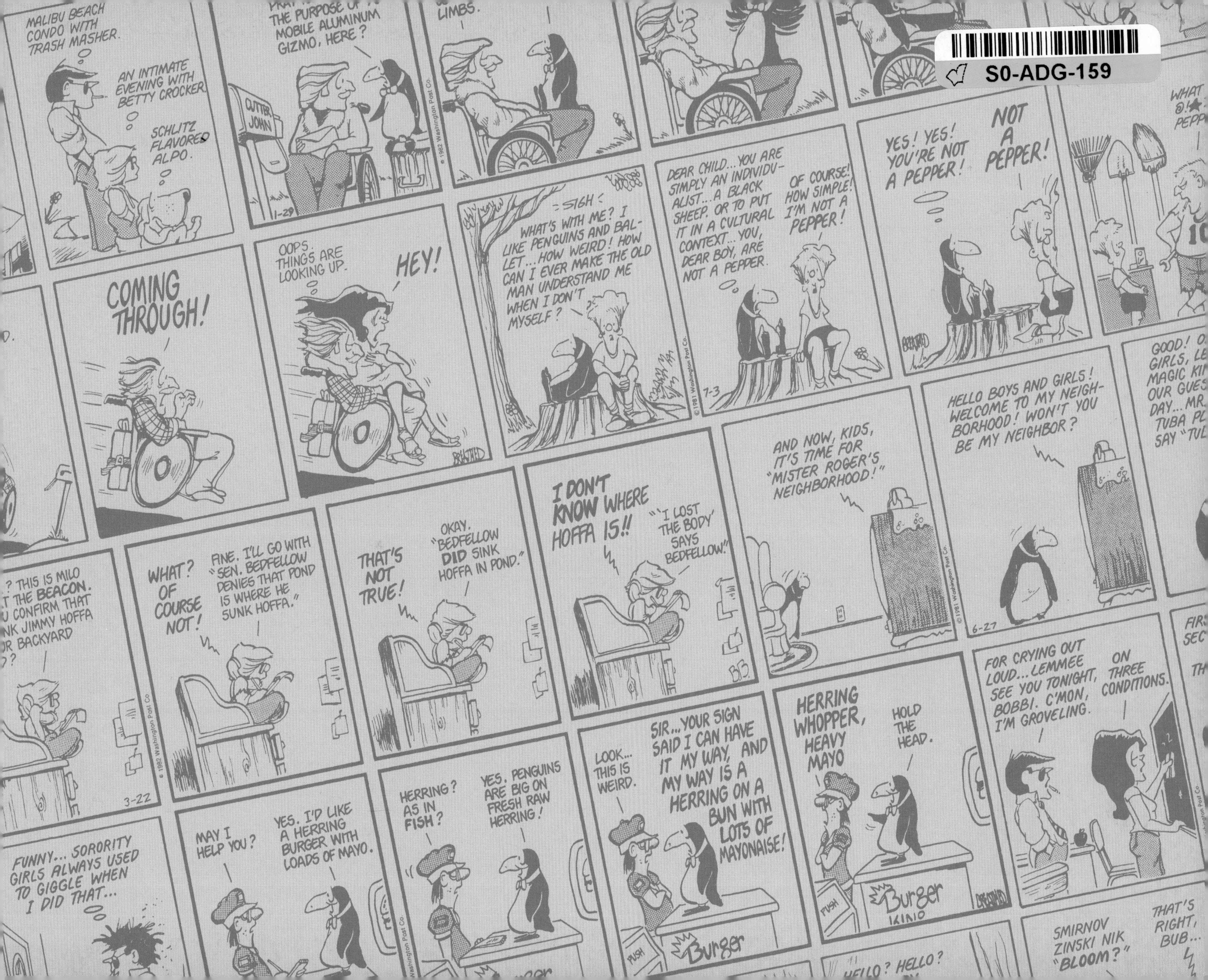

MALIBU BEACH CONDO WITH TRASH MASHER.
AN INTIMATE EVENING WITH BETTY CROCKER.
SCHLITZ FLAVORED ALPO.
THE PURPOSE OF MOBILE ALUMINUM GIZMO, HERE ?
CUTTER JOHN
1-29
© 1982 Washington Post Co.
LIMBS.
YES! YES! YOU'RE NOT A PEPPER!
NOT A PEPPER!
WHAT @!★ PEPP
COMING THROUGH!
OOPS. THINGS ARE LOOKING UP.
HEY!
=SIGH=
WHAT'S WITH ME? I LIKE PENGUINS AND BALLET... HOW WEIRD! HOW CAN I EVER MAKE THE OLD MAN UNDERSTAND ME WHEN I DON'T MYSELF ?
DEAR CHILD... YOU ARE SIMPLY AN INDIVIDUALIST... A BLACK SHEEP. OR TO PUT IT IN A CULTURAL CONTEXT... YOU, DEAR BOY, ARE NOT A PEPPER.
OF COURSE! HOW SIMPLE! I'M NOT A PEPPER!
7-3
© 1981 Washington Post Co.
GOOD! O GIRLS, LE MAGIC KI OUR GUES DAY... MR. TUBA PL SAY "TU
AND NOW, KIDS, IT'S TIME FOR "MISTER ROGER'S NEIGHBORHOOD!"
HELLO BOYS AND GIRLS! WELCOME TO MY NEIGHBORHOOD! WON'T YOU BE MY NEIGHBOR?
© 1981 Washington Post Co.
6-27
? THIS IS MILO T THE BEACON. U CONFIRM THAT NK JIMMY HOFFA R BACKYARD ?
WHAT? OF COURSE NOT!
FINE. I'LL GO WITH "SEN. BEDFELLOW DENIES THAT POND IS WHERE HE SUNK HOFFA."
THAT'S NOT TRUE!
OKAY. "BEDFELLOW DID SINK HOFFA IN POND."
I DON'T KNOW WHERE HOFFA IS!!
"'I LOST THE BODY' SAYS BEDFELLOW!"
© 1982 Washington Post Co.
3-22
FIRS SEC TH
FOR CRYING OUT LOUD... LEMMEE SEE YOU TONIGHT, BOBBI. C'MON, I'M GROVELING.
ON THREE CONDITIONS.
FUNNY... SORORITY GIRLS ALWAYS USED TO GIGGLE WHEN I DID THAT...
MAY I HELP YOU ?
YES. I'D LIKE A HERRING BURGER WITH LOADS OF MAYO.
HERRING ? AS IN FISH ?
YES. PENGUINS ARE BIG ON FRESH RAW HERRING!
LOOK... THIS IS WEIRD.
SIR... YOUR SIGN SAID I CAN HAVE IT MY WAY, AND MY WAY IS A HERRING ON A BUN WITH LOTS OF MAYONAISE!
HERRING WHOPPER, HEAVY MAYO
HOLD THE HEAD.
PUSH
Burger
Burger KING
SMIRNOV ZINSKI NIK "BLOOM?"
THAT'S RIGHT, BUB...
HELLO? HELLO?

THE
BLOOM COUNTY
LIBRARY

Other Books in The Library of American Comics

Terry and the Pirates
by Milton Caniff, vols. 1–6

Little Orphan Annie
by Harold Gray, vols. 1–3

Scorchy Smith and the Art of Noel Sickles

Dick Tracy
by Chester Gould, vols. 1–8

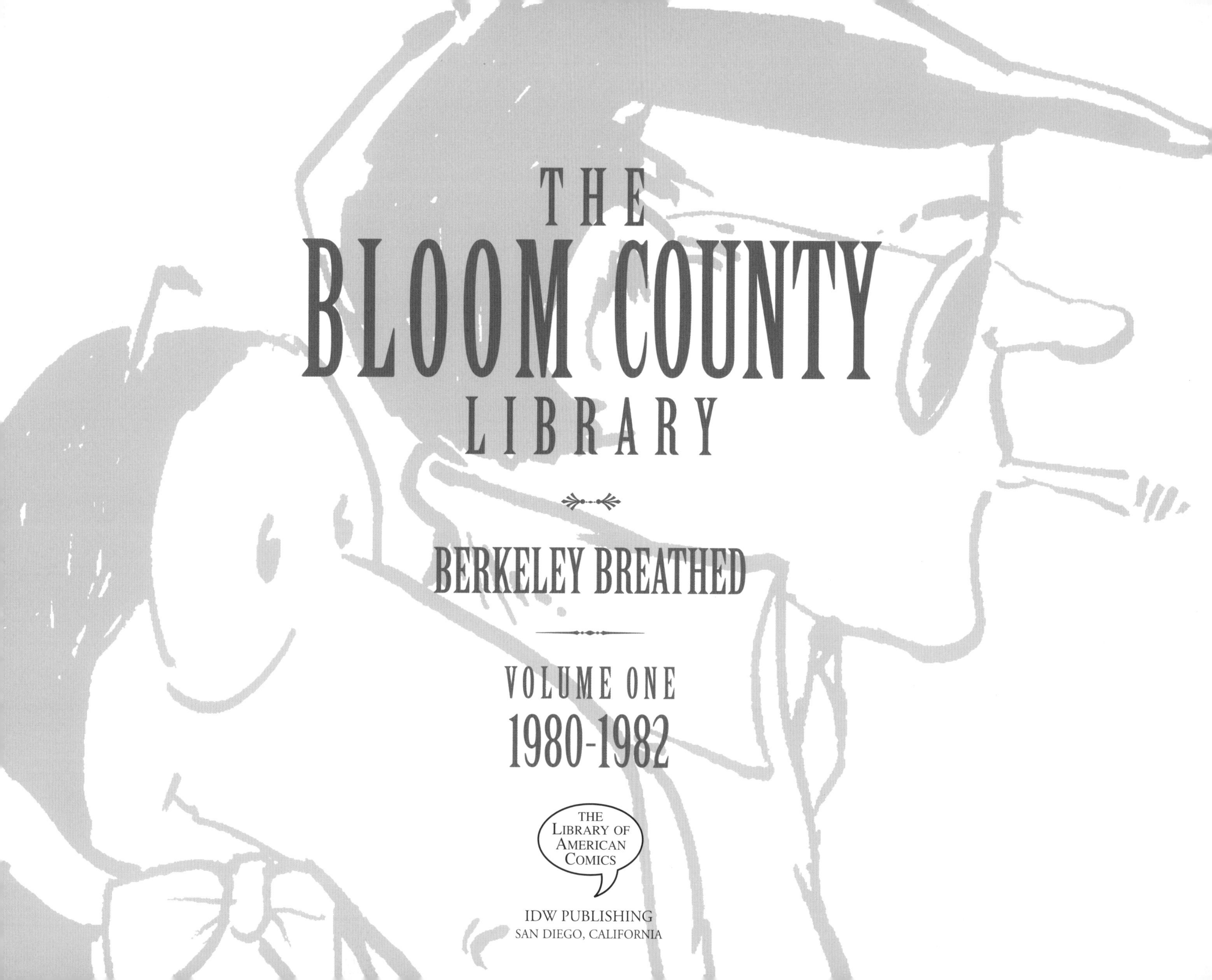

THE BLOOM COUNTY LIBRARY

BERKELEY BREATHED

VOLUME ONE
1980-1982

THE LIBRARY OF AMERICAN COMICS

IDW PUBLISHING
SAN DIEGO, CALIFORNIA

THE BLOOM COUNTY LIBRARY
VOLUME ONE: 1980–82

STORIES AND ART BY Berkeley Breathed

THE LIBRARY OF AMERICAN COMICS
EDITED BY Scott Dunbier
DESIGNED BY Dean Mullaney

COLOR RECREATION
Lorraine Turner • Joseph Ketels • Dean Mullaney

Special thanks to:
Rick Crawford and the San Diego Public Library,
Ted Adams, Kate Dobson, Amy Lago, Steve McAdoo, Rick Norwood,
David Ohman, Jeff Weber, Chris Stuart, and Scott Tipton.

ISBN: 978-1-60010-531-9
First Printing, October 2009

Distributed by Diamond Book Distributors
1-410-560-7100

IDW Publishing
a Division of Idea and Design Works, LLC
5080 Santa Fe Street
San Diego, CA 92109
www.idwpublishing.com

Operations:
Ted Adams, Chief Executive Officer
Greg Goldstein, Chief Operating Officer
Matthew Ruzicka, CPA, Chief Financial Officer
Alan Payne, VP of Sales
Lorelei Bunjes, Dir. of Digital Services
AnnaMaria White, Marketing & PR Manager
Marci Hubbard, Executive Assistant
Alonzo Simon, Shipping Manager
Angela Loggins, Staff Accountant

Editorial:
Chris Ryall, Publisher /Editor-in-Chief
Scott Dunbier, Editor, Special Projects
Andy Schmidt, Senior Editor
Justin Eisinger, Editor
Kris Oprisko, Editor/Foreign Lic.
Denton J. Tipton, Editor
Tom Waltz, Editor
Mariah Huehner, Associate Editor
Carlos Guzman, Editorial Assistant

Design:
Robbie Robbins, EVP/Sr. Graphic Artist
Neil Uyetake, Art Director
Chris Mowry, Graphic Artist
Amauri Osorio, Graphic Artist
Gilberto Lazcano, Production Assistant

INTRODUCTION

BY BERKELEY BREATHED

1981 was ripe for *Bloom County.*

In the way that 1971 was not. Or 1991. Or 2001. If I had graduated from the University of Texas at the beginning of any decade besides the Eighties, I would have had little choice but to pursue the career that I was destined and still oddly suited for: Starbucks barista.

Compiling this book reminded me of this—like so many things that only become apparent well after the fact—when the maturing brain finally catches up with the blissfully ignorant energy of youthful creativity. And hubris.

And like so many inexplicable success stories of the clueless and the out-to-lunch, my serendipitously timed cartooning career was one powered with simple luck. It would need it, because it was so lacking in other areas. I couldn't print legibly until well after a year in. Honestly, despite the rumors among my early "cult" readership, I was not stoned. Thematically, I was equally scattered. Graphically I was stuck on early *Doonesbury*. There is no easy way to explain the impact that strip would have on the newspaper comics page during that decade…

…until you take a wider look.

1981 was pretty stale. The Internet was still hiding, waiting to spring forth and send everything into chaos, like the Rebel Alliance in *Star Wars*. Young America still read newspapers and didn't feel ridiculous doing so. Cable TV had yet to find it's footing: Johnny Carson's monologue was still the place you went to for topical humor if you happened to have missed *Saturday Night Live* at midnight. The satirical pop culture landscape was plowed and fertilized but otherwise unplanted.

Bloom County, I think, was like someone dropping in marijuana seeds and then standing back to watch how the redneck farmer reacted later. The field, like I said, was desperately ripe for a little comic page locoweed, supplied by the town punk on his way to apply at, well, Starbucks.

An odd legacy for me, but I'll take it. Just as I accepted the Pulitzer Prize from the Pulitzer committee in 1987, so rattled by the thundering denunciations from the country's newspaper editorial cartoonists that Columbia University couldn't find anyone brave enough to write the fawning testimonial to my worthiness at the ceremony. I grabbed the award and ran before they asked for it back. They may have: I didn't open any official looking mail for three months after.

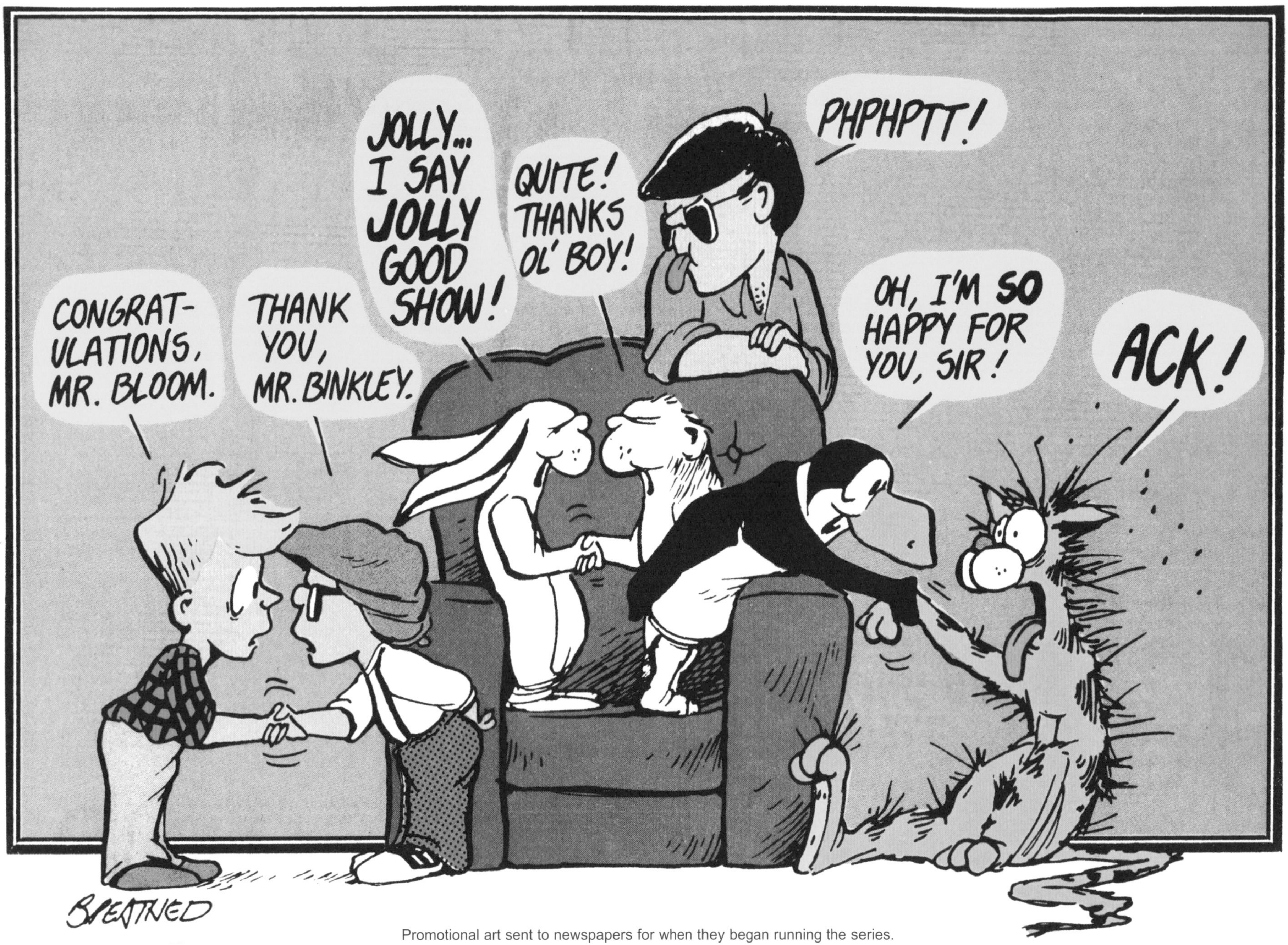
CONGRAT-ULATIONS, MR. BLOOM.
THANK YOU, MR. BINKLEY.
JOLLY... I SAY JOLLY GOOD SHOW!
QUITE! THANKS OL' BOY!
PHPHPTT!
OH, I'M SO HAPPY FOR YOU, SIR!
ACK!
BREATHED

Promotional art sent to newspapers for when they began running the series.

A bit nuts. But then—once more reminded as I reviewed the contents of this volume—so was *Bloom County*. I mean that literally. Nuts. When I wrote and drew most of these, I was mostly out of my mind. Not a single one—**NOT ONE, HE SAID IN BOLD CAPS**—was executed during a sane and lucid hour of the day. If not being drawn on the African veldt or the upper slopes of Machu Picchu during one of my frequent wanderings, they were inked in Iowa City between 2 and 5 a.m., in a sweaty, frothy, exhausted state of panic that the 5:45 a. m. plane waiting to whisk them off to their 10 a.m. deadline in Washington, D.C., would not be met in time. Several times I had no choice but to get on that plane to frantically finish inking as we descended into Washington, toothpicks propping my eyelids open, my right palm held across the open mouth of the loud passenger next to me as he inevitably inhaled to ask if cartoonists have groupies.

A perfectly preposterous manner in which to conduct a comic strip.

And in a very strange and mystical way…it was the only way for *Bloom County* to have been done. The strip's accidentally subversive attitude was born not from any shrewd calculation…but from something far more powerful:

Sleeplessness.

If my kids are reading this: take nothing from the above as you set out on your lives. As a professional, Daddy is deeply suspect. Ignore the 6 million books sold: a strange, cosmic lark, possible proof that God doesn't exist. We don't have groupies, alas, and I'll explain what that means in 2015.

So herein is the complete portrait of *Bloom County*, warts and all. And they be some big ugly ones: the gags always edited out of early volumes but contained here for the sake of historical accuracy. Like John Adams's snot stains on his letters to Abigail, they're a necessary annoyance to complete the romantic picture.

Note that some of the early strips came from incomplete copies, old crinkly yellow newspaper clippings and 6th generation Xeroxes. It was a Herculean feat of art restoration by the designer and editor of this volume, equal only to the restoration of the Sistine Chapel twenty years ago. This, and a fondness to draw nude people where they don't belong, makes me and Michelangelo kindred spirits.

So please dive into these and appreciate along with me that in any other universe more karmically punitive than this one, we're all lucky that Opus lived far beyond an otherwise alternative destiny as just a skillful swirl of milk atop a double banana mocha cappuccino.

Berkeley Breathed
Santa Barbara, California
July, 2009

THE ACADEMIA WALTZ

While an undergraduate at the University of Texas, Austin, Berkeley Breathed's *The Academia Waltz* appeared in the college newspaper, *The Daily Texan*. It caught the attention of the Washington Post Writers Group syndicate, and led to his creating *Bloom County*.

Breathed notes:
Gestational cartoons from the dim past, here only as a historical oddity. The Academia Waltz *was, like all proper college cartoon strips, far too objectionable on every conceivable level of civilized and moral discourse to be collected here. We found these barely suitable to include in this volume, out of the two years of material, circa 1978 and 1979.*

For some reason, the fact that Oscar-winner Sylvester Stallone has porn movies in his past keeps coming to mind when I see these.

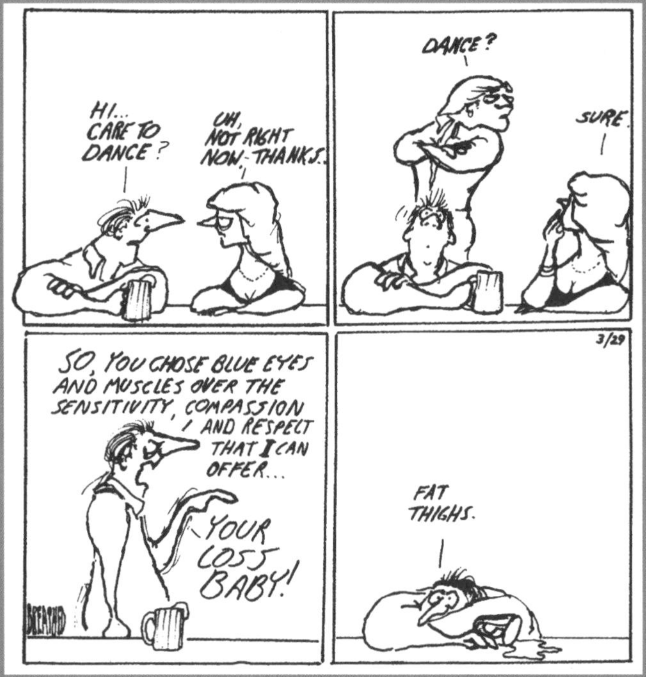
HI... CARE TO DANCE?
UH, NOT RIGHT NOW, THANKS.
DANCE?
SURE.
SO, YOU CHOSE BLUE EYES AND MUSCLES OVER THE SENSITIVITY, COMPASSION AND RESPECT THAT I CAN OFFER...
YOUR LOSS BABY!
3/29
FAT THIGHS.

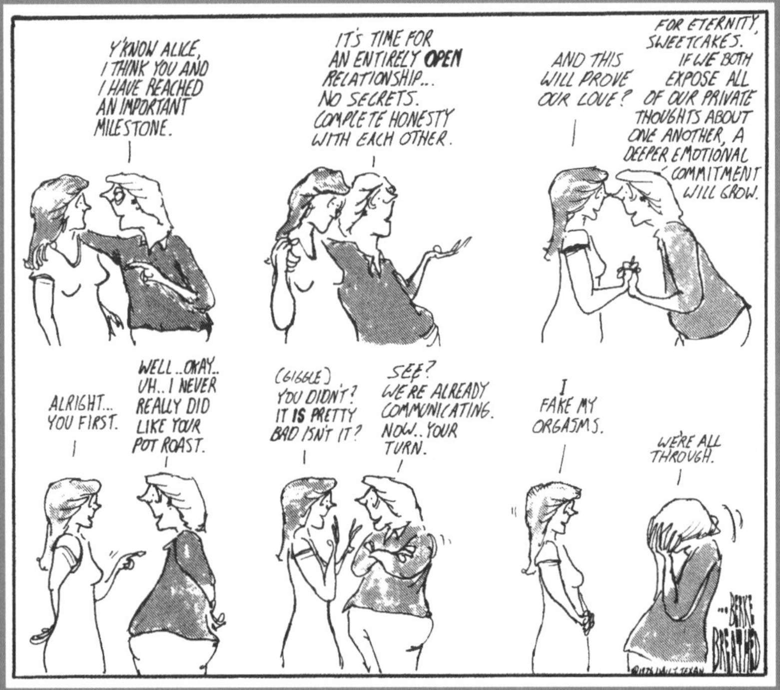
Y'KNOW ALICE, I THINK YOU AND I HAVE REACHED AN IMPORTANT MILESTONE.
IT'S TIME FOR AN ENTIRELY OPEN RELATIONSHIP... NO SECRETS. COMPLETE HONESTY WITH EACH OTHER.
AND THIS WILL PROVE OUR LOVE?
FOR ETERNITY, SWEETCAKES. IF WE BOTH EXPOSE ALL OF OUR PRIVATE THOUGHTS ABOUT ONE ANOTHER, A DEEPER EMOTIONAL COMMITMENT WILL GROW.
ALRIGHT... YOU FIRST.
WELL.. OKAY.. UH.. I NEVER REALLY DID LIKE YOUR POT ROAST.
(GIGGLE) YOU DIDN'T? IT IS PRETTY BAD ISN'T IT?
SEE? WE'RE ALREADY COMMUNICATING. NOW.. YOUR TURN.
I FAKE MY ORGASMS.
WE'RE ALL THROUGH.
BERKE BREATHED

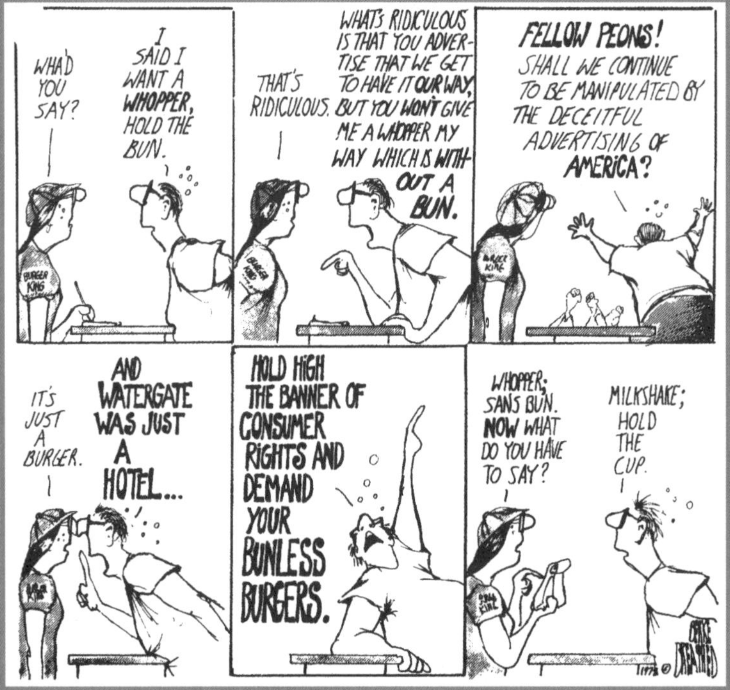
WHA'D YOU SAY?
I SAID I WANT A WHOPPER, HOLD THE BUN.
THAT'S RIDICULOUS.
WHAT'S RIDICULOUS IS THAT YOU ADVERTISE THAT WE GET TO HAVE IT OUR WAY, BUT YOU WON'T GIVE ME A WHOPPER MY WAY WHICH IS WITHOUT A BUN.
FELLOW PEONS! SHALL WE CONTINUE TO BE MANIPULATED BY THE DECEITFUL ADVERTISING OF AMERICA?
IT'S JUST A BURGER.
AND WATERGATE WAS JUST A HOTEL...
HOLD HIGH THE BANNER OF CONSUMER RIGHTS AND DEMAND YOUR BUNLESS BURGERS.
WHOPPER; SANS BUN. NOW WHAT DO YOU HAVE TO SAY?
MILKSHAKE; HOLD THE CUP.
BERKE BREATHED

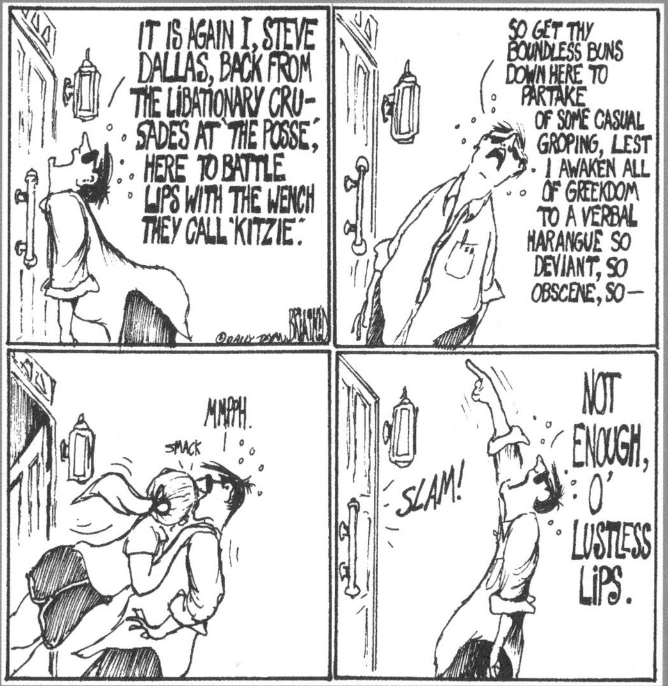
IT IS AGAIN I, STEVE DALLAS, BACK FROM THE LIBATIONARY CRU-SADES AT "THE POSSE", HERE TO BATTLE LIPS WITH THE WENCH THEY CALL "KITZIE".
SO GET THY BOUNDLESS BUNS DOWN HERE TO PARTAKE OF SOME CASUAL GROPING, LEST I AWAKEN ALL OF GREEKDOM TO A VERBAL HARANGUE SO DEVIANT, SO OBSCENE, SO—
SMACK
MMPH.
SLAM!
NOT ENOUGH, O' LUSTLESS LIPS.

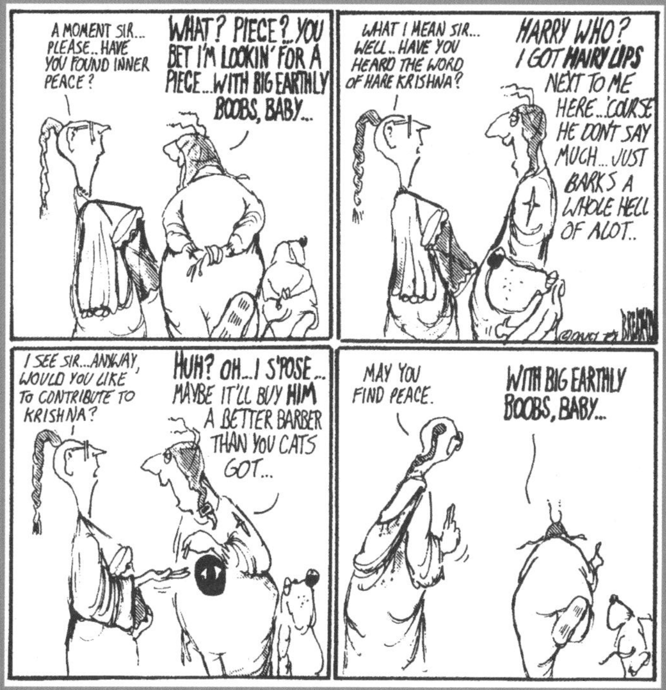
A MOMENT SIR... PLEASE.. HAVE YOU FOUND INNER PEACE?
WHAT? PIECE? YOU BET I'M LOOKIN' FOR A PIECE...WITH BIG EARTHLY BOOBS, BABY...
WHAT I MEAN SIR... WELL.. HAVE YOU HEARD THE WORD OF HARE KRISHNA?
HARRY WHO? I GOT HAIRY LIPS NEXT TO ME HERE...'COURSE HE DON'T SAY MUCH... JUST BARKS A WHOLE HELL OF ALOT..
I SEE SIR...ANYWAY, WOULD YOU LIKE TO CONTRIBUTE TO KRISHNA?
HUH? OH...I S'POSE... MAYBE IT'LL BUY HIM A BETTER BARBER THAN YOU CATS GOT...
MAY YOU FIND PEACE.
WITH BIG EARTHLY BOOBS, BABY...

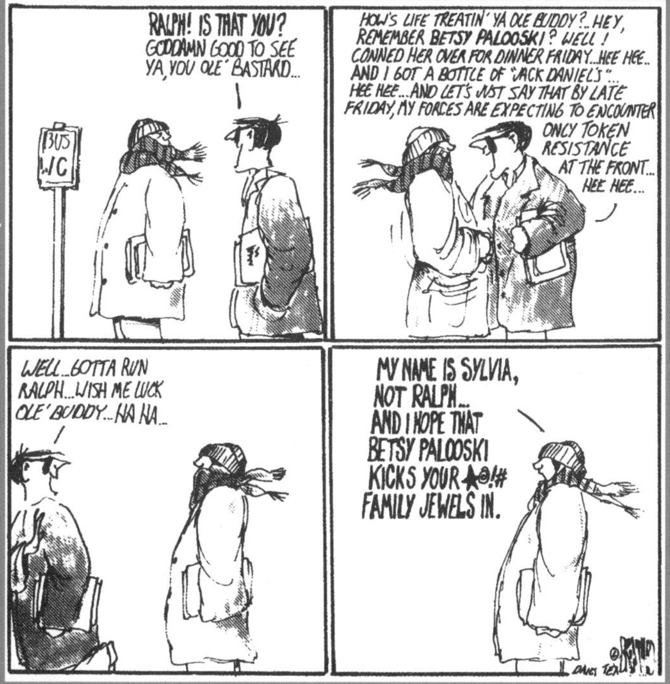
BUS
W.C
RALPH! IS THAT YOU? GODDAMN GOOD TO SEE YA, YOU OLE' BASTARD...
HOW'S LIFE TREATIN' YA OLE BUDDY?.. HEY, REMEMBER BETSY PALOOSKI? WELL! CONNED HER OVER FOR DINNER FRIDAY...HEE HEE.. AND I GOT A BOTTLE OF "JACK DANIEL'S"... HEE HEE... AND LET'S JUST SAY THAT BY LATE FRIDAY, MY FORCES ARE EXPECTING TO ENCOUNTER ONLY TOKEN RESISTANCE AT THE FRONT... HEE HEE...
WELL...GOTTA RUN RALPH...WISH ME LUCK OLE' BUDDY...HA HA...
MY NAME IS SYLVIA, NOT RALPH... AND I HOPE THAT BETSY PALOOSKI KICKS YOUR ★@!# FAMILY JEWELS IN.

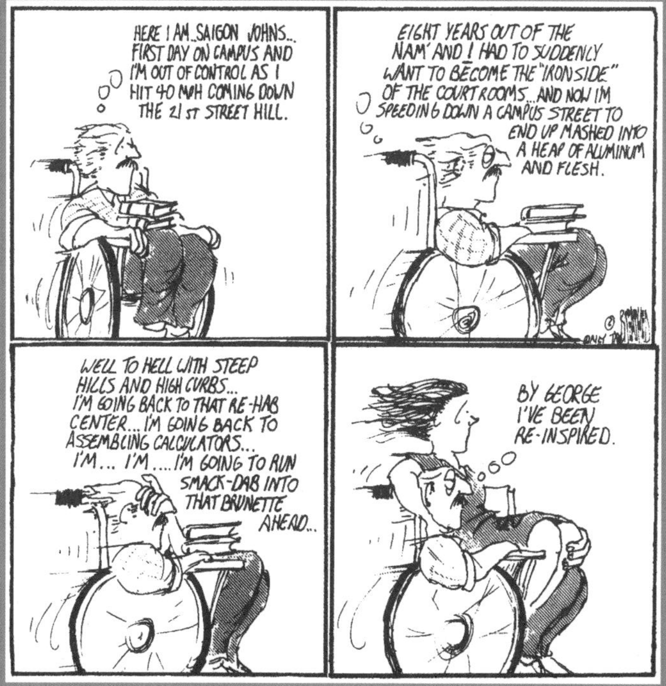
HERE I AM..SAIGON JOHNS.. FIRST DAY ON CAMPUS AND I'M OUT OF CONTROL AS I HIT 40 MPH COMING DOWN THE 21 ST STREET HILL.
EIGHT YEARS OUT OF THE 'NAM' AND I HAD TO SUDDENLY WANT TO BECOME THE "IRONSIDE" OF THE COURTROOMS...AND NOW I'M SPEEDING DOWN A CAMPUS STREET TO END UP MASHED INTO A HEAP OF ALUMINUM AND FLESH.
WELL TO HELL WITH STEEP HILLS AND HIGH CURBS... I'M GOING BACK TO THAT RE-HAB CENTER... I'M GOING BACK TO ASSEMBLING CALCULATORS... I'M... I'M.... I'M GOING TO RUN SMACK-DAB INTO THAT BRUNETTE AHEAD...
BY GEORGE I'VE BEEN RE-INSPIRED.

OPPOSITE PAGE

Top: The first strip.

Bottom right: This was reworked as the first *Bloom County* daily, December 8, 1980 (see page 20).

THIS PAGE

Bottom left: This was reworked on March 14, 1982 (see page 200).

Bottom right: The first Saigon John, later known as Cutter John. Reworked on November 9, 1981 (see page 145).

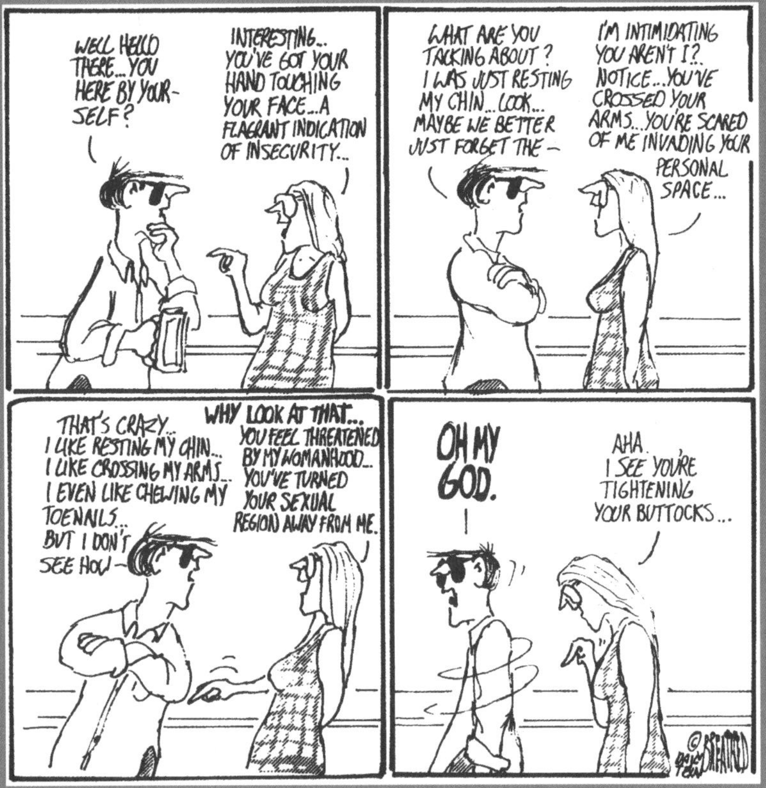
WELL HELLO THERE... YOU HERE BY YOURSELF?
INTERESTING.. YOU'VE GOT YOUR HAND TOUCHING YOUR FACE...A FLAGRANT INDICATION OF INSECURITY...
WHAT ARE YOU TALKING ABOUT? I WAS JUST RESTING MY CHIN... LOOK... MAYBE WE BETTER JUST FORGET THE —
I'M INTIMIDATING YOU AREN'T I?.. NOTICE... YOU'VE CROSSED YOUR ARMS... YOU'RE SCARED OF ME INVADING YOUR PERSONAL SPACE...
THAT'S CRAZY... I LIKE RESTING MY CHIN... I LIKE CROSSING MY ARMS... I EVEN LIKE CHEWING MY TOENAILS... BUT I DON'T SEE HOW —
WHY LOOK AT THAT... YOU FEEL THREATENED BY MY WOMANHOOD... YOU'VE TURNED YOUR SEXUAL REGION AWAY FROM ME.
OH MY GOD.
AHA. I SEE YOU'RE TIGHTENING YOUR BUTTOCKS...

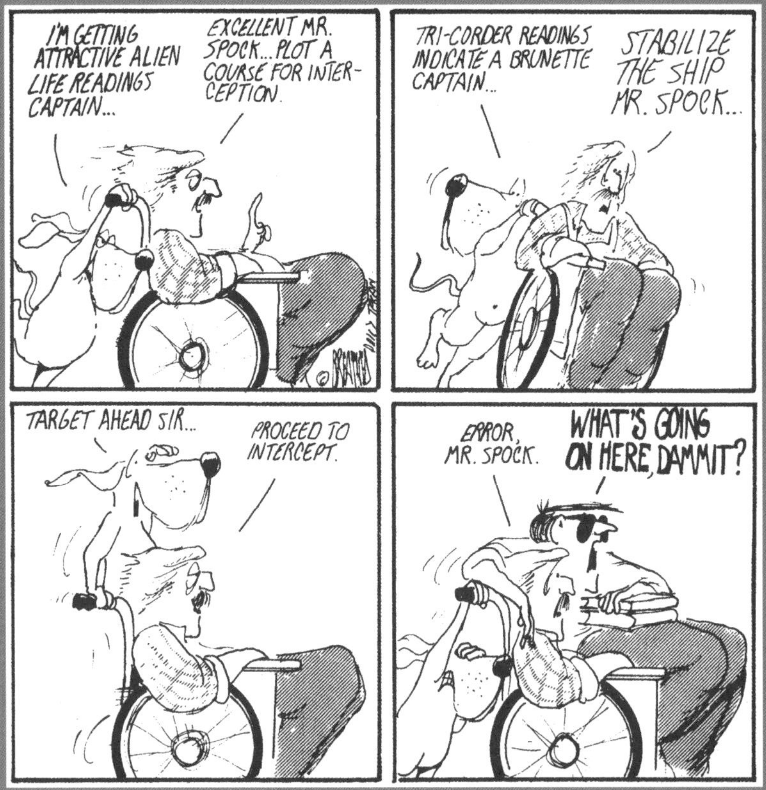
I'M GETTING ATTRACTIVE ALIEN LIFE READINGS CAPTAIN...
EXCELLENT MR. SPOCK... PLOT A COURSE FOR INTERCEPTION.
TRI-CORDER READINGS INDICATE A BRUNETTE CAPTAIN...
STABILIZE THE SHIP MR. SPOCK...
TARGET AHEAD SIR...
PROCEED TO INTERCEPT.
ERROR, MR. SPOCK.
WHAT'S GOING ON HERE, DAMMIT?

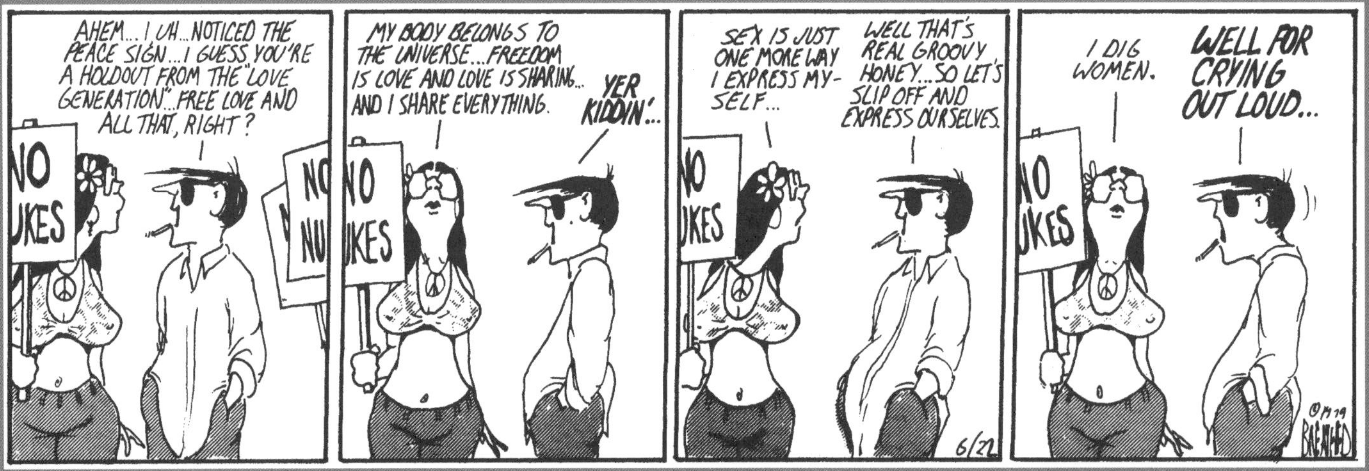
AHEM... I UH... NOTICED THE PEACE SIGN... I GUESS YOU'RE A HOLDOUT FROM THE "LOVE GENERATION"... FREE LOVE AND ALL THAT, RIGHT?
NO NUKES
MY BODY BELONGS TO THE UNIVERSE... FREEDOM IS LOVE AND LOVE IS SHARING... AND I SHARE EVERYTHING.
YER KIDDIN'...
SEX IS JUST ONE MORE WAY I EXPRESS MYSELF...
WELL THAT'S REAL GROOVY HONEY... SO LET'S SLIP OFF AND EXPRESS OURSELVES.
I DIG WOMEN.
WELL FOR CRYING OUT LOUD...

THIS PAGE

Top left: Reworked, substituting Milo in place of Steve Dallas, on December 30, 1981 (see page 166).

OPPOSITE PAGE

Bottom: The final *Academia Waltz*, and the marriage of Steve Dallas.

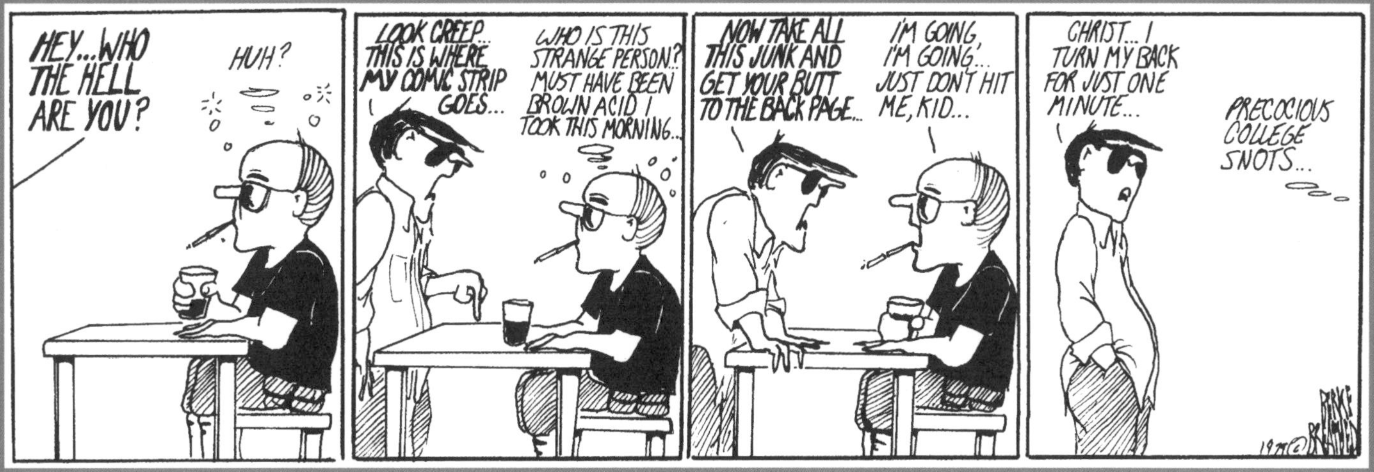
HEY...WHO THE HELL ARE YOU?
HUH?
LOOK CREEP... THIS IS WHERE MY COMIC STRIP GOES...
WHO IS THIS STRANGE PERSON?... MUST HAVE BEEN BROWN ACID I TOOK THIS MORNING...
NOW TAKE ALL THIS JUNK AND GET YOUR BUTT TO THE BACK PAGE...
I'M GOING, I'M GOING... JUST DON'T HIT ME, KID...
CHRIST... I TURN MY BACK FOR JUST ONE MINUTE...
PRECOCIOUS COLLEGE SNOTS...

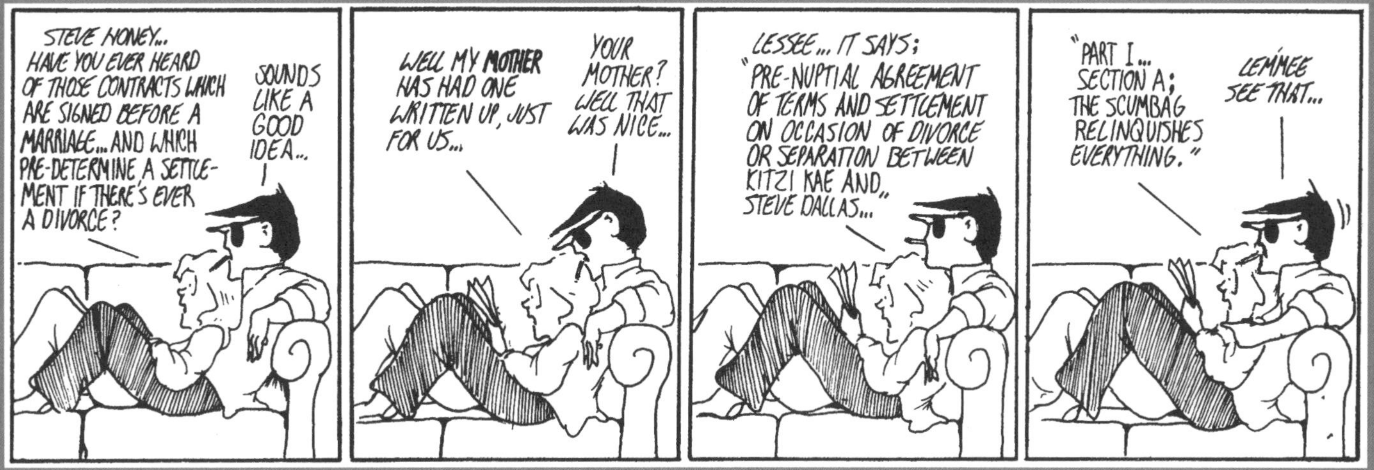
STEVE HONEY... HAVE YOU EVER HEARD OF THOSE CONTRACTS WHICH ARE SIGNED BEFORE A MARRIAGE... AND WHICH PRE-DETERMINE A SETTLE-MENT IF THERE'S EVER A DIVORCE?
SOUNDS LIKE A GOOD IDEA...
WELL MY MOTHER HAS HAD ONE WRITTEN UP, JUST FOR US...
YOUR MOTHER? WELL THAT WAS NICE...
LESSEE... IT SAYS; "PRE-NUPTIAL AGREEMENT OF TERMS AND SETTLEMENT ON OCCASION OF DIVORCE OR SEPARATION BETWEEN KITZI KAE AND STEVE DALLAS..."
"PART I... SECTION A; THE SCUMBAG RELINQUISHES EVERYTHING."
LEMMEE SEE THAT...

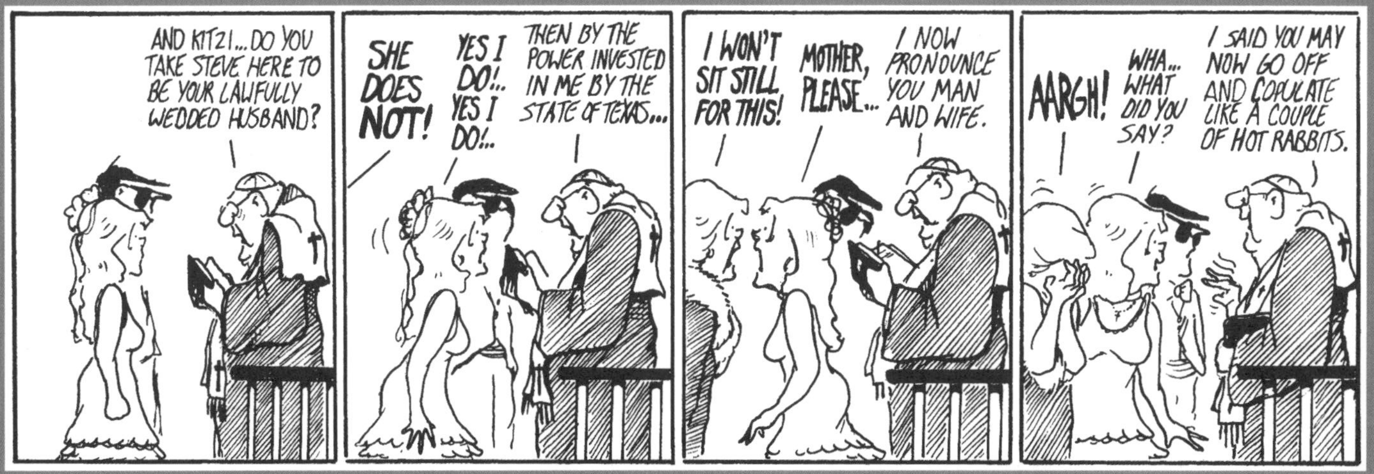
AND KITZI... DO YOU TAKE STEVE HERE TO BE YOUR LAWFULLY WEDDED HUSBAND?
SHE DOES NOT!
YES I DO!.. YES I DO!..
THEN BY THE POWER INVESTED IN ME BY THE STATE OF TEXAS...
I WON'T SIT STILL FOR THIS!
MOTHER, PLEASE...
I NOW PRONOUNCE YOU MAN AND WIFE.
AARGH!
WHA... WHAT DID YOU SAY?
I SAID YOU MAY NOW GO OFF AND COPULATE LIKE A COUPLE OF HOT RABBITS.

of us who don't know
er we're coming or going
that condition because
stood still for so long.

Copyright© 1981 Indiana
Indiana, Pennsylvania, Tuesday, January
Two Sections
—No. 170

Hostages Finally Freed

By The Associated Press

A plane carrying the 52 American hostages, freedom bound after 444 days of captivity in Iran, took off today from Tehran's Mehrabad Airport, a policeman at the airport told reporters.

There was no immediate formal announcement that the harrowing ordeal for the American captives had ended after 14½ months.

The reported departure, shortly after 11 a.m. EST, came after negotiations to wrap up final agreement exchanging the hostages for Iranian assets frozen by the United States.

The 3,000-mile flight to Algiers would take 9 to 10 hours, and it was expected that the hostages would go on to a U.S. Air Force hospital in Wiesbaden, West Germany.

In Washington, where President Carter was trying to end the hostage ordeal in the final hours of his presidency, White House press secretary Jody Powell said Algerian intermediaries had officially notified Iran.

The Bank of England confirmed that billions of dollars in frozen Iranian assets had been transferred by the United States in exchange for the hostages' freedom and put into an Algerian escrow account.

But the latest word from Algiers, where American and Algerian officials tried to wrap up the final details, was that the funds were not yet under Algerian control.

Nabavi, the Iranian negotiator, called the movement of funds a "positive step" and said as soon as the transfer was "duly completed the hostages would be released."

"The hostages are now ready to fly," Nabavi told Iran's official Pars news agency. "All pr
arations have been made and as soon as the
gerian government announces that our fro
assets have been deposited in the account of
Algerian government in the Bank of Engl
the hostages will go home to their families."

In Algiers a foreign ministry spokesmar
firmed that orders had been issued to tra
the Iranian assets, but said they were n
under Algerian control. He said America

See Page 4; Column 4

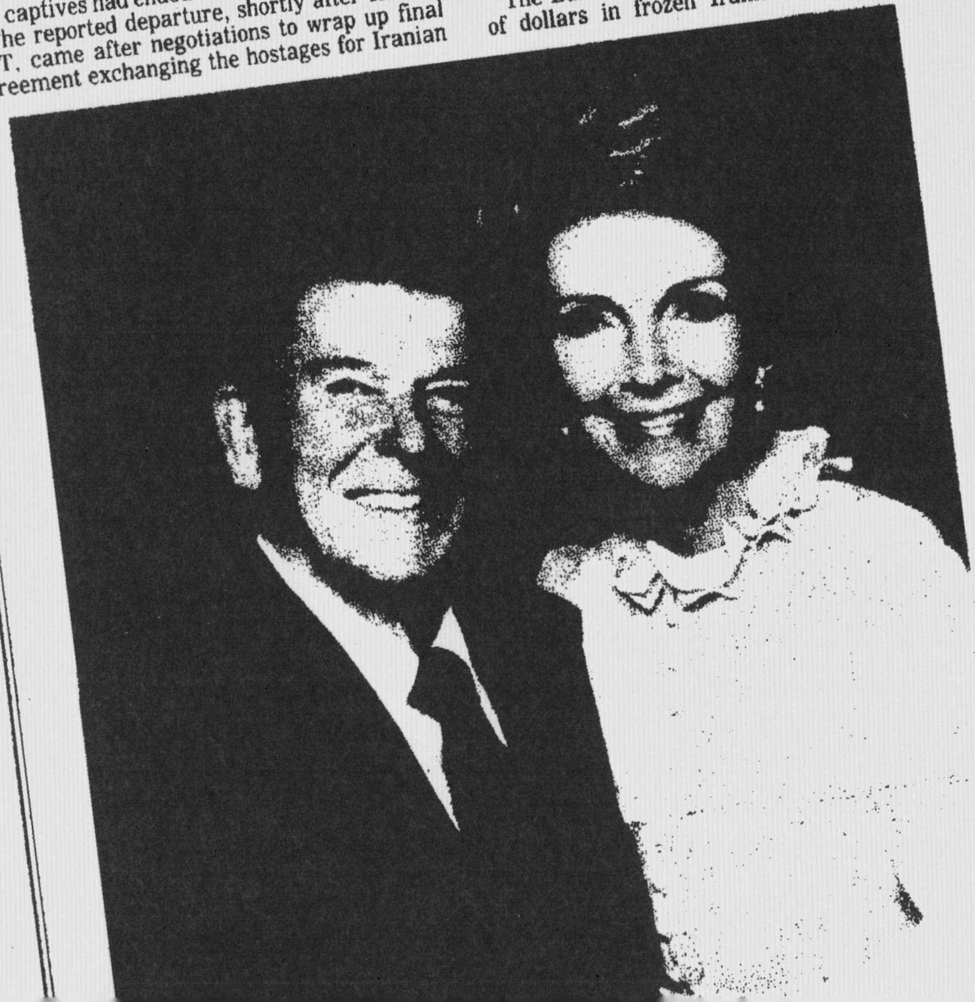

Reagan Becomes 40th President

By WALTER R. MEARS
AP Special Correspondent

WASHINGTON (AP) — Ronald Reagan was inaugurated 40th President of the United States today, his promise of a "new beginning" a hopeful clarion for 52 Americans held captive in Iran throughout his successful quest for the White House.

At noon, to the peal of bells, then a cannon salute, Reagan became the oldest man ever sworn in to the office he sought three times, over a dozen years.

So power passes from James Earl Carter Jr., Democrat of Georgia, to Ronald Wilson Reagan, 69, conservative, Republican, veteran of Hollywood, governor of California, overwhelming choice of his countrymen.

For Carter, the path led home, to the political obscurity of Plains, Ga., after a single term and a year of painstaking efforts to free the hostages.

For Reagan, it led along the ceremonial route of presidents, from the Capitol 16 blocks down Pennsylvania Avenue to the White House.

On the steps of the Capitol, the monuments to George Washington and Abraham Lincoln before him, Reagan was speaking the simple oath of all his predecessors:

"I do solemnly swear that I will faithfully execute the office of President of the United States, and will, to the best of my ability, preserve, protect and defend the Constitution of the United States."

Chief Justice Warren Burger administered the oath, as Reagan placed his left hand on a family Bible that once belonged to his mother, Nellie.

It was open to a verse of Chronicles:

"If my people, which are called by my name, shall humble themselves, and pray, and seek my face, and turn from their wicked ways: then will I hear from heave
forgive their sin, and hea

Justice Potter Stewa
tered the almost identic
dential oath to George
classmate at Yale Univ

By Constitution, pre
er passed from the de
to the victorious R
stroke of noon.

A 21-gun salute
Reagan era. Then it
president to speak
brief inaugural add
from index cards
were his trademark
er.

It was described
slice of his philoso
tion to renewal th
American spirit ar
ple rather than gov

Reagan wrote
nine pages, muc
from Washington

See Page

Orders Return Of Assets

Carter Settles One Last Account With Iranians

know they are airborne."
... night in

States resolved an 11th-hour
disagreement that delayed the
... freedom one more

ON BLOOM COUNTY

BY DEAN MULLANEY AND BRUCE CANWELL

And so a penguin walks into a bar…
or *The Bloom*, Back on the Rose

In his 1988 book, *On Bended Knee: The Press and the Reagan Presidency*, author Mark Hertsgaard argued—successfully, we might add—that during Ronald Reagan's two terms as President of the United States, the White House Press Corps "functioned less as an independent than as a palace court press," essentially giving the California Republican a ride free from objective scrutiny.

It can also be argued—again, successfully—that the media was more eager to maintain its access to the corridors of power than to investigate the policies emanating from those corridors. By doing so, in turn, they failed the country. A free press is all well and good, but when that freedom ignores the important issues of the day and instead opts to fill the airwaves and newspaper column inches with an inane obsession with the arranged marriage between a foreign prince and a mate presumably chosen solely for her ability to incubate heirs to the throne, the balance of power is undeniably out of kilter. (That Princess Diana would use her fame to promote good and humanitarian causes was something no one could have anticipated.)

Thankfully for us, Ronald Reagan's landslide 1980 victory coincided with the debut of a new comic strip in America's funny pages: *Bloom County* by Berkeley Breathed.

The year 1980 was staggering to a close as *Bloom County* debuted on December 8th. Walter Cronkite reminded his *CBS Evening News* viewers that it was Day 401 of the Iranian hostage crisis. For more than a year, 52 Americans were held captive by Iranian fundamentalists who had stormed the American embassy in Tehran. President Jimmy Carter could not extricate the hostages through means of force—in the form of a disastrously botched military operation—or diplomacy. The

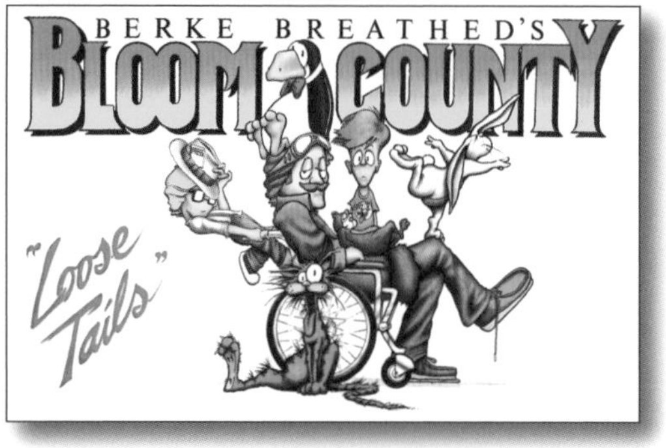
BERKE BREATHED'S
BLOOM COUNTY
"Loose Tails"

Loose Tails, the first *Bloom County* book.

perception of the United States as a laughing stock in the eyes of the world, coupled with a 12.5% domestic inflation rate, helped sweep Ronald Reagan to the Presidency in November's elections. Reagan carried 44 states and won 489 of the available 538 electoral votes. America was ready for change, and during the eight years of the Reagan administration, that change would encompass both good (relief from double-digit inflation, falling energy prices thanks to a glut on the world oil market, and the end of the Iranian hostage crisis on Day 444—Reagan's inauguration day) and the bad (increased national debt, a failed "war on drugs," the Iran-Contra Scandal).

Bloom County also represented change, since it was launched (before either MTV or the first space shuttle) in the *Washington Post* to replace *Doonesbury*, which had moved to a rival newspaper. Berkeley Breathed never denied the early stylistic parallels between *Doonesbury* and his own strip, yet in terms of *tone*, each strip is unique and impossible to mistake for the other. *Bloom County* possesses a consistent exuberance and manic energy the inhabitants of Walden Commune would only rarely match (usually when Duke, Garry Trudeau's drug-crazed Hunter S. Thompson *doppelgänger*, was on center stage). Each strip would build much of its reputation by being topical, and by taking on the issues of the day. Yet, while *Doonesbury* cut its targets with surgical precision, like a deftly-wielded scalpel, *Bloom County* carved a gleeful, *Texas Chainsaw Massacre*-style swath through contemporary topics as far-ranging as televangelists, apartheid, and nuclear mishaps.

America prizes intellectualism, but it *loves* enthusiasm.

Bloom County also contains fanciful and whimsical aspects. Milo is a late-20th century Billy Batson, a boy reporter with keener insights and more savvy than his adult contemporaries. And in the spectrum of cartoon animals interacting with their human counterparts, Opus and Bill the Cat stand in the crossroads between Snoopy and Woodstock of *Peanuts* fame and the irrepressible Hobbes of *Calvin &* same.

The cultural zeitgeist became increasingly fragmented as the '80s unfolded, which allowed Berkeley Breathed to hopscotch his characters from one send-up to another. He steered the *Bloom County* denizens into brushes large and small with the worlds of music and film. Billy and the Boingers toss almost loving jabs at "pop metal" bands such as Def Leppard, Mötley Crue, Poison, Twisted Sister, and Whitesnake; readers were delighted at the many references to *Star Trek*—which enjoyed a resurgence of popularity with its second-through-fourth feature films—and the hoisting of communications behemoth AT&T on its own sizable petard by comparing their corporate logo to the Death Star of *Star Wars* infamy. Breathed moved from one overstuffed windbag to another, his comedic pin primed and ready to puncture. America laughed loud and long each time he let out a little hot air.

The strip became fabulously successful, appearing in 1,200 newspapers and spawning a merchandising bonanza, as well as two spin-off strips, *Outland* and *Opus*. In 1987, Breathed was awarded the Pulitzer Prize for Editorial Cartooning. Given the woes of shrinking newspaper readership, it's fair to state that *Bloom County* may well be the last newspaper comic strip to fully capture the nation's attention.

Now, in the 21st century, we see signs that the 1980s have returned, proving once again that those who do not learn from history are doomed to repeat it. The new millennium began with eight years of Republican rule, during which Islamic aggression, as well as the U.S. response to it, shaped the way America was viewed in the international community. Economic worries plagued the citizenry, and America's automobile industry again faced woes brought on by marketing fuel-inefficient vehicles and profligate excess during a time when prices at the pump reached all-time highs. And the news media, driven by the hunger for "sexy footage," looked to such "infotainment" shows as *Entertainment Tonight* as their model. They seemed more than willing to comply with the Bush Administration's desire not to show the hundreds of flag-draped coffins bearing our dearest blood home from Iraq week after week in order to keep reporters embedded with the troops in that beleaguered country. It appeared as if all that was necessary to cover a war was night vision camerawork and close-up shots of explosions and soldiers on maneuvers in hostile territory.

In the early years of the 21st century, many things old are new again, and the national discourse has been dumbed down into strident, polarized rhetoric. It would be easy to hide in a modern-day equivalent of the anxiety closet…but how much better to be reminded that the best way to take down the stuffed shirts, the demagogues, and the greedy, is with a good, hearty belly-laugh… the kind Berkeley Breathed delivers as no one else can.

The time, my friends, is right once again to enjoy *Bloom County*. So sit back and enjoy this first of five volumes that present—for the first time—every delightful strip in chronological order. As you embark on your journey through the 1980s, you realize Milo, Opus, and their friends were peering through a crystal ball to the future—our present—and find one that would look all too familiar to them.

Dean Mullaney is the Creative Director of The Library of American Comics. Bruce Canwell is its Associate Editor.

BLOOM COUNTY®, by Berke Breathed

The following six strips were supplied by the syndicate for use in case a regular week of *Bloom County* arrived late.

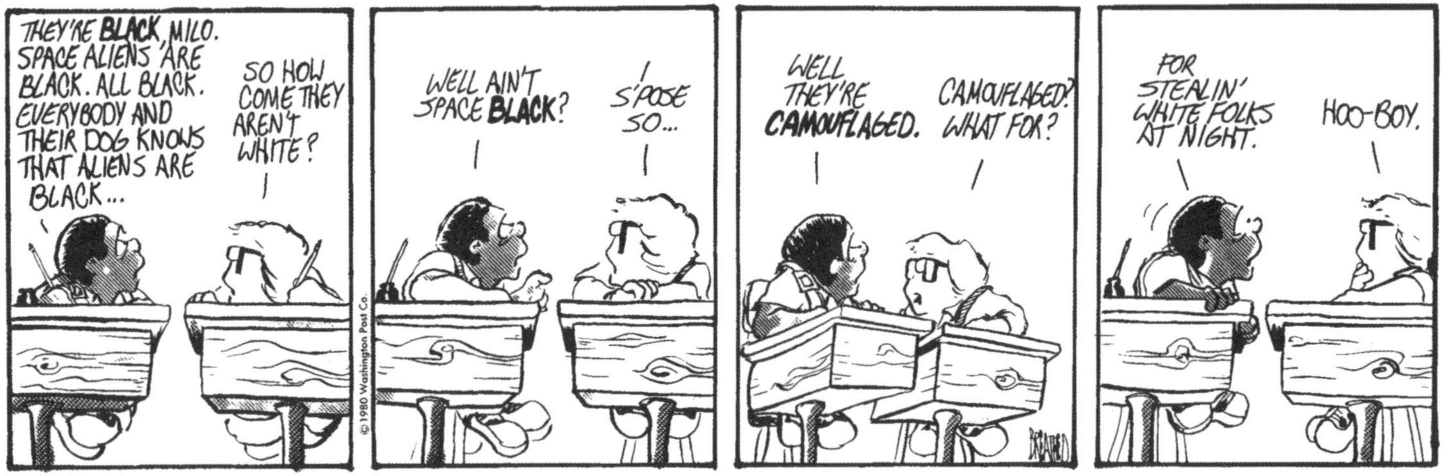
THEY'RE BLACK, MILO. SPACE ALIENS ARE BLACK. ALL BLACK. EVERYBODY AND THEIR DOG KNOWS THAT ALIENS ARE BLACK...
SO HOW COME THEY AREN'T WHITE?
WELL AIN'T SPACE BLACK?
I S'POSE SO...
WELL THEY'RE CAMOUFLAGED.
CAMOUFLAGED? WHAT FOR?
FOR STEALIN' WHITE FOLKS AT NIGHT.
HOO-BOY.
© 1980 Washington Post Co.
BREATHED

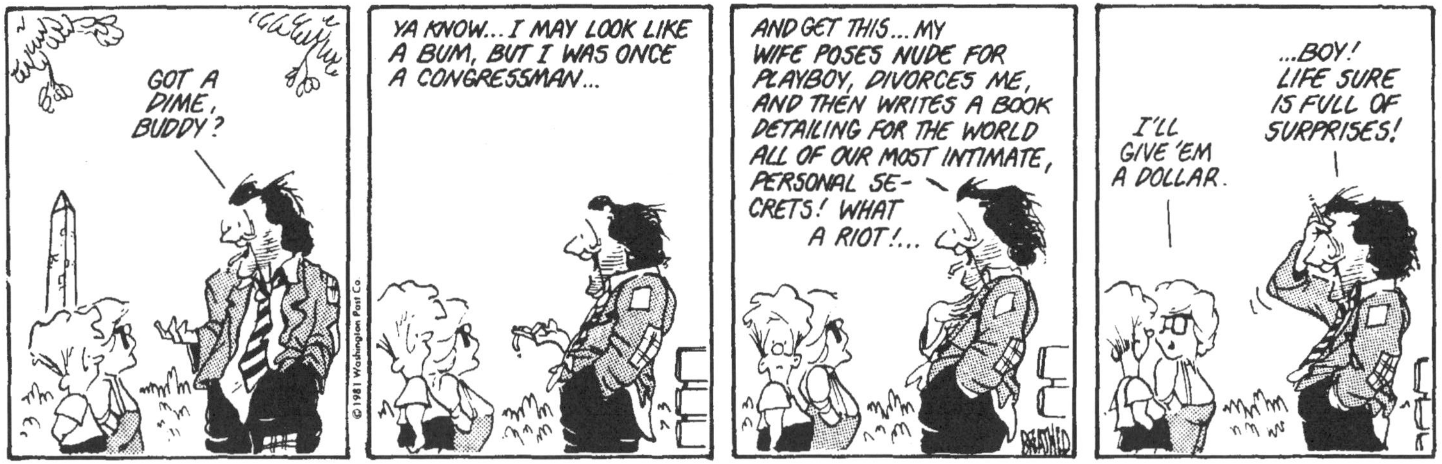
GOT A DIME, BUDDY?
YA KNOW... I MAY LOOK LIKE A BUM, BUT I WAS ONCE A CONGRESSMAN...
AND GET THIS... MY WIFE POSES NUDE FOR PLAYBOY, DIVORCES ME, AND THEN WRITES A BOOK DETAILING FOR THE WORLD ALL OF OUR MOST INTIMATE, PERSONAL SE-CRETS! WHAT A RIOT!...
I'LL GIVE 'EM A DOLLAR.
...BOY! LIFE SURE IS FULL OF SURPRISES!
© 1981 Washington Post Co.
BREATHED

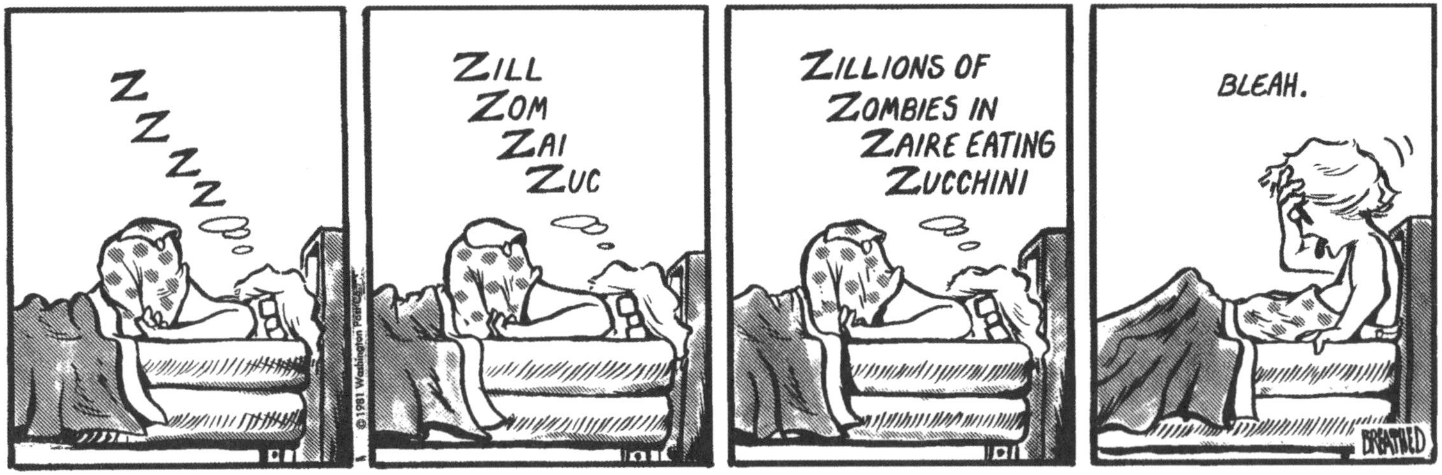
Z Z Z Z Z
ZILL
ZOM
ZAI
ZUC
ZILLIONS OF ZOMBIES IN ZAIRE EATING ZUCCHINI
BLEAH.
© 1981 Washington Post Co.
BREATHED

Berkeley Breathed prepared six non-continuity *Bloom County* dailies which could be inserted by subscribing newspapers in case of emergency. They are published here for the first time.

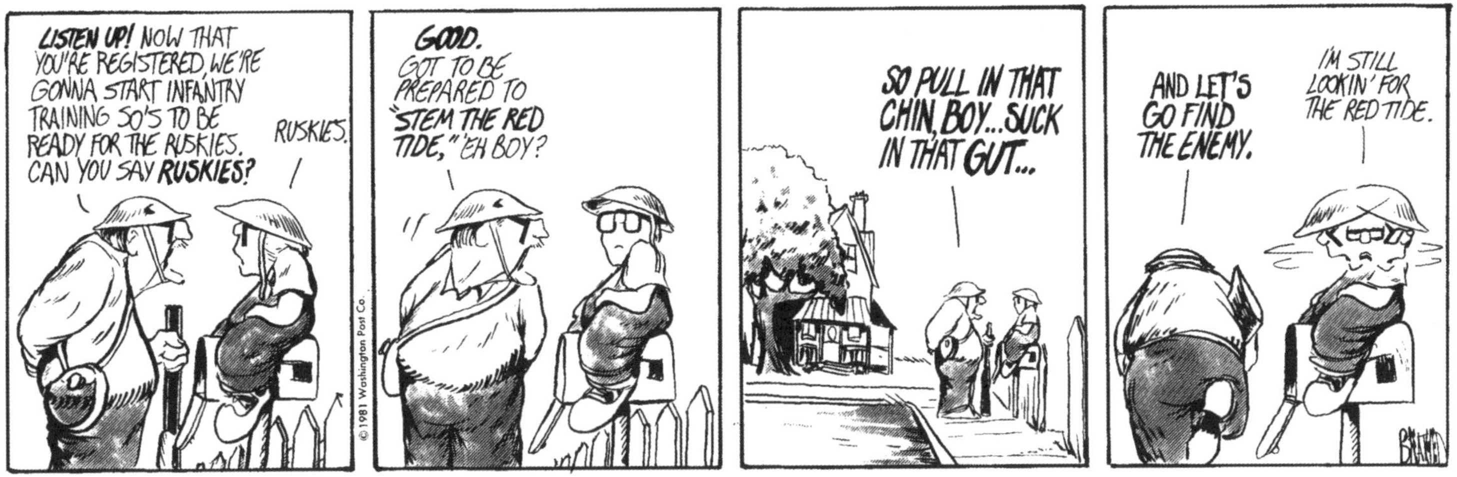
LISTEN UP! NOW THAT YOU'RE REGISTERED, WE'RE GONNA START INFANTRY TRAINING SO'S TO BE READY FOR THE RUSKIES. CAN YOU SAY RUSKIES?
RUSKIES.
© 1981 Washington Post Co.
GOOD. GOT TO BE PREPARED TO "STEM THE RED TIDE," EH BOY?
SO PULL IN THAT CHIN, BOY... SUCK IN THAT GUT...
AND LET'S GO FIND THE ENEMY.
I'M STILL LOOKIN' FOR THE RED TIDE.

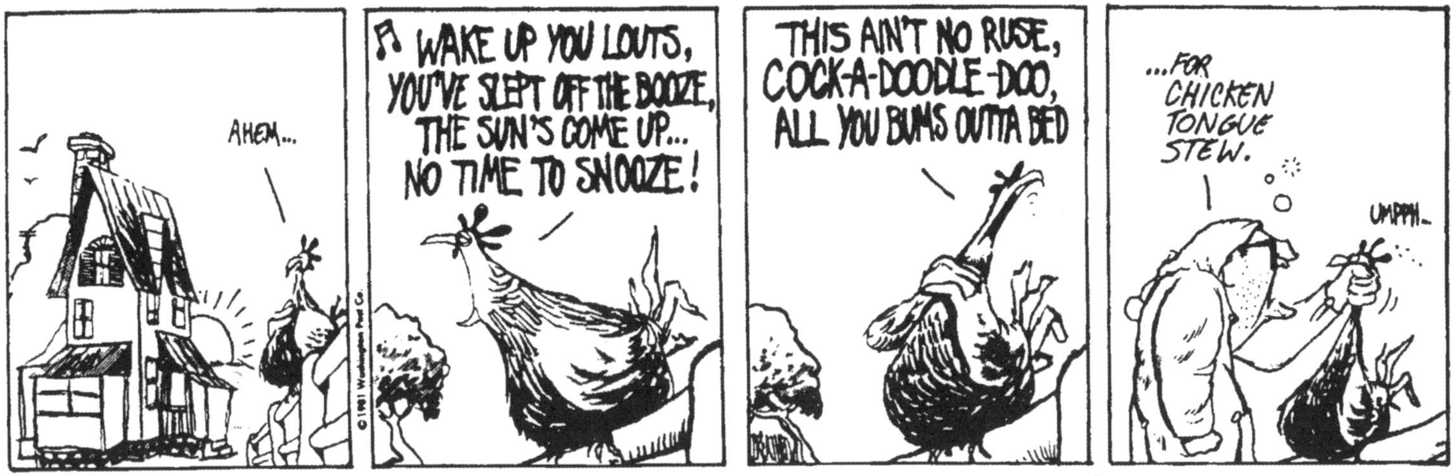
AHEM...
© 1981 Washington Post Co.
♪ WAKE UP YOU LOUTS, YOU'VE SLEPT OFF THE BOOZE, THE SUN'S COME UP... NO TIME TO SNOOZE!
THIS AIN'T NO RUSE, COCK-A-DOODLE-DOO, ALL YOU BUMS OUTTA BED
...FOR CHICKEN TONGUE STEW.
UMPPH...

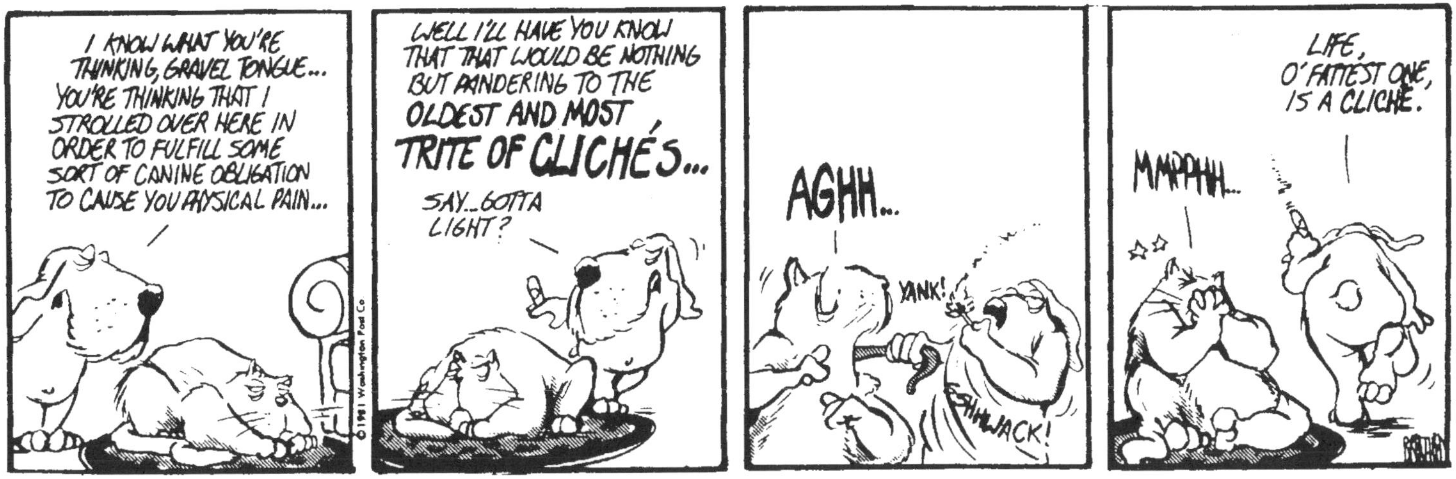
I KNOW WHAT YOU'RE THINKING, GRAVEL TONGUE... YOU'RE THINKING THAT I STROLLED OVER HERE IN ORDER TO FULFILL SOME SORT OF CANINE OBLIGATION TO CAUSE YOU PHYSICAL PAIN...
© 1981 Washington Post Co.
WELL I'LL HAVE YOU KNOW THAT THAT WOULD BE NOTHING BUT PANDERING TO THE OLDEST AND MOST TRITE OF CLICHÉS...
SAY...GOTTA LIGHT?
AGHH...
YANK!
SHWACK!
MMPPHH...
LIFE, O' FATTEST ONE, IS A CLICHÉ.

BLOOM COUNTY
1980–1982

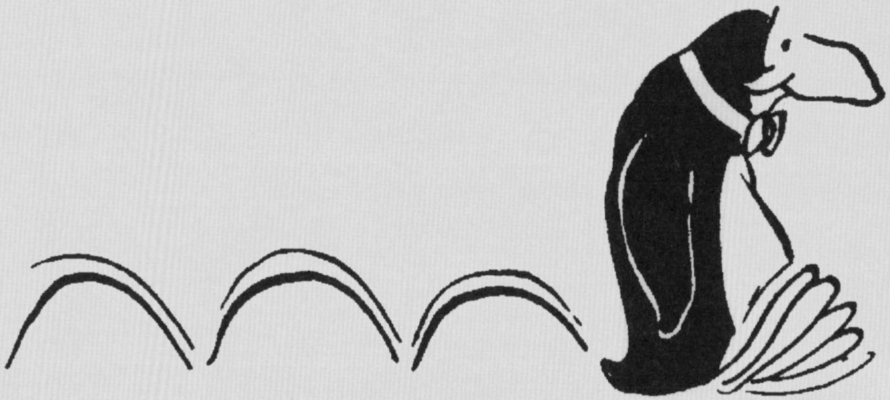

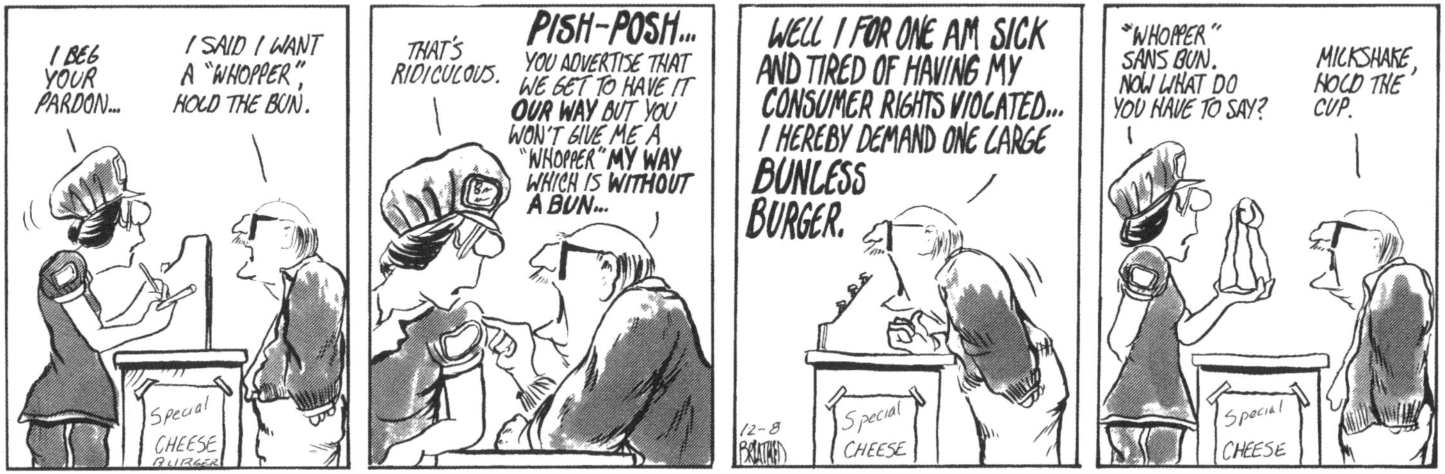
I BEG YOUR PARDON...
I SAID I WANT A "WHOPPER", HOLD THE BUN.
Special CHEESE BURGER
THAT'S RIDICULOUS.
PISH-POSH... YOU ADVERTISE THAT WE GET TO HAVE IT OUR WAY BUT YOU WON'T GIVE ME A "WHOPPER" MY WAY WHICH IS WITHOUT A BUN...
WELL I FOR ONE AM SICK AND TIRED OF HAVING MY CONSUMER RIGHTS VIOLATED... I HEREBY DEMAND ONE LARGE BUNLESS BURGER.
12-8
BREATHED
Special CHEESE
"WHOPPER" SANS BUN. NOW WHAT DO YOU HAVE TO SAY?
MILKSHAKE, HOLD THE CUP.
Special CHEESE

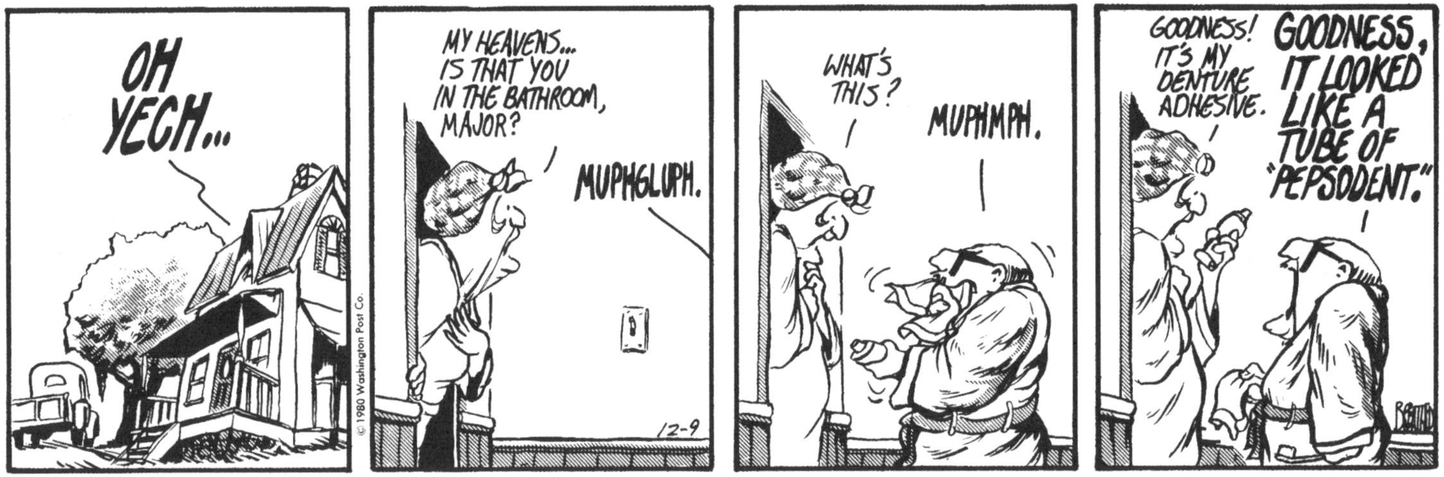
OH YECH...
© 1980 Washington Post Co.
MY HEAVENS... IS THAT YOU IN THE BATHROOM, MAJOR?
MUPHGLUPH.
12-9
WHAT'S THIS?
MUPHMPH.
GOODNESS! IT'S MY DENTURE ADHESIVE.
GOODNESS, IT LOOKED LIKE A TUBE OF "PEPSODENT."
BREATHED

"Denture adhesive" was originally "contraceptive jelly." Far funnier. The first of 30 years of comic compromise, the last finally nudging me out entirely in 2008. I'm a slow burn. —BB

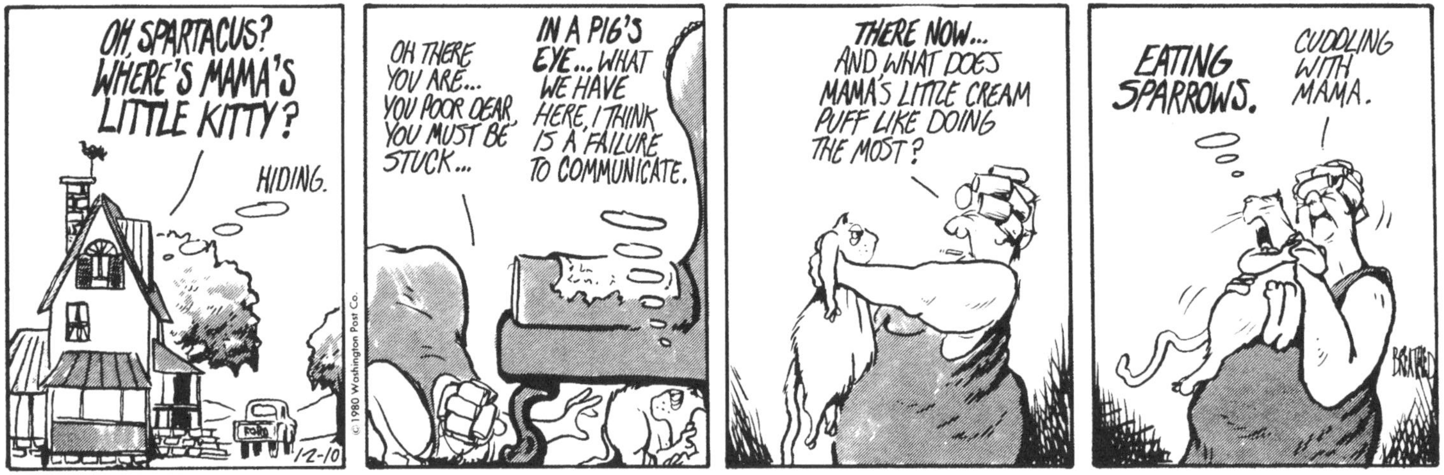
OH, SPARTACUS? WHERE'S MAMA'S LITTLE KITTY?
HIDING.
12-10
© 1980 Washington Post Co.
OH THERE YOU ARE... YOU POOR DEAR. YOU MUST BE STUCK...
IN A PIG'S EYE... WHAT WE HAVE HERE, I THINK IS A FAILURE TO COMMUNICATE.
THERE NOW... AND WHAT DOES MAMA'S LITTLE CREAM PUFF LIKE DOING THE MOST?
EATING SPARROWS.
CUDDLING WITH MAMA.
BREATHED

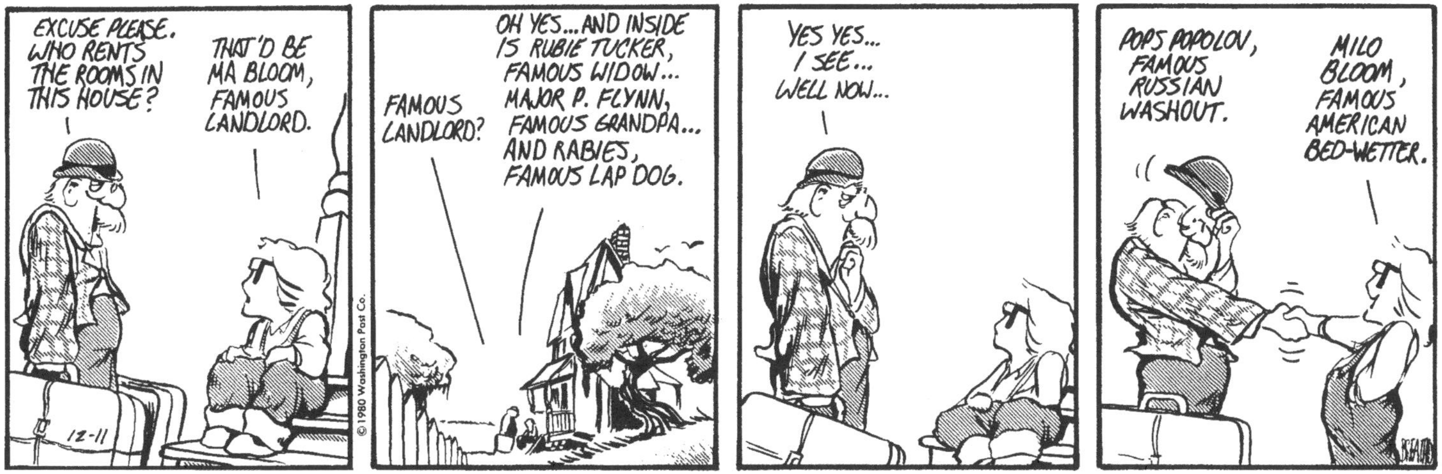
EXCUSE PLEASE. WHO RENTS THE ROOMS IN THIS HOUSE?
THAT'D BE MA BLOOM, FAMOUS LANDLORD.
12-11
FAMOUS LANDLORD?
OH YES...AND INSIDE IS RUBIE TUCKER, FAMOUS WIDOW... MAJOR P. FLYNN, FAMOUS GRANDPA... AND RABIES, FAMOUS LAP DOG.
© 1980 Washington Post Co.
YES YES... I SEE... WELL NOW...
POPS POPOLOV, FAMOUS RUSSIAN WASHOUT.
MILO BLOOM, FAMOUS AMERICAN BED-WETTER.

Enter Milo Bloom.

Milo's name came from the hero of The Phantom Tollbooth. *The first book I loved. —BB*

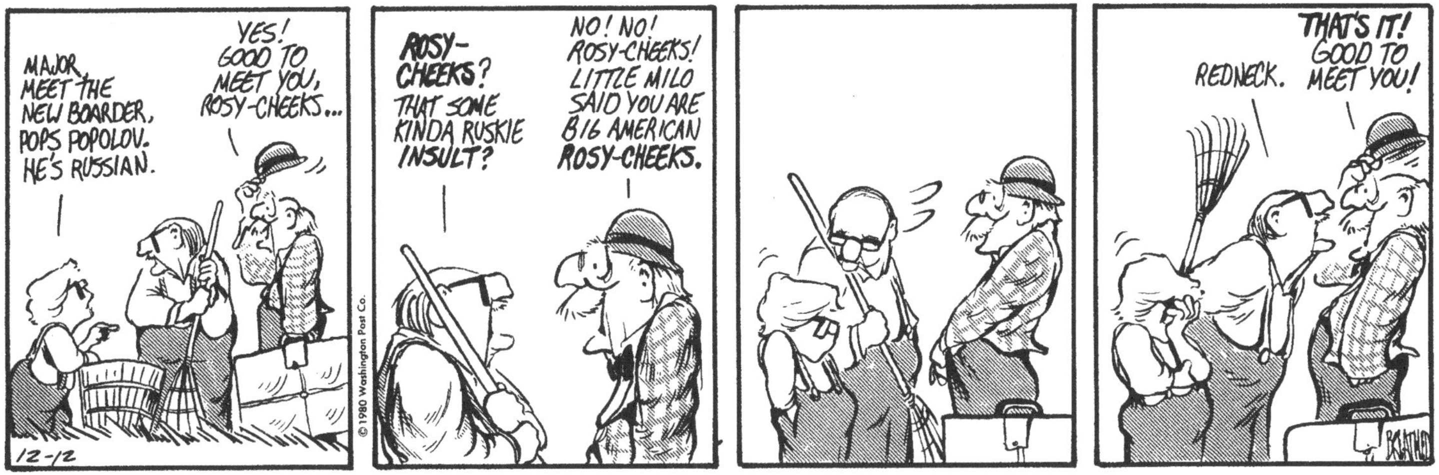
MAJOR, MEET THE NEW BOARDER, POPS POPOLOV. HE'S RUSSIAN.
YES! GOOD TO MEET YOU, ROSY-CHEEKS...
12-12
ROSY-CHEEKS? THAT SOME KINDA RUSKIE INSULT?
NO! NO! ROSY-CHEEKS! LITTLE MILO SAID YOU ARE BIG AMERICAN ROSY-CHEEKS.
© 1980 Washington Post Co.
REDNECK.
THAT'S IT! GOOD TO MEET YOU!

Note, gentle reader, that I hadn't the faintest clue what Bloom County *was going to be about at this point. I'd never read any comic besides* Doonesbury. *This is not a point of contrarian pride. It's abject embarrassment. —BB*

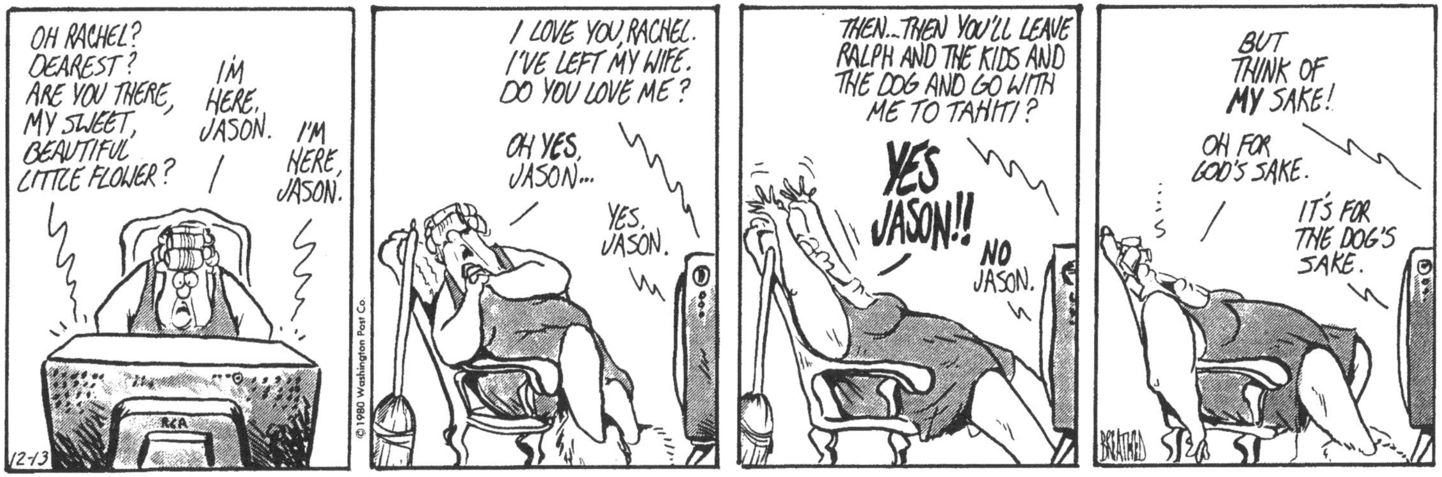
OH RACHEL? DEAREST? ARE YOU THERE, MY SWEET, BEAUTIFUL LITTLE FLOWER?
I'M HERE, JASON.
I'M HERE, JASON.
12-13
I LOVE YOU, RACHEL. I'VE LEFT MY WIFE. DO YOU LOVE ME?
OH YES, JASON...
YES, JASON.
© 1980 Washington Post Co.
THEN...THEN YOU'LL LEAVE RALPH AND THE KIDS AND THE DOG AND GO WITH ME TO TAHITI?
YES JASON!!
NO JASON.
BUT THINK OF MY SAKE!
OH FOR GOD'S SAKE.
IT'S FOR THE DOG'S SAKE.

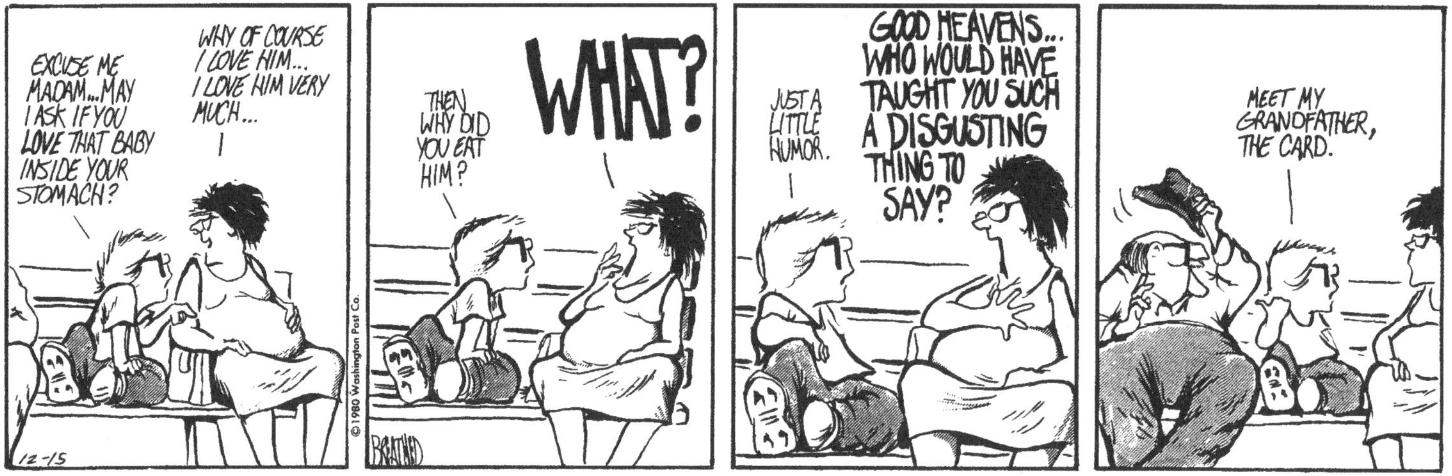
EXCUSE ME MADAM...MAY I ASK IF YOU LOVE THAT BABY INSIDE YOUR STOMACH?
WHY OF COURSE I LOVE HIM... I LOVE HIM VERY MUCH...
THEN WHY DID YOU EAT HIM?
WHAT?
JUST A LITTLE HUMOR.
GOOD HEAVENS... WHO WOULD HAVE TAUGHT YOU SUCH A DISGUSTING THING TO SAY?
MEET MY GRANDFATHER, THE CARD.
12-15
© 1980 Washington Post Co.
BREATHED

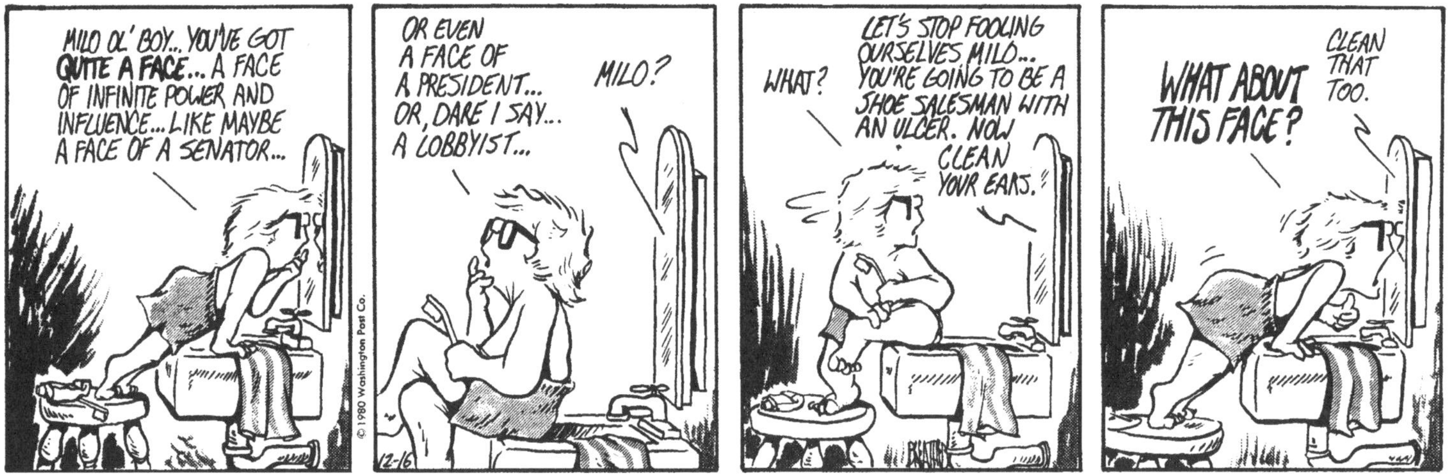
MILO OL' BOY... YOU'VE GOT QUITE A FACE... A FACE OF INFINITE POWER AND INFLUENCE... LIKE MAYBE A FACE OF A SENATOR...
OR EVEN A FACE OF A PRESIDENT... OR, DARE I SAY... A LOBBYIST...
MILO?
WHAT?
LET'S STOP FOOLING OURSELVES MILO... YOU'RE GOING TO BE A SHOE SALESMAN WITH AN ULCER. NOW CLEAN YOUR EARS.
WHAT ABOUT THIS FACE?
CLEAN THAT TOO.
12-16
© 1980 Washington Post Co.
BREATHED

If anyone can read my primordial printing, I'd love to know what it says. I honestly can't remember and I certainly can't make it out. The only clarity here is that the talking mirror is a warmed-over Garry Trudeau routine from his Yale strip, alas. I apologized some years later. —BB

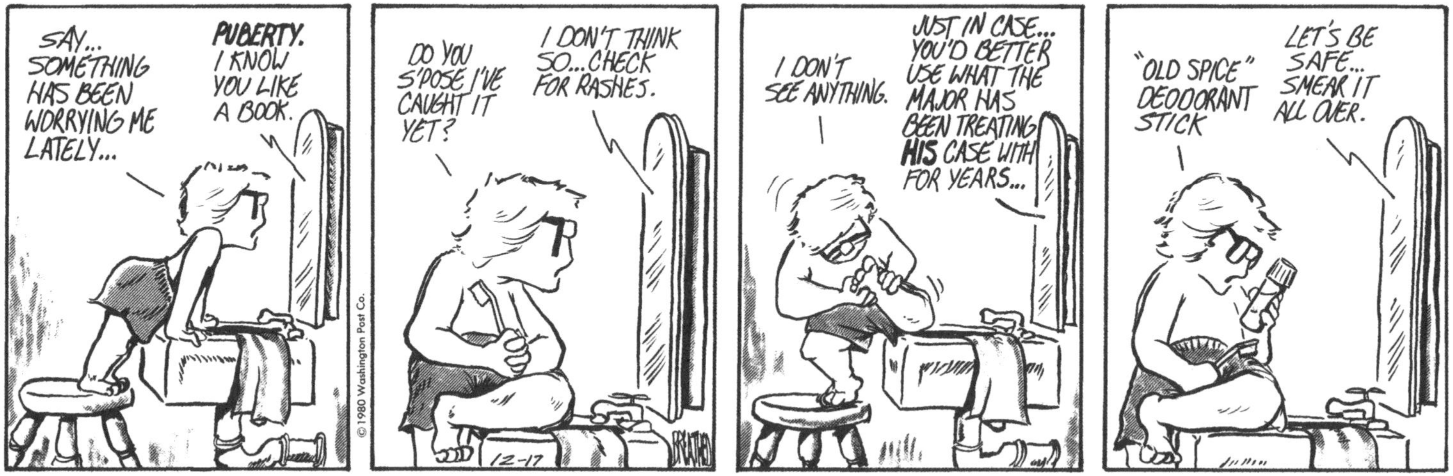
SAY... SOMETHING HAS BEEN WORRYING ME LATELY...
PUBERTY. I KNOW YOU LIKE A BOOK.
DO YOU S'POSE I'VE CAUGHT IT YET?
I DON'T THINK SO... CHECK FOR RASHES.
I DON'T SEE ANYTHING.
JUST IN CASE... YOU'D BETTER USE WHAT THE MAJOR HAS BEEN TREATING HIS CASE WITH FOR YEARS...
"OLD SPICE" DEODORANT STICK
LET'S BE SAFE... SMEAR IT ALL OVER.
12-17
© 1980 Washington Post Co.
BREATHED

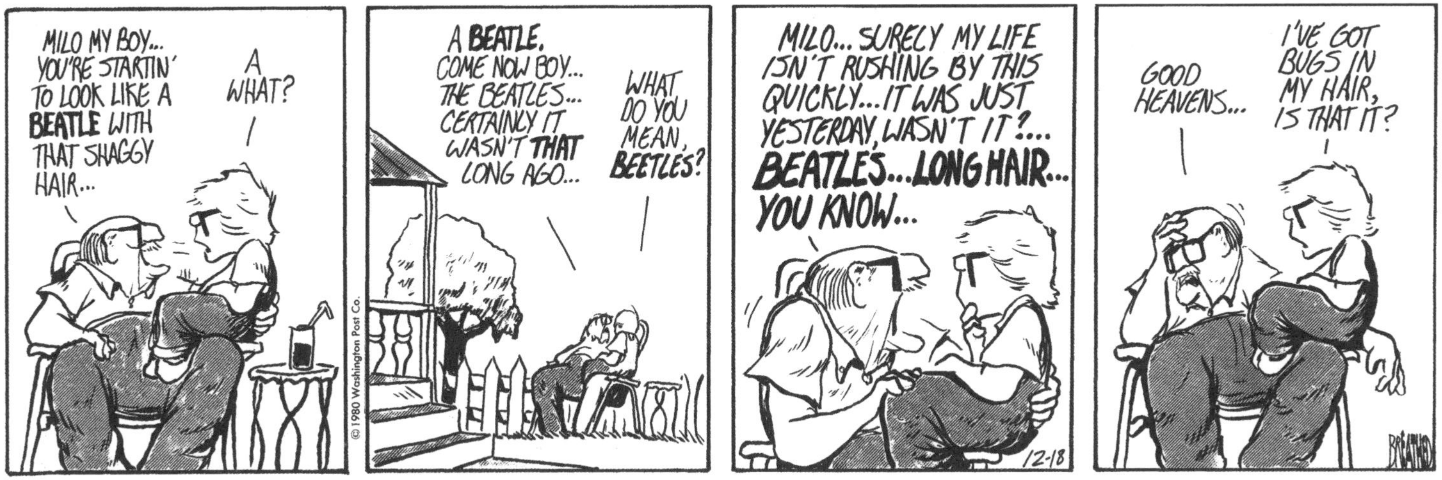
MILO MY BOY... YOU'RE STARTIN' TO LOOK LIKE A **BEATLE** WITH THAT SHAGGY HAIR...
A WHAT?
A **BEATLE.** COME NOW BOY... THE BEATLES... CERTAINLY IT WASN'T **THAT** LONG AGO...
WHAT DO YOU MEAN, **BEETLES?**
© 1980 Washington Post Co.
MILO... SURELY MY LIFE ISN'T RUSHING BY THIS QUICKLY... IT WAS JUST YESTERDAY, WASN'T IT?... **BEATLES... LONG HAIR... YOU KNOW...**
12-18
GOOD HEAVENS...
I'VE GOT BUGS IN MY HAIR, IS THAT IT?
BREATHED

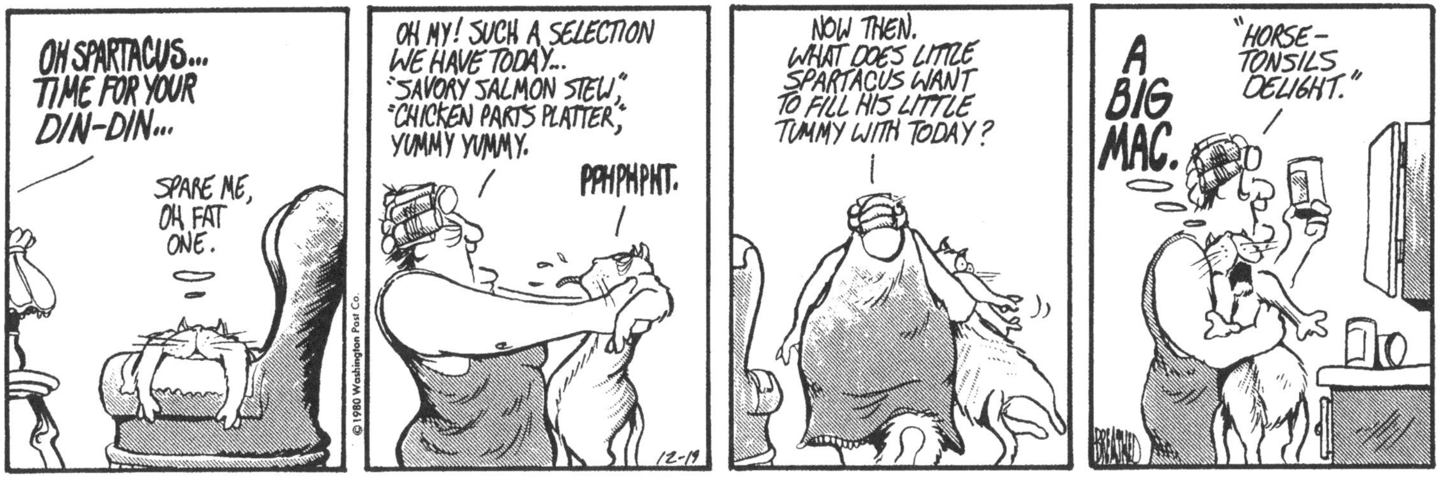
OH SPARTACUS... TIME FOR YOUR DIN-DIN...
SPARE ME, OH FAT ONE.
OH MY! SUCH A SELECTION WE HAVE TODAY... "SAVORY SALMON STEW," "CHICKEN PARTS PLATTER," YUMMY YUMMY.
PPHPHPHT.
© 1980 Washington Post Co.
12-19
NOW THEN. WHAT DOES LITTLE SPARTACUS WANT TO FILL HIS LITTLE TUMMY WITH TODAY?
"HORSE-TONSILS DELIGHT."
A BIG MAC.
BREATHED

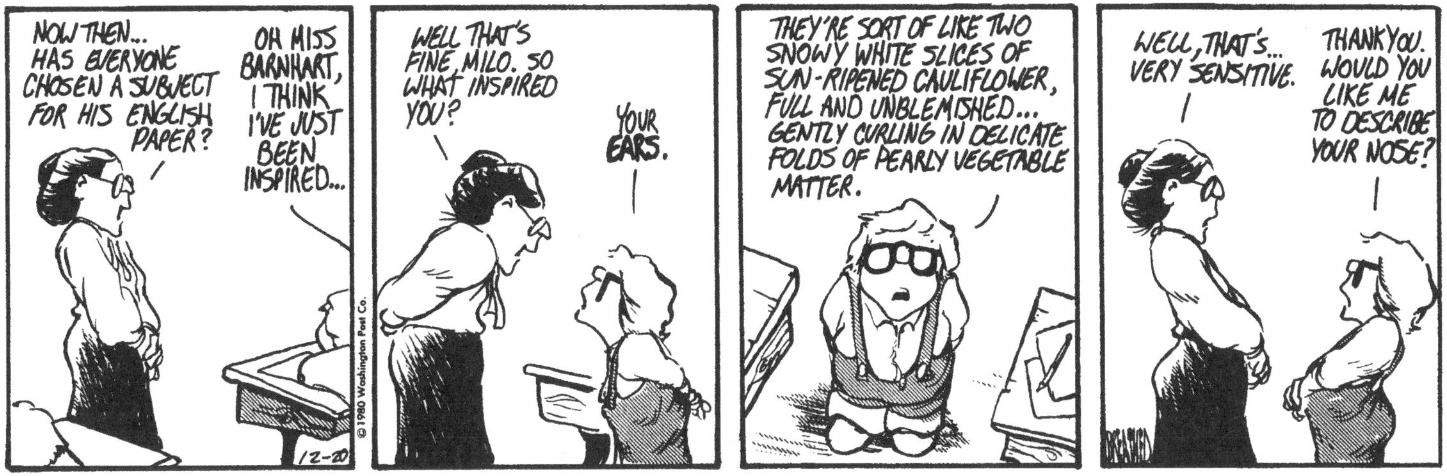
NOW THEN... HAS EVERYONE CHOSEN A SUBJECT FOR HIS ENGLISH PAPER?
OH MISS BARNHART, I THINK I'VE JUST BEEN INSPIRED...
© 1980 Washington Post Co.
12-20
WELL THAT'S FINE, MILO. SO WHAT INSPIRED YOU?
YOUR **EARS.**
THEY'RE SORT OF LIKE TWO SNOWY WHITE SLICES OF SUN-RIPENED CAULIFLOWER, FULL AND UNBLEMISHED... GENTLY CURLING IN DELICATE FOLDS OF PEARLY VEGETABLE MATTER.
WELL, THAT'S... VERY SENSITIVE.
THANK YOU. WOULD YOU LIKE ME TO DESCRIBE YOUR NOSE?
BREATHED

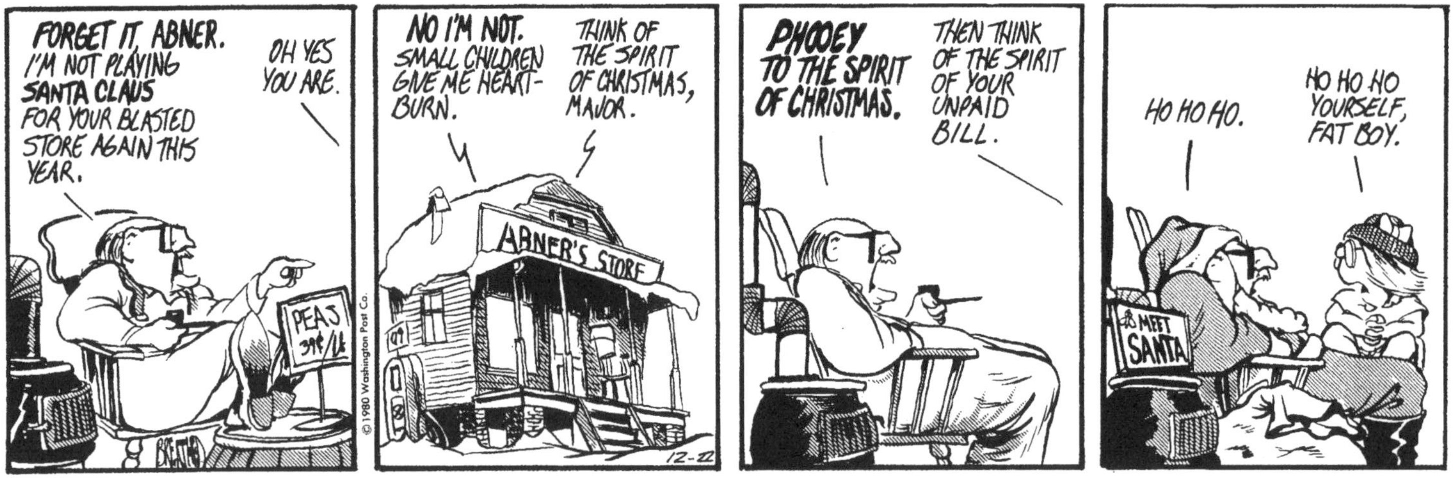
FORGET IT, ABNER. I'M NOT PLAYING SANTA CLAUS FOR YOUR BLASTED STORE AGAIN THIS YEAR.
OH YES YOU ARE.
PEAS 39¢/LB
NO I'M NOT. SMALL CHILDREN GIVE ME HEART-BURN.
THINK OF THE SPIRIT OF CHRISTMAS, MAJOR.
ABNER'S STORE
© 1980 Washington Post Co.
12-22
PHOOEY TO THE SPIRIT OF CHRISTMAS.
THEN THINK OF THE SPIRIT OF YOUR UNPAID BILL.
HO HO HO.
HO HO HO YOURSELF, FAT BOY.
MEET SANTA

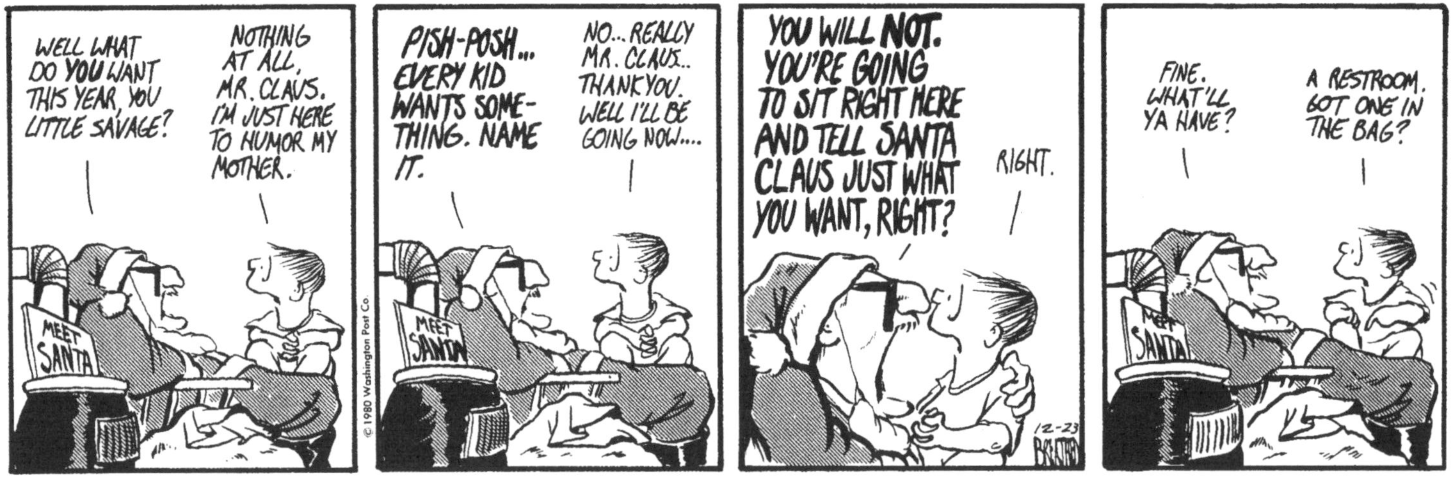
WELL WHAT DO YOU WANT THIS YEAR, YOU LITTLE SAVAGE?
NOTHING AT ALL, MR. CLAUS. I'M JUST HERE TO HUMOR MY MOTHER.
MEET SANTA
PISH-POSH... EVERY KID WANTS SOME-THING. NAME IT.
NO... REALLY MR. CLAUS.. THANK YOU. WELL I'LL BE GOING NOW....
© 1980 Washington Post Co.
YOU WILL NOT. YOU'RE GOING TO SIT RIGHT HERE AND TELL SANTA CLAUS JUST WHAT YOU WANT, RIGHT?
RIGHT.
12-23
FINE. WHAT'LL YA HAVE?
A RESTROOM. GOT ONE IN THE BAG?

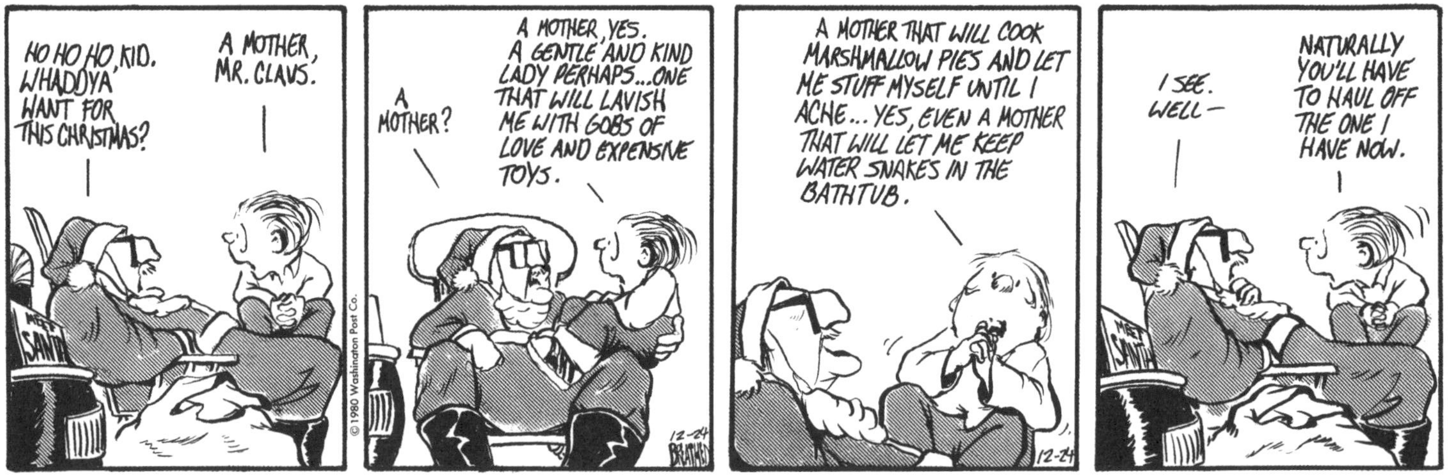
HO HO HO, KID. WHADDYA WANT FOR THIS CHRISTMAS?
A MOTHER, MR. CLAUS.
A MOTHER?
A MOTHER, YES. A GENTLE AND KIND LADY PERHAPS... ONE THAT WILL LAVISH ME WITH GOBS OF LOVE AND EXPENSIVE TOYS.
© 1980 Washington Post Co.
12-24
A MOTHER THAT WILL COOK MARSHMALLOW PIES AND LET ME STUFF MYSELF UNTIL I ACHE... YES, EVEN A MOTHER THAT WILL LET ME KEEP WATER SNAKES IN THE BATHTUB.
I SEE. WELL—
NATURALLY YOU'LL HAVE TO HAUL OFF THE ONE I HAVE NOW.

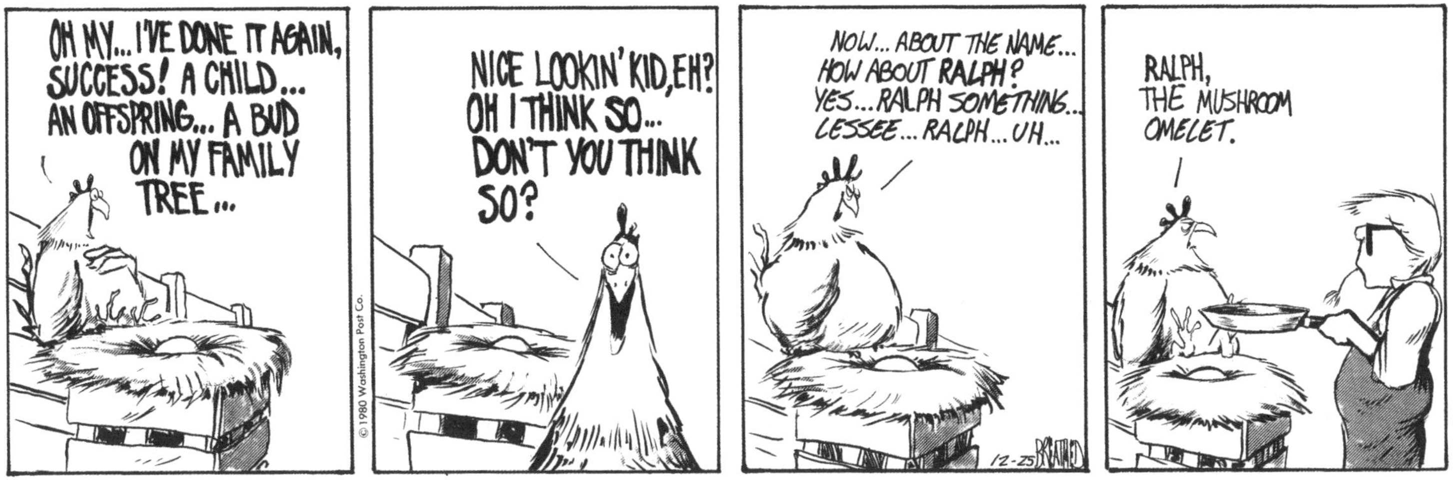
OH MY... I'VE DONE IT AGAIN, SUCCESS! A CHILD... AN OFFSPRING... A BUD ON MY FAMILY TREE...
NICE LOOKIN' KID, EH? OH I THINK SO... DON'T YOU THINK SO?
NOW... ABOUT THE NAME... HOW ABOUT RALPH? YES... RALPH SOMETHING... LESSEE... RALPH... UH...
RALPH, THE MUSHROOM OMELET.
© 1980 Washington Post Co.
12-25 BREATHED

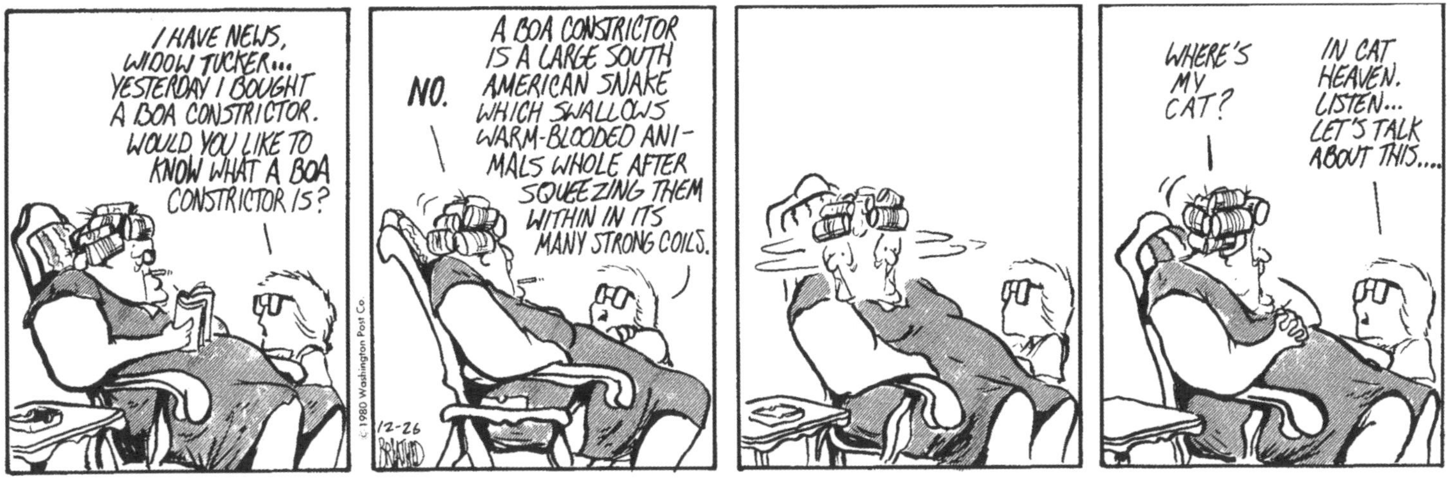
I HAVE NEWS, WIDOW TUCKER... YESTERDAY I BOUGHT A BOA CONSTRICTOR. WOULD YOU LIKE TO KNOW WHAT A BOA CONSTRICTOR IS?
NO.
A BOA CONSTRICTOR IS A LARGE SOUTH AMERICAN SNAKE WHICH SWALLOWS WARM-BLOODED ANIMALS WHOLE AFTER SQUEEZING THEM WITHIN IN ITS MANY STRONG COILS.
WHERE'S MY CAT?
IN CAT HEAVEN. LISTEN... LET'S TALK ABOUT THIS....
© 1980 Washington Post Co.
12-26 BREATHED

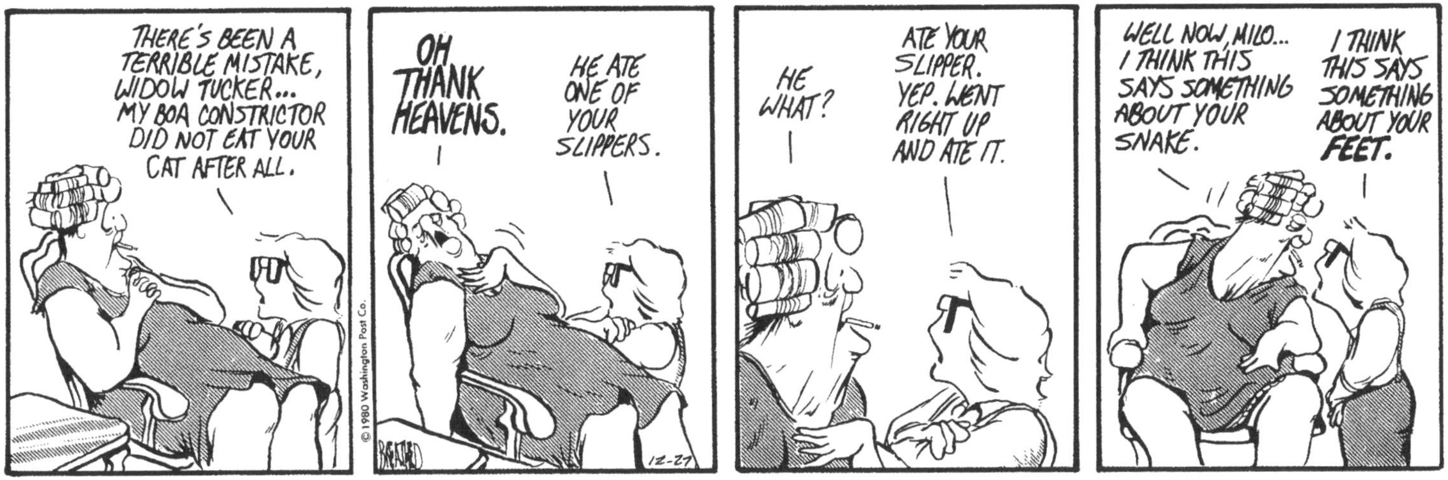
THERE'S BEEN A TERRIBLE MISTAKE, WIDOW TUCKER... MY BOA CONSTRICTOR DID NOT EAT YOUR CAT AFTER ALL.
OH THANK HEAVENS.
HE ATE ONE OF YOUR SLIPPERS.
HE WHAT?
ATE YOUR SLIPPER. YEP. WENT RIGHT UP AND ATE IT.
WELL NOW, MILO... I THINK THIS SAYS SOMETHING ABOUT YOUR SNAKE.
I THINK THIS SAYS SOMETHING ABOUT YOUR FEET.
© 1980 Washington Post Co.
BREATHED 12-27

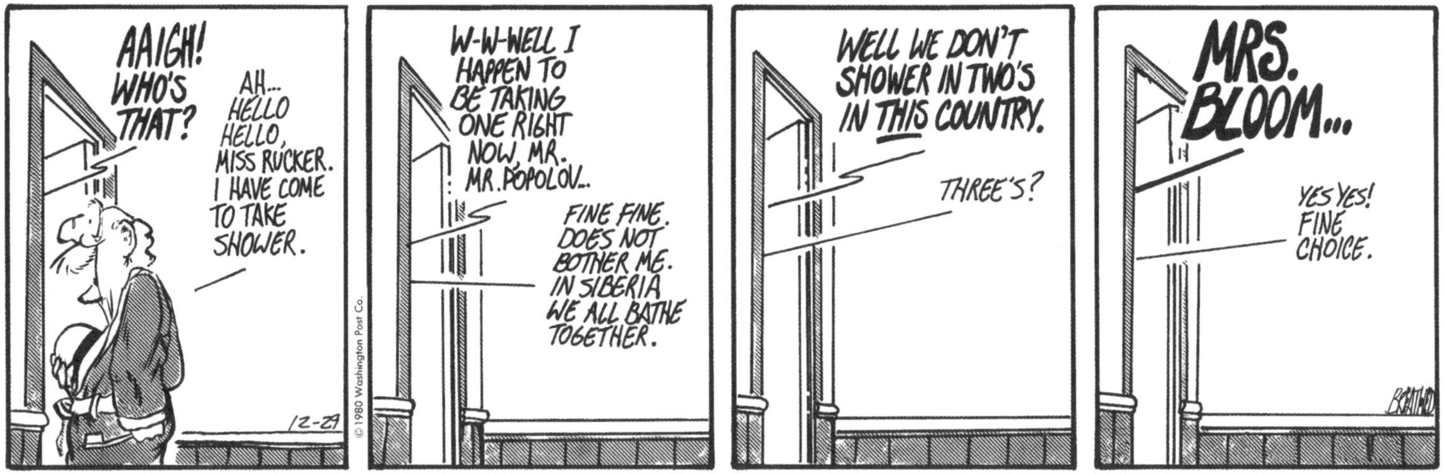
AAIGH! WHO'S THAT?
AH... HELLO HELLO, MISS RUCKER. I HAVE COME TO TAKE SHOWER.
12-29
© 1980 Washington Post Co.
W-W-WELL I HAPPEN TO BE TAKING ONE RIGHT NOW, MR. MR. POPOLOV...
FINE FINE. DOES NOT BOTHER ME. IN SIBERIA WE ALL BATHE TOGETHER.
WELL WE DON'T SHOWER IN TWO'S IN THIS COUNTRY.
THREE'S?
MRS. BLOOM...
YES YES! FINE CHOICE.

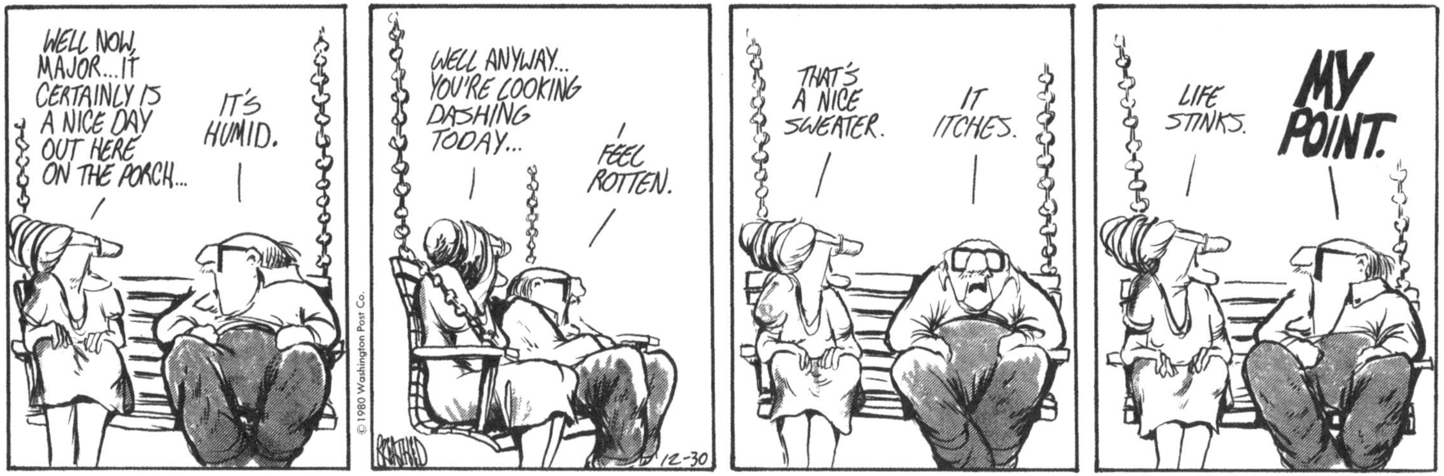
WELL NOW, MAJOR... IT CERTAINLY IS A NICE DAY OUT HERE ON THE PORCH...
IT'S HUMID.
© 1980 Washington Post Co.
WELL ANYWAY... YOU'RE LOOKING DASHING TODAY...
I FEEL ROTTEN.
12-30
THAT'S A NICE SWEATER.
IT ITCHES.
LIFE STINKS.
MY POINT.

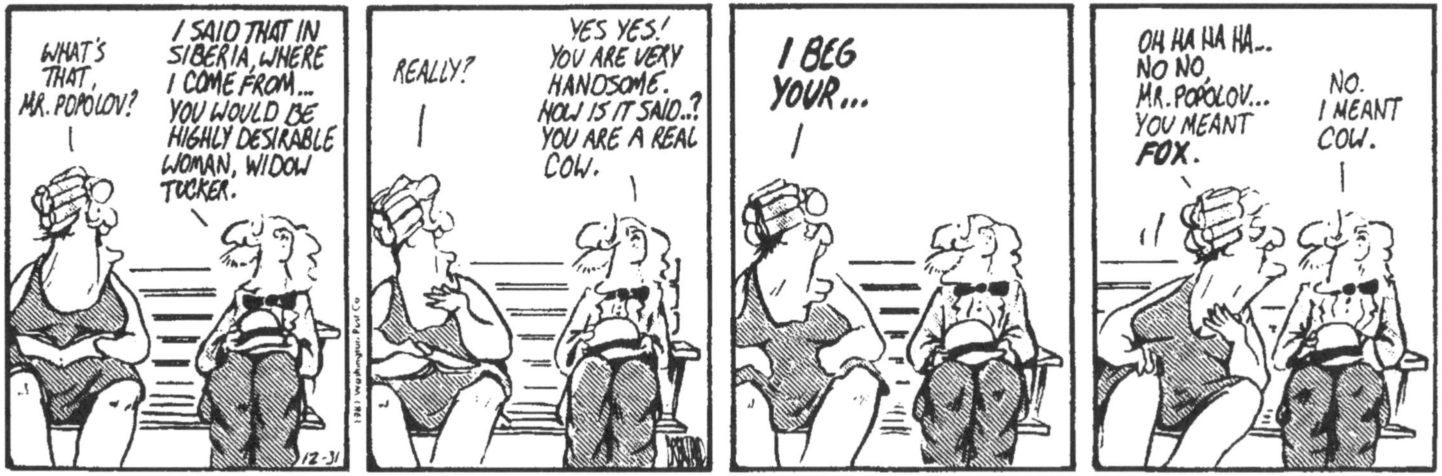
WHAT'S THAT, MR. POPOLOV?
I SAID THAT IN SIBERIA, WHERE I COME FROM... YOU WOULD BE HIGHLY DESIRABLE WOMAN, WIDOW TUCKER.
12-31
REALLY?
YES YES! YOU ARE VERY HANDSOME. HOW IS IT SAID..? YOU ARE A REAL COW.
I BEG YOUR...
OH HA HA HA... NO NO MR. POPOLOV... YOU MEANT FOX.
NO. I MEANT COW.

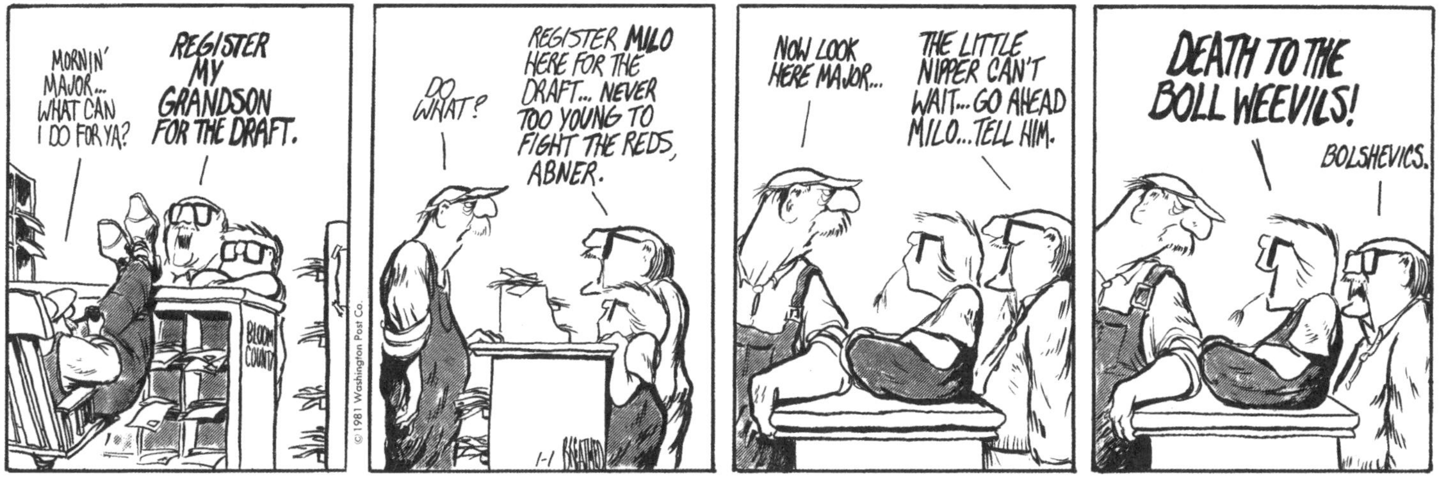
MORNIN' MAJOR... WHAT CAN I DO FOR YA?
REGISTER MY GRANDSON FOR THE DRAFT.
BLOOM COUNTY
© 1981 Washington Post Co.
DO WHAT?
REGISTER MILO HERE FOR THE DRAFT... NEVER TOO YOUNG TO FIGHT THE REDS, ABNER.
1-1
NOW LOOK HERE MAJOR...
THE LITTLE NIPPER CAN'T WAIT... GO AHEAD MILO... TELL HIM.
DEATH TO THE BOLL WEEVILS!
BOLSHEVICS.

Selective Service, compelling all men born after 1960 to register for potential military service, was re-initiated in July of 1980.

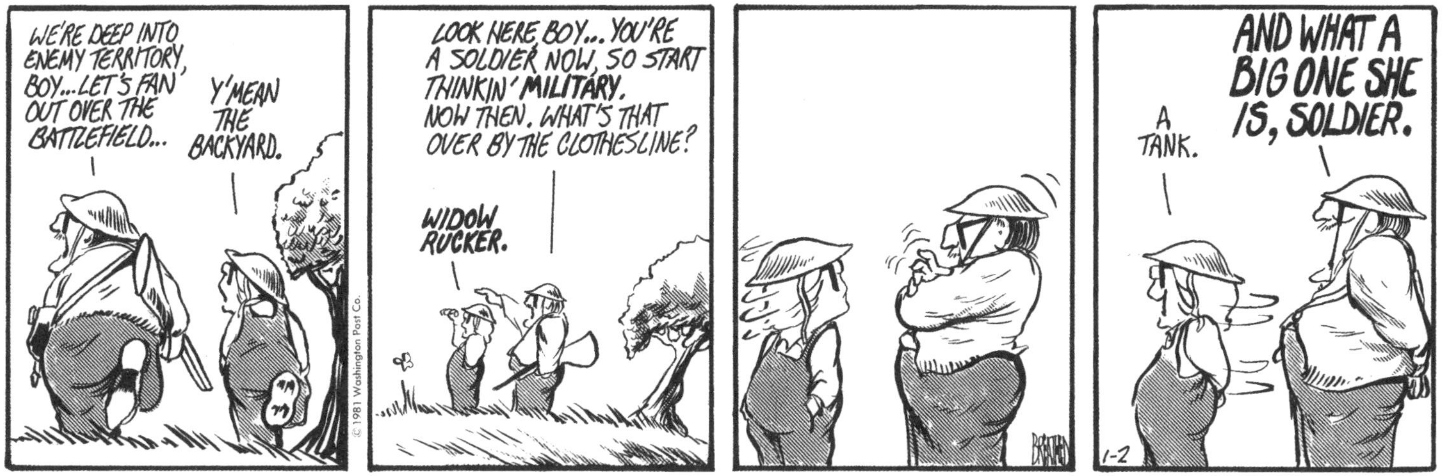
WE'RE DEEP INTO ENEMY TERRITORY, BOY... LET'S FAN OUT OVER THE BATTLEFIELD...
Y'MEAN THE BACKYARD.
© 1981 Washington Post Co.
LOOK HERE BOY... YOU'RE A SOLDIER NOW, SO START THINKIN' MILITARY. NOW THEN. WHAT'S THAT OVER BY THE CLOTHESLINE?
WIDOW RUCKER.
A TANK.
AND WHAT A BIG ONE SHE IS, SOLDIER.
1-2

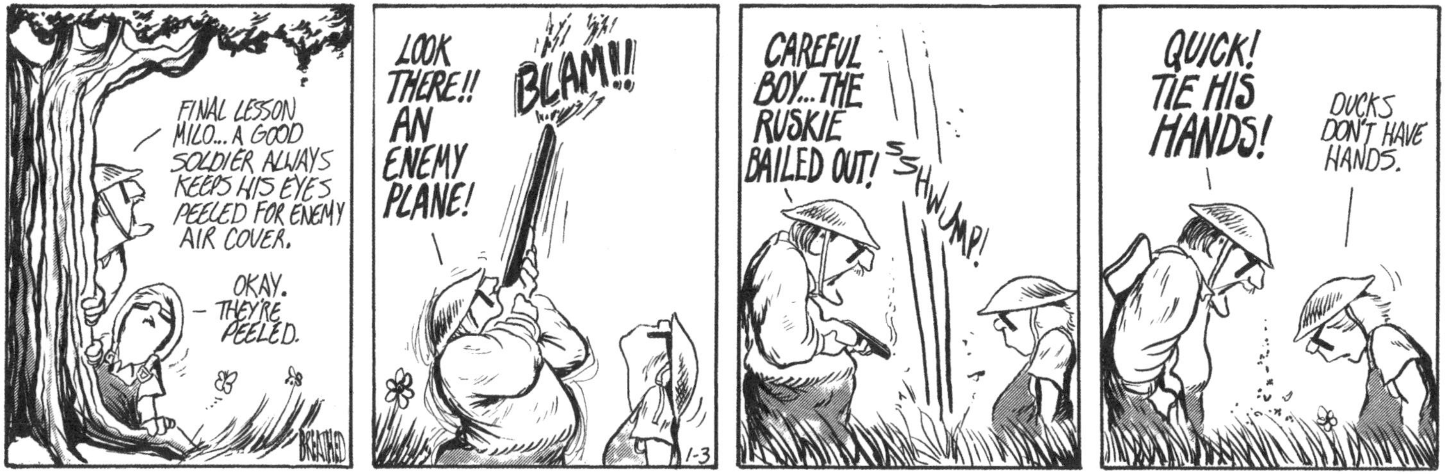
FINAL LESSON MILO... A GOOD SOLDIER ALWAYS KEEPS HIS EYES PEELED FOR ENEMY AIR COVER.
OKAY. THEY'RE PEELED.
LOOK THERE!! AN ENEMY PLANE!
BLAM!!!
1-3
CAREFUL BOY... THE RUSKIE BAILED OUT!
SSHWUMP!
QUICK! TIE HIS HANDS!
DUCKS DON'T HAVE HANDS.

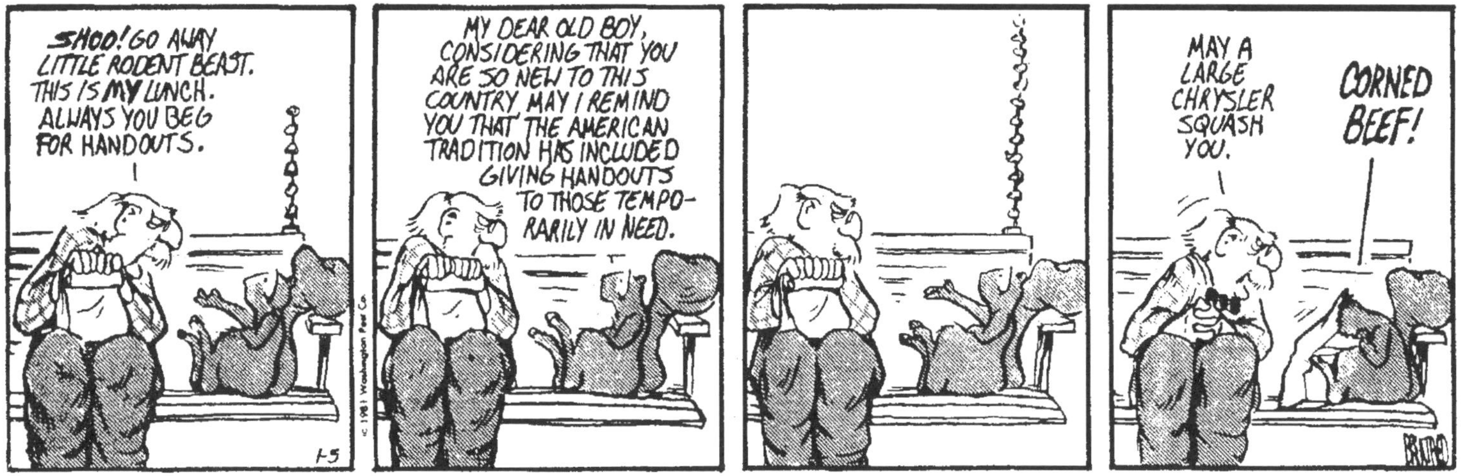
SHOO! GO AWAY LITTLE RODENT BEAST. THIS IS MY LUNCH. ALWAYS YOU BEG FOR HANDOUTS.
MY DEAR OLD BOY, CONSIDERING THAT YOU ARE SO NEW TO THIS COUNTRY MAY I REMIND YOU THAT THE AMERICAN TRADITION HAS INCLUDED GIVING HANDOUTS TO THOSE TEMPORARILY IN NEED.
MAY A LARGE CHRYSLER SQUASH YOU.
CORNED BEEF!
1-5
© 1981 Washington Post Co.

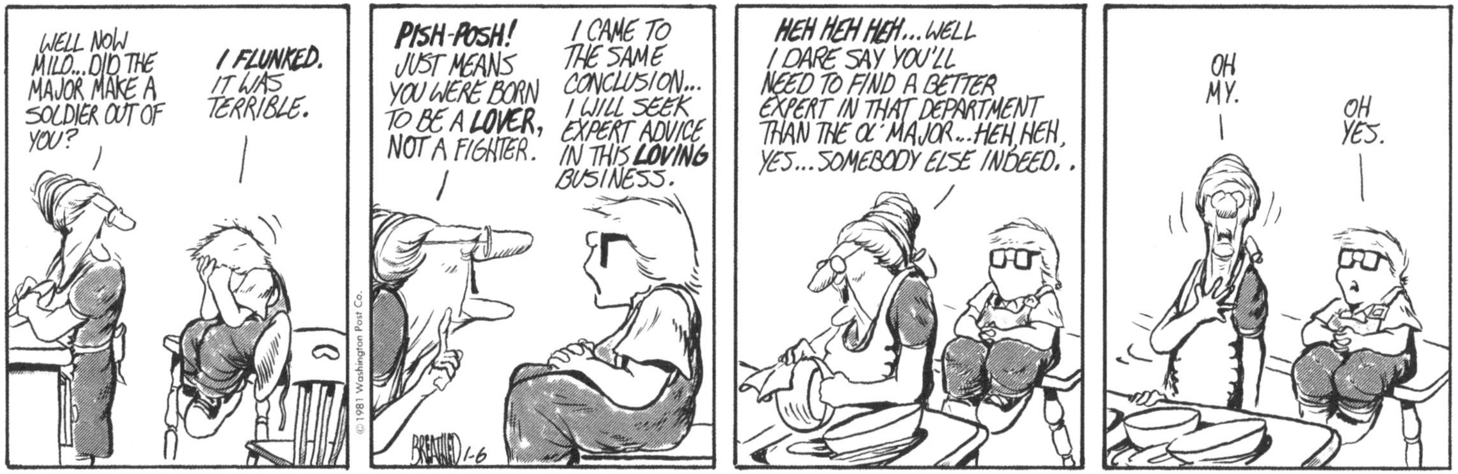
WELL NOW MILO... DID THE MAJOR MAKE A SOLDIER OUT OF YOU?
I FLUNKED. IT WAS TERRIBLE.
PISH-POSH! JUST MEANS YOU WERE BORN TO BE A LOVER, NOT A FIGHTER.
I CAME TO THE SAME CONCLUSION... I WILL SEEK EXPERT ADVICE IN THIS LOVING BUSINESS.
HEH HEH HEH... WELL I DARE SAY YOU'LL NEED TO FIND A BETTER EXPERT IN THAT DEPARTMENT THAN THE OL' MAJOR... HEH, HEH, YES... SOMEBODY ELSE INDEED.
OH MY.
OH YES.
1-6
© 1981 Washington Post Co.

In the 1960s and 1970s, communes sprang up across America. The counter-culture, or "hippie" movement, embraced the idea of a shared utopia, one that espoused spiritual and social oneness.

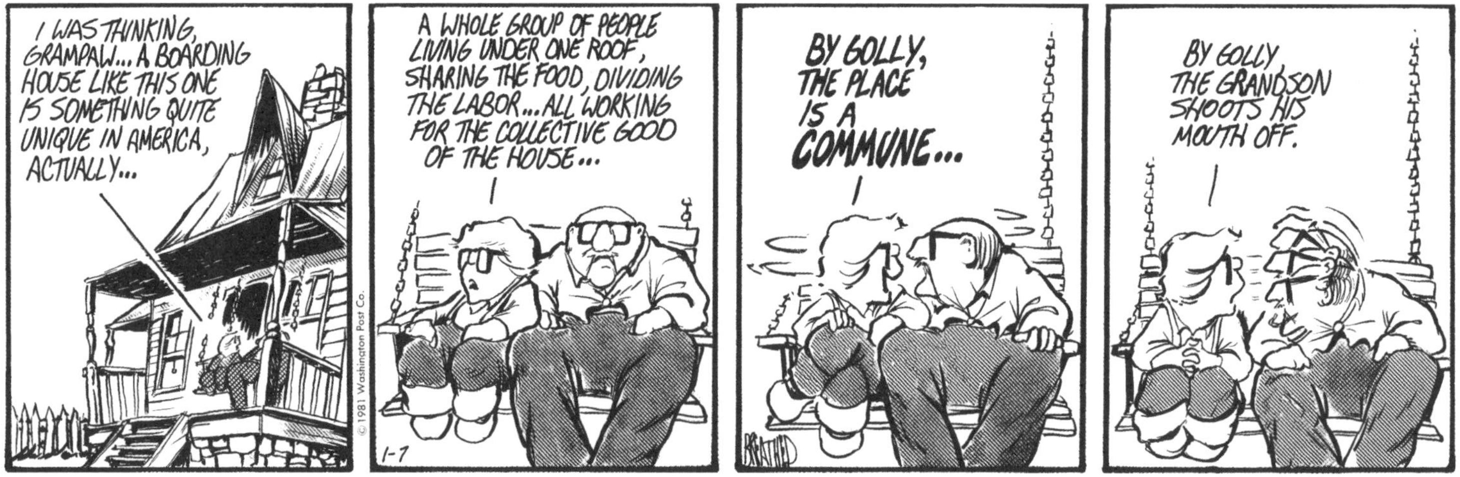
I WAS THINKING, GRAMPAW... A BOARDING HOUSE LIKE THIS ONE IS SOMETHING QUITE UNIQUE IN AMERICA, ACTUALLY...
A WHOLE GROUP OF PEOPLE LIVING UNDER ONE ROOF, SHARING THE FOOD, DIVIDING THE LABOR... ALL WORKING FOR THE COLLECTIVE GOOD OF THE HOUSE...
BY GOLLY, THE PLACE IS A COMMUNE...
BY GOLLY, THE GRANDSON SHOOTS HIS MOUTH OFF.
1-7
© 1981 Washington Post Co.

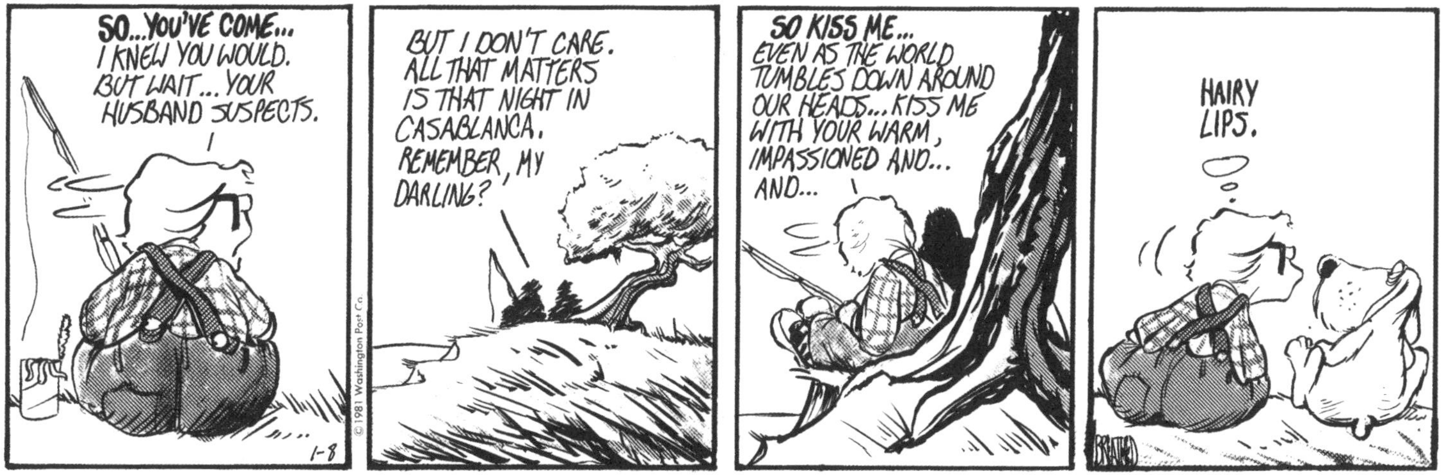
SO...YOU'VE COME... I KNEW YOU WOULD. BUT WAIT... YOUR HUSBAND SUSPECTS.
1-8
© 1981 Washington Post Co.
BUT I DON'T CARE. ALL THAT MATTERS IS THAT NIGHT IN CASABLANCA. REMEMBER, MY DARLING?
SO KISS ME... EVEN AS THE WORLD TUMBLES DOWN AROUND OUR HEADS... KISS ME WITH YOUR WARM, IMPASSIONED AND... AND...
HAIRY LIPS.

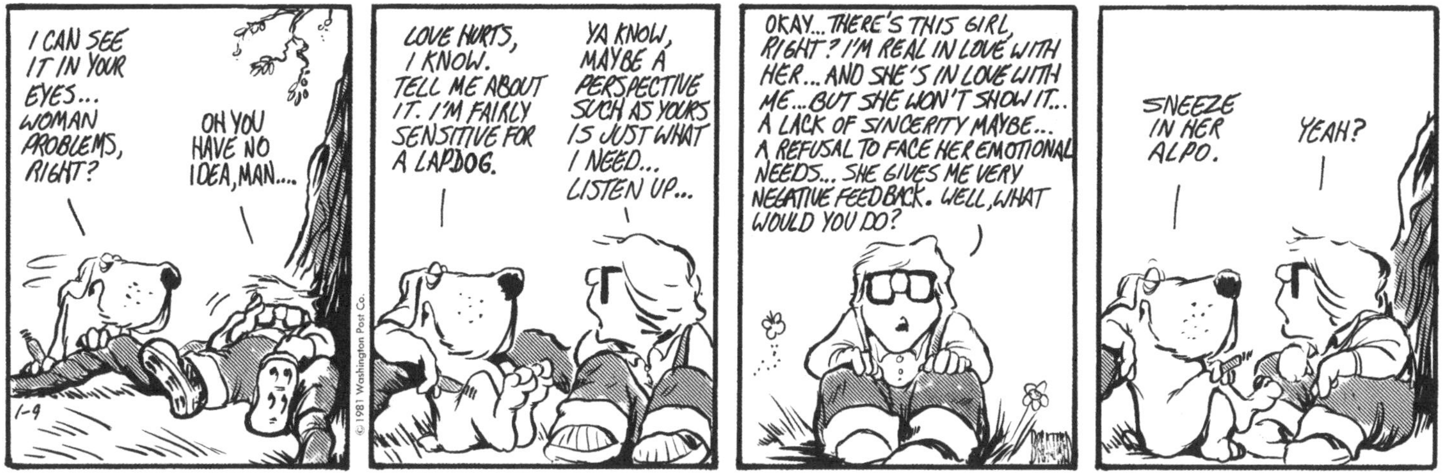
I CAN SEE IT IN YOUR EYES... WOMAN PROBLEMS, RIGHT?
OH YOU HAVE NO IDEA, MAN....
1-9
© 1981 Washington Post Co.
LOVE HURTS, I KNOW. TELL ME ABOUT IT. I'M FAIRLY SENSITIVE FOR A LAPDOG.
YA KNOW, MAYBE A PERSPECTIVE SUCH AS YOURS IS JUST WHAT I NEED... LISTEN UP...
OKAY... THERE'S THIS GIRL, RIGHT? I'M REAL IN LOVE WITH HER... AND SHE'S IN LOVE WITH ME... BUT SHE WON'T SHOW IT... A LACK OF SINCERITY MAYBE... A REFUSAL TO FACE HER EMOTIONAL NEEDS... SHE GIVES ME VERY NEGATIVE FEEDBACK. WELL, WHAT WOULD YOU DO?
SNEEZE IN HER ALPO.
YEAH?

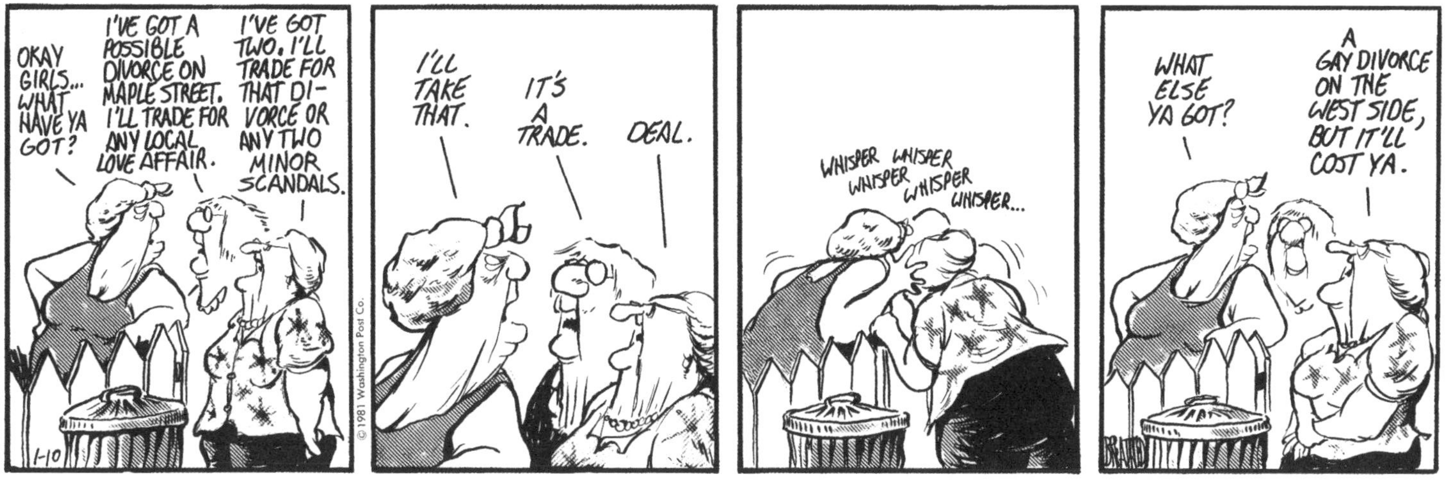
OKAY GIRLS... WHAT HAVE YA GOT?
I'VE GOT A POSSIBLE DIVORCE ON MAPLE STREET. I'LL TRADE FOR ANY LOCAL LOVE AFFAIR.
I'VE GOT TWO. I'LL TRADE FOR THAT DI-VORCE OR ANY TWO MINOR SCANDALS.
1-10
© 1981 Washington Post Co.
I'LL TAKE THAT.
IT'S A TRADE.
DEAL.
WHISPER WHISPER WHISPER WHISPER WHISPER...
WHAT ELSE YA GOT?
A GAY DIVORCE ON THE WEST SIDE, BUT IT'LL COST YA.

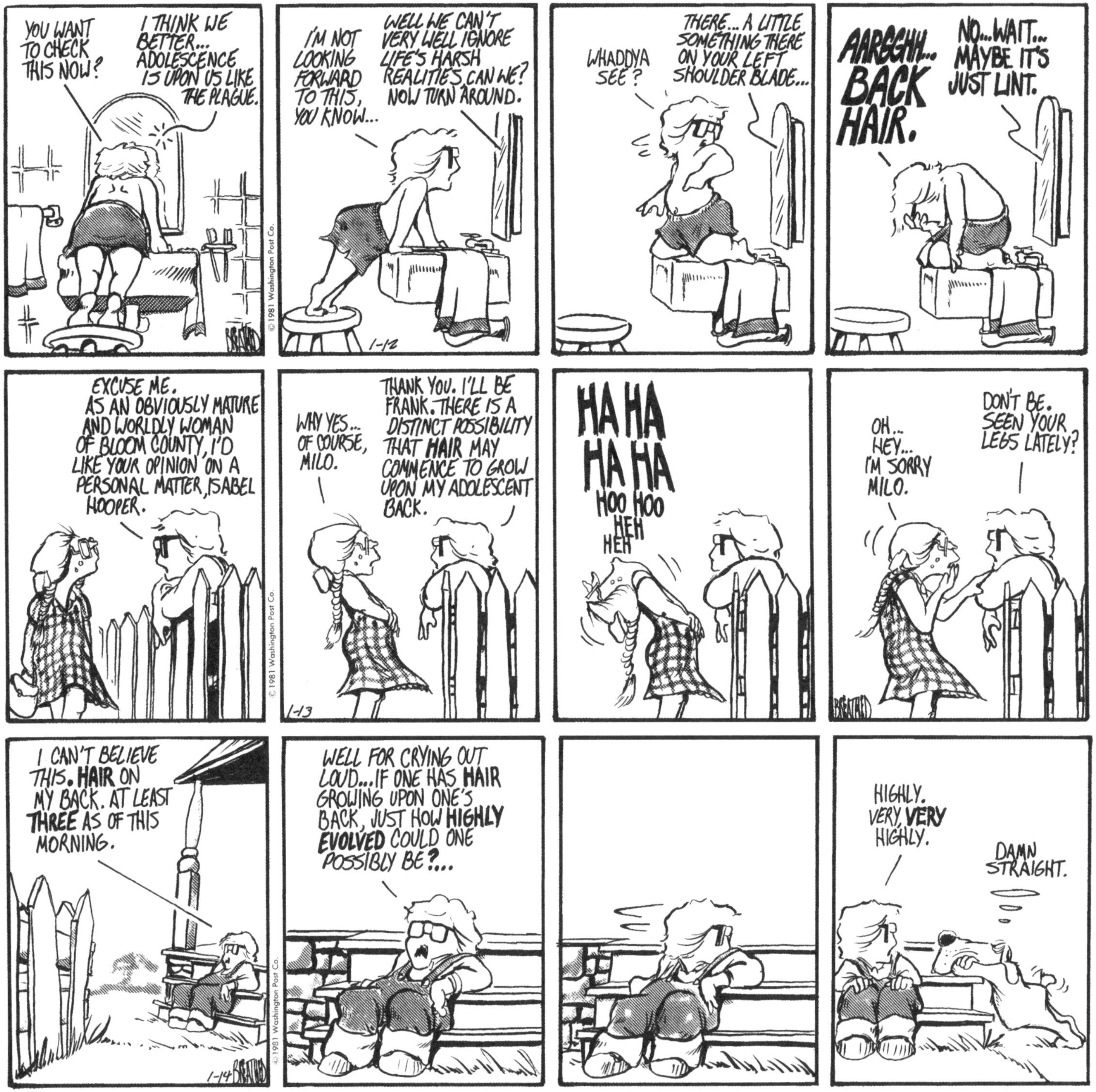
YOU WANT TO CHECK THIS NOW?
I THINK WE BETTER... ADOLESCENCE IS UPON US LIKE THE PLAGUE.
I'M NOT LOOKING FORWARD TO THIS, YOU KNOW...
WELL WE CAN'T VERY WELL IGNORE LIFE'S HARSH REALITIES, CAN WE? NOW TURN AROUND.
WHADDYA SEE?
THERE... A LITTLE SOMETHING THERE ON YOUR LEFT SHOULDER BLADE...
AARGGHH... BACK HAIR.
NO...WAIT... MAYBE IT'S JUST LINT.
1-12
© 1981 Washington Post Co.
EXCUSE ME. AS AN OBVIOUSLY MATURE AND WORLDLY WOMAN OF BLOOM COUNTY, I'D LIKE YOUR OPINION ON A PERSONAL MATTER, ISABEL HOOPER.
WHY YES... OF COURSE, MILO.
THANK YOU. I'LL BE FRANK. THERE IS A DISTINCT POSSIBILITY THAT HAIR MAY COMMENCE TO GROW UPON MY ADOLESCENT BACK.
HA HA HA HA HOO HOO HEH HEH
OH... HEY... I'M SORRY MILO.
DON'T BE. SEEN YOUR LEGS LATELY?
1-13
© 1981 Washington Post Co.
I CAN'T BELIEVE THIS. HAIR ON MY BACK. AT LEAST THREE AS OF THIS MORNING.
WELL FOR CRYING OUT LOUD... IF ONE HAS HAIR GROWING UPON ONE'S BACK, JUST HOW HIGHLY EVOLVED COULD ONE POSSIBLY BE?...
HIGHLY. VERY, VERY HIGHLY.
DAMN STRAIGHT.
1-14
© 1981 Washington Post Co.

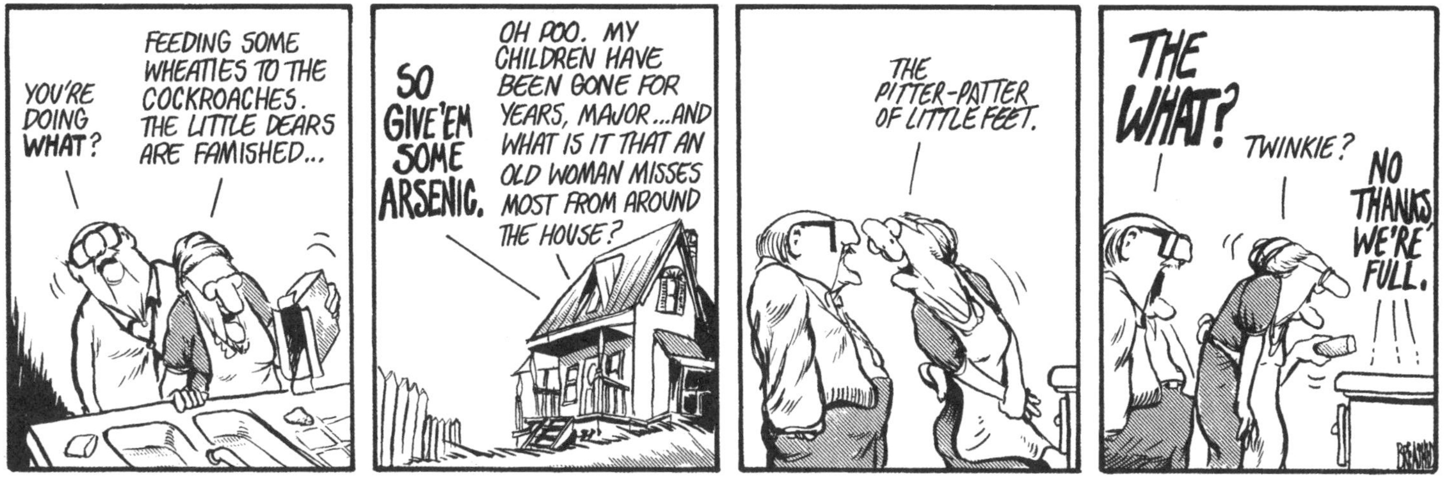
YOU'RE DOING WHAT?
FEEDING SOME WHEATIES TO THE COCKROACHES. THE LITTLE DEARS ARE FAMISHED...
SO GIVE'EM SOME ARSENIC.
OH POO. MY CHILDREN HAVE BEEN GONE FOR YEARS, MAJOR...AND WHAT IS IT THAT AN OLD WOMAN MISSES MOST FROM AROUND THE HOUSE?
THE PITTER-PATTER OF LITTLE FEET.
THE WHAT?
TWINKIE?
NO THANKS, WE'RE FULL.
BREATHED

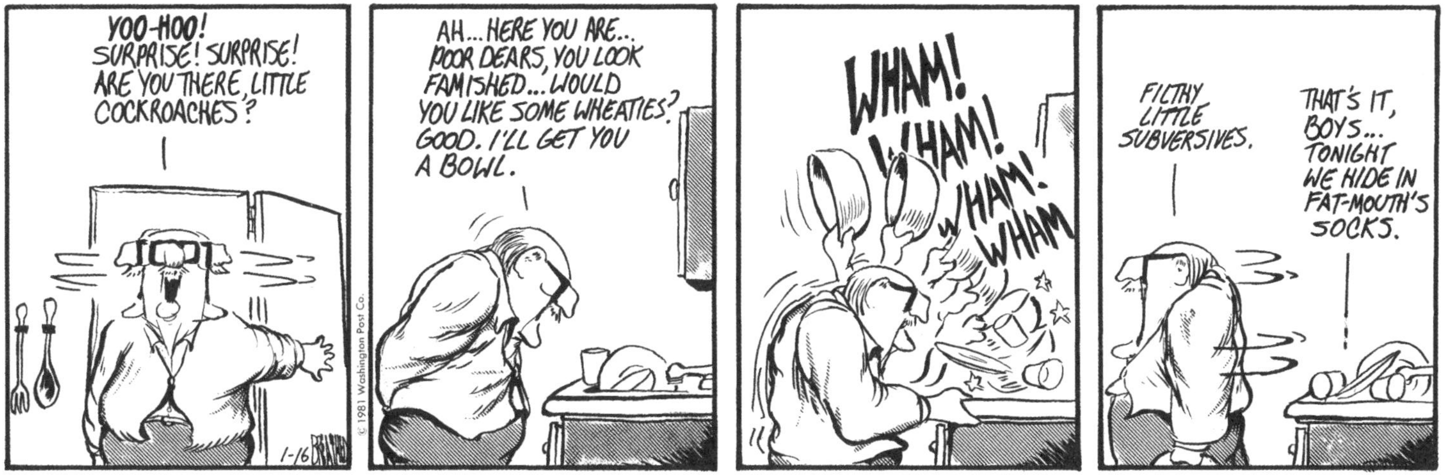
YOO-HOO! SURPRISE! SURPRISE! ARE YOU THERE, LITTLE COCKROACHES?
1-16 BREATHED
© 1981 Washington Post Co.
AH...HERE YOU ARE... POOR DEARS, YOU LOOK FAMISHED...WOULD YOU LIKE SOME WHEATIES? GOOD. I'LL GET YOU A BOWL.
WHAM! WHAM! WHAM! WHAM
FILTHY LITTLE SUBVERSIVES.
THAT'S IT, BOYS... TONIGHT WE HIDE IN FAT-MOUTH'S SOCKS.

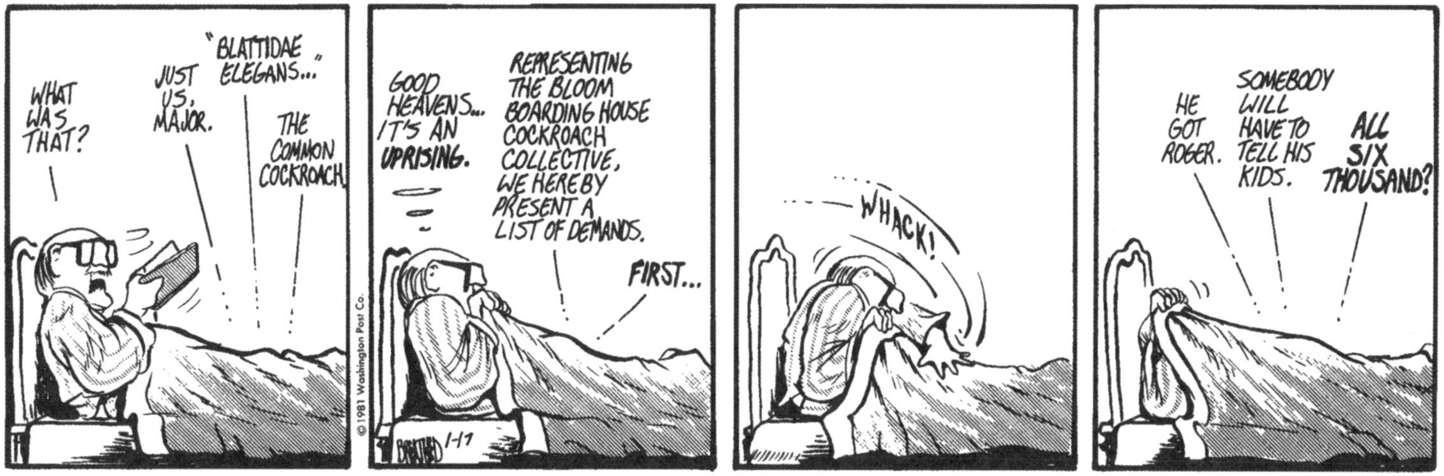
WHAT WAS THAT?
JUST US, MAJOR.
"BLATTIDAE ELEGANS..."
THE COMMON COCKROACH
© 1981 Washington Post Co.
GOOD HEAVENS... IT'S AN UPRISING.
REPRESENTING THE BLOOM BOARDING HOUSE COCKROACH COLLECTIVE, WE HEREBY PRESENT A LIST OF DEMANDS.
FIRST...
BREATHED 1-17
WHACK!
HE GOT ROGER.
SOMEBODY WILL HAVE TO TELL HIS KIDS.
ALL SIX THOUSAND?

General George S. Patton was renowned for his bravado both on and off the field of battle during World War II.

J. Edgar Hoover was the first director of the FBI and served in that capacity for nearly fifty years.

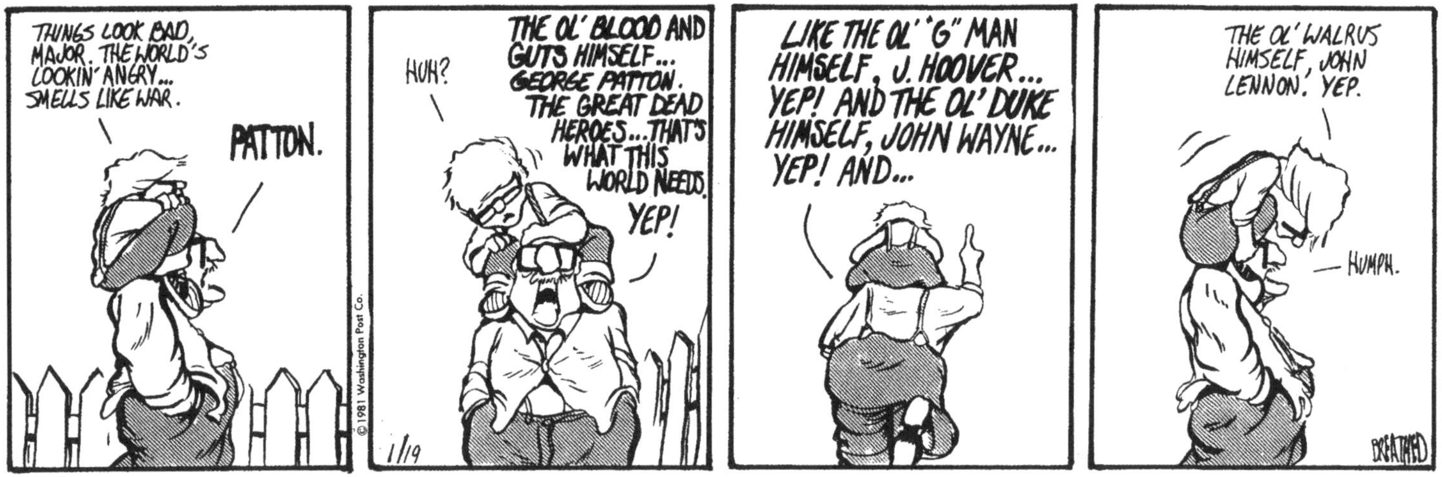
THINGS LOOK BAD, MAJOR. THE WORLD'S LOOKIN' ANGRY... SMELLS LIKE WAR.
PATTON.
HUH?
THE OL' BLOOD AND GUTS HIMSELF... GEORGE PATTON. THE GREAT DEAD HEROES... THAT'S WHAT THIS WORLD NEEDS.
YEP!
LIKE THE OL' "G" MAN HIMSELF, J. HOOVER... YEP! AND THE OL' DUKE HIMSELF, JOHN WAYNE... YEP! AND...
THE OL' WALRUS HIMSELF, JOHN LENNON. YEP.
HUMPH.
© 1981 Washington Post Co.
1/19
BREATHED

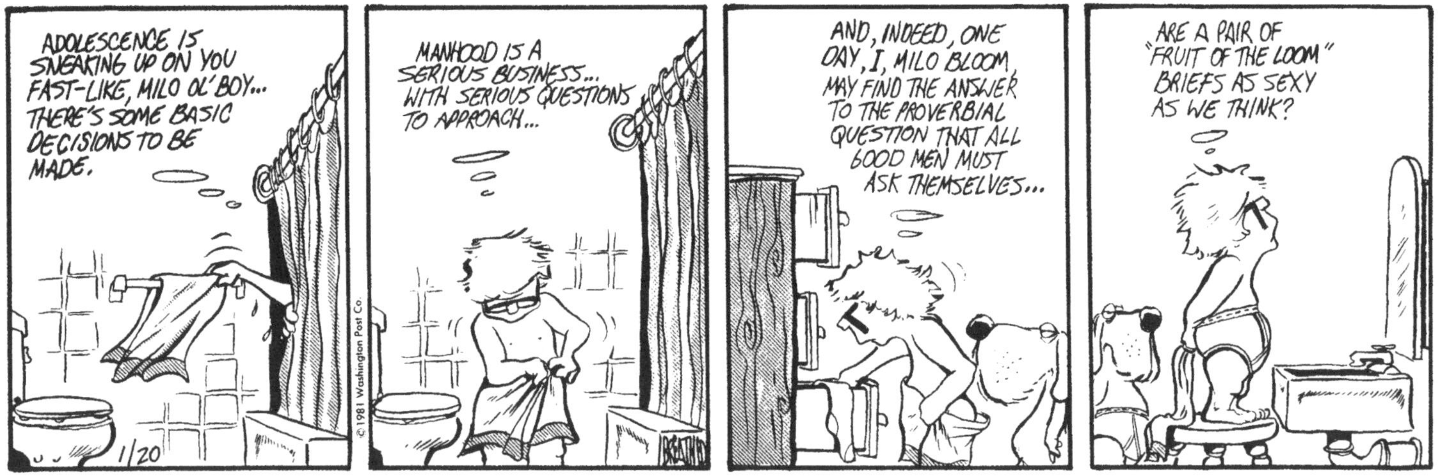
ADOLESCENCE IS SNEAKING UP ON YOU FAST-LIKE, MILO OL' BOY... THERE'S SOME BASIC DECISIONS TO BE MADE.
MANHOOD IS A SERIOUS BUSINESS... WITH SERIOUS QUESTIONS TO APPROACH...
AND, INDEED, ONE DAY, I, MILO BLOOM, MAY FIND THE ANSWER TO THE PROVERBIAL QUESTION THAT ALL GOOD MEN MUST ASK THEMSELVES...
ARE A PAIR OF "FRUIT OF THE LOOM" BRIEFS AS SEXY AS WE THINK?
1/20
© 1981 Washington Post Co.
BREATHED

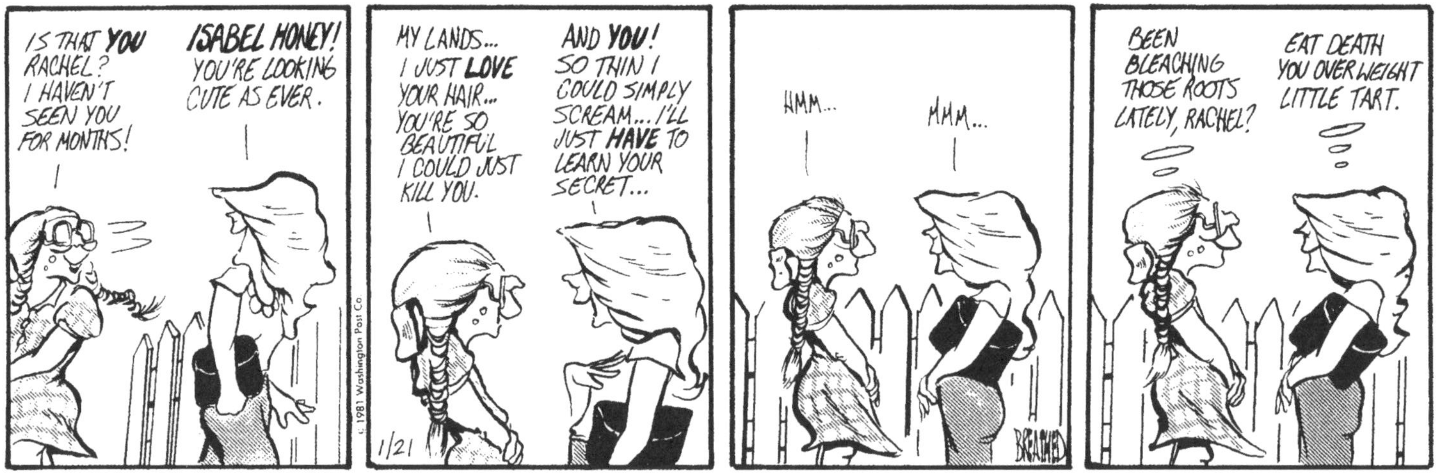
IS THAT YOU RACHEL? I HAVEN'T SEEN YOU FOR MONTHS!
ISABEL HONEY! YOU'RE LOOKING CUTE AS EVER.
MY LANDS... I JUST LOVE YOUR HAIR... YOU'RE SO BEAUTIFUL I COULD JUST KILL YOU.
AND YOU! SO THIN I COULD SIMPLY SCREAM... I'LL JUST HAVE TO LEARN YOUR SECRET...
HMM...
MMM...
BEEN BLEACHING THOSE ROOTS LATELY, RACHEL?
EAT DEATH YOU OVERWEIGHT LITTLE TART.
© 1981 Washington Post Co.
1/21
BREATHED

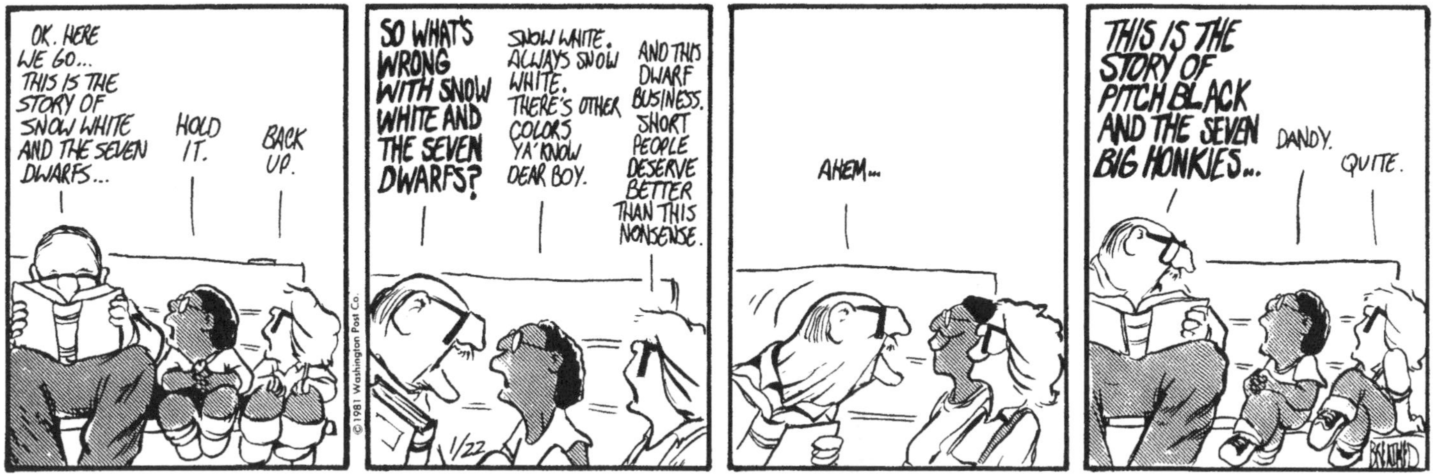
OK. HERE WE GO... THIS IS THE STORY OF SNOW WHITE AND THE SEVEN DWARFS...
HOLD IT.
BACK UP.
SO WHAT'S WRONG WITH SNOW WHITE AND THE SEVEN DWARFS?
SNOW WHITE. ALWAYS SNOW WHITE. THERE'S OTHER COLORS YA' KNOW DEAR BOY.
AND THIS DWARF BUSINESS. SHORT PEOPLE DESERVE BETTER THAN THIS NONSENSE.
©1981 Washington Post Co.
1/22
AHEM...
THIS IS THE STORY OF PITCH BLACK AND THE SEVEN BIG HONKIES...
DANDY.
QUITE.

Couldn't do this strip today. I have a lot of these ahead. Try to spot 'em. —BB

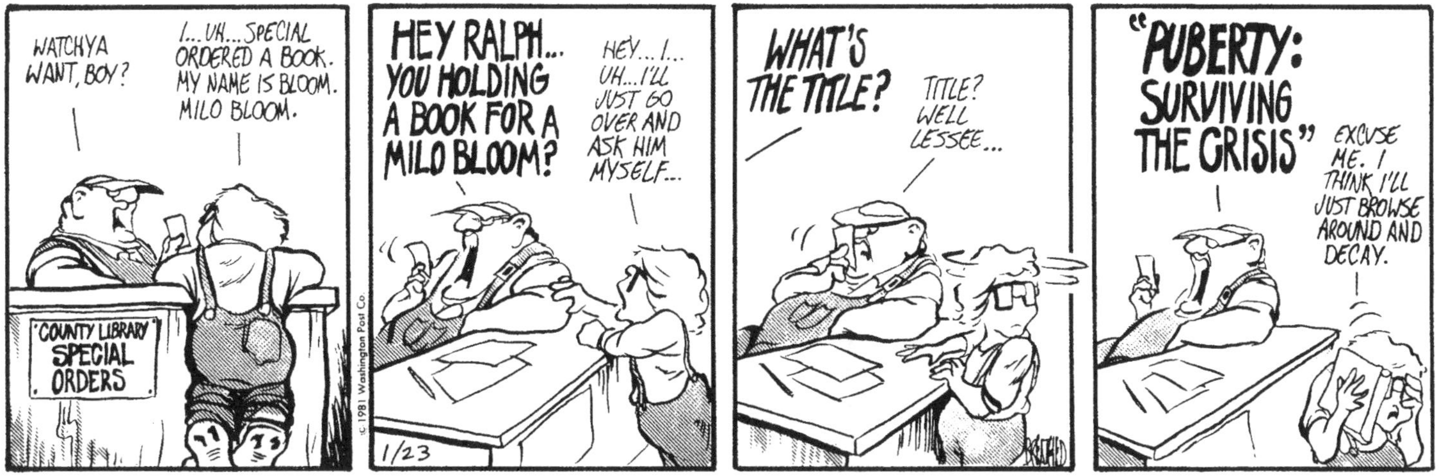
WATCHYA WANT, BOY?
I... UH... SPECIAL ORDERED A BOOK. MY NAME IS BLOOM. MILO BLOOM.
COUNTY LIBRARY
SPECIAL ORDERS
©1981 Washington Post Co.
1/23
HEY RALPH... YOU HOLDING A BOOK FOR A MILO BLOOM?
HEY... I... UH... I'LL JUST GO OVER AND ASK HIM MYSELF...
WHAT'S THE TITLE?
TITLE? WELL LESSEE...
"PUBERTY: SURVIVING THE CRISIS"
EXCUSE ME. I THINK I'LL JUST BROWSE AROUND AND DECAY.

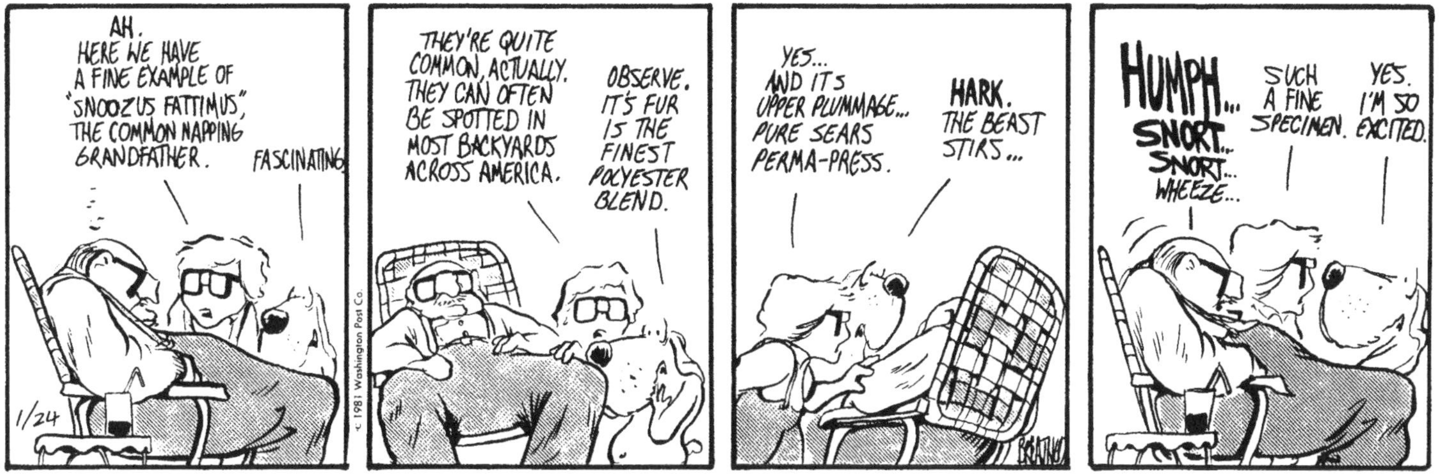
AH. HERE WE HAVE A FINE EXAMPLE OF "SNOOZUS FATTIMUS", THE COMMON NAPPING GRANDFATHER.
FASCINATING.
1/24
©1981 Washington Post Co.
THEY'RE QUITE COMMON, ACTUALLY. THEY CAN OFTEN BE SPOTTED IN MOST BACKYARDS ACROSS AMERICA.
OBSERVE. IT'S FUR IS THE FINEST POLYESTER BLEND.
YES... AND ITS UPPER PLUMMAGE... PURE SEARS PERMA-PRESS.
HARK. THE BEAST STIRS...
HUMPH... SNORT... SNORT... WHEEZE...
SUCH A FINE SPECIMEN.
YES. I'M SO EXCITED.

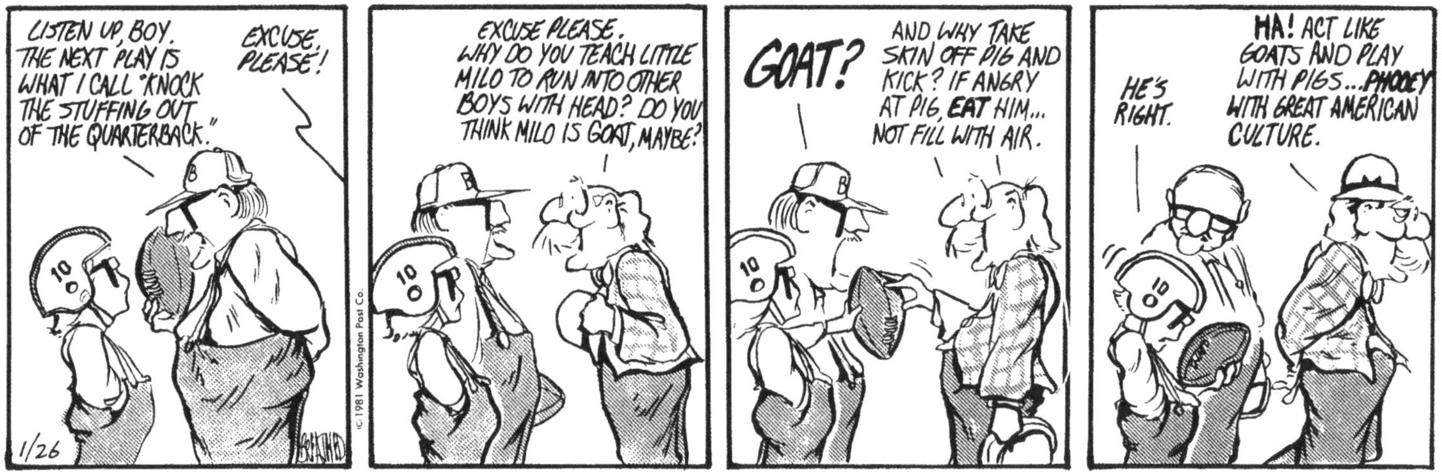
LISTEN UP, BOY. THE NEXT PLAY IS WHAT I CALL "KNOCK THE STUFFING OUT OF THE QUARTERBACK."
EXCUSE, PLEASE!
1/26
© 1981 Washington Post Co.
EXCUSE PLEASE. WHY DO YOU TEACH LITTLE MILO TO RUN INTO OTHER BOYS WITH HEAD? DO YOU THINK MILO IS GOAT, MAYBE?
GOAT?
AND WHY TAKE SKIN OFF PIG AND KICK? IF ANGRY AT PIG, EAT HIM... NOT FILL WITH AIR.
HE'S RIGHT.
HA! ACT LIKE GOATS AND PLAY WITH PIGS...PHOOEY WITH GREAT AMERICAN CULTURE.

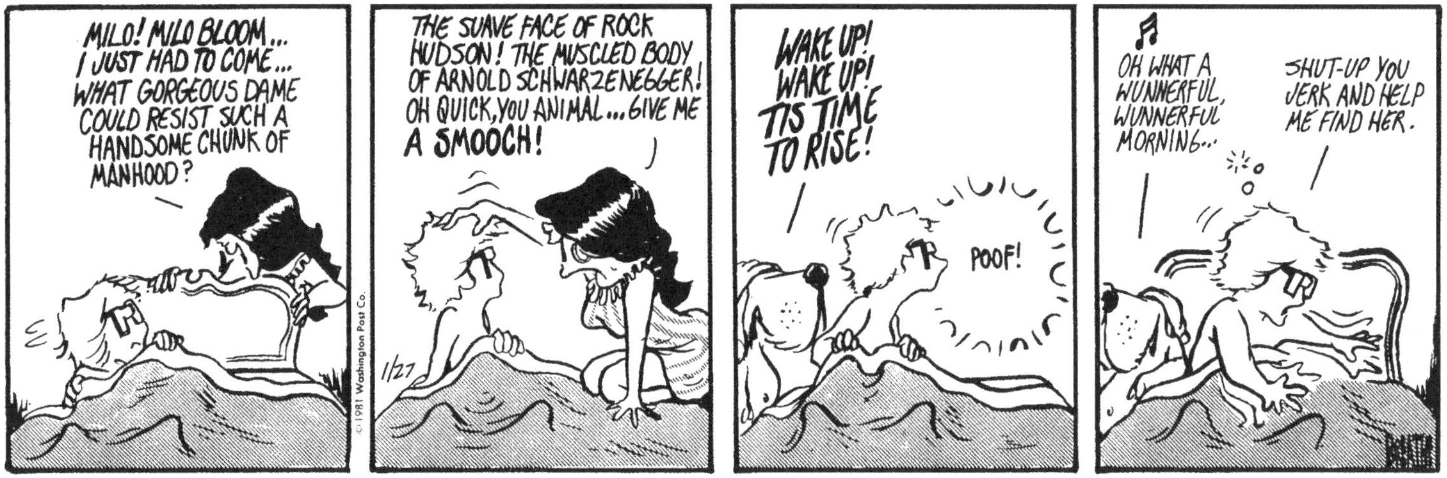
MILO! MILO BLOOM... I JUST HAD TO COME... WHAT GORGEOUS DAME COULD RESIST SUCH A HANDSOME CHUNK OF MANHOOD?
© 1981 Washington Post Co.
1/27
THE SUAVE FACE OF ROCK HUDSON! THE MUSCLED BODY OF ARNOLD SCHWARZENEGGER! OH QUICK, YOU ANIMAL... GIVE ME A SMOOCH!
WAKE UP! WAKE UP! TIS TIME TO RISE!
POOF!
OH WHAT A WUNNERFUL, WUNNERFUL MORNING...
SHUT-UP YOU JERK AND HELP ME FIND HER.

Rock Hudson was a matinee idol who starred in many romantic comedies of the 1950s and 1960s.

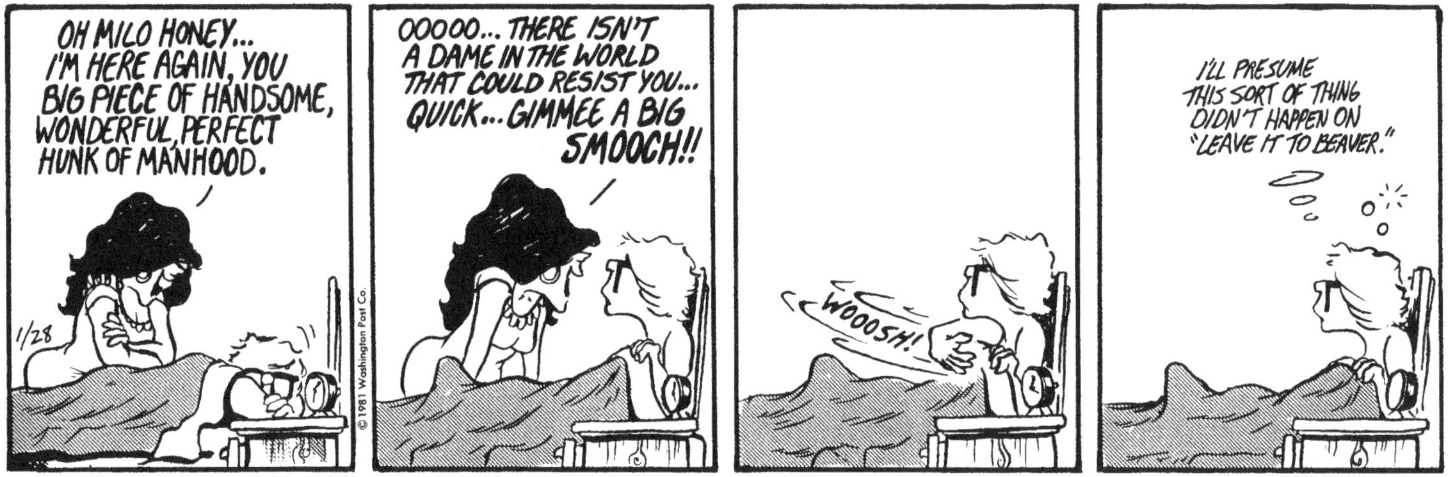
OH MILO HONEY... I'M HERE AGAIN, YOU BIG PIECE OF HANDSOME, WONDERFUL, PERFECT HUNK OF MANHOOD.
1/28
© 1981 Washington Post Co.
OOOOO... THERE ISN'T A DAME IN THE WORLD THAT COULD RESIST YOU... QUICK... GIMMEE A BIG SMOOCH!!
WOOOSH!
I'LL PRESUME THIS SORT OF THING DIDN'T HAPPEN ON "LEAVE IT TO BEAVER."

Leave it to Beaver was a popular 1950s sitcom.

An early pop-culture reference here with Leave It To Beaver. *Hard to imagine now…but this essentially was wholly unique to the American comic page in 1981. Newspaper editors were a bit flummoxed by it. They weren't even sure it was legal. Having never read a comic page, I hadn't the foggiest notion that this was something new. I was only getting started, of course. —BB*

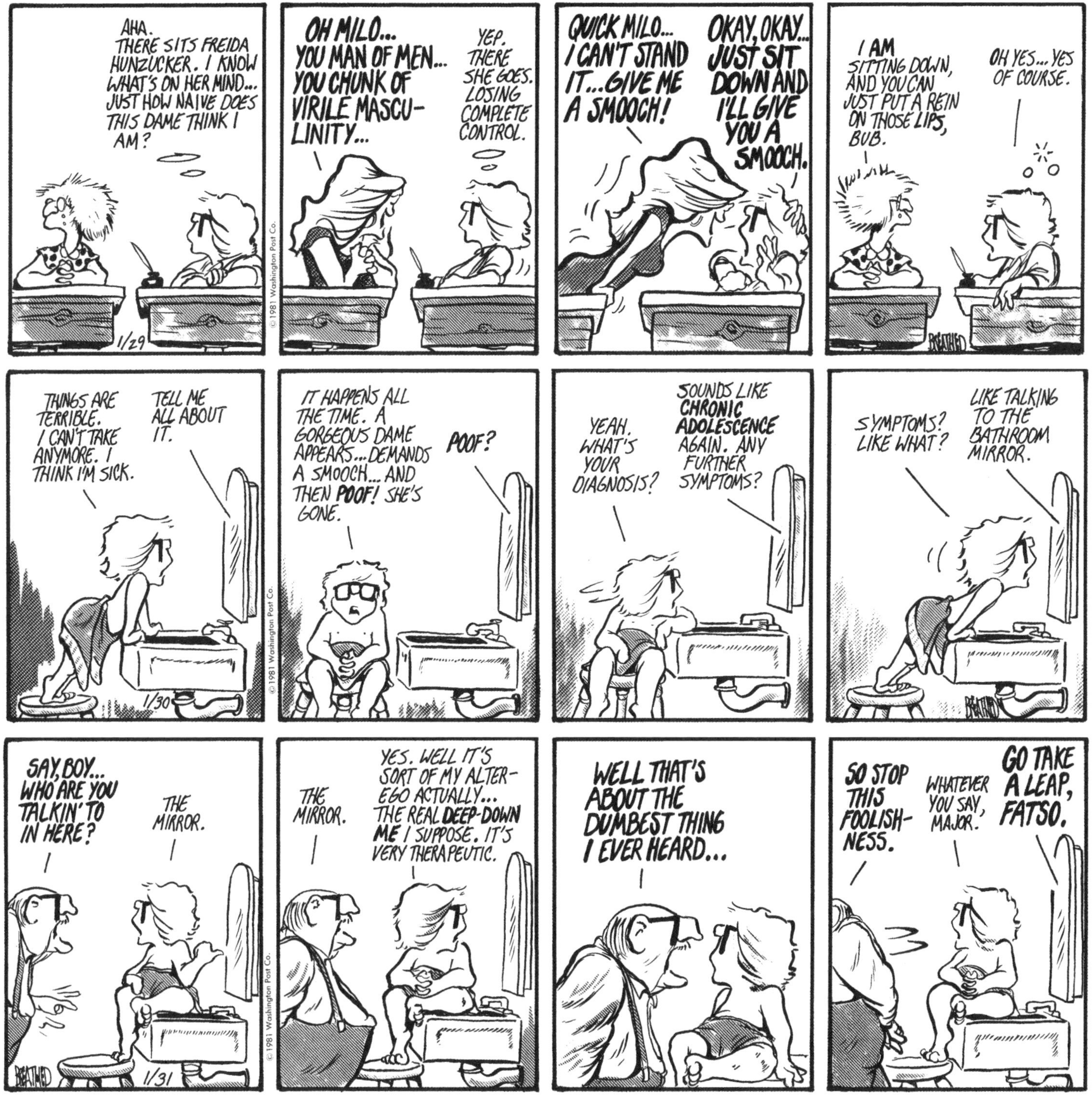
AHA. THERE SITS FREIDA HUNZUCKER. I KNOW WHAT'S ON HER MIND... JUST HOW NAIVE DOES THIS DAME THINK I AM?
1/29
OH MILO... YOU MAN OF MEN... YOU CHUNK OF VIRILE MASCU-LINITY...
YEP. THERE SHE GOES. LOSING COMPLETE CONTROL.
© 1981 Washington Post Co.
QUICK MILO... I CAN'T STAND IT...GIVE ME A SMOOCH!
OKAY, OKAY... JUST SIT DOWN AND I'LL GIVE YOU A SMOOCH.
I AM SITTING DOWN, AND YOU CAN JUST PUT A REIN ON THOSE LIPS, BUB.
OH YES... YES OF COURSE.
BREATHED
THINGS ARE TERRIBLE. I CAN'T TAKE ANYMORE. I THINK I'M SICK.
TELL ME ALL ABOUT IT.
1/30
IT HAPPENS ALL THE TIME. A GORGEOUS DAME APPEARS... DEMANDS A SMOOCH... AND THEN POOF! SHE'S GONE.
POOF?
© 1981 Washington Post Co.
YEAH. WHAT'S YOUR DIAGNOSIS?
SOUNDS LIKE CHRONIC ADOLESCENCE AGAIN. ANY FURTHER SYMPTOMS?
SYMPTOMS? LIKE WHAT?
LIKE TALKING TO THE BATHROOM MIRROR.
BREATHED
SAY, BOY... WHO ARE YOU TALKIN' TO IN HERE?
THE MIRROR.
BREATHED
1/31
THE MIRROR.
YES. WELL IT'S SORT OF MY ALTER-EGO ACTUALLY... THE REAL DEEP-DOWN ME I SUPPOSE. IT'S VERY THERAPEUTIC.
© 1981 Washington Post Co.
WELL THAT'S ABOUT THE DUMBEST THING I EVER HEARD...
SO STOP THIS FOOLISH-NESS.
WHATEVER YOU SAY, MAJOR.
GO TAKE A LEAP, FATSO.

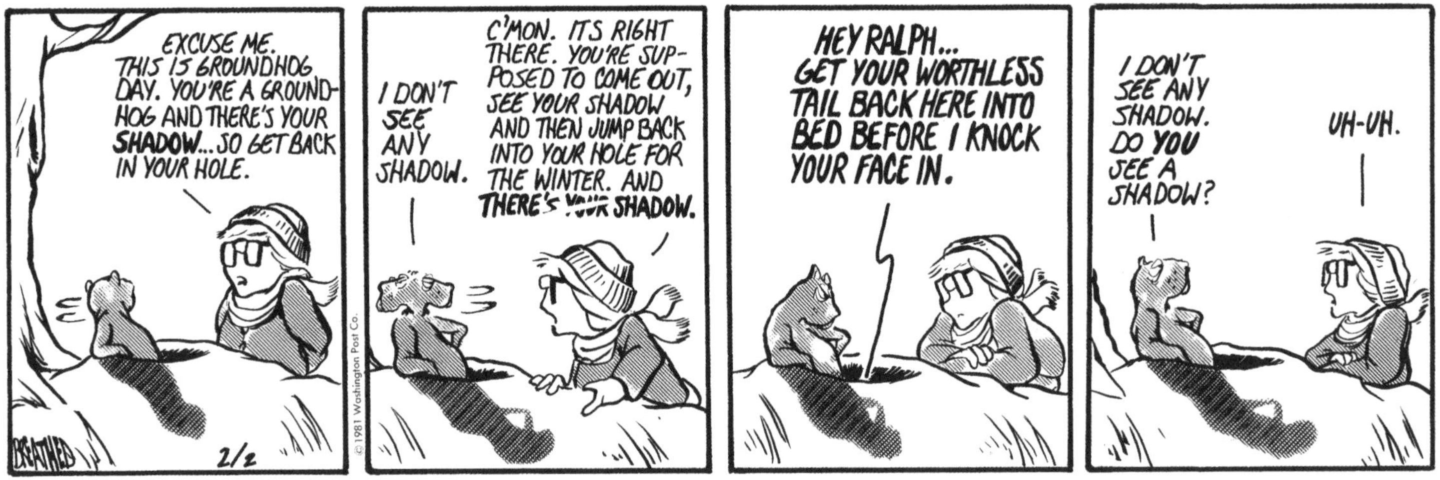
EXCUSE ME. THIS IS GROUNDHOG DAY. YOU'RE A GROUNDHOG AND THERE'S YOUR SHADOW... SO GET BACK IN YOUR HOLE.
I DON'T SEE ANY SHADOW.
C'MON. ITS RIGHT THERE. YOU'RE SUPPOSED TO COME OUT, SEE YOUR SHADOW AND THEN JUMP BACK INTO YOUR HOLE FOR THE WINTER. AND THERE'S YOUR SHADOW.
HEY RALPH... GET YOUR WORTHLESS TAIL BACK HERE INTO BED BEFORE I KNOCK YOUR FACE IN.
I DON'T SEE ANY SHADOW. DO YOU SEE A SHADOW?
UH-UH.
BREATHED
2/2
© 1981 Washington Post Co.

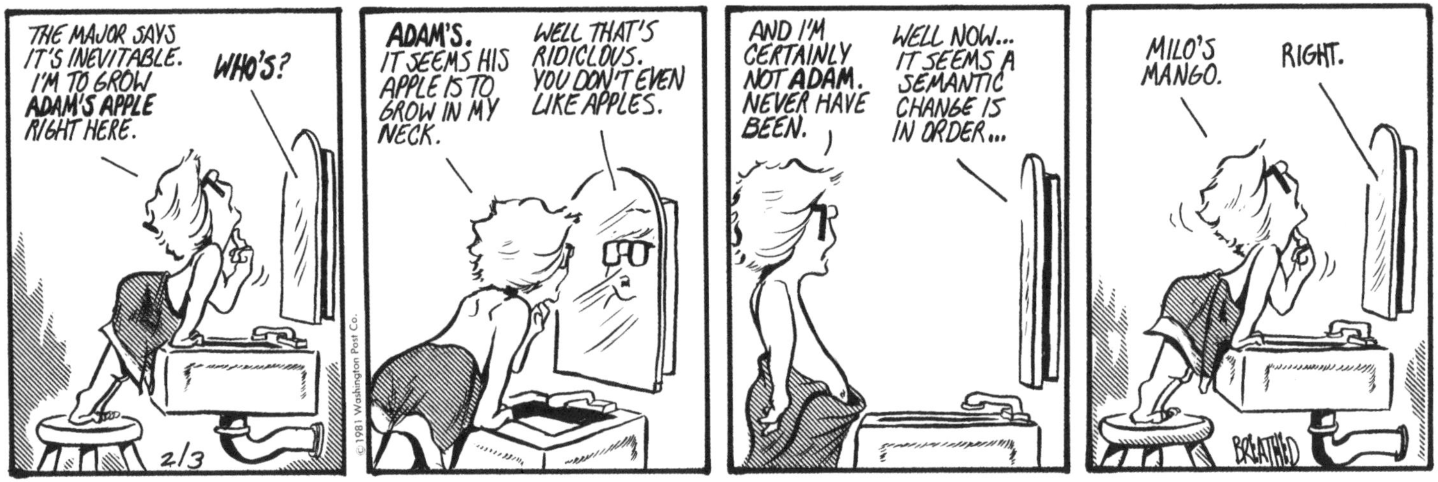
THE MAJOR SAYS IT'S INEVITABLE. I'M TO GROW ADAM'S APPLE RIGHT HERE.
WHO'S?
ADAM'S. IT SEEMS HIS APPLE IS TO GROW IN MY NECK.
WELL THAT'S RIDICLOUS. YOU DON'T EVEN LIKE APPLES.
AND I'M CERTAINLY NOT ADAM. NEVER HAVE BEEN.
WELL NOW... IT SEEMS A SEMANTIC CHANGE IS IN ORDER...
MILO'S MANGO.
RIGHT.
2/3
BREATHED
© 1981 Washington Post Co.

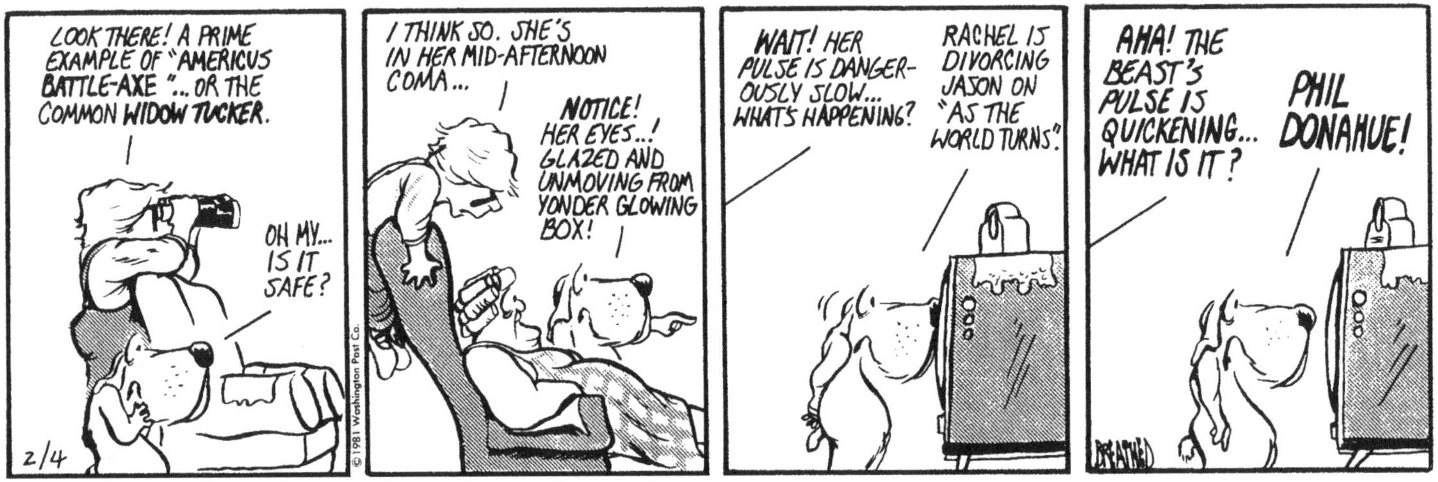
LOOK THERE! A PRIME EXAMPLE OF "AMERICUS BATTLE-AXE"... OR THE COMMON WIDOW TUCKER.
OH MY... IS IT SAFE?
I THINK SO. SHE'S IN HER MID-AFTERNOON COMA...
NOTICE! HER EYES...! GLAZED AND UNMOVING FROM YONDER GLOWING BOX!
WAIT! HER PULSE IS DANGEROUSLY SLOW... WHAT'S HAPPENING?
RACHEL IS DIVORCING JASON ON "AS THE WORLD TURNS".
AHA! THE BEAST'S PULSE IS QUICKENING... WHAT IS IT?
PHIL DONAHUE!
2/4
BREATHED
© 1981 Washington Post Co.

Phil Donahue was a popular talk show host, the Oprah of his day, whose program ran in syndication for a record 26 years.

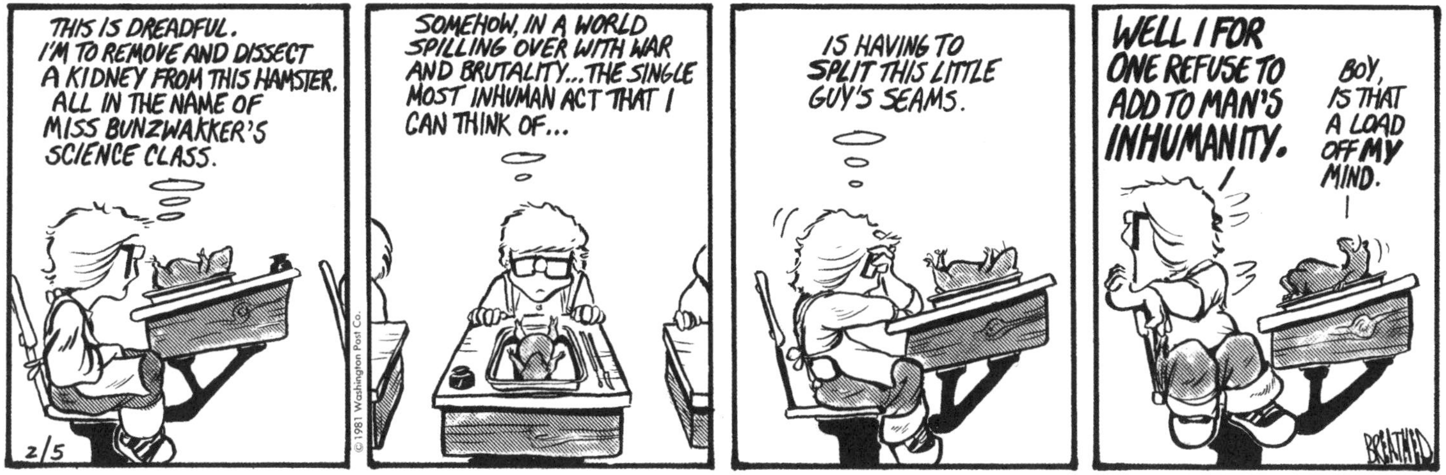
THIS IS DREADFUL. I'M TO REMOVE AND DISSECT A KIDNEY FROM THIS HAMSTER. ALL IN THE NAME OF MISS BUNZWAKKER'S SCIENCE CLASS.
2/5
© 1981 Washington Post Co.
SOMEHOW, IN A WORLD SPILLING OVER WITH WAR AND BRUTALITY... THE SINGLE MOST INHUMAN ACT THAT I CAN THINK OF...
IS HAVING TO SPLIT THIS LITTLE GUY'S SEAMS.
WELL I FOR ONE REFUSE TO ADD TO MAN'S INHUMANITY.
BOY, IS THAT A LOAD OFF MY MIND.
BREATHED

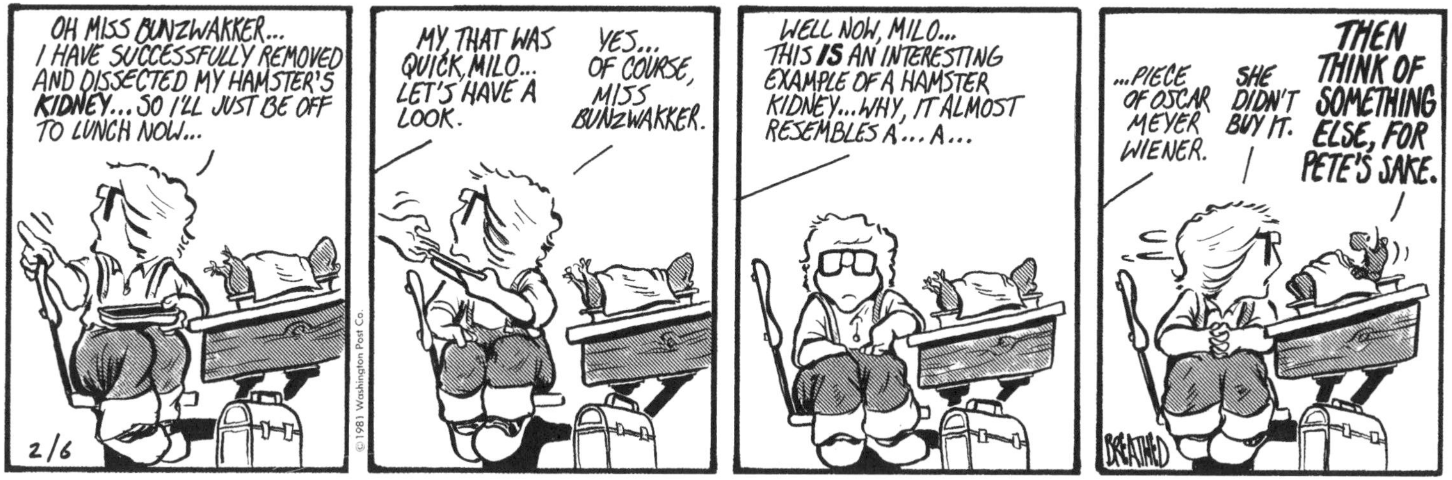
OH MISS BUNZWAKKER... I HAVE SUCCESSFULLY REMOVED AND DISSECTED MY HAMSTER'S KIDNEY... SO I'LL JUST BE OFF TO LUNCH NOW...
2/6
© 1981 Washington Post Co.
MY, THAT WAS QUICK, MILO... LET'S HAVE A LOOK.
YES... OF COURSE, MISS BUNZWAKKER.
WELL NOW, MILO... THIS IS AN INTERESTING EXAMPLE OF A HAMSTER KIDNEY... WHY, IT ALMOST RESEMBLES A... A...
...PIECE OF OSCAR MEYER WIENER.
SHE DIDN'T BUY IT.
THEN THINK OF SOMETHING ELSE, FOR PETE'S SAKE.
BREATHED

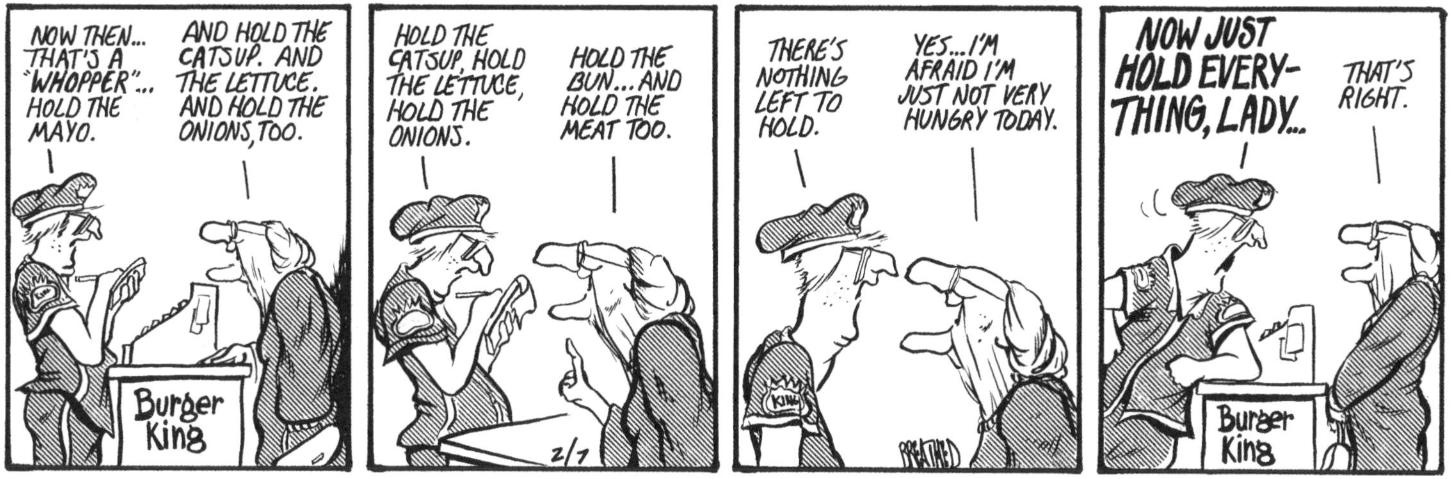
NOW THEN... THAT'S A "WHOPPER"... HOLD THE MAYO.
AND HOLD THE CATSUP. AND THE LETTUCE. AND HOLD THE ONIONS, TOO.
Burger King
HOLD THE CATSUP, HOLD THE LETTUCE, HOLD THE ONIONS.
HOLD THE BUN... AND HOLD THE MEAT TOO.
2/7
THERE'S NOTHING LEFT TO HOLD.
YES... I'M AFRAID I'M JUST NOT VERY HUNGRY TODAY.
BREATHED
NOW JUST HOLD EVERY-THING, LADY...
THAT'S RIGHT.
Burger King

Berkeley Breathed's first foray into the realm of animal rights in *Bloom County*.

February 5-7, 1981

Bella Abzug was a bombastic Democratic congresswoman from New York known for her outspoken stands on many liberal issues, including women's rights and opposition to the war in Vietnam.

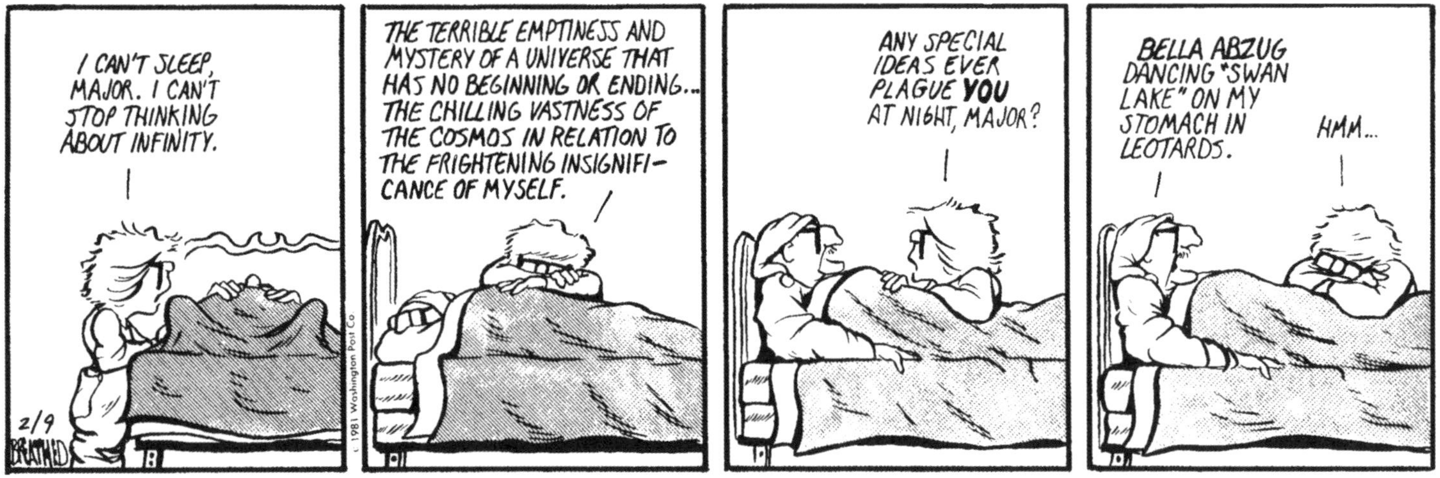
I CAN'T SLEEP, MAJOR. I CAN'T STOP THINKING ABOUT INFINITY.
2/9
BREATHED
© 1981 Washington Post Co.
THE TERRIBLE EMPTINESS AND MYSTERY OF A UNIVERSE THAT HAS NO BEGINNING OR ENDING... THE CHILLING VASTNESS OF THE COSMOS IN RELATION TO THE FRIGHTENING INSIGNIFI-CANCE OF MYSELF.
ANY SPECIAL IDEAS EVER PLAGUE **YOU** AT NIGHT, MAJOR?
BELLA ABZUG DANCING "SWAN LAKE" ON MY STOMACH IN LEOTARDS.
HMM...

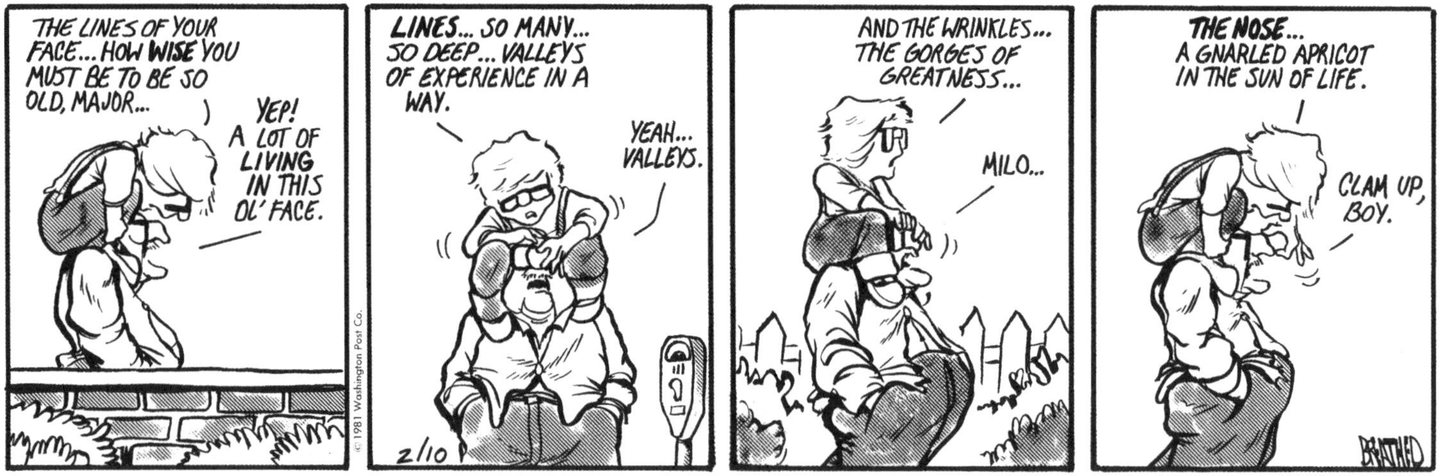
THE LINES OF YOUR FACE... HOW **WISE** YOU MUST BE TO BE SO OLD, MAJOR...
YEP! A LOT OF **LIVING** IN THIS OL' FACE.
© 1981 Washington Post Co.
LINES... SO MANY... SO DEEP... VALLEYS OF EXPERIENCE IN A WAY.
YEAH... VALLEYS.
2/10
AND THE WRINKLES... THE GORGES OF GREATNESS...
MILO...
THE NOSE... A GNARLED APRICOT IN THE SUN OF LIFE.
CLAM UP, BOY.
BREATHED

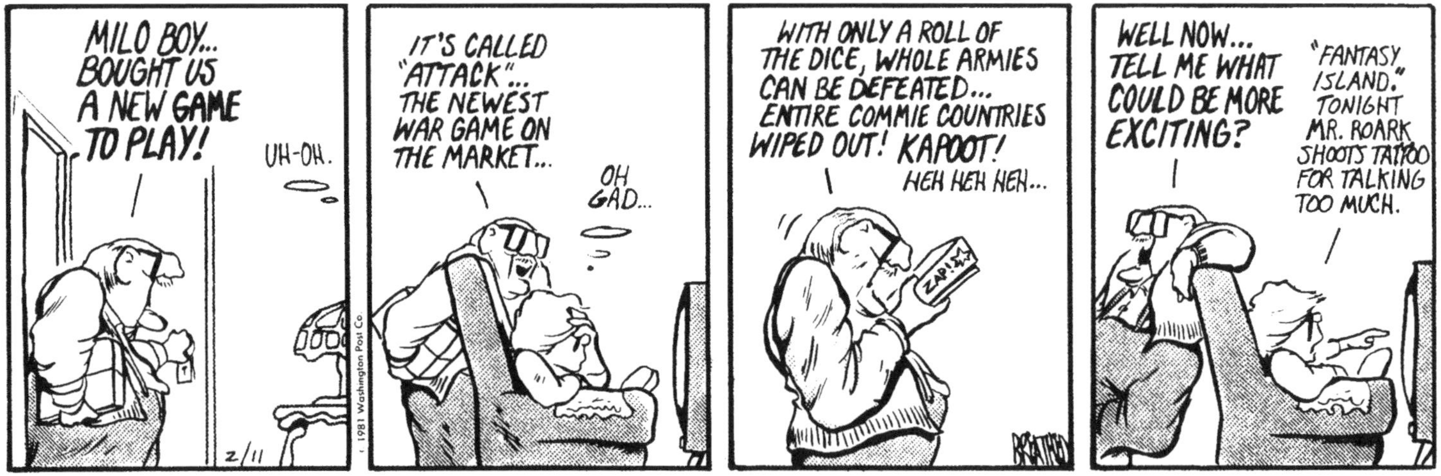
MILO BOY... BOUGHT US A NEW **GAME** TO PLAY!
UH-OH.
2/11
© 1981 Washington Post Co.
IT'S CALLED "ATTACK"... THE NEWEST WAR GAME ON THE MARKET...
OH GAD...
WITH ONLY A ROLL OF THE DICE, WHOLE ARMIES CAN BE DEFEATED... ENTIRE COMMIE COUNTRIES WIPED OUT! KAPOOT!
HEH HEH HEH...
ZAP!
BREATHED
WELL NOW... TELL ME WHAT COULD BE MORE EXCITING?
"FANTASY ISLAND." TONIGHT MR. ROARK SHOOTS TATTOO FOR TALKING TOO MUCH.

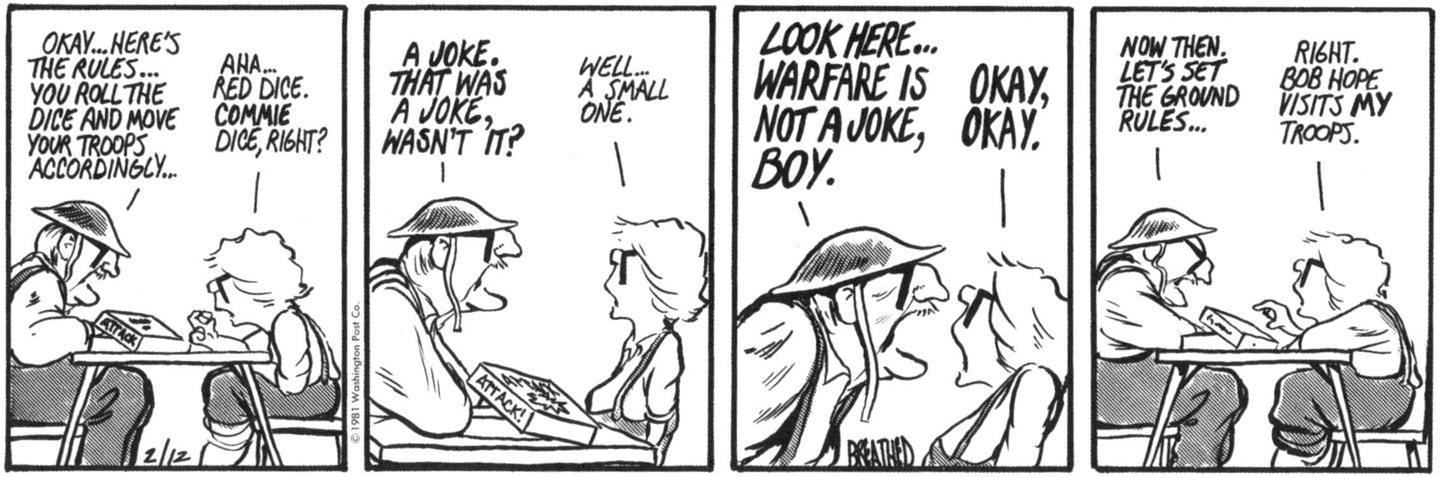
OKAY... HERE'S THE RULES... YOU ROLL THE DICE AND MOVE YOUR TROOPS ACCORDINGLY...
AHA... RED DICE. COMMIE DICE, RIGHT?
ATTACK
2/12
© 1981 Washington Post Co.
A JOKE. THAT WAS A JOKE, WASN'T IT?
WELL... A SMALL ONE.
ATTACK!
LOOK HERE... WARFARE IS NOT A JOKE, BOY.
OKAY, OKAY.
BREATHED
NOW THEN. LET'S SET THE GROUND RULES...
RIGHT. BOB HOPE VISITS MY TROOPS.

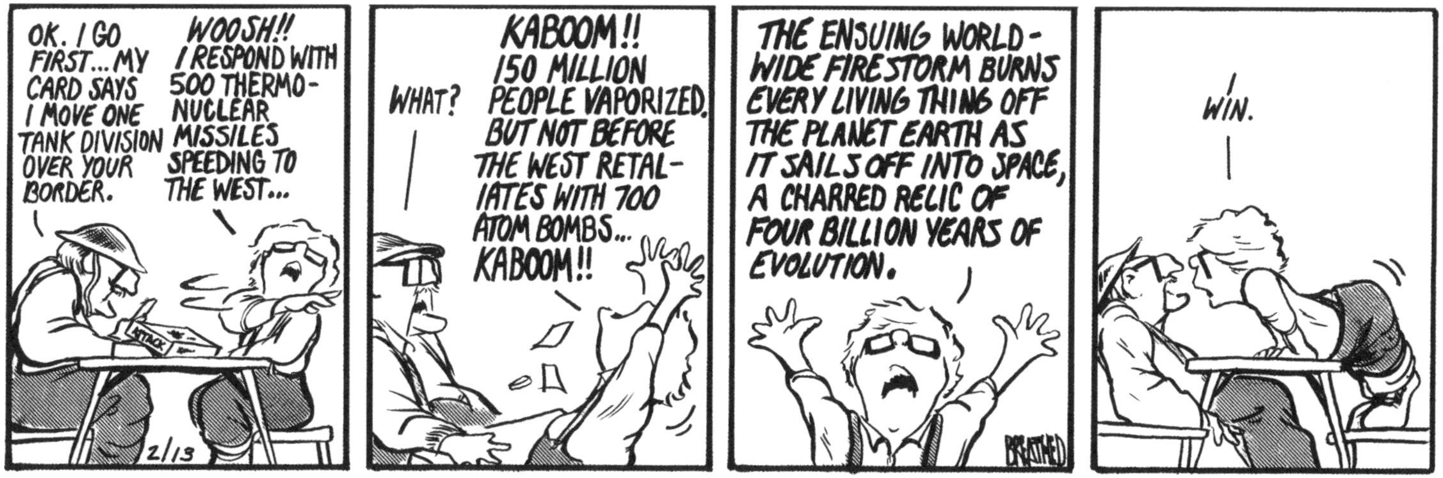
OK. I GO FIRST... MY CARD SAYS I MOVE ONE TANK DIVISION OVER YOUR BORDER.
WOOSH!! I RESPOND WITH 500 THERMO-NUCLEAR MISSILES SPEEDING TO THE WEST...
ATTACK
2/13
WHAT?
KABOOM!! 150 MILLION PEOPLE VAPORIZED. BUT NOT BEFORE THE WEST RETAL-IATES WITH 700 ATOM BOMBS... KABOOM!!
THE ENSUING WORLD-WIDE FIRESTORM BURNS EVERY LIVING THING OFF THE PLANET EARTH AS IT SAILS OFF INTO SPACE, A CHARRED RELIC OF FOUR BILLION YEARS OF EVOLUTION.
BREATHED
I WIN.

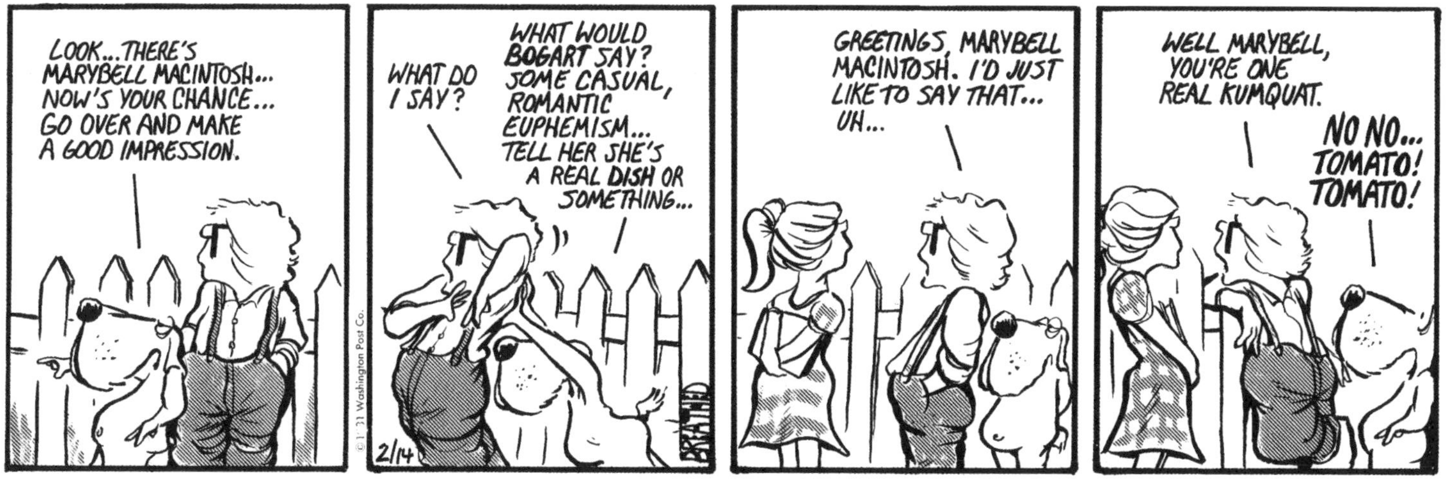
LOOK... THERE'S MARYBELL MACINTOSH... NOW'S YOUR CHANCE... GO OVER AND MAKE A GOOD IMPRESSION.
WHAT DO I SAY?
WHAT WOULD BOGART SAY? SOME CASUAL, ROMANTIC EUPHEMISM... TELL HER SHE'S A REAL DISH OR SOMETHING...
2/14
BREATHED
GREETINGS, MARYBELL MACINTOSH. I'D JUST LIKE TO SAY THAT... UH...
WELL MARYBELL, YOU'RE ONE REAL KUMQUAT.
NO NO... TOMATO! TOMATO!

Humphrey Bogart, a major film star of the '30s, '40s and '50s, played tough yet romantic leading men. Best known for his role as Rick Blaine, the saloon owner with a past in *Casablanca*, and as private eye Sam Spade in *The Maltese Falcon*.

Betty Crocker, introduced in the early 1920s, is the fictional and iconic face of General Mills. In 1945, Betty was named the second most popular woman in America, beaten only by First Lady Eleanor Roosevelt.

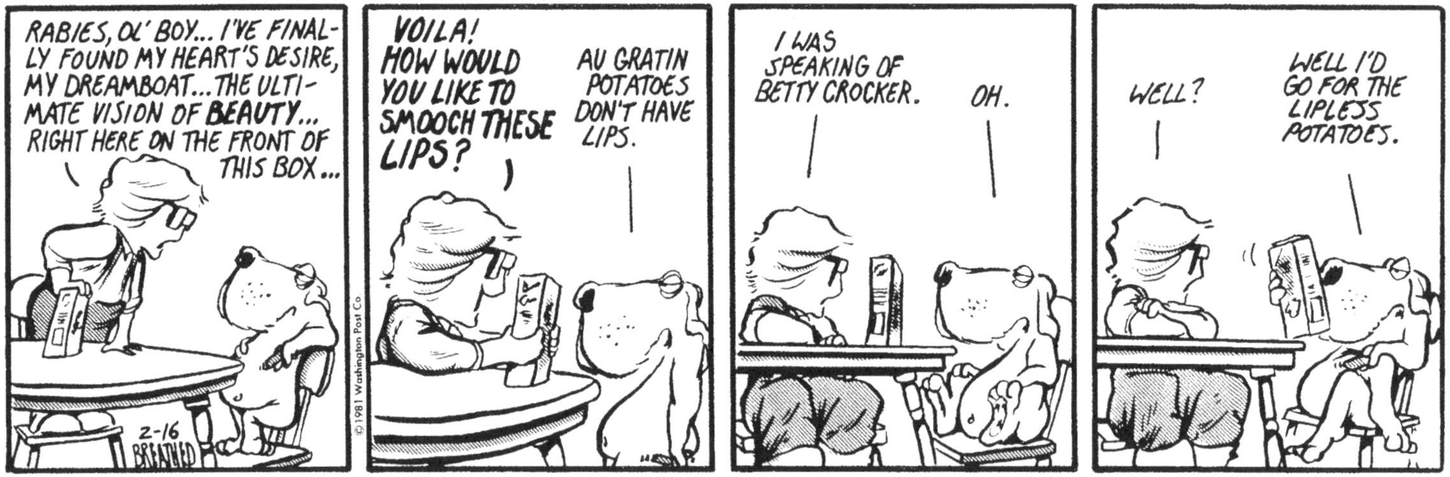

RABIES, OL' BOY... I'VE FINALLY FOUND MY HEART'S DESIRE, MY DREAMBOAT... THE ULTIMATE VISION OF BEAUTY... RIGHT HERE ON THE FRONT OF THIS BOX...
2-16
BREATHED
VOILA! HOW WOULD YOU LIKE TO SMOOCH THESE LIPS?
AU GRATIN POTATOES DON'T HAVE LIPS.
© 1981 Washington Post Co.
I WAS SPEAKING OF BETTY CROCKER.
OH.
WELL?
WELL I'D GO FOR THE LIPLESS POTATOES.

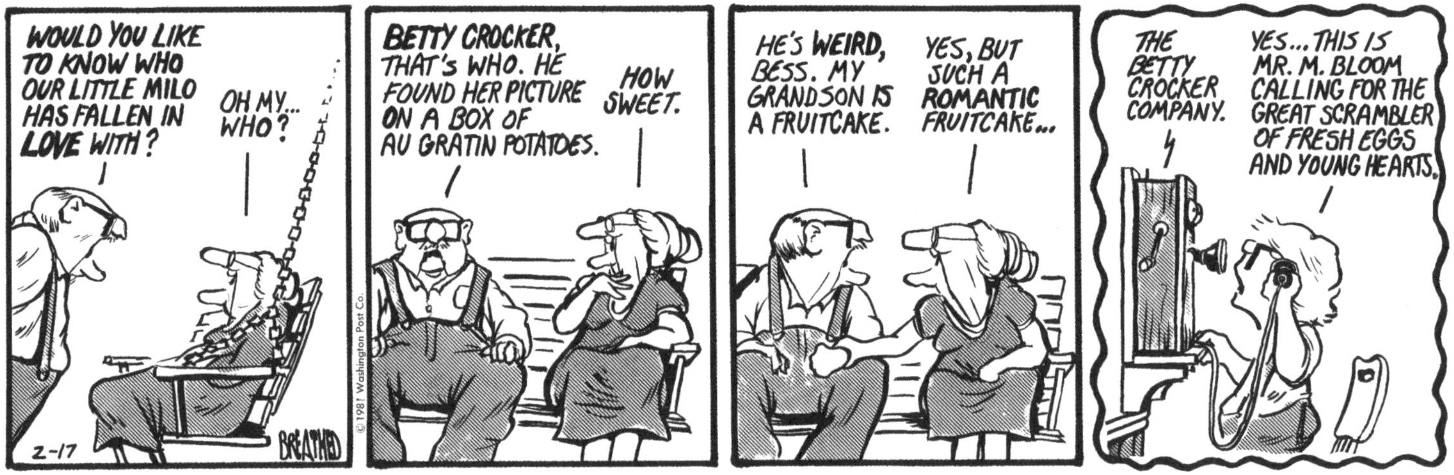

WOULD YOU LIKE TO KNOW WHO OUR LITTLE MILO HAS FALLEN IN LOVE WITH?
OH MY... WHO?
2-17
BREATHED
BETTY CROCKER, THAT'S WHO. HE FOUND HER PICTURE ON A BOX OF AU GRATIN POTATOES.
HOW SWEET.
© 1981 Washington Post Co.
HE'S WEIRD, BESS. MY GRANDSON IS A FRUITCAKE.
YES, BUT SUCH A ROMANTIC FRUITCAKE...
THE BETTY CROCKER COMPANY.
YES... THIS IS MR. M. BLOOM CALLING FOR THE GREAT SCRAMBLER OF FRESH EGGS AND YOUNG HEARTS.

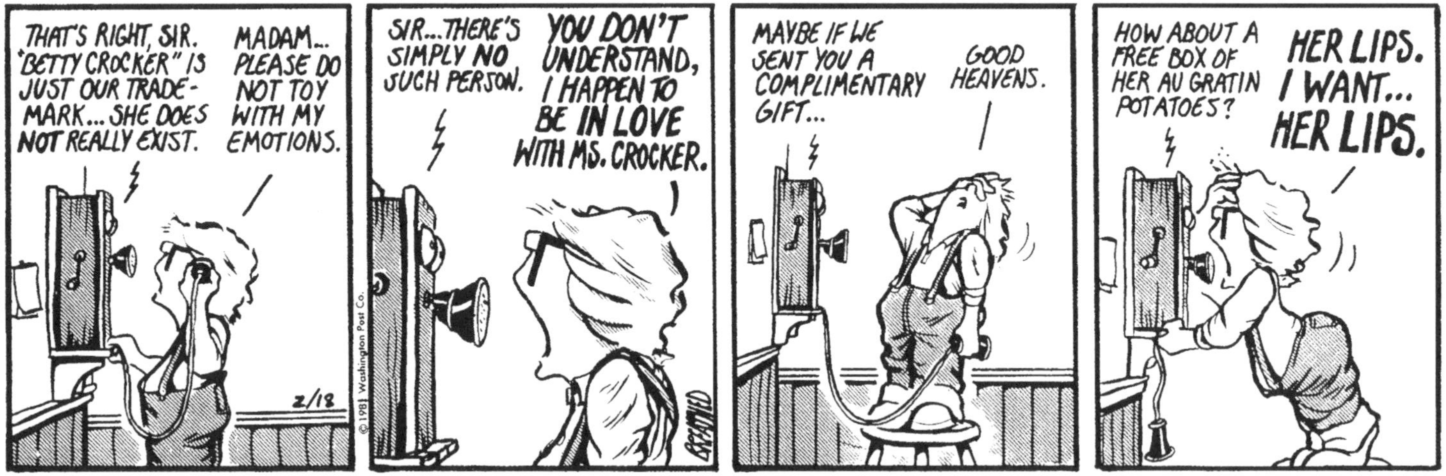

THAT'S RIGHT, SIR. "BETTY CROCKER" IS JUST OUR TRADEMARK... SHE DOES NOT REALLY EXIST.
MADAM... PLEASE DO NOT TOY WITH MY EMOTIONS.
2/18
SIR... THERE'S SIMPLY NO SUCH PERSON.
YOU DON'T UNDERSTAND, I HAPPEN TO BE IN LOVE WITH MS. CROCKER.
© 1981 Washington Post Co.
BREATHED
MAYBE IF WE SENT YOU A COMPLIMENTARY GIFT...
GOOD HEAVENS.
HOW ABOUT A FREE BOX OF HER AU GRATIN POTATOES?
HER LIPS. I WANT... HER LIPS.

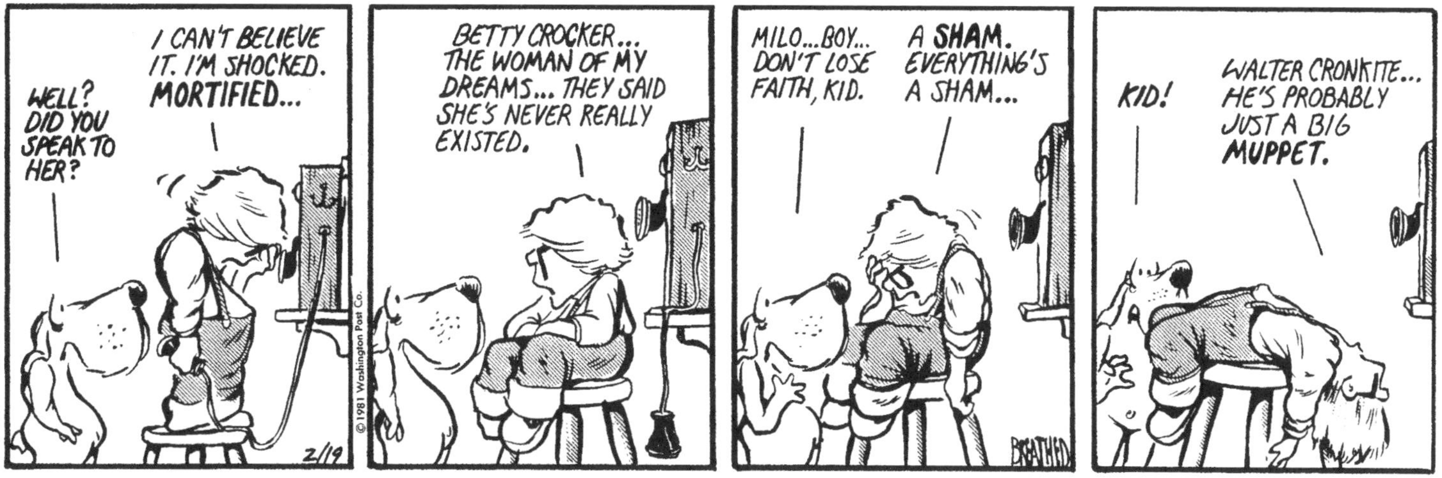
WELL? DID YOU SPEAK TO HER?
I CAN'T BELIEVE IT. I'M SHOCKED. MORTIFIED...
© 1981 Washington Post Co.
2/19
BETTY CROCKER... THE WOMAN OF MY DREAMS... THEY SAID SHE'S NEVER REALLY EXISTED.
MILO...BOY... DON'T LOSE FAITH, KID.
A SHAM. EVERYTHING'S A SHAM...
BREATHED
KID!
WALTER CRONKITE... HE'S PROBABLY JUST A BIG MUPPET.

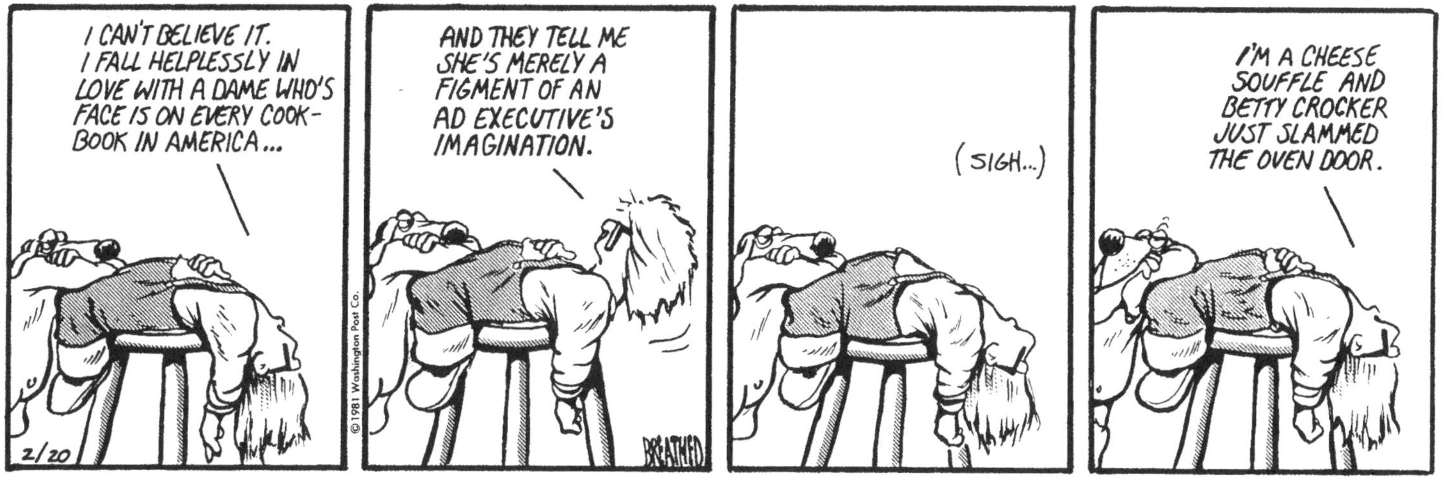
I CAN'T BELIEVE IT. I FALL HELPLESSLY IN LOVE WITH A DAME WHO'S FACE IS ON EVERY COOK-BOOK IN AMERICA...
2/20
© 1981 Washington Post Co.
AND THEY TELL ME SHE'S MERELY A FIGMENT OF AN AD EXECUTIVE'S IMAGINATION.
BREATHED
(SIGH...)
I'M A CHEESE SOUFFLE AND BETTY CROCKER JUST SLAMMED THE OVEN DOOR.

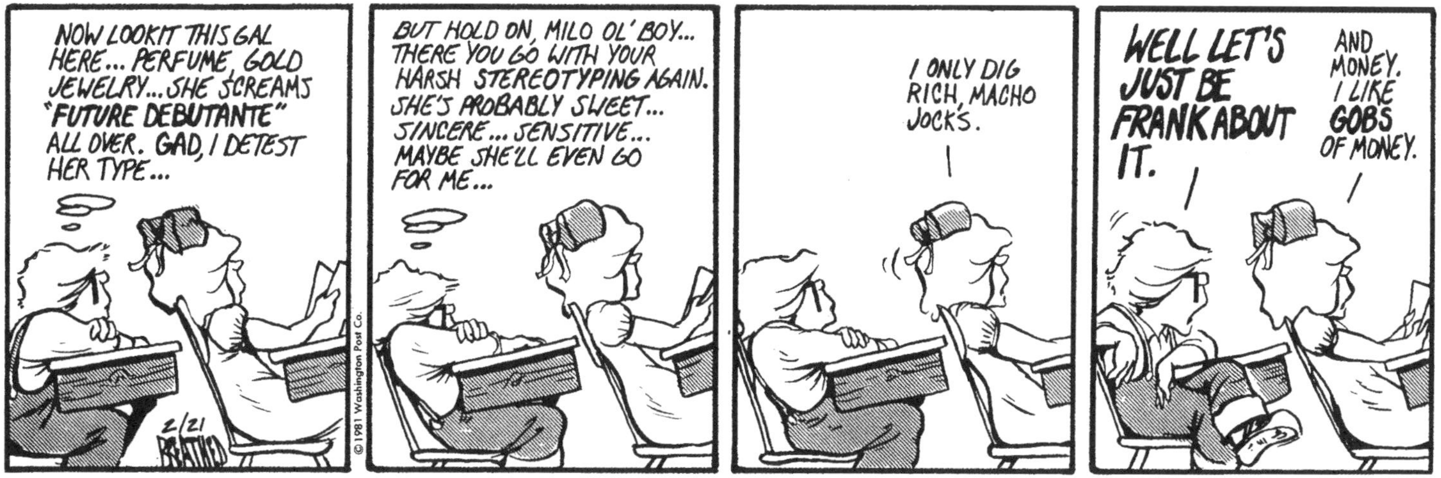
NOW LOOKIT THIS GAL HERE... PERFUME, GOLD JEWELRY...SHE SCREAMS "FUTURE DEBUTANTE" ALL OVER. GAD, I DETEST HER TYPE...
2/21
BREATHED
© 1981 Washington Post Co.
BUT HOLD ON, MILO OL' BOY... THERE YOU GO WITH YOUR HARSH STEREOTYPING AGAIN. SHE'S PROBABLY SWEET... SINCERE... SENSITIVE... MAYBE SHE'LL EVEN GO FOR ME...
I ONLY DIG RICH, MACHO JOCKS.
WELL LET'S JUST BE FRANK ABOUT IT.
AND MONEY. I LIKE GOBS OF MONEY.

Walter Cronkite was anchorman of the *CBS Evening News* from 1962 to 1981. Often cited in opinion polls of the era as "the most trusted man in America," he is vividly remembered for his live coverage of the assassination of President Kennedy in 1963.

Butch Cassidy and the Sundance Kid was the top grossing film of 1969.

Fred Silverman was the president in charge of programming for several television networks during the 1970s, and later formed his own TV production company.

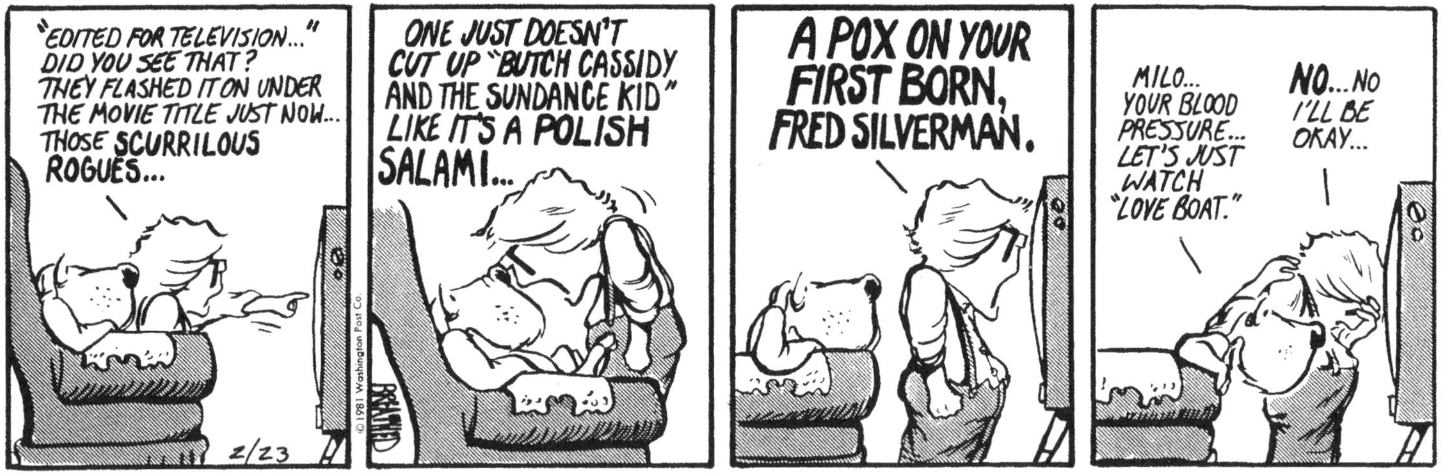

"EDITED FOR TELEVISION..." DID YOU SEE THAT? THEY FLASHED IT ON UNDER THE MOVIE TITLE JUST NOW... THOSE SCURRILOUS ROGUES...
2/23
ONE JUST DOESN'T CUT UP "BUTCH CASSIDY AND THE SUNDANCE KID" LIKE IT'S A POLISH SALAMI...
© 1981 Washington Post Co.
BREATHED
A POX ON YOUR FIRST BORN, FRED SILVERMAN.
MILO... YOUR BLOOD PRESSURE... LET'S JUST WATCH "LOVE BOAT."
NO... NO I'LL BE OKAY...

The Summer of '42 was a coming of age film released in 1971, during the height of the Vietnam conflict, and told the story of a teenage boy who embarks on a summer romance with an older woman whose husband has gone off to war.

Hee Haw was a music and comedy variety show. It ran for many years and featured a large cast of country stars playing good-natured, dim-witted hillbillies.

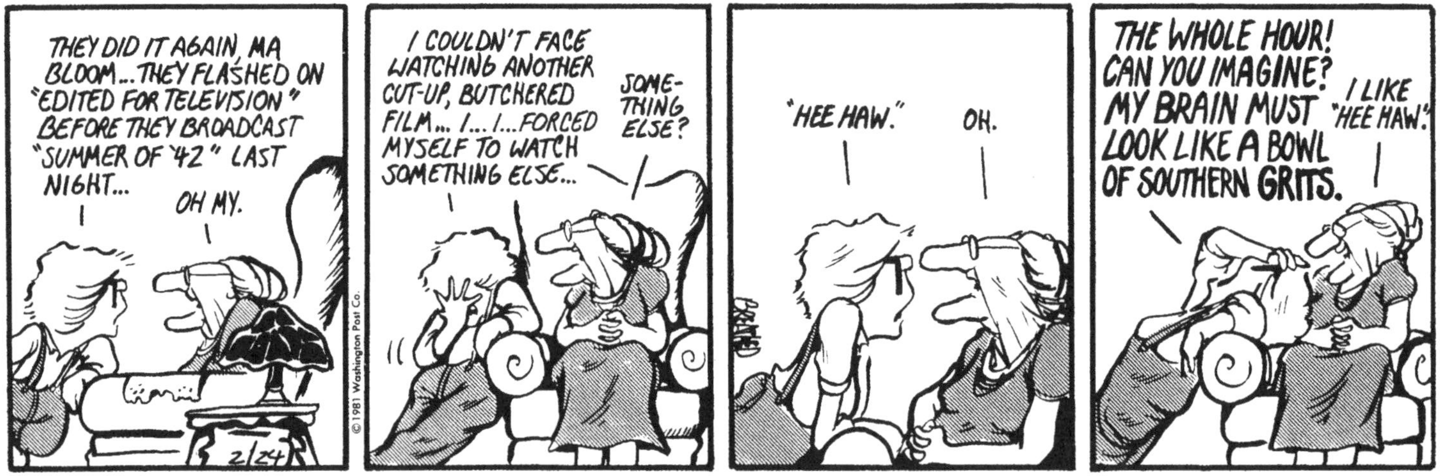

THEY DID IT AGAIN, MA BLOOM... THEY FLASHED ON "EDITED FOR TELEVISION" BEFORE THEY BROADCAST "SUMMER OF '42" LAST NIGHT...
OH MY.
2/24
© 1981 Washington Post Co.
I COULDN'T FACE WATCHING ANOTHER CUT-UP, BUTCHERED FILM... I... I... FORCED MYSELF TO WATCH SOMETHING ELSE...
SOMETHING ELSE?
"HEE HAW."
OH.
BREATHED
THE WHOLE HOUR! CAN YOU IMAGINE? MY BRAIN MUST LOOK LIKE A BOWL OF SOUTHERN GRITS.
I LIKE "HEE HAW."

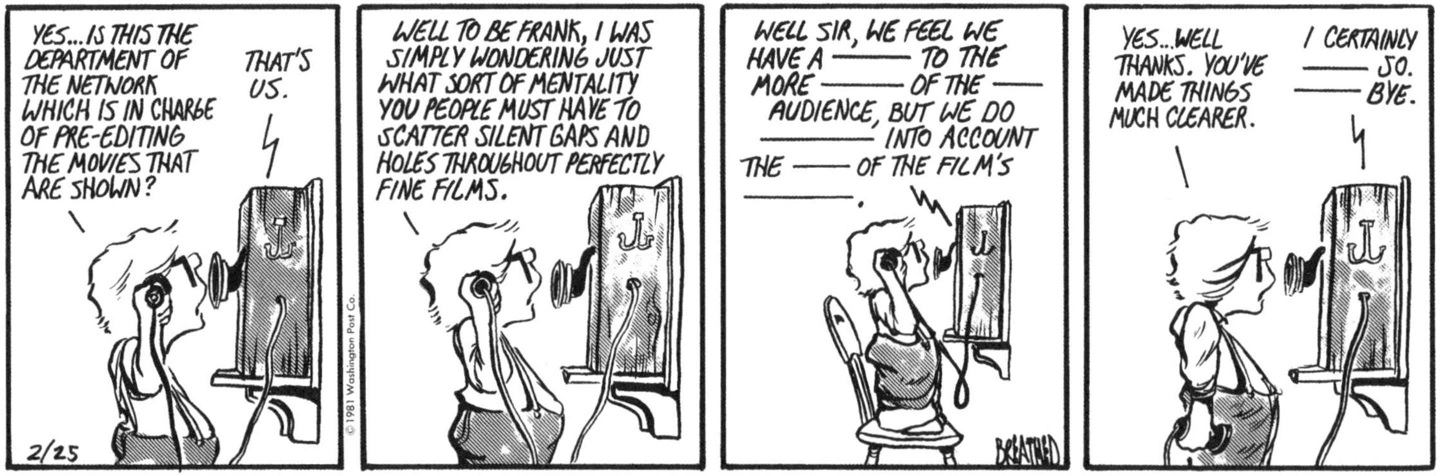

YES... IS THIS THE DEPARTMENT OF THE NETWORK WHICH IS IN CHARGE OF PRE-EDITING THE MOVIES THAT ARE SHOWN?
THAT'S US.
2/25
© 1981 Washington Post Co.
WELL TO BE FRANK, I WAS SIMPLY WONDERING JUST WHAT SORT OF MENTALITY YOU PEOPLE MUST HAVE TO SCATTER SILENT GAPS AND HOLES THROUGHOUT PERFECTLY FINE FILMS.
WELL SIR, WE FEEL WE HAVE A —— TO THE MORE —— OF THE —— AUDIENCE, BUT WE DO —— INTO ACCOUNT THE —— OF THE FILM'S ——.
BREATHED
YES... WELL THANKS. YOU'VE MADE THINGS MUCH CLEARER.
I CERTAINLY —— SO. —— BYE.

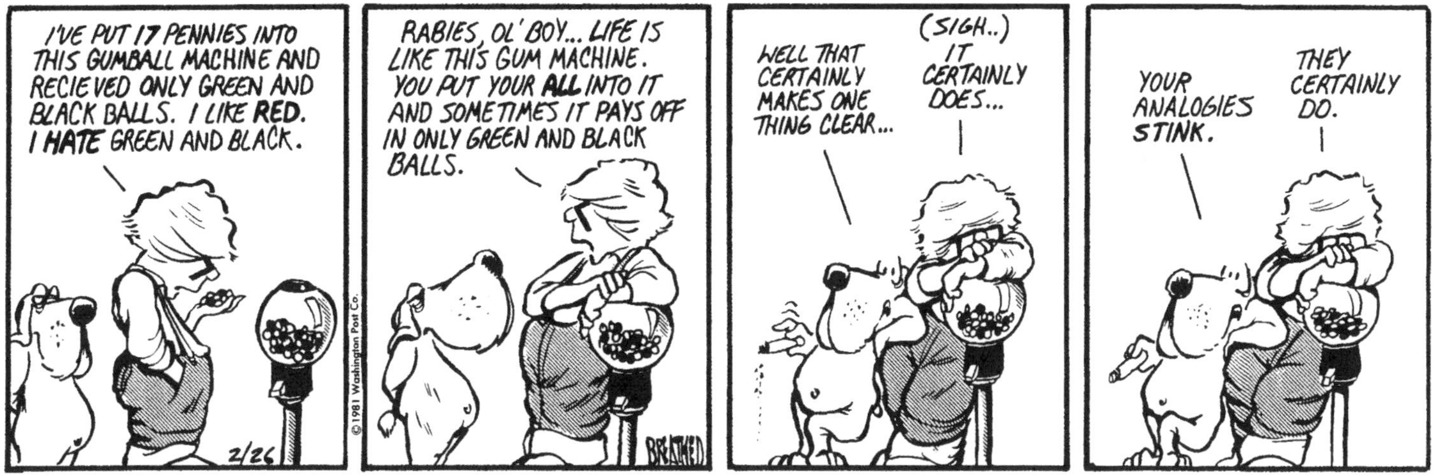
I'VE PUT 17 PENNIES INTO THIS GUMBALL MACHINE AND RECIEVED ONLY GREEN AND BLACK BALLS. I LIKE RED. I HATE GREEN AND BLACK.
2/26
©1981 Washington Post Co.
RABIES, OL' BOY... LIFE IS LIKE THIS GUM MACHINE. YOU PUT YOUR ALL INTO IT AND SOMETIMES IT PAYS OFF IN ONLY GREEN AND BLACK BALLS.
BREATHED
WELL THAT CERTAINLY MAKES ONE THING CLEAR...
(SIGH..) IT CERTAINLY DOES...
YOUR ANALOGIES STINK.
THEY CERTAINLY DO.

Rabies the dog was a carryover from my college cartoons. He was soon to be retired as there were no shortage of cartoon dogs. At this point I was beginning to look around at what animals were still left up for grabs in the cartoon world. Thought of a snake. "Opus the snake" just didn't sing, as they say. —BB

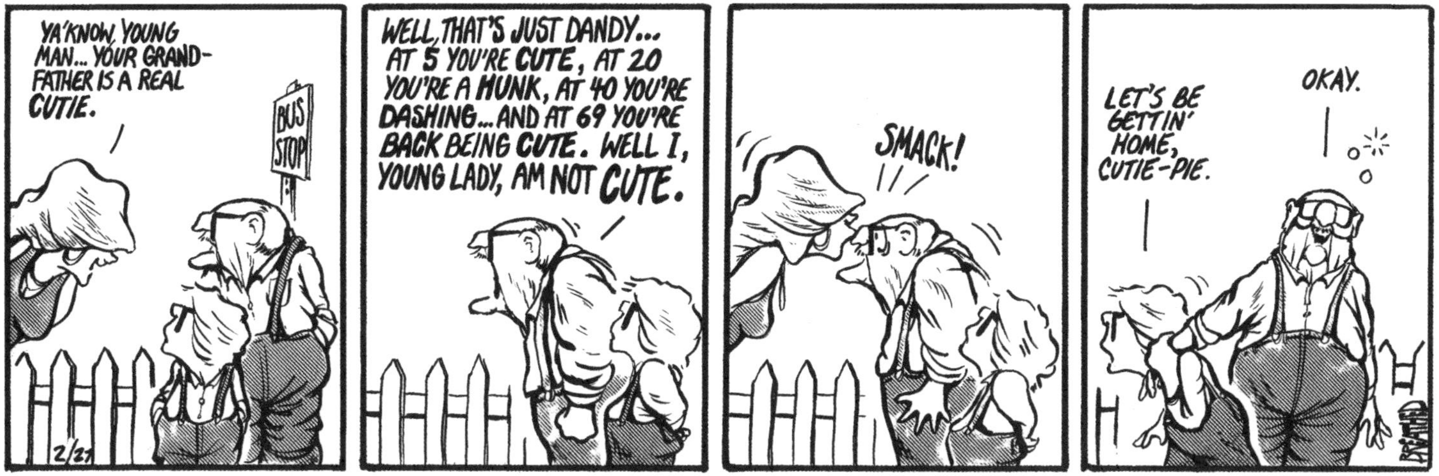
YA'KNOW, YOUNG MAN... YOUR GRAND-FATHER IS A REAL CUTIE.
BUS STOP
2/27
WELL, THAT'S JUST DANDY... AT 5 YOU'RE CUTE, AT 20 YOU'RE A HUNK, AT 40 YOU'RE DASHING... AND AT 69 YOU'RE BACK BEING CUTE. WELL I, YOUNG LADY, AM NOT CUTE.
SMACK!
LET'S BE GETTIN' HOME, CUTIE-PIE.
OKAY.
BREATHED

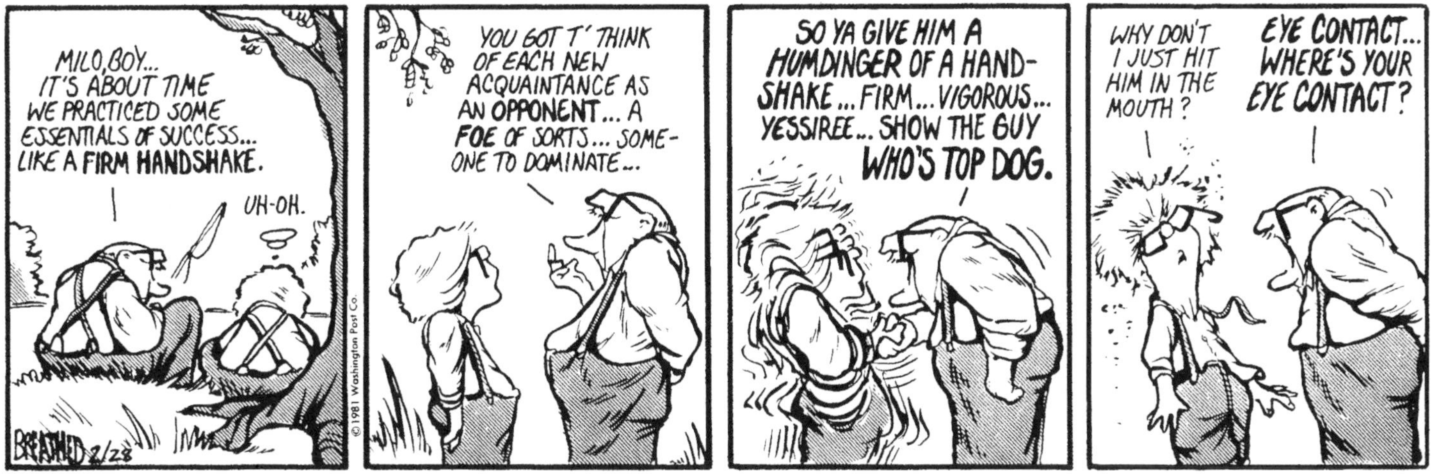
MILO, BOY... IT'S ABOUT TIME WE PRACTICED SOME ESSENTIALS OF SUCCESS... LIKE A FIRM HANDSHAKE.
UH-OH.
BREATHED 2/28
©1981 Washington Post Co.
YOU GOT T' THINK OF EACH NEW ACQUAINTANCE AS AN OPPONENT... A FOE OF SORTS... SOME-ONE TO DOMINATE...
SO YA GIVE HIM A HUMDINGER OF A HAND-SHAKE... FIRM... VIGOROUS... YESSIREE... SHOW THE GUY WHO'S TOP DOG.
WHY DON'T I JUST HIT HIM IN THE MOUTH?
EYE CONTACT... WHERE'S YOUR EYE CONTACT?

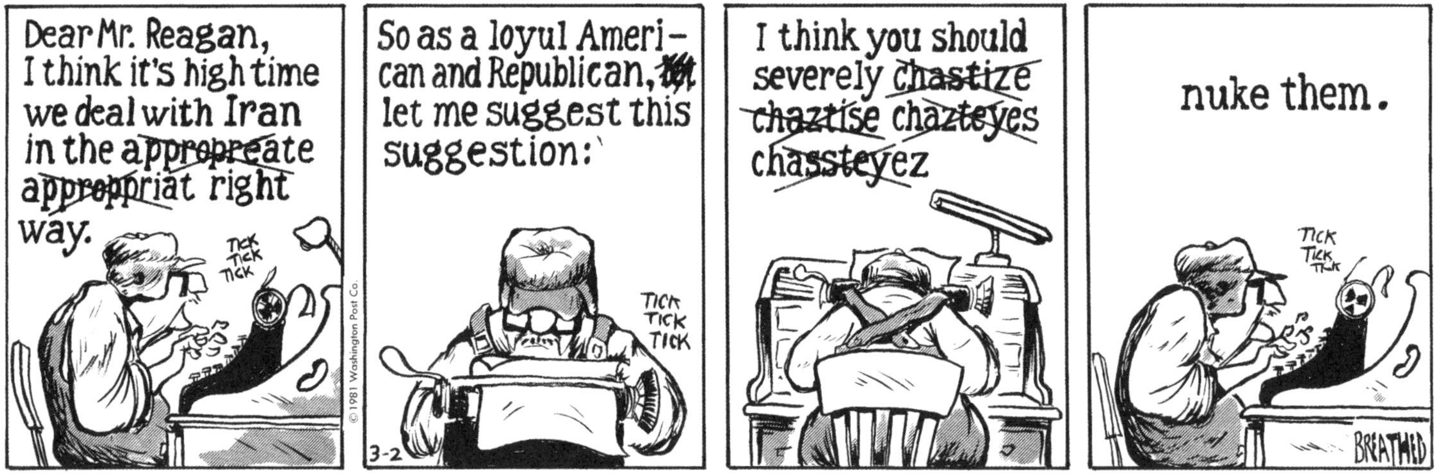
Dear Mr. Reagan, I think it's high time we deal with Iran in the ~~appropreate~~ ~~appreppriat~~ right way.
TICK TICK TICK
© 1981 Washington Post Co.
So as a loyul American and Republican, ~~let~~ let me suggest this suggestion:
TICK TICK TICK
3-2
I think you should severely ~~chastize~~ ~~chaztise~~ ~~chazteyes~~ ~~chassteyez~~
nuke them.
TICK TICK TICK
BREATHED

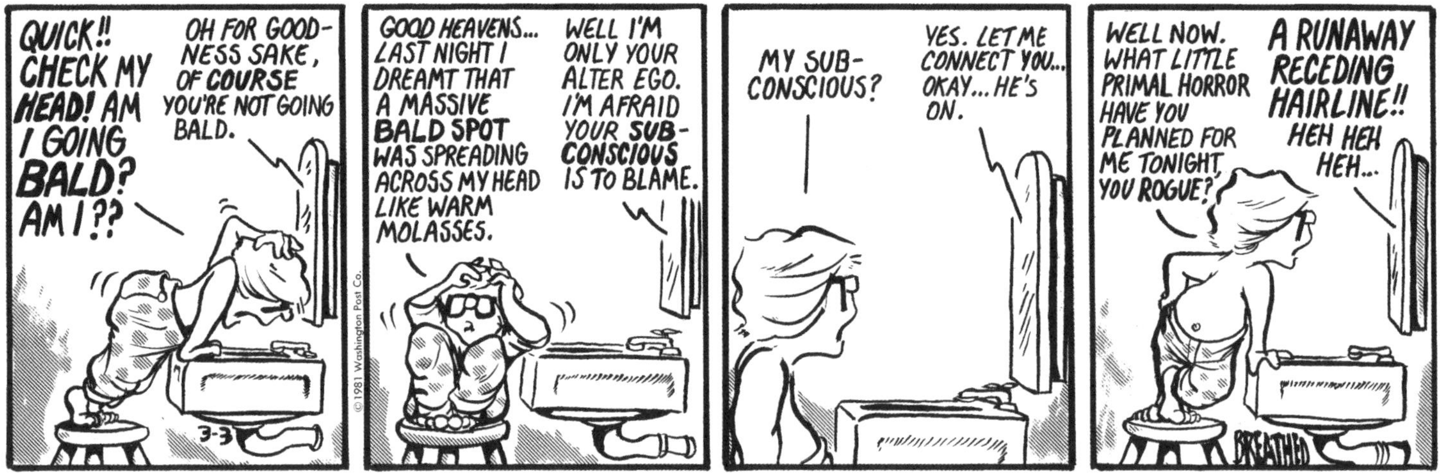
QUICK!! CHECK MY HEAD! AM I GOING BALD? AM I??
OH FOR GOODNESS SAKE, OF COURSE YOU'RE NOT GOING BALD.
3-3
© 1981 Washington Post Co.
GOOD HEAVENS... LAST NIGHT I DREAMT THAT A MASSIVE BALD SPOT WAS SPREADING ACROSS MY HEAD LIKE WARM MOLASSES.
WELL I'M ONLY YOUR ALTER EGO. I'M AFRAID YOUR SUBCONSCIOUS IS TO BLAME.
MY SUBCONSCIOUS?
YES. LET ME CONNECT YOU... OKAY... HE'S ON.
WELL NOW. WHAT LITTLE PRIMAL HORROR HAVE YOU PLANNED FOR ME TONIGHT, YOU ROGUE?
A RUNAWAY RECEDING HAIRLINE!! HEH HEH HEH...
BREATHED

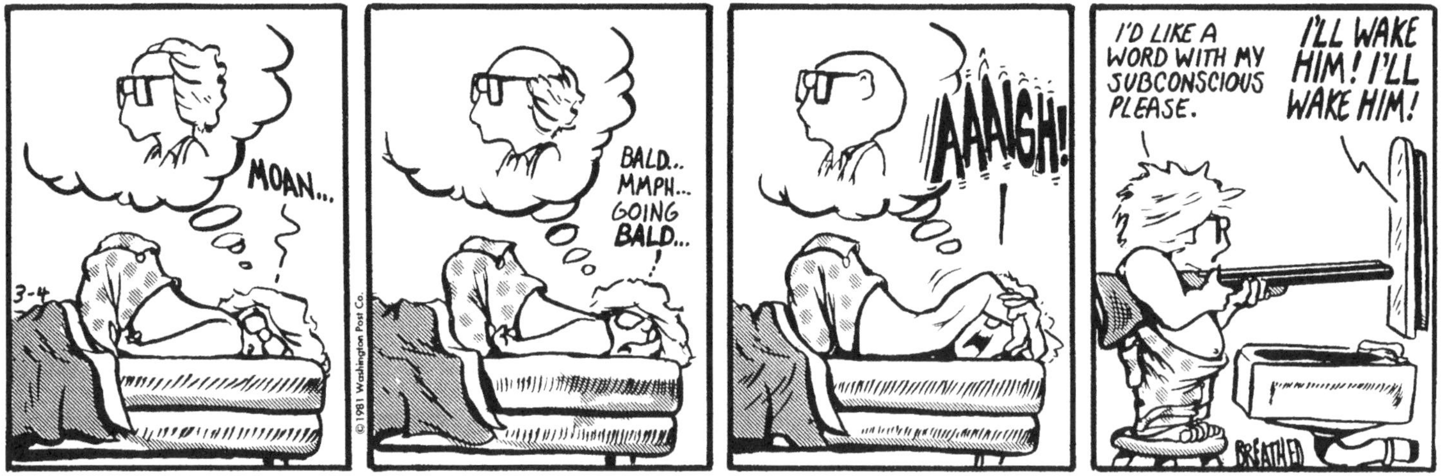
3-4
MOAN...
© 1981 Washington Post Co.
BALD.. MMPH... GOING BALD...
AAAIGH!
I'D LIKE A WORD WITH MY SUBCONSCIOUS PLEASE.
I'LL WAKE HIM! I'LL WAKE HIM!
BREATHED

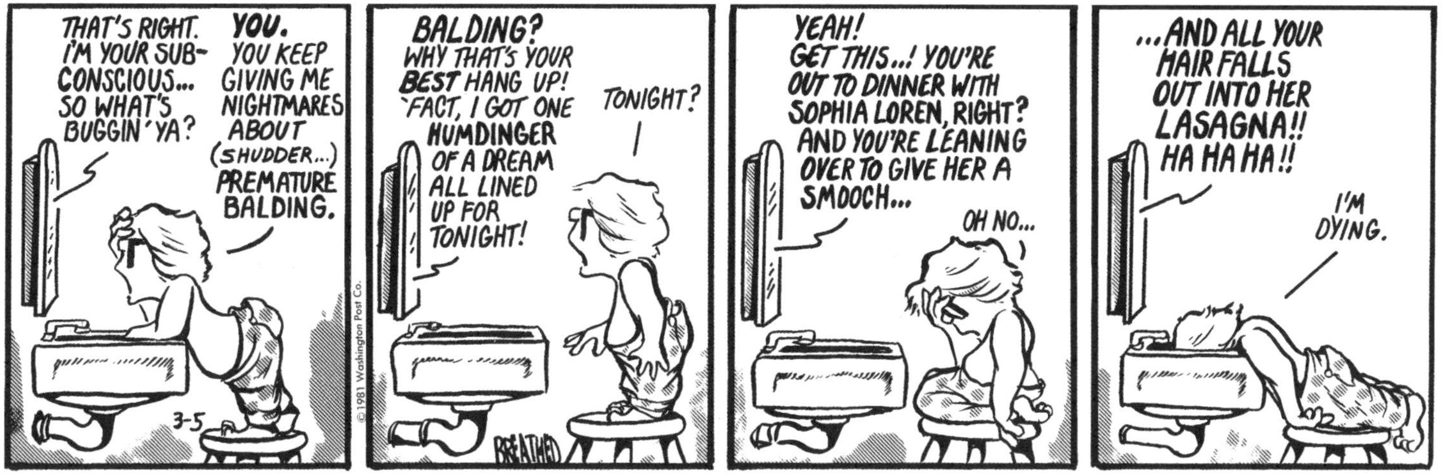
THAT'S RIGHT. I'M YOUR SUB-CONSCIOUS... SO WHAT'S BUGGIN' YA?
YOU. YOU KEEP GIVING ME NIGHTMARES ABOUT (SHUDDER...) PREMATURE BALDING.
3-5
BALDING? WHY THAT'S YOUR BEST HANG UP! 'FACT, I GOT ONE HUMDINGER OF A DREAM ALL LINED UP FOR TONIGHT!
TONIGHT?
© 1981 Washington Post Co.
BREATHED
YEAH! GET THIS...! YOU'RE OUT TO DINNER WITH SOPHIA LOREN, RIGHT? AND YOU'RE LEANING OVER TO GIVE HER A SMOOCH...
OH NO...
...AND ALL YOUR HAIR FALLS OUT INTO HER LASAGNA!! HA HA HA!!
I'M DYING.

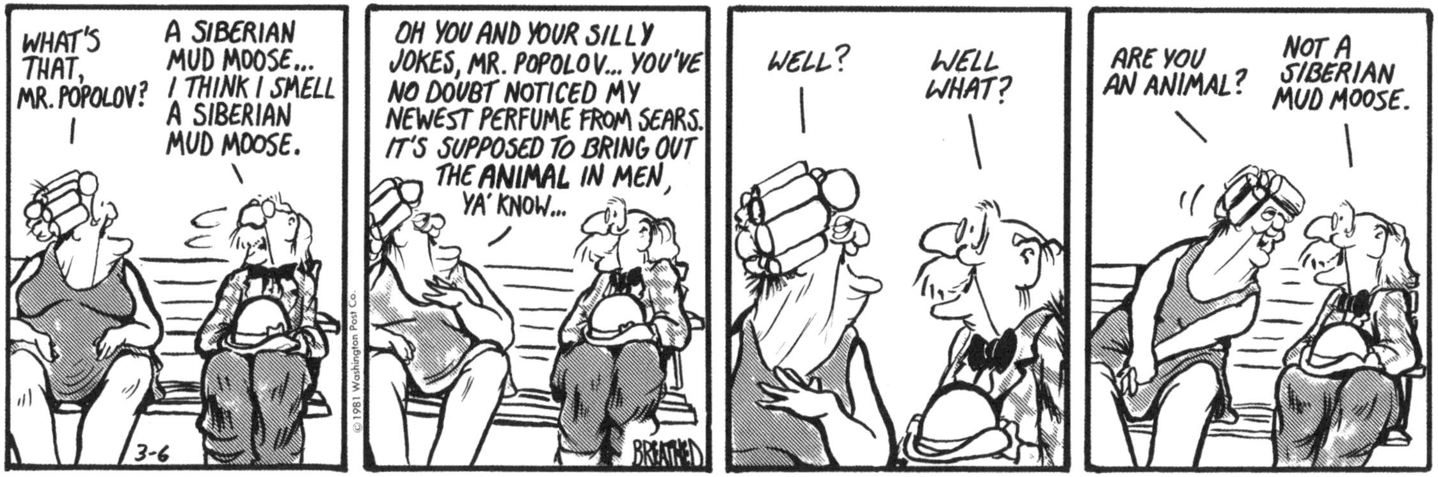
WHAT'S THAT, MR. POPOLOV?
A SIBERIAN MUD MOOSE... I THINK I SMELL A SIBERIAN MUD MOOSE.
3-6
OH YOU AND YOUR SILLY JOKES, MR. POPOLOV... YOU'VE NO DOUBT NOTICED MY NEWEST PERFUME FROM SEARS. IT'S SUPPOSED TO BRING OUT THE ANIMAL IN MEN, YA' KNOW...
© 1981 Washington Post Co.
BREATHED
WELL?
WELL WHAT?
ARE YOU AN ANIMAL?
NOT A SIBERIAN MUD MOOSE.

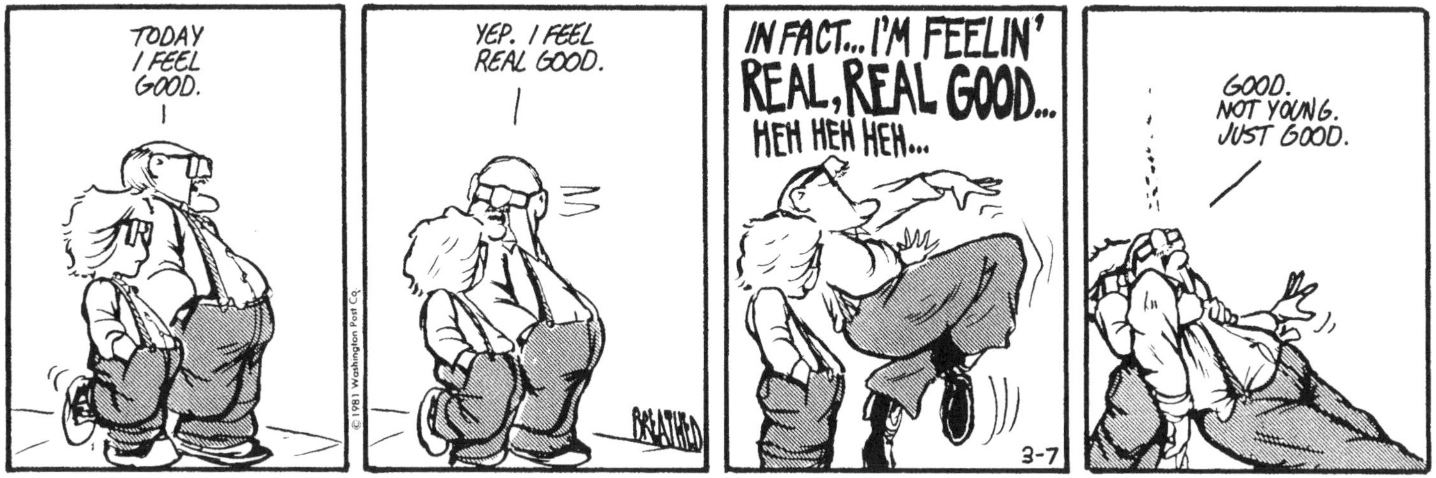
TODAY I FEEL GOOD.
YEP. I FEEL REAL GOOD.
© 1981 Washington Post Co.
BREATHED
IN FACT... I'M FEELIN' REAL, REAL GOOD... HEH HEH HEH...
3-7
GOOD. NOT YOUNG. JUST GOOD.

Limekiller: a character quickly identified by any discerning comic reader's eyes as a sloppy retread of Doonesbury's *"Duke."* Garry pointed this out in a series of spicy letters I have since locked away and ordered not to be read by my children until I am dead. The salient point is that Bloom County was still without a point of view at this late date. Being without focus, I was muddling about, looking for a center. Thievery occurs effortlessly in this state. —BB

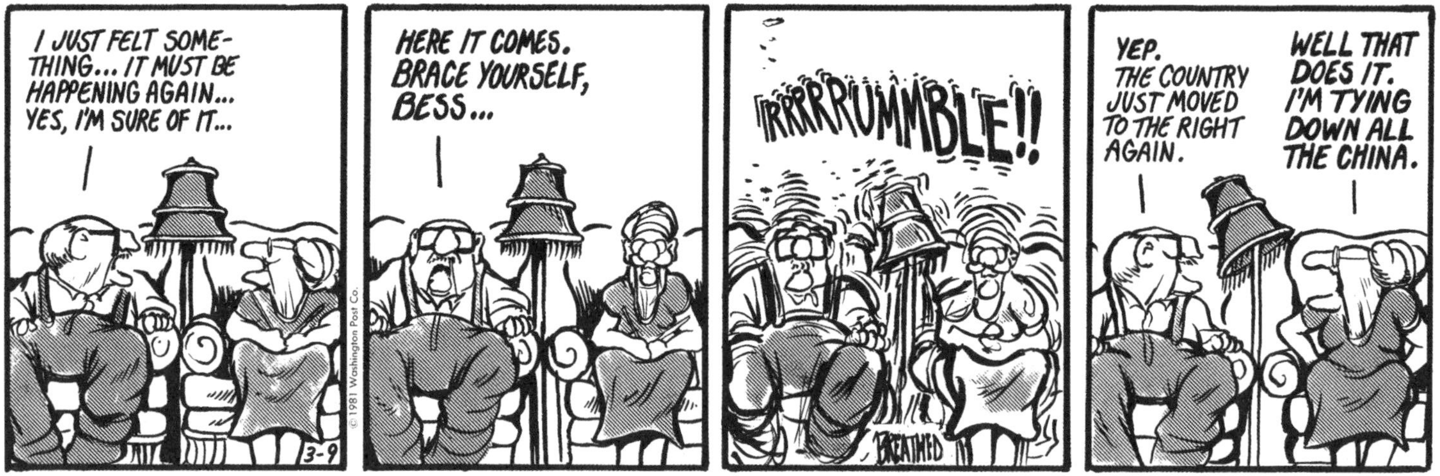

I JUST FELT SOMETHING... IT MUST BE HAPPENING AGAIN... YES, I'M SURE OF IT...
3-9
HERE IT COMES. BRACE YOURSELF, BESS...
© 1981 Washington Post Co.
RRRRRUMMBLE!!
BREATHED
YEP. THE COUNTRY JUST MOVED TO THE RIGHT AGAIN.
WELL THAT DOES IT. I'M TYING DOWN ALL THE CHINA.

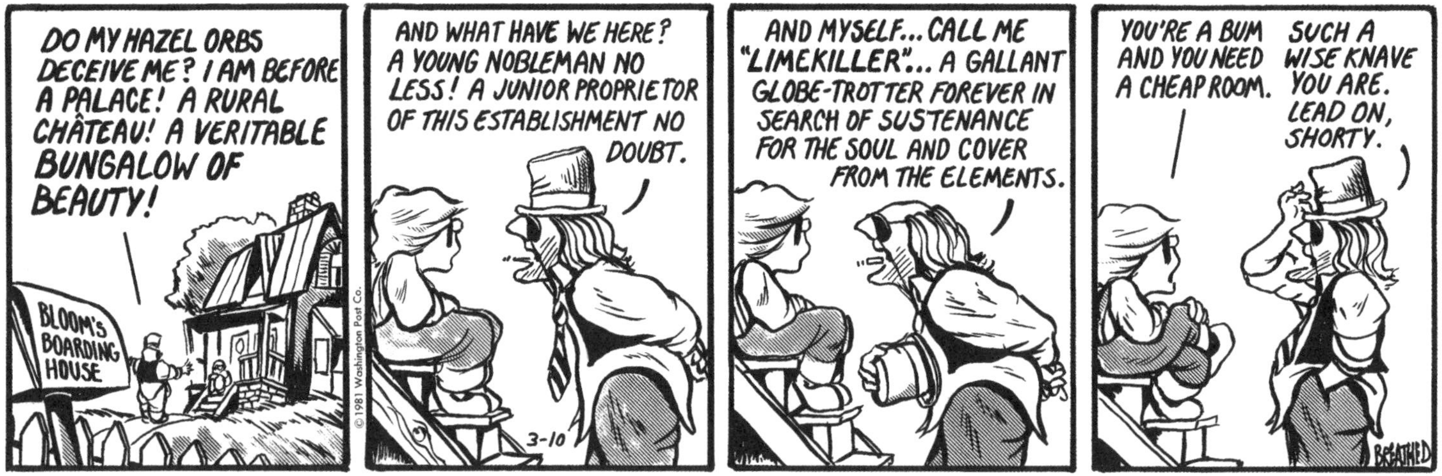

DO MY HAZEL ORBS DECEIVE ME? I AM BEFORE A PALACE! A RURAL CHÂTEAU! A VERITABLE BUNGALOW OF BEAUTY!
BLOOM'S BOARDING HOUSE
AND WHAT HAVE WE HERE? A YOUNG NOBLEMAN NO LESS! A JUNIOR PROPRIETOR OF THIS ESTABLISHMENT NO DOUBT.
© 1981 Washington Post Co.
3-10
AND MYSELF... CALL ME "LIMEKILLER"... A GALLANT GLOBE-TROTTER FOREVER IN SEARCH OF SUSTENANCE FOR THE SOUL AND COVER FROM THE ELEMENTS.
YOU'RE A BUM AND YOU NEED A CHEAP ROOM.
SUCH A WISE KNAVE YOU ARE. LEAD ON, SHORTY.
BREATHED

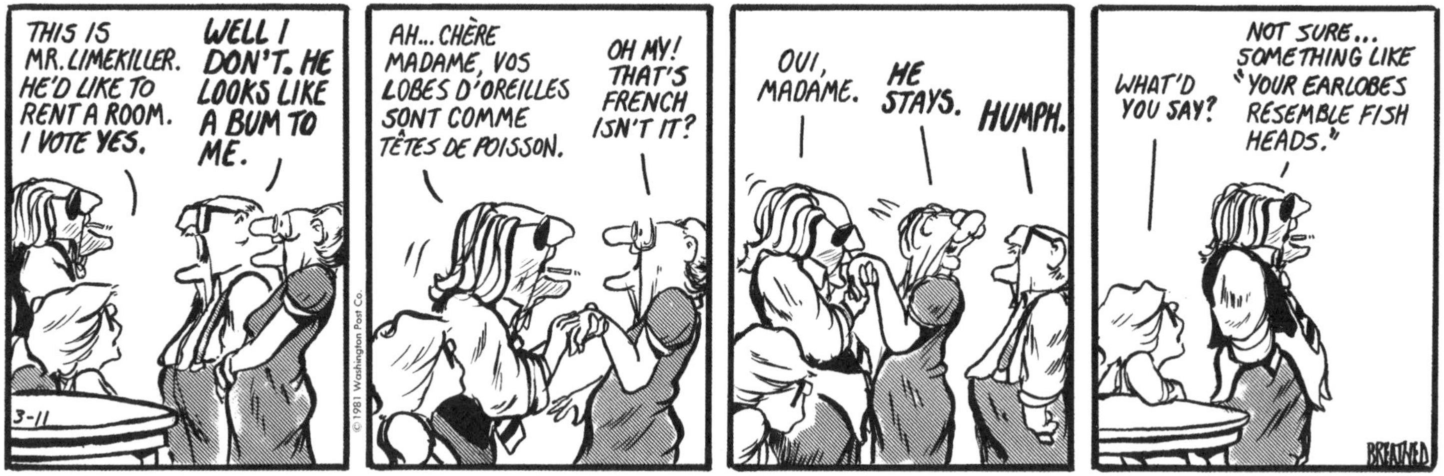

THIS IS MR. LIMEKILLER. HE'D LIKE TO RENT A ROOM. I VOTE YES.
WELL I DON'T. HE LOOKS LIKE A BUM TO ME.
3-11
AH... CHÈRE MADAME, VOS LOBES D'OREILLES SONT COMME TÊTES DE POISSON.
OH MY! THAT'S FRENCH ISN'T IT?
© 1981 Washington Post Co.
OUI, MADAME.
HE STAYS.
HUMPH.
WHAT'D YOU SAY?
NOT SURE... SOMETHING LIKE "YOUR EARLOBES RESEMBLE FISH HEADS."
BREATHED

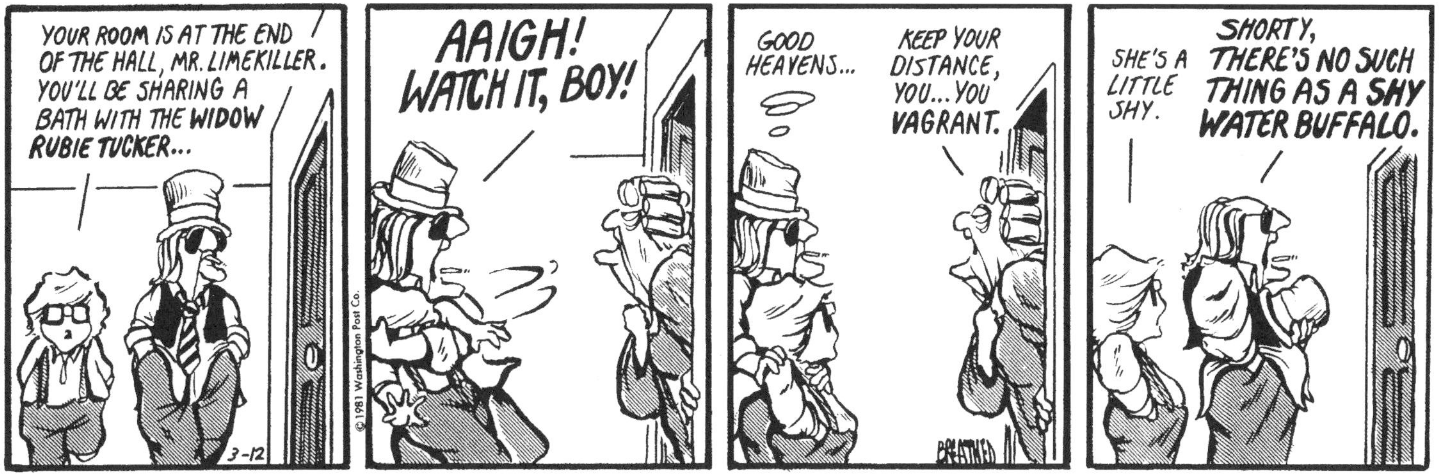
YOUR ROOM IS AT THE END OF THE HALL, MR. LIMEKILLER. YOU'LL BE SHARING A BATH WITH THE WIDOW RUBIE TUCKER...
3-12
© 1981 Washington Post Co.
AAIGH! WATCH IT, BOY!
GOOD HEAVENS...
KEEP YOUR DISTANCE, YOU... YOU VAGRANT.
BREATHED
SHE'S A LITTLE SHY.
SHORTY, THERE'S NO SUCH THING AS A SHY WATER BUFFALO.

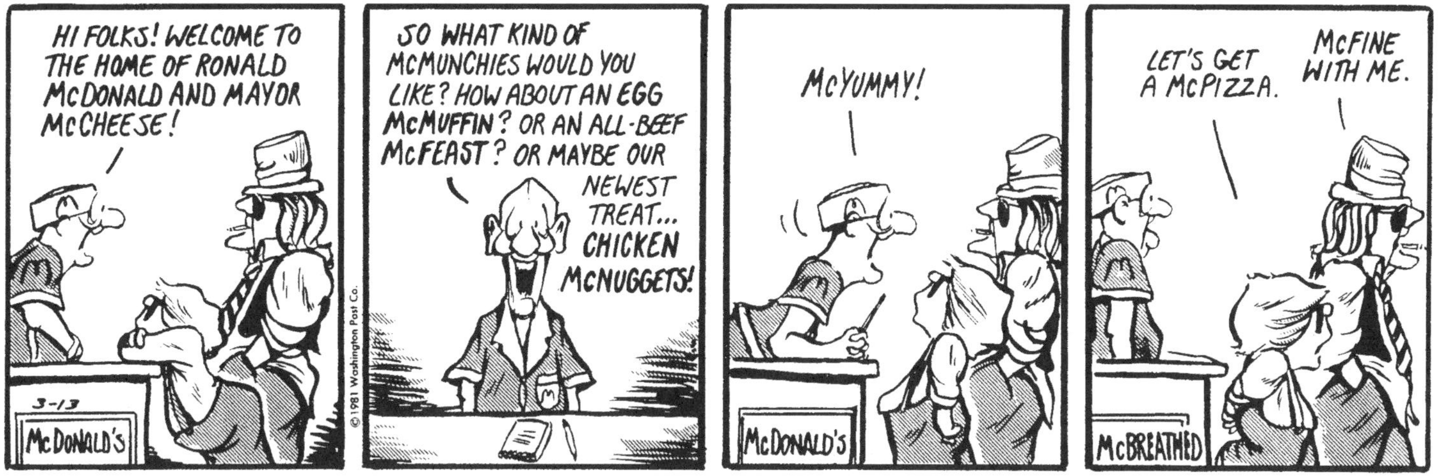
HI FOLKS! WELCOME TO THE HOME OF RONALD McDONALD AND MAYOR McCHEESE!
3-13
McDONALD'S
© 1981 Washington Post Co.
SO WHAT KIND OF McMUNCHIES WOULD YOU LIKE? HOW ABOUT AN EGG McMUFFIN? OR AN ALL-BEEF McFEAST? OR MAYBE OUR NEWEST TREAT... CHICKEN McNUGGETS!
McYUMMY!
McDONALD'S
LET'S GET A McPIZZA.
McFINE WITH ME.
McBREATHED

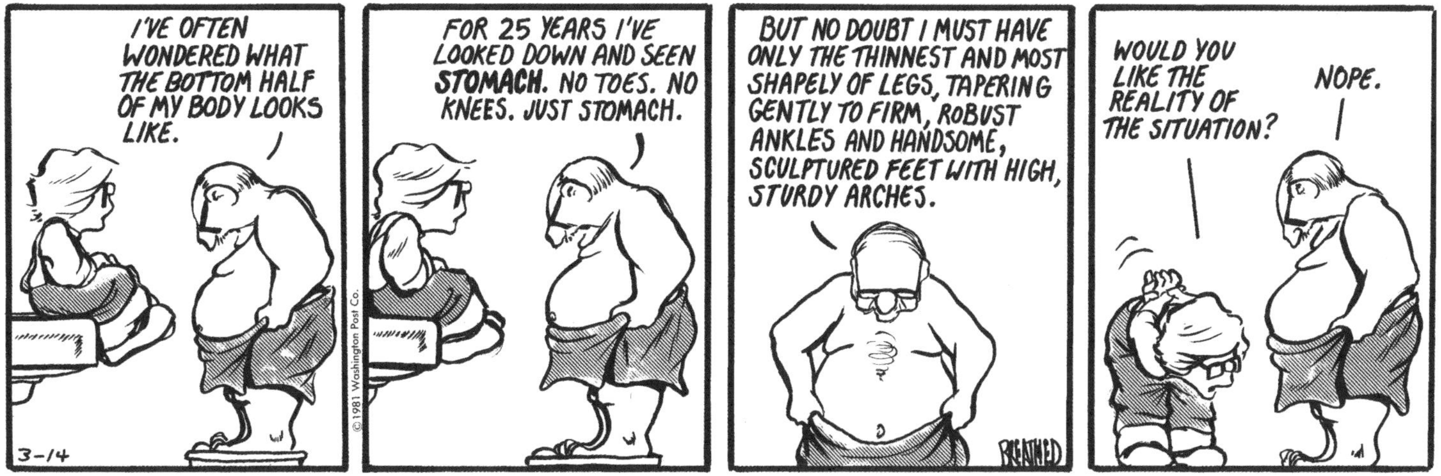
I'VE OFTEN WONDERED WHAT THE BOTTOM HALF OF MY BODY LOOKS LIKE.
3-14
© 1981 Washington Post Co.
FOR 25 YEARS I'VE LOOKED DOWN AND SEEN STOMACH. NO TOES. NO KNEES. JUST STOMACH.
BUT NO DOUBT I MUST HAVE ONLY THE THINNEST AND MOST SHAPELY OF LEGS, TAPERING GENTLY TO FIRM, ROBUST ANKLES AND HANDSOME, SCULPTURED FEET WITH HIGH, STURDY ARCHES.
BREATHED
WOULD YOU LIKE THE REALITY OF THE SITUATION?
NOPE.

Barry Manilow, a saccharine yet immensely popular singer/songwriter of the 1970s and 1980s.

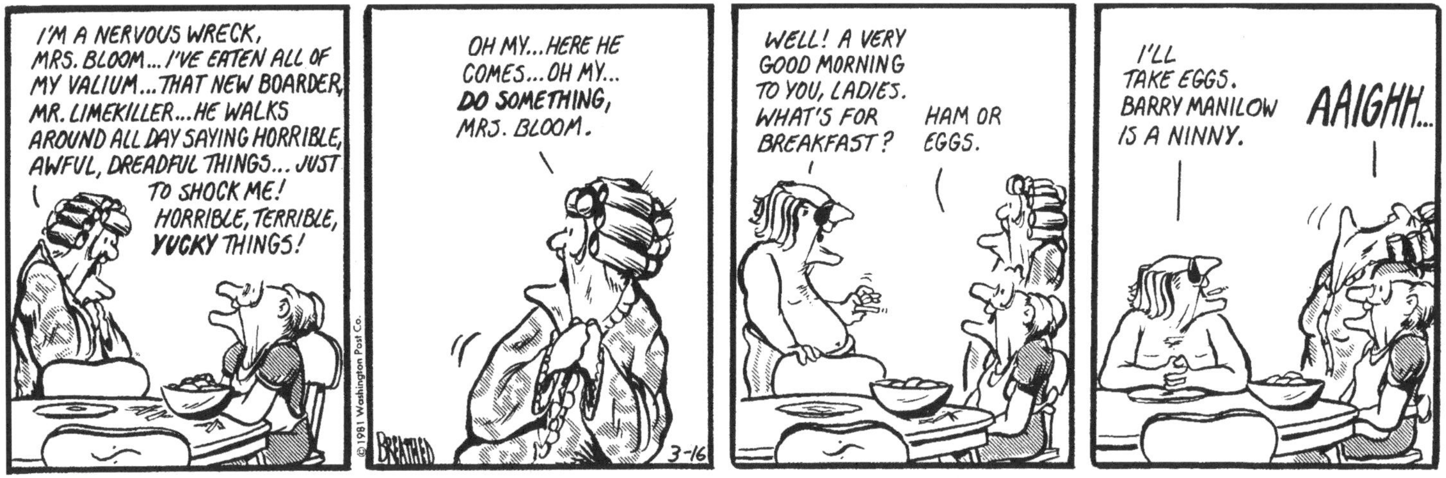
I'M A NERVOUS WRECK, MRS. BLOOM... I'VE EATEN ALL OF MY VALIUM... THAT NEW BOARDER, MR. LIMEKILLER... HE WALKS AROUND ALL DAY SAYING HORRIBLE, AWFUL, DREADFUL THINGS... JUST TO SHOCK ME!
HORRIBLE, TERRIBLE, YUCKY THINGS!
OH MY... HERE HE COMES... OH MY... DO SOMETHING, MRS. BLOOM.
© 1981 Washington Post Co.
BREATHED
3-16
WELL! A VERY GOOD MORNING TO YOU, LADIES. WHAT'S FOR BREAKFAST?
HAM OR EGGS.
I'LL TAKE EGGS. BARRY MANILOW IS A NINNY.
AAIGHH...

Alexander Haig, a United States general, was the White House chief of staff under Presidents Nixon and Ford, and served as Secretary of State under President Reagan. Haig is most remembered for asserting to reporters, "I'm in control here," after Reagan was the victim of a failed assassination attempt on March 30, 1981—less than two weeks after this strip appeared.

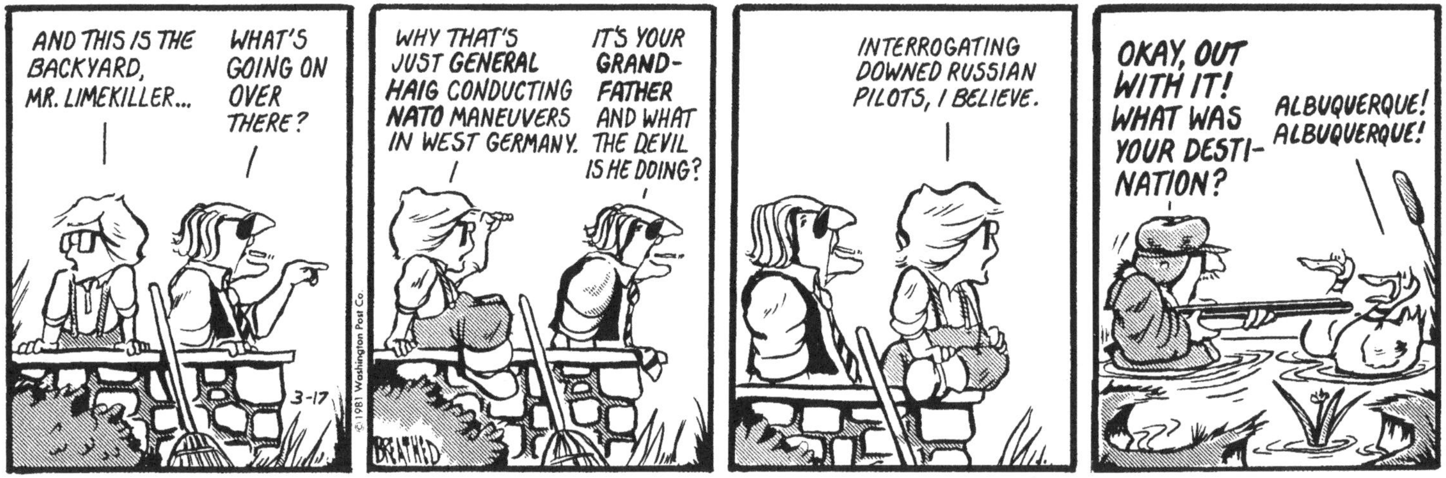
AND THIS IS THE BACKYARD, MR. LIMEKILLER...
WHAT'S GOING ON OVER THERE?
3-17
© 1981 Washington Post Co.
BREATHED
WHY THAT'S JUST GENERAL HAIG CONDUCTING NATO MANEUVERS IN WEST GERMANY.
IT'S YOUR GRANDFATHER AND WHAT THE DEVIL IS HE DOING?
INTERROGATING DOWNED RUSSIAN PILOTS, I BELIEVE.
OKAY, OUT WITH IT! WHAT WAS YOUR DESTINATION?
ALBUQUERQUE! ALBUQUERQUE!

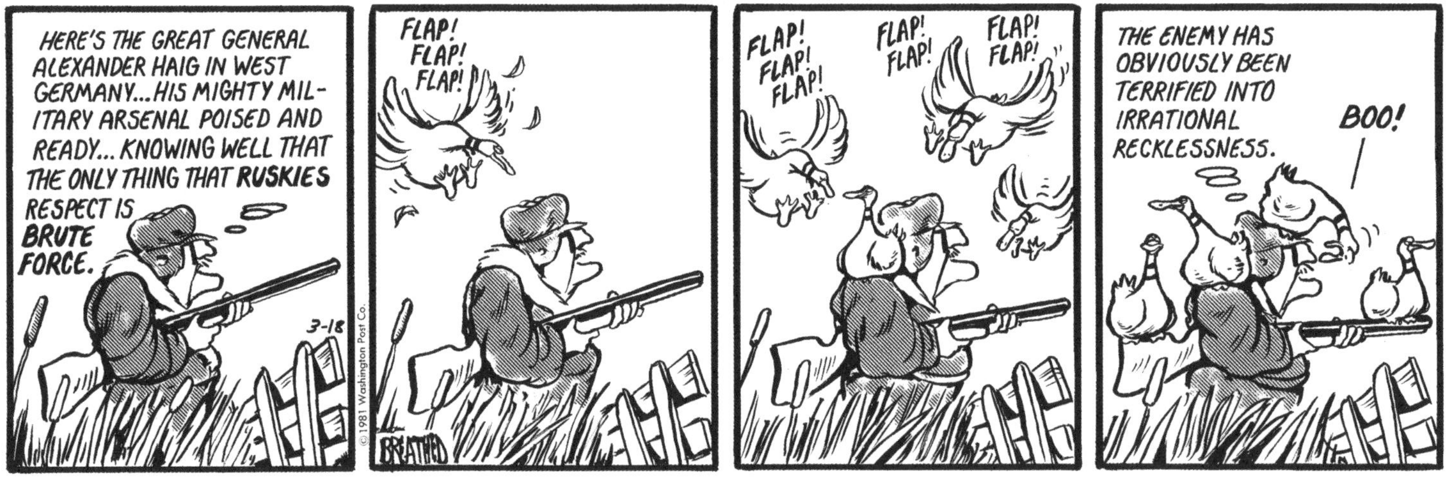
HERE'S THE GREAT GENERAL ALEXANDER HAIG IN WEST GERMANY... HIS MIGHTY MILITARY ARSENAL POISED AND READY... KNOWING WELL THAT THE ONLY THING THAT RUSKIES RESPECT IS BRUTE FORCE.
3-18
© 1981 Washington Post Co.
FLAP! FLAP! FLAP!
BREATHED
FLAP! FLAP! FLAP!
FLAP! FLAP!
FLAP! FLAP!
THE ENEMY HAS OBVIOUSLY BEEN TERRIFIED INTO IRRATIONAL RECKLESSNESS.
BOO!

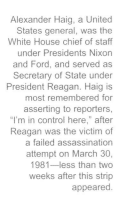

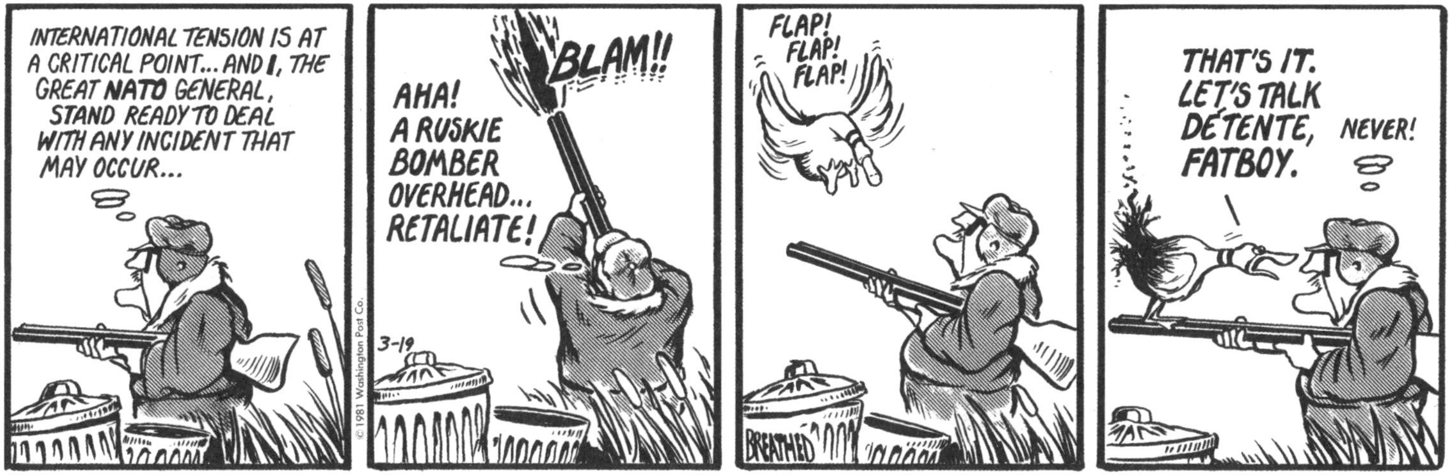
INTERNATIONAL TENSION IS AT A CRITICAL POINT... AND I, THE GREAT NATO GENERAL, STAND READY TO DEAL WITH ANY INCIDENT THAT MAY OCCUR...
© 1981 Washington Post Co.
3-19
BLAM!!
AHA! A RUSKIE BOMBER OVERHEAD... RETALIATE!
FLAP! FLAP! FLAP!
BREATHED
THAT'S IT. LET'S TALK DÉTENTE, FATBOY.
NEVER!

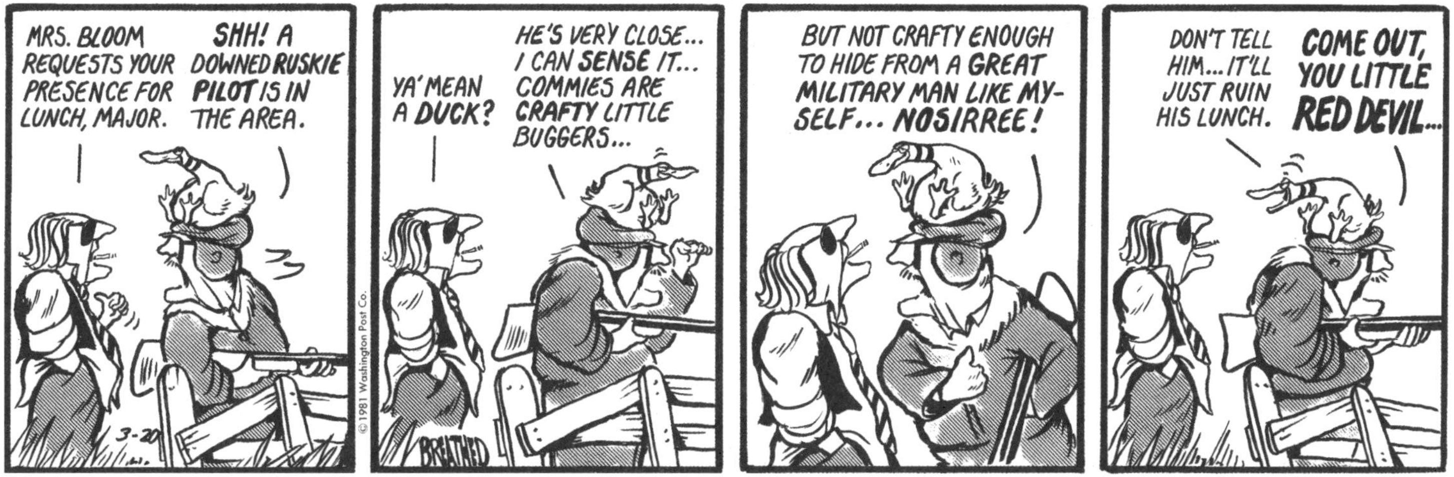
MRS. BLOOM REQUESTS YOUR PRESENCE FOR LUNCH, MAJOR.
SHH! A DOWNED RUSKIE PILOT IS IN THE AREA.
3-20
© 1981 Washington Post Co.
YA' MEAN A DUCK?
HE'S VERY CLOSE... I CAN SENSE IT... COMMIES ARE CRAFTY LITTLE BUGGERS...
BREATHED
BUT NOT CRAFTY ENOUGH TO HIDE FROM A GREAT MILITARY MAN LIKE MYSELF... NOSIRREE!
DON'T TELL HIM... IT'LL JUST RUIN HIS LUNCH.
COME OUT, YOU LITTLE RED DEVIL...

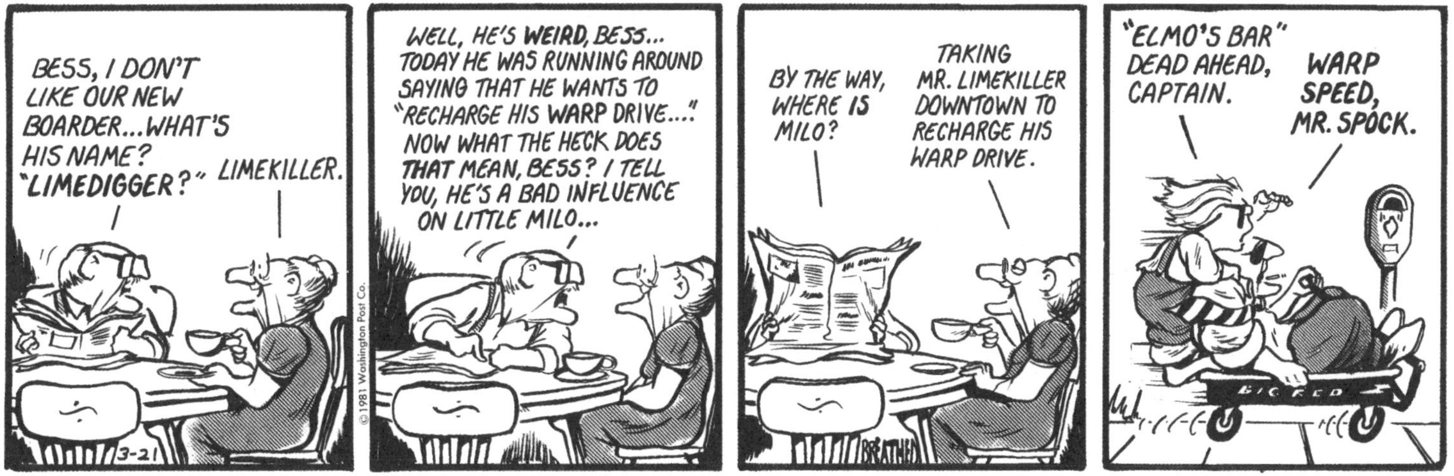
BESS, I DON'T LIKE OUR NEW BOARDER... WHAT'S HIS NAME? "LIMEDIGGER?"
LIMEKILLER.
3-21
© 1981 Washington Post Co.
WELL, HE'S WEIRD, BESS... TODAY HE WAS RUNNING AROUND SAYING THAT HE WANTS TO "RECHARGE HIS WARP DRIVE...." NOW WHAT THE HECK DOES THAT MEAN, BESS? I TELL YOU, HE'S A BAD INFLUENCE ON LITTLE MILO...
BY THE WAY, WHERE IS MILO?
TAKING MR. LIMEKILLER DOWNTOWN TO RECHARGE HIS WARP DRIVE.
BREATHED
"ELMO'S BAR" DEAD AHEAD, CAPTAIN.
WARP SPEED, MR. SPOCK.

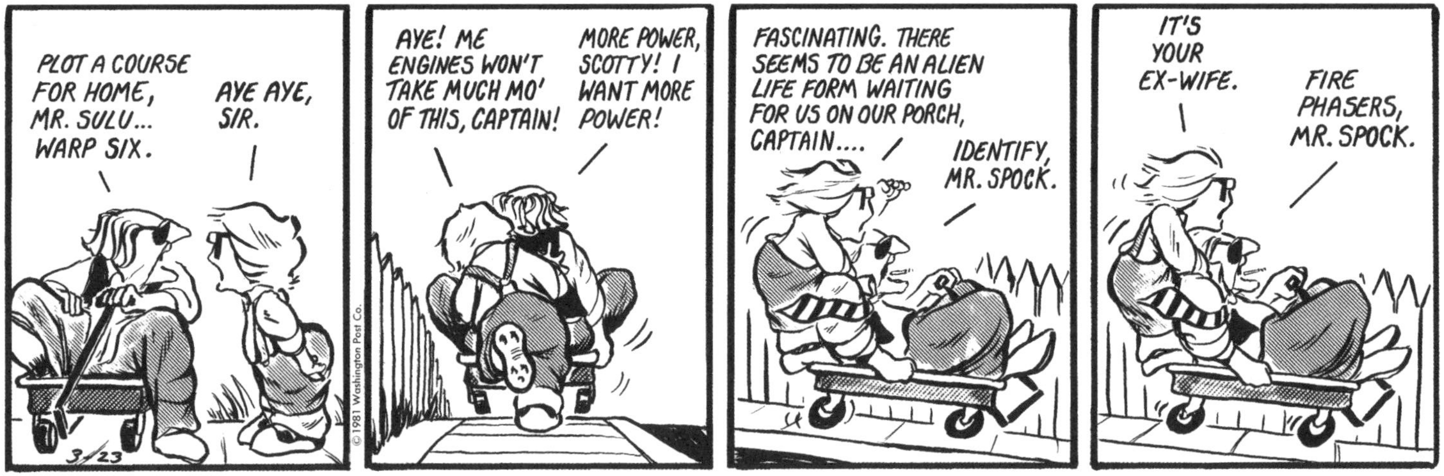
PLOT A COURSE FOR HOME, MR. SULU... WARP SIX.
AYE AYE, SIR.
3-23
© 1981 Washington Post Co.
AYE! ME ENGINES WON'T TAKE MUCH MO' OF THIS, CAPTAIN!
MORE POWER, SCOTTY! I WANT MORE POWER!
FASCINATING. THERE SEEMS TO BE AN ALIEN LIFE FORM WAITING FOR US ON OUR PORCH, CAPTAIN....
IDENTIFY, MR. SPOCK.
IT'S YOUR EX-WIFE.
FIRE PHASERS, MR. SPOCK.

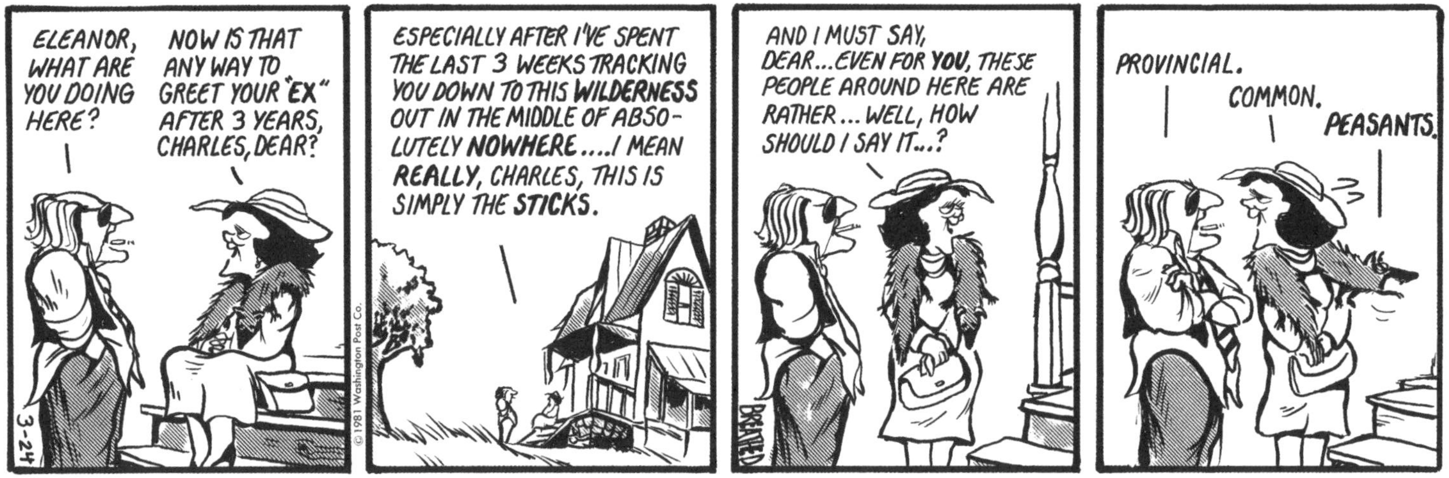
ELEANOR, WHAT ARE YOU DOING HERE?
NOW IS THAT ANY WAY TO GREET YOUR "EX" AFTER 3 YEARS, CHARLES, DEAR?
3-24
© 1981 Washington Post Co.
ESPECIALLY AFTER I'VE SPENT THE LAST 3 WEEKS TRACKING YOU DOWN TO THIS WILDERNESS OUT IN THE MIDDLE OF ABSOLUTELY NOWHERE.....I MEAN REALLY, CHARLES, THIS IS SIMPLY THE STICKS.
AND I MUST SAY, DEAR...EVEN FOR YOU, THESE PEOPLE AROUND HERE ARE RATHER... WELL, HOW SHOULD I SAY IT...?
BREATHED
PROVINCIAL.
COMMON.
PEASANTS.

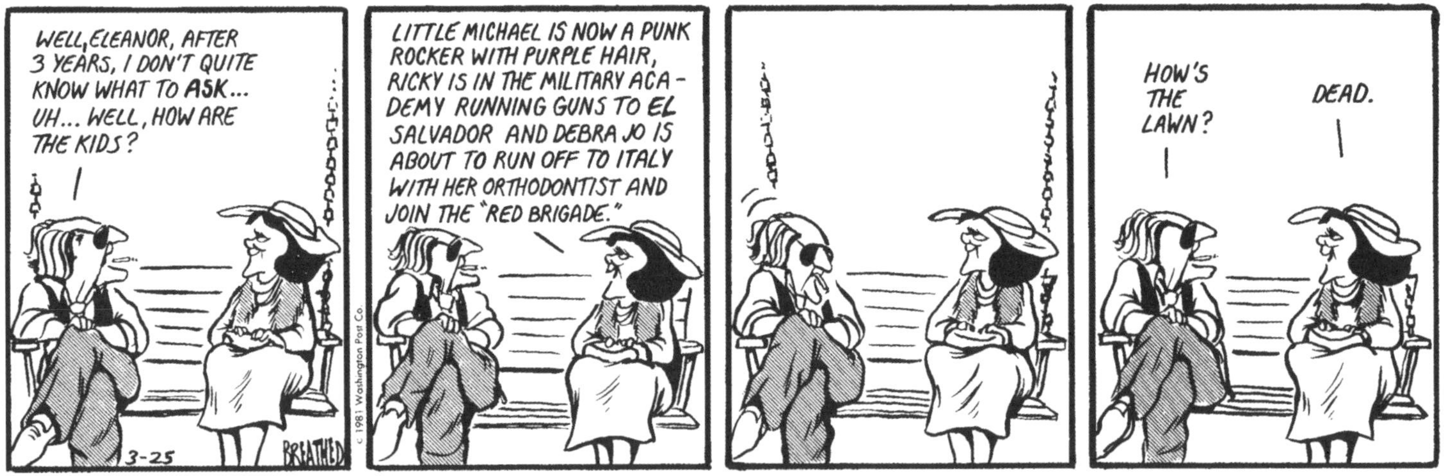
WELL, ELEANOR, AFTER 3 YEARS, I DON'T QUITE KNOW WHAT TO ASK... UH... WELL, HOW ARE THE KIDS?
3-25
BREATHED
© 1981 Washington Post Co.
LITTLE MICHAEL IS NOW A PUNK ROCKER WITH PURPLE HAIR, RICKY IS IN THE MILITARY ACADEMY RUNNING GUNS TO EL SALVADOR AND DEBRA JO IS ABOUT TO RUN OFF TO ITALY WITH HER ORTHODONTIST AND JOIN THE "RED BRIGADE."
HOW'S THE LAWN?
DEAD.

The Red Brigade was a Marxist-Leninist terrorist organization, founded in Italy in the 1970s.

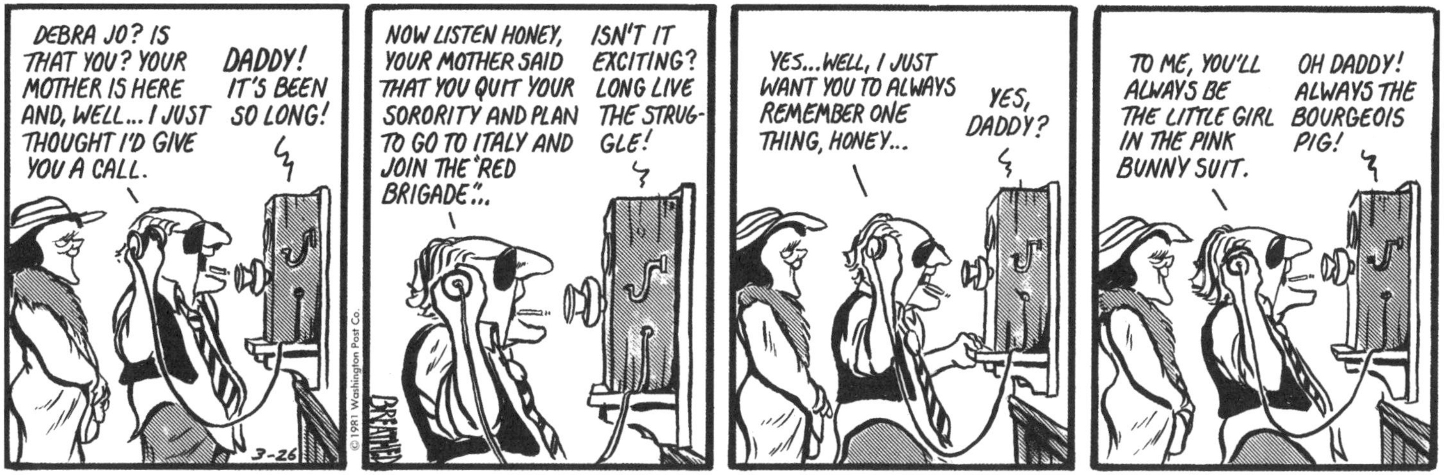
DEBRA JO? IS THAT YOU? YOUR MOTHER IS HERE AND, WELL... I JUST THOUGHT I'D GIVE YOU A CALL.
DADDY! IT'S BEEN SO LONG!
3-26
NOW LISTEN HONEY, YOUR MOTHER SAID THAT YOU QUIT YOUR SORORITY AND PLAN TO GO TO ITALY AND JOIN THE "RED BRIGADE"...
ISN'T IT EXCITING? LONG LIVE THE STRUGGLE!
© 1981 Washington Post Co.
BREATHED
YES... WELL, I JUST WANT YOU TO ALWAYS REMEMBER ONE THING, HONEY...
YES, DADDY?
TO ME, YOU'LL ALWAYS BE THE LITTLE GIRL IN THE PINK BUNNY SUIT.
OH DADDY! ALWAYS THE BOURGEOIS PIG!

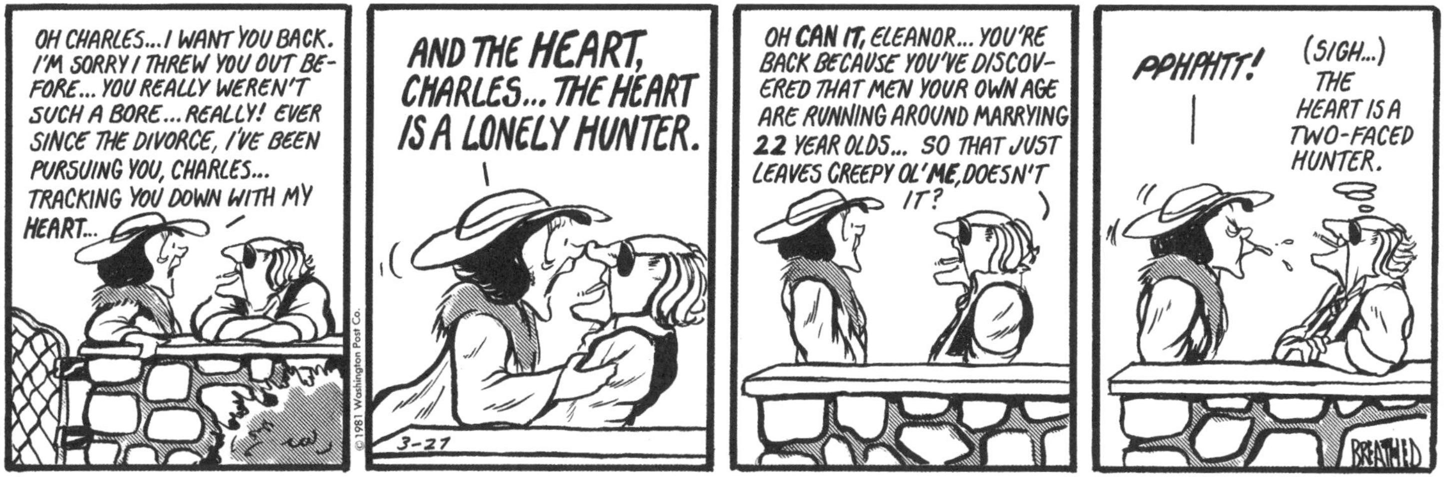
OH CHARLES... I WANT YOU BACK. I'M SORRY I THREW YOU OUT BEFORE... YOU REALLY WEREN'T SUCH A BORE... REALLY! EVER SINCE THE DIVORCE, I'VE BEEN PURSUING YOU, CHARLES... TRACKING YOU DOWN WITH MY HEART...
AND THE HEART, CHARLES... THE HEART IS A LONELY HUNTER.
© 1981 Washington Post Co.
3-27
OH CAN IT, ELEANOR... YOU'RE BACK BECAUSE YOU'VE DISCOVERED THAT MEN YOUR OWN AGE ARE RUNNING AROUND MARRYING 22 YEAR OLDS... SO THAT JUST LEAVES CREEPY OL' ME, DOESN'T IT?
PPHPHTT!
(SIGH...) THE HEART IS A TWO-FACED HUNTER.
BREATHED

The Heart is a Lonely Hunter by Carson McCullers was a best selling novel in the 1940s. It has enjoyed lasting popularity and was recently selected as one of *Time* magazine's 100 best English language novels.

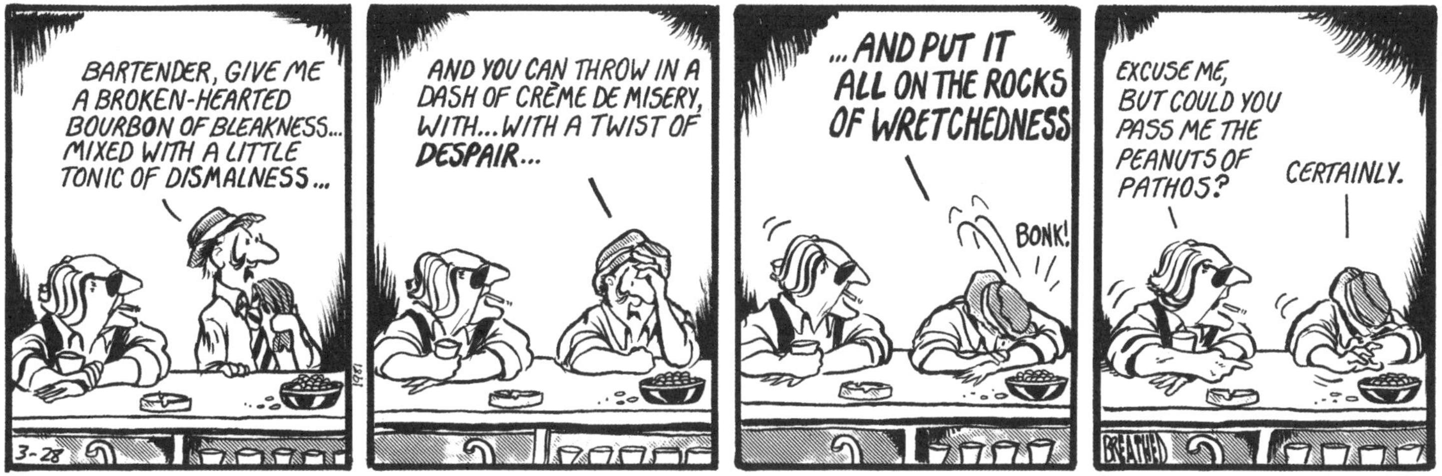
BARTENDER, GIVE ME A BROKEN-HEARTED BOURBON OF BLEAKNESS... MIXED WITH A LITTLE TONIC OF DISMALNESS...
3-28
AND YOU CAN THROW IN A DASH OF CRÈME DE MISERY, WITH... WITH A TWIST OF DESPAIR...
1981
...AND PUT IT ALL ON THE ROCKS OF WRETCHEDNESS
BONK!
EXCUSE ME, BUT COULD YOU PASS ME THE PEANUTS OF PATHOS?
CERTAINLY.
BREATHED

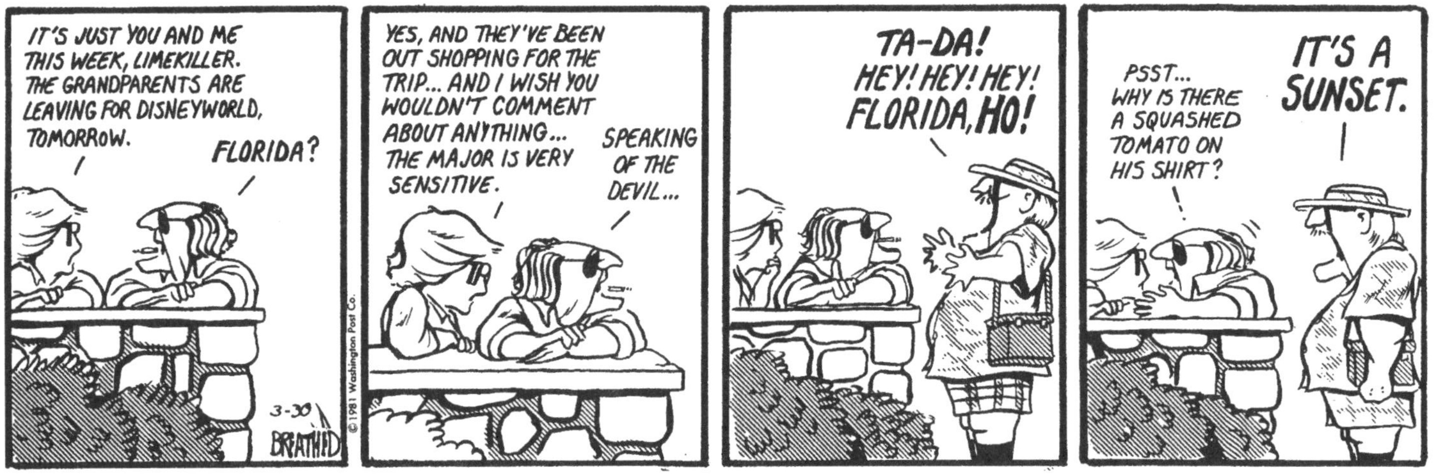
IT'S JUST YOU AND ME THIS WEEK, LIMEKILLER. THE GRANDPARENTS ARE LEAVING FOR DISNEYWORLD, TOMORROW.
FLORIDA?
3-30
BREATHED
© 1981 Washington Post Co.
YES, AND THEY'VE BEEN OUT SHOPPING FOR THE TRIP... AND I WISH YOU WOULDN'T COMMENT ABOUT ANYTHING... THE MAJOR IS VERY SENSITIVE.
SPEAKING OF THE DEVIL...
TA-DA! HEY! HEY! HEY! FLORIDA, HO!
PSST... WHY IS THERE A SQUASHED TOMATO ON HIS SHIRT?
IT'S A SUNSET.

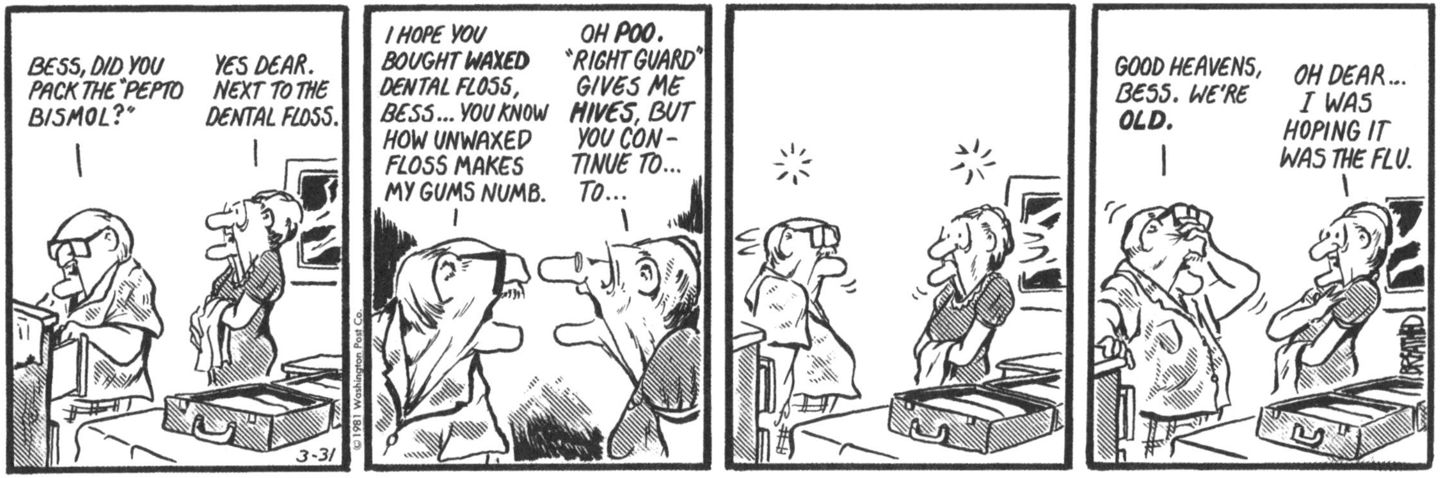
BESS, DID YOU PACK THE "PEPTO BISMOL?"
YES DEAR. NEXT TO THE DENTAL FLOSS.
3-31
© 1981 Washington Post Co.
I HOPE YOU BOUGHT WAXED DENTAL FLOSS, BESS... YOU KNOW HOW UNWAXED FLOSS MAKES MY GUMS NUMB.
OH POO. "RIGHT GUARD" GIVES ME HIVES, BUT YOU CONTINUE TO... TO...
GOOD HEAVENS, BESS. WE'RE OLD.
OH DEAR... I WAS HOPING IT WAS THE FLU.
BREATHED

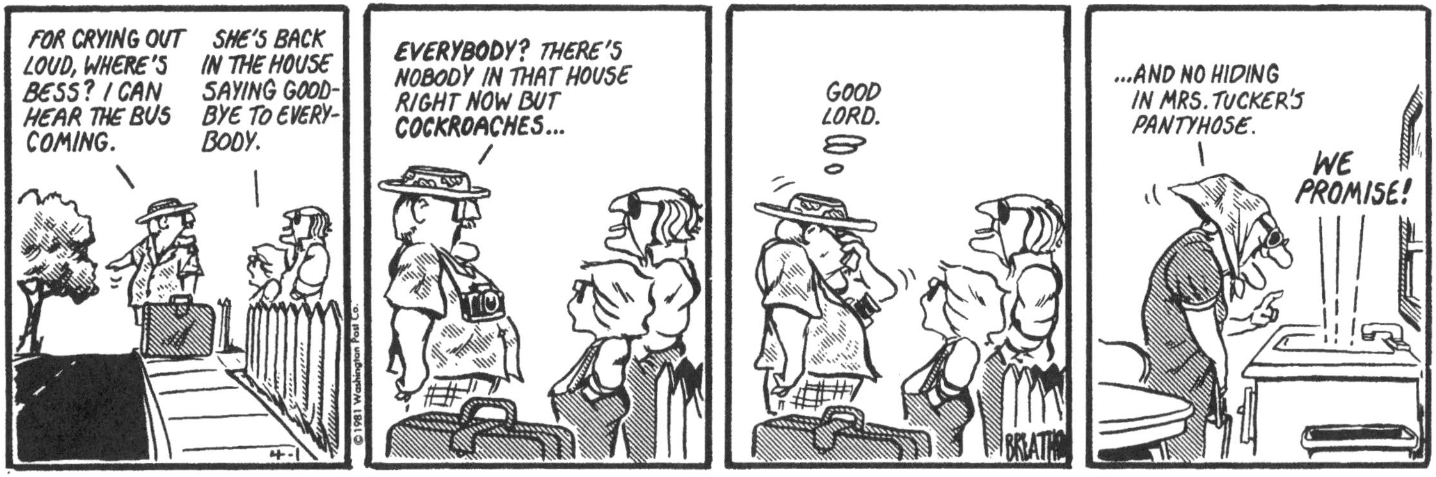
FOR CRYING OUT LOUD, WHERE'S BESS? I CAN HEAR THE BUS COMING.
SHE'S BACK IN THE HOUSE SAYING GOOD-BYE TO EVERYBODY.
4-1
© 1981 Washington Post Co.
EVERYBODY? THERE'S NOBODY IN THAT HOUSE RIGHT NOW BUT COCKROACHES...
GOOD LORD.
BREATHED
...AND NO HIDING IN MRS. TUCKER'S PANTYHOSE.
WE PROMISE!

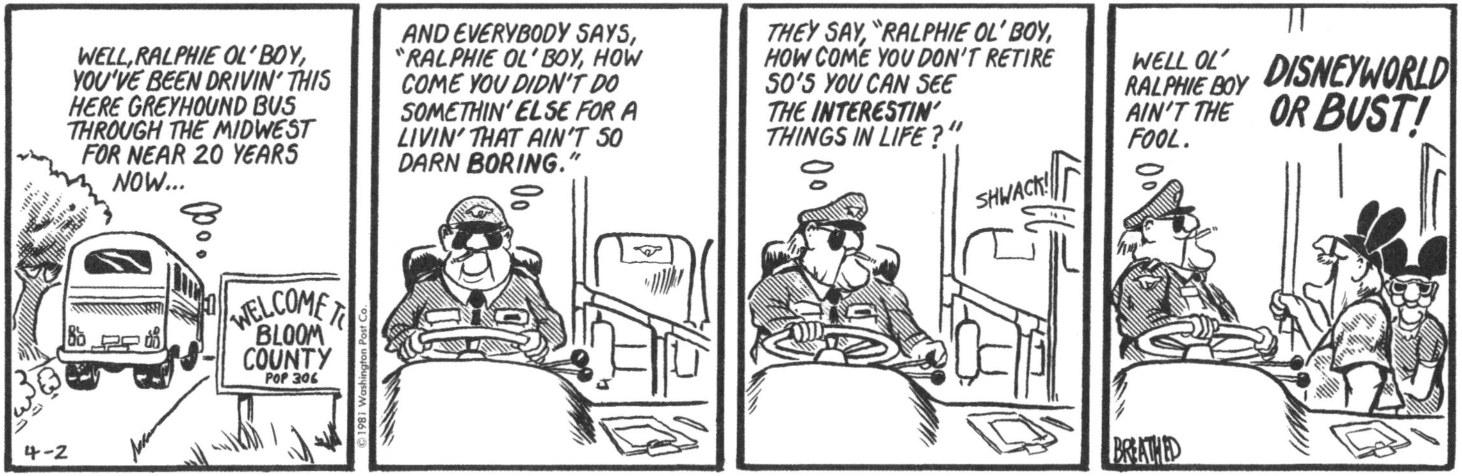
WELL, RALPHIE OL' BOY, YOU'VE BEEN DRIVIN' THIS HERE GREYHOUND BUS THROUGH THE MIDWEST FOR NEAR 20 YEARS NOW...
WELCOME TO BLOOM COUNTY POP 306
4-2
© 1981 Washington Post Co.
AND EVERYBODY SAYS, "RALPHIE OL' BOY, HOW COME YOU DIDN'T DO SOMETHIN' ELSE FOR A LIVIN' THAT AIN'T SO DARN BORING."
THEY SAY, "RALPHIE OL' BOY, HOW COME YOU DON'T RETIRE SO'S YOU CAN SEE THE INTERESTIN' THINGS IN LIFE?"
SHWACK!
WELL OL' RALPHIE BOY AIN'T THE FOOL.
DISNEYWORLD OR BUST!
BREATHED

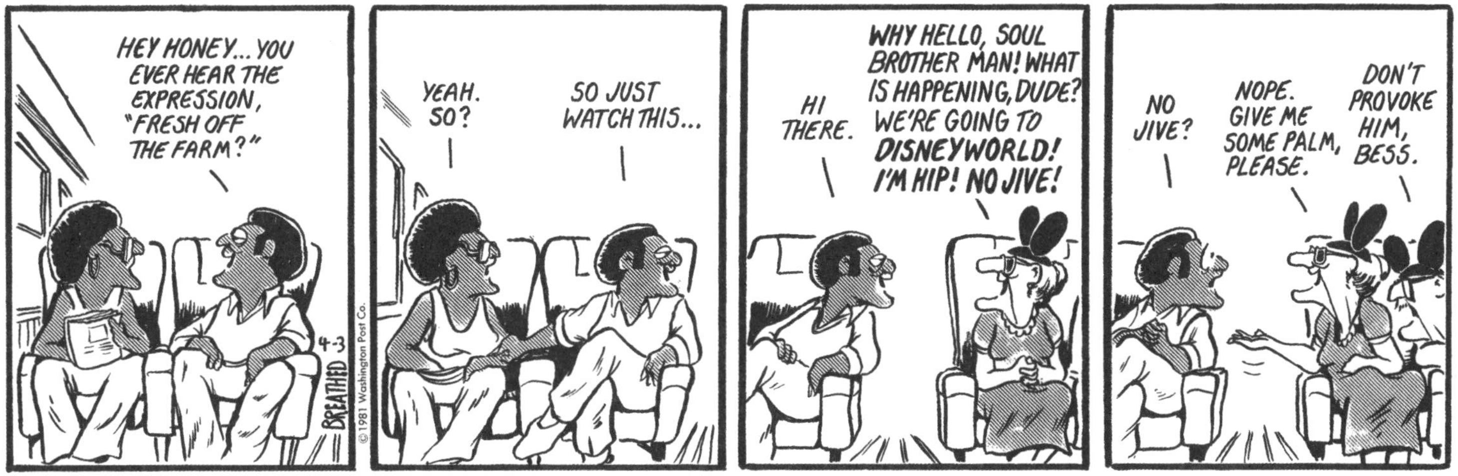
HEY HONEY... YOU EVER HEAR THE EXPRESSION, "FRESH OFF THE FARM?"
4-3
BREATHED
© 1981 Washington Post Co.
YEAH. SO?
SO JUST WATCH THIS...
HI THERE.
WHY HELLO, SOUL BROTHER MAN! WHAT IS HAPPENING, DUDE? WE'RE GOING TO DISNEYWORLD! I'M HIP! NO JIVE!
NO JIVE?
NOPE. GIVE ME SOME PALM, PLEASE.
DON'T PROVOKE HIM, BESS.

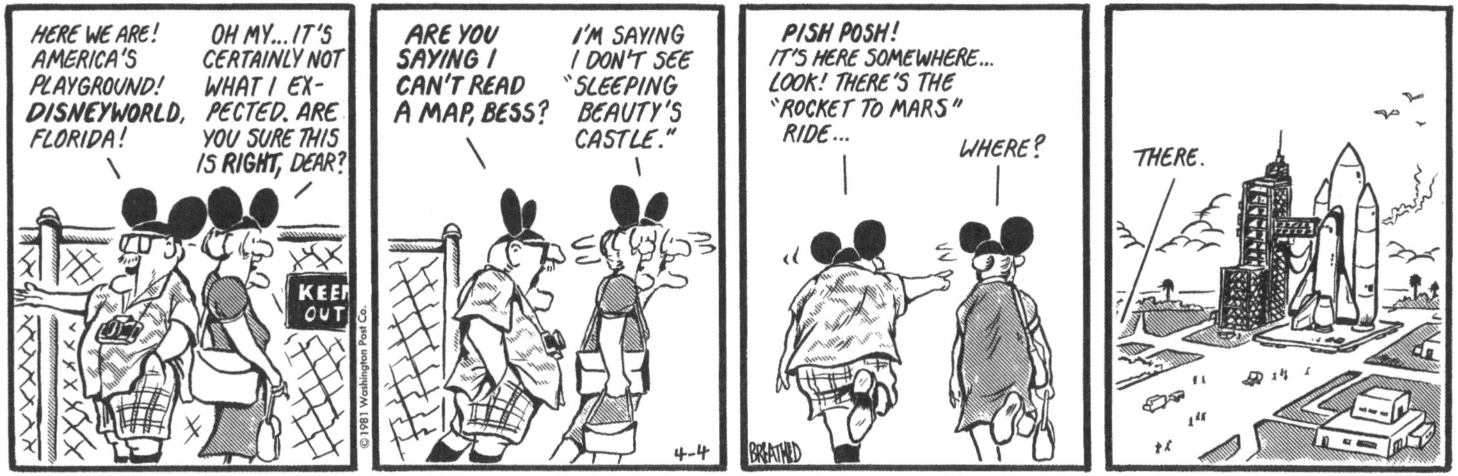
HERE WE ARE! AMERICA'S PLAYGROUND! DISNEYWORLD, FLORIDA!
OH MY... IT'S CERTAINLY NOT WHAT I EXPECTED. ARE YOU SURE THIS IS RIGHT, DEAR?
KEEP OUT
© 1981 Washington Post Co.
ARE YOU SAYING I CAN'T READ A MAP, BESS?
I'M SAYING I DON'T SEE "SLEEPING BEAUTY'S CASTLE."
4-4
PISH POSH! IT'S HERE SOMEWHERE... LOOK! THERE'S THE "ROCKET TO MARS" RIDE...
WHERE?
BREATHED
THERE.

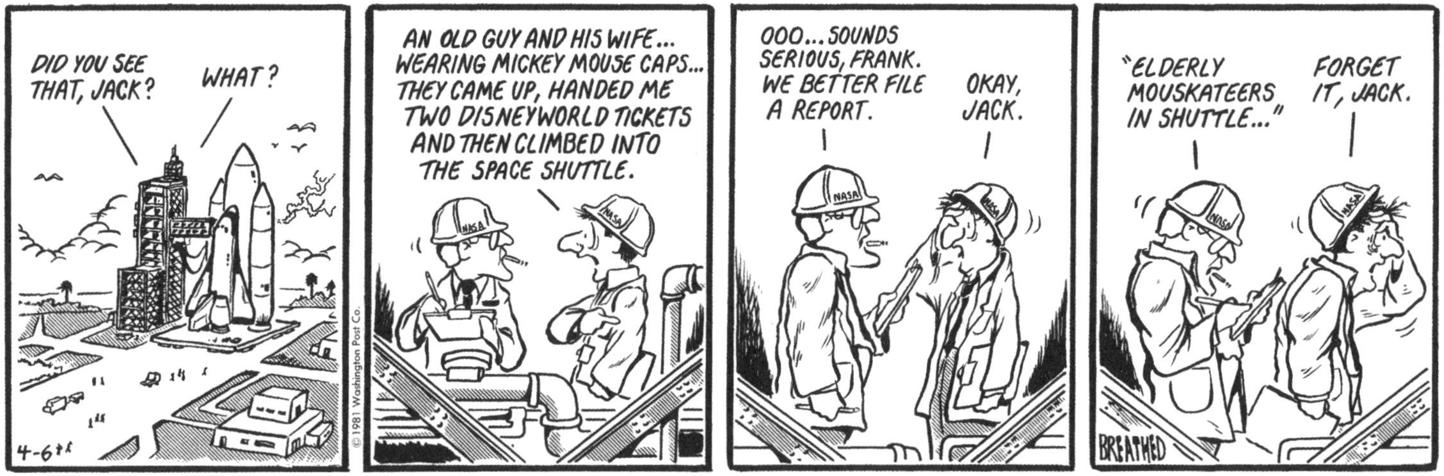
DID YOU SEE THAT, JACK?
WHAT?
4-6
© 1981 Washington Post Co.
AN OLD GUY AND HIS WIFE... WEARING MICKEY MOUSE CAPS... THEY CAME UP, HANDED ME TWO DISNEYWORLD TICKETS AND THEN CLIMBED INTO THE SPACE SHUTTLE.
NASA
OOO... SOUNDS SERIOUS, FRANK. WE BETTER FILE A REPORT.
OKAY, JACK.
"ELDERLY MOUSKATEERS IN SHUTTLE..."
FORGET IT, JACK.
BREATHED

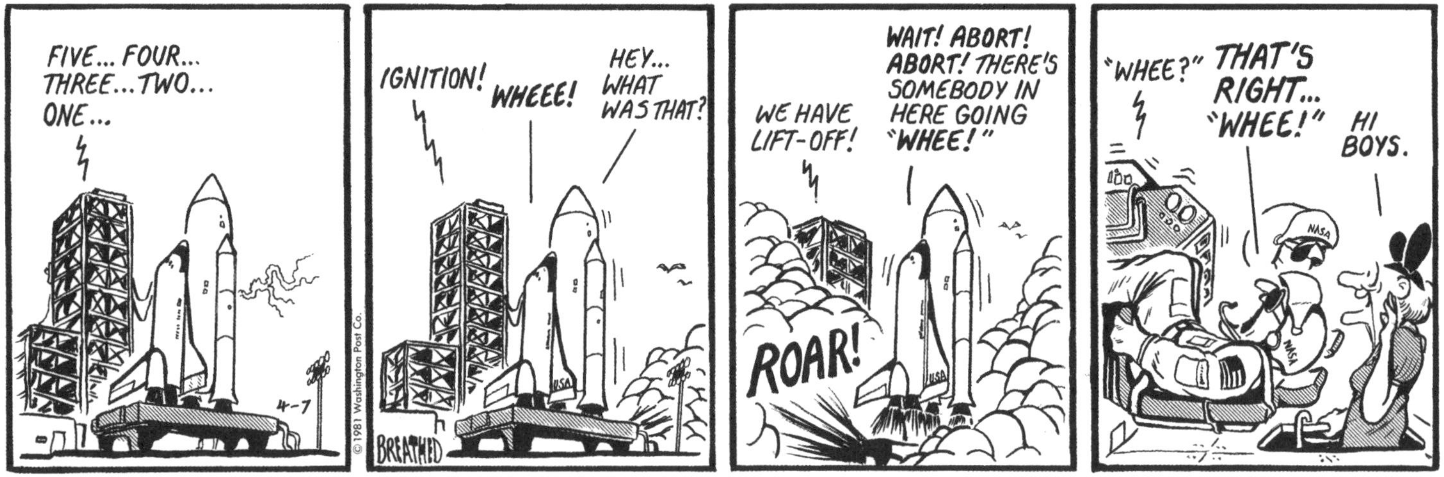
FIVE... FOUR... THREE... TWO... ONE...
4-7
© 1981 Washington Post Co.
IGNITION!
WHEEE!
HEY... WHAT WAS THAT?
BREATHED
WE HAVE LIFT-OFF!
WAIT! ABORT! ABORT! THERE'S SOMEBODY IN HERE GOING "WHEE!"
ROAR!
"WHEE?"
THAT'S RIGHT... "WHEE!"
HI BOYS.
NASA

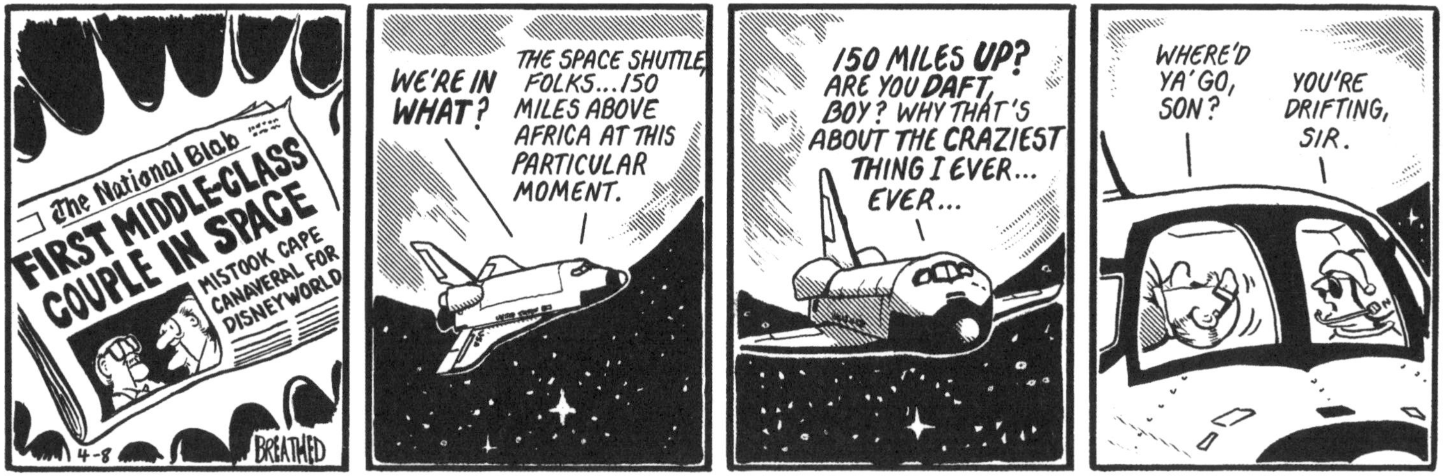
The National Blab
FIRST MIDDLE-CLASS COUPLE IN SPACE
MISTOOK CAPE CANAVERAL FOR DISNEYWORLD
4-8
BREATHED
WE'RE IN WHAT?
THE SPACE SHUTTLE, FOLKS... 150 MILES ABOVE AFRICA AT THIS PARTICULAR MOMENT.
150 MILES UP? ARE YOU DAFT, BOY? WHY THAT'S ABOUT THE CRAZIEST THING I EVER... EVER...
WHERE'D YA' GO, SON?
YOU'RE DRIFTING, SIR.

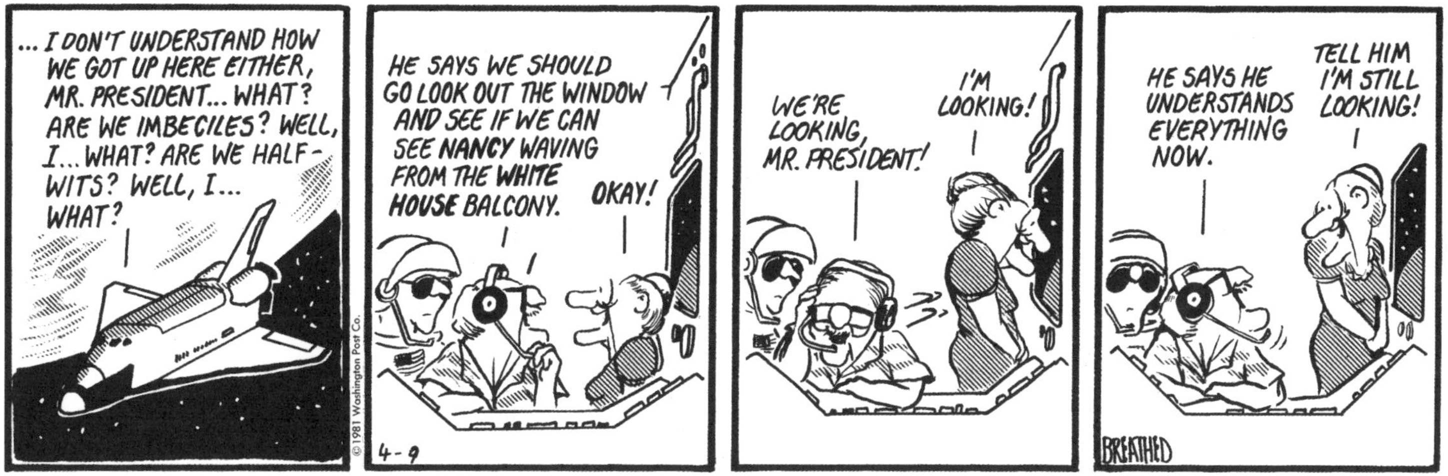
... I DON'T UNDERSTAND HOW WE GOT UP HERE EITHER, MR. PRESIDENT... WHAT? ARE WE IMBECILES? WELL, I... WHAT? ARE WE HALF-WITS? WELL, I... WHAT?
© 1981 Washington Post Co.
4-9
HE SAYS WE SHOULD GO LOOK OUT THE WINDOW AND SEE IF WE CAN SEE NANCY WAVING FROM THE WHITE HOUSE BALCONY.
OKAY!
WE'RE LOOKING, MR. PRESIDENT!
I'M LOOKING!
HE SAYS HE UNDERSTANDS EVERYTHING NOW.
TELL HIM I'M STILL LOOKING!
BREATHED

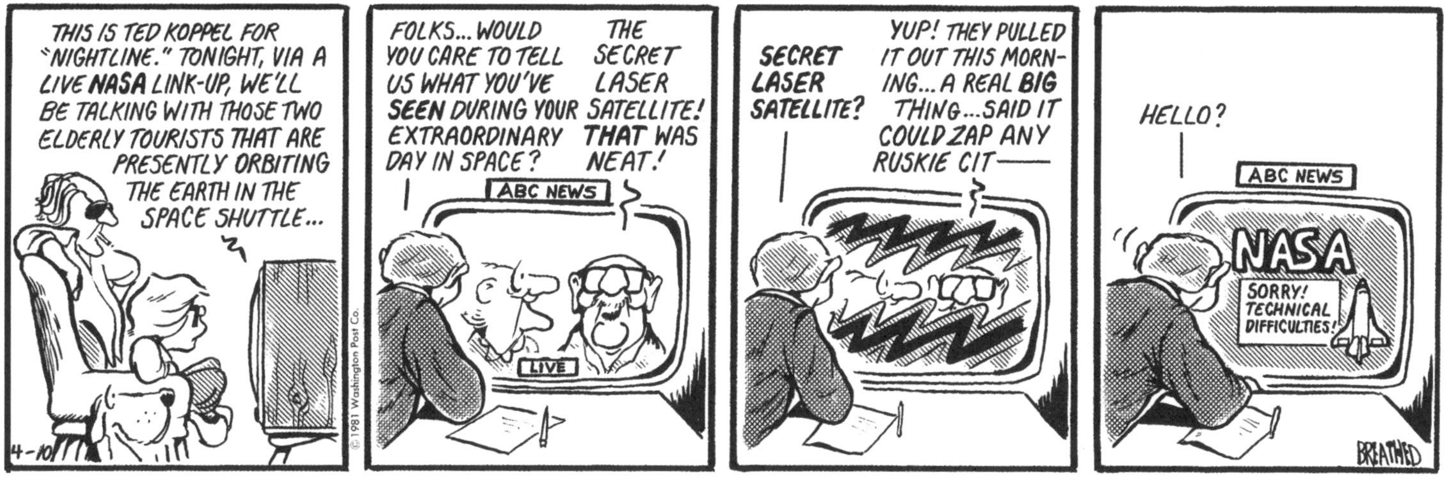
THIS IS TED KOPPEL FOR "NIGHTLINE." TONIGHT, VIA A LIVE NASA LINK-UP, WE'LL BE TALKING WITH THOSE TWO ELDERLY TOURISTS THAT ARE PRESENTLY ORBITING THE EARTH IN THE SPACE SHUTTLE...
4-10
© 1981 Washington Post Co.
FOLKS... WOULD YOU CARE TO TELL US WHAT YOU'VE SEEN DURING YOUR EXTRAORDINARY DAY IN SPACE?
THE SECRET LASER SATELLITE! THAT WAS NEAT!
ABC NEWS
LIVE
SECRET LASER SATELLITE?
YUP! THEY PULLED IT OUT THIS MORNING... A REAL BIG THING... SAID IT COULD ZAP ANY RUSKIE CIT—
HELLO?
ABC NEWS
NASA
SORRY! TECHNICAL DIFFICULTIES!
BREATHED

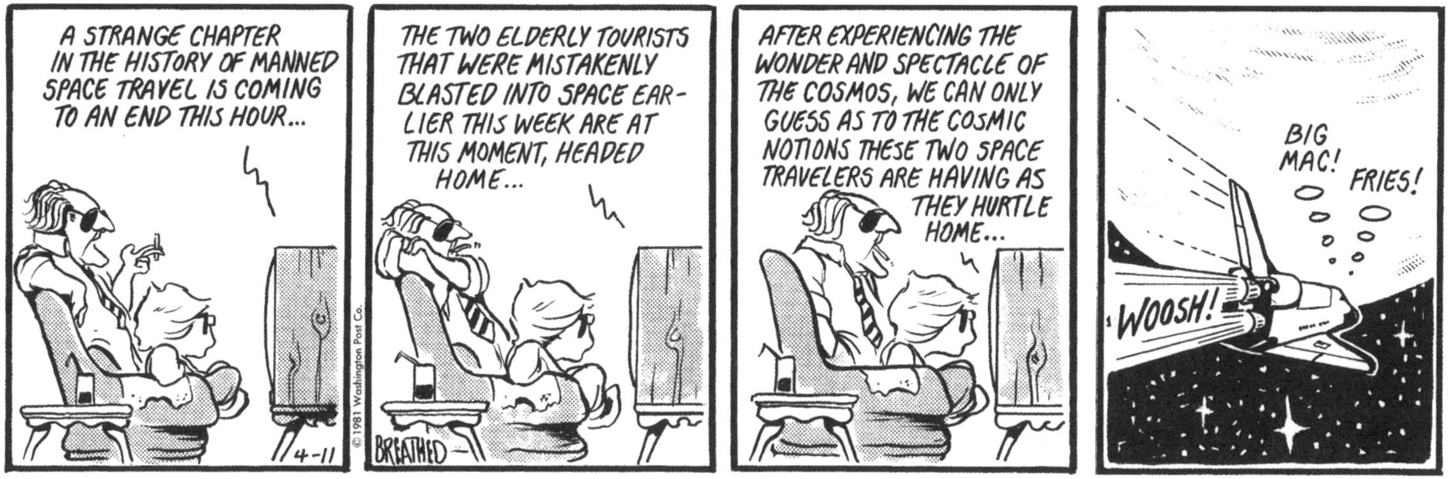
A STRANGE CHAPTER IN THE HISTORY OF MANNED SPACE TRAVEL IS COMING TO AN END THIS HOUR...
4-11
© 1981 Washington Post Co.
THE TWO ELDERLY TOURISTS THAT WERE MISTAKENLY BLASTED INTO SPACE EARLIER THIS WEEK ARE AT THIS MOMENT, HEADED HOME...
BREATHED
AFTER EXPERIENCING THE WONDER AND SPECTACLE OF THE COSMOS, WE CAN ONLY GUESS AS TO THE COSMIC NOTIONS THESE TWO SPACE TRAVELERS ARE HAVING AS THEY HURTLE HOME...
BIG MAC!
FRIES!
WOOSH!

Nancy Reagan, wife of President Ronald Reagan. As well known for her anti-drug campaign, "Just Say No," as for her contentious relationships with several White House staffers, and her faith in astrology.

Ted Koppel was the host of the critically lauded late-night news show, *Nightline*.

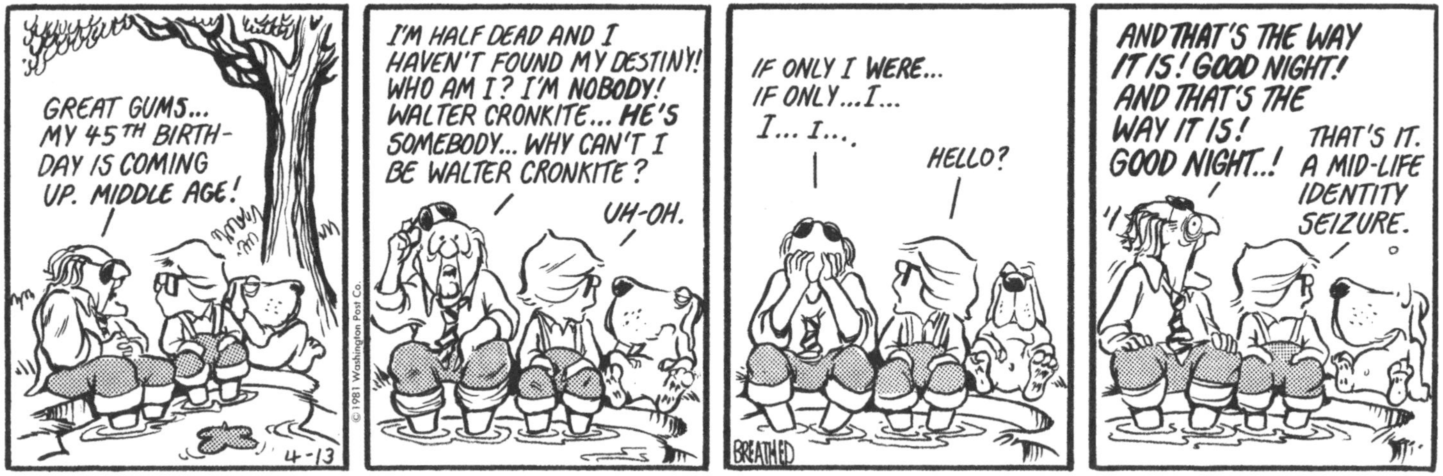
GREAT GUMS... MY 45TH BIRTHDAY IS COMING UP. MIDDLE AGE!
I'M HALF DEAD AND I HAVEN'T FOUND MY DESTINY! WHO AM I? I'M NOBODY! WALTER CRONKITE... HE'S SOMEBODY... WHY CAN'T I BE WALTER CRONKITE?
UH-OH.
IF ONLY I WERE... IF ONLY...I... I... I....
HELLO?
AND THAT'S THE WAY IT IS! GOOD NIGHT! AND THAT'S THE WAY IT IS! GOOD NIGHT..!
THAT'S IT. A MID-LIFE IDENTITY SEIZURE.
4-13
© 1981 Washington Post Co.
BREATHED

Ingrid Bergman, an Oscar-winning actress, was perhaps best known for her co-starring turn as Ilsa in *Casablanca*, opposite Humphrey Bogart.

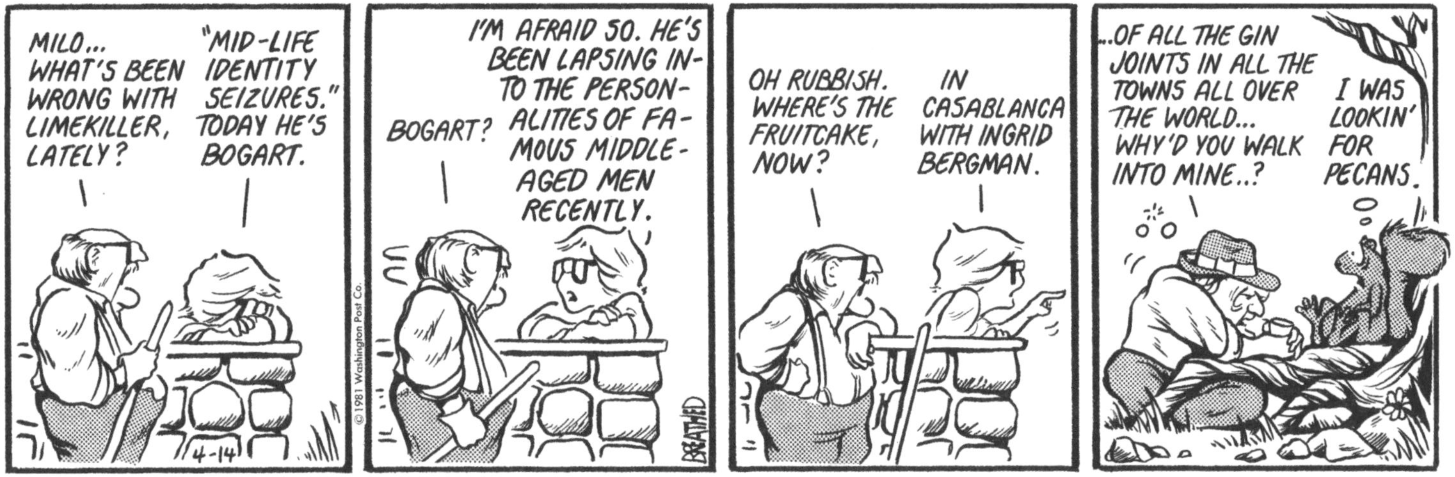
MILO... WHAT'S BEEN WRONG WITH LIMEKILLER, LATELY?
"MID-LIFE IDENTITY SEIZURES." TODAY HE'S BOGART.
BOGART?
I'M AFRAID SO. HE'S BEEN LAPSING INTO THE PERSONALITIES OF FAMOUS MIDDLE-AGED MEN RECENTLY.
OH RUBBISH. WHERE'S THE FRUITCAKE, NOW?
IN CASABLANCA WITH INGRID BERGMAN.
...OF ALL THE GIN JOINTS IN ALL THE TOWNS ALL OVER THE WORLD... WHY'D YOU WALK INTO MINE..?
I WAS LOOKIN' FOR PECANS.
4-14
© 1981 Washington Post Co.
BREATHED

Johnny Weissmuller was a gold medal-winning Olympic swimmer in the 1920s. In the 1930s and 1940s, Weissmuller starred in a dozen Tarzan films.

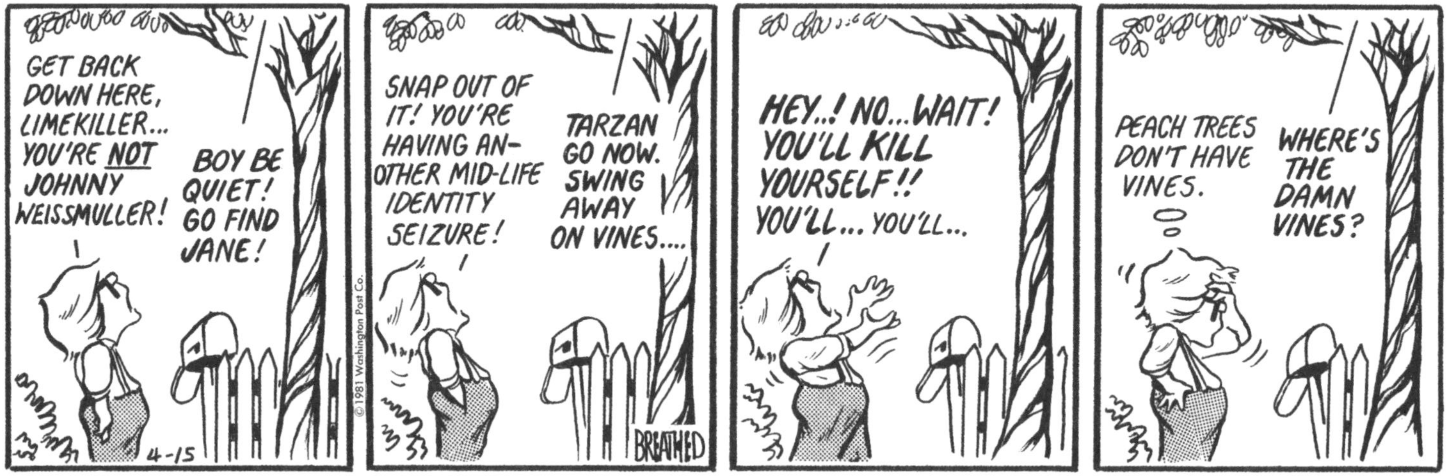
GET BACK DOWN HERE, LIMEKILLER... YOU'RE NOT JOHNNY WEISSMULLER!
BOY BE QUIET! GO FIND JANE!
SNAP OUT OF IT! YOU'RE HAVING ANOTHER MID-LIFE IDENTITY SEIZURE!
TARZAN GO NOW. SWING AWAY ON VINES....
HEY..! NO...WAIT! YOU'LL KILL YOURSELF!! YOU'LL... YOU'LL...
PEACH TREES DON'T HAVE VINES.
WHERE'S THE DAMN VINES?
4-15
© 1981 Washington Post Co.
BREATHED

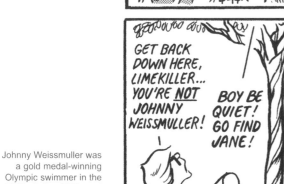

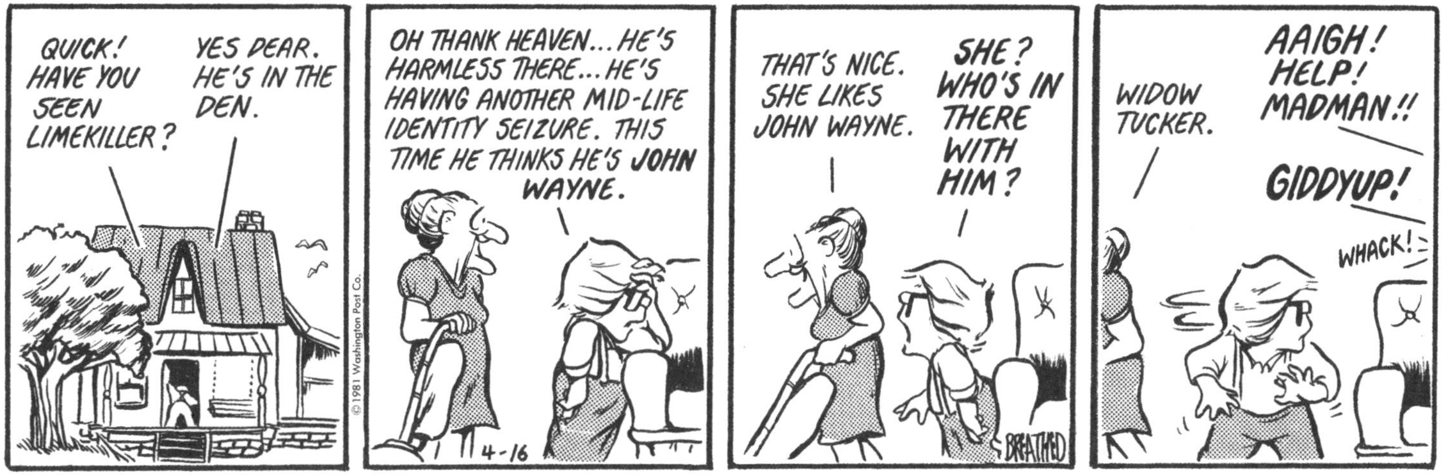
QUICK! HAVE YOU SEEN LIMEKILLER?
YES DEAR. HE'S IN THE DEN.
© 1981 Washington Post Co.
OH THANK HEAVEN... HE'S HARMLESS THERE... HE'S HAVING ANOTHER MID-LIFE IDENTITY SEIZURE. THIS TIME HE THINKS HE'S JOHN WAYNE.
4-16
THAT'S NICE. SHE LIKES JOHN WAYNE.
SHE? WHO'S IN THERE WITH HIM?
BREATHED
WIDOW TUCKER.
AAIGH! HELP! MADMAN!!
GIDDYUP!
WHACK!

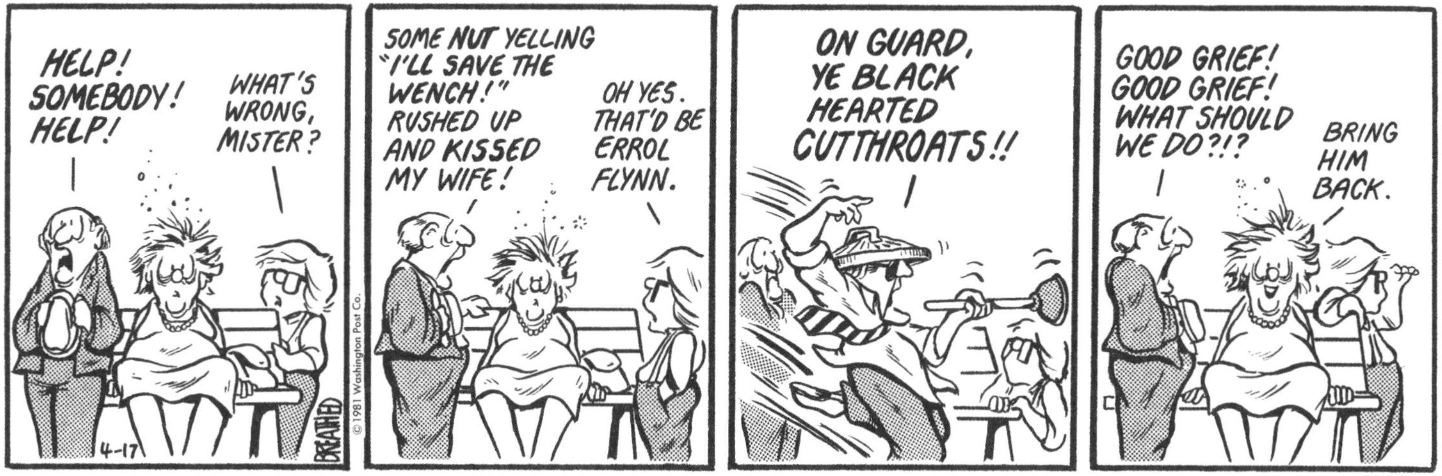
HELP! SOMEBODY! HELP!
WHAT'S WRONG, MISTER?
4-17
BREATHED
© 1981 Washington Post Co.
SOME NUT YELLING "I'LL SAVE THE WENCH!" RUSHED UP AND KISSED MY WIFE!
OH YES. THAT'D BE ERROL FLYNN.
ON GUARD, YE BLACK HEARTED CUTTHROATS!!
GOOD GRIEF! GOOD GRIEF! WHAT SHOULD WE DO?!?
BRING HIM BACK.

Errol Flynn was the definitive swashbuckling film star of the 1930s and 1940s. In addition to *Captain Blood* and *The Sea Hawk*, Flynn starred in the Technicolor classic, *The Adventures of Robin Hood*.

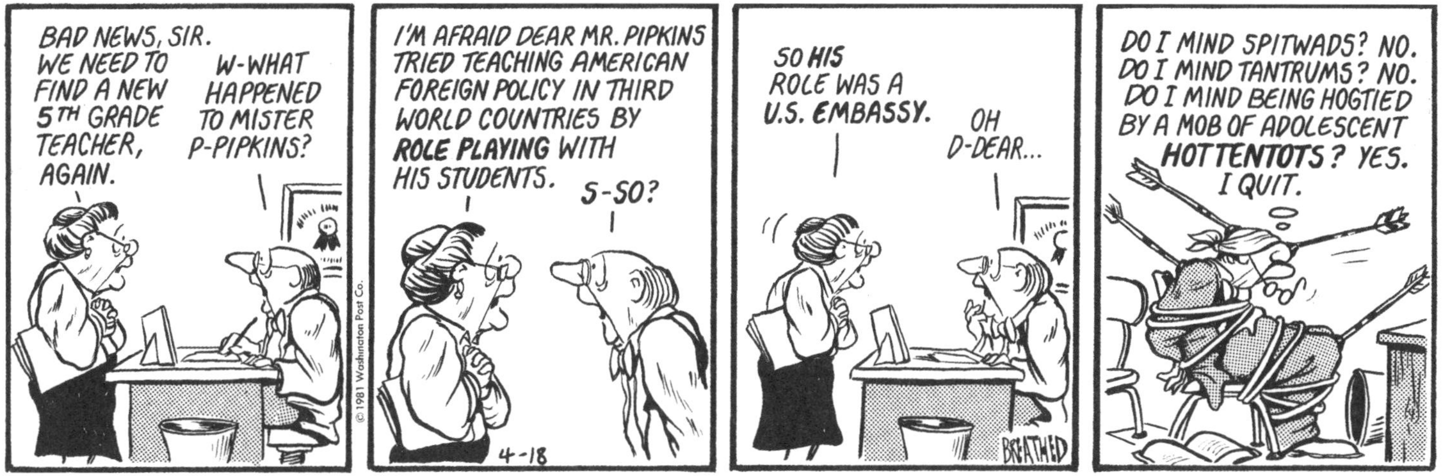
BAD NEWS, SIR. WE NEED TO FIND A NEW 5TH GRADE TEACHER, AGAIN.
W-WHAT HAPPENED TO MISTER P-PIPKINS?
© 1981 Washington Post Co.
I'M AFRAID DEAR MR. PIPKINS TRIED TEACHING AMERICAN FOREIGN POLICY IN THIRD WORLD COUNTRIES BY ROLE PLAYING WITH HIS STUDENTS.
S-SO?
4-18
SO HIS ROLE WAS A U.S. EMBASSY.
OH D-DEAR...
BREATHED
DO I MIND SPITWADS? NO. DO I MIND TANTRUMS? NO. DO I MIND BEING HOGTIED BY A MOB OF ADOLESCENT HOTTENTOTS? YES. I QUIT.

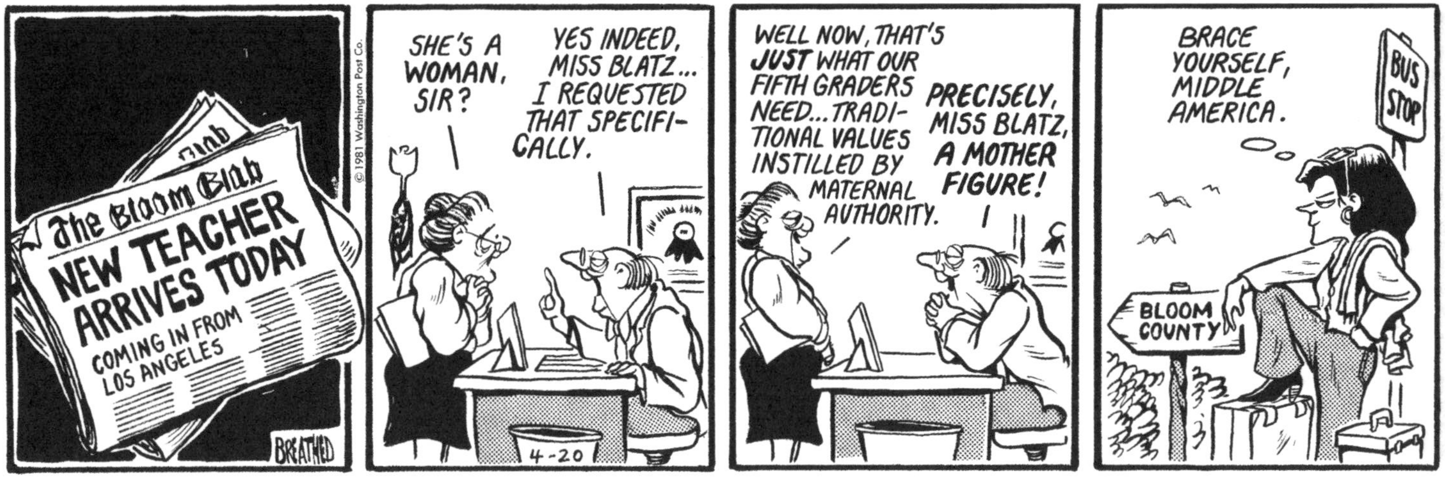
The Bloom Blab
NEW TEACHER ARRIVES TODAY
COMING IN FROM LOS ANGELES
BREATHED
© 1981 Washington Post Co.
SHE'S A WOMAN, SIR?
YES INDEED, MISS BLATZ... I REQUESTED THAT SPECIFICALLY.
4-20
WELL NOW, THAT'S JUST WHAT OUR FIFTH GRADERS NEED...TRADITIONAL VALUES INSTILLED BY MATERNAL AUTHORITY.
PRECISELY, MISS BLATZ, A MOTHER FIGURE!
BRACE YOURSELF, MIDDLE AMERICA.
BUS STOP
BLOOM COUNTY

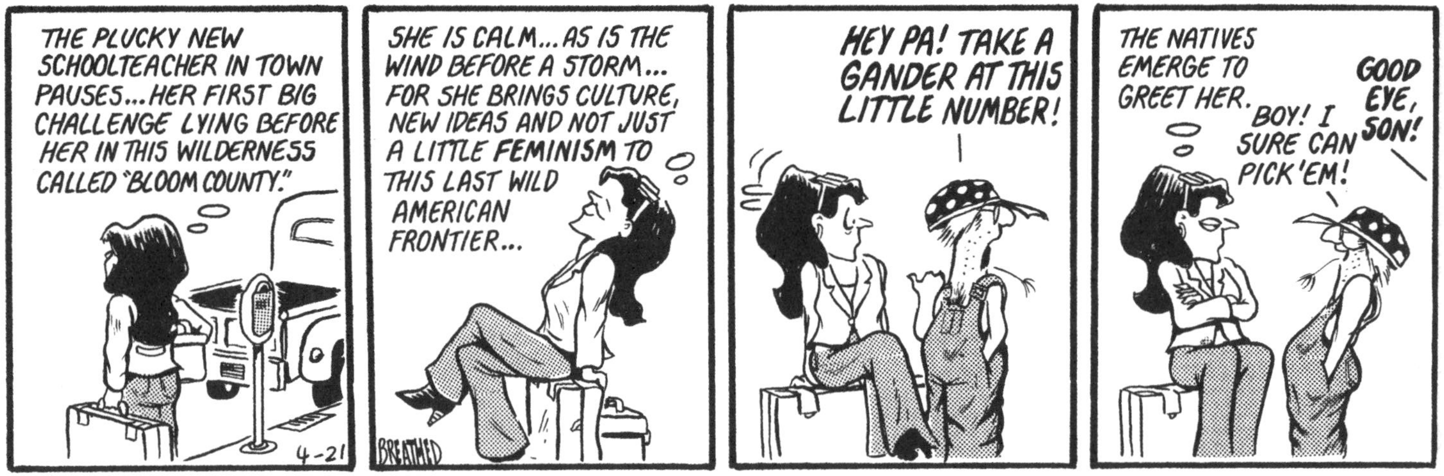
THE PLUCKY NEW SCHOOLTEACHER IN TOWN PAUSES...HER FIRST BIG CHALLENGE LYING BEFORE HER IN THIS WILDERNESS CALLED "BLOOM COUNTY."
4-21
SHE IS CALM...AS IS THE WIND BEFORE A STORM... FOR SHE BRINGS CULTURE, NEW IDEAS AND NOT JUST A LITTLE FEMINISM TO THIS LAST WILD AMERICAN FRONTIER...
BREATHED
HEY PA! TAKE A GANDER AT THIS LITTLE NUMBER!
THE NATIVES EMERGE TO GREET HER.
GOOD EYE, SON!
BOY! I SURE CAN PICK 'EM!

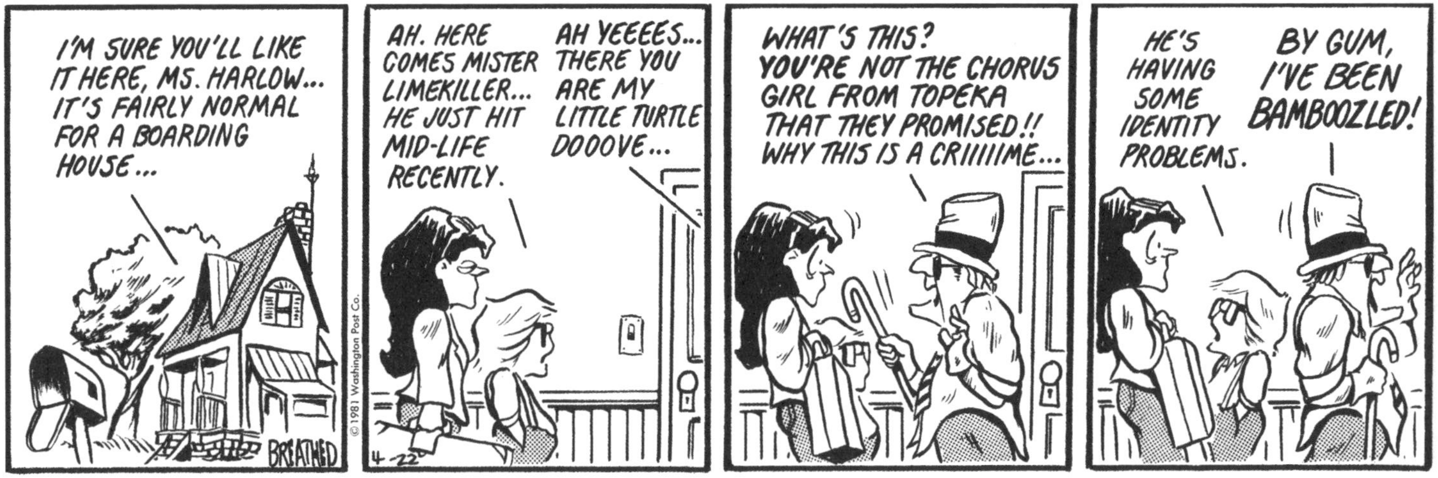
I'M SURE YOU'LL LIKE IT HERE, MS. HARLOW... IT'S FAIRLY NORMAL FOR A BOARDING HOUSE...
BREATHED
© 1981 Washington Post Co.
AH. HERE COMES MISTER LIMEKILLER... HE JUST HIT MID-LIFE RECENTLY.
AH YEEEES... THERE YOU ARE MY LITTLE TURTLE DOOOVE...
4-22
WHAT'S THIS? YOU'RE NOT THE CHORUS GIRL FROM TOPEKA THAT THEY PROMISED!! WHY THIS IS A CRIIIIIME...
HE'S HAVING SOME IDENTITY PROBLEMS.
BY GUM, I'VE BEEN BAMBOOZLED!

The first appearance of feminist schoolteacher, Bobbi Harlow.

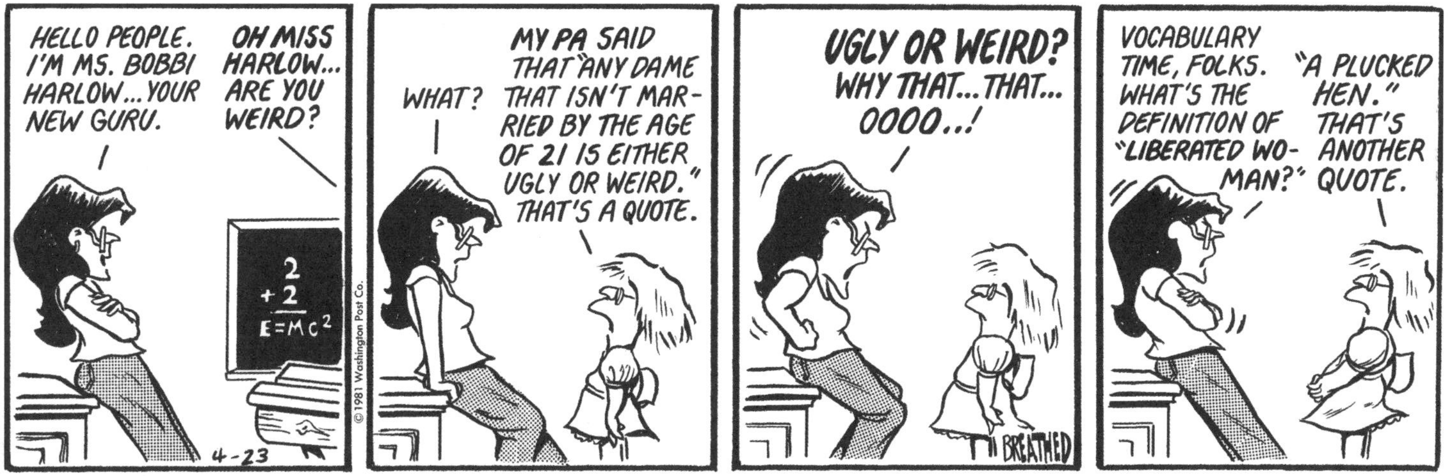
HELLO PEOPLE. I'M MS. BOBBI HARLOW...YOUR NEW GURU.
OH MISS HARLOW... ARE YOU WEIRD?
2 +2 E=MC2
4-23
© 1981 Washington Post Co.
WHAT?
MY PA SAID THAT "ANY DAME THAT ISN'T MARRIED BY THE AGE OF 21 IS EITHER UGLY OR WEIRD." THAT'S A QUOTE.
UGLY OR WEIRD? WHY THAT...THAT... OOOO..!
BREATHED
VOCABULARY TIME, FOLKS. WHAT'S THE DEFINITION OF "LIBERATED WOMAN?"
"A PLUCKED HEN." THAT'S ANOTHER QUOTE.

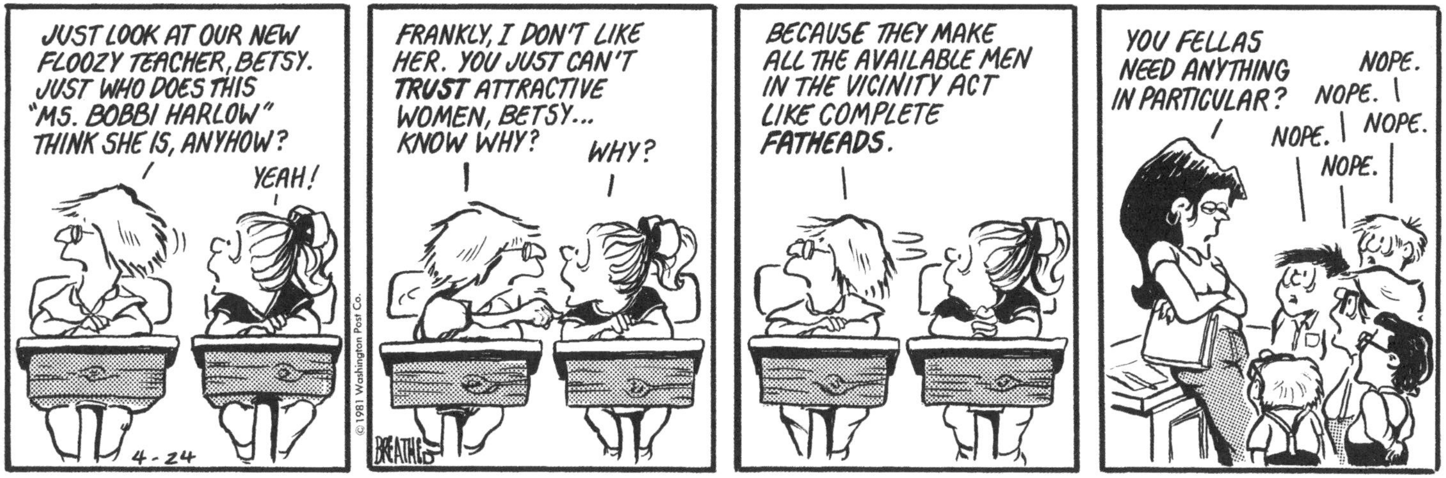
JUST LOOK AT OUR NEW FLOOZY TEACHER, BETSY. JUST WHO DOES THIS "MS. BOBBI HARLOW" THINK SHE IS, ANYHOW?
YEAH!
4-24
© 1981 Washington Post Co.
FRANKLY, I DON'T LIKE HER. YOU JUST CAN'T TRUST ATTRACTIVE WOMEN, BETSY... KNOW WHY?
WHY?
BREATHED
BECAUSE THEY MAKE ALL THE AVAILABLE MEN IN THE VICINITY ACT LIKE COMPLETE FATHEADS.
YOU FELLAS NEED ANYTHING IN PARTICULAR?
NOPE.
NOPE.
NOPE.
NOPE.
NOPE.

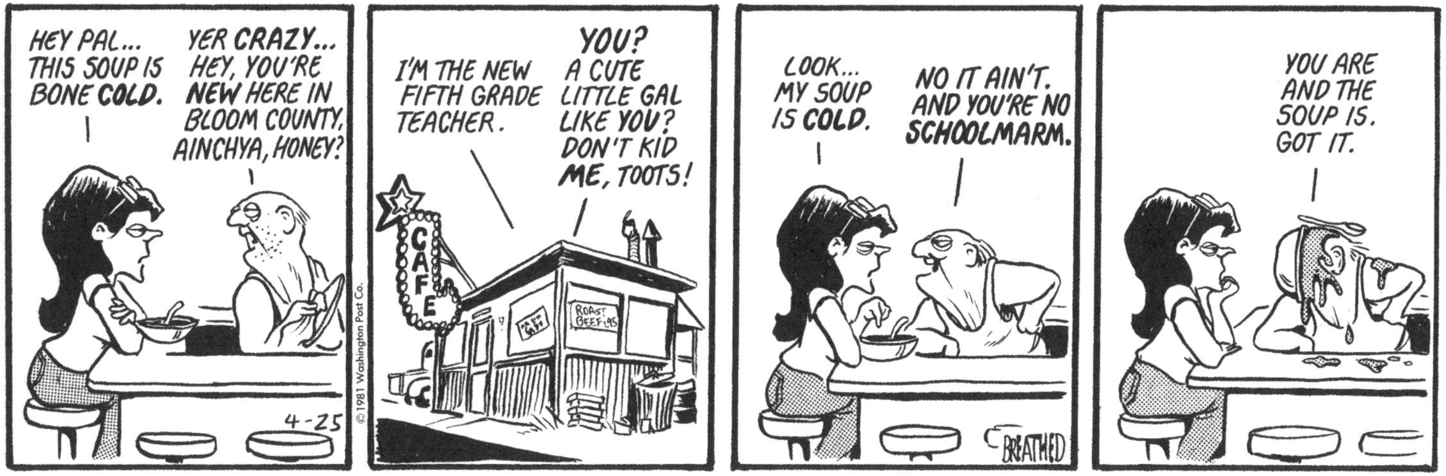
HEY PAL... THIS SOUP IS BONE COLD.
YER CRAZY... HEY, YOU'RE NEW HERE IN BLOOM COUNTY, AINCHYA, HONEY?
4-25
© 1981 Washington Post Co.
I'M THE NEW FIFTH GRADE TEACHER.
YOU? A CUTE LITTLE GAL LIKE YOU? DON'T KID ME, TOOTS!
CAFE
ROAST BEEF 1.95
LOOK... MY SOUP IS COLD.
NO IT AIN'T. AND YOU'RE NO SCHOOLMARM.
BREATHED
YOU ARE AND THE SOUP IS. GOT IT.

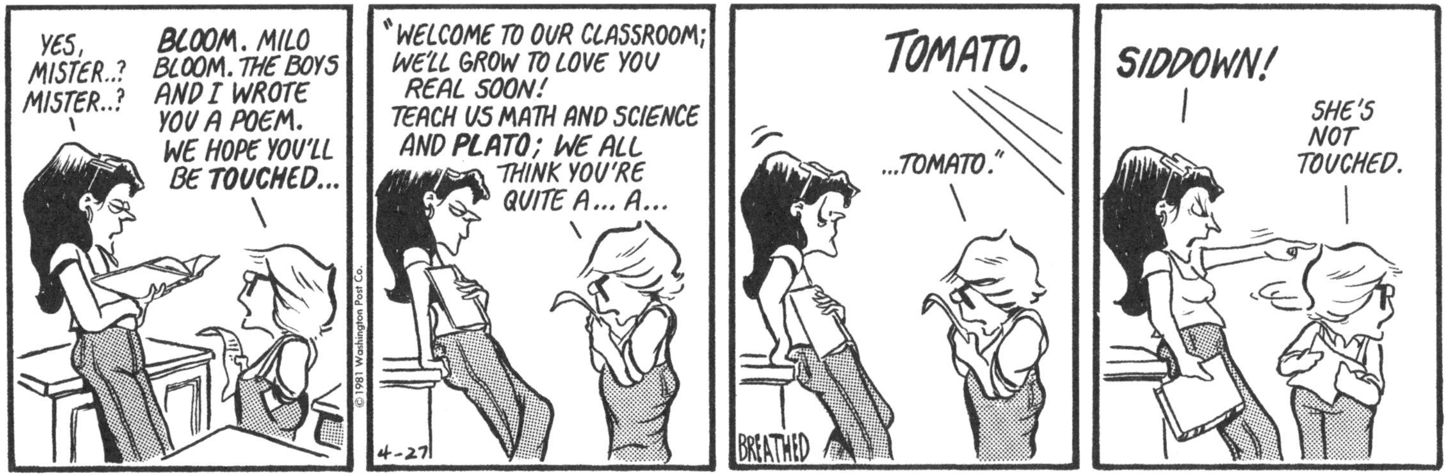
YES, MISTER..? MISTER..?
BLOOM. MILO BLOOM. THE BOYS AND I WROTE YOU A POEM. WE HOPE YOU'LL BE TOUCHED...
"WELCOME TO OUR CLASSROOM; WE'LL GROW TO LOVE YOU REAL SOON! TEACH US MATH AND SCIENCE AND PLATO; WE ALL THINK YOU'RE QUITE A... A...
© 1981 Washington Post Co.
4-27
TOMATO.
...TOMATO."
BREATHED
SIDDOWN!
SHE'S NOT TOUCHED.

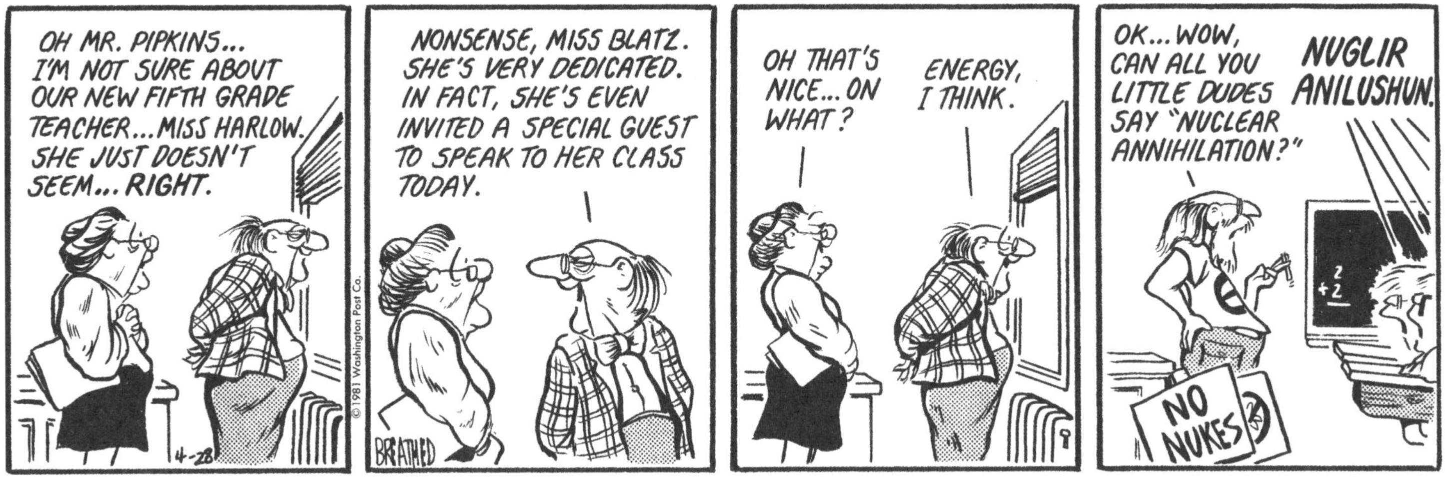
OH MR. PIPKINS... I'M NOT SURE ABOUT OUR NEW FIFTH GRADE TEACHER... MISS HARLOW. SHE JUST DOESN'T SEEM... RIGHT.
4-28
© 1981 Washington Post Co.
NONSENSE, MISS BLATZ. SHE'S VERY DEDICATED. IN FACT, SHE'S EVEN INVITED A SPECIAL GUEST TO SPEAK TO HER CLASS TODAY.
BREATHED
OH THAT'S NICE... ON WHAT?
ENERGY, I THINK.
OK... WOW, CAN ALL YOU LITTLE DUDES SAY "NUCLEAR ANNIHILATION?"
NUGLIR ANILUSHUN.
NO NUKES

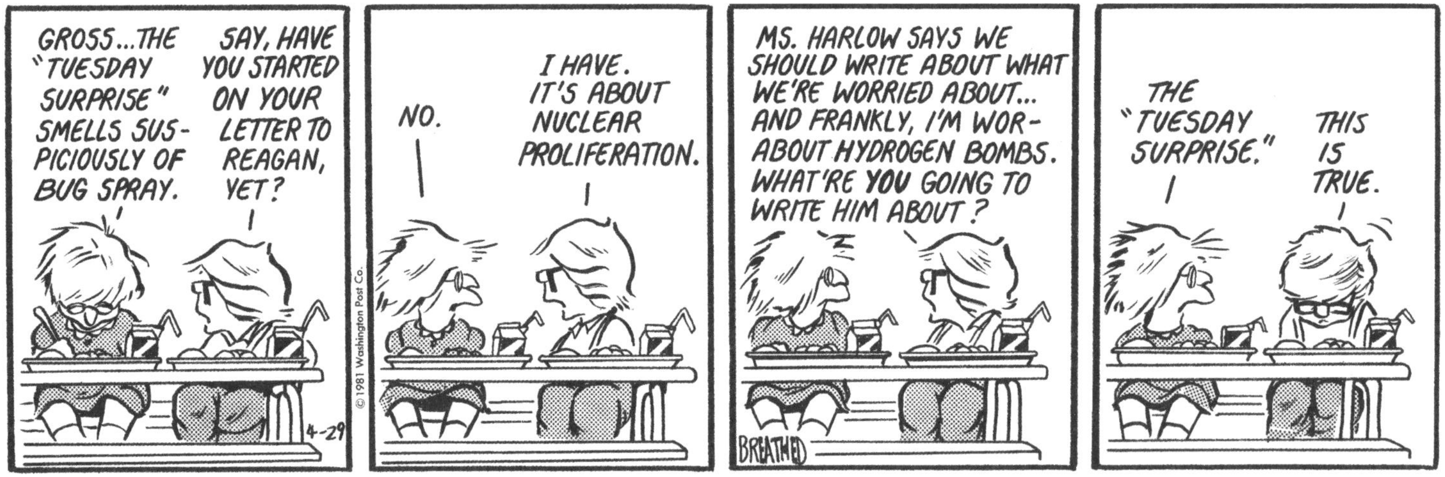
GROSS... THE "TUESDAY SURPRISE" SMELLS SUSPICIOUSLY OF BUG SPRAY.
SAY, HAVE YOU STARTED ON YOUR LETTER TO REAGAN, YET?
4-29
© 1981 Washington Post Co.
NO.
I HAVE. IT'S ABOUT NUCLEAR PROLIFERATION.
MS. HARLOW SAYS WE SHOULD WRITE ABOUT WHAT WE'RE WORRIED ABOUT... AND FRANKLY, I'M WOR- ABOUT HYDROGEN BOMBS. WHAT'RE YOU GOING TO WRITE HIM ABOUT?
BREATHED
THE "TUESDAY SURPRISE."
THIS IS TRUE.

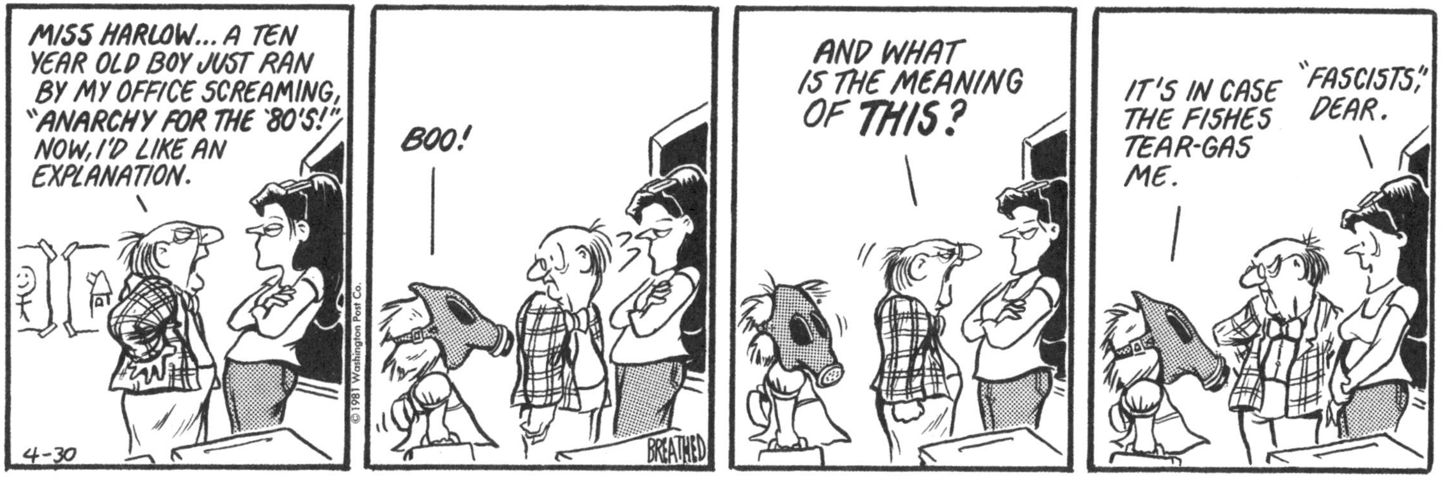
MISS HARLOW... A TEN YEAR OLD BOY JUST RAN BY MY OFFICE SCREAMING, "ANARCHY FOR THE '80'S!" NOW, I'D LIKE AN EXPLANATION.
4-30
BOO!
© 1981 Washington Post Co.
BREATHED
AND WHAT IS THE MEANING OF THIS?
IT'S IN CASE THE FISHES TEAR-GAS ME.
"FASCISTS," DEAR.

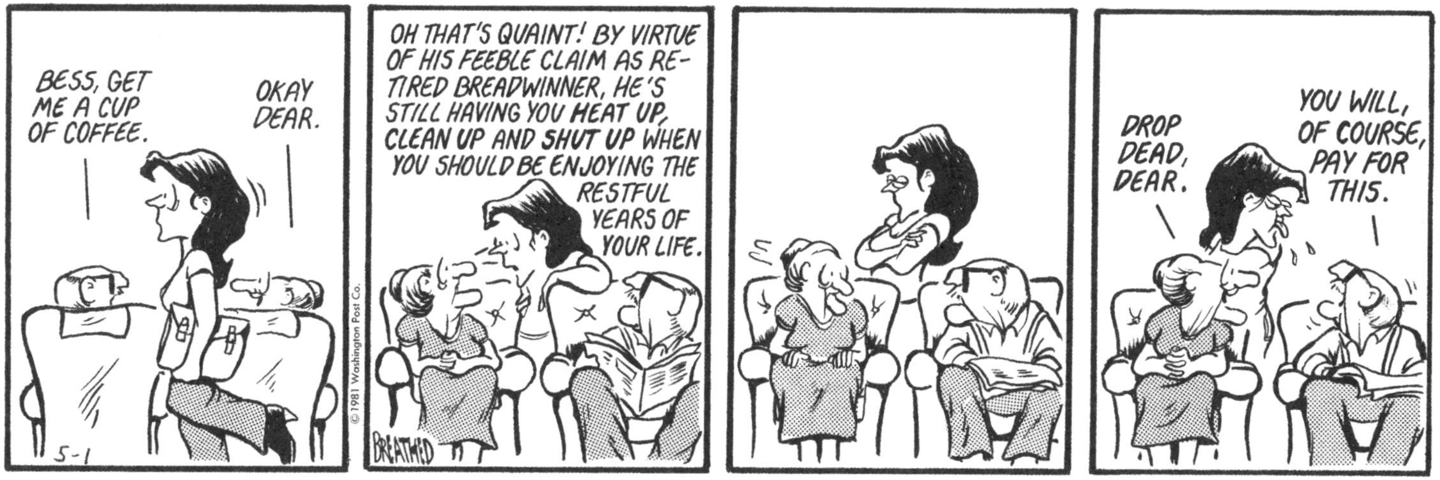
BESS, GET ME A CUP OF COFFEE.
OKAY DEAR.
5-1
© 1981 Washington Post Co.
OH THAT'S QUAINT! BY VIRTUE OF HIS FEEBLE CLAIM AS RETIRED BREADWINNER, HE'S STILL HAVING YOU HEAT UP, CLEAN UP AND SHUT UP WHEN YOU SHOULD BE ENJOYING THE RESTFUL YEARS OF YOUR LIFE.
BREATHED
DROP DEAD, DEAR.
YOU WILL, OF COURSE, PAY FOR THIS.

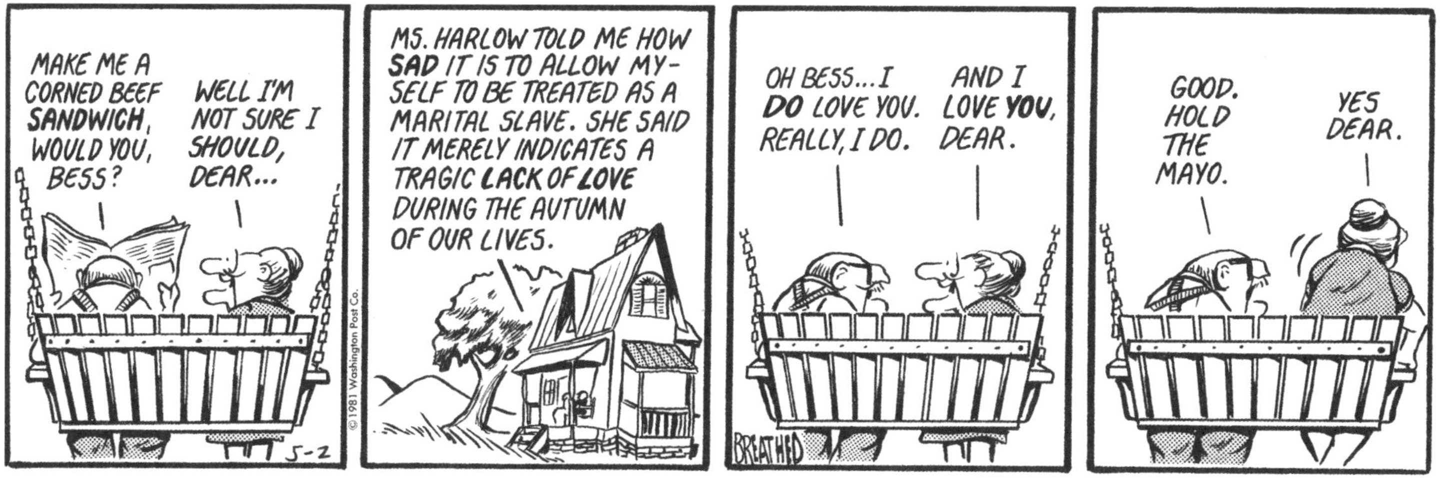
MAKE ME A CORNED BEEF SANDWICH, WOULD YOU, BESS?
WELL I'M NOT SURE I SHOULD, DEAR...
5-2
© 1981 Washington Post Co.
MS. HARLOW TOLD ME HOW SAD IT IS TO ALLOW MYSELF TO BE TREATED AS A MARITAL SLAVE. SHE SAID IT MERELY INDICATES A TRAGIC LACK OF LOVE DURING THE AUTUMN OF OUR LIVES.
OH BESS... I DO LOVE YOU. REALLY, I DO.
AND I LOVE YOU, DEAR.
BREATHED
GOOD. HOLD THE MAYO.
YES DEAR.

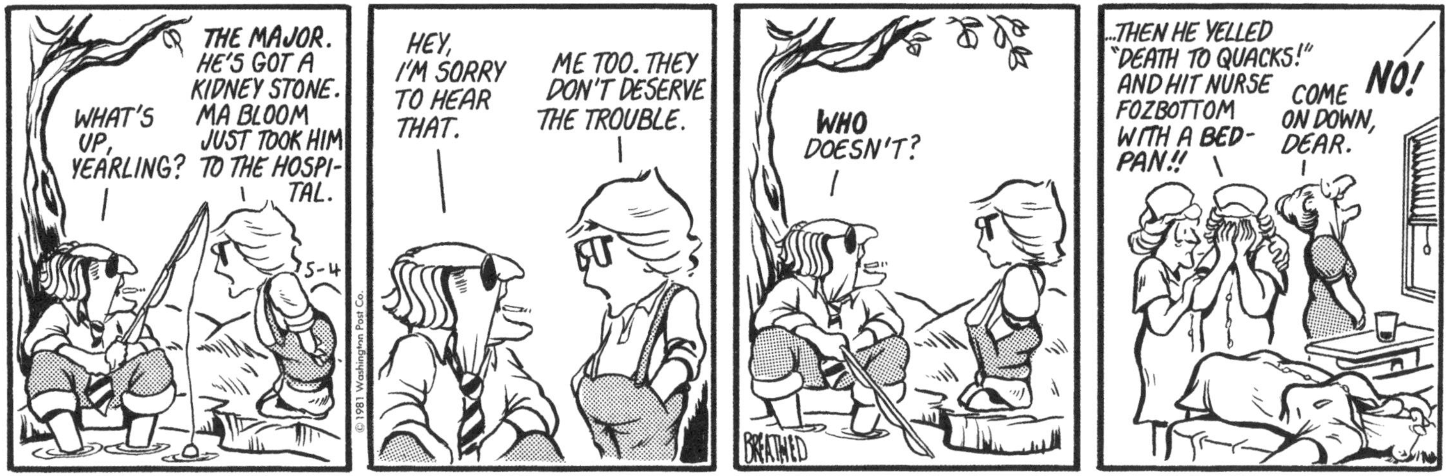
WHAT'S UP, YEARLING?
THE MAJOR. HE'S GOT A KIDNEY STONE. MA BLOOM JUST TOOK HIM TO THE HOSPITAL.
HEY, I'M SORRY TO HEAR THAT.
ME TOO. THEY DON'T DESERVE THE TROUBLE.
WHO DOESN'T?
...THEN HE YELLED "DEATH TO QUACKS!" AND HIT NURSE FOZBOTTOM WITH A BED-PAN!!
COME ON DOWN, DEAR.
NO!
© 1981 Washington Post Co.
BREATHED

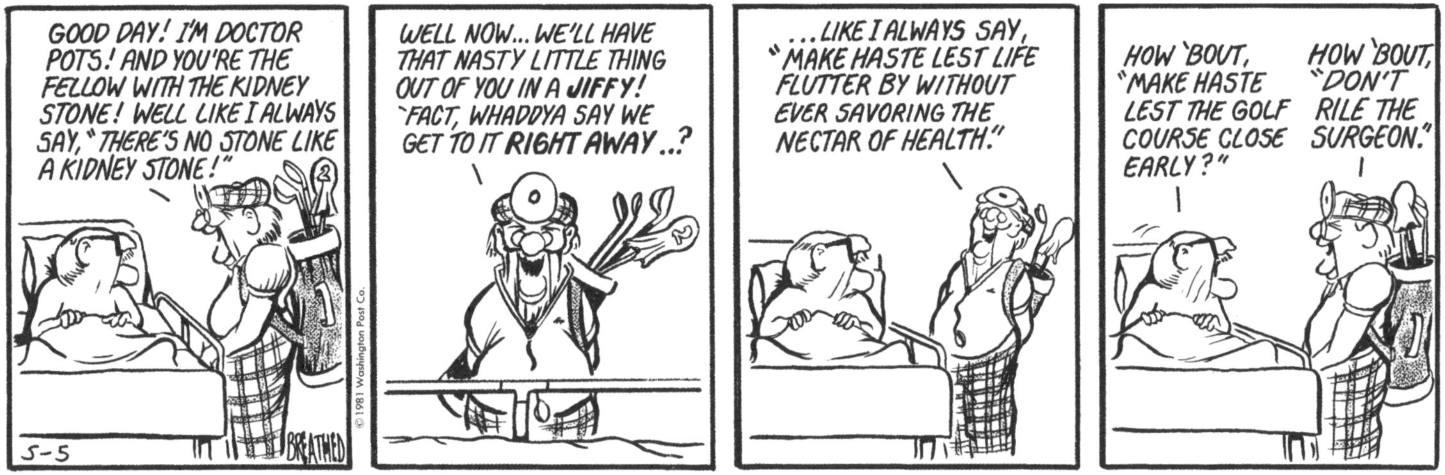
GOOD DAY! I'M DOCTOR POTS! AND YOU'RE THE FELLOW WITH THE KIDNEY STONE! WELL LIKE I ALWAYS SAY, "THERE'S NO STONE LIKE A KIDNEY STONE!"
WELL NOW... WE'LL HAVE THAT NASTY LITTLE THING OUT OF YOU IN A JIFFY! 'FACT, WHADDYA SAY WE GET TO IT RIGHT AWAY...?
"...LIKE I ALWAYS SAY, "MAKE HASTE LEST LIFE FLUTTER BY WITHOUT EVER SAVORING THE NECTAR OF HEALTH."
HOW 'BOUT, "MAKE HASTE LEST THE GOLF COURSE CLOSE EARLY?"
HOW 'BOUT, "DON'T RILE THE SURGEON."
© 1981 Washington Post Co.
BREATHED

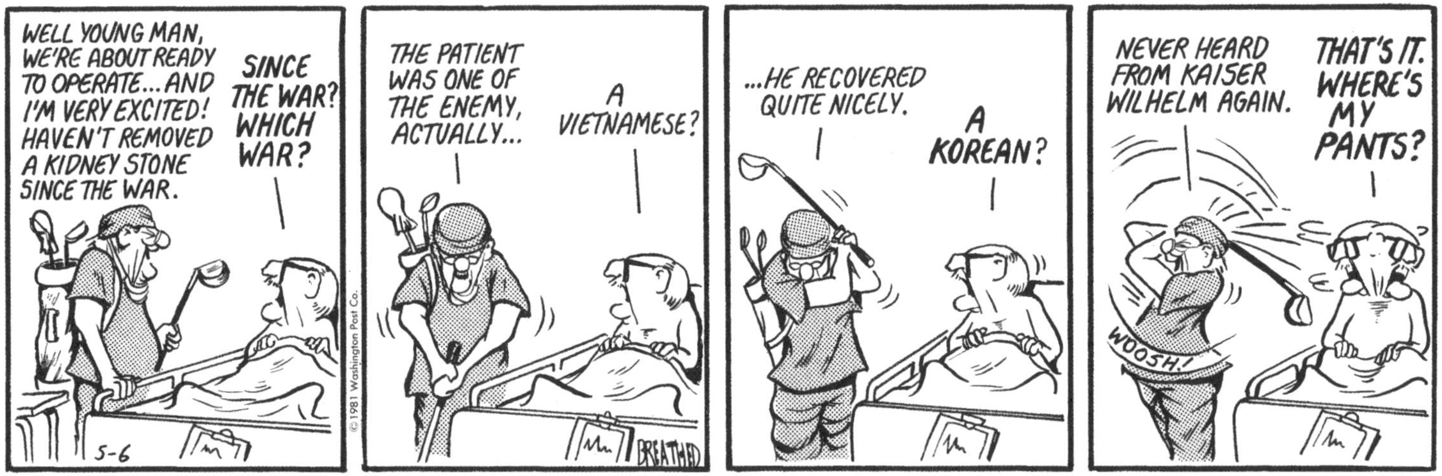
WELL YOUNG MAN, WE'RE ABOUT READY TO OPERATE... AND I'M VERY EXCITED! HAVEN'T REMOVED A KIDNEY STONE SINCE THE WAR.
SINCE THE WAR? WHICH WAR?
THE PATIENT WAS ONE OF THE ENEMY, ACTUALLY...
A VIETNAMESE?
...HE RECOVERED QUITE NICELY.
A KOREAN?
NEVER HEARD FROM KAISER WILHELM AGAIN.
THAT'S IT. WHERE'S MY PANTS?
WOOSH!
© 1981 Washington Post Co.
BREATHED

Kaiser Wilhelm II was the King of Prussia through most of World War I.

HAS MAJOR BLOOM BEEN ACTING UP, AGAIN?
HE'S A BEAST! THIS MORNING HE HIT NURSE FOZBOTTOM OVER THE HEAD WITH A BEDPAN.
5-7
© 1981 Washington Post Co.
SHOCKING! AND AFTER TOSSING JELLO AT THE X-RAY CREW LAST NIGHT!
DON'T WORRY, ETHYL... HE'S GOING INTO SURGERY IN A FEW MINUTES.
THEN HE'S SEDATED?
ASK NURSE FOZBOTTOM.
...MY FLOWER, MY ROSEBUD, MY LITTLE PETUNIA...
BREATHED

SCALPEL... SPONGE... CLAMP... #3 PUTTER...
#3 PUTTER?
5-8
TUT TUT, MAJOR... I LIKE T' THINK OF A KIDNEY STONE OPERATION AS LOOKIN' FOR A GOLFBALL IN THE ROUGH... NOW JUST RELAX AND WE'LL FIND THE LITTLE BUGGER, OKAY?
YEAH.
BREATHED
NOW THEN. LESSEE... AH, HERE IT IS...
FORE!
HELP!
SWACK!

WHAT'S ALL THIS?
ON BEHALF OF ALL THE STAFF HERE AT BLOOM COUNTY HOSPITAL, WE'D LIKE YOU TO HAVE THIS.
5-9
© 1981 Washington Post Co.
"HOSPITAL BILL: $11,836.98"
ASTOUNDING!
INCREDIBLE!
CLAP! CLAP! CLAP! CLAP!
HA! HA! VERY FUNNY FOLKS.
FINE JOB, DOCTOR!
YOU'VE OUTDONE YOURSELF!
I KNOW.
NO... REALLY, THIS IS VERY FUNNY... HO! HO!
OUT, BUB. WE NEED THE BED.
BREATHED

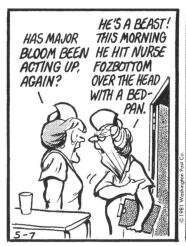

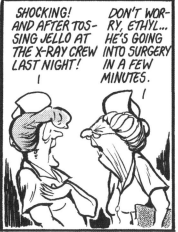

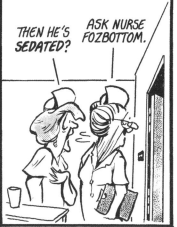

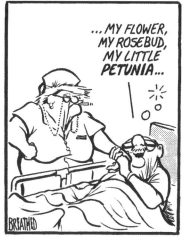

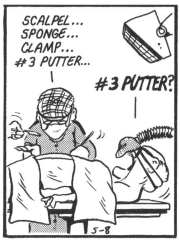

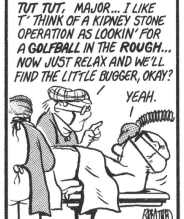

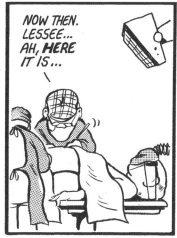

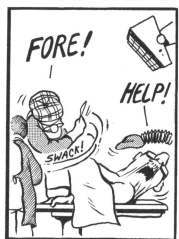

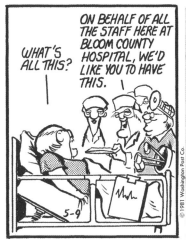

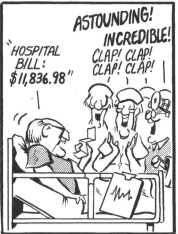

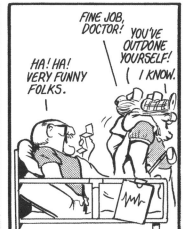

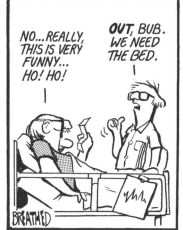

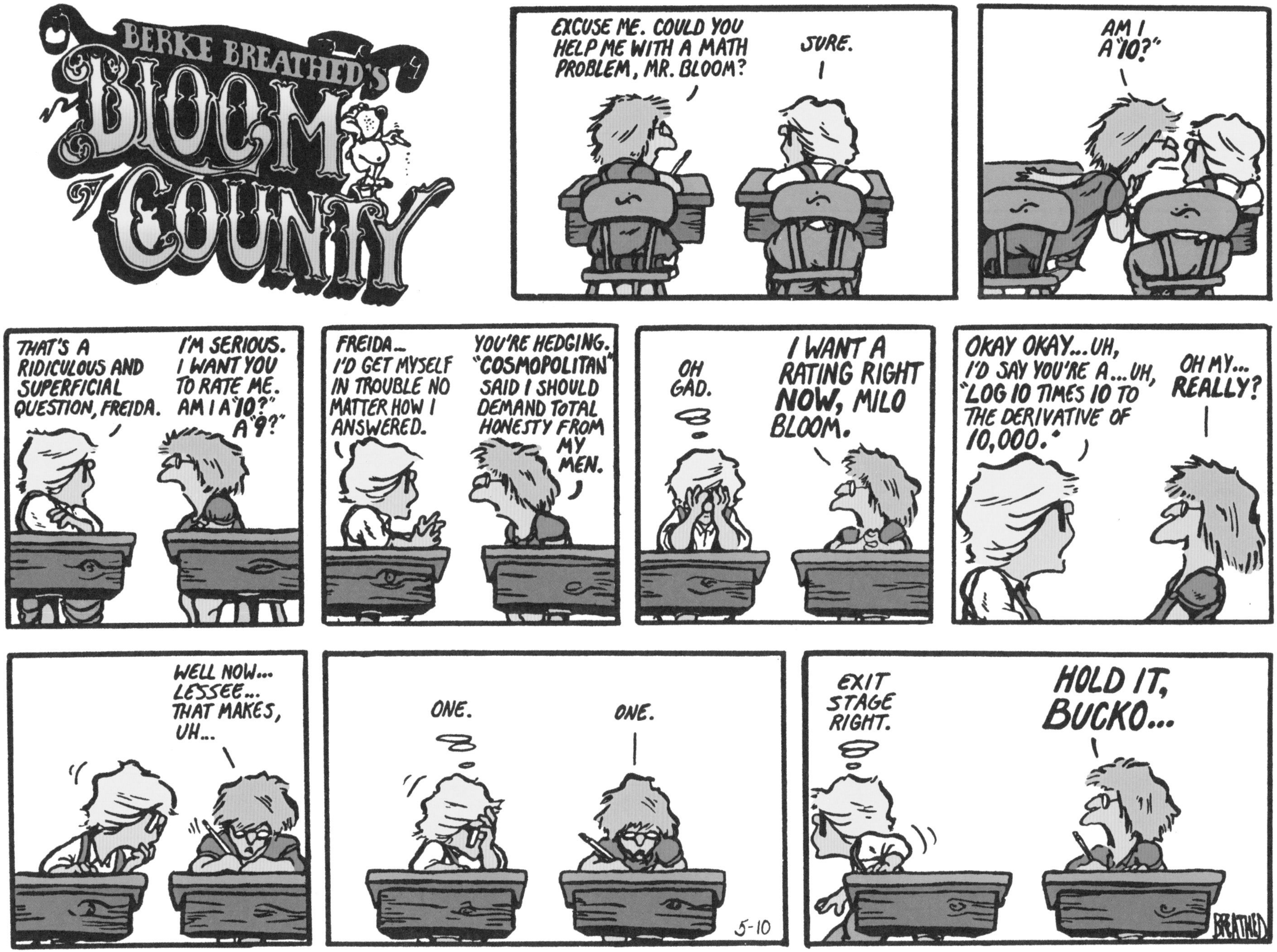
BERKE BREATHED'S
BLOOM COUNTY
EXCUSE ME. COULD YOU HELP ME WITH A MATH PROBLEM, MR. BLOOM?
SURE.
AM I A "10?"
THAT'S A RIDICULOUS AND SUPERFICIAL QUESTION, FREIDA.
I'M SERIOUS. I WANT YOU TO RATE ME. AM I A "10?" A "9?"
FREIDA... I'D GET MYSELF IN TROUBLE NO MATTER HOW I ANSWERED.
YOU'RE HEDGING. "COSMOPOLITAN" SAID I SHOULD DEMAND TOTAL HONESTY FROM MY MEN.
OH GAD.
I WANT A RATING RIGHT NOW, MILO BLOOM.
OKAY OKAY... UH, I'D SAY YOU'RE A... UH, "LOG 10 TIMES 10 TO THE DERIVATIVE OF 10,000."
OH MY... REALLY?
WELL NOW... LESSEE... THAT MAKES, UH...
ONE.
ONE.
5-10
EXIT STAGE RIGHT.
HOLD IT, BUCKO...
BREATHED

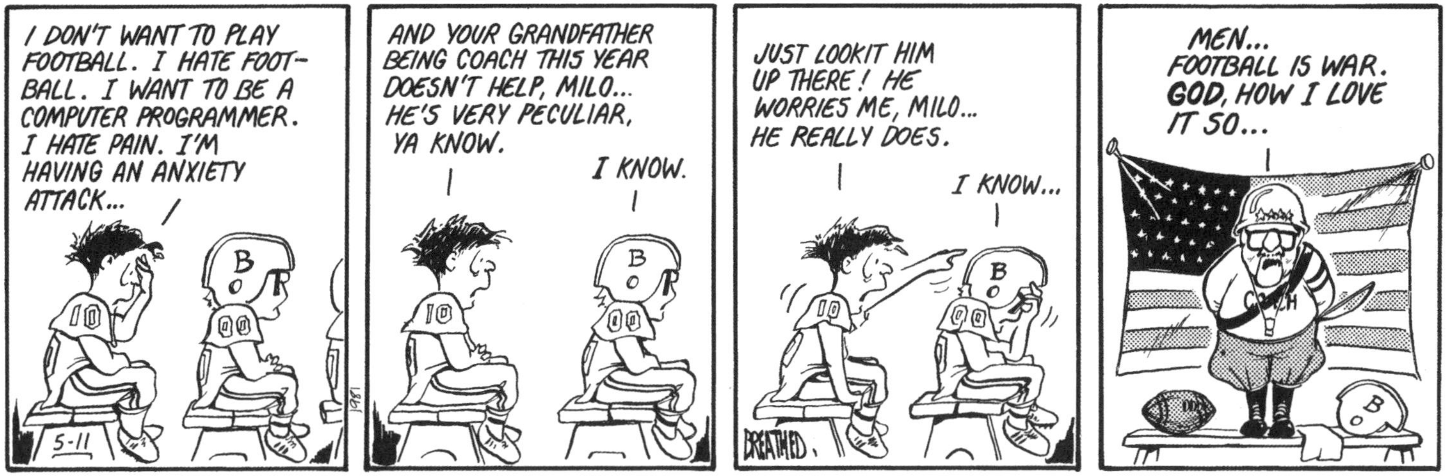
I DON'T WANT TO PLAY FOOTBALL. I HATE FOOT-BALL. I WANT TO BE A COMPUTER PROGRAMMER. I HATE PAIN. I'M HAVING AN ANXIETY ATTACK...
AND YOUR GRANDFATHER BEING COACH THIS YEAR DOESN'T HELP, MILO... HE'S VERY PECULIAR, YA KNOW.
I KNOW.
JUST LOOKIT HIM UP THERE! HE WORRIES ME, MILO... HE REALLY DOES.
I KNOW...
MEN... FOOTBALL IS WAR. **GOD**, HOW I LOVE IT SO...
5-11
1981
BREATHED

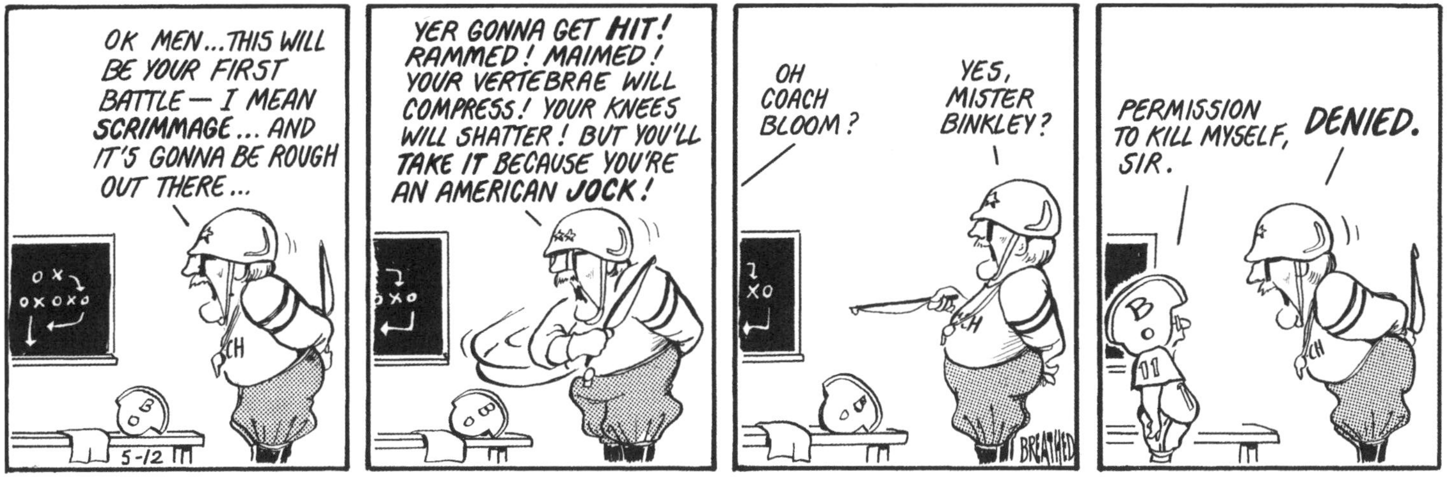
OK MEN... THIS WILL BE YOUR FIRST BATTLE — I MEAN **SCRIMMAGE**... AND IT'S GONNA BE ROUGH OUT THERE...
YER GONNA GET **HIT**! **RAMMED**! **MAIMED**! YOUR VERTEBRAE WILL COMPRESS! YOUR KNEES WILL SHATTER! BUT YOU'LL **TAKE IT** BECAUSE YOU'RE AN AMERICAN **JOCK**!
OH COACH BLOOM?
YES, MISTER BINKLEY?
PERMISSION TO KILL MYSELF, SIR.
DENIED.
5-12
BREATHED

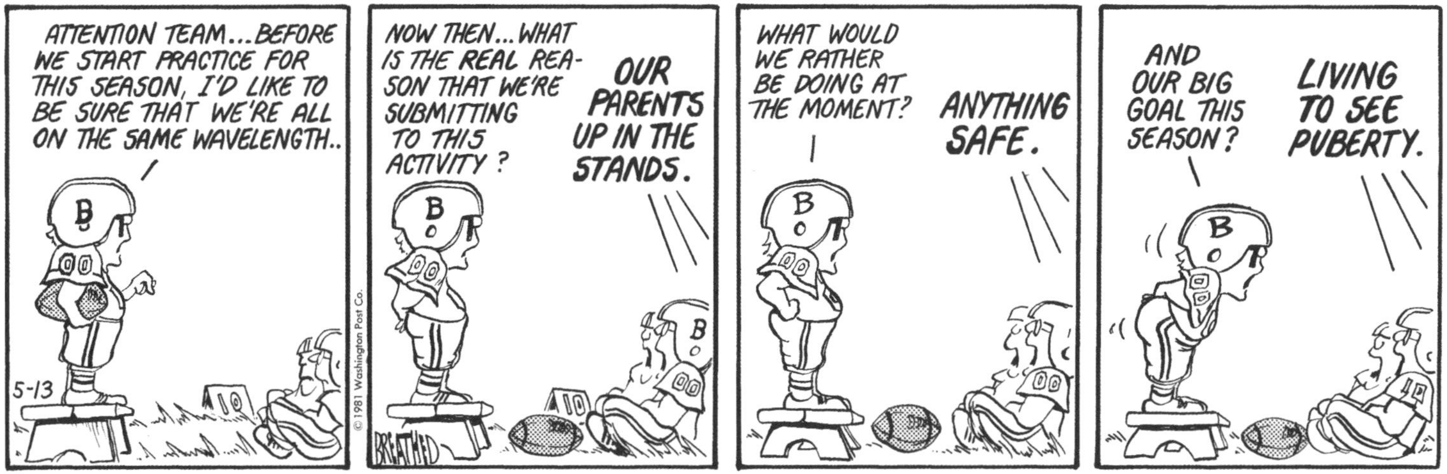
ATTENTION TEAM... BEFORE WE START PRACTICE FOR THIS SEASON, I'D LIKE TO BE SURE THAT WE'RE ALL ON THE SAME WAVELENGTH..
NOW THEN... WHAT IS THE **REAL** REASON THAT WE'RE SUBMITTING TO THIS ACTIVITY?
OUR PARENTS UP IN THE STANDS.
WHAT WOULD WE RATHER BE DOING AT THE MOMENT?
ANYTHING SAFE.
AND OUR BIG GOAL THIS SEASON?
LIVING TO SEE PUBERTY.
5-13
© 1981 Washington Post Co.
BREATHED

Michael Binkley joins the cast of *Bloom County*.

Binkley. The strip is finally moving a bit into focus... the center of expressive gravity is getting closer although I didn't know it.
—BB

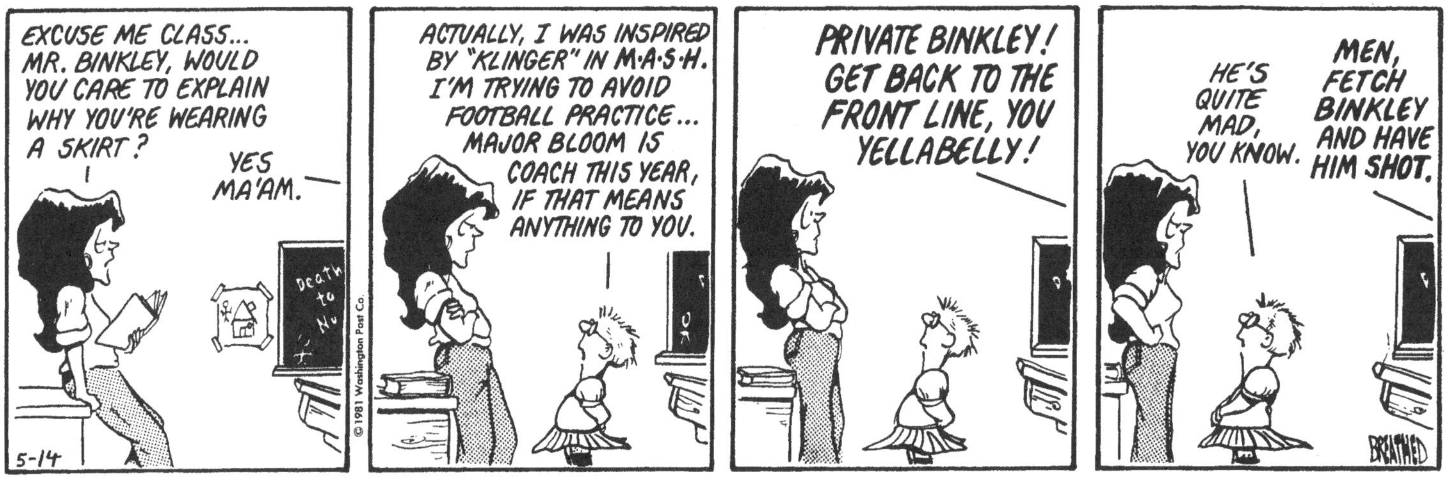
EXCUSE ME CLASS... MR. BINKLEY, WOULD YOU CARE TO EXPLAIN WHY YOU'RE WEARING A SKIRT?
YES MA'AM.
5-14
© 1981 Washington Post Co.
ACTUALLY, I WAS INSPIRED BY "KLINGER" IN M·A·S·H. I'M TRYING TO AVOID FOOTBALL PRACTICE... MAJOR BLOOM IS COACH THIS YEAR, IF THAT MEANS ANYTHING TO YOU.
PRIVATE BINKLEY! GET BACK TO THE FRONT LINE, YOU YELLABELLY!
HE'S QUITE MAD, YOU KNOW.
MEN, FETCH BINKLEY AND HAVE HIM SHOT.
BREATHED

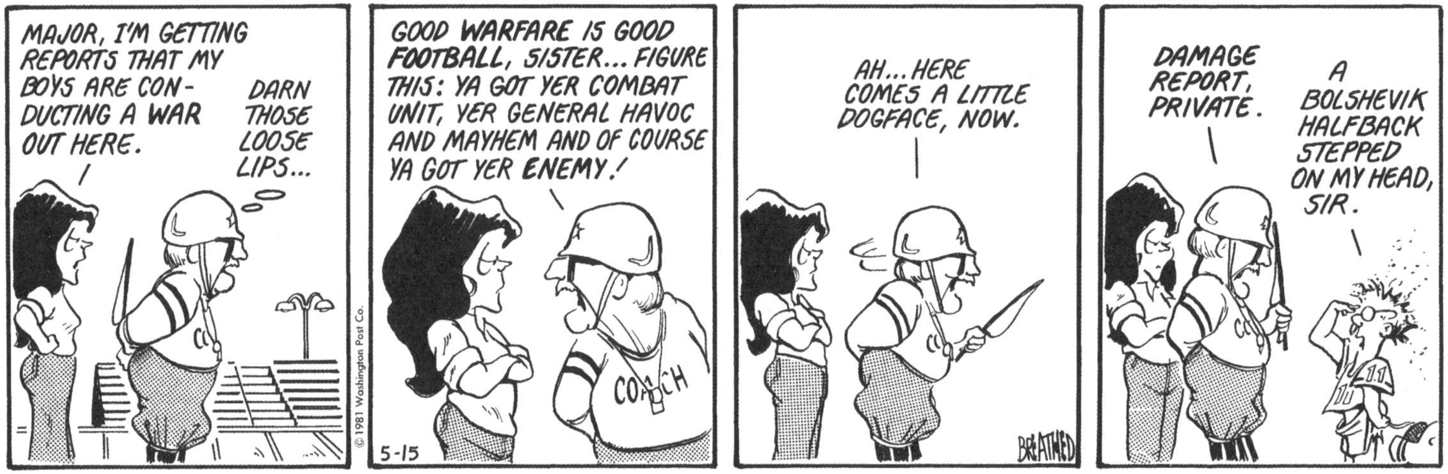
MAJOR, I'M GETTING REPORTS THAT MY BOYS ARE CONDUCTING A WAR OUT HERE.
DARN THOSE LOOSE LIPS...
© 1981 Washington Post Co.
GOOD WARFARE IS GOOD FOOTBALL, SISTER... FIGURE THIS: YA GOT YER COMBAT UNIT, YER GENERAL HAVOC AND MAYHEM AND OF COURSE YA GOT YER ENEMY!
COACH
5-15
AH... HERE COMES A LITTLE DOGFACE, NOW.
BREATHED
DAMAGE REPORT, PRIVATE.
A BOLSHEVIK HALFBACK STEPPED ON MY HEAD, SIR.

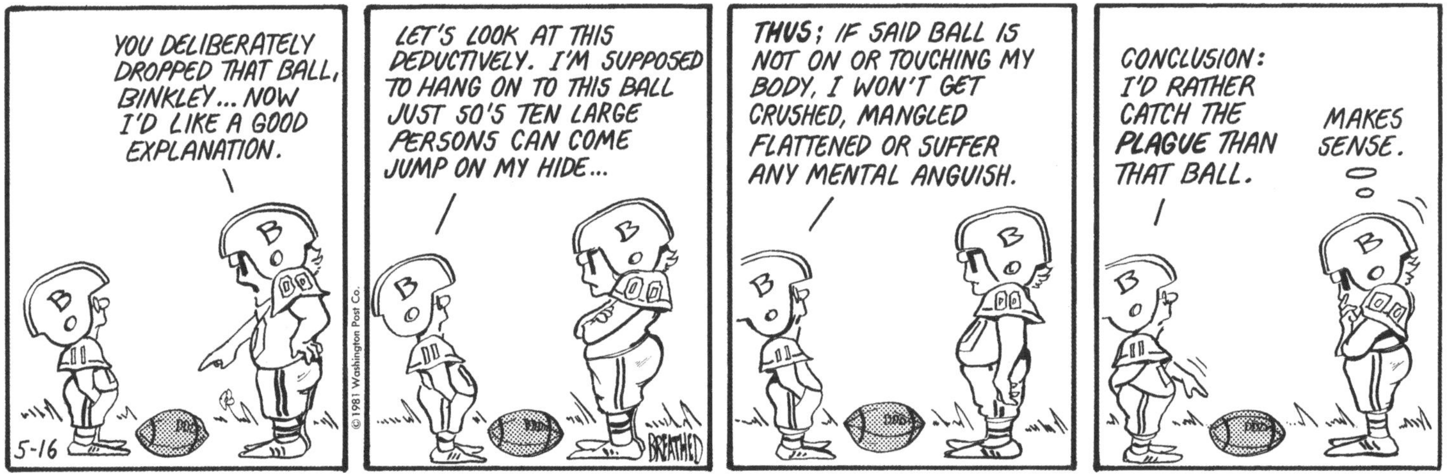
YOU DELIBERATELY DROPPED THAT BALL, BINKLEY... NOW I'D LIKE A GOOD EXPLANATION.
5-16
© 1981 Washington Post Co.
LET'S LOOK AT THIS DEDUCTIVELY. I'M SUPPOSED TO HANG ON TO THIS BALL JUST SO'S TEN LARGE PERSONS CAN COME JUMP ON MY HIDE...
BREATHED
THUS; IF SAID BALL IS NOT ON OR TOUCHING MY BODY, I WON'T GET CRUSHED, MANGLED FLATTENED OR SUFFER ANY MENTAL ANGUISH.
CONCLUSION: I'D RATHER CATCH THE PLAGUE THAN THAT BALL.
MAKES SENSE.

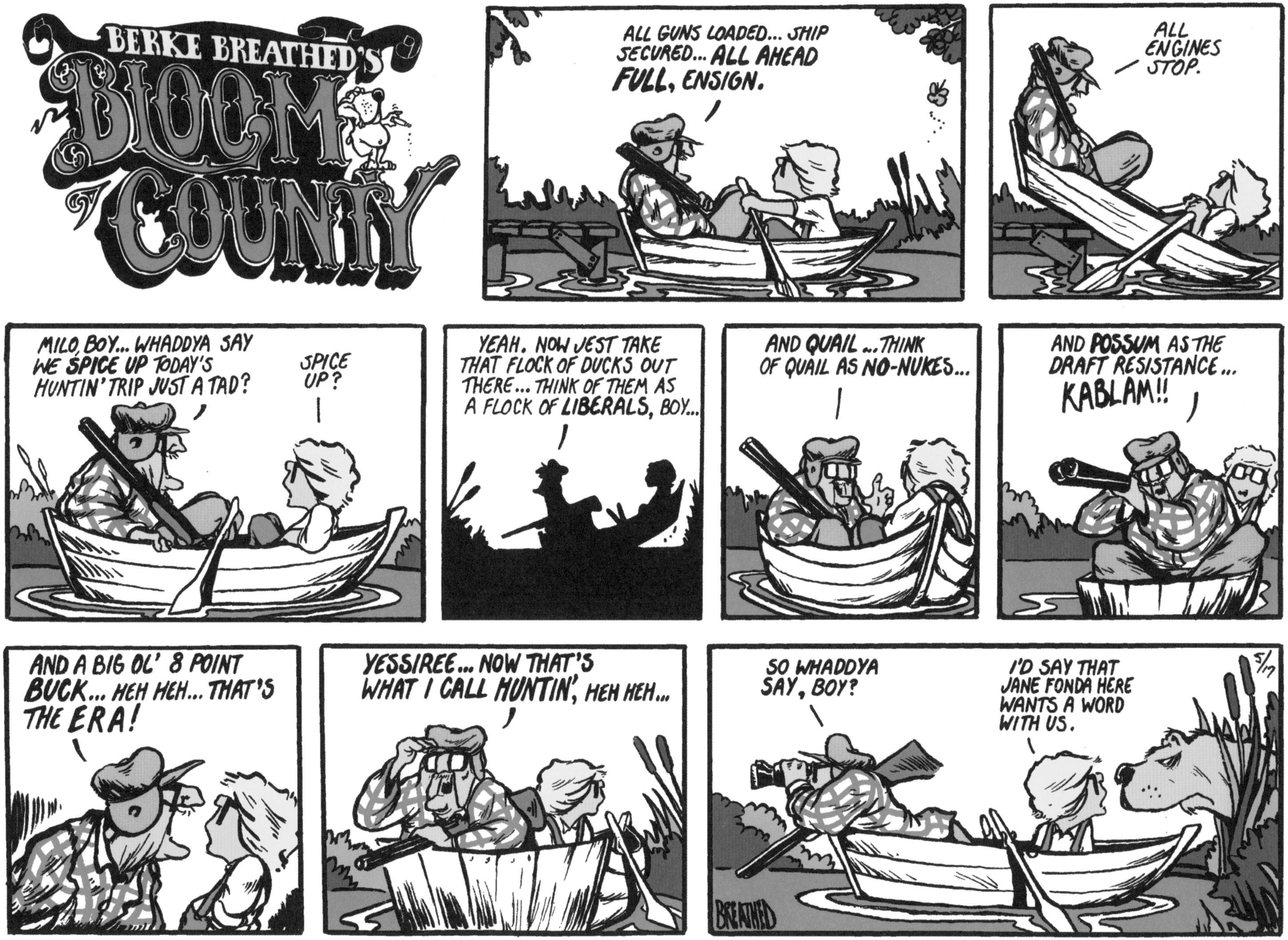
BERKE BREATHED'S
BLOOM COUNTY
ALL GUNS LOADED... SHIP SECURED... ALL AHEAD FULL, ENSIGN.
ALL ENGINES STOP.
MILO, BOY... WHADDYA SAY WE SPICE UP TODAY'S HUNTIN' TRIP JUST A TAD?
SPICE UP?
YEAH. NOW JEST TAKE THAT FLOCK OF DUCKS OUT THERE... THINK OF THEM AS A FLOCK OF LIBERALS, BOY...
AND QUAIL... THINK OF QUAIL AS NO-NUKES...
AND POSSUM AS THE DRAFT RESISTANCE... KABLAM!!
AND A BIG OL' 8 POINT BUCK... HEH HEH... THAT'S THE ERA!
YESSIREE... NOW THAT'S WHAT I CALL HUNTIN', HEH HEH...
SO WHADDYA SAY, BOY?
I'D SAY THAT JANE FONDA HERE WANTS A WORD WITH US.
5/17
BREATHED

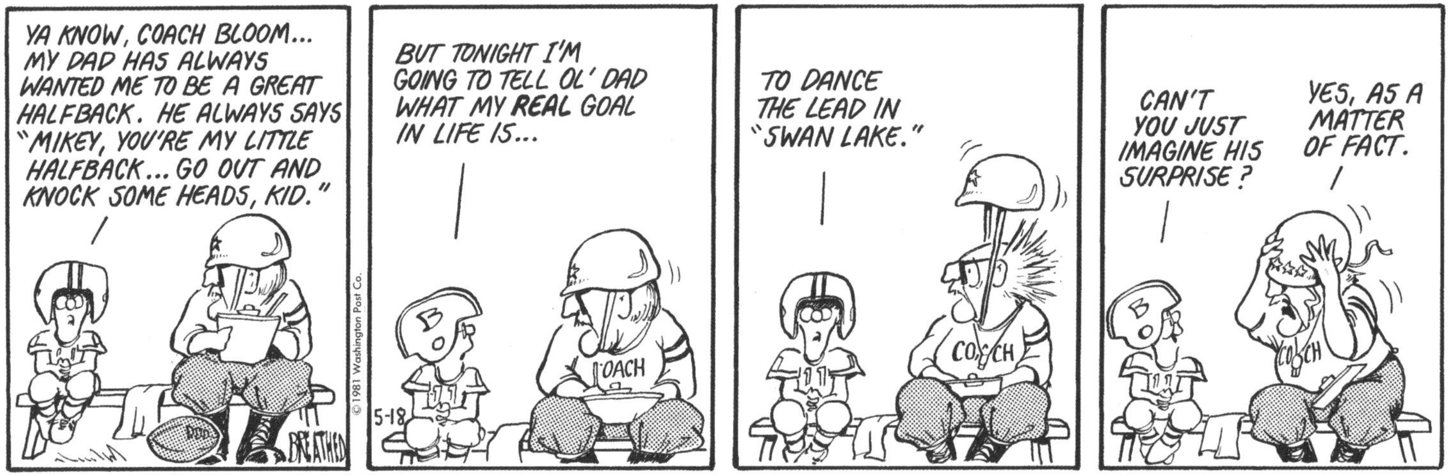
YA KNOW, COACH BLOOM... MY DAD HAS ALWAYS WANTED ME TO BE A GREAT HALFBACK. HE ALWAYS SAYS "MIKEY, YOU'RE MY LITTLE HALFBACK... GO OUT AND KNOCK SOME HEADS, KID."
BREATHED
© 1981 Washington Post Co.
5-18
BUT TONIGHT I'M GOING TO TELL OL' DAD WHAT MY **REAL** GOAL IN LIFE IS...
COACH
TO DANCE THE LEAD IN "SWAN LAKE."
COACH
CAN'T YOU JUST IMAGINE HIS SURPRISE?
YES, AS A MATTER OF FACT.
COACH

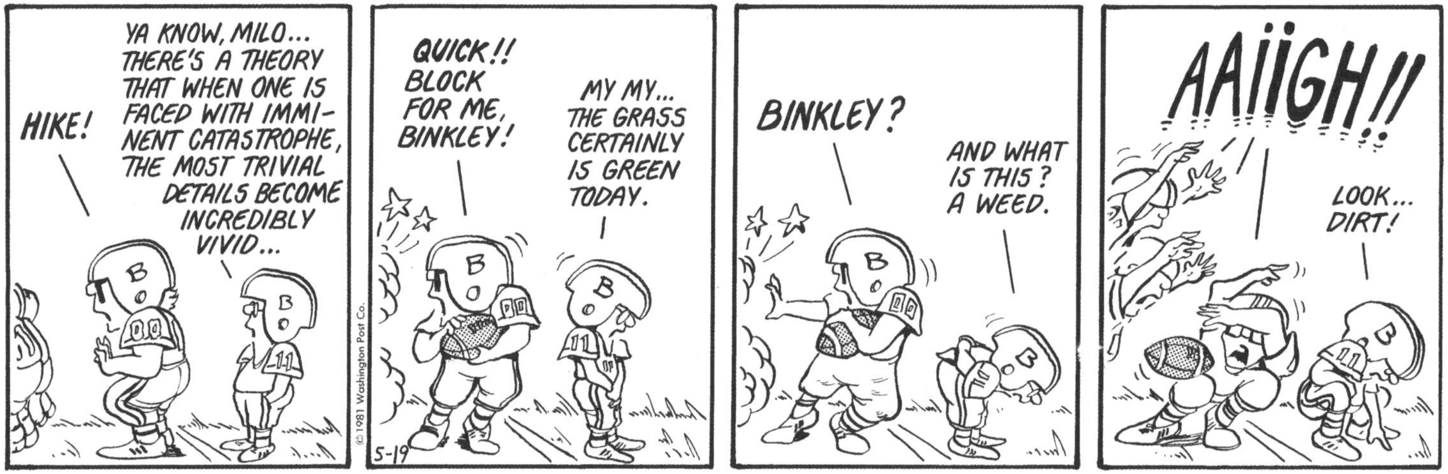
HIKE!
YA KNOW, MILO... THERE'S A THEORY THAT WHEN ONE IS FACED WITH IMMI-NENT CATASTROPHE, THE MOST TRIVIAL DETAILS BECOME INCREDIBLY VIVID...
© 1981 Washington Post Co.
5-19
QUICK!! BLOCK FOR ME, BINKLEY!
MY MY... THE GRASS CERTAINLY IS GREEN TODAY.
BINKLEY?
AND WHAT IS THIS? A WEED.
AAIIGH!!
LOOK... DIRT!

The first appearance of Steve Dallas.

Steve Dallas: the only lasting refugee from my college cartoon. A frat-boy lawyer who I knew in school. He's never written me. I suspect he was shot by an annoyed girlfriend, which saved me many legal fees. —BB

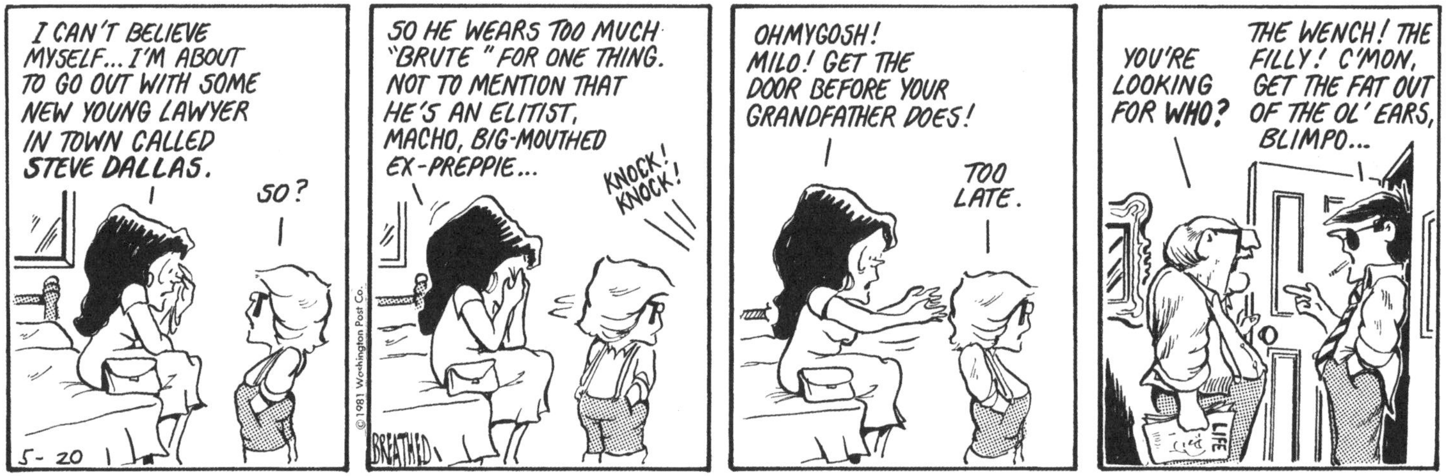
I CAN'T BELIEVE MYSELF... I'M ABOUT TO GO OUT WITH SOME NEW YOUNG LAWYER IN TOWN CALLED **STEVE DALLAS**.
SO?
5-20
SO HE WEARS TOO MUCH "BRUTE" FOR ONE THING. NOT TO MENTION THAT HE'S AN ELITIST, MACHO, BIG-MOUTHED EX-PREPPIE...
KNOCK! KNOCK!
© 1981 Washington Post Co.
BREATHED
OHMYGOSH! MILO! GET THE DOOR BEFORE YOUR GRANDFATHER DOES!
TOO LATE.
YOU'RE LOOKING FOR **WHO?**
THE WENCH! THE FILLY! C'MON, GET THE FAT OUT OF THE OL' EARS, BLIMPO...
LIFE

May 18-20, 1981

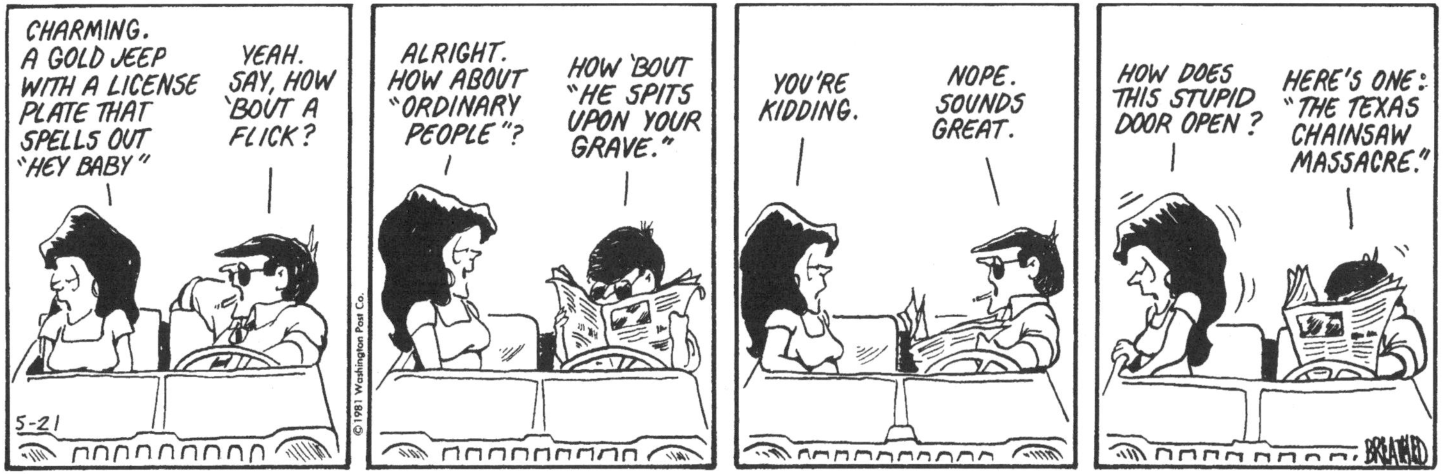
CHARMING. A GOLD JEEP WITH A LICENSE PLATE THAT SPELLS OUT "HEY BABY"
YEAH. SAY, HOW 'BOUT A FLICK?
5-21
© 1981 Washington Post Co.
ALRIGHT. HOW ABOUT "ORDINARY PEOPLE"?
HOW 'BOUT "HE SPITS UPON YOUR GRAVE."
YOU'RE KIDDING.
NOPE. SOUNDS GREAT.
HOW DOES THIS STUPID DOOR OPEN?
HERE'S ONE: "THE TEXAS CHAINSAW MASSACRE."
BREATHED

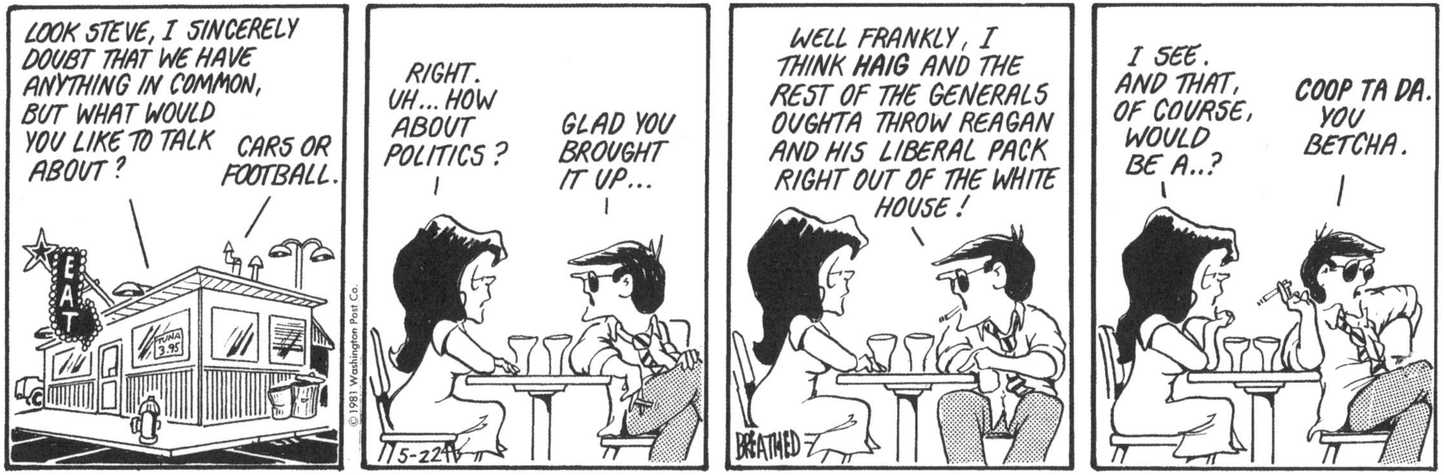
LOOK STEVE, I SINCERELY DOUBT THAT WE HAVE ANYTHING IN COMMON, BUT WHAT WOULD YOU LIKE TO TALK ABOUT?
CARS OR FOOTBALL.
EAT
TUNA 3.95
© 1981 Washington Post Co.
RIGHT. UH... HOW ABOUT POLITICS?
GLAD YOU BROUGHT IT UP...
5-22
WELL FRANKLY, I THINK HAIG AND THE REST OF THE GENERALS OUGHTA THROW REAGAN AND HIS LIBERAL PACK RIGHT OUT OF THE WHITE HOUSE!
BREATHED
I SEE. AND THAT, OF COURSE, WOULD BE A..?
COOP TA DA. YOU BETCHA.

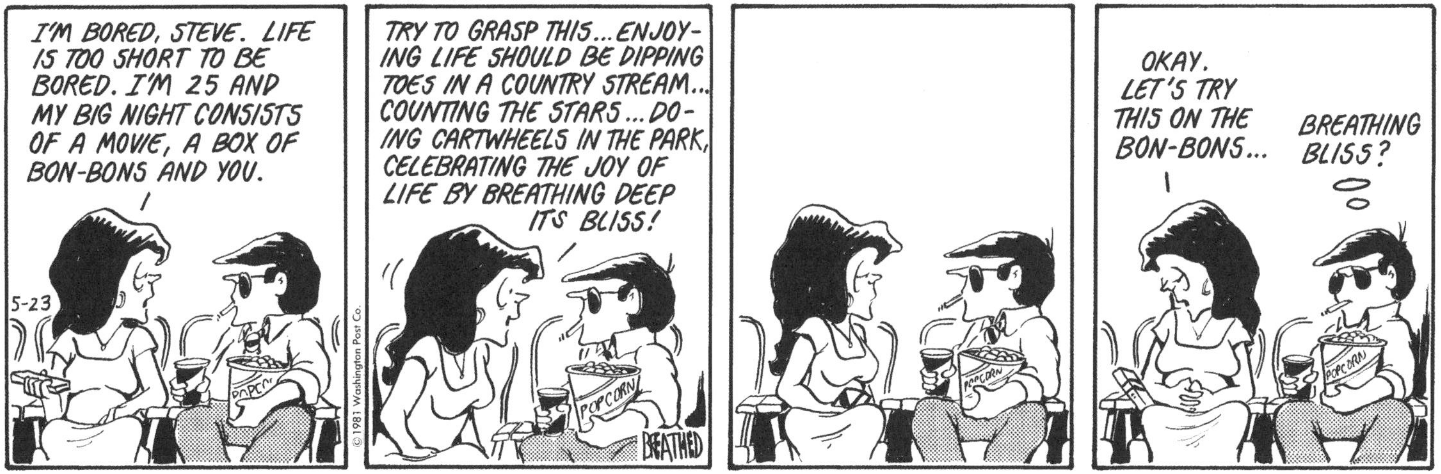
I'M BORED, STEVE. LIFE IS TOO SHORT TO BE BORED. I'M 25 AND MY BIG NIGHT CONSISTS OF A MOVIE, A BOX OF BON-BONS AND YOU.
5-23
© 1981 Washington Post Co.
TRY TO GRASP THIS... ENJOYING LIFE SHOULD BE DIPPING TOES IN A COUNTRY STREAM... COUNTING THE STARS... DOING CARTWHEELS IN THE PARK, CELEBRATING THE JOY OF LIFE BY BREATHING DEEP ITS BLISS!
POPCORN
BREATHED
OKAY. LET'S TRY THIS ON THE BON-BONS...
BREATHING BLISS?

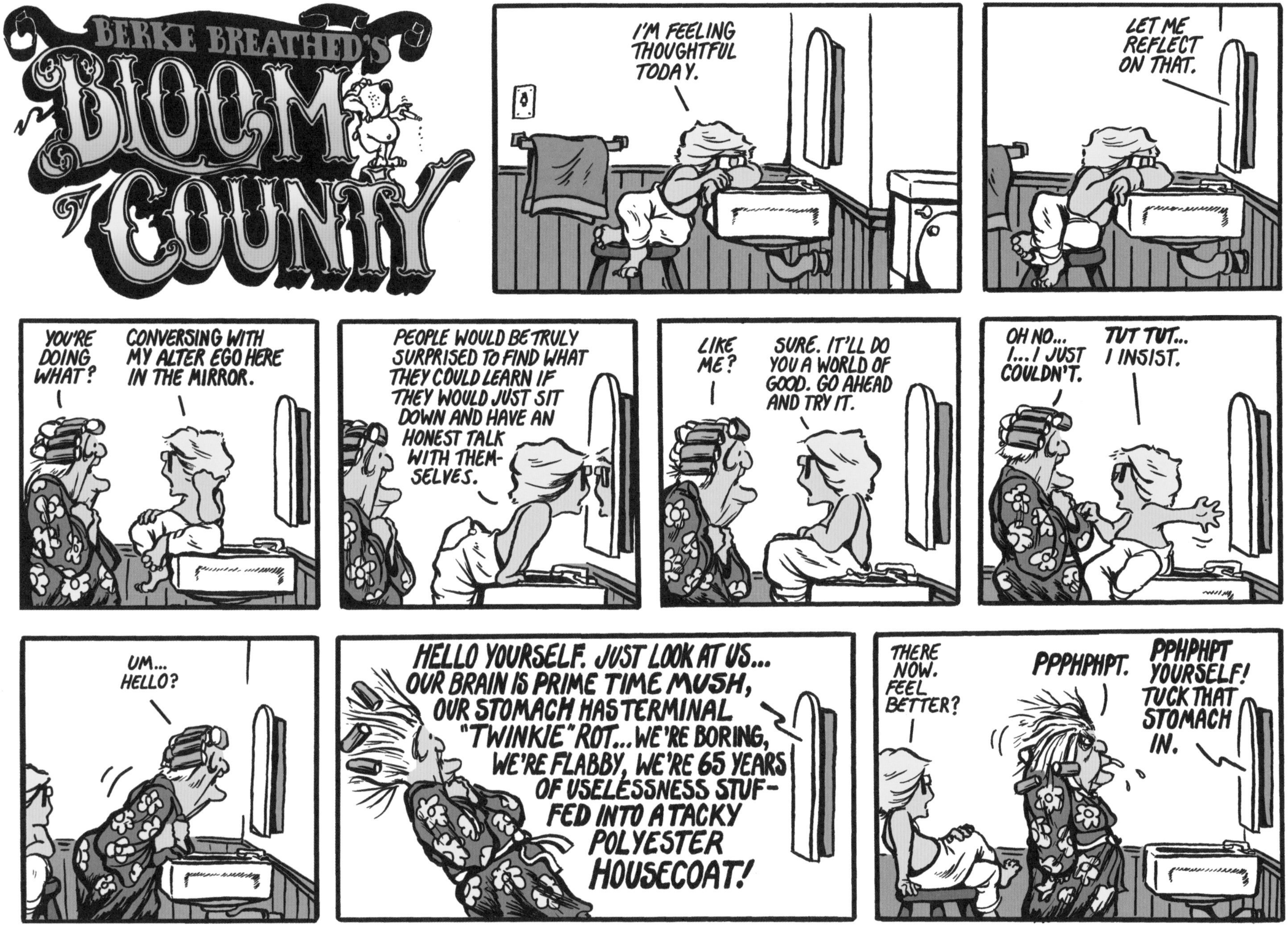
BERKE BREATHED'S
BLOOM COUNTY
I'M FEELING THOUGHTFUL TODAY.
LET ME REFLECT ON THAT.
YOU'RE DOING WHAT?
CONVERSING WITH MY ALTER EGO HERE IN THE MIRROR.
PEOPLE WOULD BE TRULY SURPRISED TO FIND WHAT THEY COULD LEARN IF THEY WOULD JUST SIT DOWN AND HAVE AN HONEST TALK WITH THEM-SELVES.
LIKE ME?
SURE. IT'LL DO YOU A WORLD OF GOOD. GO AHEAD AND TRY IT.
OH NO... I...I JUST COULDN'T.
TUT TUT... I INSIST.
UM... HELLO?
HELLO YOURSELF. JUST LOOK AT US... OUR BRAIN IS PRIME TIME MUSH, OUR STOMACH HAS TERMINAL "TWINKIE" ROT... WE'RE BORING, WE'RE FLABBY, WE'RE 65 YEARS OF USELESSNESS STUF-FED INTO A TACKY POLYESTER HOUSECOAT!
THERE NOW. FEEL BETTER?
PPPHPHPT.
PPHPHPT YOURSELF! TUCK THAT STOMACH IN.

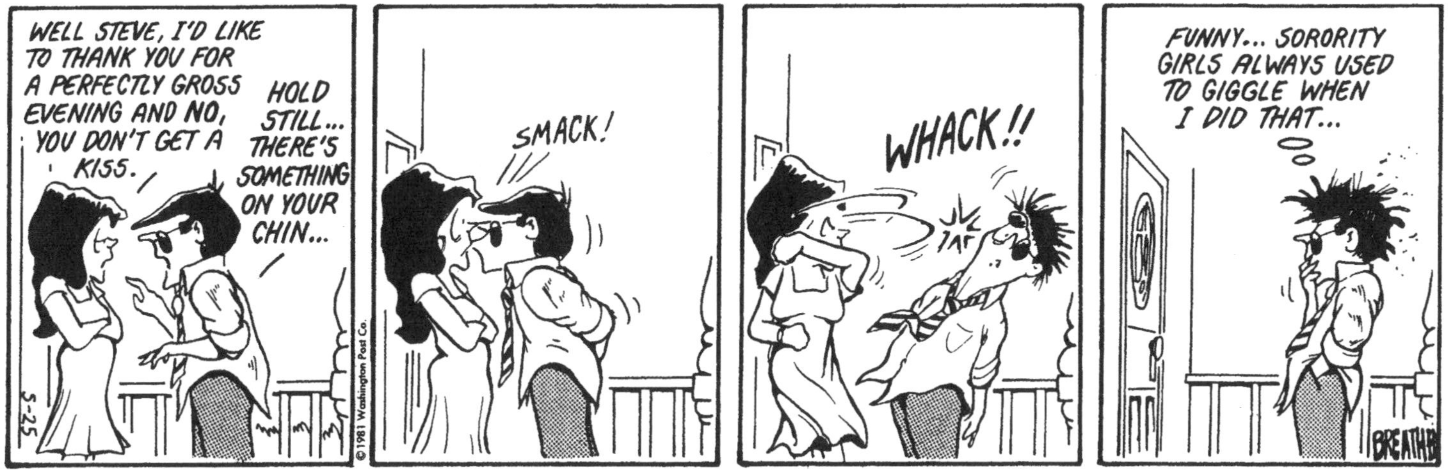
WELL STEVE, I'D LIKE TO THANK YOU FOR A PERFECTLY GROSS EVENING AND NO, YOU DON'T GET A KISS.
HOLD STILL... THERE'S SOMETHING ON YOUR CHIN...
5-25
© 1981 Washington Post Co.
SMACK!
WHACK!!
FUNNY... SORORITY GIRLS ALWAYS USED TO GIGGLE WHEN I DID THAT...
BREATHED

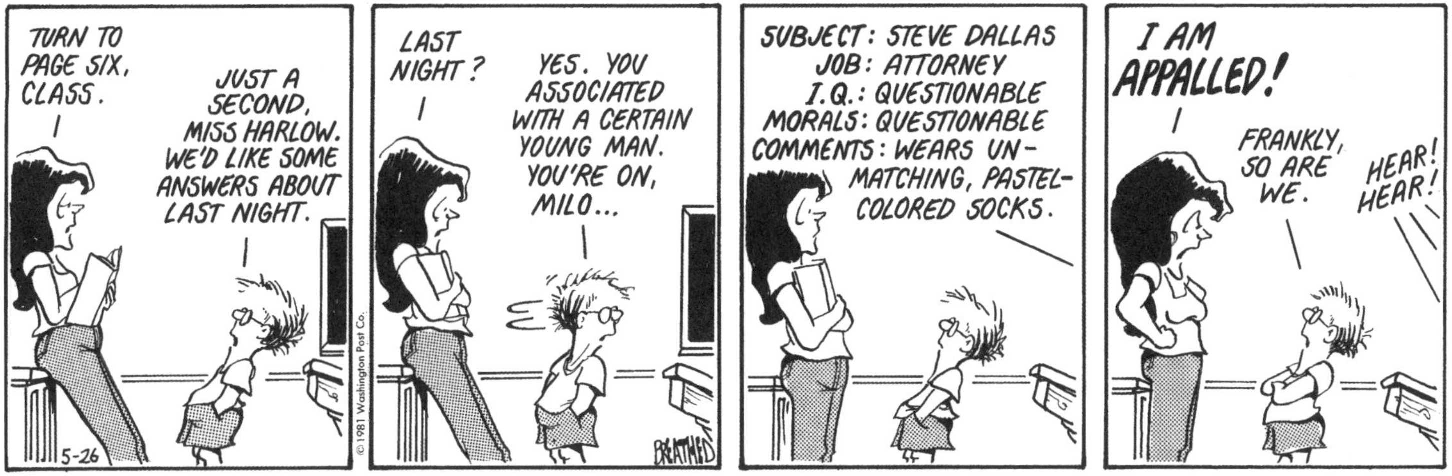
TURN TO PAGE SIX, CLASS.
JUST A SECOND, MISS HARLOW. WE'D LIKE SOME ANSWERS ABOUT LAST NIGHT.
5-26
© 1981 Washington Post Co.
LAST NIGHT?
YES. YOU ASSOCIATED WITH A CERTAIN YOUNG MAN. YOU'RE ON, MILO...
BREATHED
SUBJECT: STEVE DALLAS
JOB: ATTORNEY
I.Q.: QUESTIONABLE
MORALS: QUESTIONABLE
COMMENTS: WEARS UN-MATCHING, PASTEL-COLORED SOCKS.
I AM APPALLED!
FRANKLY, SO ARE WE.
HEAR! HEAR!

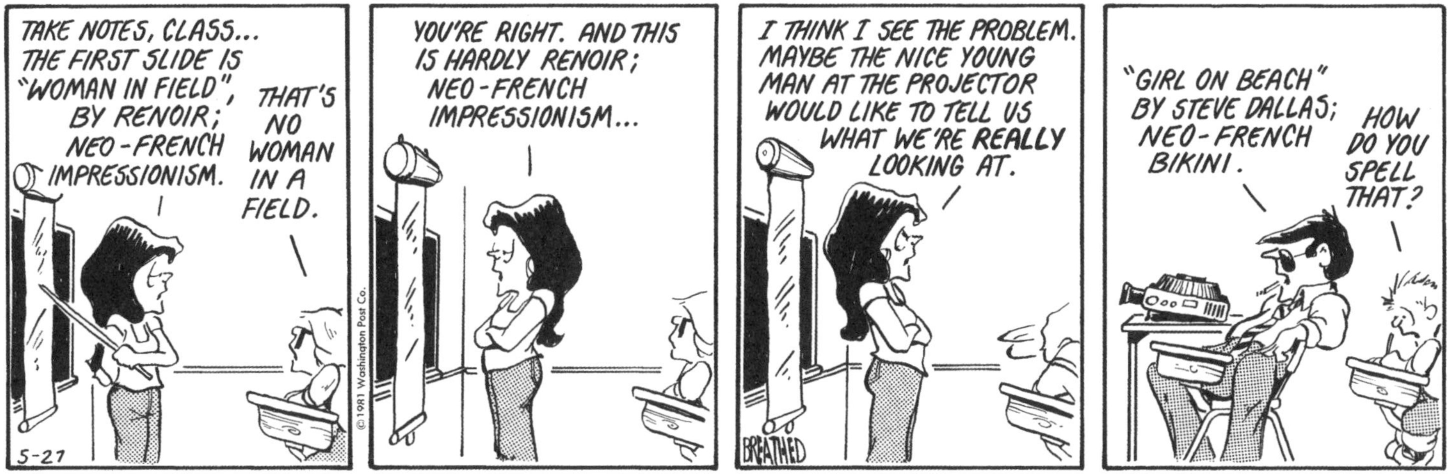
TAKE NOTES, CLASS... THE FIRST SLIDE IS "WOMAN IN FIELD", BY RENOIR; NEO-FRENCH IMPRESSIONISM.
THAT'S NO WOMAN IN A FIELD.
5-27
© 1981 Washington Post Co.
YOU'RE RIGHT. AND THIS IS HARDLY RENOIR; NEO-FRENCH IMPRESSIONISM...
I THINK I SEE THE PROBLEM. MAYBE THE NICE YOUNG MAN AT THE PROJECTOR WOULD LIKE TO TELL US WHAT WE'RE REALLY LOOKING AT.
BREATHED
"GIRL ON BEACH" BY STEVE DALLAS; NEO-FRENCH BIKINI.
HOW DO YOU SPELL THAT?

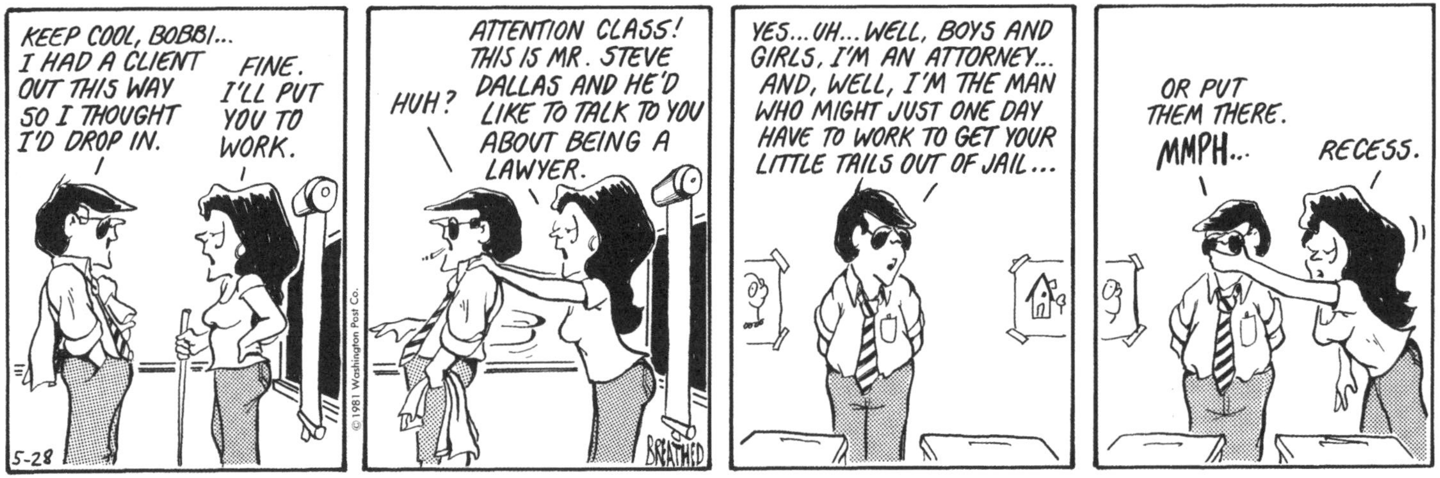
KEEP COOL, BOBBI... I HAD A CLIENT OUT THIS WAY SO I THOUGHT I'D DROP IN.
FINE. I'LL PUT YOU TO WORK.
5-28
HUH?
ATTENTION CLASS! THIS IS MR. STEVE DALLAS AND HE'D LIKE TO TALK TO YOU ABOUT BEING A LAWYER.
© 1981 Washington Post Co.
BREATHED
YES... UH... WELL, BOYS AND GIRLS, I'M AN ATTORNEY... AND, WELL, I'M THE MAN WHO MIGHT JUST ONE DAY HAVE TO WORK TO GET YOUR LITTLE TAILS OUT OF JAIL...
OR PUT THEM THERE.
MMPH...
RECESS.

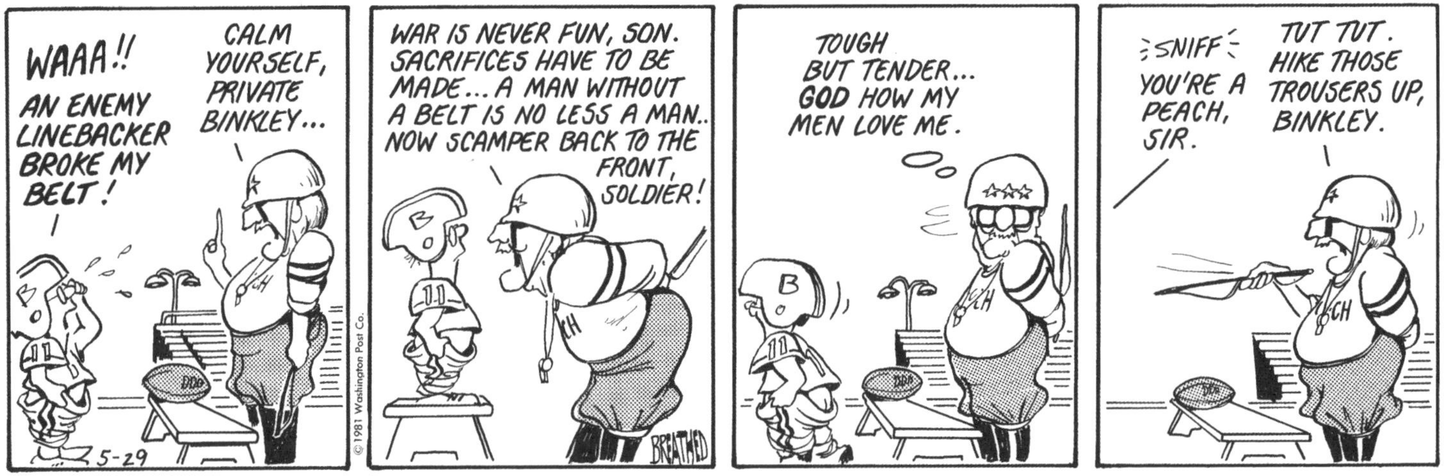
WAAA!! AN ENEMY LINEBACKER BROKE MY BELT!
CALM YOURSELF, PRIVATE BINKLEY...
5-29
WAR IS NEVER FUN, SON. SACRIFICES HAVE TO BE MADE... A MAN WITHOUT A BELT IS NO LESS A MAN.. NOW SCAMPER BACK TO THE FRONT, SOLDIER!
© 1981 Washington Post Co.
BREATHED
TOUGH BUT TENDER... GOD HOW MY MEN LOVE ME.
SNIFF
YOU'RE A PEACH, SIR.
TUT TUT. HIKE THOSE TROUSERS UP, BINKLEY.

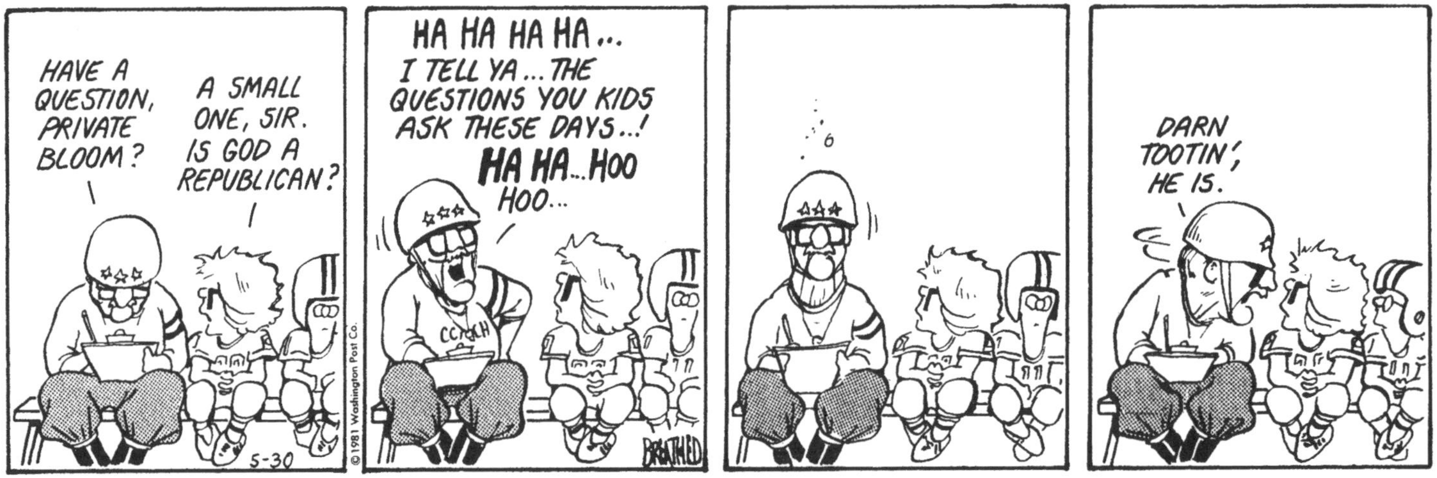
HAVE A QUESTION, PRIVATE BLOOM?
A SMALL ONE, SIR. IS GOD A REPUBLICAN?
5-30
HA HA HA HA... I TELL YA... THE QUESTIONS YOU KIDS ASK THESE DAYS...!
HA HA...HOO HOO...
© 1981 Washington Post Co.
BREATHED
DARN TOOTIN', HE IS.

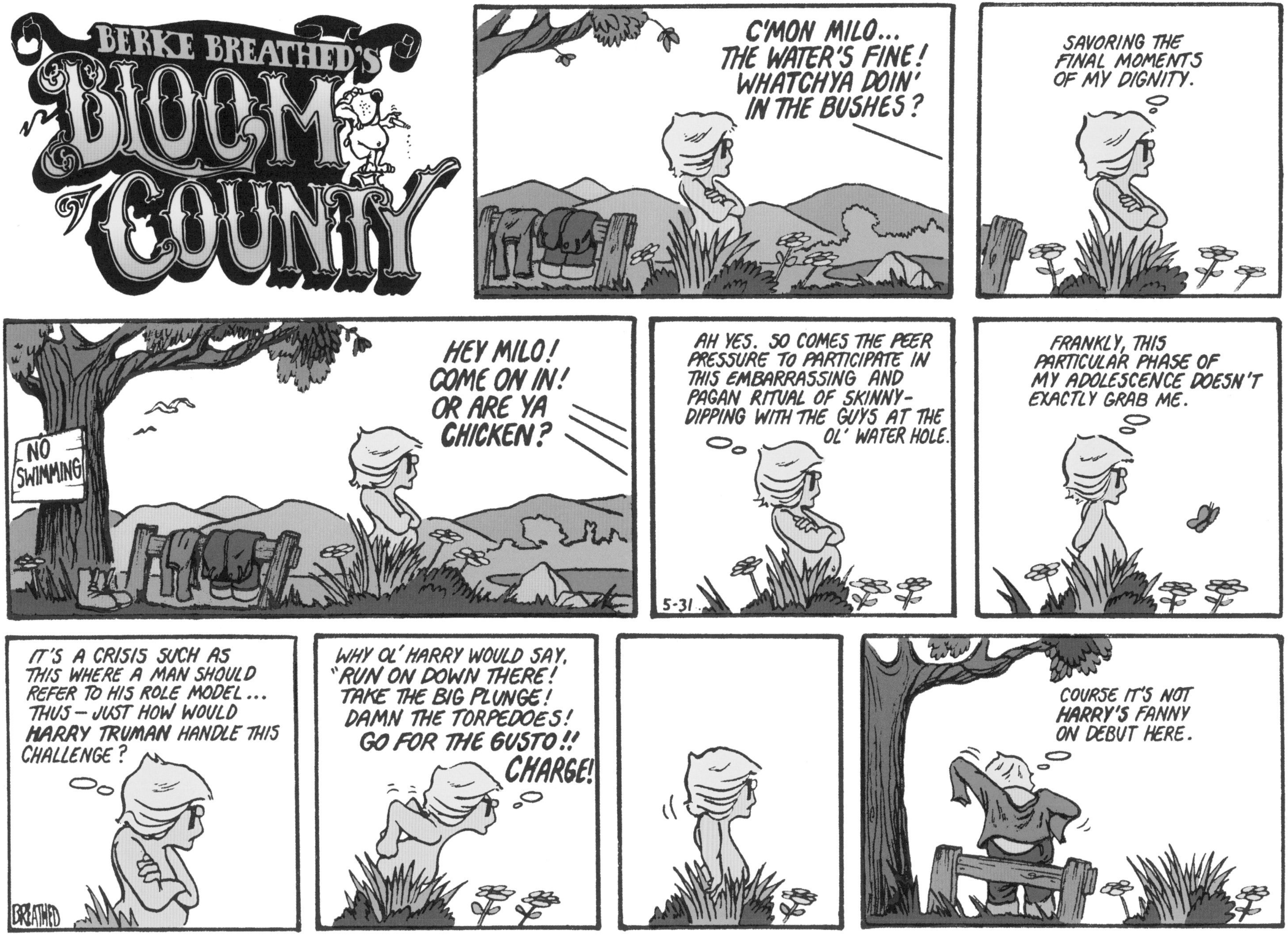
BERKE BREATHED'S
BLOOM COUNTY
C'MON MILO... THE WATER'S FINE! WHATCHYA DOIN' IN THE BUSHES?
SAVORING THE FINAL MOMENTS OF MY DIGNITY.
HEY MILO! COME ON IN! OR ARE YA CHICKEN?
NO SWIMMING
AH YES. SO COMES THE PEER PRESSURE TO PARTICIPATE IN THIS EMBARRASSING AND PAGAN RITUAL OF SKINNY-DIPPING WITH THE GUYS AT THE OL' WATER HOLE.
5-31
FRANKLY, THIS PARTICULAR PHASE OF MY ADOLESCENCE DOESN'T EXACTLY GRAB ME.
IT'S A CRISIS SUCH AS THIS WHERE A MAN SHOULD REFER TO HIS ROLE MODEL... THUS — JUST HOW WOULD HARRY TRUMAN HANDLE THIS CHALLENGE?
BREATHED
WHY OL' HARRY WOULD SAY, "RUN ON DOWN THERE! TAKE THE BIG PLUNGE! DAMN THE TORPEDOES! GO FOR THE GUSTO!! CHARGE!
COURSE IT'S NOT HARRY'S FANNY ON DEBUT HERE.

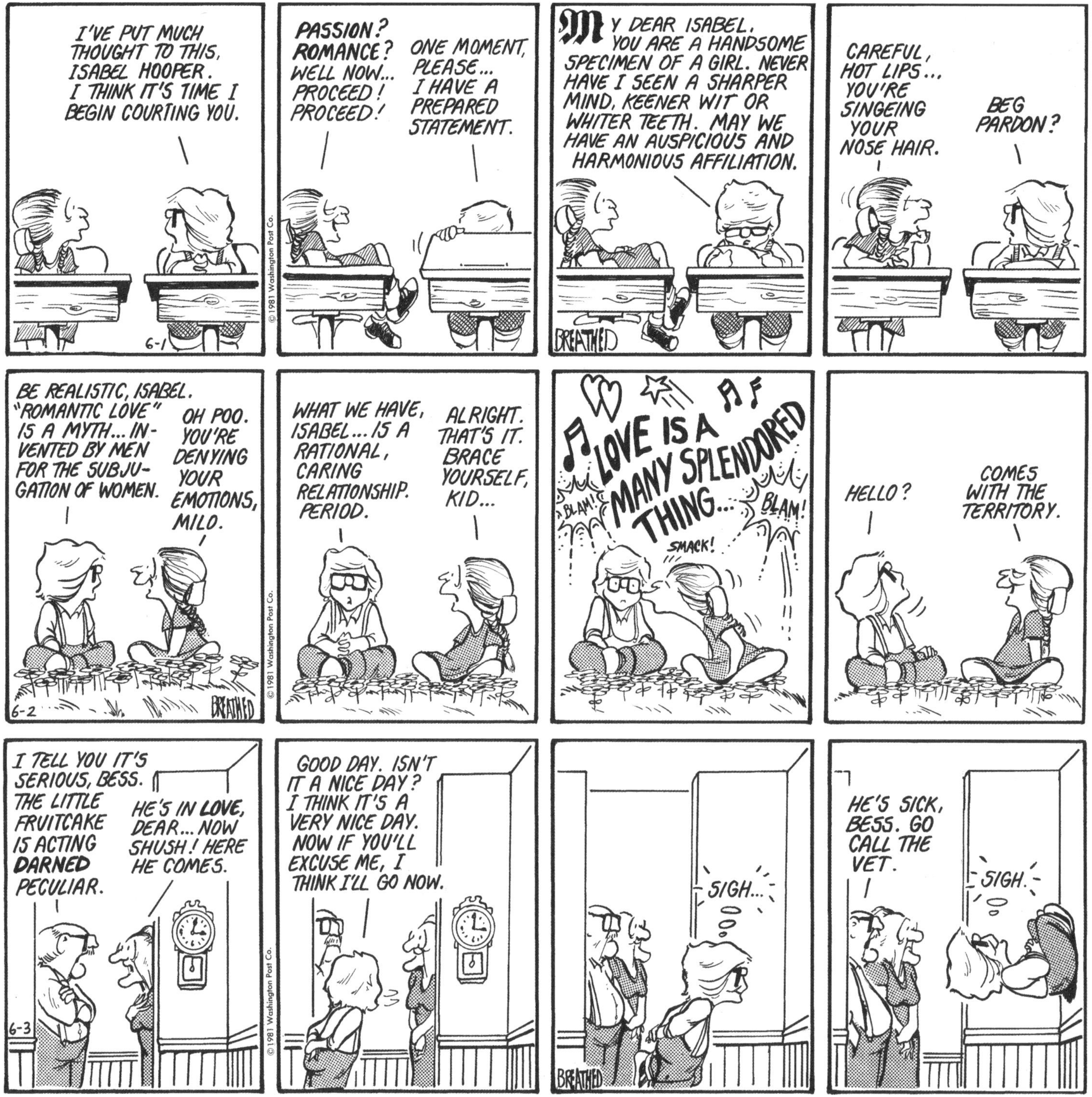
I'VE PUT MUCH THOUGHT TO THIS, ISABEL HOOPER. I THINK IT'S TIME I BEGIN COURTING YOU.
6-1
PASSION? ROMANCE? WELL NOW... PROCEED! PROCEED!
ONE MOMENT, PLEASE... I HAVE A PREPARED STATEMENT.
© 1981 Washington Post Co.
MY DEAR ISABEL, YOU ARE A HANDSOME SPECIMEN OF A GIRL. NEVER HAVE I SEEN A SHARPER MIND, KEENER WIT OR WHITER TEETH. MAY WE HAVE AN AUSPICIOUS AND HARMONIOUS AFFILIATION.
BREATHED
CAREFUL, HOT LIPS... YOU'RE SINGEING YOUR NOSE HAIR.
BEG PARDON?
BE REALISTIC, ISABEL. "ROMANTIC LOVE" IS A MYTH... INVENTED BY MEN FOR THE SUBJUGATION OF WOMEN.
OH POO. YOU'RE DENYING YOUR EMOTIONS, MILO.
6-2
BREATHED
WHAT WE HAVE, ISABEL... IS A RATIONAL, CARING RELATIONSHIP. PERIOD.
ALRIGHT. THAT'S IT. BRACE YOURSELF, KID...
© 1981 Washington Post Co.
LOVE IS A MANY SPLENDORED THING...
BLAM!
BLAM!
SMACK!
HELLO?
COMES WITH THE TERRITORY.
I TELL YOU IT'S SERIOUS, BESS. THE LITTLE FRUITCAKE IS ACTING DARNED PECULIAR.
HE'S IN LOVE, DEAR... NOW SHUSH! HERE HE COMES.
6-3
GOOD DAY. ISN'T IT A NICE DAY? I THINK IT'S A VERY NICE DAY. NOW IF YOU'LL EXCUSE ME, I THINK I'LL GO NOW.
© 1981 Washington Post Co.
SIGH...
BREATHED
HE'S SICK, BESS. GO CALL THE VET.
SIGH.

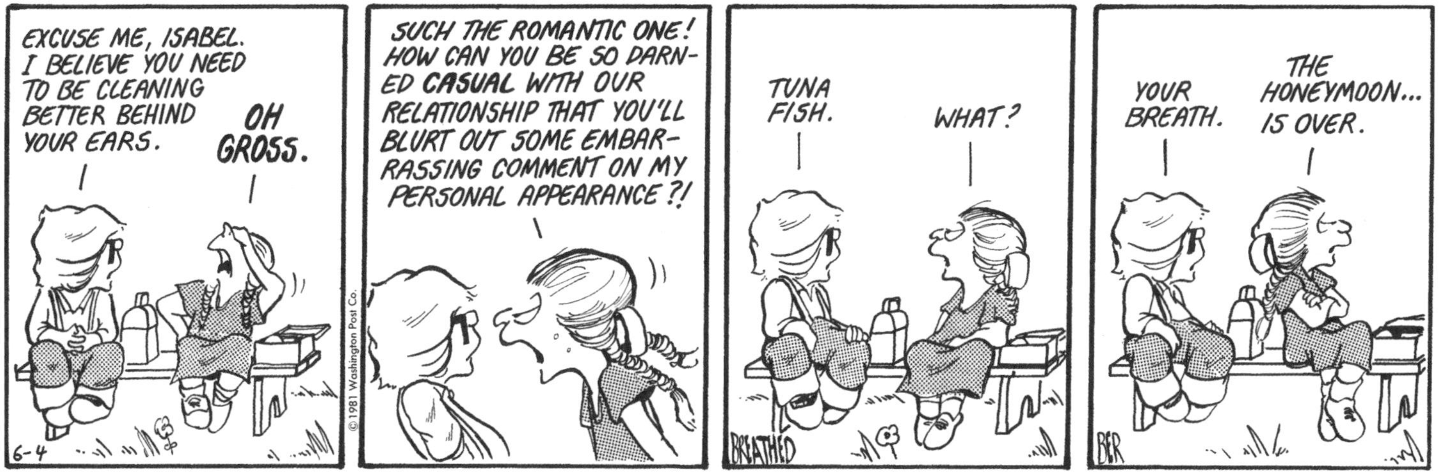
EXCUSE ME, ISABEL. I BELIEVE YOU NEED TO BE CLEANING BETTER BEHIND YOUR EARS.
OH GROSS.
6-4
SUCH THE ROMANTIC ONE! HOW CAN YOU BE SO DARNED CASUAL WITH OUR RELATIONSHIP THAT YOU'LL BLURT OUT SOME EMBARRASSING COMMENT ON MY PERSONAL APPEARANCE ?!
©1981 Washington Post Co.
TUNA FISH.
WHAT?
BREATHED
YOUR BREATH.
THE HONEYMOON... IS OVER.
BER

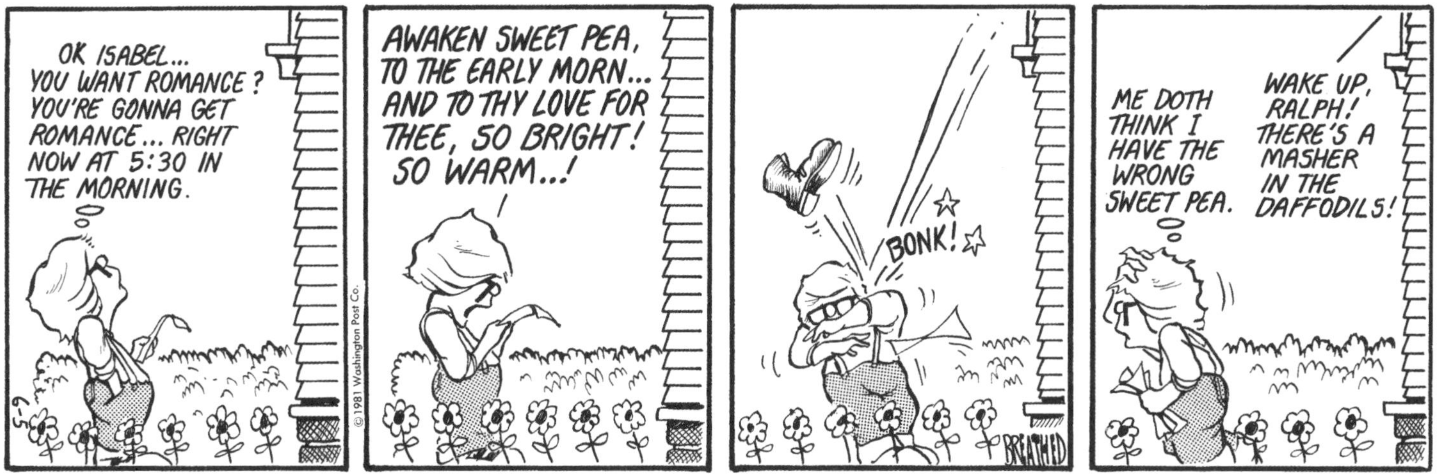
OK ISABEL... YOU WANT ROMANCE? YOU'RE GONNA GET ROMANCE... RIGHT NOW AT 5:30 IN THE MORNING.
6-5
AWAKEN SWEET PEA, TO THE EARLY MORN... AND TO THY LOVE FOR THEE, SO BRIGHT! SO WARM...!
©1981 Washington Post Co.
BONK!
BREATHED
ME DOTH THINK I HAVE THE WRONG SWEET PEA.
WAKE UP, RALPH! THERE'S A MASHER IN THE DAFFODILS!

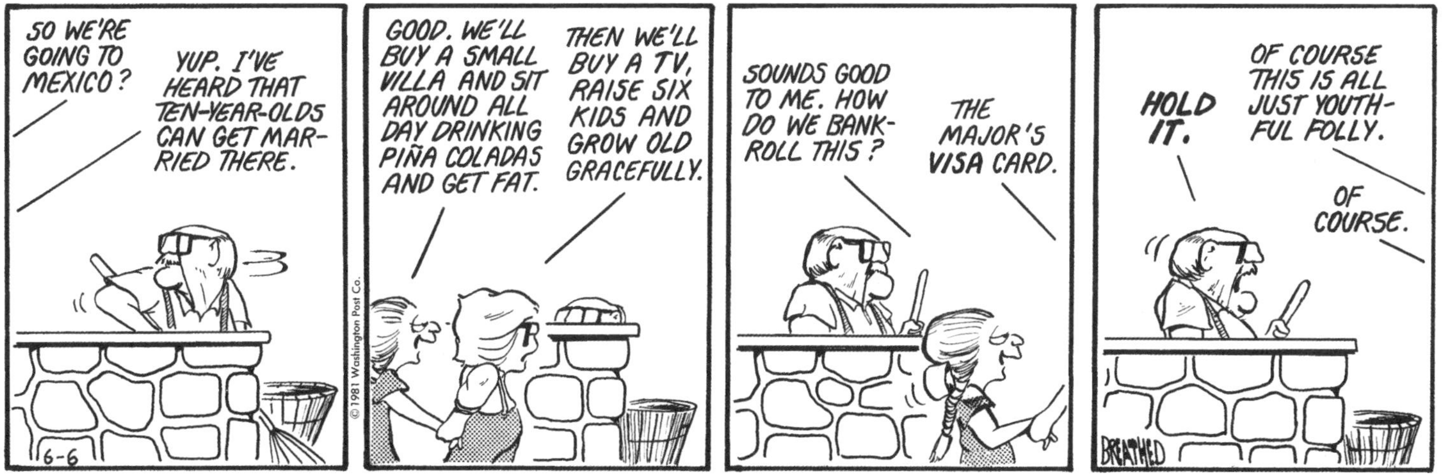
SO WE'RE GOING TO MEXICO?
YUP. I'VE HEARD THAT TEN-YEAR-OLDS CAN GET MARRIED THERE.
6-6
GOOD. WE'LL BUY A SMALL VILLA AND SIT AROUND ALL DAY DRINKING PIÑA COLADAS AND GET FAT.
THEN WE'LL BUY A TV, RAISE SIX KIDS AND GROW OLD GRACEFULLY.
©1981 Washington Post Co.
SOUNDS GOOD TO ME. HOW DO WE BANKROLL THIS?
THE MAJOR'S VISA CARD.
HOLD IT.
OF COURSE THIS IS ALL JUST YOUTHFUL FOLLY.
OF COURSE.
BREATHED

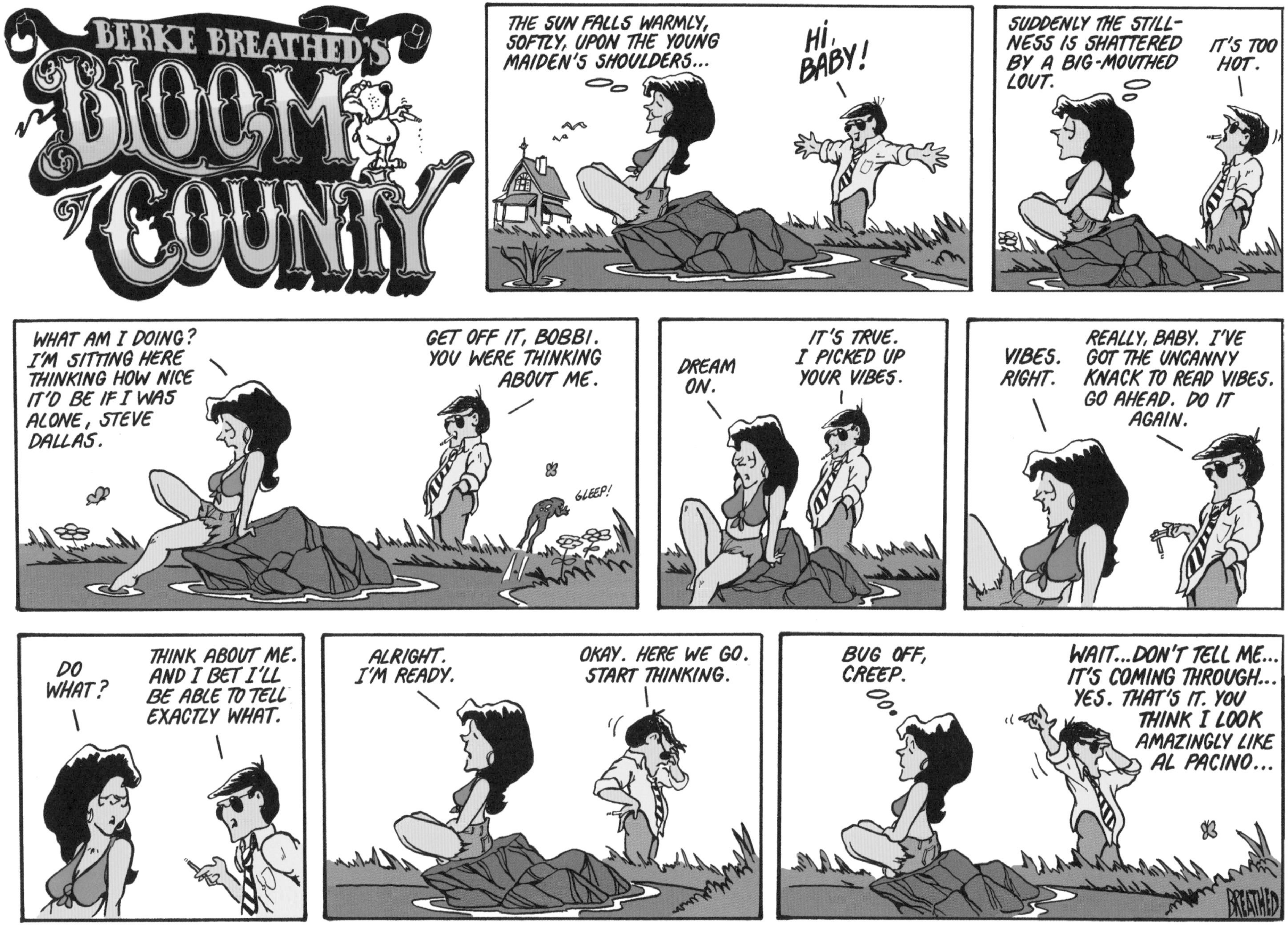
BERKE BREATHED'S
BLOOM COUNTY
THE SUN FALLS WARMLY, SOFTLY, UPON THE YOUNG MAIDEN'S SHOULDERS...
HI, BABY!
SUDDENLY THE STILLNESS IS SHATTERED BY A BIG-MOUTHED LOUT.
IT'S TOO HOT.
WHAT AM I DOING? I'M SITTING HERE THINKING HOW NICE IT'D BE IF I WAS ALONE, STEVE DALLAS.
GET OFF IT, BOBBI. YOU WERE THINKING ABOUT ME.
GLEEP!
DREAM ON.
IT'S TRUE. I PICKED UP YOUR VIBES.
VIBES. RIGHT.
REALLY, BABY. I'VE GOT THE UNCANNY KNACK TO READ VIBES. GO AHEAD. DO IT AGAIN.
DO WHAT?
THINK ABOUT ME. AND I BET I'LL BE ABLE TO TELL EXACTLY WHAT.
ALRIGHT. I'M READY.
OKAY. HERE WE GO. START THINKING.
BUG OFF, CREEP.
WAIT...DON'T TELL ME... IT'S COMING THROUGH... YES. THAT'S IT. YOU THINK I LOOK AMAZINGLY LIKE AL PACINO...
BREATHED

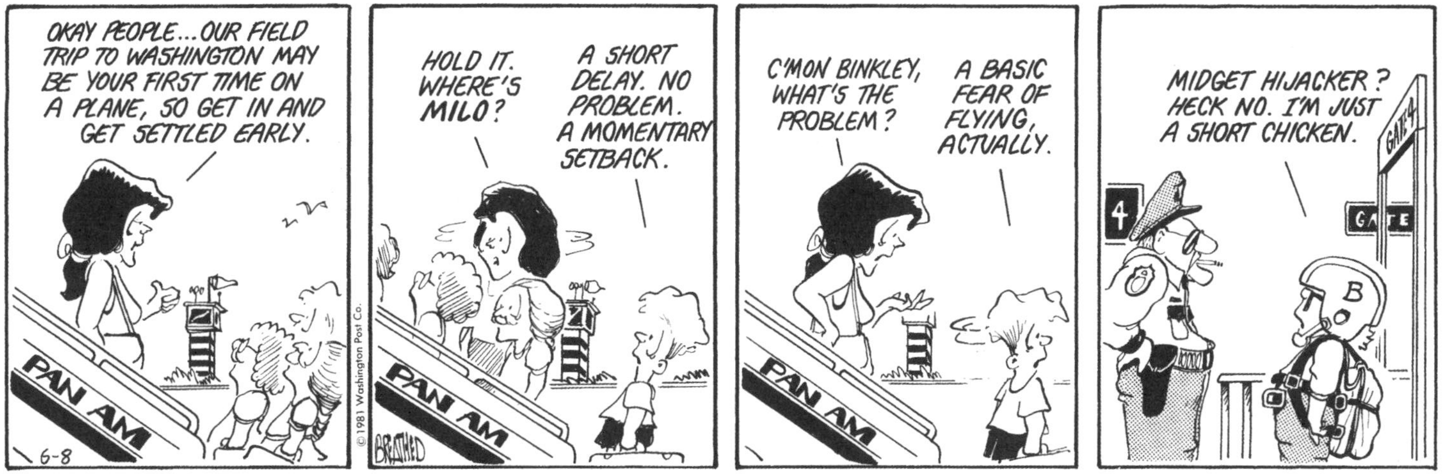
OKAY PEOPLE...OUR FIELD TRIP TO WASHINGTON MAY BE YOUR FIRST TIME ON A PLANE, SO GET IN AND GET SETTLED EARLY.
PAN AM
6-8
HOLD IT. WHERE'S MILO?
A SHORT DELAY. NO PROBLEM. A MOMENTARY SETBACK.
©1981 Washington Post Co.
BREATHED
C'MON BINKLEY, WHAT'S THE PROBLEM?
A BASIC FEAR OF FLYING, ACTUALLY.
MIDGET HIJACKER? HECK NO. I'M JUST A SHORT CHICKEN.
4
GATE 4
GATE
B

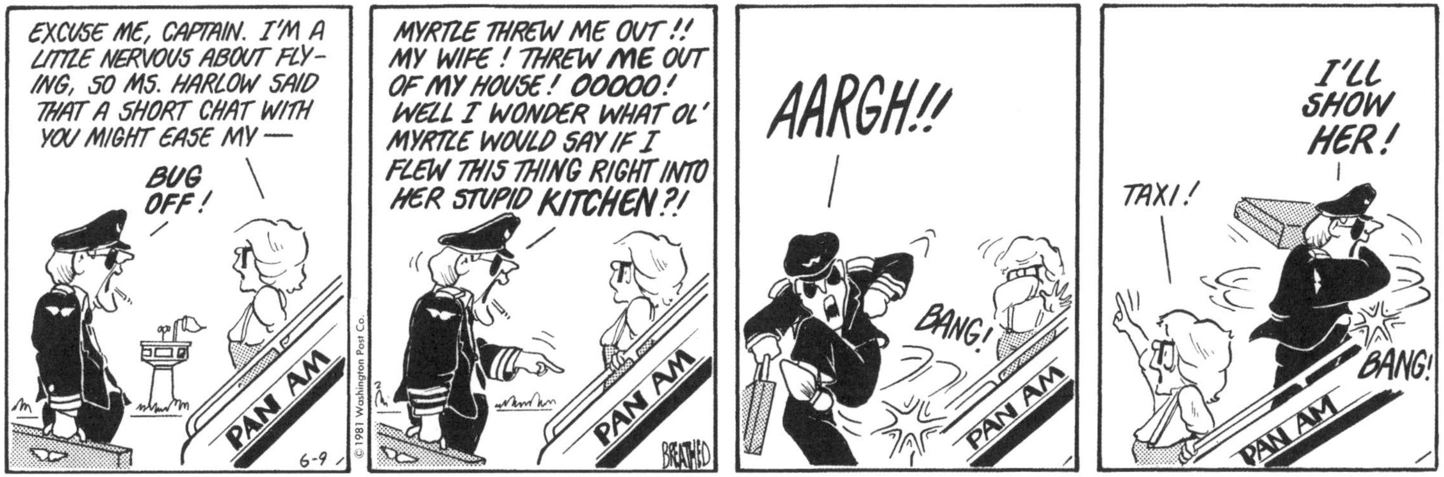
EXCUSE ME, CAPTAIN. I'M A LITTLE NERVOUS ABOUT FLY-ING, SO MS. HARLOW SAID THAT A SHORT CHAT WITH YOU MIGHT EASE MY—
BUG OFF!
PAN AM
6-9
MYRTLE THREW ME OUT!! MY WIFE! THREW ME OUT OF MY HOUSE! OOOOO! WELL I WONDER WHAT OL' MYRTLE WOULD SAY IF I FLEW THIS THING RIGHT INTO HER STUPID KITCHEN?!
©1981 Washington Post Co.
BREATHED
AARGH!!
BANG!
PAN AM
I'LL SHOW HER!
TAXI!
BANG!
PAN AM

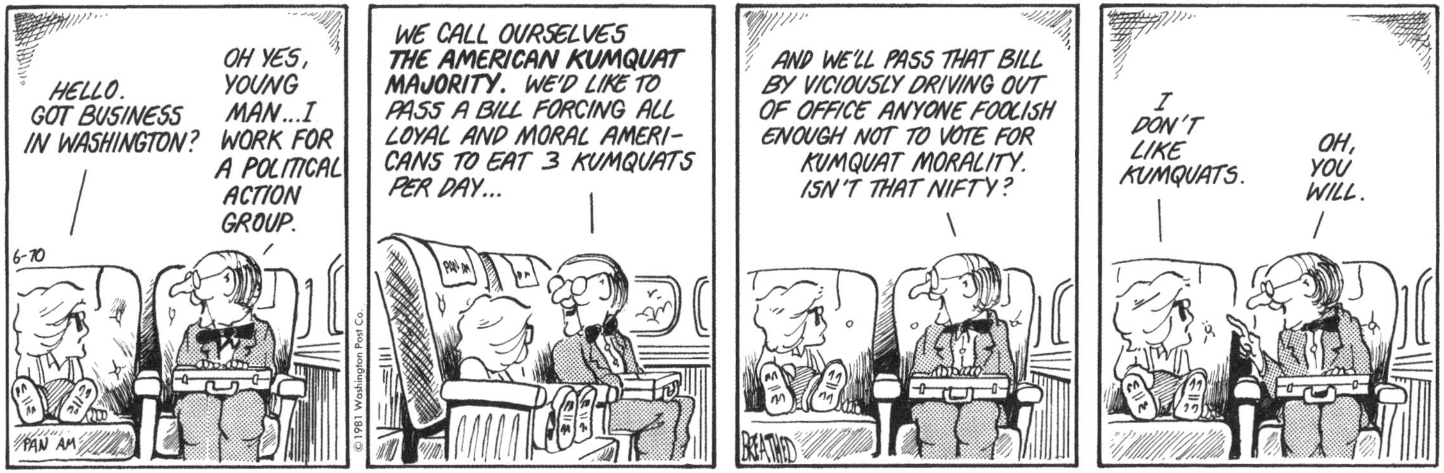
HELLO. GOT BUSINESS IN WASHINGTON?
OH YES, YOUNG MAN...I WORK FOR A POLITICAL ACTION GROUP.
6-10
PAN AM
WE CALL OURSELVES THE AMERICAN KUMQUAT MAJORITY. WE'D LIKE TO PASS A BILL FORCING ALL LOYAL AND MORAL AMERI-CANS TO EAT 3 KUMQUATS PER DAY...
©1981 Washington Post Co.
AND WE'LL PASS THAT BILL BY VICIOUSLY DRIVING OUT OF OFFICE ANYONE FOOLISH ENOUGH NOT TO VOTE FOR KUMQUAT MORALITY. ISN'T THAT NIFTY?
BREATHED
I DON'T LIKE KUMQUATS.
OH, YOU WILL.

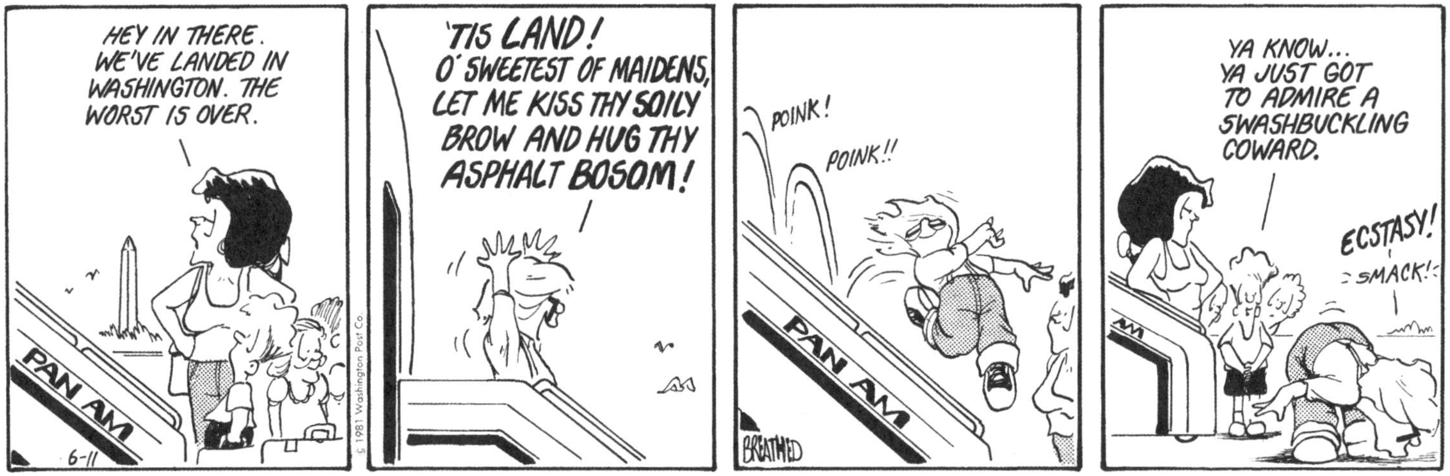
HEY IN THERE. WE'VE LANDED IN WASHINGTON. THE WORST IS OVER.
PAN AM
6-11
© 1981 Washington Post Co.
'TIS LAND! O' SWEETEST OF MAIDENS, LET ME KISS THY SOILY BROW AND HUG THY ASPHALT BOSOM!
POINK!
POINK!!
PAN AM
BREATHED
YA KNOW... YA JUST GOT TO ADMIRE A SWASHBUCKLING COWARD.
ECSTASY!
SMACK!

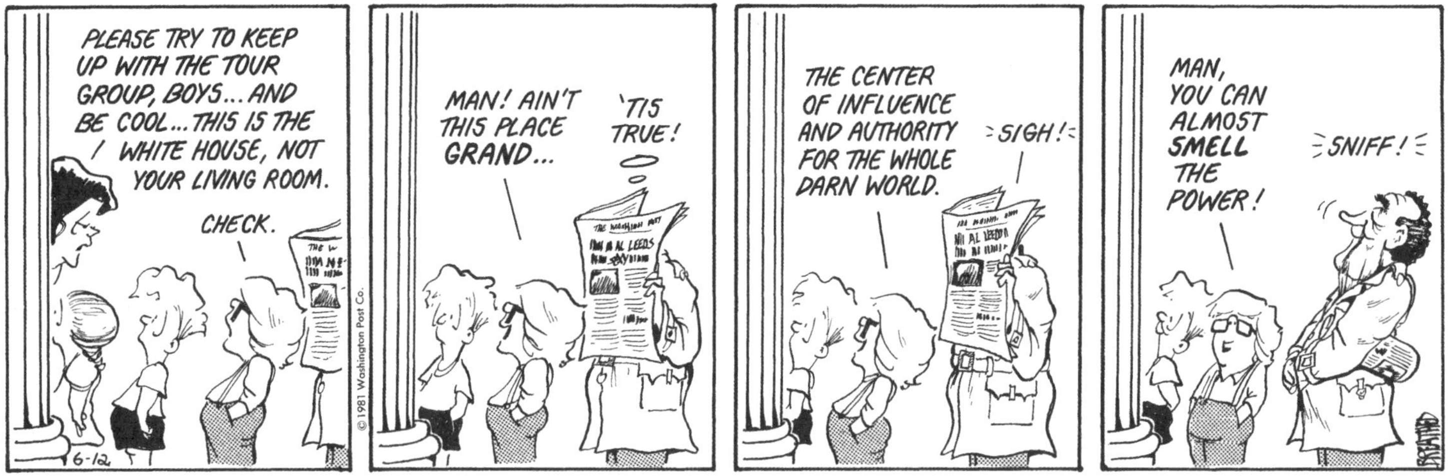
PLEASE TRY TO KEEP UP WITH THE TOUR GROUP, BOYS... AND BE COOL... THIS IS THE WHITE HOUSE, NOT YOUR LIVING ROOM.
CHECK.
6-12
© 1981 Washington Post Co.
MAN! AIN'T THIS PLACE GRAND...
'TIS TRUE!
THE CENTER OF INFLUENCE AND AUTHORITY FOR THE WHOLE DARN WORLD.
SIGH!
MAN, YOU CAN ALMOST SMELL THE POWER!
SNIFF!
BREATHED

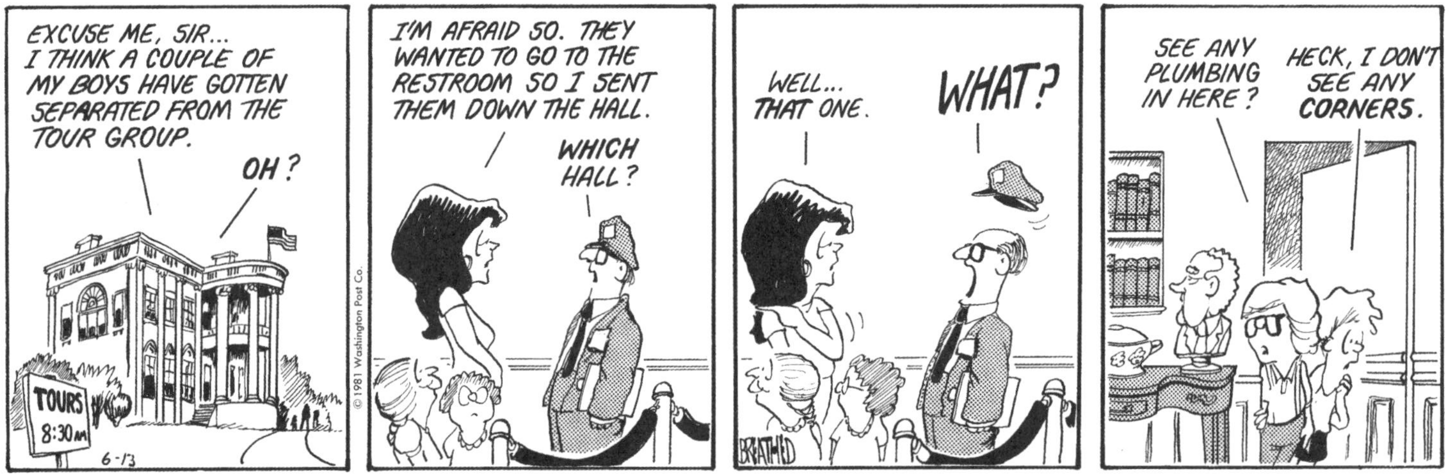
EXCUSE ME, SIR... I THINK A COUPLE OF MY BOYS HAVE GOTTEN SEPARATED FROM THE TOUR GROUP.
OH?
TOURS 8:30 AM
6-13
© 1981 Washington Post Co.
I'M AFRAID SO. THEY WANTED TO GO TO THE RESTROOM SO I SENT THEM DOWN THE HALL.
WHICH HALL?
WELL... THAT ONE.
WHAT?
BREATHED
SEE ANY PLUMBING IN HERE?
HECK, I DON'T SEE ANY CORNERS.

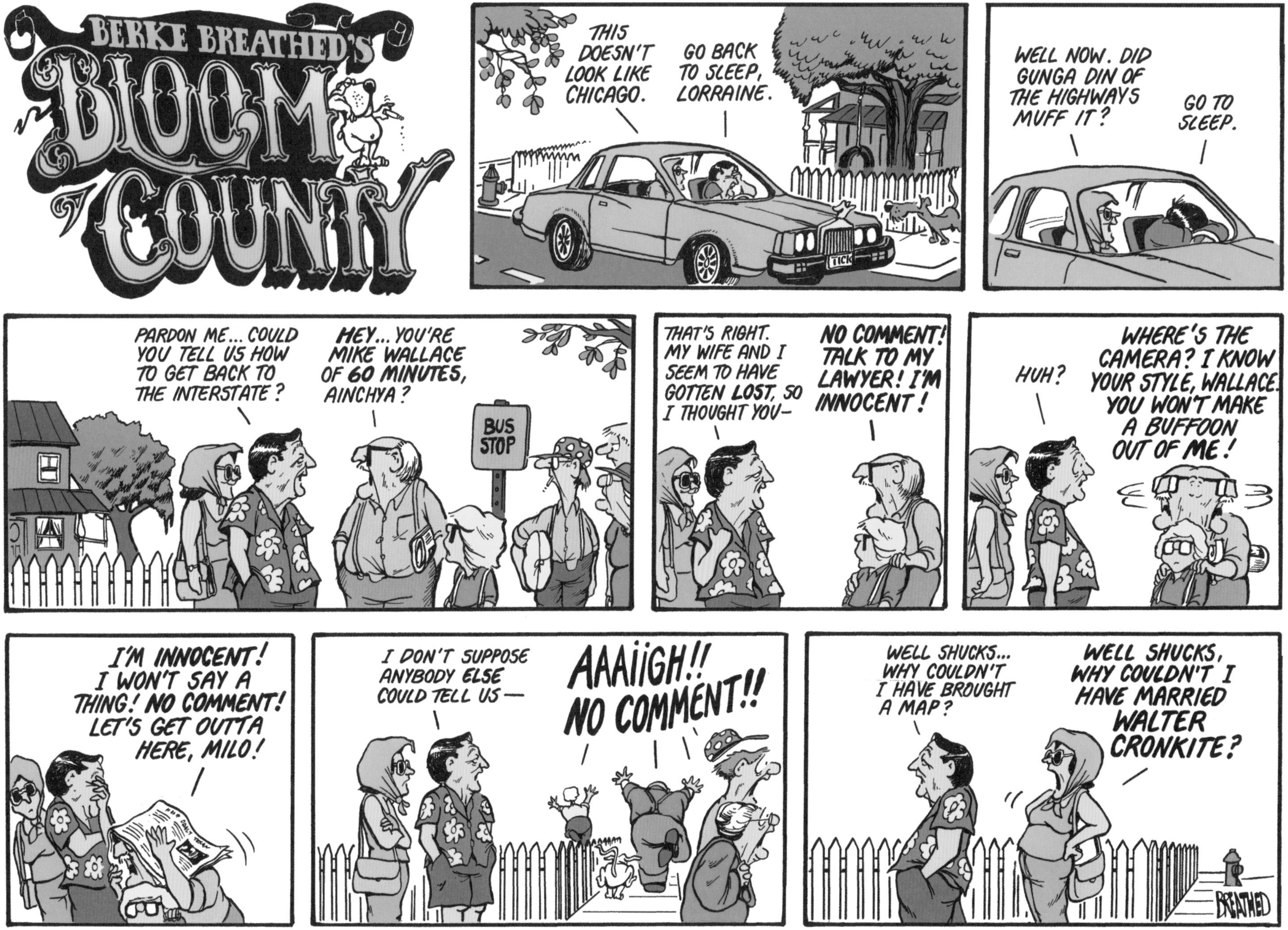
BERKE BREATHED'S
BLOOM COUNTY
THIS DOESN'T LOOK LIKE CHICAGO.
GO BACK TO SLEEP, LORRAINE.
TICK
WELL NOW. DID GUNGA DIN OF THE HIGHWAYS MUFF IT?
GO TO SLEEP.
PARDON ME... COULD YOU TELL US HOW TO GET BACK TO THE INTERSTATE?
HEY... YOU'RE MIKE WALLACE OF 60 MINUTES, AINCHYA?
BUS STOP
THAT'S RIGHT. MY WIFE AND I SEEM TO HAVE GOTTEN LOST, SO I THOUGHT YOU—
NO COMMENT! TALK TO MY LAWYER! I'M INNOCENT!
HUH?
WHERE'S THE CAMERA? I KNOW YOUR STYLE, WALLACE. YOU WON'T MAKE A BUFFOON OUT OF ME!
I'M INNOCENT! I WON'T SAY A THING! NO COMMENT! LET'S GET OUTTA HERE, MILO!
I DON'T SUPPOSE ANYBODY ELSE COULD TELL US—
AAAiiGH!! NO COMMENT!!
WELL SHUCKS... WHY COULDN'T I HAVE BROUGHT A MAP?
WELL SHUCKS, WHY COULDN'T I HAVE MARRIED WALTER CRONKITE?
BREATHED

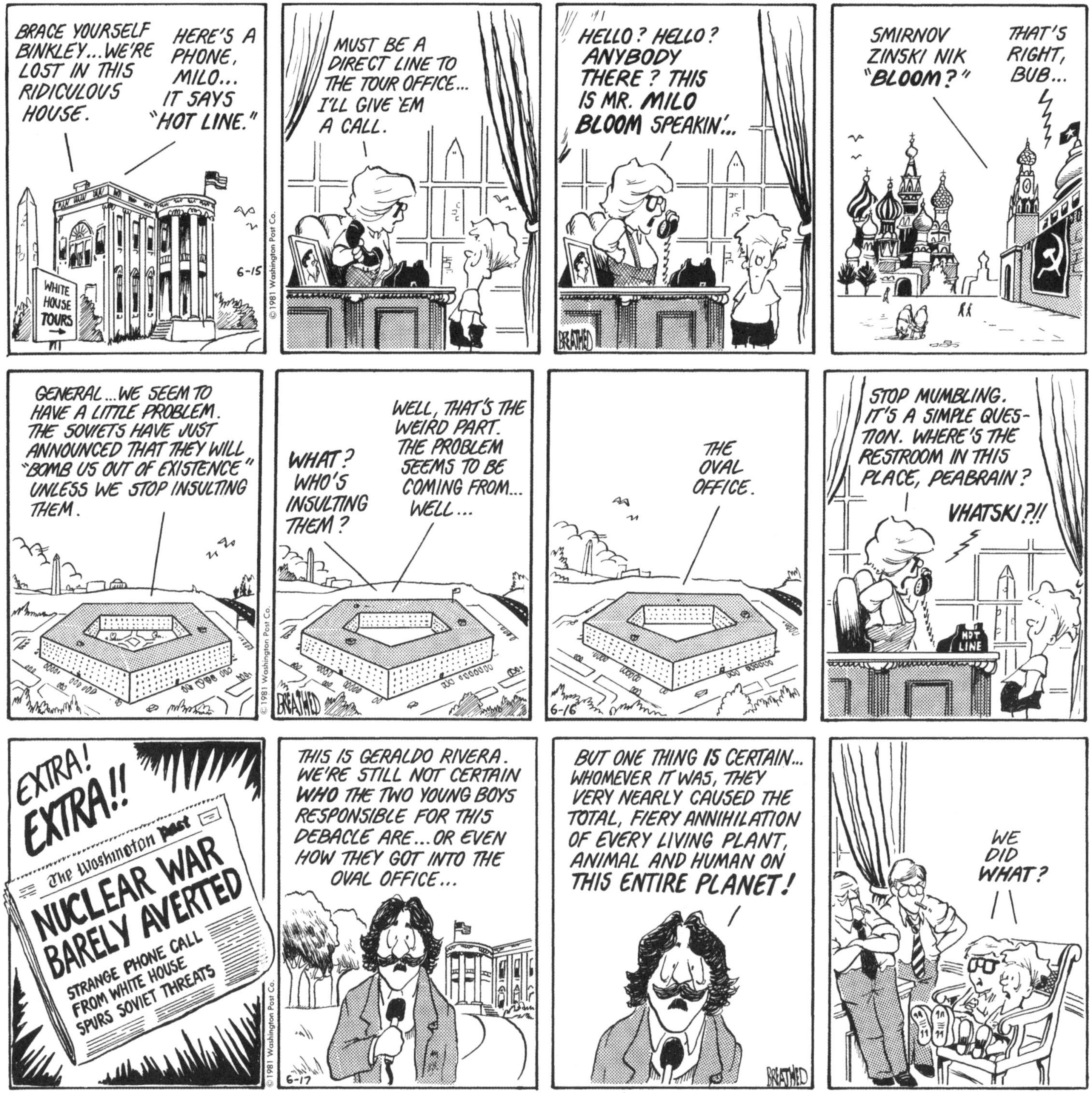
BRACE YOURSELF BINKLEY...WE'RE LOST IN THIS RIDICULOUS HOUSE.
HERE'S A PHONE, MILO... IT SAYS "HOT LINE."
WHITE HOUSE TOURS
6-15
© 1981 Washington Post Co.
MUST BE A DIRECT LINE TO THE TOUR OFFICE... I'LL GIVE 'EM A CALL.
HELLO? HELLO? ANYBODY THERE? THIS IS MR. MILO BLOOM SPEAKIN'...
BREATHED
SMIRNOV ZINSKI NIK "BLOOM?"
THAT'S RIGHT, BUB...
GENERAL...WE SEEM TO HAVE A LITTLE PROBLEM. THE SOVIETS HAVE JUST ANNOUNCED THAT THEY WILL "BOMB US OUT OF EXISTENCE" UNLESS WE STOP INSULTING THEM.
© 1981 Washington Post Co.
BREATHED
WHAT? WHO'S INSULTING THEM?
WELL, THAT'S THE WEIRD PART. THE PROBLEM SEEMS TO BE COMING FROM... WELL...
THE OVAL OFFICE.
6-16
STOP MUMBLING. IT'S A SIMPLE QUESTION. WHERE'S THE RESTROOM IN THIS PLACE, PEABRAIN?
VHATSKI?!!
HOT LINE
EXTRA! EXTRA!!
The Washington Post
NUCLEAR WAR BARELY AVERTED
STRANGE PHONE CALL FROM WHITE HOUSE SPURS SOVIET THREATS
© 1981 Washington Post Co.
THIS IS GERALDO RIVERA. WE'RE STILL NOT CERTAIN WHO THE TWO YOUNG BOYS RESPONSIBLE FOR THIS DEBACLE ARE...OR EVEN HOW THEY GOT INTO THE OVAL OFFICE...
6-17
BUT ONE THING IS CERTAIN... WHOMEVER IT WAS, THEY VERY NEARLY CAUSED THE TOTAL, FIERY ANNIHILATION OF EVERY LIVING PLANT, ANIMAL AND HUMAN ON THIS ENTIRE PLANET!
BREATHED
WE DID WHAT?

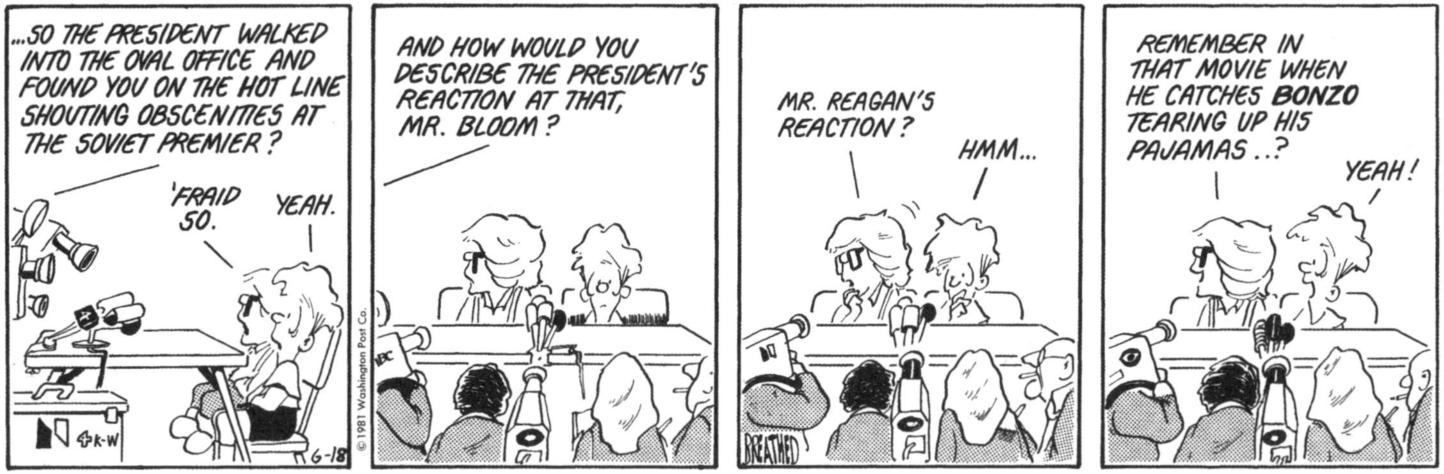
...SO THE PRESIDENT WALKED INTO THE OVAL OFFICE AND FOUND YOU ON THE HOT LINE SHOUTING OBSCENITIES AT THE SOVIET PREMIER?
'FRAID SO.
YEAH.
© 1981 Washington Post Co.
AND HOW WOULD YOU DESCRIBE THE PRESIDENT'S REACTION AT THAT, MR. BLOOM?
MR. REAGAN'S REACTION?
HMM...
REMEMBER IN THAT MOVIE WHEN HE CATCHES BONZO TEARING UP HIS PAJAMAS..?
YEAH!

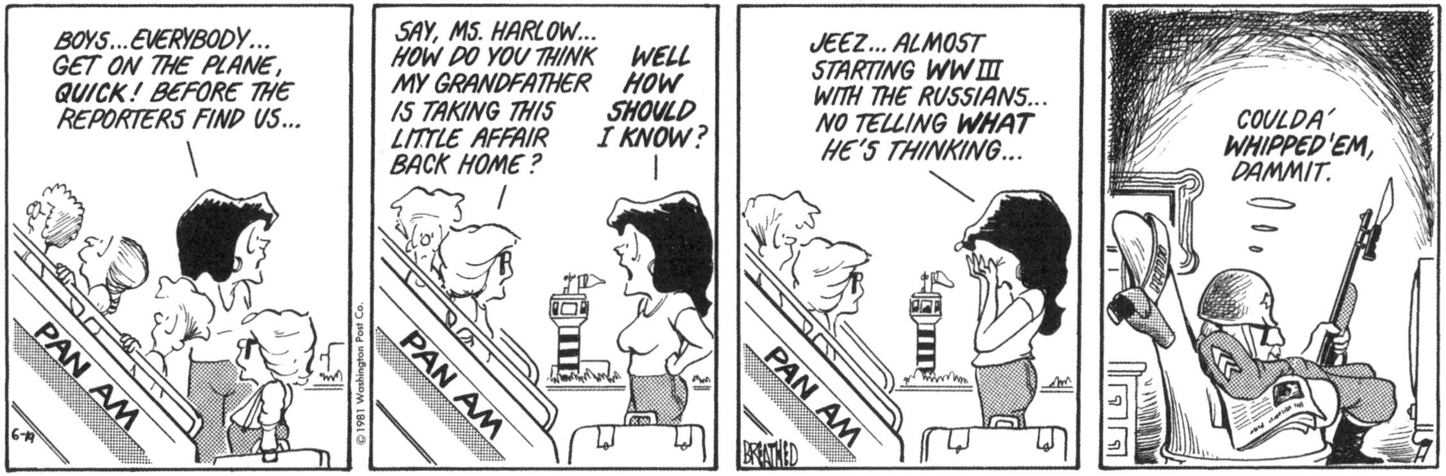
BOYS...EVERYBODY... GET ON THE PLANE, QUICK! BEFORE THE REPORTERS FIND US...
PAN AM
© 1981 Washington Post Co.
SAY, MS. HARLOW... HOW DO YOU THINK MY GRANDFATHER IS TAKING THIS LITTLE AFFAIR BACK HOME?
WELL HOW SHOULD I KNOW?
JEEZ... ALMOST STARTING WW III WITH THE RUSSIANS... NO TELLING WHAT HE'S THINKING...
COULDA' WHIPPED 'EM, DAMMIT.

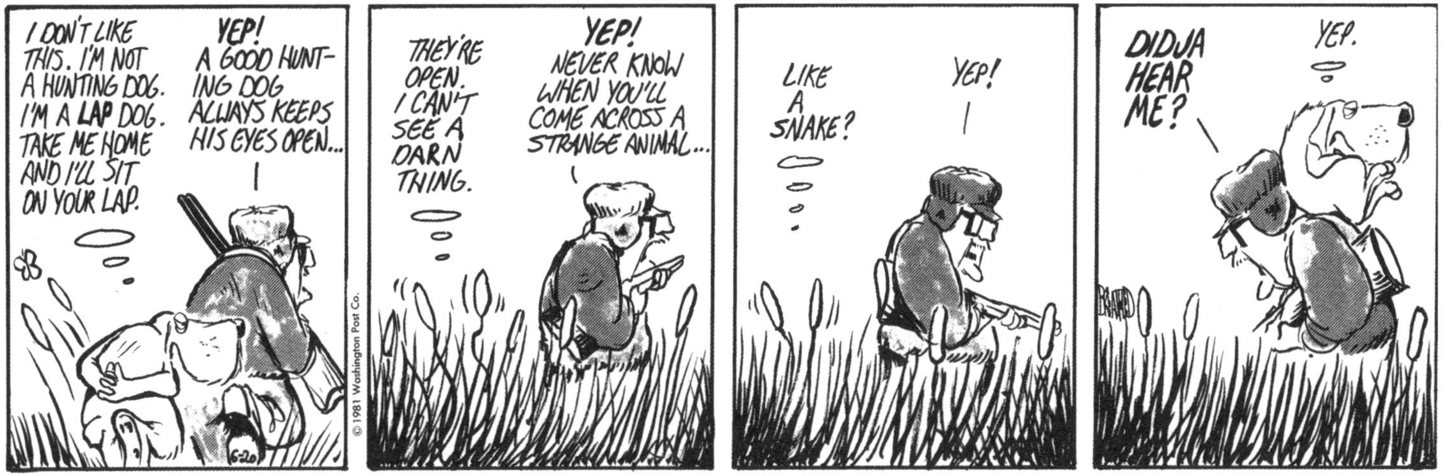
I DON'T LIKE THIS. I'M NOT A HUNTING DOG. I'M A LAP DOG. TAKE ME HOME AND I'LL SIT ON YOUR LAP.
YEP! A GOOD HUNTING DOG ALWAYS KEEPS HIS EYES OPEN...
© 1981 Washington Post Co.
THEY'RE OPEN. I CAN'T SEE A DARN THING.
YEP! NEVER KNOW WHEN YOU'LL COME ACROSS A STRANGE ANIMAL...
LIKE A SNAKE?
YEP!
DIDJA HEAR ME?
YEP.

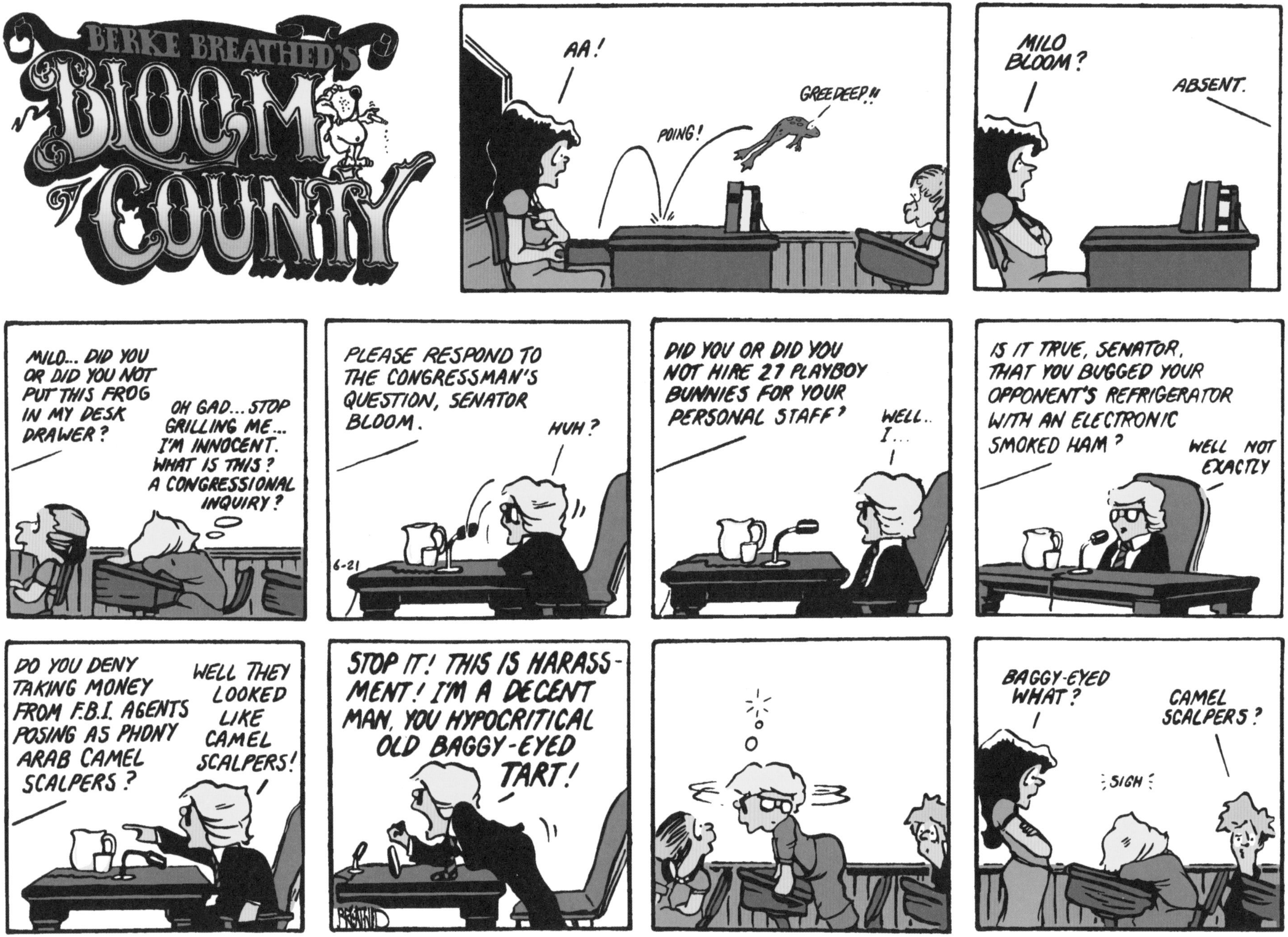
BERKE BREATHED'S
BLOOM COUNTY
AA!
POING!
GREEDEEP!!
MILO BLOOM?
ABSENT.
MILO... DID YOU OR DID YOU NOT PUT THIS FROG IN MY DESK DRAWER?
OH GAD... STOP GRILLING ME... I'M INNOCENT. WHAT IS THIS? A CONGRESSIONAL INQUIRY?
PLEASE RESPOND TO THE CONGRESSMAN'S QUESTION, SENATOR BLOOM.
HUH?
6-21
DID YOU OR DID YOU NOT HIRE 27 PLAYBOY BUNNIES FOR YOUR PERSONAL STAFF?
WELL.. I...
IS IT TRUE, SENATOR, THAT YOU BUGGED YOUR OPPONENT'S REFRIGERATOR WITH AN ELECTRONIC SMOKED HAM?
WELL NOT EXACTLY
DO YOU DENY TAKING MONEY FROM F.B.I. AGENTS POSING AS PHONY ARAB CAMEL SCALPERS?
WELL THEY LOOKED LIKE CAMEL SCALPERS!
STOP IT! THIS IS HARASS-MENT! I'M A DECENT MAN, YOU HYPOCRITICAL OLD BAGGY-EYED TART!
BREATHED
BAGGY-EYED WHAT?
SIGH
CAMEL SCALPERS?

 June 21, 1981

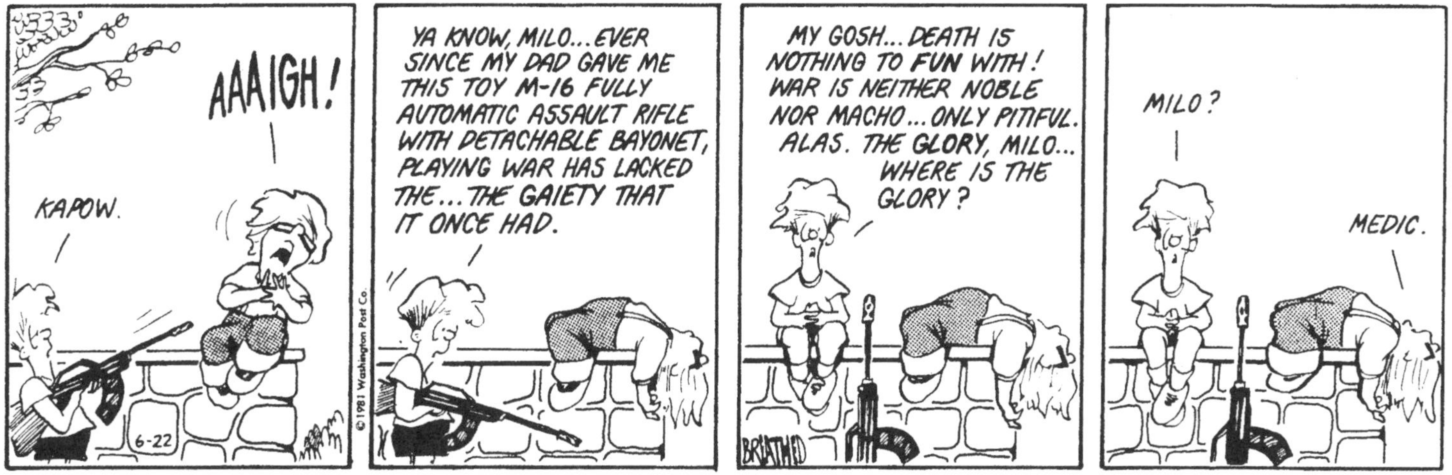
KAPOW.
AAAIGH!
6-22
© 1981 Washington Post Co.
YA KNOW, MILO... EVER SINCE MY DAD GAVE ME THIS TOY M-16 FULLY AUTOMATIC ASSAULT RIFLE WITH DETACHABLE BAYONET, PLAYING WAR HAS LACKED THE... THE GAIETY THAT IT ONCE HAD.
MY GOSH... DEATH IS NOTHING TO FUN WITH! WAR IS NEITHER NOBLE NOR MACHO... ONLY PITIFUL. ALAS. THE GLORY, MILO... WHERE IS THE GLORY?
BREATHED
MILO?
MEDIC.

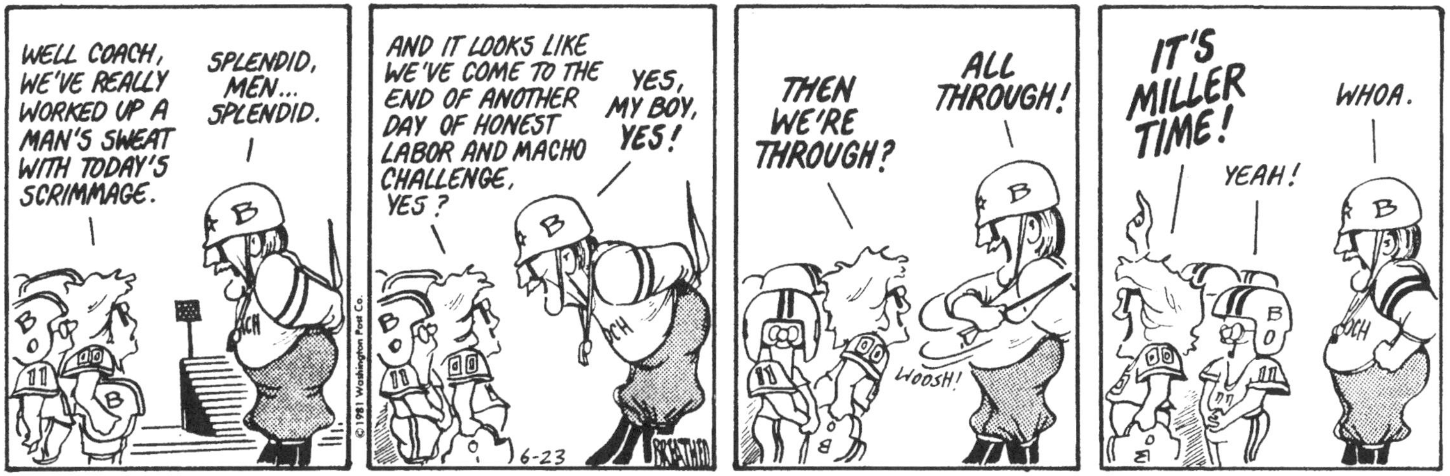
WELL COACH, WE'VE REALLY WORKED UP A MAN'S SWEAT WITH TODAY'S SCRIMMAGE.
SPLENDID, MEN... SPLENDID.
© 1981 Washington Post Co.
AND IT LOOKS LIKE WE'VE COME TO THE END OF ANOTHER DAY OF HONEST LABOR AND MACHO CHALLENGE, YES?
YES, MY BOY, YES!
6-23
BREATHED
THEN WE'RE THROUGH?
ALL THROUGH!
WOOSH!
IT'S MILLER TIME!
YEAH!
WHOA.

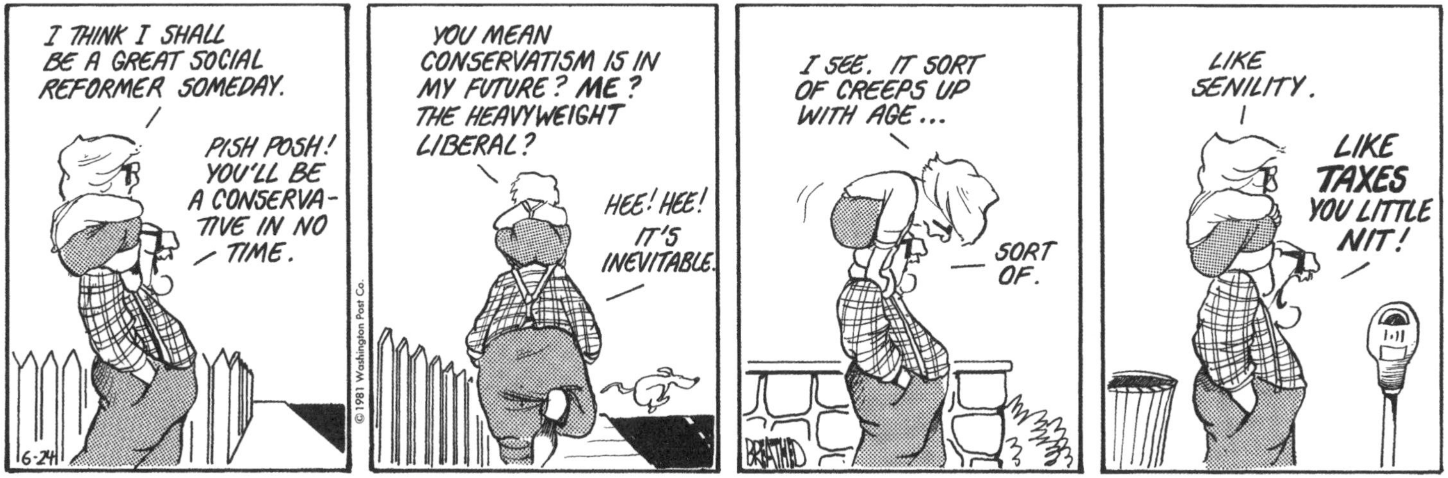
I THINK I SHALL BE A GREAT SOCIAL REFORMER SOMEDAY.
PISH POSH! YOU'LL BE A CONSERVATIVE IN NO TIME.
6-24
© 1981 Washington Post Co.
YOU MEAN CONSERVATISM IS IN MY FUTURE? ME? THE HEAVYWEIGHT LIBERAL?
HEE! HEE! IT'S INEVITABLE.
I SEE. IT SORT OF CREEPS UP WITH AGE...
SORT OF.
BREATHED
LIKE SENILITY.
LIKE TAXES YOU LITTLE NIT!

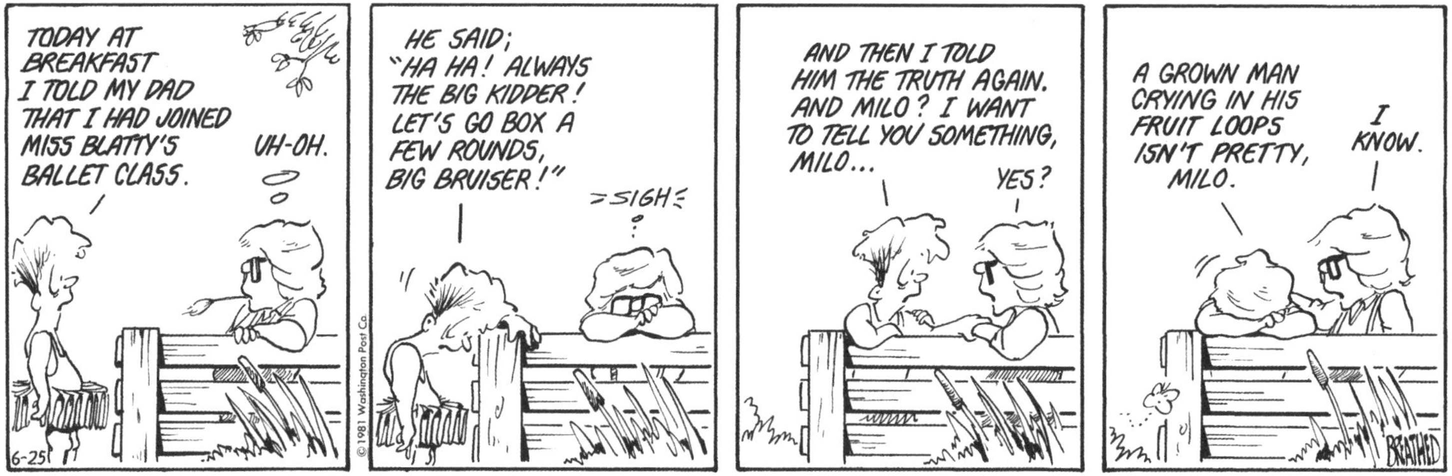
TODAY AT BREAKFAST I TOLD MY DAD THAT I HAD JOINED MISS BLATTY'S BALLET CLASS.
UH-OH.
HE SAID; "HA HA! ALWAYS THE BIG KIDDER! LET'S GO BOX A FEW ROUNDS, BIG BRUISER!"
SIGH
AND THEN I TOLD HIM THE TRUTH AGAIN. AND MILO? I WANT TO TELL YOU SOMETHING, MILO...
YES?
A GROWN MAN CRYING IN HIS FRUIT LOOPS ISN'T PRETTY, MILO.
I KNOW.
6-25
© 1981 Washington Post Co.
BREATHED

A temporary appearance of a penguin, as of yet unnamed. He was to disappear for another six months, alas. —BB

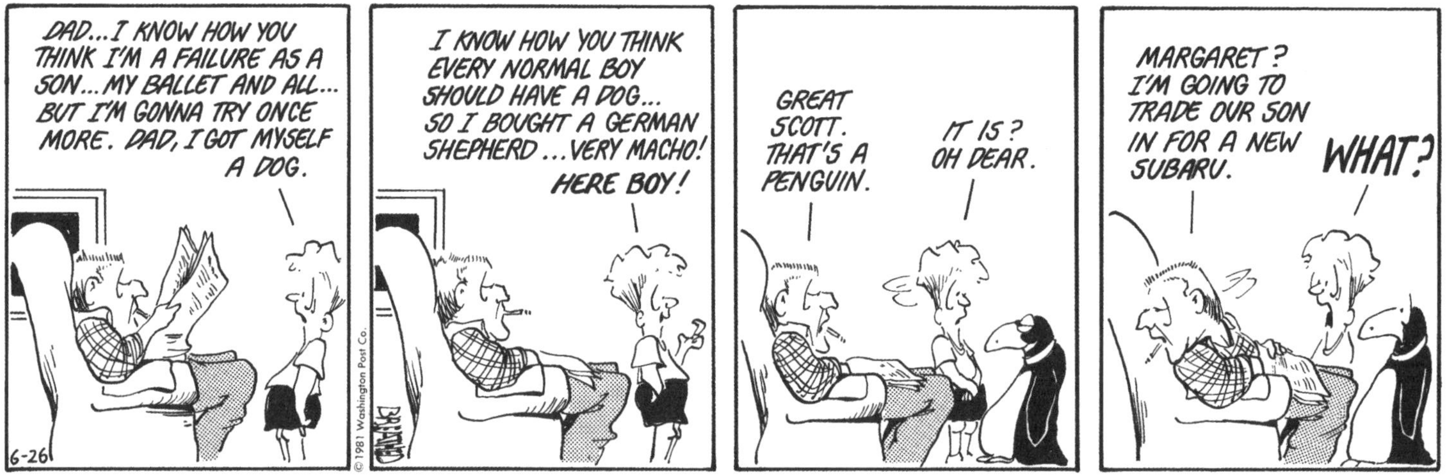
DAD...I KNOW HOW YOU THINK I'M A FAILURE AS A SON...MY BALLET AND ALL... BUT I'M GONNA TRY ONCE MORE. DAD, I GOT MYSELF A DOG.
I KNOW HOW YOU THINK EVERY NORMAL BOY SHOULD HAVE A DOG... SO I BOUGHT A GERMAN SHEPHERD ...VERY MACHO!
HERE BOY!
GREAT SCOTT. THAT'S A PENGUIN.
IT IS? OH DEAR.
MARGARET? I'M GOING TO TRADE OUR SON IN FOR A NEW SUBARU.
WHAT?
6-26
© 1981 Washington Post Co.
BREATHED

Fred Rogers, an ordained minister, was the host of the long-running PBS children's program, *Mister Roger's Neighborhood*.

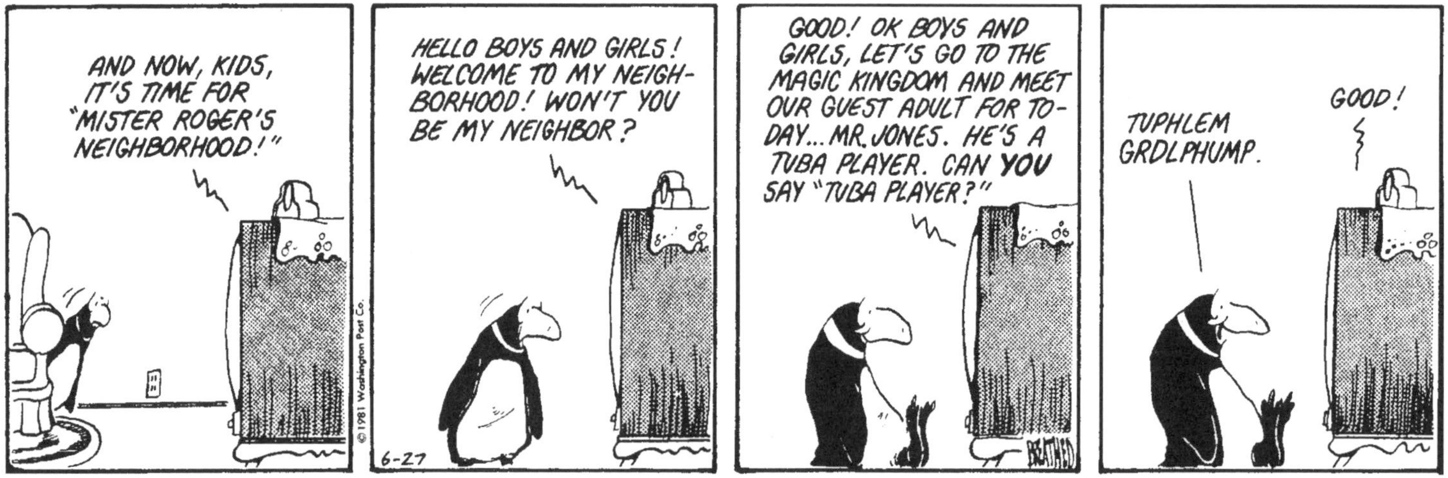
AND NOW, KIDS, IT'S TIME FOR "MISTER ROGER'S NEIGHBORHOOD!"
HELLO BOYS AND GIRLS! WELCOME TO MY NEIGHBORHOOD! WON'T YOU BE MY NEIGHBOR?
GOOD! OK BOYS AND GIRLS, LET'S GO TO THE MAGIC KINGDOM AND MEET OUR GUEST ADULT FOR TODAY... MR. JONES. HE'S A TUBA PLAYER. CAN YOU SAY "TUBA PLAYER?"
TUPHLEM GRDLPHUMP.
GOOD!
6-27
© 1981 Washington Post Co.
BREATHED

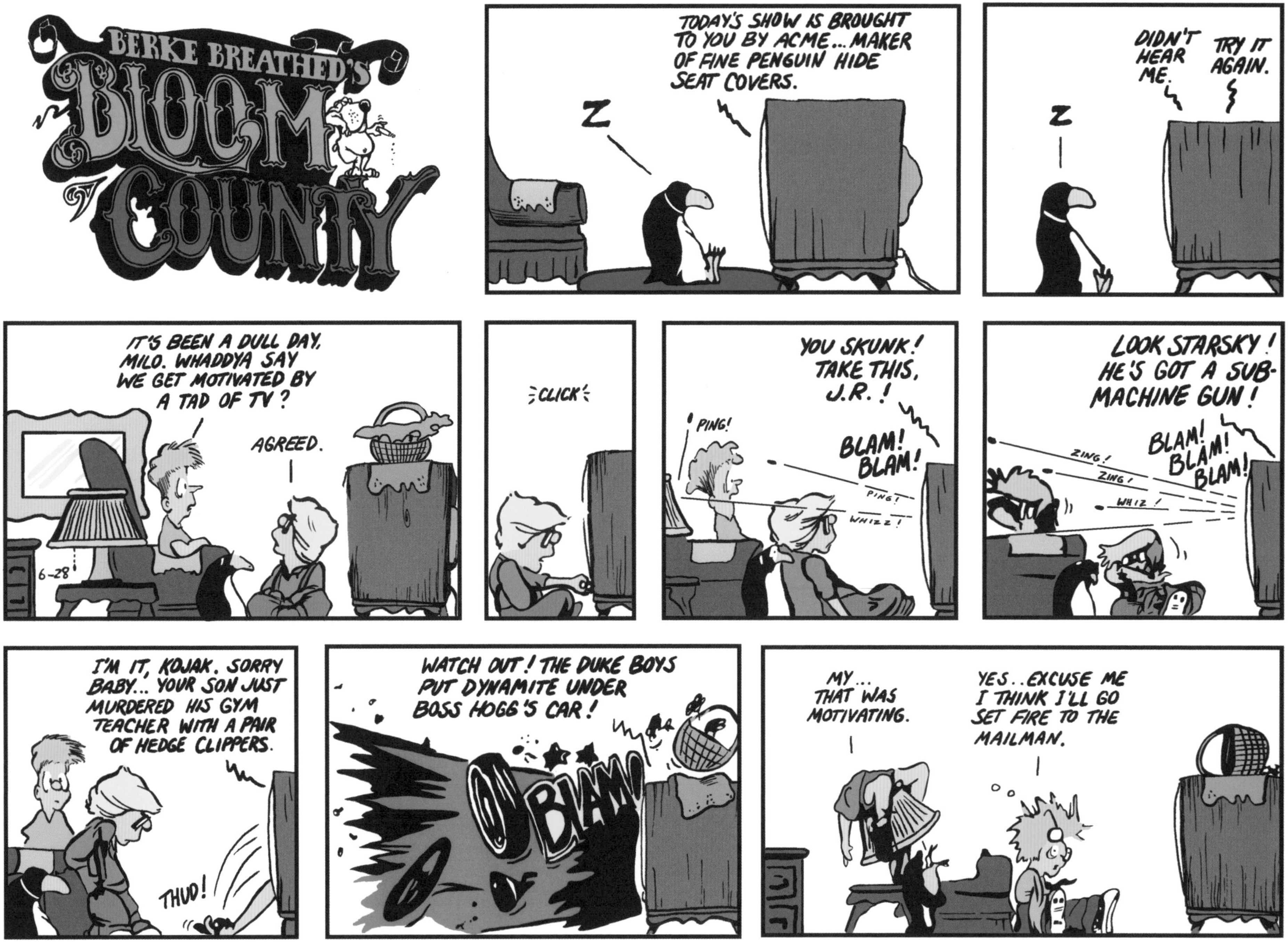
BERKE BREATHED'S
BLOOM COUNTY
Z
TODAY'S SHOW IS BROUGHT TO YOU BY ACME... MAKER OF FINE PENGUIN HIDE SEAT COVERS.
Z
DIDN'T HEAR ME.
TRY IT AGAIN.
IT'S BEEN A DULL DAY, MILO. WHADDYA SAY WE GET MOTIVATED BY A TAD OF TV?
AGREED.
6-28
CLICK
YOU SKUNK! TAKE THIS, J.R.!
PING!
BLAM! BLAM!
PING!
WHIZZ!
LOOK STARSKY! HE'S GOT A SUB-MACHINE GUN!
ZING!
ZING!
WHIZ!
BLAM! BLAM! BLAM!
I'M IT, KOJAK. SORRY BABY... YOUR SON JUST MURDERED HIS GYM TEACHER WITH A PAIR OF HEDGE CLIPPERS.
THUD!
WATCH OUT! THE DUKE BOYS PUT DYNAMITE UNDER BOSS HOGG'S CAR!
BLAM
MY... THAT WAS MOTIVATING.
YES.. EXCUSE ME I THINK I'LL GO SET FIRE TO THE MAILMAN.

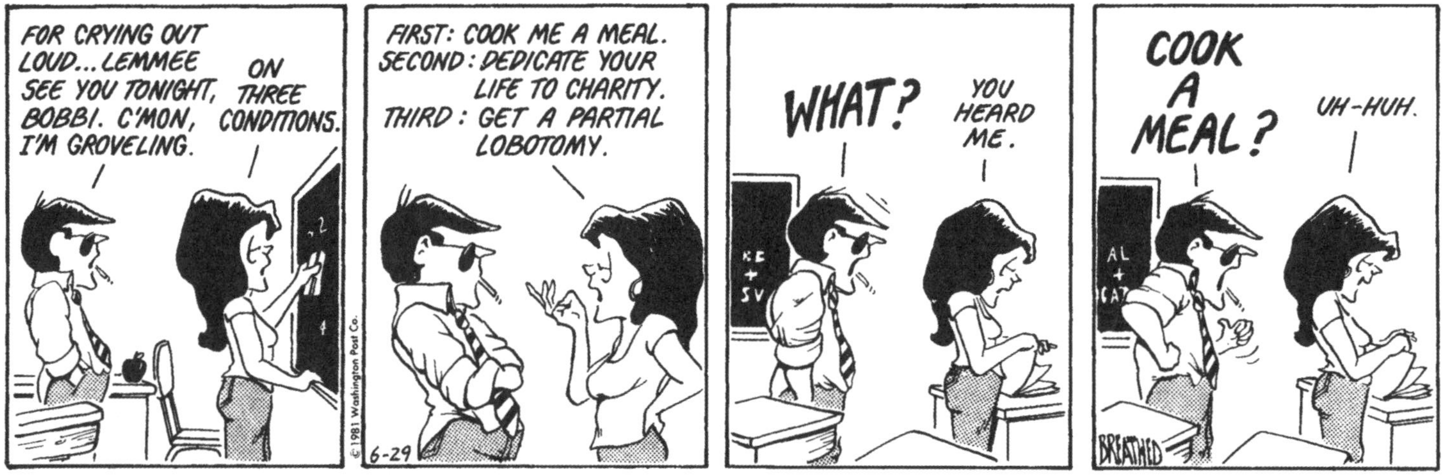
FOR CRYING OUT LOUD... LEMMEE SEE YOU TONIGHT, BOBBI. C'MON, I'M GROVELING.
ON THREE CONDITIONS.
© 1981 Washington Post Co.
6-29
FIRST: COOK ME A MEAL. SECOND: DEDICATE YOUR LIFE TO CHARITY. THIRD: GET A PARTIAL LOBOTOMY.
WHAT?
YOU HEARD ME.
COOK A MEAL?
UH-HUH.
BREATHED

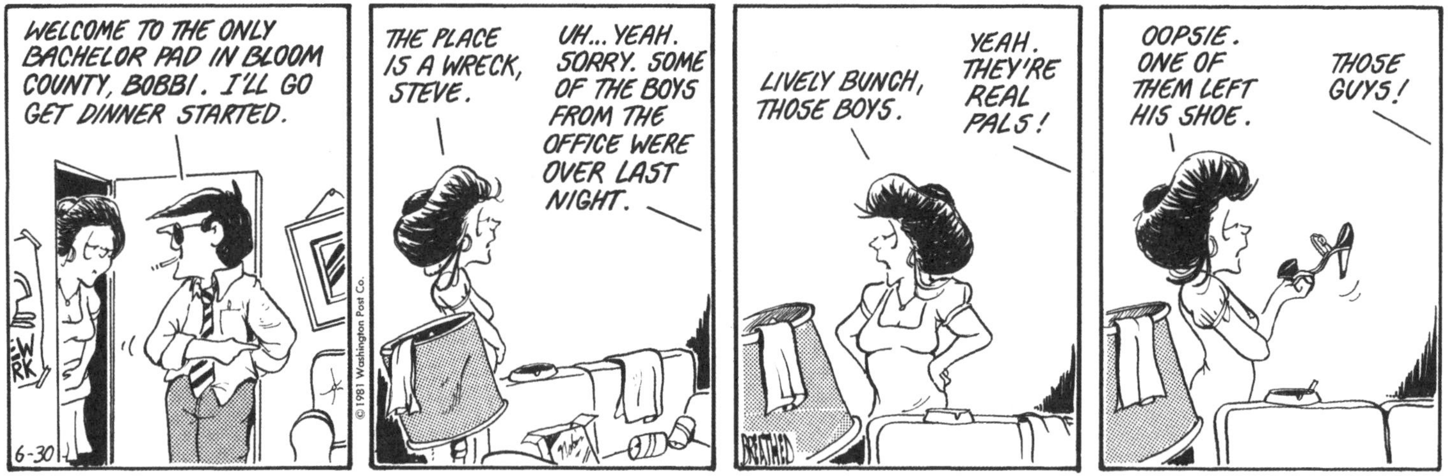
WELCOME TO THE ONLY BACHELOR PAD IN BLOOM COUNTY, BOBBI. I'LL GO GET DINNER STARTED.
6-30
© 1981 Washington Post Co.
THE PLACE IS A WRECK, STEVE.
UH... YEAH. SORRY. SOME OF THE BOYS FROM THE OFFICE WERE OVER LAST NIGHT.
LIVELY BUNCH, THOSE BOYS.
YEAH. THEY'RE REAL PALS!
BREATHED
OOPSIE. ONE OF THEM LEFT HIS SHOE.
THOSE GUYS!

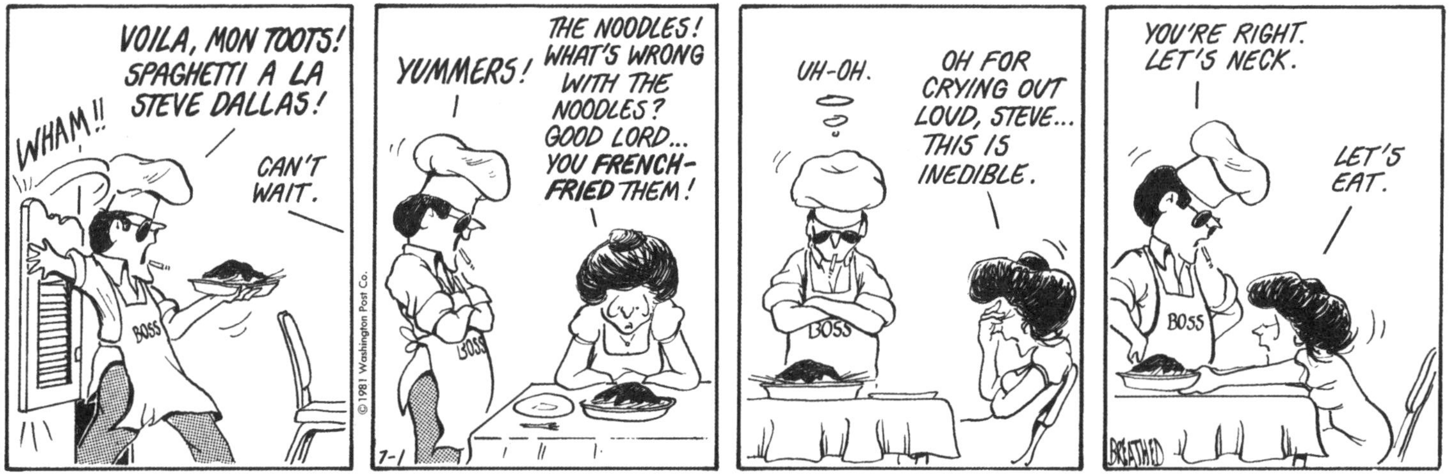
VOILA, MON TOOTS! SPAGHETTI A LA STEVE DALLAS!
WHAM!!
CAN'T WAIT.
BOSS
© 1981 Washington Post Co.
YUMMERS!
THE NOODLES! WHAT'S WRONG WITH THE NOODLES? GOOD LORD... YOU FRENCH-FRIED THEM!
7-1
UH-OH.
OH FOR CRYING OUT LOUD, STEVE... THIS IS INEDIBLE.
YOU'RE RIGHT. LET'S NECK.
LET'S EAT.
BREATHED

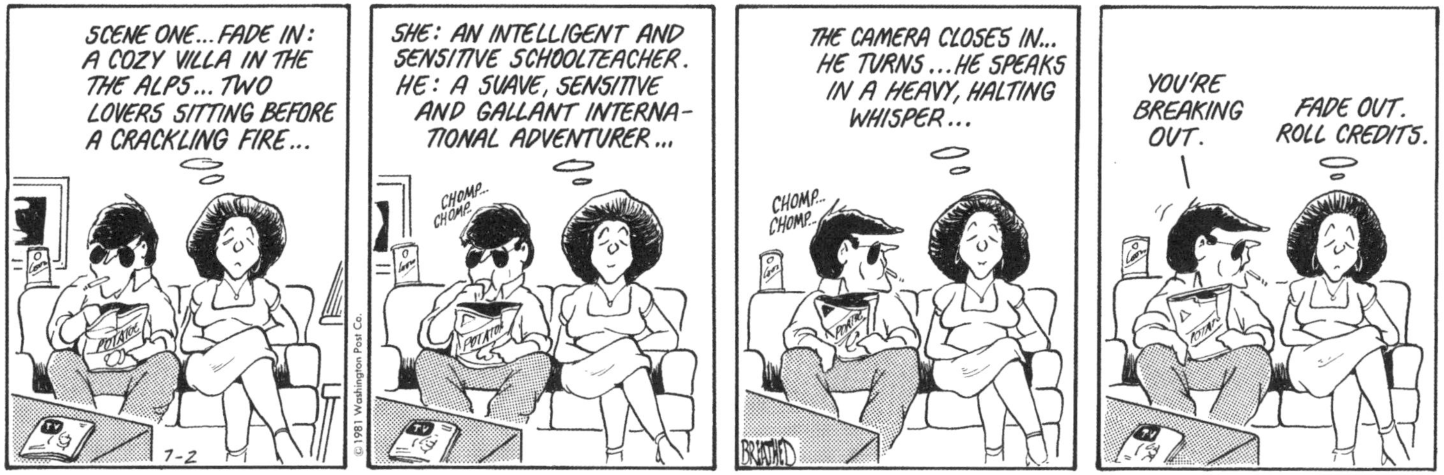
SCENE ONE... FADE IN: A COZY VILLA IN THE THE ALPS... TWO LOVERS SITTING BEFORE A CRACKLING FIRE...
7-2
SHE: AN INTELLIGENT AND SENSITIVE SCHOOLTEACHER. HE: A SUAVE, SENSITIVE AND GALLANT INTERNATIONAL ADVENTURER...
CHOMP.. CHOMP..
© 1981 Washington Post Co.
THE CAMERA CLOSES IN... HE TURNS... HE SPEAKS IN A HEAVY, HALTING WHISPER...
CHOMP.. CHOMP..
YOU'RE BREAKING OUT.
FADE OUT. ROLL CREDITS.

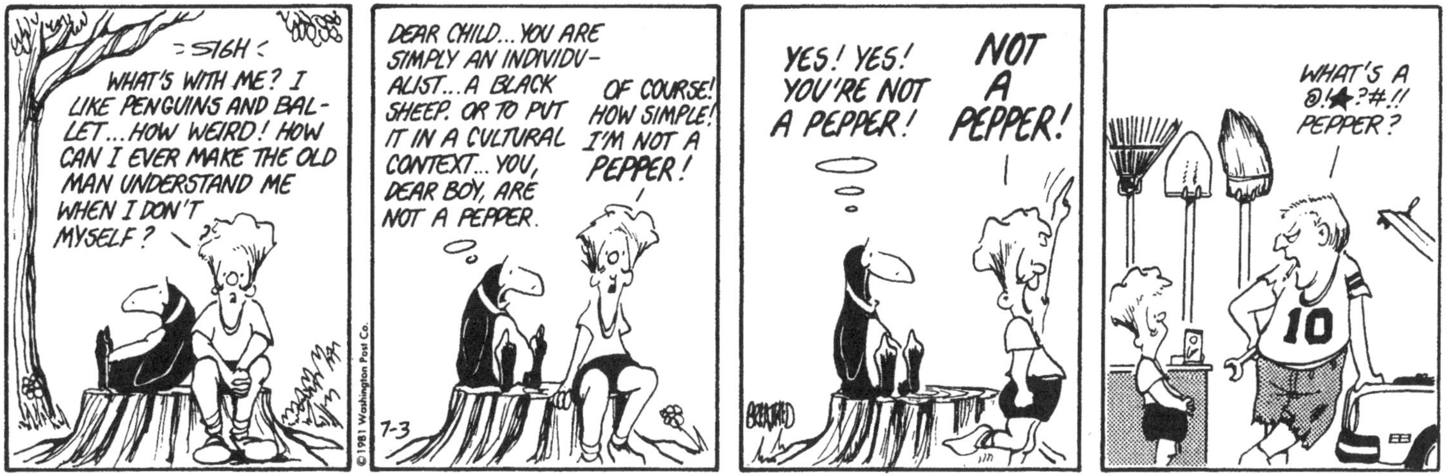
=SIGH=
WHAT'S WITH ME? I LIKE PENGUINS AND BALLET... HOW WEIRD! HOW CAN I EVER MAKE THE OLD MAN UNDERSTAND ME WHEN I DON'T MYSELF?
DEAR CHILD... YOU ARE SIMPLY AN INDIVIDUALIST... A BLACK SHEEP. OR TO PUT IT IN A CULTURAL CONTEXT... YOU, DEAR BOY, ARE NOT A PEPPER.
OF COURSE! HOW SIMPLE! I'M NOT A PEPPER!
© 1981 Washington Post Co.
7-3
YES! YES! YOU'RE NOT A PEPPER!
NOT A PEPPER!
WHAT'S A @!★?#!! PEPPER?
10

"Be a Pepper," popular catchphrase of a series of Dr. Pepper commercials preaching the virtues of soft drink conformity.

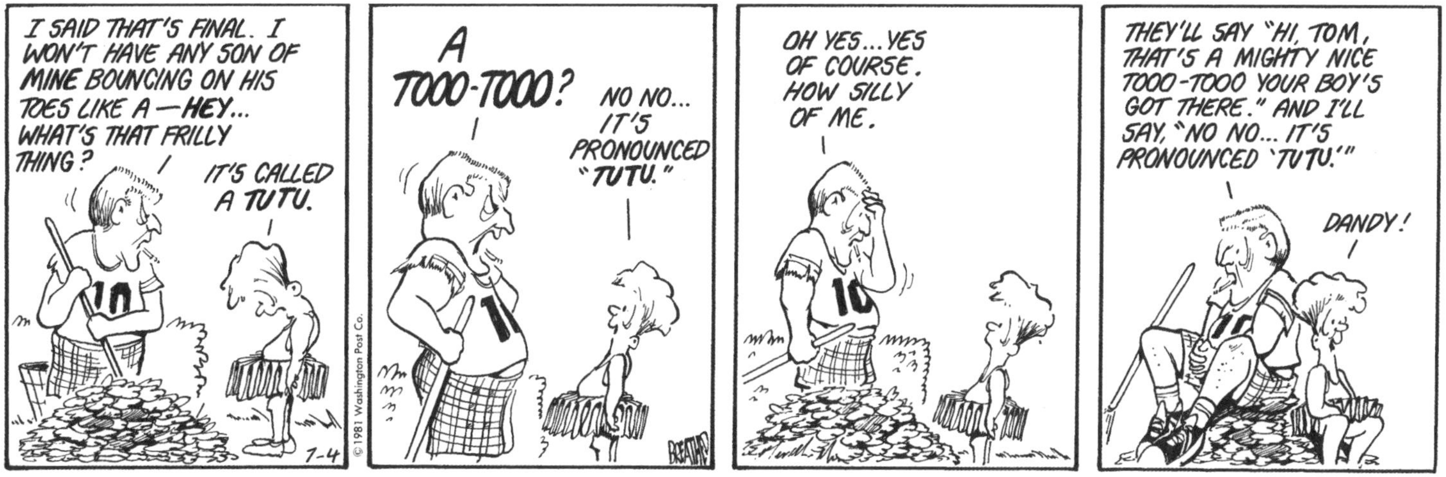
I SAID THAT'S FINAL. I WON'T HAVE ANY SON OF MINE BOUNCING ON HIS TOES LIKE A—HEY... WHAT'S THAT FRILLY THING?
IT'S CALLED A TUTU.
7-4
A TOOO-TOOO?
NO NO... IT'S PRONOUNCED "TUTU."
© 1981 Washington Post Co.
OH YES... YES OF COURSE. HOW SILLY OF ME.
THEY'LL SAY "HI, TOM, THAT'S A MIGHTY NICE TOOO-TOOO YOUR BOY'S GOT THERE." AND I'LL SAY, "NO NO... IT'S PRONOUNCED 'TUTU.'"
DANDY!

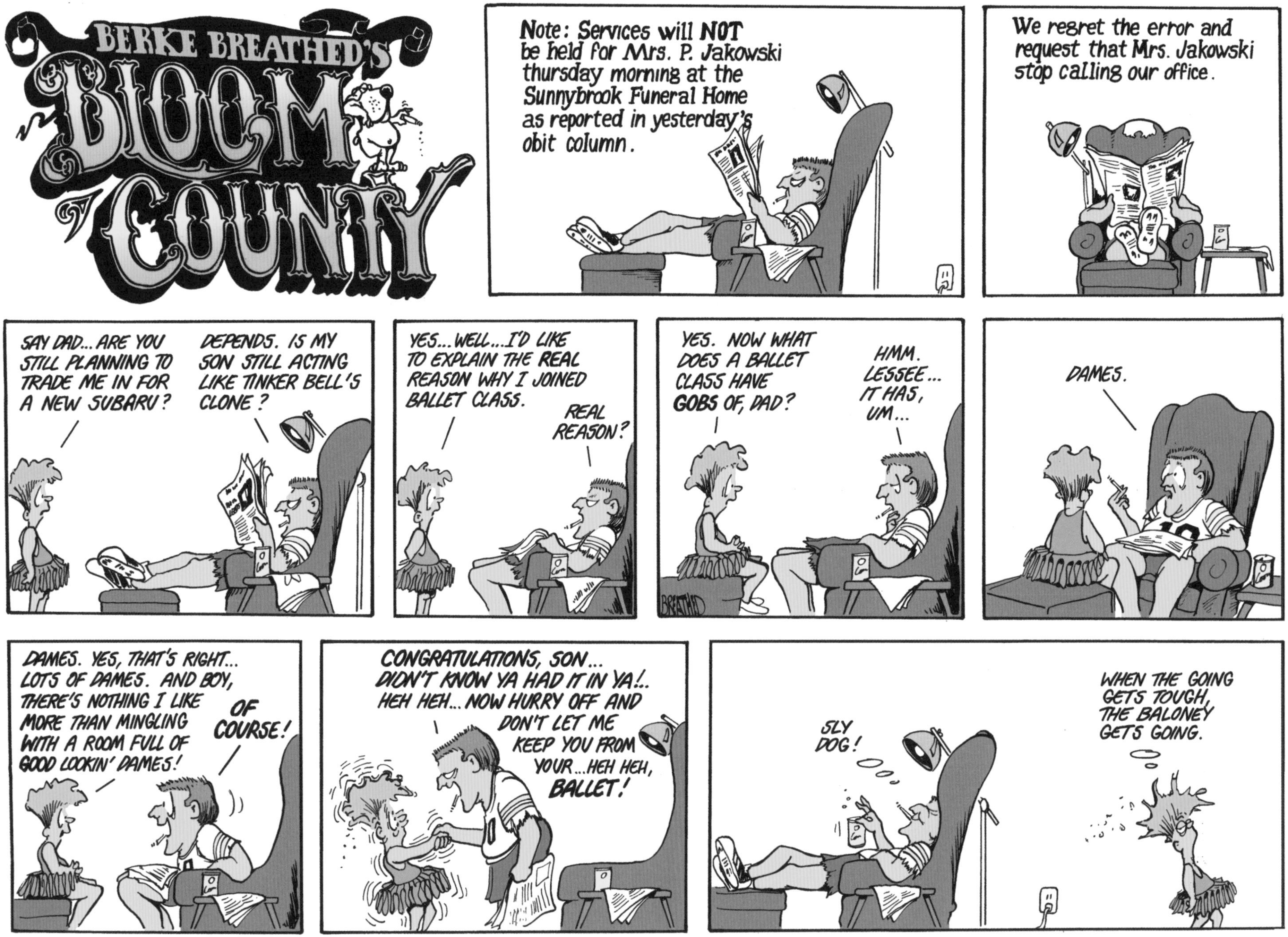

BERKE BREATHED'S
BLOOM COUNTY
Note: Services will NOT be held for Mrs. P. Jakowski thursday morning at the Sunnybrook Funeral Home as reported in yesterday's obit column.
We regret the error and request that Mrs. Jakowski stop calling our office.
SAY DAD... ARE YOU STILL PLANNING TO TRADE ME IN FOR A NEW SUBARU?
DEPENDS. IS MY SON STILL ACTING LIKE TINKER BELL'S CLONE?
YES... WELL... I'D LIKE TO EXPLAIN THE REAL REASON WHY I JOINED BALLET CLASS.
REAL REASON?
YES. NOW WHAT DOES A BALLET CLASS HAVE GOBS OF, DAD?
HMM. LESSEE... IT HAS, UM...
DAMES.
DAMES. YES, THAT'S RIGHT... LOTS OF DAMES. AND BOY, THERE'S NOTHING I LIKE MORE THAN MINGLING WITH A ROOM FULL OF GOOD LOOKIN' DAMES!
OF COURSE!
CONGRATULATIONS, SON... DIDN'T KNOW YA HAD IT IN YA!.. HEH HEH... NOW HURRY OFF AND DON'T LET ME KEEP YOU FROM YOUR... HEH HEH, BALLET!
SLY DOG!
WHEN THE GOING GETS TOUGH, THE BALONEY GETS GOING.

July 5, 1981

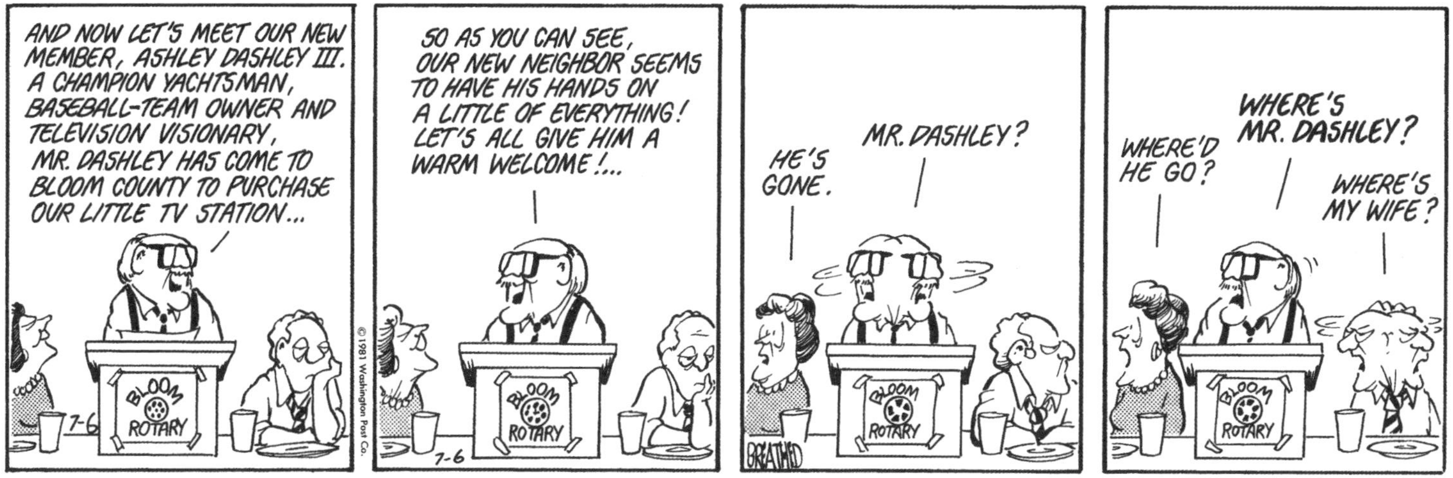
AND NOW LET'S MEET OUR NEW MEMBER, ASHLEY DASHLEY III. A CHAMPION YACHTSMAN, BASEBALL-TEAM OWNER AND TELEVISION VISIONARY, MR. DASHLEY HAS COME TO BLOOM COUNTY TO PURCHASE OUR LITTLE TV STATION...
BLOOM ROTARY
7-6
© 1981 Washington Post Co.
SO AS YOU CAN SEE, OUR NEW NEIGHBOR SEEMS TO HAVE HIS HANDS ON A LITTLE OF EVERYTHING! LET'S ALL GIVE HIM A WARM WELCOME!...
BLOOM ROTARY
7-6
HE'S GONE.
MR. DASHLEY?
BLOOM ROTARY
BREATHED
WHERE'D HE GO?
WHERE'S MR. DASHLEY?
WHERE'S MY WIFE?
BLOOM ROTARY

Ashley Dashley was a fictionalized character satirizing "champion yachtsman, baseball-team owner, and television visionary," Ted Turner.

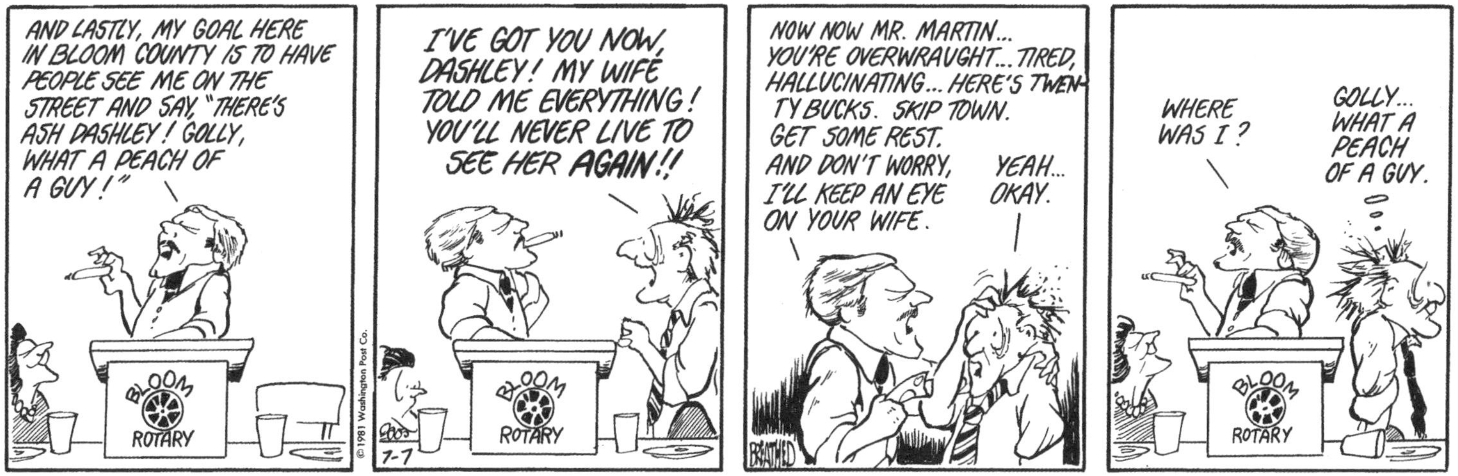
AND LASTLY, MY GOAL HERE IN BLOOM COUNTY IS TO HAVE PEOPLE SEE ME ON THE STREET AND SAY, "THERE'S ASH DASHLEY! GOLLY, WHAT A PEACH OF A GUY!"
BLOOM ROTARY
© 1981 Washington Post Co.
I'VE GOT YOU NOW, DASHLEY! MY WIFE TOLD ME EVERYTHING! YOU'LL NEVER LIVE TO SEE HER AGAIN!!
BLOOM ROTARY
7-7
NOW NOW MR. MARTIN... YOU'RE OVERWRAUGHT... TIRED, HALLUCINATING... HERE'S TWENTY BUCKS. SKIP TOWN. GET SOME REST. AND DON'T WORRY, I'LL KEEP AN EYE ON YOUR WIFE.
YEAH... OKAY.
BREATHED
WHERE WAS I?
GOLLY... WHAT A PEACH OF A GUY.
BLOOM ROTARY

Note the missing large-caliber automatic handgun in the hand of the man confronting Dashley in panel two. Time cured the syndicate's squeamishness about weaponry. That and some videos of Hopalong Cassidy *that I sent them.*
— BB

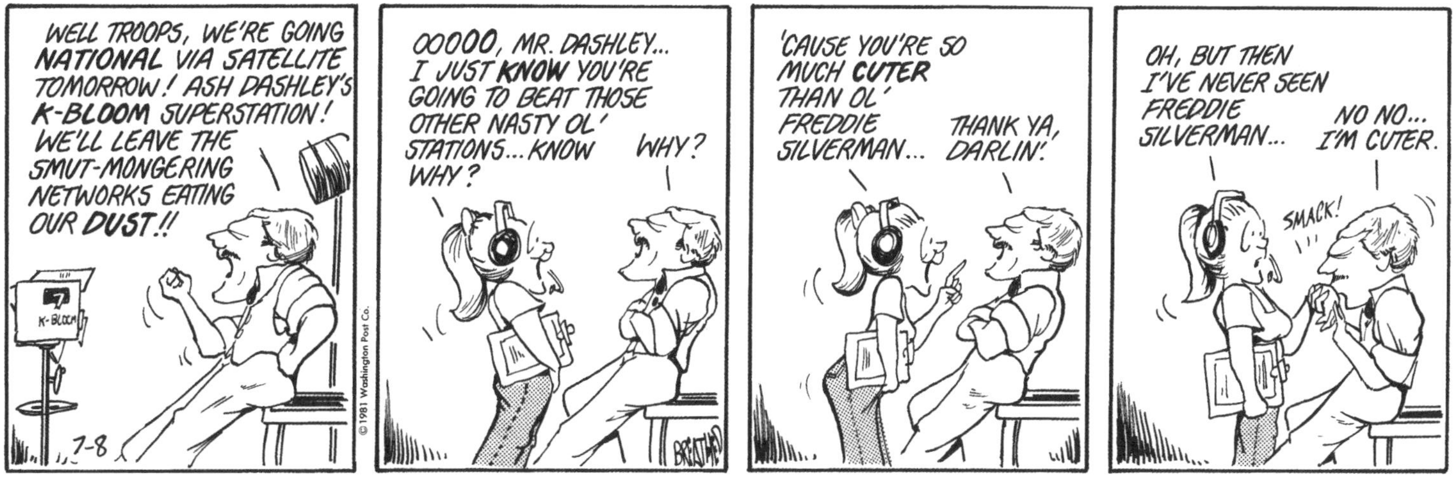
WELL TROOPS, WE'RE GOING NATIONAL VIA SATELLITE TOMORROW! ASH DASHLEY'S K-BLOOM SUPERSTATION! WE'LL LEAVE THE SMUT-MONGERING NETWORKS EATING OUR DUST!!
K-BLOOM
7-8
© 1981 Washington Post Co.
OOOOO, MR. DASHLEY... I JUST KNOW YOU'RE GOING TO BEAT THOSE OTHER NASTY OL' STATIONS... KNOW WHY?
WHY?
BREATHED
'CAUSE YOU'RE SO MUCH CUTER THAN OL' FREDDIE SILVERMAN...
THANK YA, DARLIN'.
OH, BUT THEN I'VE NEVER SEEN FREDDIE SILVERMAN...
NO NO... I'M CUTER.
SMACK!

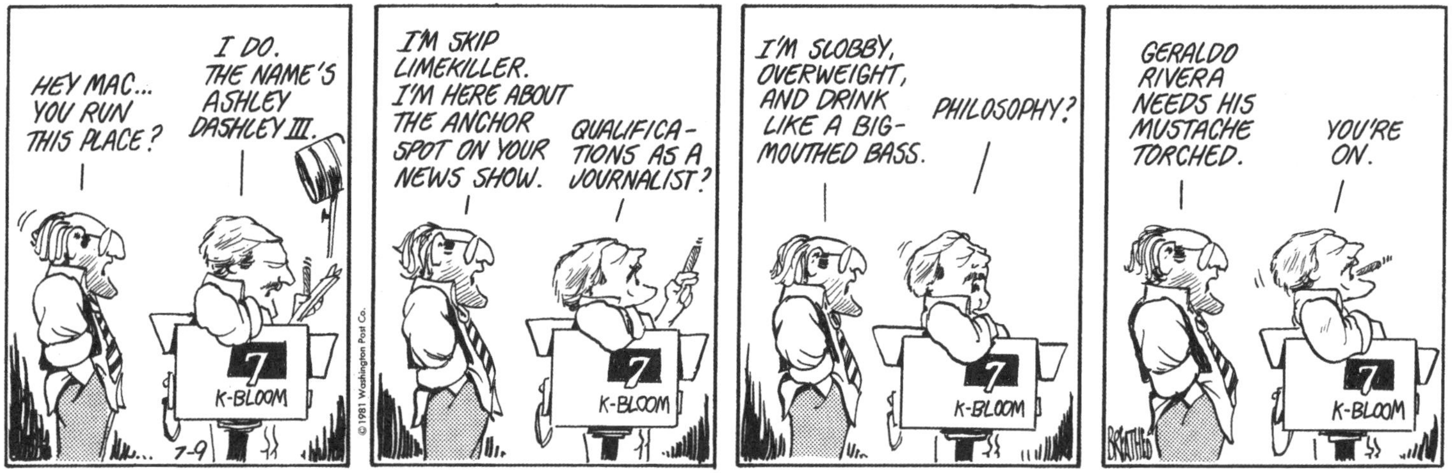
HEY MAC... YOU RUN THIS PLACE?
I DO. THE NAME'S ASHLEY DASHLEY III.
K-BLOOM
7-9
© 1981 Washington Post Co.
I'M SKIP LIMEKILLER. I'M HERE ABOUT THE ANCHOR SPOT ON YOUR NEWS SHOW.
QUALIFICA-TIONS AS A JOURNALIST?
I'M SLOBBY, OVERWEIGHT, AND DRINK LIKE A BIG-MOUTHED BASS.
PHILOSOPHY?
GERALDO RIVERA NEEDS HIS MUSTACHE TORCHED.
YOU'RE ON.
BREATHED

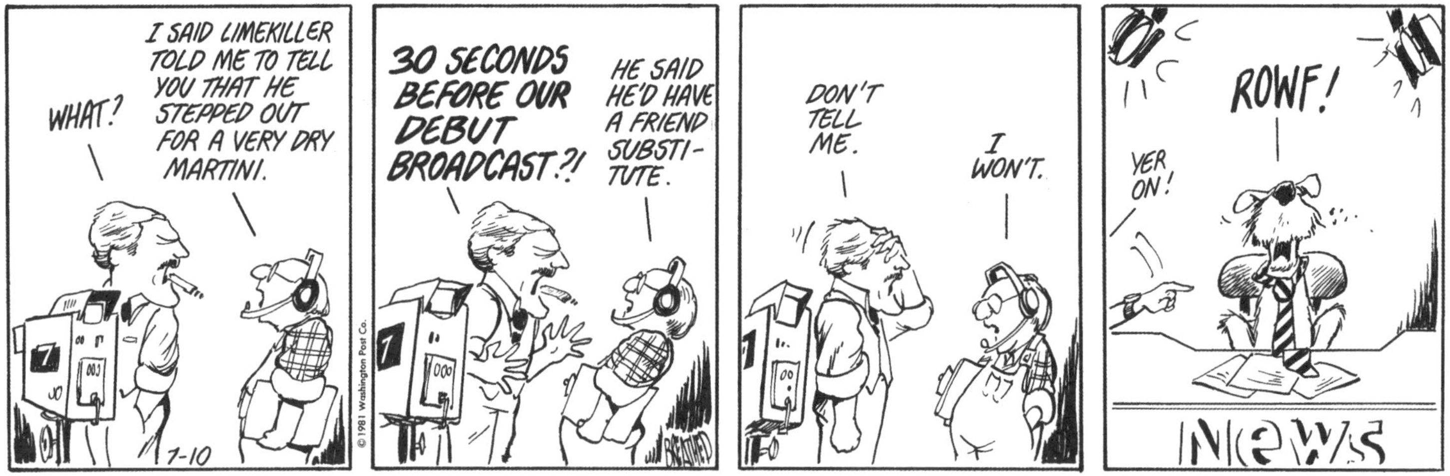
WHAT?
I SAID LIMEKILLER TOLD ME TO TELL YOU THAT HE STEPPED OUT FOR A VERY DRY MARTINI.
7-10
© 1981 Washington Post Co.
30 SECONDS BEFORE OUR DEBUT BROADCAST?!
HE SAID HE'D HAVE A FRIEND SUBSTI-TUTE.
BREATHED
DON'T TELL ME.
I WON'T.
YER ON!
ROWF!
NEWS

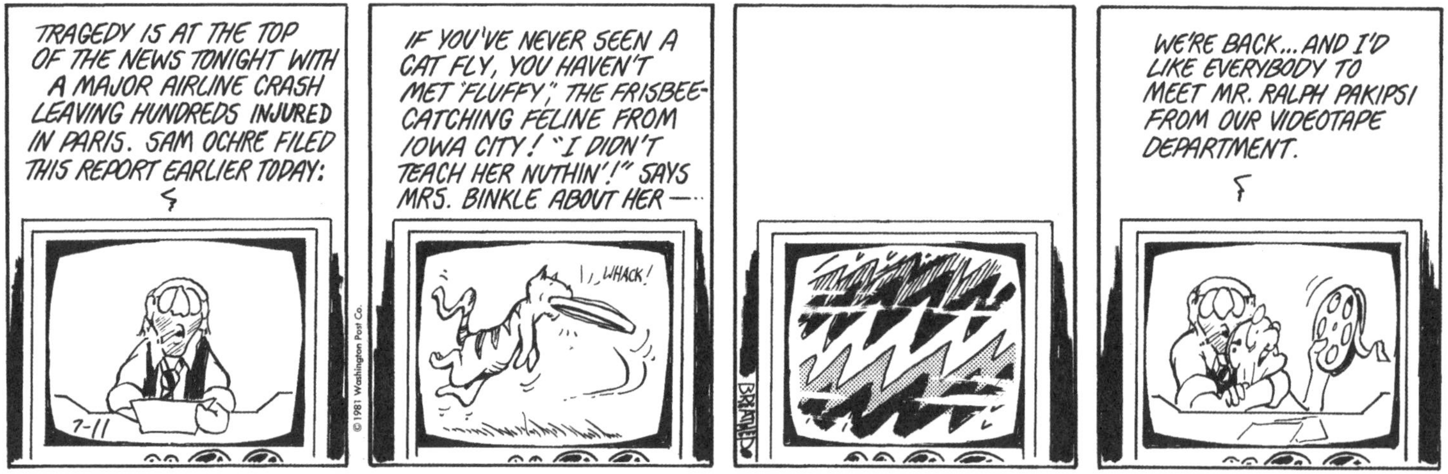
TRAGEDY IS AT THE TOP OF THE NEWS TONIGHT WITH A MAJOR AIRLINE CRASH LEAVING HUNDREDS INJURED IN PARIS. SAM OCHRE FILED THIS REPORT EARLIER TODAY:
7-11
© 1981 Washington Post Co.
IF YOU'VE NEVER SEEN A CAT FLY, YOU HAVEN'T MET "FLUFFY," THE FRISBEE-CATCHING FELINE FROM IOWA CITY! "I DIDN'T TEACH HER NUTHIN'!" SAYS MRS. BINKLE ABOUT HER—
WHACK!
BREATHED
WE'RE BACK... AND I'D LIKE EVERYBODY TO MEET MR. RALPH PAKIPSI FROM OUR VIDEOTAPE DEPARTMENT.

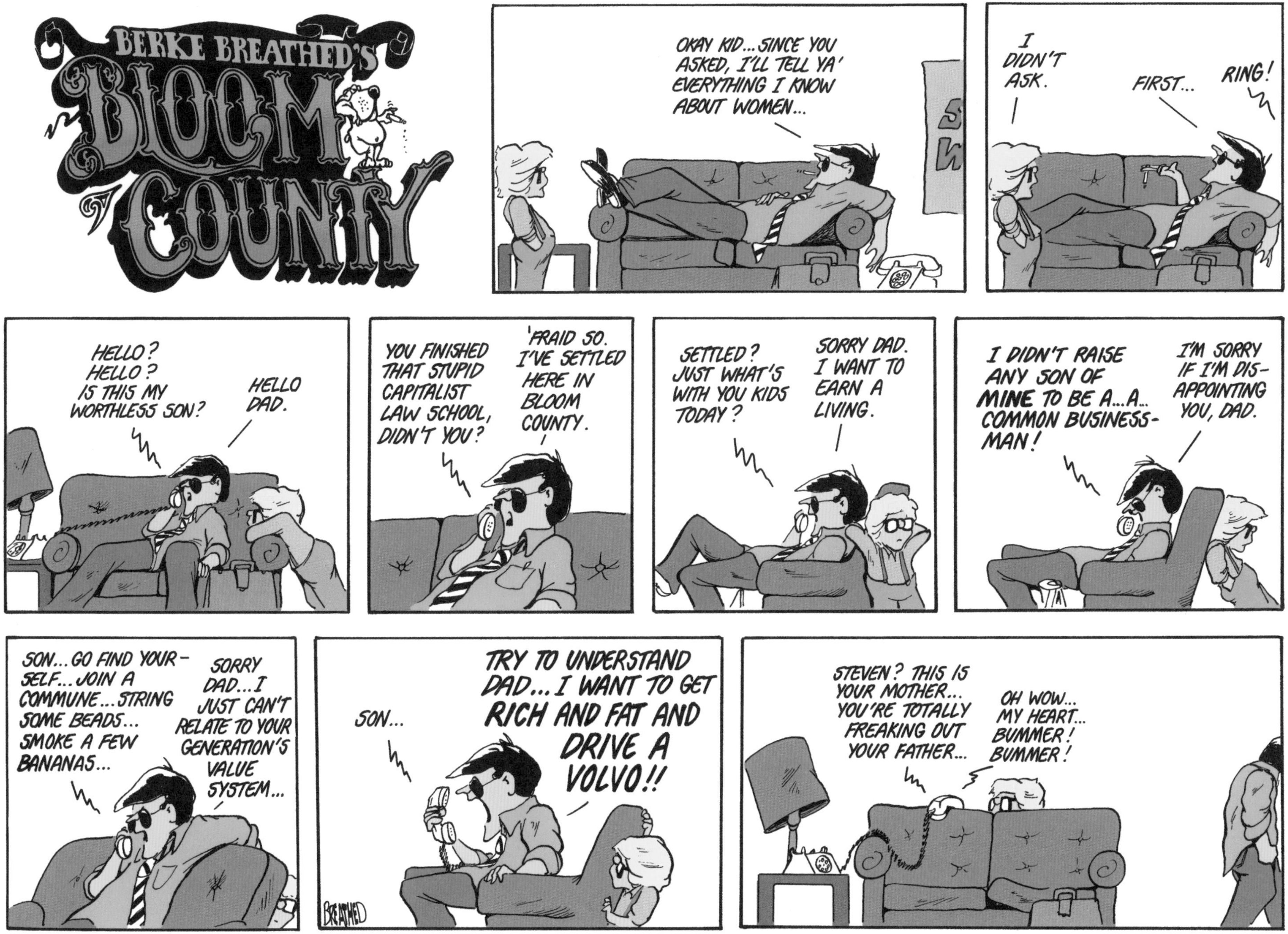
BERKE BREATHED'S
BLOOM COUNTY
OKAY KID... SINCE YOU ASKED, I'LL TELL YA' EVERYTHING I KNOW ABOUT WOMEN...
I DIDN'T ASK.
FIRST...
RING!
HELLO? HELLO? IS THIS MY WORTHLESS SON?
HELLO DAD.
YOU FINISHED THAT STUPID CAPITALIST LAW SCHOOL, DIDN'T YOU?
'FRAID SO. I'VE SETTLED HERE IN BLOOM COUNTY.
SETTLED? JUST WHAT'S WITH YOU KIDS TODAY?
SORRY DAD. I WANT TO EARN A LIVING.
I DIDN'T RAISE ANY SON OF MINE TO BE A...A... COMMON BUSINESS-MAN!
I'M SORRY IF I'M DIS-APPOINTING YOU, DAD.
SON... GO FIND YOUR-SELF... JOIN A COMMUNE... STRING SOME BEADS... SMOKE A FEW BANANAS...
SORRY DAD... I JUST CAN'T RELATE TO YOUR GENERATION'S VALUE SYSTEM...
SON...
TRY TO UNDERSTAND DAD... I WANT TO GET RICH AND FAT AND DRIVE A VOLVO!!
BREATHED
STEVEN? THIS IS YOUR MOTHER... YOU'RE TOTALLY FREAKING OUT YOUR FATHER...
OH WOW... MY HEART... BUMMER! BUMMER!

July 12, 1981

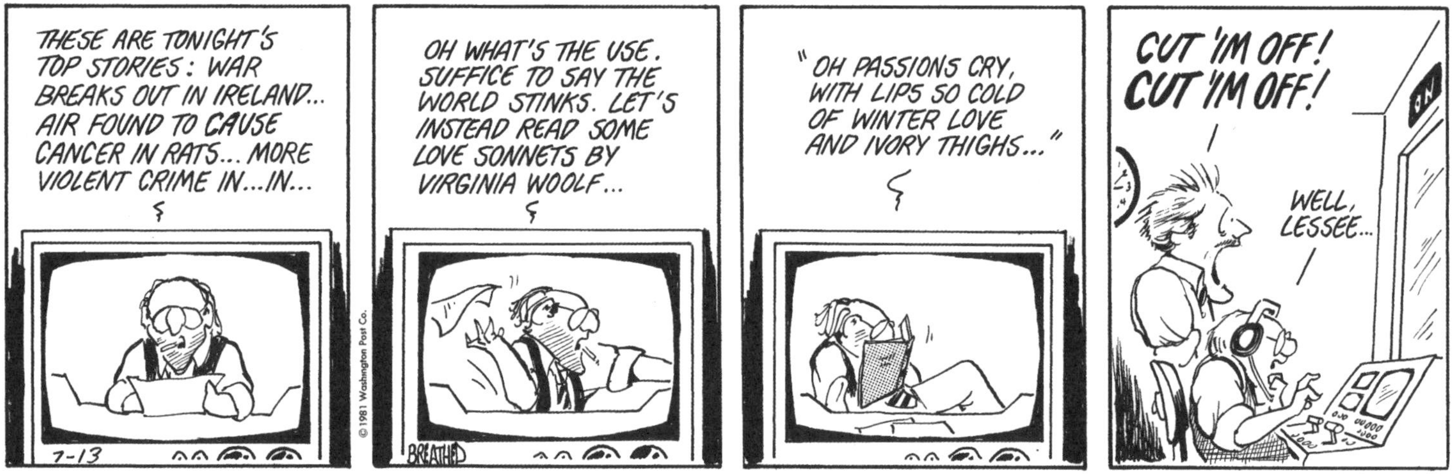
THESE ARE TONIGHT'S TOP STORIES: WAR BREAKS OUT IN IRELAND... AIR FOUND TO CAUSE CANCER IN RATS... MORE VIOLENT CRIME IN...IN...
7-13
OH WHAT'S THE USE. SUFFICE TO SAY THE WORLD STINKS. LET'S INSTEAD READ SOME LOVE SONNETS BY VIRGINIA WOOLF...
© 1981 Washington Post Co.
BREATHED
"OH PASSIONS CRY, WITH LIPS SO COLD OF WINTER LOVE AND IVORY THIGHS..."
CUT 'IM OFF! CUT 'IM OFF!
WELL, LESSEE...
ON

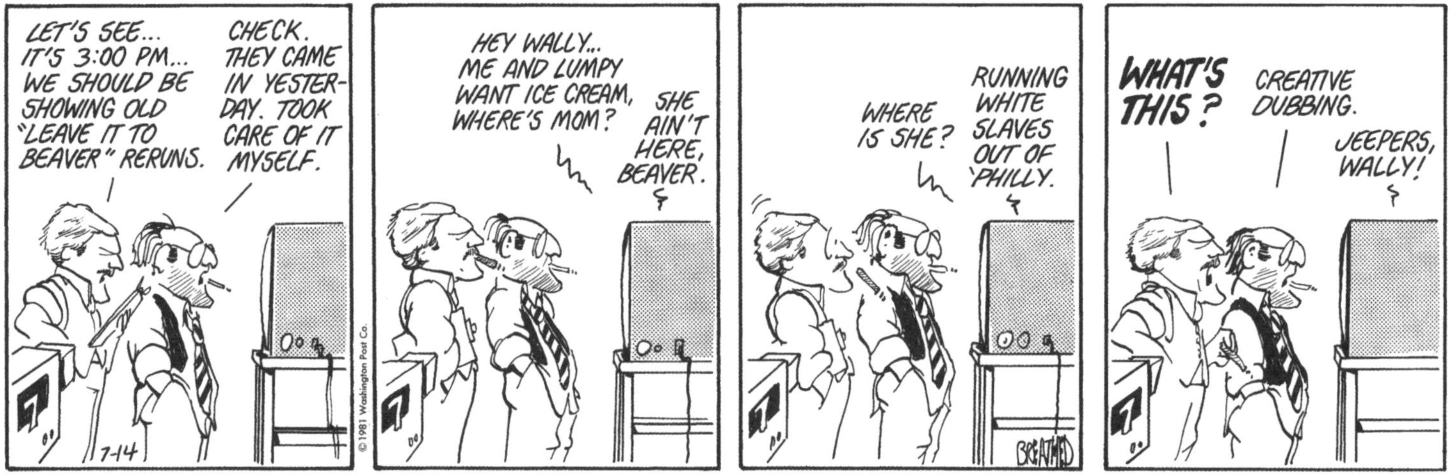
LET'S SEE... IT'S 3:00 PM... WE SHOULD BE SHOWING OLD "LEAVE IT TO BEAVER" RERUNS.
CHECK. THEY CAME IN YESTERDAY. TOOK CARE OF IT MYSELF.
7-14
© 1981 Washington Post Co.
HEY WALLY... ME AND LUMPY WANT ICE CREAM. WHERE'S MOM?
SHE AIN'T HERE, BEAVER.
WHERE IS SHE?
RUNNING WHITE SLAVES OUT OF 'PHILLY.
BREATHED
WHAT'S THIS?
CREATIVE DUBBING.
JEEPERS, WALLY!

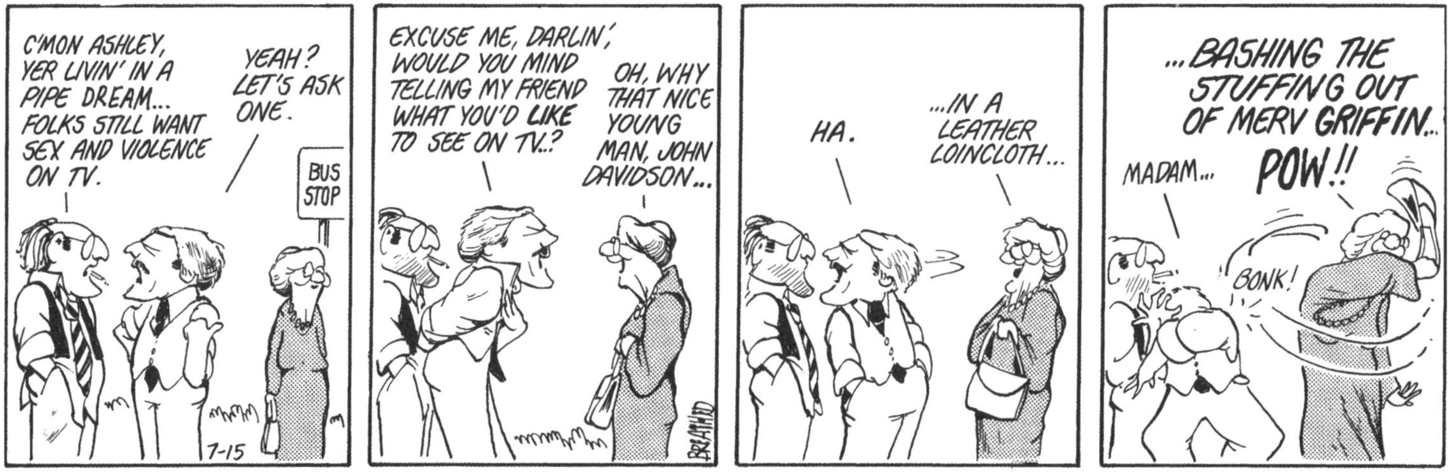
C'MON ASHLEY, YER LIVIN' IN A PIPE DREAM... FOLKS STILL WANT SEX AND VIOLENCE ON TV.
YEAH? LET'S ASK ONE.
BUS STOP
7-15
EXCUSE ME, DARLIN', WOULD YOU MIND TELLING MY FRIEND WHAT YOU'D LIKE TO SEE ON TV..?
OH, WHY THAT NICE YOUNG MAN, JOHN DAVIDSON...
BREATHED
HA.
...IN A LEATHER LOINCLOTH...
...BASHING THE STUFFING OUT OF MERV GRIFFIN...
MADAM...
POW!!
BONK!

Davidson was a pretty-boy actor and game show host, popular in the 1970s and 1980s.

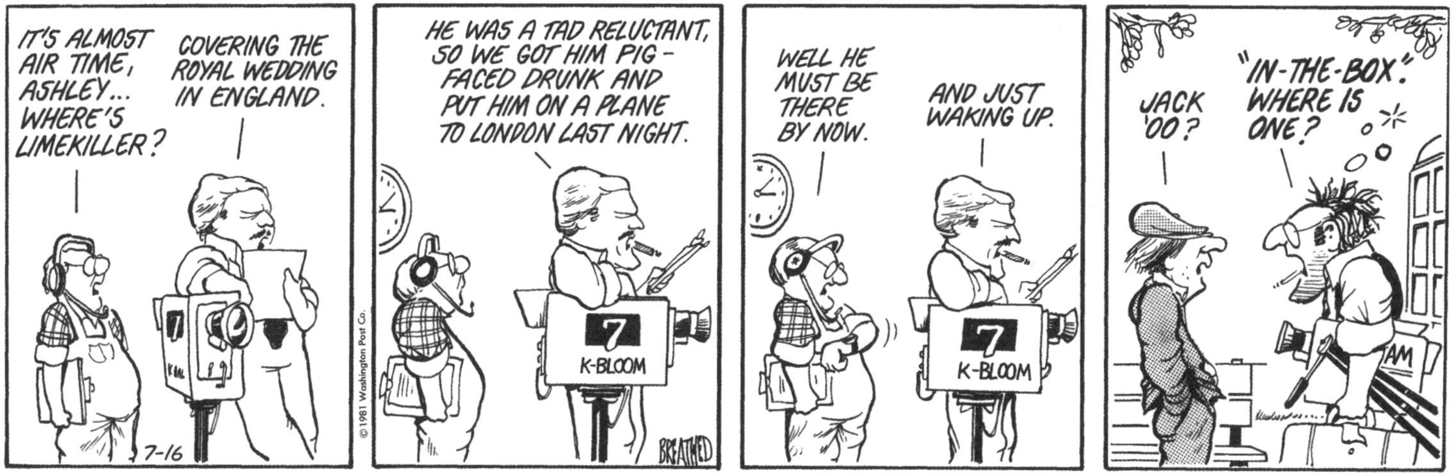
IT'S ALMOST AIR TIME, ASHLEY... WHERE'S LIMEKILLER?
COVERING THE ROYAL WEDDING IN ENGLAND.
7-16
© 1981 Washington Post Co.
HE WAS A TAD RELUCTANT, SO WE GOT HIM PIG-FACED DRUNK AND PUT HIM ON A PLANE TO LONDON LAST NIGHT.
7
K-BLOOM
BREATHED
WELL HE MUST BE THERE BY NOW.
AND JUST WAKING UP.
7
K-BLOOM
JACK 'OO?
"IN-THE-BOX". WHERE IS ONE?

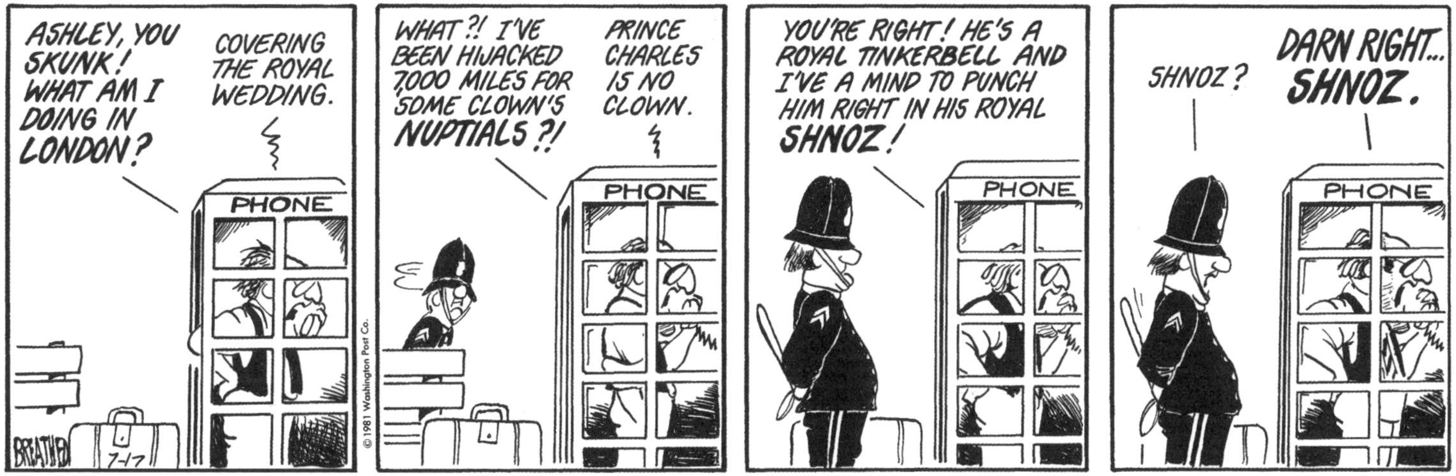
ASHLEY, YOU SKUNK! WHAT AM I DOING IN LONDON?
COVERING THE ROYAL WEDDING.
PHONE
BREATHED
7-17
© 1981 Washington Post Co.
WHAT?! I'VE BEEN HIJACKED 7,000 MILES FOR SOME CLOWN'S NUPTIALS?!
PRINCE CHARLES IS NO CLOWN.
PHONE
YOU'RE RIGHT! HE'S A ROYAL TINKERBELL AND I'VE A MIND TO PUNCH HIM RIGHT IN HIS ROYAL SHNOZ!
PHONE
SHNOZ?
DARN RIGHT... SHNOZ.
PHONE

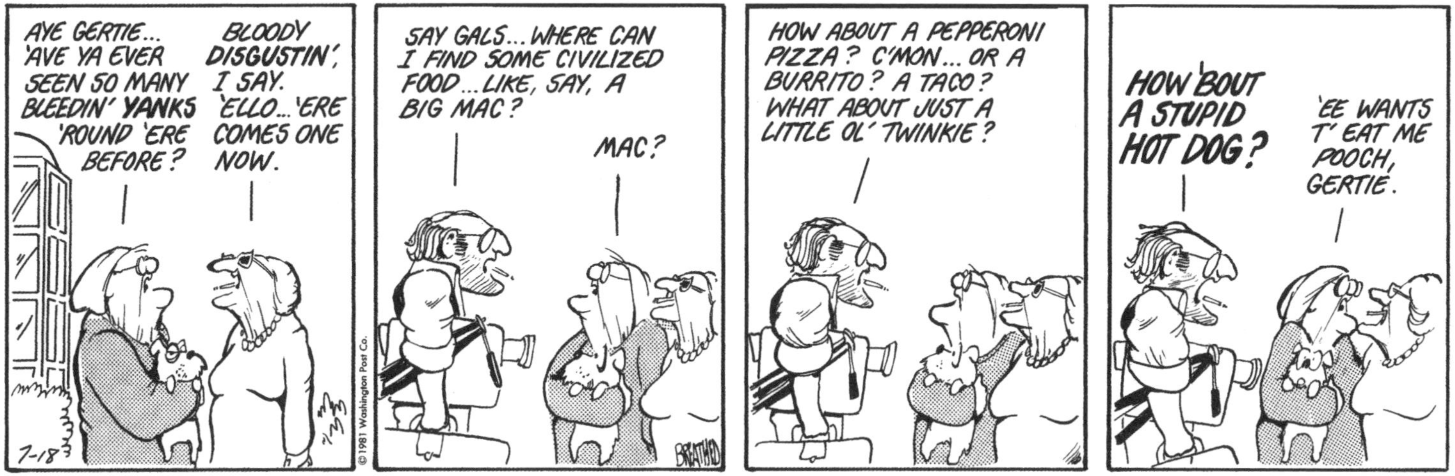
AYE GERTIE... 'AVE YA EVER SEEN SO MANY BLEEDIN' YANKS 'ROUND 'ERE BEFORE?
BLOODY DISGUSTIN', I SAY. 'ELLO...'ERE COMES ONE NOW.
7-18
© 1981 Washington Post Co.
SAY GALS... WHERE CAN I FIND SOME CIVILIZED FOOD... LIKE, SAY, A BIG MAC?
MAC?
BREATHED
HOW ABOUT A PEPPERONI PIZZA? C'MON... OR A BURRITO? A TACO? WHAT ABOUT JUST A LITTLE OL' TWINKIE?
HOW 'BOUT A STUPID HOT DOG?
'EE WANTS T' EAT ME POOCH, GERTIE.

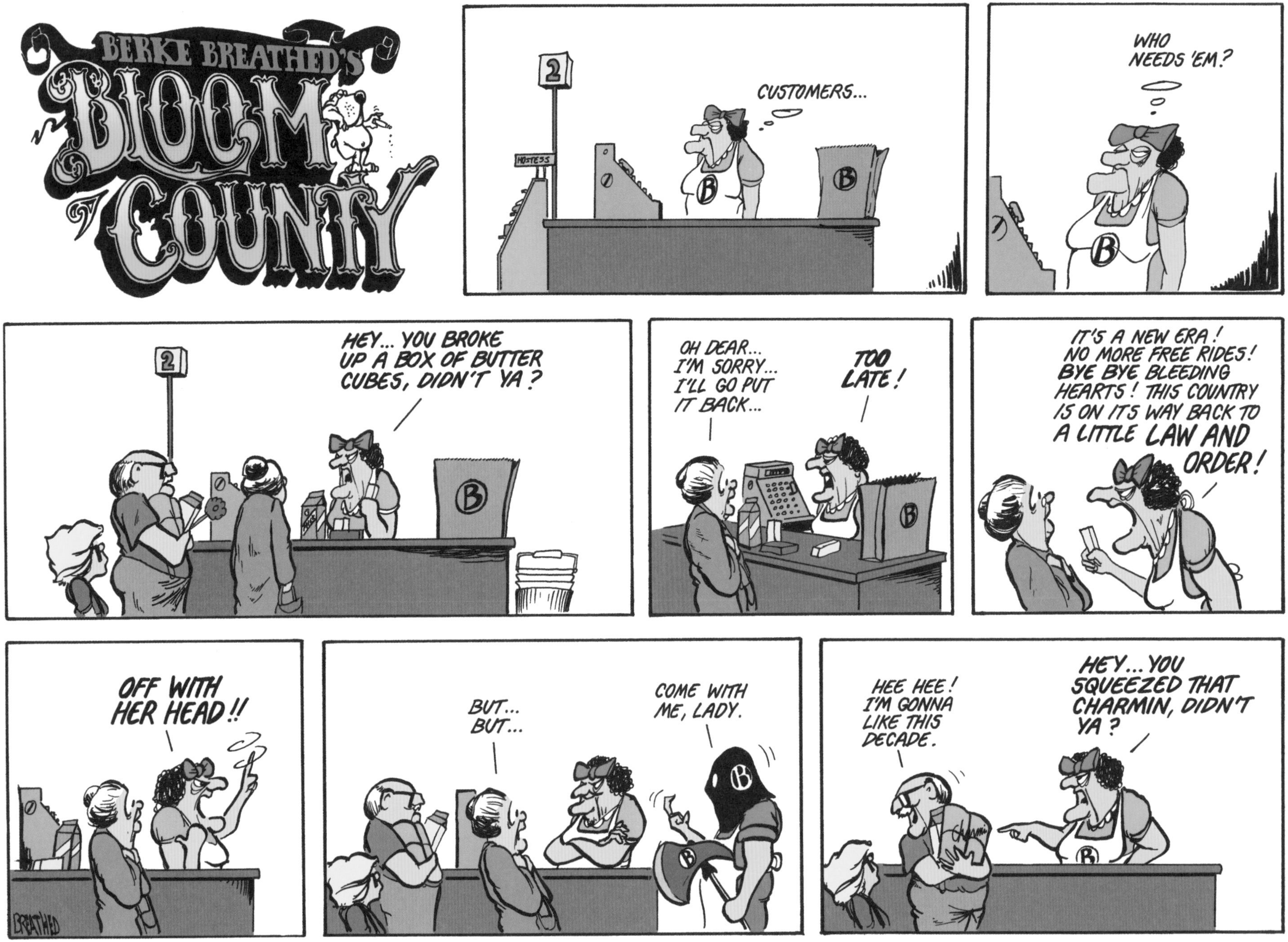
BERKE BREATHED'S
BLOOM COUNTY
2
HOSTESS
CUSTOMERS...
WHO NEEDS 'EM?
2
HEY... YOU BROKE UP A BOX OF BUTTER CUBES, DIDN'T YA?
OH DEAR... I'M SORRY... I'LL GO PUT IT BACK...
TOO LATE!
IT'S A NEW ERA! NO MORE FREE RIDES! BYE BYE BLEEDING HEARTS! THIS COUNTRY IS ON ITS WAY BACK TO A LITTLE LAW AND ORDER!
OFF WITH HER HEAD!!
BREATHED
BUT... BUT...
COME WITH ME, LADY.
HEE HEE! I'M GONNA LIKE THIS DECADE.
HEY... YOU SQUEEZED THAT CHARMIN, DIDN'T YA?

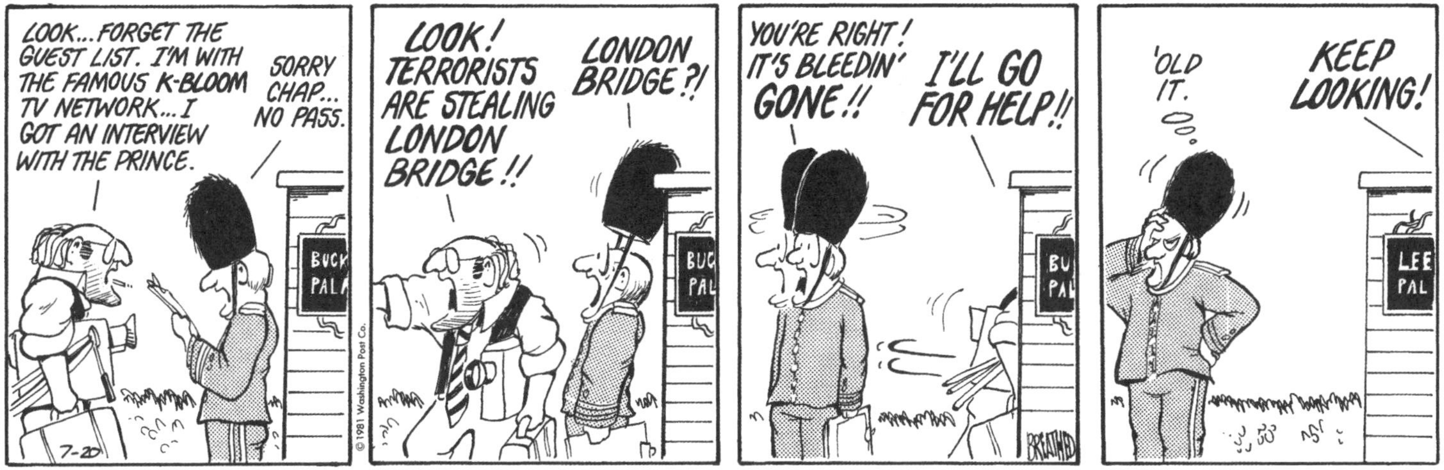
LOOK... FORGET THE GUEST LIST. I'M WITH THE FAMOUS K-BLOOM TV NETWORK... I GOT AN INTERVIEW WITH THE PRINCE.
SORRY CHAP... NO PASS.
LOOK! TERRORISTS ARE STEALING LONDON BRIDGE!!
LONDON BRIDGE?!
YOU'RE RIGHT! IT'S BLEEDIN' GONE!!
I'LL GO FOR HELP!!
'OLD IT.
KEEP LOOKING!
7-20
© 1981 Washington Post Co.
BREATHED

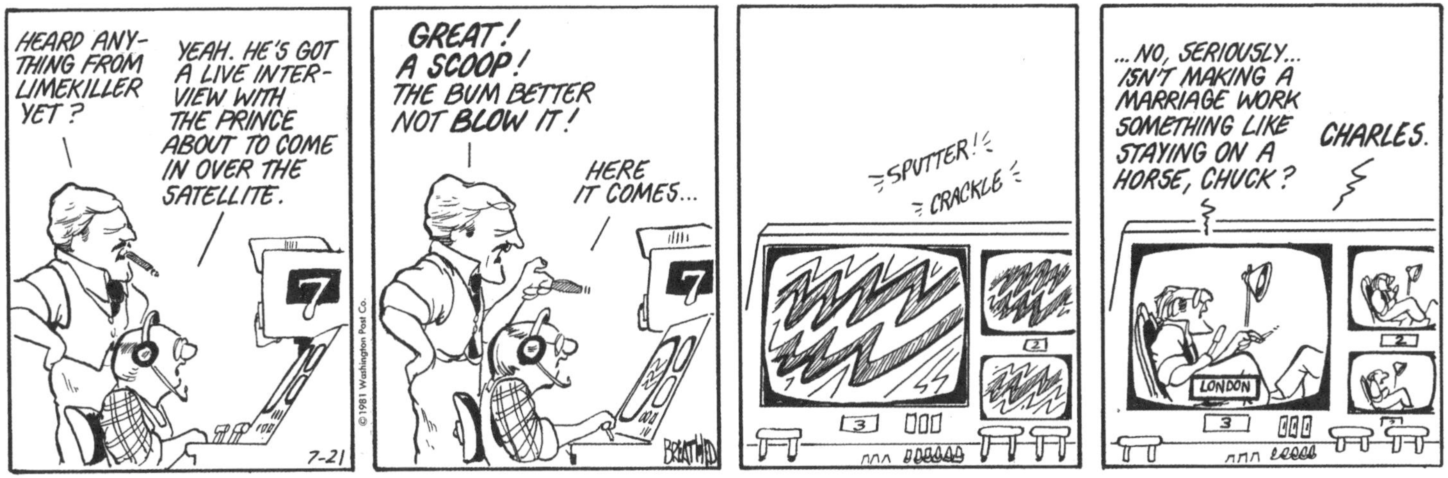
HEARD ANY-THING FROM LIMEKILLER YET?
YEAH. HE'S GOT A LIVE INTER-VIEW WITH THE PRINCE ABOUT TO COME IN OVER THE SATELLITE.
GREAT! A SCOOP! THE BUM BETTER NOT BLOW IT!
HERE IT COMES...
SPUTTER!
CRACKLE
...NO, SERIOUSLY... ISN'T MAKING A MARRIAGE WORK SOMETHING LIKE STAYING ON A HORSE, CHUCK?
CHARLES.
LONDON
7-21
© 1981 Washington Post Co.
BREATHED

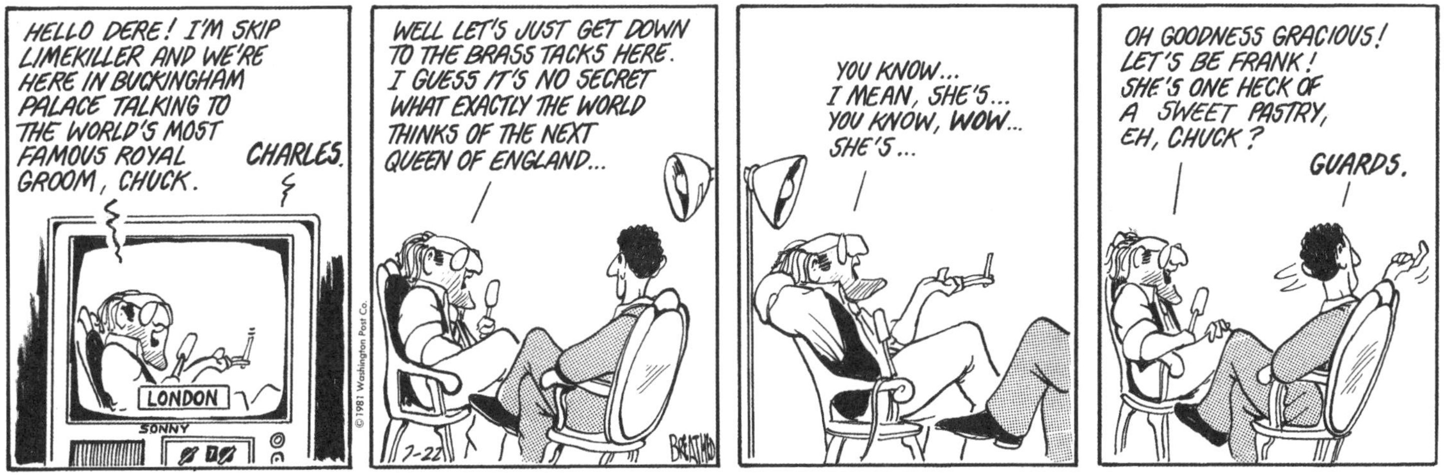
HELLO DERE! I'M SKIP LIMEKILLER AND WE'RE HERE IN BUCKINGHAM PALACE TALKING TO THE WORLD'S MOST FAMOUS ROYAL GROOM, CHUCK.
CHARLES.
LONDON
SONNY
WELL LET'S JUST GET DOWN TO THE BRASS TACKS HERE. I GUESS IT'S NO SECRET WHAT EXACTLY THE WORLD THINKS OF THE NEXT QUEEN OF ENGLAND...
YOU KNOW... I MEAN, SHE'S... YOU KNOW, WOW... SHE'S...
OH GOODNESS GRACIOUS! LET'S BE FRANK! SHE'S ONE HECK OF A SWEET PASTRY, EH, CHUCK?
GUARDS.
7-22
© 1981 Washington Post Co.
BREATHED

The storybook wedding of Prince Charles and Lady Diana Spencer captivated the world in 1981, and was possibly the biggest news story of the year.

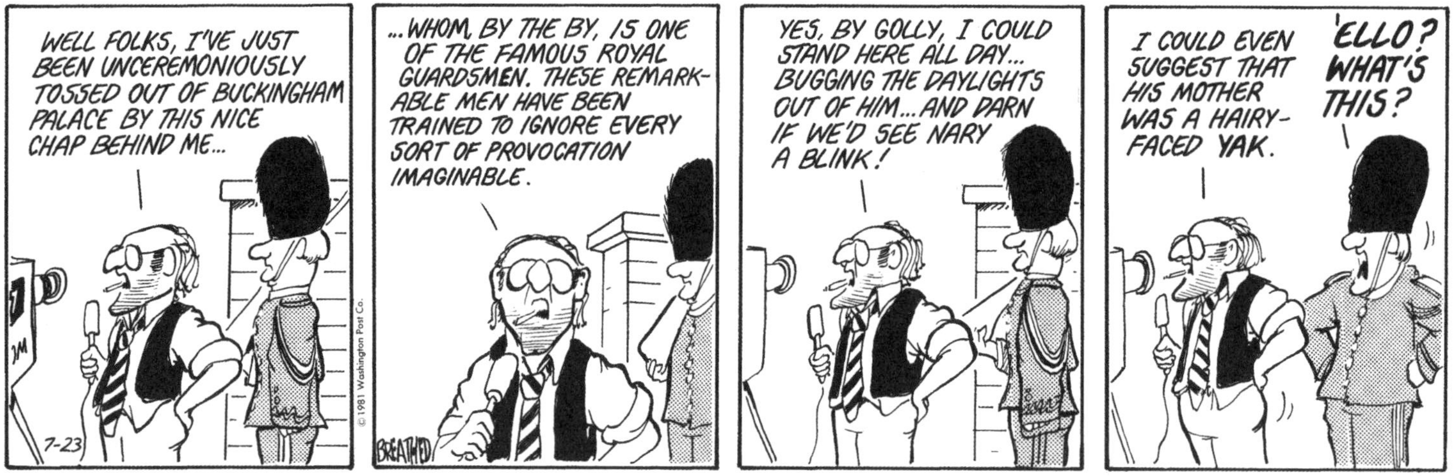
WELL FOLKS, I'VE JUST BEEN UNCEREMONIOUSLY TOSSED OUT OF BUCKINGHAM PALACE BY THIS NICE CHAP BEHIND ME...
7-23
...WHOM, BY THE BY, IS ONE OF THE FAMOUS ROYAL GUARDSMEN. THESE REMARKABLE MEN HAVE BEEN TRAINED TO IGNORE EVERY SORT OF PROVOCATION IMAGINABLE.
© 1981 Washington Post Co.
BREATHED
YES, BY GOLLY, I COULD STAND HERE ALL DAY... BUGGING THE DAYLIGHTS OUT OF HIM... AND DARN IF WE'D SEE NARY A BLINK!
I COULD EVEN SUGGEST THAT HIS MOTHER WAS A HAIRY-FACED YAK.
'ELLO? WHAT'S THIS?

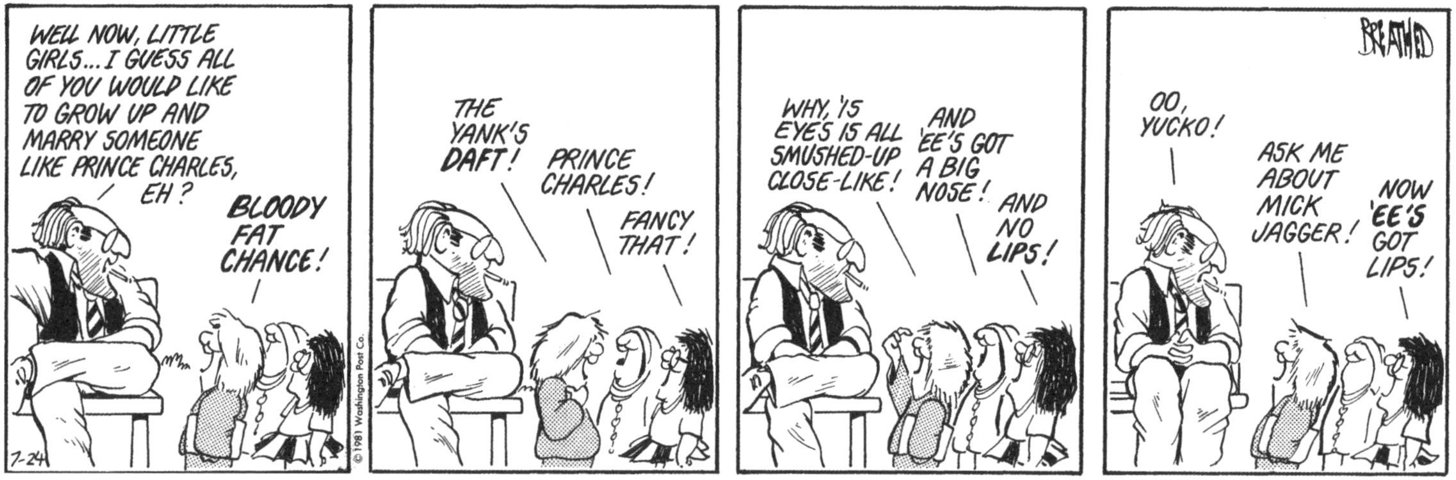
WELL NOW, LITTLE GIRLS... I GUESS ALL OF YOU WOULD LIKE TO GROW UP AND MARRY SOMEONE LIKE PRINCE CHARLES, EH?
BLOODY FAT CHANCE!
7-24
© 1981 Washington Post Co.
THE YANK'S DAFT!
PRINCE CHARLES!
FANCY THAT!
WHY, 'IS EYE'S IS ALL SMUSHED-UP CLOSE-LIKE!
AND 'EE'S GOT A BIG NOSE!
AND NO LIPS!
BREATHED
OO, YUCKO!
ASK ME ABOUT MICK JAGGER!
NOW 'EE'S GOT LIPS!

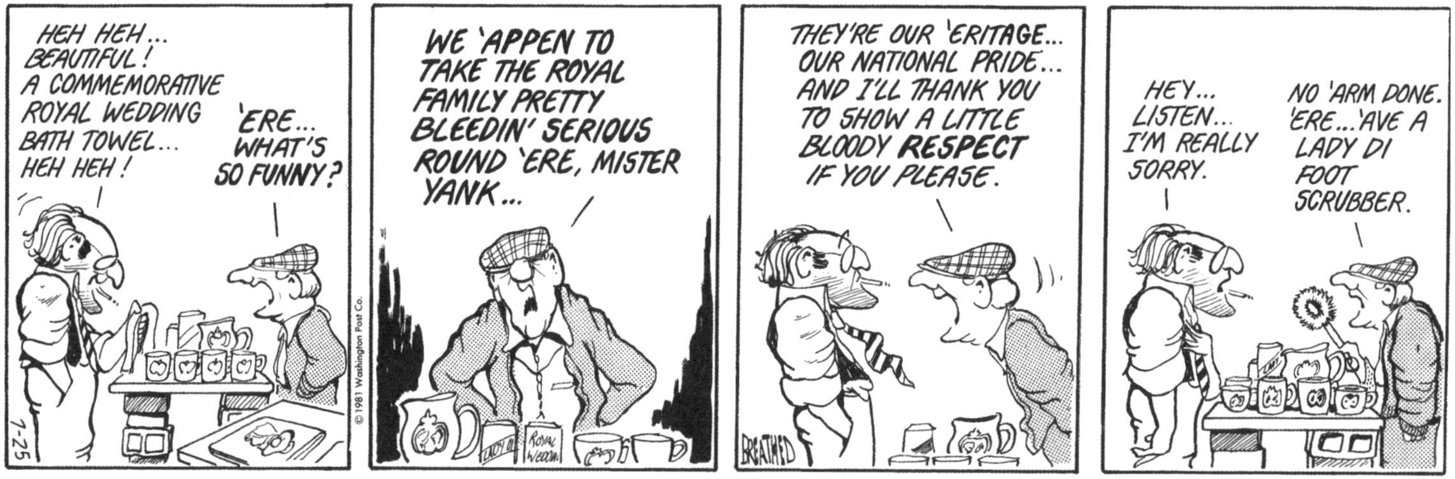
HEH HEH... BEAUTIFUL! A COMMEMORATIVE ROYAL WEDDING BATH TOWEL... HEH HEH!
'ERE... WHAT'S SO FUNNY?
7-25
© 1981 Washington Post Co.
WE 'APPEN TO TAKE THE ROYAL FAMILY PRETTY BLEEDIN' SERIOUS ROUND 'ERE, MISTER YANK...
THEY'RE OUR 'ERITAGE... OUR NATIONAL PRIDE... AND I'LL THANK YOU TO SHOW A LITTLE BLOODY RESPECT IF YOU PLEASE.
BREATHED
HEY... LISTEN... I'M REALLY SORRY.
NO 'ARM DONE. 'ERE... 'AVE A LADY DI FOOT SCRUBBER.

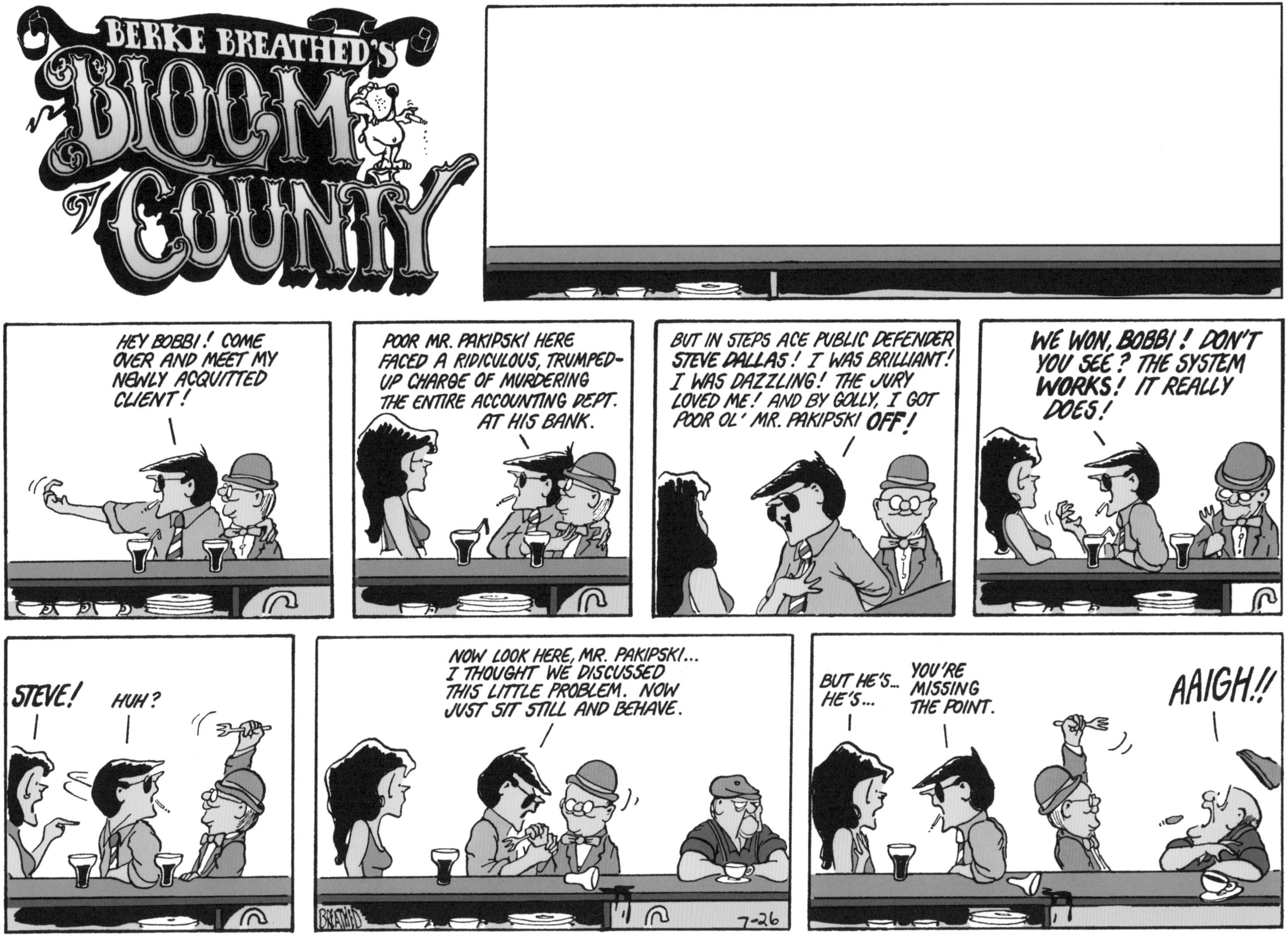
BERKE BREATHED'S
BLOOM COUNTY
HEY BOBBI! COME OVER AND MEET MY NEWLY ACQUITTED CLIENT!
POOR MR. PAKIPSKI HERE FACED A RIDICULOUS, TRUMPED-UP CHARGE OF MURDERING THE ENTIRE ACCOUNTING DEPT. AT HIS BANK.
BUT IN STEPS ACE PUBLIC DEFENDER STEVE DALLAS! I WAS BRILLIANT! I WAS DAZZLING! THE JURY LOVED ME! AND BY GOLLY, I GOT POOR OL' MR. PAKIPSKI OFF!
WE WON, BOBBI! DON'T YOU SEE? THE SYSTEM WORKS! IT REALLY DOES!
STEVE!
HUH?
NOW LOOK HERE, MR. PAKIPSKI... I THOUGHT WE DISCUSSED THIS LITTLE PROBLEM. NOW JUST SIT STILL AND BEHAVE.
BREATHED
7-26
BUT HE'S... HE'S...
YOU'RE MISSING THE POINT.
AAIGH!!

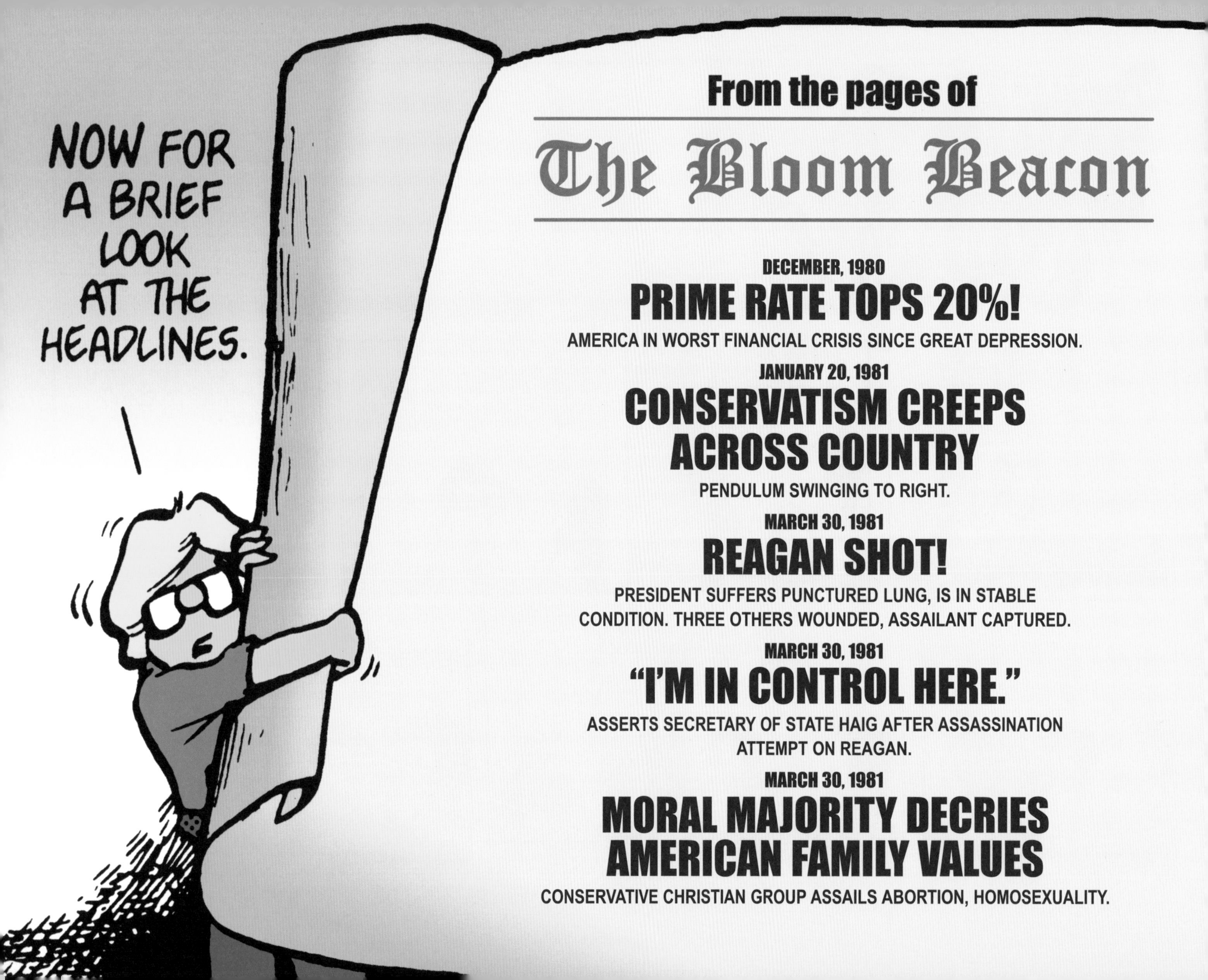
NOW FOR A BRIEF LOOK AT THE HEADLINES.
From the pages of
The Bloom Beacon
DECEMBER, 1980
PRIME RATE TOPS 20%!
AMERICA IN WORST FINANCIAL CRISIS SINCE GREAT DEPRESSION.
JANUARY 20, 1981
CONSERVATISM CREEPS ACROSS COUNTRY
PENDULUM SWINGING TO RIGHT.
MARCH 30, 1981
REAGAN SHOT!
PRESIDENT SUFFERS PUNCTURED LUNG, IS IN STABLE CONDITION. THREE OTHERS WOUNDED, ASSAILANT CAPTURED.
MARCH 30, 1981
"I'M IN CONTROL HERE."
ASSERTS SECRETARY OF STATE HAIG AFTER ASSASSINATION ATTEMPT ON REAGAN.
MARCH 30, 1981
MORAL MAJORITY DECRIES AMERICAN FAMILY VALUES
CONSERVATIVE CHRISTIAN GROUP ASSAILS ABORTION, HOMOSEXUALITY.

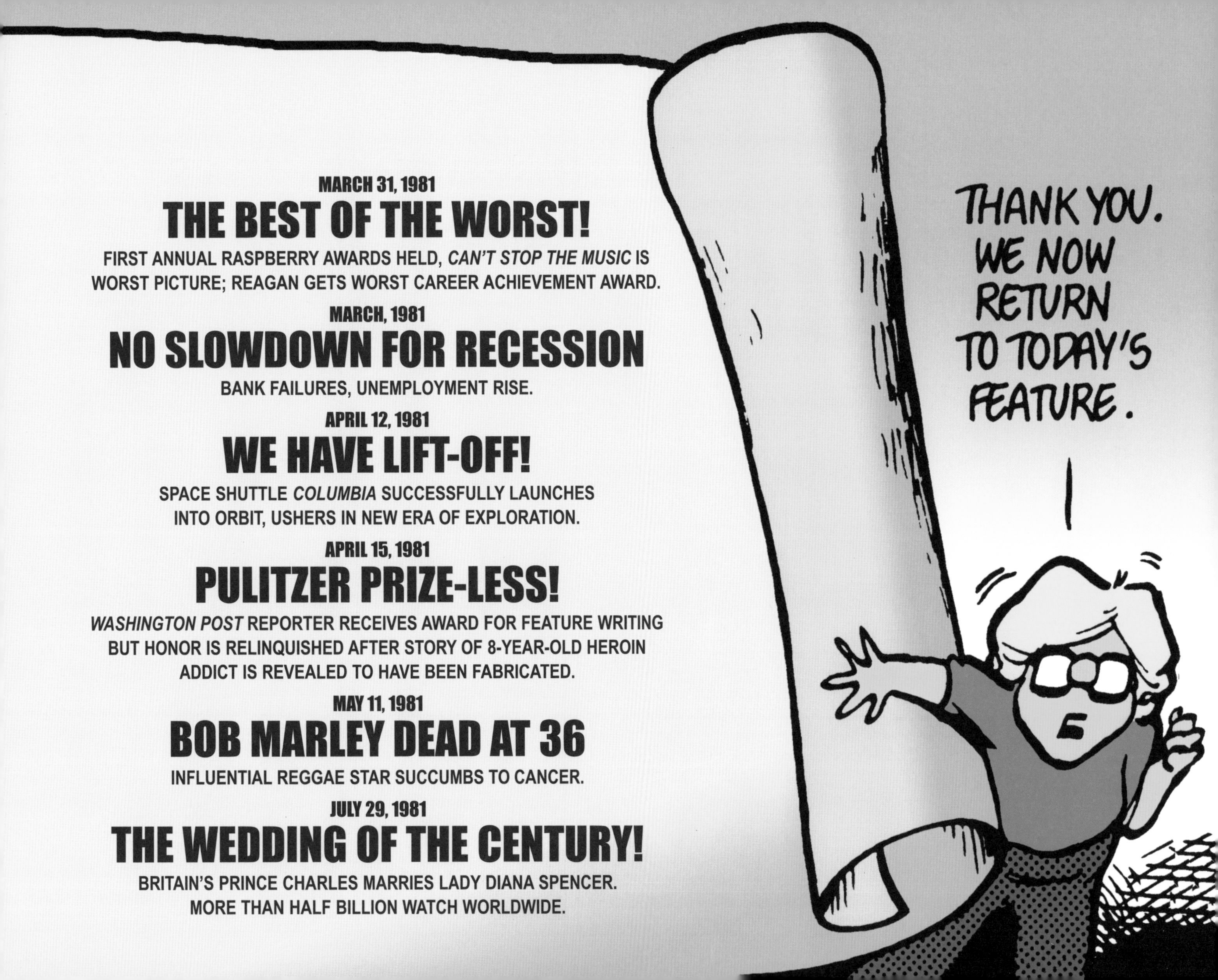
MARCH 31, 1981
THE BEST OF THE WORST!
FIRST ANNUAL RASPBERRY AWARDS HELD, *CAN'T STOP THE MUSIC* IS WORST PICTURE; REAGAN GETS WORST CAREER ACHIEVEMENT AWARD.
MARCH, 1981
NO SLOWDOWN FOR RECESSION
BANK FAILURES, UNEMPLOYMENT RISE.
APRIL 12, 1981
WE HAVE LIFT-OFF!
SPACE SHUTTLE *COLUMBIA* SUCCESSFULLY LAUNCHES INTO ORBIT, USHERS IN NEW ERA OF EXPLORATION.
APRIL 15, 1981
PULITZER PRIZE-LESS!
WASHINGTON POST REPORTER RECEIVES AWARD FOR FEATURE WRITING BUT HONOR IS RELINQUISHED AFTER STORY OF 8-YEAR-OLD HEROIN ADDICT IS REVEALED TO HAVE BEEN FABRICATED.
MAY 11, 1981
BOB MARLEY DEAD AT 36
INFLUENTIAL REGGAE STAR SUCCUMBS TO CANCER.
JULY 29, 1981
THE WEDDING OF THE CENTURY!
BRITAIN'S PRINCE CHARLES MARRIES LADY DIANA SPENCER. MORE THAN HALF BILLION WATCH WORLDWIDE.
THANK YOU. WE NOW RETURN TO TODAY'S FEATURE.

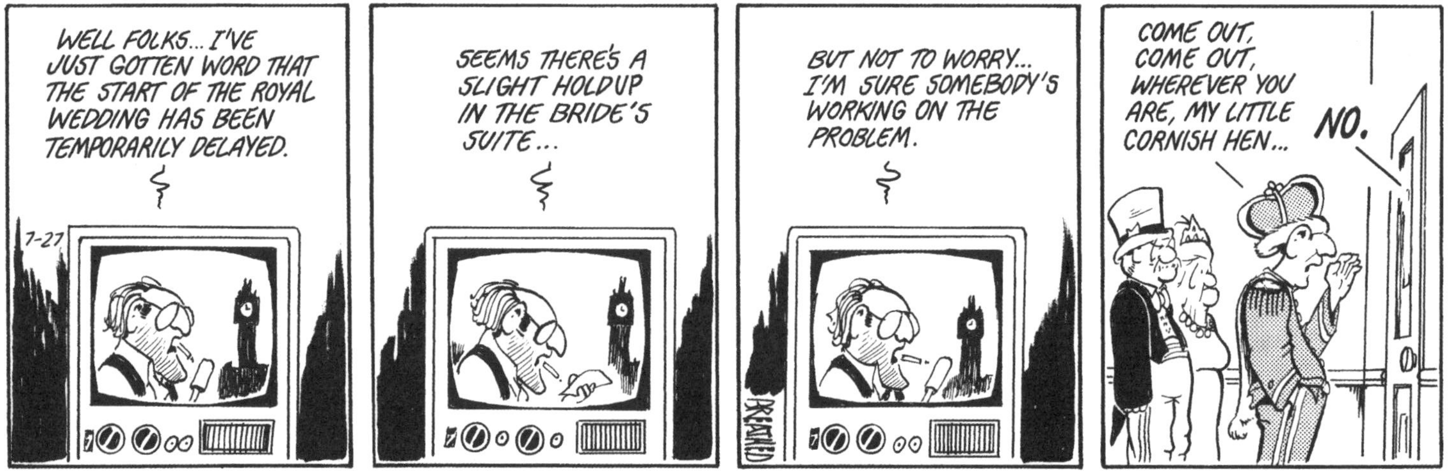
WELL FOLKS... I'VE JUST GOTTEN WORD THAT THE START OF THE ROYAL WEDDING HAS BEEN TEMPORARILY DELAYED.
7-27
SEEMS THERE'S A SLIGHT HOLDUP IN THE BRIDE'S SUITE...
BUT NOT TO WORRY... I'M SURE SOMEBODY'S WORKING ON THE PROBLEM.
BREATHED
COME OUT, COME OUT, WHEREVER YOU ARE, MY LITTLE CORNISH HEN...
NO.

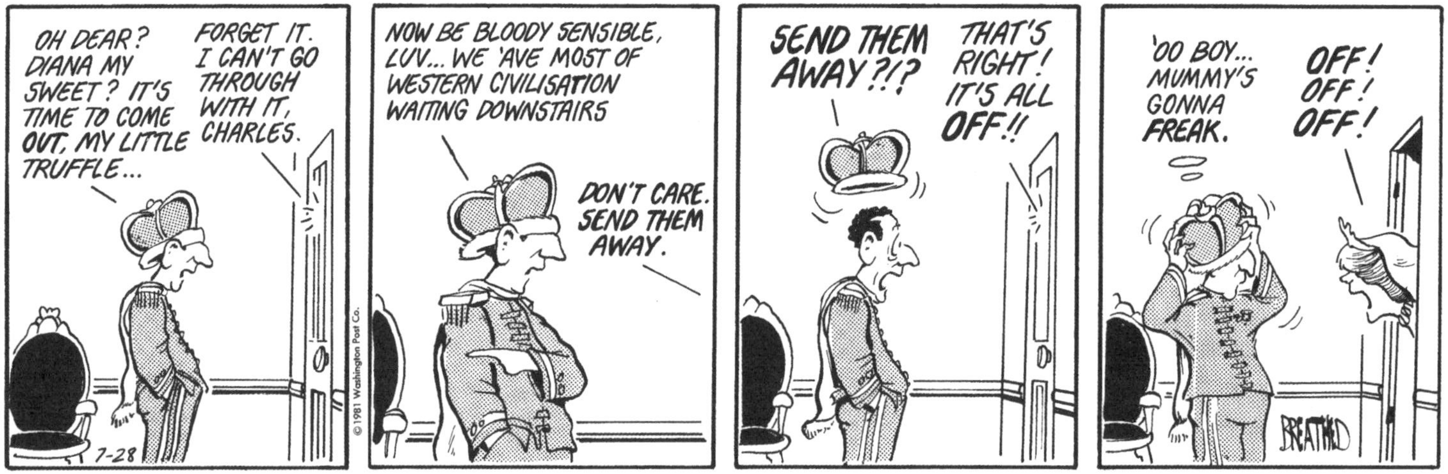
OH DEAR? DIANA MY SWEET? IT'S TIME TO COME OUT, MY LITTLE TRUFFLE...
FORGET IT. I CAN'T GO THROUGH WITH IT, CHARLES.
7-28
© 1981 Washington Post Co.
NOW BE BLOODY SENSIBLE, LUV... WE 'AVE MOST OF WESTERN CIVILISATION WAITING DOWNSTAIRS
DON'T CARE. SEND THEM AWAY.
SEND THEM AWAY?!?
THAT'S RIGHT! IT'S ALL OFF!!
'OO BOY... MUMMY'S GONNA FREAK.
OFF! OFF! OFF!
BREATHED

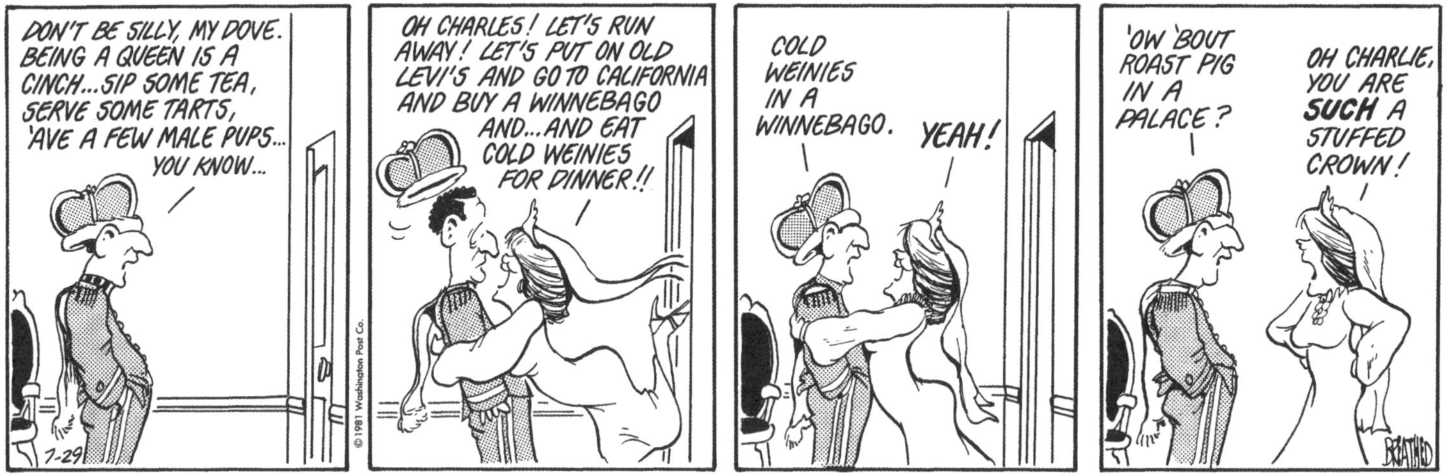
DON'T BE SILLY, MY DOVE. BEING A QUEEN IS A CINCH...SIP SOME TEA, SERVE SOME TARTS, 'AVE A FEW MALE PUPS... YOU KNOW...
7-29
© 1981 Washington Post Co.
OH CHARLES! LET'S RUN AWAY! LET'S PUT ON OLD LEVI'S AND GO TO CALIFORNIA AND BUY A WINNEBAGO AND...AND EAT COLD WEINIES FOR DINNER!!
COLD WEINIES IN A WINNEBAGO.
YEAH!
'OW 'BOUT ROAST PIG IN A PALACE?
OH CHARLIE, YOU ARE SUCH A STUFFED CROWN!
BREATHED

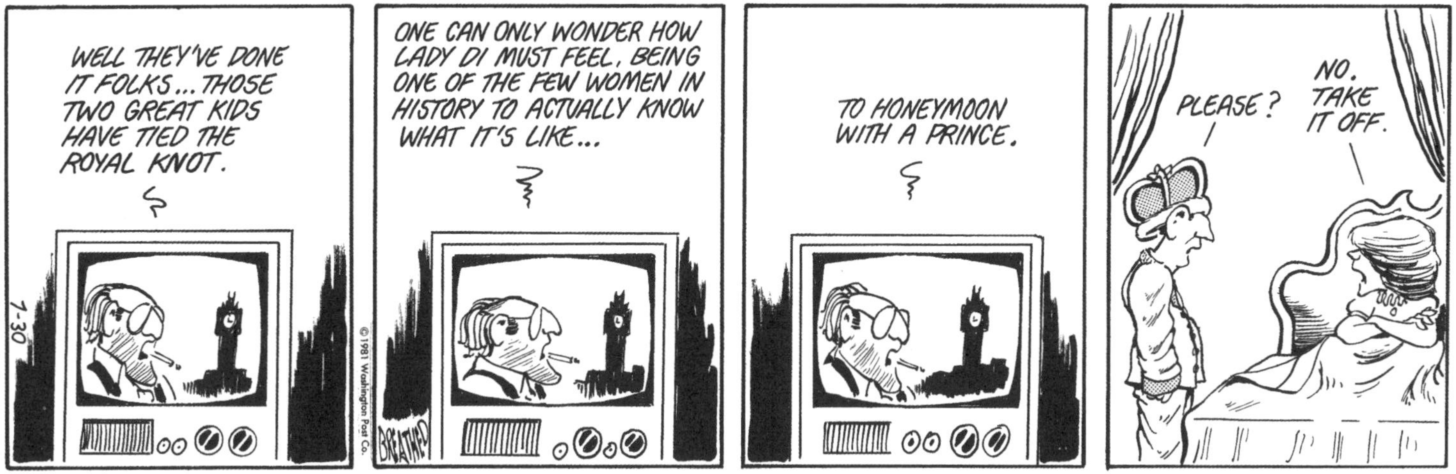
7-30
WELL THEY'VE DONE IT FOLKS... THOSE TWO GREAT KIDS HAVE TIED THE ROYAL KNOT.
© 1981 Washington Post Co.
ONE CAN ONLY WONDER HOW LADY DI MUST FEEL, BEING ONE OF THE FEW WOMEN IN HISTORY TO ACTUALLY KNOW WHAT IT'S LIKE...
TO HONEYMOON WITH A PRINCE.
PLEASE?
NO. TAKE IT OFF.

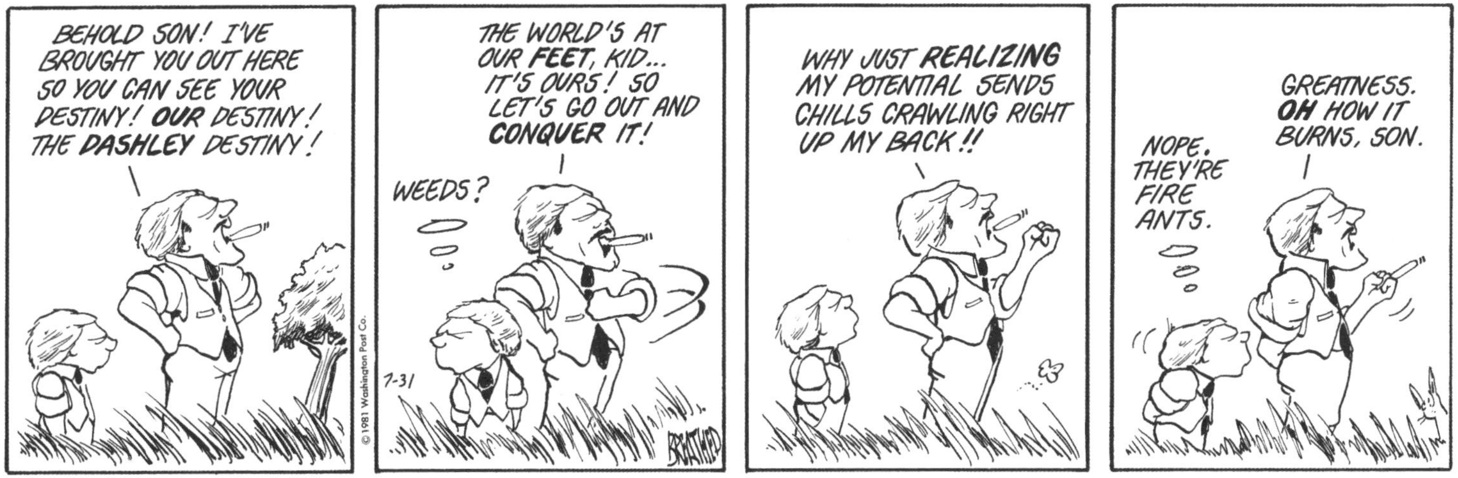
BEHOLD SON! I'VE BROUGHT YOU OUT HERE SO YOU CAN SEE YOUR DESTINY! OUR DESTINY! THE DASHLEY DESTINY!
© 1981 Washington Post Co.
7-31
THE WORLD'S AT OUR FEET, KID... IT'S OURS! SO LET'S GO OUT AND CONQUER IT!
WEEDS?
WHY JUST REALIZING MY POTENTIAL SENDS CHILLS CRAWLING RIGHT UP MY BACK!!
NOPE. THEY'RE FIRE ANTS.
GREATNESS. OH HOW IT BURNS, SON.

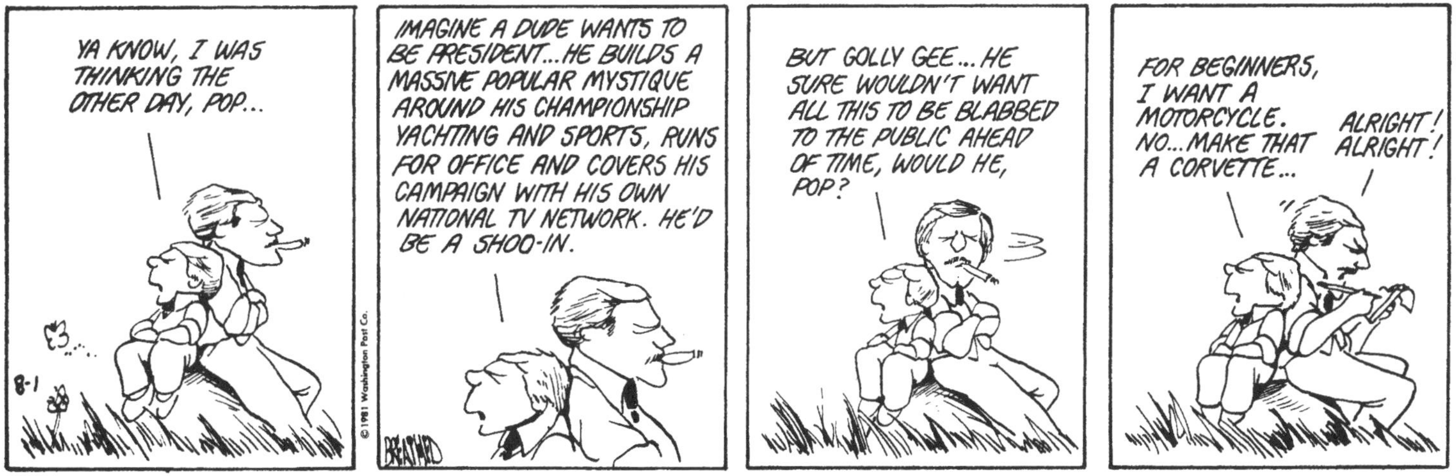
8-1
YA KNOW, I WAS THINKING THE OTHER DAY, POP...
© 1981 Washington Post Co.
IMAGINE A DUDE WANTS TO BE PRESIDENT... HE BUILDS A MASSIVE POPULAR MYSTIQUE AROUND HIS CHAMPIONSHIP YACHTING AND SPORTS, RUNS FOR OFFICE AND COVERS HIS CAMPAIGN WITH HIS OWN NATIONAL TV NETWORK. HE'D BE A SHOO-IN.
BUT GOLLY GEE... HE SURE WOULDN'T WANT ALL THIS TO BE BLABBED TO THE PUBLIC AHEAD OF TIME, WOULD HE, POP?
FOR BEGINNERS, I WANT A MOTORCYCLE. NO... MAKE THAT A CORVETTE...
ALRIGHT! ALRIGHT!

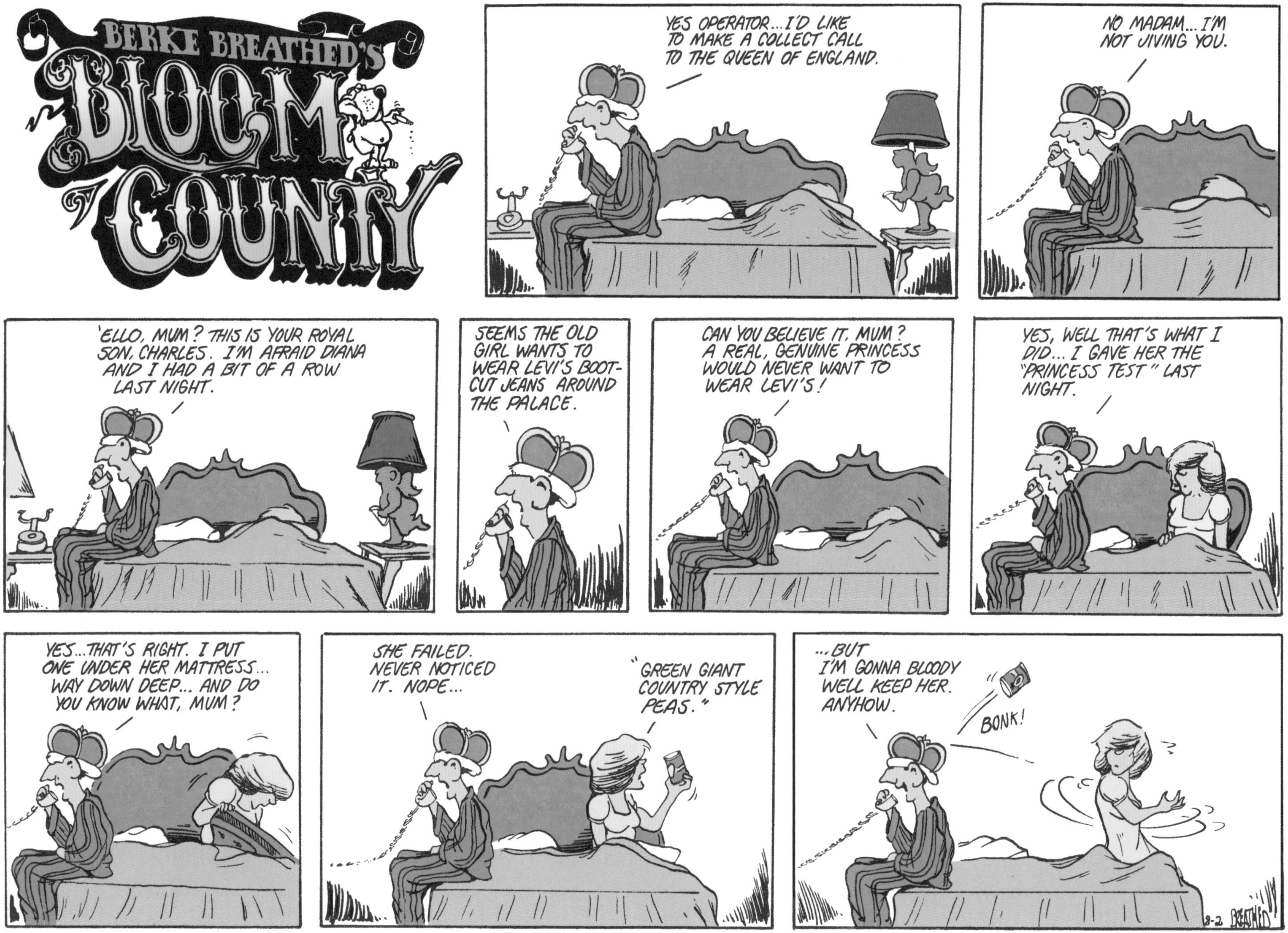
BERKE BREATHED'S
BLOOM COUNTY
YES OPERATOR...I'D LIKE TO MAKE A COLLECT CALL TO THE QUEEN OF ENGLAND.
NO MADAM... I'M NOT JIVING YOU.
'ELLO, MUM? THIS IS YOUR ROYAL SON, CHARLES. I'M AFRAID DIANA AND I HAD A BIT OF A ROW LAST NIGHT.
SEEMS THE OLD GIRL WANTS TO WEAR LEVI'S BOOT-CUT JEANS AROUND THE PALACE.
CAN YOU BELIEVE IT, MUM? A REAL, GENUINE PRINCESS WOULD NEVER WANT TO WEAR LEVI'S!
YES, WELL THAT'S WHAT I DID... I GAVE HER THE "PRINCESS TEST" LAST NIGHT.
YES...THAT'S RIGHT. I PUT ONE UNDER HER MATTRESS... WAY DOWN DEEP... AND DO YOU KNOW WHAT, MUM?
SHE FAILED. NEVER NOTICED IT. NOPE...
"GREEN GIANT COUNTRY STYLE PEAS."
...BUT I'M GONNA BLOODY WELL KEEP HER. ANYHOW.
BONK!
8-2 BREATHED

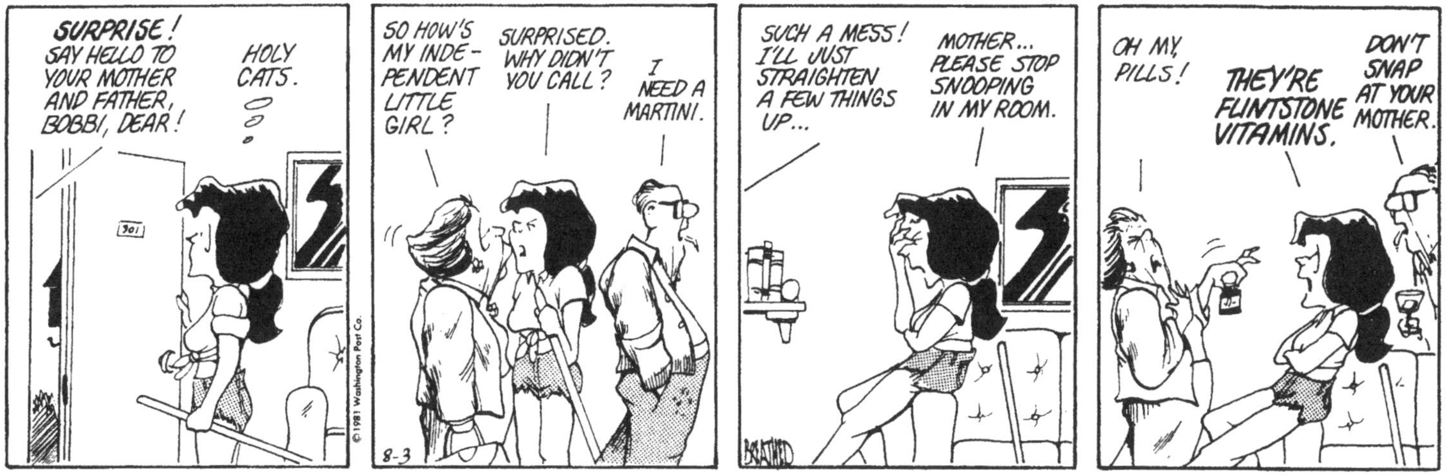
SURPRISE! SAY HELLO TO YOUR MOTHER AND FATHER, BOBBI, DEAR!
HOLY CATS.
SO HOW'S MY INDEPENDENT LITTLE GIRL?
SURPRISED. WHY DIDN'T YOU CALL?
I NEED A MARTINI.
© 1981 Washington Post Co.
8-3
SUCH A MESS! I'LL JUST STRAIGHTEN A FEW THINGS UP...
MOTHER... PLEASE STOP SNOOPING IN MY ROOM.
OH MY PILLS!
THEY'RE FLINTSTONE VITAMINS.
DON'T SNAP AT YOUR MOTHER.

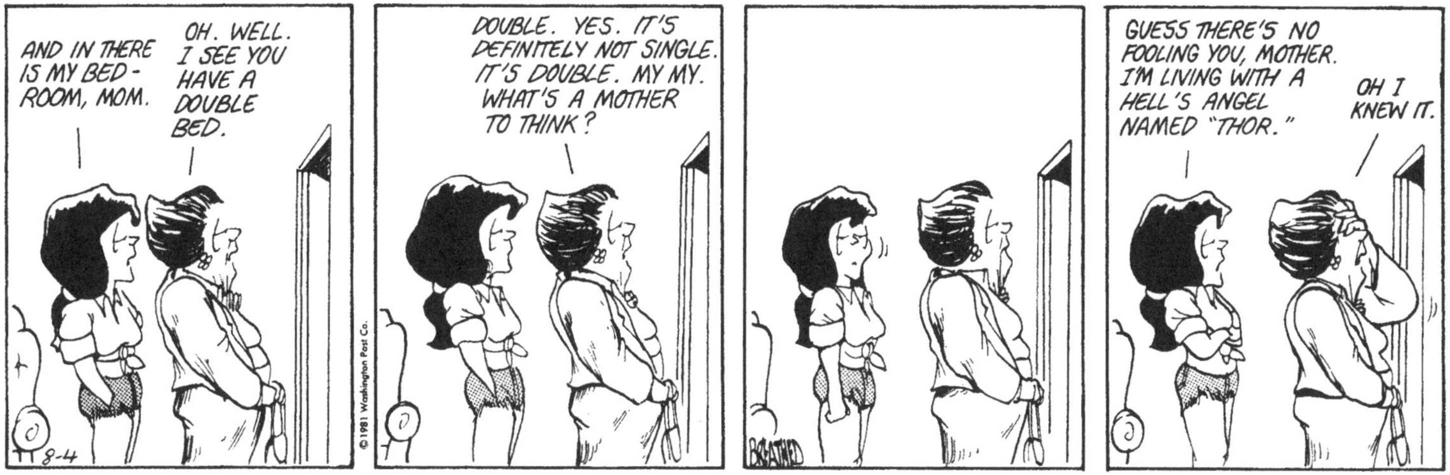
AND IN THERE IS MY BEDROOM, MOM.
OH. WELL. I SEE YOU HAVE A DOUBLE BED.
8-4
© 1981 Washington Post Co.
DOUBLE. YES. IT'S DEFINITELY NOT SINGLE. IT'S DOUBLE. MY MY. WHAT'S A MOTHER TO THINK?
GUESS THERE'S NO FOOLING YOU, MOTHER. I'M LIVING WITH A HELL'S ANGEL NAMED "THOR."
OH I KNEW IT.

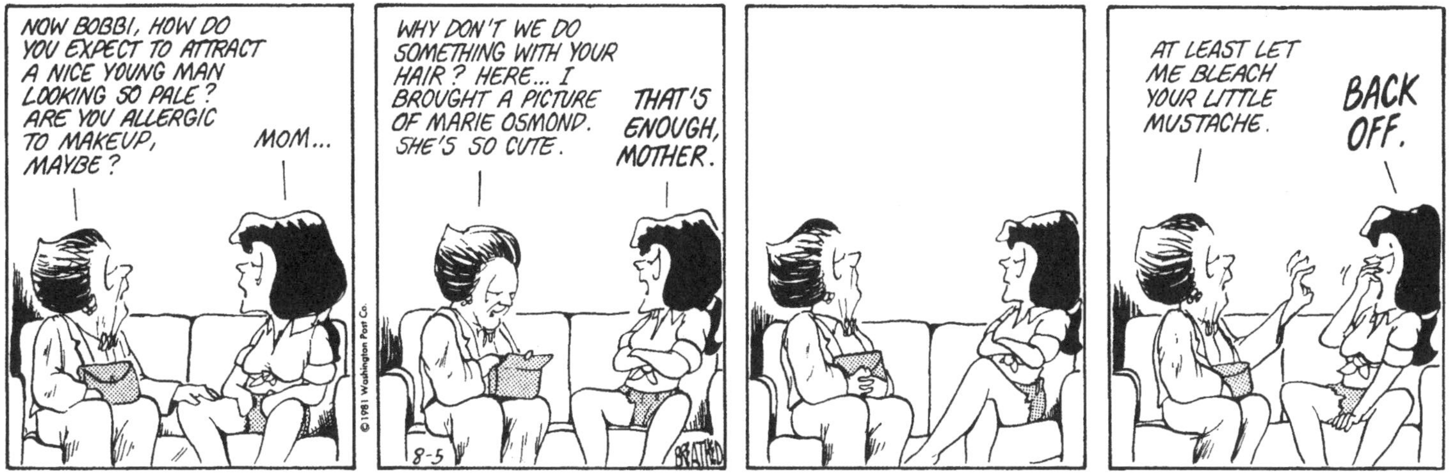
NOW BOBBI, HOW DO YOU EXPECT TO ATTRACT A NICE YOUNG MAN LOOKING SO PALE? ARE YOU ALLERGIC TO MAKEUP, MAYBE?
MOM...
© 1981 Washington Post Co.
WHY DON'T WE DO SOMETHING WITH YOUR HAIR? HERE... I BROUGHT A PICTURE OF MARIE OSMOND. SHE'S SO CUTE.
THAT'S ENOUGH, MOTHER.
8-5
AT LEAST LET ME BLEACH YOUR LITTLE MUSTACHE.
BACK OFF.

Marie Osmond was a pop and country music singer in the '70s and '80s, and co-hosted a TV variety show with her brother, Donny.

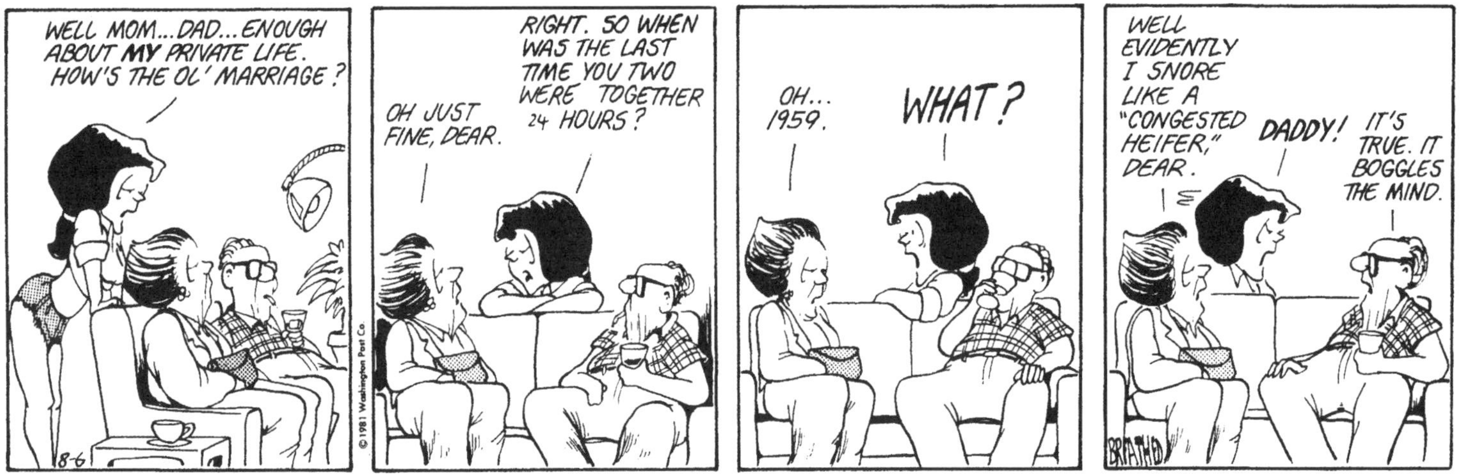
WELL MOM...DAD...ENOUGH ABOUT **MY** PRIVATE LIFE. HOW'S THE OL' MARRIAGE?
OH JUST FINE, DEAR.
RIGHT. SO WHEN WAS THE LAST TIME YOU TWO WERE TOGETHER 24 HOURS?
OH... 1959.
WHAT?
WELL EVIDENTLY I SNORE LIKE A "CONGESTED HEIFER," DEAR.
DADDY!
IT'S TRUE. IT BOGGLES THE MIND.

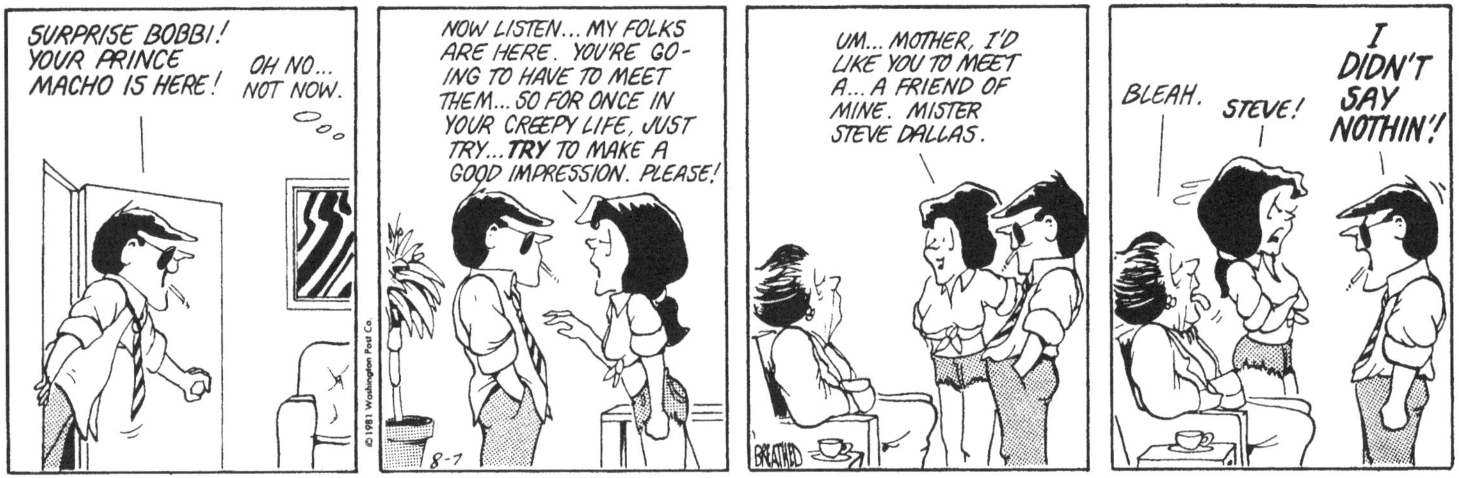
SURPRISE BOBBI! YOUR PRINCE MACHO IS HERE!
OH NO... NOT NOW.
NOW LISTEN... MY FOLKS ARE HERE. YOU'RE GOING TO HAVE TO MEET THEM... SO FOR ONCE IN YOUR CREEPY LIFE, JUST TRY...**TRY** TO MAKE A GOOD IMPRESSION. PLEASE!
UM... MOTHER, I'D LIKE YOU TO MEET A... A FRIEND OF MINE. MISTER STEVE DALLAS.
BLEAH.
STEVE!
I DIDN'T SAY NOTHIN'!

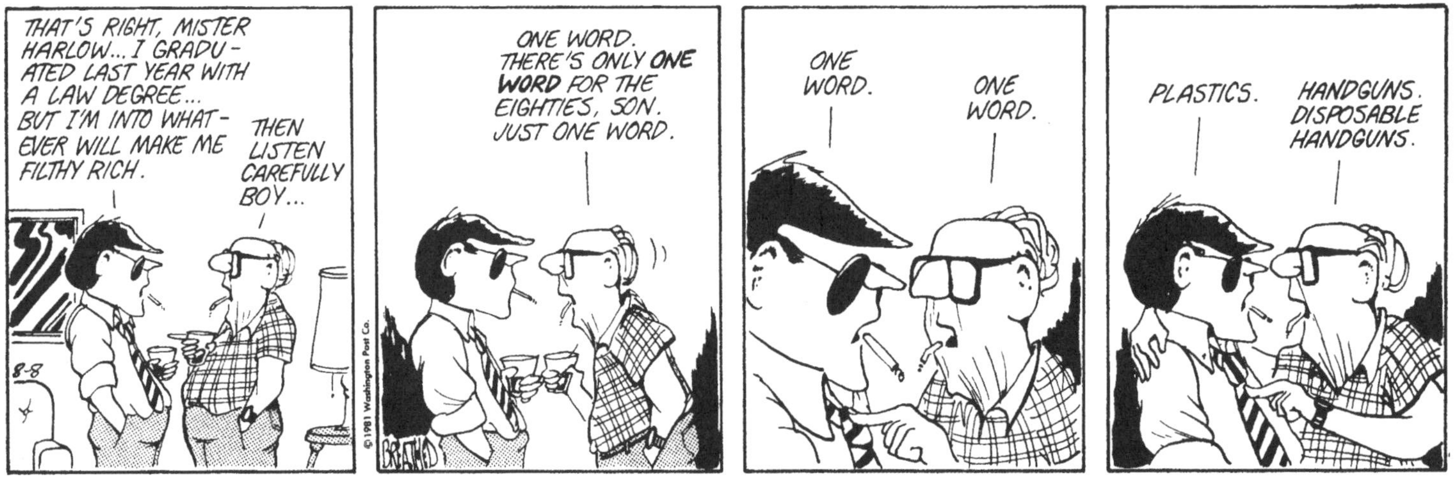
THAT'S RIGHT, MISTER HARLOW...I GRADUATED LAST YEAR WITH A LAW DEGREE... BUT I'M INTO WHATEVER WILL MAKE ME FILTHY RICH.
THEN LISTEN CAREFULLY BOY...
ONE WORD. THERE'S ONLY **ONE WORD** FOR THE EIGHTIES, SON. JUST ONE WORD.
ONE WORD.
ONE WORD.
PLASTICS.
HANDGUNS. DISPOSABLE HANDGUNS.

"Plastics" alludes to career advice Dustin Hoffman's character received in the 1967 film, *The Graduate*.

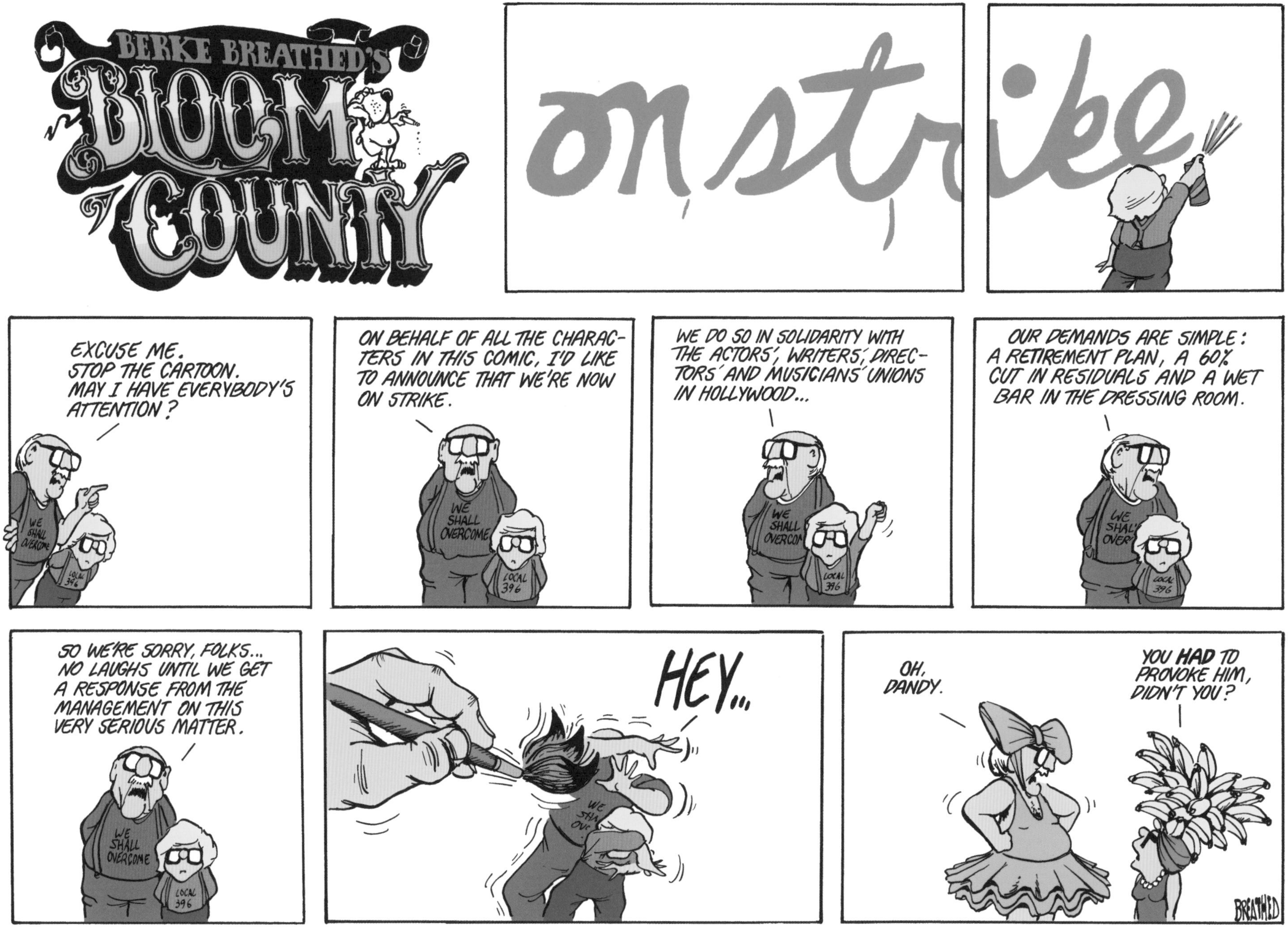
BERKE BREATHED'S
BLOOM COUNTY
on strike
EXCUSE ME. STOP THE CARTOON. MAY I HAVE EVERYBODY'S ATTENTION?
WE SHALL OVERCOME
LOCAL 396
ON BEHALF OF ALL THE CHARACTERS IN THIS COMIC, I'D LIKE TO ANNOUNCE THAT WE'RE NOW ON STRIKE.
WE SHALL OVERCOME
LOCAL 396
WE DO SO IN SOLIDARITY WITH THE ACTORS', WRITERS', DIRECTORS' AND MUSICIANS' UNIONS IN HOLLYWOOD...
OUR DEMANDS ARE SIMPLE: A RETIREMENT PLAN, A 60% CUT IN RESIDUALS AND A WET BAR IN THE DRESSING ROOM.
SO WE'RE SORRY, FOLKS... NO LAUGHS UNTIL WE GET A RESPONSE FROM THE MANAGEMENT ON THIS VERY SERIOUS MATTER.
WE SHALL OVERCOME
LOCAL 396
HEY...
OH, DANDY.
YOU **HAD** TO PROVOKE HIM, DIDN'T YOU?
BREATHED

August 9, 1981

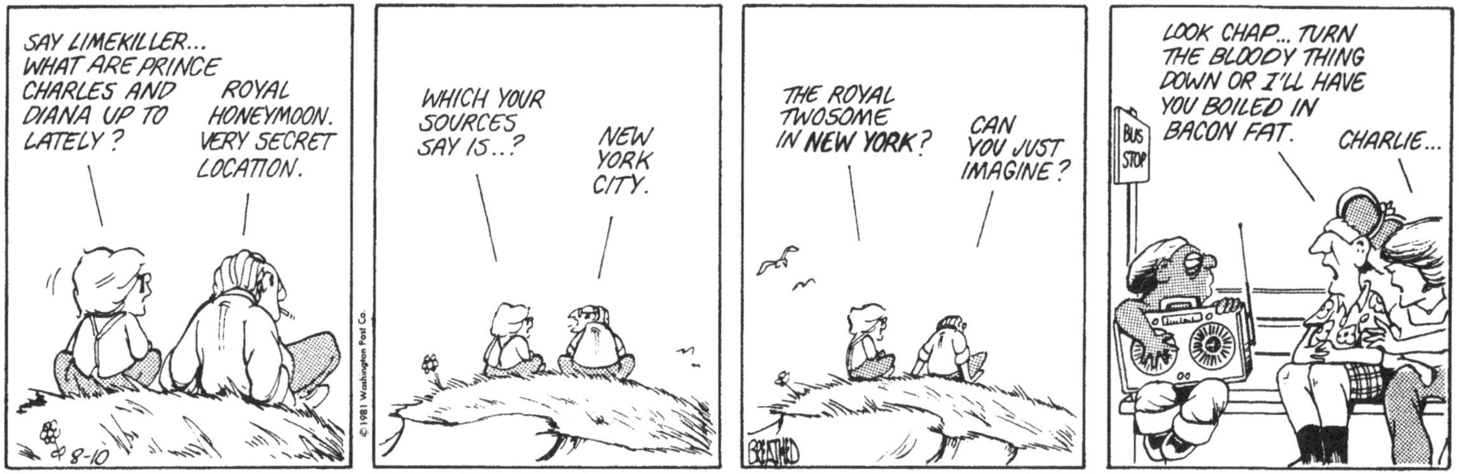
SAY LIMEKILLER... WHAT ARE PRINCE CHARLES AND DIANA UP TO LATELY?
ROYAL HONEYMOON. VERY SECRET LOCATION.
8-10
© 1981 Washington Post Co.
WHICH YOUR SOURCES SAY IS...?
NEW YORK CITY.
THE ROYAL TWOSOME IN NEW YORK?
CAN YOU JUST IMAGINE?
BREATHED
LOOK CHAP... TURN THE BLOODY THING DOWN OR I'LL HAVE YOU BOILED IN BACON FAT.
CHARLIE...
BUS STOP

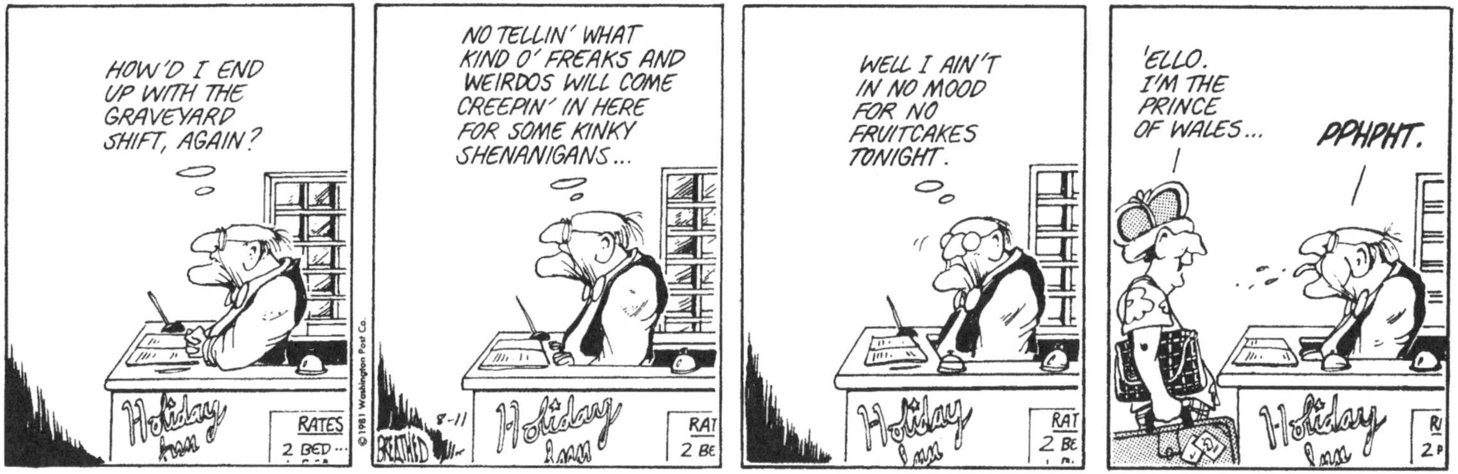
HOW'D I END UP WITH THE GRAVEYARD SHIFT, AGAIN?
Holiday Inn
RATES 2 BED...
© 1981 Washington Post Co.
BREATHED
8-11
NO TELLIN' WHAT KIND O' FREAKS AND WEIRDOS WILL COME CREEPIN' IN HERE FOR SOME KINKY SHENANIGANS...
WELL I AIN'T IN NO MOOD FOR NO FRUITCAKES TONIGHT.
'ELLO. I'M THE PRINCE OF WALES...
PPHPHT.

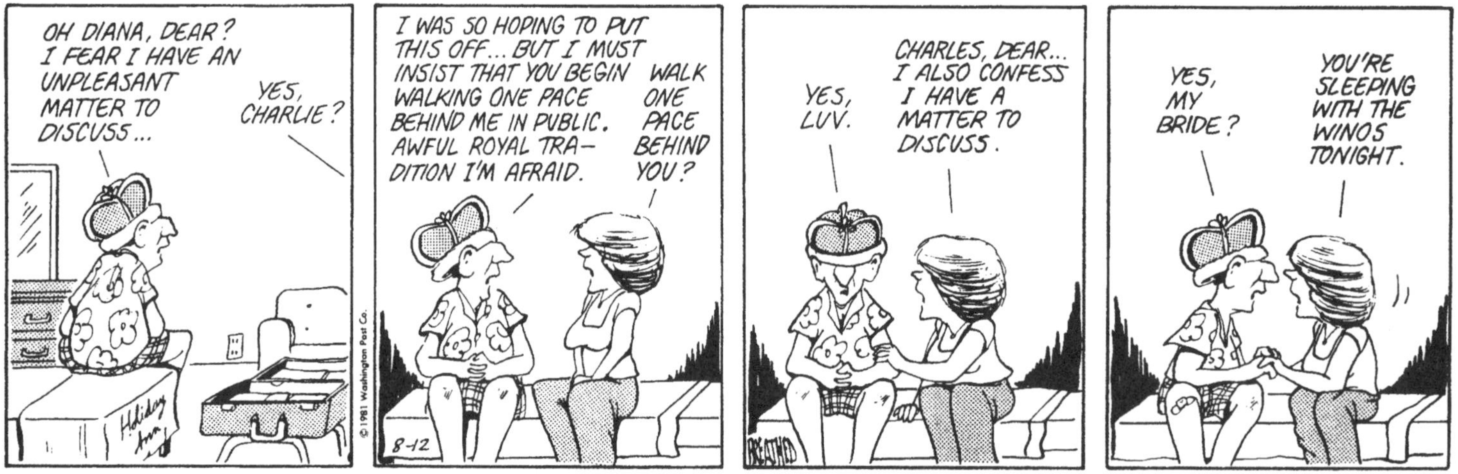
OH DIANA, DEAR? I FEAR I HAVE AN UNPLEASANT MATTER TO DISCUSS...
YES, CHARLIE?
Holiday Inn
© 1981 Washington Post Co.
I WAS SO HOPING TO PUT THIS OFF... BUT I MUST INSIST THAT YOU BEGIN WALKING ONE PACE BEHIND ME IN PUBLIC. AWFUL ROYAL TRADITION I'M AFRAID.
WALK ONE PACE BEHIND YOU?
8-12
YES, LUV.
CHARLES, DEAR... I ALSO CONFESS I HAVE A MATTER TO DISCUSS.
BREATHED
YES, MY BRIDE?
YOU'RE SLEEPING WITH THE WINOS TONIGHT.

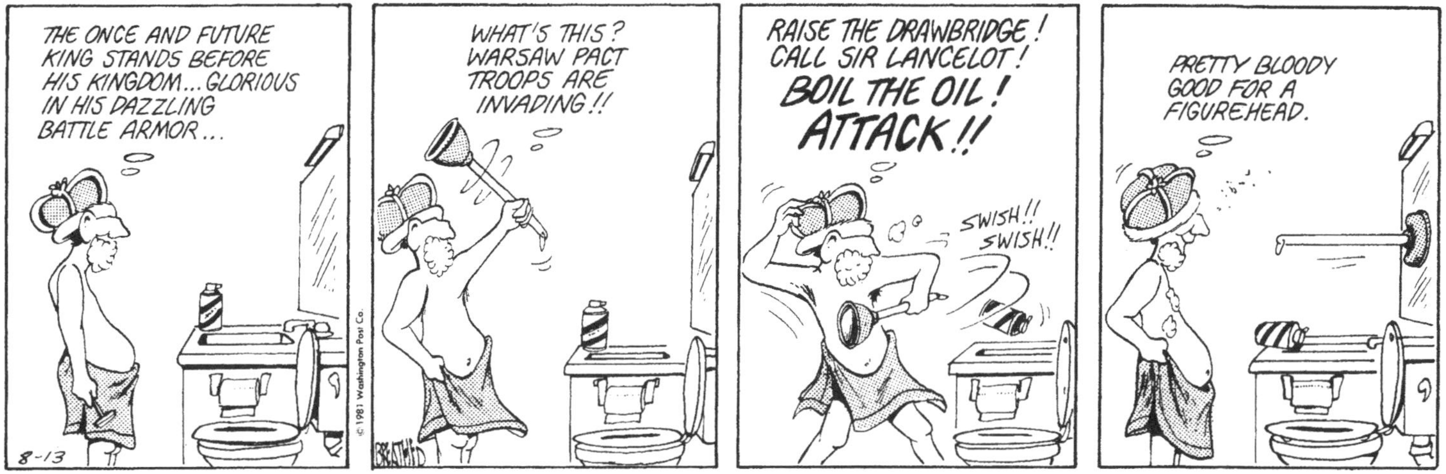
THE ONCE AND FUTURE KING STANDS BEFORE HIS KINGDOM... GLORIOUS IN HIS DAZZLING BATTLE ARMOR...
8-13
© 1981 Washington Post Co.
WHAT'S THIS? WARSAW PACT TROOPS ARE INVADING!!
BREATHED
RAISE THE DRAWBRIDGE! CALL SIR LANCELOT! BOIL THE OIL! ATTACK!!
SWISH!! SWISH!!
PRETTY BLOODY GOOD FOR A FIGUREHEAD.

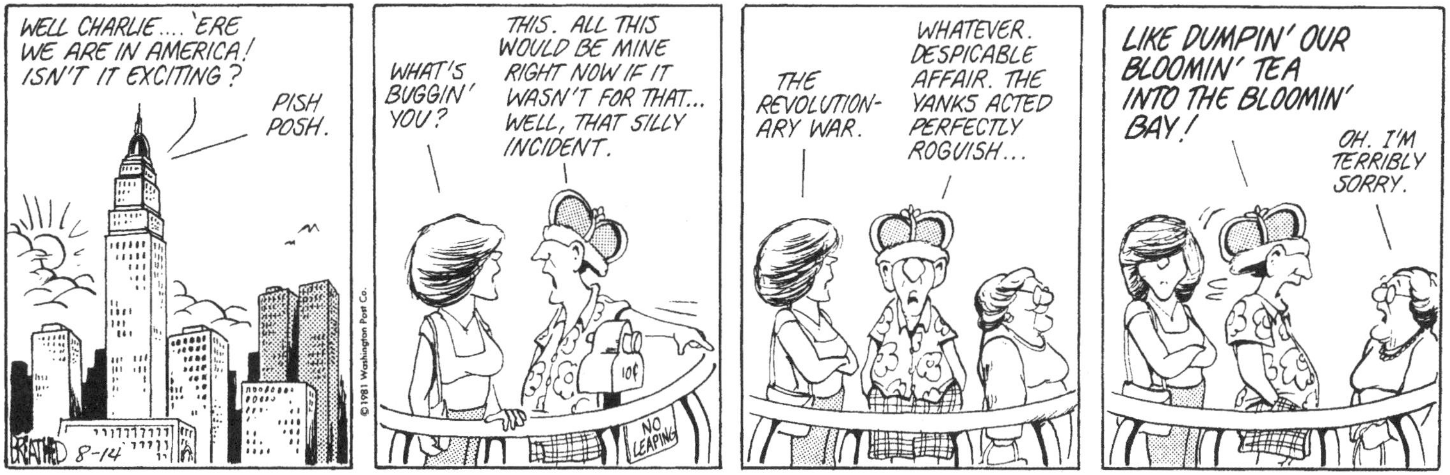
WELL CHARLIE.... 'ERE WE ARE IN AMERICA! ISN'T IT EXCITING?
PISH POSH.
BREATHED 8-14
© 1981 Washington Post Co.
WHAT'S BUGGIN' YOU?
THIS. ALL THIS WOULD BE MINE RIGHT NOW IF IT WASN'T FOR THAT... WELL, THAT SILLY INCIDENT.
10¢
NO LEAPING
THE REVOLUTIONARY WAR.
WHATEVER. DESPICABLE AFFAIR. THE YANKS ACTED PERFECTLY ROGUISH...
LIKE DUMPIN' OUR BLOOMIN' TEA INTO THE BLOOMIN' BAY!
OH. I'M TERRIBLY SORRY.

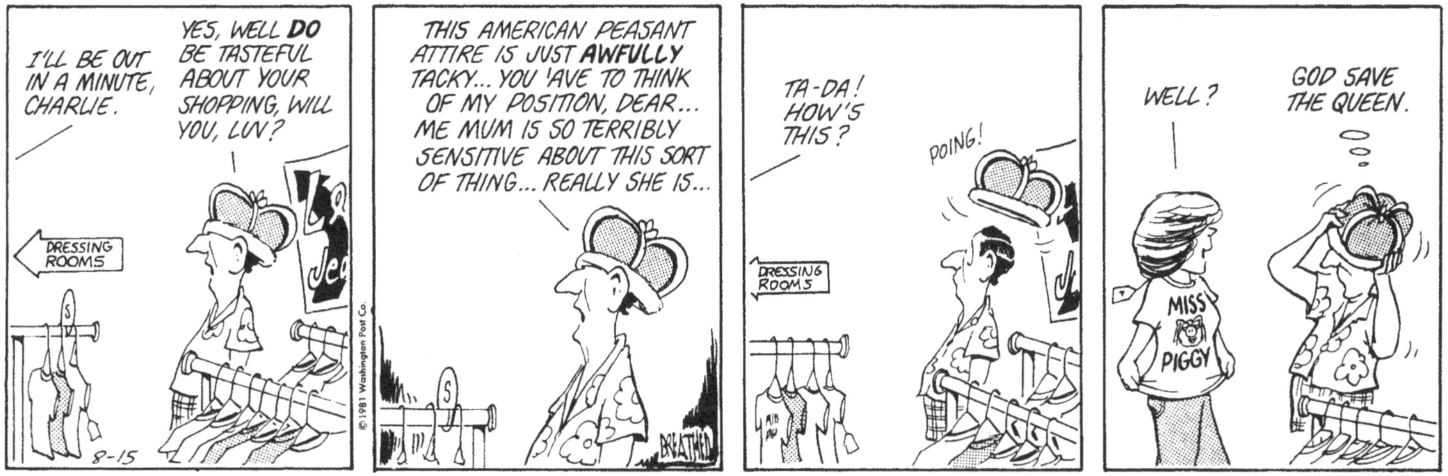
I'LL BE OUT IN A MINUTE, CHARLIE.
YES, WELL DO BE TASTEFUL ABOUT YOUR SHOPPING, WILL YOU, LUV?
DRESSING ROOMS
8-15
© 1981 Washington Post Co.
THIS AMERICAN PEASANT ATTIRE IS JUST AWFULLY TACKY... YOU 'AVE TO THINK OF MY POSITION, DEAR... ME MUM IS SO TERRIBLY SENSITIVE ABOUT THIS SORT OF THING... REALLY SHE IS...
BREATHED
TA-DA! HOW'S THIS?
POING!
DRESSING ROOMS
WELL?
GOD SAVE THE QUEEN.
MISS PIGGY

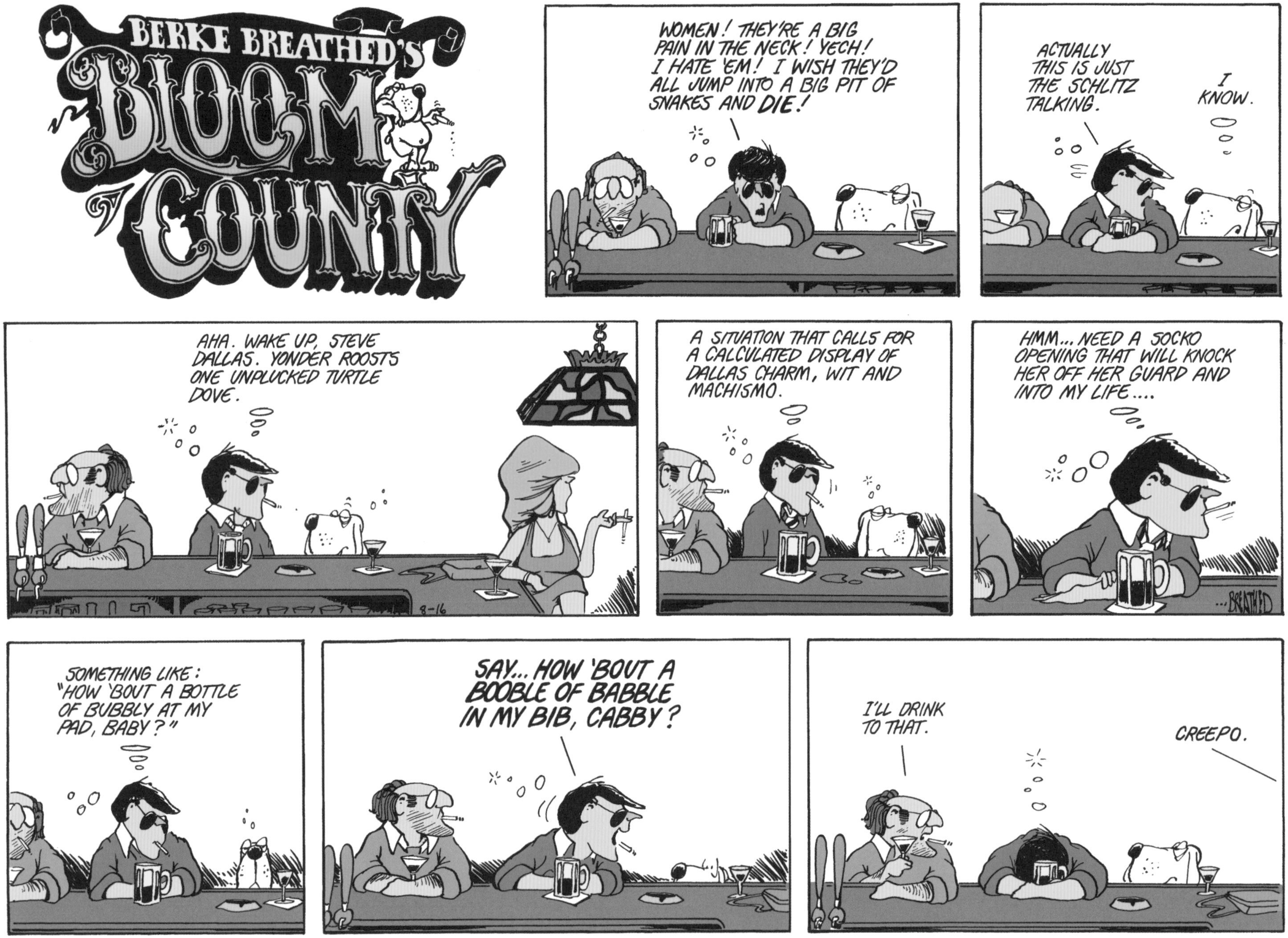
BERKE BREATHED'S
BLOOM COUNTY
WOMEN! THEY'RE A BIG PAIN IN THE NECK! YECH! I HATE 'EM! I WISH THEY'D ALL JUMP INTO A BIG PIT OF SNAKES AND DIE!
ACTUALLY THIS IS JUST THE SCHLITZ TALKING.
I KNOW.
AHA. WAKE UP, STEVE DALLAS. YONDER ROOSTS ONE UNPLUCKED TURTLE DOVE.
8-16
A SITUATION THAT CALLS FOR A CALCULATED DISPLAY OF DALLAS CHARM, WIT AND MACHISMO.
HMM... NEED A SOCKO OPENING THAT WILL KNOCK HER OFF HER GUARD AND INTO MY LIFE....
...BREATHED
SOMETHING LIKE: "HOW 'BOUT A BOTTLE OF BUBBLY AT MY PAD, BABY?"
SAY... HOW 'BOUT A BOOBLE OF BABBLE IN MY BIB, CABBY?
I'LL DRINK TO THAT.
CREEPO.

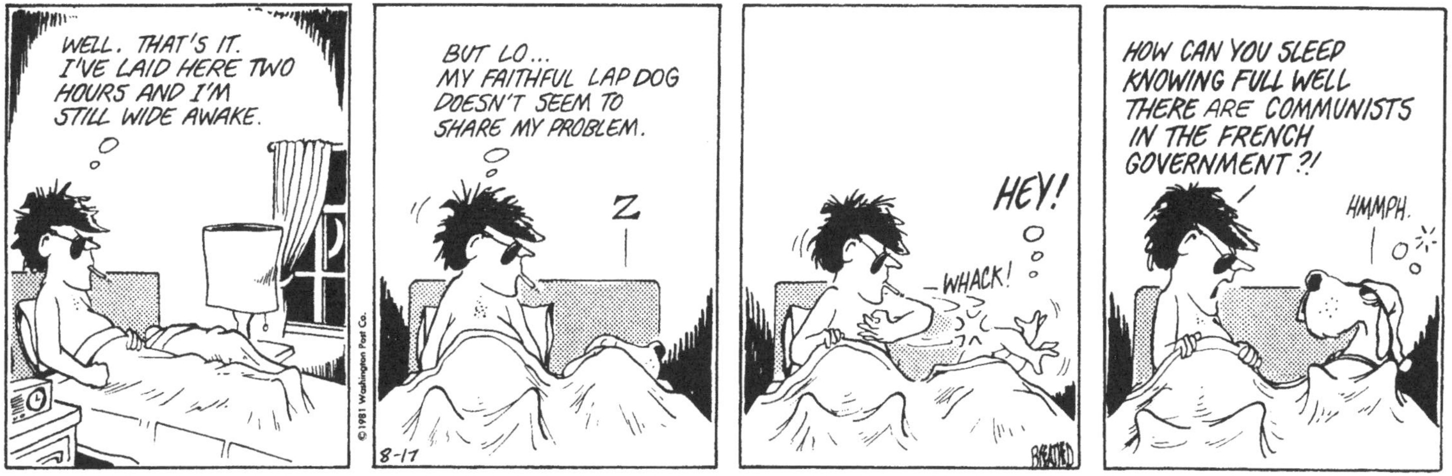
WELL. THAT'S IT. I'VE LAID HERE TWO HOURS AND I'M STILL WIDE AWAKE.
BUT LO... MY FAITHFUL LAP DOG DOESN'T SEEM TO SHARE MY PROBLEM.
Z
HEY!
WHACK!
HOW CAN YOU SLEEP KNOWING FULL WELL THERE ARE COMMUNISTS IN THE FRENCH GOVERNMENT ?!
HMMPH.
©1981 Washington Post Co.
8-17
BREATHED

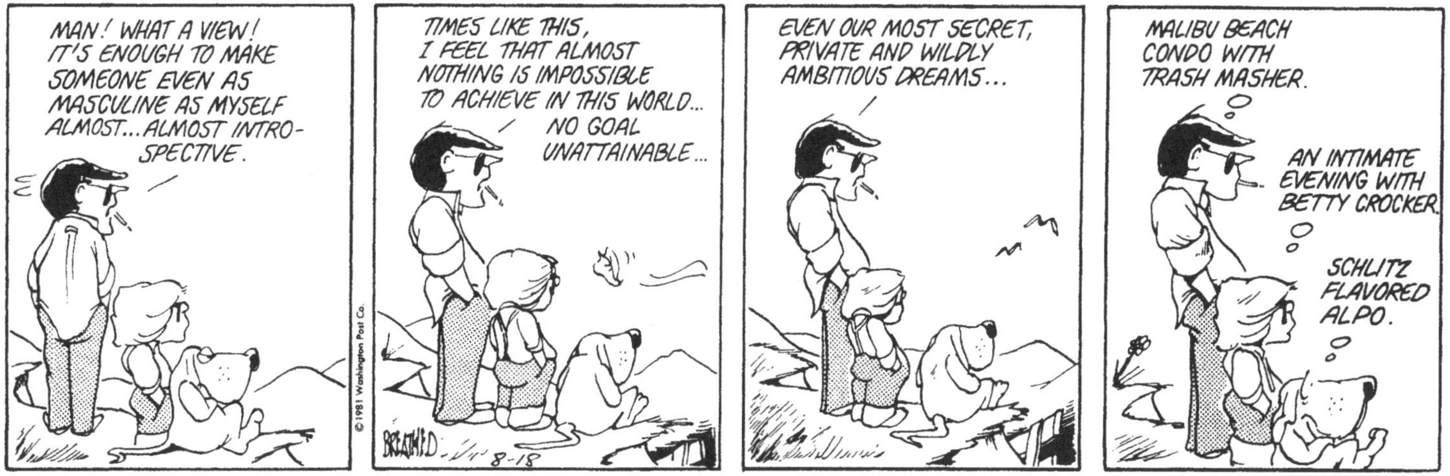
MAN! WHAT A VIEW! IT'S ENOUGH TO MAKE SOMEONE EVEN AS MASCULINE AS MYSELF ALMOST... ALMOST INTRO-SPECTIVE.
TIMES LIKE THIS, I FEEL THAT ALMOST NOTHING IS IMPOSSIBLE TO ACHIEVE IN THIS WORLD...
NO GOAL UNATTAINABLE...
EVEN OUR MOST SECRET, PRIVATE AND WILDLY AMBITIOUS DREAMS...
MALIBU BEACH CONDO WITH TRASH MASHER.
AN INTIMATE EVENING WITH BETTY CROCKER.
SCHLITZ FLAVORED ALPO.
©1981 Washington Post Co.
BREATHED
8-18

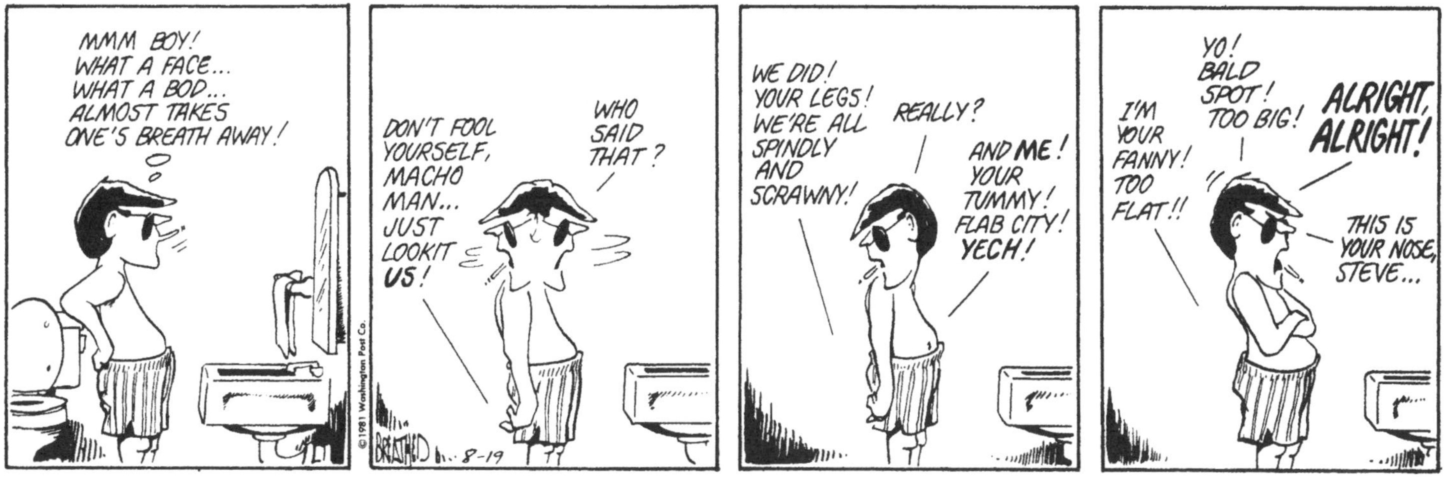
MMM BOY! WHAT A FACE... WHAT A BOD... ALMOST TAKES ONE'S BREATH AWAY!
DON'T FOOL YOURSELF, MACHO MAN... JUST LOOKIT US!
WHO SAID THAT?
WE DID! YOUR LEGS! WE'RE ALL SPINDLY AND SCRAWNY!
REALLY?
AND ME! YOUR TUMMY! FLAB CITY! YECH!
I'M YOUR FANNY! TOO FLAT!!
YO! BALD SPOT! TOO BIG!
ALRIGHT, ALRIGHT!
THIS IS YOUR NOSE, STEVE...
©1981 Washington Post Co.
BREATHED
8-19

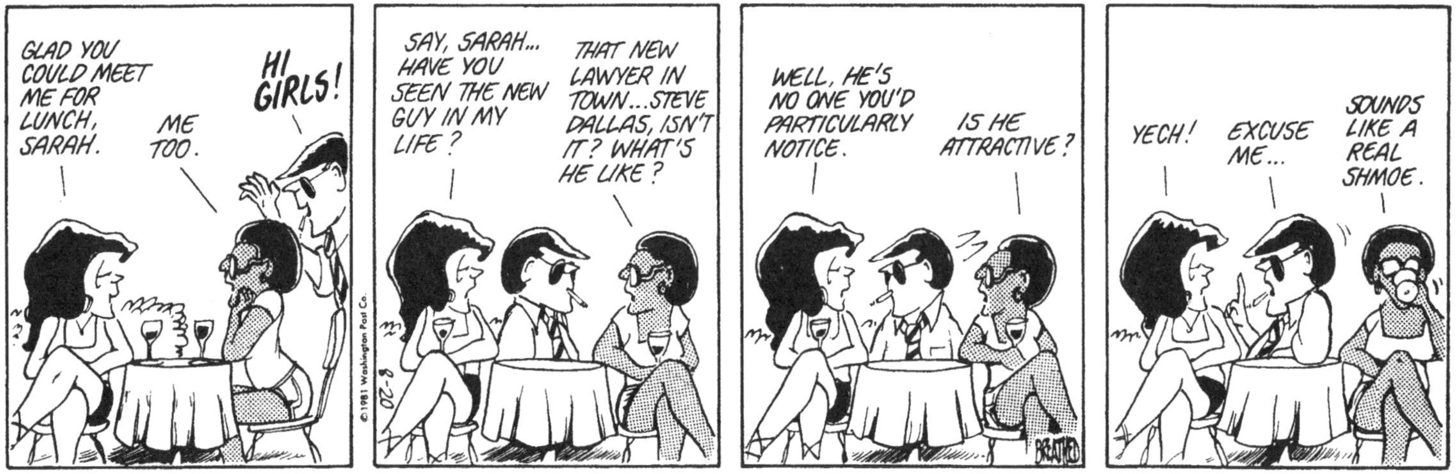
GLAD YOU COULD MEET ME FOR LUNCH, SARAH.
ME TOO.
HI GIRLS!
SAY, SARAH... HAVE YOU SEEN THE NEW GUY IN MY LIFE?
THAT NEW LAWYER IN TOWN...STEVE DALLAS, ISN'T IT? WHAT'S HE LIKE?
WELL, HE'S NO ONE YOU'D PARTICULARLY NOTICE.
IS HE ATTRACTIVE?
YECH!
EXCUSE ME...
SOUNDS LIKE A REAL SHMOE.
© 1981 Washington Post Co.
8-20
BREATHED

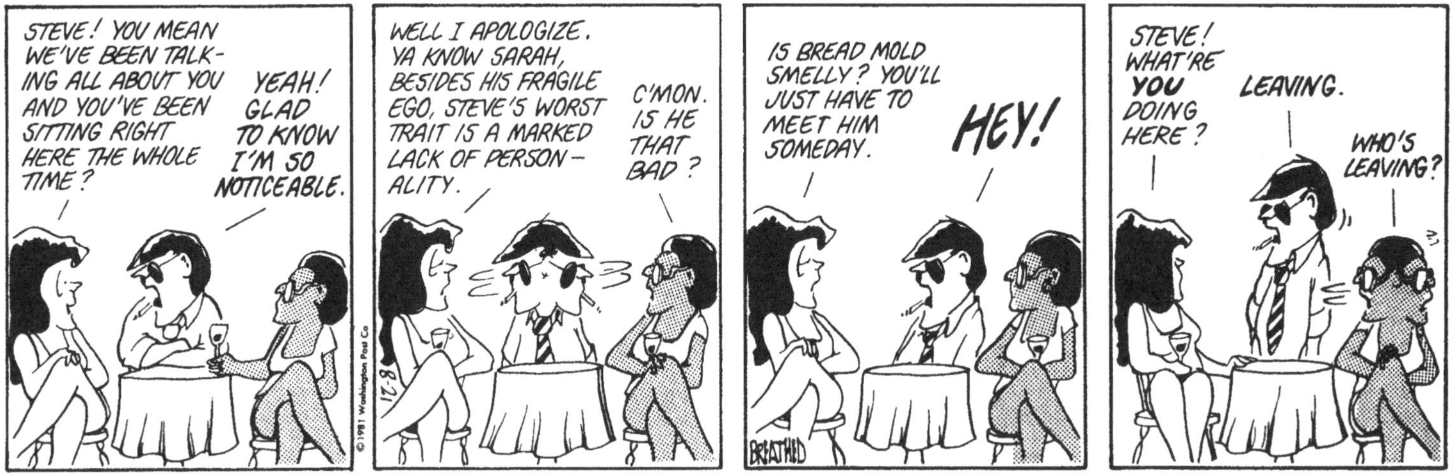
STEVE! YOU MEAN WE'VE BEEN TALKING ALL ABOUT YOU AND YOU'VE BEEN SITTING RIGHT HERE THE WHOLE TIME?
YEAH! GLAD TO KNOW I'M SO NOTICEABLE.
WELL I APOLOGIZE. YA KNOW SARAH, BESIDES HIS FRAGILE EGO, STEVE'S WORST TRAIT IS A MARKED LACK OF PERSONALITY.
C'MON. IS HE THAT BAD?
IS BREAD MOLD SMELLY? YOU'LL JUST HAVE TO MEET HIM SOMEDAY.
HEY!
STEVE! WHAT'RE YOU DOING HERE?
LEAVING.
WHO'S LEAVING?
© 1981 Washington Post Co.
8-21
BREATHED

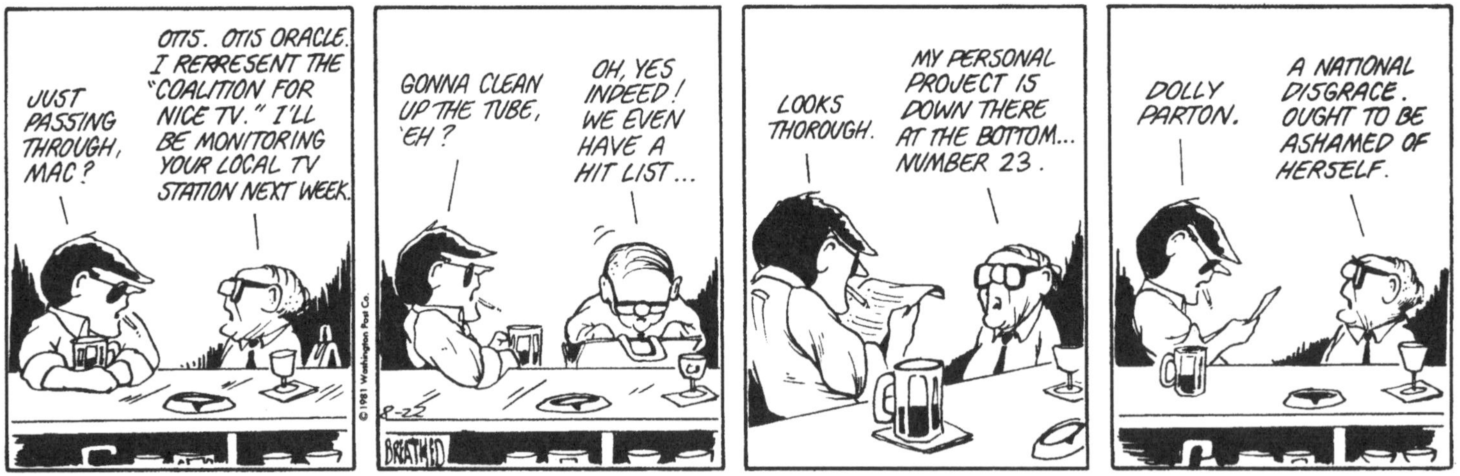
JUST PASSING THROUGH, MAC?
OTIS. OTIS ORACLE. I RERRESENT THE "COALITION FOR NICE TV." I'LL BE MONITORING YOUR LOCAL TV STATION NEXT WEEK.
GONNA CLEAN UP THE TUBE, 'EH?
OH, YES INDEED! WE EVEN HAVE A HIT LIST...
LOOKS THOROUGH.
MY PERSONAL PROJECT IS DOWN THERE AT THE BOTTOM... NUMBER 23.
DOLLY PARTON.
A NATIONAL DISGRACE. OUGHT TO BE ASHAMED OF HERSELF.
© 1981 Washington Post Co.
8-22
BREATHED

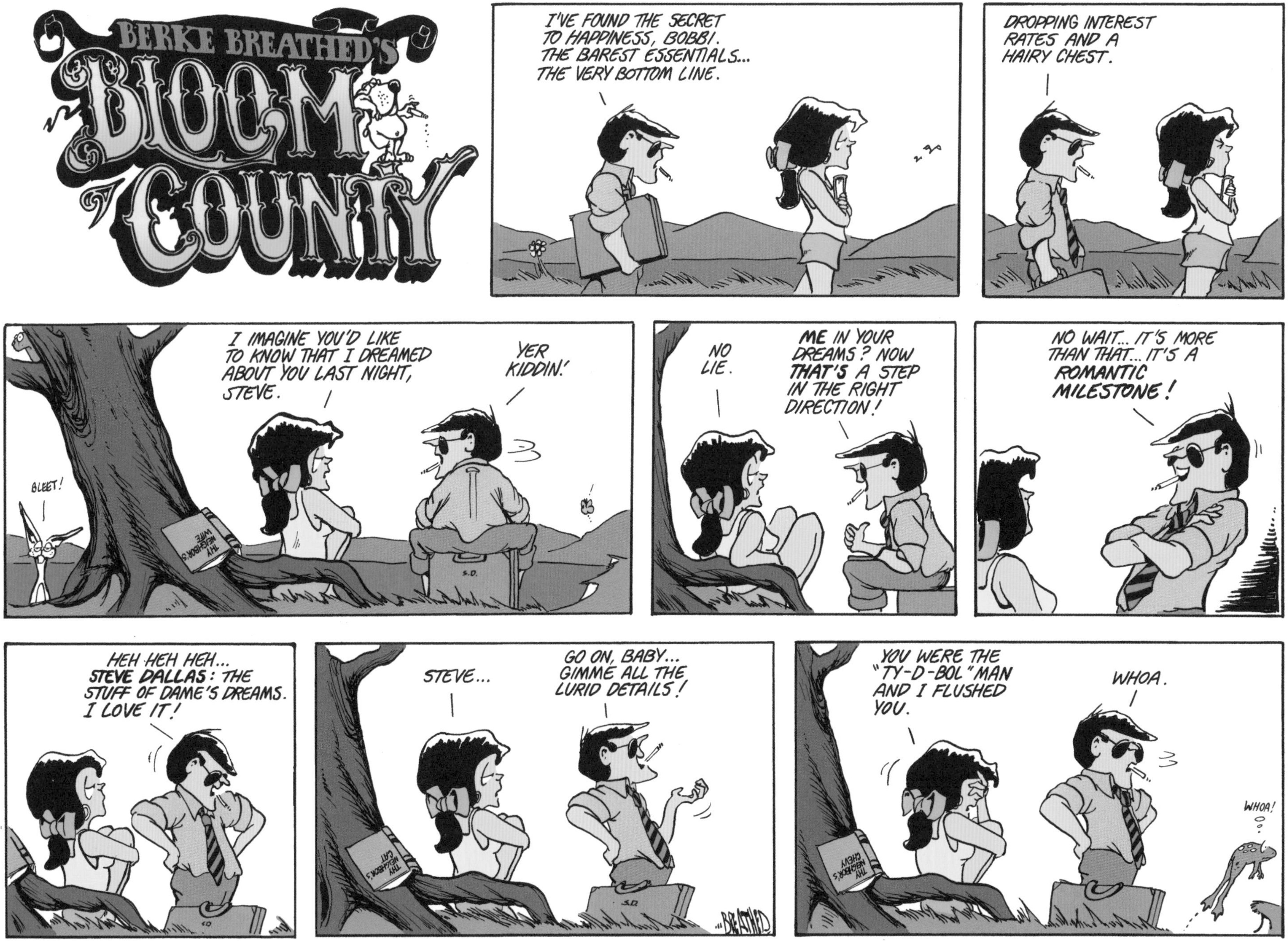
BERKE BREATHED'S
BLOOM COUNTY
I'VE FOUND THE SECRET TO HAPPINESS, BOBBI. THE BAREST ESSENTIALS... THE VERY BOTTOM LINE.
DROPPING INTEREST RATES AND A HAIRY CHEST.
I IMAGINE YOU'D LIKE TO KNOW THAT I DREAMED ABOUT YOU LAST NIGHT, STEVE.
YER KIDDIN'!
BLEET!
THY NEIGHBOR'S WIFE
S.D.
NO LIE.
ME IN YOUR DREAMS? NOW THAT'S A STEP IN THE RIGHT DIRECTION!
NO WAIT... IT'S MORE THAN THAT... IT'S A ROMANTIC MILESTONE!
HEH HEH HEH... STEVE DALLAS: THE STUFF OF DAME'S DREAMS. I LOVE IT!
STEVE...
GO ON, BABY... GIMME ALL THE LURID DETAILS!
THY NEIGHBOR'S CAT
S.D.
BREATHED
YOU WERE THE "TY-D-BOL" MAN AND I FLUSHED YOU.
WHOA.
THY NEIGHBOR'S CHEVY
WHOA!

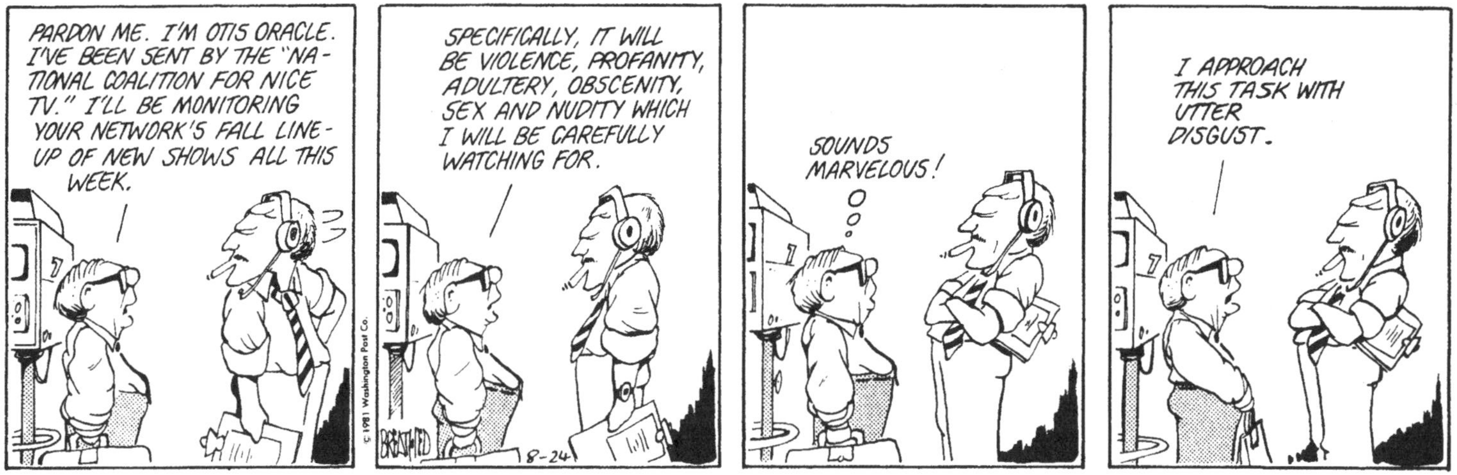
PARDON ME. I'M OTIS ORACLE. I'VE BEEN SENT BY THE "NATIONAL COALITION FOR NICE TV." I'LL BE MONITORING YOUR NETWORK'S FALL LINE-UP OF NEW SHOWS ALL THIS WEEK.
SPECIFICALLY, IT WILL BE VIOLENCE, PROFANITY, ADULTERY, OBSCENITY, SEX AND NUDITY WHICH I WILL BE CAREFULLY WATCHING FOR.
© 1981 Washington Post Co.
BREATHED
8-24
SOUNDS MARVELOUS!
I APPROACH THIS TASK WITH UTTER DISGUST.

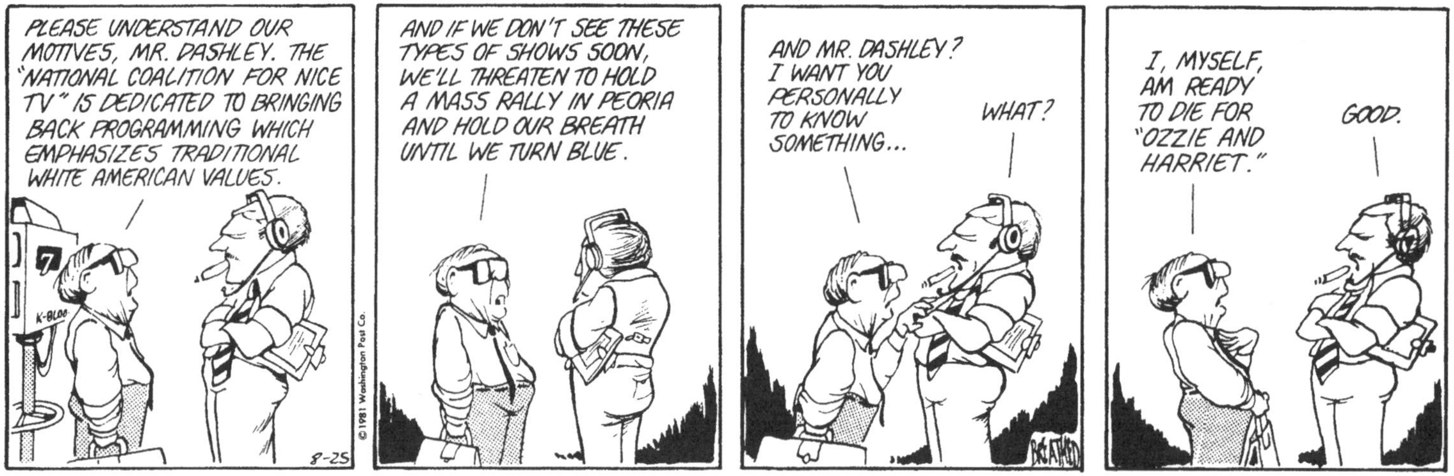
PLEASE UNDERSTAND OUR MOTIVES, MR. DASHLEY. THE "NATIONAL COALITION FOR NICE TV" IS DEDICATED TO BRINGING BACK PROGRAMMING WHICH EMPHASIZES TRADITIONAL WHITE AMERICAN VALUES.
7
8-25
© 1981 Washington Post Co.
AND IF WE DON'T SEE THESE TYPES OF SHOWS SOON, WE'LL THREATEN TO HOLD A MASS RALLY IN PEORIA AND HOLD OUR BREATH UNTIL WE TURN BLUE.
AND MR. DASHLEY? I WANT YOU PERSONALLY TO KNOW SOMETHING...
WHAT?
BREATHED
I, MYSELF, AM READY TO DIE FOR "OZZIE AND HARRIET."
GOOD.

Ozzie and Harriet Nelson were the quintessential "white-bread" American television family from the early 1950s until the mid-1960s.

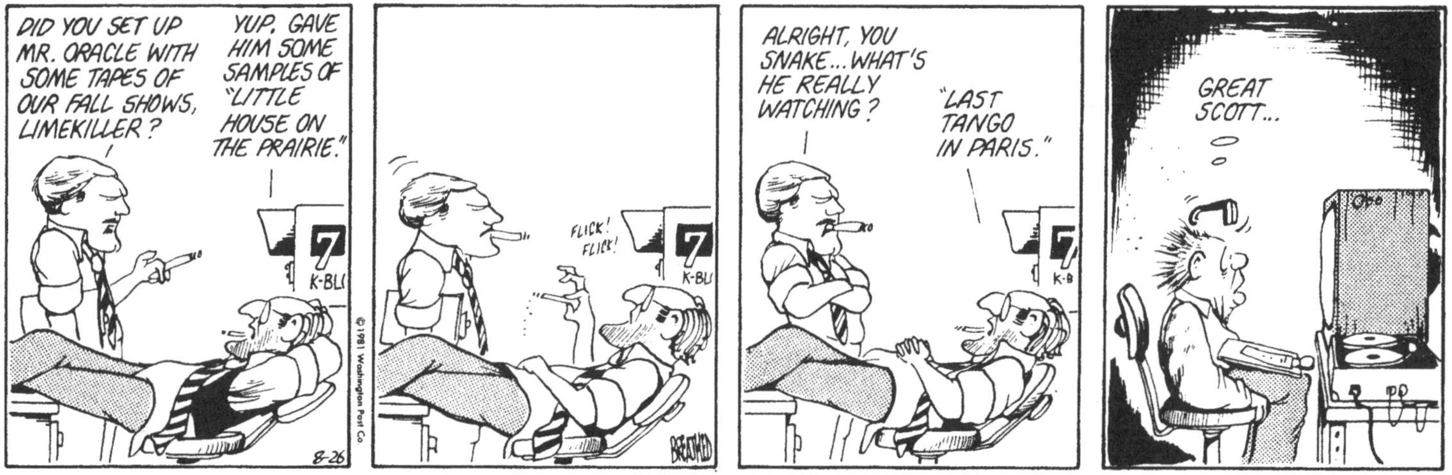
DID YOU SET UP MR. ORACLE WITH SOME TAPES OF OUR FALL SHOWS, LIMEKILLER?
YUP. GAVE HIM SOME SAMPLES OF "LITTLE HOUSE ON THE PRAIRIE."
7
8-26
© 1981 Washington Post Co.
FLICK! FLICK!
BREATHED
ALRIGHT, YOU SNAKE... WHAT'S HE REALLY WATCHING?
"LAST TANGO IN PARIS."
GREAT SCOTT...

Last Tango in Paris, a 1973 film starring Marlon Brando, set off a storm of controversy because of its frank portrayals of sex and violence. It is one of the few non-pornographic films of the era to receive an X rating.

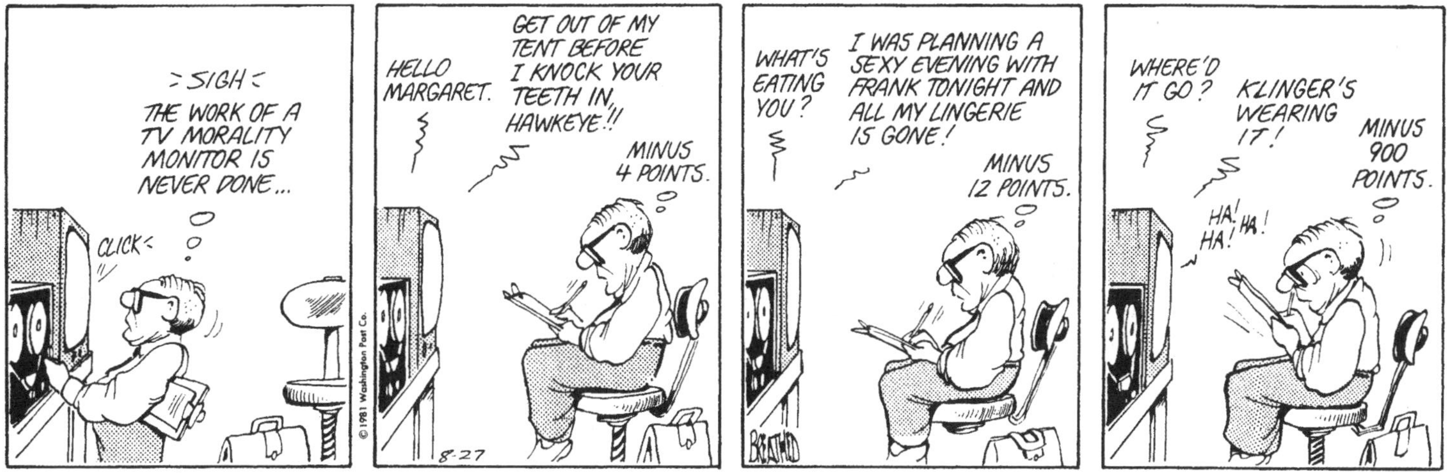
>SIGH<
THE WORK OF A TV MORALITY MONITOR IS NEVER DONE...
CLICK<
© 1981 Washington Post Co.
HELLO MARGARET.
GET OUT OF MY TENT BEFORE I KNOCK YOUR TEETH IN, HAWKEYE!!
MINUS 4 POINTS.
8-27
WHAT'S EATING YOU?
I WAS PLANNING A SEXY EVENING WITH FRANK TONIGHT AND ALL MY LINGERIE IS GONE!
MINUS 12 POINTS.
WHERE'D IT GO?
KLINGER'S WEARING IT!
HA! HA! HA!
MINUS 900 POINTS.

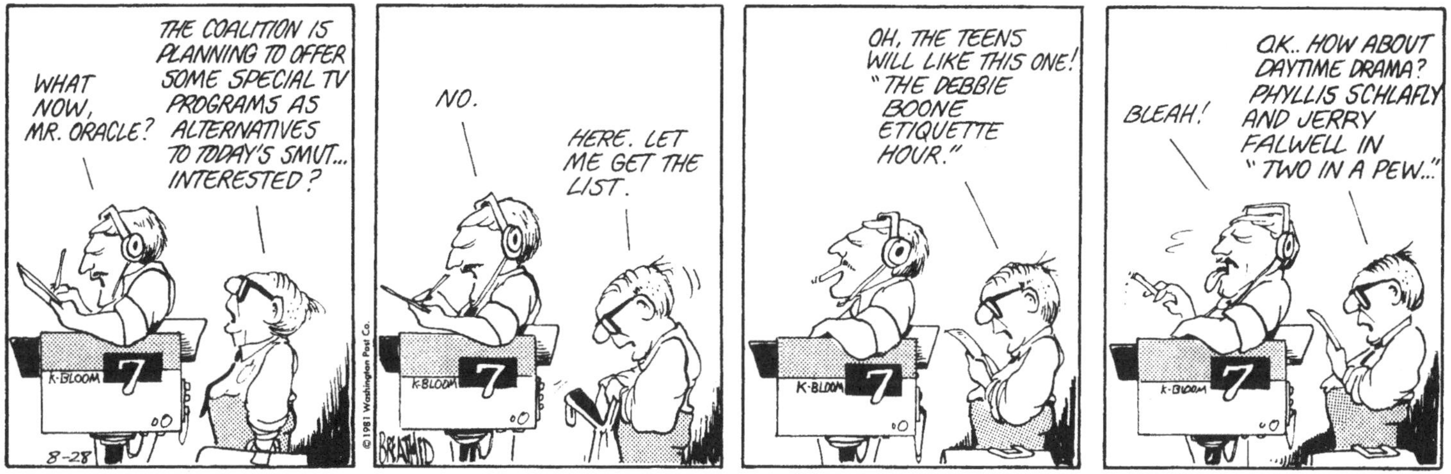
WHAT NOW, MR. ORACLE?
THE COALITION IS PLANNING TO OFFER SOME SPECIAL TV PROGRAMS AS ALTERNATIVES TO TODAY'S SMUT... INTERESTED?
K-BLOOM 7
8-28
© 1981 Washington Post Co.
NO.
HERE. LET ME GET THE LIST.
OH, THE TEENS WILL LIKE THIS ONE! "THE DEBBIE BOONE ETIQUETTE HOUR."
BLEAH!
O.K.. HOW ABOUT DAYTIME DRAMA? PHYLLIS SCHLAFLY AND JERRY FALWELL IN "TWO IN A PEW..."

Debbie Boone, daughter of Pat, is a singer best known for her late '70s hit, "You Light Up My Life."

Phyllis Schlafly is a conservative political consultant who earnestly opposed ratification of the Equal Rights Amendment.

Jerry Falwell was a televangelist and co-founder of the Moral Majority.

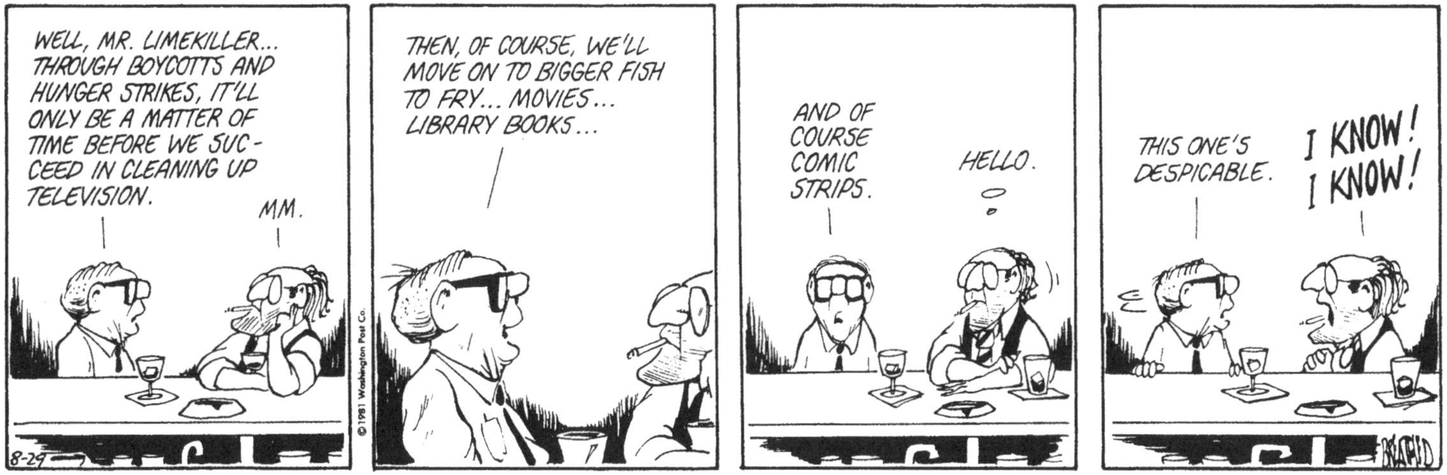
WELL, MR. LIMEKILLER... THROUGH BOYCOTTS AND HUNGER STRIKES, IT'LL ONLY BE A MATTER OF TIME BEFORE WE SUCCEED IN CLEANING UP TELEVISION.
MM.
8-29
© 1981 Washington Post Co.
THEN, OF COURSE, WE'LL MOVE ON TO BIGGER FISH TO FRY... MOVIES... LIBRARY BOOKS...
AND OF COURSE COMIC STRIPS.
HELLO.
THIS ONE'S DESPICABLE.
I KNOW! I KNOW!

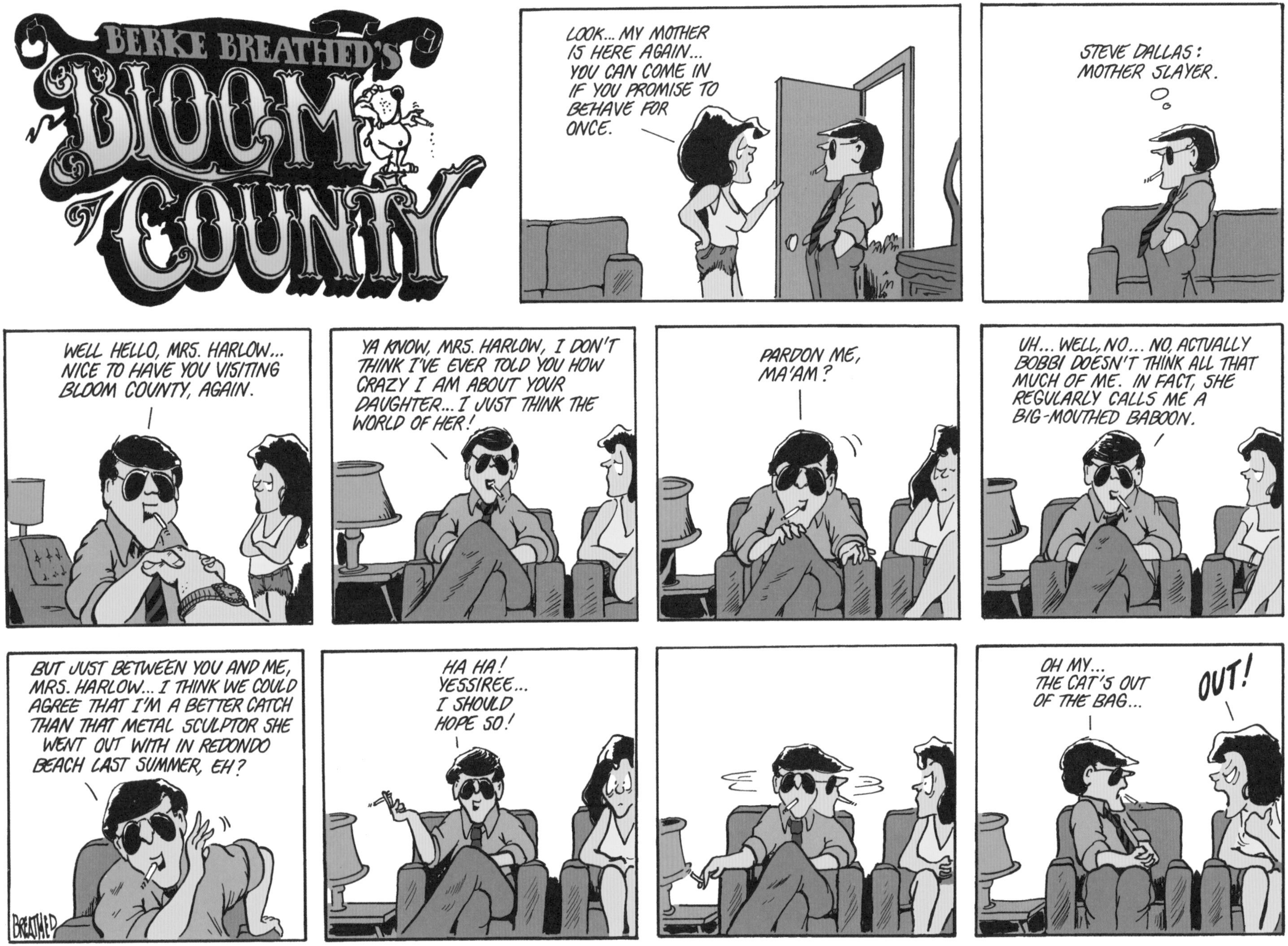
BERKE BREATHED'S
BLOOM COUNTY
LOOK... MY MOTHER IS HERE AGAIN... YOU CAN COME IN IF YOU PROMISE TO BEHAVE FOR ONCE.
STEVE DALLAS: MOTHER SLAYER.
WELL HELLO, MRS. HARLOW... NICE TO HAVE YOU VISITING BLOOM COUNTY, AGAIN.
YA KNOW, MRS. HARLOW, I DON'T THINK I'VE EVER TOLD YOU HOW CRAZY I AM ABOUT YOUR DAUGHTER... I JUST THINK THE WORLD OF HER!
PARDON ME, MA'AM?
UH... WELL, NO... NO, ACTUALLY BOBBI DOESN'T THINK ALL THAT MUCH OF ME. IN FACT, SHE REGULARLY CALLS ME A BIG-MOUTHED BABOON.
BUT JUST BETWEEN YOU AND ME, MRS. HARLOW... I THINK WE COULD AGREE THAT I'M A BETTER CATCH THAN THAT METAL SCULPTOR SHE WENT OUT WITH IN REDONDO BEACH LAST SUMMER, EH?
BREATHED
HA HA! YESSIREE... I SHOULD HOPE SO!
OH MY... THE CAT'S OUT OF THE BAG...
OUT!

 August 30, 1981

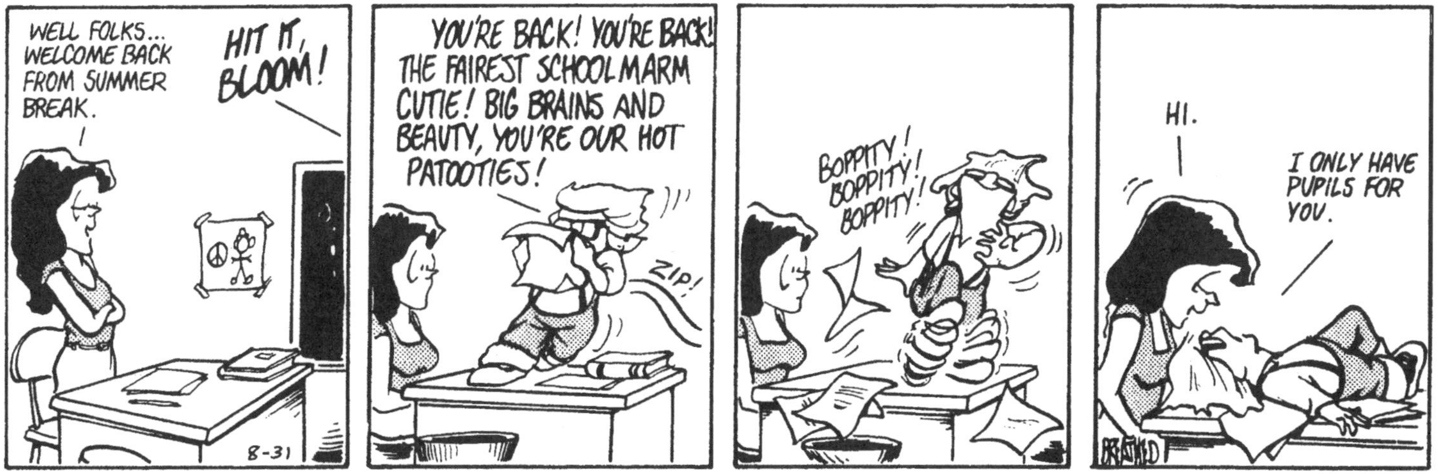
WELL FOLKS... WELCOME BACK FROM SUMMER BREAK.
HIT IT, BLOOM!
8-31
YOU'RE BACK! YOU'RE BACK! THE FAIREST SCHOOLMARM CUTIE! BIG BRAINS AND BEAUTY, YOU'RE OUR HOT PATOOTIES!
ZIP!
BOPPITY! BOPPITY! BOPPITY!
HI.
I ONLY HAVE PUPILS FOR YOU.
BREATHED

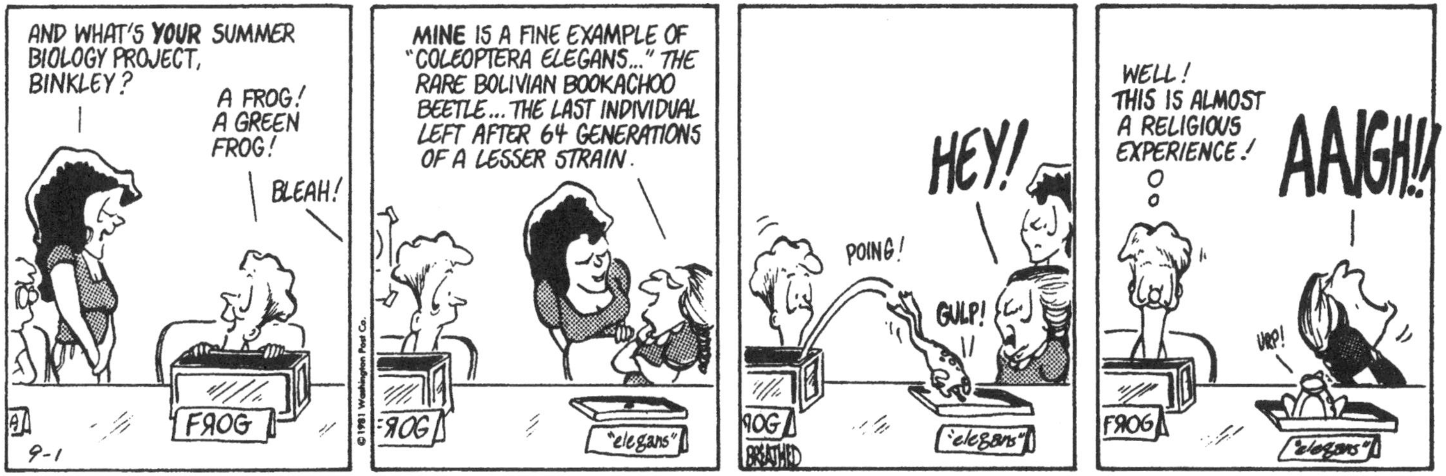
AND WHAT'S YOUR SUMMER BIOLOGY PROJECT, BINKLEY?
A FROG! A GREEN FROG!
BLEAH!
FROG
9-1
© 1981 Washington Post Co.
MINE IS A FINE EXAMPLE OF "COLEOPTERA ELEGANS..." THE RARE BOLIVIAN BOOKACHOO BEETLE... THE LAST INDIVIDUAL LEFT AFTER 64 GENERATIONS OF A LESSER STRAIN.
"elegans"
HEY!
POING!
GULP!
BREATHED
WELL! THIS IS ALMOST A RELIGIOUS EXPERIENCE!
AAIGH!!
URP!
FROG
"elegans"

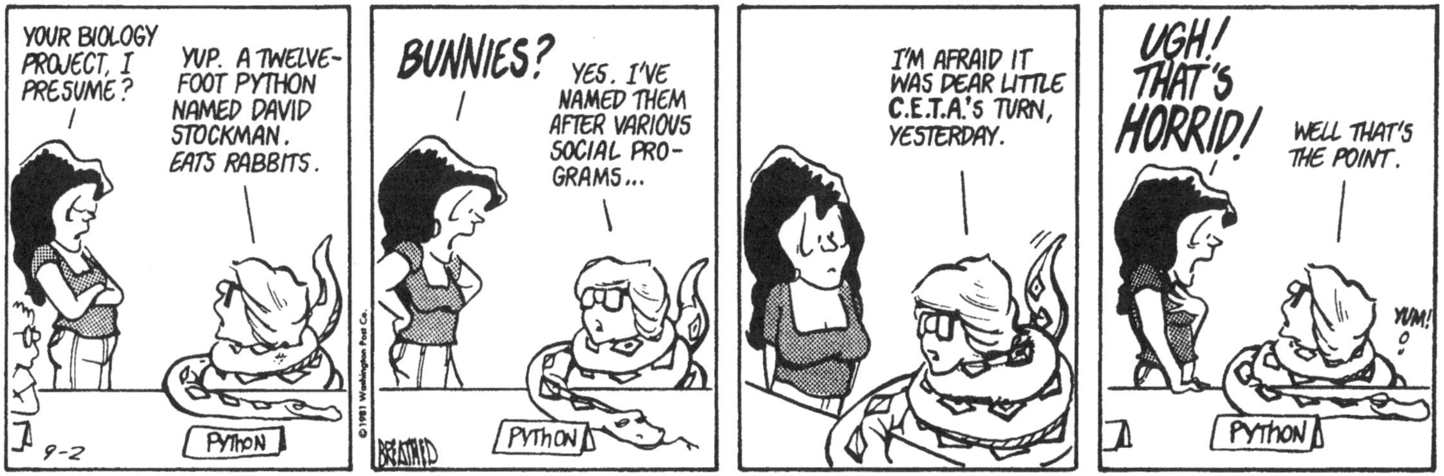
YOUR BIOLOGY PROJECT, I PRESUME?
YUP. A TWELVE-FOOT PYTHON NAMED DAVID STOCKMAN. EATS RABBITS.
PYTHON
9-2
© 1981 Washington Post Co.
BUNNIES?
YES. I'VE NAMED THEM AFTER VARIOUS SOCIAL PROGRAMS...
PYTHON
BREATHED
I'M AFRAID IT WAS DEAR LITTLE C.E.T.A.'S TURN, YESTERDAY.
UGH! THAT'S HORRID!
WELL THAT'S THE POINT.
YUM!
PYTHON

David Stockman was a Republican representative from Michigan until appointed head of the Office of Management and Budget during the Reagan administration.

CETA, the Comprehensive Employment and Training Act, was a federal program initiated to help unemployed workers find jobs.

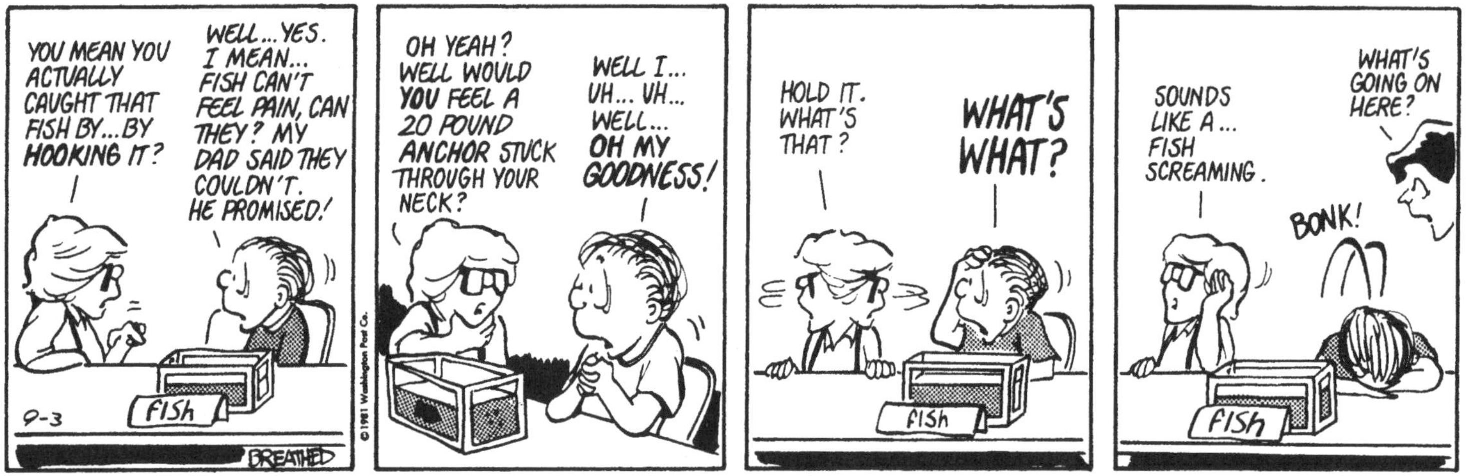
YOU MEAN YOU ACTUALLY CAUGHT THAT FISH BY...BY HOOKING IT?
WELL...YES. I MEAN... FISH CAN'T FEEL PAIN, CAN THEY? MY DAD SAID THEY COULDN'T. HE PROMISED!
FISH
9-3
BREATHED
OH YEAH? WELL WOULD YOU FEEL A 20 POUND ANCHOR STUCK THROUGH YOUR NECK?
WELL I... UH... UH... WELL... OH MY GOODNESS!
© 1981 Washington Post Co.
HOLD IT. WHAT'S THAT?
WHAT'S WHAT?
FISH
SOUNDS LIKE A... FISH SCREAMING.
WHAT'S GOING ON HERE?
BONK!
FISH

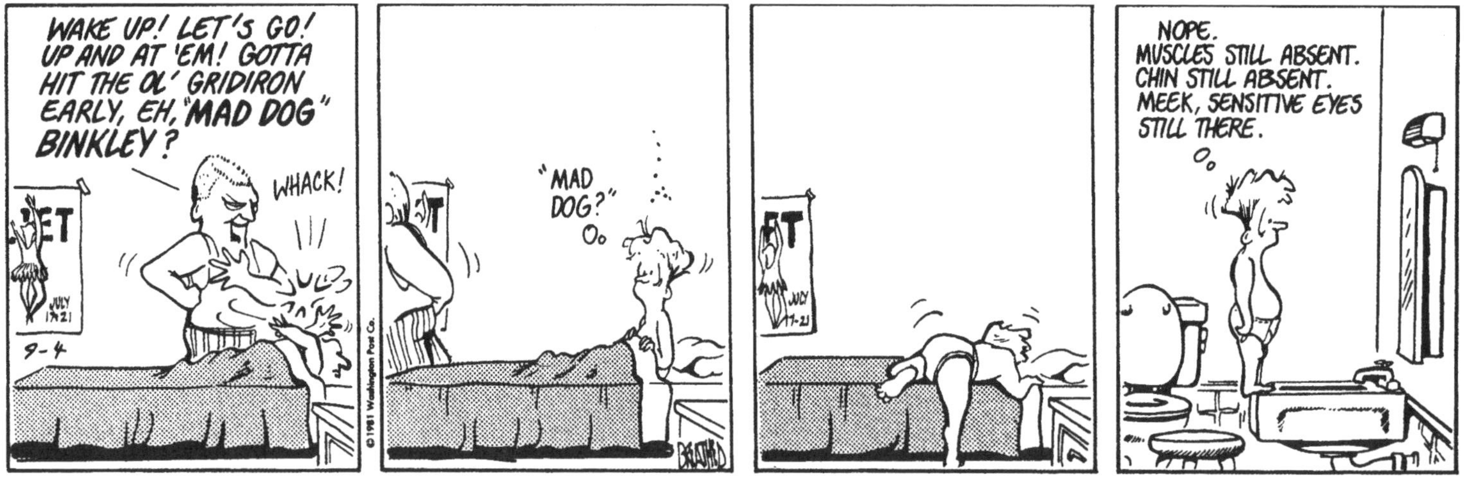
WAKE UP! LET'S GO! UP AND AT 'EM! GOTTA HIT THE OL' GRIDIRON EARLY, EH, "MAD DOG" BINKLEY?
WHACK!
9-4
"MAD DOG?"
© 1981 Washington Post Co.
BREATHED
NOPE. MUSCLES STILL ABSENT. CHIN STILL ABSENT. MEEK, SENSITIVE EYES STILL THERE.

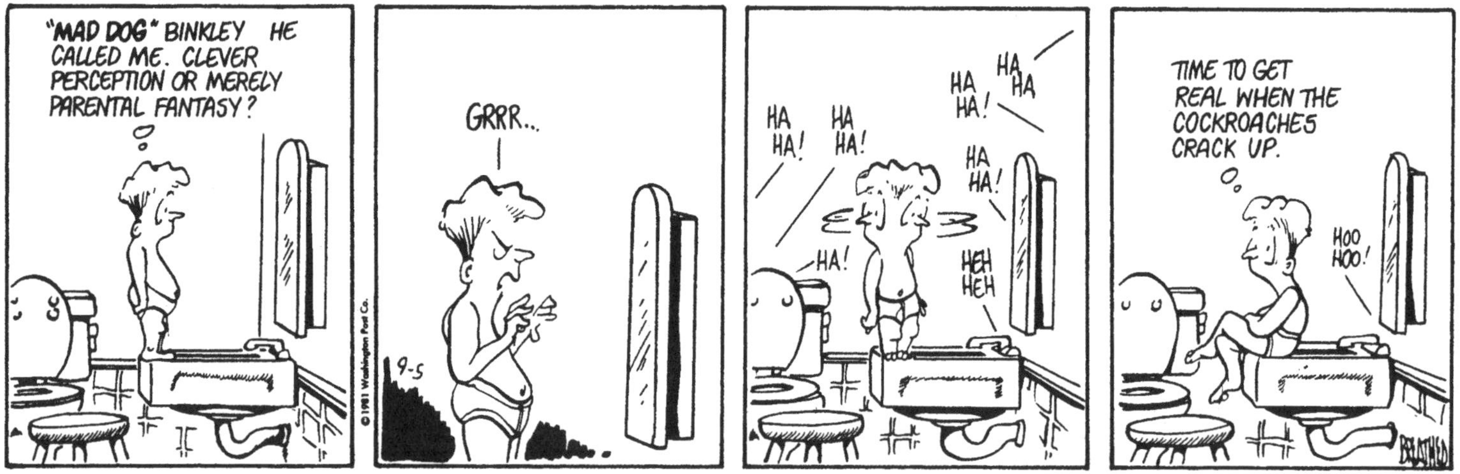
"MAD DOG" BINKLEY HE CALLED ME. CLEVER PERCEPTION OR MERELY PARENTAL FANTASY?
GRRR...
9-5
© 1981 Washington Post Co.
HA HA! HA HA! HA HA! HA HA HA HA! HA! HEH HEH
TIME TO GET REAL WHEN THE COCKROACHES CRACK UP.
HOO HOO!
BREATHED

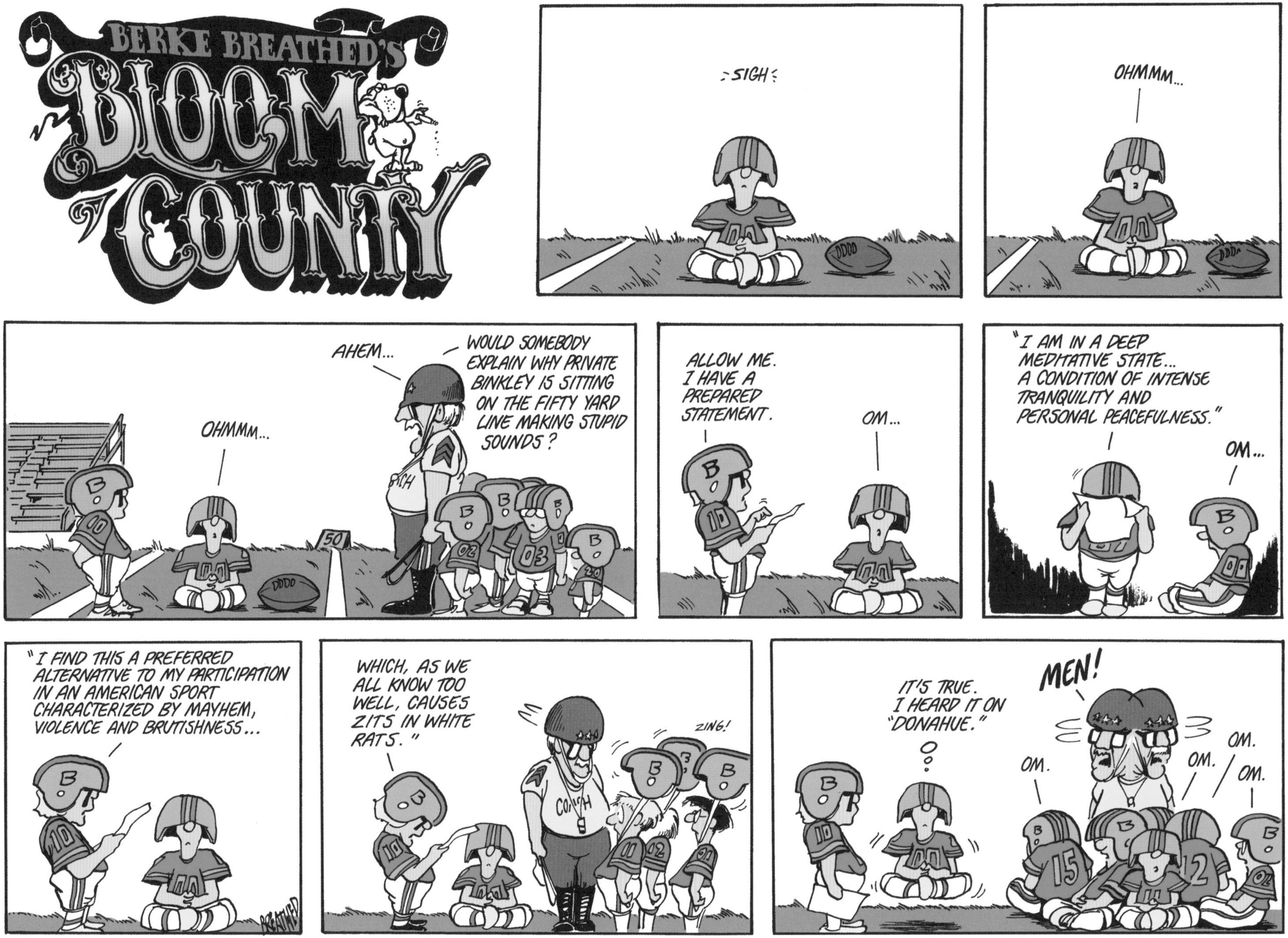
BERKE BREATHED'S
BLOOM COUNTY
SIGH
OHMMM...
OHMMM...
AHEM...
WOULD SOMEBODY EXPLAIN WHY PRIVATE BINKLEY IS SITTING ON THE FIFTY YARD LINE MAKING STUPID SOUNDS?
ALLOW ME. I HAVE A PREPARED STATEMENT.
OM...
"I AM IN A DEEP MEDITATIVE STATE... A CONDITION OF INTENSE TRANQUILITY AND PERSONAL PEACEFULNESS."
OM...
"I FIND THIS A PREFERRED ALTERNATIVE TO MY PARTICIPATION IN AN AMERICAN SPORT CHARACTERIZED BY MAYHEM, VIOLENCE AND BRUTISHNESS...
WHICH, AS WE ALL KNOW TOO WELL, CAUSES ZITS IN WHITE RATS."
ZING!
IT'S TRUE. I HEARD IT ON "DONAHUE."
MEN!
OM.
OM.
OM.
OM.

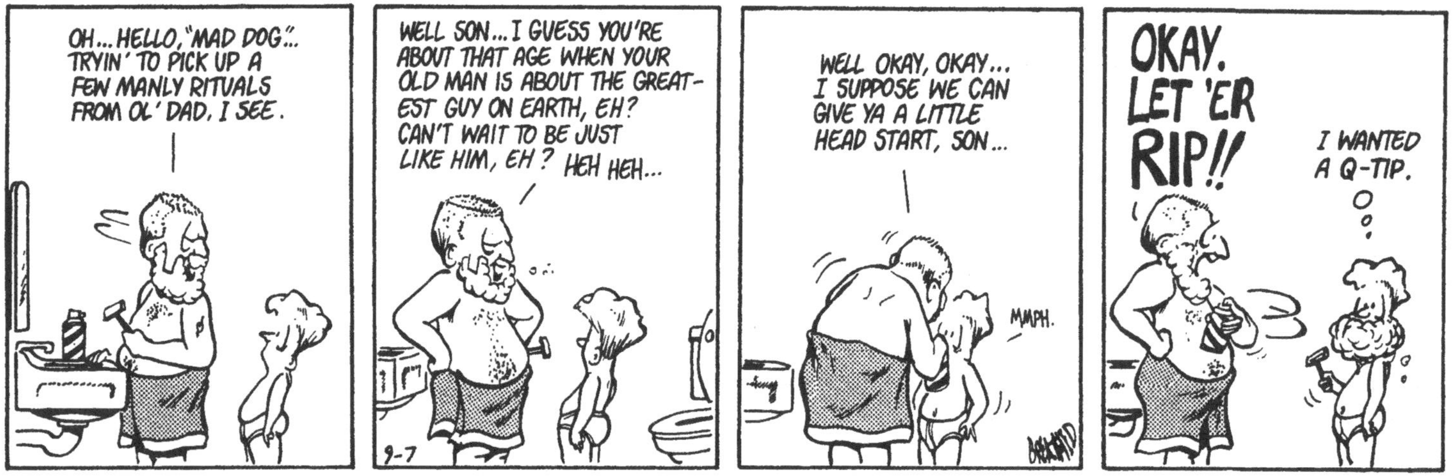
OH... HELLO, "MAD DOG"... TRYIN' TO PICK UP A FEW MANLY RITUALS FROM OL' DAD, I SEE.
WELL SON... I GUESS YOU'RE ABOUT THAT AGE WHEN YOUR OLD MAN IS ABOUT THE GREATEST GUY ON EARTH, EH? CAN'T WAIT TO BE JUST LIKE HIM, EH?
HEH HEH...
9-7
WELL OKAY, OKAY... I SUPPOSE WE CAN GIVE YA A LITTLE HEAD START, SON...
MMPH.
OKAY. LET 'ER RIP!!
I WANTED A Q-TIP.

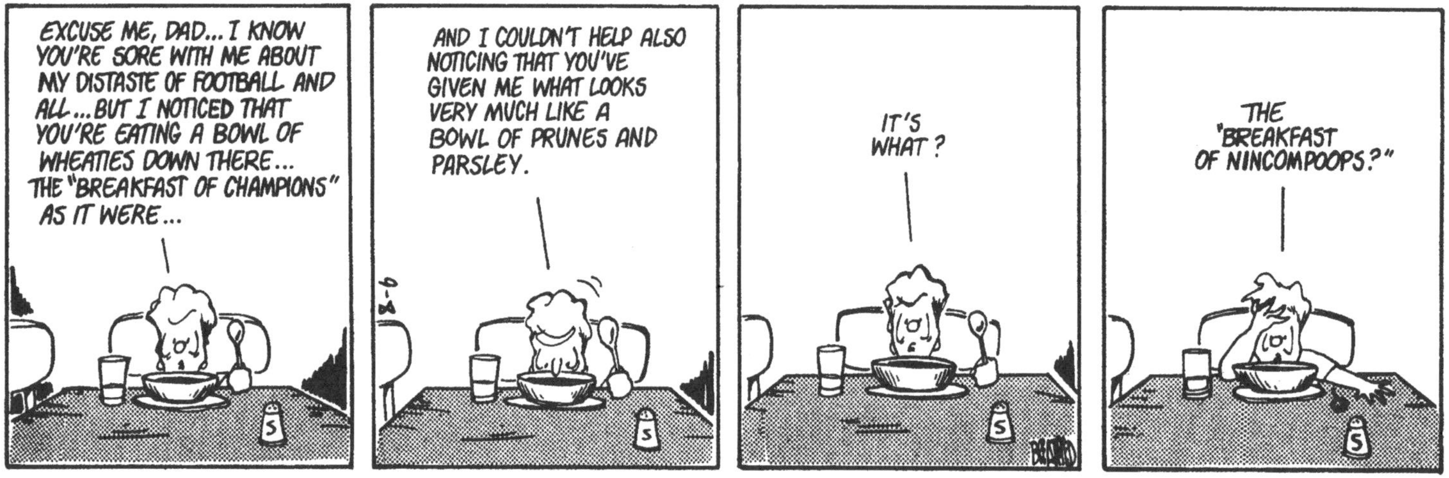
EXCUSE ME, DAD... I KNOW YOU'RE SORE WITH ME ABOUT MY DISTASTE OF FOOTBALL AND ALL... BUT I NOTICED THAT YOU'RE EATING A BOWL OF WHEATIES DOWN THERE... THE "BREAKFAST OF CHAMPIONS" AS IT WERE...
AND I COULDN'T HELP ALSO NOTICING THAT YOU'VE GIVEN ME WHAT LOOKS VERY MUCH LIKE A BOWL OF PRUNES AND PARSLEY.
IT'S WHAT?
THE "BREAKFAST OF NINCOMPOOPS?"

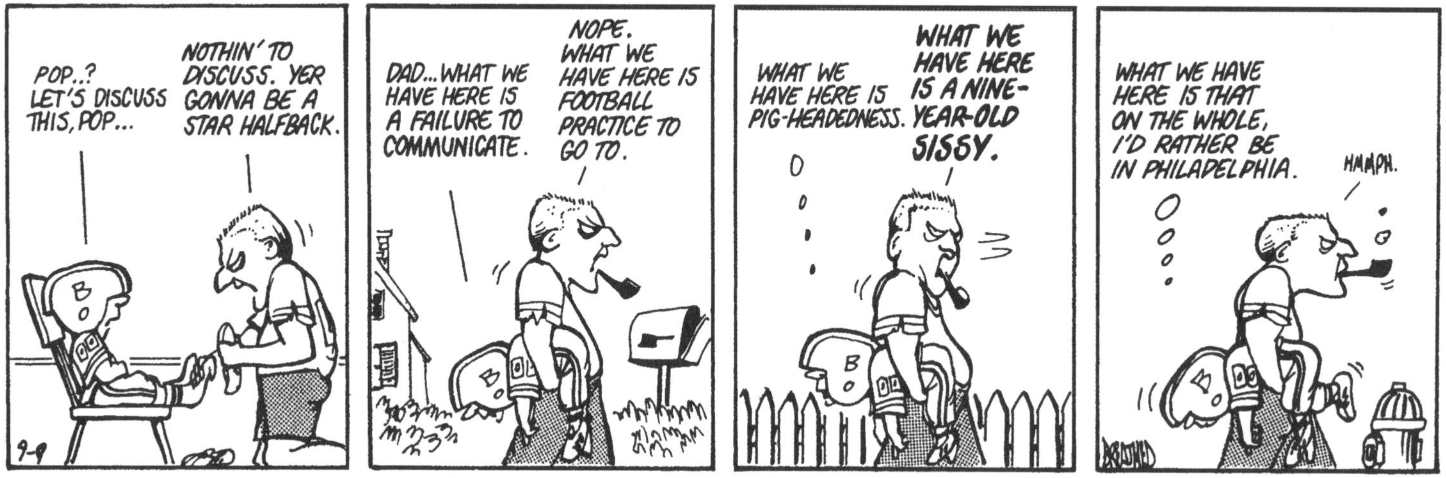
POP..? LET'S DISCUSS THIS, POP...
NOTHIN' TO DISCUSS. YER GONNA BE A STAR HALFBACK.
9-9
DAD... WHAT WE HAVE HERE IS A FAILURE TO COMMUNICATE.
NOPE. WHAT WE HAVE HERE IS FOOTBALL PRACTICE TO GO TO.
WHAT WE HAVE HERE IS PIG-HEADEDNESS.
WHAT WE HAVE HERE IS A NINE-YEAR-OLD SISSY.
WHAT WE HAVE HERE IS THAT ON THE WHOLE, I'D RATHER BE IN PHILADELPHIA.
HMMPH.

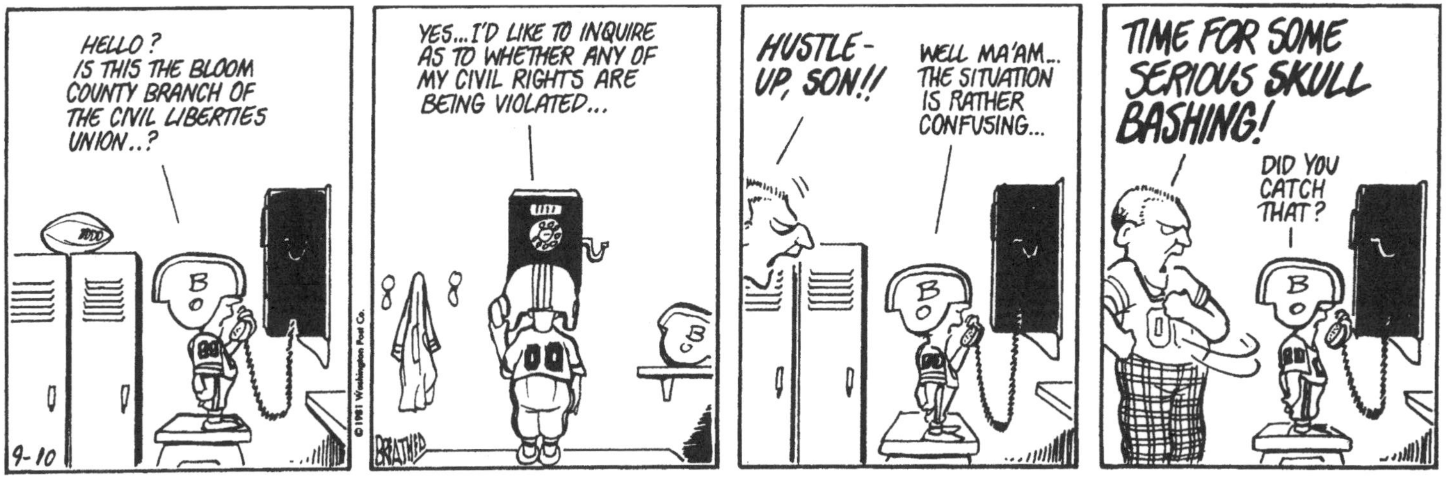
HELLO? IS THIS THE BLOOM COUNTY BRANCH OF THE CIVIL LIBERTIES UNION..?
9-10
YES...I'D LIKE TO INQUIRE AS TO WHETHER ANY OF MY CIVIL RIGHTS ARE BEING VIOLATED...
© 1981 Washington Post Co.
BREATHED
HUSTLE-UP, SON!!
WELL MA'AM... THE SITUATION IS RATHER CONFUSING...
TIME FOR SOME SERIOUS SKULL BASHING!
DID YOU CATCH THAT?

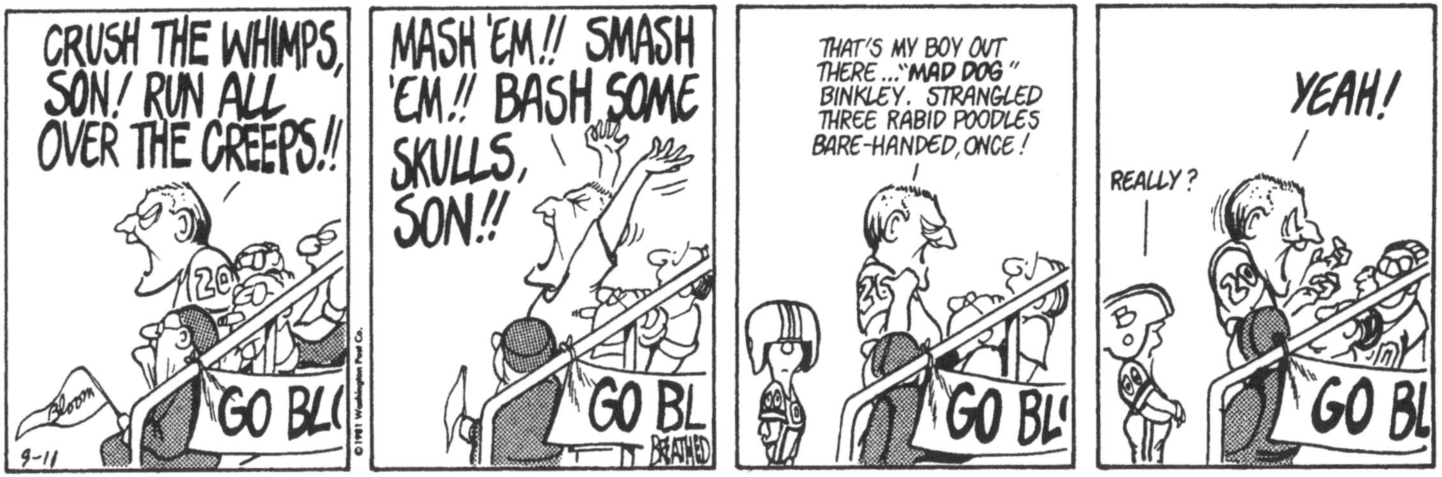
CRUSH THE WHIMPS, SON! RUN ALL OVER THE CREEPS!!
9-11
GO BL
MASH 'EM!! SMASH 'EM!! BASH SOME SKULLS, SON!!
© 1981 Washington Post Co.
GO BL
BREATHED
THAT'S MY BOY OUT THERE..."MAD DOG" BINKLEY. STRANGLED THREE RABID POODLES BARE-HANDED, ONCE!
GO BL
REALLY?
YEAH!
GO BL

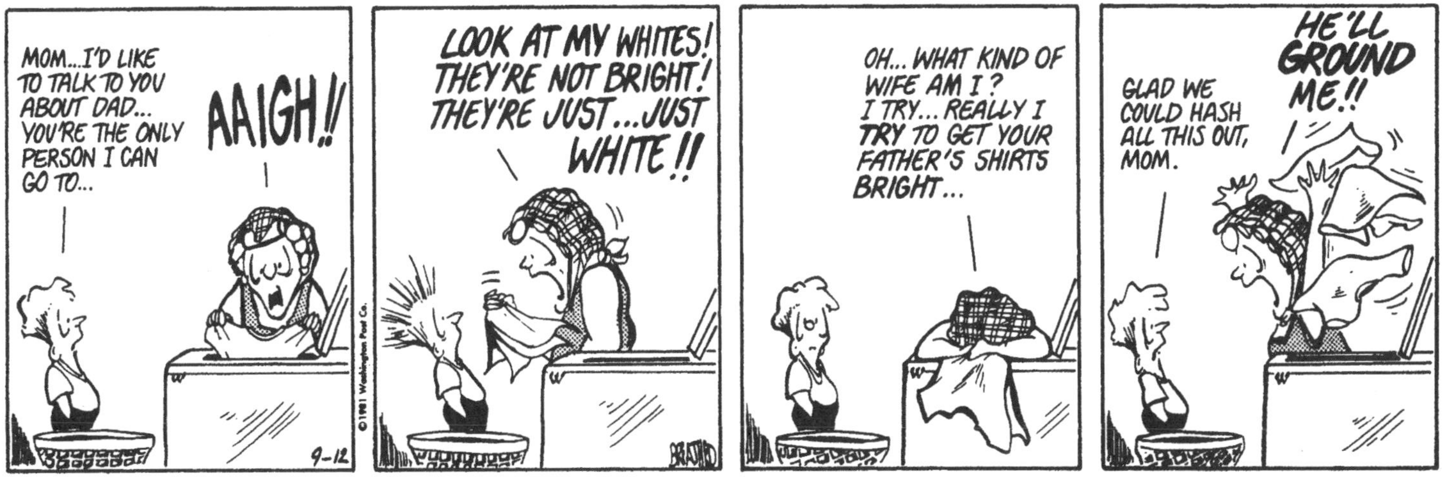
MOM...I'D LIKE TO TALK TO YOU ABOUT DAD... YOU'RE THE ONLY PERSON I CAN GO TO...
AAIGH!!
9-12
LOOK AT MY WHITES! THEY'RE NOT BRIGHT! THEY'RE JUST...JUST WHITE!!
© 1981 Washington Post Co.
BREATHED
OH... WHAT KIND OF WIFE AM I? I TRY... REALLY I TRY TO GET YOUR FATHER'S SHIRTS BRIGHT...
GLAD WE COULD HASH ALL THIS OUT, MOM.
HE'LL GROUND ME!!

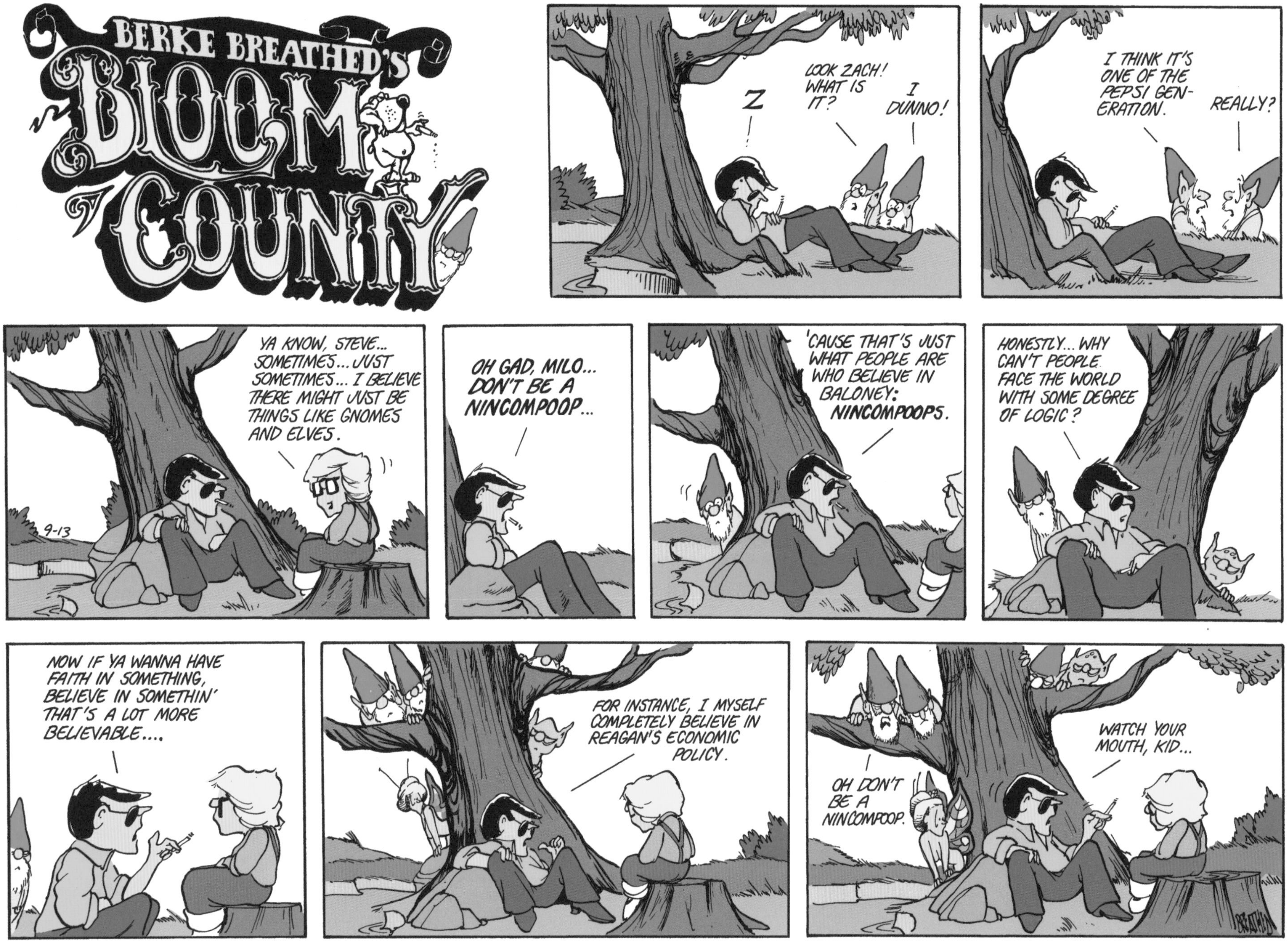
BERKE BREATHED'S
BLOOM COUNTY
Z
LOOK ZACH! WHAT IS IT?
I DUNNO!
I THINK IT'S ONE OF THE PEPSI GEN-ERATION.
REALLY?
9-13
YA KNOW, STEVE... SOMETIMES... JUST SOMETIMES... I BELIEVE THERE MIGHT JUST BE THINGS LIKE GNOMES AND ELVES.
OH GAD, MILO... DON'T BE A NINCOMPOOP...
'CAUSE THAT'S JUST WHAT PEOPLE ARE WHO BELIEVE IN BALONEY: NINCOMPOOPS.
HONESTLY... WHY CAN'T PEOPLE FACE THE WORLD WITH SOME DEGREE OF LOGIC?
NOW IF YA WANNA HAVE FAITH IN SOMETHING, BELIEVE IN SOMETHIN' THAT'S A LOT MORE BELIEVABLE....
FOR INSTANCE, I MYSELF COMPLETELY BELIEVE IN REAGAN'S ECONOMIC POLICY.
OH DON'T BE A NINCOMPOOP.
WATCH YOUR MOUTH, KID...
BREATHED

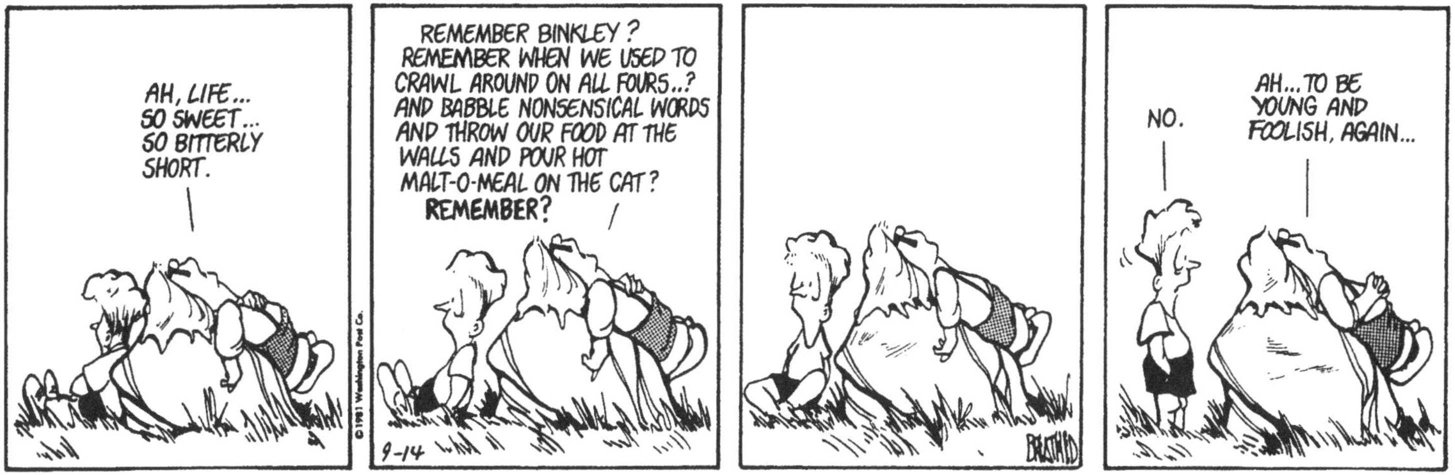
AH, LIFE... SO SWEET... SO BITTERLY SHORT.
9-14
REMEMBER BINKLEY? REMEMBER WHEN WE USED TO CRAWL AROUND ON ALL FOURS..? AND BABBLE NONSENSICAL WORDS AND THROW OUR FOOD AT THE WALLS AND POUR HOT MALT-O-MEAL ON THE CAT? REMEMBER?
NO.
AH...TO BE YOUNG AND FOOLISH, AGAIN...

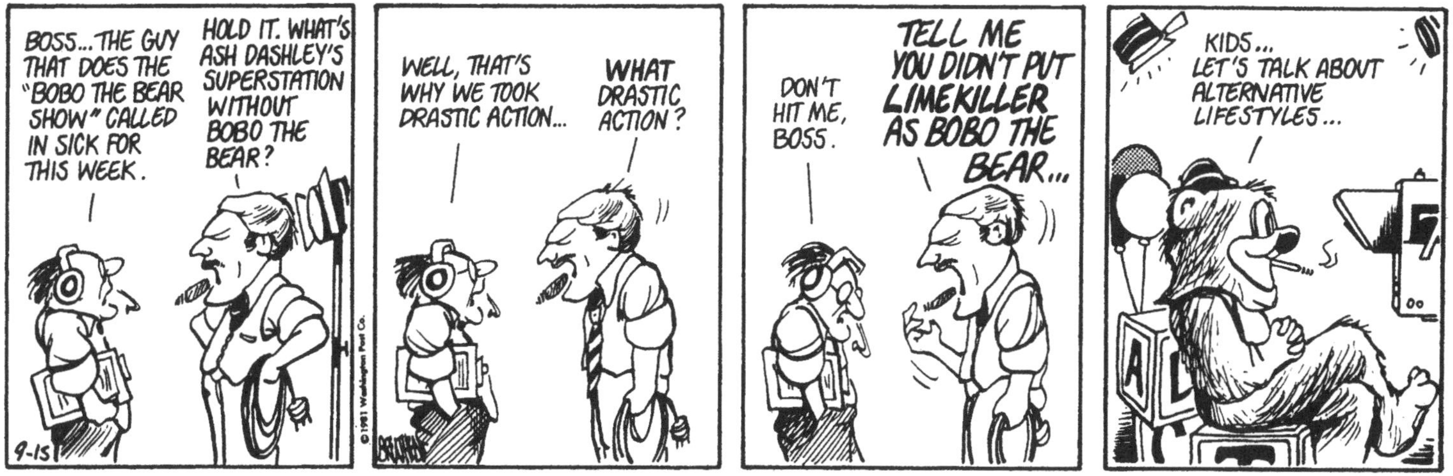
BOSS... THE GUY THAT DOES THE "BOBO THE BEAR SHOW" CALLED IN SICK FOR THIS WEEK.
HOLD IT. WHAT'S ASH DASHLEY'S SUPERSTATION WITHOUT BOBO THE BEAR?
9-15
WELL, THAT'S WHY WE TOOK DRASTIC ACTION...
WHAT DRASTIC ACTION?
DON'T HIT ME, BOSS.
TELL ME YOU DIDN'T PUT LIMEKILLER AS BOBO THE BEAR...
KIDS... LET'S TALK ABOUT ALTERNATIVE LIFESTYLES...

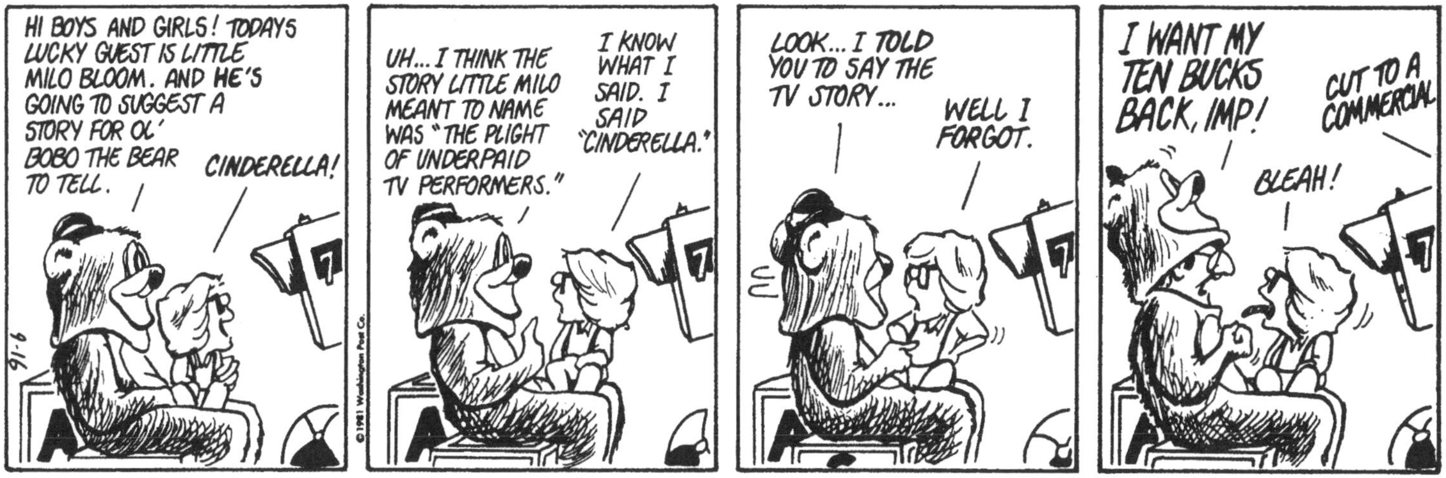
HI BOYS AND GIRLS! TODAYS LUCKY GUEST IS LITTLE MILO BLOOM. AND HE'S GOING TO SUGGEST A STORY FOR OL' BOBO THE BEAR TO TELL.
CINDERELLA!
9-16
UH... I THINK THE STORY LITTLE MILO MEANT TO NAME WAS "THE PLIGHT OF UNDERPAID TV PERFORMERS."
I KNOW WHAT I SAID. I SAID "CINDERELLA."
LOOK... I TOLD YOU TO SAY THE TV STORY...
WELL I FORGOT.
I WANT MY TEN BUCKS BACK, IMP!
BLEAH!
CUT TO A COMMERCIAL

Founded in 1979 by Jerry Falwell, the Moral Majority was a right-wing Christian organization that opposed abortion rights, the ERA and homosexuality, while promoting "anti-family" censorship in the media.

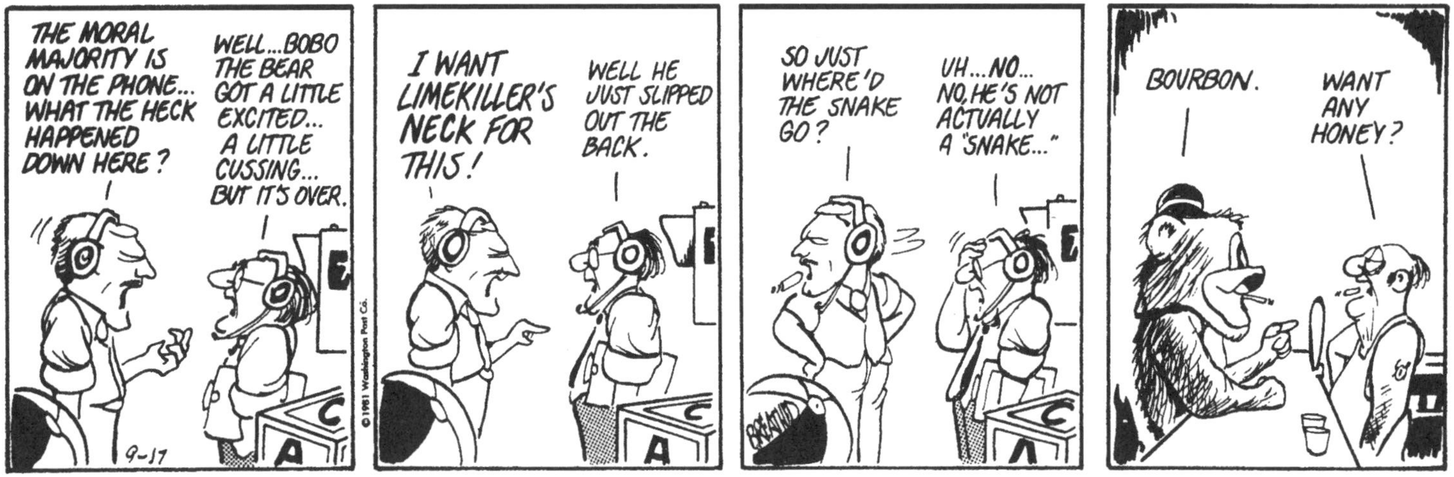
THE MORAL MAJORITY IS ON THE PHONE... WHAT THE HECK HAPPENED DOWN HERE?
WELL...BOBO THE BEAR GOT A LITTLE EXCITED... A LITTLE CUSSING... BUT IT'S OVER.
I WANT LIMEKILLER'S NECK FOR THIS!
WELL HE JUST SLIPPED OUT THE BACK.
SO JUST WHERE'D THE SNAKE GO?
UH...NO... NO, HE'S NOT ACTUALLY A "SNAKE..."
BOURBON.
WANT ANY HONEY?
9-17

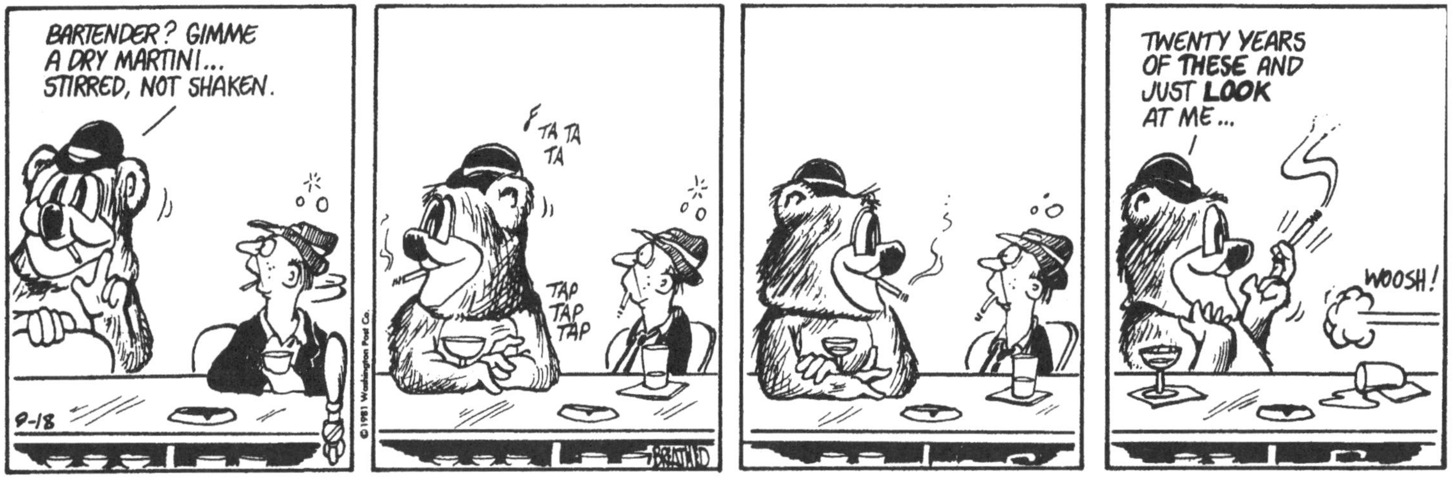
BARTENDER? GIMME A DRY MARTINI... STIRRED, NOT SHAKEN.
TA TA TA
TAP TAP TAP
TWENTY YEARS OF THESE AND JUST LOOK AT ME...
WOOSH!
9-18

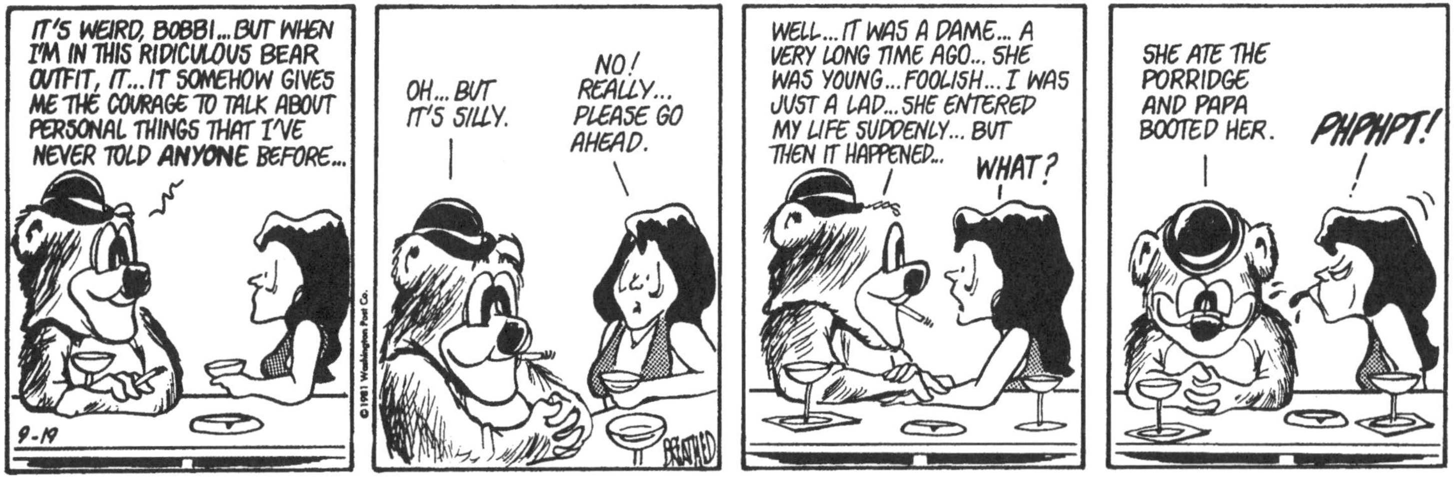
IT'S WEIRD, BOBBI...BUT WHEN I'M IN THIS RIDICULOUS BEAR OUTFIT, IT...IT SOMEHOW GIVES ME THE COURAGE TO TALK ABOUT PERSONAL THINGS THAT I'VE NEVER TOLD ANYONE BEFORE...
OH... BUT IT'S SILLY.
NO! REALLY... PLEASE GO AHEAD.
WELL... IT WAS A DAME... A VERY LONG TIME AGO... SHE WAS YOUNG...FOOLISH... I WAS JUST A LAD...SHE ENTERED MY LIFE SUDDENLY... BUT THEN IT HAPPENED...
WHAT?
SHE ATE THE PORRIDGE AND PAPA BOOTED HER.
PHPHPT!
9-19

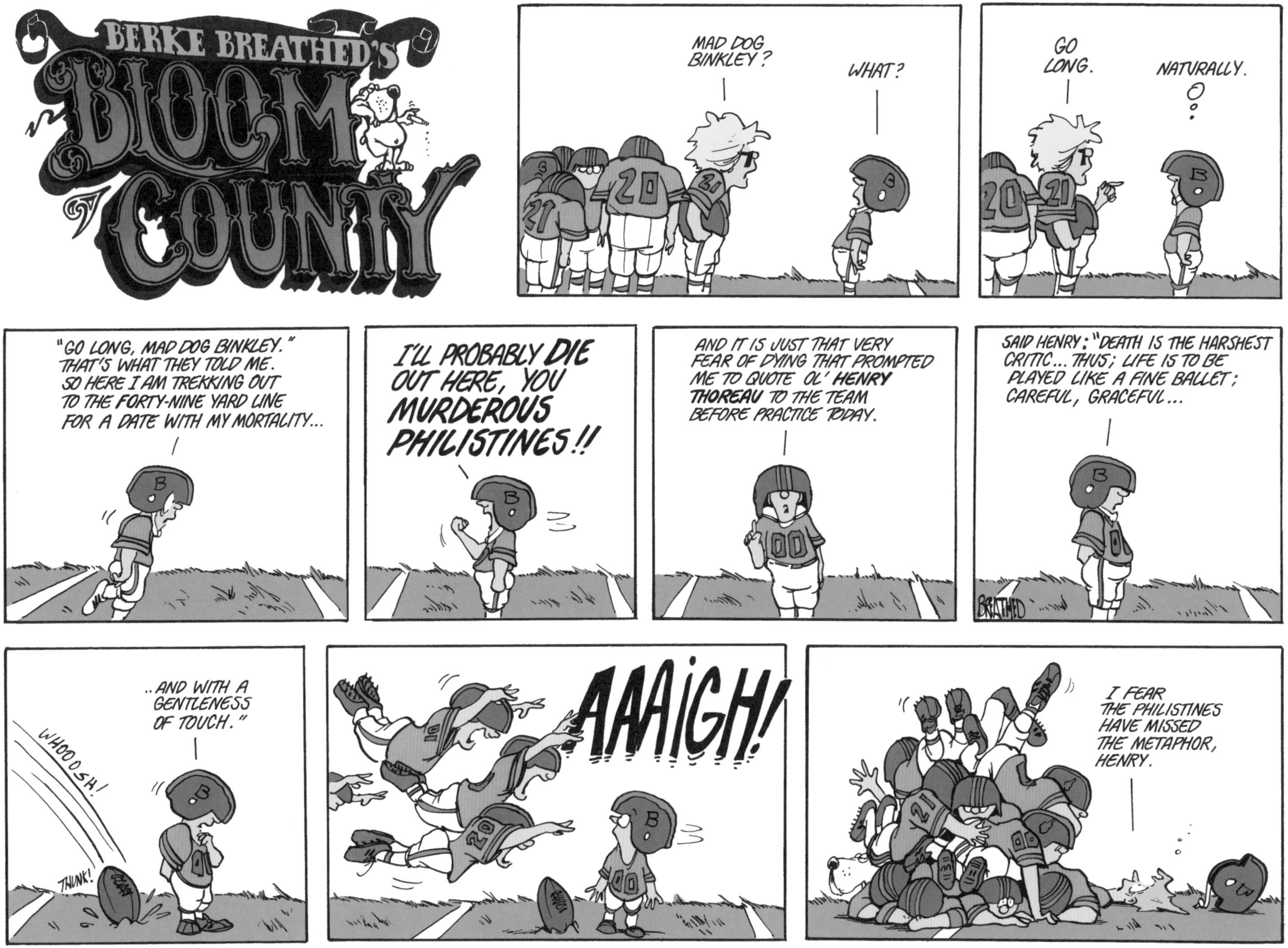
BERKE BREATHED'S
BLOOM COUNTY
MAD DOG BINKLEY?
WHAT?
GO LONG.
NATURALLY.
"GO LONG, MAD DOG BINKLEY." THAT'S WHAT THEY TOLD ME. SO HERE I AM TREKKING OUT TO THE FORTY-NINE YARD LINE FOR A DATE WITH MY MORTALITY...
I'LL PROBABLY DIE OUT HERE, YOU MURDEROUS PHILISTINES!!
AND IT IS JUST THAT VERY FEAR OF DYING THAT PROMPTED ME TO QUOTE 'OL' HENRY THOREAU TO THE TEAM BEFORE PRACTICE TODAY.
SAID HENRY: "DEATH IS THE HARSHEST CRITIC... THUS; LIFE IS TO BE PLAYED LIKE A FINE BALLET; CAREFUL, GRACEFUL...
BREATHED
..AND WITH A GENTLENESS OF TOUCH."
WHOOOSH!
THUNK!
AAAIGH!
I FEAR THE PHILISTINES HAVE MISSED THE METAPHOR, HENRY.

Henry Thoreau, famed 19th century philosopher and writer, best known for his novel, *Walden*, espousing the simple joys of life.

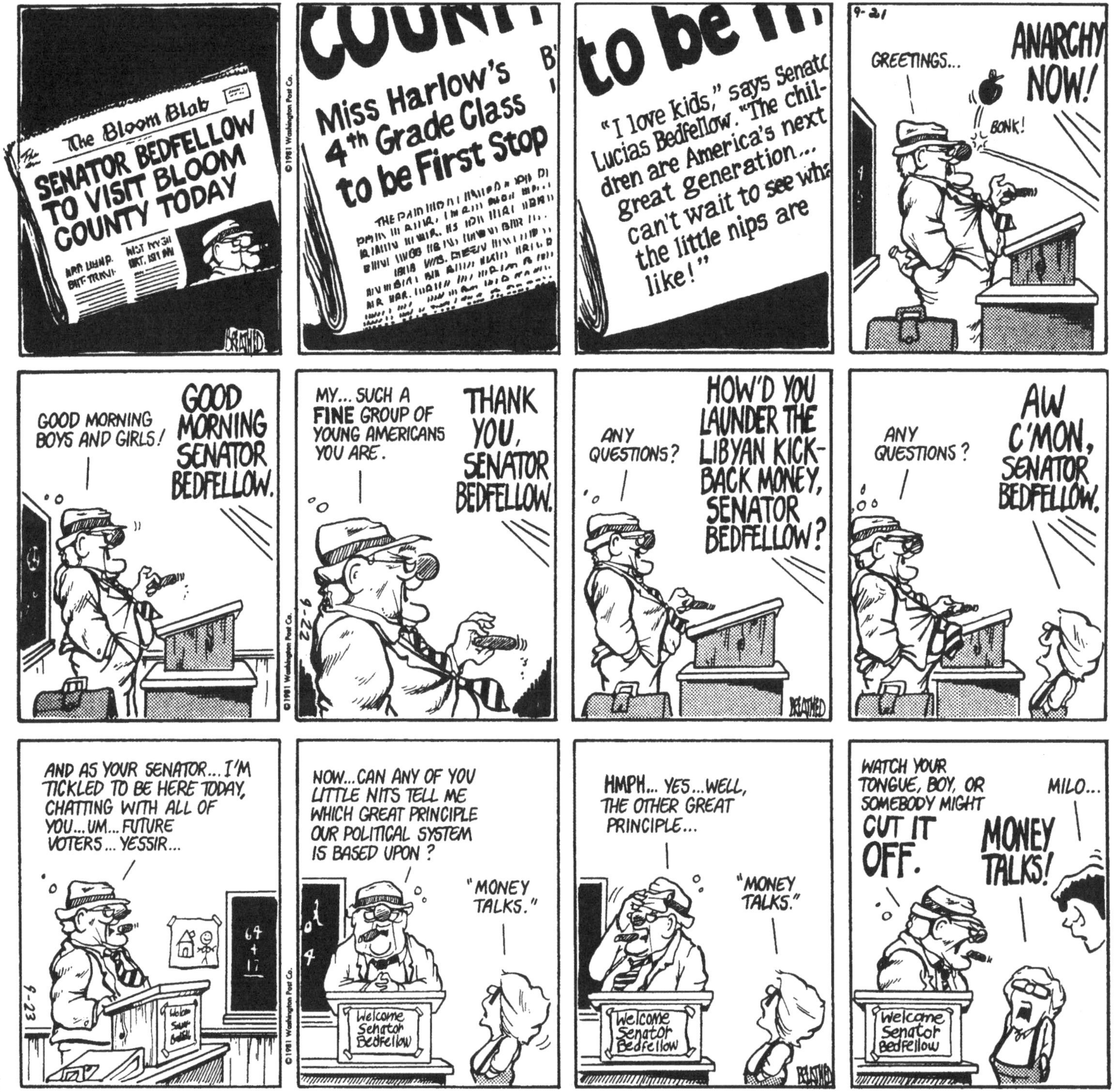

The Bloom Blab
SENATOR BEDFELLOW TO VISIT BLOOM COUNTY TODAY
COUNT
Miss Harlow's 4th Grade Class to be First Stop
to be fi
"I love kids," says Senato Lucias Bedfellow. "The children are America's next great generation... can't wait to see wha the little nips are like!"
9-21
GREETINGS...
ANARCHY NOW!
BONK!
GOOD MORNING BOYS AND GIRLS!
GOOD MORNING SENATOR BEDFELLOW.
MY... SUCH A FINE GROUP OF YOUNG AMERICANS YOU ARE.
THANK YOU, SENATOR BEDFELLOW.
9-22
ANY QUESTIONS?
HOW'D YOU LAUNDER THE LIBYAN KICK-BACK MONEY, SENATOR BEDFELLOW?
ANY QUESTIONS?
AW C'MON, SENATOR BEDFELLOW.
AND AS YOUR SENATOR... I'M TICKLED TO BE HERE TODAY, CHATTING WITH ALL OF YOU... UM... FUTURE VOTERS... YESSIR...
9-23
NOW... CAN ANY OF YOU LITTLE NITS TELL ME WHICH GREAT PRINCIPLE OUR POLITICAL SYSTEM IS BASED UPON?
"MONEY TALKS."
Welcome Senator Bedfellow
HMPH... YES... WELL, THE OTHER GREAT PRINCIPLE...
"MONEY TALKS."
Welcome Senator Bedfellow
WATCH YOUR TONGUE, BOY, OR SOMEBODY MIGHT CUT IT OFF.
MILO...
MONEY TALKS!
Welcome Senator Bedfellow

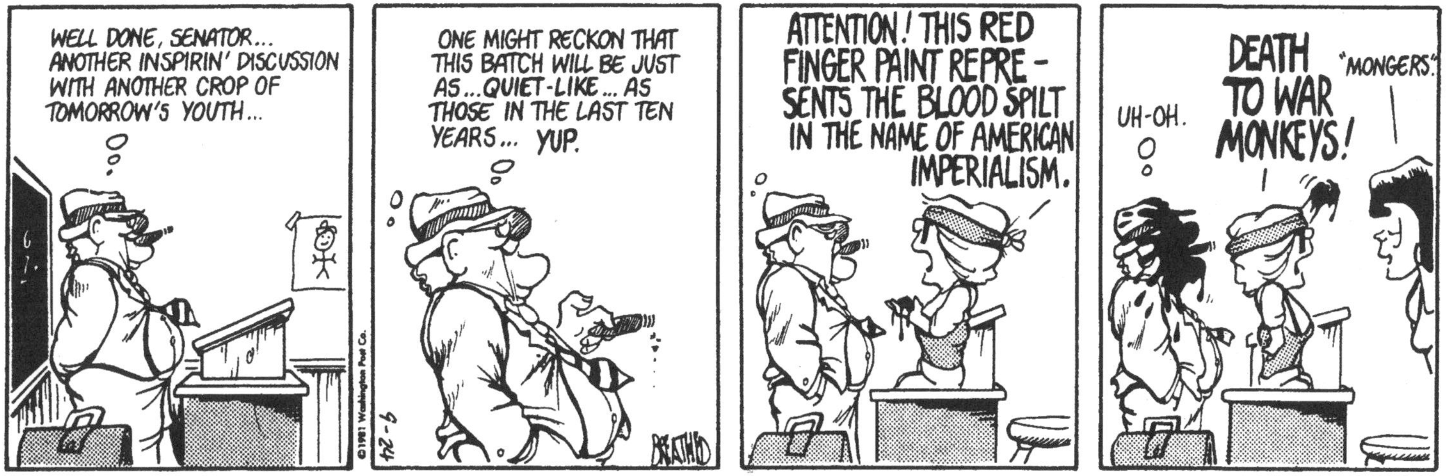
WELL DONE, SENATOR... ANOTHER INSPIRIN' DISCUSSION WITH ANOTHER CROP OF TOMORROW'S YOUTH...
ONE MIGHT RECKON THAT THIS BATCH WILL BE JUST AS...QUIET-LIKE... AS THOSE IN THE LAST TEN YEARS... YUP.
© 1981 Washington Post Co.
9-24
BREATHED
ATTENTION! THIS RED FINGER PAINT REPRESENTS THE BLOOD SPILT IN THE NAME OF AMERICAN IMPERIALISM.
UH-OH.
DEATH TO WAR MONKEYS!
"MONGERS."

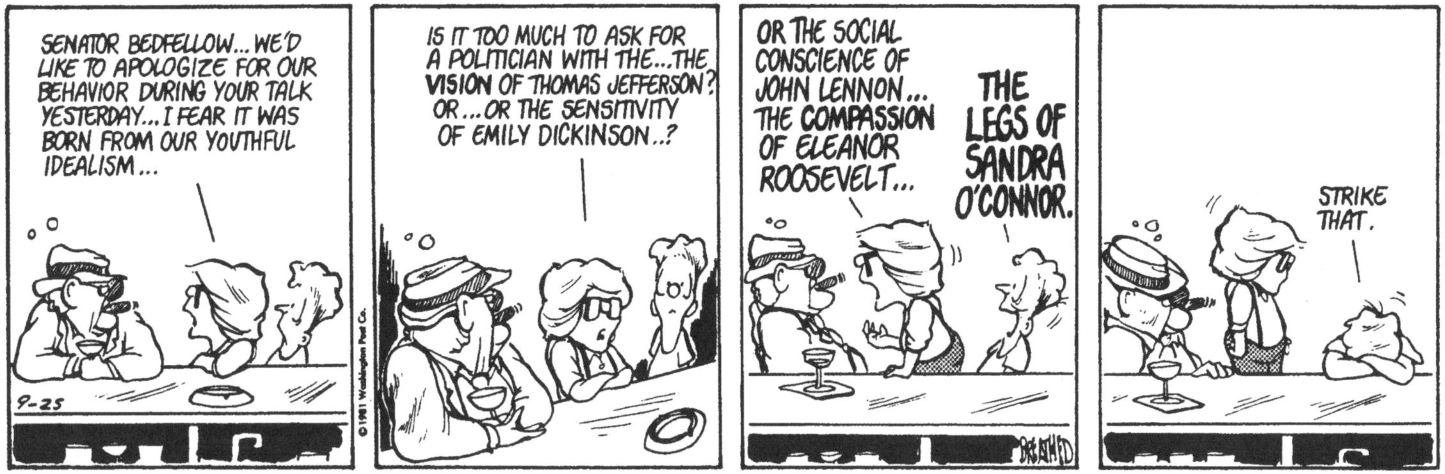
SENATOR BEDFELLOW... WE'D LIKE TO APOLOGIZE FOR OUR BEHAVIOR DURING YOUR TALK YESTERDAY... I FEAR IT WAS BORN FROM OUR YOUTHFUL IDEALISM...
9-25
IS IT TOO MUCH TO ASK FOR A POLITICIAN WITH THE...THE VISION OF THOMAS JEFFERSON? OR...OR THE SENSITIVITY OF EMILY DICKINSON..?
© 1981 Washington Post Co.
OR THE SOCIAL CONSCIENCE OF JOHN LENNON... THE COMPASSION OF ELEANOR ROOSEVELT...
THE LEGS OF SANDRA O'CONNOR.
BREATHED
STRIKE THAT.

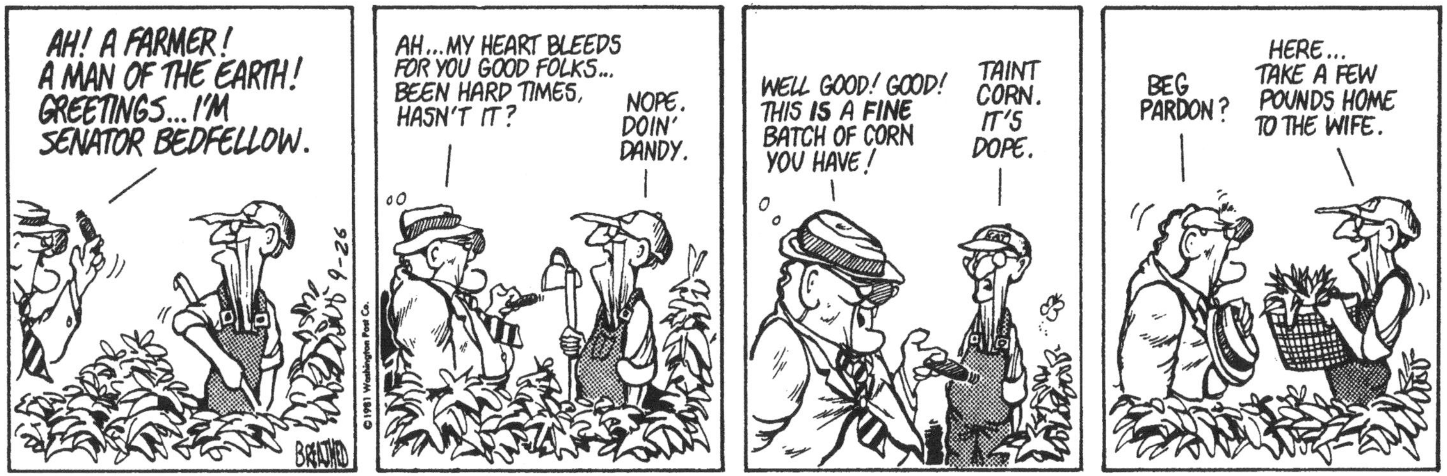
AH! A FARMER! A MAN OF THE EARTH! GREETINGS...I'M SENATOR BEDFELLOW.
9-26
BREATHED
AH...MY HEART BLEEDS FOR YOU GOOD FOLKS... BEEN HARD TIMES, HASN'T IT?
NOPE. DOIN' DANDY.
© 1981 Washington Post Co.
WELL GOOD! GOOD! THIS IS A FINE BATCH OF CORN YOU HAVE!
TAINT CORN. IT'S DOPE.
BEG PARDON?
HERE... TAKE A FEW POUNDS HOME TO THE WIFE.

Almost 30 years later and I still get this one quoted to me. I believe we quadrupled our college newspaper clients the next week. Potheads. —BB

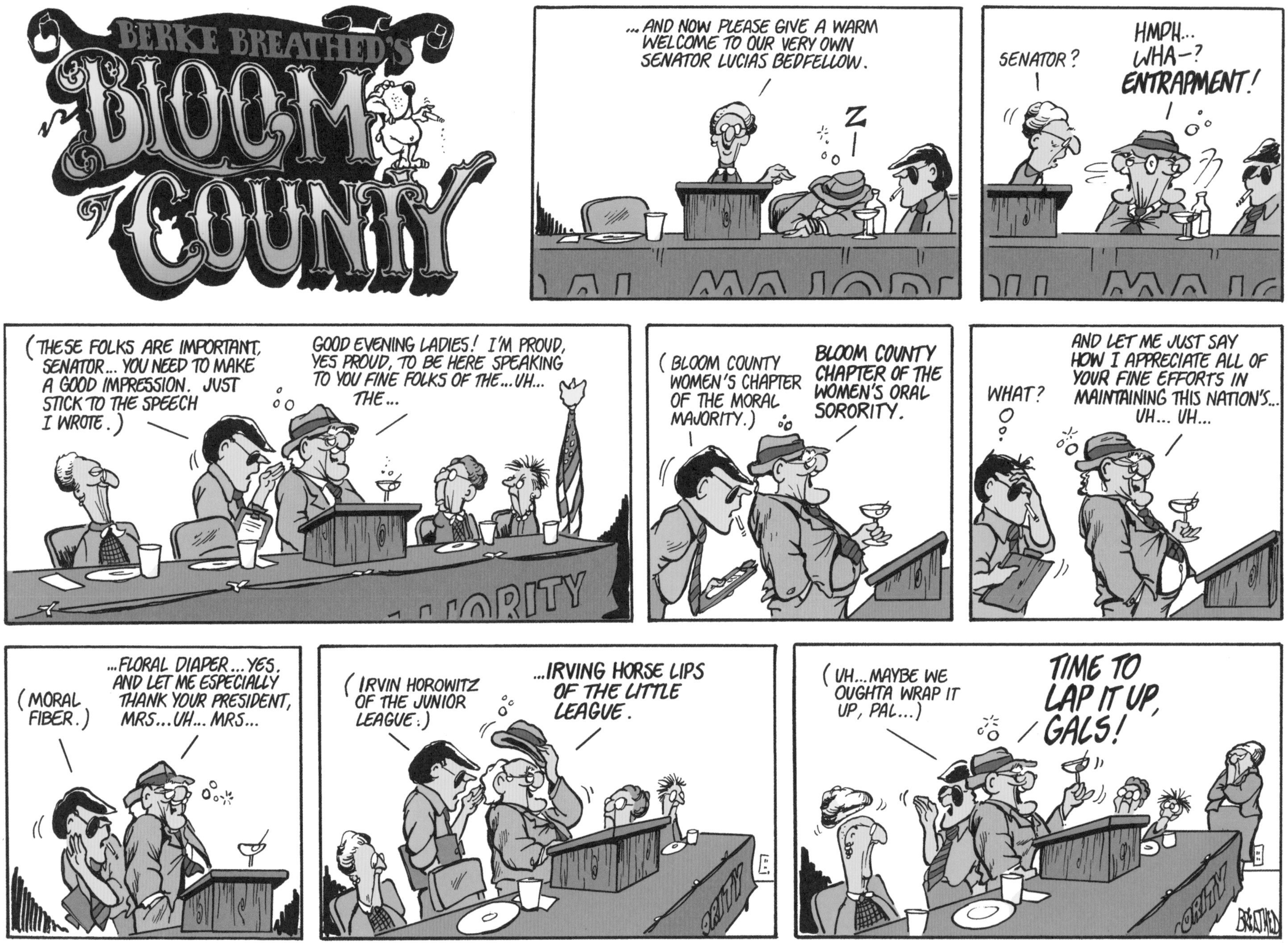
BERKE BREATHED'S
BLOOM COUNTY
...AND NOW PLEASE GIVE A WARM WELCOME TO OUR VERY OWN SENATOR LUCIAS BEDFELLOW.
Z
SENATOR?
HMPH... WHA-? ENTRAPMENT!
(THESE FOLKS ARE IMPORTANT, SENATOR... YOU NEED TO MAKE A GOOD IMPRESSION. JUST STICK TO THE SPEECH I WROTE.)
GOOD EVENING LADIES! I'M PROUD, YES PROUD, TO BE HERE SPEAKING TO YOU FINE FOLKS OF THE...UH... THE...
(BLOOM COUNTY WOMEN'S CHAPTER OF THE MORAL MAJORITY.)
BLOOM COUNTY CHAPTER OF THE WOMEN'S ORAL SORORITY.
WHAT?
AND LET ME JUST SAY HOW I APPRECIATE ALL OF YOUR FINE EFFORTS IN MAINTAINING THIS NATION'S... UH... UH...
(MORAL FIBER.)
...FLORAL DIAPER... YES. AND LET ME ESPECIALLY THANK YOUR PRESIDENT, MRS...UH... MRS...
(IRVIN HOROWITZ OF THE JUNIOR LEAGUE.)
...IRVING HORSE LIPS OF THE LITTLE LEAGUE.
(UH...MAYBE WE OUGHTA WRAP IT UP, PAL...)
TIME TO LAP IT UP, GALS!
BREATHED

Panel 1: BINKLEY! WHAT'S WRONG WITH MILO? / LOVE! HE'S SICK WITH IT, AGAIN.

9-28

Panel 2: ≈SIGH≈ OH BETTY... I ALWAYS KNEW YOU WERE ALIVE, YOU CULINARY CUTIE...

Panel 3: BETTY? HE DOESN'T MEAN BETTY CROCKER? / YEAH! SHE'S ALIVE AND WELL. THE "NATIONAL ENQUIRER" RAN A STORY. LOOK!

Panel 4: "FABLED HOMEMAKER DISCOVERED IN SECRET LOVE NEST WITH IDI AMIN'S CLONE" / WOW. / ALMOST UNBELIEVABLE.

Panel 5: MILO? LET'S TALK ABOUT THIS BETTY CROCKER BUSINESS. / NO GOOD. HE'S STILL SEMI-COMATOSE WITH PASSION.

9-29

Panel 6: MILO... SHE'S NO GOOD FOR YA, KID. SHE ONLY EXISTS ON PACKAGES OF DRIED POTATOES. THERE'RE OTHERS.... / NOPE. HE SAYS HE'S ONLY GOT TASTE BUDS FOR HER.

Panel 7: THIS IS RIDICULOUS.

Panel 8: HOW ABOUT BROOKE SHIELDS? / BLEAH! TOO LEGGY.

Panel 9: OUR GRANDSON IS AT IT AGAIN, BESS! HE THINKS HE'S IN LOVE WITH BETTY CROCKER. DIDYA HEAR ME? BETTY CROCKER, AGAIN!

9-30

Panel 10: NOW NOW... DEAR MILO IS JUST A LITTLE ROMANTIC. / HE'S A WALKING LOON, THAT'S WHAT HE IS!

Panel 11: OH POO. WHAT'S THE LITTLE RASCAL DOING NOW? / TAKE A GUESS!

Panel 12: Oh Betty, I live ~~die~~ for your Glazed Beef Tongue.

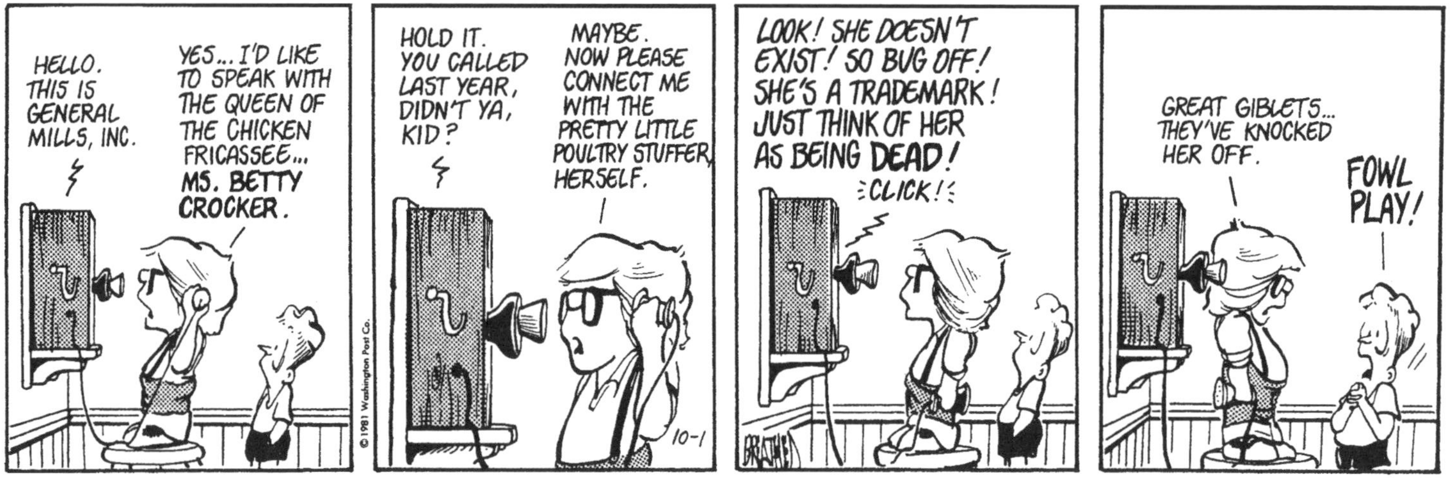
HELLO. THIS IS GENERAL MILLS, INC.
YES... I'D LIKE TO SPEAK WITH THE QUEEN OF THE CHICKEN FRICASSEE... MS. BETTY CROCKER.
© 1981 Washington Post Co.
HOLD IT. YOU CALLED LAST YEAR, DIDN'T YA, KID?
MAYBE. NOW PLEASE CONNECT ME WITH THE PRETTY LITTLE POULTRY STUFFER, HERSELF.
10-1
LOOK! SHE DOESN'T EXIST! SO BUG OFF! SHE'S A TRADEMARK! JUST THINK OF HER AS BEING DEAD!
CLICK!
GREAT GIBLETS... THEY'VE KNOCKED HER OFF.
FOWL PLAY!

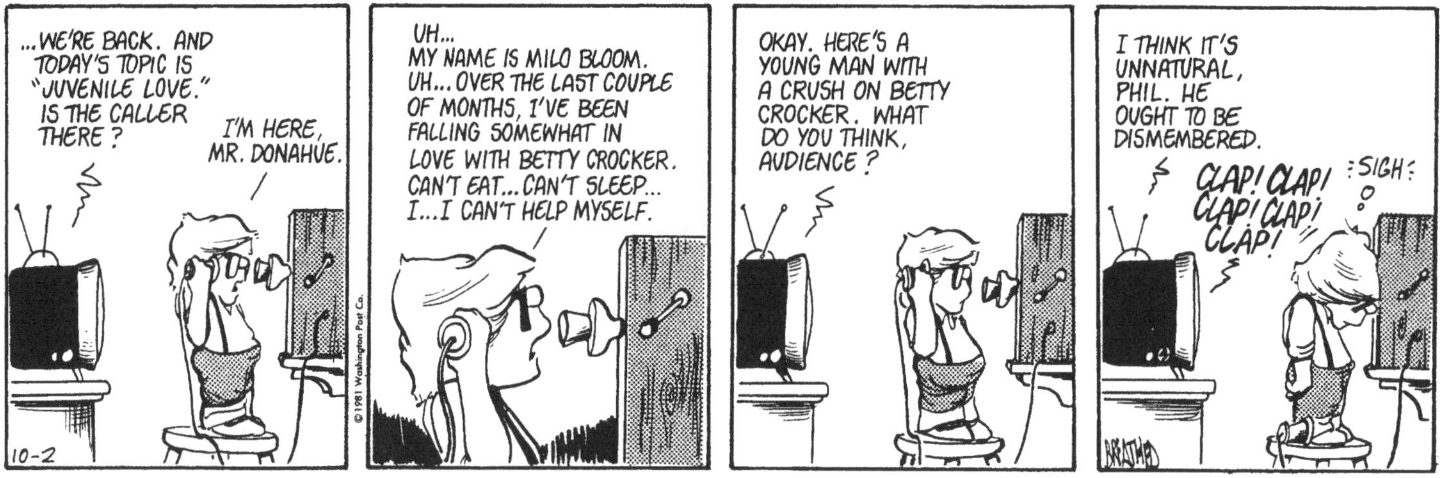
...WE'RE BACK. AND TODAY'S TOPIC IS "JUVENILE LOVE." IS THE CALLER THERE?
I'M HERE, MR. DONAHUE.
10-2
© 1981 Washington Post Co.
UH... MY NAME IS MILO BLOOM. UH... OVER THE LAST COUPLE OF MONTHS, I'VE BEEN FALLING SOMEWHAT IN LOVE WITH BETTY CROCKER. CAN'T EAT... CAN'T SLEEP... I... I CAN'T HELP MYSELF.
OKAY. HERE'S A YOUNG MAN WITH A CRUSH ON BETTY CROCKER. WHAT DO YOU THINK, AUDIENCE?
I THINK IT'S UNNATURAL, PHIL. HE OUGHT TO BE DISMEMBERED.
CLAP! CLAP! CLAP! CLAP! CLAP!
SIGH

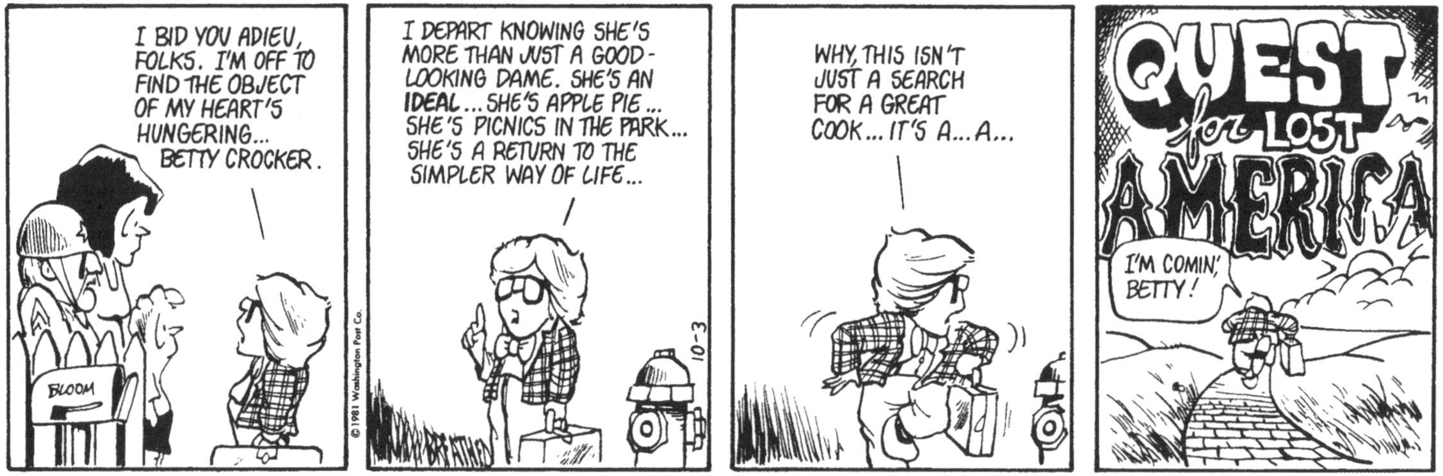
I BID YOU ADIEU, FOLKS. I'M OFF TO FIND THE OBJECT OF MY HEART'S HUNGERING... BETTY CROCKER.
BLOOM
© 1981 Washington Post Co.
I DEPART KNOWING SHE'S MORE THAN JUST A GOOD-LOOKING DAME. SHE'S AN IDEAL... SHE'S APPLE PIE... SHE'S PICNICS IN THE PARK... SHE'S A RETURN TO THE SIMPLER WAY OF LIFE...
10-3
WHY, THIS ISN'T JUST A SEARCH FOR A GREAT COOK... IT'S A... A...
QUEST for LOST AMERICA
I'M COMIN', BETTY!

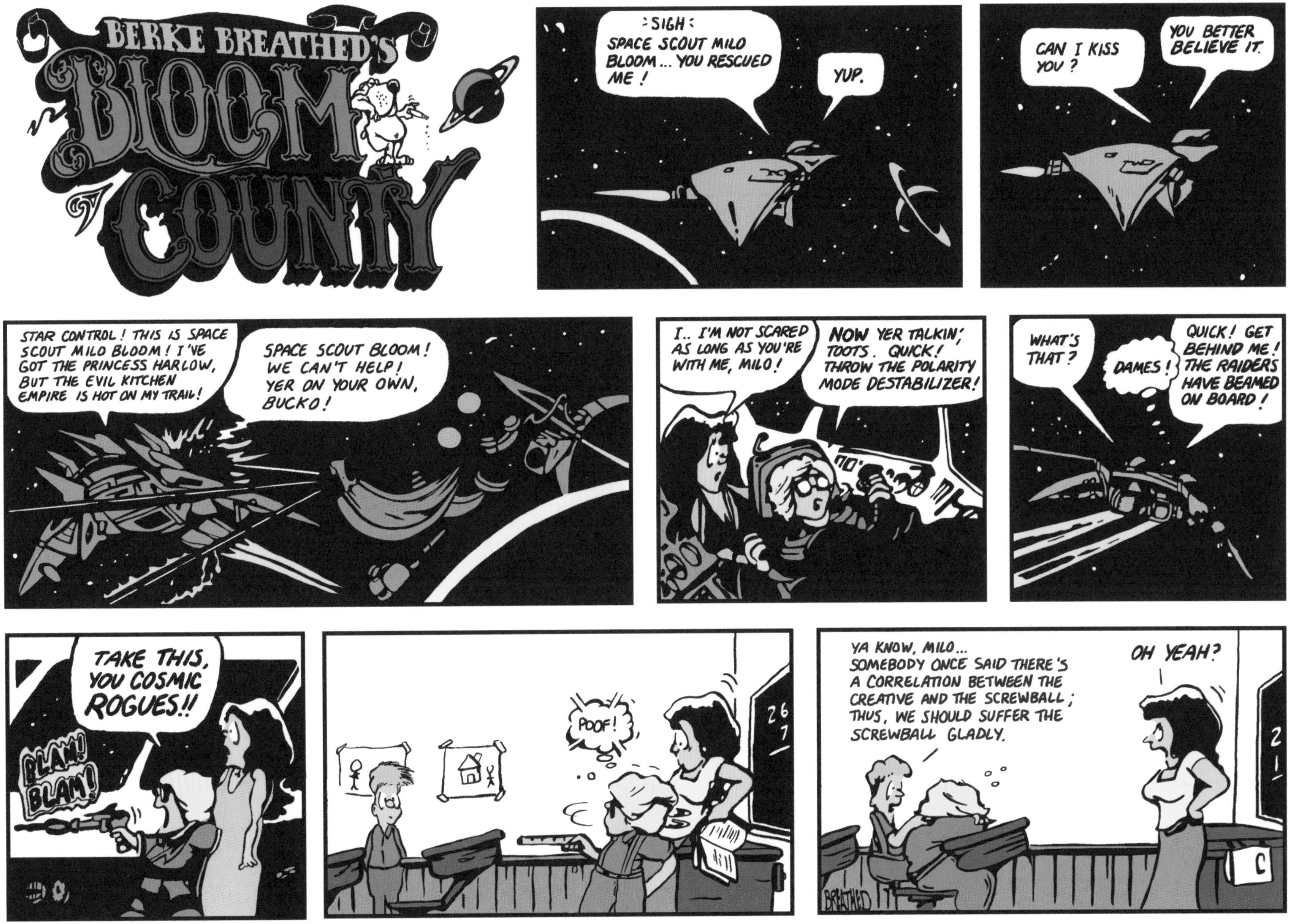
BERKE BREATHED'S
BLOOM COUNTY
:SIGH: SPACE SCOUT MILO BLOOM... YOU RESCUED ME!
YUP.
CAN I KISS YOU?
YOU BETTER BELIEVE IT.
STAR CONTROL! THIS IS SPACE SCOUT MILO BLOOM! I'VE GOT THE PRINCESS HARLOW, BUT THE EVIL KITCHEN EMPIRE IS HOT ON MY TRAIL!
SPACE SCOUT BLOOM! WE CAN'T HELP! YER ON YOUR OWN, BUCKO!
I.. I'M NOT SCARED AS LONG AS YOU'RE WITH ME, MILO!
NOW YER TALKIN', TOOTS. QUICK! THROW THE POLARITY MODE DESTABILIZER!
WHAT'S THAT?
DAMES!
QUICK! GET BEHIND ME! THE RAIDERS HAVE BEAMED ON BOARD!
TAKE THIS, YOU COSMIC ROGUES!!
BLAM! BLAM!
POOF!
YA KNOW, MILO... SOMEBODY ONCE SAID THERE'S A CORRELATION BETWEEN THE CREATIVE AND THE SCREWBALL; THUS, WE SHOULD SUFFER THE SCREWBALL GLADLY.
OH YEAH?
BREATHED

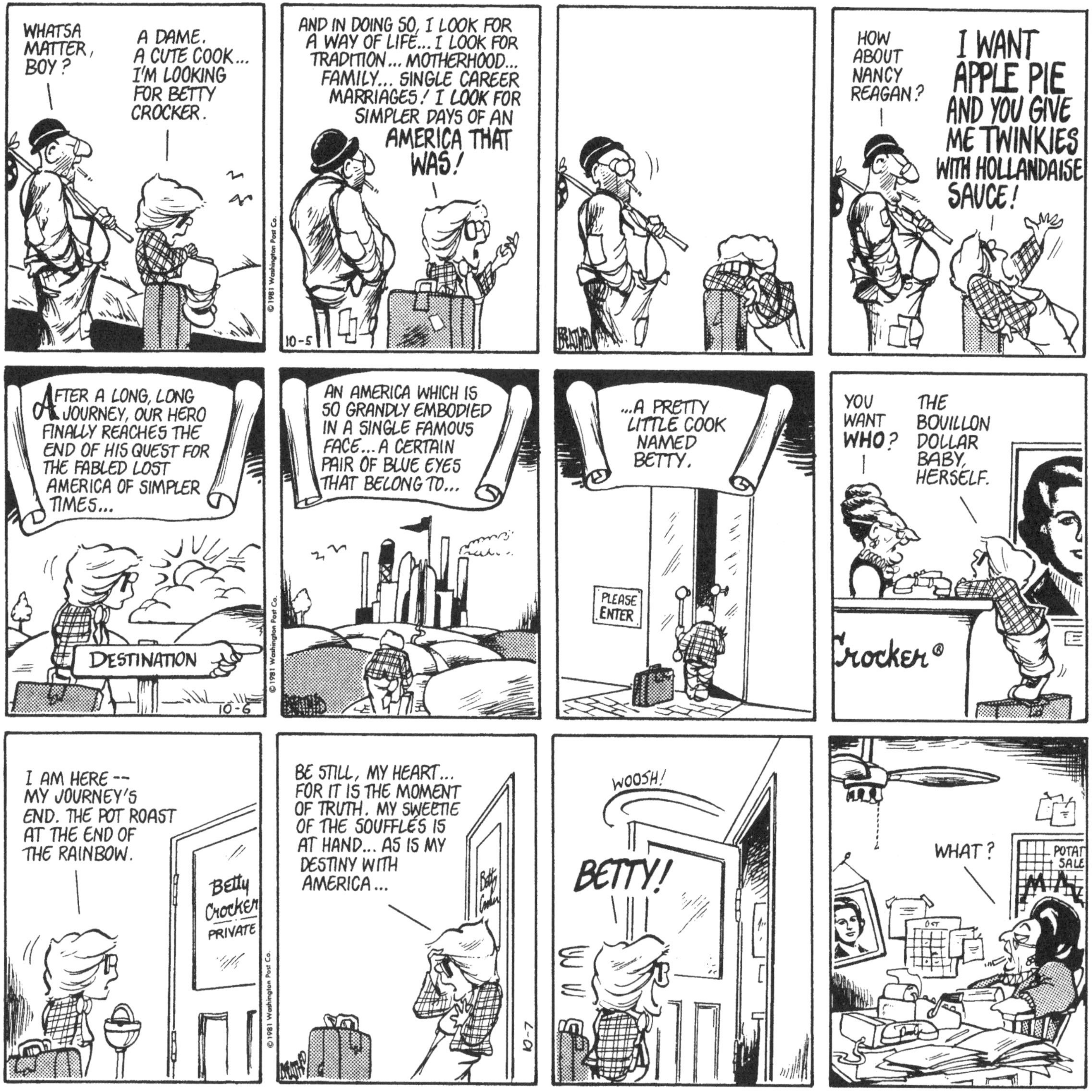

WHATSA MATTER, BOY?
A DAME. A CUTE COOK... I'M LOOKING FOR BETTY CROCKER.
AND IN DOING SO, I LOOK FOR A WAY OF LIFE... I LOOK FOR TRADITION... MOTHERHOOD... FAMILY... SINGLE CAREER MARRIAGES! I LOOK FOR SIMPLER DAYS OF AN AMERICA THAT WAS!
© 1981 Washington Post Co.
10-5
HOW ABOUT NANCY REAGAN?
I WANT APPLE PIE AND YOU GIVE ME TWINKIES WITH HOLLANDAISE SAUCE!
AFTER A LONG, LONG JOURNEY, OUR HERO FINALLY REACHES THE END OF HIS QUEST FOR THE FABLED LOST AMERICA OF SIMPLER TIMES...
DESTINATION
10-6
© 1981 Washington Post Co.
AN AMERICA WHICH IS SO GRANDLY EMBODIED IN A SINGLE FAMOUS FACE... A CERTAIN PAIR OF BLUE EYES THAT BELONG TO...
...A PRETTY LITTLE COOK NAMED BETTY.
PLEASE ENTER
YOU WANT WHO?
THE BOUILLON DOLLAR BABY, HERSELF.
Crocker®
I AM HERE -- MY JOURNEY'S END. THE POT ROAST AT THE END OF THE RAINBOW.
Betty Crocker
PRIVATE
© 1981 Washington Post Co.
BE STILL, MY HEART... FOR IT IS THE MOMENT OF TRUTH. MY SWEETIE OF THE SOUFFLÉS IS AT HAND... AS IS MY DESTINY WITH AMERICA...
10-7
WOOSH!
BETTY!
WHAT?

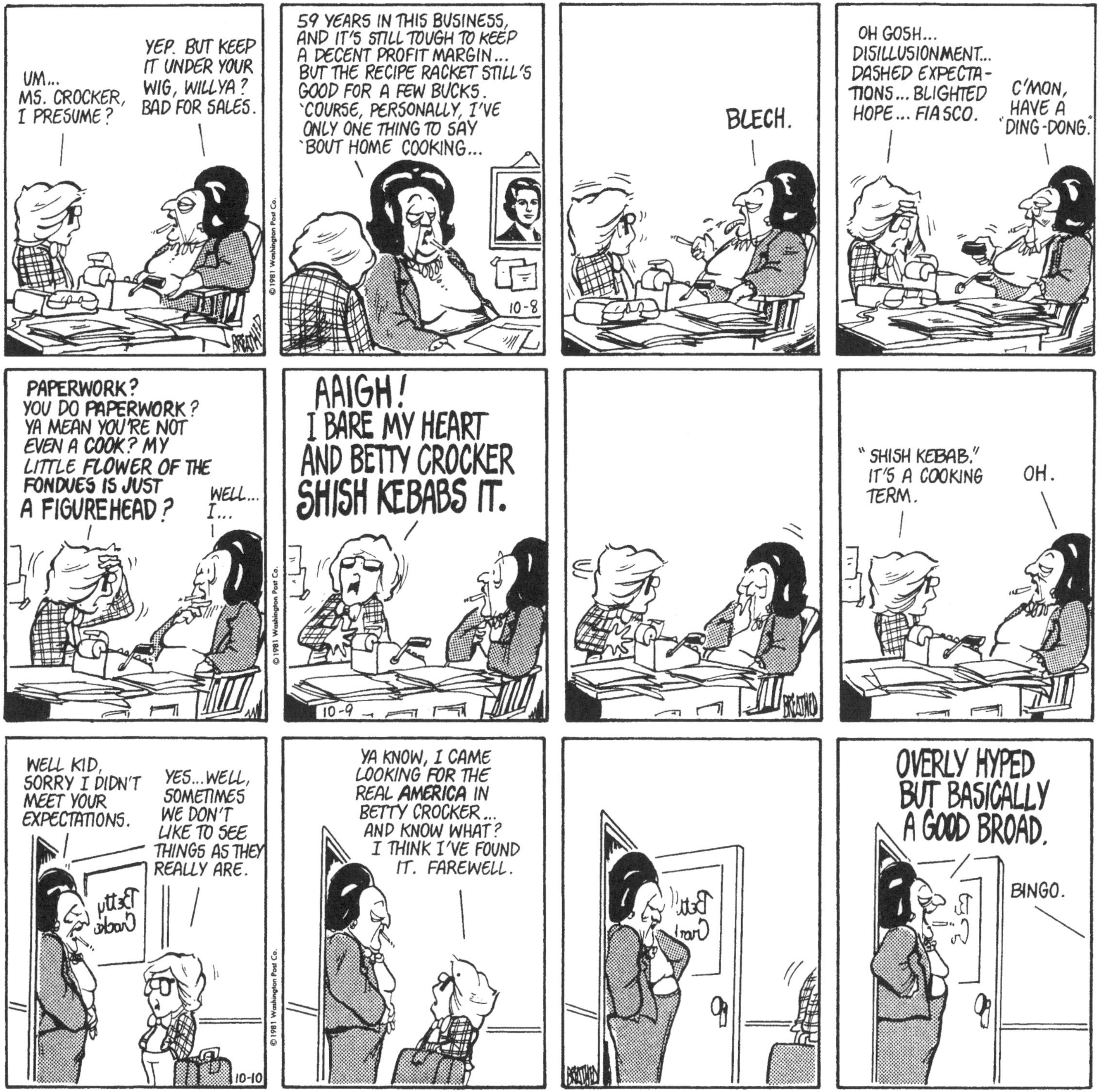
UM... MS. CROCKER, I PRESUME?
YEP. BUT KEEP IT UNDER YOUR WIG, WILLYA? BAD FOR SALES.
59 YEARS IN THIS BUSINESS, AND IT'S STILL TOUGH TO KEEP A DECENT PROFIT MARGIN... BUT THE RECIPE RACKET STILL'S GOOD FOR A FEW BUCKS. `COURSE, PERSONALLY, I'VE ONLY ONE THING TO SAY `BOUT HOME COOKING...
BLECH.
OH GOSH... DISILLUSIONMENT... DASHED EXPECTATIONS... BLIGHTED HOPE... FIASCO.
C'MON, HAVE A "DING-DONG."
PAPERWORK? YOU DO PAPERWORK? YA MEAN YOU'RE NOT EVEN A COOK? MY LITTLE FLOWER OF THE FONDUES IS JUST A FIGUREHEAD?
WELL... I...
AAIGH! I BARE MY HEART AND BETTY CROCKER SHISH KEBABS IT.
"SHISH KEBAB." IT'S A COOKING TERM.
OH.
WELL KID, SORRY I DIDN'T MEET YOUR EXPECTATIONS.
YES... WELL, SOMETIMES WE DON'T LIKE TO SEE THINGS AS THEY REALLY ARE.
YA KNOW, I CAME LOOKING FOR THE REAL AMERICA IN BETTY CROCKER... AND KNOW WHAT? I THINK I'VE FOUND IT. FAREWELL.
OVERLY HYPED BUT BASICALLY A GOOD BROAD.
BINGO.

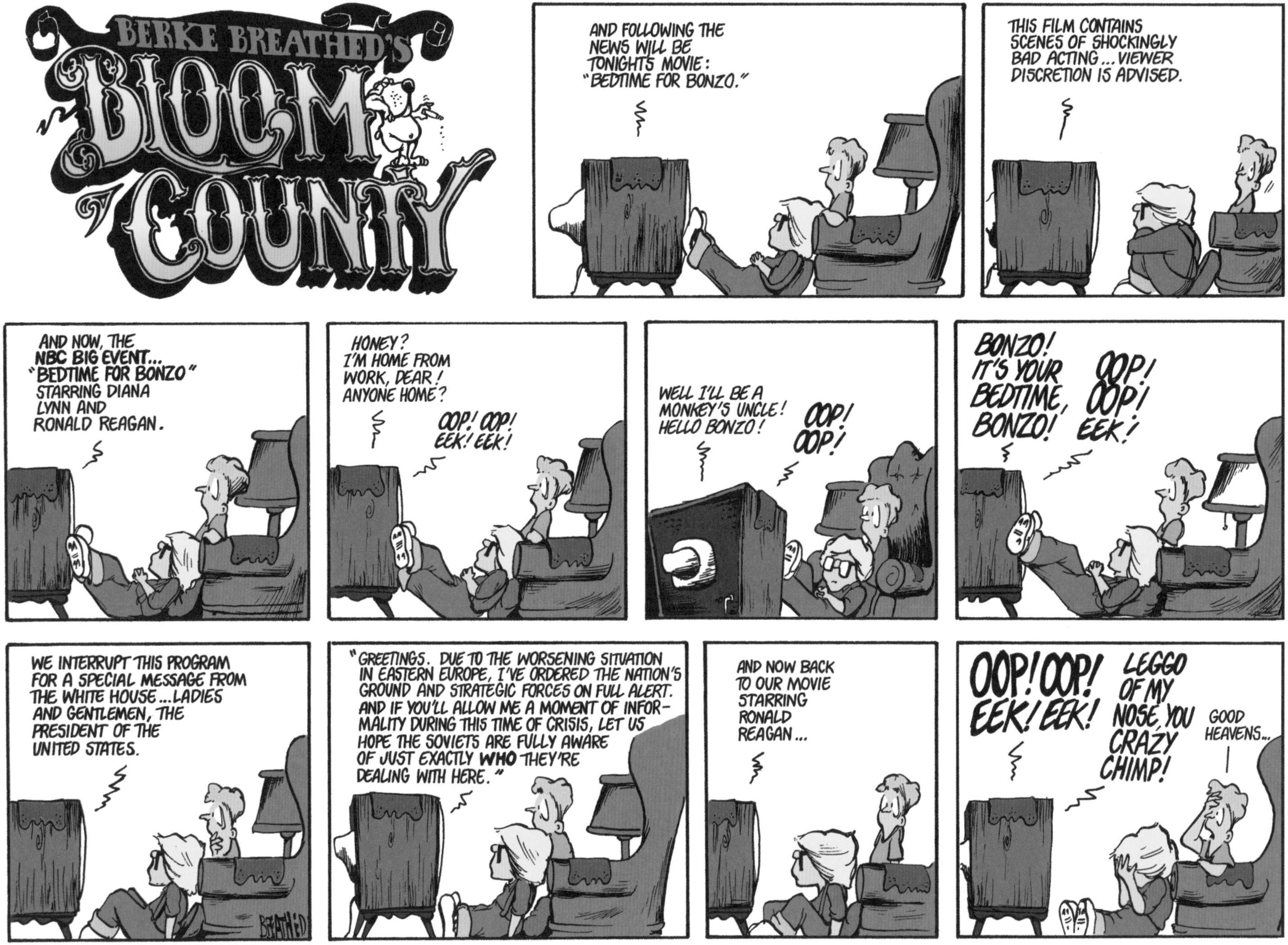
BERKE BREATHED'S
BLOOM COUNTY
AND FOLLOWING THE NEWS WILL BE TONIGHT'S MOVIE: "BEDTIME FOR BONZO."
THIS FILM CONTAINS SCENES OF SHOCKINGLY BAD ACTING ... VIEWER DISCRETION IS ADVISED.
AND NOW, THE NBC BIG EVENT... "BEDTIME FOR BONZO" STARRING DIANA LYNN AND RONALD REAGAN.
HONEY? I'M HOME FROM WORK, DEAR! ANYONE HOME?
OOP! OOP! EEK! EEK!
WELL I'LL BE A MONKEY'S UNCLE! HELLO BONZO!
OOP! OOP!
BONZO! IT'S YOUR BEDTIME, BONZO!
OOP! OOP! EEK!
WE INTERRUPT THIS PROGRAM FOR A SPECIAL MESSAGE FROM THE WHITE HOUSE ... LADIES AND GENTLEMEN, THE PRESIDENT OF THE UNITED STATES.
BREATHED
"GREETINGS. DUE TO THE WORSENING SITUATION IN EASTERN EUROPE, I'VE ORDERED THE NATION'S GROUND AND STRATEGIC FORCES ON FULL ALERT. AND IF YOU'LL ALLOW ME A MOMENT OF INFORMALITY DURING THIS TIME OF CRISIS, LET US HOPE THE SOVIETS ARE FULLY AWARE OF JUST EXACTLY WHO THEY'RE DEALING WITH HERE."
AND NOW BACK TO OUR MOVIE STARRING RONALD REAGAN ...
OOP! OOP! EEK! EEK!
LEGGO OF MY NOSE, YOU CRAZY CHIMP!
GOOD HEAVENS...

 October 11, 1981

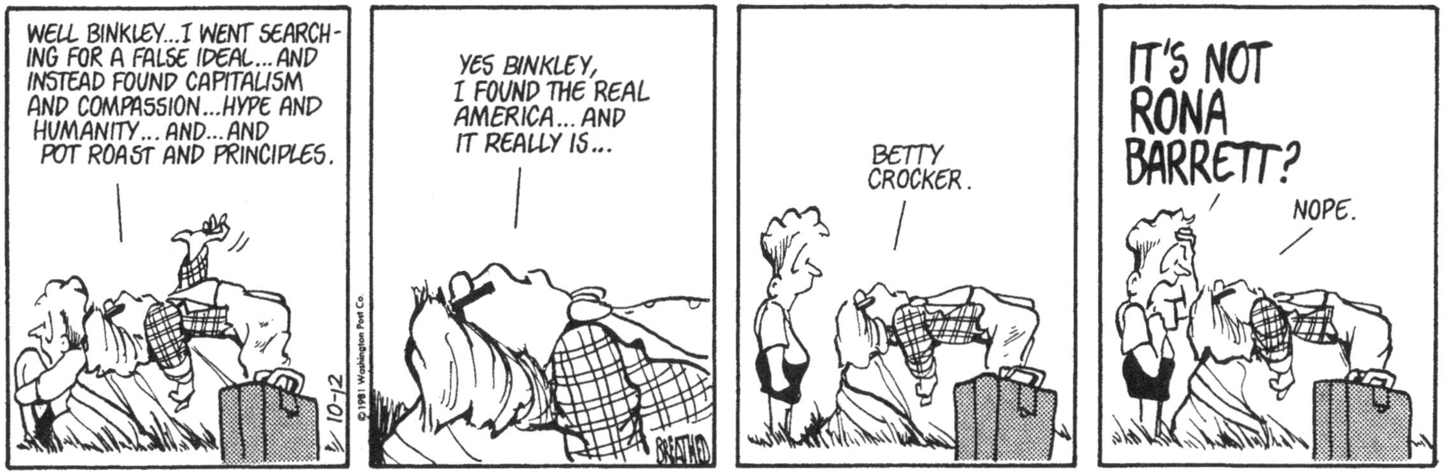
WELL BINKLEY...I WENT SEARCHING FOR A FALSE IDEAL... AND INSTEAD FOUND CAPITALISM AND COMPASSION...HYPE AND HUMANITY... AND...AND POT ROAST AND PRINCIPLES.
10-12
© 1981 Washington Post Co.
YES BINKLEY, I FOUND THE REAL AMERICA... AND IT REALLY IS...
BETTY CROCKER.
IT'S NOT RONA BARRETT?
NOPE.

Rona Barrett was a well-known television gossip columnist in the 1970s and 1980s.

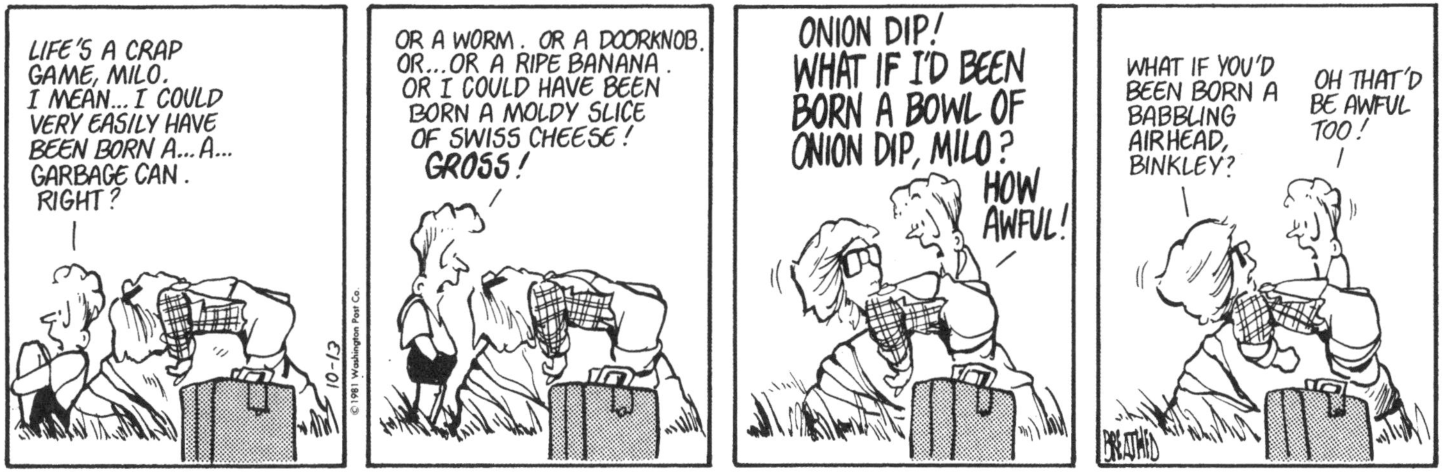
LIFE'S A CRAP GAME, MILO. I MEAN... I COULD VERY EASILY HAVE BEEN BORN A... A... GARBAGE CAN. RIGHT?
10-13
© 1981 Washington Post Co.
OR A WORM. OR A DOORKNOB. OR...OR A RIPE BANANA. OR I COULD HAVE BEEN BORN A MOLDY SLICE OF SWISS CHEESE! GROSS!
ONION DIP! WHAT IF I'D BEEN BORN A BOWL OF ONION DIP, MILO?
HOW AWFUL!
WHAT IF YOU'D BEEN BORN A BABBLING AIRHEAD, BINKLEY?
OH THAT'D BE AWFUL TOO!

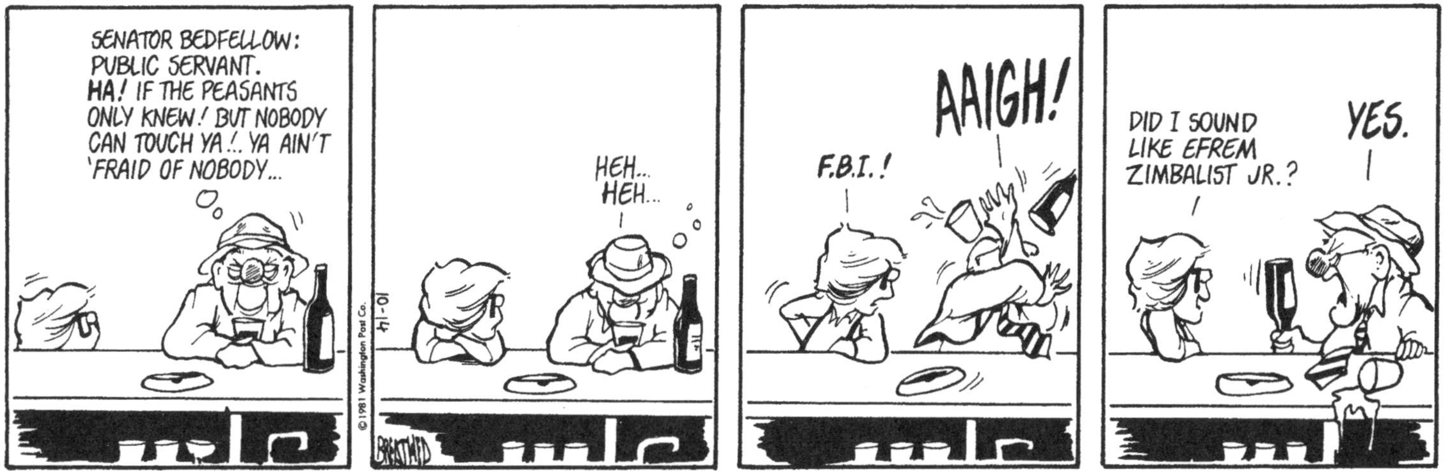
SENATOR BEDFELLOW: PUBLIC SERVANT. HA! IF THE PEASANTS ONLY KNEW! BUT NOBODY CAN TOUCH YA!.. YA AIN'T 'FRAID OF NOBODY...
10-14
© 1981 Washington Post Co.
HEH.. HEH..
F.B.I.!
AAIGH!
DID I SOUND LIKE EFREM ZIMBALIST JR.?
YES.

Efrem Zimbalist, Jr. is an actor best known for his role as Inspector Lewis Erskine in the late '60s, early '70s TV drama, *The F.B.I.*

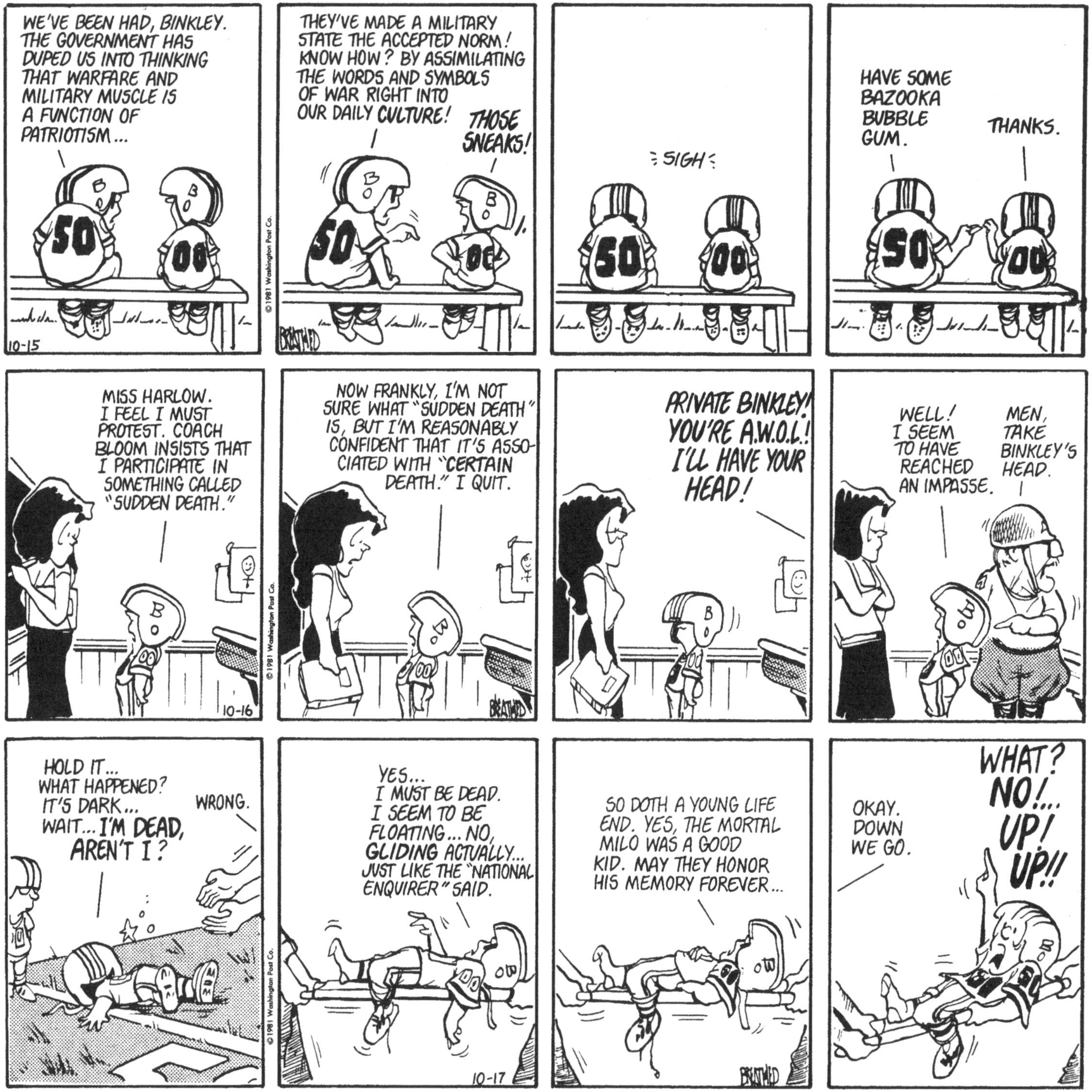
WE'VE BEEN HAD, BINKLEY. THE GOVERNMENT HAS DUPED US INTO THINKING THAT WARFARE AND MILITARY MUSCLE IS A FUNCTION OF PATRIOTISM...
10-15
THEY'VE MADE A MILITARY STATE THE ACCEPTED NORM! KNOW HOW? BY ASSIMILATING THE WORDS AND SYMBOLS OF WAR RIGHT INTO OUR DAILY CULTURE!
THOSE SNEAKS!
© 1981 Washington Post Co.
SIGH
HAVE SOME BAZOOKA BUBBLE GUM.
THANKS.
MISS HARLOW. I FEEL I MUST PROTEST. COACH BLOOM INSISTS THAT I PARTICIPATE IN SOMETHING CALLED "SUDDEN DEATH."
10-16
NOW FRANKLY, I'M NOT SURE WHAT "SUDDEN DEATH" IS, BUT I'M REASONABLY CONFIDENT THAT IT'S ASSOCIATED WITH "CERTAIN DEATH." I QUIT.
© 1981 Washington Post Co.
PRIVATE BINKLEY! YOU'RE A.W.O.L.! I'LL HAVE YOUR HEAD!
WELL! I SEEM TO HAVE REACHED AN IMPASSE.
MEN, TAKE BINKLEY'S HEAD.
HOLD IT... WHAT HAPPENED? IT'S DARK... WAIT... I'M DEAD, AREN'T I?
WRONG.
© 1981 Washington Post Co.
YES... I MUST BE DEAD. I SEEM TO BE FLOATING... NO, GLIDING ACTUALLY... JUST LIKE THE "NATIONAL ENQUIRER" SAID.
10-17
SO DOTH A YOUNG LIFE END. YES, THE MORTAL MILO WAS A GOOD KID. MAY THEY HONOR HIS MEMORY FOREVER...
OKAY. DOWN WE GO.
WHAT? NO!... UP! UP!!

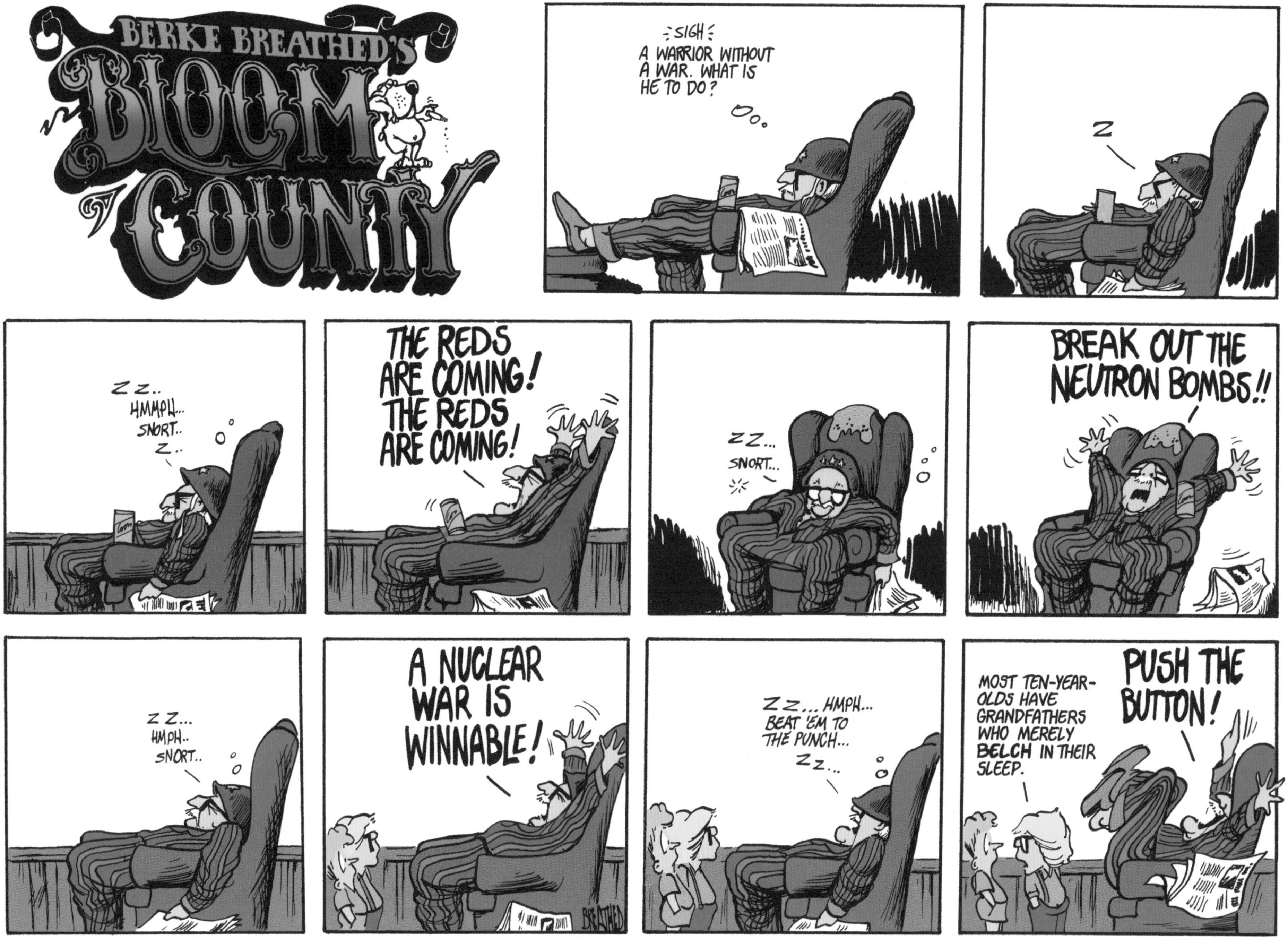
BERKE BREATHED'S
BLOOM COUNTY
SIGH
A WARRIOR WITHOUT A WAR. WHAT IS HE TO DO?
Z
Z Z.. HMMPH... SNORT.. Z..
THE REDS ARE COMING! THE REDS ARE COMING!
Z Z... SNORT...
BREAK OUT THE NEUTRON BOMBS!!
Z Z... HMPH.. SNORT..
A NUCLEAR WAR IS WINNABLE!
Z Z... HMPH... BEAT 'EM TO THE PUNCH... Z Z...
MOST TEN-YEAR-OLDS HAVE GRANDFATHERS WHO MERELY BELCH IN THEIR SLEEP.
PUSH THE BUTTON!
BREATHED

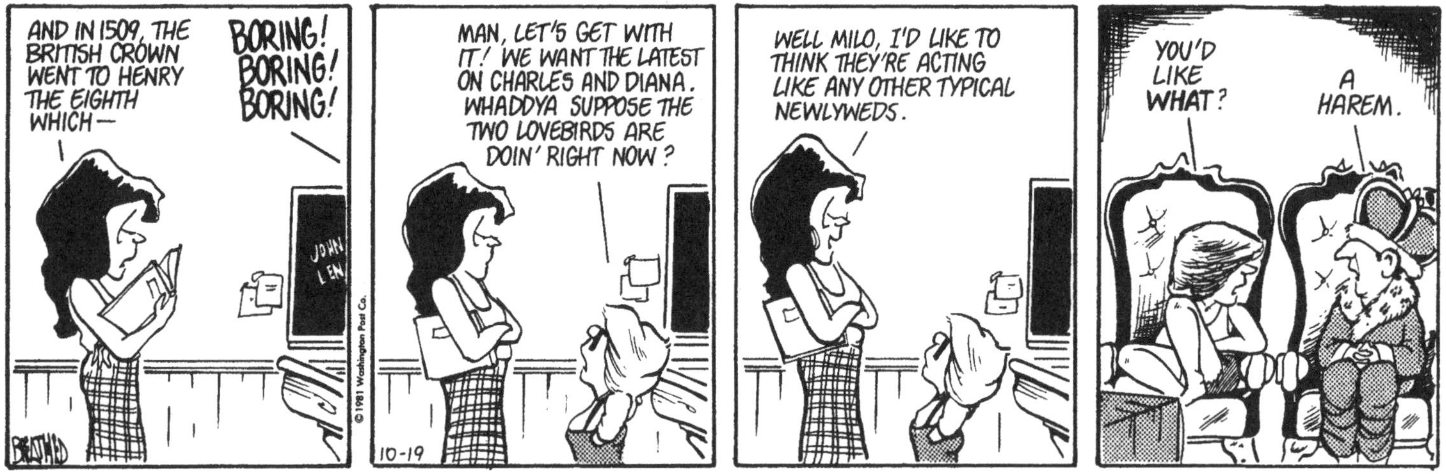
AND IN 1509, THE BRITISH CROWN WENT TO HENRY THE EIGHTH WHICH—
BORING! BORING! BORING!
MAN, LET'S GET WITH IT! WE WANT THE LATEST ON CHARLES AND DIANA. WHADDYA SUPPOSE THE TWO LOVEBIRDS ARE DOIN' RIGHT NOW?
WELL MILO, I'D LIKE TO THINK THEY'RE ACTING LIKE ANY OTHER TYPICAL NEWLYWEDS.
YOU'D LIKE WHAT?
A HAREM.
© 1981 Washington Post Co.
10-19

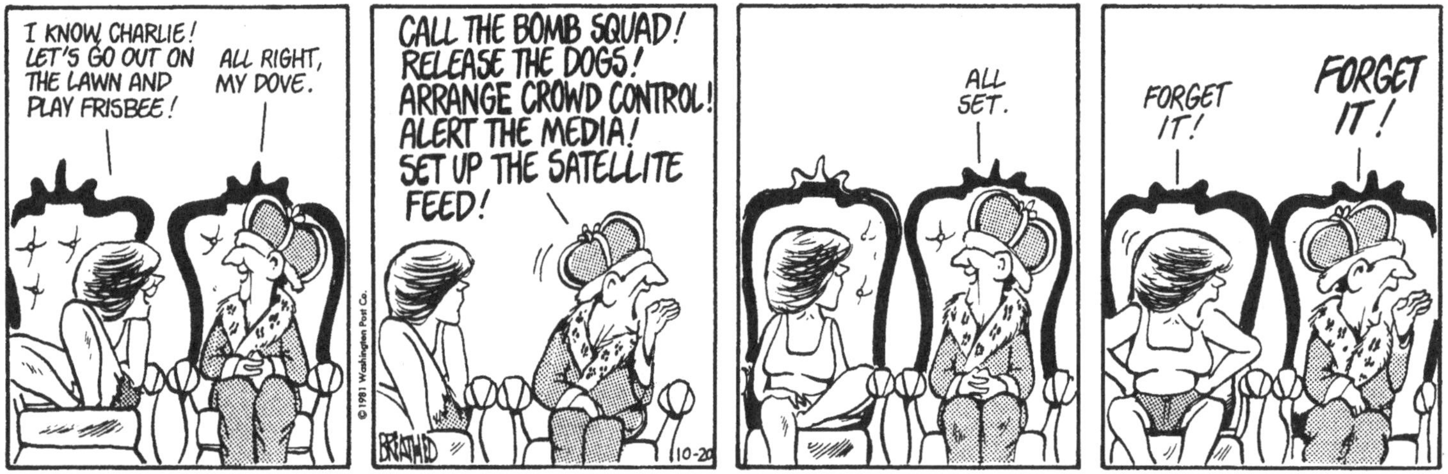
I KNOW, CHARLIE! LET'S GO OUT ON THE LAWN AND PLAY FRISBEE!
ALL RIGHT, MY DOVE.
CALL THE BOMB SQUAD! RELEASE THE DOGS! ARRANGE CROWD CONTROL! ALERT THE MEDIA! SET UP THE SATELLITE FEED!
ALL SET.
FORGET IT!
FORGET IT!
© 1981 Washington Post Co.
10-20

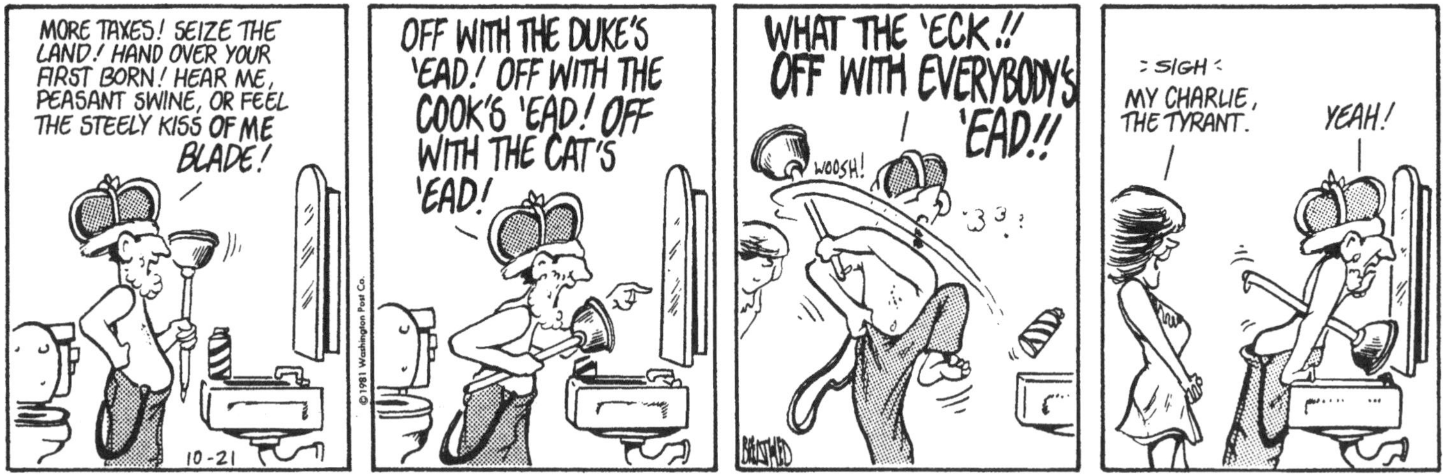
MORE TAXES! SEIZE THE LAND! HAND OVER YOUR FIRST BORN! HEAR ME, PEASANT SWINE, OR FEEL THE STEELY KISS OF ME BLADE!
OFF WITH THE DUKE'S 'EAD! OFF WITH THE COOK'S 'EAD! OFF WITH THE CAT'S 'EAD!
WHAT THE 'ECK!! OFF WITH EVERYBODY'S 'EAD!!
WOOSH!
: SIGH :
MY CHARLIE, THE TYRANT.
YEAH!
© 1981 Washington Post Co.
10-21

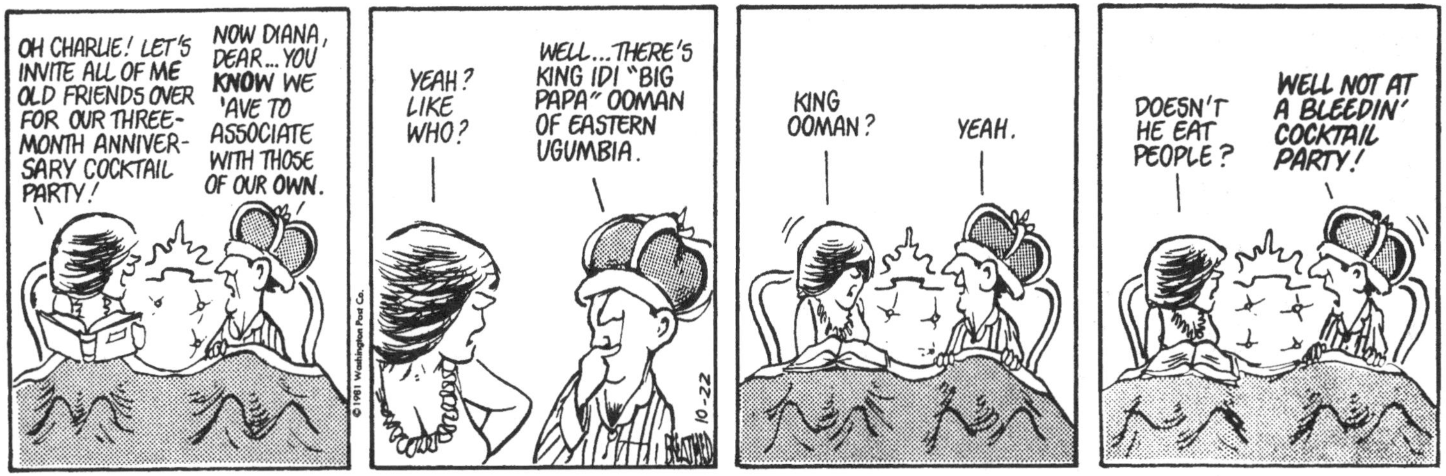
OH CHARLIE! LET'S INVITE ALL OF ME OLD FRIENDS OVER FOR OUR THREE-MONTH ANNIVERSARY COCKTAIL PARTY!
NOW DIANA, DEAR... YOU KNOW WE 'AVE TO ASSOCIATE WITH THOSE OF OUR OWN.
YEAH? LIKE WHO?
WELL... THERE'S KING IDI "BIG PAPA" OOMAN OF EASTERN UGUMBIA.
© 1981 Washington Post Co.
10-22
BREATHED
KING OOMAN?
YEAH.
DOESN'T HE EAT PEOPLE?
WELL NOT AT A BLEEDIN' COCKTAIL PARTY!

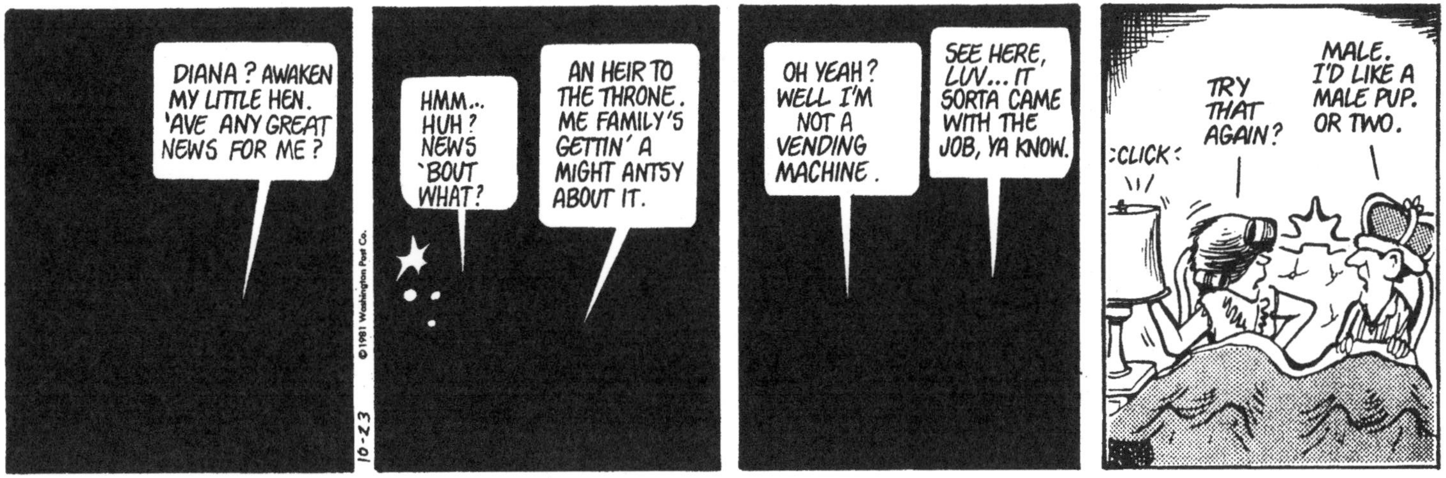
DIANA? AWAKEN MY LITTLE HEN. 'AVE ANY GREAT NEWS FOR ME?
10-23
© 1981 Washington Post Co.
HMM... HUH? NEWS 'BOUT WHAT?
AN HEIR TO THE THRONE. ME FAMILY'S GETTIN' A MIGHT ANTSY ABOUT IT.
OH YEAH? WELL I'M NOT A VENDING MACHINE.
SEE HERE, LUV... IT SORTA CAME WITH THE JOB, YA KNOW.
CLICK
TRY THAT AGAIN?
MALE. I'D LIKE A MALE PUP. OR TWO.

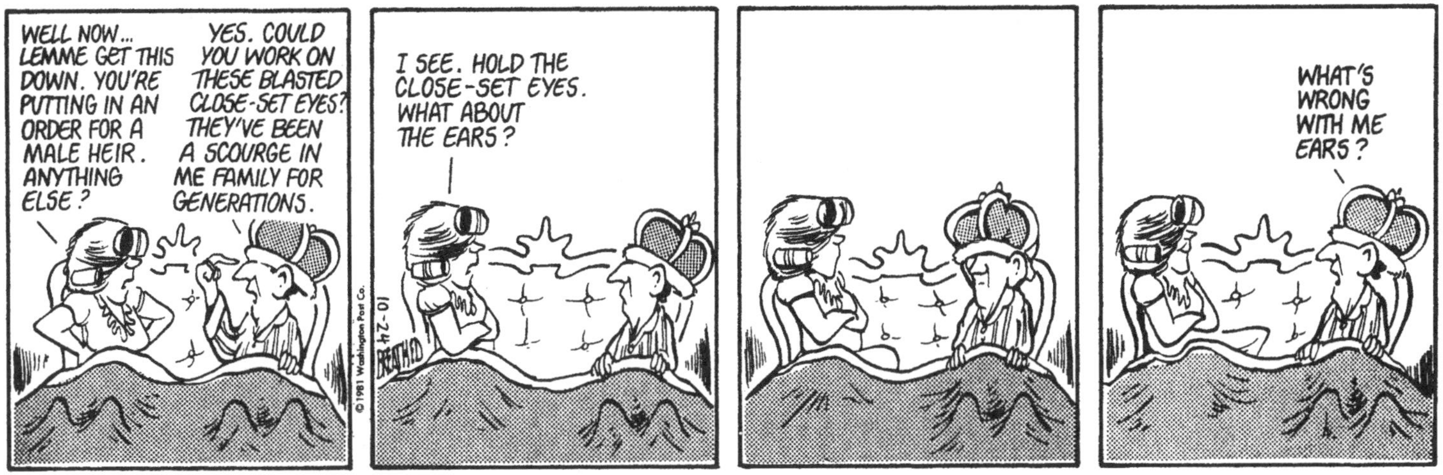
WELL NOW... LEMME GET THIS DOWN. YOU'RE PUTTING IN AN ORDER FOR A MALE HEIR. ANYTHING ELSE?
YES. COULD YOU WORK ON THESE BLASTED CLOSE-SET EYES? THEY'VE BEEN A SCOURGE IN ME FAMILY FOR GENERATIONS.
© 1981 Washington Post Co.
10-24
BREATHED
I SEE. HOLD THE CLOSE-SET EYES. WHAT ABOUT THE EARS?
WHAT'S WRONG WITH ME EARS?

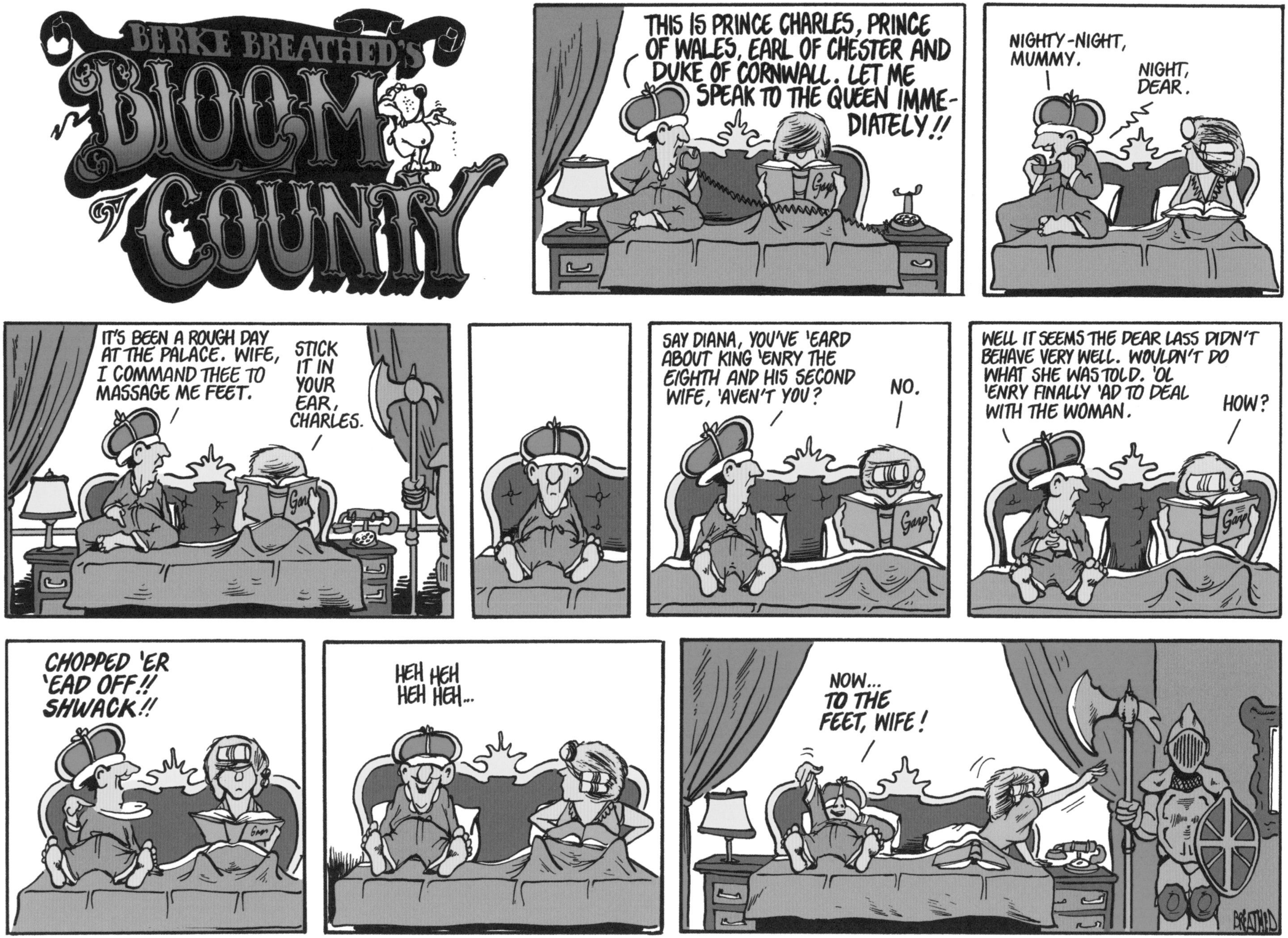
BERKE BREATHED'S
BLOOM COUNTY
THIS IS PRINCE CHARLES, PRINCE OF WALES, EARL OF CHESTER AND DUKE OF CORNWALL. LET ME SPEAK TO THE QUEEN IMMEDIATELY!!
NIGHTY-NIGHT, MUMMY.
NIGHT, DEAR.
IT'S BEEN A ROUGH DAY AT THE PALACE. WIFE, I COMMAND THEE TO MASSAGE ME FEET.
STICK IT IN YOUR EAR, CHARLES.
SAY DIANA, YOU'VE 'EARD ABOUT KING 'ENRY THE EIGHTH AND HIS SECOND WIFE, 'AVEN'T YOU?
NO.
WELL IT SEEMS THE DEAR LASS DIDN'T BEHAVE VERY WELL. WOULDN'T DO WHAT SHE WAS TOLD. 'OL 'ENRY FINALLY 'AD TO DEAL WITH THE WOMAN.
HOW?
CHOPPED 'ER 'EAD OFF!! SHWACK!!
HEH HEH HEH HEH...
NOW... TO THE FEET, WIFE!
BREATHED

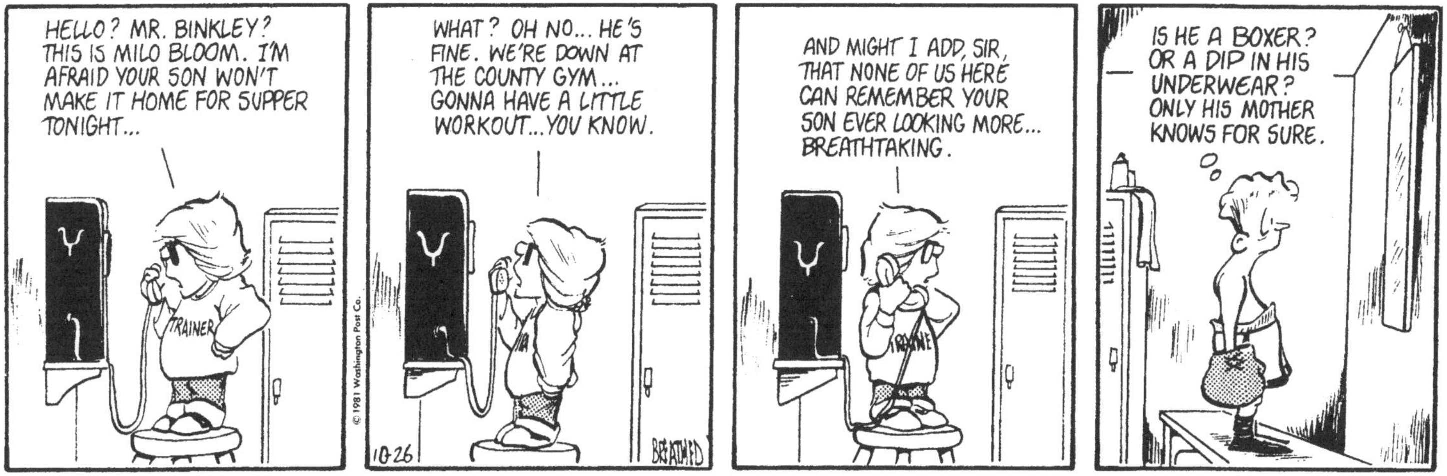
HELLO? MR. BINKLEY? THIS IS MILO BLOOM. I'M AFRAID YOUR SON WON'T MAKE IT HOME FOR SUPPER TONIGHT...
TRAINER
WHAT? OH NO... HE'S FINE. WE'RE DOWN AT THE COUNTY GYM... GONNA HAVE A LITTLE WORKOUT... YOU KNOW.
© 1981 Washington Post Co.
10-26
BREATHED
AND MIGHT I ADD, SIR, THAT NONE OF US HERE CAN REMEMBER YOUR SON EVER LOOKING MORE... BREATHTAKING.
IS HE A BOXER? OR A DIP IN HIS UNDERWEAR? ONLY HIS MOTHER KNOWS FOR SURE.

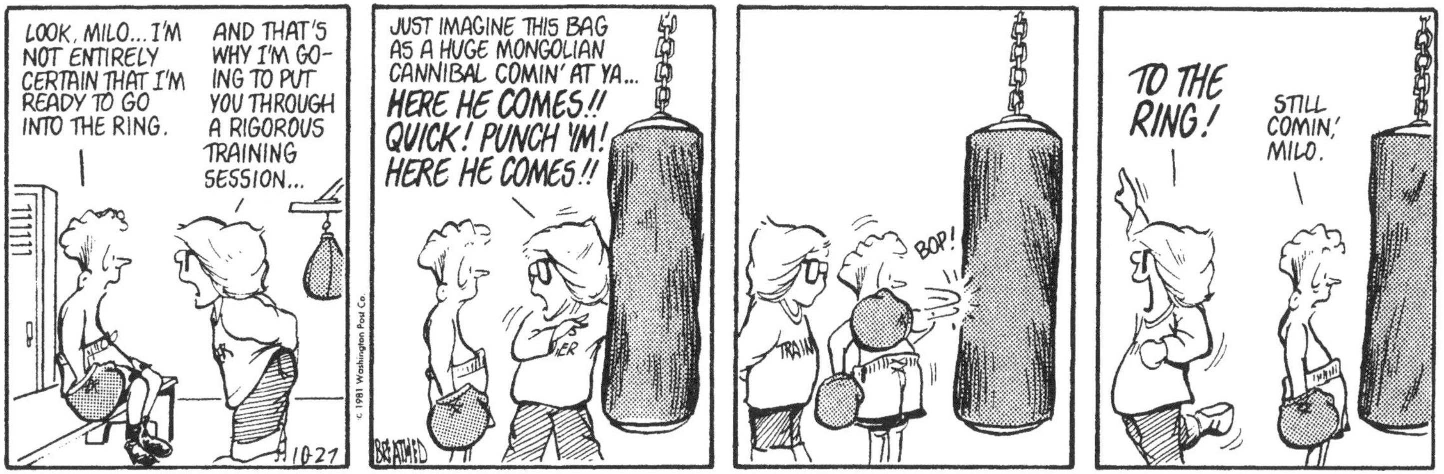
LOOK, MILO... I'M NOT ENTIRELY CERTAIN THAT I'M READY TO GO INTO THE RING.
AND THAT'S WHY I'M GOING TO PUT YOU THROUGH A RIGOROUS TRAINING SESSION...
10-27
© 1981 Washington Post Co.
JUST IMAGINE THIS BAG AS A HUGE MONGOLIAN CANNIBAL COMIN' AT YA... HERE HE COMES!! QUICK! PUNCH 'IM! HERE HE COMES!!
BREATHED
BOP!
TO THE RING!
STILL COMIN,' MILO.

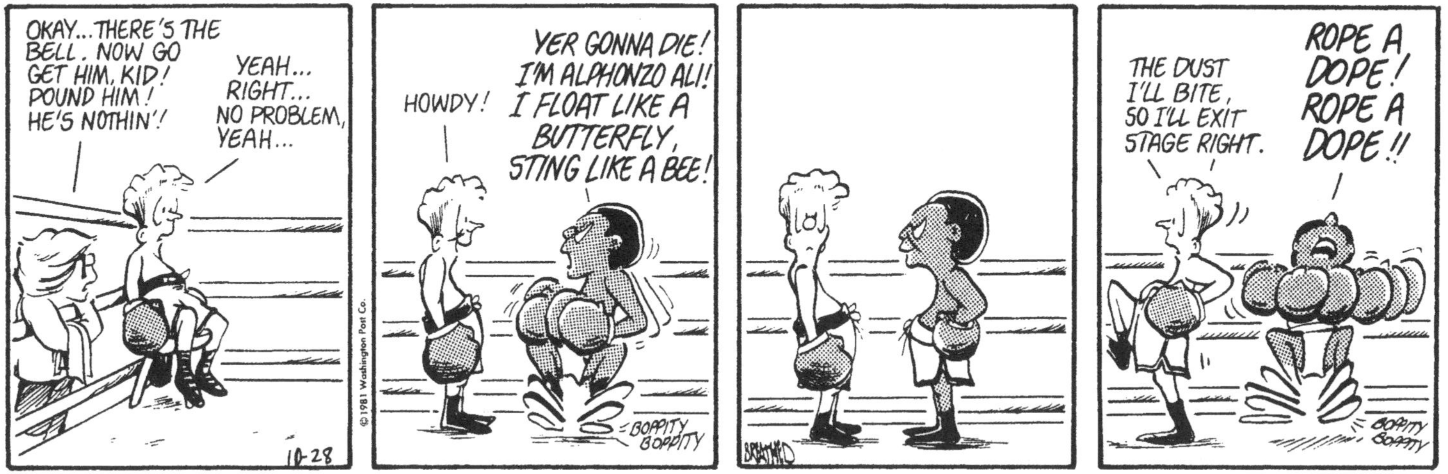
OKAY... THERE'S THE BELL. NOW GO GET HIM, KID! POUND HIM! HE'S NOTHIN'!
YEAH... RIGHT... NO PROBLEM, YEAH...
10-28
© 1981 Washington Post Co.
HOWDY!
YER GONNA DIE! I'M ALPHONZO ALI! I FLOAT LIKE A BUTTERFLY, STING LIKE A BEE!
BOPPITY BOPPITY
BREATHED
THE DUST I'LL BITE, SO I'LL EXIT STAGE RIGHT.
ROPE A DOPE! ROPE A DOPE!!
BOPPITY BOPPITY

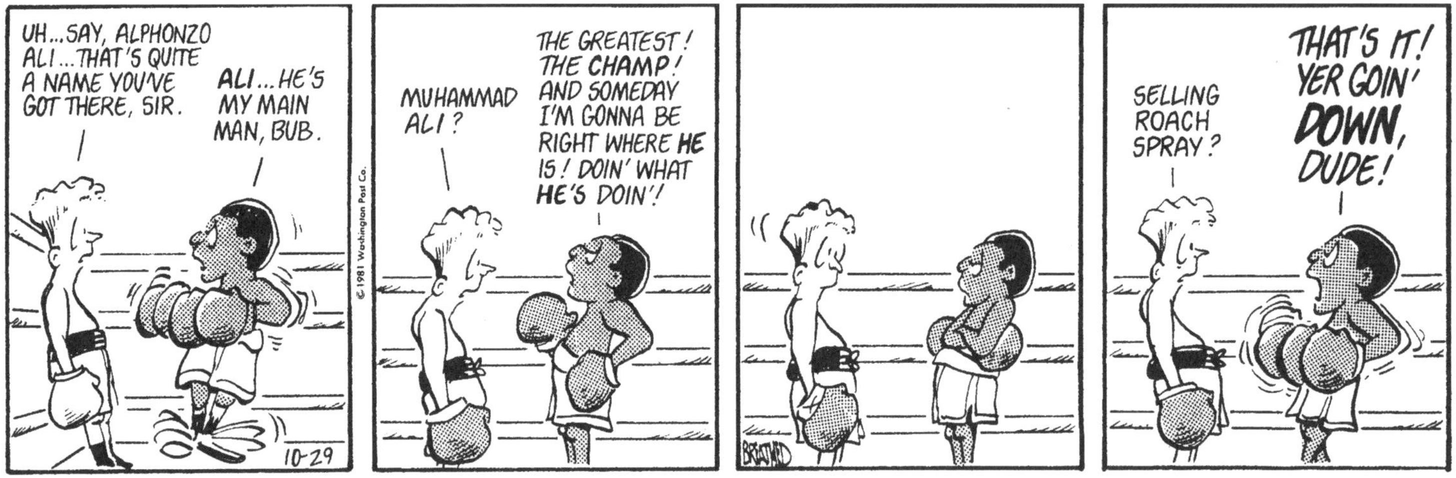
UH...SAY, ALPHONZO ALI...THAT'S QUITE A NAME YOU'VE GOT THERE, SIR.
ALI...HE'S MY MAIN MAN, BUB.
10-29
© 1981 Washington Post Co.
MUHAMMAD ALI?
THE GREATEST! THE CHAMP! AND SOMEDAY I'M GONNA BE RIGHT WHERE HE IS! DOIN' WHAT HE'S DOIN'!
BREATHED
SELLING ROACH SPRAY?
THAT'S IT! YER GOIN' DOWN, DUDE!

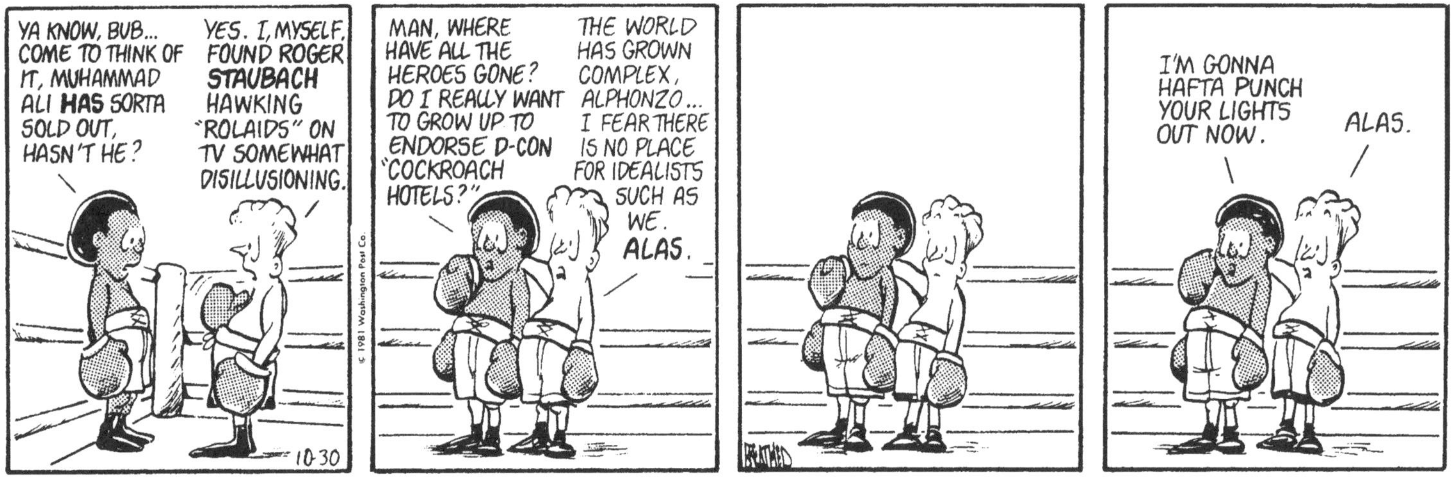
YA KNOW, BUB... COME TO THINK OF IT, MUHAMMAD ALI HAS SORTA SOLD OUT, HASN'T HE?
YES. I, MYSELF, FOUND ROGER STAUBACH HAWKING "ROLAIDS" ON TV SOMEWHAT DISILLUSIONING.
10-30
© 1981 Washington Post Co.
MAN, WHERE HAVE ALL THE HEROES GONE? DO I REALLY WANT TO GROW UP TO ENDORSE D-CON "COCKROACH HOTELS?"
THE WORLD HAS GROWN COMPLEX, ALPHONZO... I FEAR THERE IS NO PLACE FOR IDEALISTS SUCH AS WE. ALAS.
BREATHED
I'M GONNA HAFTA PUNCH YOUR LIGHTS OUT NOW.
ALAS.

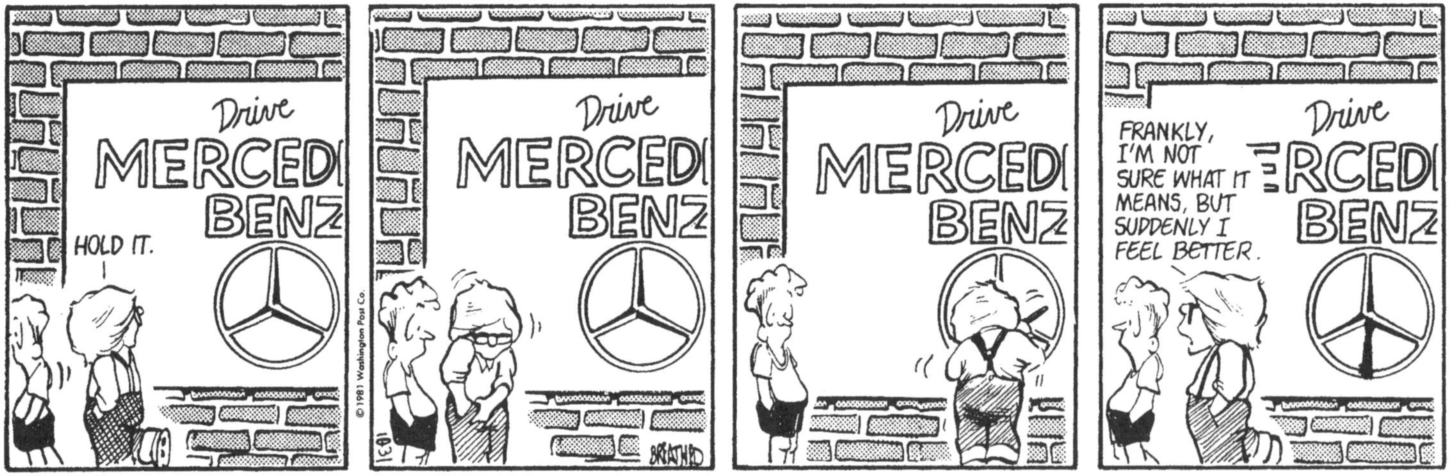
Drive
MERCED
BENZ
HOLD IT.
© 1981 Washington Post Co.
10-31
Drive
MERCED
BENZ
BREATHED
Drive
MERCED
BENZ
FRANKLY, I'M NOT SURE WHAT IT MEANS, BUT SUDDENLY I FEEL BETTER.
Drive
RCED
BENZ

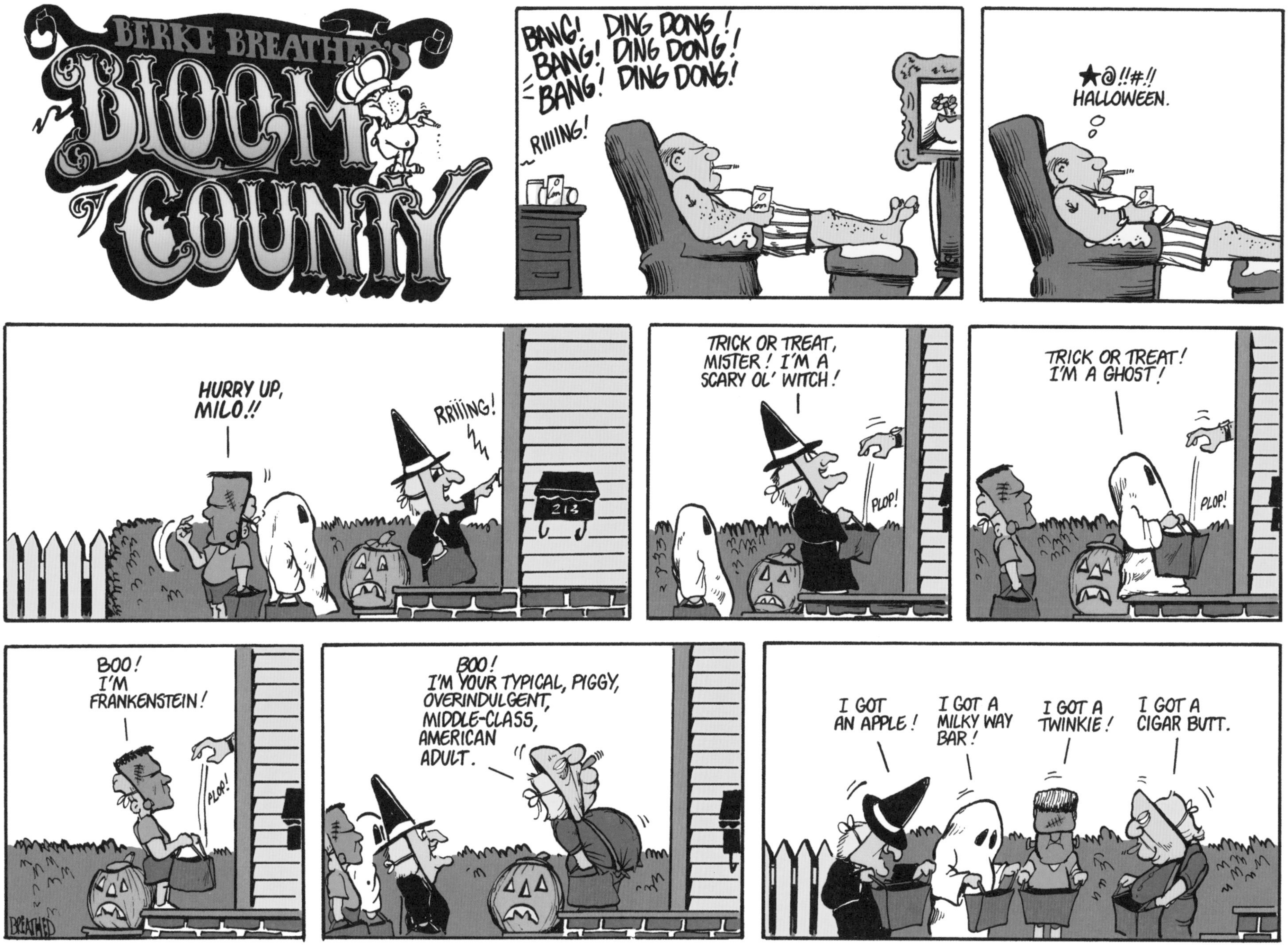
BERKE BREATHED'S
BLOOM COUNTY
BANG! BANG! BANG!
DING DONG! DING DONG! DING DONG!
RIIIING!
★@!!#!! HALLOWEEN.
HURRY UP, MILO.!!
RRIIING!
213
TRICK OR TREAT, MISTER! I'M A SCARY OL' WITCH!
PLOP!
TRICK OR TREAT! I'M A GHOST!
PLOP!
BOO! I'M FRANKENSTEIN!
PLOP!
BOO! I'M YOUR TYPICAL, PIGGY, OVERINDULGENT, MIDDLE-CLASS, AMERICAN ADULT.
I GOT AN APPLE!
I GOT A MILKY WAY BAR!
I GOT A TWINKIE!
I GOT A CIGAR BUTT.
BREATHED

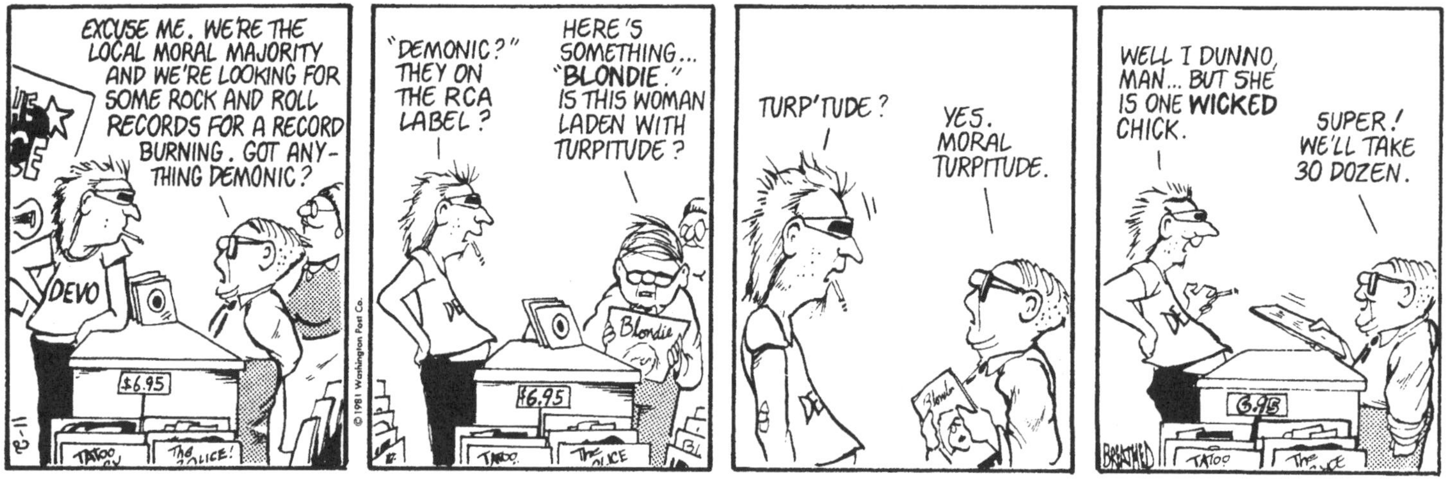
EXCUSE ME. WE'RE THE LOCAL MORAL MAJORITY AND WE'RE LOOKING FOR SOME ROCK AND ROLL RECORDS FOR A RECORD BURNING. GOT ANYTHING DEMONIC?
DEVO
$6.95
"DEMONIC?" THEY ON THE RCA LABEL?
HERE'S SOMETHING... "**BLONDIE**." IS THIS WOMAN LADEN WITH TURPITUDE?
Blondie
© 1981 Washington Post Co.
TURP'TUDE?
YES. MORAL TURPITUDE.
WELL I DUNNO, MAN... BUT SHE IS ONE **WICKED** CHICK.
SUPER! WE'LL TAKE 30 DOZEN.
BREATHED
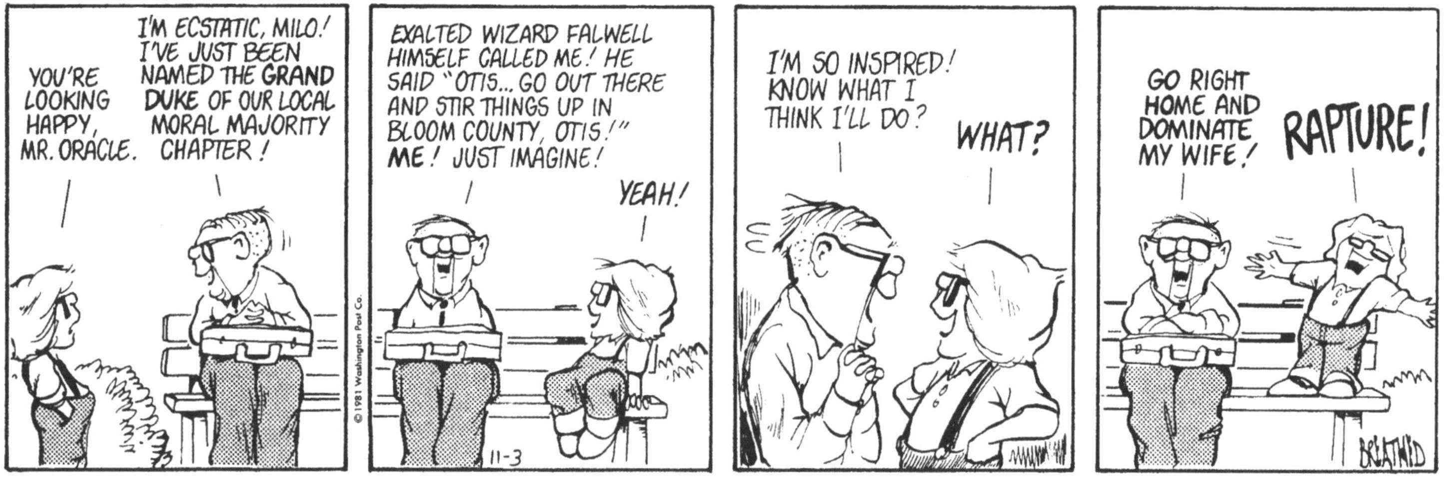
YOU'RE LOOKING HAPPY, MR. ORACLE.
I'M ECSTATIC, MILO! I'VE JUST BEEN NAMED THE **GRAND DUKE** OF OUR LOCAL MORAL MAJORITY CHAPTER!
© 1981 Washington Post Co.
EXALTED WIZARD FALWELL HIMSELF CALLED ME! HE SAID "OTIS... GO OUT THERE AND STIR THINGS UP IN BLOOM COUNTY, OTIS!" **ME**! JUST IMAGINE!
YEAH!
11-3
I'M SO INSPIRED! KNOW WHAT I THINK I'LL DO?
WHAT?
GO RIGHT **HOME** AND **DOMINATE** MY WIFE!
RAPTURE!
BREATHED
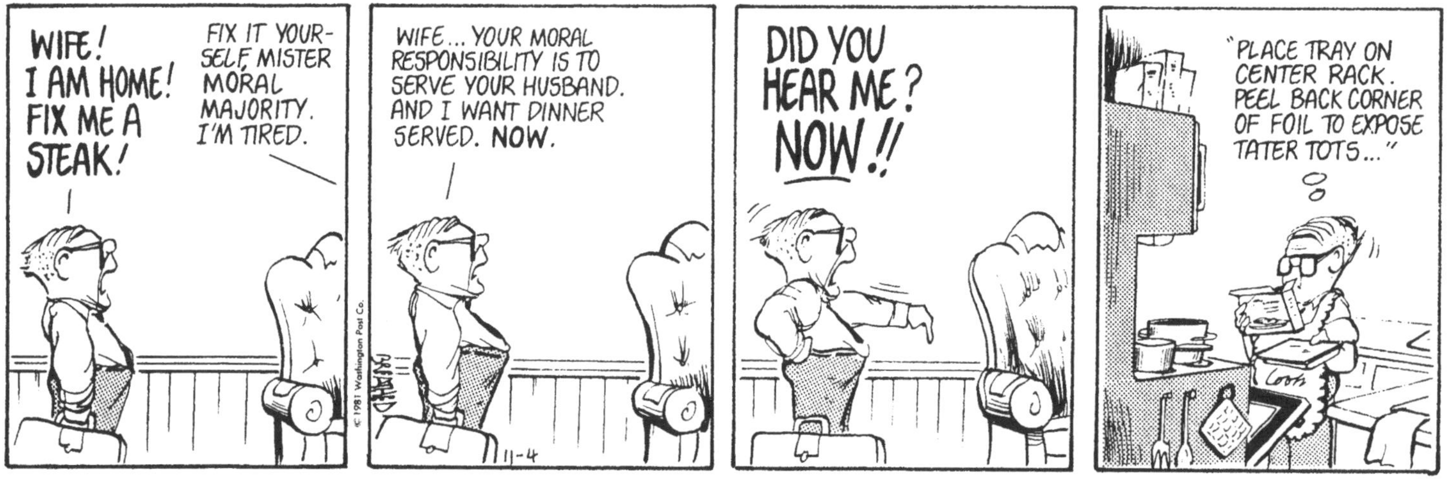
WIFE! I AM HOME! FIX ME A STEAK!
FIX IT YOURSELF, MISTER MORAL MAJORITY. I'M TIRED.
© 1981 Washington Post Co.
WIFE... YOUR MORAL RESPONSIBILITY IS TO SERVE YOUR HUSBAND. AND I WANT DINNER SERVED. **NOW**.
11-4
DID YOU HEAR ME? NOW!!
"PLACE TRAY ON CENTER RACK. PEEL BACK CORNER OF FOIL TO EXPOSE TATER TOTS..."

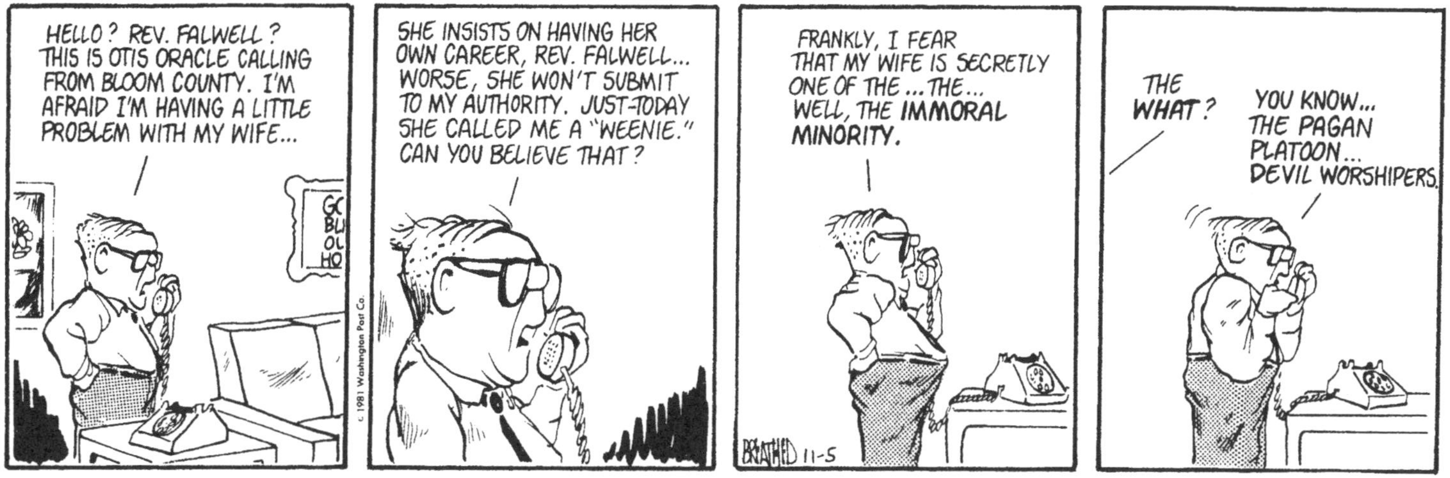
HELLO? REV. FALWELL? THIS IS OTIS ORACLE CALLING FROM BLOOM COUNTY. I'M AFRAID I'M HAVING A LITTLE PROBLEM WITH MY WIFE...
SHE INSISTS ON HAVING HER OWN CAREER, REV. FALWELL... WORSE, SHE WON'T SUBMIT TO MY AUTHORITY. JUST TODAY SHE CALLED ME A "WEENIE." CAN YOU BELIEVE THAT?
© 1981 Washington Post Co.
FRANKLY, I FEAR THAT MY WIFE IS SECRETLY ONE OF THE ... THE... WELL, THE **IMMORAL MINORITY.**
BREATHED 11-5
THE **WHAT**?
YOU KNOW... THE PAGAN PLATOON... DEVIL WORSHIPERS.

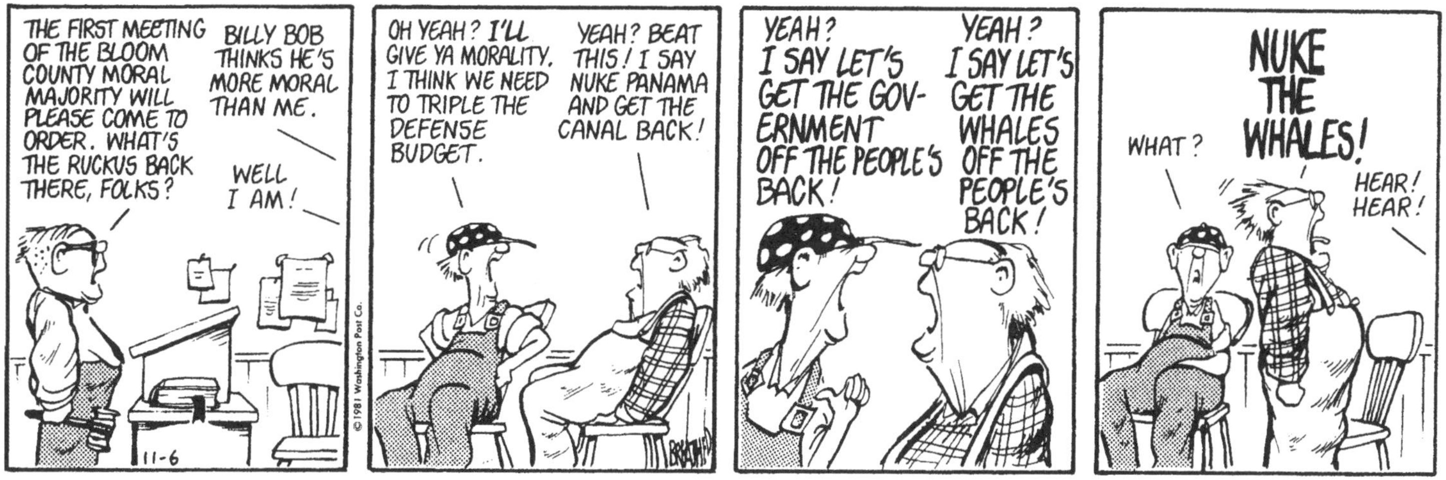
THE FIRST MEETING OF THE BLOOM COUNTY MORAL MAJORITY WILL PLEASE COME TO ORDER. WHAT'S THE RUCKUS BACK THERE, FOLKS?
BILLY BOB THINKS HE'S MORE MORAL THAN ME.
WELL I AM!
11-6
© 1981 Washington Post Co.
OH YEAH? **I'LL** GIVE YA MORALITY. I THINK WE NEED TO TRIPLE THE DEFENSE BUDGET.
YEAH? BEAT THIS! I SAY NUKE PANAMA AND GET THE CANAL BACK!
BREATHED
YEAH? I SAY LET'S GET THE GOVERNMENT OFF THE PEOPLE'S BACK!
YEAH? I SAY LET'S GET THE WHALES OFF THE PEOPLE'S BACK!
NUKE THE WHALES!
WHAT?
HEAR! HEAR!

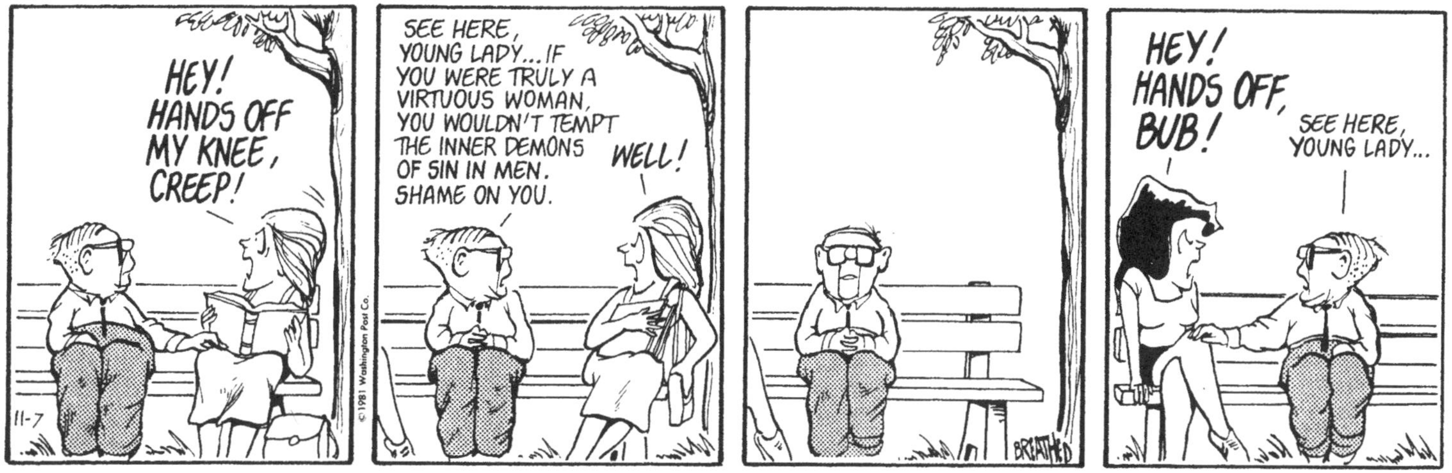
HEY! HANDS OFF MY KNEE, CREEP!
11-7
© 1981 Washington Post Co.
SEE HERE, YOUNG LADY... IF YOU WERE TRULY A VIRTUOUS WOMAN, YOU WOULDN'T TEMPT THE INNER DEMONS OF SIN IN MEN. SHAME ON YOU.
WELL!
BREATHED
HEY! HANDS OFF, BUB!
SEE HERE, YOUNG LADY...

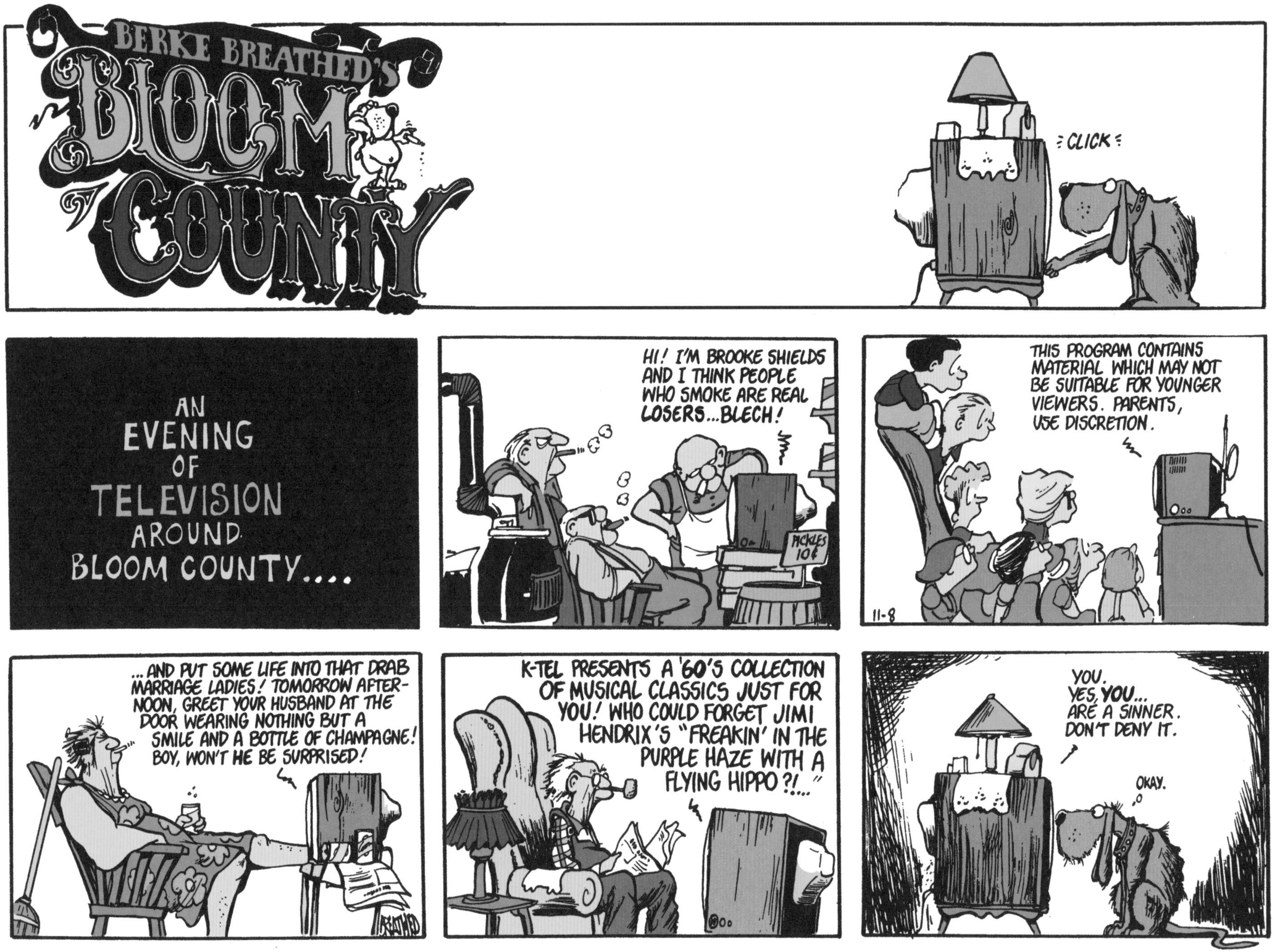
BERKE BREATHED'S
BLOOM COUNTY
CLICK
AN EVENING OF TELEVISION AROUND BLOOM COUNTY....
HI! I'M BROOKE SHIELDS AND I THINK PEOPLE WHO SMOKE ARE REAL LOSERS...BLECH!
PICKLES 10¢
THIS PROGRAM CONTAINS MATERIAL WHICH MAY NOT BE SUITABLE FOR YOUNGER VIEWERS. PARENTS, USE DISCRETION.
11-8
...AND PUT SOME LIFE INTO THAT DRAB MARRIAGE LADIES! TOMORROW AFTERNOON, GREET YOUR HUSBAND AT THE DOOR WEARING NOTHING BUT A SMILE AND A BOTTLE OF CHAMPAGNE! BOY, WON'T HE BE SURPRISED!
K-TEL PRESENTS A '60'S COLLECTION OF MUSICAL CLASSICS JUST FOR YOU! WHO COULD FORGET JIMI HENDRIX'S "FREAKIN' IN THE PURPLE HAZE WITH A FLYING HIPPO?!..."
YOU. YES, YOU... ARE A SINNER. DON'T DENY IT.
OKAY.

 November 8, 1981

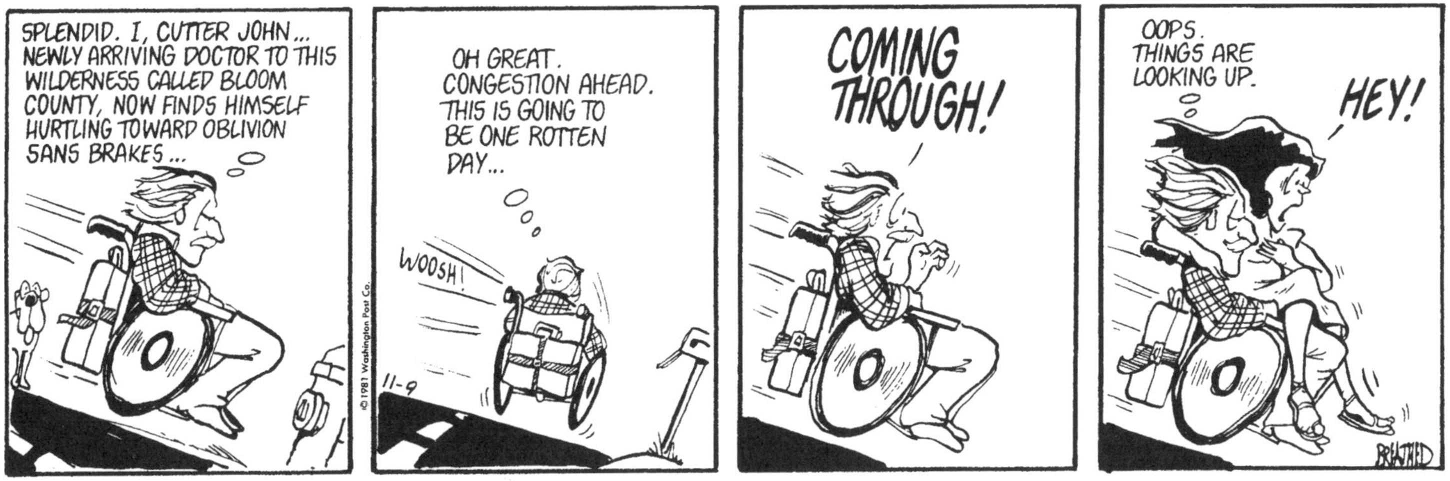
SPLENDID. I, CUTTER JOHN... NEWLY ARRIVING DOCTOR TO THIS WILDERNESS CALLED BLOOM COUNTY, NOW FINDS HIMSELF HURTLING TOWARD OBLIVION SANS BRAKES...
© 1981 Washington Post Co.
11-9
WOOSH!
OH GREAT. CONGESTION AHEAD. THIS IS GOING TO BE ONE ROTTEN DAY...
COMING THROUGH!
OOPS. THINGS ARE LOOKING UP.
HEY!
BREATHED

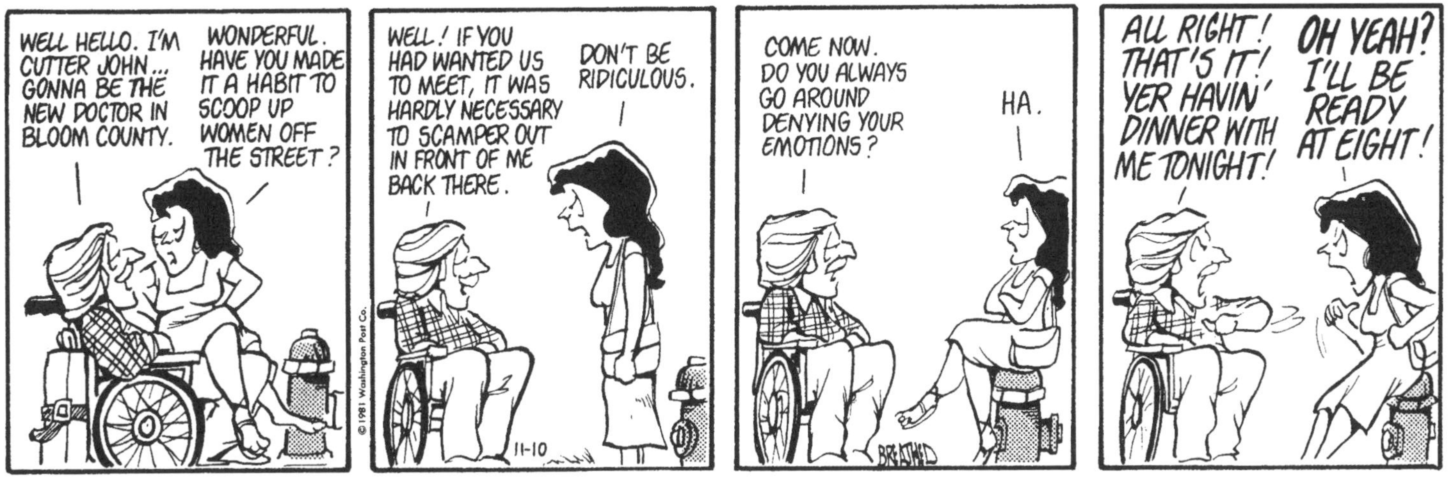
WELL HELLO. I'M CUTTER JOHN... GONNA BE THE NEW DOCTOR IN BLOOM COUNTY.
WONDERFUL. HAVE YOU MADE IT A HABIT TO SCOOP UP WOMEN OFF THE STREET?
© 1981 Washington Post Co.
WELL! IF YOU HAD WANTED US TO MEET, IT WAS HARDLY NECESSARY TO SCAMPER OUT IN FRONT OF ME BACK THERE.
DON'T BE RIDICULOUS.
11-10
COME NOW. DO YOU ALWAYS GO AROUND DENYING YOUR EMOTIONS?
HA.
BREATHED
ALL RIGHT! THAT'S IT! YER HAVIN' DINNER WITH ME TONIGHT!
OH YEAH? I'LL BE READY AT EIGHT!

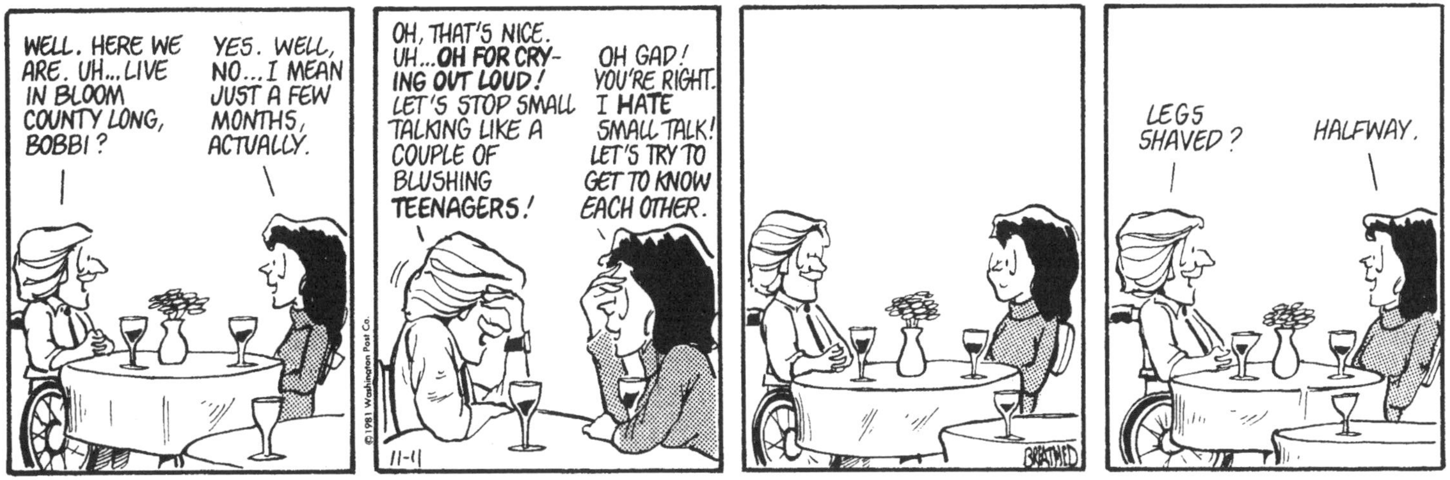
WELL. HERE WE ARE. UH...LIVE IN BLOOM COUNTY LONG, BOBBI?
YES. WELL, NO...I MEAN JUST A FEW MONTHS, ACTUALLY.
© 1981 Washington Post Co.
OH, THAT'S NICE. UH...OH FOR CRYING OUT LOUD! LET'S STOP SMALL TALKING LIKE A COUPLE OF BLUSHING TEENAGERS!
OH GAD! YOU'RE RIGHT. I HATE SMALL TALK! LET'S TRY TO GET TO KNOW EACH OTHER.
11-11
BREATHED
LEGS SHAVED?
HALFWAY.

Cutter John rolls in for the first time.

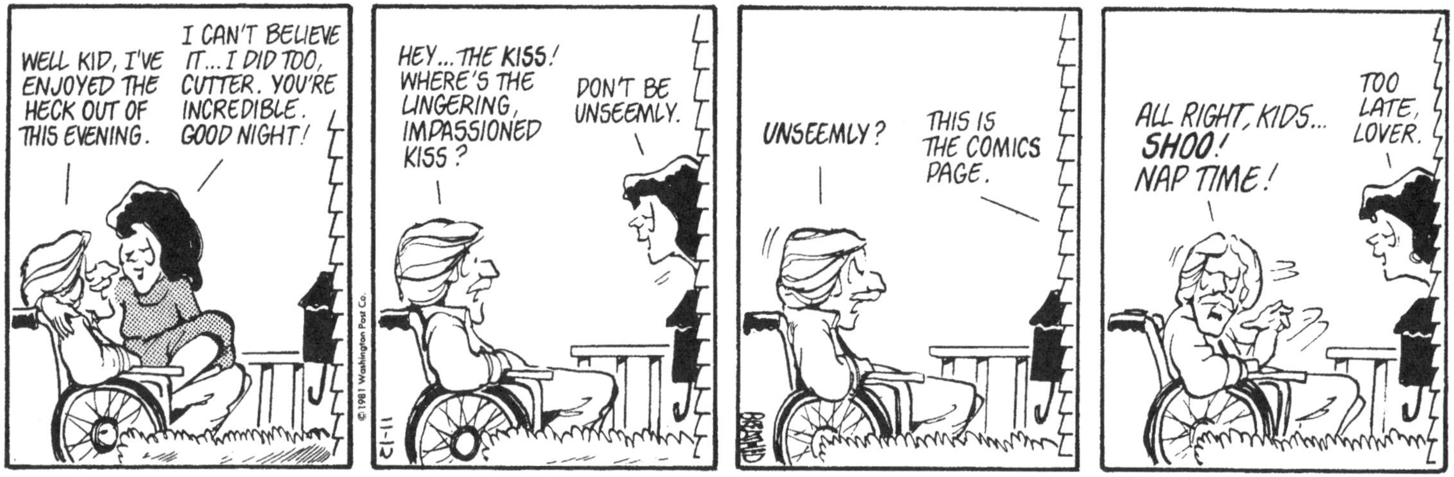
WELL KID, I'VE ENJOYED THE HECK OUT OF THIS EVENING.
I CAN'T BELIEVE IT... I DID TOO, CUTTER. YOU'RE INCREDIBLE. GOOD NIGHT!
© 1981 Washington Post Co.
11-12
HEY... THE KISS! WHERE'S THE LINGERING, IMPASSIONED KISS?
DON'T BE UNSEEMLY.
UNSEEMLY?
THIS IS THE COMICS PAGE.
BREATHED
ALL RIGHT, KIDS... SHOO! NAP TIME!
TOO LATE, LOVER.

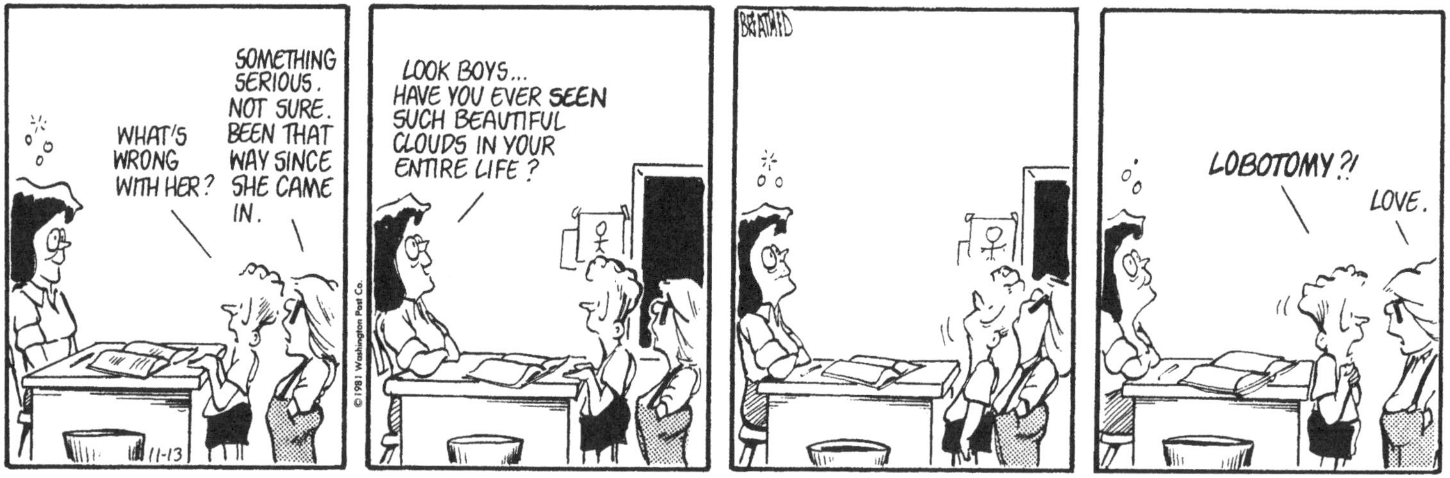
WHAT'S WRONG WITH HER?
SOMETHING SERIOUS. NOT SURE. BEEN THAT WAY SINCE SHE CAME IN.
11-13
© 1981 Washington Post Co.
LOOK BOYS... HAVE YOU EVER SEEN SUCH BEAUTIFUL CLOUDS IN YOUR ENTIRE LIFE?
BREATHED
LOBOTOMY?!
LOVE.

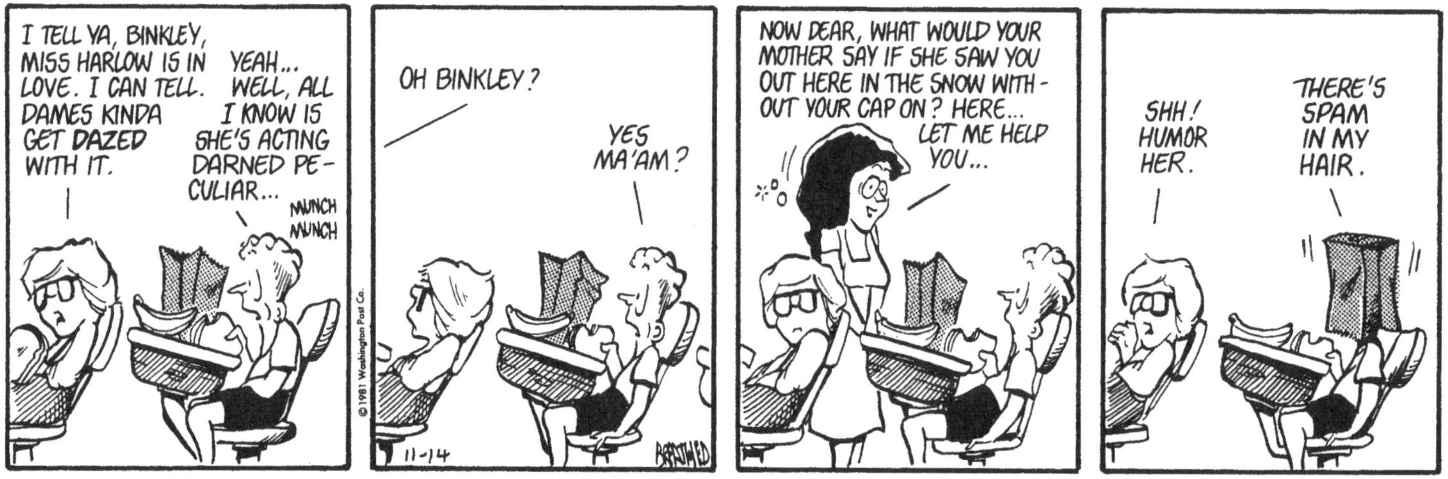
I TELL YA, BINKLEY, MISS HARLOW IS IN LOVE. I CAN TELL. DAMES KINDA GET DAZED WITH IT.
YEAH... WELL, ALL I KNOW IS SHE'S ACTING DARNED PECULIAR...
MUNCH MUNCH
© 1981 Washington Post Co.
OH BINKLEY?
YES MA'AM?
11-14
BREATHED
NOW DEAR, WHAT WOULD YOUR MOTHER SAY IF SHE SAW YOU OUT HERE IN THE SNOW WITHOUT YOUR CAP ON? HERE... LET ME HELP YOU...
SHH! HUMOR HER.
THERE'S SPAM IN MY HAIR.

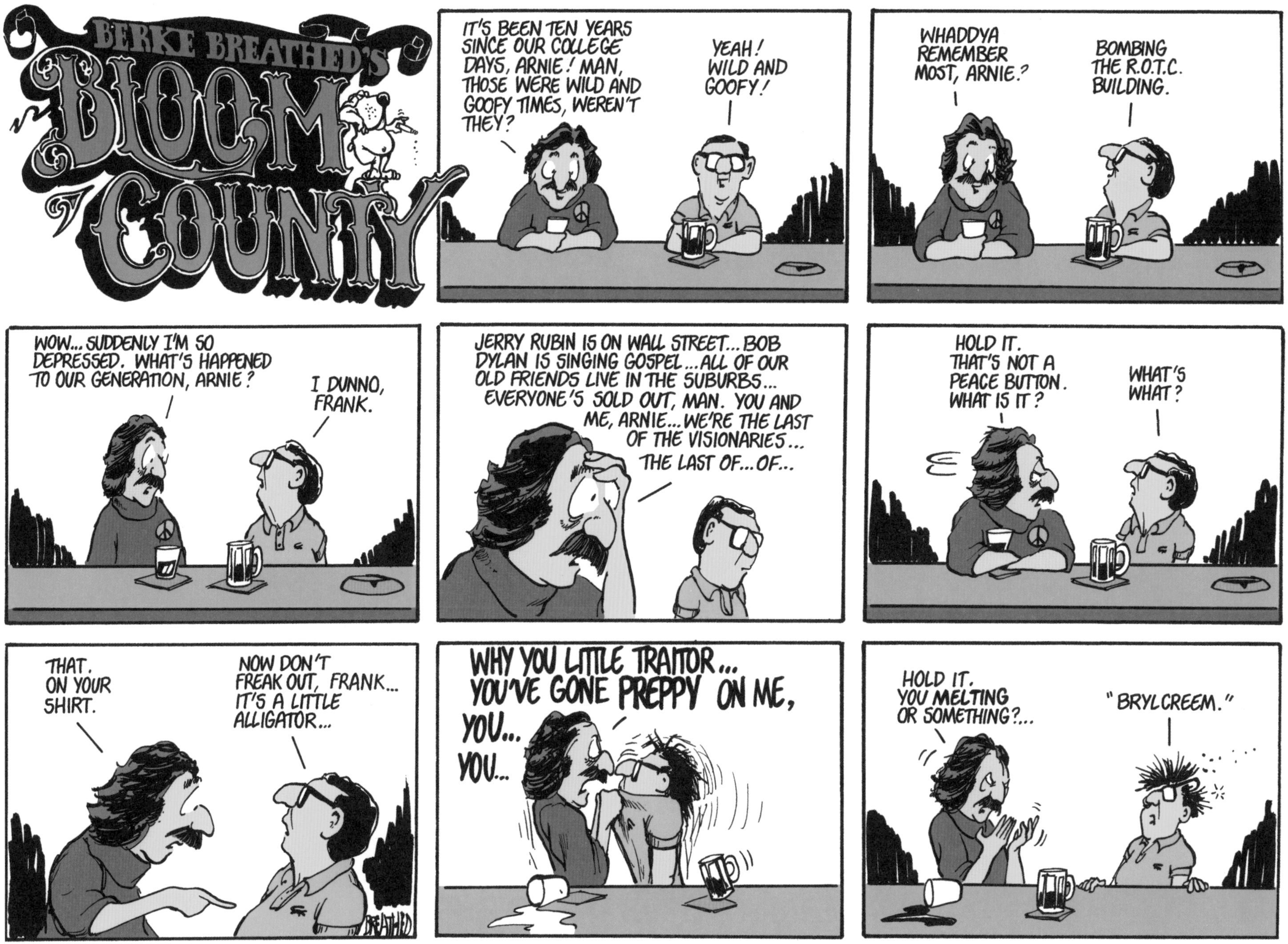
BERKE BREATHED'S
BLOOM COUNTY
IT'S BEEN TEN YEARS SINCE OUR COLLEGE DAYS, ARNIE! MAN, THOSE WERE WILD AND GOOFY TIMES, WEREN'T THEY?
YEAH! WILD AND GOOFY!
WHADDYA REMEMBER MOST, ARNIE?
BOMBING THE R.O.T.C. BUILDING.
WOW... SUDDENLY I'M SO DEPRESSED. WHAT'S HAPPENED TO OUR GENERATION, ARNIE?
I DUNNO, FRANK.
JERRY RUBIN IS ON WALL STREET... BOB DYLAN IS SINGING GOSPEL... ALL OF OUR OLD FRIENDS LIVE IN THE SUBURBS... EVERYONE'S SOLD OUT, MAN. YOU AND ME, ARNIE... WE'RE THE LAST OF THE VISIONARIES... THE LAST OF... OF...
HOLD IT. THAT'S NOT A PEACE BUTTON. WHAT IS IT?
WHAT'S WHAT?
THAT. ON YOUR SHIRT.
NOW DON'T FREAK OUT, FRANK... IT'S A LITTLE ALLIGATOR...
WHY YOU LITTLE TRAITOR... YOU'VE GONE PREPPY ON ME, YOU... YOU...
HOLD IT. YOU MELTING OR SOMETHING?...
"BRYLCREEM."
BREATHED

Jerry Rubin, 1960s political and anti-war activist, and founding member of the Youth International Party, aka, YIPPIES.

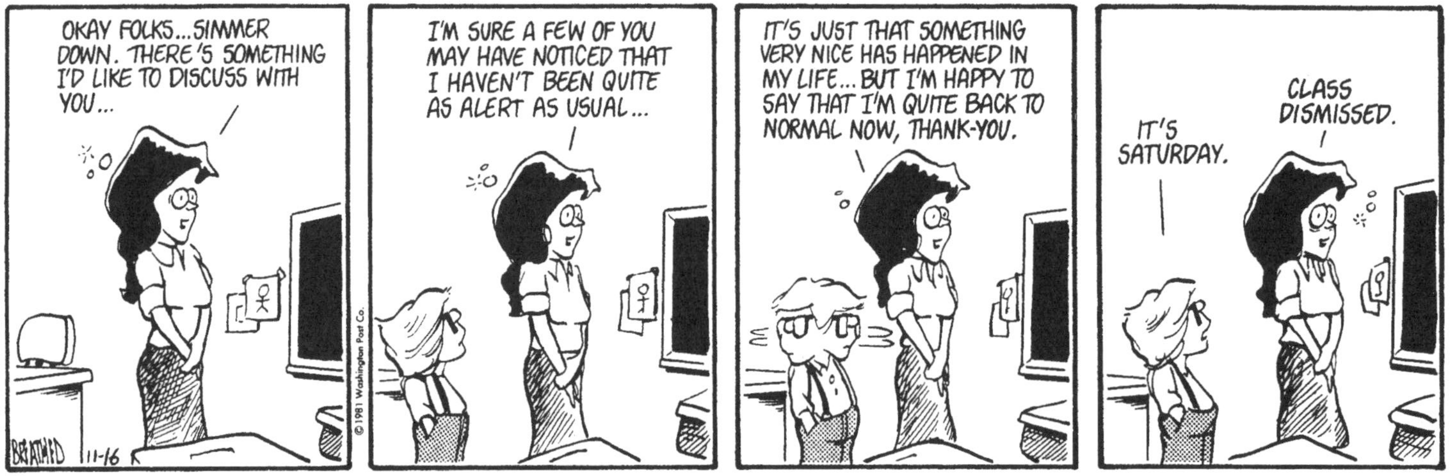
OKAY FOLKS...SIMMER DOWN. THERE'S SOMETHING I'D LIKE TO DISCUSS WITH YOU...
I'M SURE A FEW OF YOU MAY HAVE NOTICED THAT I HAVEN'T BEEN QUITE AS ALERT AS USUAL...
IT'S JUST THAT SOMETHING VERY NICE HAS HAPPENED IN MY LIFE... BUT I'M HAPPY TO SAY THAT I'M QUITE BACK TO NORMAL NOW, THANK-YOU.
IT'S SATURDAY.
CLASS DISMISSED.

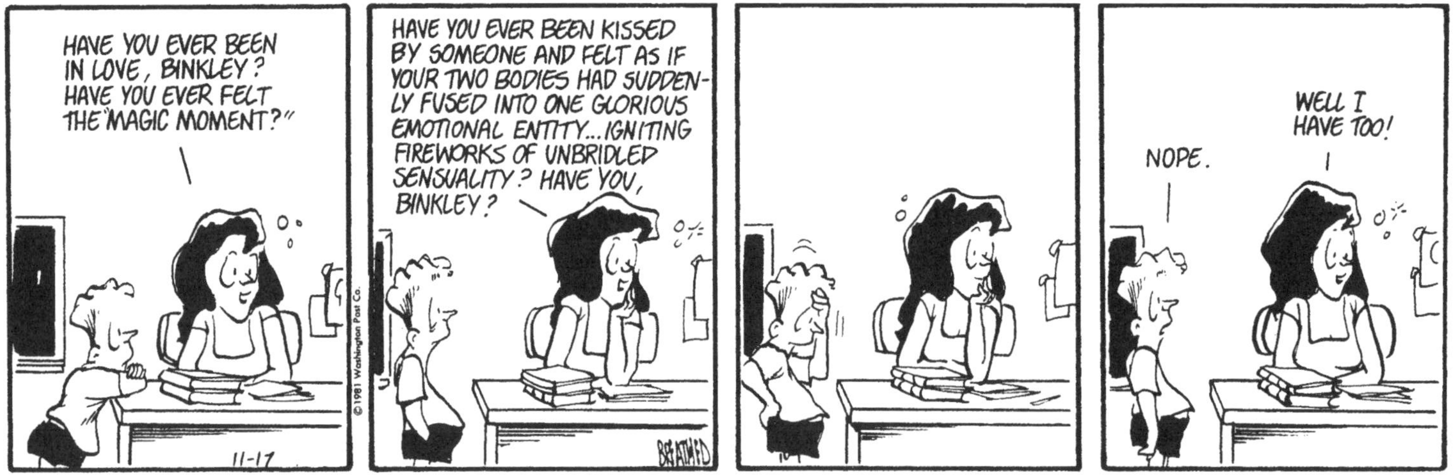
HAVE YOU EVER BEEN IN LOVE, BINKLEY? HAVE YOU EVER FELT THE "MAGIC MOMENT?"
HAVE YOU EVER BEEN KISSED BY SOMEONE AND FELT AS IF YOUR TWO BODIES HAD SUDDENLY FUSED INTO ONE GLORIOUS EMOTIONAL ENTITY...IGNITING FIREWORKS OF UNBRIDLED SENSUALITY? HAVE YOU, BINKLEY?
NOPE.
WELL I HAVE TOO!

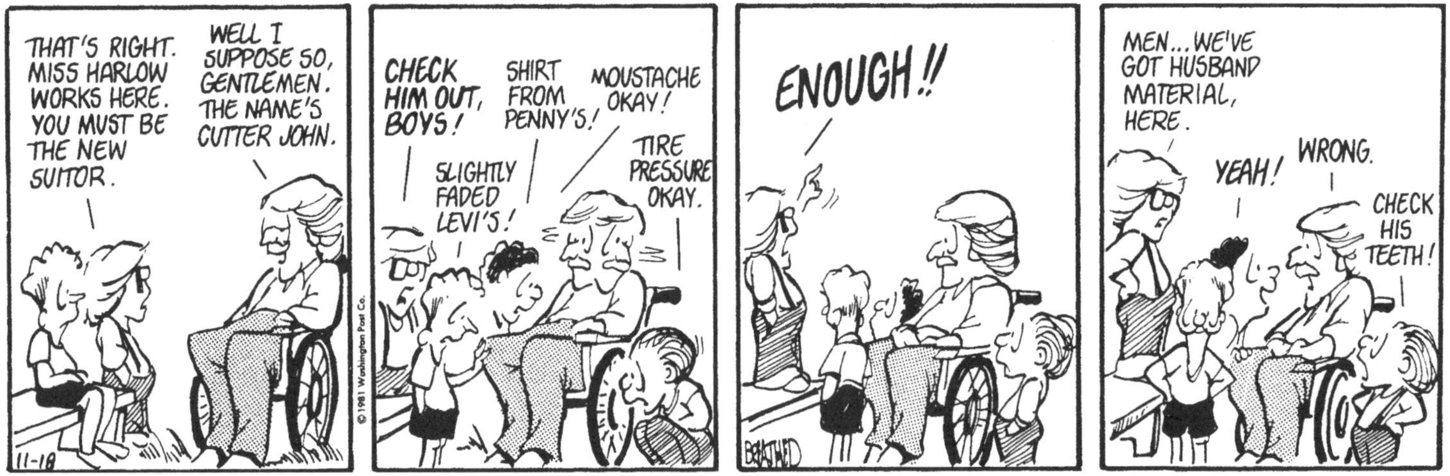
THAT'S RIGHT. MISS HARLOW WORKS HERE. YOU MUST BE THE NEW SUITOR.
WELL I SUPPOSE SO, GENTLEMEN. THE NAME'S CUTTER JOHN.
CHECK HIM OUT, BOYS!
SLIGHTLY FADED LEVI'S!
SHIRT FROM PENNY'S!
MOUSTACHE OKAY!
TIRE PRESSURE OKAY.
ENOUGH!!
MEN... WE'VE GOT HUSBAND MATERIAL, HERE.
YEAH!
WRONG.
CHECK HIS TEETH!

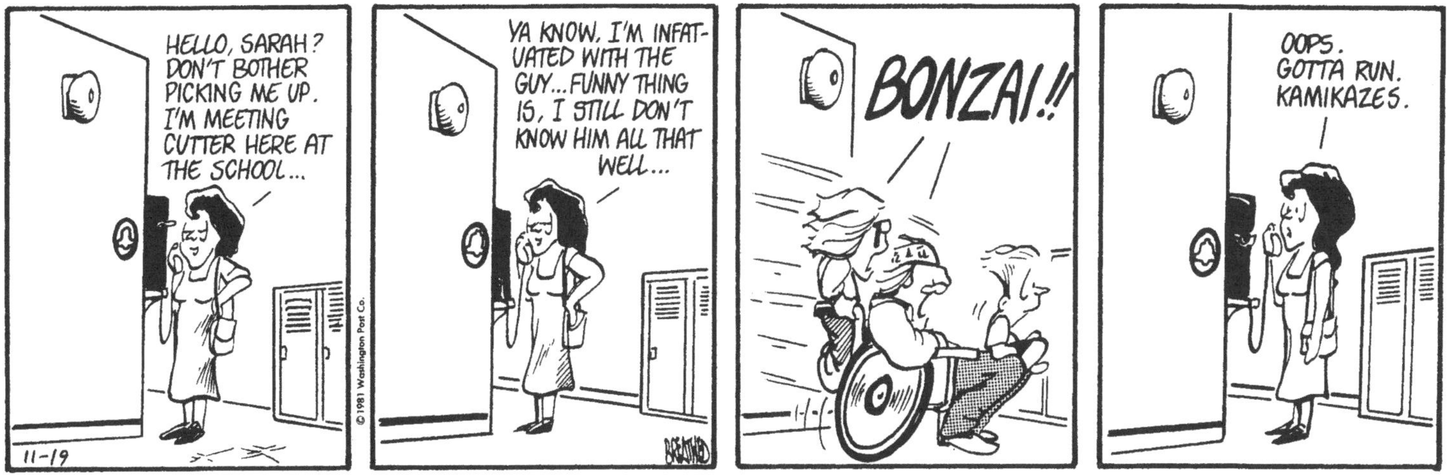
HELLO, SARAH? DON'T BOTHER PICKING ME UP. I'M MEETING CUTTER HERE AT THE SCHOOL...
11-19
YA KNOW, I'M INFATUATED WITH THE GUY...FUNNY THING IS, I STILL DON'T KNOW HIM ALL THAT WELL...
© 1981 Washington Post Co.
BONZAI!!
OOPS. GOTTA RUN. KAMIKAZES.
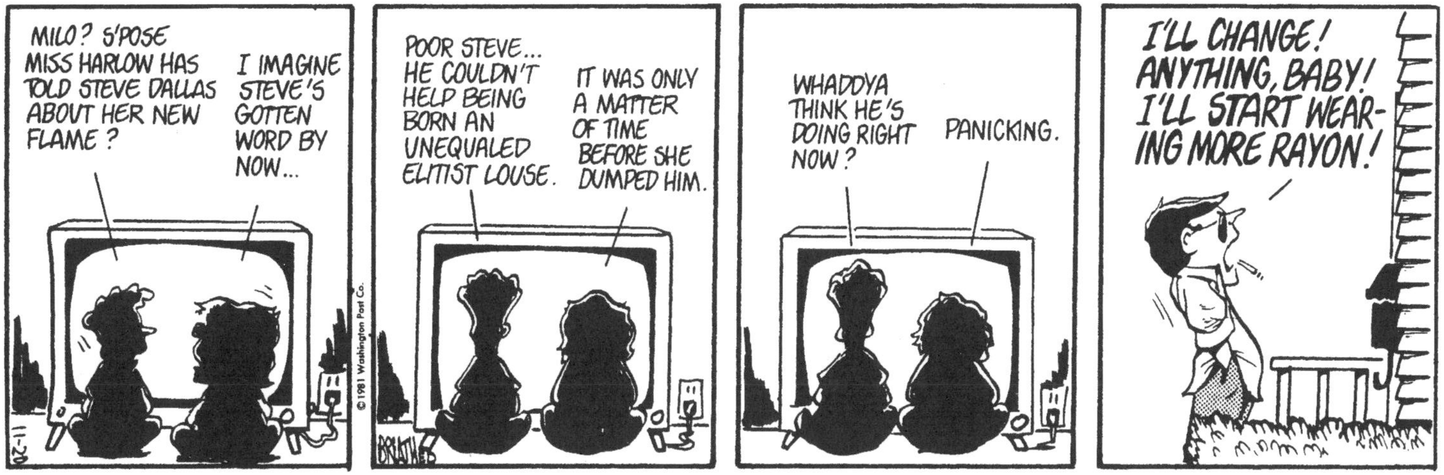
MILO? S'POSE MISS HARLOW HAS TOLD STEVE DALLAS ABOUT HER NEW FLAME?
I IMAGINE STEVE'S GOTTEN WORD BY NOW...
© 1981 Washington Post Co.
POOR STEVE... HE COULDN'T HELP BEING BORN AN UNEQUALED ELITIST LOUSE.
IT WAS ONLY A MATTER OF TIME BEFORE SHE DUMPED HIM.
WHADDYA THINK HE'S DOING RIGHT NOW?
PANICKING.
I'LL CHANGE! ANYTHING, BABY! I'LL START WEARING MORE RAYON!
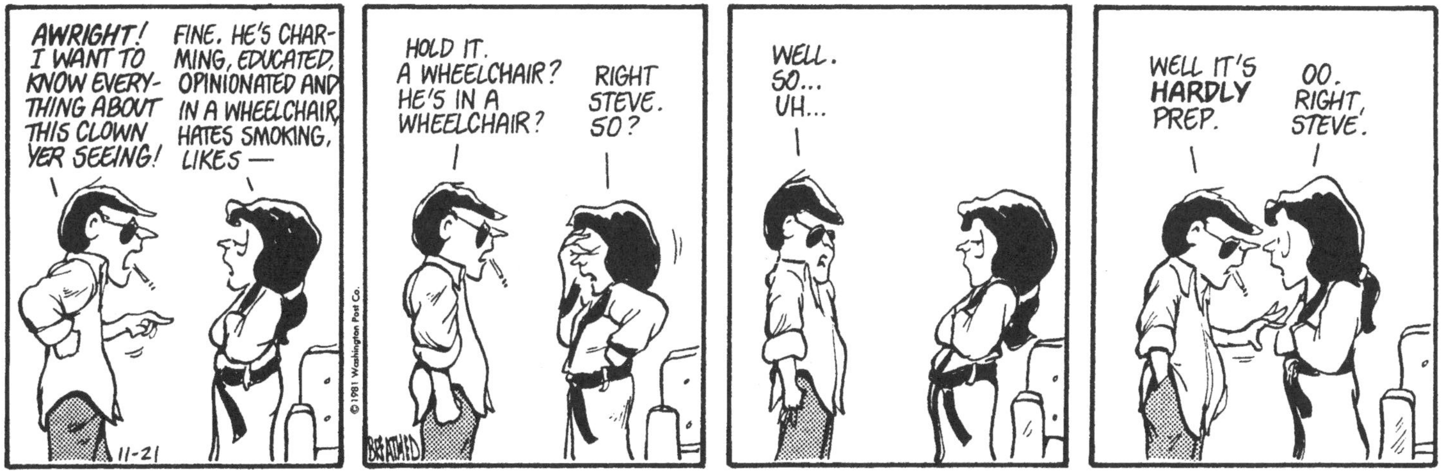
AWRIGHT! I WANT TO KNOW EVERYTHING ABOUT THIS CLOWN YER SEEING!
FINE. HE'S CHARMING, EDUCATED, OPINIONATED AND IN A WHEELCHAIR, HATES SMOKING, LIKES —
11-21
© 1981 Washington Post Co.
HOLD IT. A WHEELCHAIR? HE'S IN A WHEELCHAIR?
RIGHT STEVE. SO?
WELL. SO... UH...
WELL IT'S HARDLY PREP.
OO. RIGHT, STEVE.

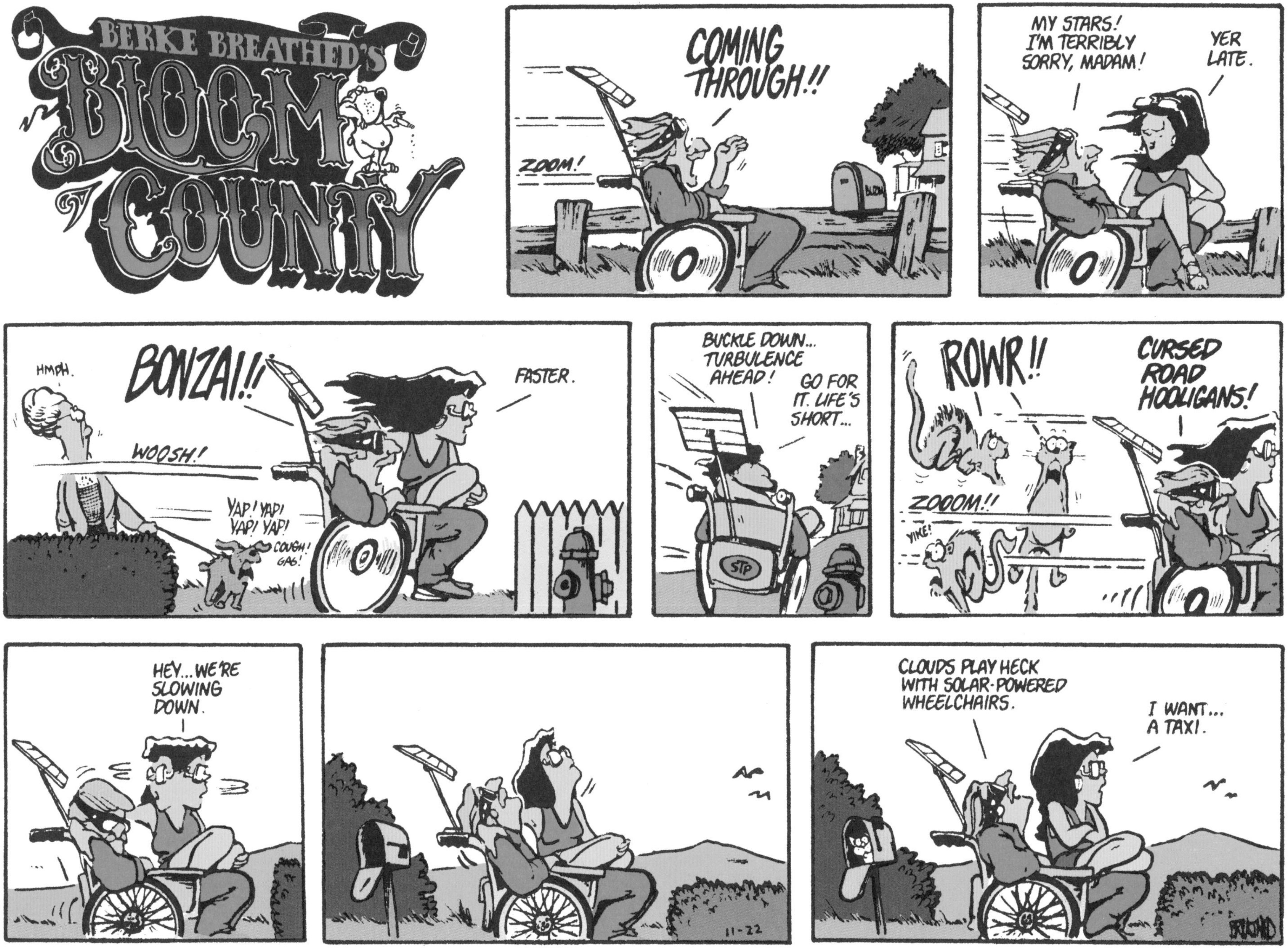
BERKE BREATHED'S
BLOOM COUNTY
COMING THROUGH!!
ZOOM!
MY STARS! I'M TERRIBLY SORRY, MADAM!
YER LATE.
HMPH.
BONZAI!!
FASTER.
WOOSH!
YAP! YAP! YAP! YAP!
COUGH! GAG!
BUCKLE DOWN... TURBULENCE AHEAD!
GO FOR IT. LIFE'S SHORT...
STP
ROWR!!
CURSED ROAD HOOLIGANS!
ZOOOM!!
YIKE!
HEY... WE'RE SLOWING DOWN.
11-22
CLOUDS PLAY HECK WITH SOLAR-POWERED WHEELCHAIRS.
I WANT... A TAXI.

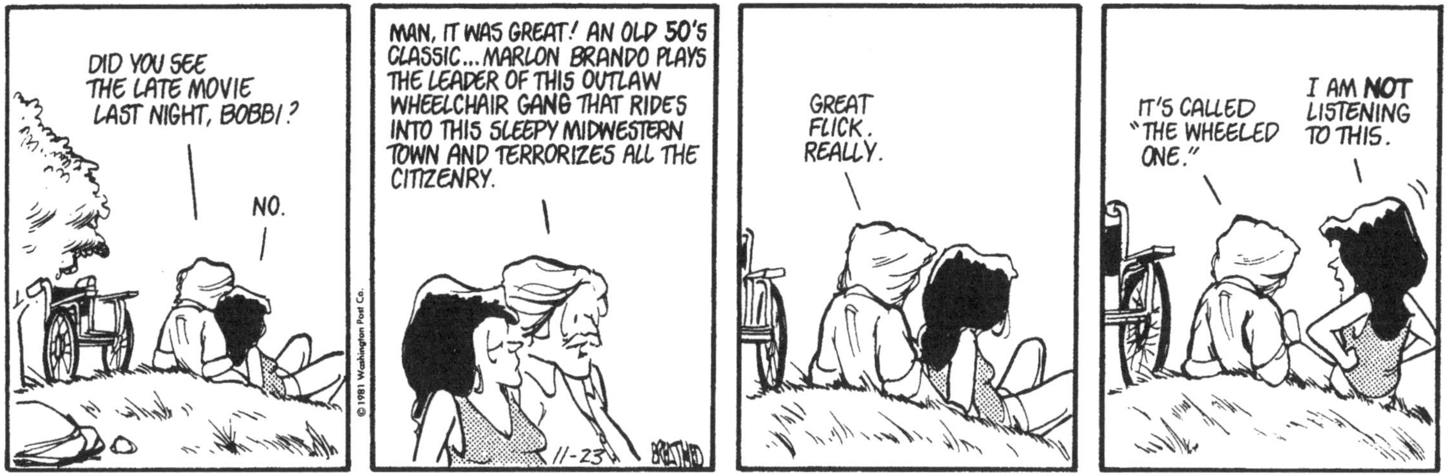
DID YOU SEE THE LATE MOVIE LAST NIGHT, BOBBI?
NO.
MAN, IT WAS GREAT! AN OLD 50'S CLASSIC... MARLON BRANDO PLAYS THE LEADER OF THIS OUTLAW WHEELCHAIR GANG THAT RIDES INTO THIS SLEEPY MIDWESTERN TOWN AND TERRORIZES ALL THE CITIZENRY.
GREAT FLICK. REALLY.
IT'S CALLED "THE WHEELED ONE."
I AM **NOT** LISTENING TO THIS.

A reference to *The Wild One*, the classic 1953 film starring Marlon Brando as the leader of a motorcycle gang.

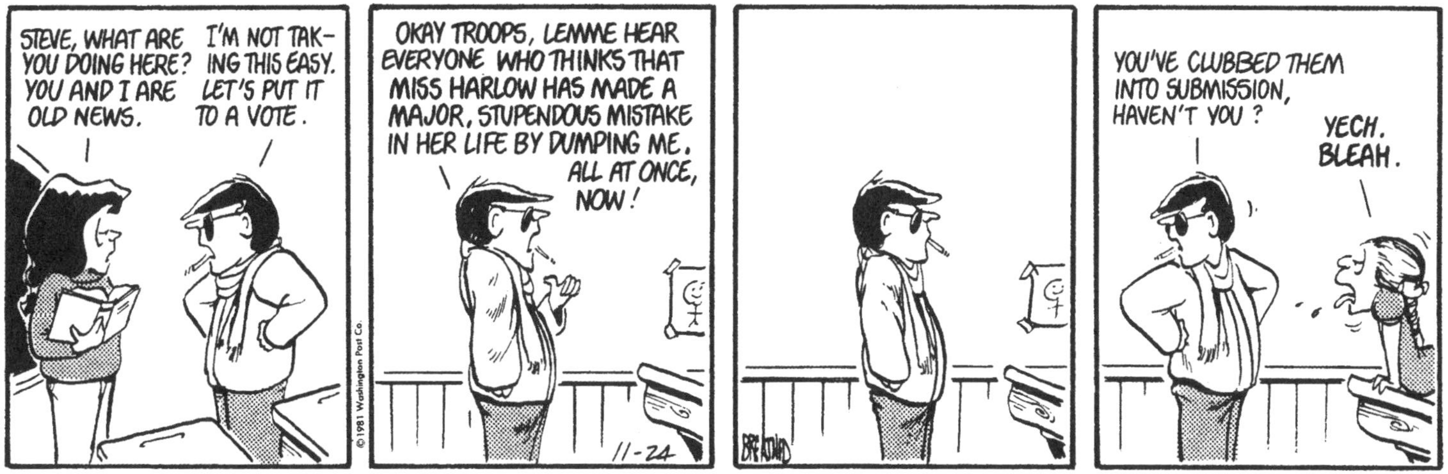
STEVE, WHAT ARE YOU DOING HERE? YOU AND I ARE OLD NEWS.
I'M NOT TAKING THIS EASY. LET'S PUT IT TO A VOTE.
OKAY TROOPS, LEMME HEAR EVERYONE WHO THINKS THAT MISS HARLOW HAS MADE A MAJOR, STUPENDOUS MISTAKE IN HER LIFE BY DUMPING ME.
ALL AT ONCE, NOW!
YOU'VE CLUBBED THEM INTO SUBMISSION, HAVEN'T YOU?
YECH. BLEAH.

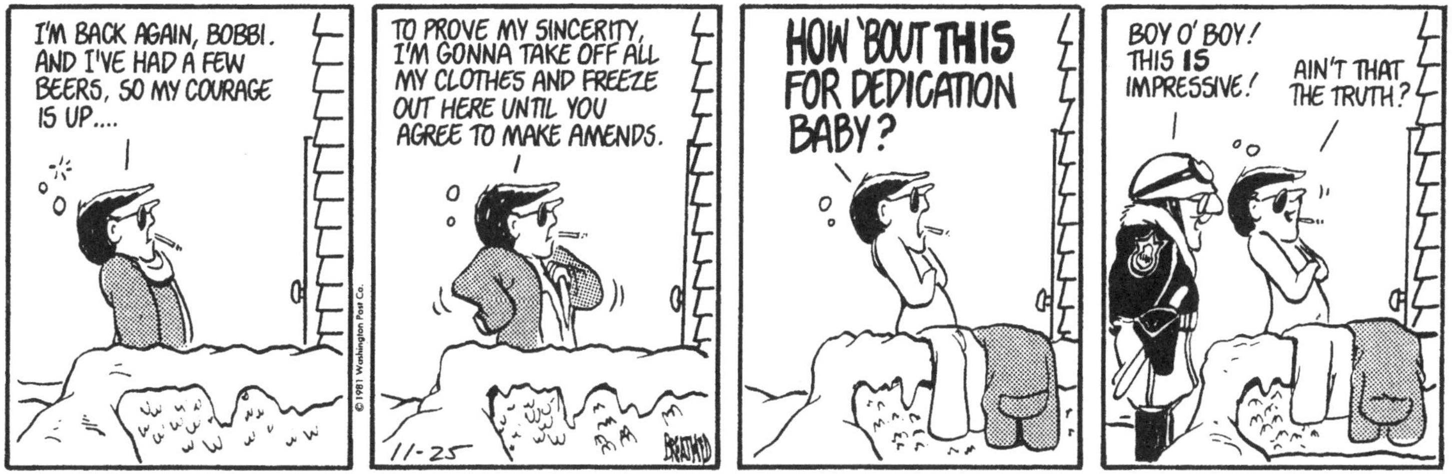
I'M BACK AGAIN, BOBBI. AND I'VE HAD A FEW BEERS, SO MY COURAGE IS UP....
TO PROVE MY SINCERITY, I'M GONNA TAKE OFF ALL MY CLOTHES AND FREEZE OUT HERE UNTIL YOU AGREE TO MAKE AMENDS.
HOW 'BOUT **THIS** FOR DEDICATION BABY?
BOY O' BOY! THIS **IS** IMPRESSIVE!
AIN'T THAT THE TRUTH?

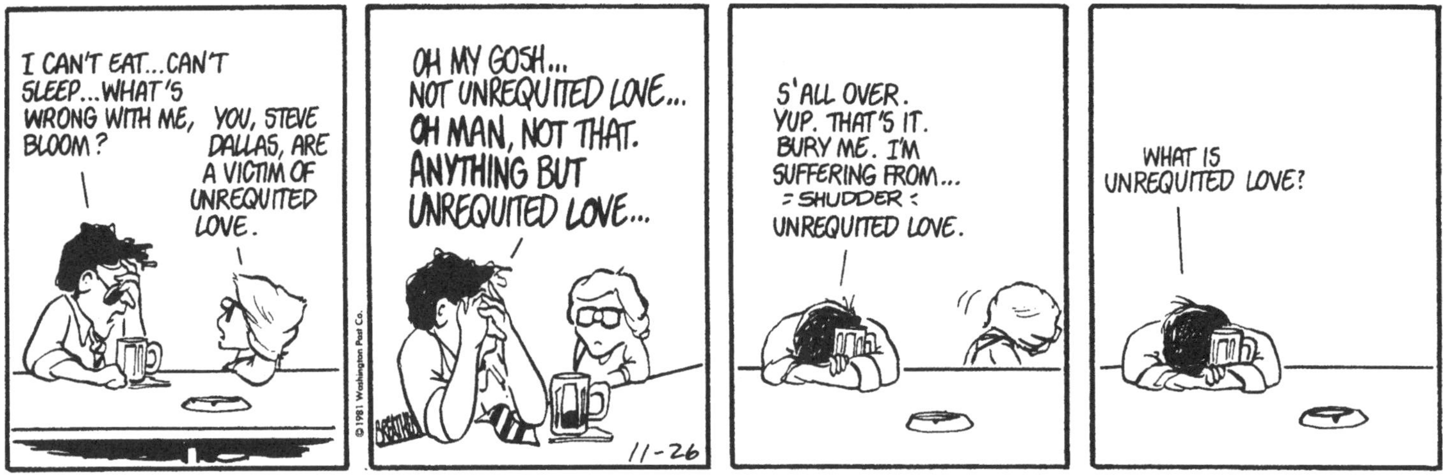
I CAN'T EAT...CAN'T SLEEP...WHAT'S WRONG WITH ME, BLOOM?
YOU, STEVE DALLAS, ARE A VICTIM OF UNREQUITED LOVE.
OH MY GOSH... NOT UNREQUITED LOVE... OH MAN, NOT THAT. ANYTHING BUT UNREQUITED LOVE...
© 1981 Washington Post Co.
BREATHED
11-26
S'ALL OVER. YUP. THAT'S IT. BURY ME. I'M SUFFERING FROM... :SHUDDER: UNREQUITED LOVE.
WHAT IS UNREQUITED LOVE?

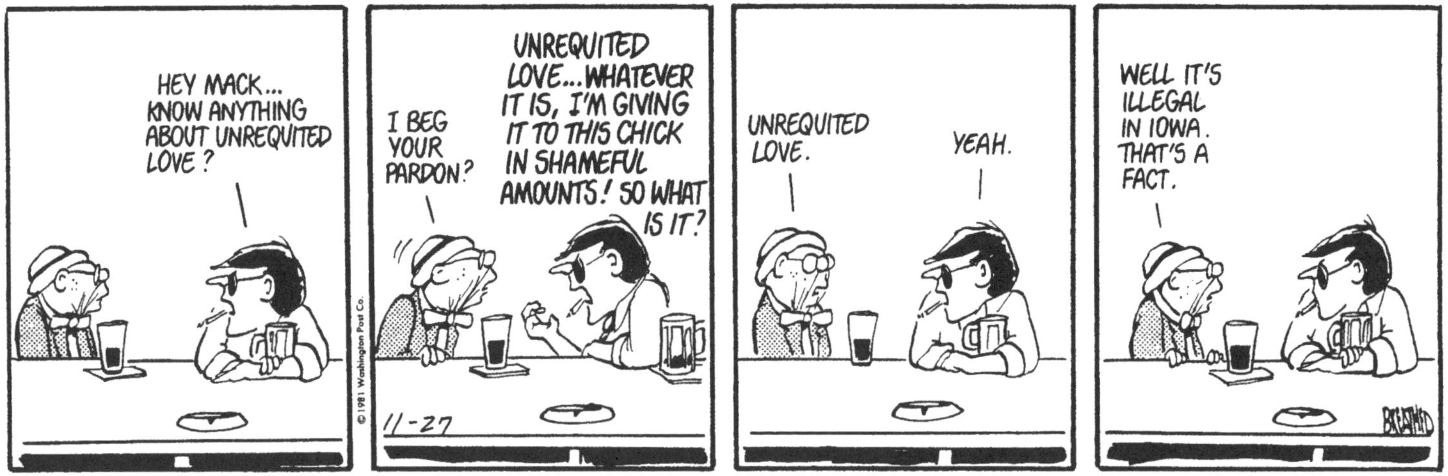
HEY MACK... KNOW ANYTHING ABOUT UNREQUITED LOVE?
© 1981 Washington Post Co.
I BEG YOUR PARDON?
UNREQUITED LOVE...WHATEVER IT IS, I'M GIVING IT TO THIS CHICK IN SHAMEFUL AMOUNTS! SO WHAT IS IT?
11-27
UNREQUITED LOVE.
YEAH.
WELL IT'S ILLEGAL IN IOWA. THAT'S A FACT.
BREATHED

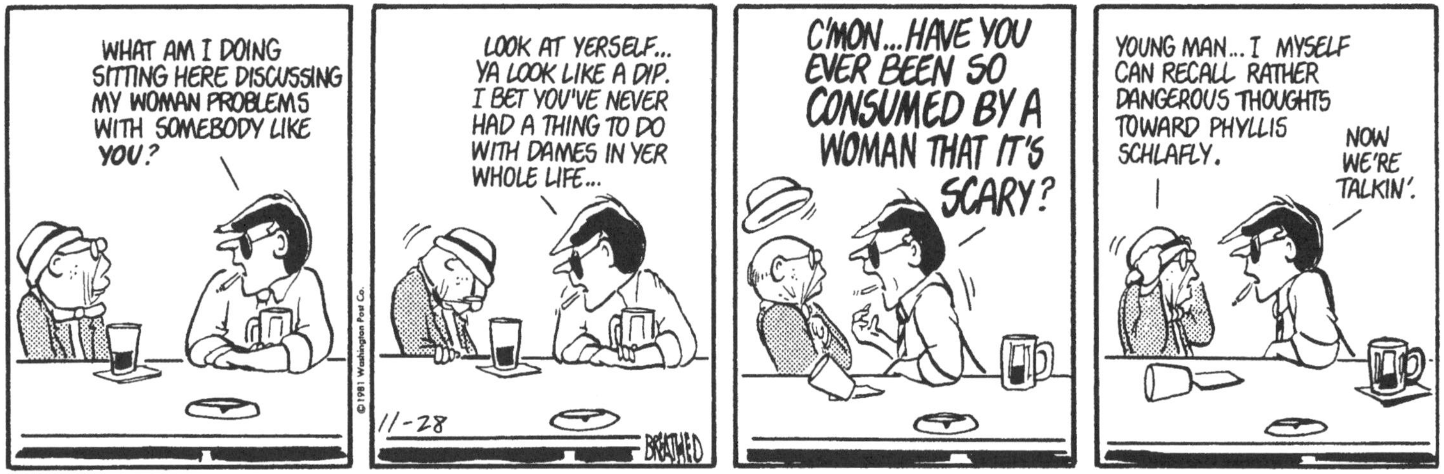
WHAT AM I DOING SITTING HERE DISCUSSING MY WOMAN PROBLEMS WITH SOMEBODY LIKE YOU?
© 1981 Washington Post Co.
LOOK AT YERSELF... YA LOOK LIKE A DIP. I BET YOU'VE NEVER HAD A THING TO DO WITH DAMES IN YER WHOLE LIFE...
11-28
BREATHED
C'MON...HAVE YOU EVER BEEN SO CONSUMED BY A WOMAN THAT IT'S SCARY?
YOUNG MAN... I MYSELF CAN RECALL RATHER DANGEROUS THOUGHTS TOWARD PHYLLIS SCHLAFLY.
NOW WE'RE TALKIN'.

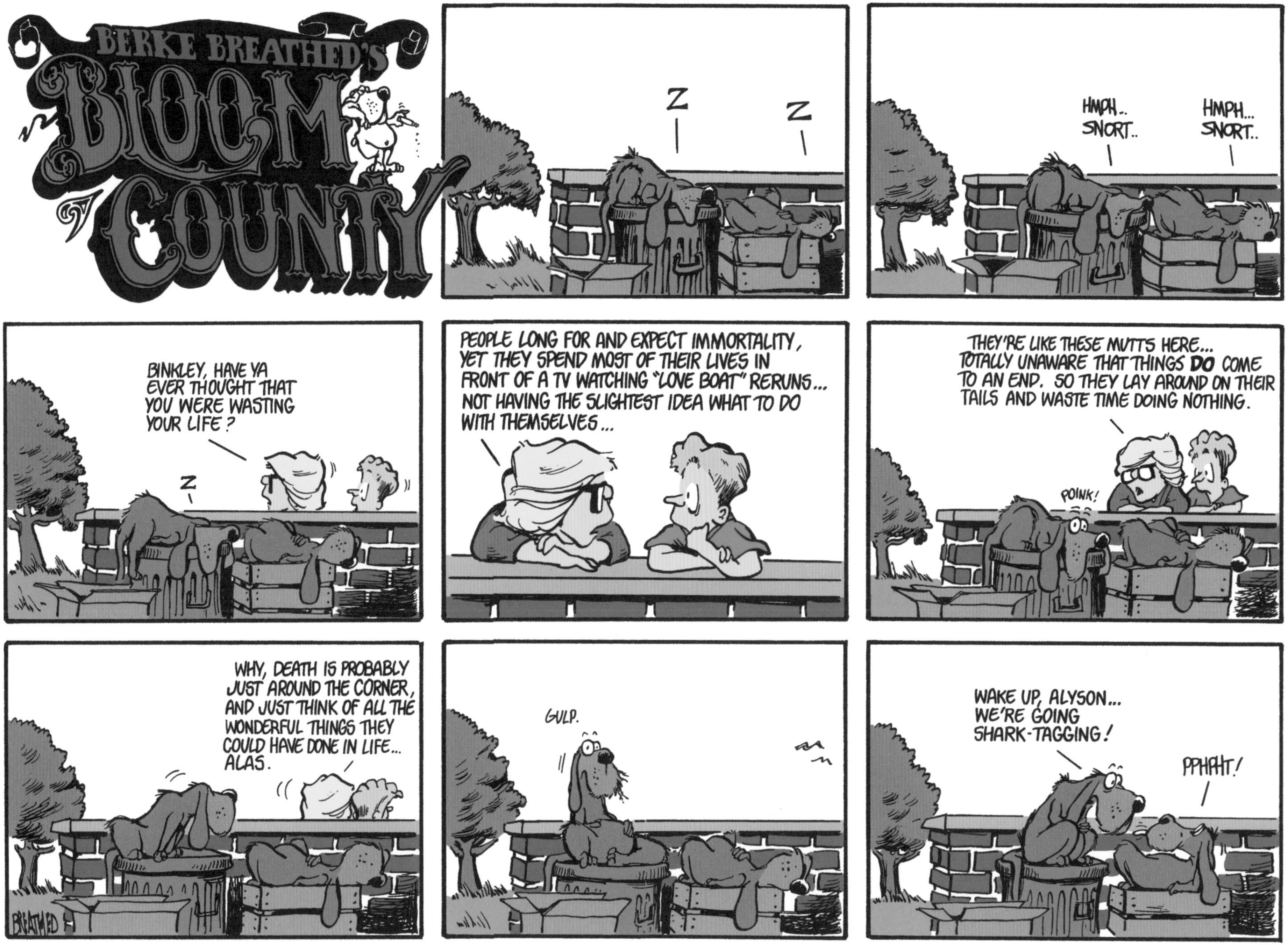
BERKE BREATHED'S
BLOOM COUNTY
Z
Z
HMPH.. SNORT..
HMPH... SNORT..
BINKLEY, HAVE YA EVER THOUGHT THAT YOU WERE WASTING YOUR LIFE?
Z
PEOPLE LONG FOR AND EXPECT IMMORTALITY, YET THEY SPEND MOST OF THEIR LIVES IN FRONT OF A TV WATCHING "LOVE BOAT" RERUNS... NOT HAVING THE SLIGHTEST IDEA WHAT TO DO WITH THEMSELVES...
THEY'RE LIKE THESE MUTTS HERE... TOTALLY UNAWARE THAT THINGS DO COME TO AN END. SO THEY LAY AROUND ON THEIR TAILS AND WASTE TIME DOING NOTHING.
POINK!
WHY, DEATH IS PROBABLY JUST AROUND THE CORNER, AND JUST THINK OF ALL THE WONDERFUL THINGS THEY COULD HAVE DONE IN LIFE... ALAS.
BREATHED
GULP.
WAKE UP, ALYSON... WE'RE GOING SHARK-TAGGING!
PPHFHT!

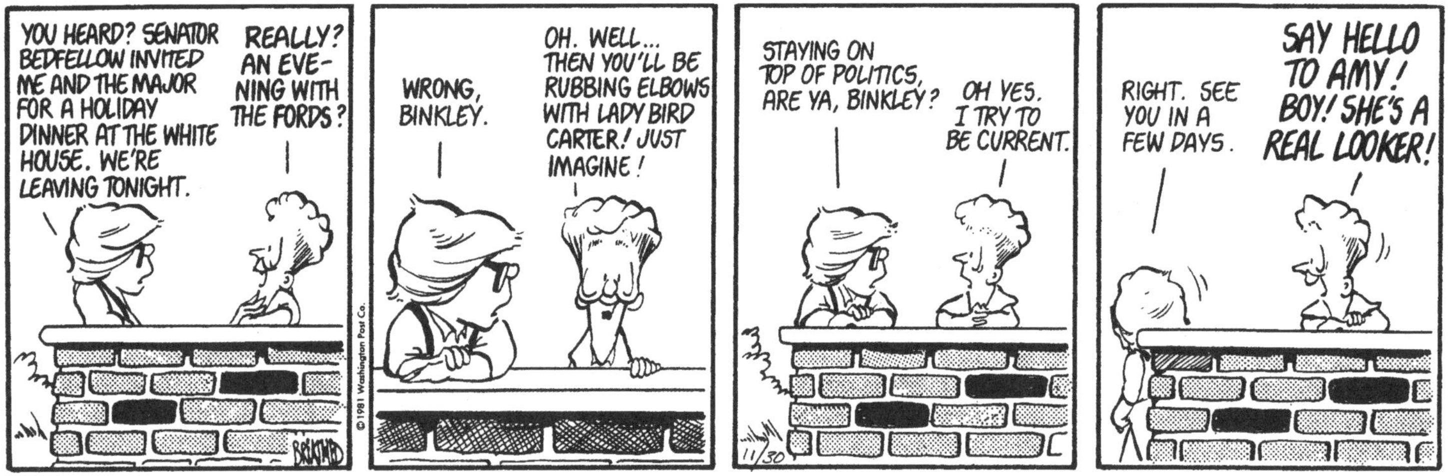
YOU HEARD? SENATOR BEDFELLOW INVITED ME AND THE MAJOR FOR A HOLIDAY DINNER AT THE WHITE HOUSE. WE'RE LEAVING TONIGHT.
REALLY? AN EVENING WITH THE FORDS?
WRONG, BINKLEY.
OH. WELL... THEN YOU'LL BE RUBBING ELBOWS WITH LADY BIRD CARTER! JUST IMAGINE!
STAYING ON TOP OF POLITICS, ARE YA, BINKLEY?
OH YES. I TRY TO BE CURRENT.
RIGHT. SEE YOU IN A FEW DAYS.
SAY HELLO TO AMY! BOY! SHE'S A REAL LOOKER!

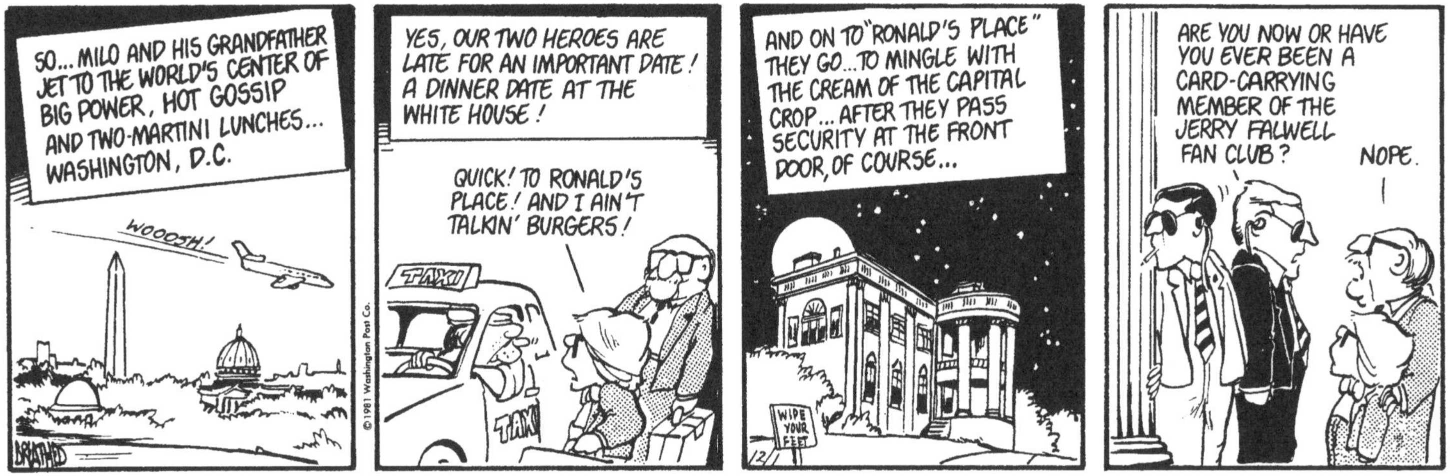
SO... MILO AND HIS GRANDFATHER JET TO THE WORLD'S CENTER OF BIG POWER, HOT GOSSIP AND TWO-MARTINI LUNCHES... WASHINGTON, D.C.
WOOOSH!
YES, OUR TWO HEROES ARE LATE FOR AN IMPORTANT DATE! A DINNER DATE AT THE WHITE HOUSE!
QUICK! TO RONALD'S PLACE! AND I AIN'T TALKIN' BURGERS!
TAXI
AND ON TO "RONALD'S PLACE" THEY GO... TO MINGLE WITH THE CREAM OF THE CAPITAL CROP... AFTER THEY PASS SECURITY AT THE FRONT DOOR, OF COURSE...
WIPE YOUR FEET
ARE YOU NOW OR HAVE YOU EVER BEEN A CARD-CARRYING MEMBER OF THE JERRY FALWELL FAN CLUB?
NOPE.

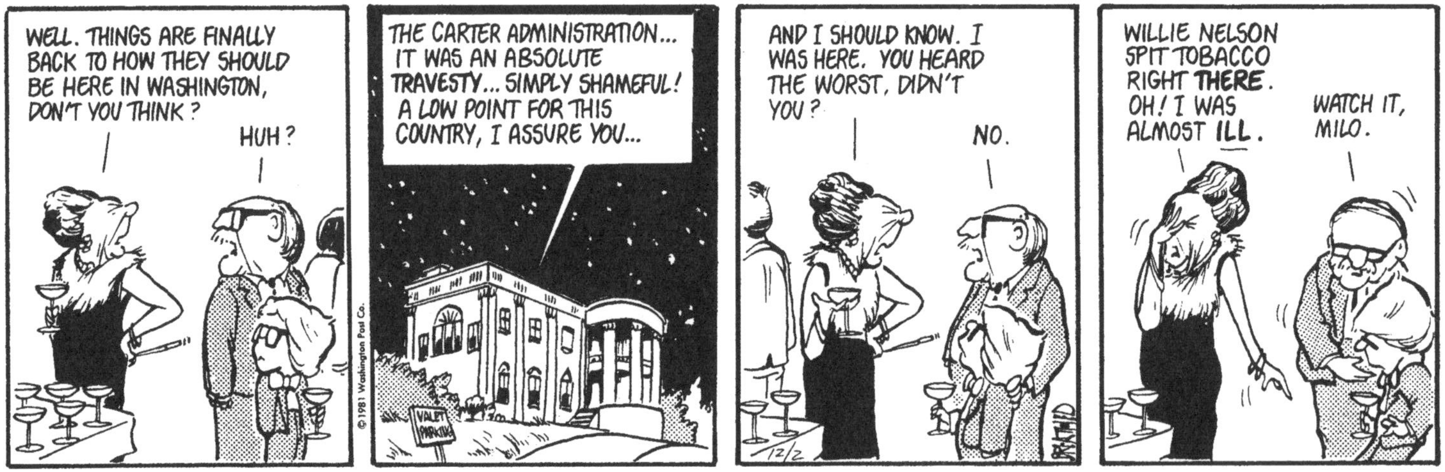
WELL. THINGS ARE FINALLY BACK TO HOW THEY SHOULD BE HERE IN WASHINGTON, DON'T YOU THINK?
HUH?
THE CARTER ADMINISTRATION... IT WAS AN ABSOLUTE TRAVESTY... SIMPLY SHAMEFUL! A LOW POINT FOR THIS COUNTRY, I ASSURE YOU...
VALET PARKING
AND I SHOULD KNOW. I WAS HERE. YOU HEARD THE WORST, DIDN'T YOU?
NO.
WILLIE NELSON SPIT TOBACCO RIGHT THERE. OH! I WAS ALMOST ILL.
WATCH IT, MILO.

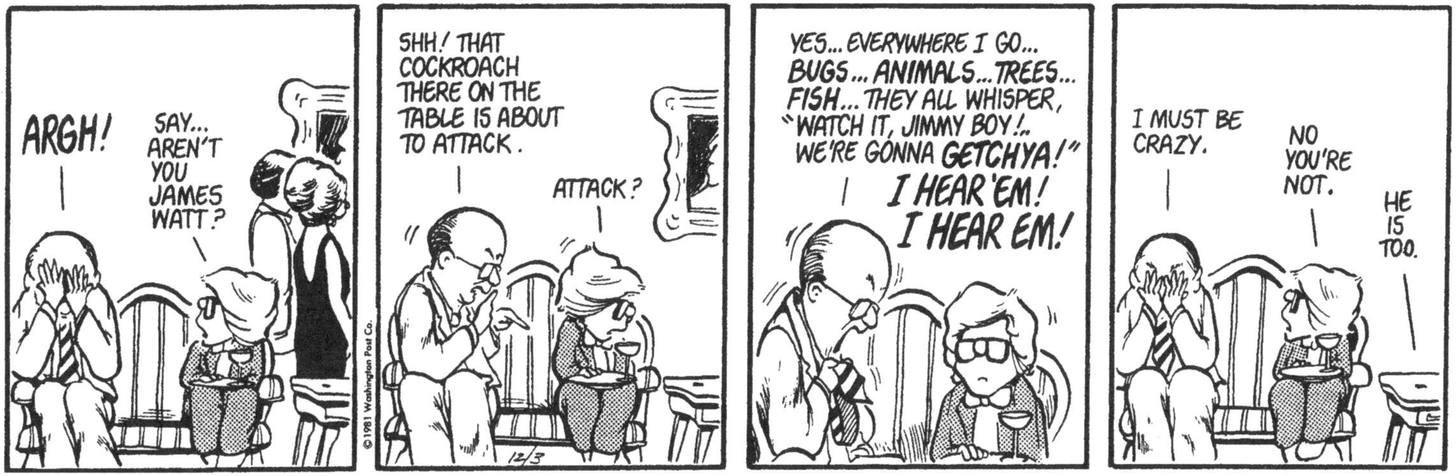
ARGH!
SAY... AREN'T YOU JAMES WATT?
SHH! THAT COCKROACH THERE ON THE TABLE IS ABOUT TO ATTACK.
ATTACK?
YES... EVERYWHERE I GO... BUGS... ANIMALS... TREES... FISH... THEY ALL WHISPER, "WATCH IT, JIMMY BOY!.. WE'RE GONNA GETCHYA!"
I HEAR 'EM! I HEAR EM!
I MUST BE CRAZY.
NO YOU'RE NOT.
HE IS TOO.

James Watt was Secretary of the Interior for nearly the first three years of the Reagan administration. He suggested that all undeveloped public land eventually be exploited by oil and coal interests, and sought to abolish the Land and Water Conservation Fund.

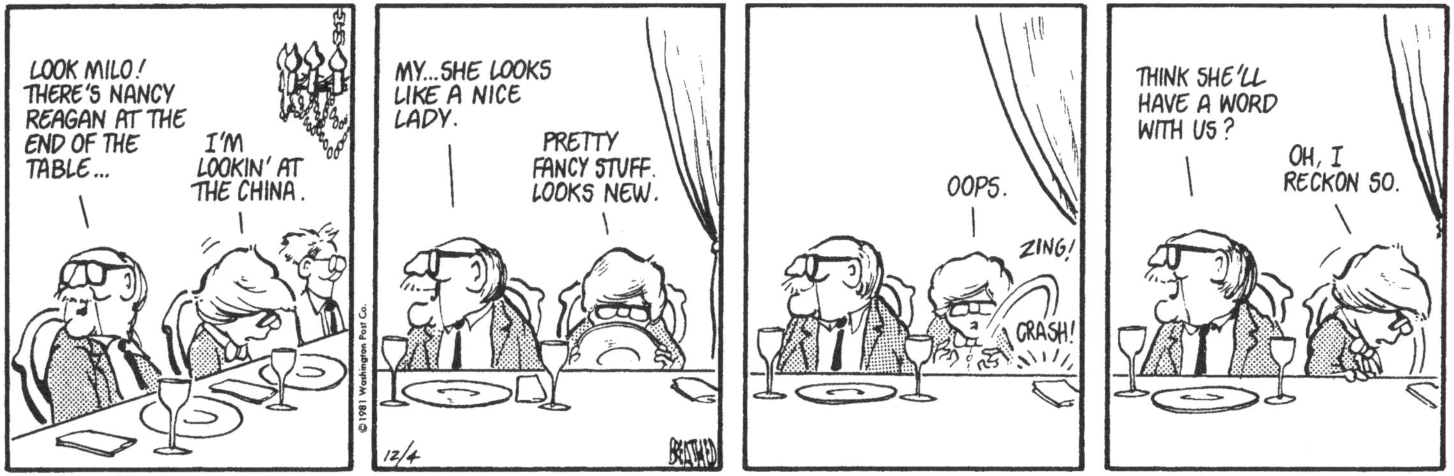
LOOK MILO! THERE'S NANCY REAGAN AT THE END OF THE TABLE...
I'M LOOKIN' AT THE CHINA.
MY... SHE LOOKS LIKE A NICE LADY.
PRETTY FANCY STUFF. LOOKS NEW.
OOPS.
ZING!
CRASH!
THINK SHE'LL HAVE A WORD WITH US?
OH, I RECKON SO.

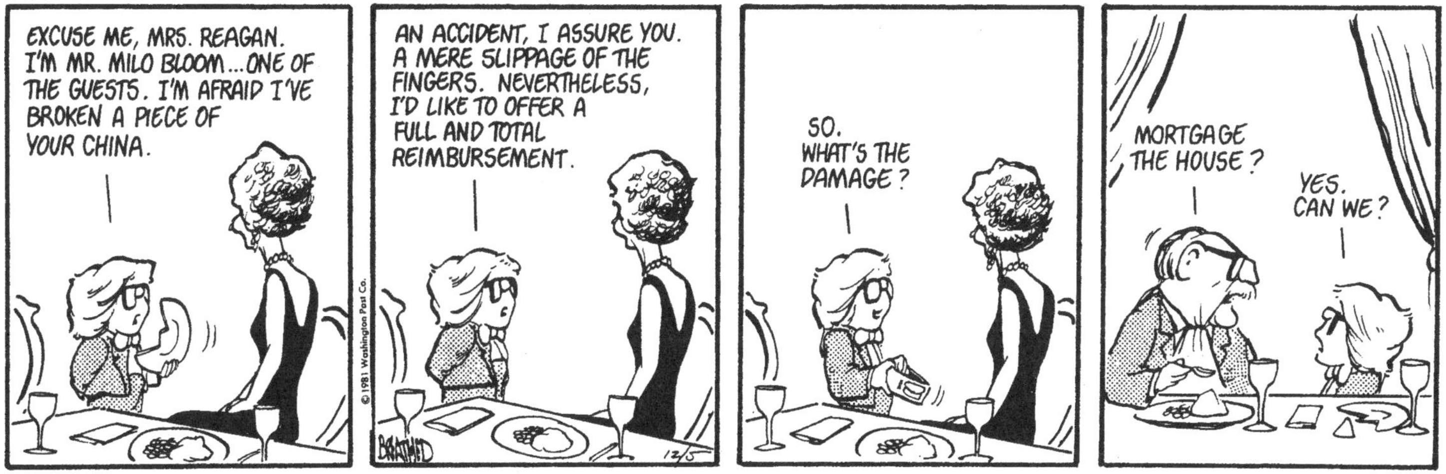
EXCUSE ME, MRS. REAGAN. I'M MR. MILO BLOOM... ONE OF THE GUESTS. I'M AFRAID I'VE BROKEN A PIECE OF YOUR CHINA.
AN ACCIDENT, I ASSURE YOU. A MERE SLIPPAGE OF THE FINGERS. NEVERTHELESS, I'D LIKE TO OFFER A FULL AND TOTAL REIMBURSEMENT.
SO. WHAT'S THE DAMAGE?
MORTGAGE THE HOUSE?
YES. CAN WE?

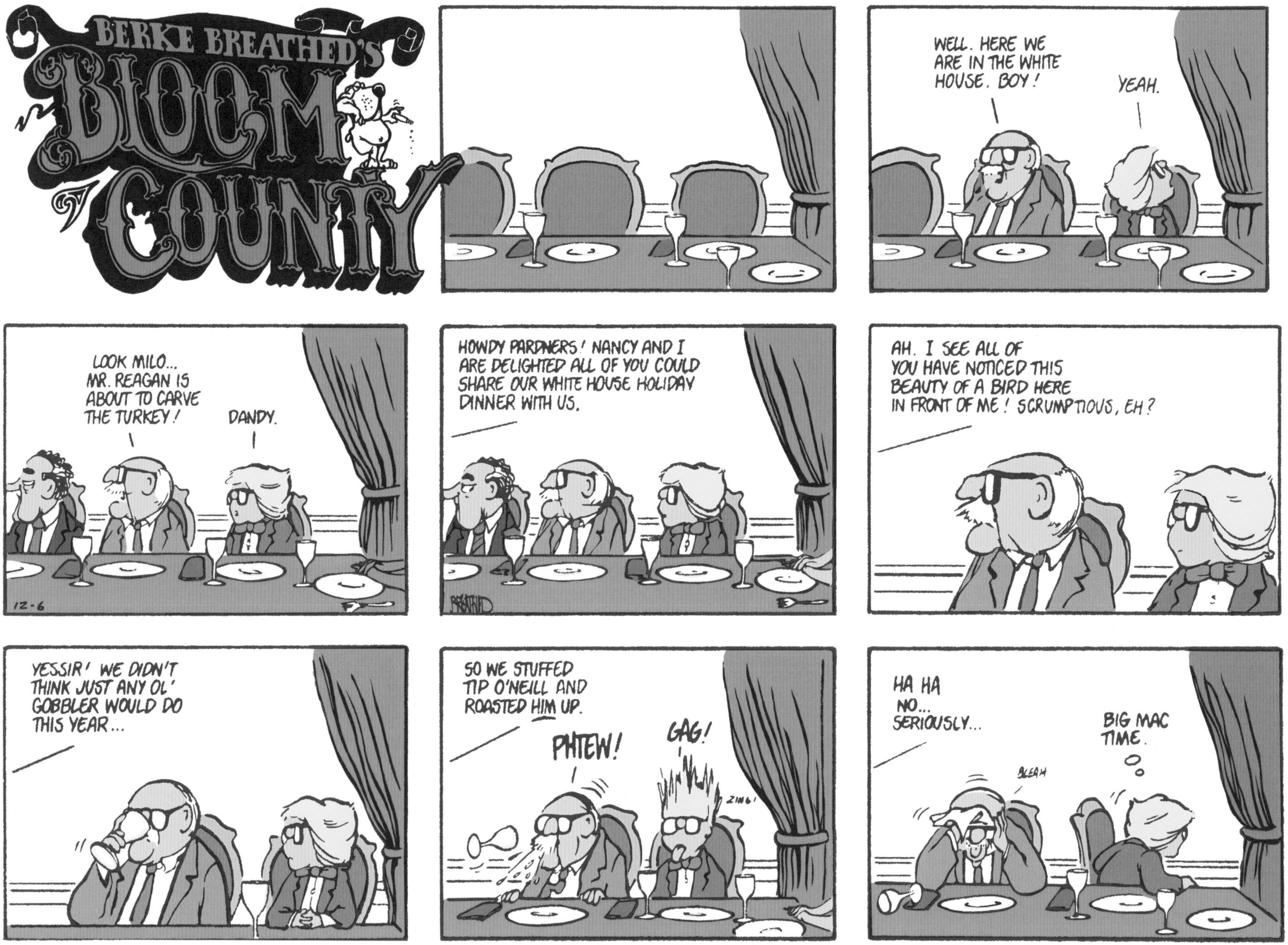

BERKE BREATHED'S
BLOOM COUNTY
WELL. HERE WE ARE IN THE WHITE HOUSE. BOY!
YEAH.
LOOK MILO... MR. REAGAN IS ABOUT TO CARVE THE TURKEY!
DANDY.
12-6
HOWDY PARDNERS! NANCY AND I ARE DELIGHTED ALL OF YOU COULD SHARE OUR WHITE HOUSE HOLIDAY DINNER WITH US.
BREATHED
AH. I SEE ALL OF YOU HAVE NOTICED THIS BEAUTY OF A BIRD HERE IN FRONT OF ME! SCRUMPTIOUS, EH?
YESSIR! WE DIDN'T THINK JUST ANY OL' GOBBLER WOULD DO THIS YEAR...
SO WE STUFFED TIP O'NEILL AND ROASTED HIM UP.
PHTEW!
GAG!
ZING!
HA HA NO... SERIOUSLY...
BLEAH
BIG MAC TIME.

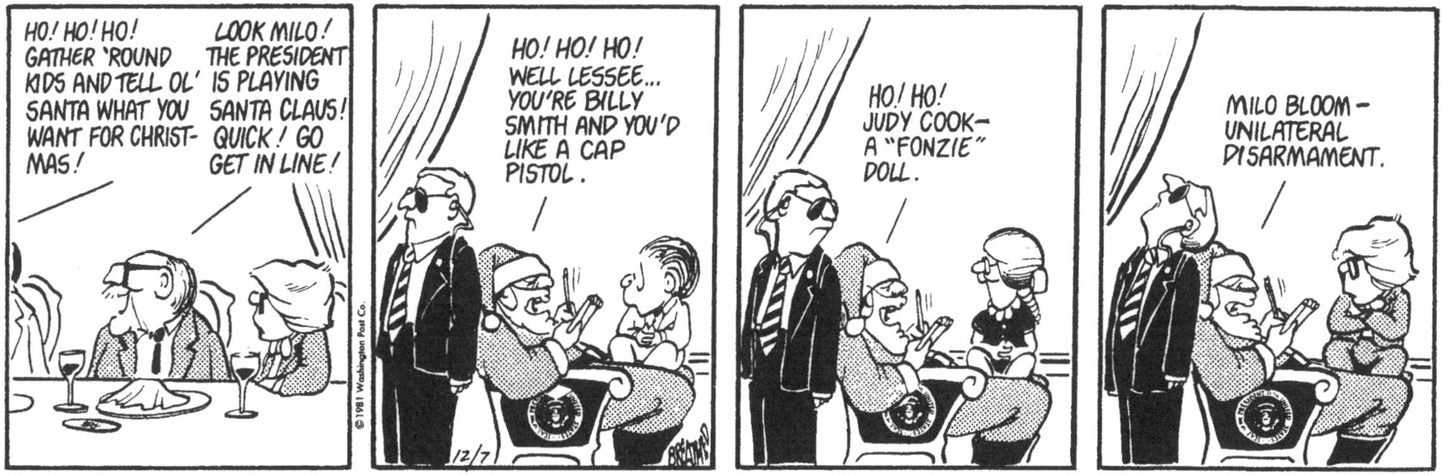
HO! HO! HO! GATHER 'ROUND KIDS AND TELL OL' SANTA WHAT YOU WANT FOR CHRISTMAS!
LOOK MILO! THE PRESIDENT IS PLAYING SANTA CLAUS! QUICK! GO GET IN LINE!
© 1981 Washington Post Co.
HO! HO! HO! WELL LESSEE... YOU'RE BILLY SMITH AND YOU'D LIKE A CAP PISTOL.
12/7
BREATHED
HO! HO! JUDY COOK— A "FONZIE" DOLL.
MILO BLOOM— UNILATERAL DISARMAMENT.

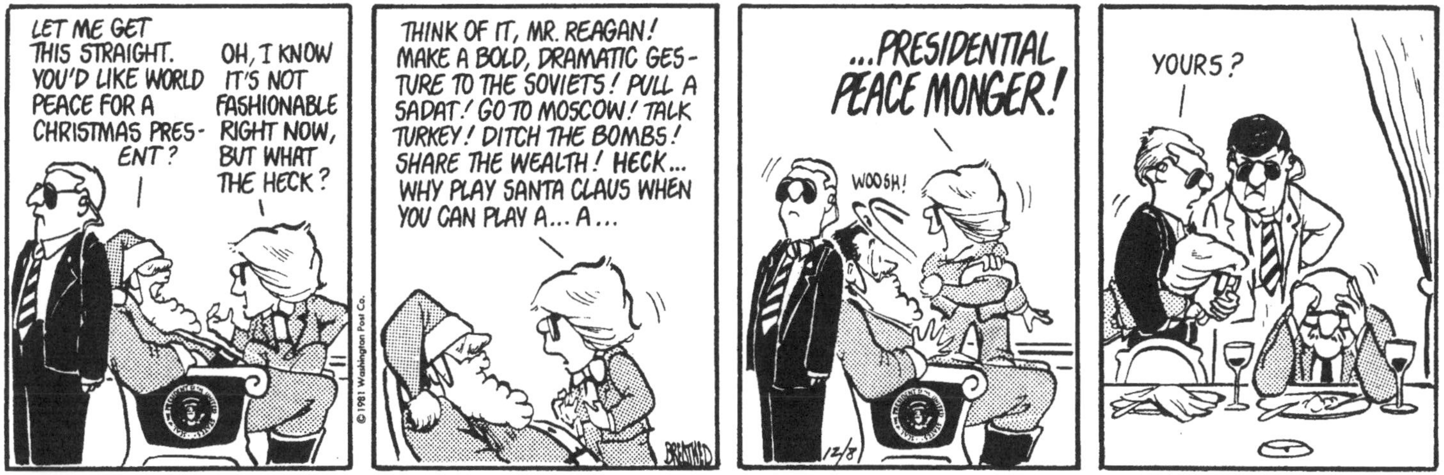
LET ME GET THIS STRAIGHT. YOU'D LIKE WORLD PEACE FOR A CHRISTMAS PRESENT?
OH, I KNOW IT'S NOT FASHIONABLE RIGHT NOW, BUT WHAT THE HECK?
© 1981 Washington Post Co.
THINK OF IT, MR. REAGAN! MAKE A BOLD, DRAMATIC GESTURE TO THE SOVIETS! PULL A SADAT! GO TO MOSCOW! TALK TURKEY! DITCH THE BOMBS! SHARE THE WEALTH! HECK... WHY PLAY SANTA CLAUS WHEN YOU CAN PLAY A... A...
BREATHED
...PRESIDENTIAL PEACE MONGER!
WOOSH!
12/8
YOURS?

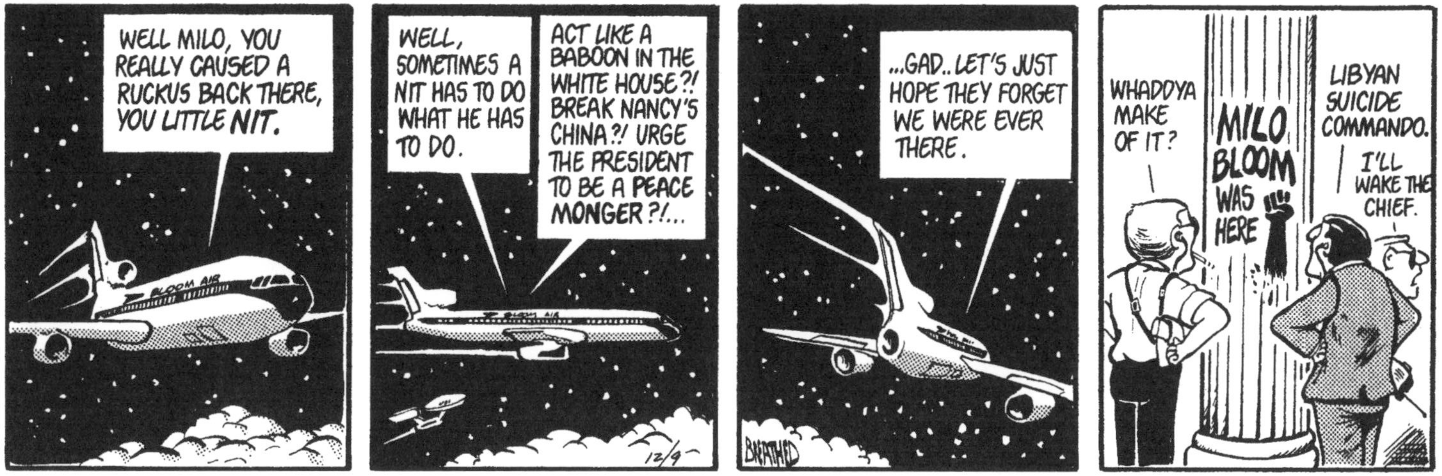
WELL MILO, YOU REALLY CAUSED A RUCKUS BACK THERE, YOU LITTLE NIT.
BLOOM AIR
WELL, SOMETIMES A NIT HAS TO DO WHAT HE HAS TO DO.
ACT LIKE A BABOON IN THE WHITE HOUSE?! BREAK NANCY'S CHINA?! URGE THE PRESIDENT TO BE A PEACE MONGER?!...
12/9
...GAD.. LET'S JUST HOPE THEY FORGET WE WERE EVER THERE.
BREATHED
WHADDYA MAKE OF IT?
MILO BLOOM WAS HERE
LIBYAN SUICIDE COMMANDO.
I'LL WAKE THE CHIEF.

Anwar Sadat, the third president of Egypt, was assassinated on October 6, 1981, shortly before this strip ran. In 1978, Sadat, along with Israel's Menachem Begin, was awarded the Nobel Peace Prize for negotiating a peace agreement between their two countries.

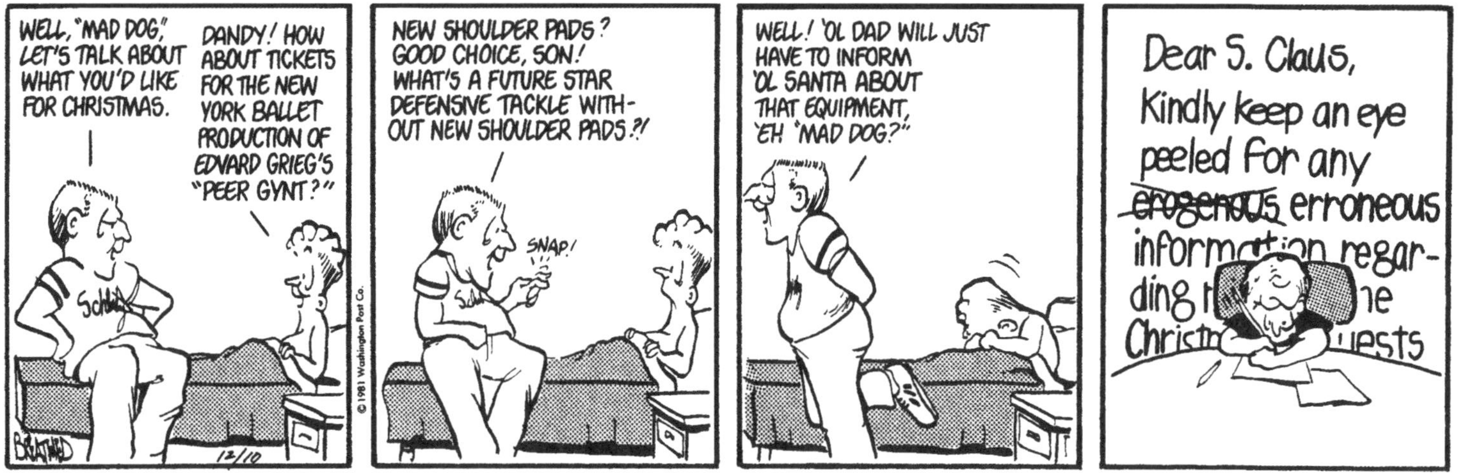
WELL, "MAD DOG," LET'S TALK ABOUT WHAT YOU'D LIKE FOR CHRISTMAS.
DANDY! HOW ABOUT TICKETS FOR THE NEW YORK BALLET PRODUCTION OF EDVARD GRIEG'S "PEER GYNT?"
NEW SHOULDER PADS? GOOD CHOICE, SON! WHAT'S A FUTURE STAR DEFENSIVE TACKLE WITHOUT NEW SHOULDER PADS?!
SNAP!
WELL! 'OL DAD WILL JUST HAVE TO INFORM 'OL SANTA ABOUT THAT EQUIPMENT, 'EH "MAD DOG?"
Dear S. Claus,
Kindly keep an eye peeled for any ~~erogenous~~ erroneous information regar-
© 1981 Washington Post Co.
12/10

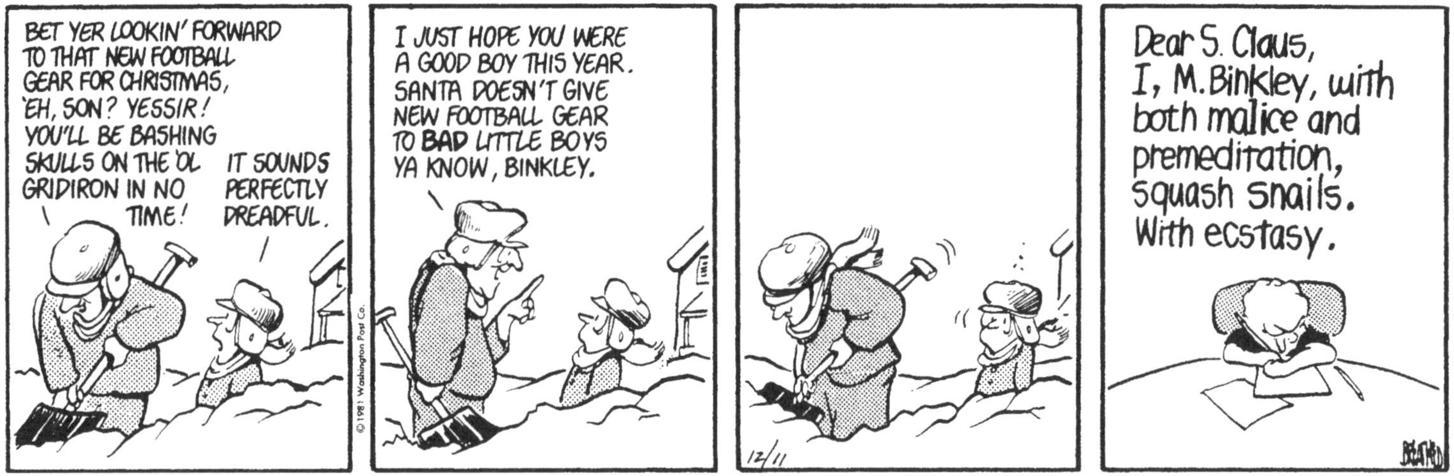
BET YER LOOKIN' FORWARD TO THAT NEW FOOTBALL GEAR FOR CHRISTMAS, 'EH, SON? YESSIR! YOU'LL BE BASHING SKULLS ON THE 'OL GRIDIRON IN NO TIME!
IT SOUNDS PERFECTLY DREADFUL.
I JUST HOPE YOU WERE A GOOD BOY THIS YEAR. SANTA DOESN'T GIVE NEW FOOTBALL GEAR TO **BAD** LITTLE BOYS YA KNOW, BINKLEY.
Dear S. Claus,
I, M. Binkley, with both malice and premeditation, squash snails. With ecstasy.
© 1981 Washington Post Co.
12/11

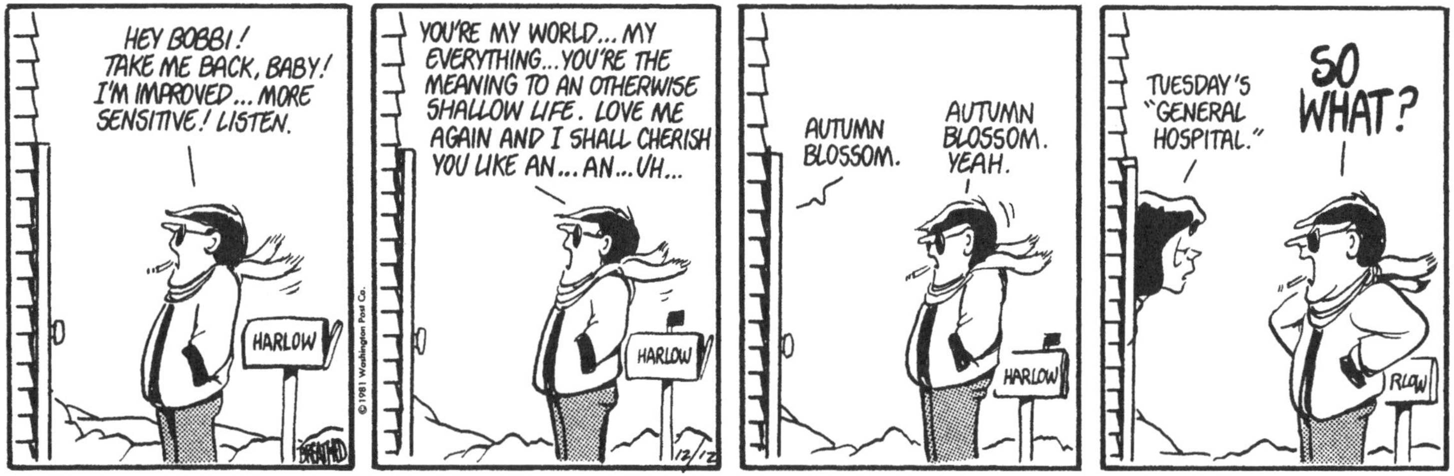
HEY BOBBI! TAKE ME BACK, BABY! I'M IMPROVED... MORE SENSITIVE! LISTEN.
HARLOW
YOU'RE MY WORLD... MY EVERYTHING... YOU'RE THE MEANING TO AN OTHERWISE SHALLOW LIFE. LOVE ME AGAIN AND I SHALL CHERISH YOU LIKE AN... AN... UH...
AUTUMN BLOSSOM.
AUTUMN BLOSSOM. YEAH.
TUESDAY'S "GENERAL HOSPITAL."
SO WHAT?
© 1981 Washington Post Co.
12/12

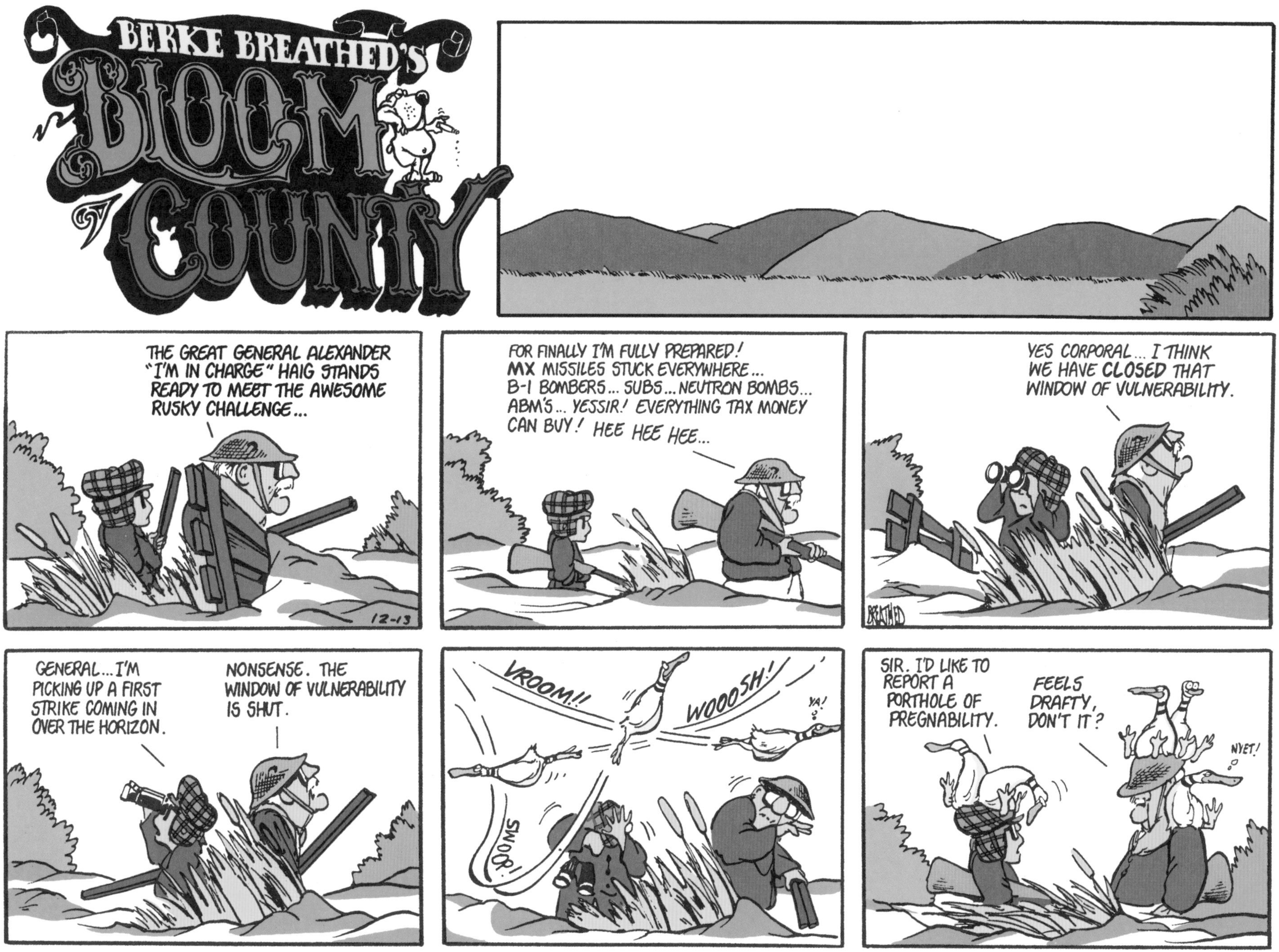
BERKE BREATHED'S
BLOOM COUNTY
THE GREAT GENERAL ALEXANDER "I'M IN CHARGE" HAIG STANDS READY TO MEET THE AWESOME RUSKY CHALLENGE...
12-13
FOR FINALLY I'M FULLY PREPARED! MX MISSILES STUCK EVERYWHERE... B-1 BOMBERS... SUBS... NEUTRON BOMBS... ABM'S... YESSIR! EVERYTHING TAX MONEY CAN BUY! HEE HEE HEE...
YES CORPORAL... I THINK WE HAVE CLOSED THAT WINDOW OF VULNERABILITY.
BREATHED
GENERAL... I'M PICKING UP A FIRST STRIKE COMING IN OVER THE HORIZON.
NONSENSE. THE WINDOW OF VULNERABILITY IS SHUT.
VROOM!!
WOOOSH!
YA!
SWOOP!
SIR. I'D LIKE TO REPORT A PORTHOLE OF PREGNABILITY.
FEELS DRAFTY, DON'T IT?
NYET!

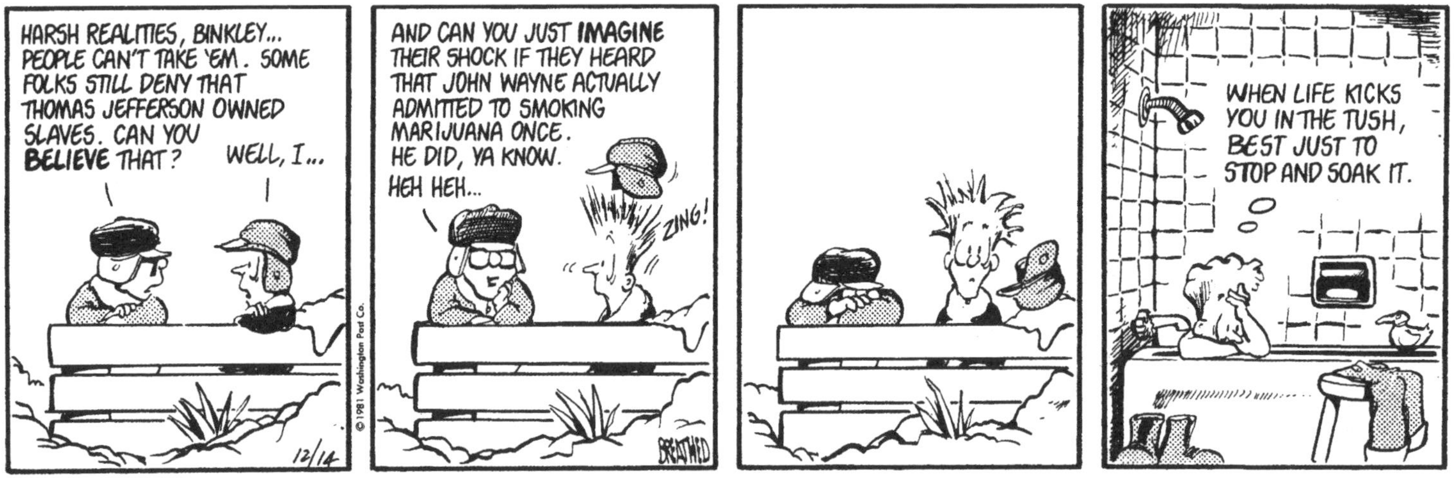
HARSH REALITIES, BINKLEY... PEOPLE CAN'T TAKE 'EM. SOME FOLKS STILL DENY THAT THOMAS JEFFERSON OWNED SLAVES. CAN YOU **BELIEVE** THAT?
WELL, I...
12/14
© 1981 Washington Post Co.
AND CAN YOU JUST **IMAGINE** THEIR SHOCK IF THEY HEARD THAT JOHN WAYNE ACTUALLY ADMITTED TO SMOKING MARIJUANA ONCE. HE DID, YA KNOW.
HEH HEH...
ZING!
BREATHED
WHEN LIFE KICKS YOU IN THE TUSH, BEST JUST TO STOP AND SOAK IT.

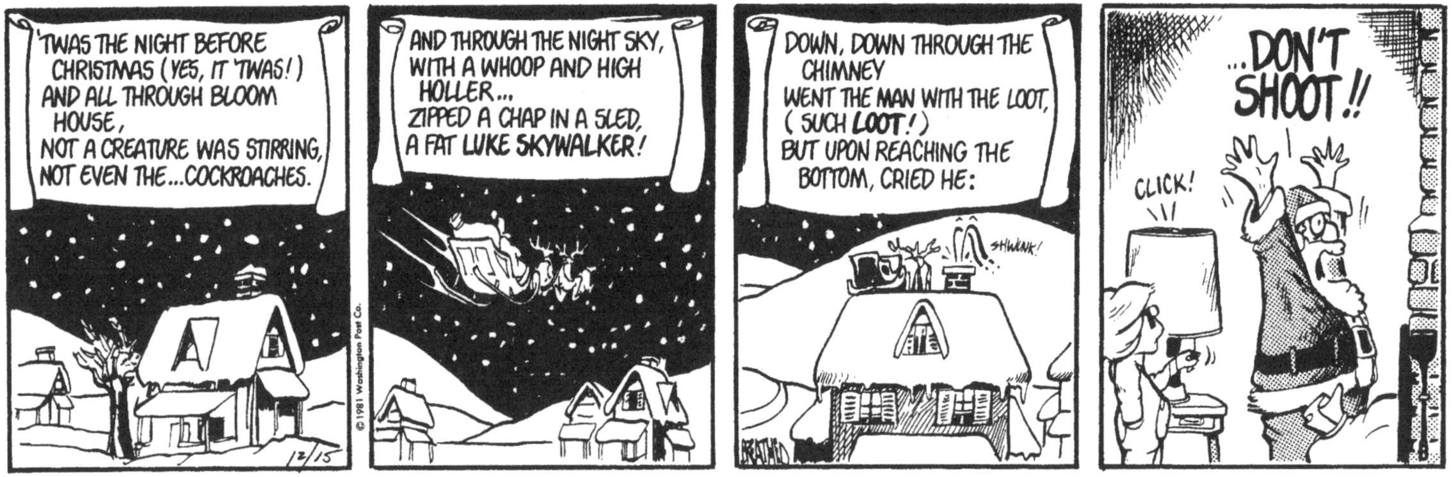
'TWAS THE NIGHT BEFORE CHRISTMAS (YES, IT 'TWAS!) AND ALL THROUGH BLOOM HOUSE, NOT A CREATURE WAS STIRRING, NOT EVEN THE...COCKROACHES.
12/15
© 1981 Washington Post Co.
AND THROUGH THE NIGHT SKY, WITH A WHOOP AND HIGH HOLLER... ZIPPED A CHAP IN A SLED, A FAT **LUKE SKYWALKER**!
DOWN, DOWN THROUGH THE CHIMNEY WENT THE **MAN** WITH THE LOOT, (SUCH **LOOT**!) BUT UPON REACHING THE BOTTOM, CRIED HE:
SHWINK!
BREATHED
CLICK!
...DON'T SHOOT!!

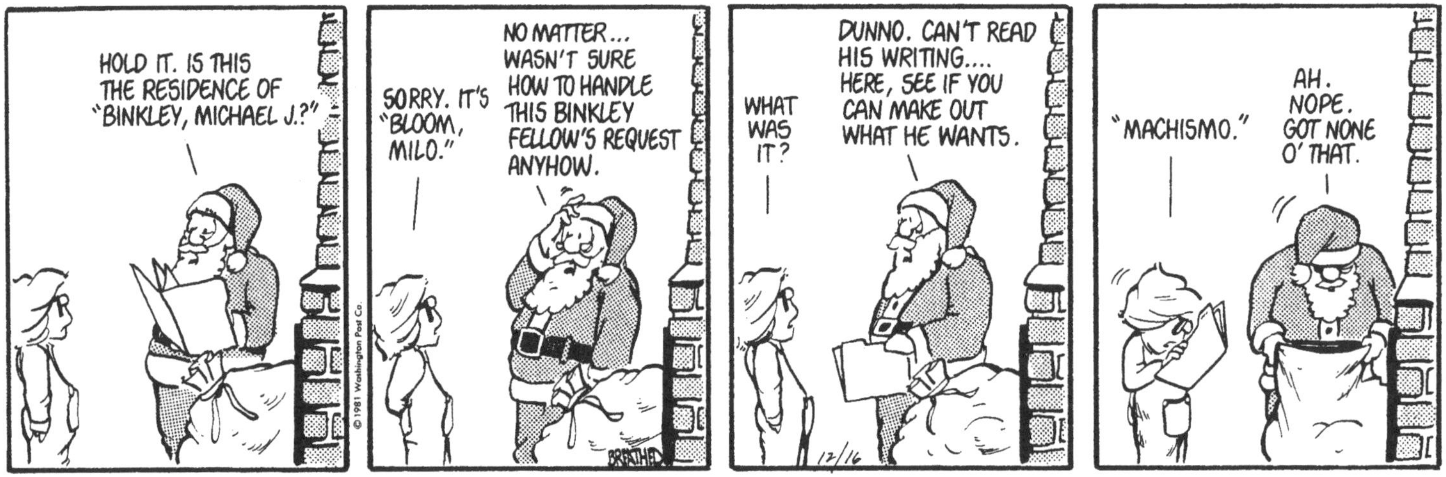
HOLD IT. IS THIS THE RESIDENCE OF "BINKLEY, MICHAEL J.?"
© 1981 Washington Post Co.
SORRY. IT'S "BLOOM, MILO."
NO MATTER... WASN'T SURE HOW TO HANDLE THIS BINKLEY FELLOW'S REQUEST ANYHOW.
BREATHED
WHAT WAS IT?
DUNNO. CAN'T READ HIS WRITING.... HERE, SEE IF YOU CAN MAKE OUT WHAT HE WANTS.
12/16
"MACHISMO."
AH. NOPE. GOT NONE O' THAT.

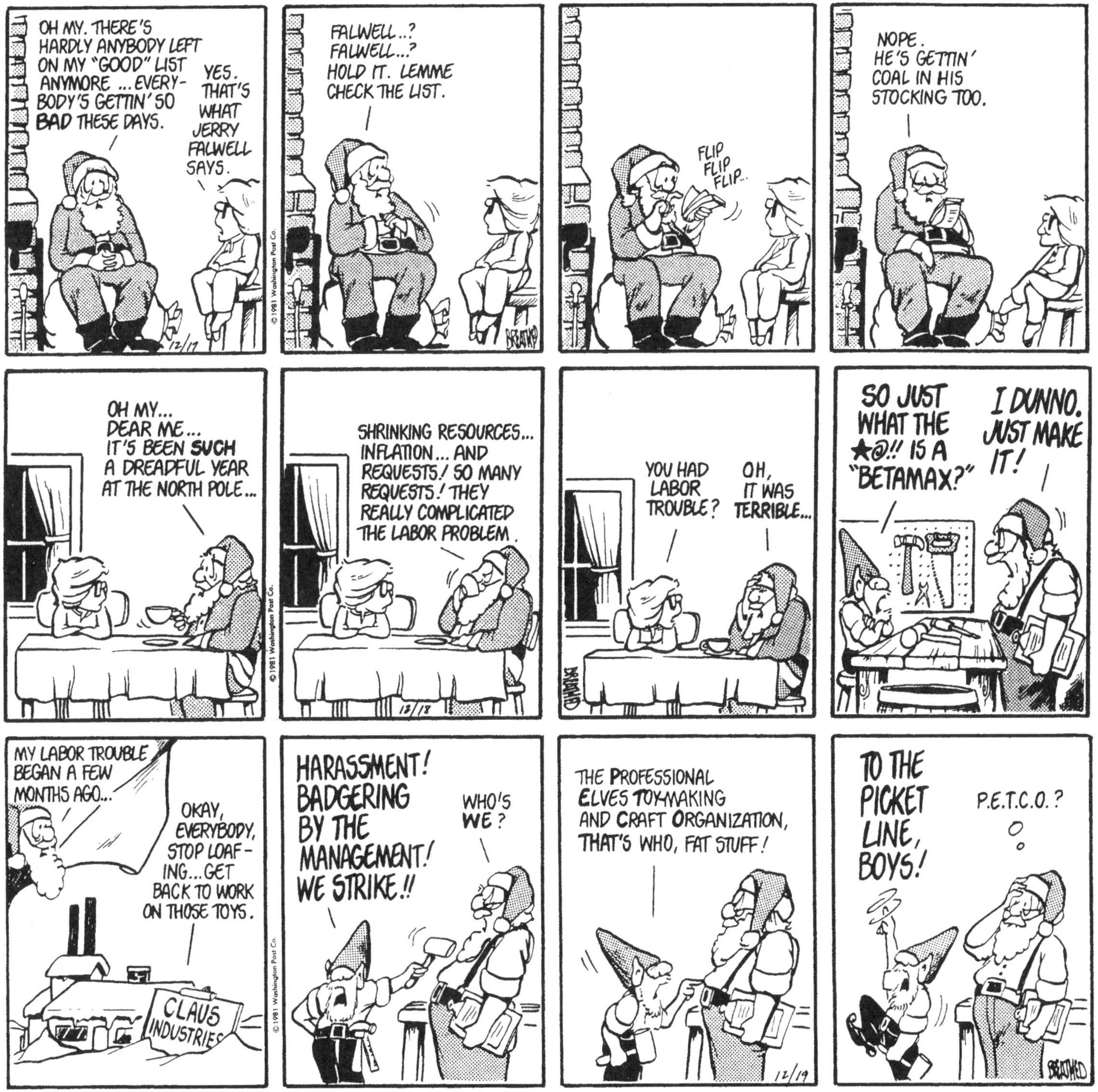
OH MY. THERE'S HARDLY ANYBODY LEFT ON MY "GOOD" LIST ANYMORE ... EVERYBODY'S GETTIN' SO BAD THESE DAYS.
YES. THAT'S WHAT JERRY FALWELL SAYS.
12/17
© 1981 Washington Post Co.
FALWELL..? FALWELL...? HOLD IT. LEMME CHECK THE LIST.
FLIP FLIP FLIP...
NOPE. HE'S GETTIN' COAL IN HIS STOCKING TOO.
OH MY... DEAR ME... IT'S BEEN SUCH A DREADFUL YEAR AT THE NORTH POLE...
© 1981 Washington Post Co.
SHRINKING RESOURCES... INFLATION... AND REQUESTS! SO MANY REQUESTS! THEY REALLY COMPLICATED THE LABOR PROBLEM.
12/18
YOU HAD LABOR TROUBLE?
OH, IT WAS TERRIBLE...
SO JUST WHAT THE ★@!! IS A "BETAMAX?"
I DUNNO. JUST MAKE IT!
MY LABOR TROUBLE BEGAN A FEW MONTHS AGO...
OKAY, EVERYBODY, STOP LOAFING...GET BACK TO WORK ON THOSE TOYS.
CLAUS INDUSTRIES
© 1981 Washington Post Co.
HARASSMENT! BADGERING BY THE MANAGEMENT! WE STRIKE!!
WHO'S WE?
THE PROFESSIONAL ELVES TOY-MAKING AND CRAFT ORGANIZATION, THAT'S WHO, FAT STUFF!
12/19
TO THE PICKET LINE, BOYS!
P.E.T.C.O.?

Betamax was the rival of VHS in the videocassette format battle for market supremacy. Generally regarded as a superior product, by the late 1980s Betamax conceded defeat to VHS.

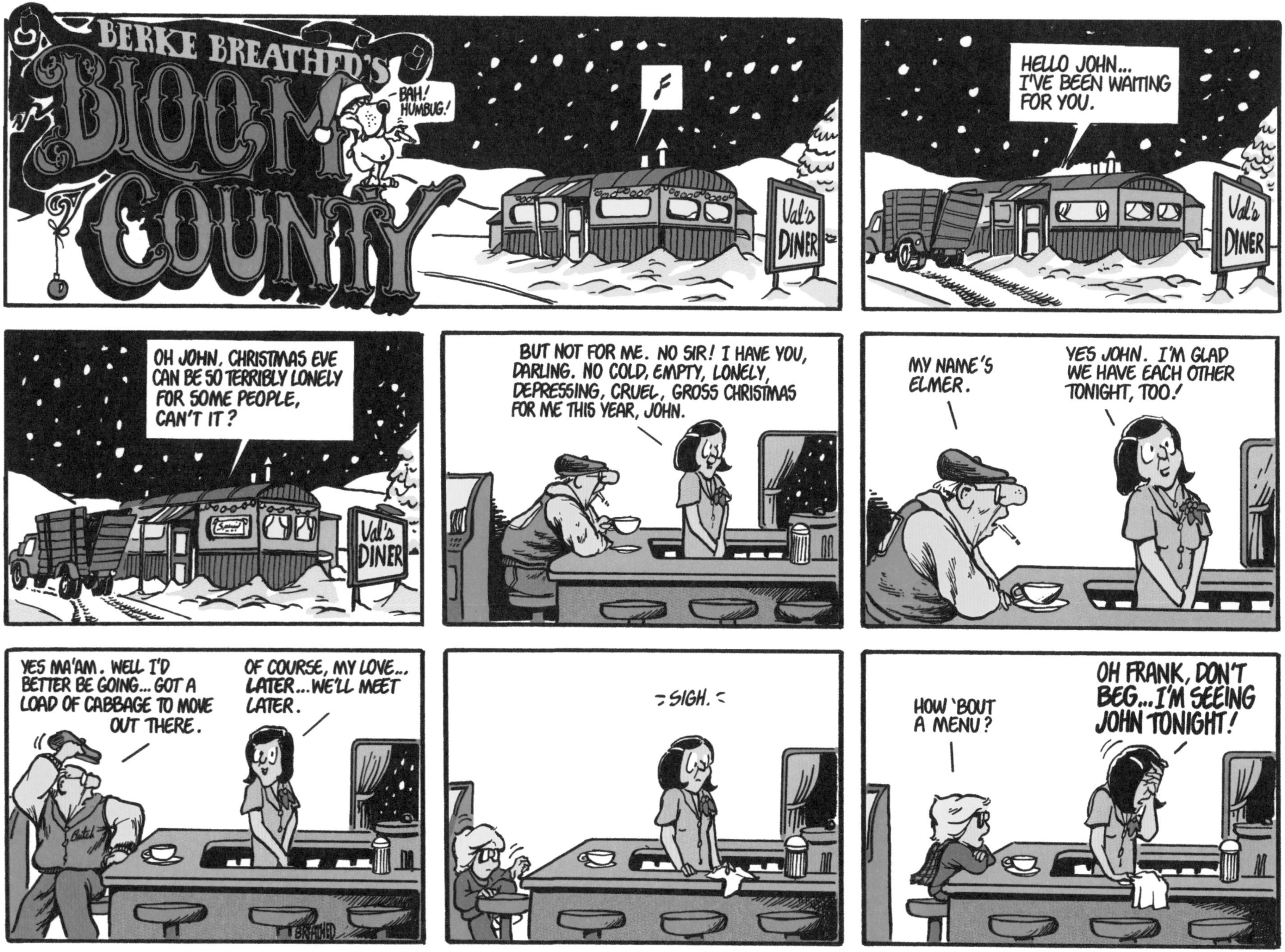
BERKE BREATHED'S
BLOOM COUNTY
BAH! HUMBUG!
Val's DINER
HELLO JOHN... I'VE BEEN WAITING FOR YOU.
Val's DINER
OH JOHN, CHRISTMAS EVE CAN BE SO TERRIBLY LONELY FOR SOME PEOPLE, CAN'T IT?
Val's DINER
BUT NOT FOR ME. NO SIR! I HAVE YOU, DARLING. NO COLD, EMPTY, LONELY, DEPRESSING, CRUEL, GROSS CHRISTMAS FOR ME THIS YEAR, JOHN.
MY NAME'S ELMER.
YES JOHN. I'M GLAD WE HAVE EACH OTHER TONIGHT, TOO!
YES MA'AM. WELL I'D BETTER BE GOING... GOT A LOAD OF CABBAGE TO MOVE OUT THERE.
OF COURSE, MY LOVE... LATER... WE'LL MEET LATER.
BREATHED
SIGH.
HOW 'BOUT A MENU?
OH FRANK, DON'T BEG... I'M SEEING JOHN TONIGHT!

 December 20, 1981

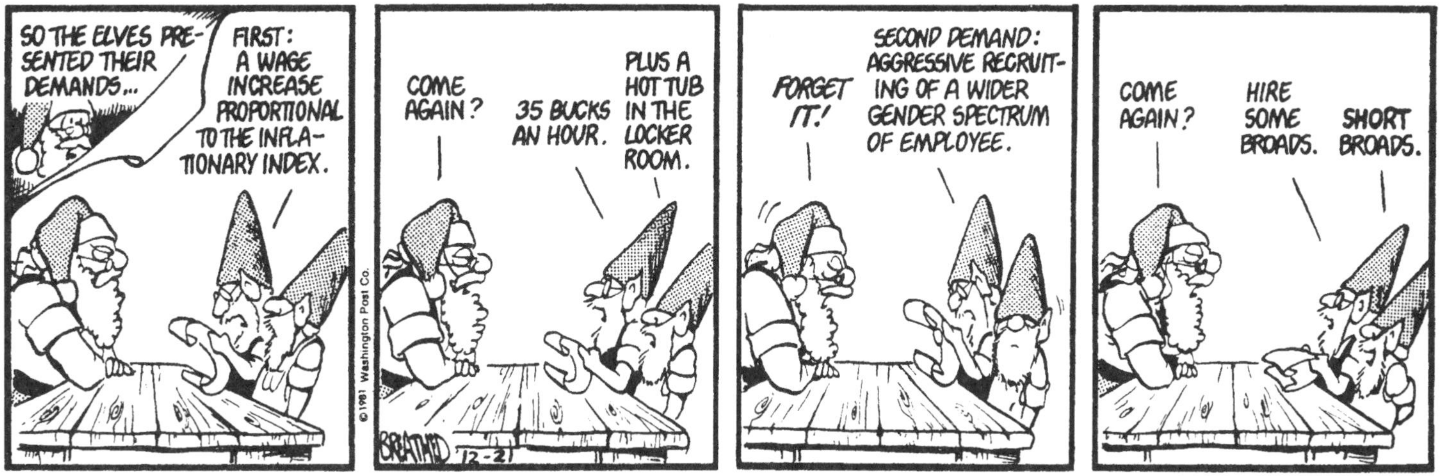
SO THE ELVES PRESENTED THEIR DEMANDS...
FIRST: A WAGE INCREASE PROPORTIONAL TO THE INFLATIONARY INDEX.
COME AGAIN?
35 BUCKS AN HOUR.
PLUS A HOT TUB IN THE LOCKER ROOM.
FORGET IT!
SECOND DEMAND: AGGRESSIVE RECRUITING OF A WIDER GENDER SPECTRUM OF EMPLOYEE.
COME AGAIN?
HIRE SOME BROADS.
SHORT BROADS.
© 1981 Washington Post Co.
BREATHED 12-21

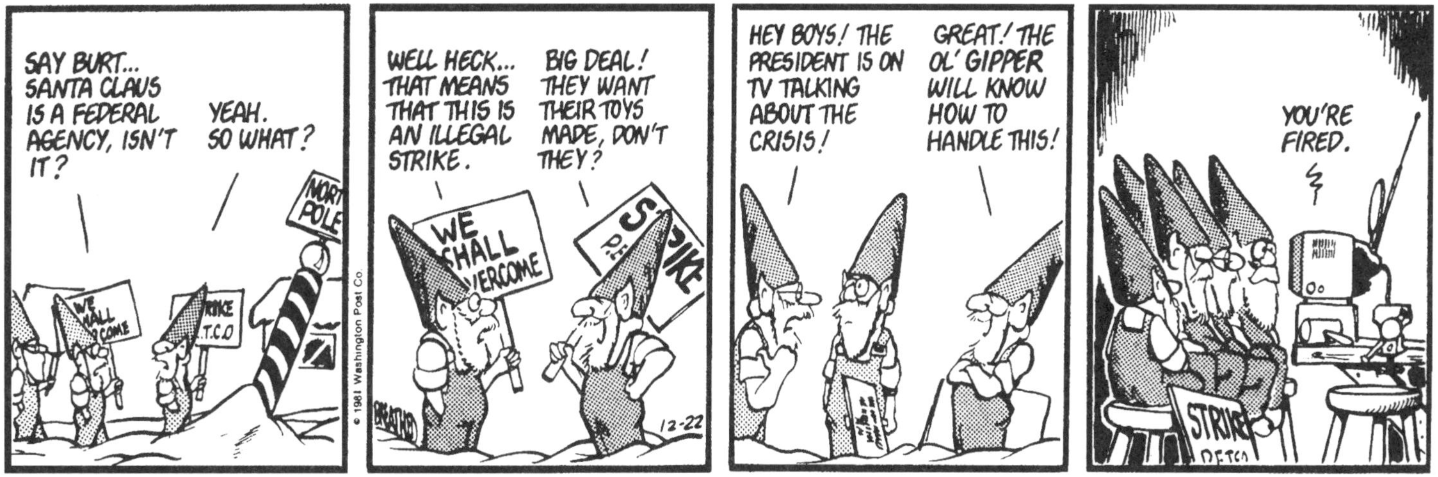
SAY BURT... SANTA CLAUS IS A FEDERAL AGENCY, ISN'T IT?
YEAH. SO WHAT?
NORTH POLE
WELL HECK... THAT MEANS THAT THIS IS AN ILLEGAL STRIKE.
BIG DEAL! THEY WANT THEIR TOYS MADE, DON'T THEY?
© 1981 Washington Post Co.
BREATHED 12-22
HEY BOYS! THE PRESIDENT IS ON TV TALKING ABOUT THE CRISIS!
GREAT! THE OL' GIPPER WILL KNOW HOW TO HANDLE THIS!
YOU'RE FIRED.
STRIKE

The Gipper was a nickname of President Reagan, one he received after the then-actor portrayed dying Notre Dame football legend George Gipp in a 1940 film.

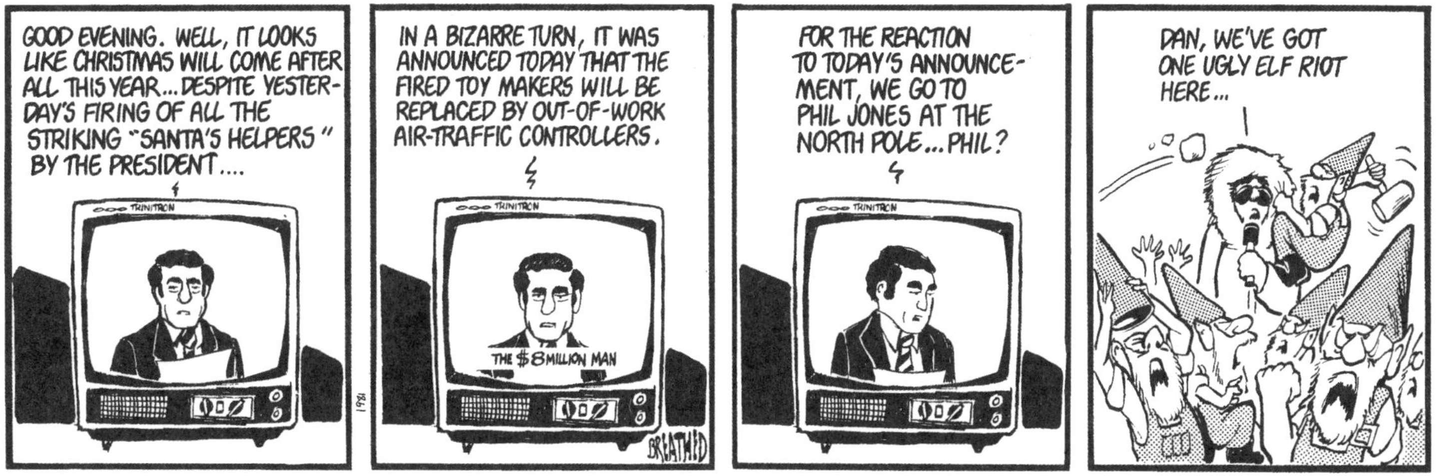
GOOD EVENING. WELL, IT LOOKS LIKE CHRISTMAS WILL COME AFTER ALL THIS YEAR... DESPITE YESTERDAY'S FIRING OF ALL THE STRIKING "SANTA'S HELPERS" BY THE PRESIDENT....
TRINITRON
IN A BIZARRE TURN, IT WAS ANNOUNCED TODAY THAT THE FIRED TOY MAKERS WILL BE REPLACED BY OUT-OF-WORK AIR-TRAFFIC CONTROLLERS.
THE $8 MILLION MAN
FOR THE REACTION TO TODAY'S ANNOUNCEMENT, WE GO TO PHIL JONES AT THE NORTH POLE... PHIL?
DAN, WE'VE GOT ONE UGLY ELF RIOT HERE...
1981
BREATHED

Dan Rather replaced Walter Cronkite as anchorman of the *CBS Evening News* in 1981.

The air traffic controllers' strike began August 3, 1981. President Reagan declared the strike illegal, saying it was a "peril to national safety," and ordered the strikers back to work. More than 11,000 workers refused to comply and were fired on August 5.

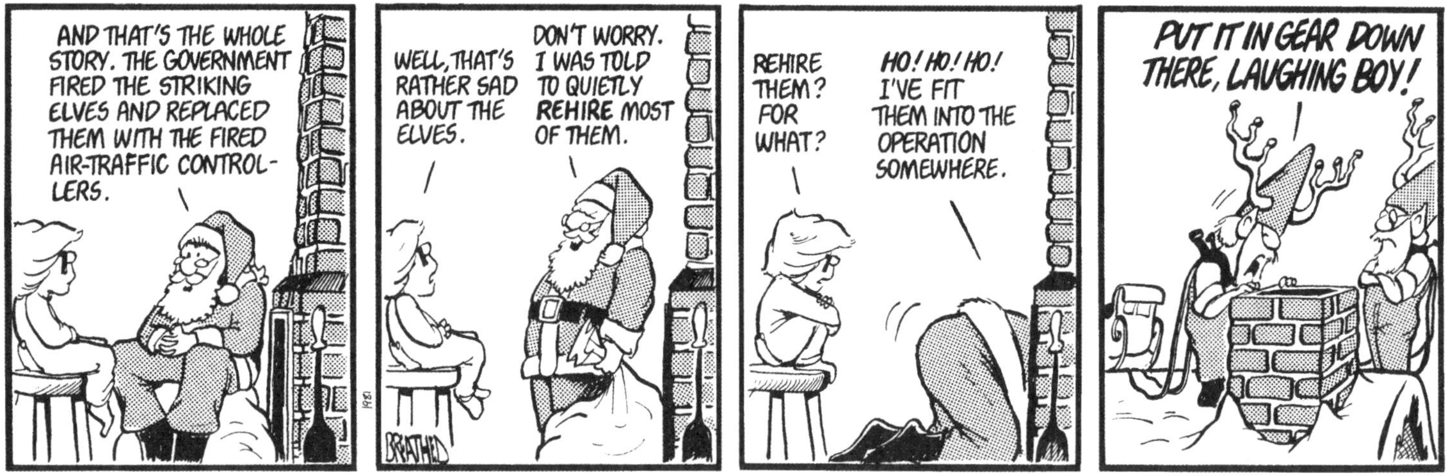
AND THAT'S THE WHOLE STORY. THE GOVERNMENT FIRED THE STRIKING ELVES AND REPLACED THEM WITH THE FIRED AIR-TRAFFIC CONTROLLERS.
WELL, THAT'S RATHER SAD ABOUT THE ELVES.
DON'T WORRY. I WAS TOLD TO QUIETLY REHIRE MOST OF THEM.
REHIRE THEM? FOR WHAT?
HO! HO! HO! I'VE FIT THEM INTO THE OPERATION SOMEWHERE.
PUT IT IN GEAR DOWN THERE, LAUGHING BOY!

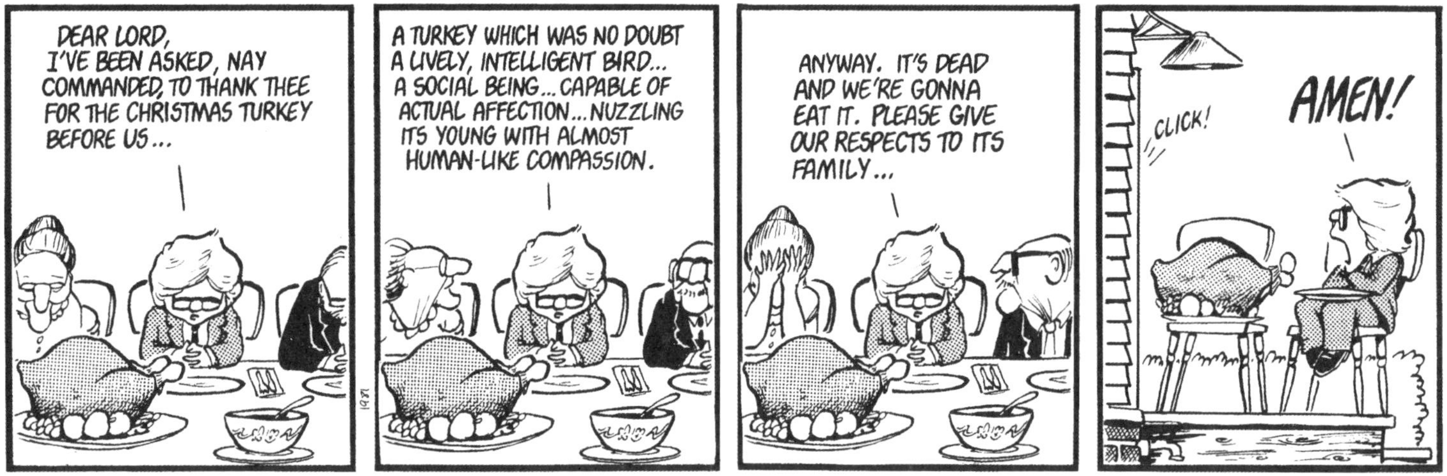
DEAR LORD, I'VE BEEN ASKED, NAY COMMANDED, TO THANK THEE FOR THE CHRISTMAS TURKEY BEFORE US...
A TURKEY WHICH WAS NO DOUBT A LIVELY, INTELLIGENT BIRD... A SOCIAL BEING... CAPABLE OF ACTUAL AFFECTION... NUZZLING ITS YOUNG WITH ALMOST HUMAN-LIKE COMPASSION.
ANYWAY. IT'S DEAD AND WE'RE GONNA EAT IT. PLEASE GIVE OUR RESPECTS TO ITS FAMILY...
CLICK!
AMEN!

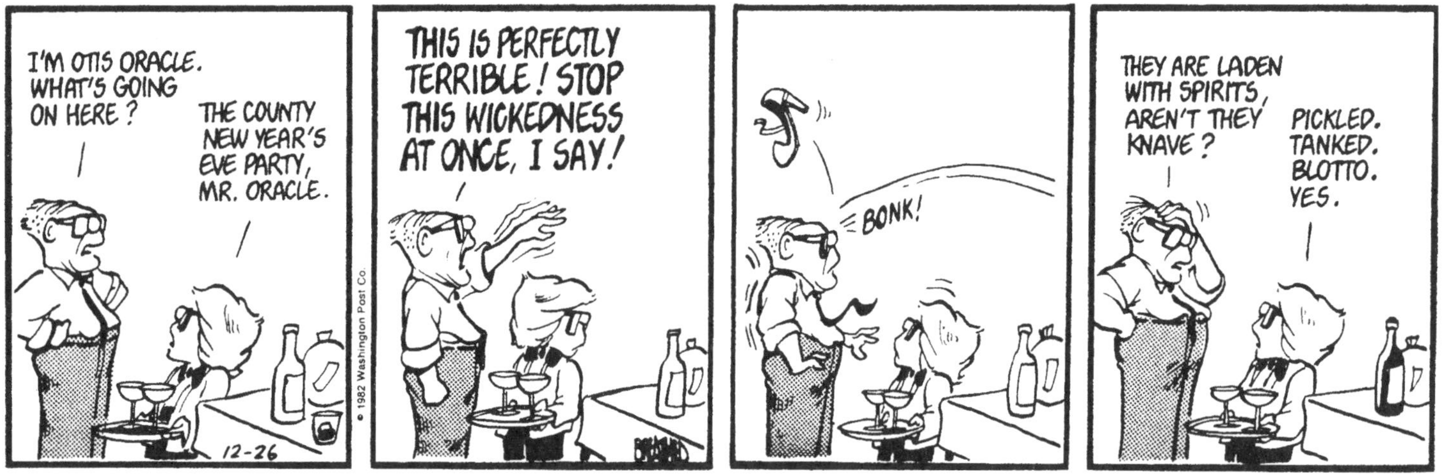
I'M OTIS ORACLE. WHAT'S GOING ON HERE?
THE COUNTY NEW YEAR'S EVE PARTY, MR. ORACLE.
12-26
© 1982 Washington Post Co.
THIS IS PERFECTLY TERRIBLE! STOP THIS WICKEDNESS AT ONCE, I SAY!
BONK!
THEY ARE LADEN WITH SPIRITS, AREN'T THEY KNAVE?
PICKLED. TANKED. BLOTTO. YES.

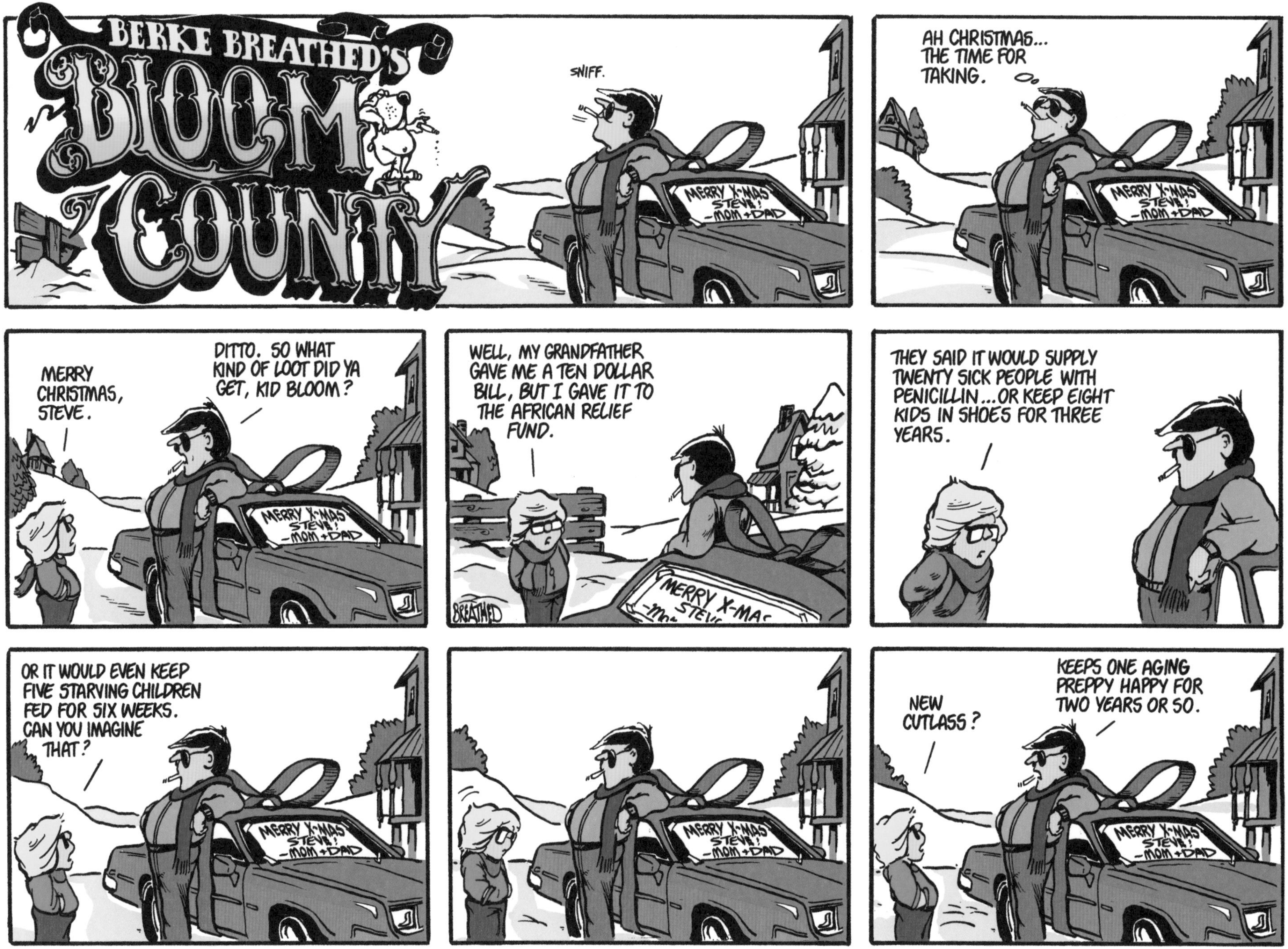
BERKE BREATHED'S
BLOOM COUNTY
SNIFF.
MERRY X-MAS STEVE! -MOM + DAD
AH CHRISTMAS... THE TIME FOR TAKING.
MERRY X-MAS STEVE! -MOM + DAD
MERRY CHRISTMAS, STEVE.
DITTO. SO WHAT KIND OF LOOT DID YA GET, KID BLOOM?
MERRY X-MAS STEVE! -MOM + DAD
WELL, MY GRANDFATHER GAVE ME A TEN DOLLAR BILL, BUT I GAVE IT TO THE AFRICAN RELIEF FUND.
BREATHED
THEY SAID IT WOULD SUPPLY TWENTY SICK PEOPLE WITH PENICILLIN...OR KEEP EIGHT KIDS IN SHOES FOR THREE YEARS.
OR IT WOULD EVEN KEEP FIVE STARVING CHILDREN FED FOR SIX WEEKS. CAN YOU IMAGINE THAT?
MERRY X-MAS STEVE! -MOM + DAD
MERRY X-MAS STEVE! -MOM + DAD
NEW CUTLASS?
KEEPS ONE AGING PREPPY HAPPY FOR TWO YEARS OR SO.
MERRY X-MAS STEVE! -MOM + DAD

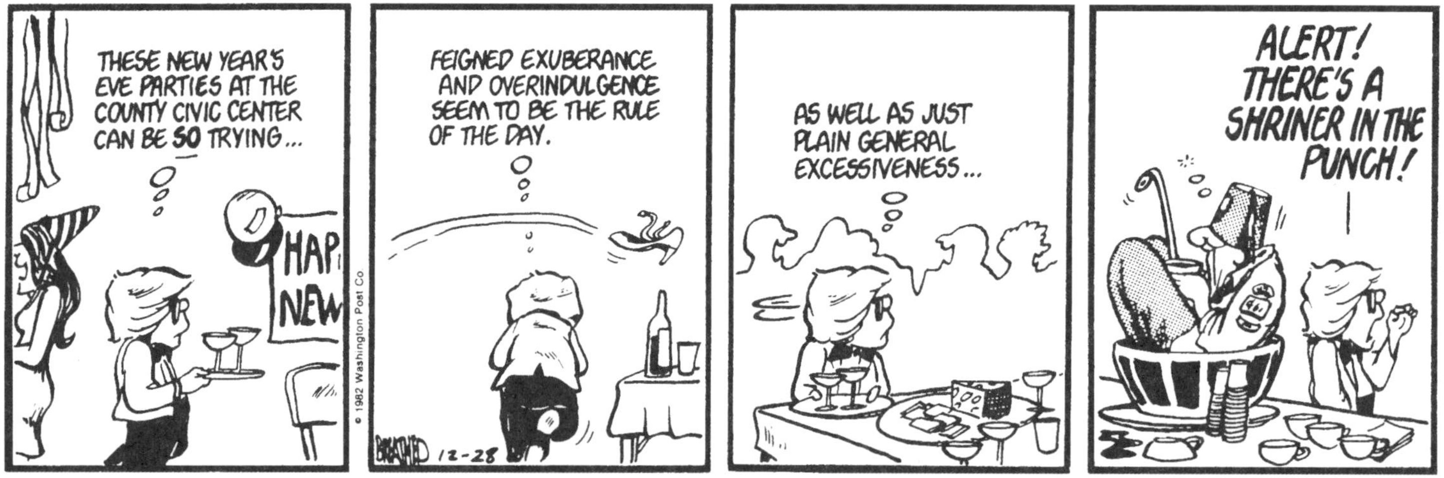
THESE NEW YEAR'S EVE PARTIES AT THE COUNTY CIVIC CENTER CAN BE SO TRYING...
HAP NEW
© 1982 Washington Post Co.
FEIGNED EXUBERANCE AND OVERINDULGENCE SEEM TO BE THE RULE OF THE DAY.
12-28
AS WELL AS JUST PLAIN GENERAL EXCESSIVENESS...
ALERT! THERE'S A SHRINER IN THE PUNCH!

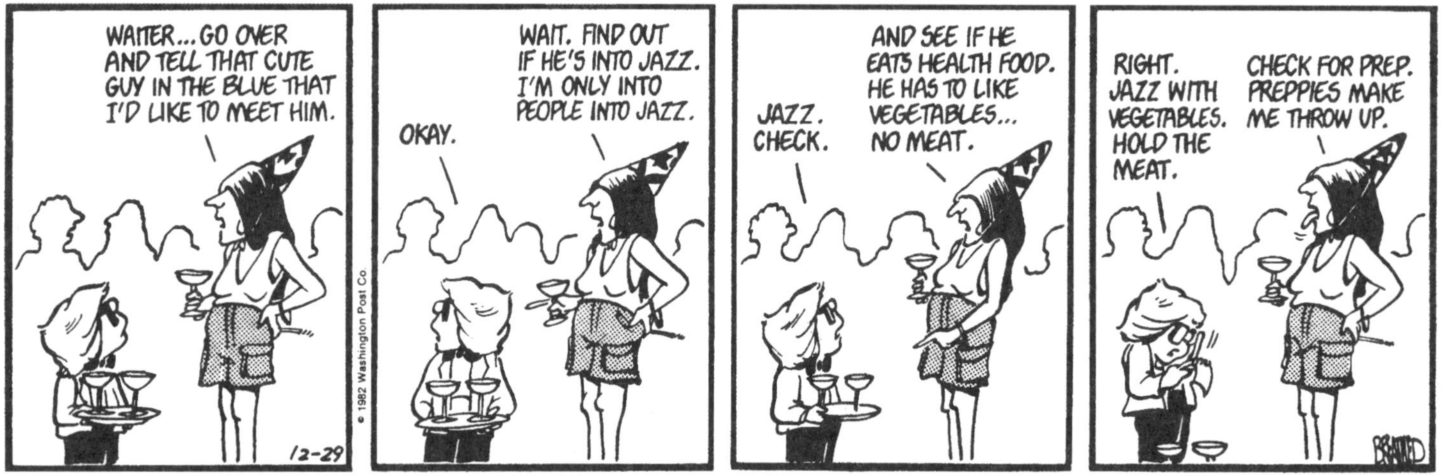
WAITER... GO OVER AND TELL THAT CUTE GUY IN THE BLUE THAT I'D LIKE TO MEET HIM.
12-29
© 1982 Washington Post Co.
OKAY.
WAIT. FIND OUT IF HE'S INTO JAZZ. I'M ONLY INTO PEOPLE INTO JAZZ.
JAZZ. CHECK.
AND SEE IF HE EATS HEALTH FOOD. HE HAS TO LIKE VEGETABLES... NO MEAT.
RIGHT. JAZZ WITH VEGETABLES. HOLD THE MEAT.
CHECK FOR PREP. PREPPIES MAKE ME THROW UP.

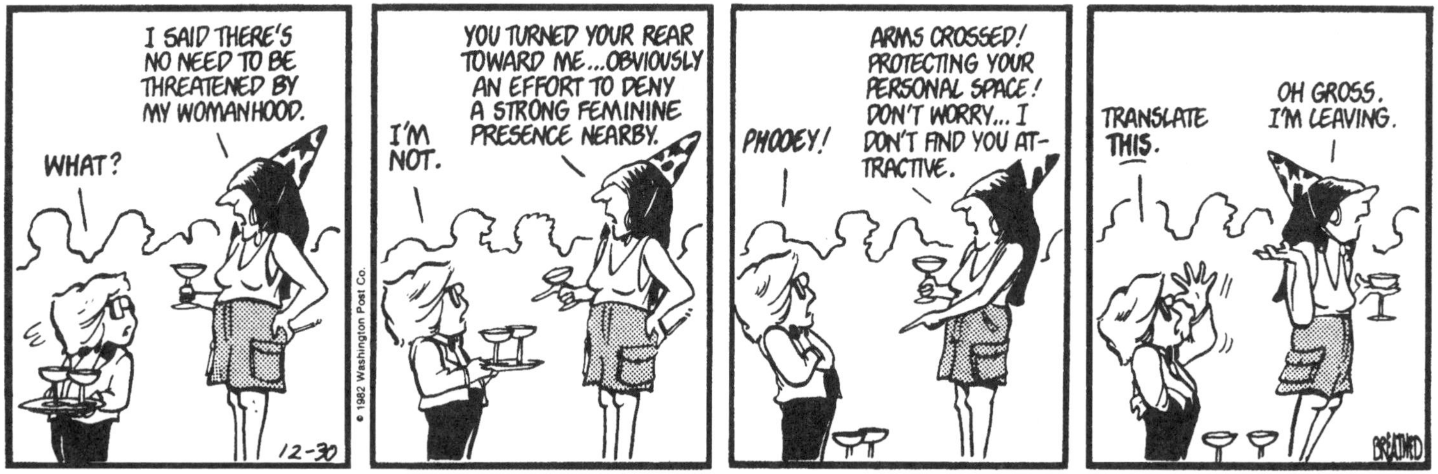
WHAT?
I SAID THERE'S NO NEED TO BE THREATENED BY MY WOMANHOOD.
12-30
© 1982 Washington Post Co.
I'M NOT.
YOU TURNED YOUR REAR TOWARD ME...OBVIOUSLY AN EFFORT TO DENY A STRONG FEMININE PRESENCE NEARBY.
PHOOEY!
ARMS CROSSED! PROTECTING YOUR PERSONAL SPACE! DON'T WORRY... I DON'T FIND YOU ATTRACTIVE.
TRANSLATE THIS.
OH GROSS. I'M LEAVING.

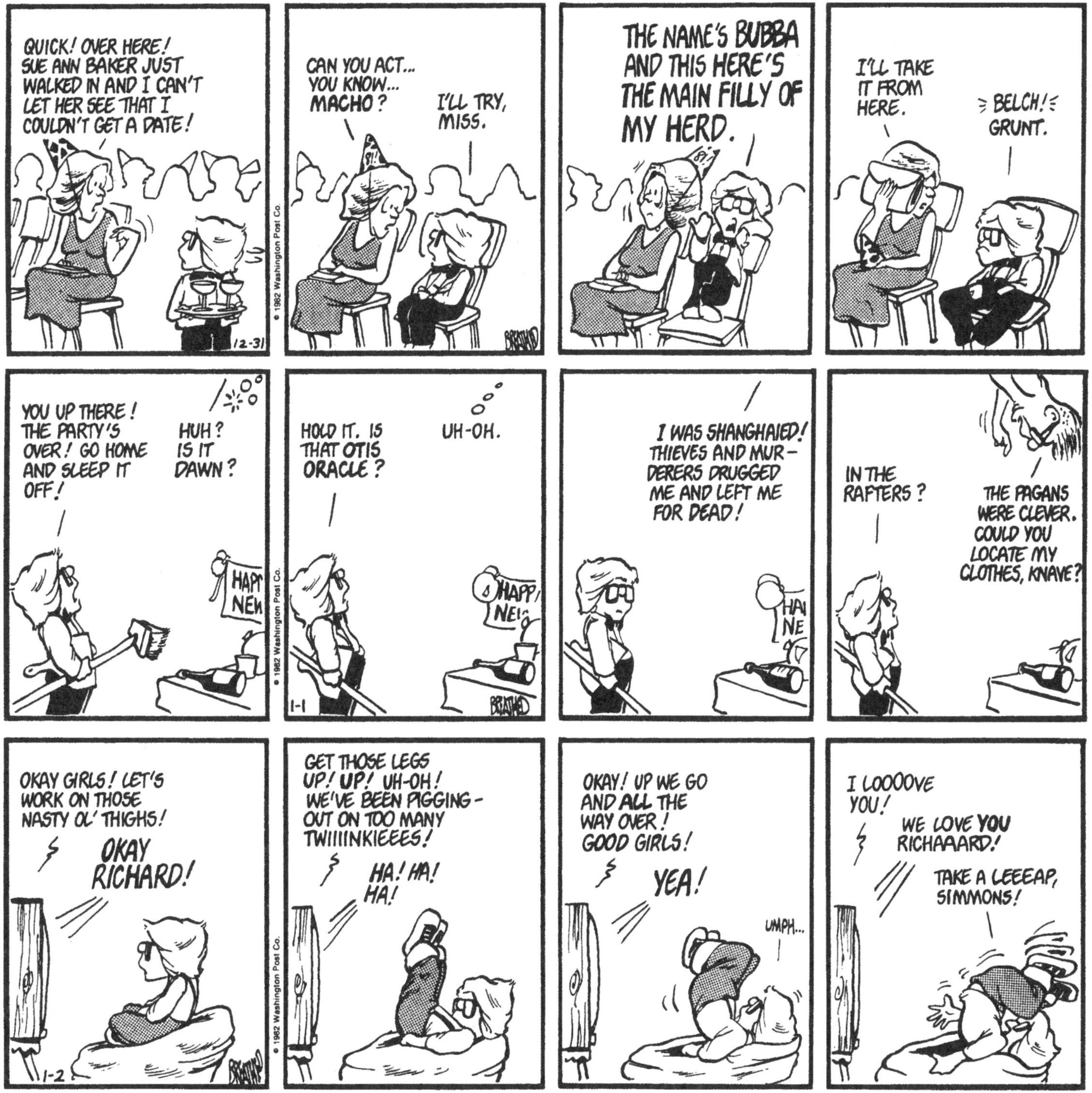
QUICK! OVER HERE! SUE ANN BAKER JUST WALKED IN AND I CAN'T LET HER SEE THAT I COULDN'T GET A DATE!
12-31
© 1982 Washington Post Co.
CAN YOU ACT... YOU KNOW... MACHO?
I'LL TRY, MISS.
THE NAME'S BUBBA AND THIS HERE'S THE MAIN FILLY OF MY HERD.
I'LL TAKE IT FROM HERE.
BELCH! GRUNT.
YOU UP THERE! THE PARTY'S OVER! GO HOME AND SLEEP IT OFF!
HUH? IS IT DAWN?
HOLD IT. IS THAT OTIS ORACLE?
UH-OH.
1-1
© 1982 Washington Post Co.
I WAS SHANGHAIED! THIEVES AND MURDERERS DRUGGED ME AND LEFT ME FOR DEAD!
IN THE RAFTERS?
THE PAGANS WERE CLEVER. COULD YOU LOCATE MY CLOTHES, KNAVE?
OKAY GIRLS! LET'S WORK ON THOSE NASTY OL' THIGHS!
OKAY RICHARD!
1-2
© 1982 Washington Post Co.
GET THOSE LEGS UP! UP! UH-OH! WE'VE BEEN PIGGING-OUT ON TOO MANY TWIIIINKIEEES!
HA! HA! HA!
OKAY! UP WE GO AND ALL THE WAY OVER! GOOD GIRLS!
YEA!
UMPH...
I LOOOOVE YOU!
WE LOVE YOU RICHAAARD!
TAKE A LEEEAP, SIMMONS!

December 31, 1981-
January 2, 1982

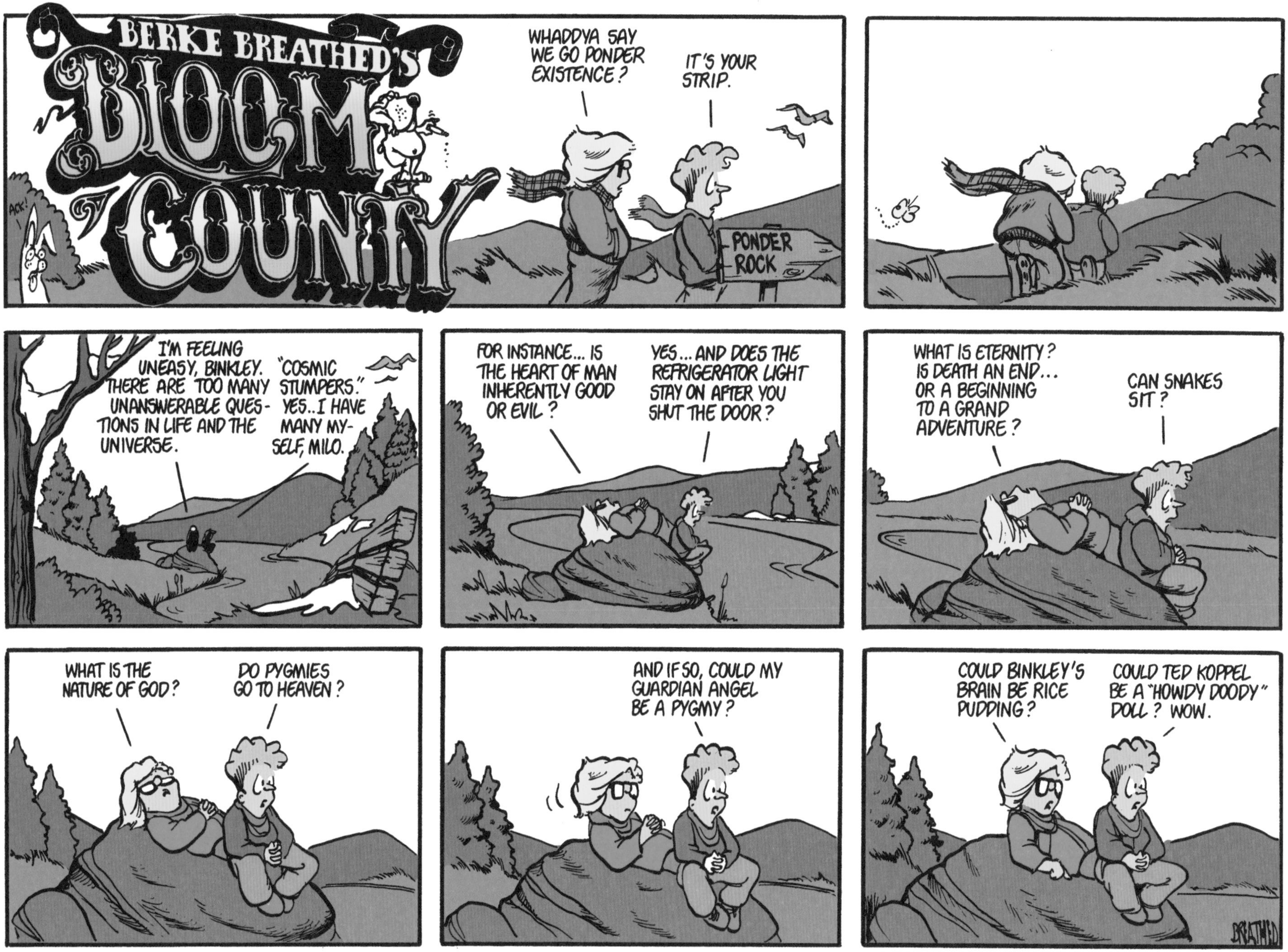
BERKE BREATHED'S
BLOOM COUNTY
ACK!
WHADDYA SAY WE GO PONDER EXISTENCE?
IT'S YOUR STRIP.
PONDER ROCK
I'M FEELING UNEASY, BINKLEY. THERE ARE TOO MANY UNANSWERABLE QUESTIONS IN LIFE AND THE UNIVERSE.
"COSMIC STUMPERS." YES.. I HAVE MANY MYSELF, MILO.
FOR INSTANCE... IS THE HEART OF MAN INHERENTLY GOOD OR EVIL?
YES... AND DOES THE REFRIGERATOR LIGHT STAY ON AFTER YOU SHUT THE DOOR?
WHAT IS ETERNITY? IS DEATH AN END... OR A BEGINNING TO A GRAND ADVENTURE?
CAN SNAKES SIT?
WHAT IS THE NATURE OF GOD?
DO PYGMIES GO TO HEAVEN?
AND IF SO, COULD MY GUARDIAN ANGEL BE A PYGMY?
COULD BINKLEY'S BRAIN BE RICE PUDDING?
COULD TED KOPPEL BE A "HOWDY DOODY" DOLL? WOW.
BREATHED

Howdy Doody, the star of his own 1950s children's television program, was a marionette.

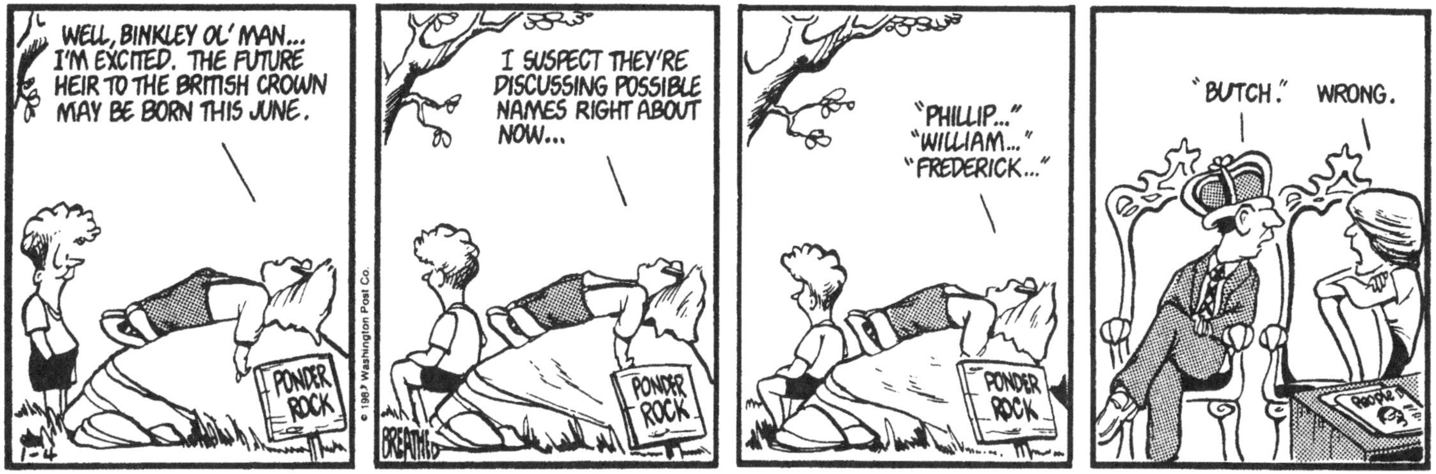
WELL, BINKLEY OL' MAN... I'M EXCITED. THE FUTURE HEIR TO THE BRITISH CROWN MAY BE BORN THIS JUNE.
PONDER ROCK
1-4
I SUSPECT THEY'RE DISCUSSING POSSIBLE NAMES RIGHT ABOUT NOW...
BREATHED
"PHILLIP..." "WILLIAM..." "FREDERICK..."
"BUTCH."
WRONG.

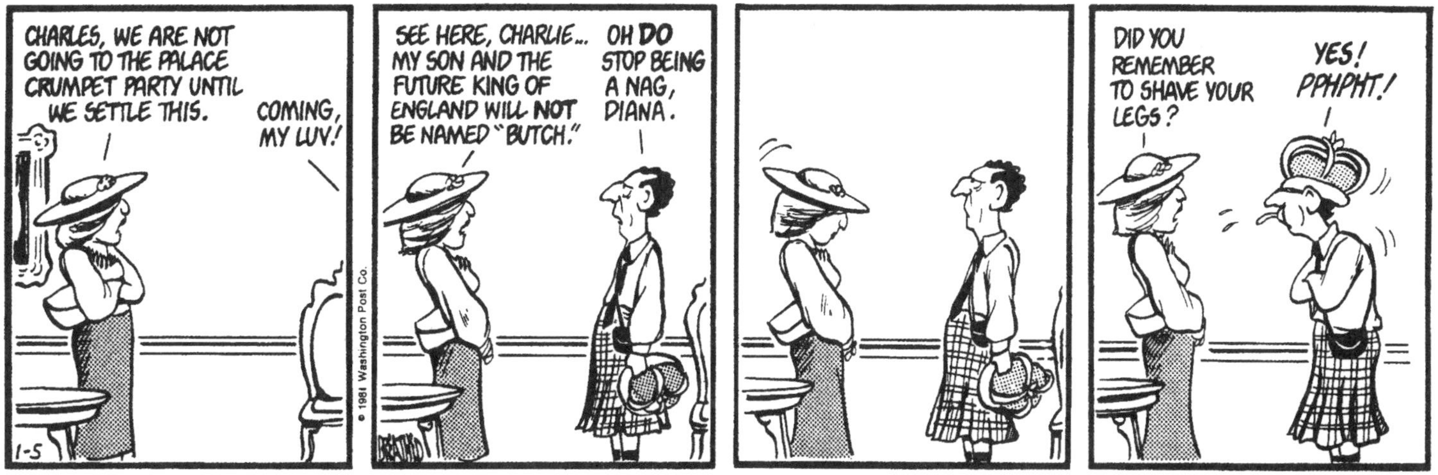
CHARLES, WE ARE NOT GOING TO THE PALACE CRUMPET PARTY UNTIL WE SETTLE THIS.
COMING, MY LUV!
1-5
© 1981 Washington Post Co.
SEE HERE, CHARLIE... MY SON AND THE FUTURE KING OF ENGLAND WILL NOT BE NAMED "BUTCH."
OH DO STOP BEING A NAG, DIANA.
BREATHED
DID YOU REMEMBER TO SHAVE YOUR LEGS?
YES! PPHPHT!

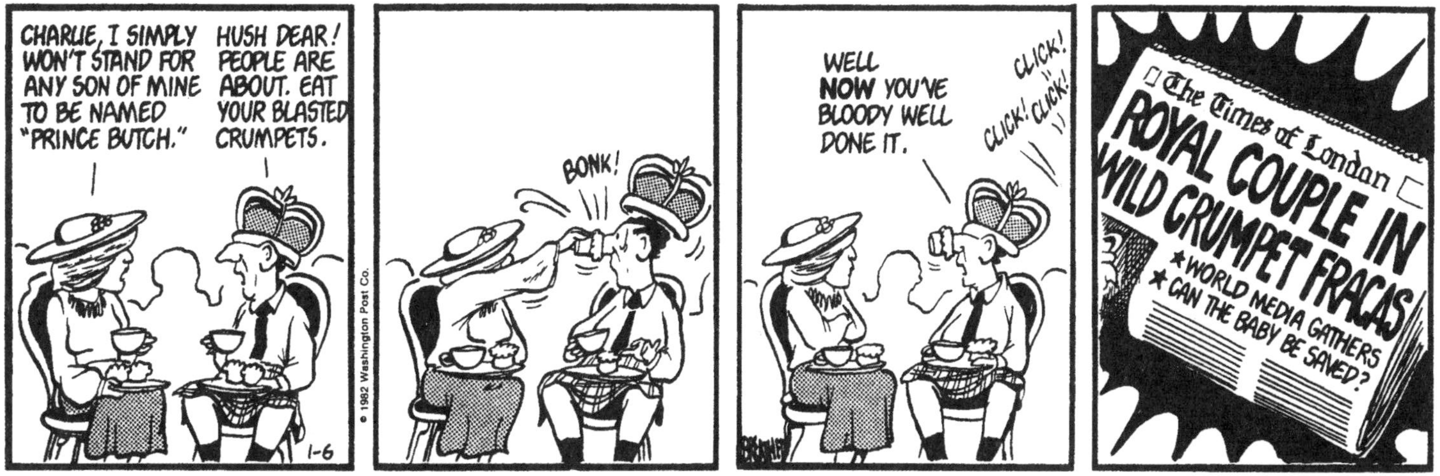
CHARLIE, I SIMPLY WON'T STAND FOR ANY SON OF MINE TO BE NAMED "PRINCE BUTCH."
HUSH DEAR! PEOPLE ARE ABOUT. EAT YOUR BLASTED CRUMPETS.
1-6
© 1982 Washington Post Co.
BONK!
WELL NOW YOU'VE BLOODY WELL DONE IT.
CLICK! CLICK! CLICK!
The Times of London
ROYAL COUPLE IN WILD CRUMPET FRACAS
★WORLD MEDIA GATHERS
★CAN THE BABY BE SAVED?

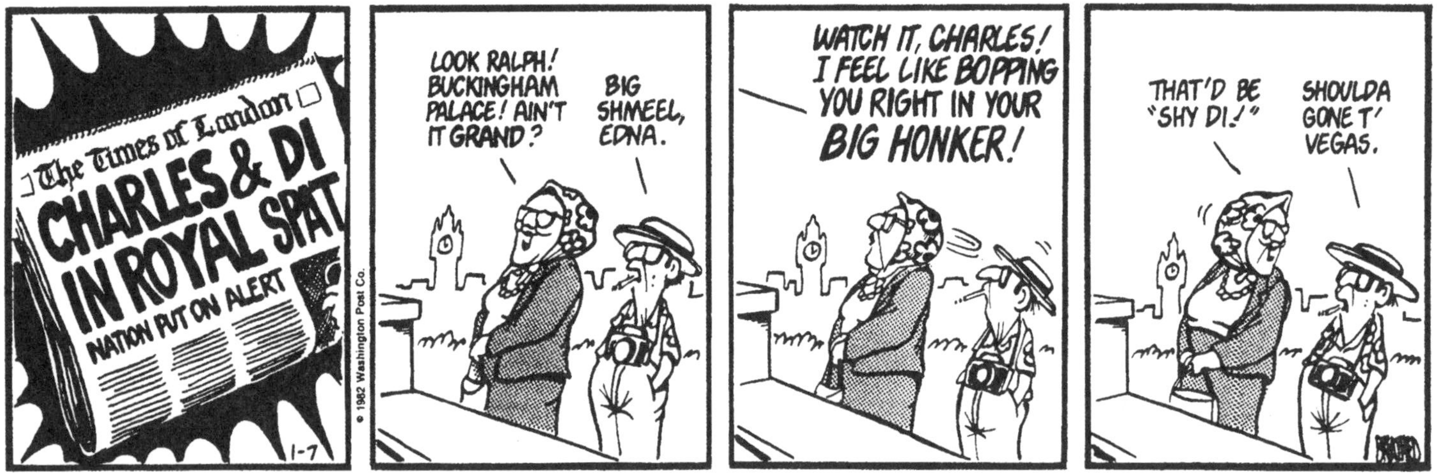
The Times of London
CHARLES & DI IN ROYAL SPAT
NATION PUT ON ALERT
1-7
© 1982 Washington Post Co.
LOOK RALPH! BUCKINGHAM PALACE! AIN'T IT GRAND?
BIG SHMEEL, EDNA.
WATCH IT, CHARLES! I FEEL LIKE BOPPING YOU RIGHT IN YOUR BIG HONKER!
THAT'D BE "SHY DI!"
SHOULDA GONE T' VEGAS.

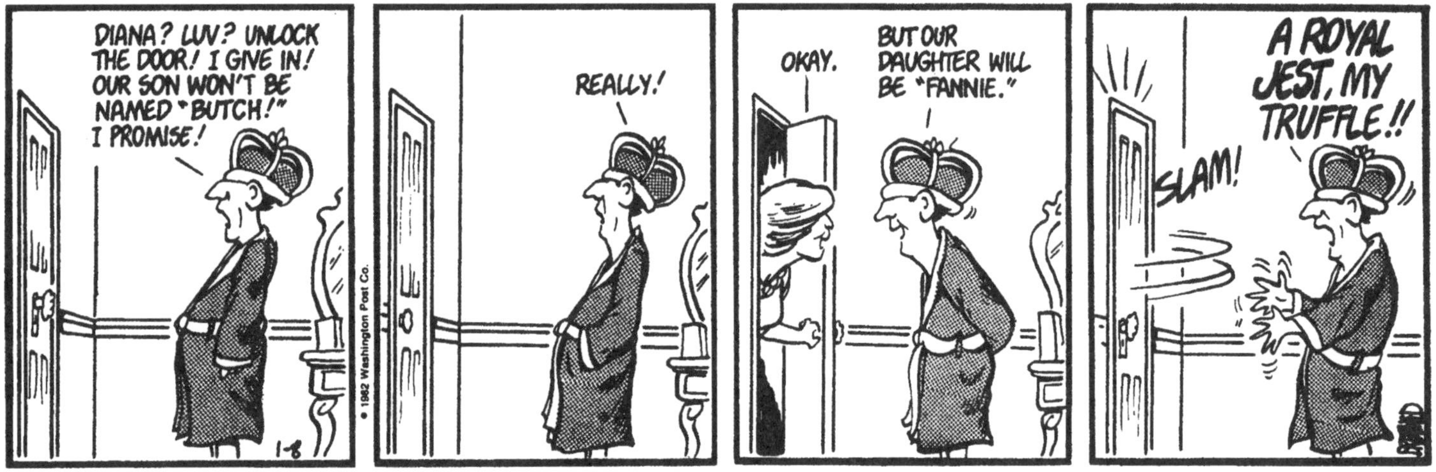
DIANA? LUV? UNLOCK THE DOOR! I GIVE IN! OUR SON WON'T BE NAMED "BUTCH!" I PROMISE!
1-8
© 1982 Washington Post Co.
REALLY!
OKAY.
BUT OUR DAUGHTER WILL BE "FANNIE."
SLAM!
A ROYAL JEST, MY TRUFFLE!!

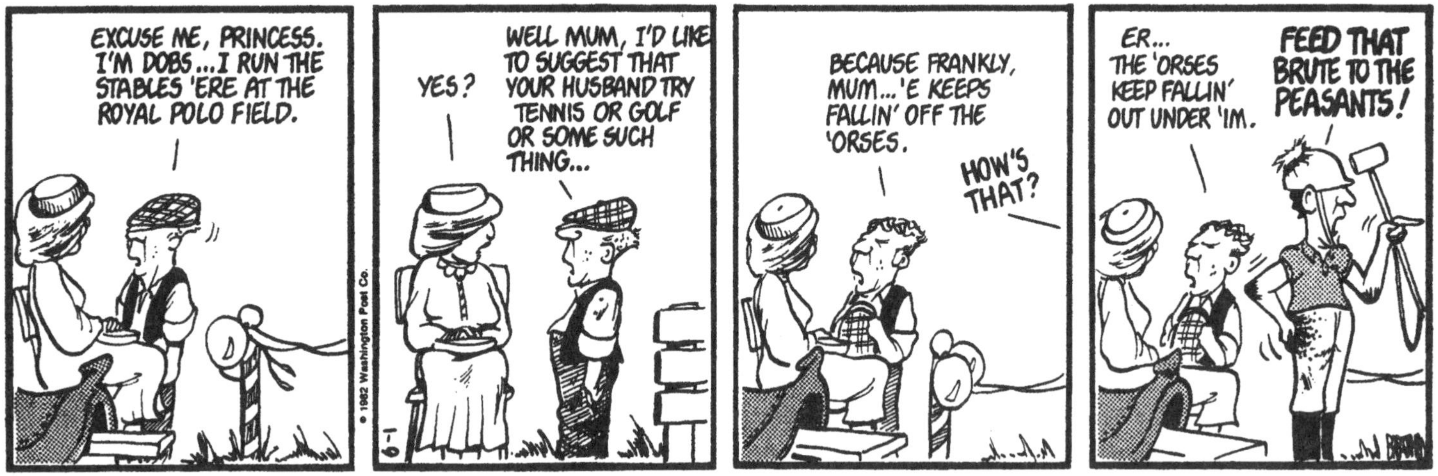
EXCUSE ME, PRINCESS. I'M DOBS...I RUN THE STABLES 'ERE AT THE ROYAL POLO FIELD.
© 1982 Washington Post Co.
1-9
YES?
WELL MUM, I'D LIKE TO SUGGEST THAT YOUR HUSBAND TRY TENNIS OR GOLF OR SOME SUCH THING...
BECAUSE FRANKLY, MUM...'E KEEPS FALLIN' OFF THE 'ORSES.
HOW'S THAT?
ER... THE 'ORSES KEEP FALLIN' OUT UNDER 'IM.
FEED THAT BRUTE TO THE PEASANTS!

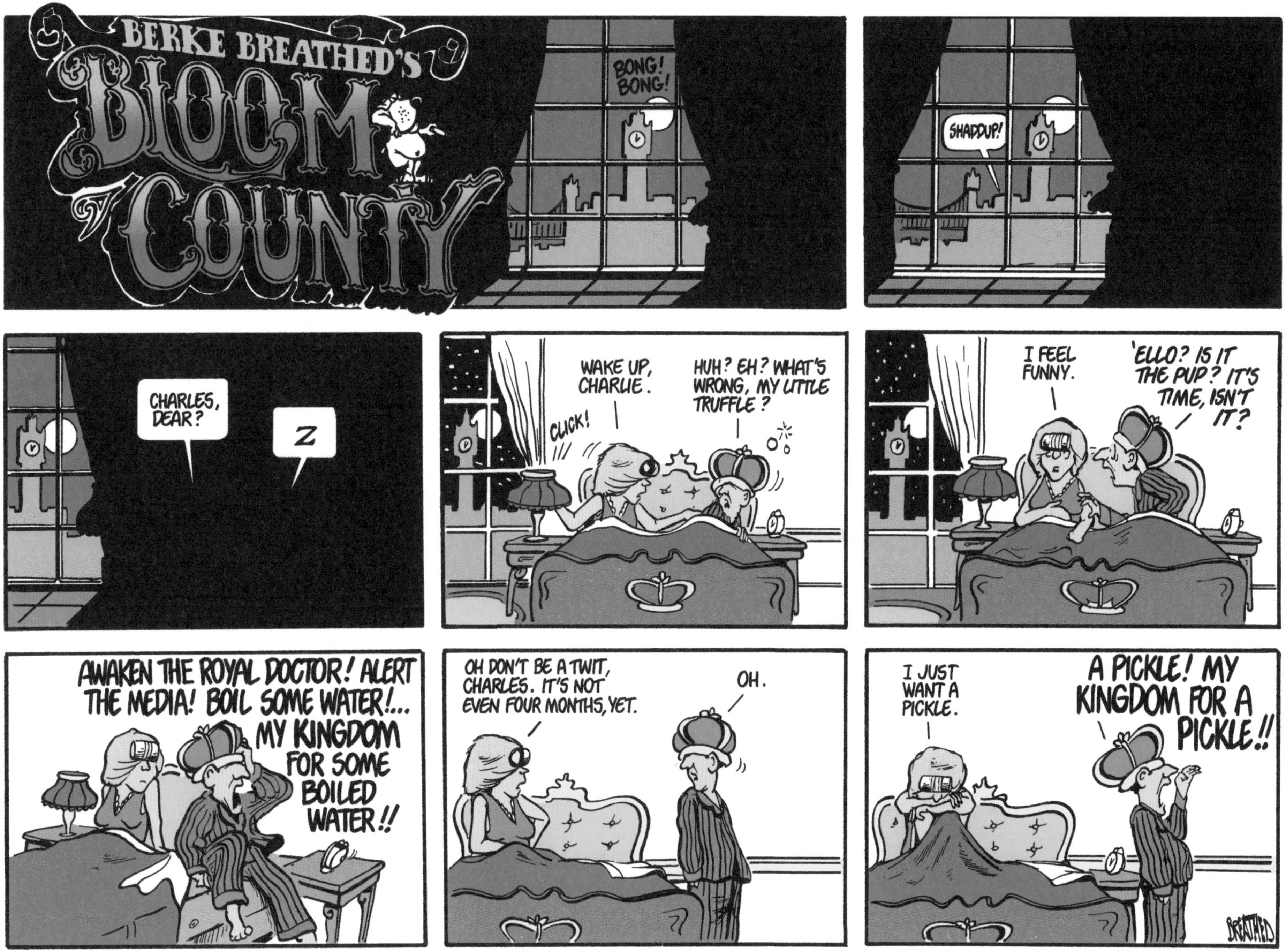
BERKE BREATHED'S
BLOOM COUNTY
BONG! BONG!
SHADDUP!
CHARLES, DEAR?
Z
CLICK!
WAKE UP, CHARLIE.
HUH? EH? WHAT'S WRONG, MY LITTLE TRUFFLE?
I FEEL FUNNY.
'ELLO? IS IT THE PUP? IT'S TIME, ISN'T IT?
AWAKEN THE ROYAL DOCTOR! ALERT THE MEDIA! BOIL SOME WATER!... MY KINGDOM FOR SOME BOILED WATER!!
OH DON'T BE A TWIT, CHARLES. IT'S NOT EVEN FOUR MONTHS, YET.
OH.
I JUST WANT A PICKLE.
A PICKLE! MY KINGDOM FOR A PICKLE!!
BREATHED

Tip O'Neill, liberal Democratic representative from Massachusetts, assumed office in 1963. He served as Speaker of the House from 1977 until his retirement in 1987.

Jesse Helms, conservative Republican senator from North Carolina, opposed school integration, the Civil Rights Act, gay and abortion rights, and the NEA.

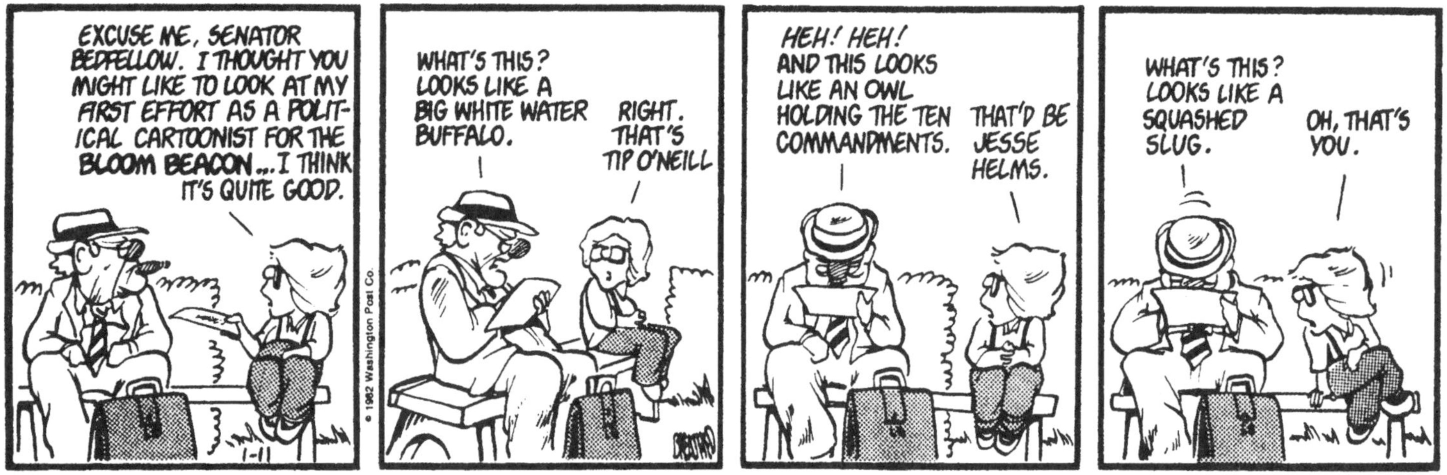
EXCUSE ME, SENATOR BEDFELLOW. I THOUGHT YOU MIGHT LIKE TO LOOK AT MY FIRST EFFORT AS A POLITICAL CARTOONIST FOR THE BLOOM BEACON... I THINK IT'S QUITE GOOD.
1-11
WHAT'S THIS? LOOKS LIKE A BIG WHITE WATER BUFFALO.
RIGHT. THAT'S TIP O'NEILL
© 1982 Washington Post Co.
HEH! HEH! AND THIS LOOKS LIKE AN OWL HOLDING THE TEN COMMANDMENTS.
THAT'D BE JESSE HELMS.
WHAT'S THIS? LOOKS LIKE A SQUASHED SLUG.
OH, THAT'S YOU.

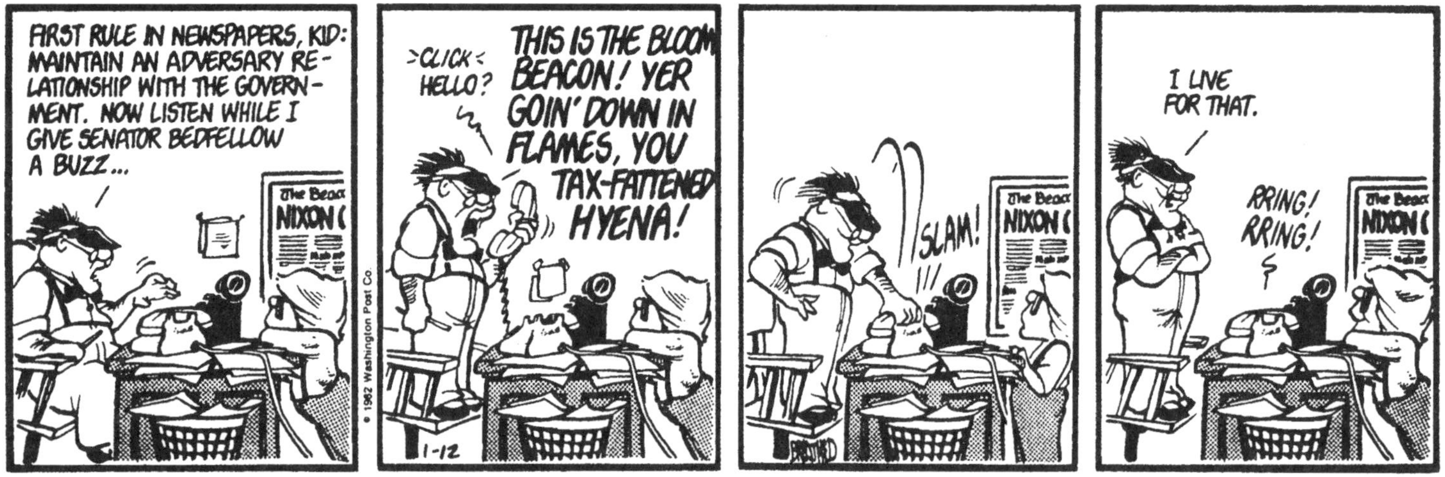
FIRST RULE IN NEWSPAPERS, KID: MAINTAIN AN ADVERSARY RELATIONSHIP WITH THE GOVERNMENT. NOW LISTEN WHILE I GIVE SENATOR BEDFELLOW A BUZZ...
The Beac
NIXON (
>CLICK< HELLO?
THIS IS THE BLOOM BEACON! YER GOIN' DOWN IN FLAMES, YOU TAX-FATTENED HYENA!
© 1982 Washington Post Co.
1-12
SLAM!
I LIVE FOR THAT.
RRING! RRING!

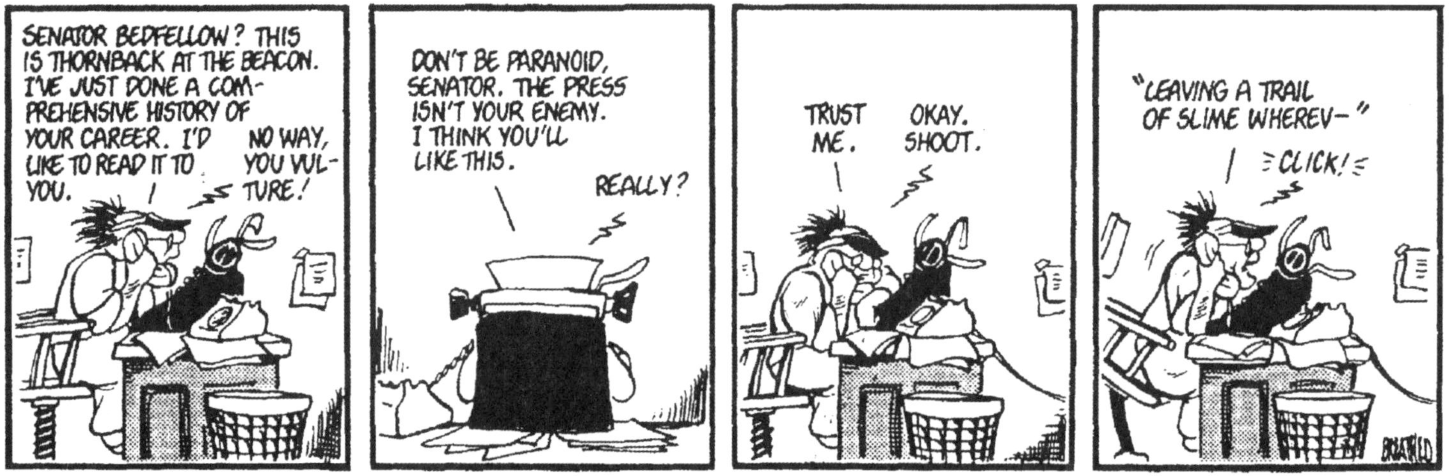
SENATOR BEDFELLOW? THIS IS THORNBACK AT THE BEACON. I'VE JUST DONE A COMPREHENSIVE HISTORY OF YOUR CAREER. I'D LIKE TO READ IT TO YOU.
NO WAY, YOU VULTURE!
DON'T BE PARANOID, SENATOR. THE PRESS ISN'T YOUR ENEMY. I THINK YOU'LL LIKE THIS.
REALLY?
TRUST ME.
OKAY. SHOOT.
"LEAVING A TRAIL OF SLIME WHEREV–"
>CLICK!<

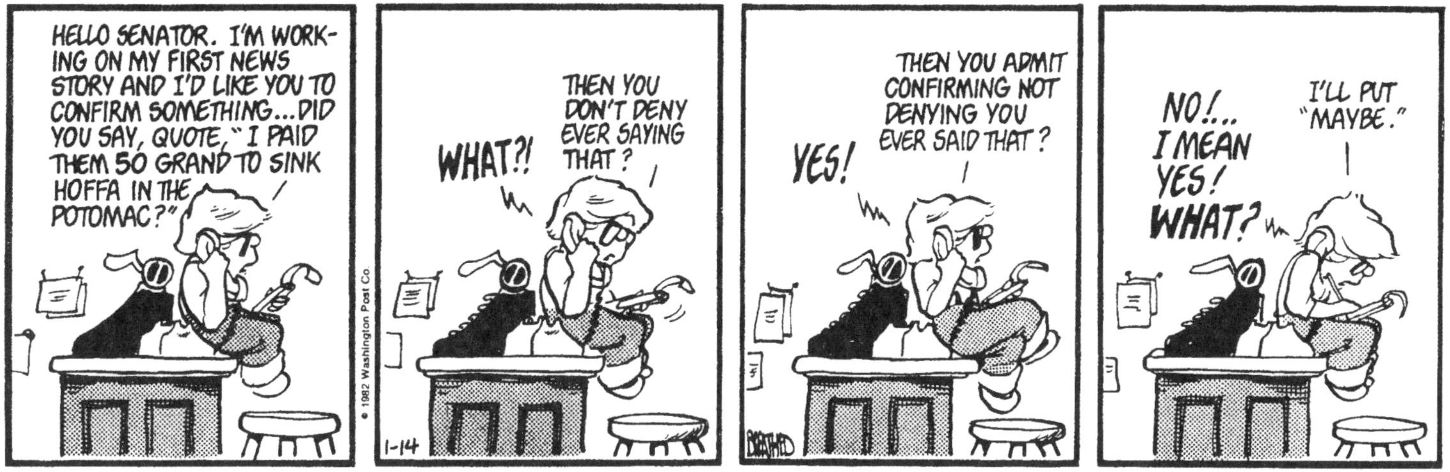
HELLO SENATOR. I'M WORKING ON MY FIRST NEWS STORY AND I'D LIKE YOU TO CONFIRM SOMETHING...DID YOU SAY, QUOTE, "I PAID THEM 50 GRAND TO SINK HOFFA IN THE POTOMAC?"
© 1982 Washington Post Co.
WHAT?!
THEN YOU DON'T DENY EVER SAYING THAT?
1-14
YES!
THEN YOU ADMIT CONFIRMING NOT DENYING YOU EVER SAID THAT?
BREATHED
NO!... I MEAN YES! WHAT?
I'LL PUT "MAYBE."

Jimmy Hoffa, the combative and powerful Teamsters union leader, disappeared in 1975, and is presumed dead.

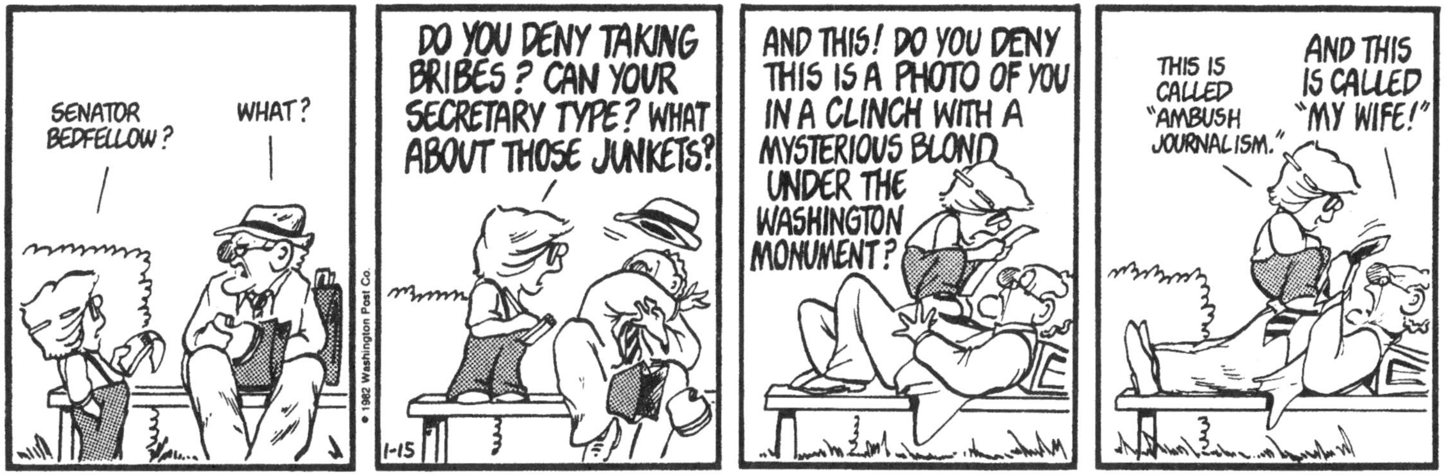
SENATOR BEDFELLOW?
WHAT?
© 1982 Washington Post Co.
DO YOU DENY TAKING BRIBES? CAN YOUR SECRETARY TYPE? WHAT ABOUT THOSE JUNKETS?
1-15
AND THIS! DO YOU DENY THIS IS A PHOTO OF YOU IN A CLINCH WITH A MYSTERIOUS BLOND UNDER THE WASHINGTON MONUMENT?
THIS IS CALLED "AMBUSH JOURNALISM."
AND THIS IS CALLED "MY WIFE!"

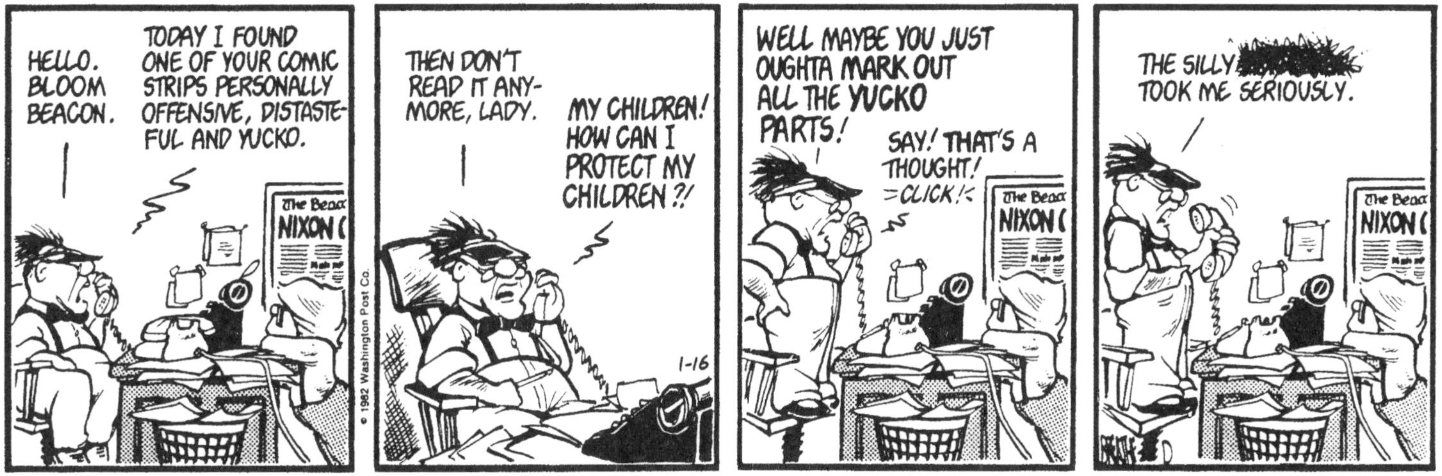
HELLO. BLOOM BEACON.
TODAY I FOUND ONE OF YOUR COMIC STRIPS PERSONALLY OFFENSIVE, DISTASTEFUL AND YUCKO.
The Beac
NIXON (
© 1982 Washington Post Co.
THEN DON'T READ IT ANYMORE, LADY.
MY CHILDREN! HOW CAN I PROTECT MY CHILDREN?!
1-16
WELL MAYBE YOU JUST OUGHTA MARK OUT ALL THE YUCKO PARTS!
SAY! THAT'S A THOUGHT!
CLICK!
THE SILLY [redacted] TOOK ME SERIOUSLY.
BREATHED

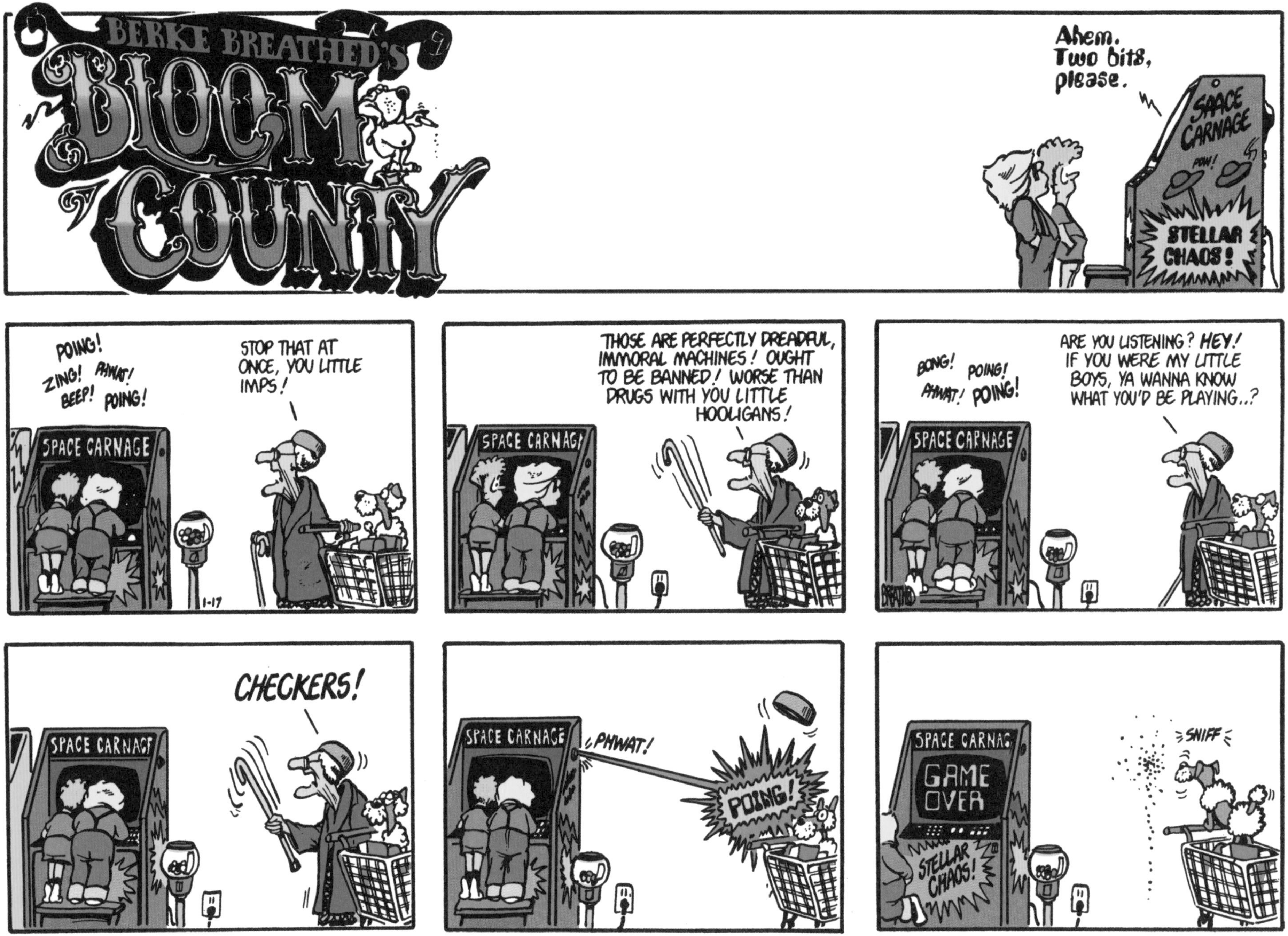
BERKE BREATHED'S
BLOOM COUNTY
Ahem. Two bits, please.
SPACE CARNAGE
POW!
STELLAR CHAOS!
POING!
ZING! PHWAT!
BEEP! POING!
STOP THAT AT ONCE, YOU LITTLE IMPS!
SPACE CARNAGE
1-17
THOSE ARE PERFECTLY DREADFUL, IMMORAL MACHINES! OUGHT TO BE BANNED! WORSE THAN DRUGS WITH YOU LITTLE HOOLIGANS!
BONG! POING!
PHWAT! POING!
ARE YOU LISTENING? HEY! IF YOU WERE MY LITTLE BOYS, YA WANNA KNOW WHAT YOU'D BE PLAYING..?
SPACE CARNAGE
CHECKERS!
PHWAT!
POING!
SNIFF
GAME OVER
STELLAR CHAOS!

January 17, 1981

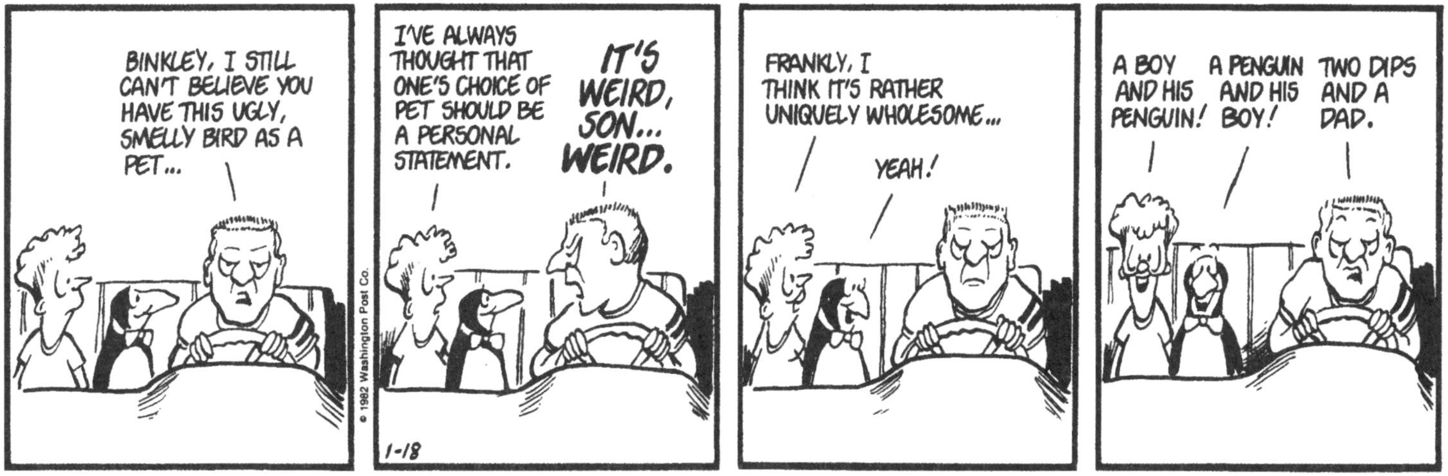
BINKLEY, I STILL CAN'T BELIEVE YOU HAVE THIS UGLY, SMELLY BIRD AS A PET...
I'VE ALWAYS THOUGHT THAT ONE'S CHOICE OF PET SHOULD BE A PERSONAL STATEMENT.
IT'S WEIRD, SON... WEIRD.
© 1982 Washington Post Co.
1-18
FRANKLY, I THINK IT'S RATHER UNIQUELY WHOLESOME...
YEAH!
A BOY AND HIS PENGUIN!
A PENGUIN AND HIS BOY!
TWO DIPS AND A DAD.

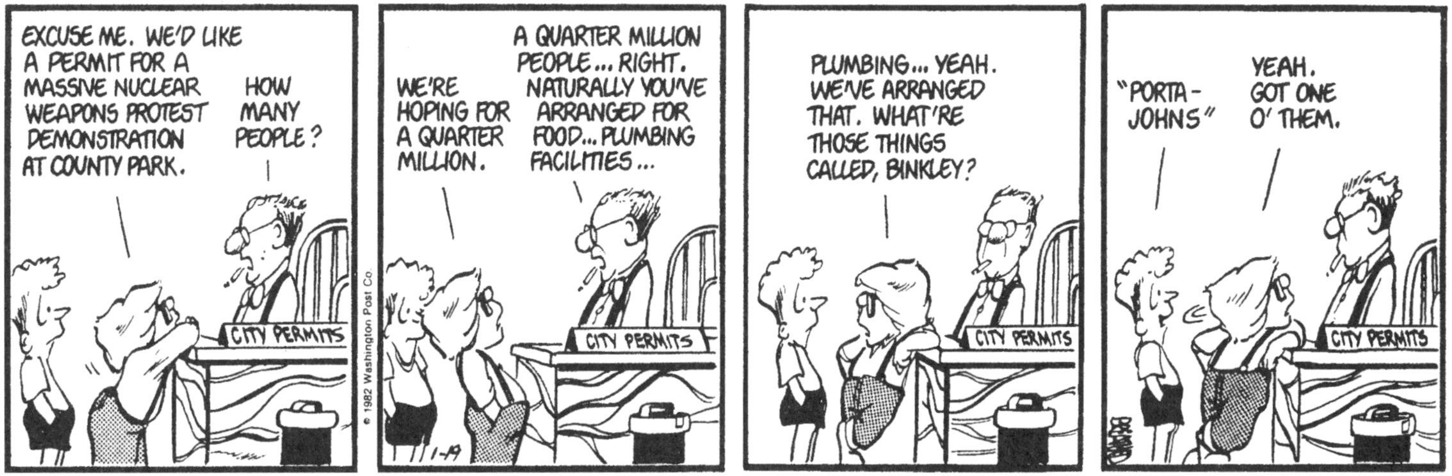
EXCUSE ME. WE'D LIKE A PERMIT FOR A MASSIVE NUCLEAR WEAPONS PROTEST DEMONSTRATION AT COUNTY PARK.
HOW MANY PEOPLE?
CITY PERMITS
© 1982 Washington Post Co.
WE'RE HOPING FOR A QUARTER MILLION.
A QUARTER MILLION PEOPLE... RIGHT. NATURALLY YOU'VE ARRANGED FOR FOOD... PLUMBING FACILITIES...
CITY PERMITS
1-19
PLUMBING... YEAH. WE'VE ARRANGED THAT. WHAT'RE THOSE THINGS CALLED, BINKLEY?
CITY PERMITS
"PORTA-JOHNS"
YEAH. GOT ONE O' THEM.
CITY PERMITS

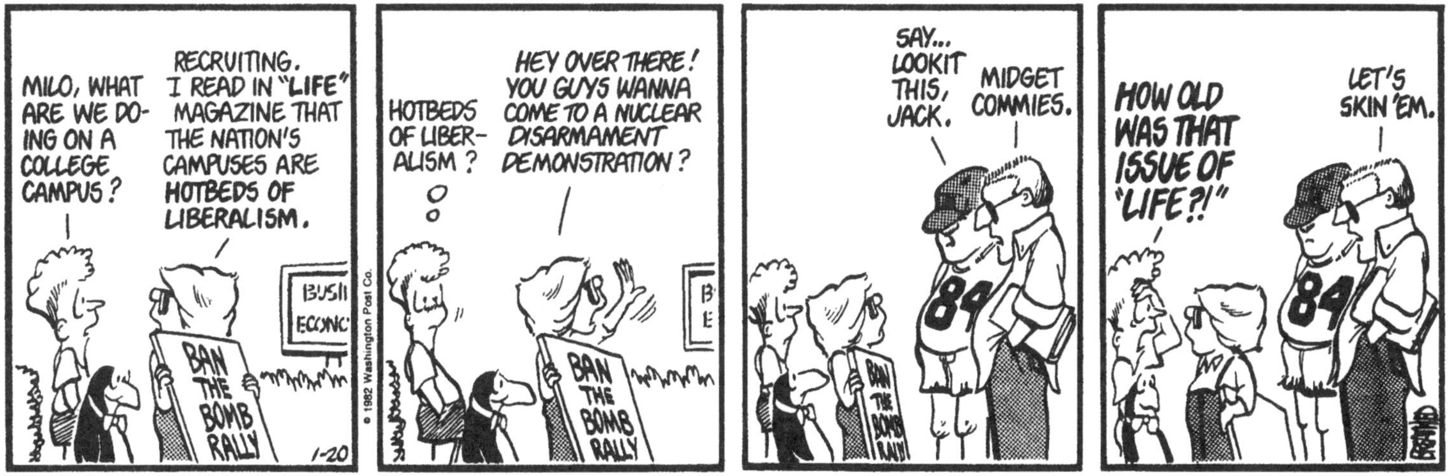
MILO, WHAT ARE WE DOING ON A COLLEGE CAMPUS?
RECRUITING. I READ IN "LIFE" MAGAZINE THAT THE NATION'S CAMPUSES ARE HOTBEDS OF LIBERALISM.
BAN THE BOMB RALLY
1-20
© 1982 Washington Post Co.
HOTBEDS OF LIBERALISM?
HEY OVER THERE! YOU GUYS WANNA COME TO A NUCLEAR DISARMAMENT DEMONSTRATION?
BAN THE BOMB RALLY
SAY... LOOKIT THIS, JACK.
MIDGET COMMIES.
84
HOW OLD WAS THAT ISSUE OF "LIFE?!"
LET'S SKIN 'EM.
84
BREATHED

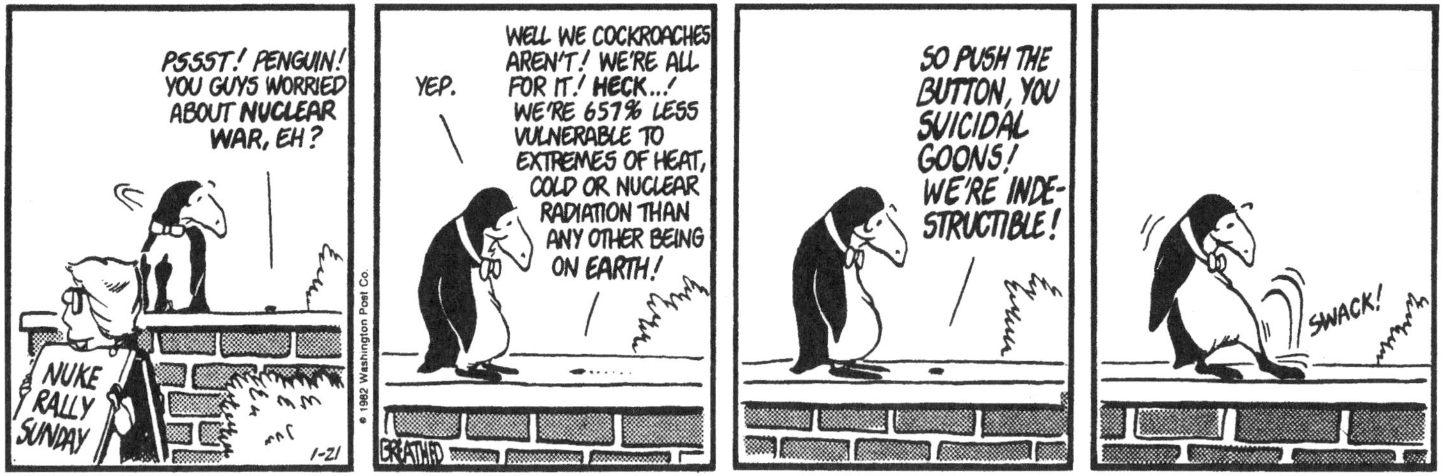
PSSST! PENGUIN! YOU GUYS WORRIED ABOUT NUCLEAR WAR, EH?
NUKE RALLY SUNDAY
1-21
YEP.
WELL WE COCKROACHES AREN'T! WE'RE ALL FOR IT! HECK...! WE'RE 657% LESS VULNERABLE TO EXTREMES OF HEAT, COLD OR NUCLEAR RADIATION THAN ANY OTHER BEING ON EARTH!
© 1982 Washington Post Co.
BREATHED
SO PUSH THE BUTTON, YOU SUICIDAL GOONS! WE'RE INDESTRUCTIBLE!
SWACK!

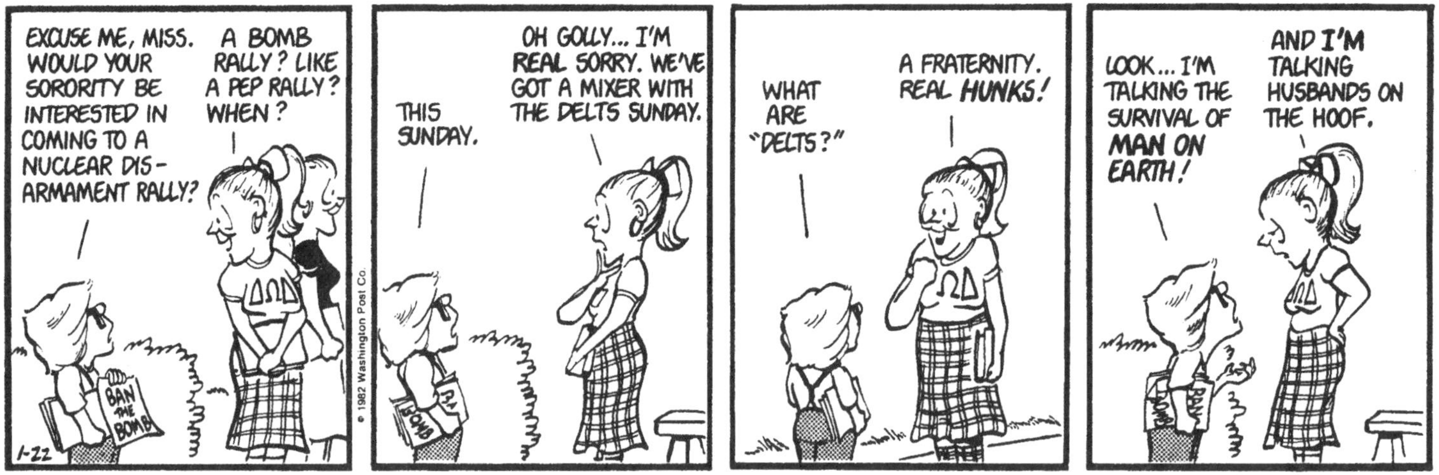
EXCUSE ME, MISS. WOULD YOUR SORORITY BE INTERESTED IN COMING TO A NUCLEAR DISARMAMENT RALLY?
A BOMB RALLY? LIKE A PEP RALLY? WHEN?
BAN THE BOMB
1-22
THIS SUNDAY.
OH GOLLY... I'M REAL SORRY. WE'VE GOT A MIXER WITH THE DELTS SUNDAY.
© 1982 Washington Post Co.
WHAT ARE "DELTS?"
A FRATERNITY. REAL HUNKS!
LOOK... I'M TALKING THE SURVIVAL OF MAN ON EARTH!
AND I'M TALKING HUSBANDS ON THE HOOF.

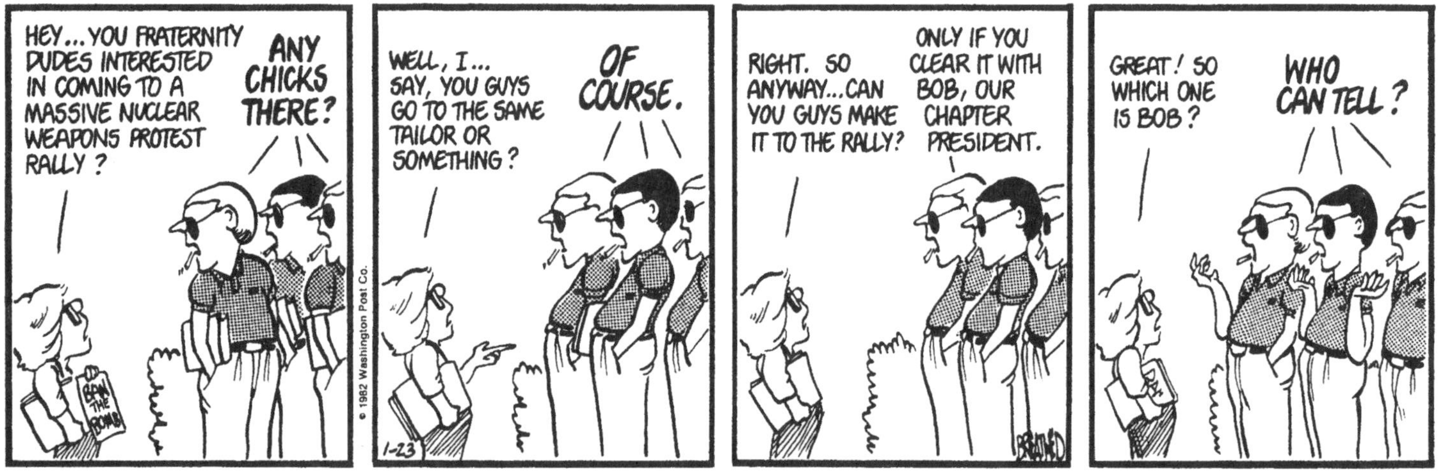
HEY... YOU FRATERNITY DUDES INTERESTED IN COMING TO A MASSIVE NUCLEAR WEAPONS PROTEST RALLY?
ANY CHICKS THERE?
BAN THE BOMB
WELL, I... SAY, YOU GUYS GO TO THE SAME TAILOR OR SOMETHING?
OF COURSE.
© 1982 Washington Post Co.
1-23
RIGHT. SO ANYWAY...CAN YOU GUYS MAKE IT TO THE RALLY?
ONLY IF YOU CLEAR IT WITH BOB, OUR CHAPTER PRESIDENT.
BREATHED
GREAT! SO WHICH ONE IS BOB?
WHO CAN TELL?

BERKE BREATHED'S BLOOM COUNT

DITCH THE BOMB!

OKAY, FOLKS... WE'RE READY TO START. QUIET PLEASE.

PSST. THERE'S NOBODY HERE.

HEY. WHO'S RUNNING THIS SHOW, BUB?

I'D LIKE TO WELCOME, UH... ALL OF YOU TO AMERICA'S FIRST MASSIVE DEMONSTRATION AGAINST NUCLEAR WEAPONS.

IMPEACH NIXON

OUR GOAL, FELLOW CITIZENS, IS TO BUILD A HUGE GRASS ROOTS RESISTANCE TO THIS RUSH INTO NUCLEAR SUICIDE...

A RESISTANCE MADE OF COMMON, EVERYDAY PEOPLE OF MAINSTREAM AMERICA... PEOPLE LIKE ME AND... UH... YOU.

RIGHT! DIG IT!

AHEM. FURTHERMORE...

C'MON! BRING ON FONDA! BREAK OUT THE FRISBEES!

WAIT! CATCH THIS! LITTLE MX MISSILES PAINTED ON THE BOTTOM OF MY FEET! DIG IT!

THIS AIN'T GONNA PLAY IN PEORIA.!!

MAN, OL' RONALD RAY-GUNS IS GONNA FLIP FAR FREAKIN' **OUT** AT THIS!

Jane Fonda, Academy Award-winning actress and liberal cause activist.

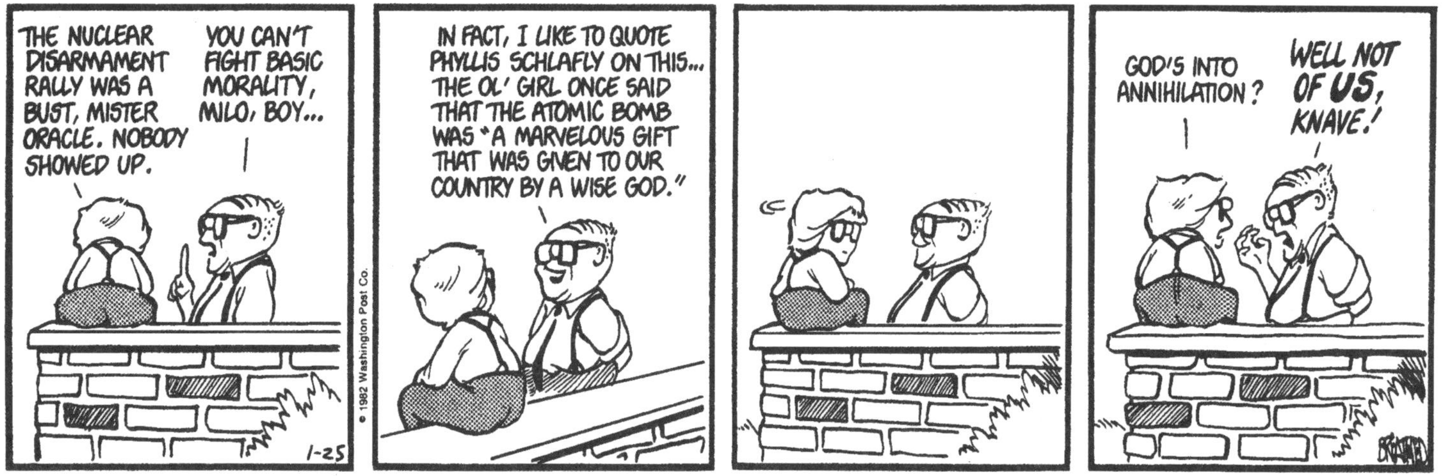
THE NUCLEAR DISARMAMENT RALLY WAS A BUST, MISTER ORACLE. NOBODY SHOWED UP.
YOU CAN'T FIGHT BASIC MORALITY, MILO, BOY...
IN FACT, I LIKE TO QUOTE PHYLLIS SCHLAFLY ON THIS... THE OL' GIRL ONCE SAID THAT THE ATOMIC BOMB WAS "A MARVELOUS GIFT THAT WAS GIVEN TO OUR COUNTRY BY A WISE GOD."
GOD'S INTO ANNIHILATION?
WELL NOT OF **US**, KNAVE!
1-25
© 1982 Washington Post Co.

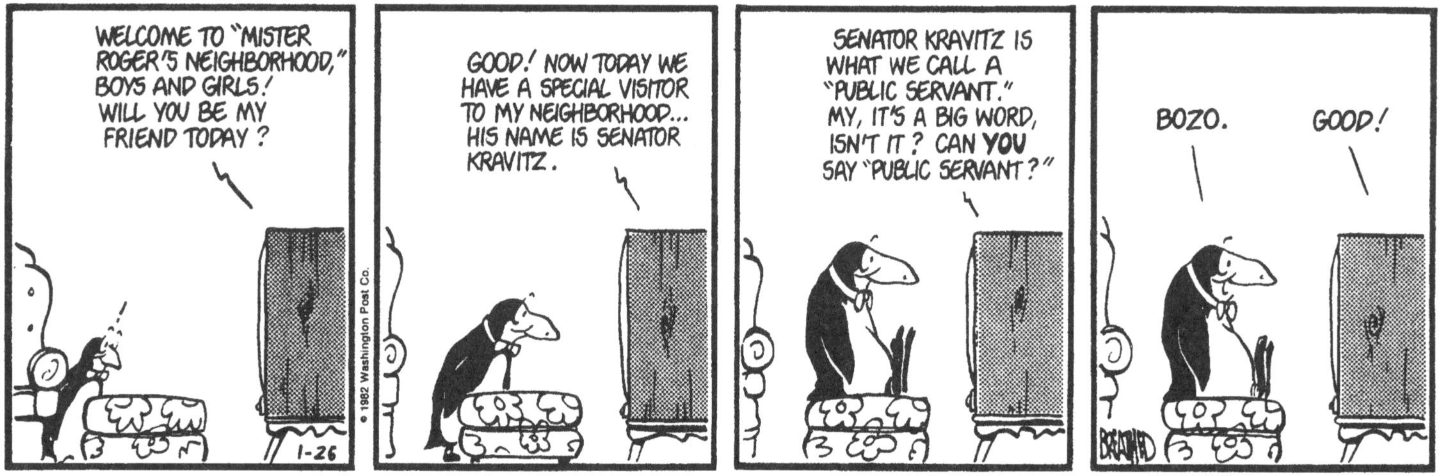
WELCOME TO "MISTER ROGER'S NEIGHBORHOOD," BOYS AND GIRLS! WILL YOU BE MY FRIEND TODAY?
GOOD! NOW TODAY WE HAVE A SPECIAL VISITOR TO MY NEIGHBORHOOD... HIS NAME IS SENATOR KRAVITZ.
SENATOR KRAVITZ IS WHAT WE CALL A "PUBLIC SERVANT." MY, IT'S A BIG WORD, ISN'T IT? CAN **YOU** SAY "PUBLIC SERVANT?"
BOZO.
GOOD!
1-26
© 1982 Washington Post Co.

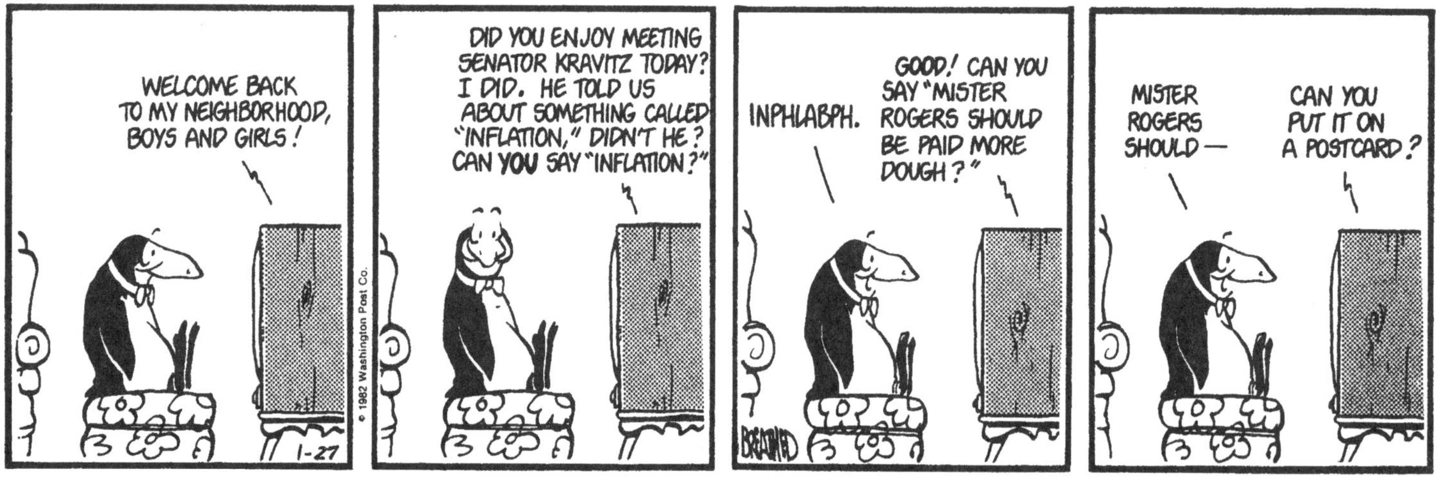
WELCOME BACK TO MY NEIGHBORHOOD, BOYS AND GIRLS!
DID YOU ENJOY MEETING SENATOR KRAVITZ TODAY? I DID. HE TOLD US ABOUT SOMETHING CALLED "INFLATION," DIDN'T HE? CAN **YOU** SAY "INFLATION?"
INPHLABPH.
GOOD! CAN YOU SAY "MISTER ROGERS SHOULD BE PAID MORE DOUGH?"
MISTER ROGERS SHOULD—
CAN YOU PUT IT ON A POSTCARD?
1-27
© 1982 Washington Post Co.

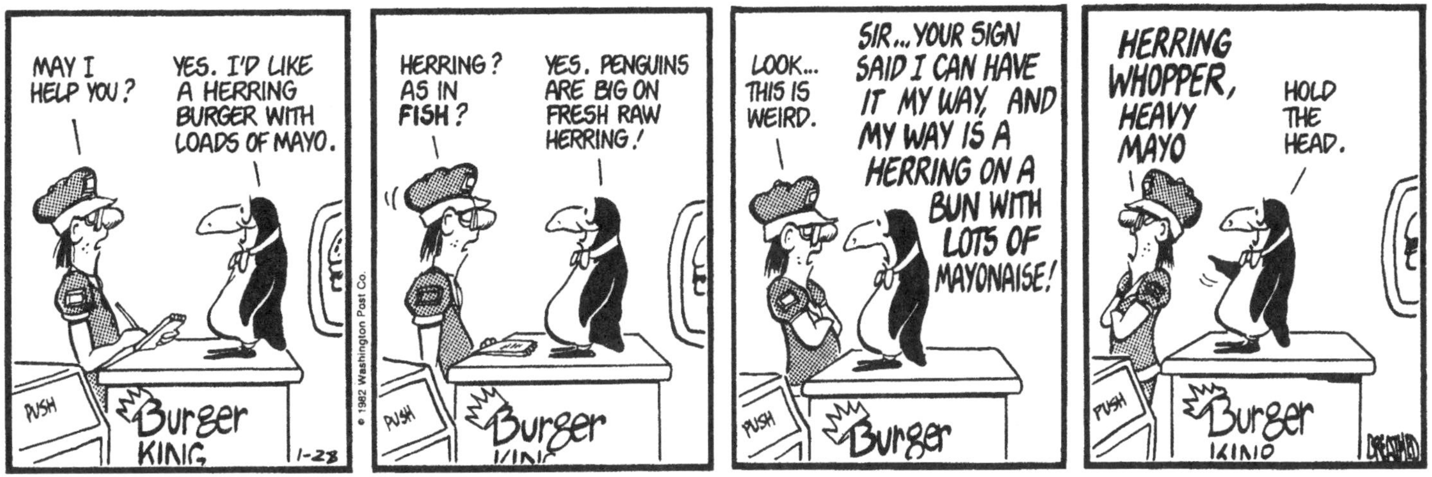
MAY I HELP YOU?
YES. I'D LIKE A HERRING BURGER WITH LOADS OF MAYO.
PUSH
Burger King
1-28
HERRING? AS IN FISH?
YES. PENGUINS ARE BIG ON FRESH RAW HERRING!
© 1982 Washington Post Co.
LOOK... THIS IS WEIRD.
SIR... YOUR SIGN SAID I CAN HAVE IT MY WAY, AND MY WAY IS A HERRING ON A BUN WITH LOTS OF MAYONAISE!
HERRING WHOPPER, HEAVY MAYO
HOLD THE HEAD.
BREATHED

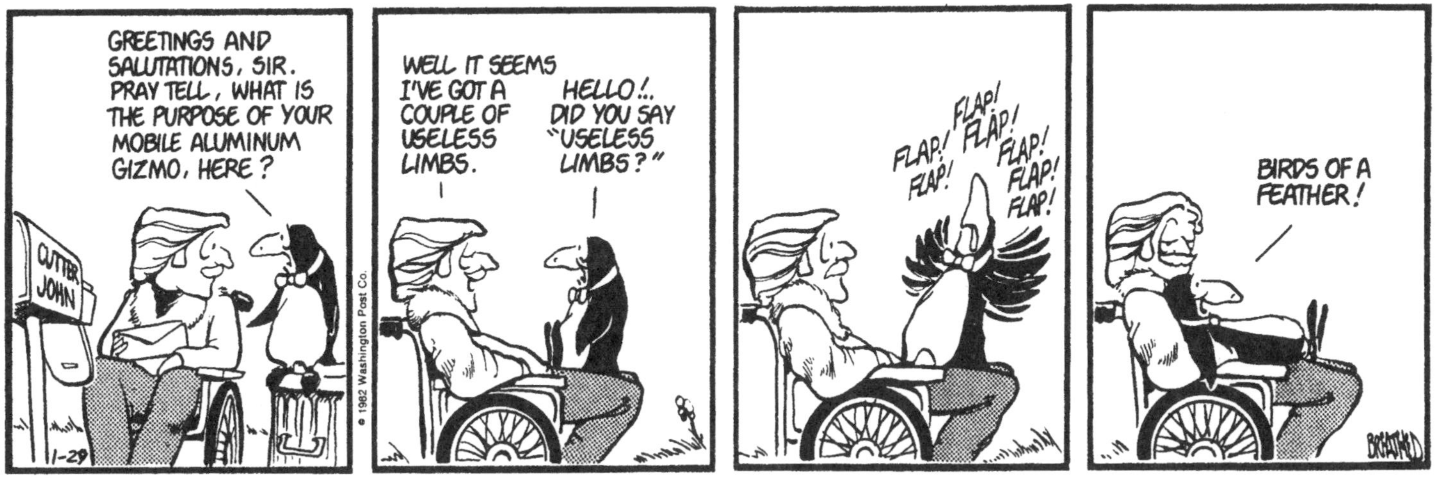
GREETINGS AND SALUTATIONS, SIR. PRAY TELL, WHAT IS THE PURPOSE OF YOUR MOBILE ALUMINUM GIZMO, HERE?
CUTTER JOHN
1-29
© 1982 Washington Post Co.
WELL IT SEEMS I'VE GOT A COUPLE OF USELESS LIMBS.
HELLO!.. DID YOU SAY "USELESS LIMBS?"
FLAP! FLAP! FLAP! FLAP! FLAP! FLAP! FLAP!
BIRDS OF A FEATHER!
BREATHED

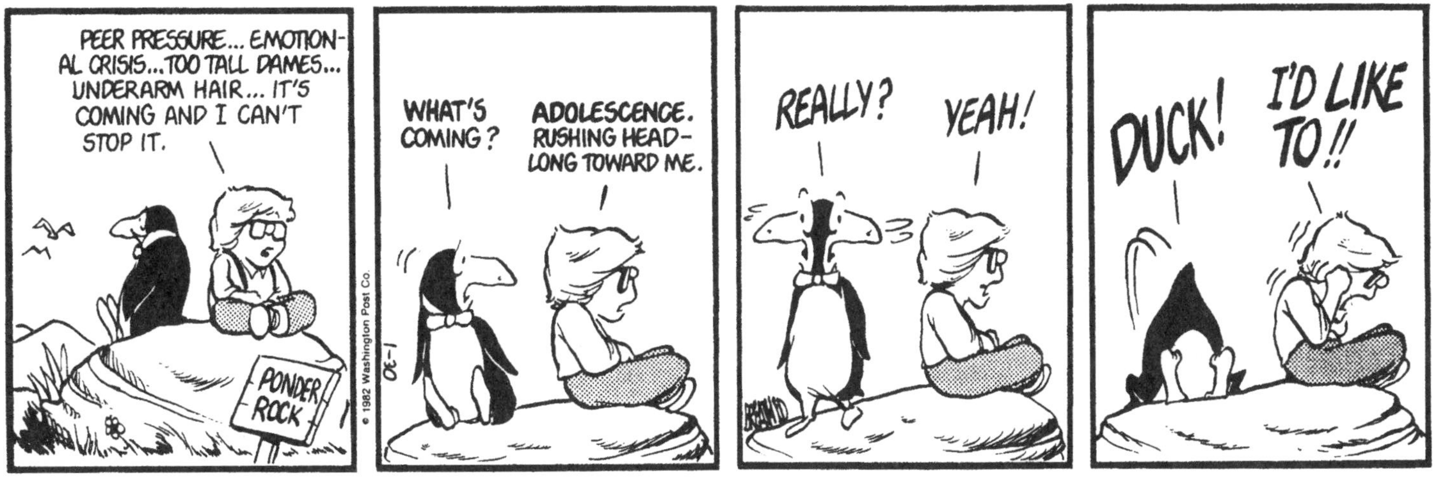
PEER PRESSURE... EMOTIONAL CRISIS... TOO TALL DAMES... UNDERARM HAIR... IT'S COMING AND I CAN'T STOP IT.
PONDER ROCK
© 1982 Washington Post Co.
1-30
WHAT'S COMING?
ADOLESCENCE. RUSHING HEADLONG TOWARD ME.
REALLY?
YEAH!
BREATHED
DUCK!
I'D LIKE TO!!

Opus. Center found, the fog clearing. The strip had found its voice, its tone and its point of view. People and comic strips are alike in needing this. —BB

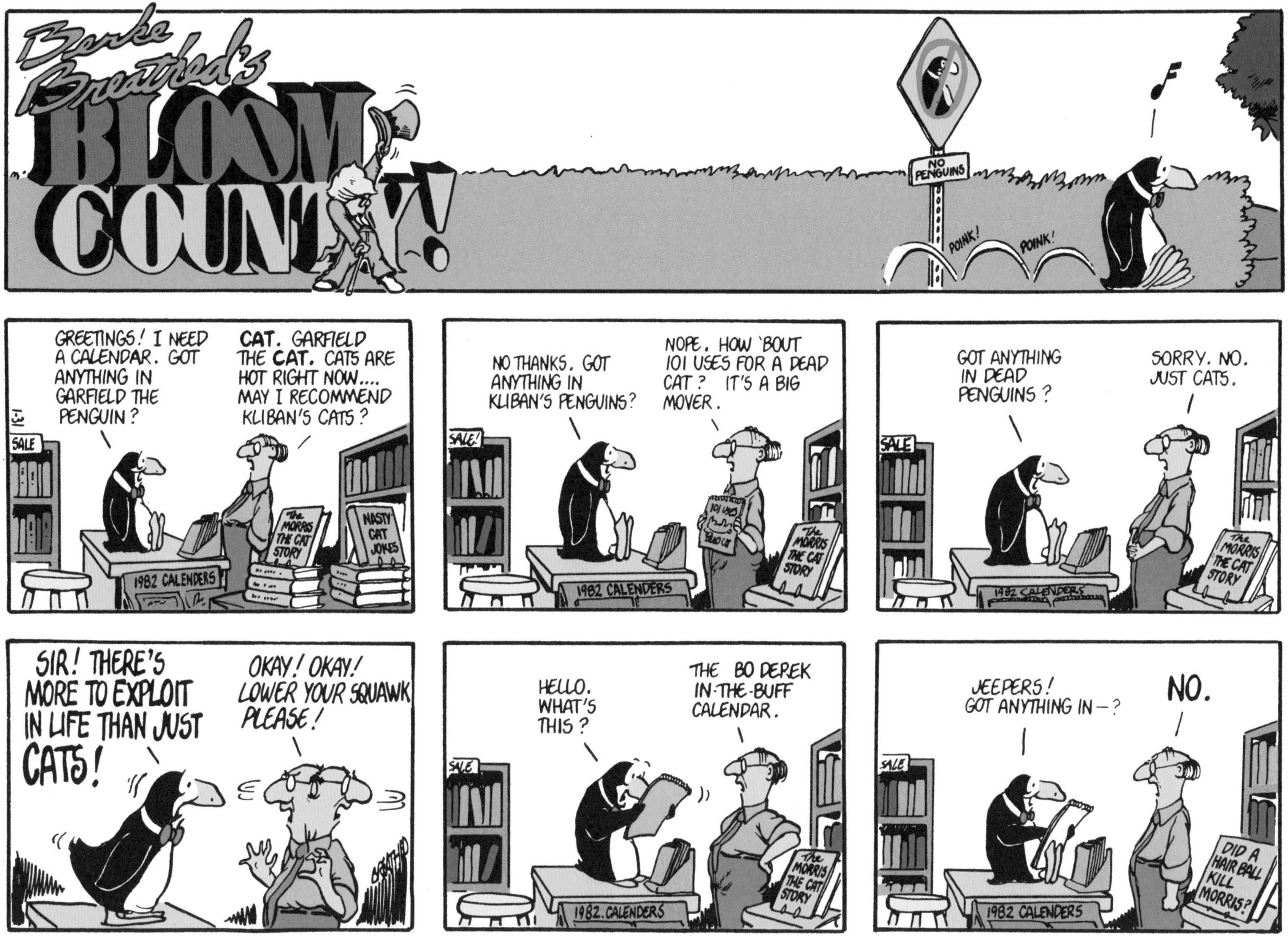
Berke Breathed's
BLOOM COUNTY!
NO PENGUINS
POINK!
POINK!
GREETINGS! I NEED A CALENDAR. GOT ANYTHING IN GARFIELD THE PENGUIN?
CAT. GARFIELD THE CAT. CATS ARE HOT RIGHT NOW.... MAY I RECOMMEND KLIBAN'S CATS?
SALE
1982 CALENDERS
The MORRIS THE CAT STORY
NASTY CAT JOKES
NO THANKS. GOT ANYTHING IN KLIBAN'S PENGUINS?
NOPE. HOW 'BOUT 101 USES FOR A DEAD CAT? IT'S A BIG MOVER.
SALE!
1982 CALENDERS
GOT ANYTHING IN DEAD PENGUINS?
SORRY. NO. JUST CATS.
SALE
1982 CALENDERS
The MORRIS THE CAT STORY
SIR! THERE'S MORE TO EXPLOIT IN LIFE THAN JUST CATS!
OKAY! OKAY! LOWER YOUR SQUAWK PLEASE!
HELLO. WHAT'S THIS?
THE BO DEREK IN-THE-BUFF CALENDAR.
SALE
1982. CALENDERS
The MORRIS THE CAT STORY
JEEPERS! GOT ANYTHING IN —?
NO.
SALE
1982 CALENDERS
DID A HAIR BALL KILL MORRIS?

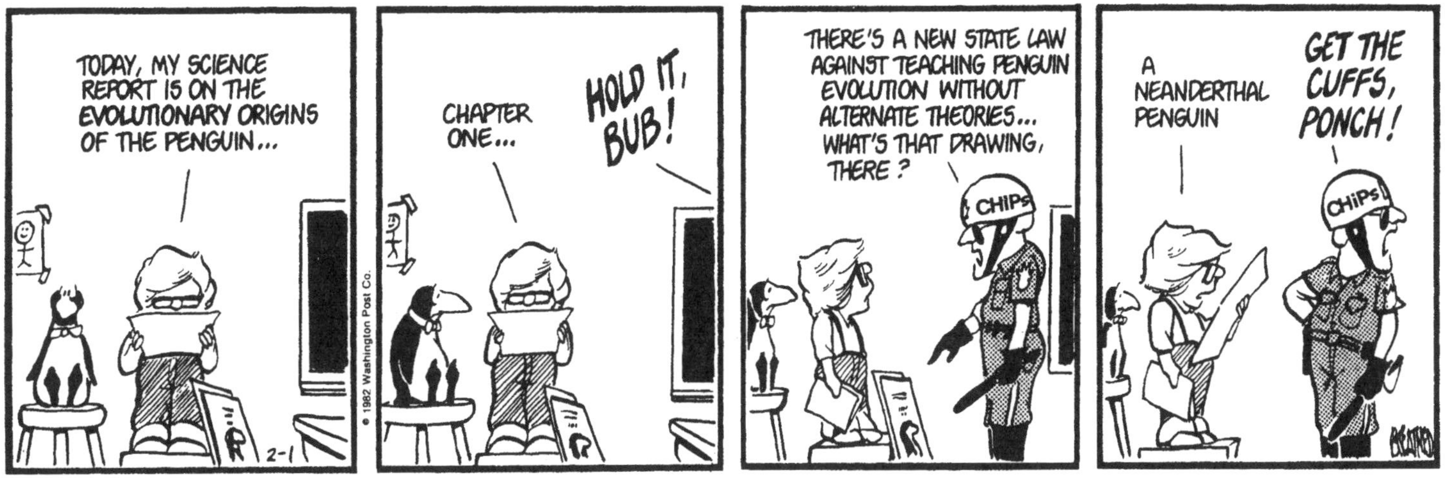
TODAY, MY SCIENCE REPORT IS ON THE EVOLUTIONARY ORIGINS OF THE PENGUIN...
2-1
© 1982 Washington Post Co.
CHAPTER ONE...
HOLD IT, BUB!
THERE'S A NEW STATE LAW AGAINST TEACHING PENGUIN EVOLUTION WITHOUT ALTERNATE THEORIES... WHAT'S THAT DRAWING, THERE?
CHiPs
A NEANDERTHAL PENGUIN
GET THE CUFFS, PONCH!
CHiPs

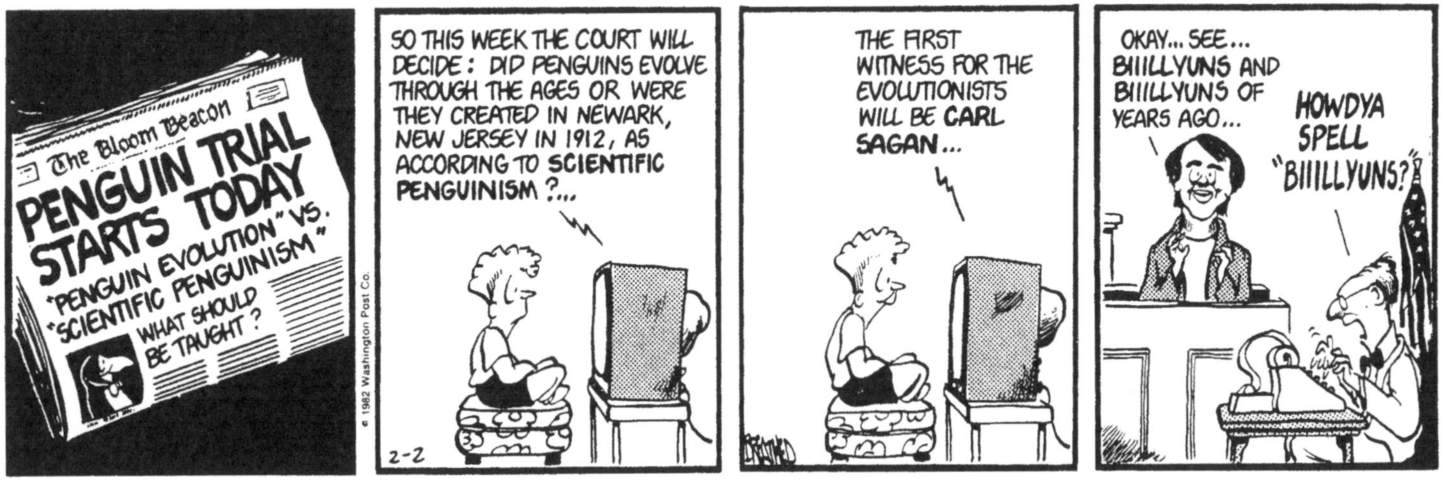
The Bloom Beacon
PENGUIN TRIAL STARTS TODAY
"PENGUIN EVOLUTION" VS. "SCIENTIFIC PENGUINISM"
WHAT SHOULD BE TAUGHT?
© 1982 Washington Post Co.
SO THIS WEEK THE COURT WILL DECIDE: DID PENGUINS EVOLVE THROUGH THE AGES OR WERE THEY CREATED IN NEWARK, NEW JERSEY IN 1912, AS ACCORDING TO SCIENTIFIC PENGUINISM?...
2-2
THE FIRST WITNESS FOR THE EVOLUTIONISTS WILL BE CARL SAGAN...
OKAY... SEE... BIIILLYUNS AND BIIILLYUNS OF YEARS AGO...
HOWDYA SPELL "BIIILLYUNS?"

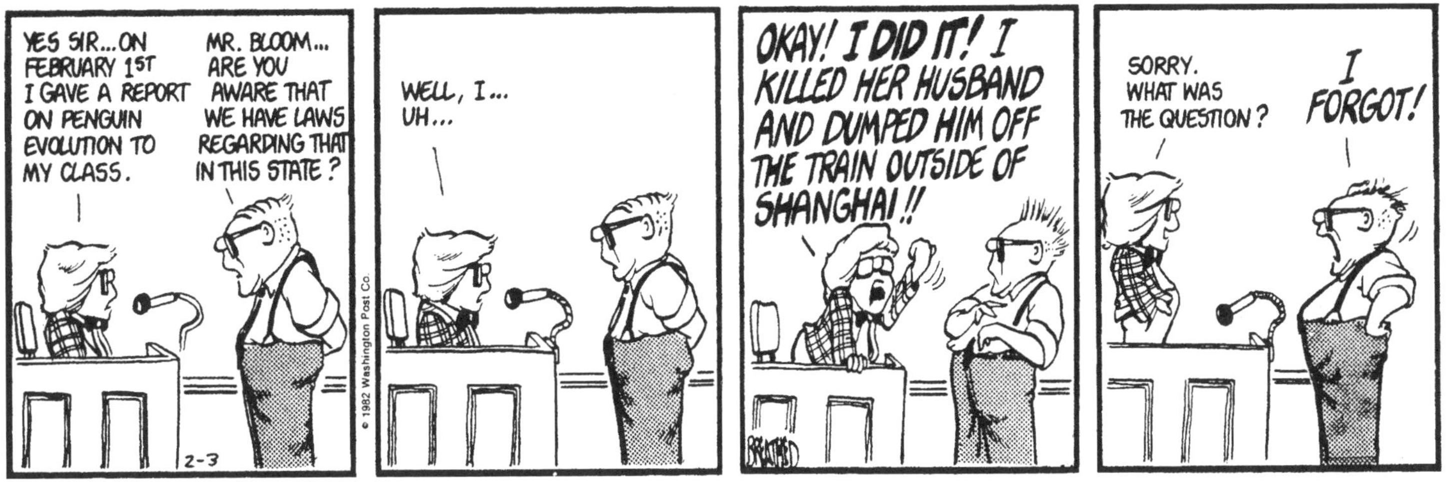
YES SIR... ON FEBRUARY 1ST I GAVE A REPORT ON PENGUIN EVOLUTION TO MY CLASS.
MR. BLOOM... ARE YOU AWARE THAT WE HAVE LAWS REGARDING THAT IN THIS STATE?
2-3
© 1982 Washington Post Co.
WELL, I... UH...
OKAY! I DID IT! I KILLED HER HUSBAND AND DUMPED HIM OFF THE TRAIN OUTSIDE OF SHANGHAI!!
SORRY. WHAT WAS THE QUESTION?
I FORGOT!

Carl Sagan helped popularize astronomy and other sciences through his many books, as well as the acclaimed PBS television series, *Cosmos*, which Sagan co-wrote and narrated.

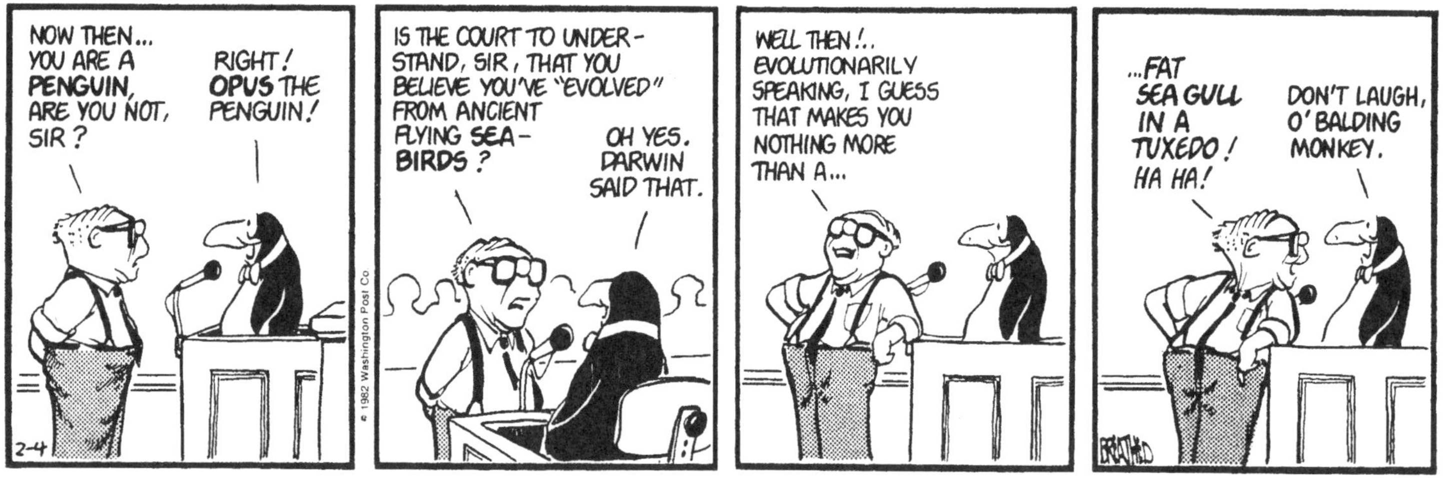
NOW THEN... YOU ARE A **PENGUIN**, ARE YOU NOT, SIR?
RIGHT! **OPUS** THE PENGUIN!
IS THE COURT TO UNDER-STAND, SIR, THAT YOU BELIEVE YOU'VE "EVOLVED" FROM ANCIENT FLYING **SEA-BIRDS**?
OH YES. DARWIN SAID THAT.
WELL THEN!.. EVOLUTIONARILY SPEAKING, I GUESS THAT MAKES YOU NOTHING MORE THAN A...
...**FAT SEA GULL IN A TUXEDO!** HA HA!
DON'T LAUGH, O' BALDING MONKEY.
2-4
© 1982 Washington Post Co.
BREATHED

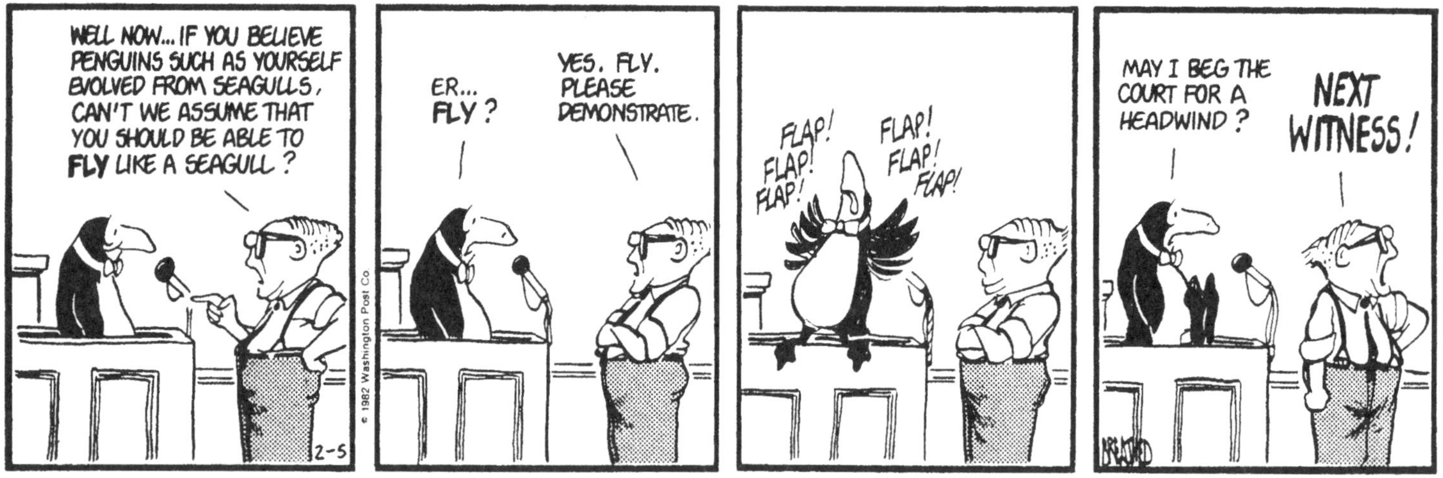
WELL NOW... IF YOU BELIEVE PENGUINS SUCH AS YOURSELF EVOLVED FROM SEAGULLS, CAN'T WE ASSUME THAT YOU SHOULD BE ABLE TO **FLY** LIKE A SEAGULL?
ER... **FLY**?
YES. FLY. PLEASE DEMONSTRATE.
FLAP! FLAP! FLAP!
FLAP! FLAP! FLAP!
MAY I BEG THE COURT FOR A HEADWIND?
NEXT WITNESS!
2-5
© 1982 Washington Post Co.
BREATHED

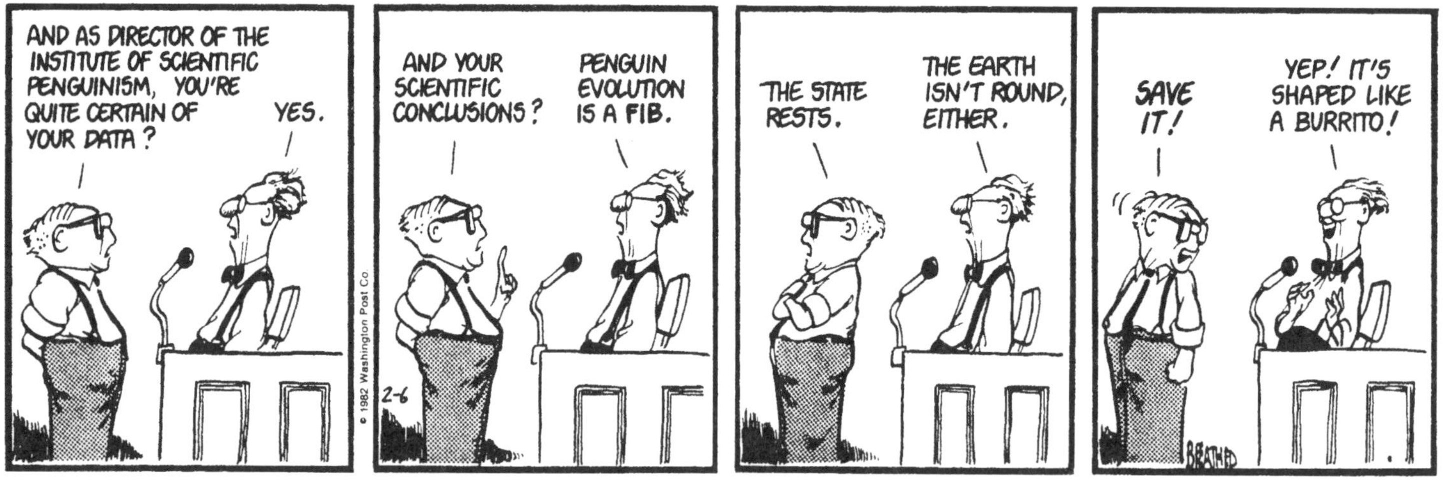
AND AS DIRECTOR OF THE INSTITUTE OF SCIENTIFIC PENGUINISM, YOU'RE QUITE CERTAIN OF YOUR DATA?
YES.
AND YOUR SCIENTIFIC CONCLUSIONS?
PENGUIN EVOLUTION IS A **FIB**.
THE STATE RESTS.
THE EARTH ISN'T ROUND, EITHER.
SAVE IT!
YEP! IT'S SHAPED LIKE A BURRITO!
2-6
© 1982 Washington Post Co.
BREATHED

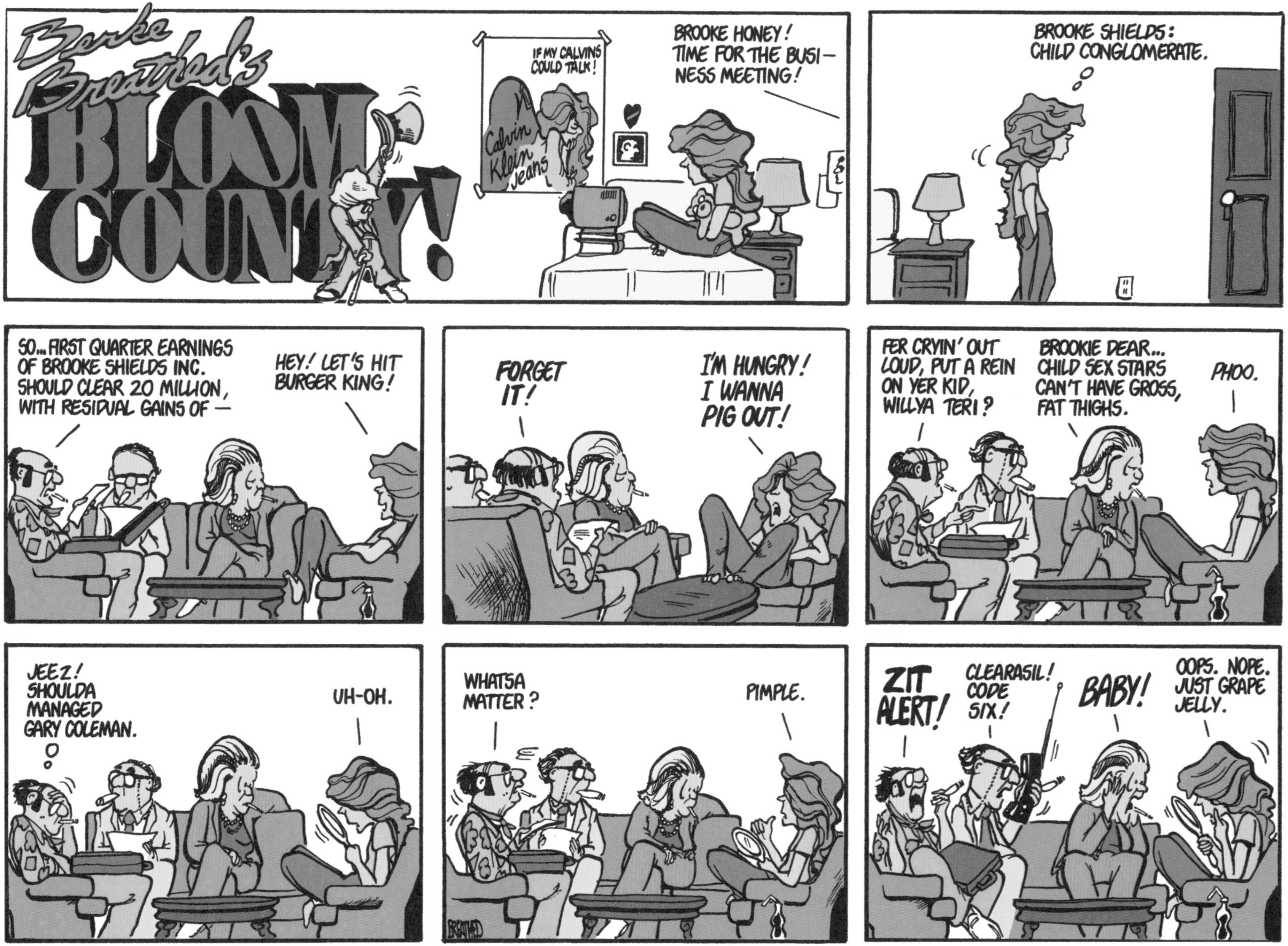
Berke Breathed's
BLOOM COUNTY!
IF MY CALVINS COULD TALK!
Calvin Klein jeans
BROOKE HONEY! TIME FOR THE BUSINESS MEETING!
BROOKE SHIELDS: CHILD CONGLOMERATE.
SO... FIRST QUARTER EARNINGS OF BROOKE SHIELDS INC. SHOULD CLEAR 20 MILLION, WITH RESIDUAL GAINS OF —
HEY! LET'S HIT BURGER KING!
FORGET IT!
I'M HUNGRY! I WANNA PIG OUT!
FER CRYIN' OUT LOUD, PUT A REIN ON YER KID, WILLYA TERI?
BROOKIE DEAR... CHILD SEX STARS CAN'T HAVE GROSS, FAT THIGHS.
PHOO.
JEEZ! SHOULDA MANAGED GARY COLEMAN.
UH-OH.
WHATSA MATTER?
PIMPLE.
ZIT ALERT!
CLEARASIL! CODE SIX!
BABY!
OOPS. NOPE. JUST GRAPE JELLY.
BREATHED

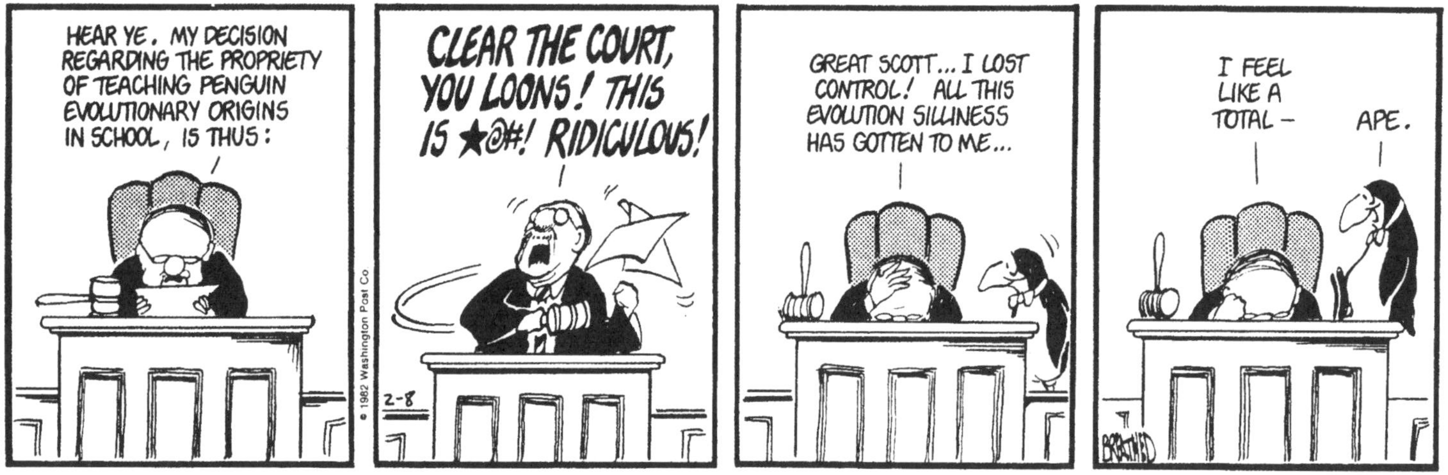
HEAR YE. MY DECISION REGARDING THE PROPRIETY OF TEACHING PENGUIN EVOLUTIONARY ORIGINS IN SCHOOL, IS THUS:
CLEAR THE COURT, YOU LOONS! THIS IS ★@#! RIDICULOUS!
© 1982 Washington Post Co.
2-8
GREAT SCOTT... I LOST CONTROL! ALL THIS EVOLUTION SILLINESS HAS GOTTEN TO ME...
I FEEL LIKE A TOTAL –
APE.
BREATHED

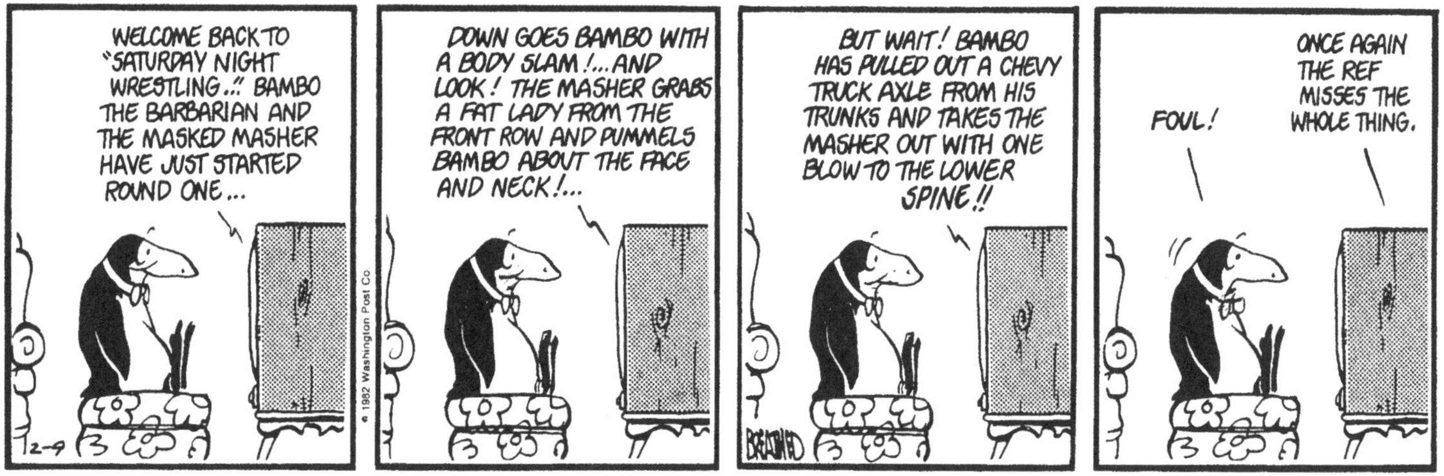
WELCOME BACK TO "SATURDAY NIGHT WRESTLING..!" BAMBO THE BARBARIAN AND THE MASKED MASHER HAVE JUST STARTED ROUND ONE...
2-9
DOWN GOES BAMBO WITH A BODY SLAM!... AND LOOK! THE MASHER GRABS A FAT LADY FROM THE FRONT ROW AND PUMMELS BAMBO ABOUT THE FACE AND NECK!...
© 1982 Washington Post Co.
BUT WAIT! BAMBO HAS PULLED OUT A CHEVY TRUCK AXLE FROM HIS TRUNKS AND TAKES THE MASHER OUT WITH ONE BLOW TO THE LOWER SPINE!!
BREATHED
FOUL!
ONCE AGAIN THE REF MISSES THE WHOLE THING.

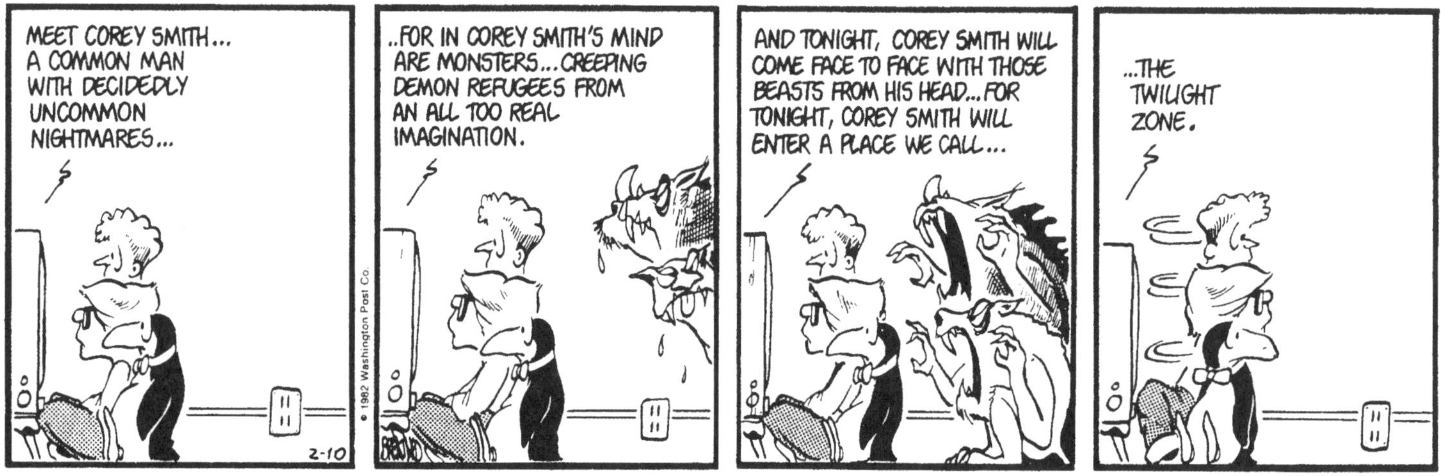
MEET COREY SMITH... A COMMON MAN WITH DECIDEDLY UNCOMMON NIGHTMARES...
2-10
..FOR IN COREY SMITH'S MIND ARE MONSTERS... CREEPING DEMON REFUGEES FROM AN ALL TOO REAL IMAGINATION.
© 1982 Washington Post Co.
AND TONIGHT, COREY SMITH WILL COME FACE TO FACE WITH THOSE BEASTS FROM HIS HEAD... FOR TONIGHT, COREY SMITH WILL ENTER A PLACE WE CALL...
...THE TWILIGHT ZONE.

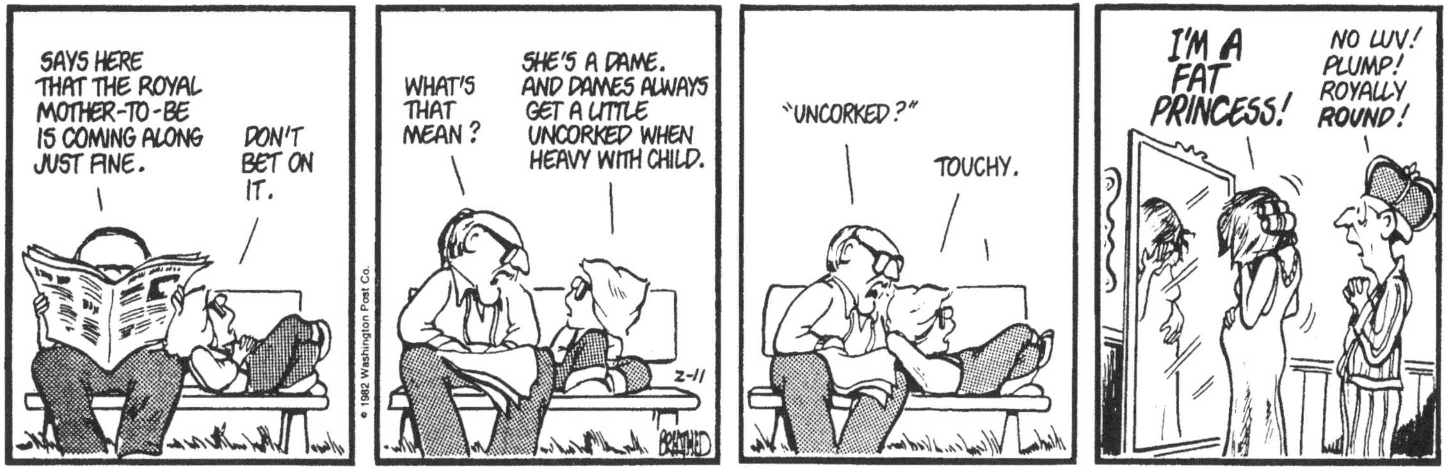
SAYS HERE THAT THE ROYAL MOTHER-TO-BE IS COMING ALONG JUST FINE.
DON'T BET ON IT.
© 1982 Washington Post Co.
WHAT'S THAT MEAN?
SHE'S A DAME. AND DAMES ALWAYS GET A LITTLE UNCORKED WHEN HEAVY WITH CHILD.
2-11
"UNCORKED?"
TOUCHY.
I'M A FAT PRINCESS!
NO LUV! PLUMP! ROYALLY **ROUND**!

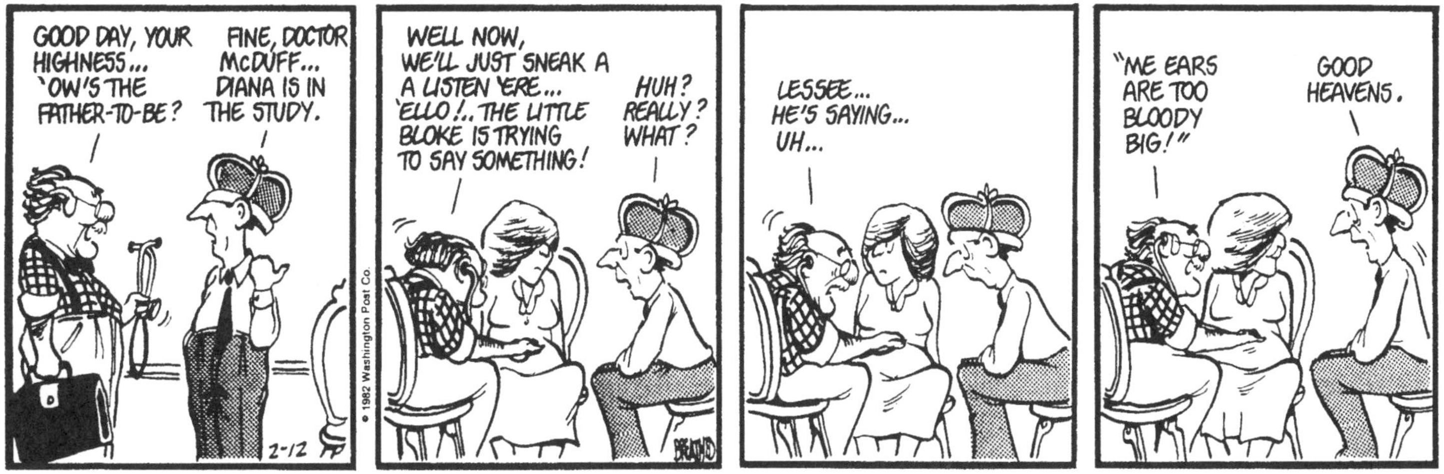
GOOD DAY, YOUR HIGHNESS... 'OW'S THE FATHER-TO-BE?
FINE, DOCTOR McDUFF... DIANA IS IN THE STUDY.
2-12
© 1982 Washington Post Co.
WELL NOW, WE'LL JUST SNEAK A A LISTEN 'ERE... 'ELLO!.. THE LITTLE BLOKE IS TRYING TO SAY SOMETHING!
HUH? REALLY? WHAT?
LESSEE... HE'S SAYING... UH...
"ME EARS ARE TOO BLOODY BIG!"
GOOD HEAVENS.

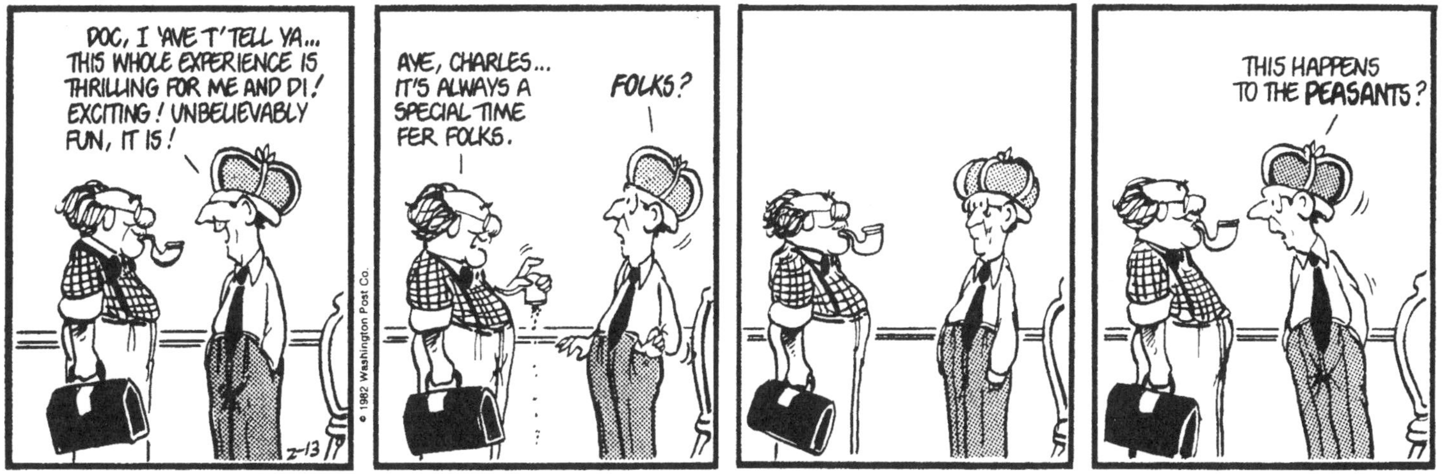
DOC, I 'AVE T' TELL YA... THIS WHOLE EXPERIENCE IS THRILLING FOR ME AND DI! EXCITING! UNBELIEVABLY FUN, IT IS!
2-13
© 1982 Washington Post Co.
AYE, CHARLES... IT'S ALWAYS A SPECIAL TIME FER FOLKS.
FOLKS?
THIS HAPPENS TO THE **PEASANTS**?

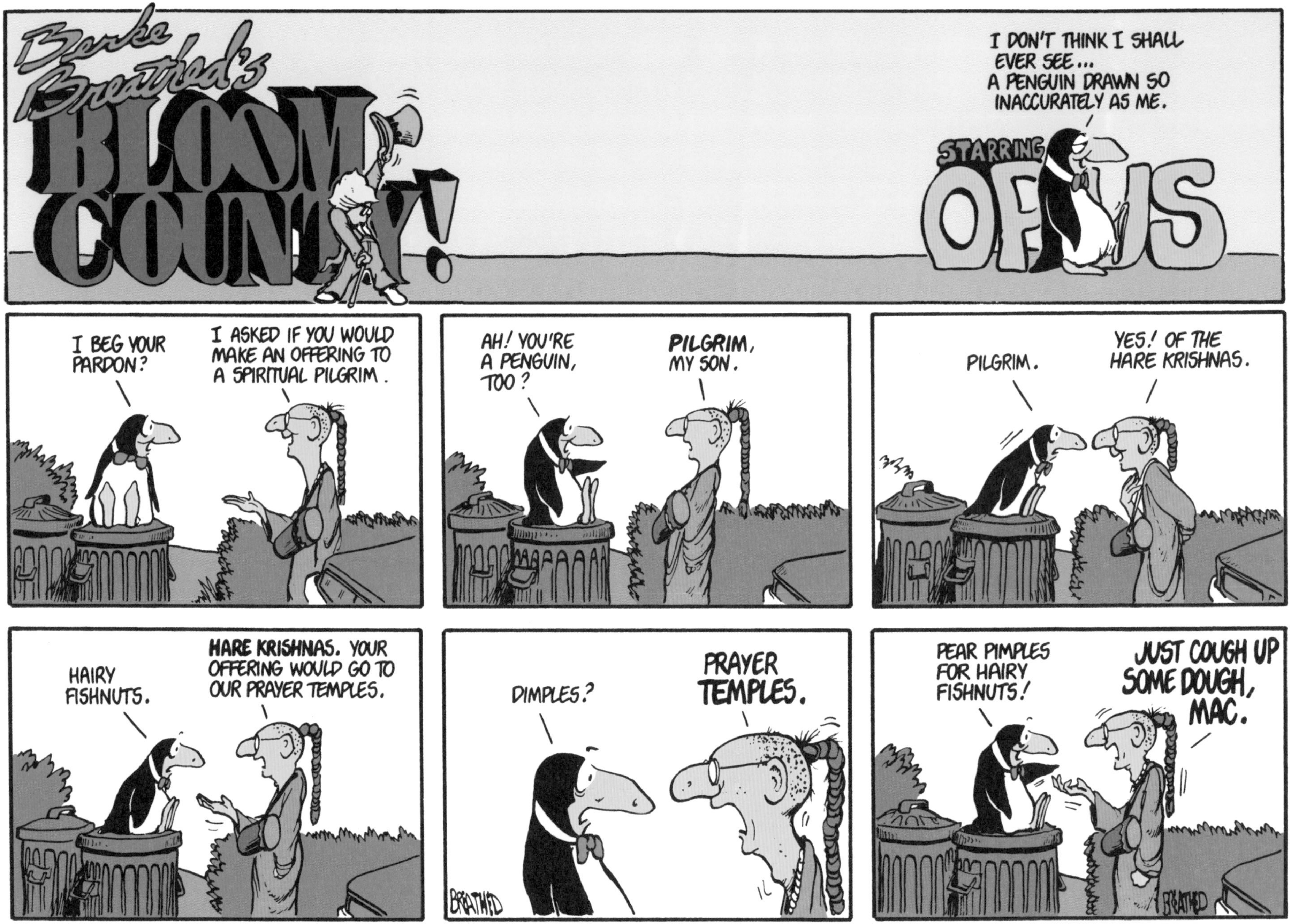
Berke Breathed's
BLOOM COUNTY!
I DON'T THINK I SHALL EVER SEE... A PENGUIN DRAWN SO INACCURATELY AS ME.
STARRING OPUS
I BEG YOUR PARDON?
I ASKED IF YOU WOULD MAKE AN OFFERING TO A SPIRITUAL PILGRIM.
AH! YOU'RE A PENGUIN, TOO?
PILGRIM, MY SON.
PILGRIM.
YES! OF THE HARE KRISHNAS.
HAIRY FISHNUTS.
HARE KRISHNAS. YOUR OFFERING WOULD GO TO OUR PRAYER TEMPLES.
DIMPLES?
PRAYER TEMPLES.
PEAR PIMPLES FOR HAIRY FISHNUTS!
JUST COUGH UP SOME DOUGH, MAC.

Kids don't know who Hare Krishnas are today. This is a tragedy for the world of comedy. Side note: The Washington Post *would not allow this strip now. The publisher shut down my gentle mockery of Scientology in 2008. The poor dears are terrified as I write this. Less so in 1982. —BB*

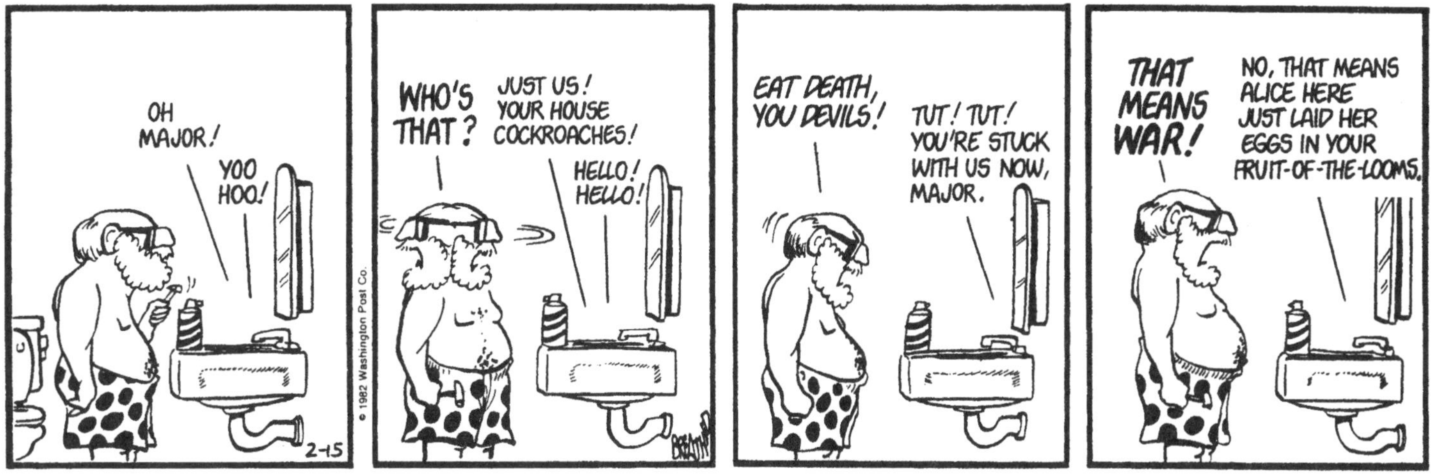
OH MAJOR!
YOO HOO!
2-15
© 1982 Washington Post Co.
WHO'S THAT?
JUST US! YOUR HOUSE COCKROACHES!
HELLO! HELLO!
EAT DEATH, YOU DEVILS!
TUT! TUT! YOU'RE STUCK WITH US NOW, MAJOR.
THAT MEANS WAR!
NO, THAT MEANS ALICE HERE JUST LAID HER EGGS IN YOUR FRUIT-OF-THE-LOOMS.

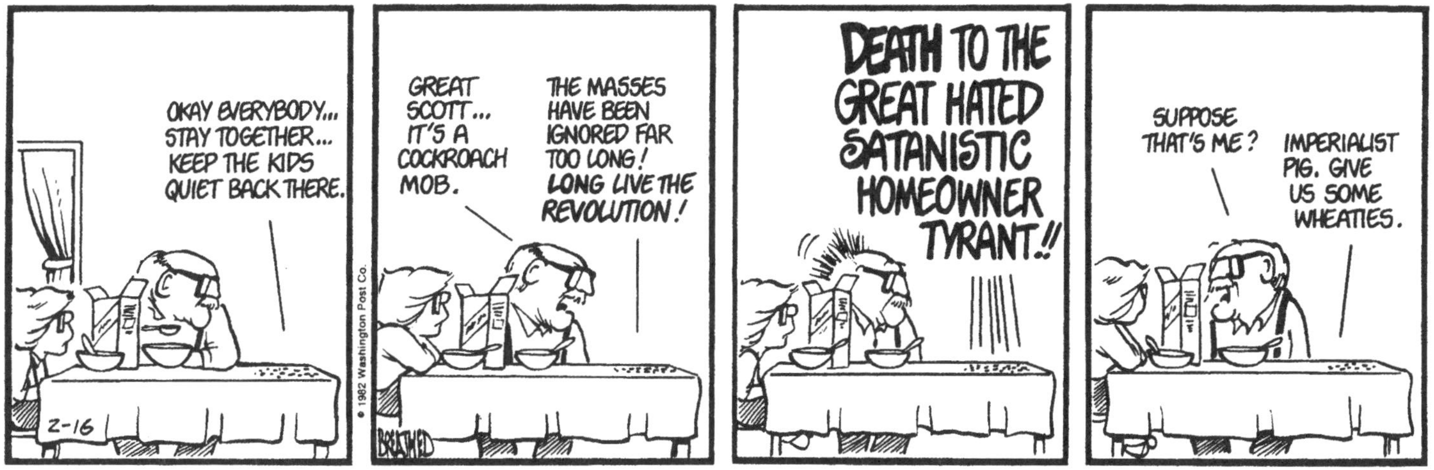
OKAY EVERYBODY... STAY TOGETHER... KEEP THE KIDS QUIET BACK THERE.
2-16
© 1982 Washington Post Co.
GREAT SCOTT... IT'S A COCKROACH MOB.
THE MASSES HAVE BEEN IGNORED FAR TOO LONG! LONG LIVE THE REVOLUTION!
DEATH TO THE GREAT HATED SATANISTIC HOMEOWNER TYRANT!!
SUPPOSE THAT'S ME?
IMPERIALIST PIG. GIVE US SOME WHEATIES.

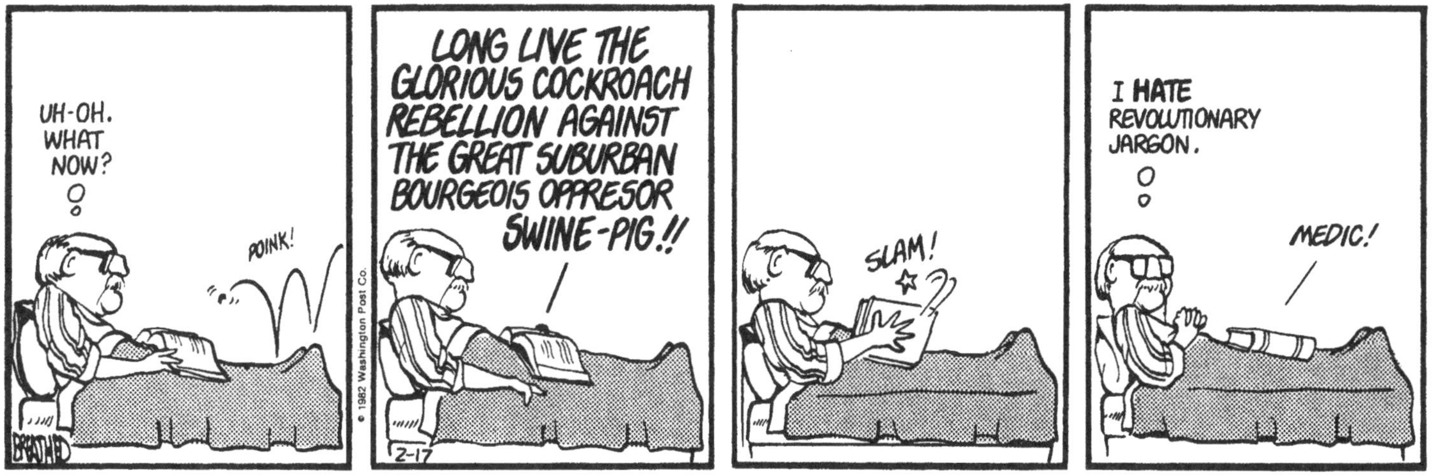
UH-OH. WHAT NOW?
POINK!
© 1982 Washington Post Co.
LONG LIVE THE GLORIOUS COCKROACH REBELLION AGAINST THE GREAT SUBURBAN BOURGEOIS OPPRESOR SWINE-PIG!!
2-17
SLAM!
I HATE REVOLUTIONARY JARGON.
MEDIC!

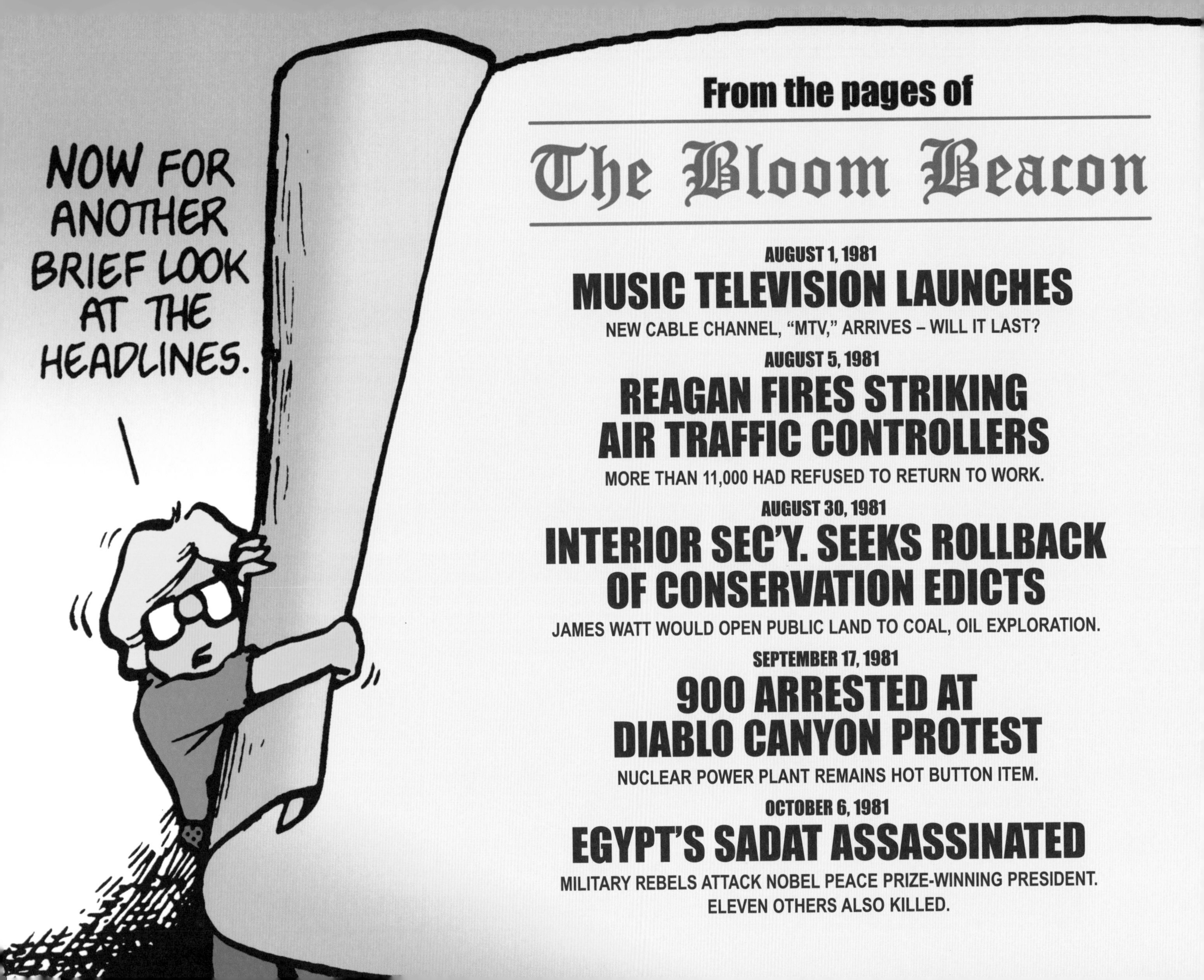
NOW FOR ANOTHER BRIEF LOOK AT THE HEADLINES.
From the pages of
The Bloom Beacon
AUGUST 1, 1981
MUSIC TELEVISION LAUNCHES
NEW CABLE CHANNEL, "MTV," ARRIVES – WILL IT LAST?
AUGUST 5, 1981
REAGAN FIRES STRIKING AIR TRAFFIC CONTROLLERS
MORE THAN 11,000 HAD REFUSED TO RETURN TO WORK.
AUGUST 30, 1981
INTERIOR SEC'Y. SEEKS ROLLBACK OF CONSERVATION EDICTS
JAMES WATT WOULD OPEN PUBLIC LAND TO COAL, OIL EXPLORATION.
SEPTEMBER 17, 1981
900 ARRESTED AT DIABLO CANYON PROTEST
NUCLEAR POWER PLANT REMAINS HOT BUTTON ITEM.
OCTOBER 6, 1981
EGYPT'S SADAT ASSASSINATED
MILITARY REBELS ATTACK NOBEL PEACE PRIZE-WINNING PRESIDENT. ELEVEN OTHERS ALSO KILLED.

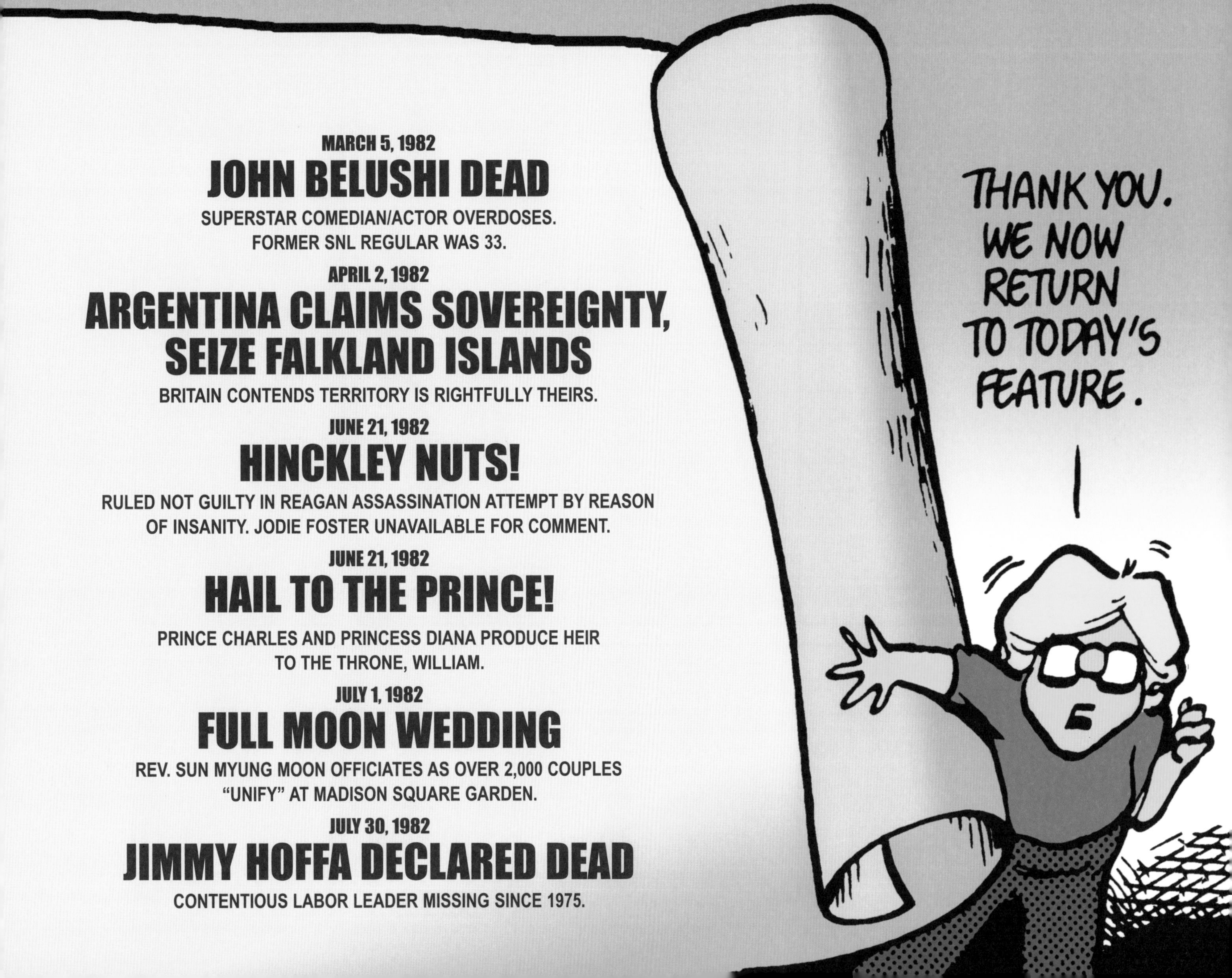
MARCH 5, 1982
JOHN BELUSHI DEAD
SUPERSTAR COMEDIAN/ACTOR OVERDOSES. FORMER SNL REGULAR WAS 33.
APRIL 2, 1982
ARGENTINA CLAIMS SOVEREIGNTY, SEIZE FALKLAND ISLANDS
BRITAIN CONTENDS TERRITORY IS RIGHTFULLY THEIRS.
JUNE 21, 1982
HINCKLEY NUTS!
RULED NOT GUILTY IN REAGAN ASSASSINATION ATTEMPT BY REASON OF INSANITY. JODIE FOSTER UNAVAILABLE FOR COMMENT.
JUNE 21, 1982
HAIL TO THE PRINCE!
PRINCE CHARLES AND PRINCESS DIANA PRODUCE HEIR TO THE THRONE, WILLIAM.
JULY 1, 1982
FULL MOON WEDDING
REV. SUN MYUNG MOON OFFICIATES AS OVER 2,000 COUPLES "UNIFY" AT MADISON SQUARE GARDEN.
JULY 30, 1982
JIMMY HOFFA DECLARED DEAD
CONTENTIOUS LABOR LEADER MISSING SINCE 1975.
THANK YOU. WE NOW RETURN TO TODAY'S FEATURE.

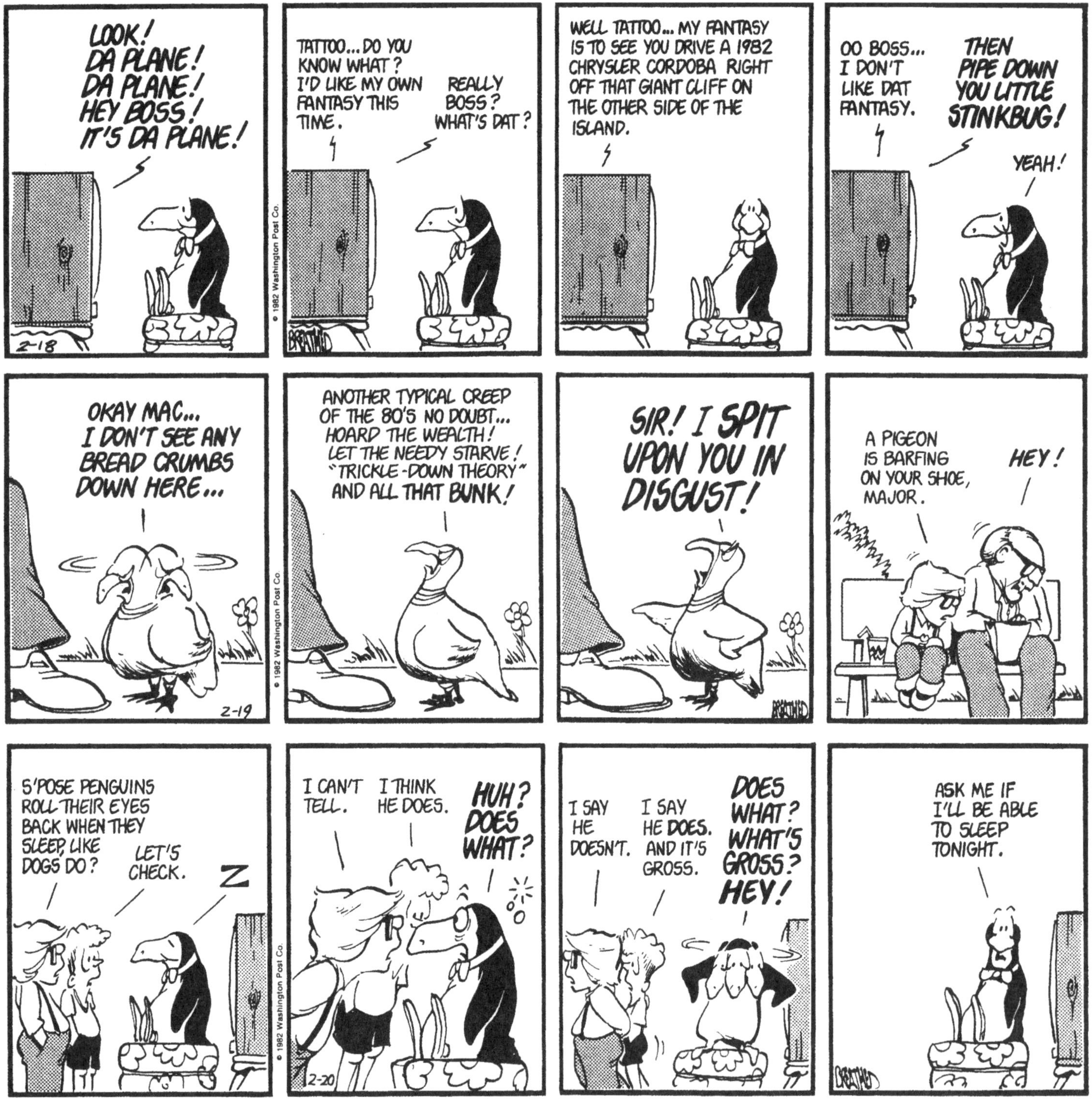
LOOK! DA PLANE! DA PLANE! HEY BOSS! IT'S DA PLANE!
2-18
TATTOO... DO YOU KNOW WHAT? I'D LIKE MY OWN FANTASY THIS TIME.
REALLY BOSS? WHAT'S DAT?
© 1982 Washington Post Co.
BREATHED
WELL TATTOO... MY FANTASY IS TO SEE YOU DRIVE A 1982 CHRYSLER CORDOBA RIGHT OFF THAT GIANT CLIFF ON THE OTHER SIDE OF THE ISLAND.
OO BOSS... I DON'T LIKE DAT FANTASY.
THEN PIPE DOWN YOU LITTLE STINKBUG!
YEAH!
OKAY MAC... I DON'T SEE ANY BREAD CRUMBS DOWN HERE...
2-19
ANOTHER TYPICAL CREEP OF THE 80'S NO DOUBT... HOARD THE WEALTH! LET THE NEEDY STARVE! "TRICKLE-DOWN THEORY" AND ALL THAT BUNK!
© 1982 Washington Post Co.
SIR! I SPIT UPON YOU IN DISGUST!
BREATHED
A PIGEON IS BARFING ON YOUR SHOE, MAJOR.
HEY!
S'POSE PENGUINS ROLL THEIR EYES BACK WHEN THEY SLEEP, LIKE DOGS DO?
LET'S CHECK.
Z
I CAN'T TELL.
I THINK HE DOES.
HUH? DOES WHAT?
2-20
© 1982 Washington Post Co.
I SAY HE DOESN'T.
I SAY HE DOES. AND IT'S GROSS.
DOES WHAT? WHAT'S GROSS? HEY!
ASK ME IF I'LL BE ABLE TO SLEEP TONIGHT.
BREATHED

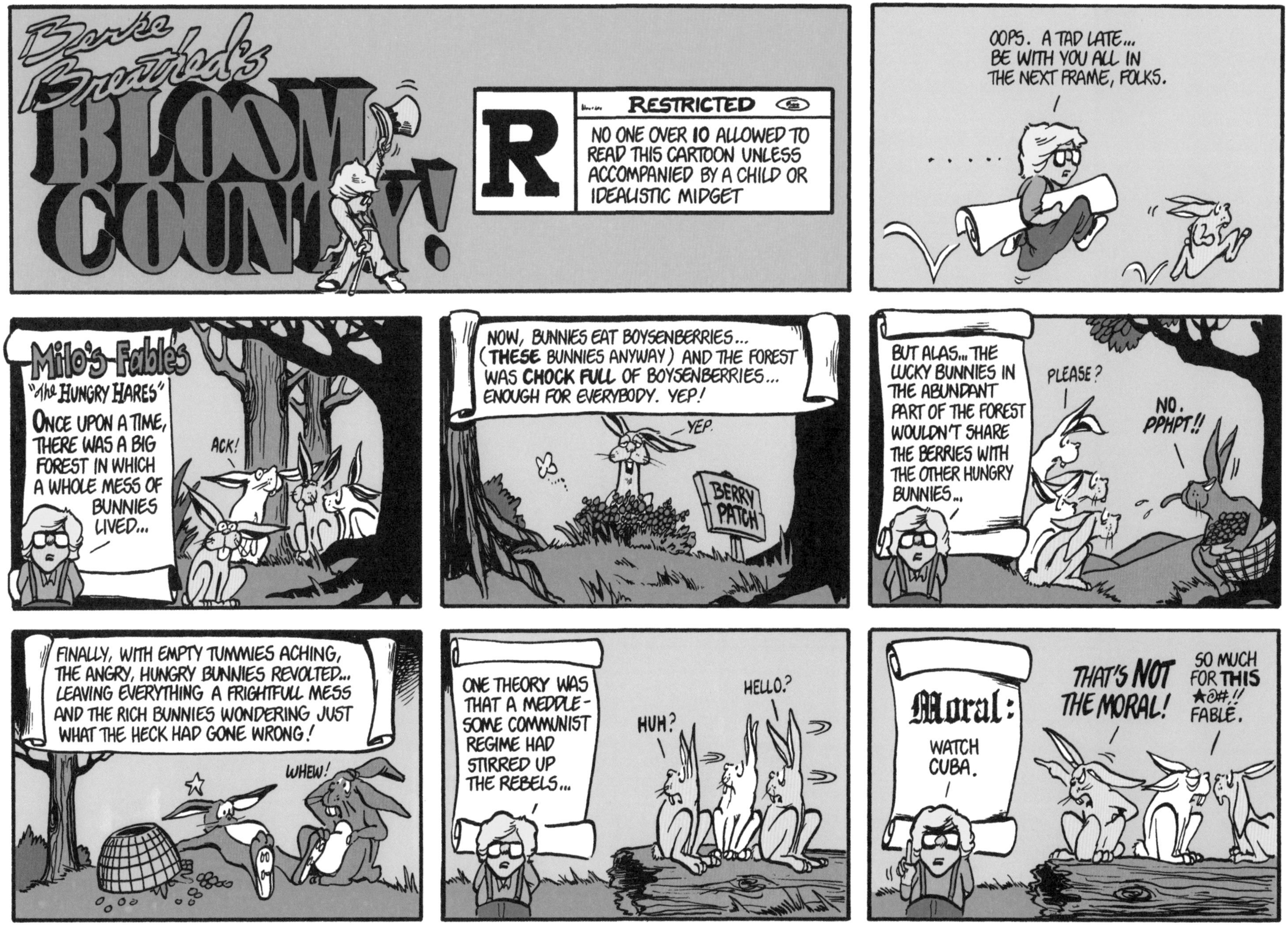
Berke Breathed's
BLOOM COUNTY!
R
RESTRICTED
NO ONE OVER 10 ALLOWED TO READ THIS CARTOON UNLESS ACCOMPANIED BY A CHILD OR IDEALISTIC MIDGET
OOPS. A TAD LATE... BE WITH YOU ALL IN THE NEXT FRAME, FOLKS.
Milo's Fables
"the HUNGRY HARES"
ONCE UPON A TIME, THERE WAS A BIG FOREST IN WHICH A WHOLE MESS OF BUNNIES LIVED...
ACK!
NOW, BUNNIES EAT BOYSENBERRIES... (THESE BUNNIES ANYWAY) AND THE FOREST WAS CHOCK FULL OF BOYSENBERRIES... ENOUGH FOR EVERYBODY. YEP!
YEP.
BERRY PATCH
BUT ALAS... THE LUCKY BUNNIES IN THE ABUNDANT PART OF THE FOREST WOULDN'T SHARE THE BERRIES WITH THE OTHER HUNGRY BUNNIES...
PLEASE?
NO. PPHPT!!
FINALLY, WITH EMPTY TUMMIES ACHING, THE ANGRY, HUNGRY BUNNIES REVOLTED... LEAVING EVERYTHING A FRIGHTFULL MESS AND THE RICH BUNNIES WONDERING JUST WHAT THE HECK HAD GONE WRONG!
WHEW!
ONE THEORY WAS THAT A MEDDLESOME COMMUNIST REGIME HAD STIRRED UP THE REBELS...
HUH?
HELLO.?
Moral:
WATCH CUBA.
THAT'S NOT THE MORAL!
SO MUCH FOR THIS ★@#.!! FABLE.

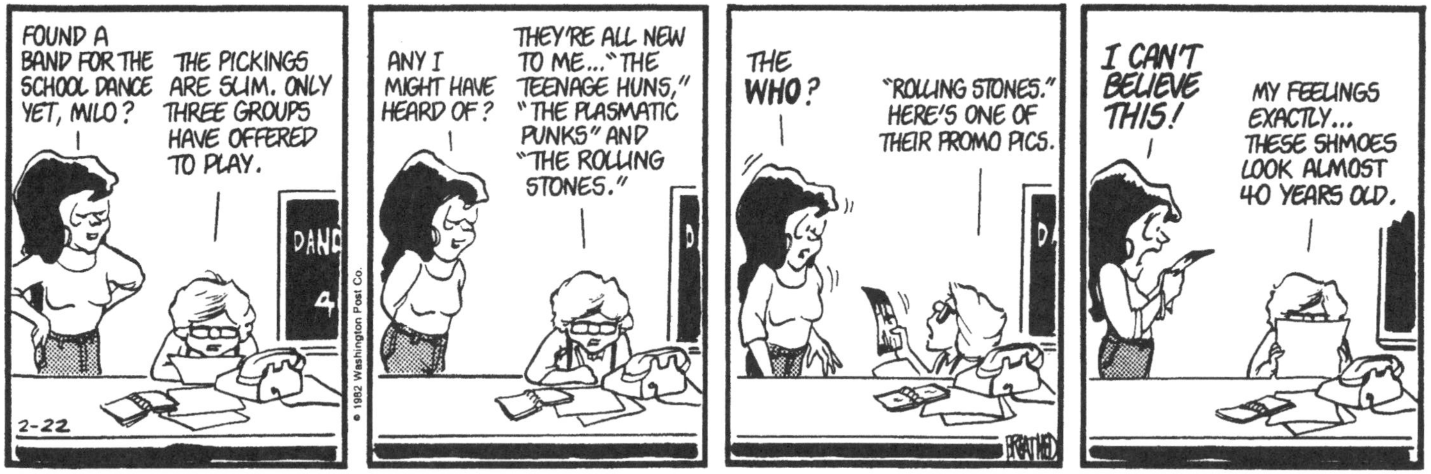
FOUND A BAND FOR THE SCHOOL DANCE YET, MILO?
THE PICKINGS ARE SLIM. ONLY THREE GROUPS HAVE OFFERED TO PLAY.
2-22
© 1982 Washington Post Co.
ANY I MIGHT HAVE HEARD OF?
THEY'RE ALL NEW TO ME... "THE TEENAGE HUNS," "THE PLASMATIC PUNKS" AND "THE ROLLING STONES."
THE WHO?
"ROLLING STONES." HERE'S ONE OF THEIR PROMO PICS.
I CAN'T BELIEVE THIS!
MY FEELINGS EXACTLY... THESE SHMOES LOOK ALMOST 40 YEARS OLD.

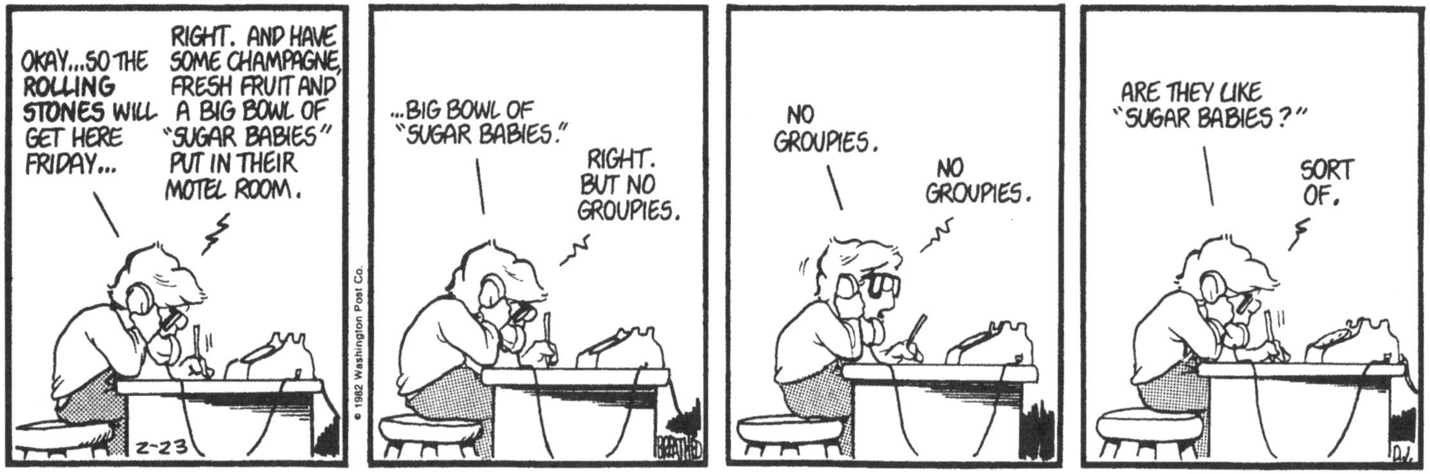
OKAY...SO THE ROLLING STONES WILL GET HERE FRIDAY...
RIGHT. AND HAVE SOME CHAMPAGNE, FRESH FRUIT AND A BIG BOWL OF "SUGAR BABIES" PUT IN THEIR MOTEL ROOM.
2-23
© 1982 Washington Post Co.
...BIG BOWL OF "SUGAR BABIES."
RIGHT. BUT NO GROUPIES.
NO GROUPIES.
NO GROUPIES.
ARE THEY LIKE "SUGAR BABIES?"
SORT OF.

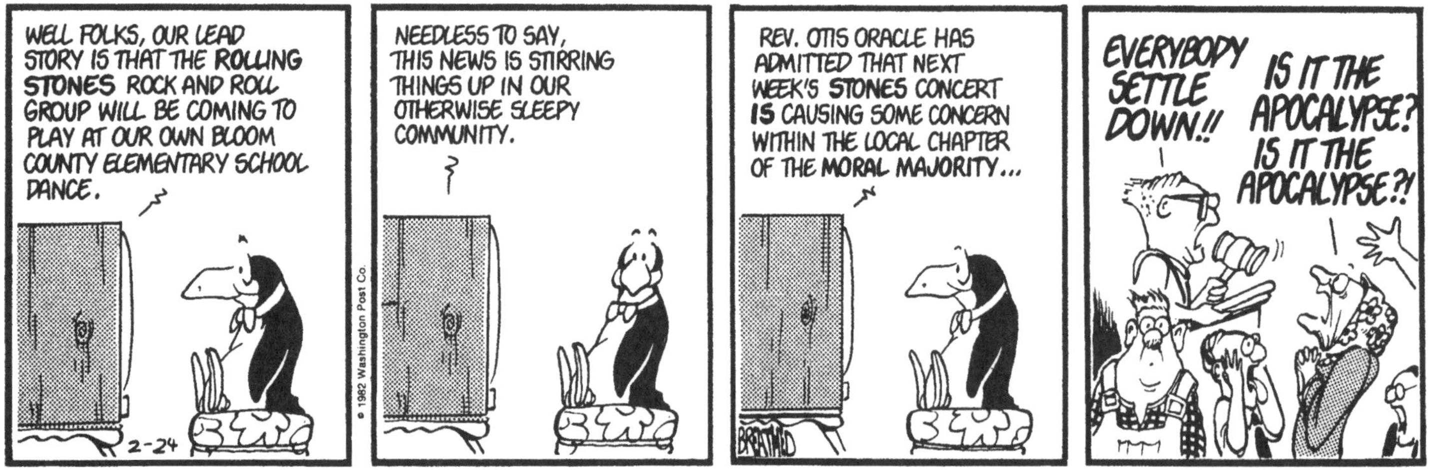
WELL FOLKS, OUR LEAD STORY IS THAT THE ROLLING STONES ROCK AND ROLL GROUP WILL BE COMING TO PLAY AT OUR OWN BLOOM COUNTY ELEMENTARY SCHOOL DANCE.
2-24
© 1982 Washington Post Co.
NEEDLESS TO SAY, THIS NEWS IS STIRRING THINGS UP IN OUR OTHERWISE SLEEPY COMMUNITY.
REV. OTIS ORACLE HAS ADMITTED THAT NEXT WEEK'S STONES CONCERT IS CAUSING SOME CONCERN WITHIN THE LOCAL CHAPTER OF THE MORAL MAJORITY...
EVERYBODY SETTLE DOWN!!
IS IT THE APOCALYPSE? IS IT THE APOCALYPSE?!

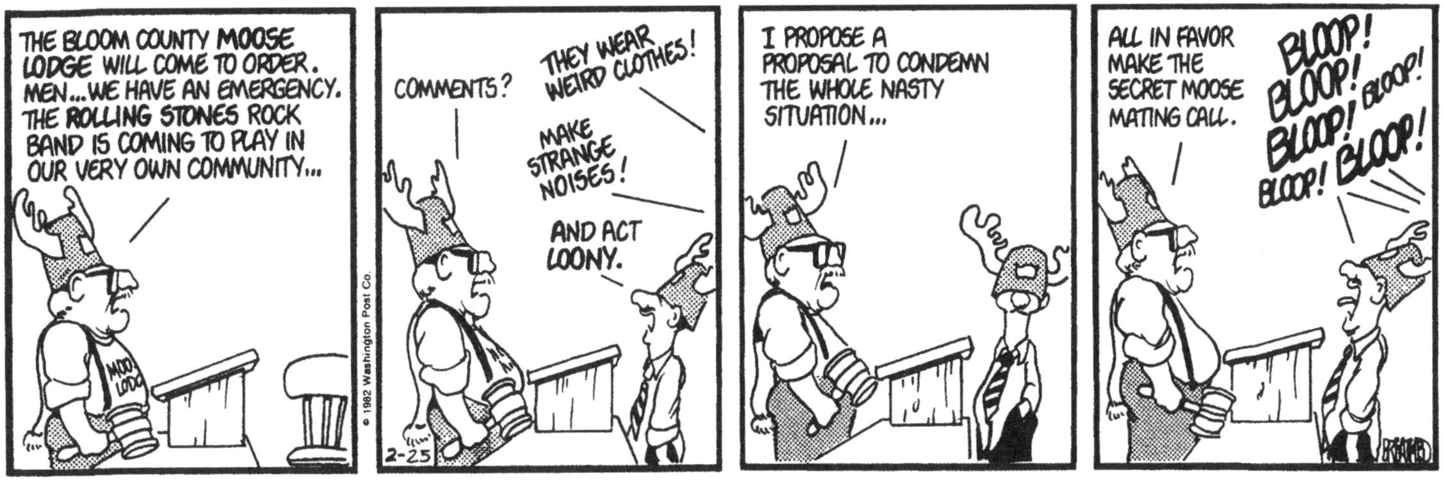
THE BLOOM COUNTY MOOSE LODGE WILL COME TO ORDER. MEN...WE HAVE AN EMERGENCY. THE ROLLING STONES ROCK BAND IS COMING TO PLAY IN OUR VERY OWN COMMUNITY...
MOO LODG
© 1982 Washington Post Co.
2-25
COMMENTS?
THEY WEAR WEIRD CLOTHES!
MAKE STRANGE NOISES!
AND ACT LOONY.
I PROPOSE A PROPOSAL TO CONDEMN THE WHOLE NASTY SITUATION...
ALL IN FAVOR MAKE THE SECRET MOOSE MATING CALL.
BLOOP! BLOOP! BLOOP! BLOOP! BLOOP! BLOOP!
BREATHED

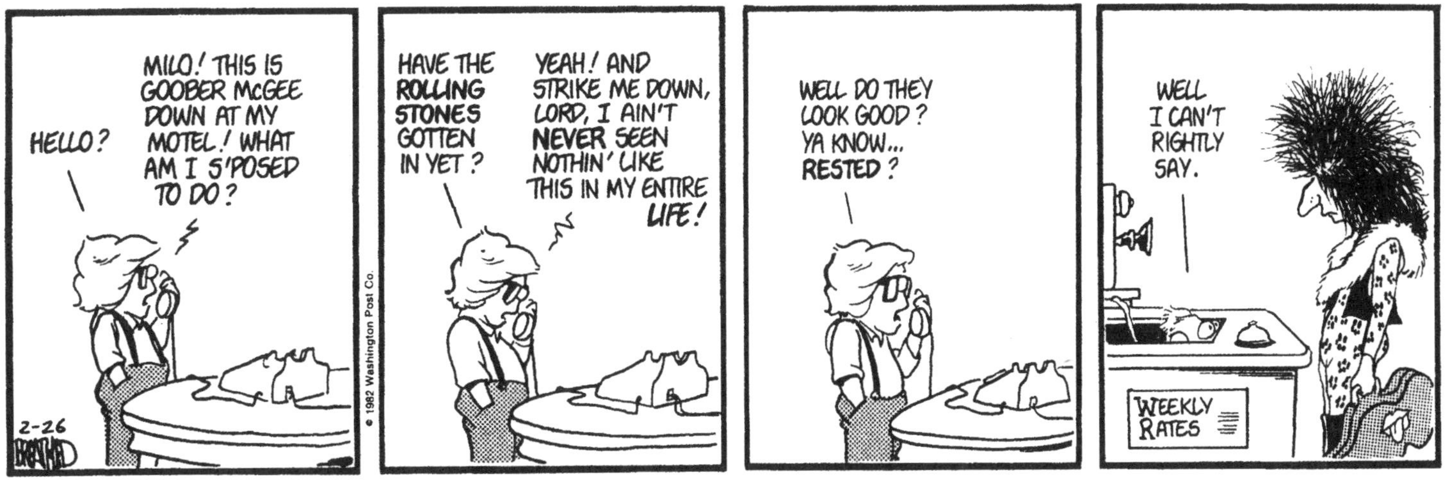
HELLO?
MILO! THIS IS GOOBER McGEE DOWN AT MY MOTEL! WHAT AM I S'POSED TO DO?
2-26
BREATHED
© 1982 Washington Post Co.
HAVE THE ROLLING STONES GOTTEN IN YET?
YEAH! AND STRIKE ME DOWN, LORD, I AIN'T NEVER SEEN NOTHIN' LIKE THIS IN MY ENTIRE LIFE!
WELL DO THEY LOOK GOOD? YA KNOW... RESTED?
WELL I CAN'T RIGHTLY SAY.
WEEKLY RATES

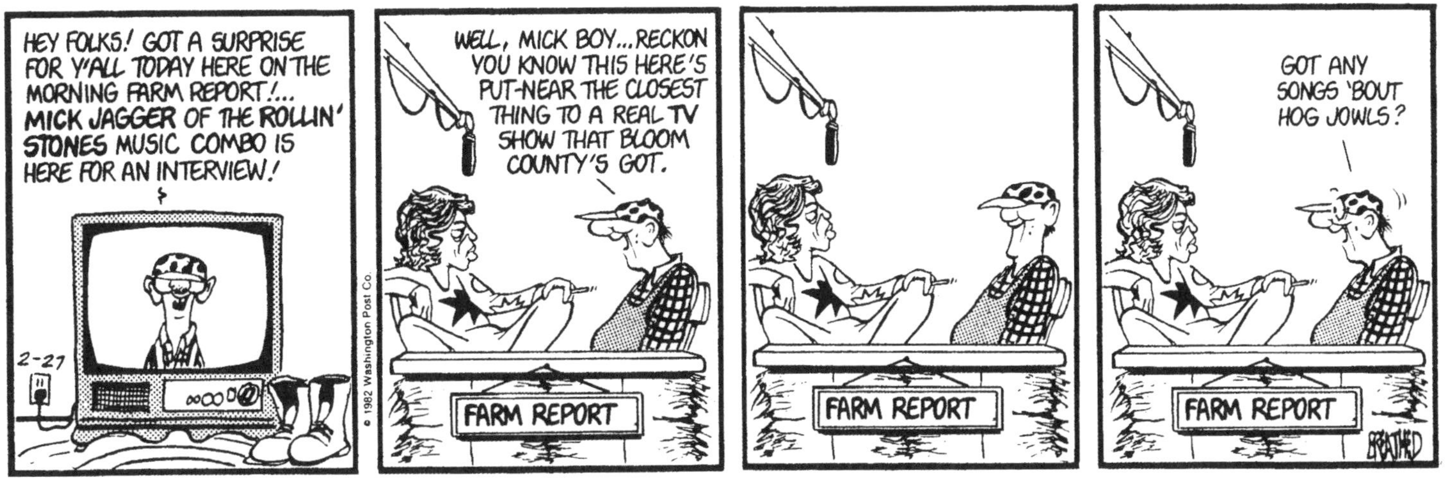
HEY FOLKS! GOT A SURPRISE FOR Y'ALL TODAY HERE ON THE MORNING FARM REPORT!... MICK JAGGER OF THE ROLLIN' STONES MUSIC COMBO IS HERE FOR AN INTERVIEW!
2-27
© 1982 Washington Post Co.
WELL, MICK BOY...RECKON YOU KNOW THIS HERE'S PUT-NEAR THE CLOSEST THING TO A REAL TV SHOW THAT BLOOM COUNTY'S GOT.
FARM REPORT
FARM REPORT
GOT ANY SONGS 'BOUT HOG JOWLS?
FARM REPORT
BREATHED

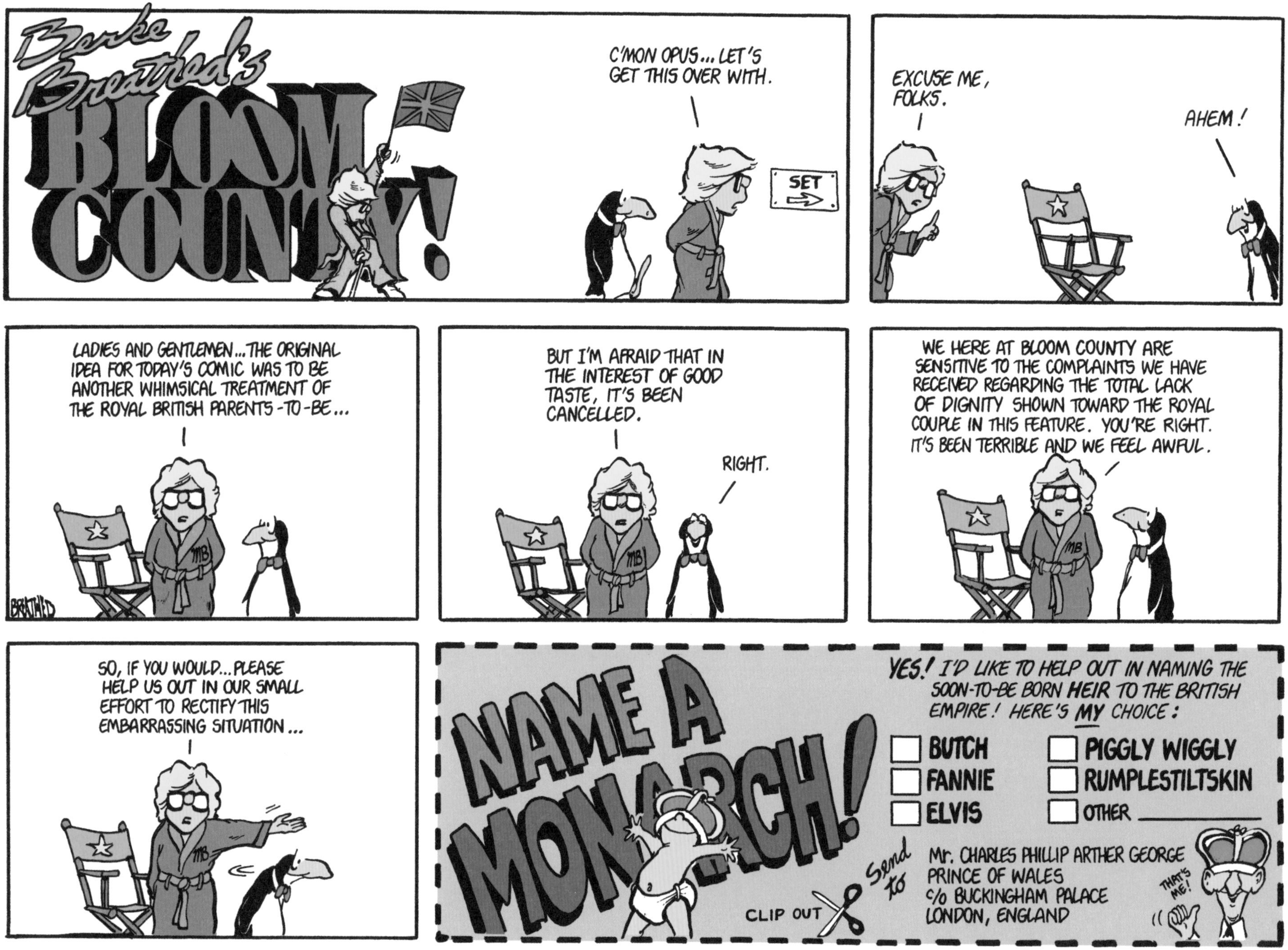
Berke Breathed's
BLOOM COUNTY!
C'MON OPUS... LET'S GET THIS OVER WITH.
SET
EXCUSE ME, FOLKS.
AHEM!
LADIES AND GENTLEMEN...THE ORIGINAL IDEA FOR TODAY'S COMIC WAS TO BE ANOTHER WHIMSICAL TREATMENT OF THE ROYAL BRITISH PARENTS-TO-BE...
BREATHED
BUT I'M AFRAID THAT IN THE INTEREST OF GOOD TASTE, IT'S BEEN CANCELLED.
RIGHT.
WE HERE AT BLOOM COUNTY ARE SENSITIVE TO THE COMPLAINTS WE HAVE RECEIVED REGARDING THE TOTAL LACK OF DIGNITY SHOWN TOWARD THE ROYAL COUPLE IN THIS FEATURE. YOU'RE RIGHT. IT'S BEEN TERRIBLE AND WE FEEL AWFUL.
SO, IF YOU WOULD... PLEASE HELP US OUT IN OUR SMALL EFFORT TO RECTIFY THIS EMBARRASSING SITUATION...
NAME A MONARCH!
YES! I'D LIKE TO HELP OUT IN NAMING THE SOON-TO-BE BORN HEIR TO THE BRITISH EMPIRE! HERE'S MY CHOICE:
BUTCH
PIGGLY WIGGLY
FANNIE
RUMPLESTILTSKIN
ELVIS
OTHER
Send to
Mr. CHARLES PHILLIP ARTHER GEORGE
PRINCE OF WALES
c/o BUCKINGHAM PALACE
LONDON, ENGLAND
CLIP OUT
THAT'S ME!

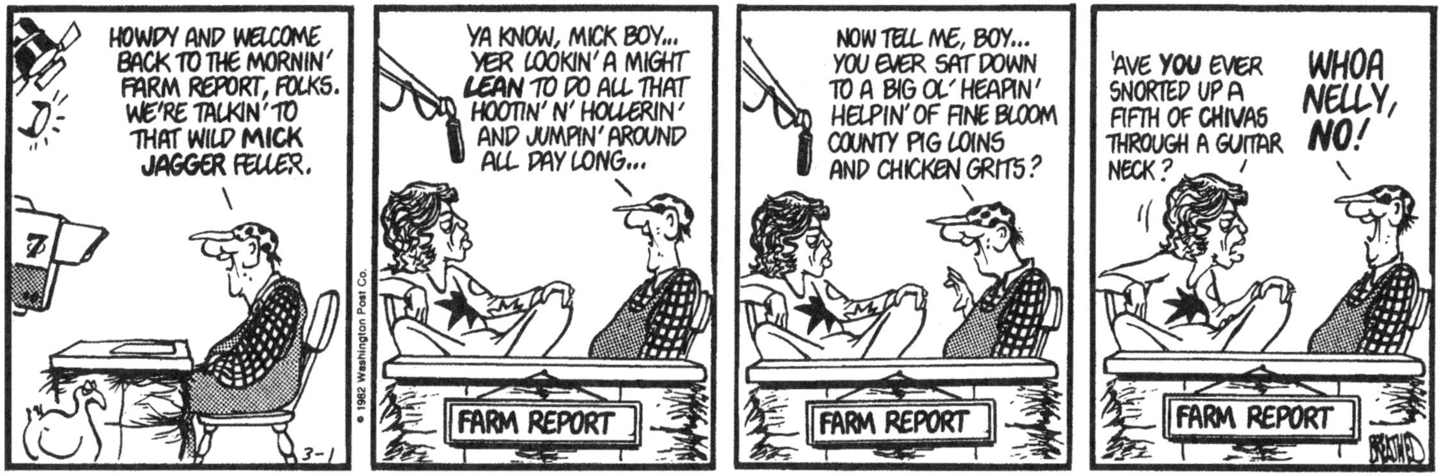
HOWDY AND WELCOME BACK TO THE MORNIN' FARM REPORT, FOLKS. WE'RE TALKIN' TO THAT WILD **MICK JAGGER** FELLER.
3-1
© 1982 Washington Post Co.
YA KNOW, MICK BOY... YER LOOKIN' A MIGHT **LEAN** TO DO ALL THAT HOOTIN' N' HOLLERIN' AND JUMPIN' AROUND ALL DAY LONG...
FARM REPORT
NOW TELL ME, BOY... YOU EVER SAT DOWN TO A BIG OL' HEAPIN' HELPIN' OF FINE BLOOM COUNTY PIG LOINS AND CHICKEN GRITS?
FARM REPORT
'AVE **YOU** EVER SNORTED UP A FIFTH OF CHIVAS THROUGH A GUITAR NECK?
WHOA NELLY, NO!
FARM REPORT

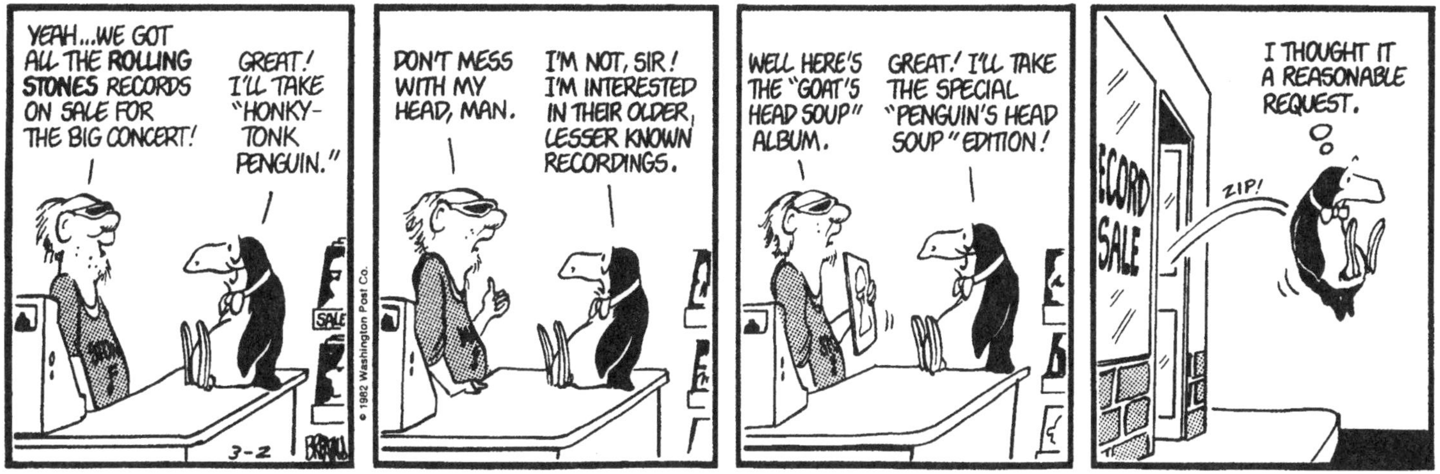
YEAH...WE GOT ALL THE **ROLLING STONES** RECORDS ON SALE FOR THE BIG CONCERT!
GREAT! I'LL TAKE "HONKY-TONK PENGUIN."
SALE
3-2
© 1982 Washington Post Co.
DON'T MESS WITH MY HEAD, MAN.
I'M NOT, SIR! I'M INTERESTED IN THEIR OLDER, LESSER KNOWN RECORDINGS.
WELL HERE'S THE "GOAT'S HEAD SOUP" ALBUM.
GREAT! I'LL TAKE THE SPECIAL "PENGUIN'S HEAD SOUP" EDITION!
I THOUGHT IT A REASONABLE REQUEST.
ZIP!
ECORD SALE

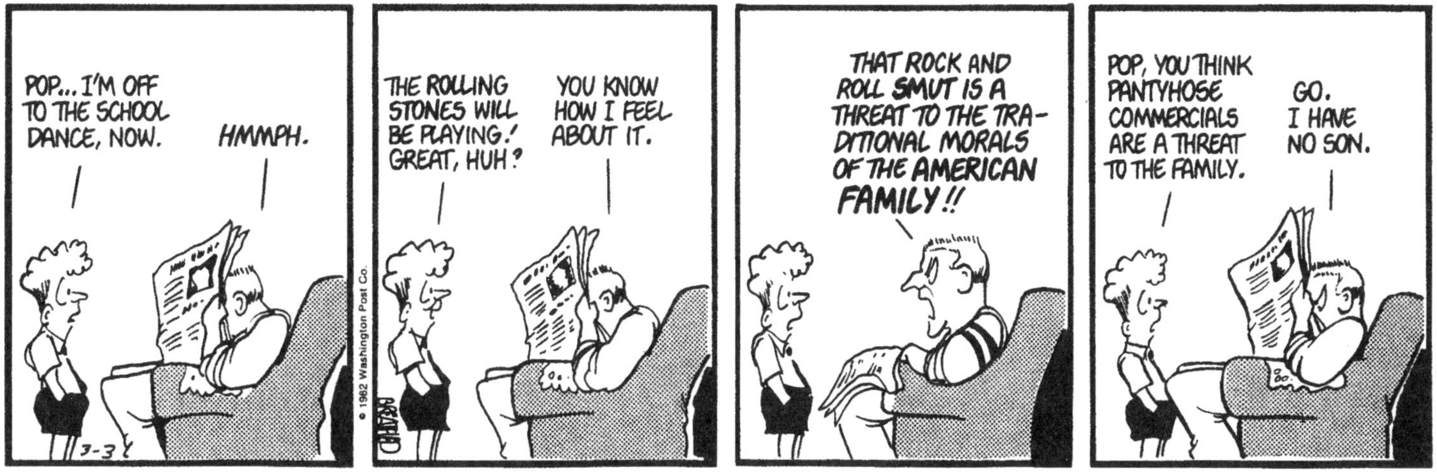
POP... I'M OFF TO THE SCHOOL DANCE, NOW.
HMMPH.
3-3
© 1982 Washington Post Co.
THE ROLLING STONES WILL BE PLAYING! GREAT, HUH?
YOU KNOW HOW I FEEL ABOUT IT.
THAT ROCK AND ROLL **SMUT** IS A THREAT TO THE TRADITIONAL MORALS OF THE **AMERICAN FAMILY**!!
POP, YOU THINK PANTYHOSE COMMERCIALS ARE A THREAT TO THE FAMILY.
GO. I HAVE NO SON.

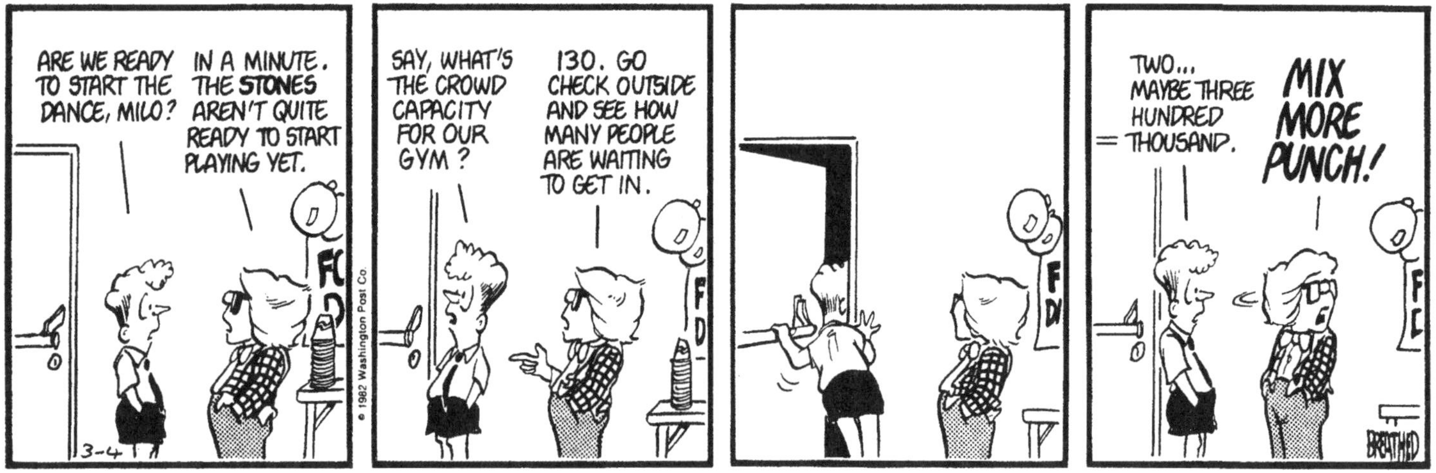
ARE WE READY TO START THE DANCE, MILO?
IN A MINUTE. THE **STONES** AREN'T QUITE READY TO START PLAYING YET.
3-4
© 1982 Washington Post Co.
SAY, WHAT'S THE CROWD CAPACITY FOR OUR GYM?
130. GO CHECK OUTSIDE AND SEE HOW MANY PEOPLE ARE WAITING TO GET IN.
TWO... MAYBE THREE HUNDRED THOUSAND.
MIX MORE PUNCH!
BREATHED

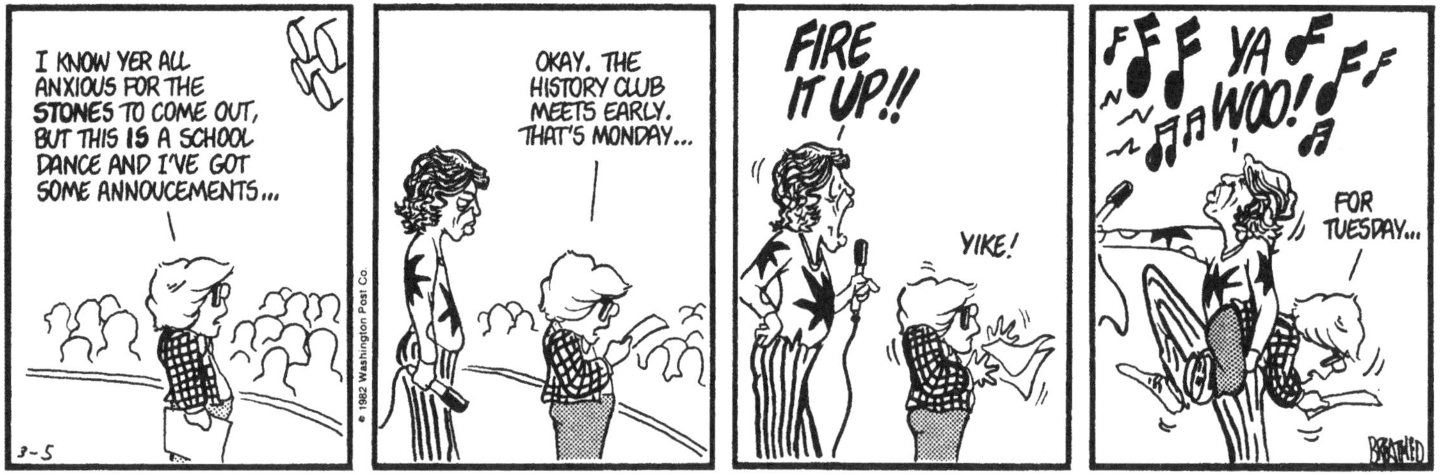
I KNOW YER ALL ANXIOUS FOR THE **STONES** TO COME OUT, BUT THIS **IS** A SCHOOL DANCE AND I'VE GOT SOME ANNOUCEMENTS...
3-5
© 1982 Washington Post Co.
OKAY. THE HISTORY CLUB MEETS EARLY. THAT'S MONDAY...
FIRE IT UP!!
YIKE!
YA WOO!
FOR TUESDAY...
BREATHED

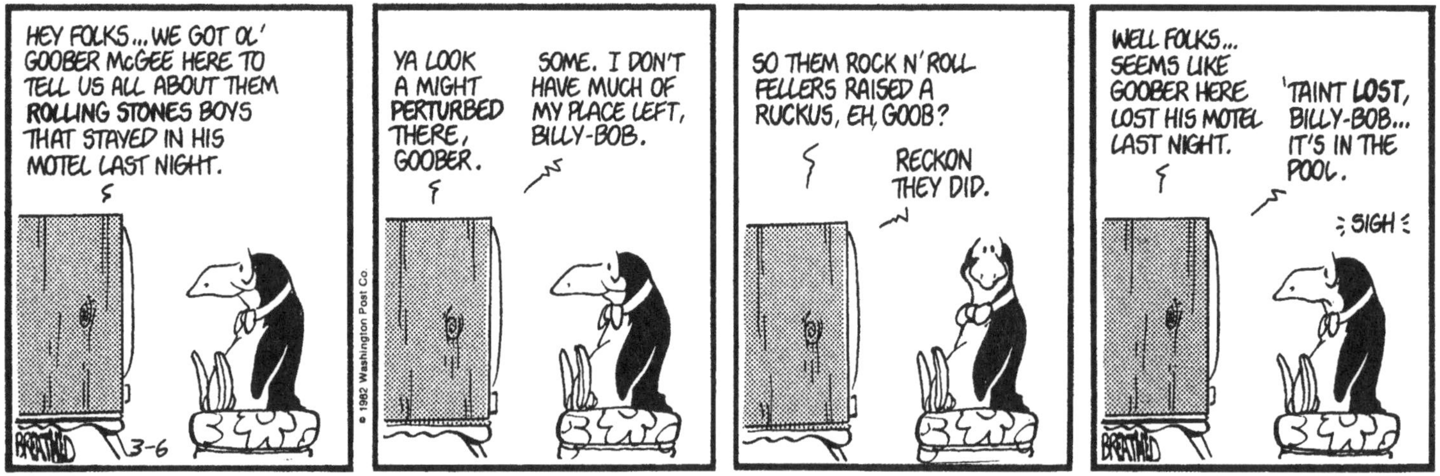
HEY FOLKS... WE GOT OL' GOOBER McGEE HERE TO TELL US ALL ABOUT THEM **ROLLING STONES** BOYS THAT STAYED IN HIS MOTEL LAST NIGHT.
BREATHED
3-6
© 1982 Washington Post Co.
YA LOOK A MIGHT **PERTURBED** THERE, GOOBER.
SOME. I DON'T HAVE MUCH OF MY PLACE LEFT, BILLY-BOB.
SO THEM ROCK N' ROLL FELLERS RAISED A RUCKUS, EH, GOOB?
RECKON THEY DID.
WELL FOLKS... SEEMS LIKE GOOBER HERE LOST HIS MOTEL LAST NIGHT.
'TAINT **LOST**, BILLY-BOB... IT'S IN THE POOL.
SIGH
BREATHED

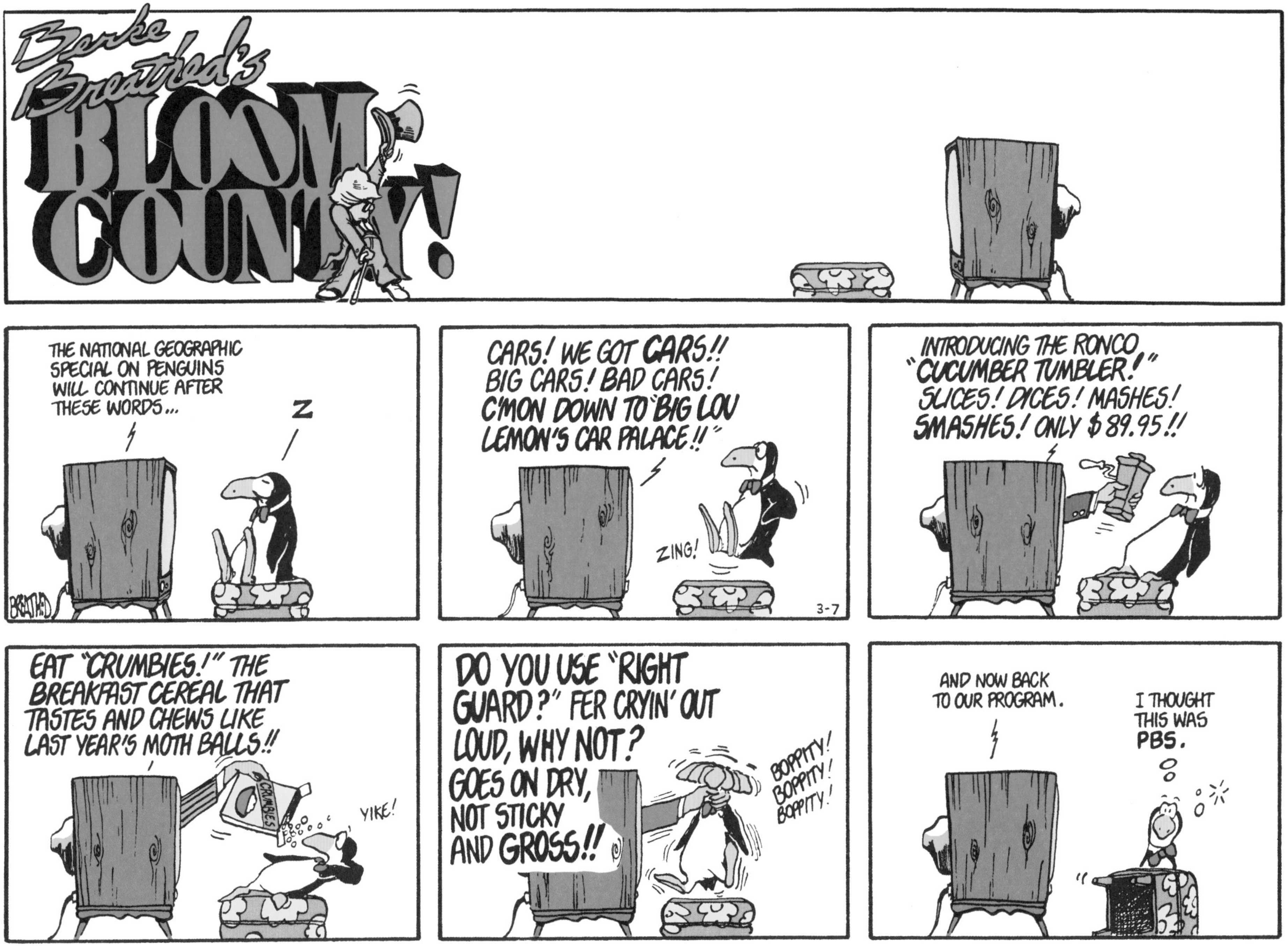
Berke Breathed's
BLOOM COUNTY!
THE NATIONAL GEOGRAPHIC SPECIAL ON PENGUINS WILL CONTINUE AFTER THESE WORDS...
Z
BREATHED
CARS! WE GOT CARS!! BIG CARS! BAD CARS! C'MON DOWN TO "BIG LOU LEMON'S CAR PALACE!!"
ZING!
3-7
INTRODUCING THE RONCO "CUCUMBER TUMBLER!" SLICES! DICES! MASHES! SMASHES! ONLY $89.95!!
EAT "CRUMBIES!" THE BREAKFAST CEREAL THAT TASTES AND CHEWS LIKE LAST YEAR'S MOTH BALLS!!
CRUMBIES
YIKE!
DO YOU USE "RIGHT GUARD?" FER CRYIN' OUT LOUD, WHY NOT? GOES ON DRY, NOT STICKY AND GROSS!!
BOPPITY! BOPPITY! BOPPITY!
AND NOW BACK TO OUR PROGRAM.
I THOUGHT THIS WAS PBS.

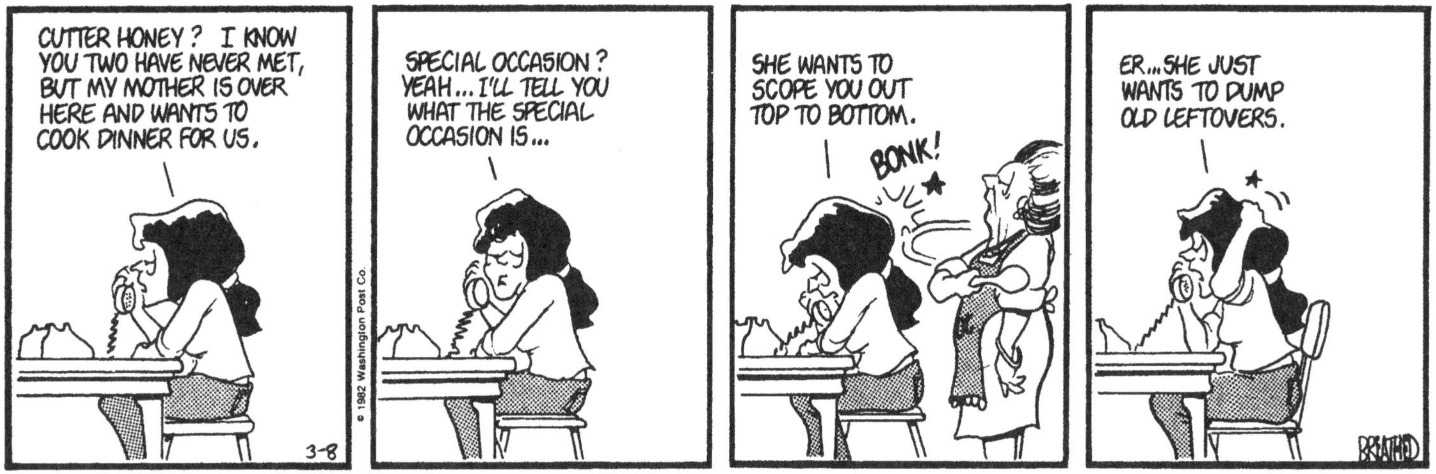
CUTTER HONEY? I KNOW YOU TWO HAVE NEVER MET, BUT MY MOTHER IS OVER HERE AND WANTS TO COOK DINNER FOR US.
3-8
© 1982 Washington Post Co.
SPECIAL OCCASION? YEAH... I'LL TELL YOU WHAT THE SPECIAL OCCASION IS...
SHE WANTS TO SCOPE YOU OUT TOP TO BOTTOM.
BONK!
ER... SHE JUST WANTS TO DUMP OLD LEFTOVERS.
BREATHED

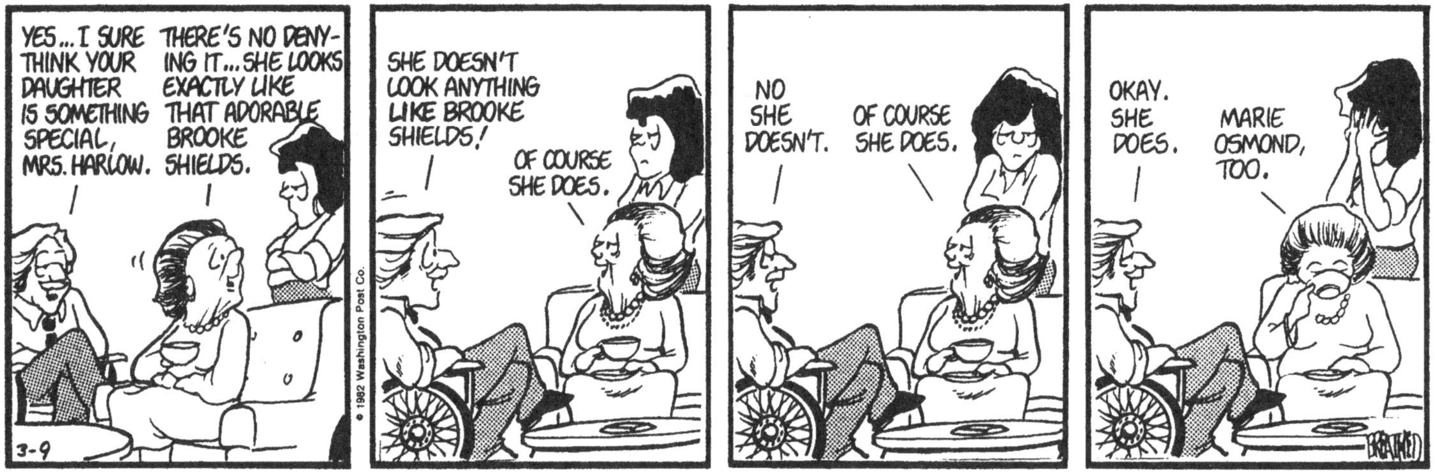
YES... I SURE THINK YOUR DAUGHTER IS SOMETHING SPECIAL, MRS. HARLOW.
THERE'S NO DENYING IT... SHE LOOKS EXACTLY LIKE THAT ADORABLE BROOKE SHIELDS.
3-9
© 1982 Washington Post Co.
SHE DOESN'T LOOK ANYTHING LIKE BROOKE SHIELDS!
OF COURSE SHE DOES.
NO SHE DOESN'T.
OF COURSE SHE DOES.
OKAY. SHE DOES.
MARIE OSMOND, TOO.
BREATHED

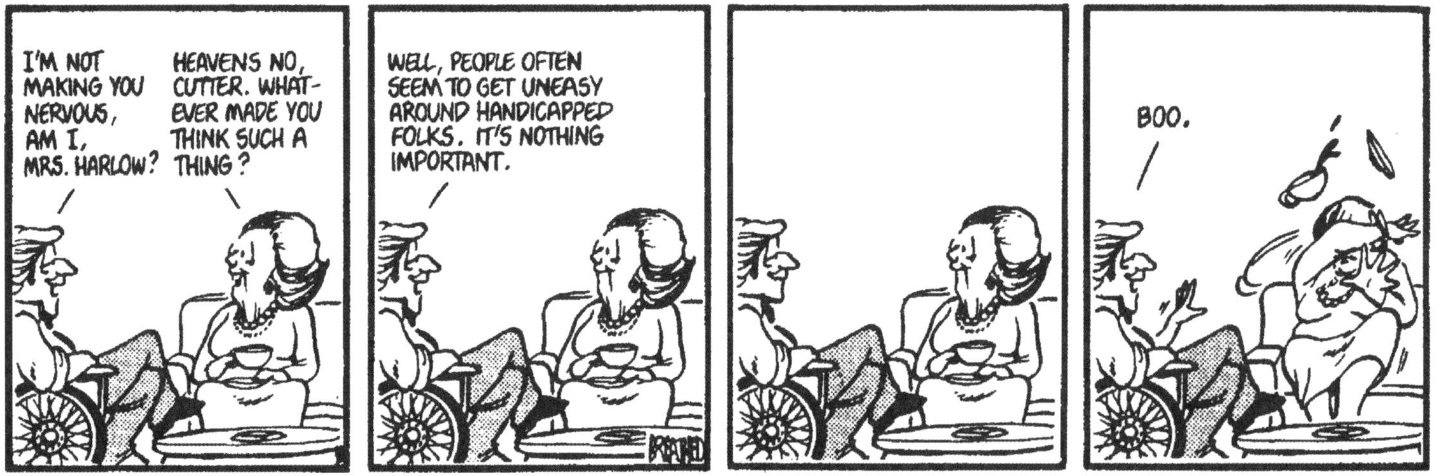
I'M NOT MAKING YOU NERVOUS, AM I, MRS. HARLOW?
HEAVENS NO, CUTTER. WHATEVER MADE YOU THINK SUCH A THING?
WELL, PEOPLE OFTEN SEEM TO GET UNEASY AROUND HANDICAPPED FOLKS. IT'S NOTHING IMPORTANT.
BREATHED
BOO.

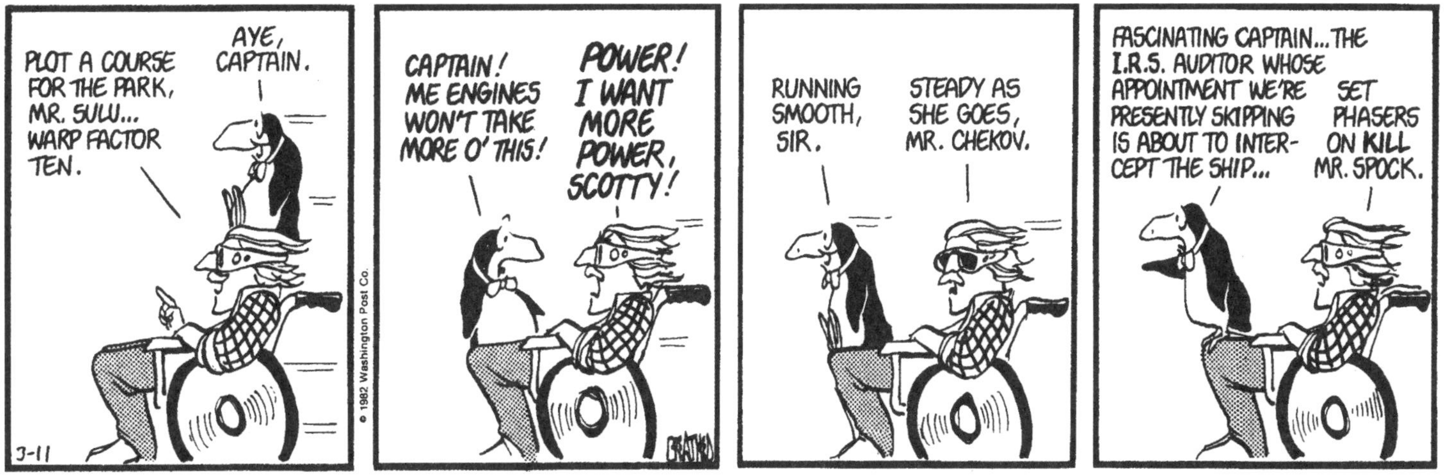
PLOT A COURSE FOR THE PARK, MR. SULU... WARP FACTOR TEN.
AYE, CAPTAIN.
3-11
© 1982 Washington Post Co.
CAPTAIN! ME ENGINES WON'T TAKE MORE O' THIS!
POWER! I WANT MORE POWER, SCOTTY!
BREATHED
RUNNING SMOOTH, SIR.
STEADY AS SHE GOES, MR. CHEKOV.
FASCINATING CAPTAIN... THE I.R.S. AUDITOR WHOSE APPOINTMENT WE'RE PRESENTLY SKIPPING IS ABOUT TO INTERCEPT THE SHIP...
SET PHASERS ON KILL MR. SPOCK.

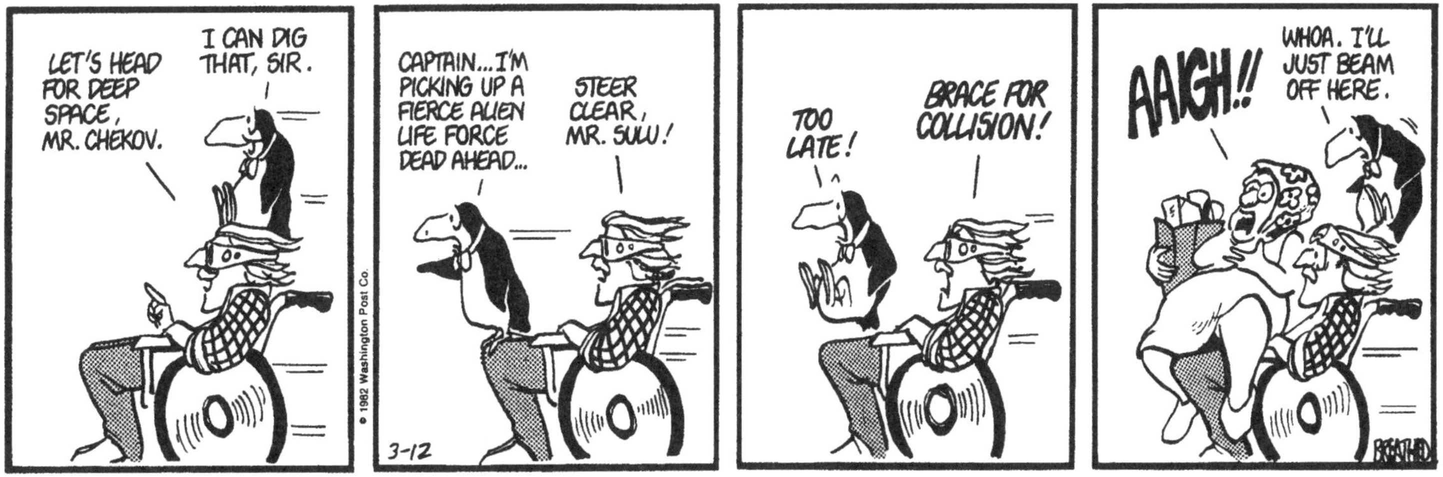
LET'S HEAD FOR DEEP SPACE, MR. CHEKOV.
I CAN DIG THAT, SIR.
© 1982 Washington Post Co.
CAPTAIN... I'M PICKING UP A FIERCE ALIEN LIFE FORCE DEAD AHEAD...
STEER CLEAR, MR. SULU!
3-12
TOO LATE!
BRACE FOR COLLISION!
AAIGH!!
WHOA. I'LL JUST BEAM OFF HERE.
BREATHED

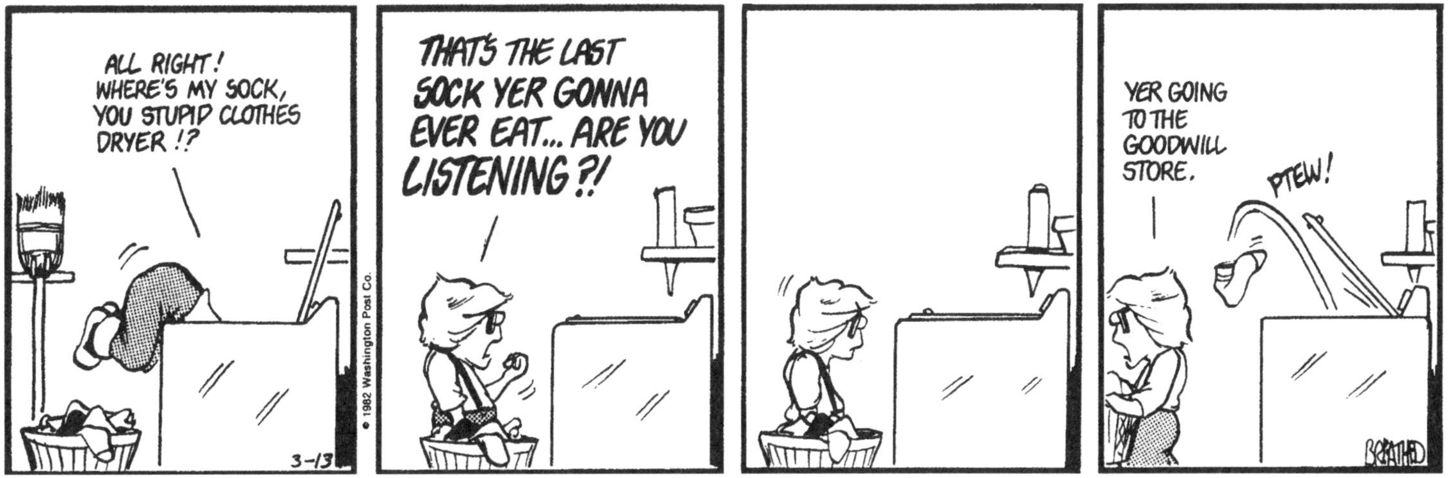
ALL RIGHT! WHERE'S MY SOCK, YOU STUPID CLOTHES DRYER!?
3-13
© 1982 Washington Post Co.
THAT'S THE LAST SOCK YER GONNA EVER EAT... ARE YOU LISTENING?!
YER GOING TO THE GOODWILL STORE.
PTEW!
BREATHED

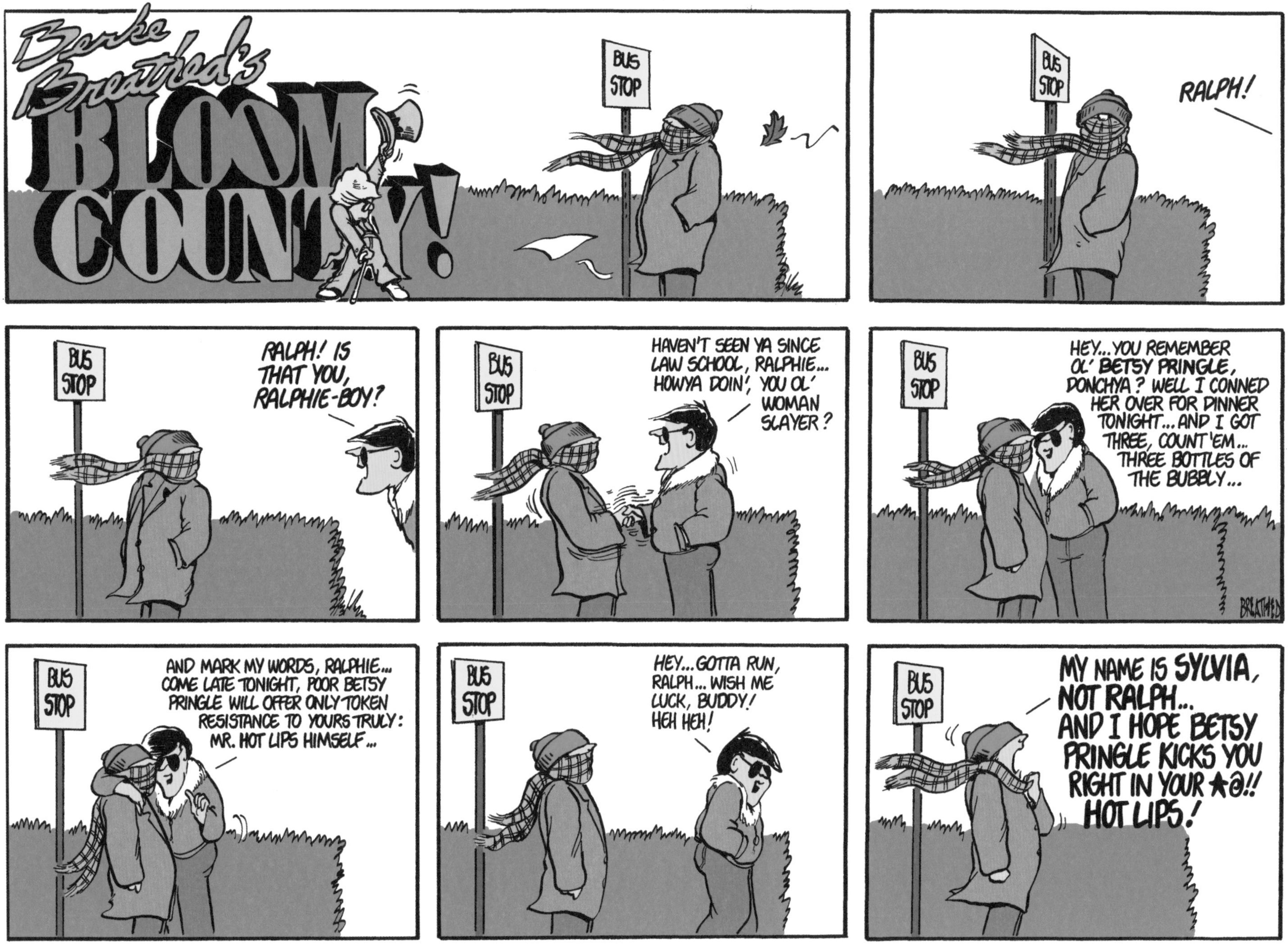
Berke Breathed's
BLOOM COUNTY!
BUS STOP
RALPH!
RALPH! IS THAT YOU, RALPHIE-BOY?
HAVEN'T SEEN YA SINCE LAW SCHOOL, RALPHIE... HOWYA DOIN', YOU OL' WOMAN SLAYER?
HEY... YOU REMEMBER OL' BETSY PRINGLE, DONCHYA? WELL I CONNED HER OVER FOR DINNER TONIGHT... AND I GOT THREE, COUNT 'EM... THREE BOTTLES OF THE BUBBLY...
BREATHED
AND MARK MY WORDS, RALPHIE... COME LATE TONIGHT, POOR BETSY PRINGLE WILL OFFER ONLY TOKEN RESISTANCE TO YOURS TRULY: MR. HOT LIPS HIMSELF...
HEY... GOTTA RUN, RALPH... WISH ME LUCK, BUDDY! HEH HEH!
MY NAME IS SYLVIA, NOT RALPH... AND I HOPE BETSY PRINGLE KICKS YOU RIGHT IN YOUR ★@!! HOT LIPS!

 March 14, 1982

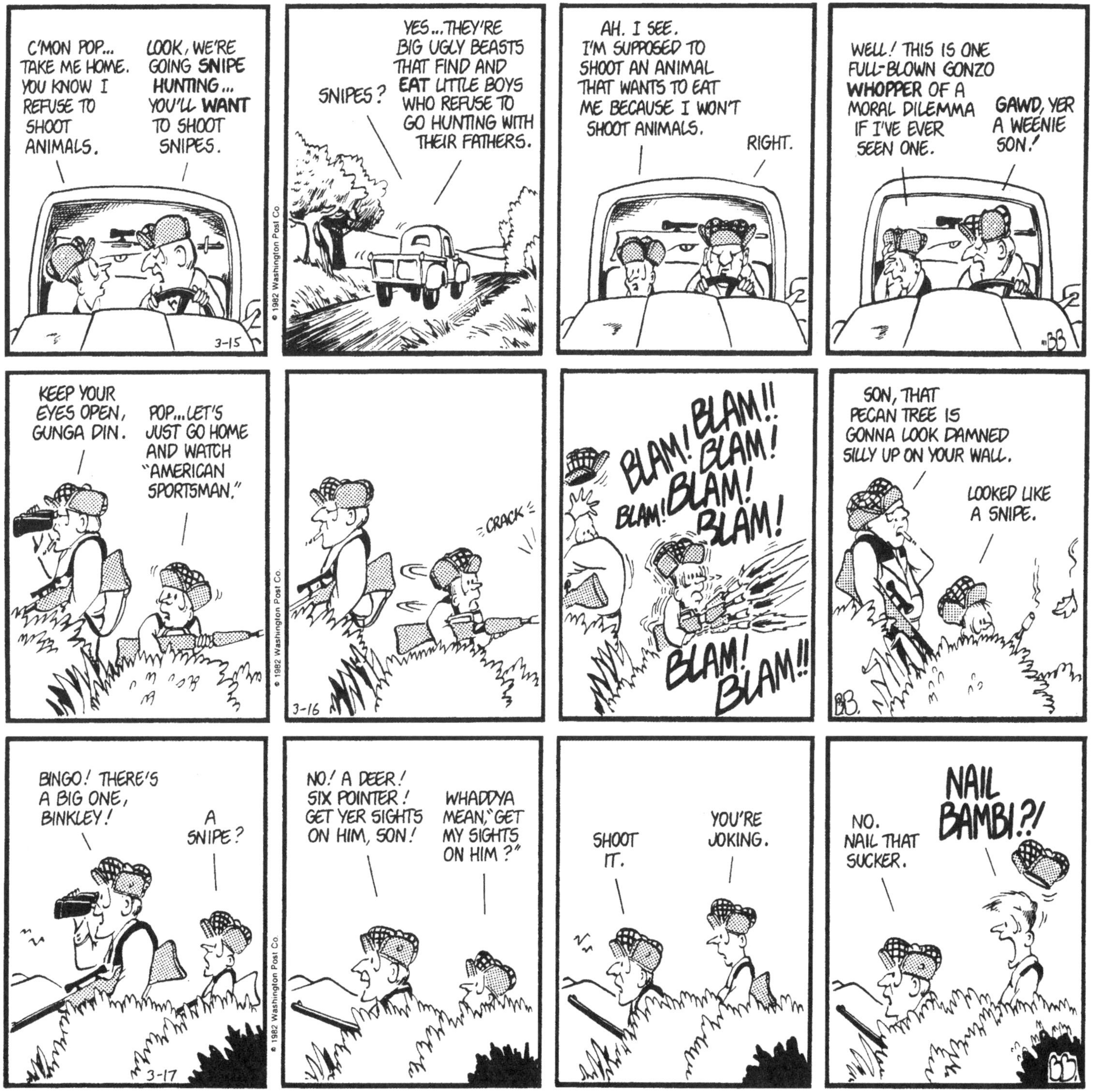
C'MON POP... TAKE ME HOME. YOU KNOW I REFUSE TO SHOOT ANIMALS.
LOOK, WE'RE GOING **SNIPE HUNTING**... YOU'LL **WANT** TO SHOOT SNIPES.
3-15
SNIPES?
YES... THEY'RE BIG UGLY BEASTS THAT FIND AND **EAT** LITTLE BOYS WHO REFUSE TO GO HUNTING WITH THEIR FATHERS.
© 1982 Washington Post Co.
AH. I SEE. I'M SUPPOSED TO SHOOT AN ANIMAL THAT WANTS TO EAT ME BECAUSE I WON'T SHOOT ANIMALS.
RIGHT.
WELL! THIS IS ONE FULL-BLOWN GONZO **WHOPPER** OF A MORAL DILEMMA IF I'VE EVER SEEN ONE.
GAWD, YER A WEENIE SON!
BB
KEEP YOUR EYES OPEN, GUNGA DIN.
POP... LET'S JUST GO HOME AND WATCH "AMERICAN SPORTSMAN."
© 1982 Washington Post Co.
CRACK
3-16
BLAM! BLAM!! BLAM! BLAM! BLAM! BLAM!
BLAM! BLAM!!
SON, THAT PECAN TREE IS GONNA LOOK DAMNED SILLY UP ON YOUR WALL.
LOOKED LIKE A SNIPE.
BB.
BINGO! THERE'S A BIG ONE, BINKLEY!
A SNIPE?
3-17
© 1982 Washington Post Co.
NO! A DEER! SIX POINTER! GET YER SIGHTS ON HIM, SON!
WHADDYA MEAN, "GET MY SIGHTS ON HIM?"
SHOOT IT.
YOU'RE JOKING.
NO. NAIL THAT SUCKER.
NAIL BAMBI?!
BB.

Breathed's first use of his initials as a signature.

March 15-17, 1982

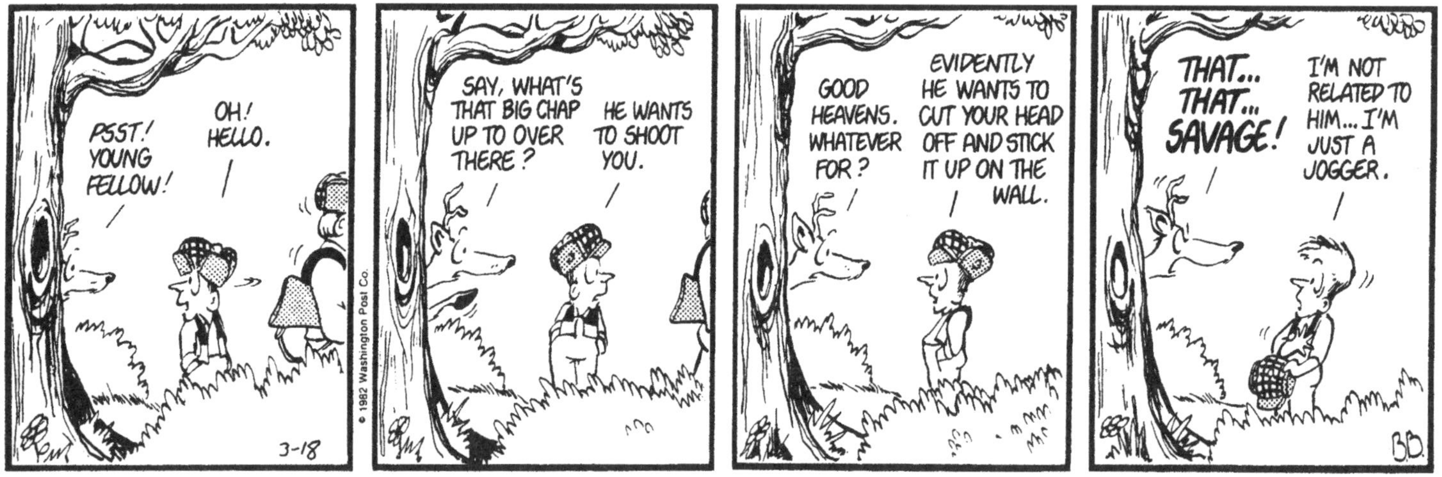
PSST! YOUNG FELLOW!
OH! HELLO.
3-18
© 1982 Washington Post Co.
SAY, WHAT'S THAT BIG CHAP UP TO OVER THERE?
HE WANTS TO SHOOT YOU.
GOOD HEAVENS. WHATEVER FOR?
EVIDENTLY HE WANTS TO CUT YOUR HEAD OFF AND STICK IT UP ON THE WALL.
THAT... THAT... SAVAGE!
I'M NOT RELATED TO HIM... I'M JUST A JOGGER.
B.B.

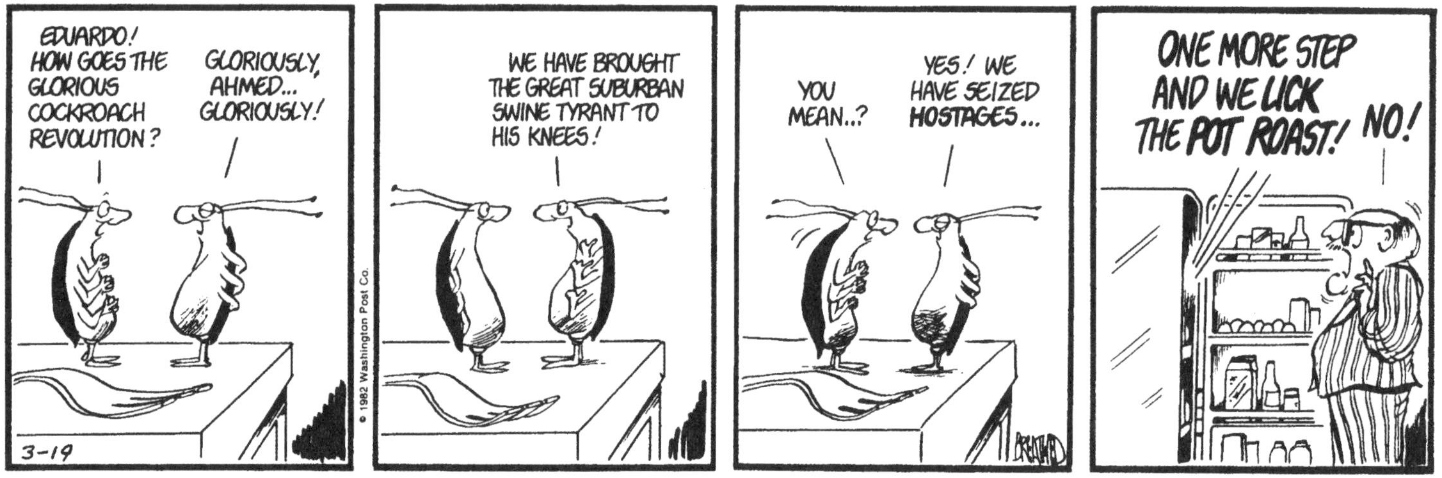
EDUARDO! HOW GOES THE GLORIOUS COCKROACH REVOLUTION?
GLORIOUSLY, AHMED... GLORIOUSLY!
3-19
© 1982 Washington Post Co.
WE HAVE BROUGHT THE GREAT SUBURBAN SWINE TYRANT TO HIS KNEES!
YOU MEAN..?
YES! WE HAVE SEIZED HOSTAGES...
ONE MORE STEP AND WE LICK THE POT ROAST!
NO!

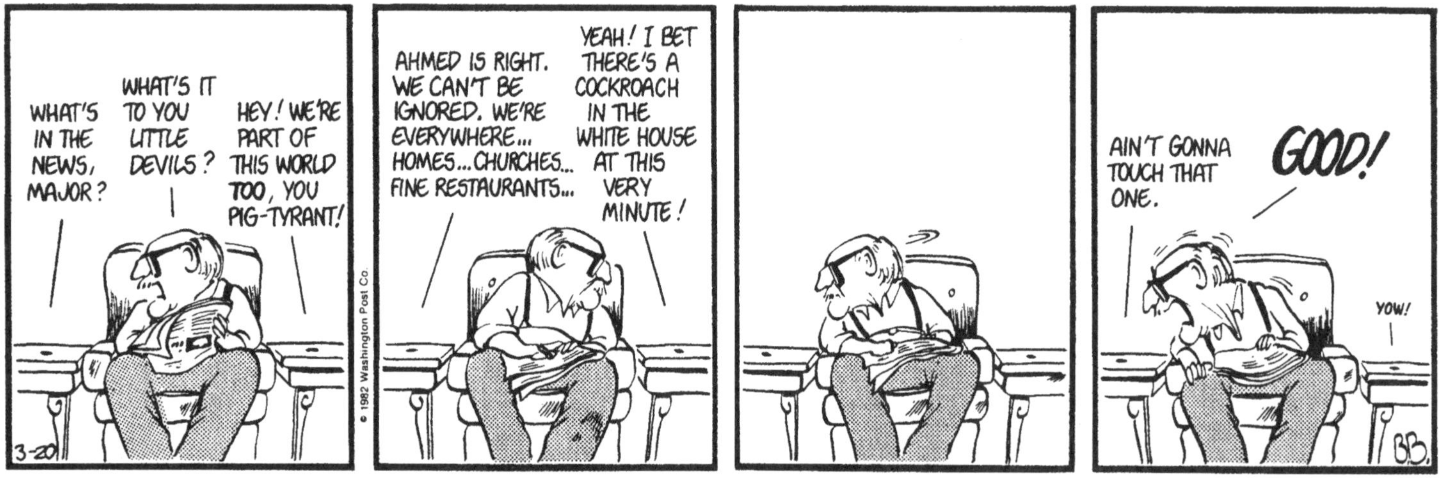
WHAT'S IN THE NEWS, MAJOR?
WHAT'S IT TO YOU LITTLE DEVILS?
HEY! WE'RE PART OF THIS WORLD TOO, YOU PIG-TYRANT!
3-20
© 1982 Washington Post Co.
AHMED IS RIGHT. WE CAN'T BE IGNORED. WE'RE EVERYWHERE... HOMES... CHURCHES... FINE RESTAURANTS...
YEAH! I BET THERE'S A COCKROACH IN THE WHITE HOUSE AT THIS VERY MINUTE!
AIN'T GONNA TOUCH THAT ONE.
GOOD!
YOW!
B.B.

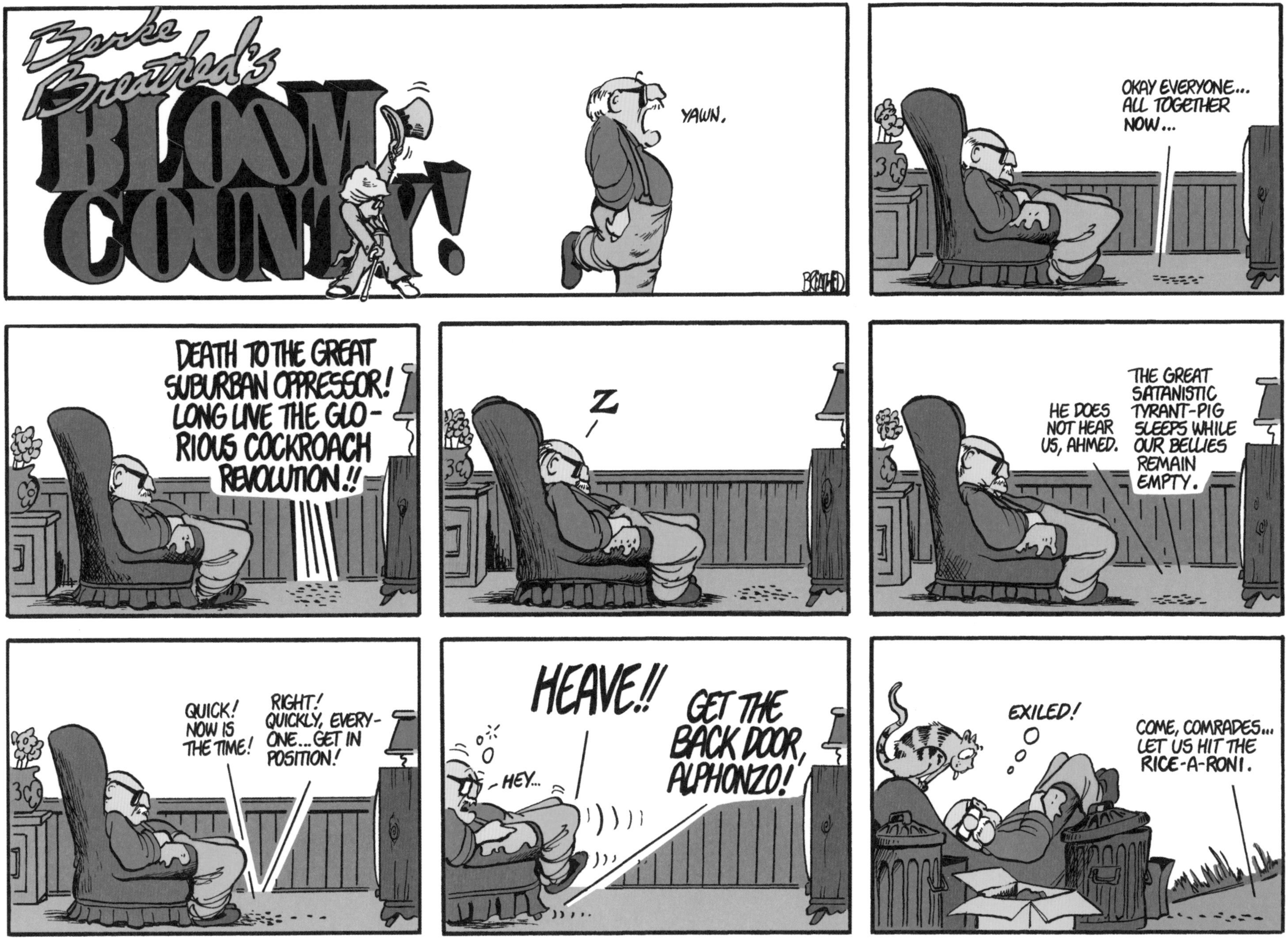

Berke Breathed's
BLOOM COUNTY!
YAWN.
BREATHED
OKAY EVERYONE... ALL TOGETHER NOW...
DEATH TO THE GREAT SUBURBAN OPPRESSOR! LONG LIVE THE GLORIOUS COCKROACH REVOLUTION!!
Z
HE DOES NOT HEAR US, AHMED.
THE GREAT SATANISTIC TYRANT-PIG SLEEPS WHILE OUR BELLIES REMAIN EMPTY.
QUICK! NOW IS THE TIME!
RIGHT! QUICKLY, EVERYONE... GET IN POSITION!
HEAVE!!
HEY...
GET THE BACK DOOR, ALPHONZO!
EXILED!
COME, COMRADES... LET US HIT THE RICE-A-RONI.

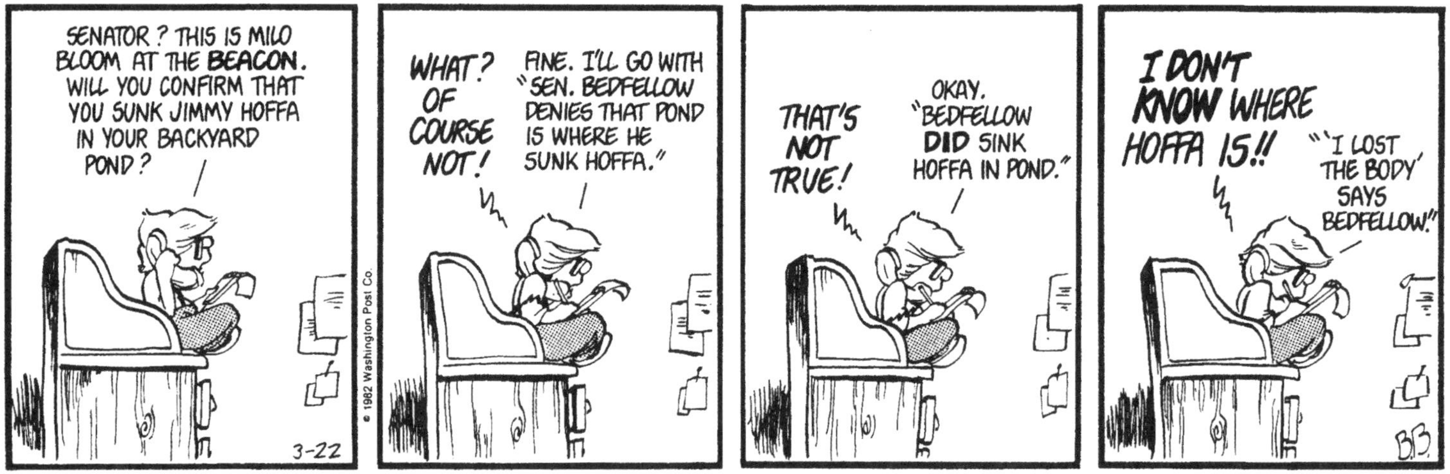
SENATOR? THIS IS MILO BLOOM AT THE **BEACON**. WILL YOU CONFIRM THAT YOU SUNK JIMMY HOFFA IN YOUR BACKYARD POND?
WHAT? OF COURSE NOT!
FINE. I'LL GO WITH "SEN. BEDFELLOW DENIES THAT POND IS WHERE HE SUNK HOFFA."
THAT'S NOT TRUE!
OKAY. "BEDFELLOW **DID** SINK HOFFA IN POND."
I DON'T KNOW WHERE HOFFA IS!!
"'I LOST THE BODY' SAYS BEDFELLOW."
3-22
© 1982 Washington Post Co.
B.B.

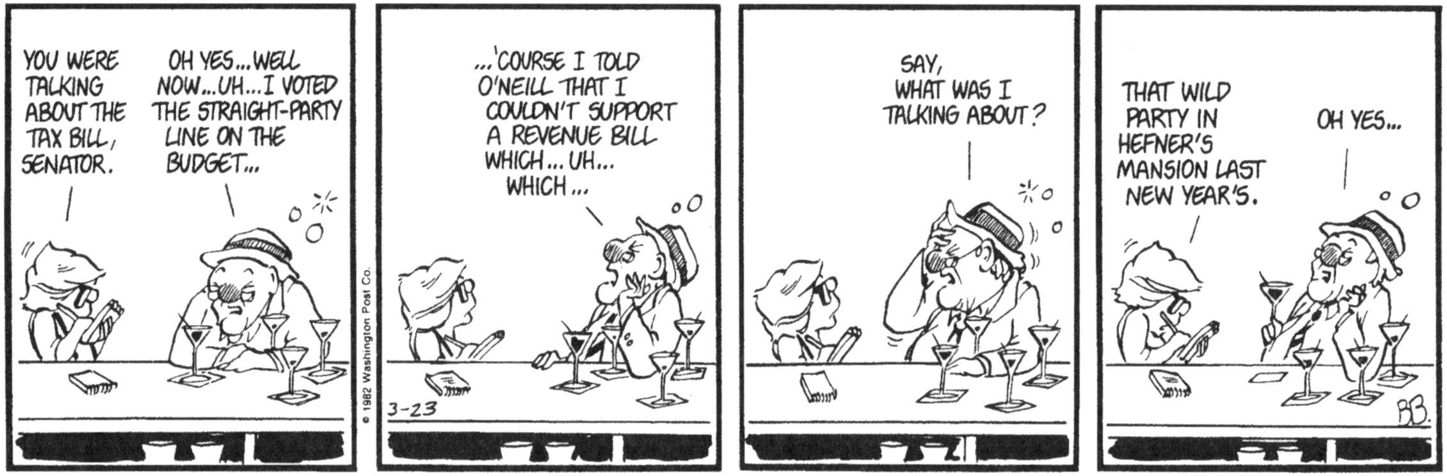
YOU WERE TALKING ABOUT THE TAX BILL, SENATOR.
OH YES...WELL NOW...UH...I VOTED THE STRAIGHT-PARTY LINE ON THE BUDGET...
...'COURSE I TOLD O'NEILL THAT I COULDN'T SUPPORT A REVENUE BILL WHICH...UH... WHICH...
SAY, WHAT WAS I TALKING ABOUT?
THAT WILD PARTY IN HEFNER'S MANSION LAST NEW YEAR'S.
OH YES...
3-23
© 1982 Washington Post Co.
B.B.

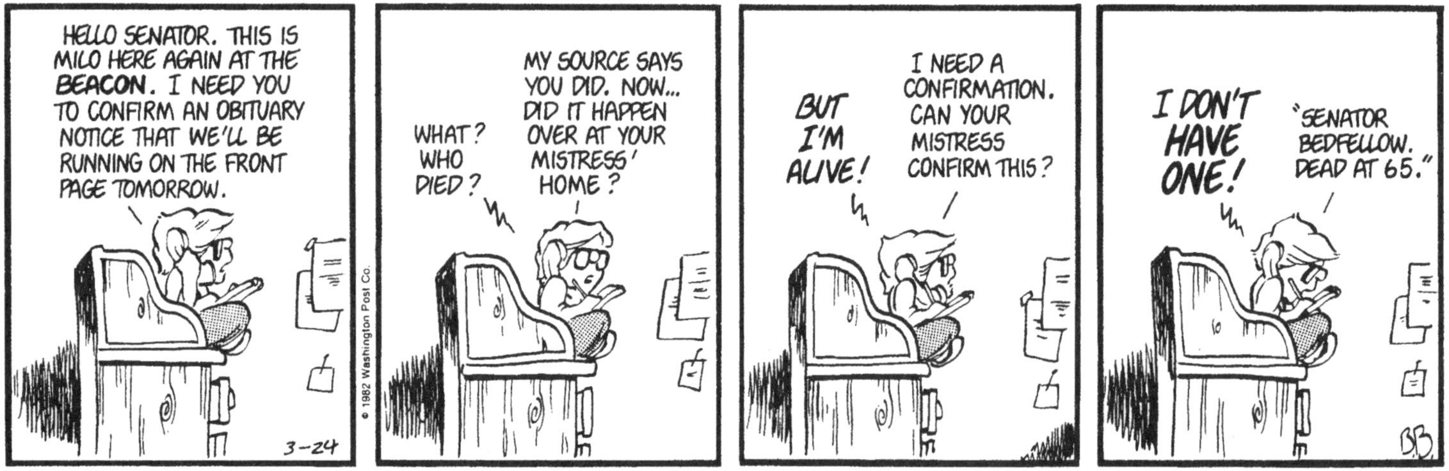
HELLO SENATOR. THIS IS MILO HERE AGAIN AT THE **BEACON**. I NEED YOU TO CONFIRM AN OBITUARY NOTICE THAT WE'LL BE RUNNING ON THE FRONT PAGE TOMORROW.
WHAT? WHO DIED?
MY SOURCE SAYS YOU DID. NOW... DID IT HAPPEN OVER AT YOUR MISTRESS' HOME?
BUT I'M ALIVE!
I NEED A CONFIRMATION. CAN YOUR MISTRESS CONFIRM THIS?
I DON'T HAVE ONE!
"SENATOR BEDFELLOW. DEAD AT 65."
3-24
© 1982 Washington Post Co.
B.B.

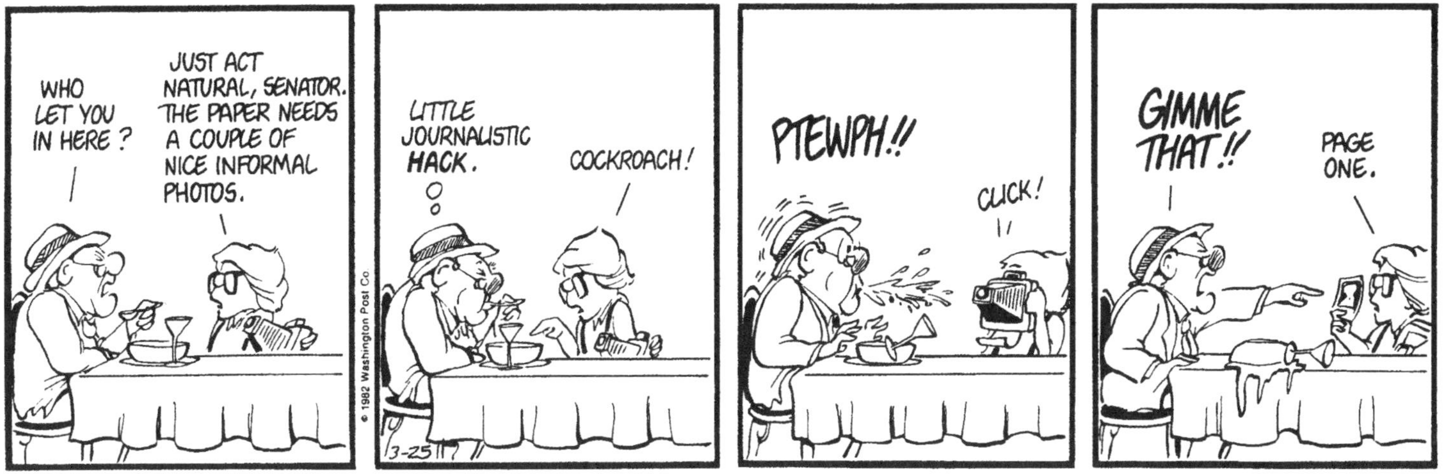
WHO LET YOU IN HERE?
JUST ACT NATURAL, SENATOR. THE PAPER NEEDS A COUPLE OF NICE INFORMAL PHOTOS.
© 1982 Washington Post Co.
LITTLE JOURNALISTIC **HACK**.
COCKROACH!
3-25
PTEWPH!!
CLICK!
GIMME THAT!!
PAGE ONE.

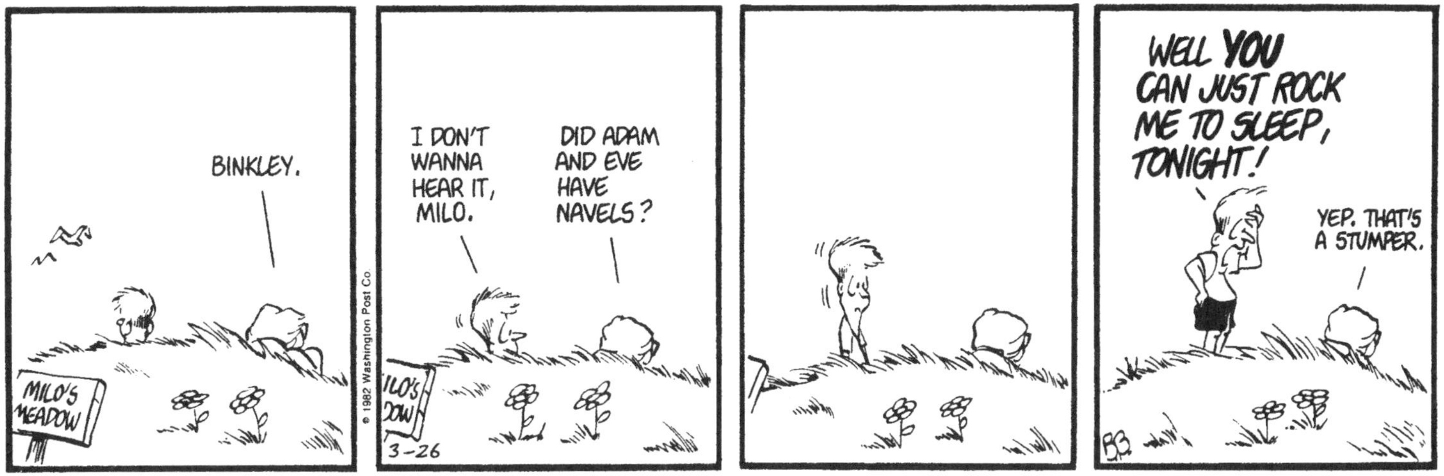
BINKLEY.
MILO'S MEADOW
© 1982 Washington Post Co.
I DON'T WANNA HEAR IT, MILO.
DID ADAM AND EVE HAVE NAVELS?
3-26
WELL **YOU** CAN JUST ROCK ME TO SLEEP, TONIGHT!
YEP. THAT'S A STUMPER.
BB.

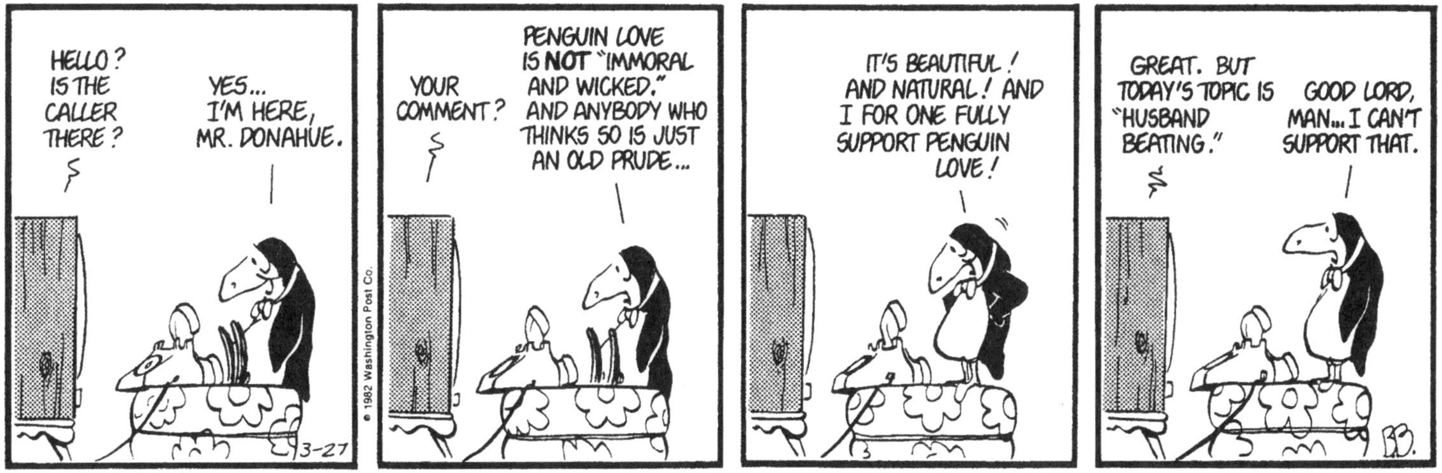
HELLO? IS THE CALLER THERE?
YES... I'M HERE, MR. DONAHUE.
3-27
© 1982 Washington Post Co.
YOUR COMMENT?
PENGUIN LOVE IS **NOT** "IMMORAL AND WICKED." AND ANYBODY WHO THINKS SO IS JUST AN OLD PRUDE...
IT'S BEAUTIFUL! AND NATURAL! AND I FOR ONE FULLY SUPPORT PENGUIN LOVE!
GREAT. BUT TODAY'S TOPIC IS "HUSBAND BEATING."
GOOD LORD, MAN... I CAN'T SUPPORT THAT.
BB.

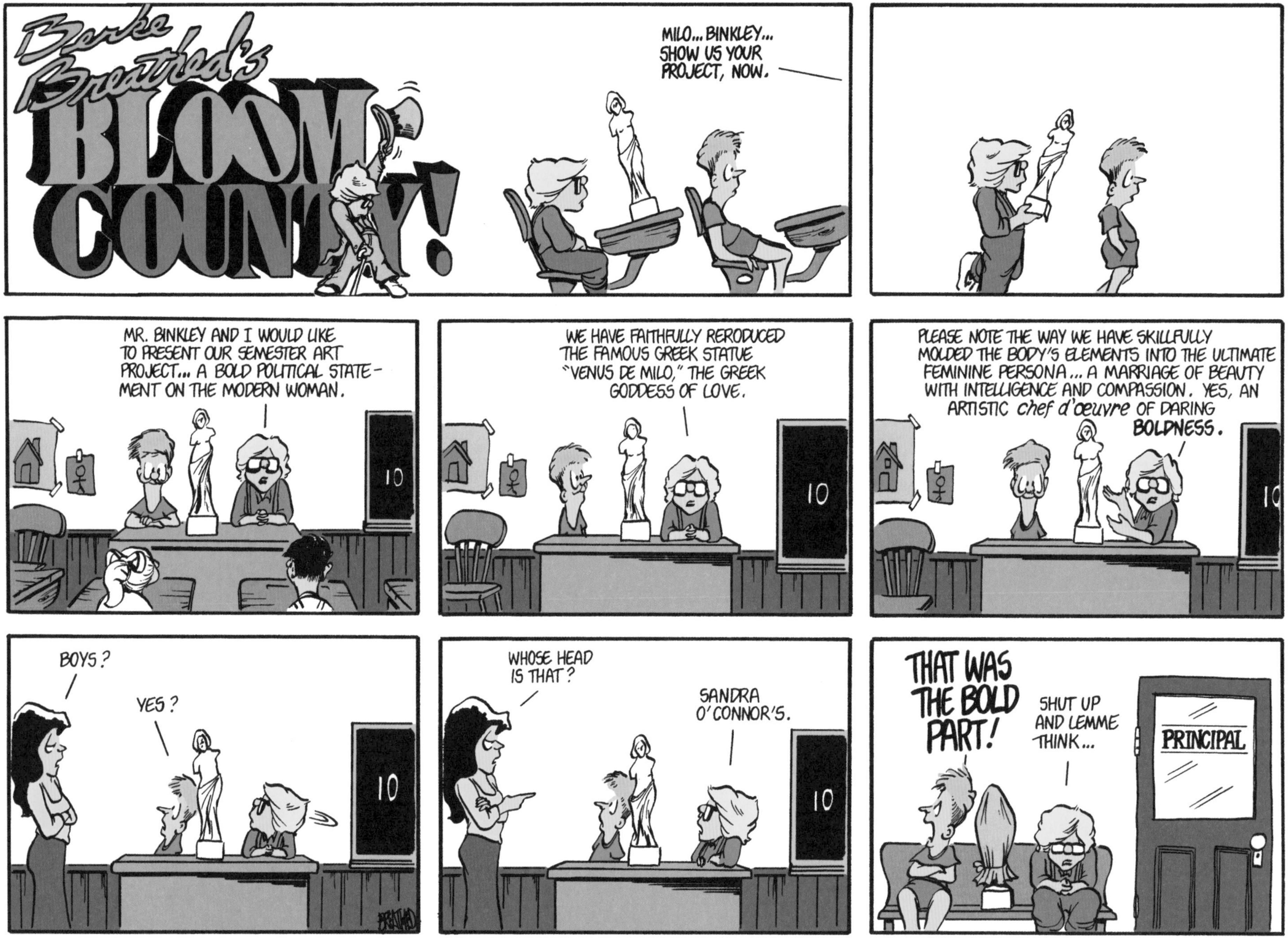

Berke Breathed's
BLOOM COUNTY!
MILO... BINKLEY... SHOW US YOUR PROJECT, NOW.
MR. BINKLEY AND I WOULD LIKE TO PRESENT OUR SEMESTER ART PROJECT... A BOLD POLITICAL STATEMENT ON THE MODERN WOMAN.
10
WE HAVE FAITHFULLY RERODUCED THE FAMOUS GREEK STATUE "VENUS DE MILO," THE GREEK GODDESS OF LOVE.
10
PLEASE NOTE THE WAY WE HAVE SKILLFULLY MOLDED THE BODY'S ELEMENTS INTO THE ULTIMATE FEMININE PERSONA... A MARRIAGE OF BEAUTY WITH INTELLIGENCE AND COMPASSION. YES, AN ARTISTIC *chef d'œuvre* OF DARING **BOLDNESS.**
BOYS?
YES?
10
WHOSE HEAD IS THAT?
SANDRA O'CONNOR'S.
10
THAT WAS THE BOLD PART!
SHUT UP AND LEMME THINK...
PRINCIPAL

Judge Sandra Day O'Connor, in 1981, was the first woman appointed to serve as an Associate Justice of the Supreme Court.

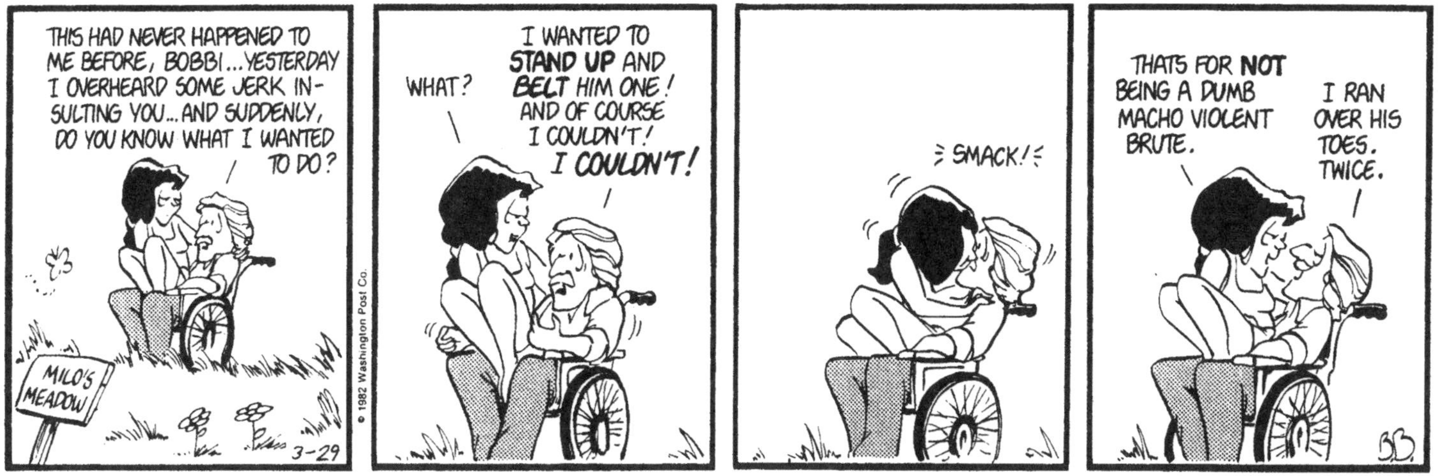
THIS HAD NEVER HAPPENED TO ME BEFORE, BOBBI...YESTERDAY I OVERHEARD SOME JERK IN-SULTING YOU...AND SUDDENLY, DO YOU KNOW WHAT I WANTED TO DO?
MILO'S MEADOW
3-29
WHAT?
I WANTED TO STAND UP AND BELT HIM ONE! AND OF COURSE I COULDN'T! I COULDN'T!
© 1982 Washington Post Co.
SMACK!
THATS FOR NOT BEING A DUMB MACHO VIOLENT BRUTE.
I RAN OVER HIS TOES. TWICE.
BB.

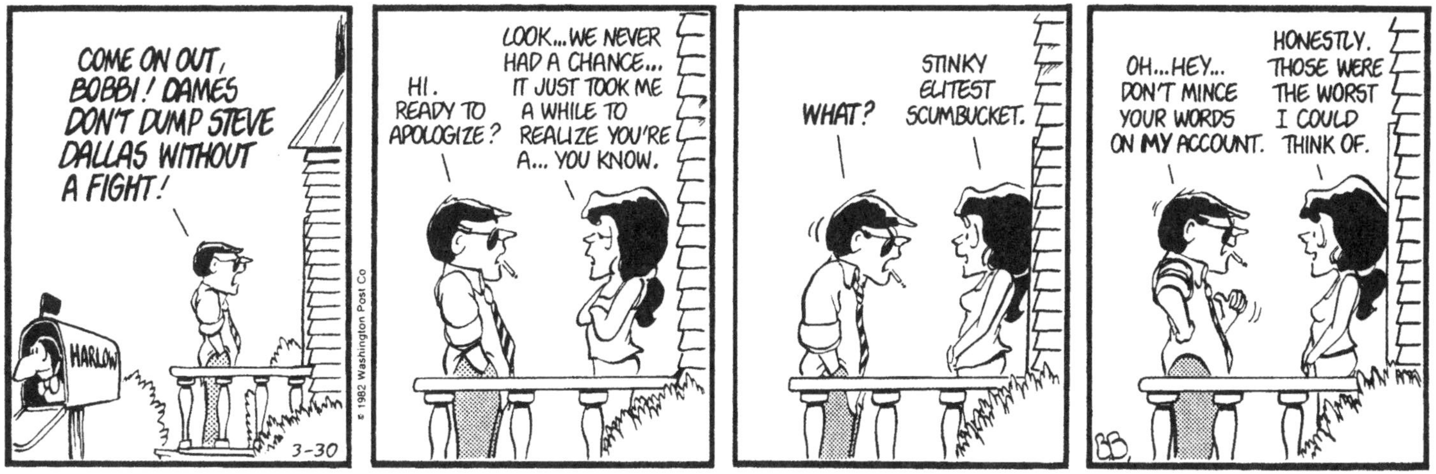
COME ON OUT, BOBBI! DAMES DON'T DUMP STEVE DALLAS WITHOUT A FIGHT!
HARLOW
3-30
HI. READY TO APOLOGIZE?
LOOK...WE NEVER HAD A CHANCE... IT JUST TOOK ME A WHILE TO REALIZE YOU'RE A... YOU KNOW.
© 1982 Washington Post Co.
WHAT?
STINKY ELITEST SCUMBUCKET.
OH...HEY... DON'T MINCE YOUR WORDS ON MY ACCOUNT.
HONESTLY. THOSE WERE THE WORST I COULD THINK OF.
BB.

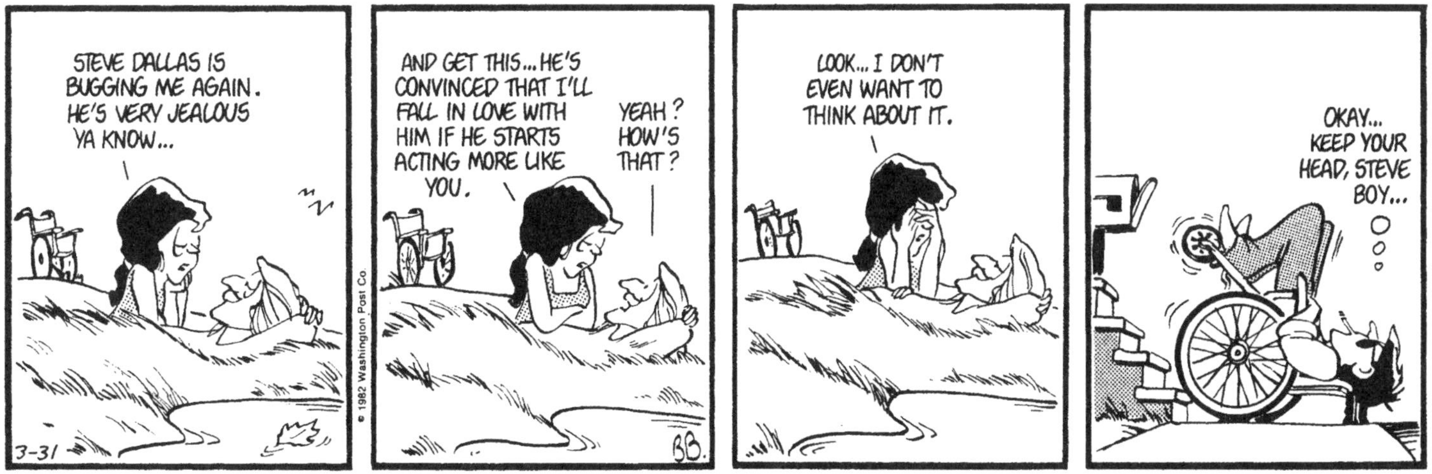
STEVE DALLAS IS BUGGING ME AGAIN. HE'S VERY JEALOUS YA KNOW...
3-31
AND GET THIS...HE'S CONVINCED THAT I'LL FALL IN LOVE WITH HIM IF HE STARTS ACTING MORE LIKE YOU.
YEAH? HOW'S THAT?
© 1982 Washington Post Co.
BB.
LOOK... I DON'T EVEN WANT TO THINK ABOUT IT.
OKAY... KEEP YOUR HEAD, STEVE BOY...

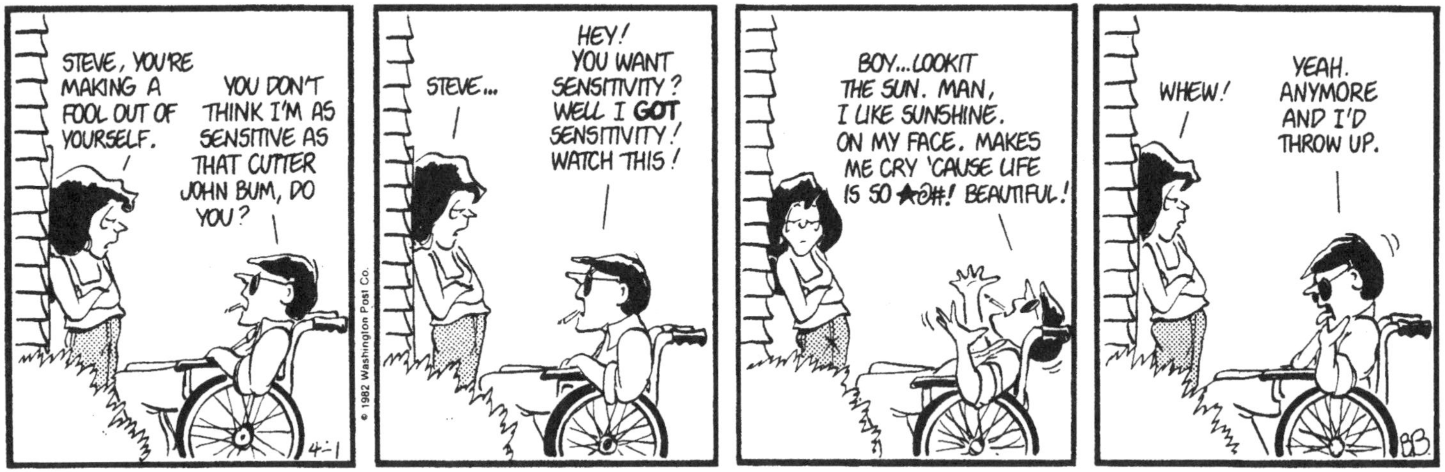
STEVE, YOU'RE MAKING A FOOL OUT OF YOURSELF.
YOU DON'T THINK I'M AS SENSITIVE AS THAT CUTTER JOHN BUM, DO YOU?
4-1
© 1982 Washington Post Co.
STEVE...
HEY! YOU WANT SENSITIVITY? WELL I GOT SENSITIVITY! WATCH THIS!
BOY...LOOKIT THE SUN. MAN, I LIKE SUNSHINE. ON MY FACE. MAKES ME CRY 'CAUSE LIFE IS SO ★@#! BEAUTIFUL!
WHEW!
YEAH. ANYMORE AND I'D THROW UP.
BB.

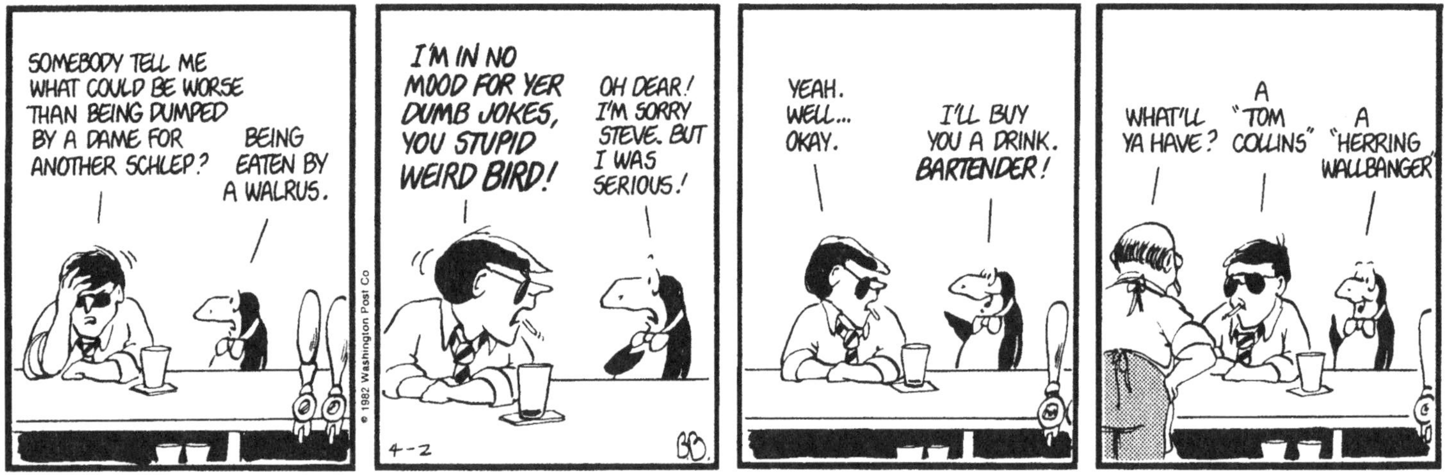
SOMEBODY TELL ME WHAT COULD BE WORSE THAN BEING DUMPED BY A DAME FOR ANOTHER SCHLEP?
BEING EATEN BY A WALRUS.
© 1982 Washington Post Co.
I'M IN NO MOOD FOR YER DUMB JOKES, YOU STUPID WEIRD BIRD!
OH DEAR! I'M SORRY STEVE. BUT I WAS SERIOUS!
4-2
BB.
YEAH. WELL... OKAY.
I'LL BUY YOU A DRINK. BARTENDER!
WHAT'LL YA HAVE?
A "TOM COLLINS"
A "HERRING WALLBANGER"

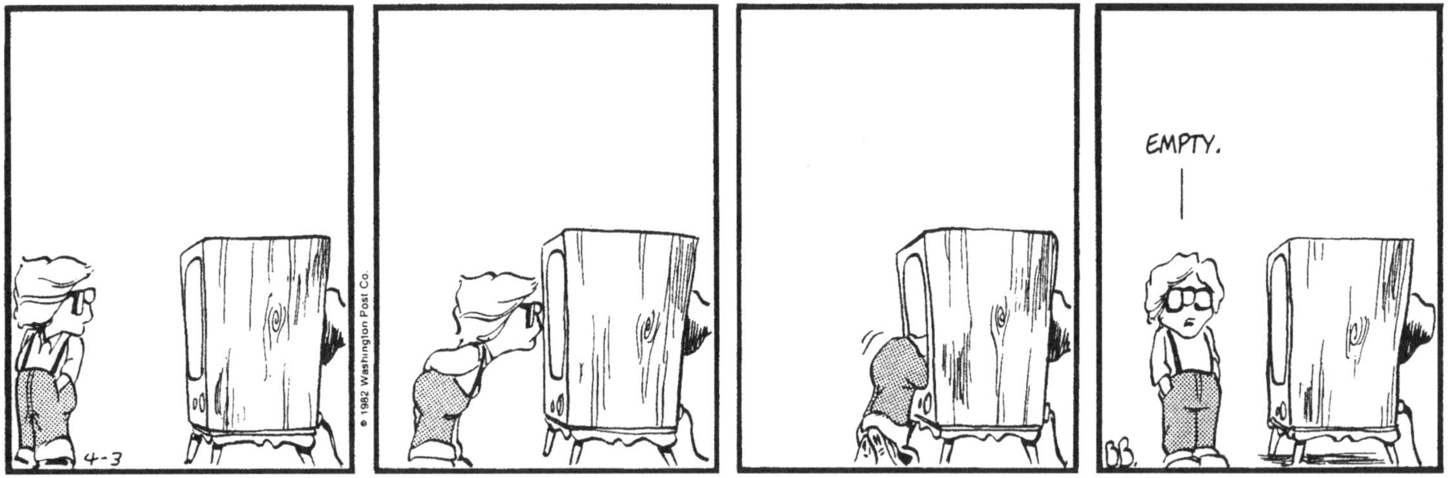
4-3
© 1982 Washington Post Co.
EMPTY.
BB.

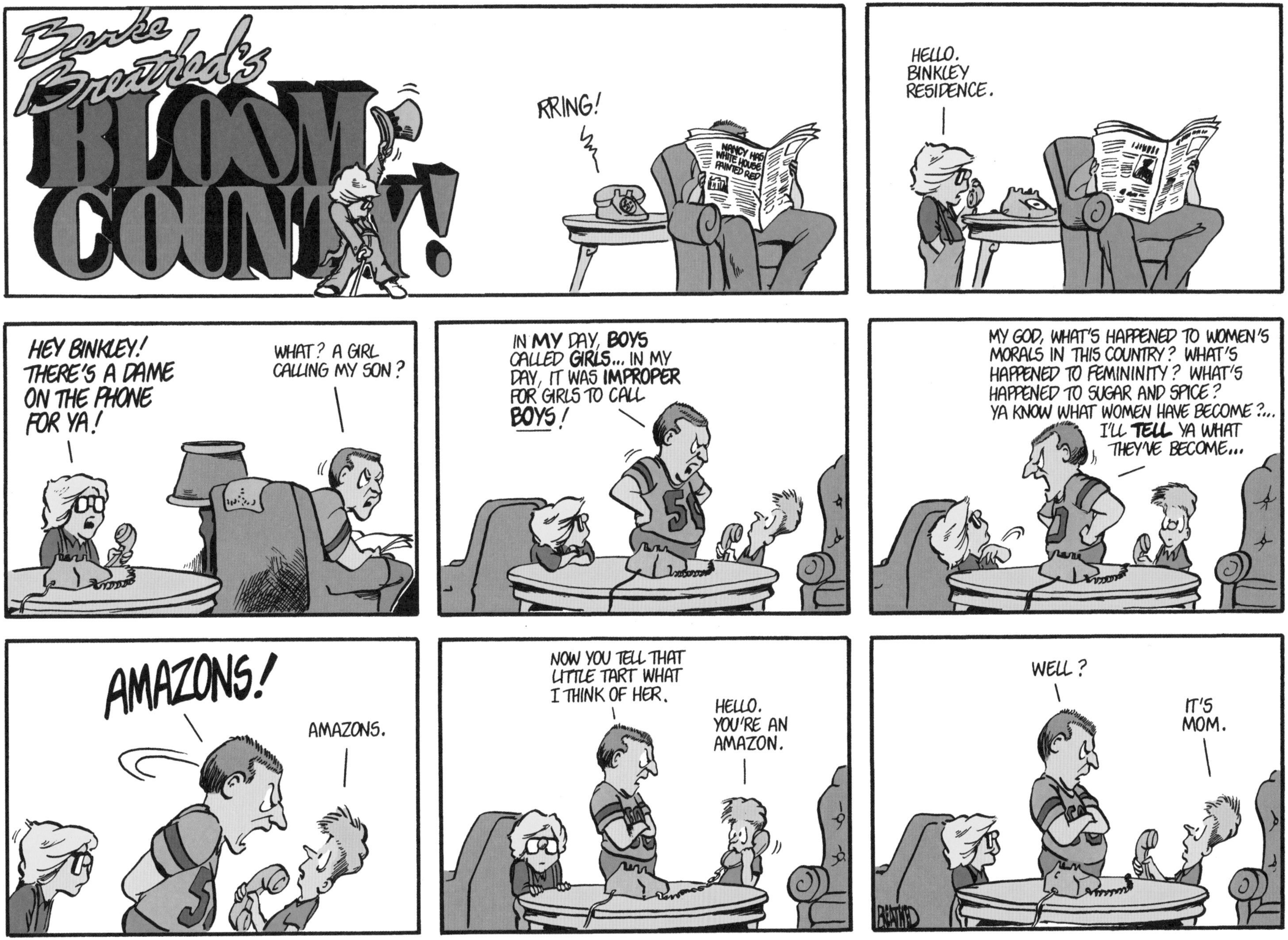
Berke Breathed's
BLOOM COUNTY!
RRING!
NANCY HAS WHITE HOUSE PAINTED RED
HELLO. BINKLEY RESIDENCE.
HEY BINKLEY! THERE'S A DAME ON THE PHONE FOR YA!
WHAT? A GIRL CALLING MY SON?
IN MY DAY, BOYS CALLED GIRLS... IN MY DAY, IT WAS IMPROPER FOR GIRLS TO CALL BOYS!
MY GOD, WHAT'S HAPPENED TO WOMEN'S MORALS IN THIS COUNTRY? WHAT'S HAPPENED TO FEMININITY? WHAT'S HAPPENED TO SUGAR AND SPICE? YA KNOW WHAT WOMEN HAVE BECOME?... I'LL TELL YA WHAT THEY'VE BECOME...
AMAZONS!
AMAZONS.
NOW YOU TELL THAT LITTLE TART WHAT I THINK OF HER.
HELLO. YOU'RE AN AMAZON.
BREATHED
WELL?
IT'S MOM.

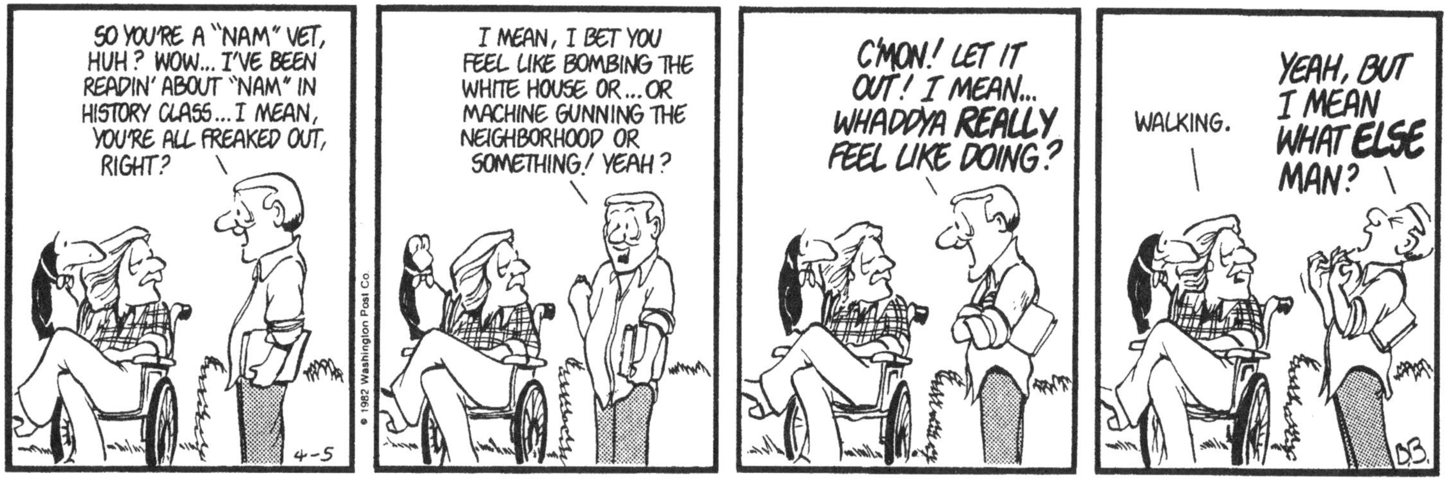
SO YOU'RE A "NAM" VET, HUH? WOW... I'VE BEEN READIN' ABOUT "NAM" IN HISTORY CLASS... I MEAN, YOU'RE ALL FREAKED OUT, RIGHT?
4-5
© 1982 Washington Post Co.
I MEAN, I BET YOU FEEL LIKE BOMBING THE WHITE HOUSE OR... OR MACHINE GUNNING THE NEIGHBORHOOD OR SOMETHING! YEAH?
C'MON! LET IT OUT! I MEAN... WHADDYA REALLY FEEL LIKE DOING?
WALKING.
YEAH, BUT I MEAN WHAT ELSE MAN?
B.B.

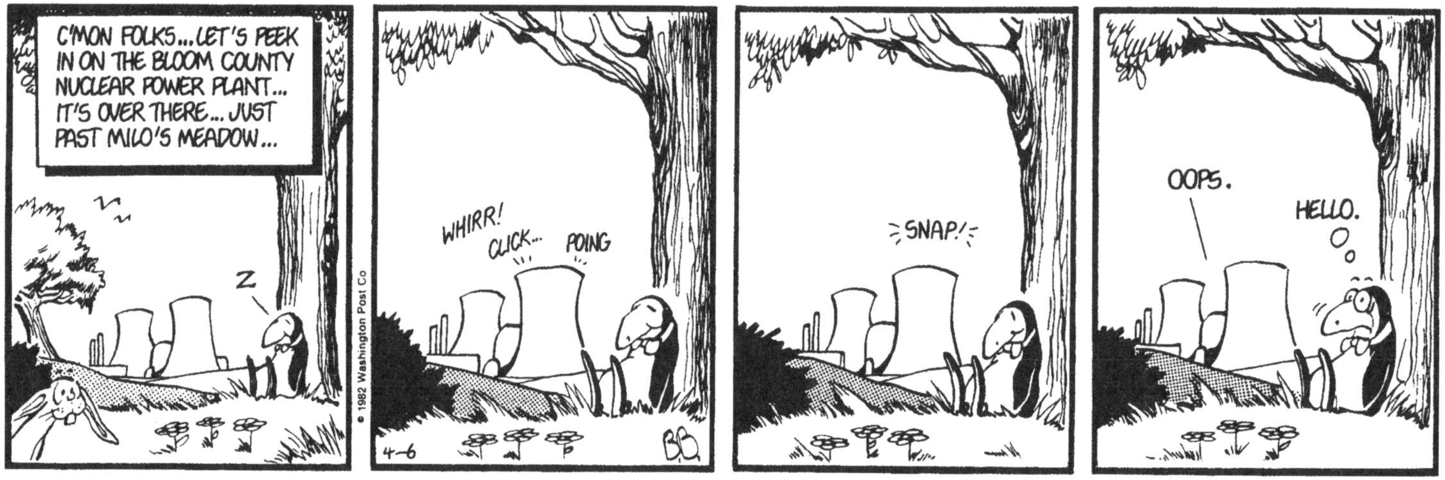
C'MON FOLKS... LET'S PEEK IN ON THE BLOOM COUNTY NUCLEAR POWER PLANT... IT'S OVER THERE... JUST PAST MILO'S MEADOW...
Z
© 1982 Washington Post Co.
WHIRR!
CLICK...
POING
4-6
B.B.
SNAP!
OOPS.
HELLO.

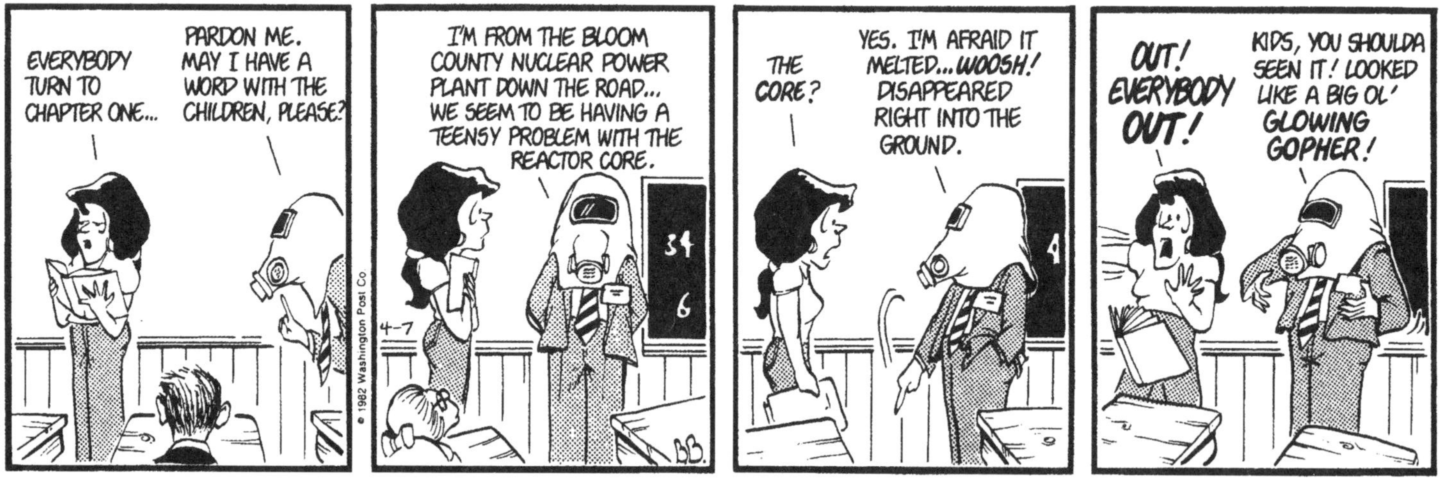
EVERYBODY TURN TO CHAPTER ONE...
PARDON ME. MAY I HAVE A WORD WITH THE CHILDREN, PLEASE?
© 1982 Washington Post Co.
4-7
I'M FROM THE BLOOM COUNTY NUCLEAR POWER PLANT DOWN THE ROAD... WE SEEM TO BE HAVING A TEENSY PROBLEM WITH THE REACTOR CORE.
THE CORE?
YES. I'M AFRAID IT MELTED... WOOSH! DISAPPEARED RIGHT INTO THE GROUND.
OUT! EVERYBODY OUT!
KIDS, YOU SHOULDA SEEN IT! LOOKED LIKE A BIG OL' GLOWING GOPHER!
B.B.

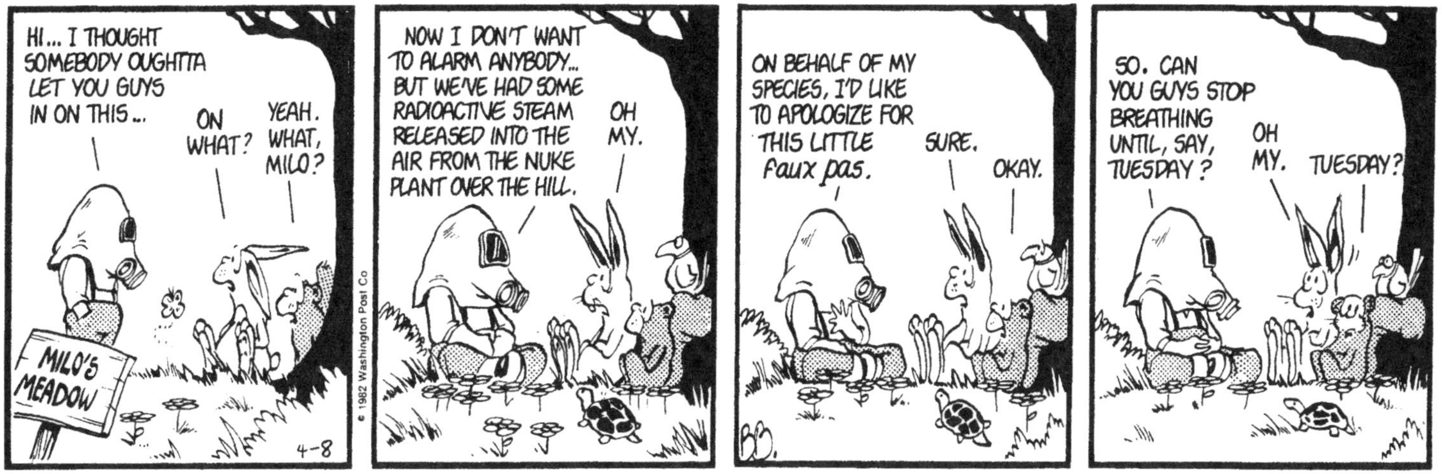
HI... I THOUGHT SOMEBODY OUGHTTA LET YOU GUYS IN ON THIS...
ON WHAT?
YEAH. WHAT, MILO?
MILO'S MEADOW
4-8
© 1982 Washington Post Co.
NOW I DON'T WANT TO ALARM ANYBODY... BUT WE'VE HAD SOME RADIOACTIVE STEAM RELEASED INTO THE AIR FROM THE NUKE PLANT OVER THE HILL.
OH MY.
ON BEHALF OF MY SPECIES, I'D LIKE TO APOLOGIZE FOR THIS LITTLE *faux pas*.
SURE.
OKAY.
SO. CAN YOU GUYS STOP BREATHING UNTIL, SAY, TUESDAY?
OH MY.
TUESDAY?

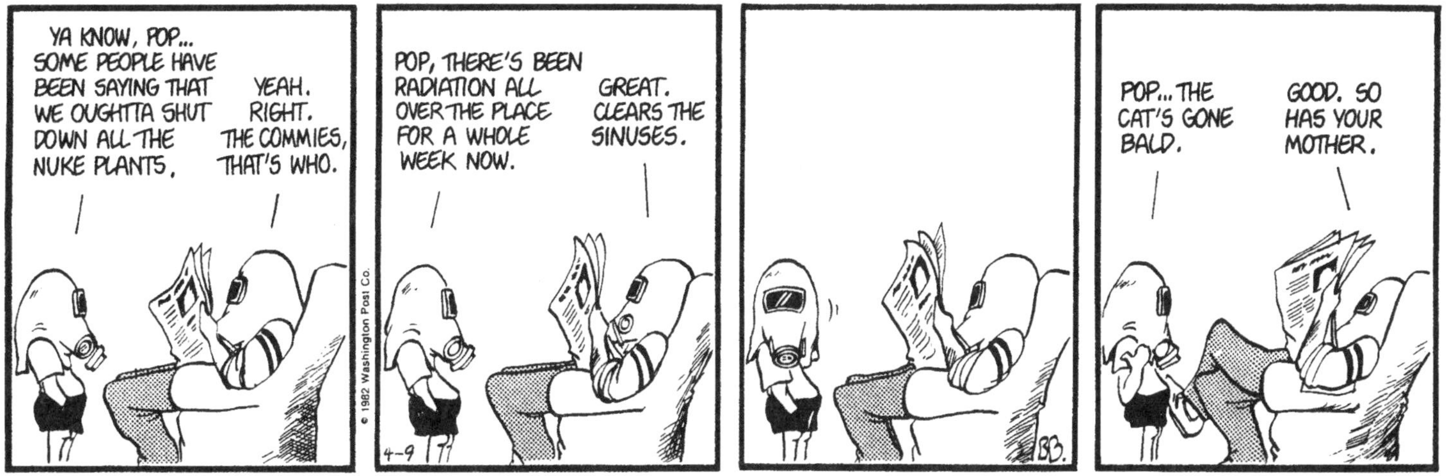
YA KNOW, POP... SOME PEOPLE HAVE BEEN SAYING THAT WE OUGHTTA SHUT DOWN ALL THE NUKE PLANTS.
YEAH. RIGHT. THE COMMIES, THAT'S WHO.
© 1982 Washington Post Co.
POP, THERE'S BEEN RADIATION ALL OVER THE PLACE FOR A WHOLE WEEK NOW.
GREAT. CLEARS THE SINUSES.
4-9
POP... THE CAT'S GONE BALD.
GOOD. SO HAS YOUR MOTHER.

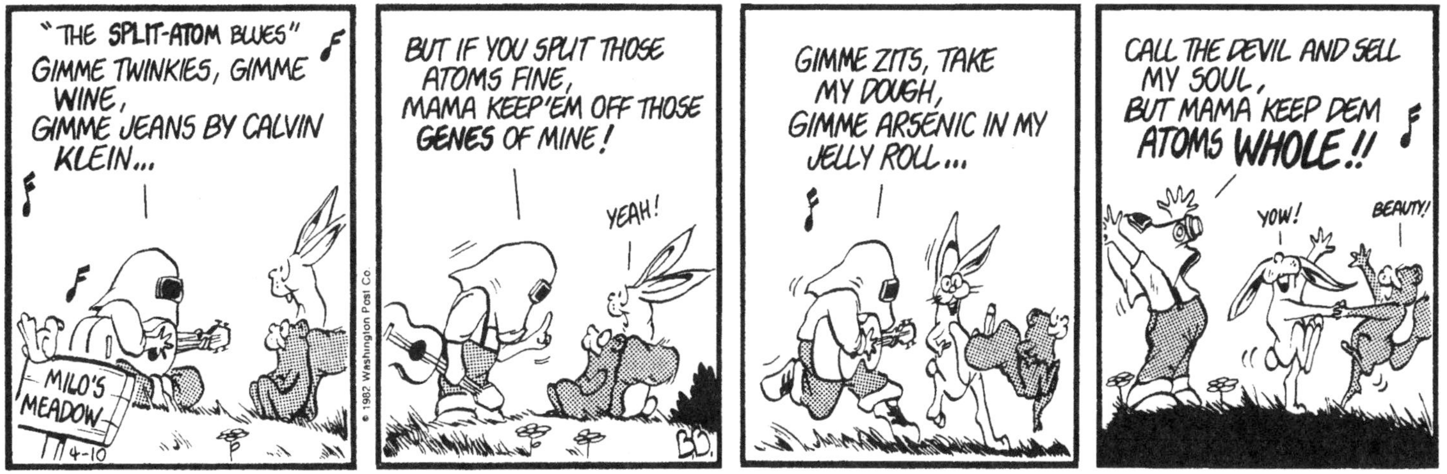
"THE SPLIT-ATOM BLUES"
GIMME TWINKIES, GIMME WINE, GIMME JEANS BY CALVIN KLEIN...
MILO'S MEADOW
4-10
© 1982 Washington Post Co.
BUT IF YOU SPLIT THOSE ATOMS FINE, MAMA KEEP'EM OFF THOSE GENES OF MINE!
YEAH!
GIMME ZITS, TAKE MY DOUGH, GIMME ARSENIC IN MY JELLY ROLL...
CALL THE DEVIL AND SELL MY SOUL, BUT MAMA KEEP DEM ATOMS WHOLE!!
YOW!
BEAUTY!

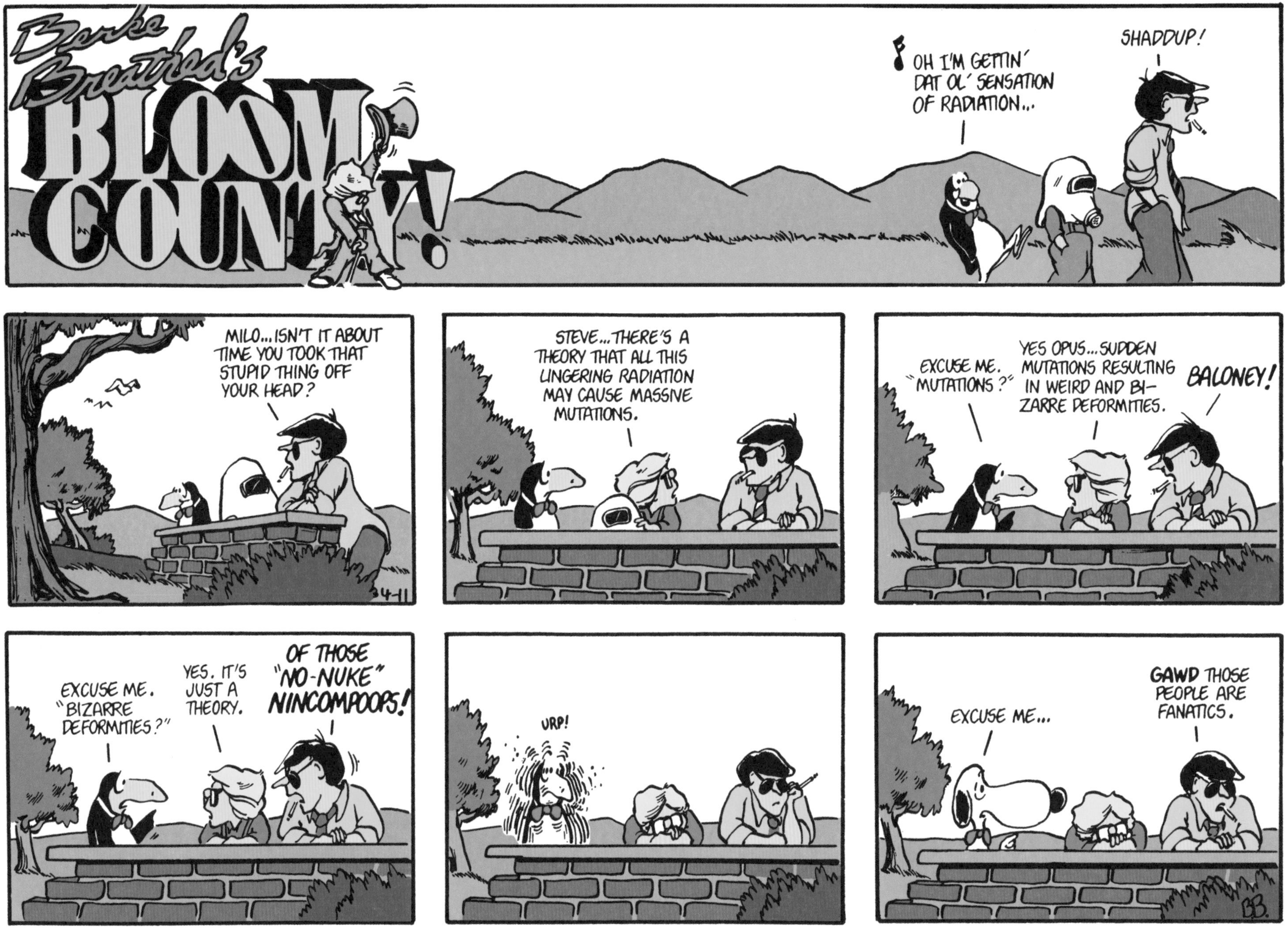
Berke Breathed's
BLOOM COUNTY!
OH I'M GETTIN' DAT OL' SENSATION OF RADIATION...
SHADDUP!
MILO...ISN'T IT ABOUT TIME YOU TOOK THAT STUPID THING OFF YOUR HEAD?
4-11
STEVE...THERE'S A THEORY THAT ALL THIS LINGERING RADIATION MAY CAUSE MASSIVE MUTATIONS.
EXCUSE ME. "MUTATIONS?"
YES OPUS...SUDDEN MUTATIONS RESULTING IN WEIRD AND BIZARRE DEFORMITIES.
BALONEY!
EXCUSE ME. "BIZARRE DEFORMITIES?"
YES. IT'S JUST A THEORY.
OF THOSE "NO-NUKE" NINCOMPOOPS!
URP!
EXCUSE ME...
GAWD THOSE PEOPLE ARE FANATICS.
B.B.

April 11, 1982

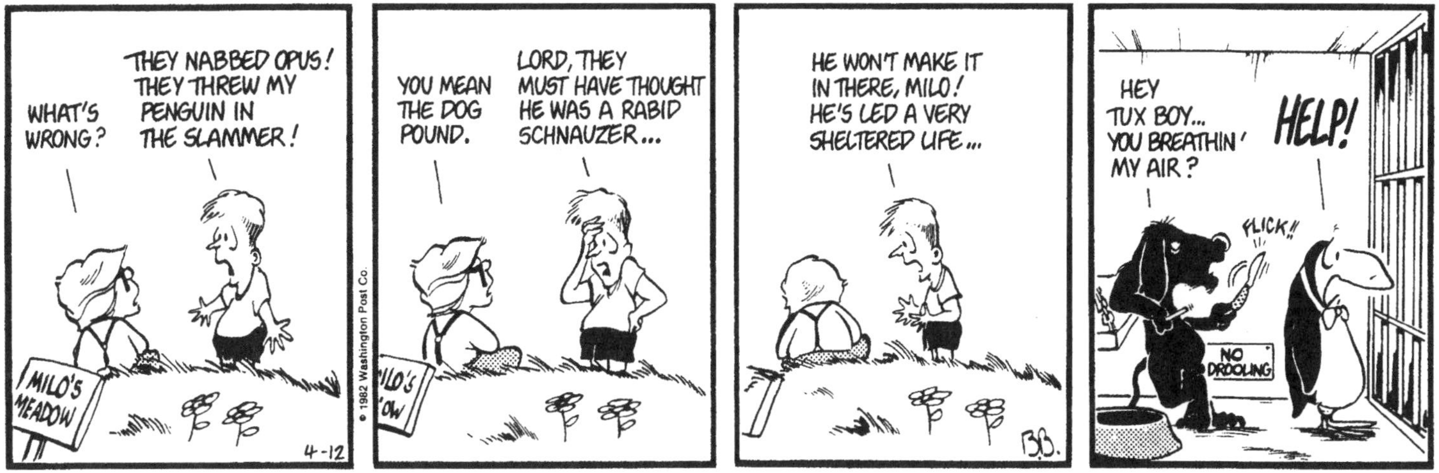
WHAT'S WRONG?
THEY NABBED OPUS! THEY THREW MY PENGUIN IN THE SLAMMER!
MILO'S MEADOW
4-12
© 1982 Washington Post Co.
YOU MEAN THE DOG POUND.
LORD, THEY MUST HAVE THOUGHT HE WAS A RABID SCHNAUZER...
HE WON'T MAKE IT IN THERE, MILO! HE'S LED A VERY SHELTERED LIFE...
B.B.
HEY TUX BOY... YOU BREATHIN' MY AIR?
HELP!
FLICK!!
NO DROOLING

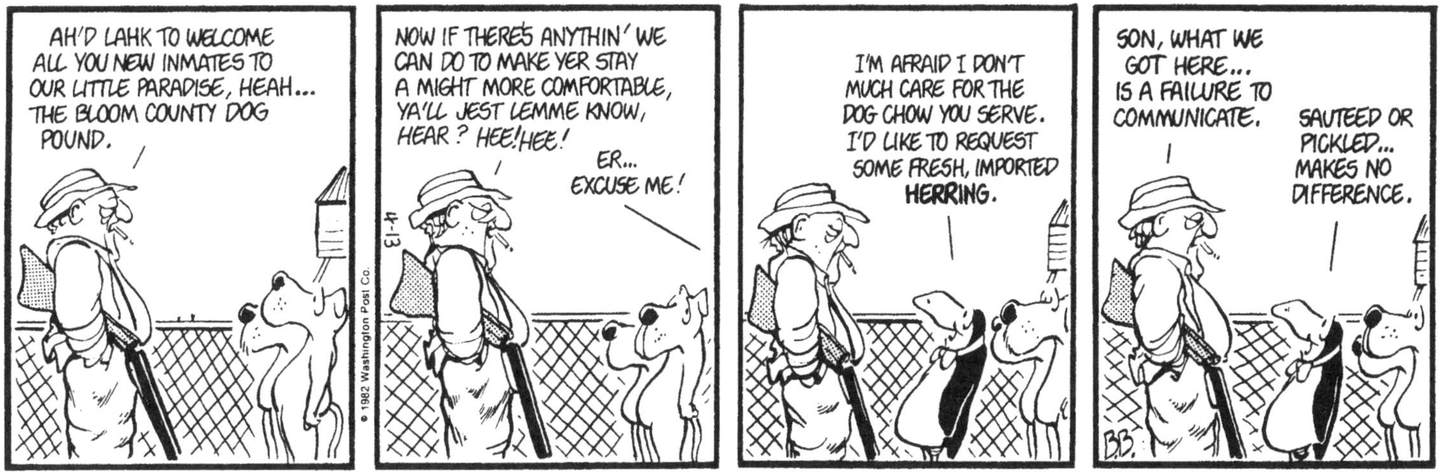
AH'D LAHK TO WELCOME ALL YOU NEW INMATES TO OUR LITTLE PARADISE, HEAH... THE BLOOM COUNTY DOG POUND.
NOW IF THERE'S ANYTHIN' WE CAN DO TO MAKE YER STAY A MIGHT MORE COMFORTABLE, YA'LL JEST LEMME KNOW, HEAR? HEE! HEE!
4-13
© 1982 Washington Post Co.
ER... EXCUSE ME!
I'M AFRAID I DON'T MUCH CARE FOR THE DOG CHOW YOU SERVE. I'D LIKE TO REQUEST SOME FRESH, IMPORTED HERRING.
SON, WHAT WE GOT HERE... IS A FAILURE TO COMMUNICATE.
SAUTEED OR PICKLED... MAKES NO DIFFERENCE.
B.B.

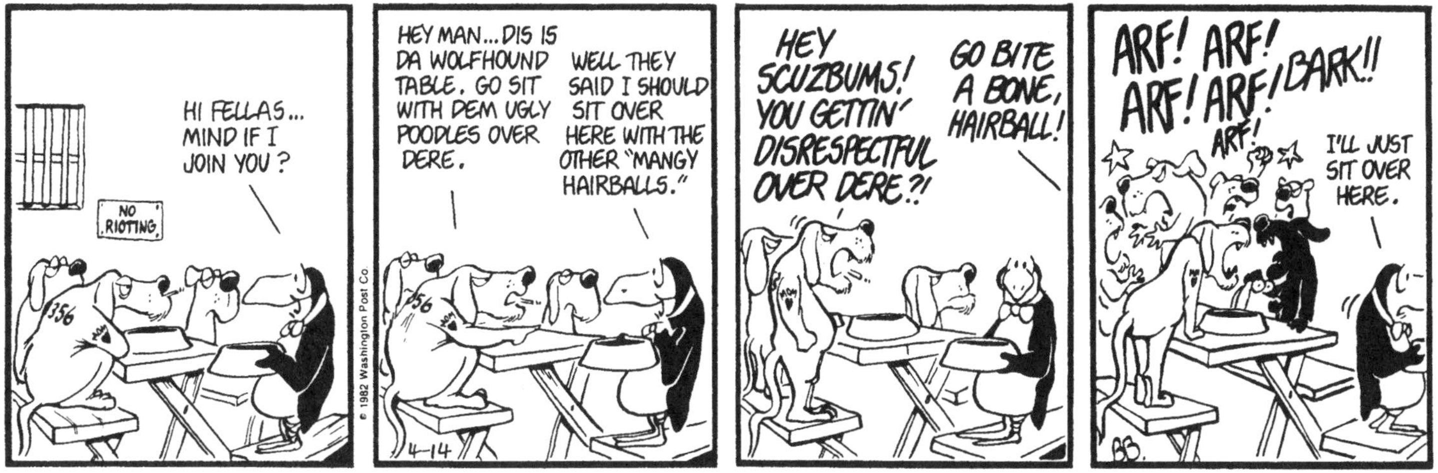
HI FELLAS... MIND IF I JOIN YOU?
NO RIOTING
356
© 1982 Washington Post Co.
HEY MAN... DIS IS DA WOLFHOUND TABLE. GO SIT WITH DEM UGLY POODLES OVER DERE.
WELL THEY SAID I SHOULD SIT OVER HERE WITH THE OTHER "MANGY HAIRBALLS."
4-14
HEY SCUZBUMS! YOU GETTIN' DISRESPECTFUL OVER DERE?!
GO BITE A BONE, HAIRBALL!
ARF! ARF! ARF! ARF! BARK!!
ARF!
I'LL JUST SIT OVER HERE.
B.B.

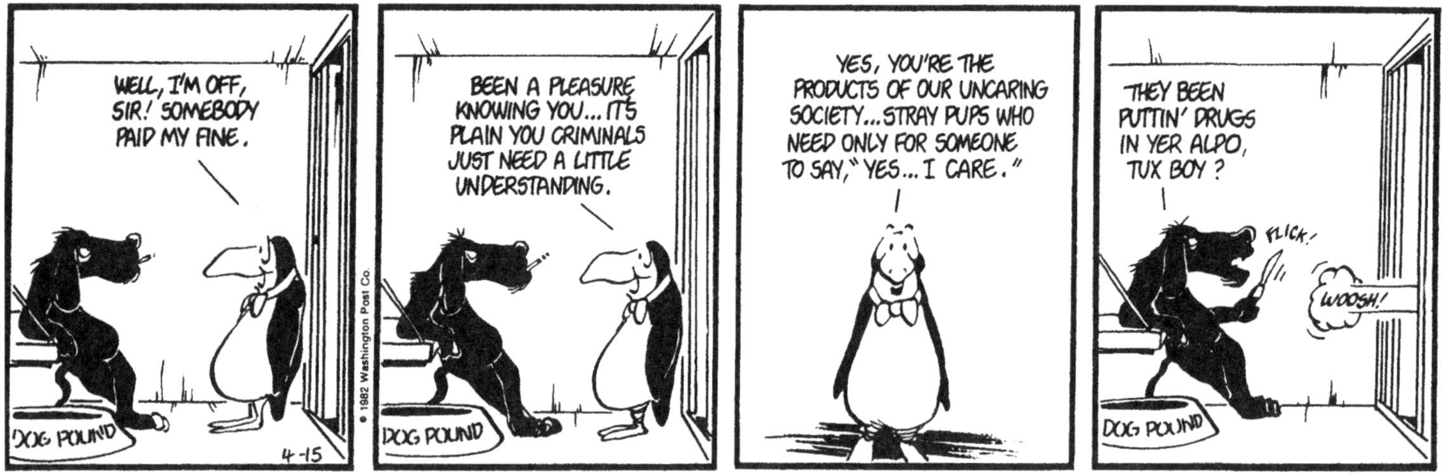
WELL, I'M OFF, SIR! SOMEBODY PAID MY FINE.
DOG POUND
4-15
© 1982 Washington Post Co.
BEEN A PLEASURE KNOWING YOU... IT'S PLAIN YOU CRIMINALS JUST NEED A LITTLE UNDERSTANDING.
DOG POUND
YES, YOU'RE THE PRODUCTS OF OUR UNCARING SOCIETY... STRAY PUPS WHO NEED ONLY FOR SOMEONE TO SAY, "YES... I CARE."
THEY BEEN PUTTIN' DRUGS IN YER ALPO, TUX BOY ?
FLICK!
WOOSH!
DOG POUND

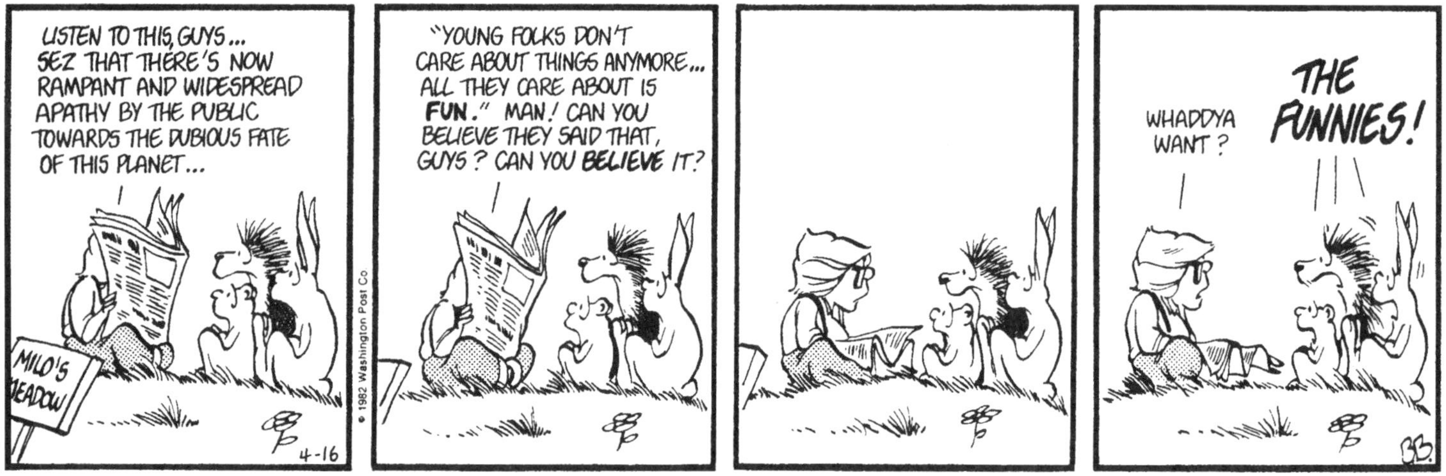
LISTEN TO THIS, GUYS... SEZ THAT THERE'S NOW RAMPANT AND WIDESPREAD APATHY BY THE PUBLIC TOWARDS THE DUBIOUS FATE OF THIS PLANET...
MILO'S MEADOW
4-16
© 1982 Washington Post Co.
"YOUNG FOLKS DON'T CARE ABOUT THINGS ANYMORE... ALL THEY CARE ABOUT IS **FUN**." MAN! CAN YOU BELIEVE THEY SAID THAT, GUYS ? CAN YOU **BELIEVE** IT?
WHADDYA WANT ?
THE FUNNIES!
B.B.

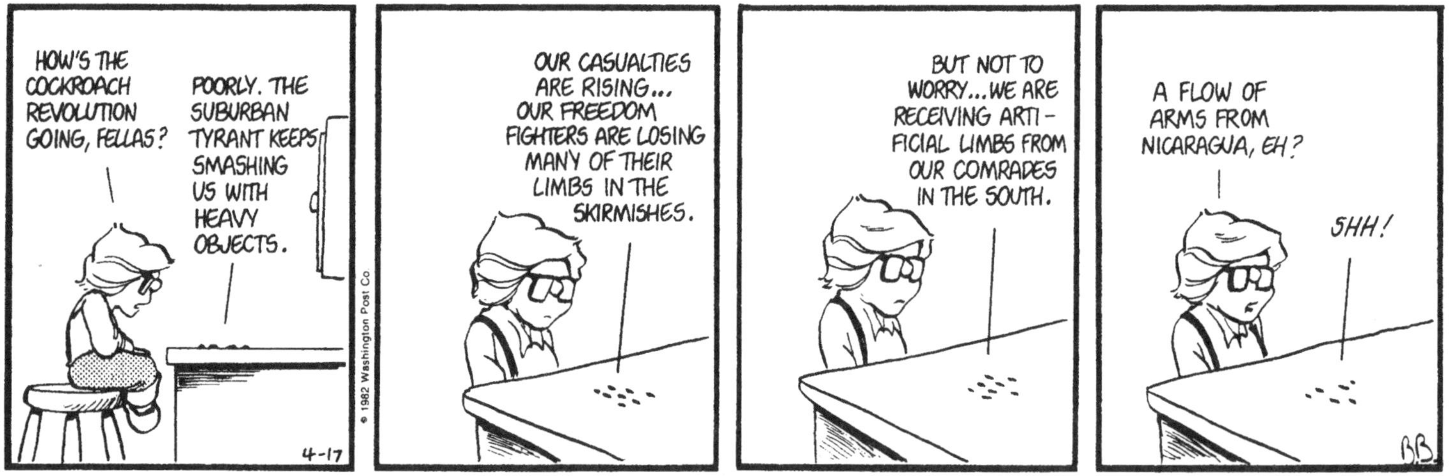
HOW'S THE COCKROACH REVOLUTION GOING, FELLAS?
POORLY. THE SUBURBAN TYRANT KEEPS SMASHING US WITH HEAVY OBJECTS.
4-17
© 1982 Washington Post Co.
OUR CASUALTIES ARE RISING... OUR FREEDOM FIGHTERS ARE LOSING MANY OF THEIR LIMBS IN THE SKIRMISHES.
BUT NOT TO WORRY... WE ARE RECEIVING ARTI-FICIAL LIMBS FROM OUR COMRADES IN THE SOUTH.
A FLOW OF ARMS FROM NICARAGUA, EH?
SHH!
B.B.

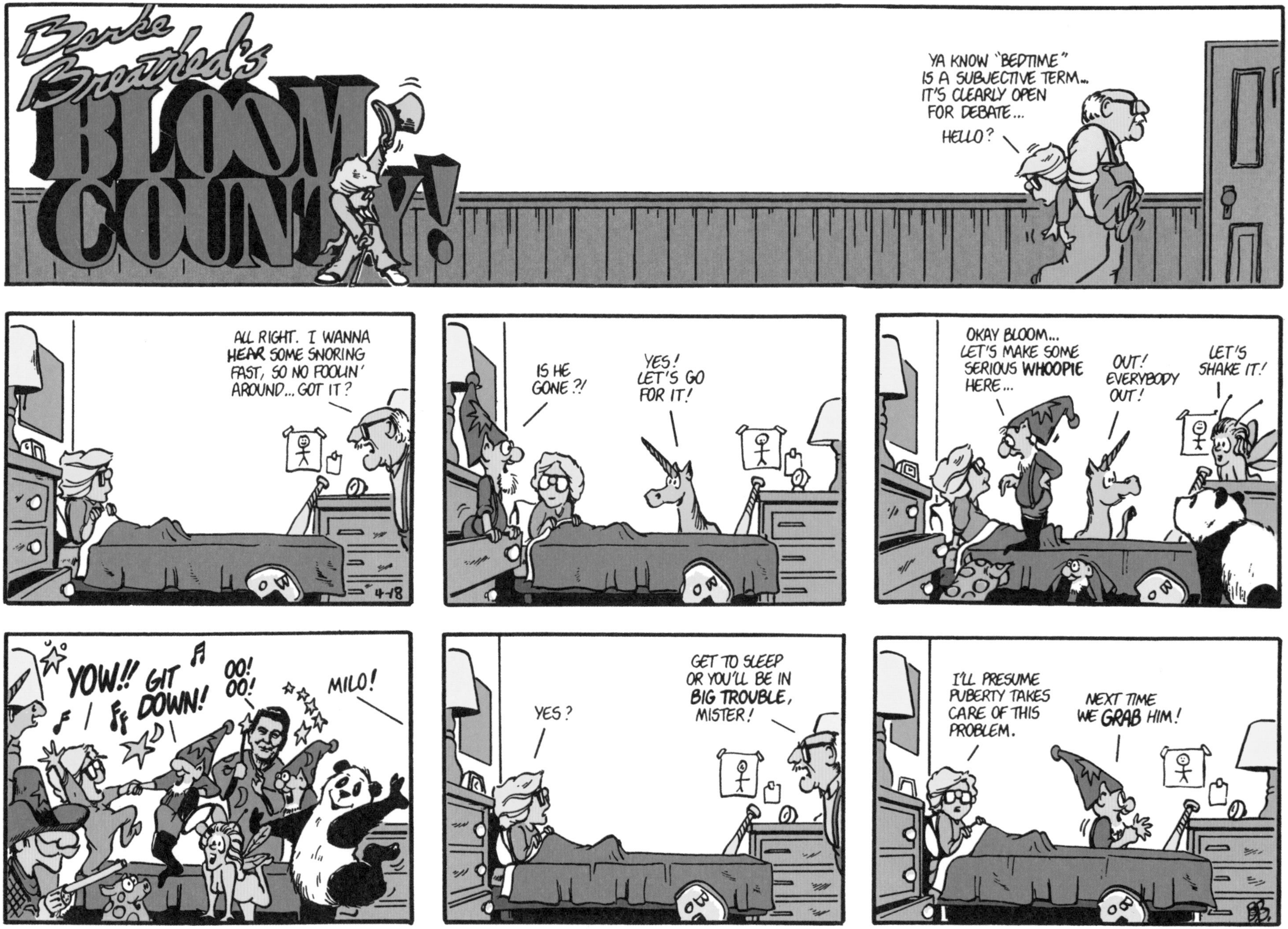
Berke Breathed's
BLOOM COUNTY!
YA KNOW "BEDTIME" IS A SUBJECTIVE TERM... IT'S CLEARLY OPEN FOR DEBATE...
HELLO?
ALL RIGHT. I WANNA HEAR SOME SNORING FAST, SO NO FOOLIN' AROUND... GOT IT?
4-18
IS HE GONE?!
YES! LET'S GO FOR IT!
OKAY BLOOM... LET'S MAKE SOME SERIOUS WHOOPIE HERE...
OUT! EVERYBODY OUT!
LET'S SHAKE IT!
YOW!!
GIT DOWN!
OO! OO!
MILO!
YES?
GET TO SLEEP OR YOU'LL BE IN BIG TROUBLE, MISTER!
I'LL PRESUME PUBERTY TAKES CARE OF THIS PROBLEM.
NEXT TIME WE GRAB HIM!

April 18, 1982

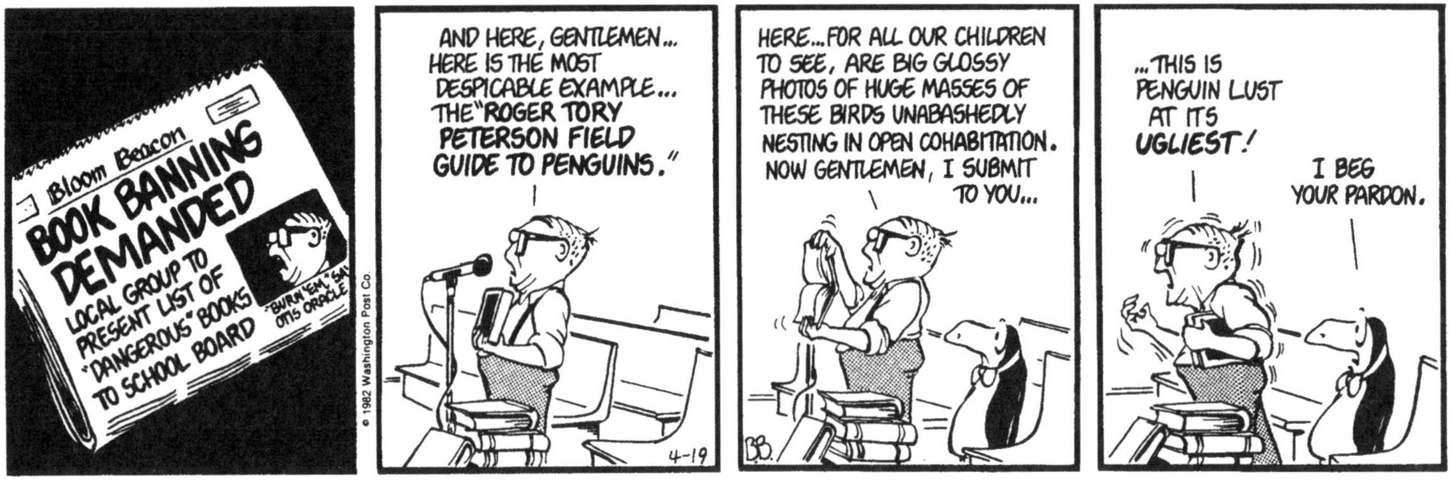
Bloom Beacon
BOOK BANNING DEMANDED
LOCAL GROUP TO PRESENT LIST OF "DANGEROUS" BOOKS TO SCHOOL BOARD
"BURN 'EM,"
OTIS ORACLE
© 1982 Washington Post Co.
AND HERE, GENTLEMEN... HERE IS THE MOST DESPICABLE EXAMPLE... THE "**ROGER TORY PETERSON FIELD GUIDE TO PENGUINS**."
HERE... FOR ALL OUR CHILDREN TO SEE, ARE BIG GLOSSY PHOTOS OF HUGE MASSES OF THESE BIRDS UNABASHEDLY NESTING IN OPEN COHABITATION. NOW GENTLEMEN, I SUBMIT TO YOU...
...THIS IS PENGUIN LUST AT ITS **UGLIEST**!
I BEG YOUR PARDON.
4-19
BB.

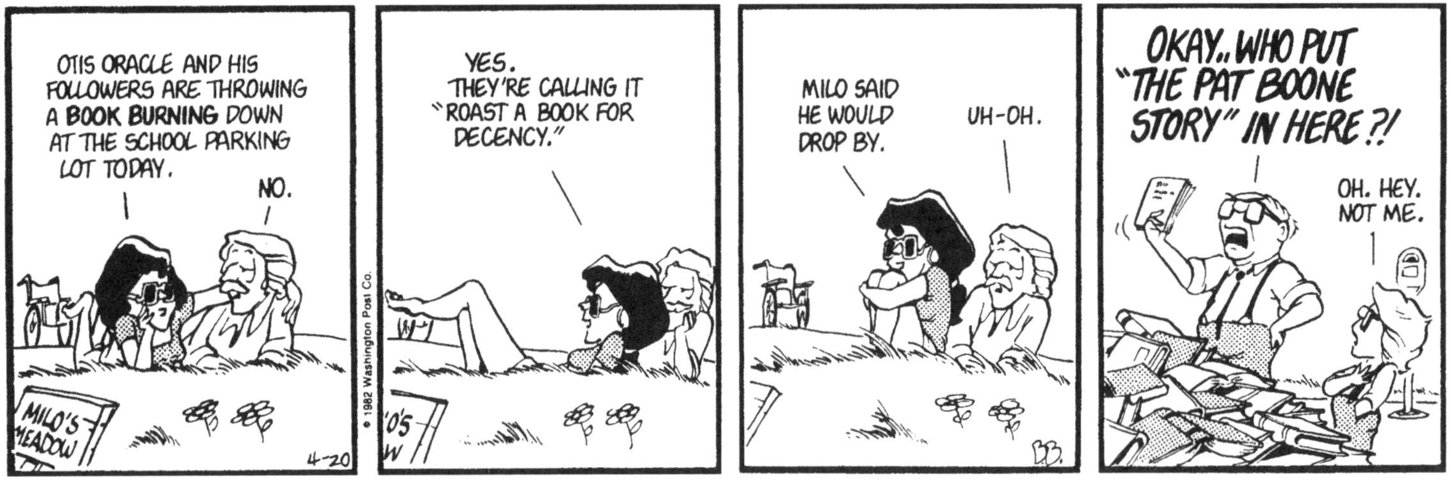
OTIS ORACLE AND HIS FOLLOWERS ARE THROWING A **BOOK BURNING** DOWN AT THE SCHOOL PARKING LOT TODAY.
NO.
MILO'S MEADOW
4-20
© 1982 Washington Post Co.
YES. THEY'RE CALLING IT "ROAST A BOOK FOR DECENCY."
MILO SAID HE WOULD DROP BY.
UH-OH.
BB.
OKAY.. WHO PUT "THE PAT BOONE STORY" IN HERE ?!
OH. HEY. NOT ME.

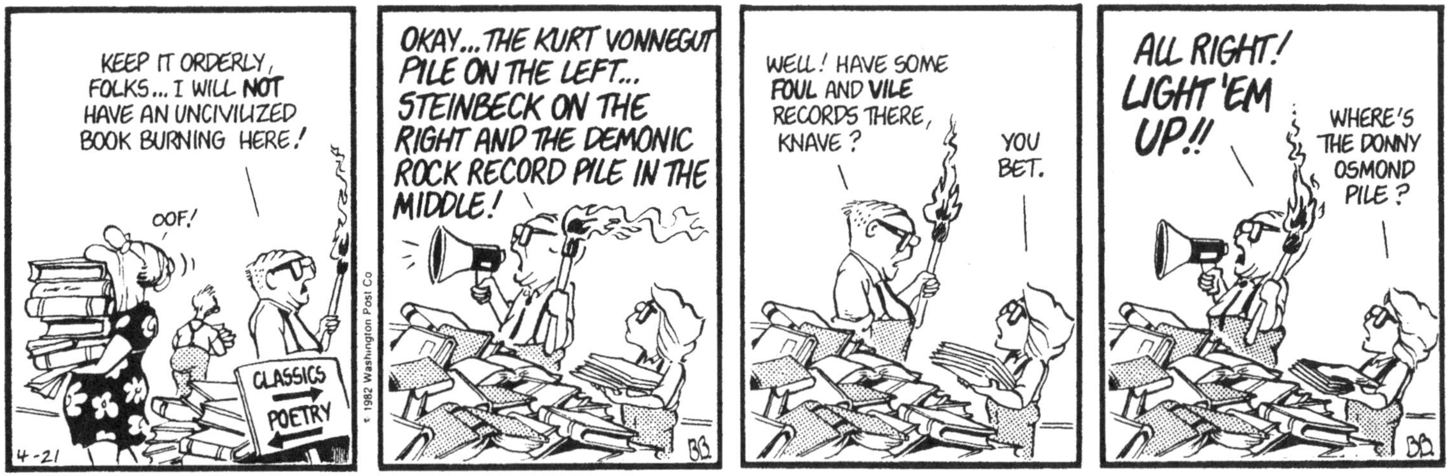
KEEP IT ORDERLY, FOLKS... I WILL **NOT** HAVE AN UNCIVILIZED BOOK BURNING HERE!
OOF!
CLASSICS
POETRY
4-21
© 1982 Washington Post Co.
OKAY... THE KURT VONNEGUT PILE ON THE LEFT... STEINBECK ON THE RIGHT AND THE DEMONIC ROCK RECORD PILE IN THE MIDDLE!
BB.
WELL! HAVE SOME **FOUL** AND **VILE** RECORDS THERE, KNAVE?
YOU BET.
ALL RIGHT! LIGHT 'EM UP!!
WHERE'S THE DONNY OSMOND PILE?
BB.

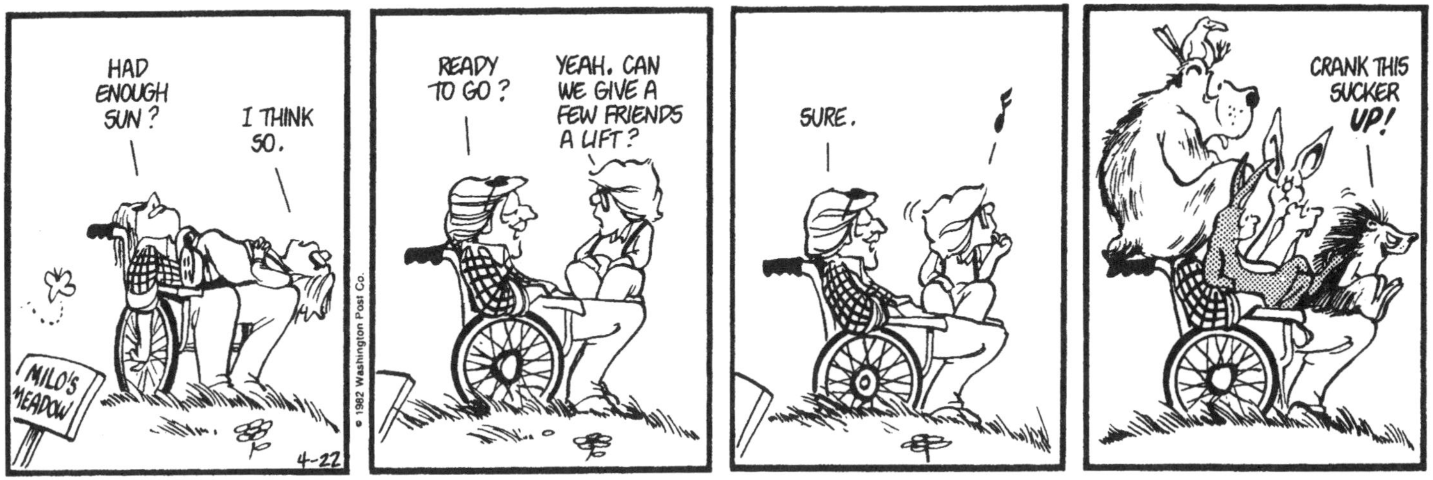
HAD ENOUGH SUN?
I THINK SO.
MILO'S MEADOW
4-22
© 1982 Washington Post Co.
READY TO GO?
YEAH. CAN WE GIVE A FEW FRIENDS A LIFT?
SURE.
CRANK THIS SUCKER UP!

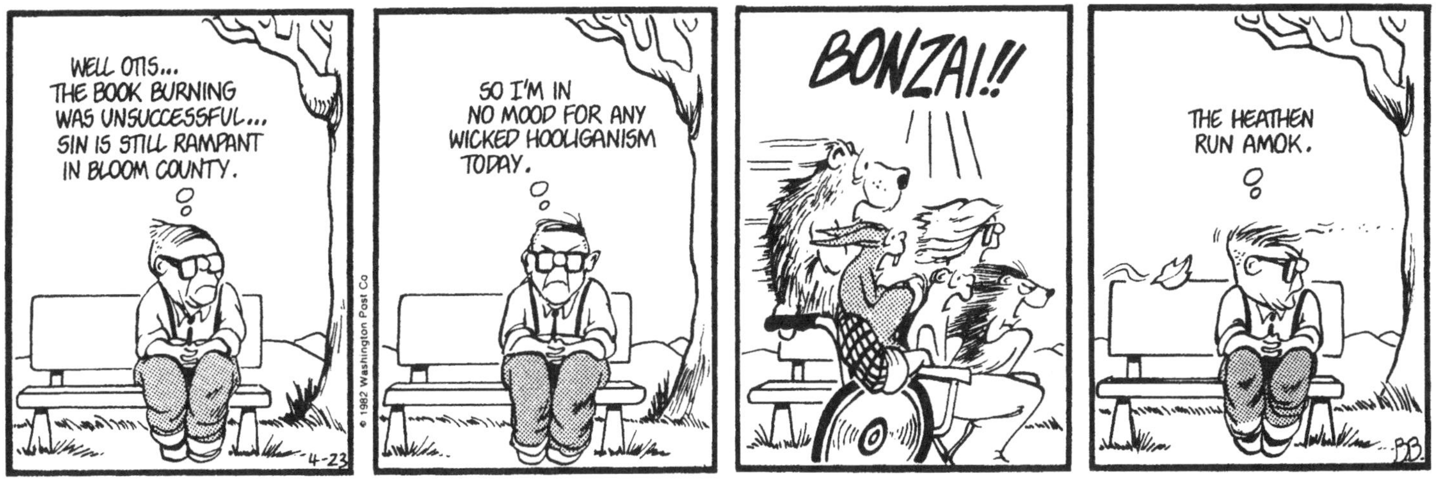
WELL OTIS... THE BOOK BURNING WAS UNSUCCESSFUL... SIN IS STILL RAMPANT IN BLOOM COUNTY.
4-23
© 1982 Washington Post Co.
SO I'M IN NO MOOD FOR ANY WICKED HOOLIGANISM TODAY.
BONZAI!!
THE HEATHEN RUN AMOK.
B.B.

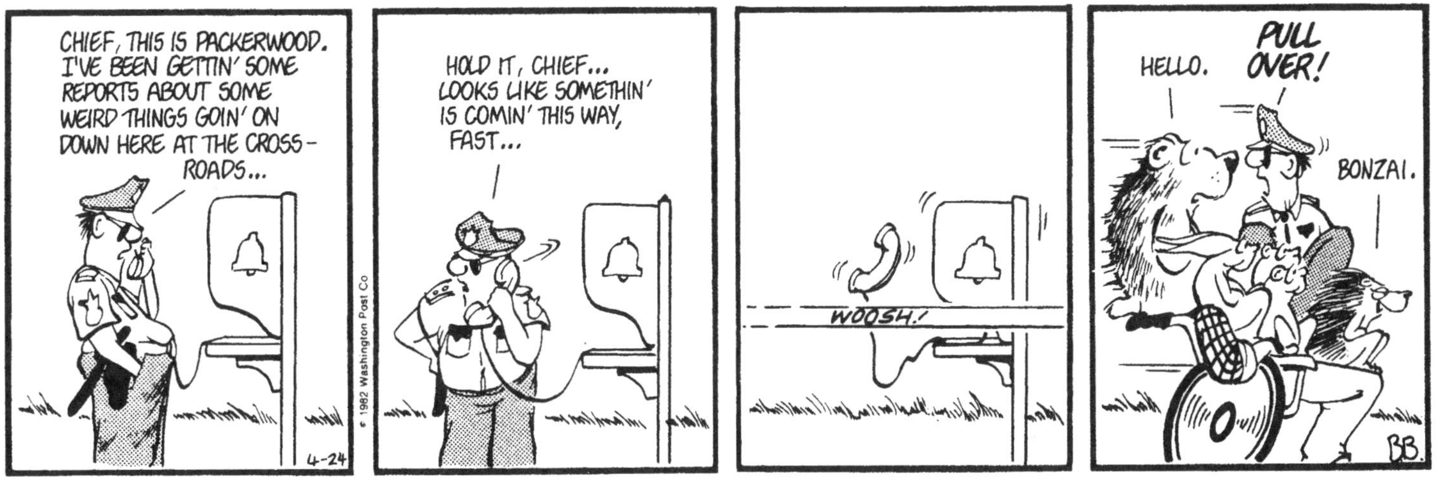
CHIEF, THIS IS PACKERWOOD. I'VE BEEN GETTIN' SOME REPORTS ABOUT SOME WEIRD THINGS GOIN' ON DOWN HERE AT THE CROSS-ROADS...
4-24
© 1982 Washington Post Co.
HOLD IT, CHIEF... LOOKS LIKE SOMETHIN' IS COMIN' THIS WAY, FAST...
WOOSH!
HELLO.
PULL OVER!
BONZAI.
B.B.

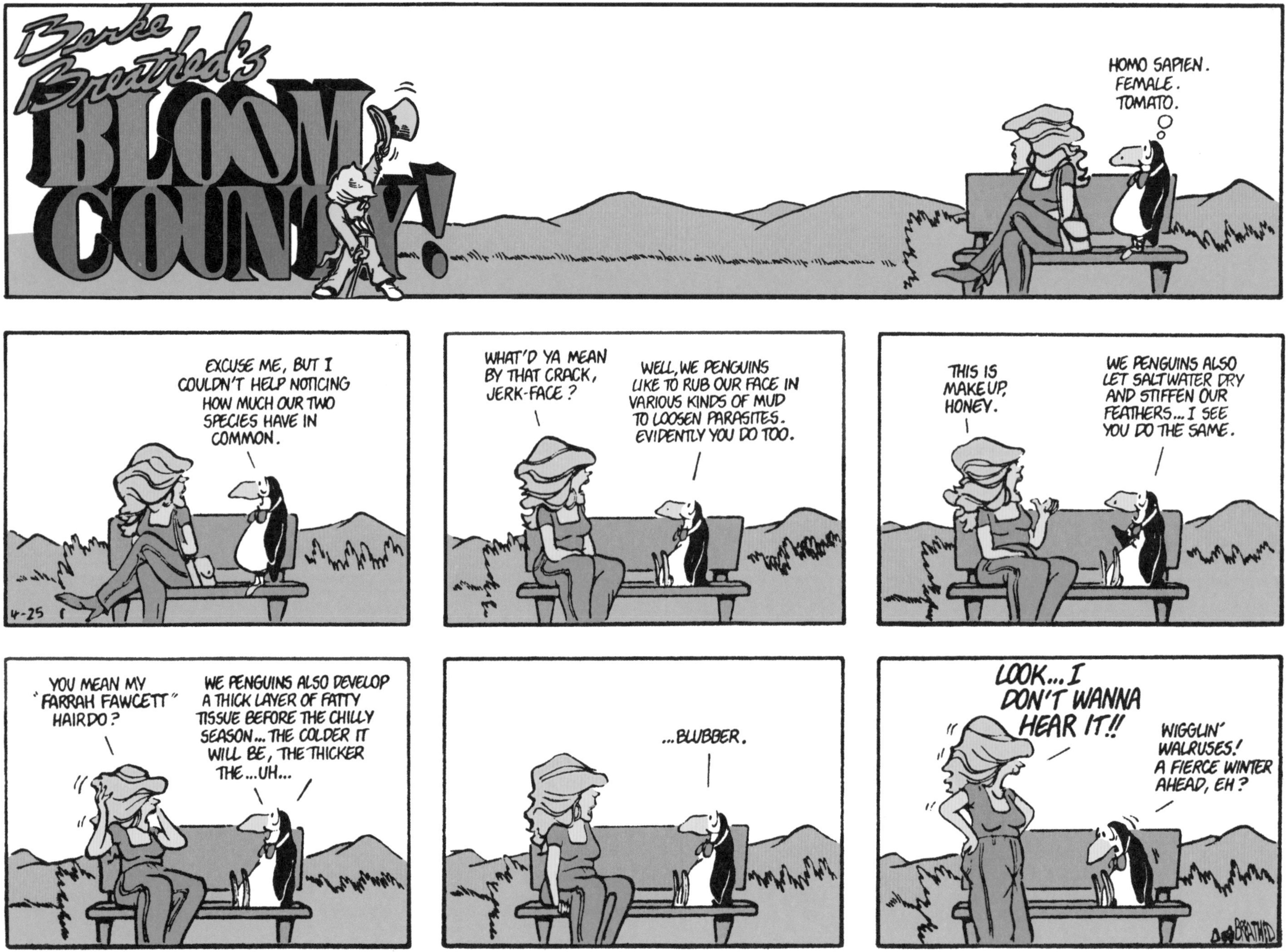
Berke Breathed's
BLOOM COUNTY!
HOMO SAPIEN. FEMALE. TOMATO.
4-25
EXCUSE ME, BUT I COULDN'T HELP NOTICING HOW MUCH OUR TWO SPECIES HAVE IN COMMON.
WHAT'D YA MEAN BY THAT CRACK, JERK-FACE?
WELL, WE PENGUINS LIKE TO RUB OUR FACE IN VARIOUS KINDS OF MUD TO LOOSEN PARASITES. EVIDENTLY YOU DO TOO.
THIS IS MAKEUP, HONEY.
WE PENGUINS ALSO LET SALTWATER DRY AND STIFFEN OUR FEATHERS... I SEE YOU DO THE SAME.
YOU MEAN MY "FARRAH FAWCETT" HAIRDO?
WE PENGUINS ALSO DEVELOP A THICK LAYER OF FATTY TISSUE BEFORE THE CHILLY SEASON... THE COLDER IT WILL BE, THE THICKER THE... UH...
...BLUBBER.
LOOK... I DON'T WANNA HEAR IT!!
WIGGLIN' WALRUSES! A FIERCE WINTER AHEAD, EH?
BREATHED

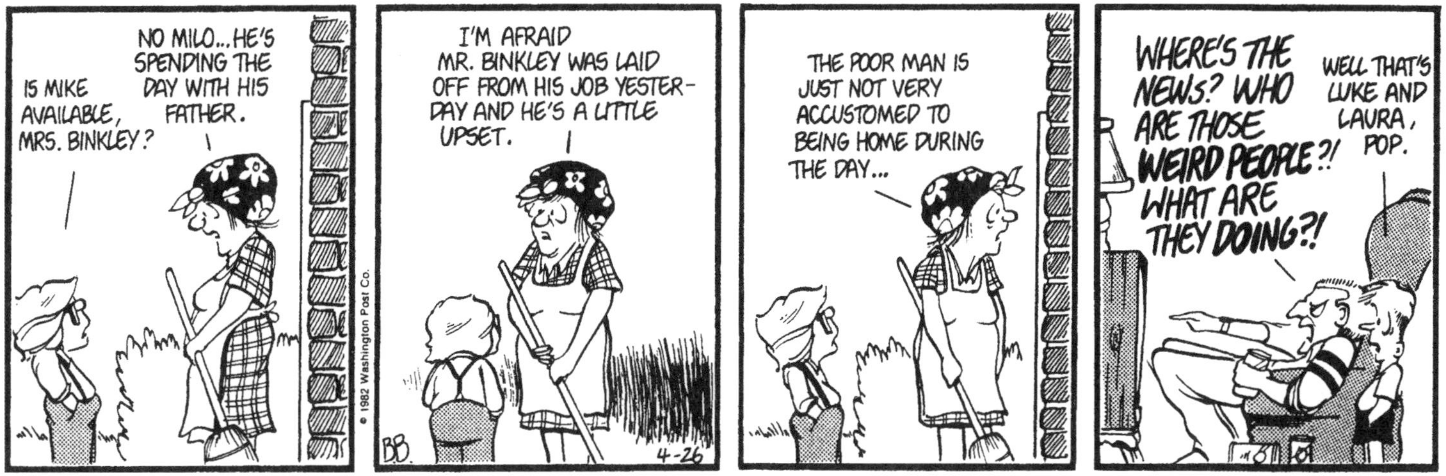
IS MIKE AVAILABLE, MRS. BINKLEY?
NO MILO...HE'S SPENDING THE DAY WITH HIS FATHER.
© 1982 Washington Post Co.
I'M AFRAID MR. BINKLEY WAS LAID OFF FROM HIS JOB YESTERDAY AND HE'S A LITTLE UPSET.
BB.
4-26
THE POOR MAN IS JUST NOT VERY ACCUSTOMED TO BEING HOME DURING THE DAY...
WHERE'S THE NEWS? WHO ARE THOSE WEIRD PEOPLE?! WHAT ARE THEY DOING?!
WELL THAT'S LUKE AND LAURA, POP.

Luke and Laura Spencer, the most popular lovers in soap opera history, boasted 30 million viewers in 1981 when they were wed on *General Hospital*.

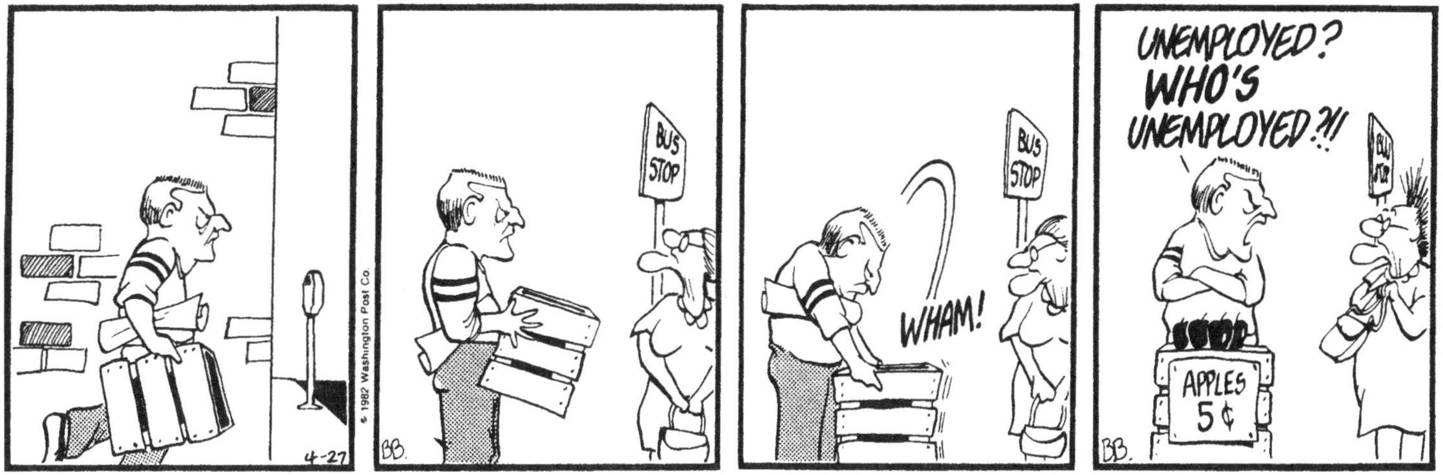
4-27
© 1982 Washington Post Co.
BB.
BUS STOP
WHAM!
BUS STOP
UNEMPLOYED? WHO'S UNEMPLOYED?!!
APPLES 5¢
BB.

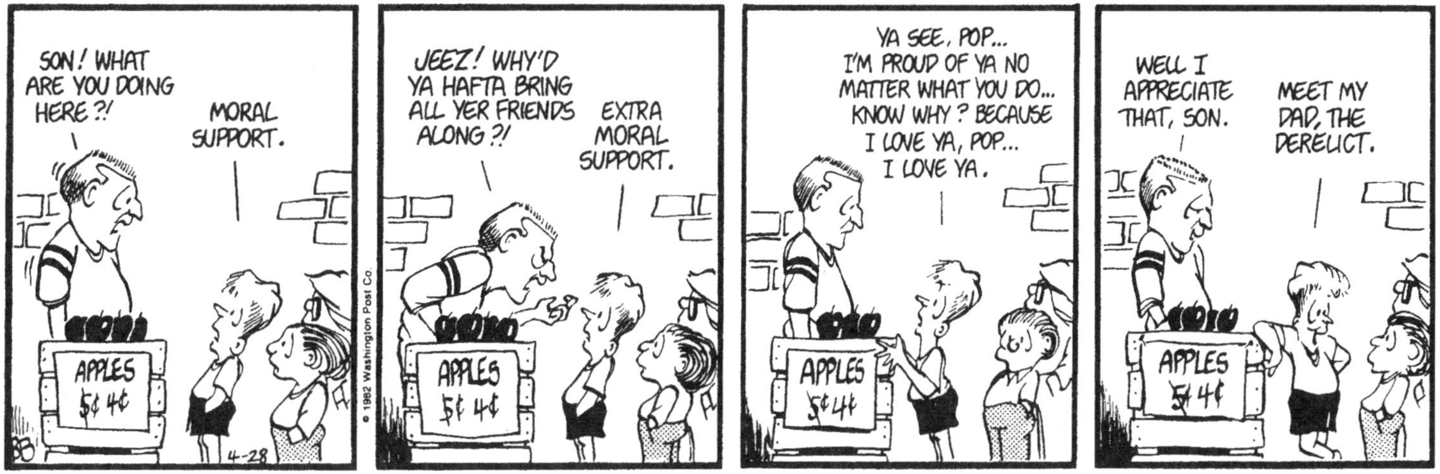
SON! WHAT ARE YOU DOING HERE?!
MORAL SUPPORT.
APPLES 5¢ 4¢
BB
4-28
© 1982 Washington Post Co.
JEEZ! WHY'D YA HAFTA BRING ALL YER FRIENDS ALONG?!
EXTRA MORAL SUPPORT.
APPLES 5¢ 4¢
YA SEE, POP... I'M PROUD OF YA NO MATTER WHAT YOU DO... KNOW WHY? BECAUSE I LOVE YA, POP... I LOVE YA.
APPLES 5¢ 4¢
WELL I APPRECIATE THAT, SON.
MEET MY DAD, THE DERELICT.
APPLES 5¢ 4¢

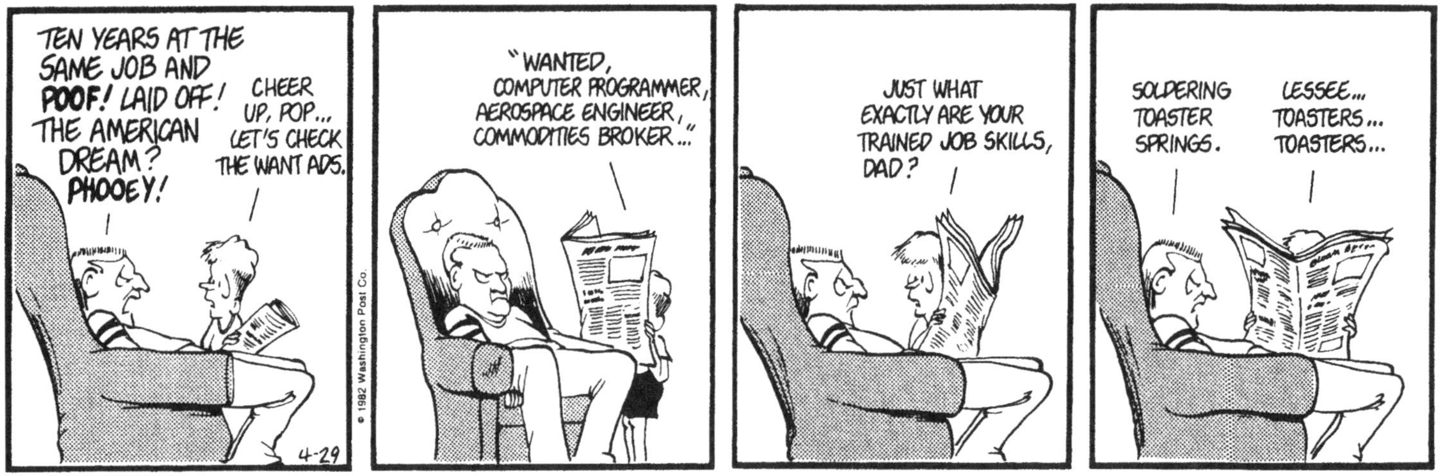
TEN YEARS AT THE SAME JOB AND POOF! LAID OFF! THE AMERICAN DREAM? PHOOEY!
CHEER UP, POP... LET'S CHECK THE WANT ADS.
4-29
© 1982 Washington Post Co
"WANTED, COMPUTER PROGRAMMER, AEROSPACE ENGINEER, COMMODITIES BROKER..."
JUST WHAT EXACTLY ARE YOUR TRAINED JOB SKILLS, DAD?
SOLDERING TOASTER SPRINGS.
LESSEE... TOASTERS... TOASTERS...

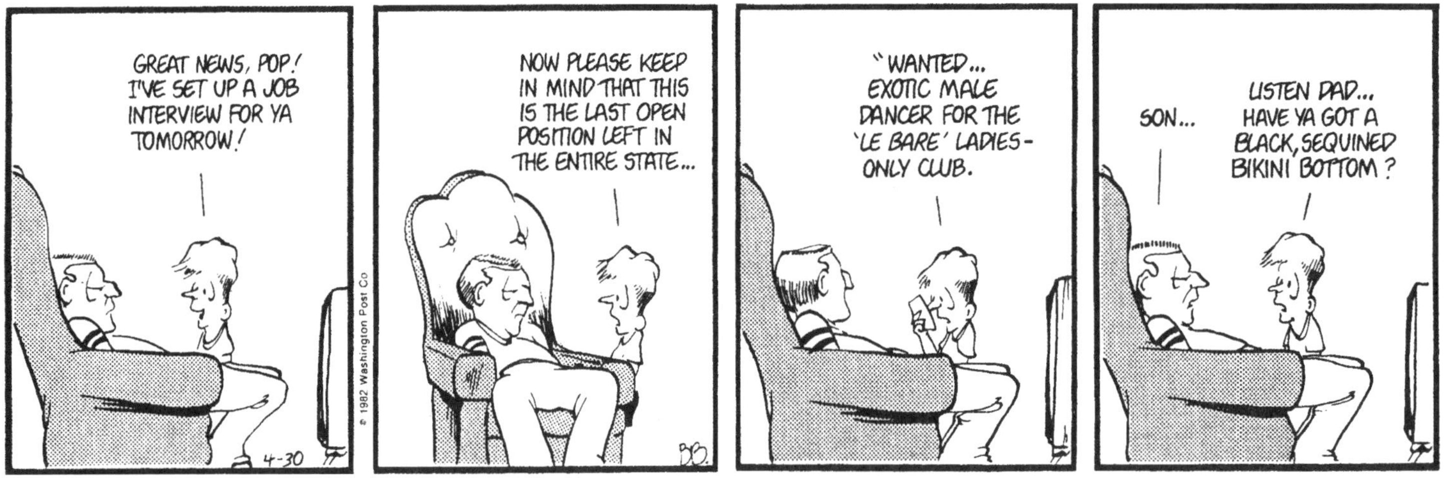
GREAT NEWS, POP! I'VE SET UP A JOB INTERVIEW FOR YA TOMORROW!
4-30
© 1982 Washington Post Co
NOW PLEASE KEEP IN MIND THAT THIS IS THE LAST OPEN POSITION LEFT IN THE ENTIRE STATE...
"WANTED... EXOTIC MALE DANCER FOR THE 'LE BARE' LADIES-ONLY CLUB.
SON...
LISTEN DAD... HAVE YA GOT A BLACK, SEQUINED BIKINI BOTTOM?

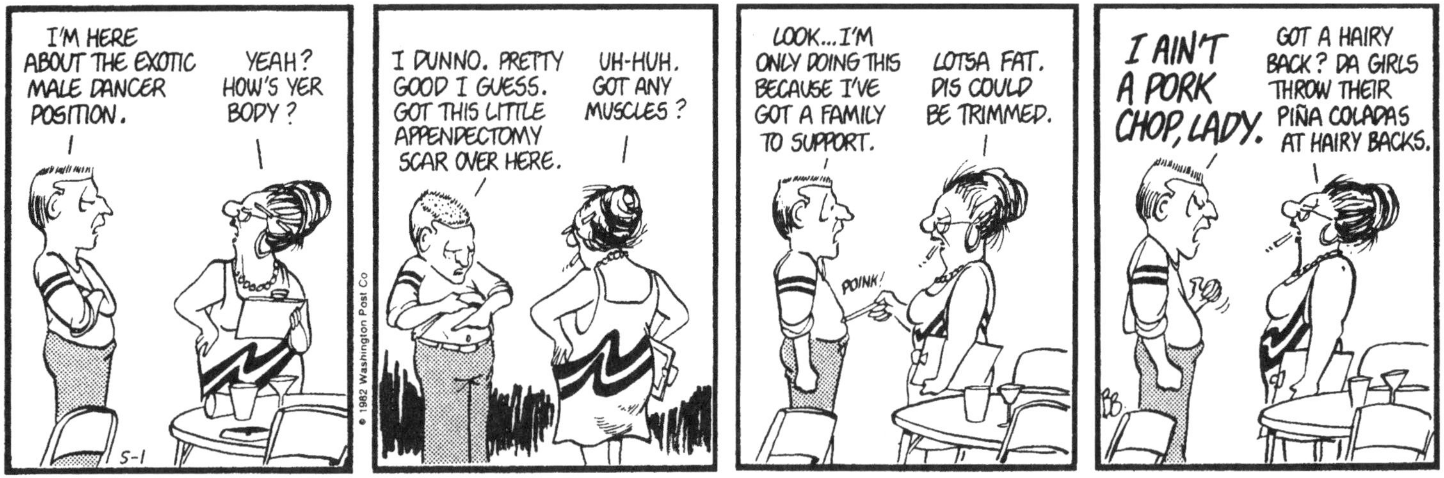
I'M HERE ABOUT THE EXOTIC MALE DANCER POSITION.
YEAH? HOW'S YER BODY?
5-1
© 1982 Washington Post Co
I DUNNO. PRETTY GOOD I GUESS. GOT THIS LITTLE APPENDECTOMY SCAR OVER HERE.
UH-HUH. GOT ANY MUSCLES?
LOOK... I'M ONLY DOING THIS BECAUSE I'VE GOT A FAMILY TO SUPPORT.
LOTSA FAT. DIS COULD BE TRIMMED.
POINK!
I AIN'T A PORK CHOP, LADY.
GOT A HAIRY BACK? DA GIRLS THROW THEIR PIÑA COLADAS AT HAIRY BACKS.

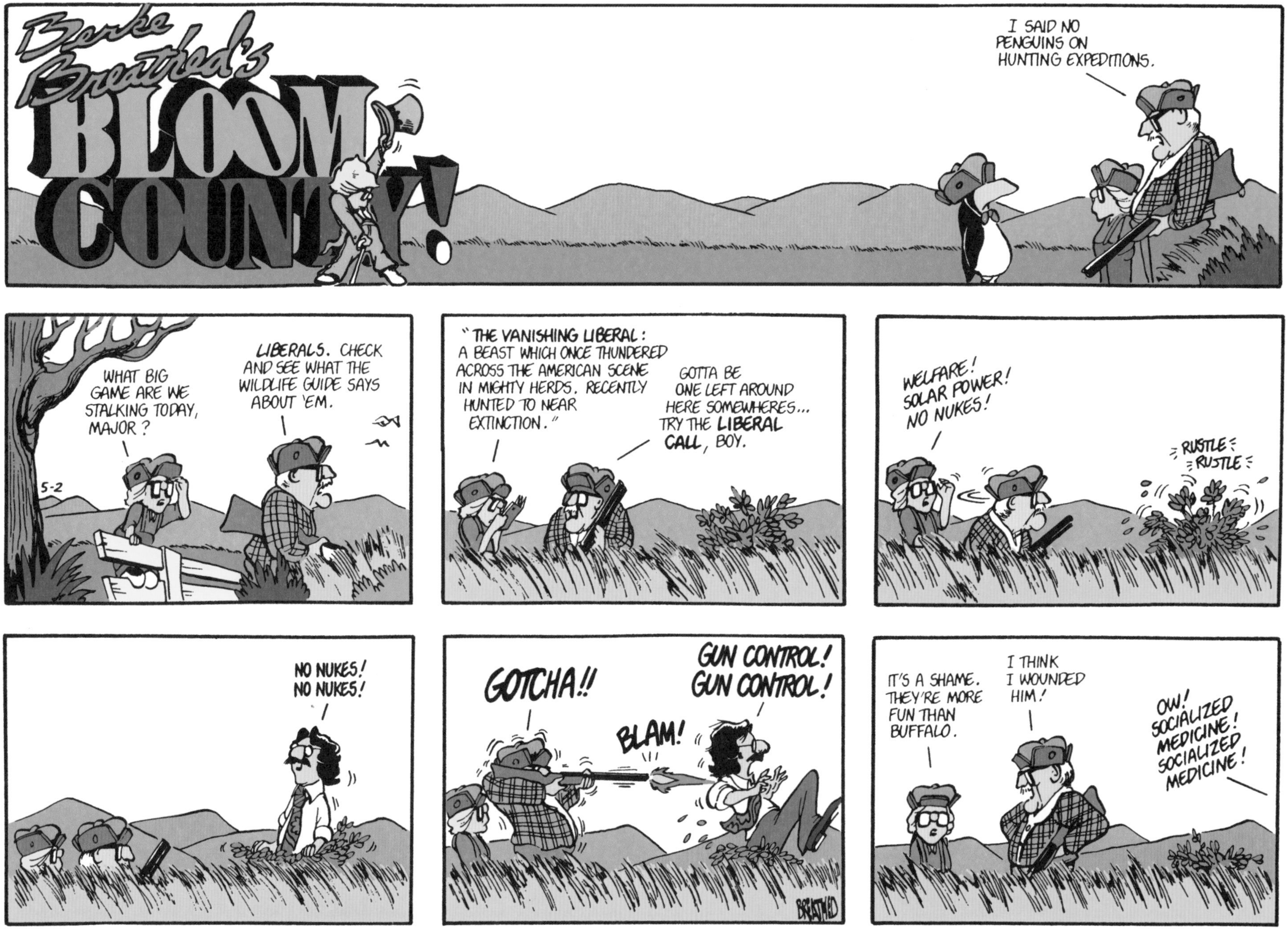
Berke Breathed's
BLOOM COUNTY!
I SAID NO PENGUINS ON HUNTING EXPEDITIONS.
5-2
WHAT BIG GAME ARE WE STALKING TODAY, MAJOR?
LIBERALS. CHECK AND SEE WHAT THE WILDLIFE GUIDE SAYS ABOUT 'EM.
"THE VANISHING LIBERAL: A BEAST WHICH ONCE THUNDERED ACROSS THE AMERICAN SCENE IN MIGHTY HERDS. RECENTLY HUNTED TO NEAR EXTINCTION."
GOTTA BE ONE LEFT AROUND HERE SOMEWHERES... TRY THE LIBERAL CALL, BOY.
WELFARE! SOLAR POWER! NO NUKES!
RUSTLE RUSTLE
NO NUKES! NO NUKES!
GOTCHA!!
BLAM!
GUN CONTROL! GUN CONTROL!
BREATHED
IT'S A SHAME. THEY'RE MORE FUN THAN BUFFALO.
I THINK I WOUNDED HIM!
OW! SOCIALIZED MEDICINE! SOCIALIZED MEDICINE!

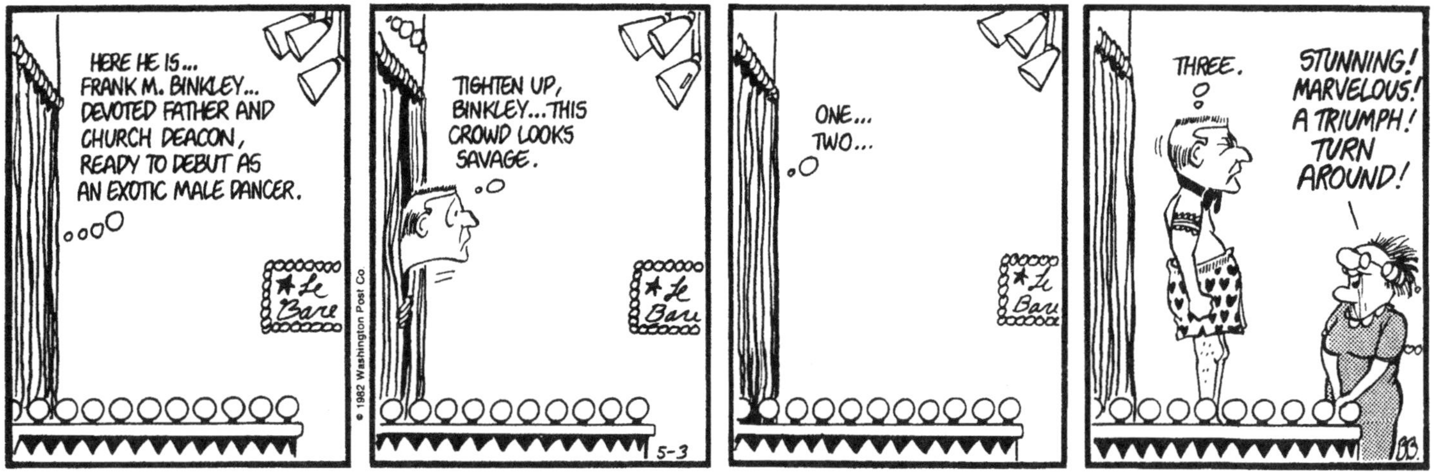
HERE HE IS... FRANK M. BINKLEY... DEVOTED FATHER AND CHURCH DEACON, READY TO DEBUT AS AN EXOTIC MALE DANCER.
Le Bare
© 1982 Washington Post Co.
TIGHTEN UP, BINKLEY... THIS CROWD LOOKS SAVAGE.
5-3
ONE... TWO...
THREE.
STUNNING! MARVELOUS! A TRIUMPH! TURN AROUND!
B.B.

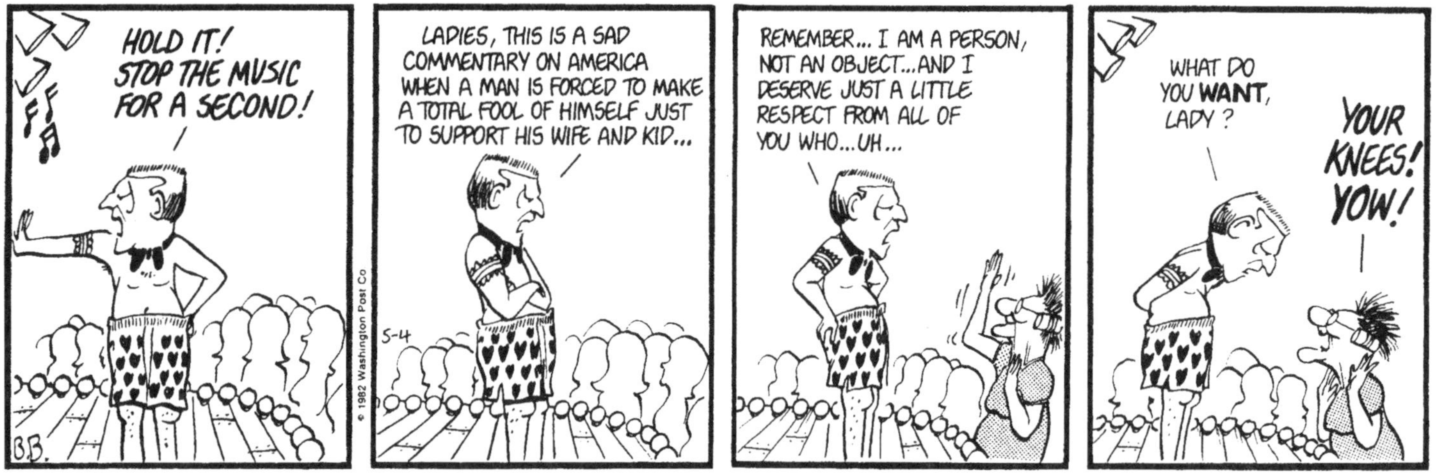
HOLD IT! STOP THE MUSIC FOR A SECOND!
B.B.
© 1982 Washington Post Co.
5-4
LADIES, THIS IS A SAD COMMENTARY ON AMERICA WHEN A MAN IS FORCED TO MAKE A TOTAL FOOL OF HIMSELF JUST TO SUPPORT HIS WIFE AND KID...
REMEMBER... I AM A PERSON, NOT AN OBJECT... AND I DESERVE JUST A LITTLE RESPECT FROM ALL OF YOU WHO... UH...
WHAT DO YOU **WANT**, LADY?
YOUR KNEES! YOW!

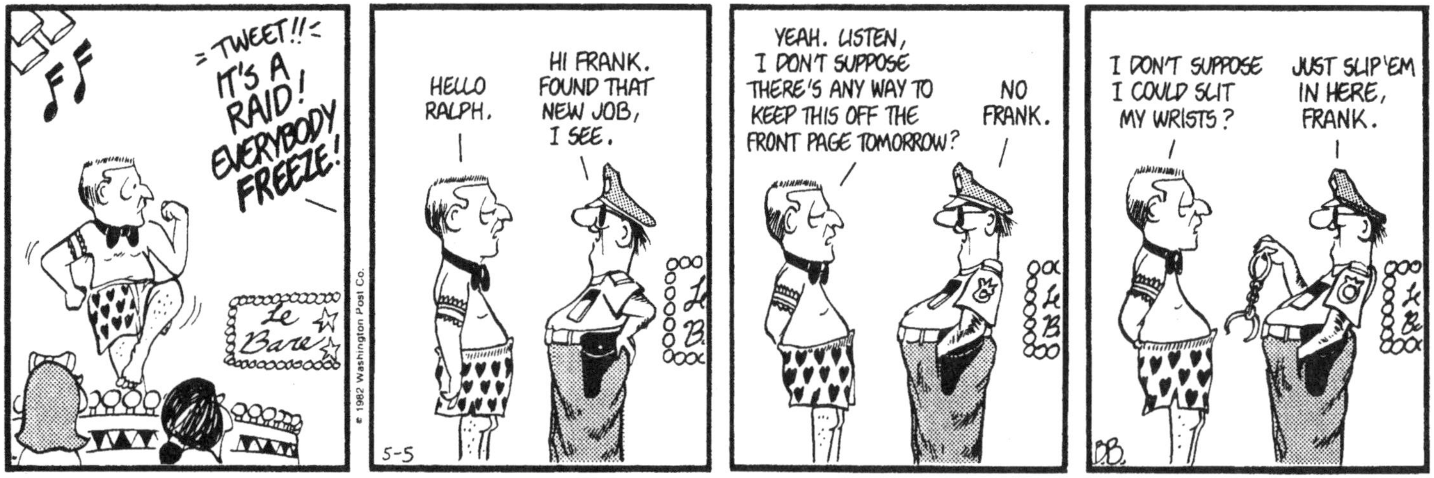
TWEET!!
IT'S A RAID! EVERYBODY FREEZE!
Le Bare
© 1982 Washington Post Co.
HELLO RALPH.
HI FRANK. FOUND THAT NEW JOB, I SEE.
5-5
YEAH. LISTEN, I DON'T SUPPOSE THERE'S ANY WAY TO KEEP THIS OFF THE FRONT PAGE TOMORROW?
NO FRANK.
I DON'T SUPPOSE I COULD SLIT MY WRISTS?
JUST SLIP 'EM IN HERE, FRANK.
B.B.

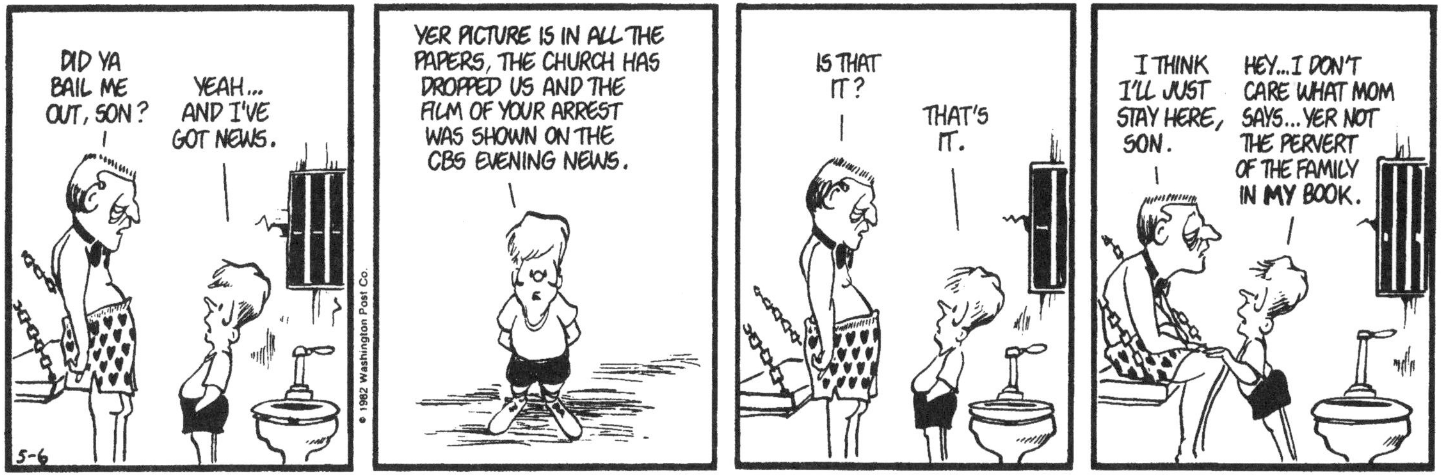
DID YA BAIL ME OUT, SON?
YEAH... AND I'VE GOT NEWS.
5-6
© 1982 Washington Post Co.
YER PICTURE IS IN ALL THE PAPERS, THE CHURCH HAS DROPPED US AND THE FILM OF YOUR ARREST WAS SHOWN ON THE CBS EVENING NEWS.
IS THAT IT?
THAT'S IT.
I THINK I'LL JUST STAY HERE, SON.
HEY... I DON'T CARE WHAT MOM SAYS... YER NOT THE PERVERT OF THE FAMILY IN MY BOOK.

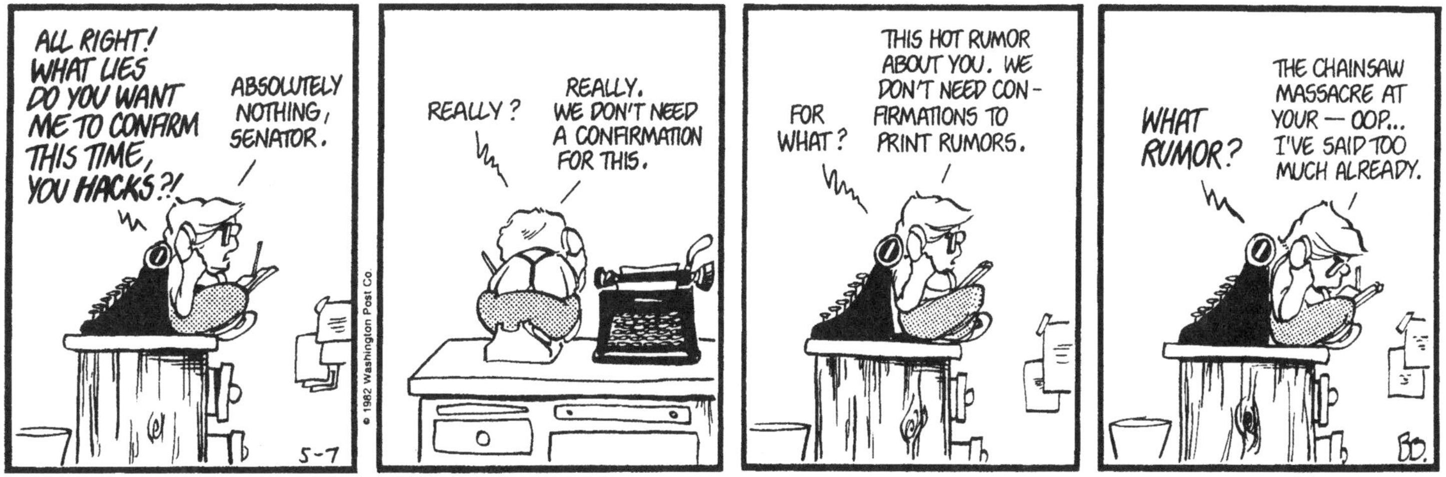
ALL RIGHT! WHAT LIES DO YOU WANT ME TO CONFIRM THIS TIME, YOU HACKS?!
ABSOLUTELY NOTHING, SENATOR.
5-7
© 1982 Washington Post Co.
REALLY?
REALLY. WE DON'T NEED A CONFIRMATION FOR THIS.
FOR WHAT?
THIS HOT RUMOR ABOUT YOU. WE DON'T NEED CONFIRMATIONS TO PRINT RUMORS.
WHAT RUMOR?
THE CHAINSAW MASSACRE AT YOUR — OOP... I'VE SAID TOO MUCH ALREADY.
BB.

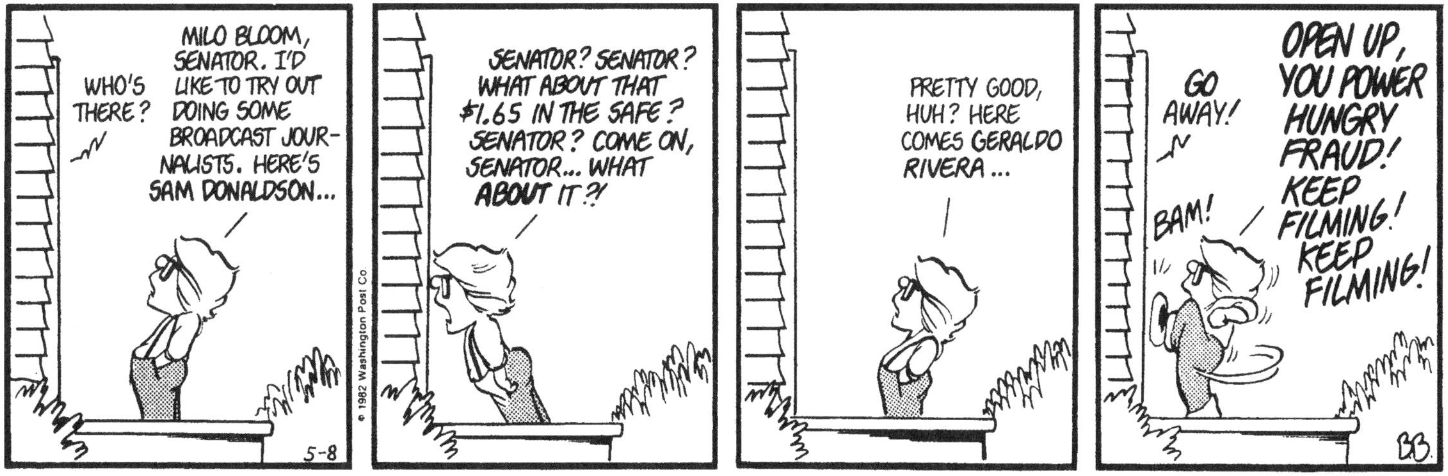
WHO'S THERE?
MILO BLOOM, SENATOR. I'D LIKE TO TRY OUT DOING SOME BROADCAST JOURNALISTS. HERE'S SAM DONALDSON...
5-8
© 1982 Washington Post Co.
SENATOR? SENATOR? WHAT ABOUT THAT $1.65 IN THE SAFE? SENATOR? COME ON, SENATOR... WHAT ABOUT IT?!
PRETTY GOOD, HUH? HERE COMES GERALDO RIVERA...
GO AWAY!
BAM!
OPEN UP, YOU POWER HUNGRY FRAUD! KEEP FILMING! KEEP FILMING!
BB.

Sam Donaldson is a longtime anchorman and correspondent for ABC News.

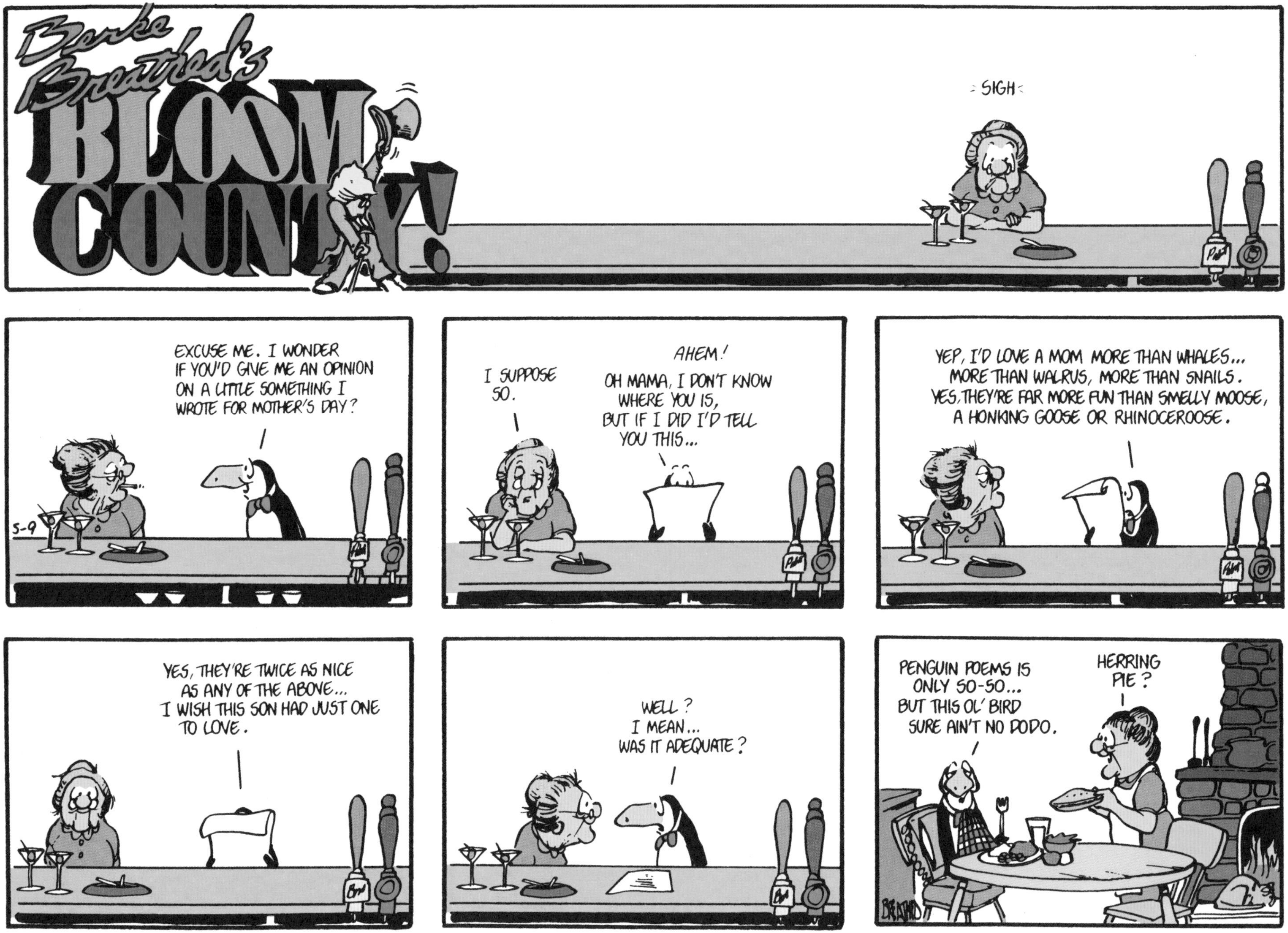
Berke Breathed's
BLOOM COUNTY!
SIGH
5-9
EXCUSE ME. I WONDER IF YOU'D GIVE ME AN OPINION ON A LITTLE SOMETHING I WROTE FOR MOTHER'S DAY?
I SUPPOSE SO.
AHEM!
OH MAMA, I DON'T KNOW WHERE YOU IS, BUT IF I DID I'D TELL YOU THIS...
YEP, I'D LOVE A MOM MORE THAN WHALES... MORE THAN WALRUS, MORE THAN SNAILS. YES, THEY'RE FAR MORE FUN THAN SMELLY MOOSE, A HONKING GOOSE OR RHINOCEROOSE.
YES, THEY'RE TWICE AS NICE AS ANY OF THE ABOVE... I WISH THIS SON HAD JUST ONE TO LOVE.
WELL? I MEAN... WAS IT ADEQUATE?
PENGUIN POEMS IS ONLY SO-SO... BUT THIS OL' BIRD SURE AIN'T NO DODO.
HERRING PIE?
BREATHED

May 9, 1982

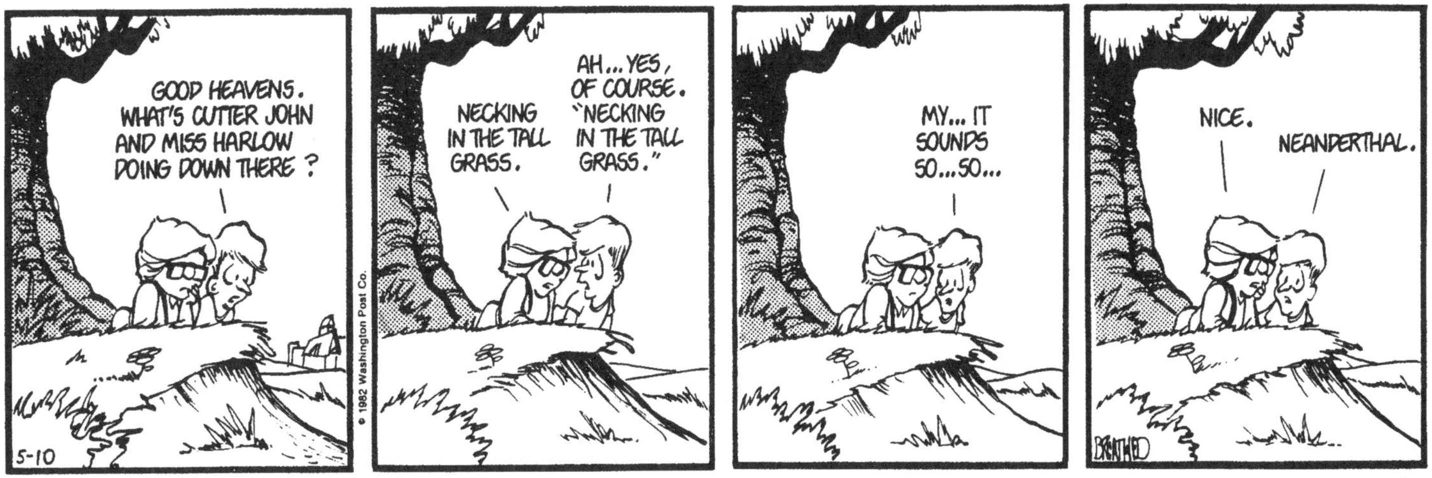
GOOD HEAVENS. WHAT'S CUTTER JOHN AND MISS HARLOW DOING DOWN THERE ?
NECKING IN THE TALL GRASS.
AH... YES, OF COURSE. "NECKING IN THE TALL GRASS."
MY... IT SOUNDS SO... SO...
NICE.
NEANDERTHAL.
© 1982 Washington Post Co.
5-10
BREATHED

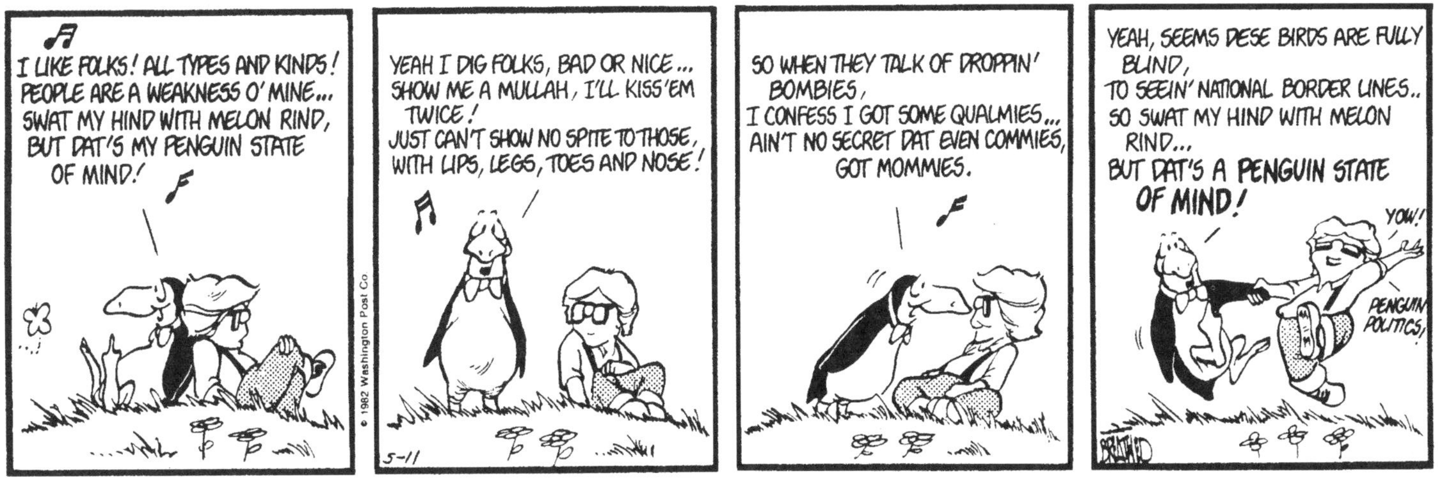
I LIKE FOLKS! ALL TYPES AND KINDS! PEOPLE ARE A WEAKNESS O' MINE... SWAT MY HIND WITH MELON RIND, BUT DAT'S MY PENGUIN STATE OF MIND!
YEAH I DIG FOLKS, BAD OR NICE... SHOW ME A MULLAH, I'LL KISS'EM TWICE! JUST CAN'T SHOW NO SPITE TO THOSE, WITH LIPS, LEGS, TOES AND NOSE!
SO WHEN THEY TALK OF DROPPIN' BOMBIES, I CONFESS I GOT SOME QUALMIES... AIN'T NO SECRET DAT EVEN COMMIES, GOT MOMMIES.
YEAH, SEEMS DESE BIRDS ARE FULLY BLIND, TO SEEIN' NATIONAL BORDER LINES.. SO SWAT MY HIND WITH MELON RIND... BUT DAT'S A PENGUIN STATE OF MIND!
YOW!
PENGUIN POLITICS!
© 1982 Washington Post Co.
5-11
BREATHED

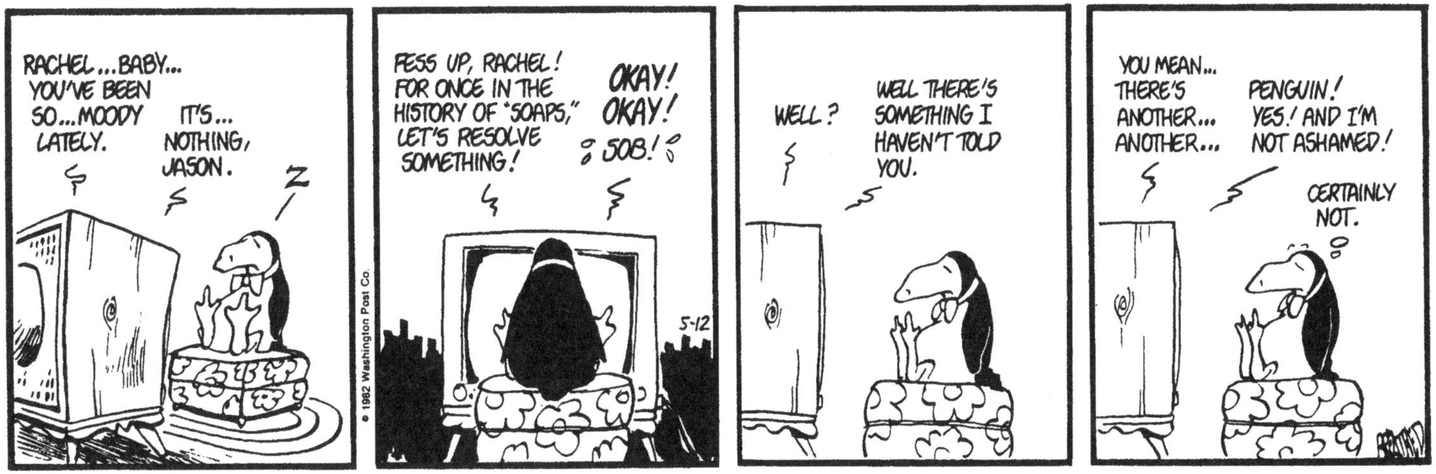
RACHEL... BABY... YOU'VE BEEN SO... MOODY LATELY.
IT'S... NOTHING, JASON.
Z
FESS UP, RACHEL! FOR ONCE IN THE HISTORY OF "SOAPS," LET'S RESOLVE SOMETHING!
OKAY! OKAY! SOB!
WELL ?
WELL THERE'S SOMETHING I HAVEN'T TOLD YOU.
YOU MEAN... THERE'S ANOTHER... ANOTHER...
PENGUIN! YES! AND I'M NOT ASHAMED!
CERTAINLY NOT.
© 1982 Washington Post Co.
5-12
BREATHED

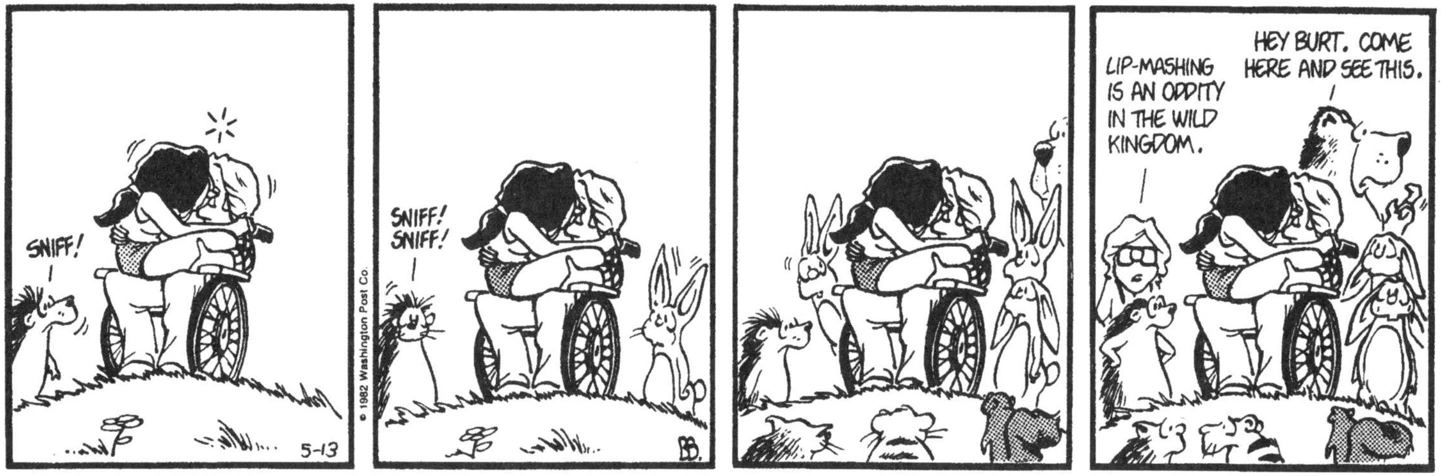
SNIFF!
5-13
© 1982 Washington Post Co.
SNIFF! SNIFF!
LIP-MASHING IS AN ODDITY IN THE WILD KINGDOM.
HEY BURT. COME HERE AND SEE THIS.

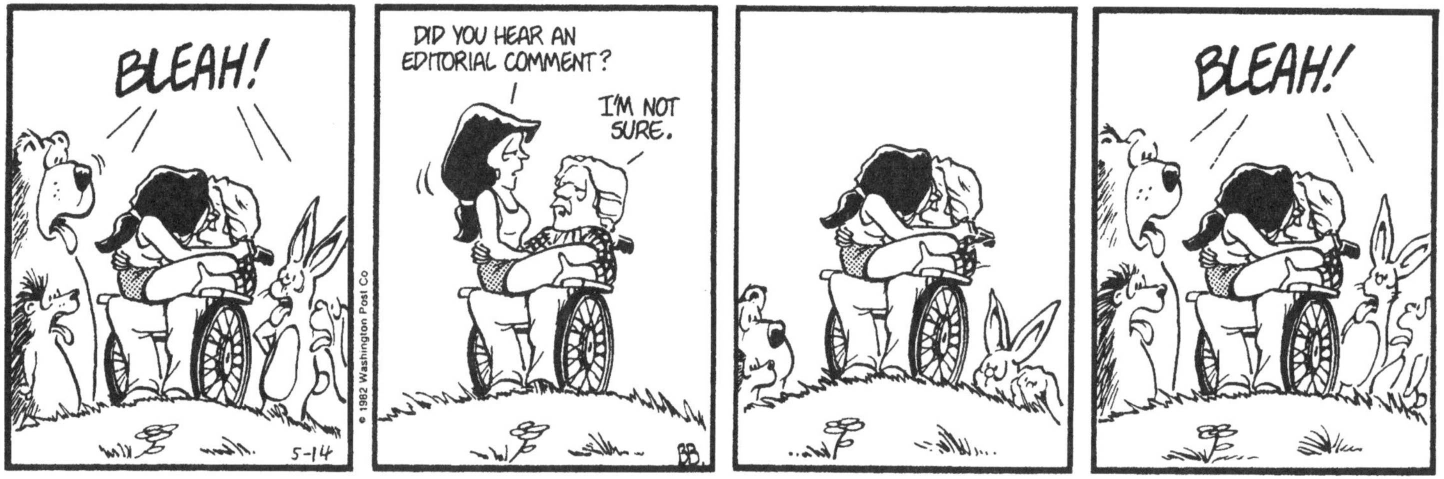
BLEAH!
5-14
© 1982 Washington Post Co.
DID YOU HEAR AN EDITORIAL COMMENT?
I'M NOT SURE.
BLEAH!

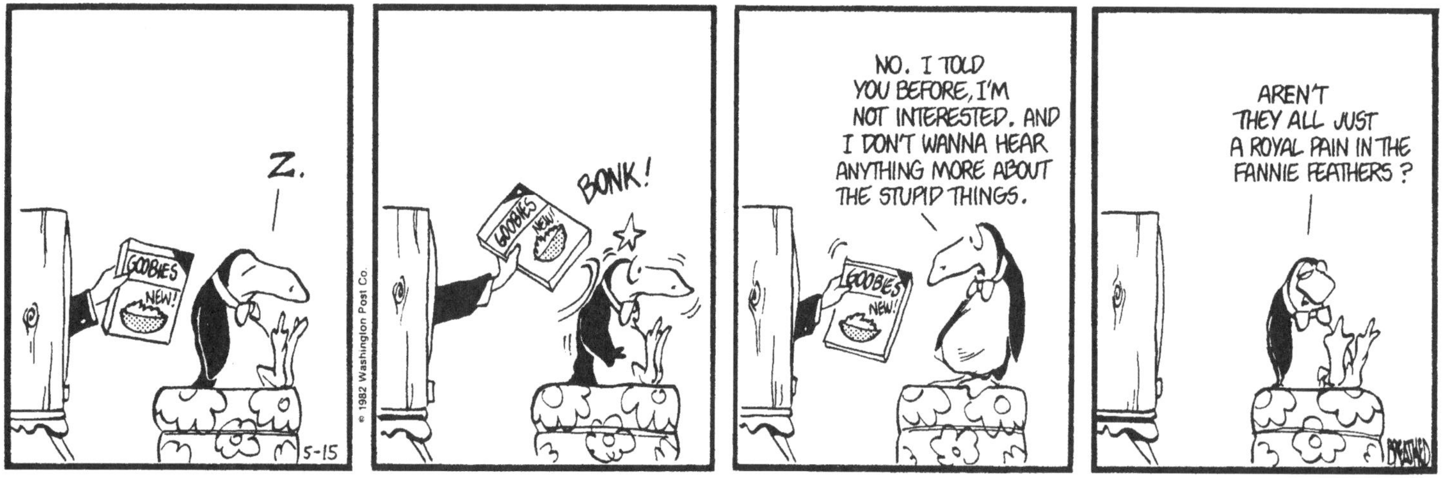
Z.
GOOBIES
NEW!
5-15
© 1982 Washington Post Co.
BONK!
NO. I TOLD YOU BEFORE, I'M NOT INTERESTED. AND I DON'T WANNA HEAR ANYTHING MORE ABOUT THE STUPID THINGS.
AREN'T THEY ALL JUST A ROYAL PAIN IN THE FANNIE FEATHERS?

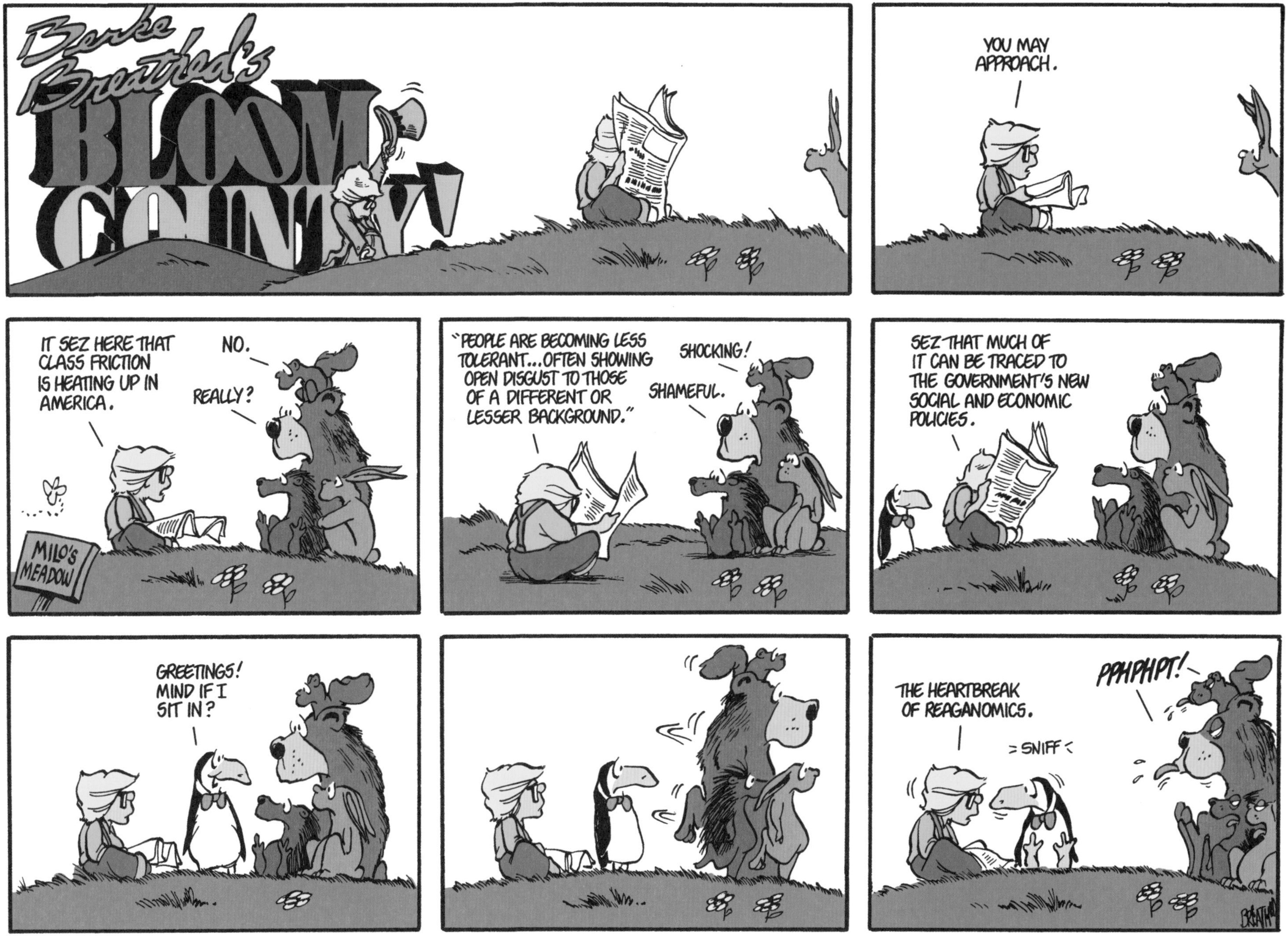
Berke Breathed's
BLOOM COUNTY
YOU MAY APPROACH.
IT SEZ HERE THAT CLASS FRICTION IS HEATING UP IN AMERICA.
NO.
REALLY?
MILO'S MEADOW
"PEOPLE ARE BECOMING LESS TOLERANT...OFTEN SHOWING OPEN DISGUST TO THOSE OF A DIFFERENT OR LESSER BACKGROUND."
SHOCKING!
SHAMEFUL.
SEZ THAT MUCH OF IT CAN BE TRACED TO THE GOVERNMENT'S NEW SOCIAL AND ECONOMIC POLICIES.
GREETINGS! MIND IF I SIT IN?
THE HEARTBREAK OF REAGANOMICS.
SNIFF
PPHPHPT!

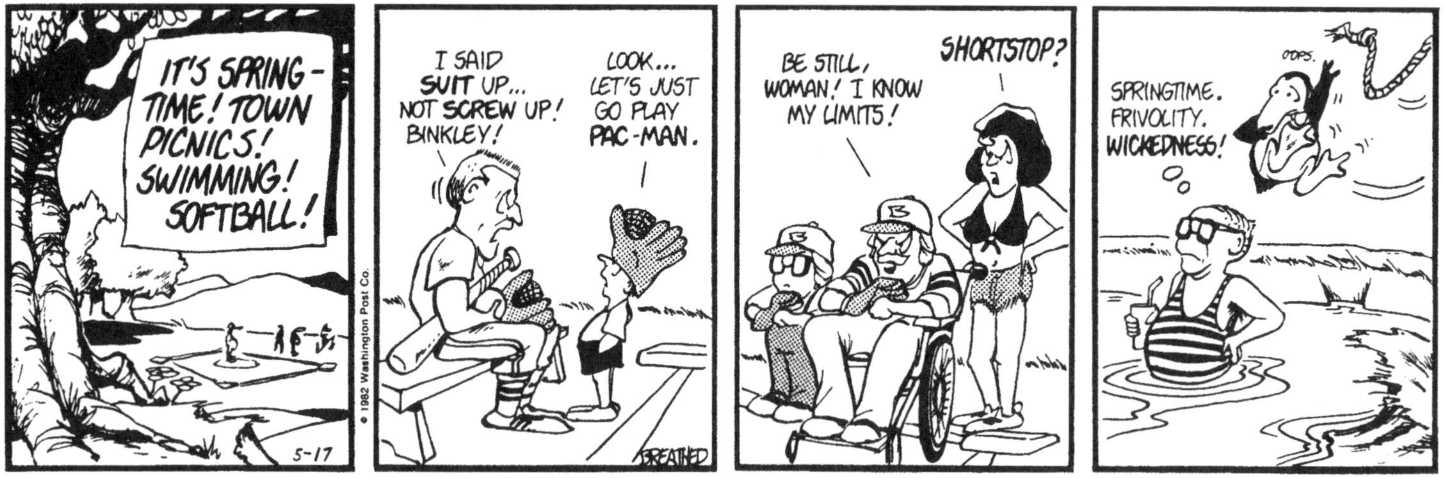
IT'S SPRING-TIME! TOWN PICNICS! SWIMMING! SOFTBALL!
5-17
I SAID SUIT UP... NOT SCREW UP! BINKLEY!
LOOK... LET'S JUST GO PLAY PAC-MAN.
© 1982 Washington Post Co.
BREATHED
BE STILL, WOMAN! I KNOW MY LIMITS!
SHORTSTOP?
SPRINGTIME. FRIVOLITY. WICKEDNESS!
OOPS.

Benito Mussolini was leader of the ruling Fascist Party in Italy prior to and during World War II.

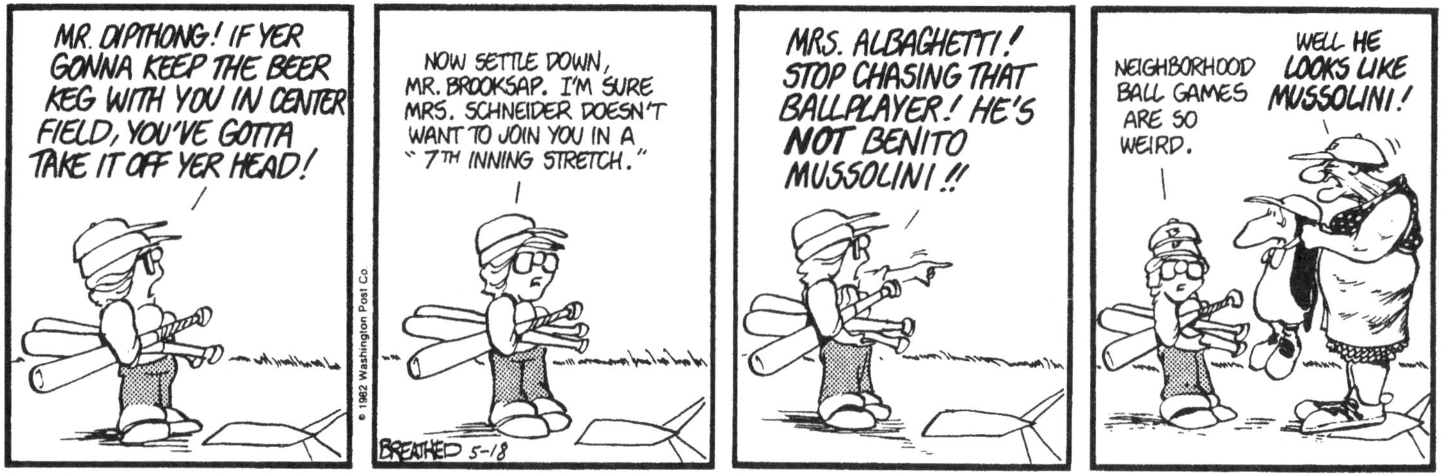
MR. DIPTHONG! IF YER GONNA KEEP THE BEER KEG WITH YOU IN CENTER FIELD, YOU'VE GOTTA TAKE IT OFF YER HEAD!
NOW SETTLE DOWN, MR. BROOKSAP. I'M SURE MRS. SCHNEIDER DOESN'T WANT TO JOIN YOU IN A "7TH INNING STRETCH."
© 1982 Washington Post Co.
BREATHED 5-18
MRS. ALBAGHETTI! STOP CHASING THAT BALLPLAYER! HE'S NOT BENITO MUSSOLINI!!
NEIGHBORHOOD BALL GAMES ARE SO WEIRD.
WELL HE LOOKS LIKE MUSSOLINI!

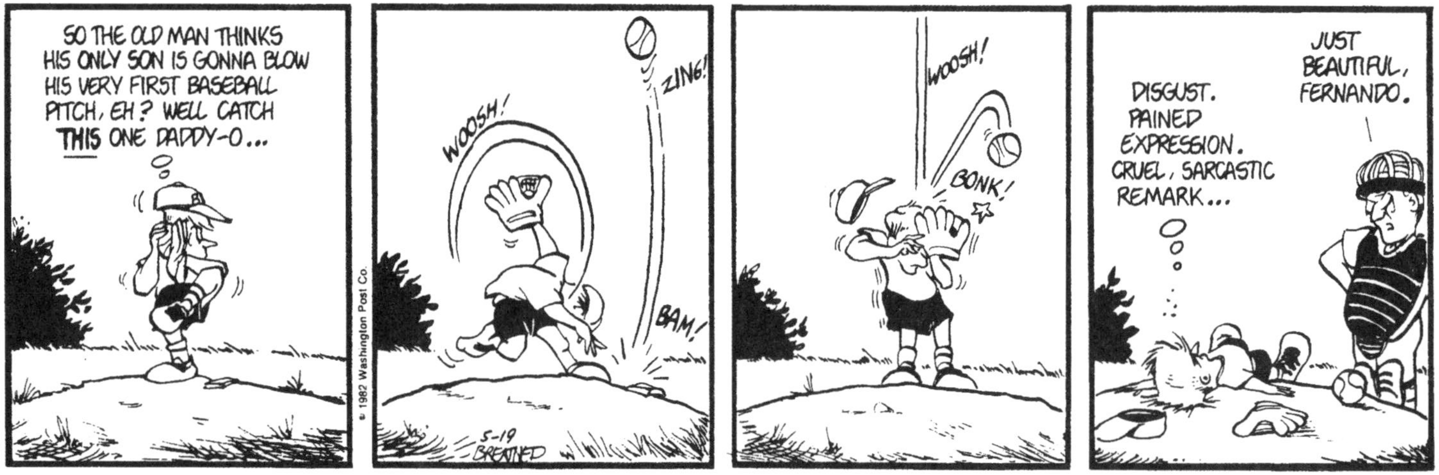
SO THE OLD MAN THINKS HIS ONLY SON IS GONNA BLOW HIS VERY FIRST BASEBALL PITCH, EH? WELL CATCH THIS ONE DADDY-O...
WOOSH!
ZING!
BAM!
© 1982 Washington Post Co.
5-19 BREATHED
WOOSH!
BONK!
DISGUST. PAINED EXPRESSION. CRUEL, SARCASTIC REMARK...
JUST BEAUTIFUL, FERNANDO.

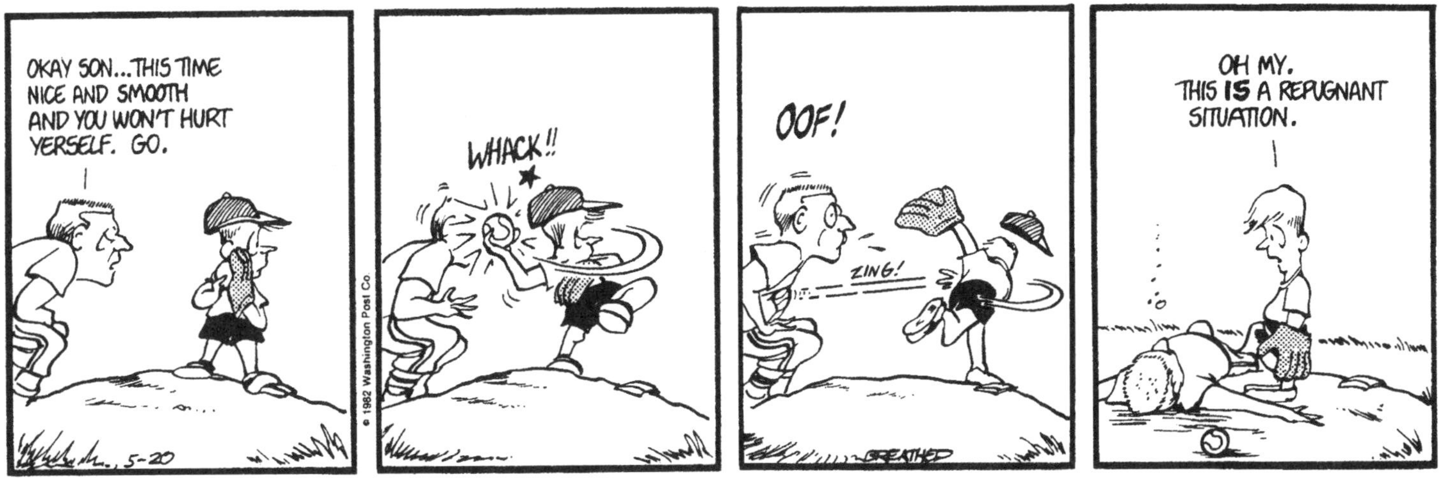
OKAY SON...THIS TIME NICE AND SMOOTH AND YOU WON'T HURT YERSELF. GO.
WHACK!!
OOF!
ZING!
OH MY. THIS **IS** A REPUGNANT SITUATION.
5-20
© 1982 Washington Post Co.
BREATHED

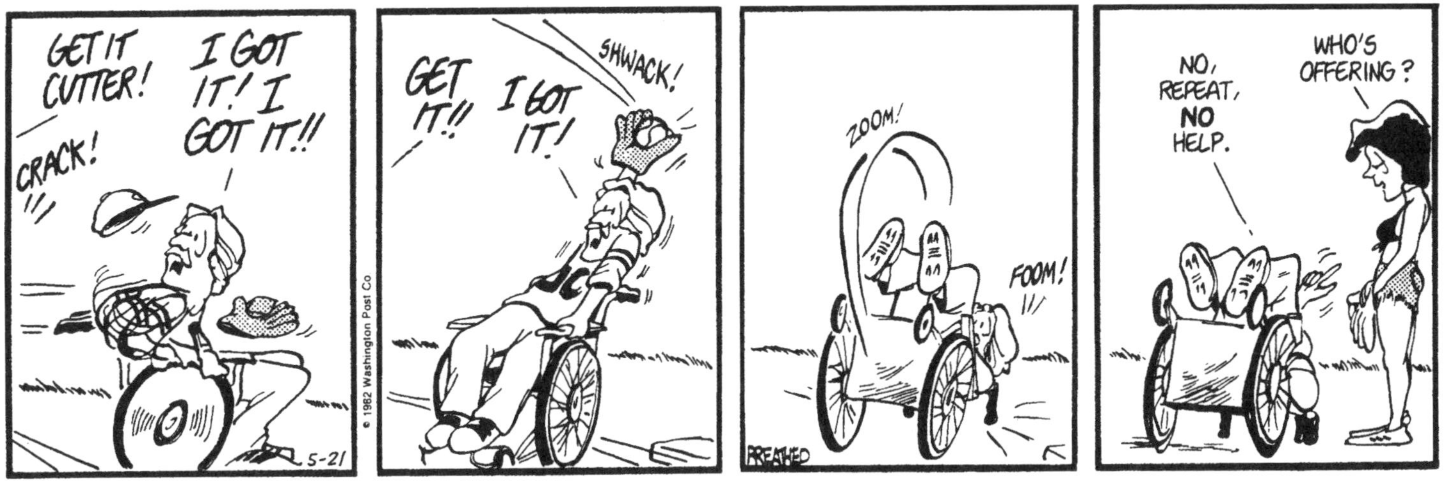
GET IT CUTTER!
I GOT IT! I GOT IT!!
CRACK!
GET IT!!
I GOT IT!
SHWACK!
ZOOM!
FOOM!
NO, REPEAT, **NO** HELP.
WHO'S OFFERING?
5-21
© 1982 Washington Post Co.
BREATHED

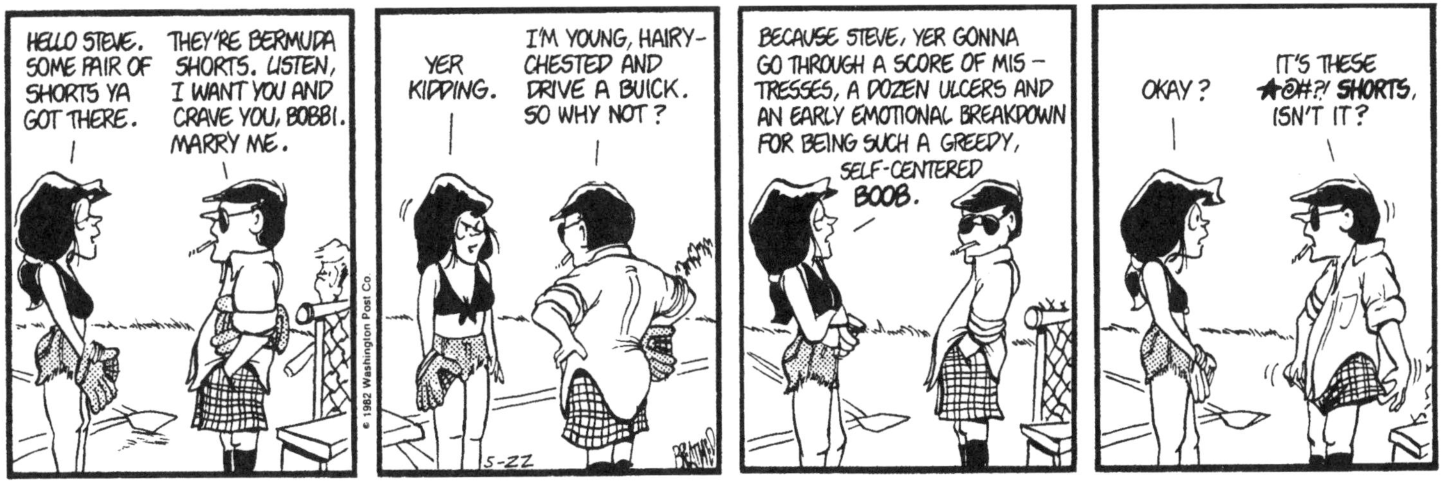
HELLO STEVE. SOME PAIR OF SHORTS YA GOT THERE.
THEY'RE BERMUDA SHORTS. LISTEN, I WANT YOU AND CRAVE YOU, BOBBI. MARRY ME.
YER KIDDING.
I'M YOUNG, HAIRY-CHESTED AND DRIVE A BUICK. SO WHY NOT?
BECAUSE STEVE, YER GONNA GO THROUGH A SCORE OF MIS-TRESSES, A DOZEN ULCERS AND AN EARLY EMOTIONAL BREAKDOWN FOR BEING SUCH A GREEDY, SELF-CENTERED **BOOB**.
OKAY?
IT'S THESE ★@#?! **SHORTS**, ISN'T IT?
5-22
© 1982 Washington Post Co.

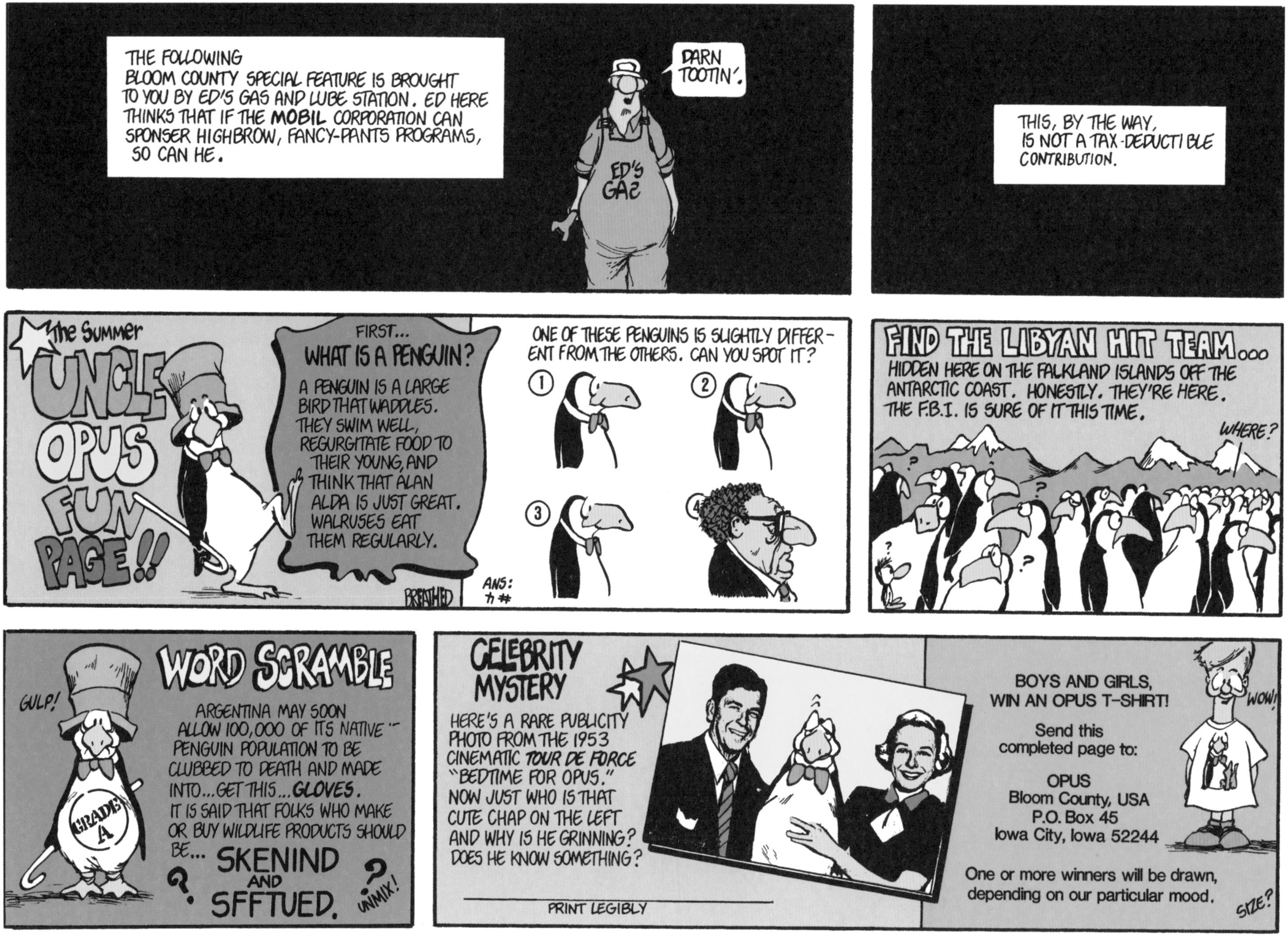
THE FOLLOWING BLOOM COUNTY SPECIAL FEATURE IS BROUGHT TO YOU BY ED'S GAS AND LUBE STATION. ED HERE THINKS THAT IF THE MOBIL CORPORATION CAN SPONSER HIGHBROW, FANCY-PANTS PROGRAMS, SO CAN HE.
DARN TOOTIN'.
ED'S GAS
THIS, BY THE WAY, IS NOT A TAX-DEDUCTIBLE CONTRIBUTION.
The Summer UNCLE OPUS FUN PAGE!!
FIRST... WHAT IS A PENGUIN?
A PENGUIN IS A LARGE BIRD THAT WADDLES. THEY SWIM WELL, REGURGITATE FOOD TO THEIR YOUNG, AND THINK THAT ALAN ALDA IS JUST GREAT. WALRUSES EAT THEM REGULARLY.
BREATHED
ONE OF THESE PENGUINS IS SLIGHTLY DIFFERENT FROM THE OTHERS. CAN YOU SPOT IT?
1
2
3
4
ANS:
FIND THE LIBYAN HIT TEAM...
HIDDEN HERE ON THE FALKLAND ISLANDS OFF THE ANTARCTIC COAST. HONESTLY. THEY'RE HERE. THE F.B.I. IS SURE OF IT THIS TIME.
WHERE?
WORD SCRAMBLE
GULP!
GRADE A
ARGENTINA MAY SOON ALLOW 100,000 OF ITS NATIVE PENGUIN POPULATION TO BE CLUBBED TO DEATH AND MADE INTO... GET THIS... GLOVES. IT IS SAID THAT FOLKS WHO MAKE OR BUY WILDLIFE PRODUCTS SHOULD BE... SKENIND AND SFFTUED.
UNMIX!
CELEBRITY MYSTERY
HERE'S A RARE PUBLICITY PHOTO FROM THE 1953 CINEMATIC TOUR DE FORCE "BEDTIME FOR OPUS." NOW JUST WHO IS THAT CUTE CHAP ON THE LEFT AND WHY IS HE GRINNING? DOES HE KNOW SOMETHING?
PRINT LEGIBLY
BOYS AND GIRLS, WIN AN OPUS T-SHIRT!
Send this completed page to:
OPUS
Bloom County, USA
P.O. Box 45
Iowa City, Iowa 52244
One or more winners will be drawn, depending on our particular mood.
WOW!
SIZE?

Alan Alda, star of the long-running *M*A*S*H* television series, was the "sensitive male" poster child.

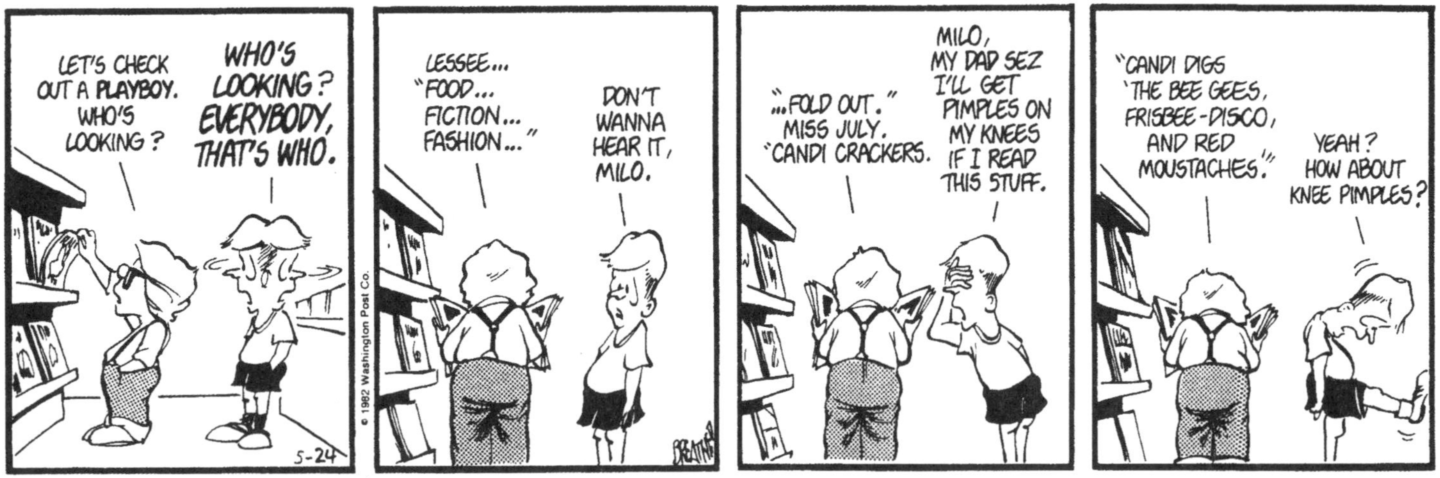
LET'S CHECK OUT A PLAYBOY. WHO'S LOOKING?
WHO'S LOOKING? EVERYBODY, THAT'S WHO.
5-24
© 1982 Washington Post Co.
LESSEE... "FOOD... FICTION... FASHION..."
DON'T WANNA HEAR IT, MILO.
BREATHED
"...FOLD OUT." MISS JULY. "CANDI CRACKERS.
MILO, MY DAD SEZ I'LL GET PIMPLES ON MY KNEES IF I READ THIS STUFF.
"CANDI DIGS 'THE BEE GEES, FRISBEE-DISCO, AND RED MOUSTACHES.'"
YEAH? HOW ABOUT KNEE PIMPLES?

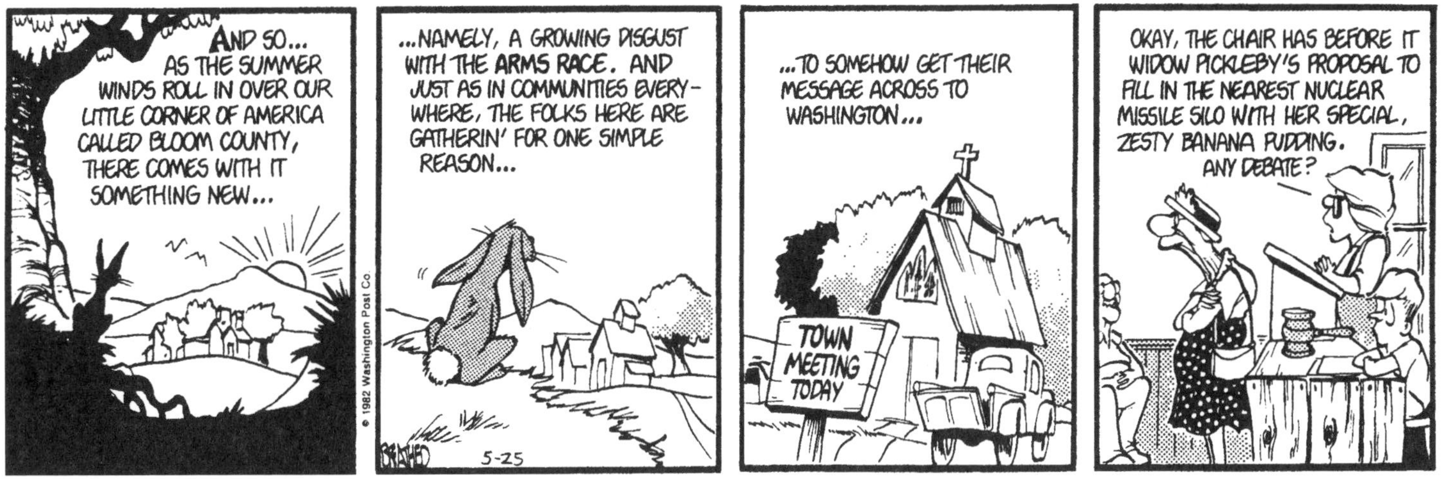
AND SO... AS THE SUMMER WINDS ROLL IN OVER OUR LITTLE CORNER OF AMERICA CALLED BLOOM COUNTY, THERE COMES WITH IT SOMETHING NEW...
...NAMELY, A GROWING DISGUST WITH THE ARMS RACE. AND JUST AS IN COMMUNITIES EVERYWHERE, THE FOLKS HERE ARE GATHERIN' FOR ONE SIMPLE REASON...
© 1982 Washington Post Co.
BREATHED
5-25
...TO SOMEHOW GET THEIR MESSAGE ACROSS TO WASHINGTON...
TOWN MEETING TODAY
OKAY, THE CHAIR HAS BEFORE IT WIDOW PICKLEBY'S PROPOSAL TO FILL IN THE NEAREST NUCLEAR MISSILE SILO WITH HER SPECIAL, ZESTY BANANA PUDDING. ANY DEBATE?

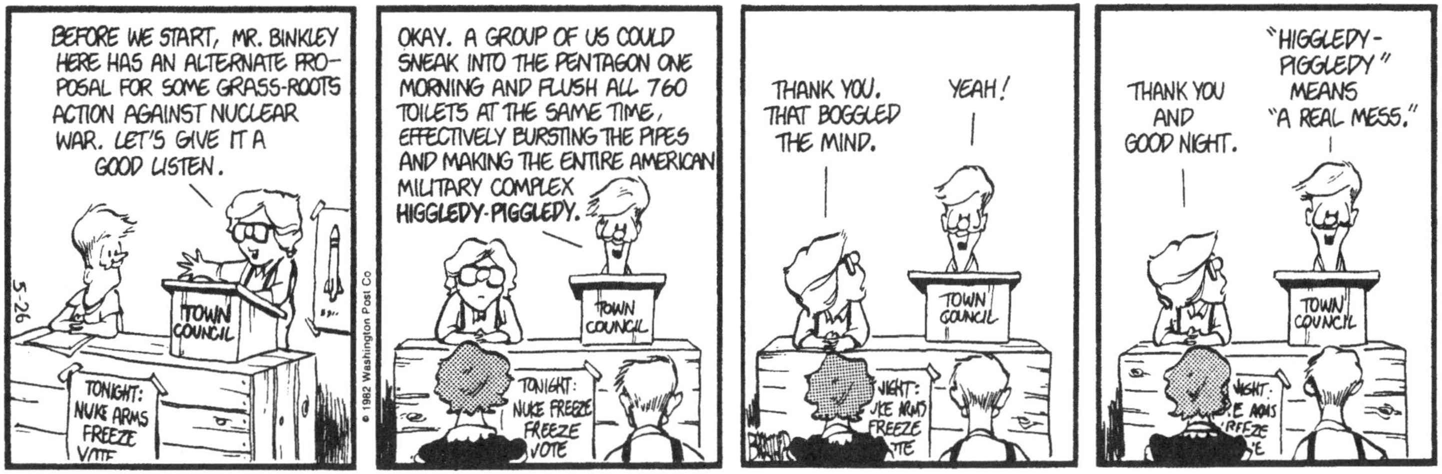
BEFORE WE START, MR. BINKLEY HERE HAS AN ALTERNATE PROPOSAL FOR SOME GRASS-ROOTS ACTION AGAINST NUCLEAR WAR. LET'S GIVE IT A GOOD LISTEN.
5-26
TOWN COUNCIL
TONIGHT: NUKE ARMS FREEZE VOTE
© 1982 Washington Post Co.
OKAY. A GROUP OF US COULD SNEAK INTO THE PENTAGON ONE MORNING AND FLUSH ALL 760 TOILETS AT THE SAME TIME, EFFECTIVELY BURSTING THE PIPES AND MAKING THE ENTIRE AMERICAN MILITARY COMPLEX HIGGLEDY-PIGGLEDY.
TOWN COUNCIL
TONIGHT: NUKE FREEZE VOTE
THANK YOU. THAT BOGGLED THE MIND.
YEAH!
TOWN COUNCIL
THANK YOU AND GOOD NIGHT.
"HIGGLEDY-PIGGLEDY" MEANS "A REAL MESS."
TOWN COUNCIL

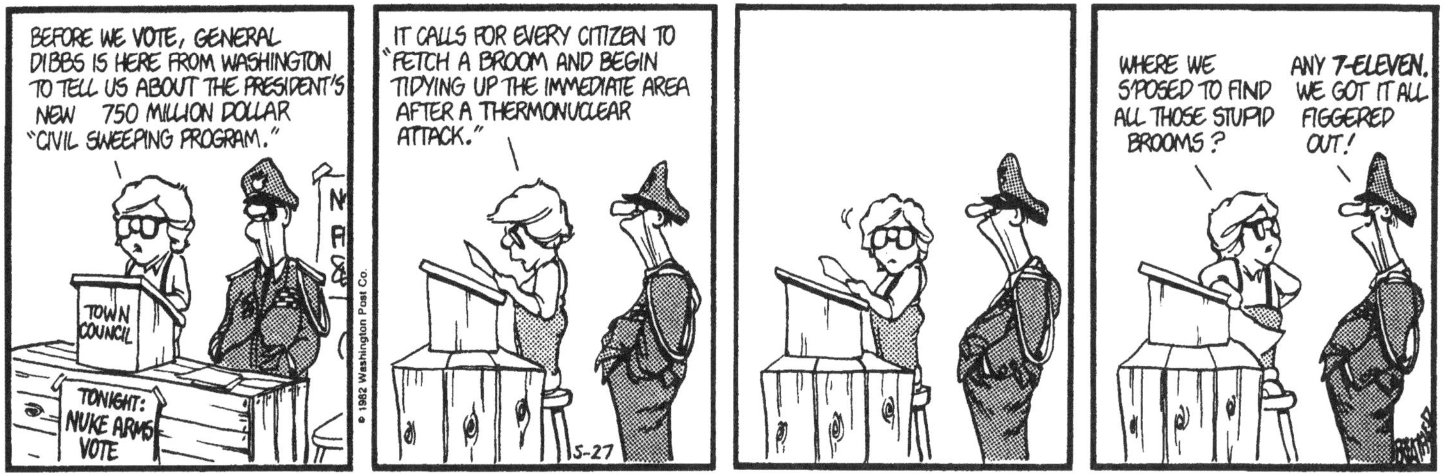
BEFORE WE VOTE, GENERAL DIBBS IS HERE FROM WASHINGTON TO TELL US ABOUT THE PRESIDENT'S NEW 750 MILLION DOLLAR "CIVIL SWEEPING PROGRAM."
TOWN COUNCIL
TONIGHT: NUKE ARMS VOTE
© 1982 Washington Post Co.
IT CALLS FOR EVERY CITIZEN TO FETCH A BROOM AND BEGIN TIDYING UP THE IMMEDIATE AREA AFTER A THERMONUCLEAR ATTACK."
5-27
WHERE WE S'POSED TO FIND ALL THOSE STUPID BROOMS?
ANY 7-ELEVEN. WE GOT IT ALL FIGGERED OUT!

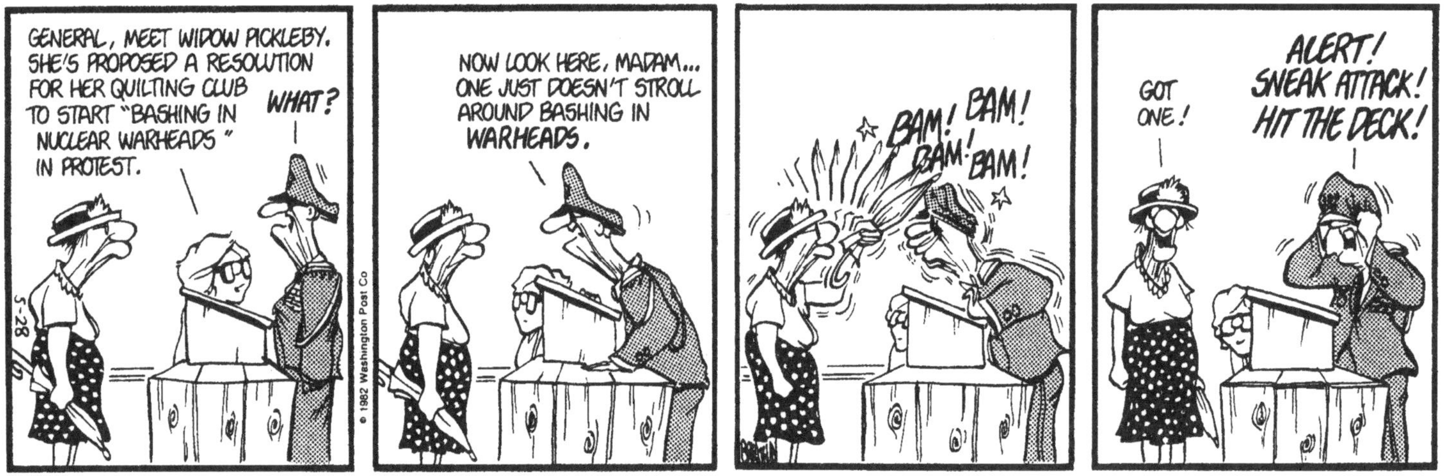
GENERAL, MEET WIDOW PICKLEBY. SHE'S PROPOSED A RESOLUTION FOR HER QUILTING CLUB TO START "BASHING IN NUCLEAR WARHEADS" IN PROTEST.
WHAT?
5-28
© 1982 Washington Post Co.
NOW LOOK HERE, MADAM... ONE JUST DOESN'T STROLL AROUND BASHING IN WARHEADS.
BAM! BAM! BAM! BAM!
GOT ONE!
ALERT! SNEAK ATTACK! HIT THE DECK!

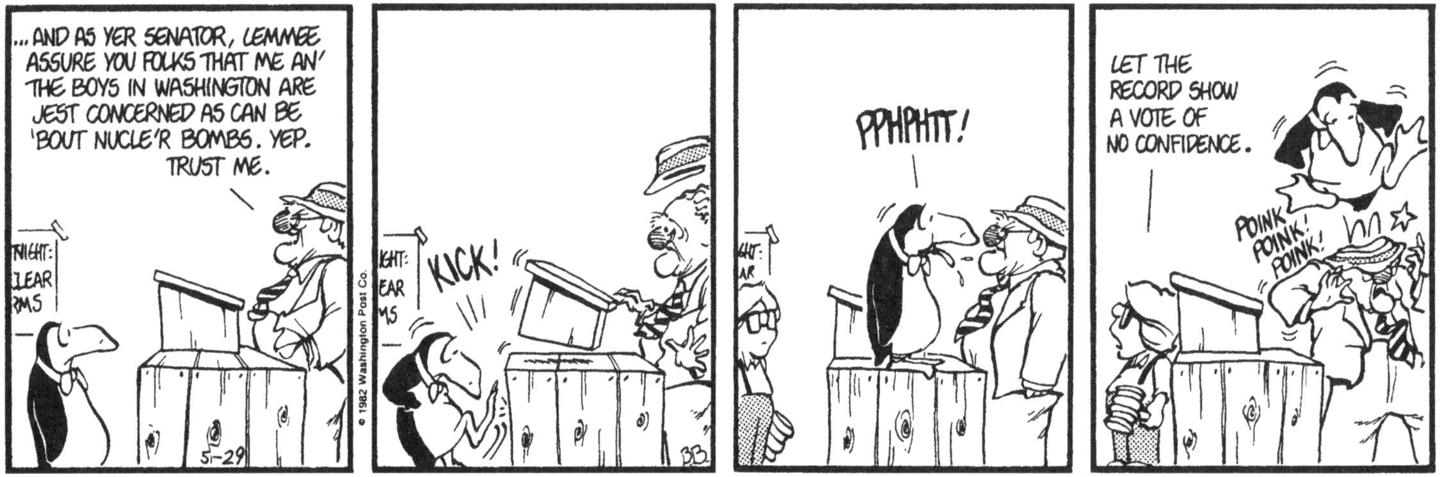
...AND AS YER SENATOR, LEMMEE ASSURE YOU FOLKS THAT ME AN' THE BOYS IN WASHINGTON ARE JEST CONCERNED AS CAN BE 'BOUT NUCLE'R BOMBS. YEP. TRUST ME.
5-29
© 1982 Washington Post Co.
KICK!
PPHPHTT!
LET THE RECORD SHOW A VOTE OF NO CONFIDENCE.
POINK! POINK! POINK!

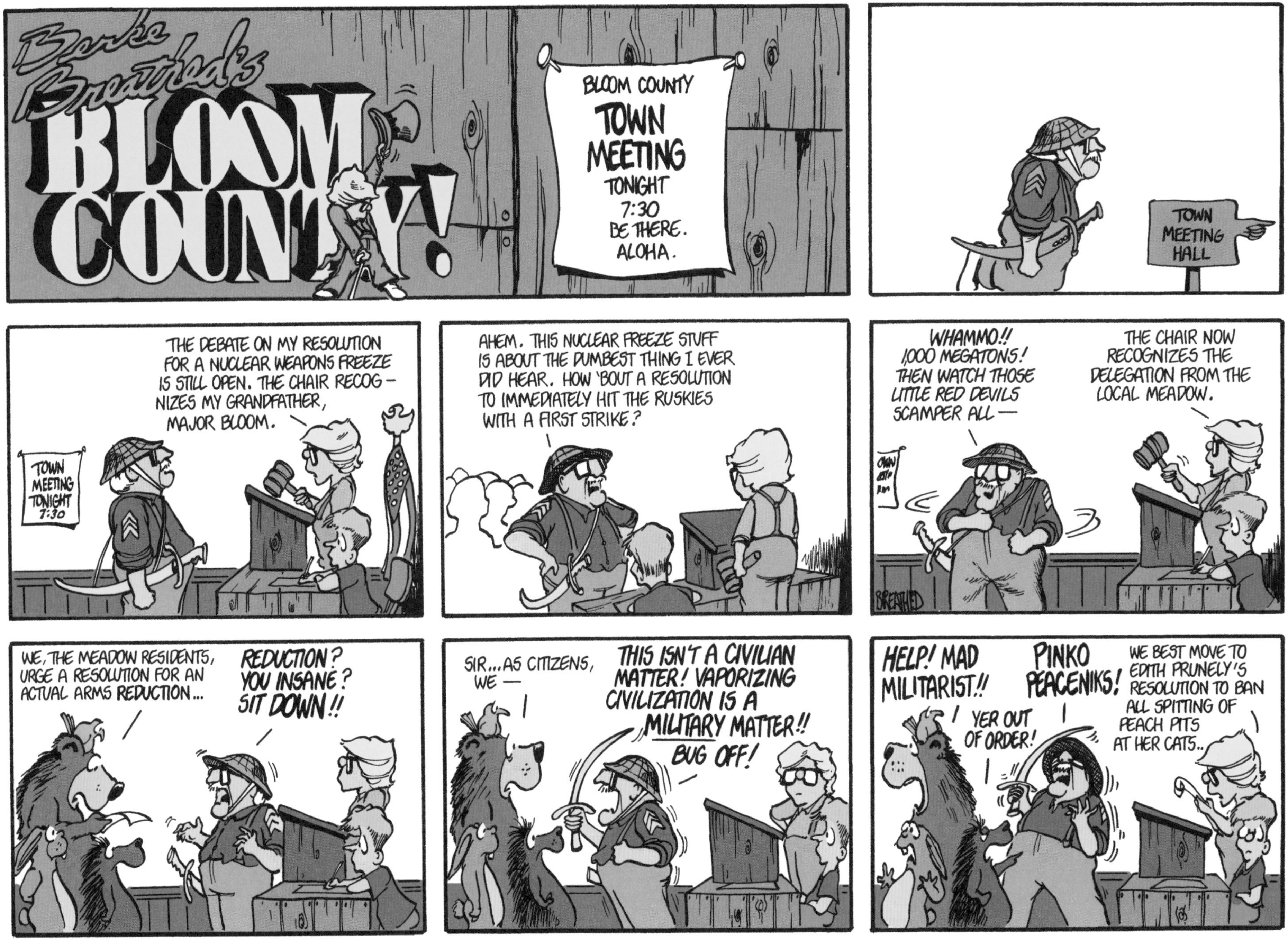
Berke Breathed's
BLOOM COUNTY!
BLOOM COUNTY
TOWN MEETING
TONIGHT
7:30
BE THERE.
ALOHA.
TOWN MEETING HALL
TOWN MEETING TONIGHT 7:30
THE DEBATE ON MY RESOLUTION FOR A NUCLEAR WEAPONS FREEZE IS STILL OPEN. THE CHAIR RECOG-NIZES MY GRANDFATHER, MAJOR BLOOM.
AHEM. THIS NUCLEAR FREEZE STUFF IS ABOUT THE DUMBEST THING I EVER DID HEAR. HOW 'BOUT A RESOLUTION TO IMMEDIATELY HIT THE RUSKIES WITH A FIRST STRIKE?
WHAMMO!! 1,000 MEGATONS! THEN WATCH THOSE LITTLE RED DEVILS SCAMPER ALL —
THE CHAIR NOW RECOGNIZES THE DELEGATION FROM THE LOCAL MEADOW.
BREATHED
WE, THE MEADOW RESIDENTS, URGE A RESOLUTION FOR AN ACTUAL ARMS REDUCTION...
REDUCTION? YOU INSANE? SIT DOWN!!
SIR...AS CITIZENS, WE —
THIS ISN'T A CIVILIAN MATTER! VAPORIZING CIVILIZATION IS A MILITARY MATTER!! BUG OFF!
HELP! MAD MILITARIST!!
YER OUT OF ORDER!
PINKO PEACENIKS!
WE BEST MOVE TO EDITH PRUNELY'S RESOLUTION TO BAN ALL SPITTING OF PEACH PITS AT HER CATS..

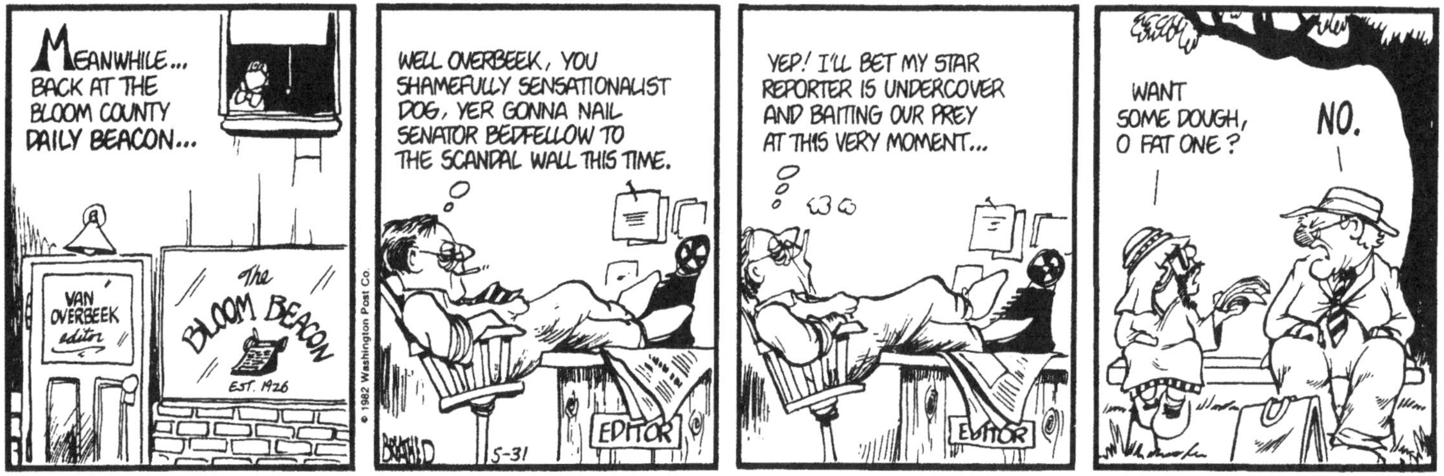
MEANWHILE... BACK AT THE BLOOM COUNTY DAILY BEACON...
VAN OVERBEEK editor
The BLOOM BEACON EST. 1926
© 1982 Washington Post Co.
WELL OVERBEEK, YOU SHAMEFULLY SENSATIONALIST DOG, YER GONNA NAIL SENATOR BEDFELLOW TO THE SCANDAL WALL THIS TIME.
5-31
EDITOR
YEP! I'LL BET MY STAR REPORTER IS UNDERCOVER AND BAITING OUR PREY AT THIS VERY MOMENT...
EDITOR
WANT SOME DOUGH, O FAT ONE?
NO.

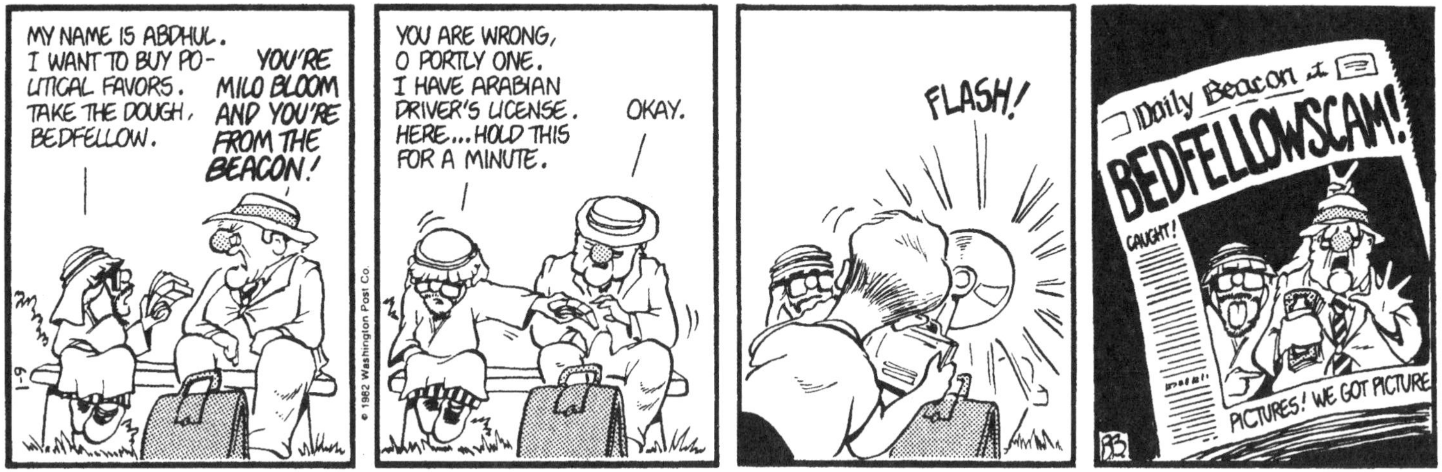
MY NAME IS ABDHUL. I WANT TO BUY POLITICAL FAVORS. TAKE THE DOUGH, BEDFELLOW.
YOU'RE MILO BLOOM AND YOU'RE FROM THE BEACON!
6-1
© 1982 Washington Post Co.
YOU ARE WRONG, O PORTLY ONE. I HAVE ARABIAN DRIVER'S LICENSE. HERE...HOLD THIS FOR A MINUTE.
OKAY.
FLASH!
Daily Beacon
BEDFELLOWSCAM!
CAUGHT!
PICTURES! WE GOT PICTURE

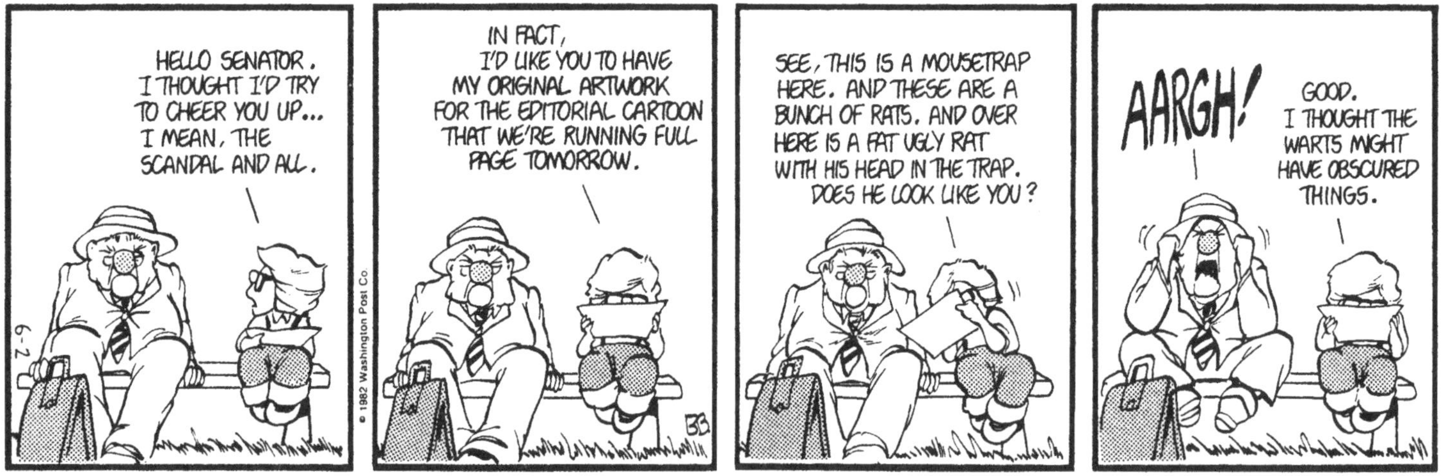
HELLO SENATOR. I THOUGHT I'D TRY TO CHEER YOU UP... I MEAN, THE SCANDAL AND ALL.
6-2
© 1982 Washington Post Co.
IN FACT, I'D LIKE YOU TO HAVE MY ORIGINAL ARTWORK FOR THE EDITORIAL CARTOON THAT WE'RE RUNNING FULL PAGE TOMORROW.
SEE, THIS IS A MOUSETRAP HERE. AND THESE ARE A BUNCH OF RATS. AND OVER HERE IS A FAT UGLY RAT WITH HIS HEAD IN THE TRAP. DOES HE LOOK LIKE YOU?
AARGH!
GOOD. I THOUGHT THE WARTS MIGHT HAVE OBSCURED THINGS.

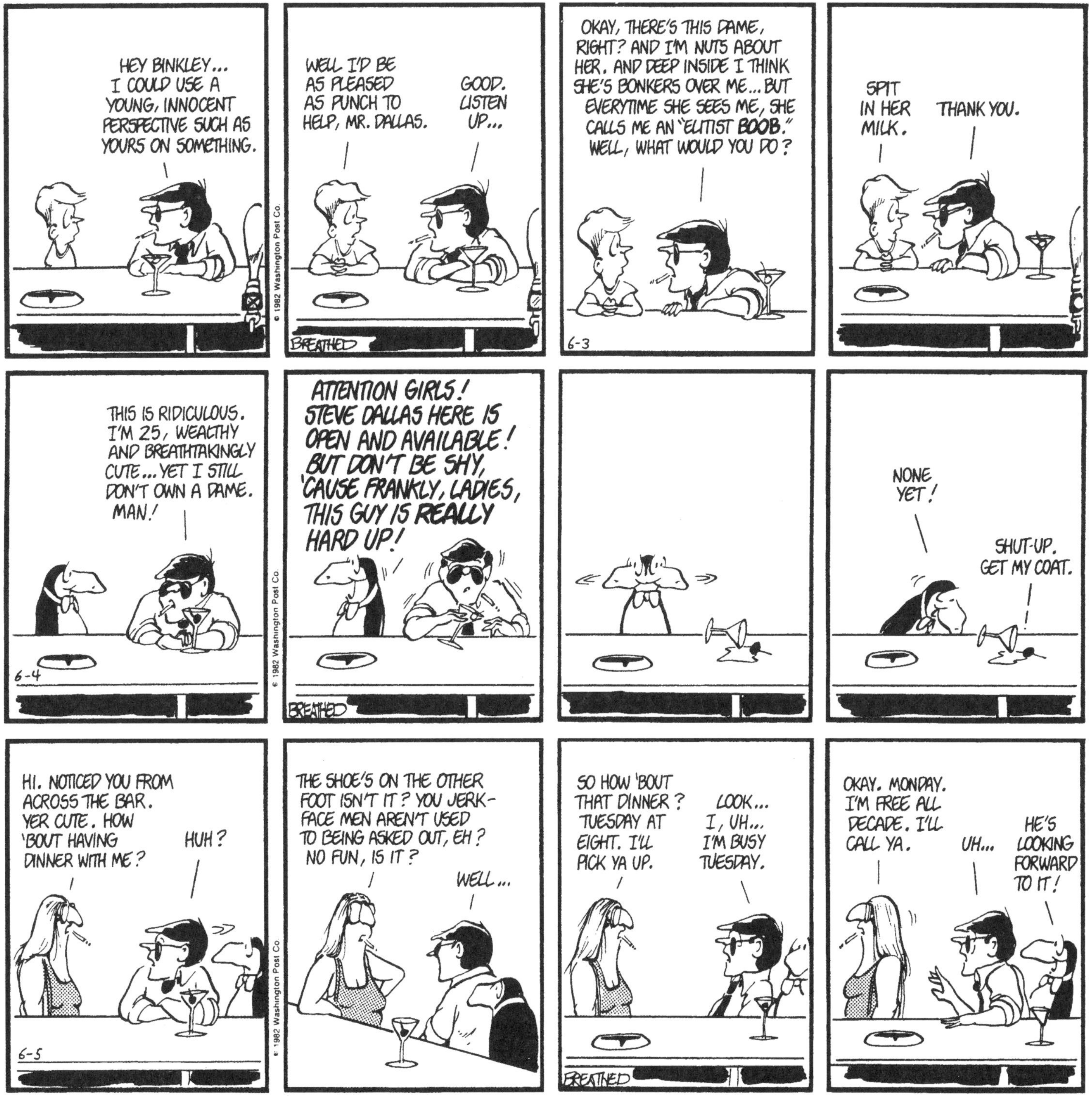
HEY BINKLEY... I COULD USE A YOUNG, INNOCENT PERSPECTIVE SUCH AS YOURS ON SOMETHING.
WELL I'D BE AS PLEASED AS PUNCH TO HELP, MR. DALLAS.
GOOD. LISTEN UP...
OKAY, THERE'S THIS DAME, RIGHT? AND I'M NUTS ABOUT HER. AND DEEP INSIDE I THINK SHE'S BONKERS OVER ME... BUT EVERYTIME SHE SEES ME, SHE CALLS ME AN "ELITIST **BOOB**." WELL, WHAT WOULD YOU DO?
SPIT IN HER MILK.
THANK YOU.
© 1982 Washington Post Co.
BREATHED
6-3
THIS IS RIDICULOUS. I'M 25, WEALTHY AND BREATHTAKINGLY CUTE... YET I STILL DON'T OWN A DAME. MAN!
ATTENTION GIRLS! STEVE DALLAS HERE IS OPEN AND AVAILABLE! BUT DON'T BE SHY, 'CAUSE FRANKLY, LADIES, THIS GUY IS **REALLY** HARD UP!
NONE YET!
SHUT-UP. GET MY COAT.
6-4
© 1982 Washington Post Co.
BREATHED
HI. NOTICED YOU FROM ACROSS THE BAR. YER CUTE. HOW 'BOUT HAVING DINNER WITH ME?
HUH?
THE SHOE'S ON THE OTHER FOOT ISN'T IT? YOU JERK-FACE MEN AREN'T USED TO BEING ASKED OUT, EH? NO FUN, IS IT?
WELL...
SO HOW 'BOUT THAT DINNER? TUESDAY AT EIGHT. I'LL PICK YA UP.
LOOK... I, UH... I'M BUSY TUESDAY.
OKAY. MONDAY. I'M FREE ALL DECADE. I'LL CALL YA.
UH...
HE'S LOOKING FORWARD TO IT!
6-5
© 1982 Washington Post Co.
BREATHED

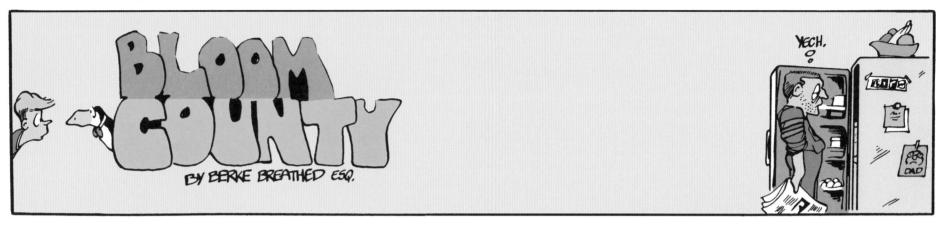

BLOOM COUNTY

BY BERKE BREATHED ESQ.

YECH.

WELL, TOM BINKLEY... AT THE ANCIENT AGE OF 35, YER LIFE, FAMILY AND AMERICAN DREAM ARE IN SHAMBLES.

LAID OFF. DEEP IN DEBT. AND ONLY A '74 VEGA IN THE GARAGE...

PLUS A WIFE WHO IS PROBABLY THINKING DIVORCE AND A SON WHO IS PURELY INCAPABLE OF THROWING A BASEBALL.

DAD!

WELL THERE'S AT LEAST ONE SMALL COMFORT IN BEING AT THE VERY BOTTOM...

NO MORE AWFUL SURPRISES.

DAD, I WANNA BE A HAIRDRESSER.

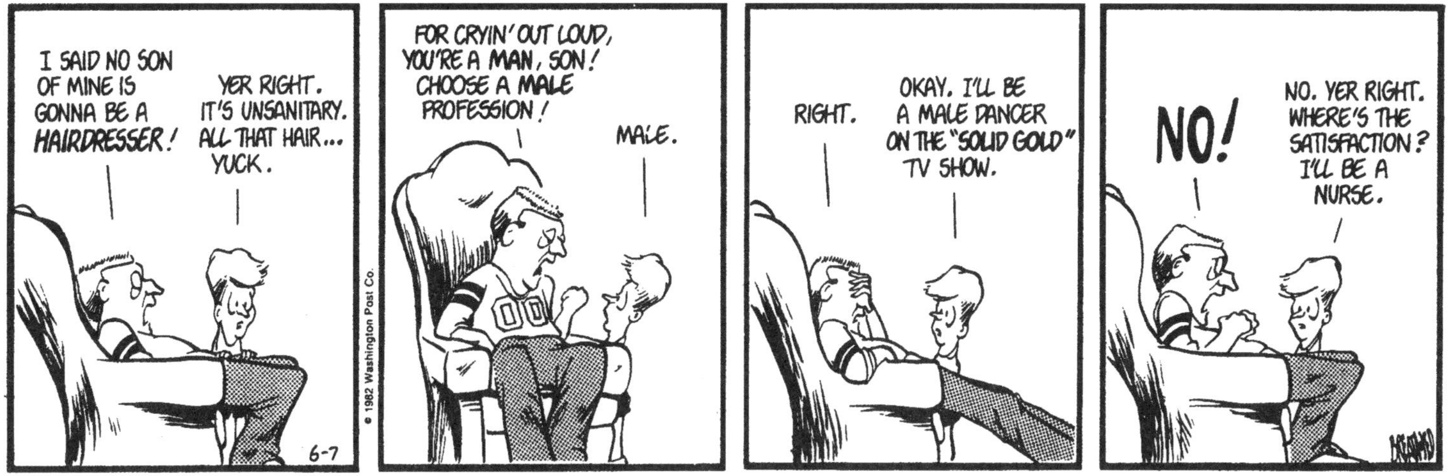
I SAID NO SON OF MINE IS GONNA BE A **HAIRDRESSER**!
YER RIGHT. IT'S UNSANITARY. ALL THAT HAIR... YUCK.
6-7
© 1982 Washington Post Co.
FOR CRYIN' OUT LOUD, YOU'RE A **MAN**, SON! CHOOSE A **MALE** PROFESSION!
MALE.
RIGHT.
OKAY. I'LL BE A MALE DANCER ON THE "SOLID GOLD" TV SHOW.
NO!
NO. YER RIGHT. WHERE'S THE SATISFACTION? I'LL BE A NURSE.

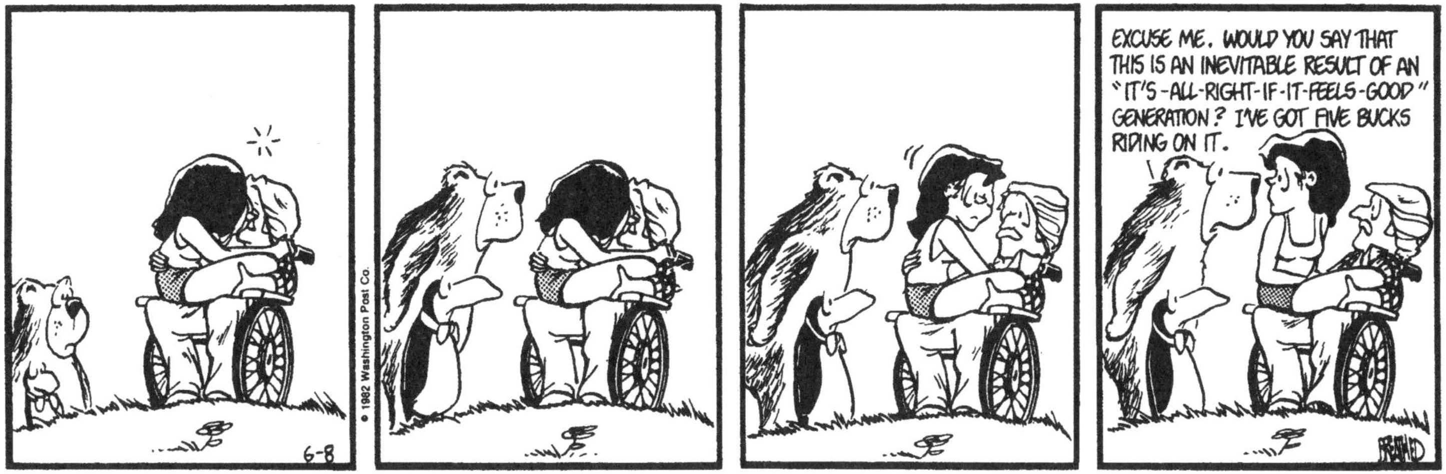
6-8
© 1982 Washington Post Co.
EXCUSE ME. WOULD YOU SAY THAT THIS IS AN INEVITABLE RESULT OF AN "IT'S-ALL-RIGHT-IF-IT-FEELS-GOOD" GENERATION? I'VE GOT FIVE BUCKS RIDING ON IT.

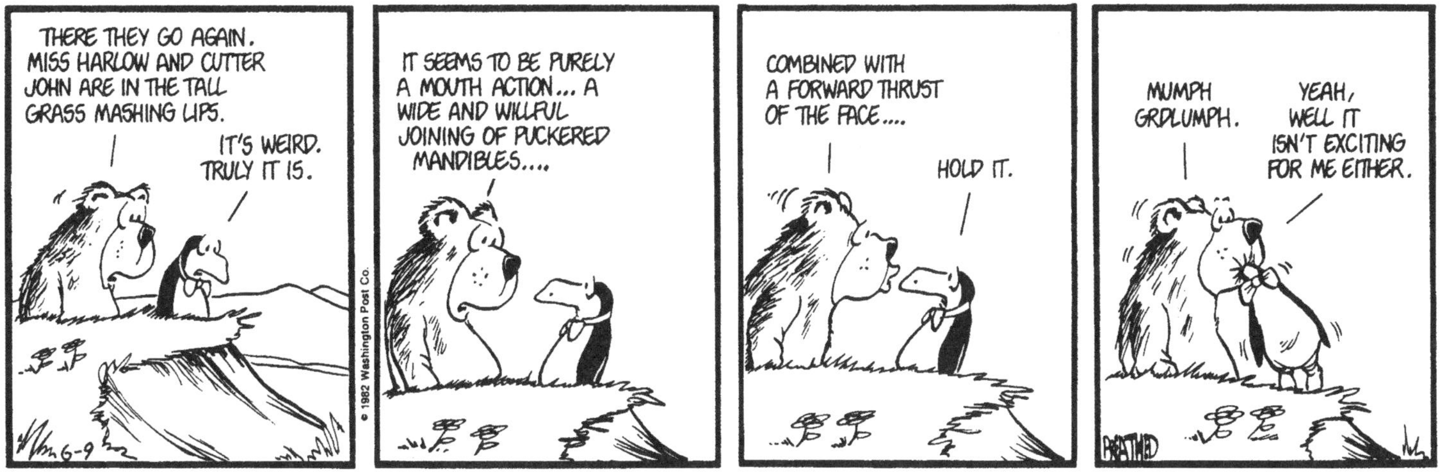
THERE THEY GO AGAIN. MISS HARLOW AND CUTTER JOHN ARE IN THE TALL GRASS MASHING LIPS.
IT'S WEIRD. TRULY IT IS.
6-9
© 1982 Washington Post Co.
IT SEEMS TO BE PURELY A MOUTH ACTION... A WIDE AND WILLFUL JOINING OF PUCKERED MANDIBLES....
COMBINED WITH A FORWARD THRUST OF THE FACE....
HOLD IT.
MUMPH GRDLUMPH.
YEAH, WELL IT ISN'T EXCITING FOR ME EITHER.

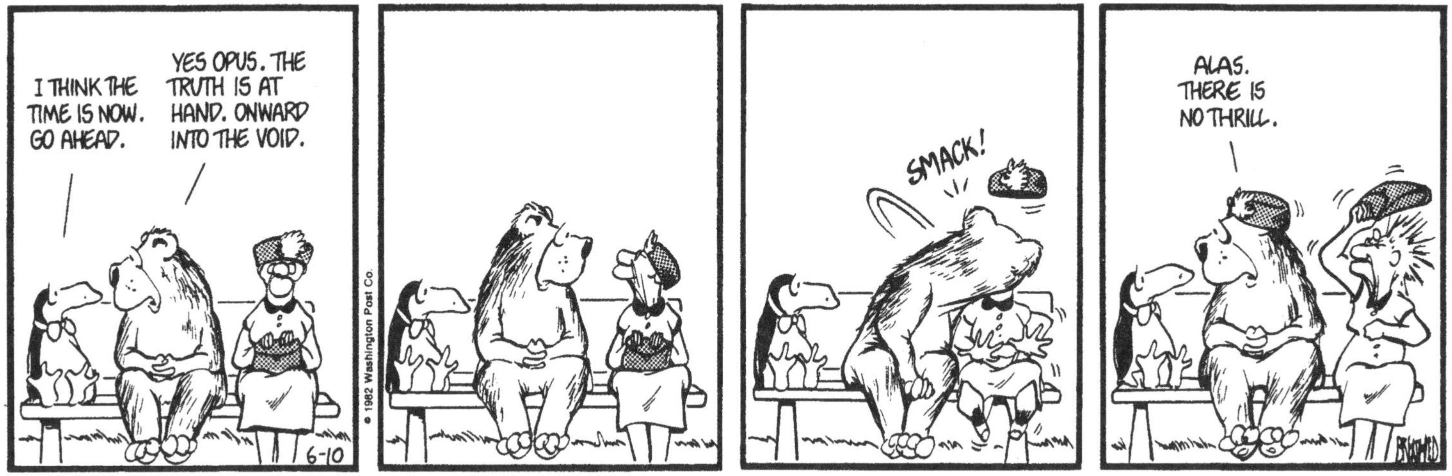
I THINK THE TIME IS NOW. GO AHEAD.
YES OPUS. THE TRUTH IS AT HAND. ONWARD INTO THE VOID.
6-10
© 1982 Washington Post Co.
SMACK!
ALAS. THERE IS NO THRILL.
BREATHED

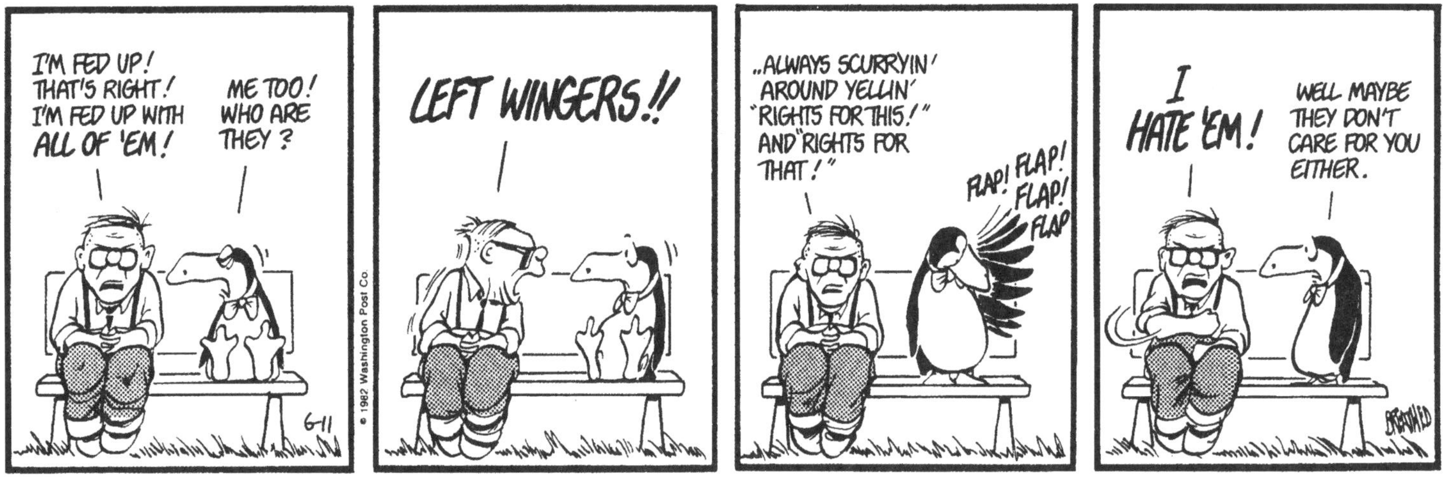
I'M FED UP! THAT'S RIGHT! I'M FED UP WITH ALL OF 'EM!
ME TOO! WHO ARE THEY?
6-11
© 1982 Washington Post Co.
LEFT WINGERS!!
..ALWAYS SCURRYIN' AROUND YELLIN' "RIGHTS FOR THIS!" AND "RIGHTS FOR THAT!"
FLAP! FLAP! FLAP! FLAP
I HATE 'EM!
WELL MAYBE THEY DON'T CARE FOR YOU EITHER.
BREATHED

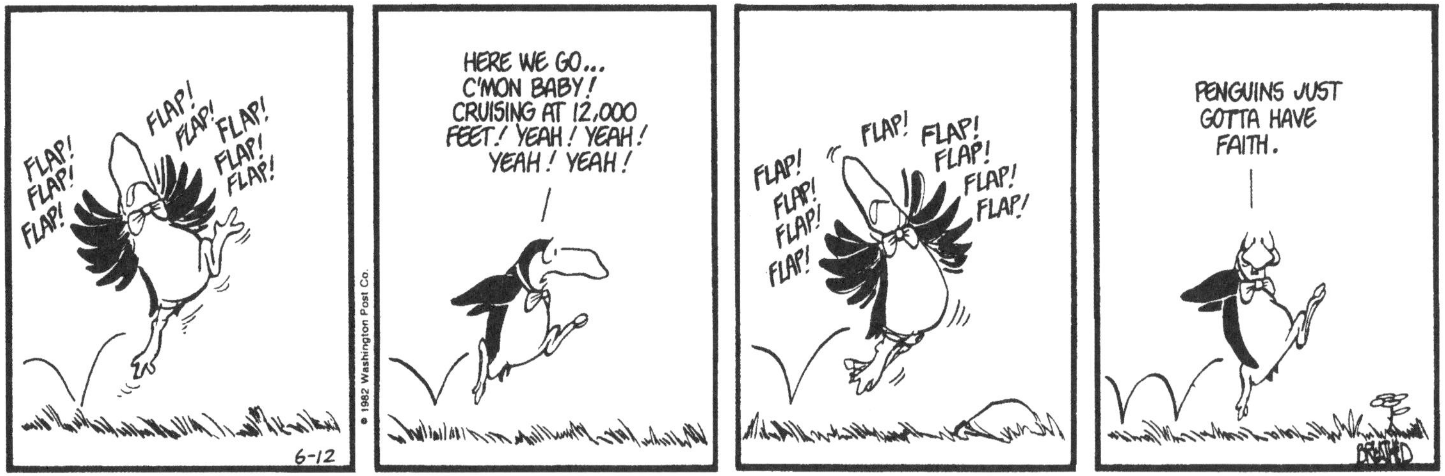
FLAP! FLAP! FLAP!
FLAP! FLAP! FLAP! FLAP! FLAP!
6-12
© 1982 Washington Post Co.
HERE WE GO... C'MON BABY! CRUISING AT 12,000 FEET! YEAH! YEAH! YEAH! YEAH!
FLAP! FLAP! FLAP! FLAP!
FLAP! FLAP! FLAP! FLAP! FLAP!
PENGUINS JUST GOTTA HAVE FAITH.
BREATHED

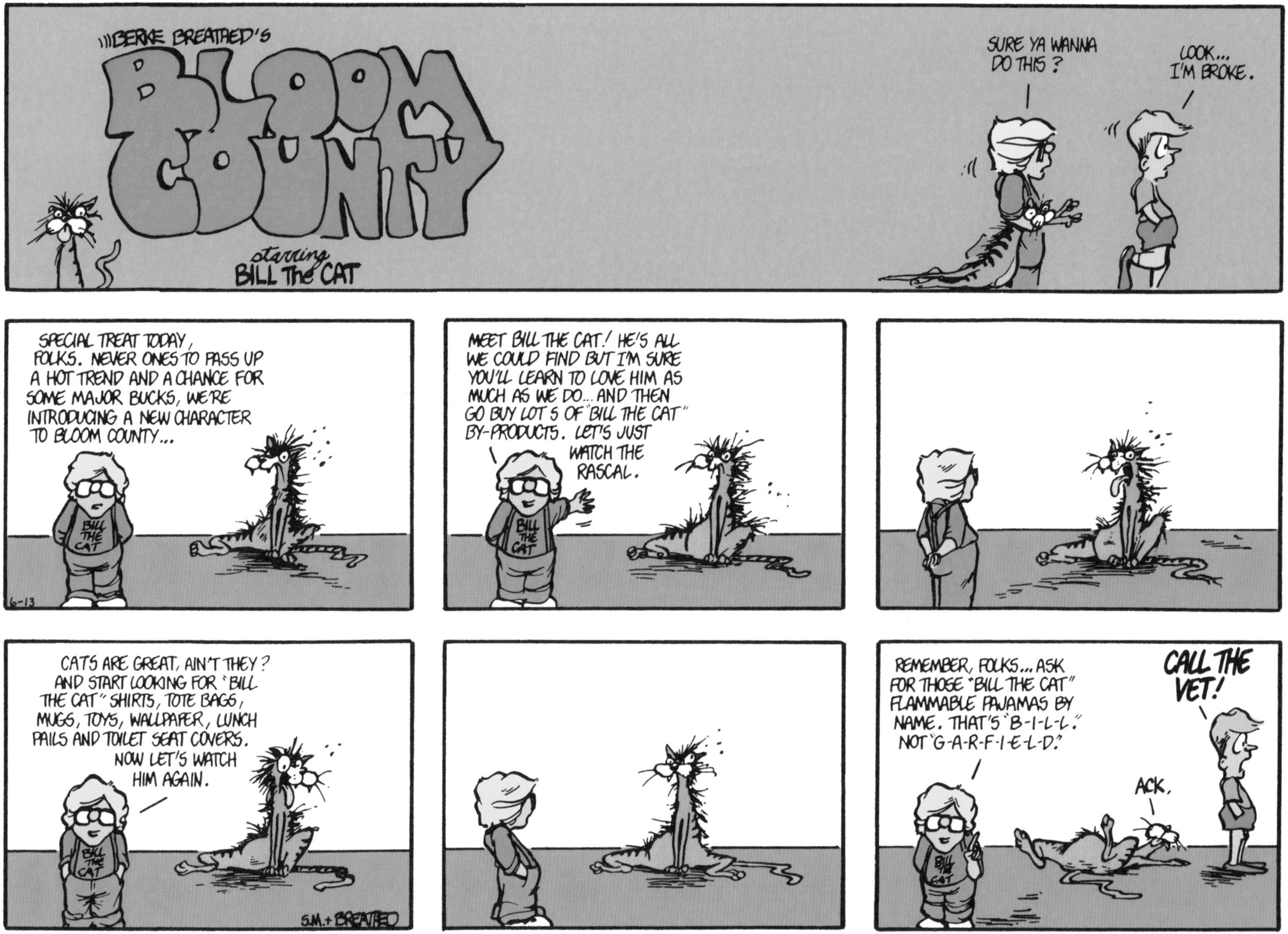
BERKE BREATHED'S
BLOOM COUNTY
starring BILL The CAT
SURE YA WANNA DO THIS ?
LOOK... I'M BROKE.
SPECIAL TREAT TODAY, FOLKS. NEVER ONES TO PASS UP A HOT TREND AND A CHANCE FOR SOME MAJOR BUCKS, WE'RE INTRODUCING A NEW CHARACTER TO BLOOM COUNTY...
BILL THE CAT
6-13
MEET BILL THE CAT! HE'S ALL WE COULD FIND BUT I'M SURE YOU'LL LEARN TO LOVE HIM AS MUCH AS WE DO... AND THEN GO BUY LOTS OF "BILL THE CAT" BY-PRODUCTS. LET'S JUST WATCH THE RASCAL.
BILL THE CAT
CATS ARE GREAT, AIN'T THEY? AND START LOOKING FOR "BILL THE CAT" SHIRTS, TOTE BAGS, MUGS, TOYS, WALLPAPER, LUNCH PAILS AND TOILET SEAT COVERS. NOW LET'S WATCH HIM AGAIN.
BILL THE CAT
S.M. + BREATHED
REMEMBER, FOLKS... ASK FOR THOSE "BILL THE CAT" FLAMMABLE PAJAMAS BY NAME. THAT'S "B-I-L-L." NOT "G-A-R-F-I-E-L-D."
CALL THE VET!
ACK.
BILL THE CAT

Bill debuts. I think you'll agree that it's almost as exciting to see this as those grainy old 8mm movies of Michael Jackson singing with his brothers in his basement in 1966. Curiously, plastic surgery was to play similar roles in both tragic lives. —BB

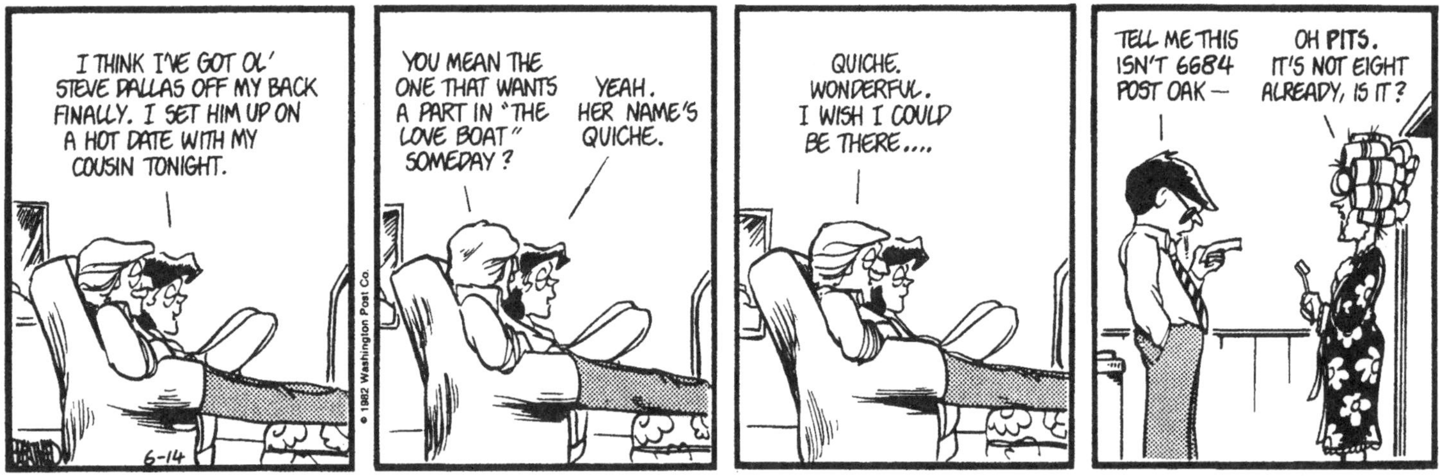

I THINK I'VE GOT OL' STEVE DALLAS OFF MY BACK FINALLY. I SET HIM UP ON A HOT DATE WITH MY COUSIN TONIGHT.
6-14
© 1982 Washington Post Co.
YOU MEAN THE ONE THAT WANTS A PART IN "THE LOVE BOAT" SOMEDAY?
YEAH. HER NAME'S QUICHE.
QUICHE. WONDERFUL. I WISH I COULD BE THERE....
TELL ME THIS ISN'T 6684 POST OAK —
OH PITS. IT'S NOT EIGHT ALREADY, IS IT?

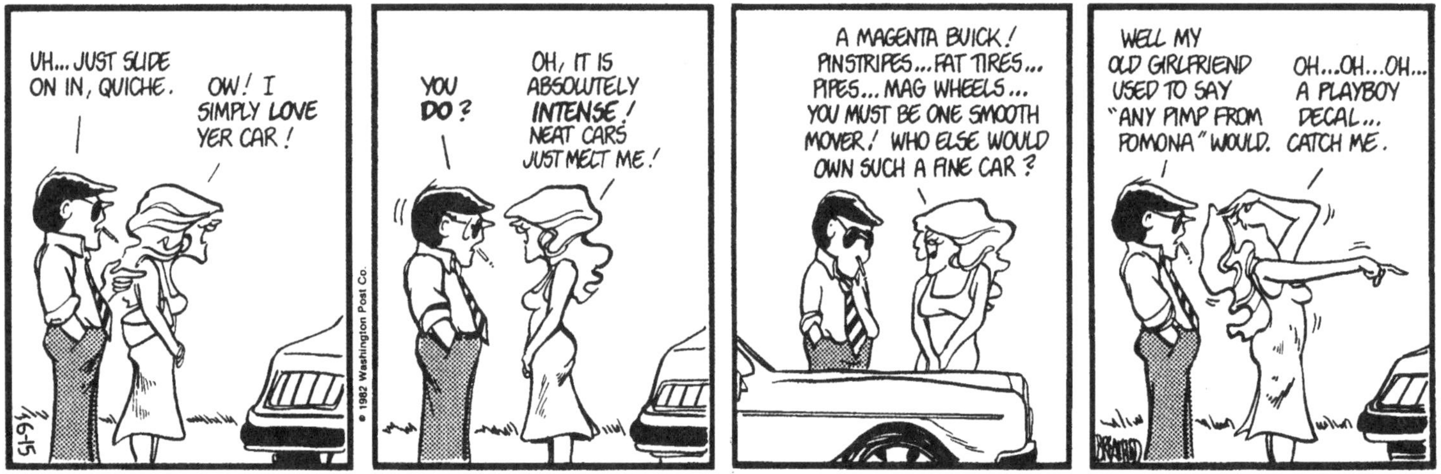

UH... JUST SLIDE ON IN, QUICHE.
OW! I SIMPLY LOVE YER CAR!
6-15
© 1982 Washington Post Co.
YOU DO?
OH, IT IS ABSOLUTELY INTENSE! NEAT CARS JUST MELT ME!
A MAGENTA BUICK! PINSTRIPES... FAT TIRES... PIPES... MAG WHEELS... YOU MUST BE ONE SMOOTH MOVER! WHO ELSE WOULD OWN SUCH A FINE CAR?
WELL MY OLD GIRLFRIEND USED TO SAY "ANY PIMP FROM POMONA" WOULD.
OH...OH...OH... A PLAYBOY DECAL... CATCH ME.

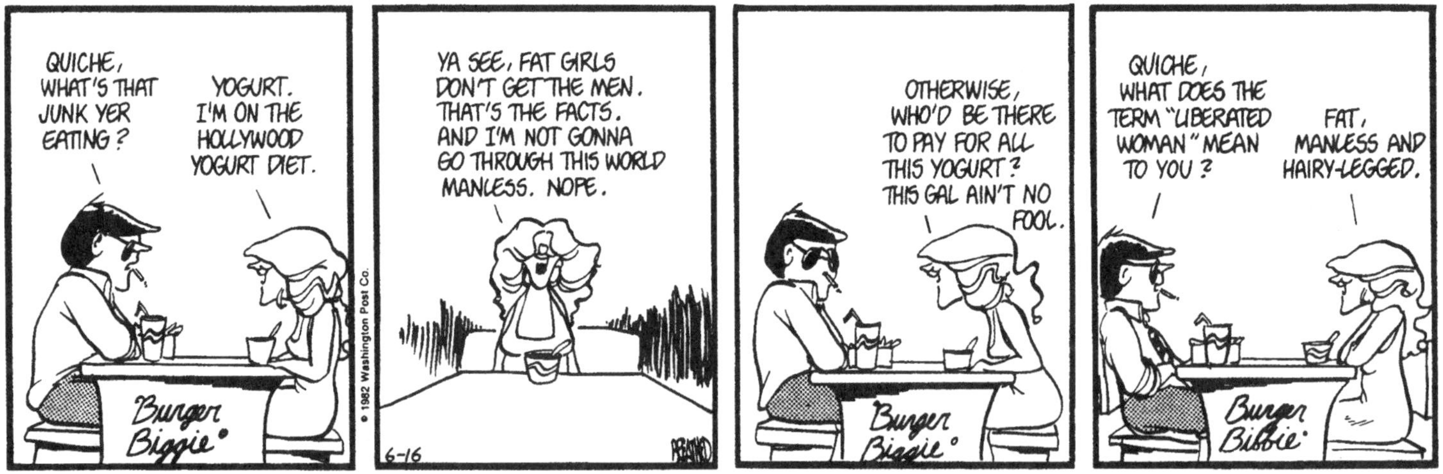

QUICHE, WHAT'S THAT JUNK YER EATING?
YOGURT. I'M ON THE HOLLYWOOD YOGURT DIET.
Burger Biggie
© 1982 Washington Post Co.
YA SEE, FAT GIRLS DON'T GET THE MEN. THAT'S THE FACTS. AND I'M NOT GONNA GO THROUGH THIS WORLD MANLESS. NOPE.
6-16
OTHERWISE, WHO'D BE THERE TO PAY FOR ALL THIS YOGURT? THIS GAL AIN'T NO FOOL.
Burger Biggie
QUICHE, WHAT DOES THE TERM "LIBERATED WOMAN" MEAN TO YOU?
FAT, MANLESS AND HAIRY-LEGGED.
Burger Biggie

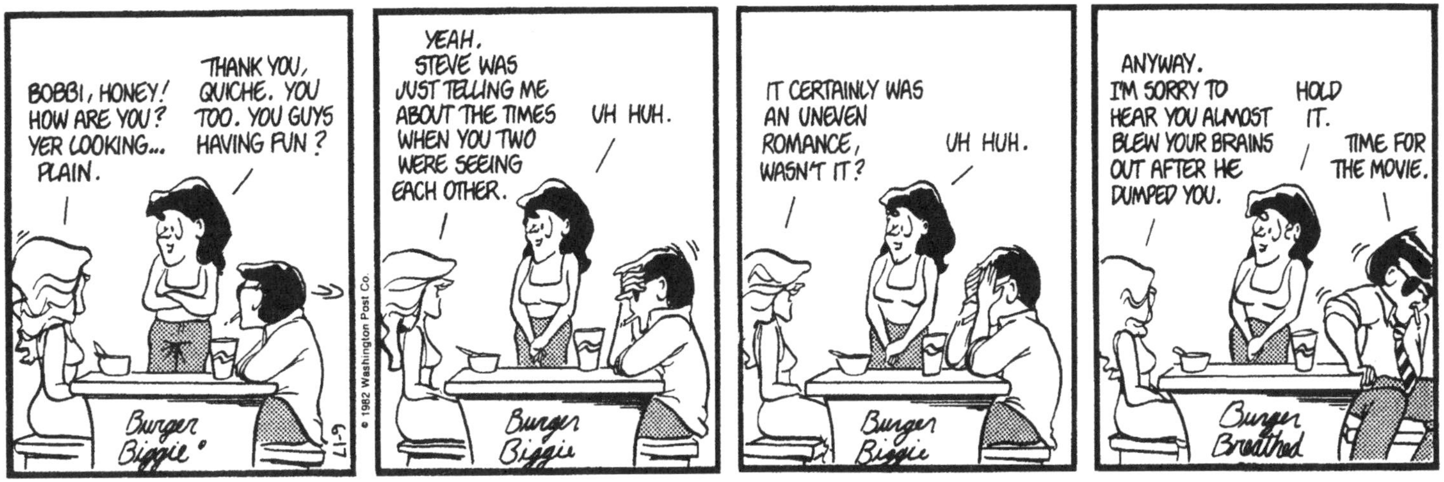
BOBBI, HONEY! HOW ARE YOU? YER LOOKING... PLAIN.
THANK YOU, QUICHE. YOU TOO. YOU GUYS HAVING FUN?
Burger Biggie
6-17
© 1982 Washington Post Co.
YEAH. STEVE WAS JUST TELLING ME ABOUT THE TIMES WHEN YOU TWO WERE SEEING EACH OTHER.
UH HUH.
Burger Biggie
IT CERTAINLY WAS AN UNEVEN ROMANCE, WASN'T IT?
UH HUH.
Burger Biggie
ANYWAY. I'M SORRY TO HEAR YOU ALMOST BLEW YOUR BRAINS OUT AFTER HE DUMPED YOU.
HOLD IT.
TIME FOR THE MOVIE.
Burger Breathed

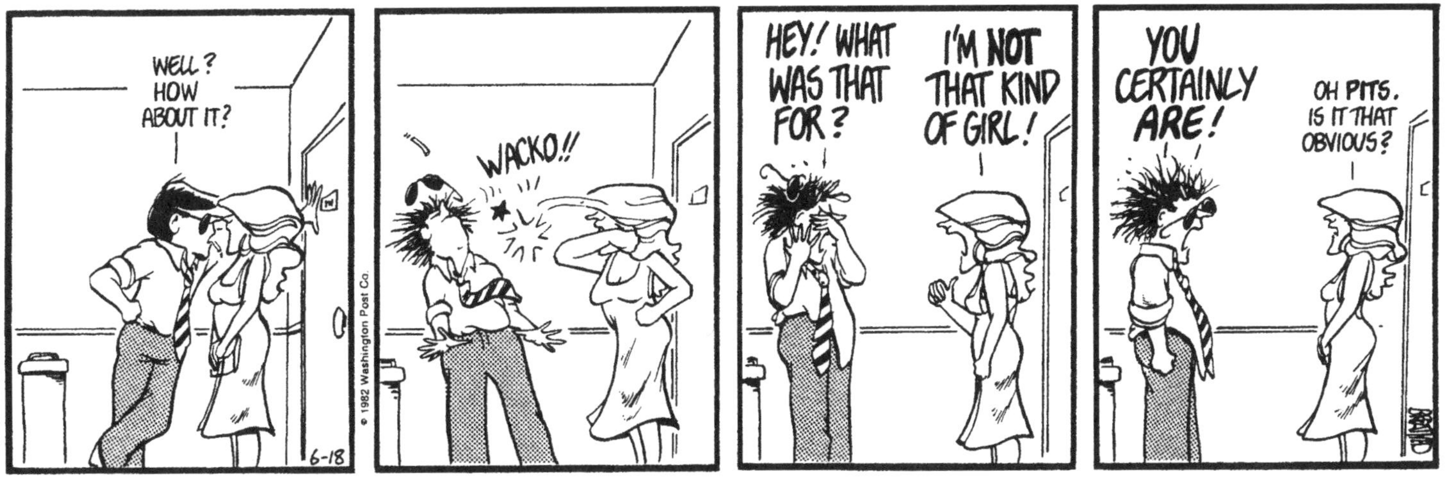
WELL? HOW ABOUT IT?
6-18
© 1982 Washington Post Co.
WACKO!!
HEY! WHAT WAS THAT FOR?
I'M NOT THAT KIND OF GIRL!
YOU CERTAINLY ARE!
OH PITS. IS IT THAT OBVIOUS?

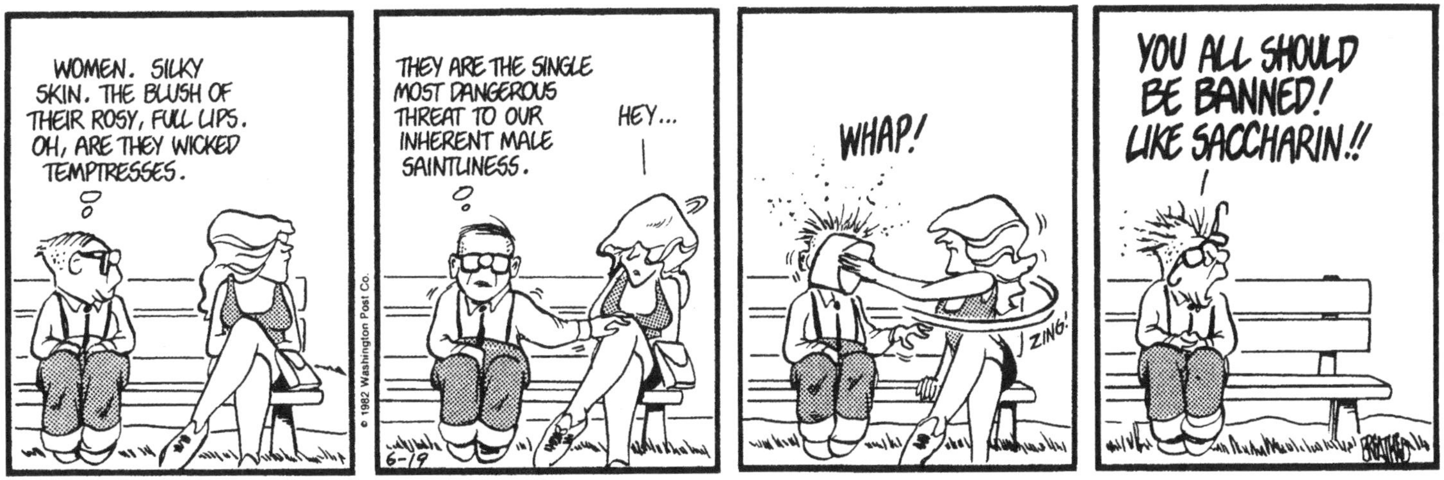
WOMEN. SILKY SKIN. THE BLUSH OF THEIR ROSY, FULL LIPS. OH, ARE THEY WICKED TEMPTRESSES.
© 1982 Washington Post Co.
THEY ARE THE SINGLE MOST DANGEROUS THREAT TO OUR INHERENT MALE SAINTLINESS.
HEY...
6-19
WHAP!
ZING!
YOU ALL SHOULD BE BANNED! LIKE SACCHARIN!!
BREATHED

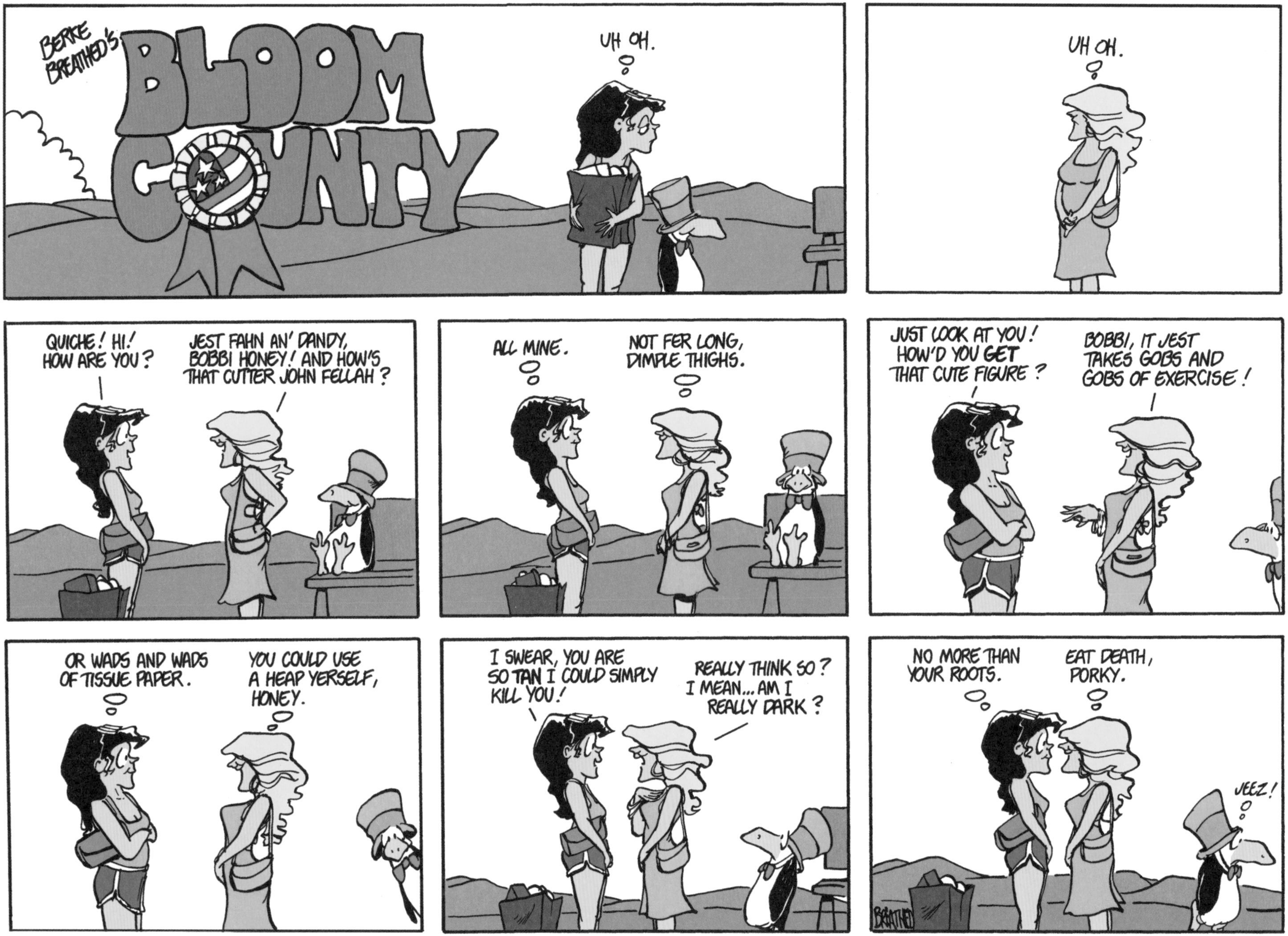
BERKE BREATHED'S
BLOOM COUNTY
UH OH.
UH OH.
QUICHE! HI! HOW ARE YOU?
JEST FAHN AN' DANDY, BOBBI HONEY! AND HOW'S THAT CUTTER JOHN FELLAH?
ALL MINE.
NOT FER LONG, DIMPLE THIGHS.
JUST LOOK AT YOU! HOW'D YOU GET THAT CUTE FIGURE?
BOBBI, IT JEST TAKES GOBS AND GOBS OF EXERCISE!
OR WADS AND WADS OF TISSUE PAPER.
YOU COULD USE A HEAP YERSELF, HONEY.
I SWEAR, YOU ARE SO TAN I COULD SIMPLY KILL YOU!
REALLY THINK SO? I MEAN... AM I REALLY DARK?
NO MORE THAN YOUR ROOTS.
EAT DEATH, PORKY.
JEEZ!
BREATHED

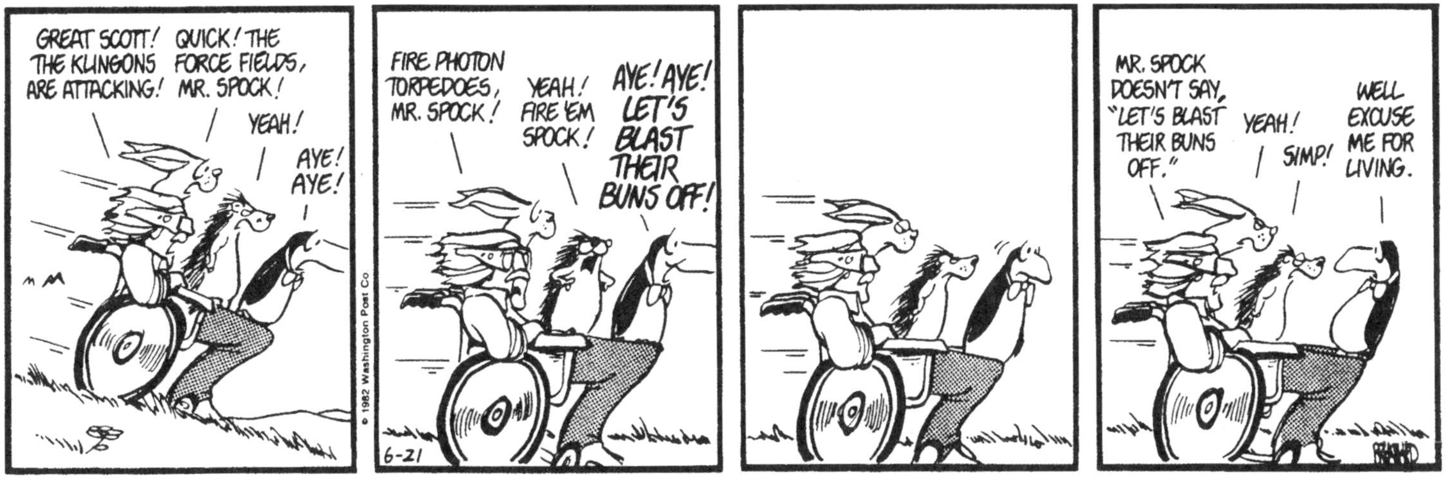
GREAT SCOTT! THE KLINGONS ARE ATTACKING!
QUICK! THE FORCE FIELDS, MR. SPOCK!
YEAH!
AYE! AYE!
© 1982 Washington Post Co.
6-21
FIRE PHOTON TORPEDOES, MR. SPOCK!
YEAH! FIRE 'EM SPOCK!
AYE! AYE! LET'S BLAST THEIR BUNS OFF!
MR. SPOCK DOESN'T SAY, "LET'S BLAST THEIR BUNS OFF."
YEAH!
SIMP!
WELL EXCUSE ME FOR LIVING.
BREATHED

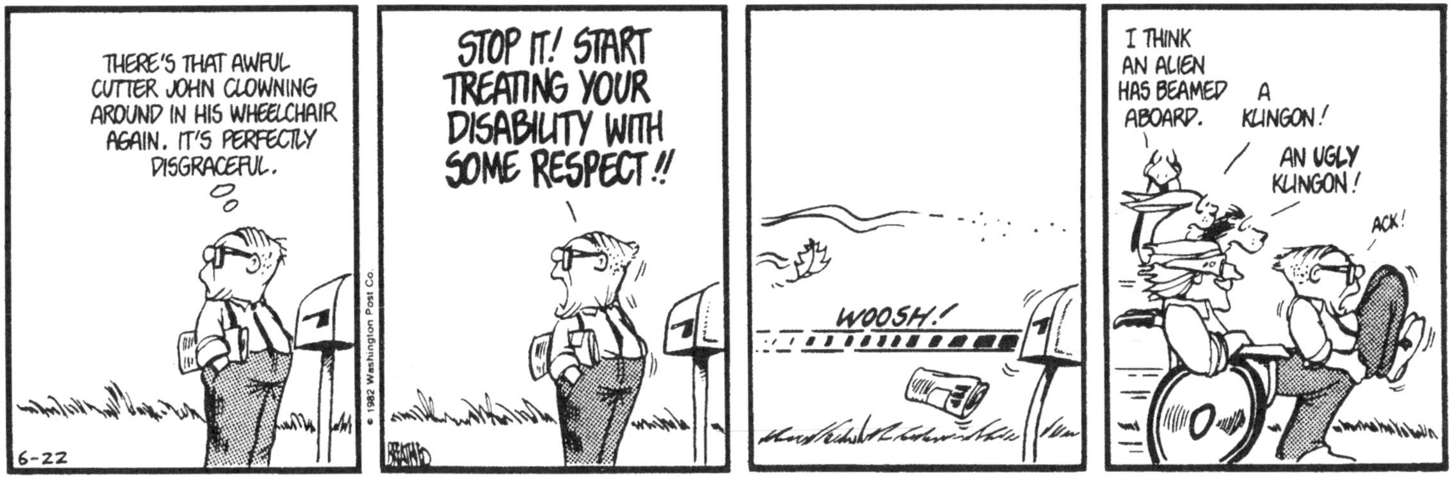
6-22
THERE'S THAT AWFUL CUTTER JOHN CLOWNING AROUND IN HIS WHEELCHAIR AGAIN. IT'S PERFECTLY DISGRACEFUL.
© 1982 Washington Post Co.
STOP IT! START TREATING YOUR DISABILITY WITH SOME RESPECT!!
BREATHED
WOOSH!
I THINK AN ALIEN HAS BEAMED ABOARD.
A KLINGON!
AN UGLY KLINGON!
ACK!

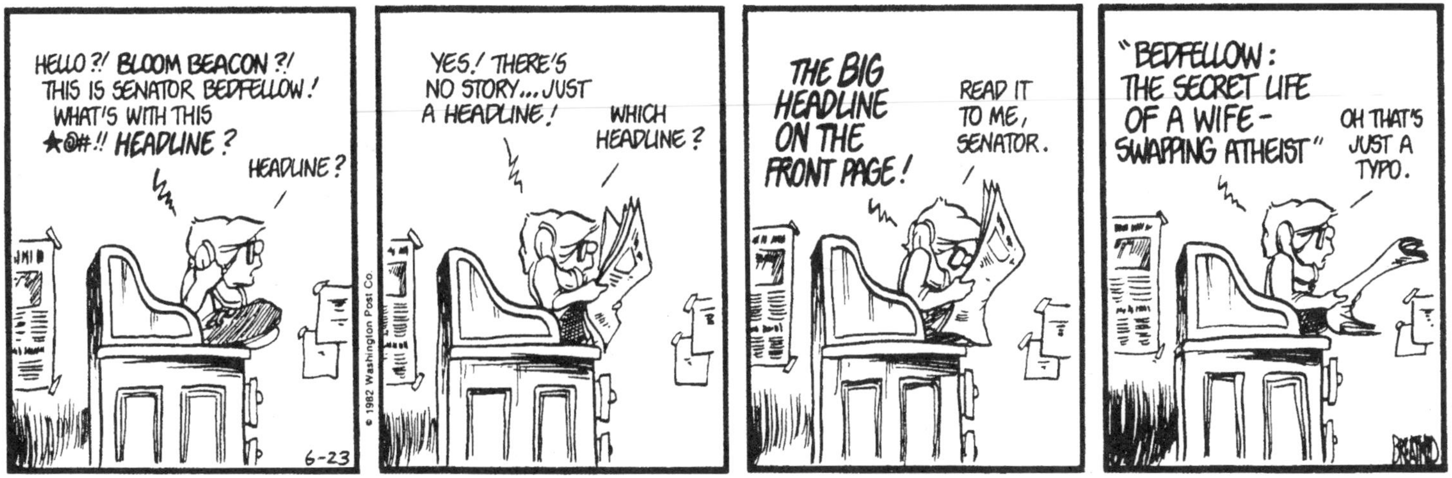
HELLO?! BLOOM BEACON?! THIS IS SENATOR BEDFELLOW! WHAT'S WITH THIS ★@#!! HEADLINE?
HEADLINE?
6-23
© 1982 Washington Post Co.
YES! THERE'S NO STORY... JUST A HEADLINE!
WHICH HEADLINE?
THE BIG HEADLINE ON THE FRONT PAGE!
READ IT TO ME, SENATOR.
"BEDFELLOW: THE SECRET LIFE OF A WIFE-SWAPPING ATHEIST"
OH THAT'S JUST A TYPO.
BREATHED

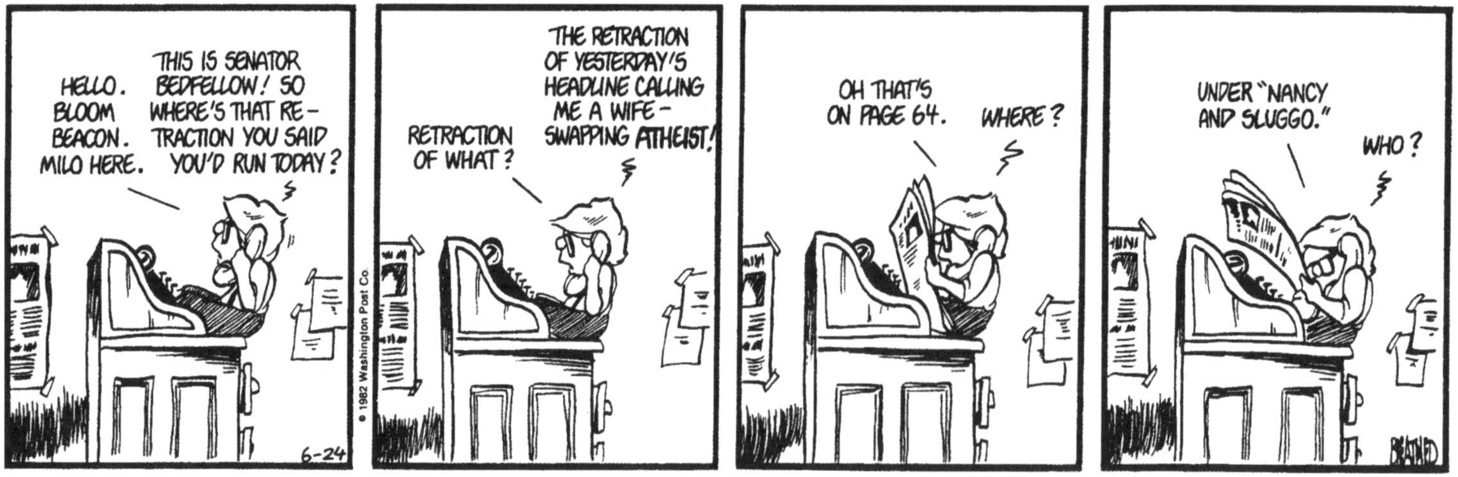
HELLO. BLOOM BEACON. MILO HERE.
THIS IS SENATOR BEDFELLOW! SO WHERE'S THAT RETRACTION YOU SAID YOU'D RUN TODAY?
RETRACTION OF WHAT?
THE RETRACTION OF YESTERDAY'S HEADLINE CALLING ME A WIFE-SWAPPING ATHEIST!
OH THAT'S ON PAGE 64.
WHERE?
UNDER "NANCY AND SLUGGO."
WHO?
6-24
© 1982 Washington Post Co.
BREATHED

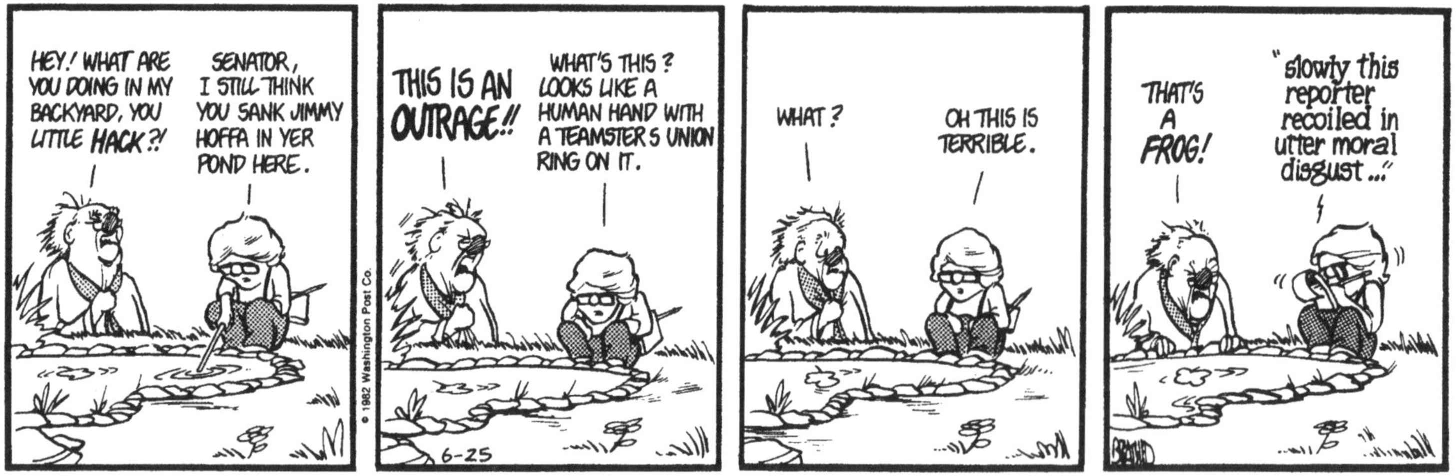
HEY! WHAT ARE YOU DOING IN MY BACKYARD, YOU LITTLE HACK?!
SENATOR, I STILL THINK YOU SANK JIMMY HOFFA IN YER POND HERE.
THIS IS AN OUTRAGE!!
WHAT'S THIS? LOOKS LIKE A HUMAN HAND WITH A TEAMSTER'S UNION RING ON IT.
WHAT?
OH THIS IS TERRIBLE.
THAT'S A FROG!
"slowly this reporter recoiled in utter moral disgust..."
6-25
© 1982 Washington Post Co.
BREATHED

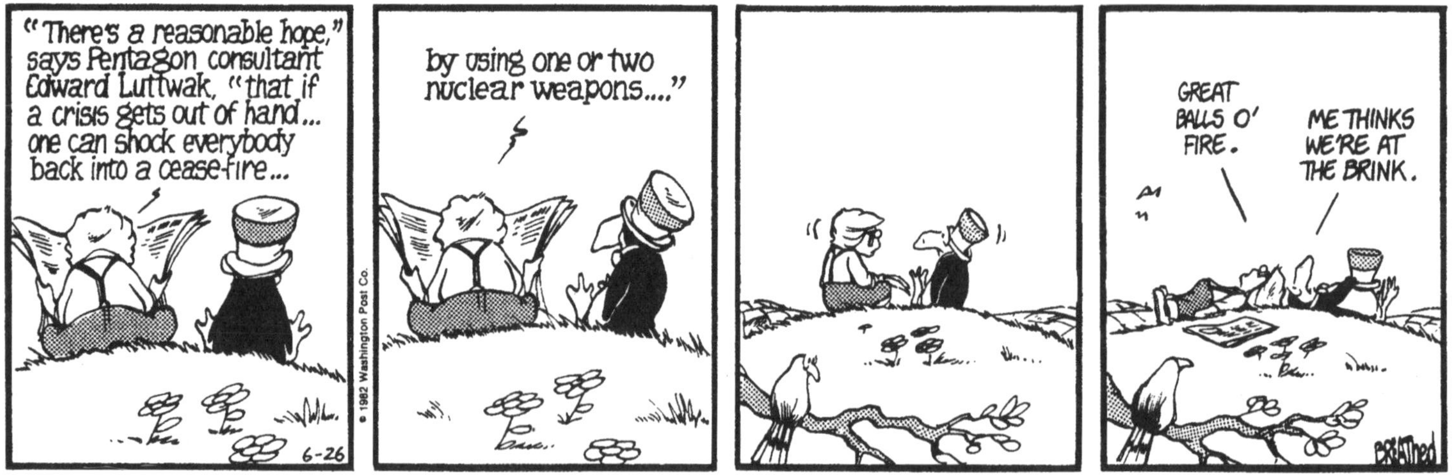
"There's a reasonable hope," says Pentagon consultant Edward Luttwak, "that if a crisis gets out of hand... one can shock everybody back into a cease-fire...
by using one or two nuclear weapons...."
GREAT BALLS O' FIRE.
ME THINKS WE'RE AT THE BRINK.
6-26
© 1982 Washington Post Co.
BREATHED

Edward Luttwak is a controversial military strategist and consultant, known for his unorthodox and occasionally inflammatory views.

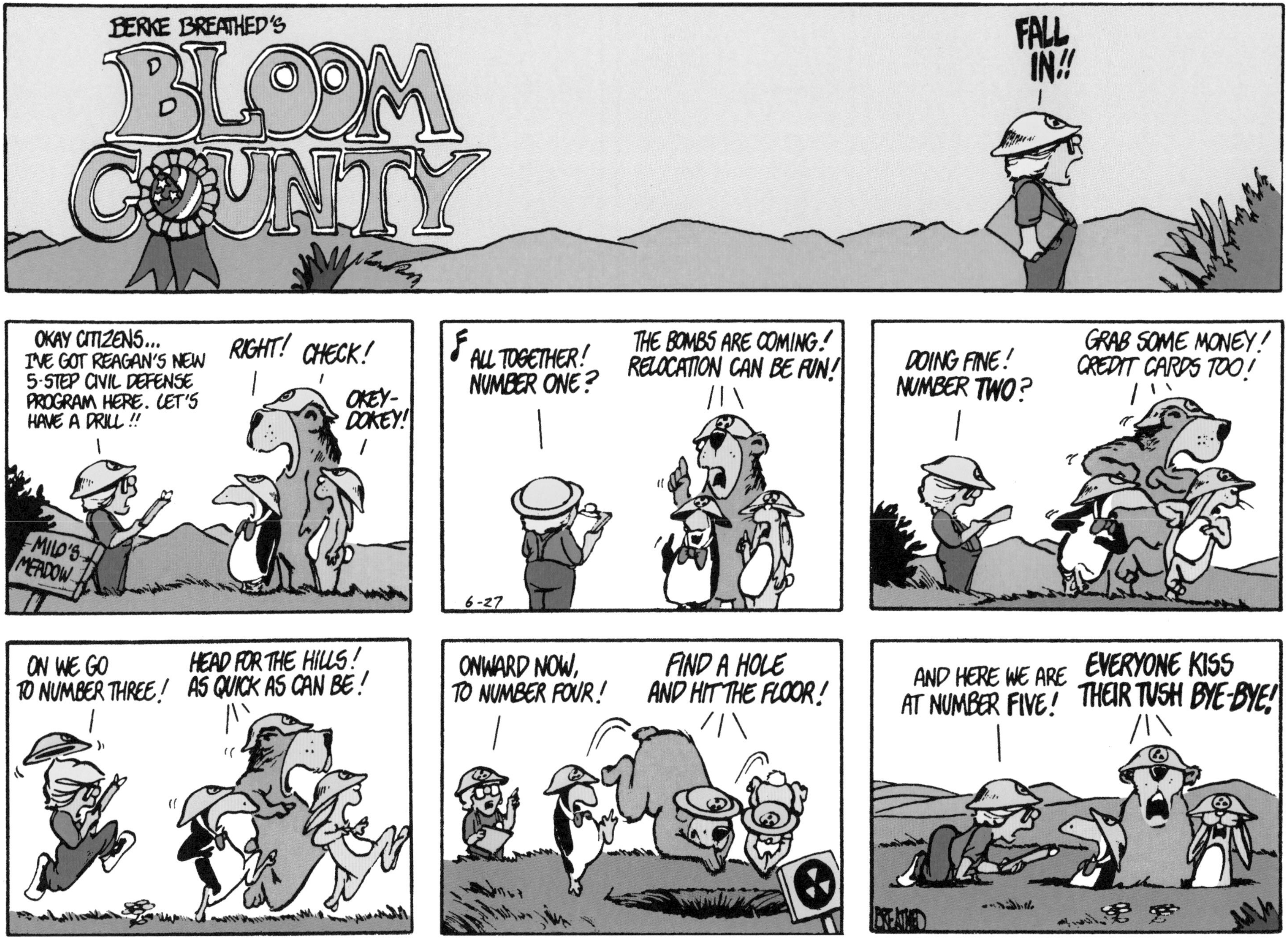
BERKE BREATHED'S
BLOOM COUNTY
FALL IN!!
OKAY CITIZENS... I'VE GOT REAGAN'S NEW 5-STEP CIVIL DEFENSE PROGRAM HERE. LET'S HAVE A DRILL!!
RIGHT!
CHECK!
OKEY-DOKEY!
MILO'S MEADOW
ALL TOGETHER! NUMBER ONE?
THE BOMBS ARE COMING! RELOCATION CAN BE FUN!
6-27
DOING FINE! NUMBER TWO?
GRAB SOME MONEY! CREDIT CARDS TOO!
ON WE GO TO NUMBER THREE!
HEAD FOR THE HILLS! AS QUICK AS CAN BE!
ONWARD NOW, TO NUMBER FOUR!
FIND A HOLE AND HIT THE FLOOR!
AND HERE WE ARE AT NUMBER FIVE!
EVERYONE KISS THEIR TUSH BYE-BYE!
BREATHED

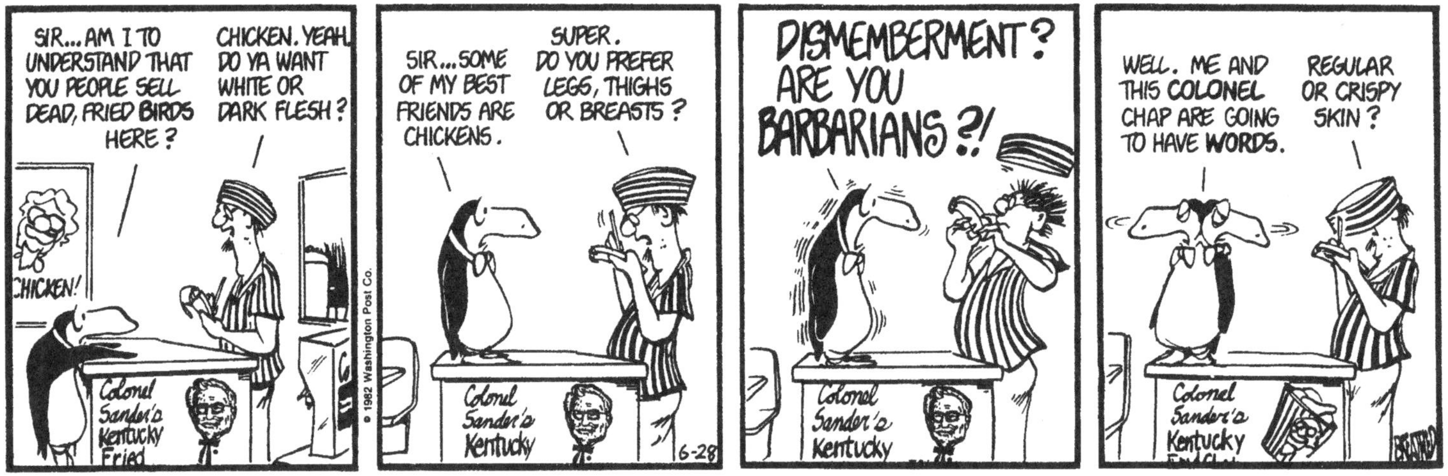
SIR... AM I TO UNDERSTAND THAT YOU PEOPLE SELL DEAD, FRIED BIRDS HERE?
CHICKEN. YEAH. DO YA WANT WHITE OR DARK FLESH?
CHICKEN!
Colonel Sander's Kentucky Fried
© 1982 Washington Post Co.
SIR... SOME OF MY BEST FRIENDS ARE CHICKENS.
SUPER. DO YOU PREFER LEGS, THIGHS OR BREASTS?
Colonel Sander's Kentucky
6-28
DISMEMBERMENT? ARE YOU BARBARIANS ?!
Colonel Sander's Kentucky
WELL. ME AND THIS COLONEL CHAP ARE GOING TO HAVE WORDS.
REGULAR OR CRISPY SKIN?
Colonel Sander's Kentucky
BREATHED

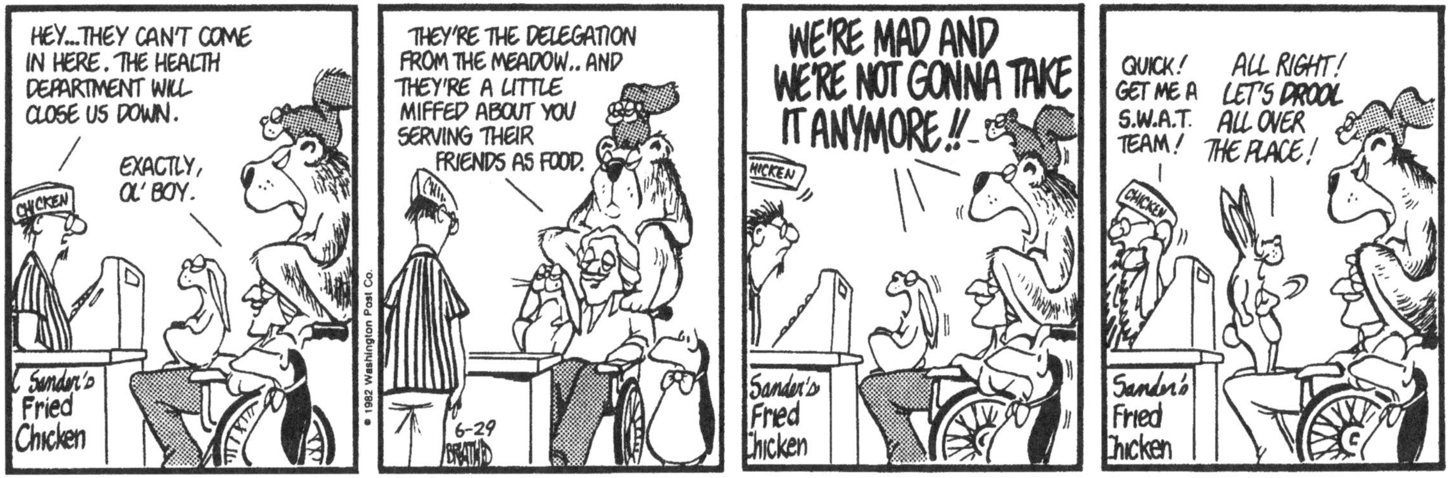
HEY... THEY CAN'T COME IN HERE. THE HEALTH DEPARTMENT WILL CLOSE US DOWN.
EXACTLY, OL' BOY.
CHICKEN
Sander's Fried Chicken
© 1982 Washington Post Co.
THEY'RE THE DELEGATION FROM THE MEADOW.. AND THEY'RE A LITTLE MIFFED ABOUT YOU SERVING THEIR FRIENDS AS FOOD.
6-29
BREATHED
WE'RE MAD AND WE'RE NOT GONNA TAKE IT ANYMORE!!
HICKEN
Sander's Fried Chicken
QUICK! GET ME A S.W.A.T. TEAM!
ALL RIGHT! LET'S DROOL ALL OVER THE PLACE!
CHICKEN
Sander's Fried Chicken

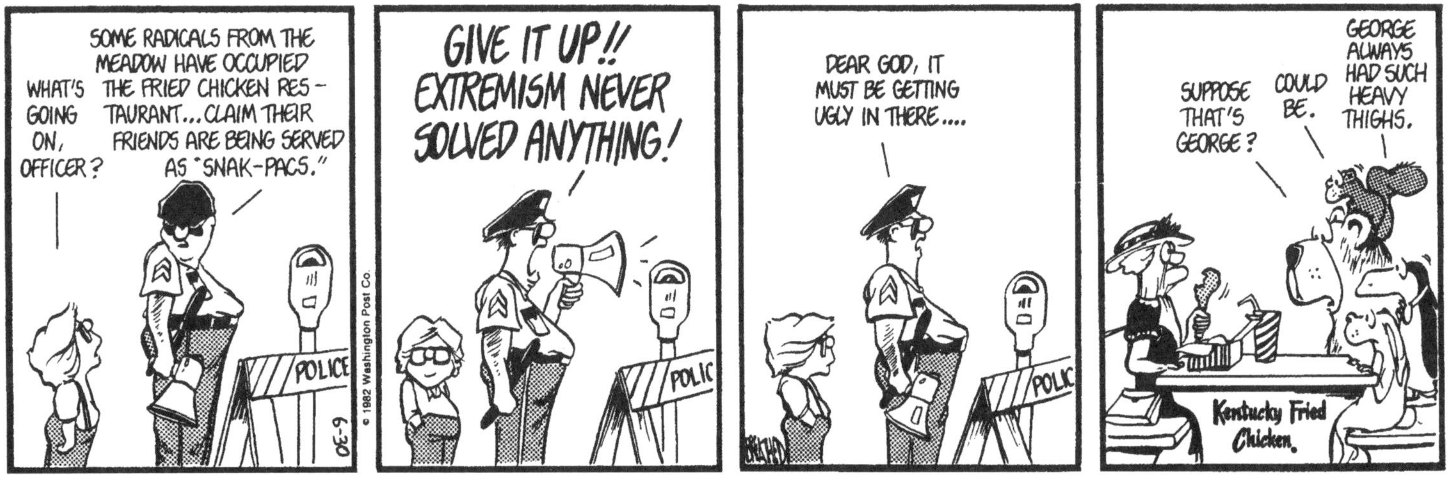
WHAT'S GOING ON, OFFICER?
SOME RADICALS FROM THE MEADOW HAVE OCCUPIED THE FRIED CHICKEN RES-TAURANT... CLAIM THEIR FRIENDS ARE BEING SERVED AS "SNAK-PACS."
POLICE
6-30
© 1982 Washington Post Co.
GIVE IT UP!! EXTREMISM NEVER SOLVED ANYTHING!
POLIC
DEAR GOD, IT MUST BE GETTING UGLY IN THERE....
POLIC
BREATHED
SUPPOSE THAT'S GEORGE?
COULD BE.
GEORGE ALWAYS HAD SUCH HEAVY THIGHS.
Kentucky Fried Chicken

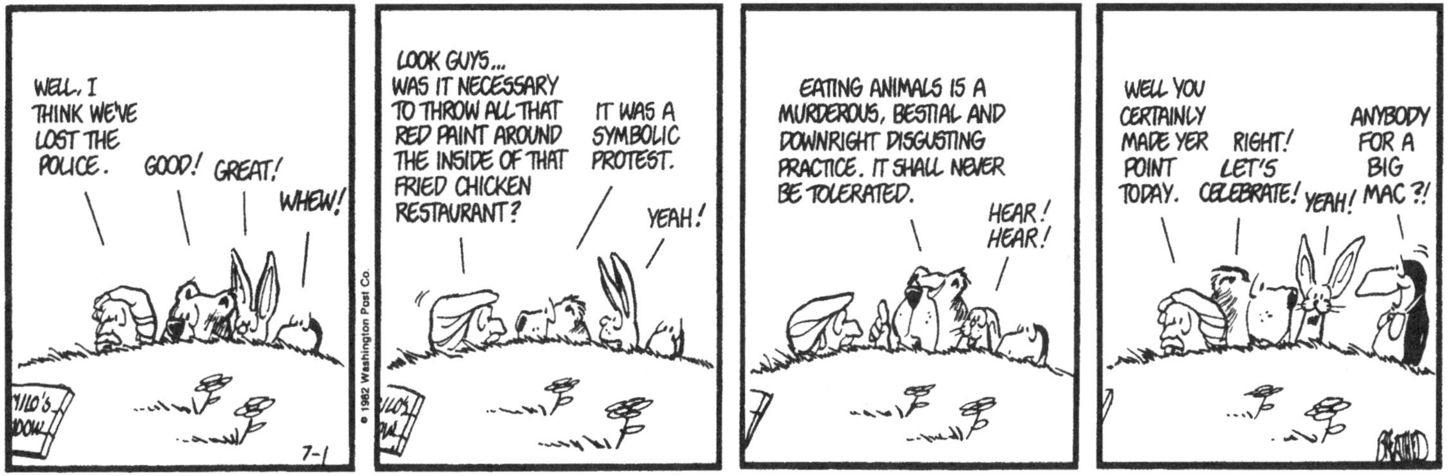
WELL, I THINK WE'VE LOST THE POLICE.
GOOD!
GREAT!
WHEW!
7-1
© 1982 Washington Post Co.
LOOK GUYS... WAS IT NECESSARY TO THROW ALL THAT RED PAINT AROUND THE INSIDE OF THAT FRIED CHICKEN RESTAURANT?
IT WAS A SYMBOLIC PROTEST.
YEAH!
EATING ANIMALS IS A MURDEROUS, BESTIAL AND DOWNRIGHT DISGUSTING PRACTICE. IT SHALL NEVER BE TOLERATED.
HEAR! HEAR!
WELL YOU CERTAINLY MADE YER POINT TODAY.
RIGHT! LET'S CELEBRATE!
YEAH!
ANYBODY FOR A BIG MAC ?!

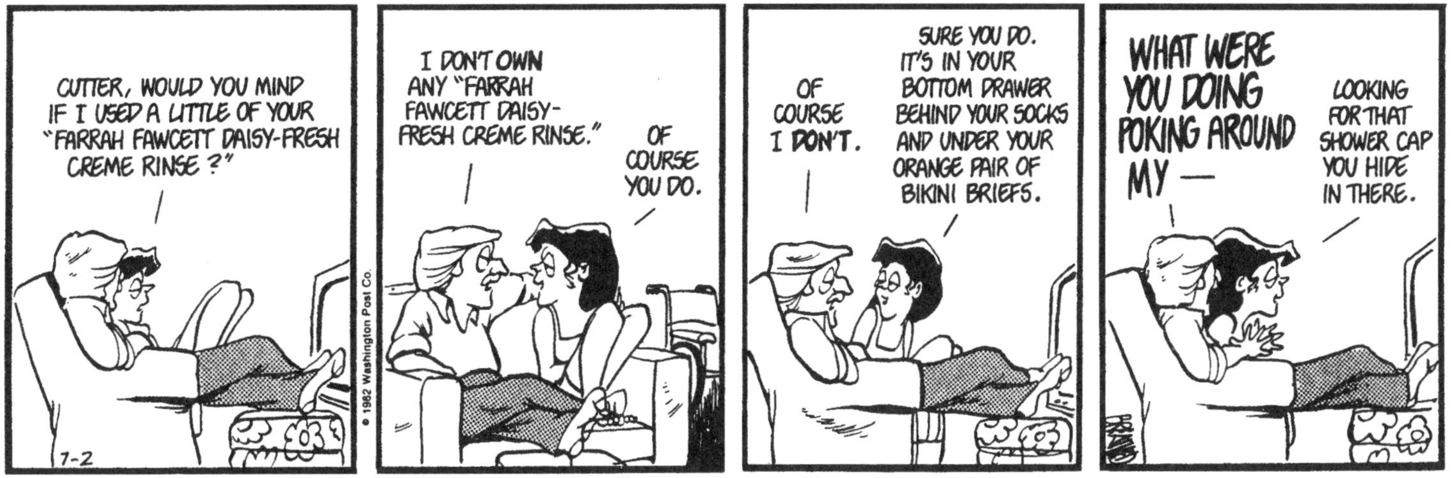
CUTTER, WOULD YOU MIND IF I USED A LITTLE OF YOUR "FARRAH FAWCETT DAISY-FRESH CREME RINSE?"
7-2
© 1982 Washington Post Co.
I DON'T OWN ANY "FARRAH FAWCETT DAISY-FRESH CREME RINSE."
OF COURSE YOU DO.
OF COURSE I DON'T.
SURE YOU DO. IT'S IN YOUR BOTTOM DRAWER BEHIND YOUR SOCKS AND UNDER YOUR ORANGE PAIR OF BIKINI BRIEFS.
WHAT WERE YOU DOING POKING AROUND MY —
LOOKING FOR THAT SHOWER CAP YOU HIDE IN THERE.

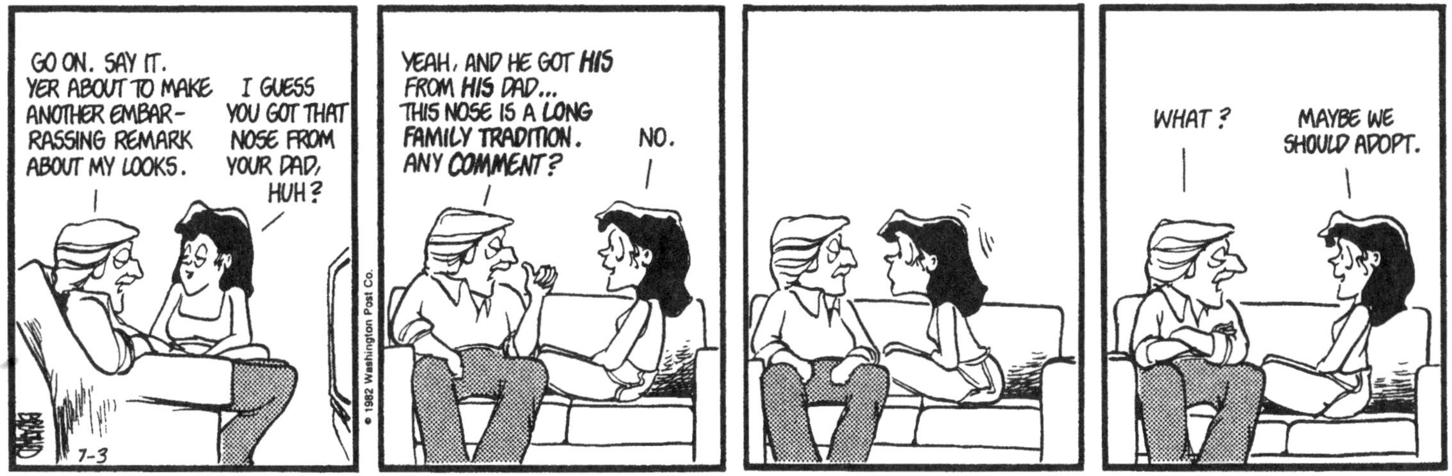
GO ON. SAY IT. YER ABOUT TO MAKE ANOTHER EMBARRASSING REMARK ABOUT MY LOOKS.
I GUESS YOU GOT THAT NOSE FROM YOUR DAD, HUH?
7-3
© 1982 Washington Post Co.
YEAH, AND HE GOT HIS FROM HIS DAD... THIS NOSE IS A LONG FAMILY TRADITION. ANY COMMENT?
NO.
WHAT?
MAYBE WE SHOULD ADOPT.

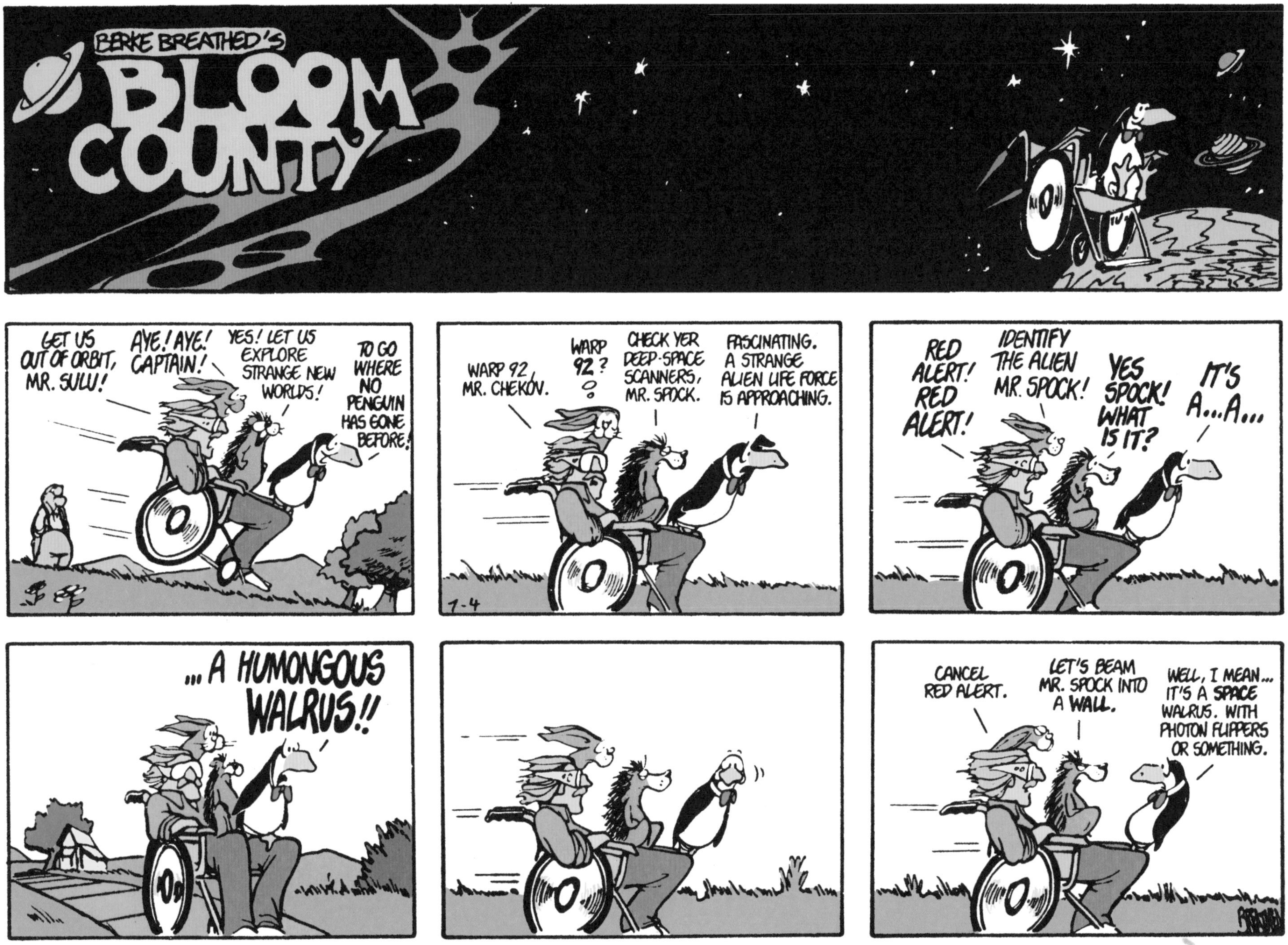
BERKE BREATHED'S
BLOOM COUNTY
GET US OUT OF ORBIT, MR. SULU!
AYE! AYE! CAPTAIN!
YES! LET US EXPLORE STRANGE NEW WORLDS!
TO GO WHERE NO PENGUIN HAS GONE BEFORE!
7-4
WARP 92, MR. CHEKOV.
WARP 92?
CHECK YER DEEP-SPACE SCANNERS, MR. SPOCK.
FASCINATING. A STRANGE ALIEN LIFE FORCE IS APPROACHING.
RED ALERT! RED ALERT!
IDENTIFY THE ALIEN MR. SPOCK!
YES SPOCK! WHAT IS IT?
IT'S A...A...
...A HUMONGOUS WALRUS!!
CANCEL RED ALERT.
LET'S BEAM MR. SPOCK INTO A WALL.
WELL, I MEAN... IT'S A SPACE WALRUS. WITH PHOTON FLIPPERS OR SOMETHING.

The hoary pop reference material of Star Trek aside (fresh still in 1982), I might point out that it was about here that I actually began to start amusing myself with these. Again, up to this point, I was new enough to the medium that it was more task than pleasure. Never a virtue in writing. But I smile at this gag now, as I remembered doing all those years ago. A tipping point of sorts. Fun is good in creative pursuits. You can increasingly see me having it. —BB

July 4, 1982

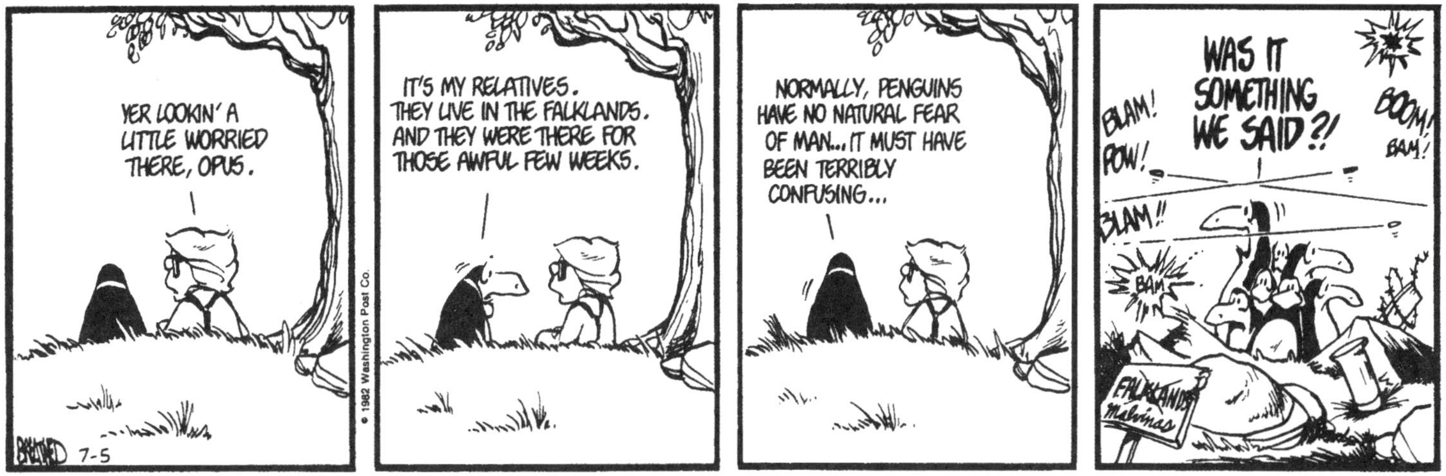
YER LOOKIN' A LITTLE WORRIED THERE, OPUS.
IT'S MY RELATIVES. THEY LIVE IN THE FALKLANDS. AND THEY WERE THERE FOR THOSE AWFUL FEW WEEKS.
NORMALLY, PENGUINS HAVE NO NATURAL FEAR OF MAN... IT MUST HAVE BEEN TERRIBLY CONFUSING...
BLAM!
POW!
WAS IT SOMETHING WE SAID?!
BOOM!
BAM!
BLAM!!
BAM
FALKLANDS Malvinas
© 1982 Washington Post Co.
7-5

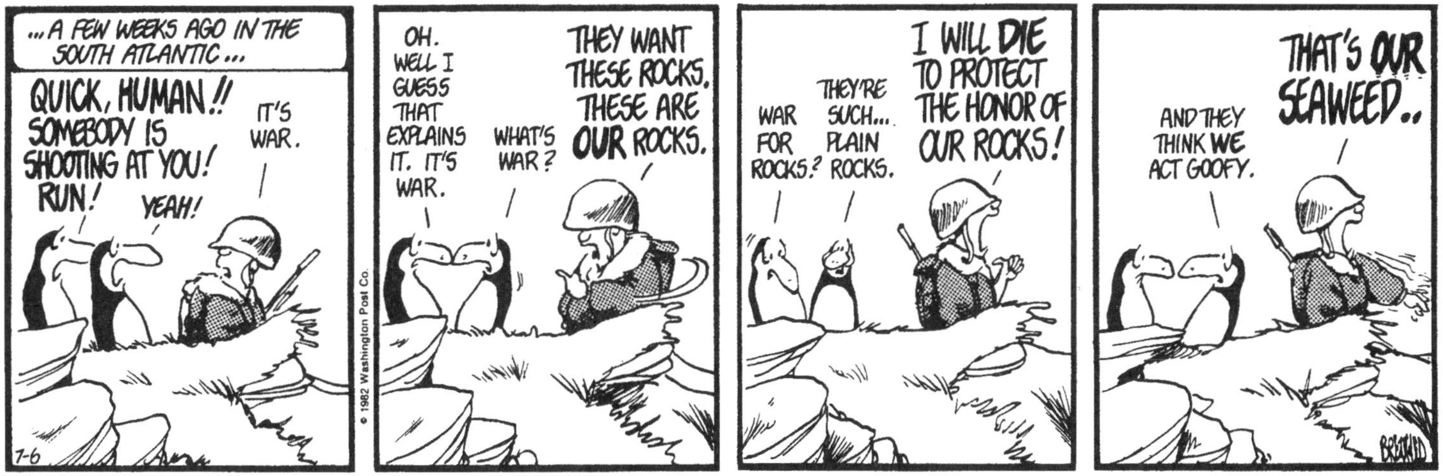
...A FEW WEEKS AGO IN THE SOUTH ATLANTIC...
QUICK, HUMAN!! SOMEBODY IS SHOOTING AT YOU! RUN!
YEAH!
IT'S WAR.
OH. WELL I GUESS THAT EXPLAINS IT. IT'S WAR.
WHAT'S WAR?
THEY WANT THESE ROCKS. THESE ARE OUR ROCKS.
WAR FOR ROCKS?
THEY'RE SUCH... PLAIN ROCKS.
I WILL DIE TO PROTECT THE HONOR OF OUR ROCKS!
AND THEY THINK WE ACT GOOFY.
THAT'S OUR SEAWEED..
© 1982 Washington Post Co.
7-6

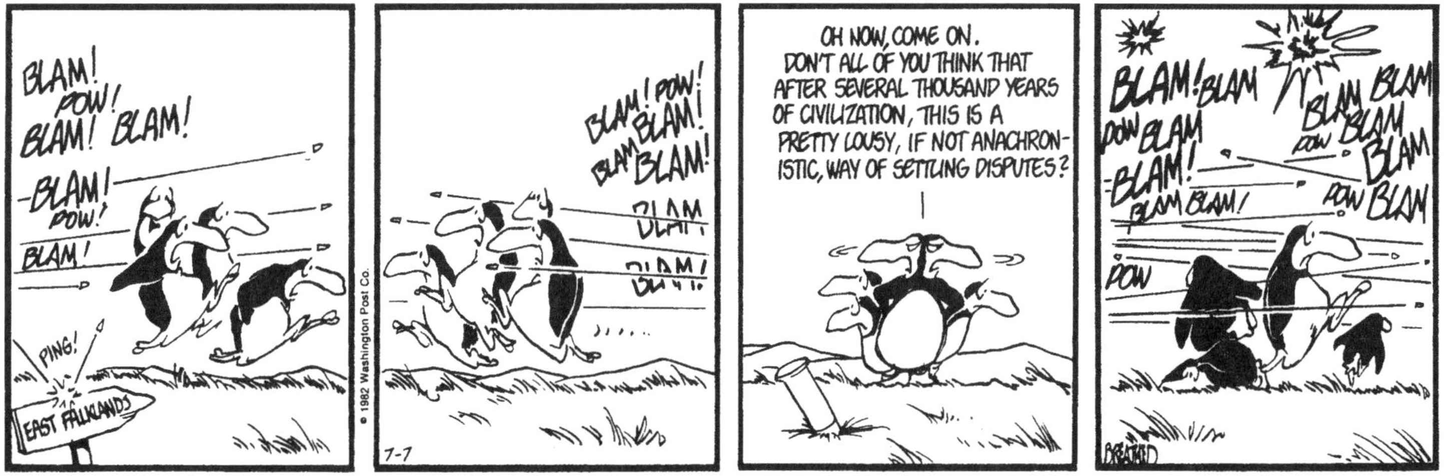
BLAM! POW! BLAM! BLAM!
BLAM! POW!
BLAM!
PING!
EAST FALKLANDS
BLAM! POW! BLAM! BLAM BLAM!
OH NOW, COME ON. DON'T ALL OF YOU THINK THAT AFTER SEVERAL THOUSAND YEARS OF CIVILIZATION, THIS IS A PRETTY LOUSY, IF NOT ANACHRONISTIC, WAY OF SETTLING DISPUTES?
BLAM! BLAM BLAM BLAM
POW BLAM
BLAM! BLAM BLAM!
POW
© 1982 Washington Post Co.
7-7

The contested sovereignty of the Falkland Islands, between England and Argentina, erupted into war in April of 1982. Ten weeks, and nearly 1,000 casualties later, Britain prevailed. The territory remains disputed to this day.

EXCUSE ME. MAY I MAKE AN OBSERVATION ON ALL THIS ? THANK YOU.

FALKLANDS
Malvinas

WELL SIR.. THIS LOOKS LIKE YET ANOTHER TRAGIC EXAMPLE OF THE OLD SENDING OUT THE YOUNG TO SPILL THEIR GUTS IN SOME STUPID POLITICAL MOVE DISGUISED AS A NATIONAL HONOR.

© 1982 Washington Post Co.

7-8

HEY MELENDEZ. COME AND HEAR THIS.

I MEAN.. EVEN A HERRING COULD SEE THAT.

WELL MAYBE NOT A HERRING.

BERKE

OH MY. THE HUMANS SEEM TO HAVE KILLED A GREAT NUMBER OF EACH OTHER DOWN THERE.

A TRULY CURIOUS SPECIES...

MALVINAS
FALKLANDS

7-9

NORMAL ACTIVITY SEEMS TO BE A SORT OF PERPETUAL ACT OF SELF-MASSACRE.

SAVAGE... PRIMITIVE... ALMOST ANIMALISTIC BEHAVIOR.

© 1982 Washington Post Co.

YOU DON'T SUPPOSE WE EVOLVED FROM *THEM* ?

I, MYSELF, AM PHYSICALLY REPULSED AT THE IDEA.

BERKE

AAIGH!!

7-10

© 1982 Washington Post Co.

THERE'S A PENGUIN IN THE FREEZER!

WOULD YOU PREFER A HIPPO IN THE TUB ?

BERKE

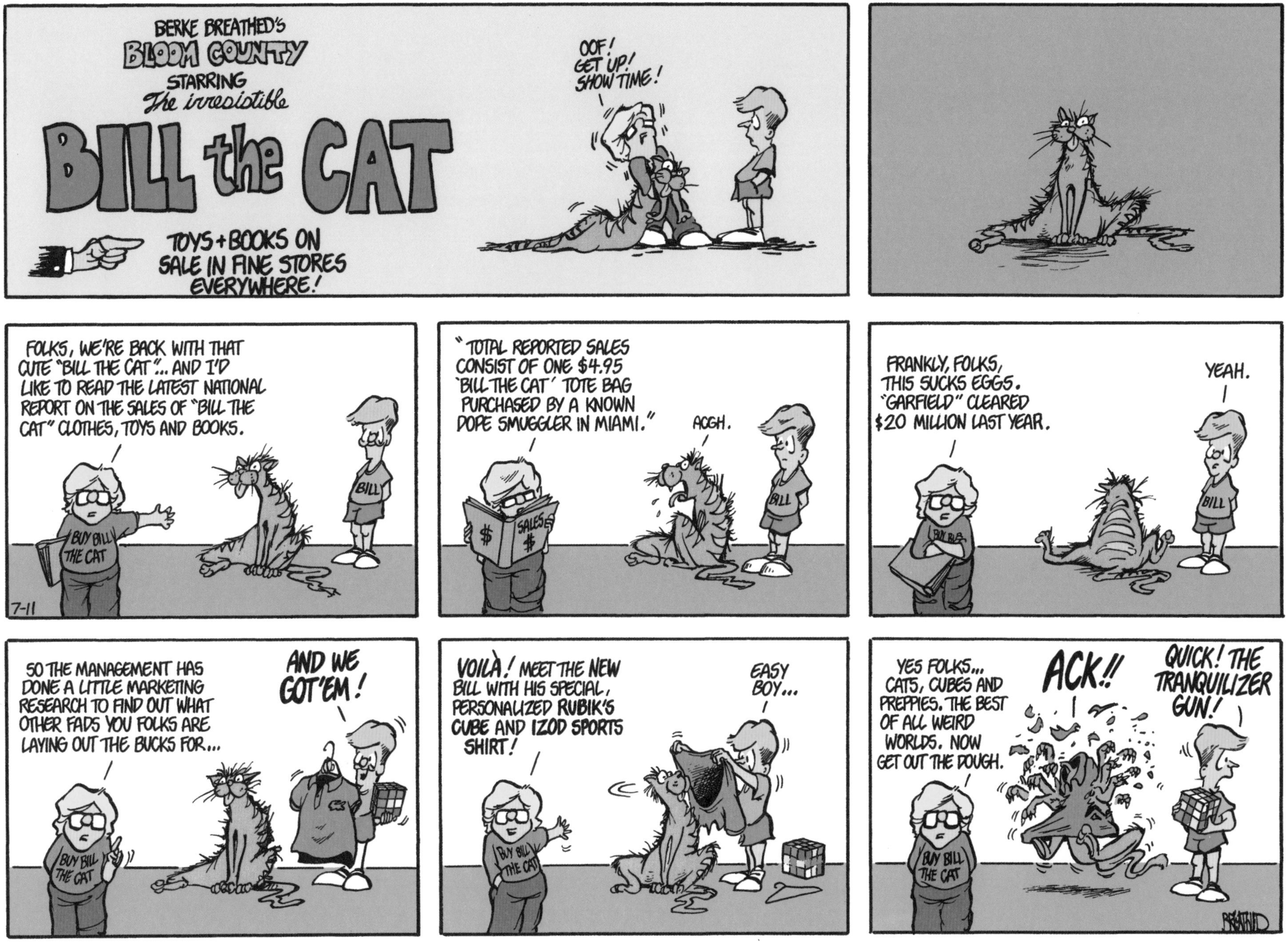
BERKE BREATHED'S
BLOOM COUNTY
STARRING
The irresistible
BILL the CAT
TOYS + BOOKS ON SALE IN FINE STORES EVERYWHERE!
OOF! GET UP! SHOW TIME!
7-11
FOLKS, WE'RE BACK WITH THAT CUTE "BILL THE CAT"... AND I'D LIKE TO READ THE LATEST NATIONAL REPORT ON THE SALES OF "BILL THE CAT" CLOTHES, TOYS AND BOOKS.
BUY BILL THE CAT
BILL
"TOTAL REPORTED SALES CONSIST OF ONE $4.95 'BILL THE CAT' TOTE BAG PURCHASED BY A KNOWN DOPE SMUGGLER IN MIAMI."
AOGH.
SALES $ $
BILL
FRANKLY, FOLKS, THIS SUCKS EGGS. "GARFIELD" CLEARED $20 MILLION LAST YEAR.
YEAH.
BILL
SO THE MANAGEMENT HAS DONE A LITTLE MARKETING RESEARCH TO FIND OUT WHAT OTHER FADS YOU FOLKS ARE LAYING OUT THE BUCKS FOR...
AND WE GOT'EM!
BUY BILL THE CAT
VOILÀ! MEET THE NEW BILL WITH HIS SPECIAL, PERSONALIZED RUBIK'S CUBE AND IZOD SPORTS SHIRT!
EASY BOY...
BUY BILL THE CAT
YES FOLKS... CATS, CUBES AND PREPPIES. THE BEST OF ALL WEIRD WORLDS. NOW GET OUT THE DOUGH.
ACK!!
QUICK! THE TRANQUILIZER GUN!
BUY BILL THE CAT
BREATHED

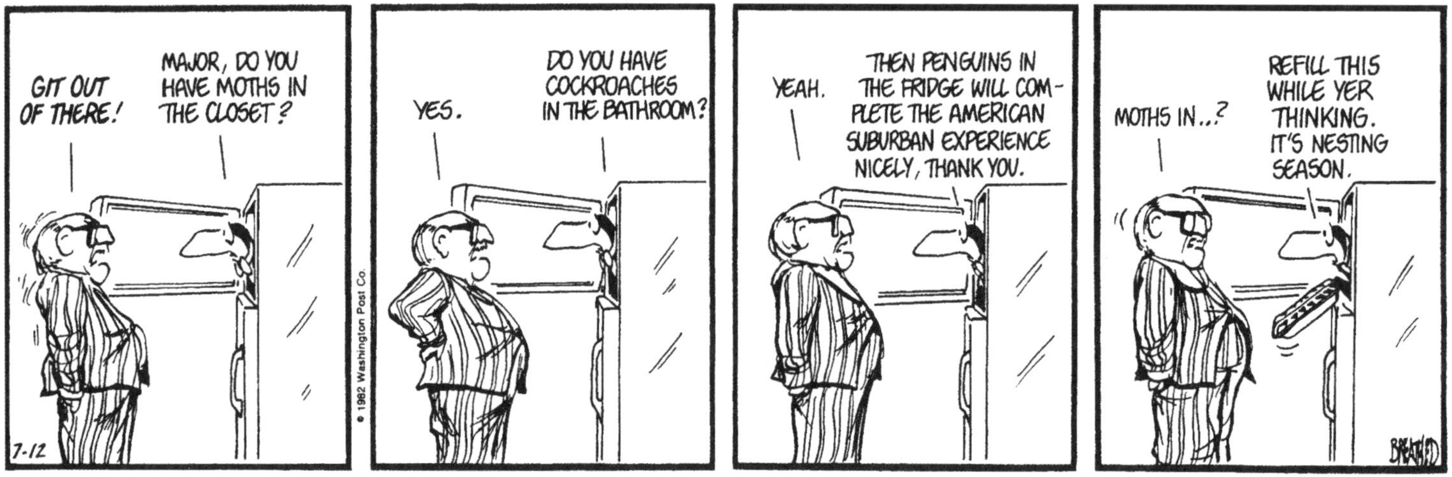

GIT OUT OF THERE!
MAJOR, DO YOU HAVE MOTHS IN THE CLOSET?
7-12
YES.
DO YOU HAVE COCKROACHES IN THE BATHROOM?
© 1982 Washington Post Co.
YEAH.
THEN PENGUINS IN THE FRIDGE WILL COMPLETE THE AMERICAN SUBURBAN EXPERIENCE NICELY, THANK YOU.
MOTHS IN...?
REFILL THIS WHILE YER THINKING. IT'S NESTING SEASON.

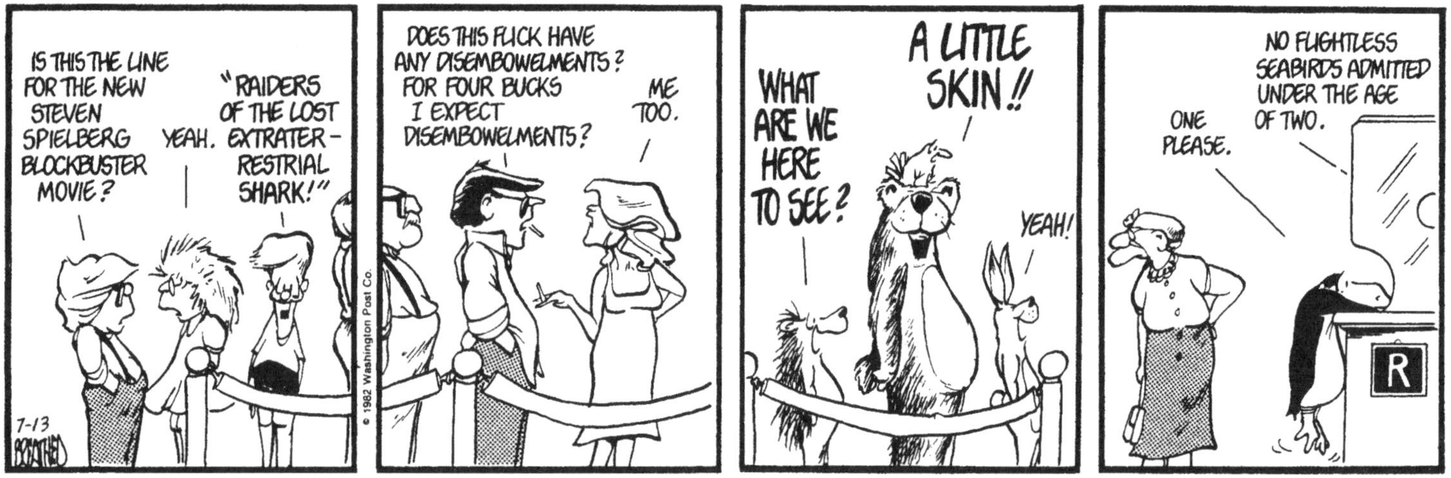

IS THIS THE LINE FOR THE NEW STEVEN SPIELBERG BLOCKBUSTER MOVIE?
YEAH.
"RAIDERS OF THE LOST EXTRATERRESTRIAL SHARK!"
7-13
© 1982 Washington Post Co.
DOES THIS FLICK HAVE ANY DISEMBOWELMENTS? FOR FOUR BUCKS I EXPECT DISEMBOWELMENTS?
ME TOO.
WHAT ARE WE HERE TO SEE?
A LITTLE SKIN!!
YEAH!
ONE PLEASE.
NO FLIGHTLESS SEABIRDS ADMITTED UNDER THE AGE OF TWO.
R

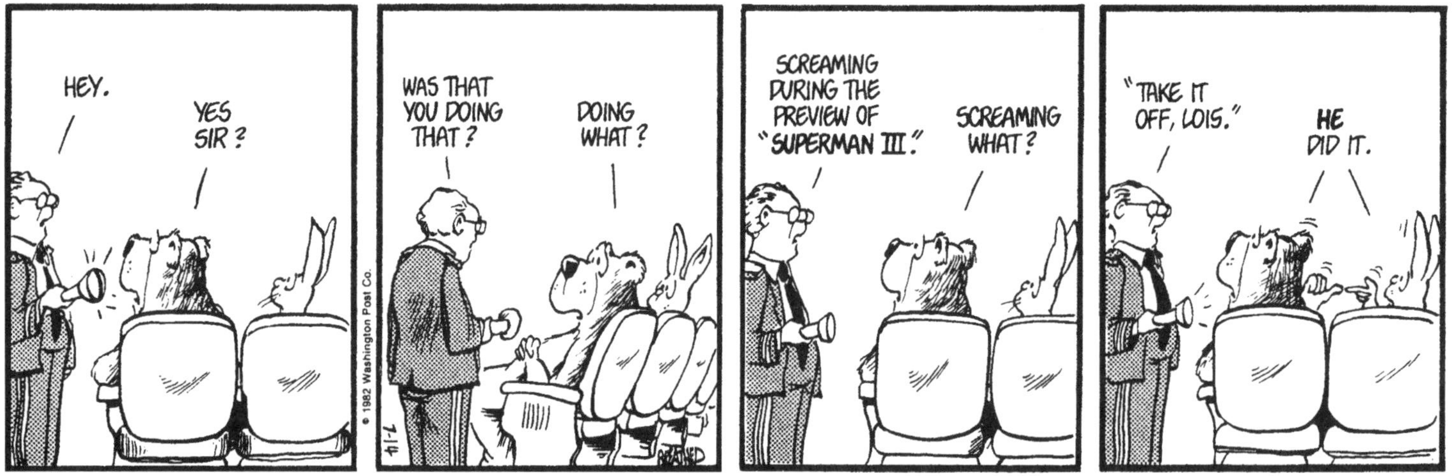

HEY.
YES SIR?
© 1982 Washington Post Co.
7-14
WAS THAT YOU DOING THAT?
DOING WHAT?
SCREAMING DURING THE PREVIEW OF "SUPERMAN III."
SCREAMING WHAT?
"TAKE IT OFF, LOIS."
HE DID IT.

A good place to point out what often isn't obvious to pop-culture fans: there had rarely been comic strip animals that talked to people. Take a moment and consider this (I never did, not surprisingly). In movies and comics, animals talked to each other... but hardly ever to us. Aside from Bugs Bunny (slapstick license, one supposes) and Winnie the Pooh (the imagination of Christopher Robin) it remained, with very few exceptions, an invisible wall where suspension of reality never dared to go. When Miramax Films began developing Opus as a movie in 2002, my first note from the top was that Opus shouldn't talk to people. I knew it would never become a film at that moment, as providence would bear out. —BB

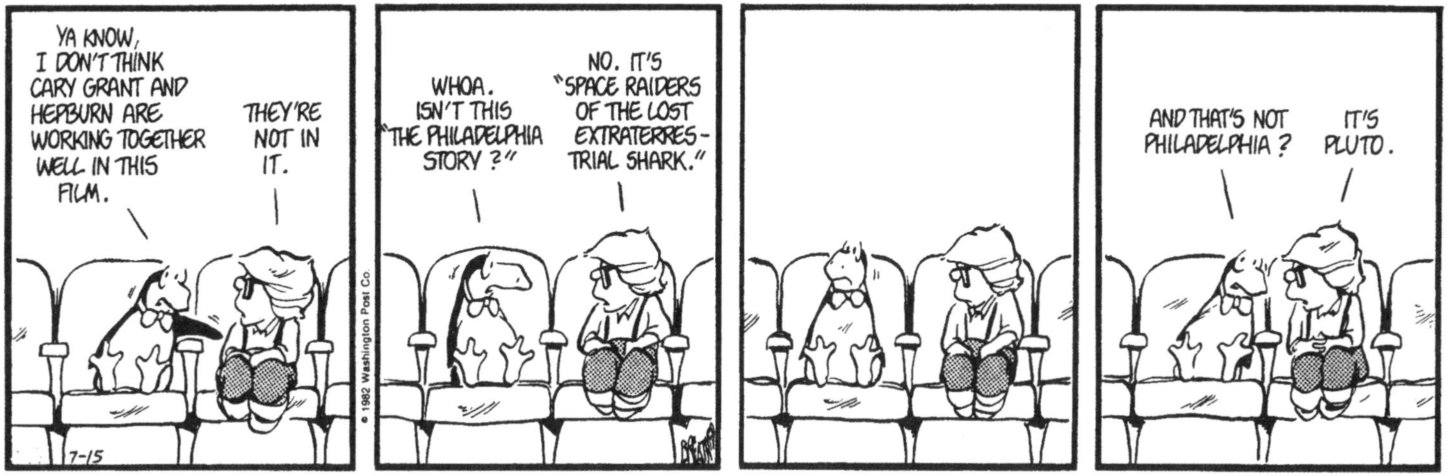
YA KNOW, I DON'T THINK CARY GRANT AND HEPBURN ARE WORKING TOGETHER WELL IN THIS FILM.
THEY'RE NOT IN IT.
7-15
© 1982 Washington Post Co.
WHOA. ISN'T THIS "THE PHILADELPHIA STORY?"
NO. IT'S "SPACE RAIDERS OF THE LOST EXTRATERRESTRIAL SHARK."
AND THAT'S NOT PHILADELPHIA?
IT'S PLUTO.

Cary Grant and Katharine Hepburn co-starred in the quintessential screwball comedy, *The Philadelphia Story*. Both had careers spanning decades and were revered by fans and critics alike.

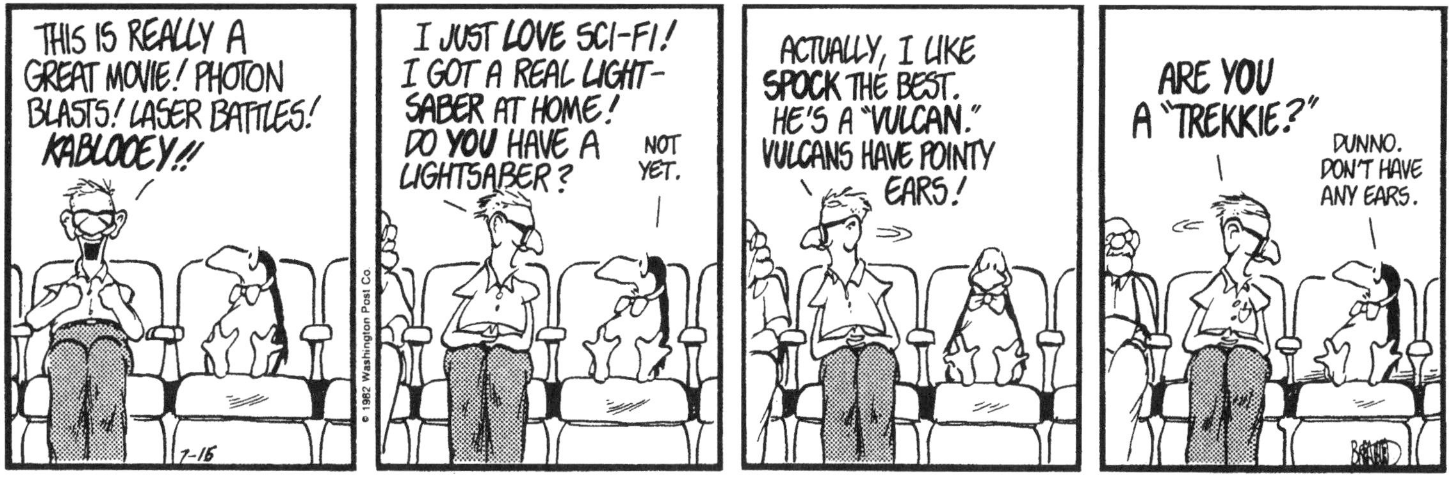
THIS IS REALLY A GREAT MOVIE! PHOTON BLASTS! LASER BATTLES! KABLOOEY!!
7-16
© 1982 Washington Post Co.
I JUST LOVE SCI-FI! I GOT A REAL LIGHT-SABER AT HOME! DO YOU HAVE A LIGHTSABER?
NOT YET.
ACTUALLY, I LIKE SPOCK THE BEST. HE'S A "VULCAN." VULCANS HAVE POINTY EARS!
ARE YOU A "TREKKIE?"
DUNNO. DON'T HAVE ANY EARS.

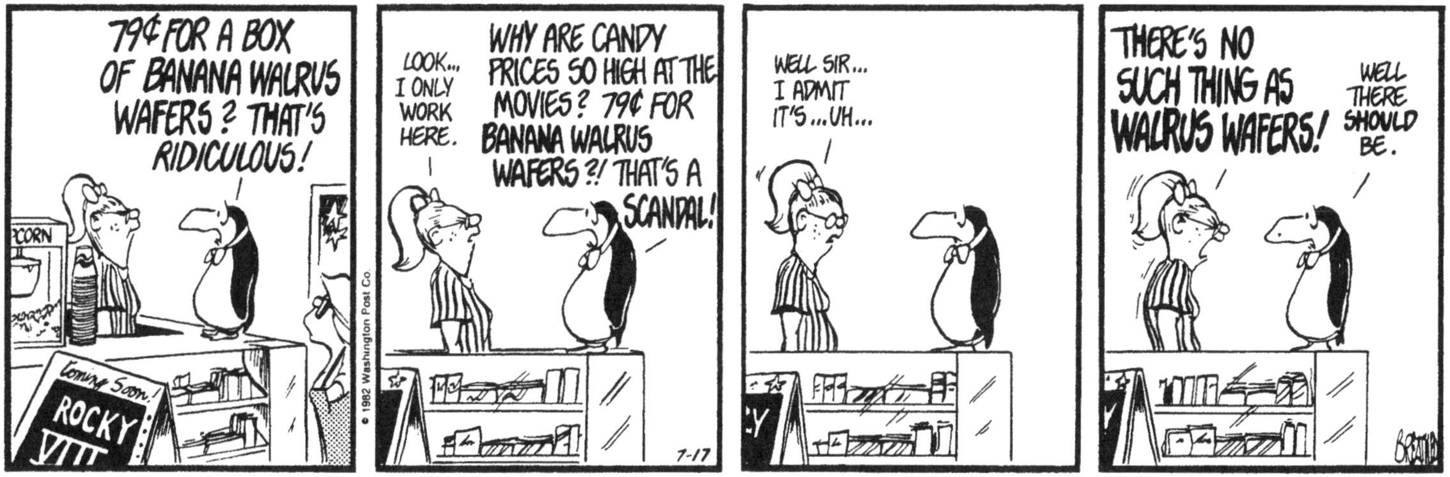
79¢ FOR A BOX OF BANANA WALRUS WAFERS? THAT'S RIDICULOUS!
Coming Soon!
ROCKY VIII
© 1982 Washington Post Co.
LOOK... I ONLY WORK HERE.
WHY ARE CANDY PRICES SO HIGH AT THE MOVIES? 79¢ FOR BANANA WALRUS WAFERS?! THAT'S A SCANDAL!
7-17
WELL SIR... I ADMIT IT'S...UH...
THERE'S NO SUCH THING AS WALRUS WAFERS!
WELL THERE SHOULD BE.

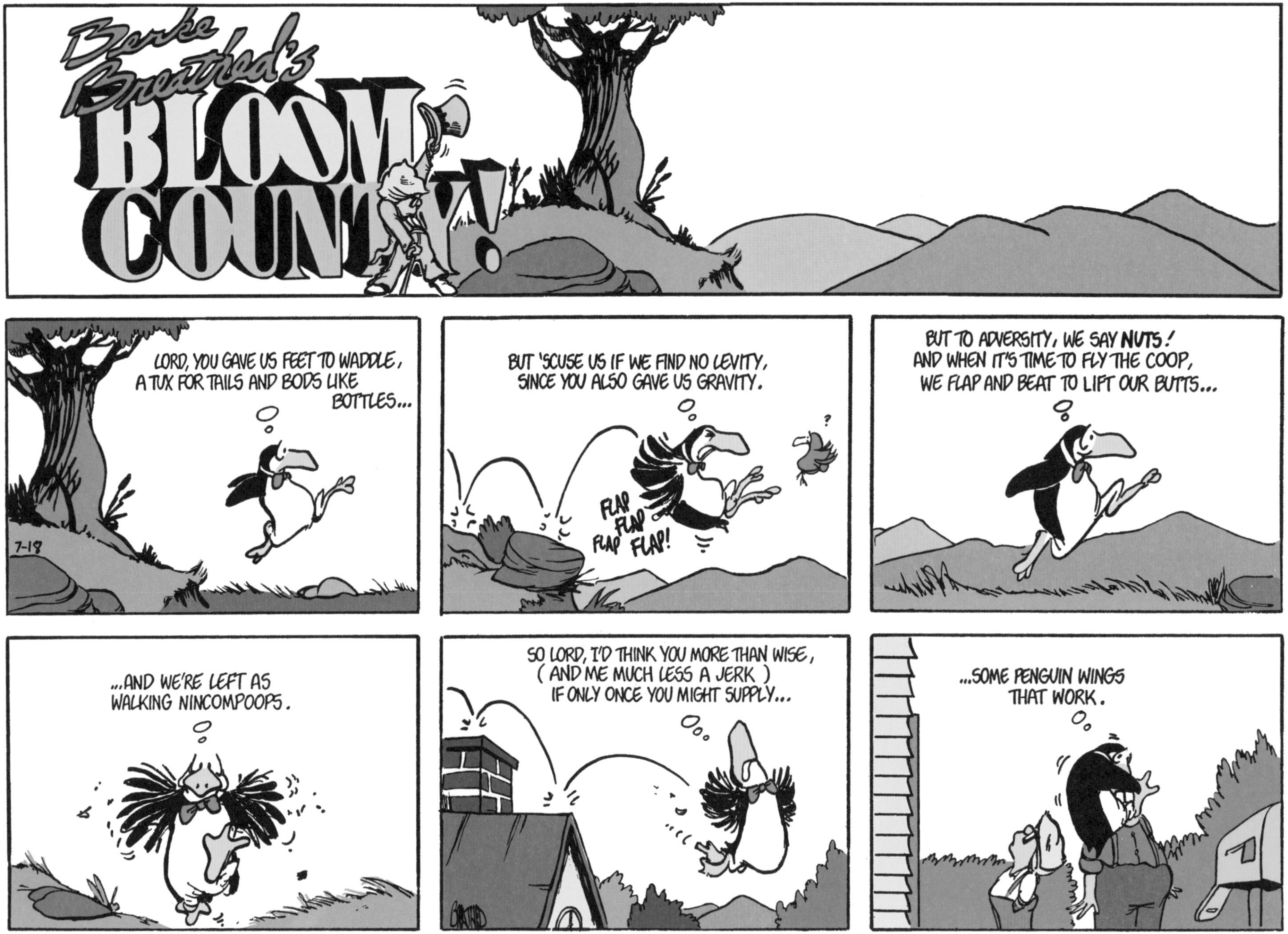
Berke Breathed's
BLOOM COUNTY!
7-18
LORD, YOU GAVE US FEET TO WADDLE, A TUX FOR TAILS AND BODS LIKE BOTTLES...
BUT 'SCUSE US IF WE FIND NO LEVITY, SINCE YOU ALSO GAVE US GRAVITY.
FLAP FLAP FLAP FLAP!
BUT TO ADVERSITY, WE SAY NUTS! AND WHEN IT'S TIME TO FLY THE COOP, WE FLAP AND BEAT TO LIFT OUR BUTTS...
...AND WE'RE LEFT AS WALKING NINCOMPOOPS.
SO LORD, I'D THINK YOU MORE THAN WISE, (AND ME MUCH LESS A JERK) IF ONLY ONCE YOU MIGHT SUPPLY...
...SOME PENGUIN WINGS THAT WORK.

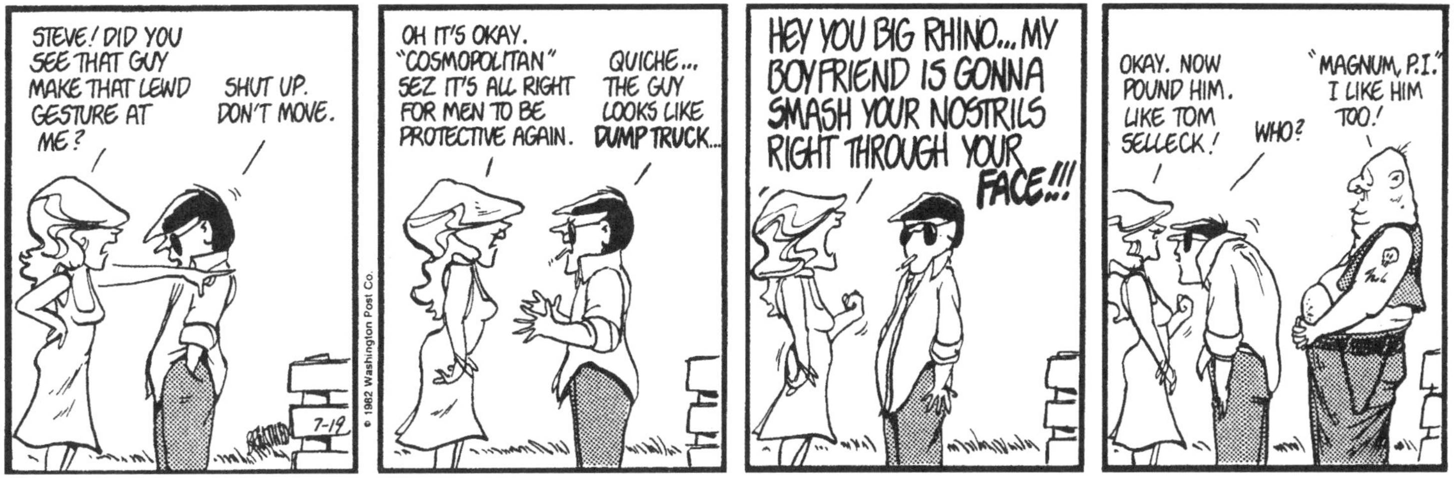
STEVE! DID YOU SEE THAT GUY MAKE THAT LEWD GESTURE AT ME?
SHUT UP. DON'T MOVE.
7-19
© 1982 Washington Post Co.
OH IT'S OKAY. "COSMOPOLITAN" SEZ IT'S ALL RIGHT FOR MEN TO BE PROTECTIVE AGAIN.
QUICHE... THE GUY LOOKS LIKE DUMP TRUCK...
HEY YOU BIG RHINO... MY BOYFRIEND IS GONNA SMASH YOUR NOSTRILS RIGHT THROUGH YOUR FACE!!!
OKAY. NOW POUND HIM. LIKE TOM SELLECK!
WHO?
"MAGNUM, P.I." I LIKE HIM TOO!

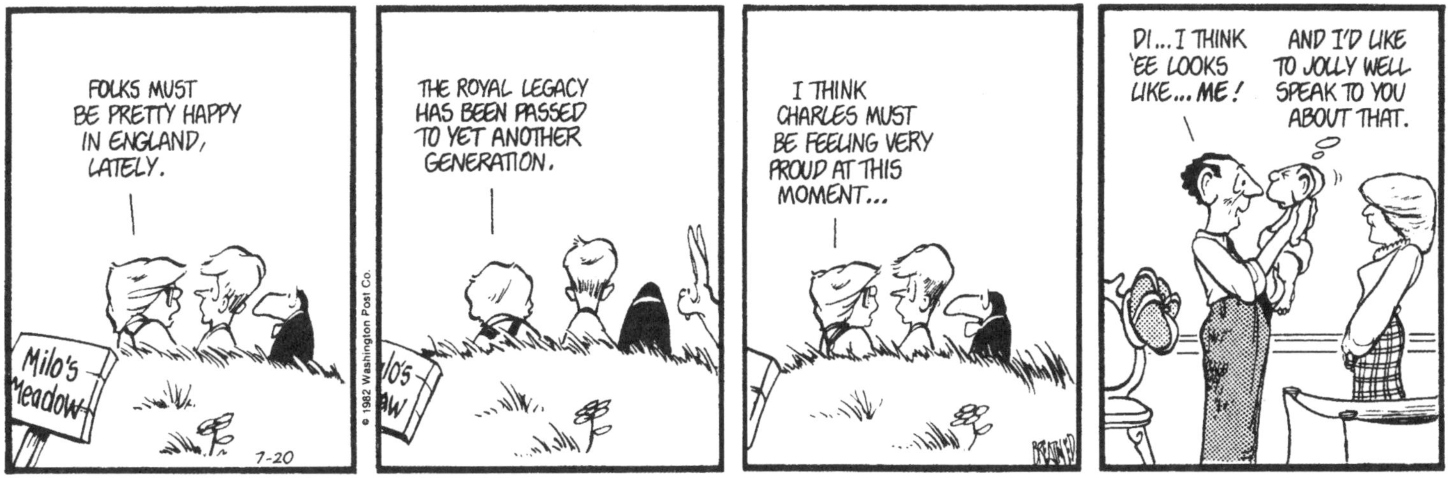
FOLKS MUST BE PRETTY HAPPY IN ENGLAND, LATELY.
Milo's Meadow
7-20
© 1982 Washington Post Co.
THE ROYAL LEGACY HAS BEEN PASSED TO YET ANOTHER GENERATION.
I THINK CHARLES MUST BE FEELING VERY PROUD AT THIS MOMENT...
DI... I THINK 'EE LOOKS LIKE... ME!
AND I'D LIKE TO JOLLY WELL SPEAK TO YOU ABOUT THAT.

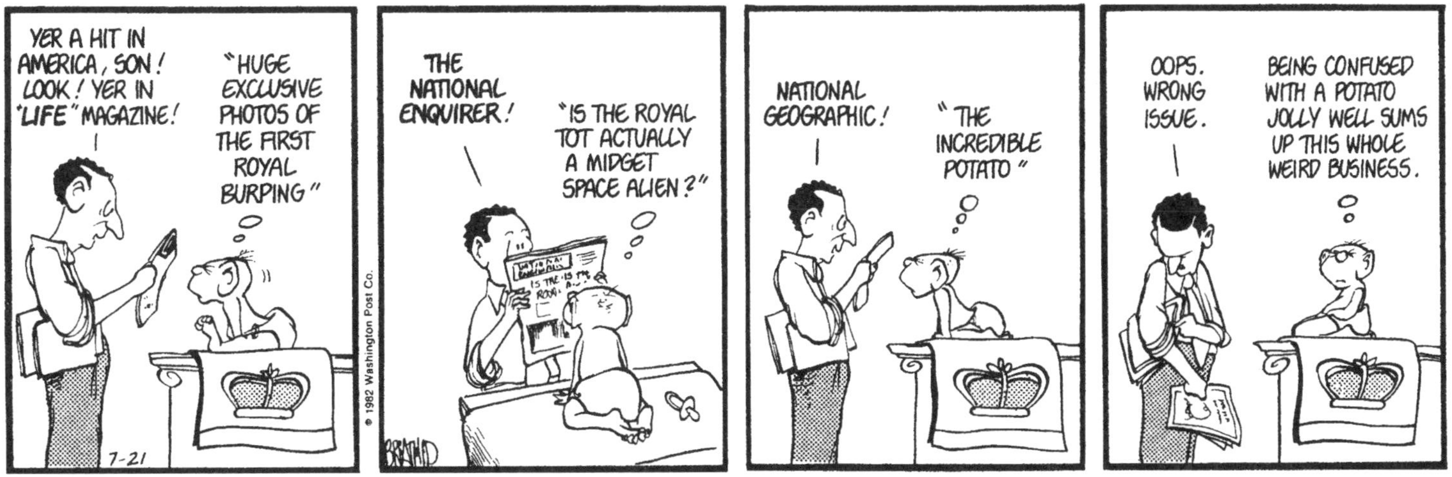
YER A HIT IN AMERICA, SON! LOOK! YER IN "LIFE" MAGAZINE!
"HUGE EXCLUSIVE PHOTOS OF THE FIRST ROYAL BURPING"
7-21
© 1982 Washington Post Co.
THE NATIONAL ENQUIRER!
"IS THE ROYAL TOT ACTUALLY A MIDGET SPACE ALIEN?"
NATIONAL GEOGRAPHIC!
"THE INCREDIBLE POTATO"
OOPS. WRONG ISSUE.
BEING CONFUSED WITH A POTATO JOLLY WELL SUMS UP THIS WHOLE WEIRD BUSINESS.

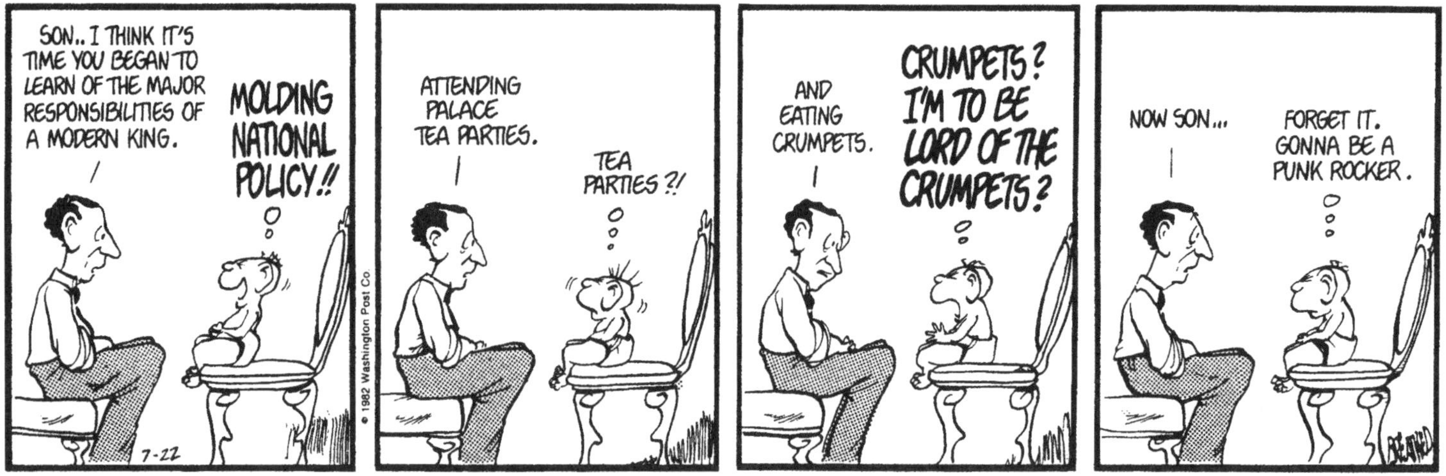
SON.. I THINK IT'S TIME YOU BEGAN TO LEARN OF THE MAJOR RESPONSIBILITIES OF A MODERN KING.
MOLDING NATIONAL POLICY!!
7-22
© 1982 Washington Post Co.
ATTENDING PALACE TEA PARTIES.
TEA PARTIES ?!
AND EATING CRUMPETS.
CRUMPETS? I'M TO BE LORD OF THE CRUMPETS?
NOW SON...
FORGET IT. GONNA BE A PUNK ROCKER.

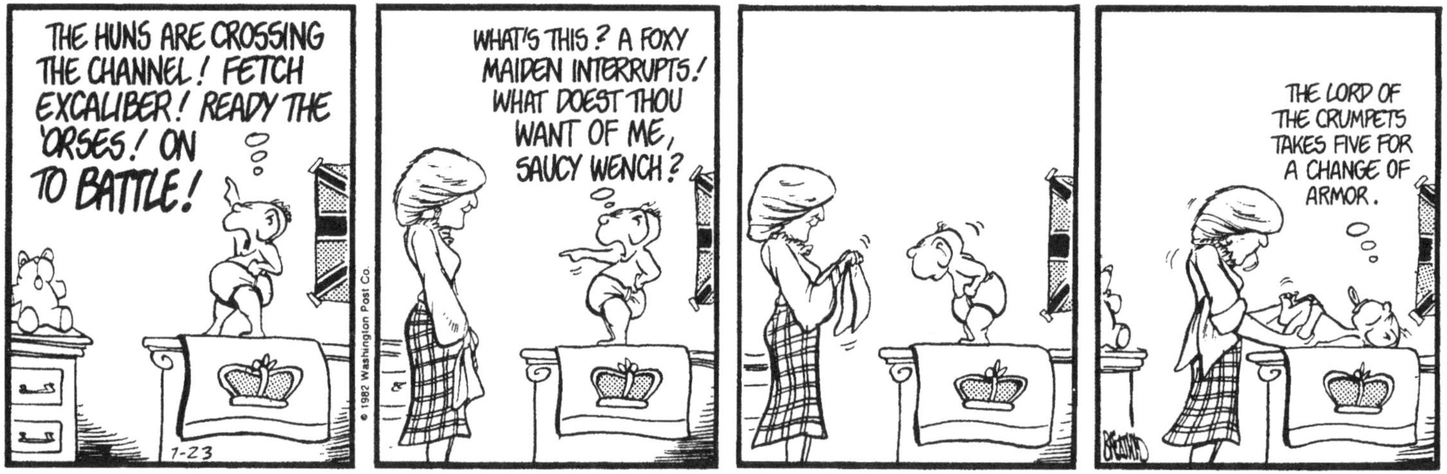
THE HUNS ARE CROSSING THE CHANNEL! FETCH EXCALIBER! READY THE 'ORSES! ON TO BATTLE!
7-23
© 1982 Washington Post Co.
WHAT'S THIS? A FOXY MAIDEN INTERRUPTS! WHAT DOEST THOU WANT OF ME, SAUCY WENCH?
THE LORD OF THE CRUMPETS TAKES FIVE FOR A CHANGE OF ARMOR.

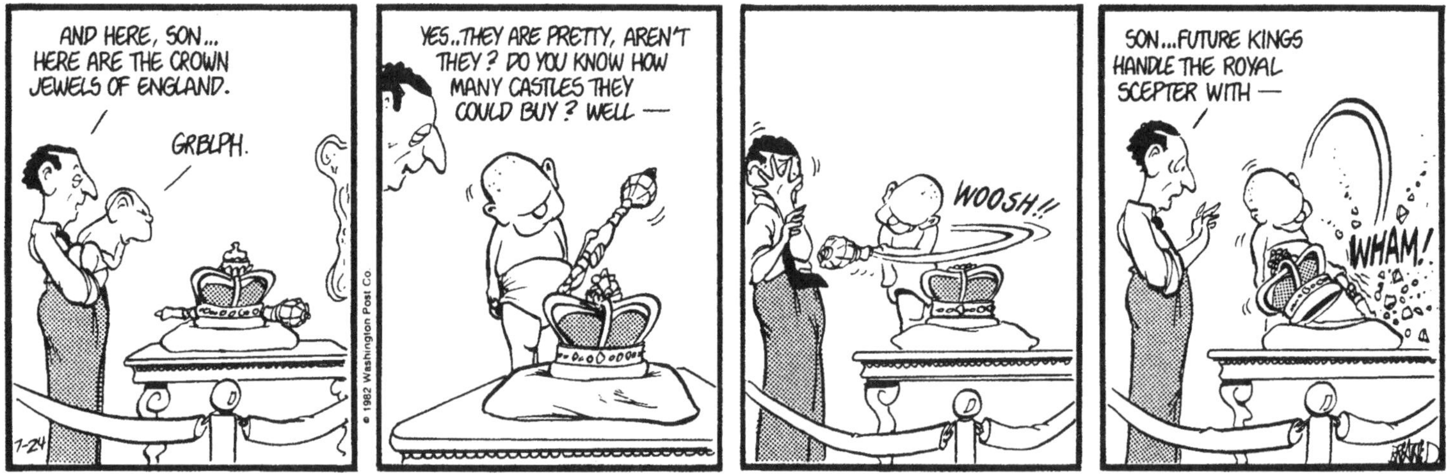
AND HERE, SON... HERE ARE THE CROWN JEWELS OF ENGLAND.
GRBLPH.
7-24
© 1982 Washington Post Co.
YES..THEY ARE PRETTY, AREN'T THEY? DO YOU KNOW HOW MANY CASTLES THEY COULD BUY? WELL —
WOOSH!!
SON...FUTURE KINGS HANDLE THE ROYAL SCEPTER WITH —
WHAM!

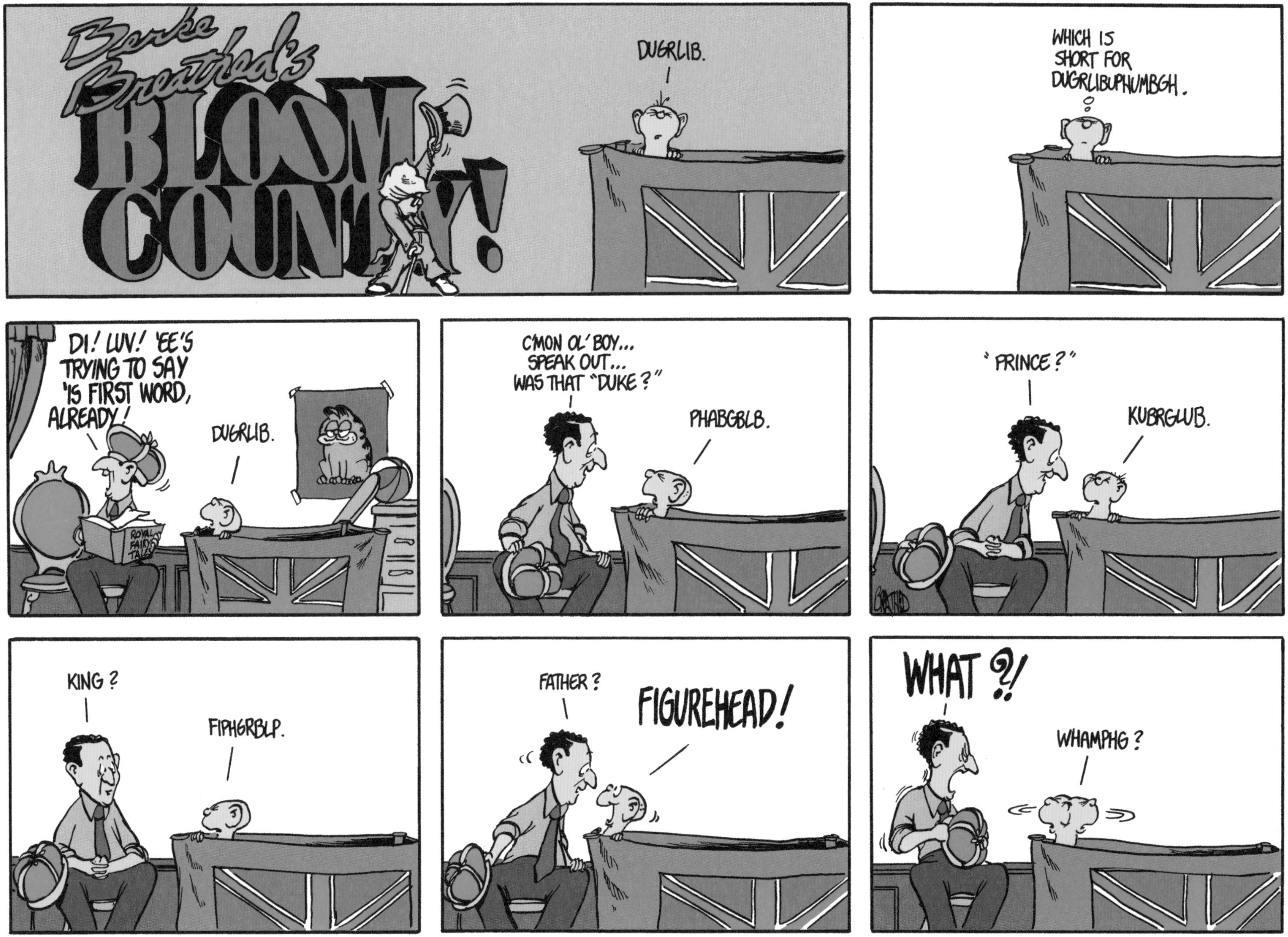
Berke Breathed's
BLOOM COUNTY!
DUGRLIB.
WHICH IS SHORT FOR DUGRLIBUPHUMBGH.
DI! LUV! 'EE'S TRYING TO SAY 'IS FIRST WORD, ALREADY!
ROYAL FAIRY TALES
DUGRLIB.
C'MON OL' BOY... SPEAK OUT... WAS THAT "DUKE?"
PHABGBLB.
"PRINCE?"
KUBRGLUB.
KING?
FIPHGRBLP.
FATHER?
FIGUREHEAD!
WHAT?!
WHAMPHG?

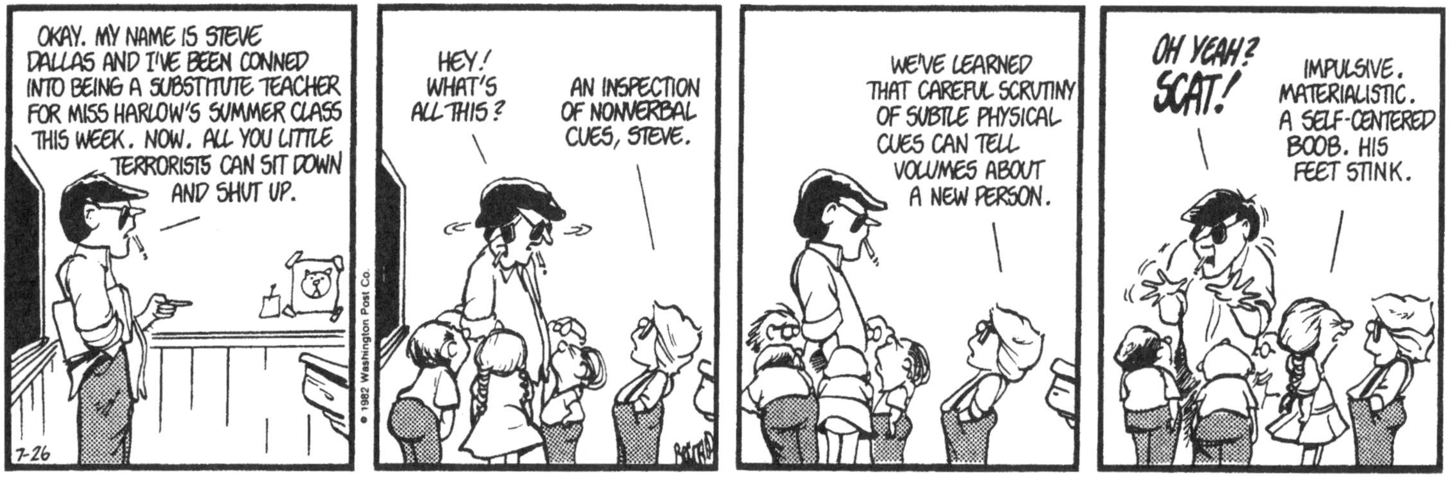
OKAY. MY NAME IS STEVE DALLAS AND I'VE BEEN CONNED INTO BEING A SUBSTITUTE TEACHER FOR MISS HARLOW'S SUMMER CLASS THIS WEEK. NOW. ALL YOU LITTLE TERRORISTS CAN SIT DOWN AND SHUT UP.
HEY! WHAT'S ALL THIS?
AN INSPECTION OF NONVERBAL CUES, STEVE.
WE'VE LEARNED THAT CAREFUL SCRUTINY OF SUBTLE PHYSICAL CUES CAN TELL VOLUMES ABOUT A NEW PERSON.
OH YEAH? SCAT!
IMPULSIVE. MATERIALISTIC. A SELF-CENTERED BOOB. HIS FEET STINK.

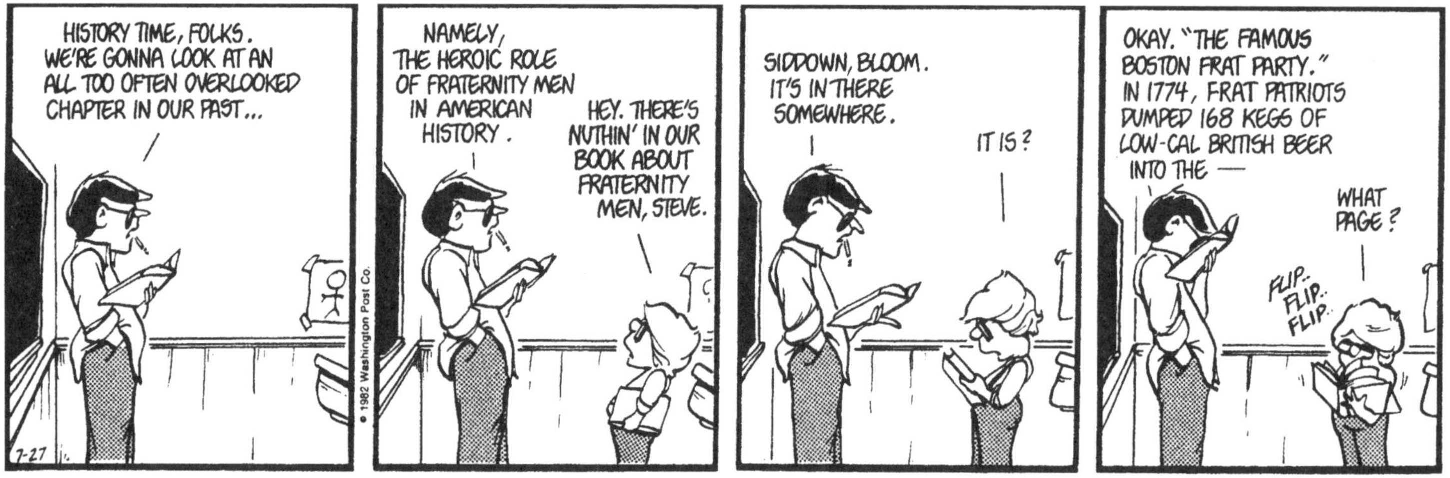
HISTORY TIME, FOLKS. WE'RE GONNA LOOK AT AN ALL TOO OFTEN OVERLOOKED CHAPTER IN OUR PAST...
NAMELY, THE HEROIC ROLE OF FRATERNITY MEN IN AMERICAN HISTORY.
HEY. THERE'S NUTHIN' IN OUR BOOK ABOUT FRATERNITY MEN, STEVE.
SIDDOWN, BLOOM. IT'S IN THERE SOMEWHERE.
IT IS?
OKAY. "THE FAMOUS BOSTON FRAT PARTY." IN 1774, FRAT PATRIOTS DUMPED 168 KEGS OF LOW-CAL BRITISH BEER INTO THE —
WHAT PAGE?
FLIP.. FLIP.. FLIP..

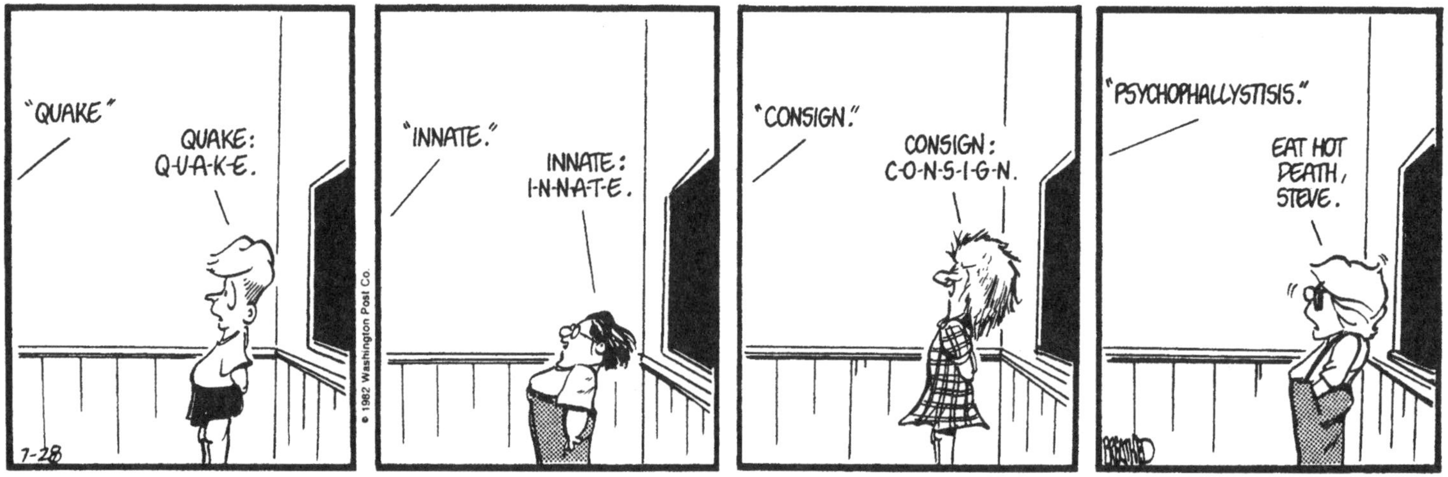
"QUAKE"
QUAKE: Q-U-A-K-E.
"INNATE."
INNATE: I-N-N-A-T-E.
"CONSIGN."
CONSIGN: C-O-N-S-I-G-N.
"PSYCHOPHALLYSTISIS."
EAT HOT DEATH, STEVE.

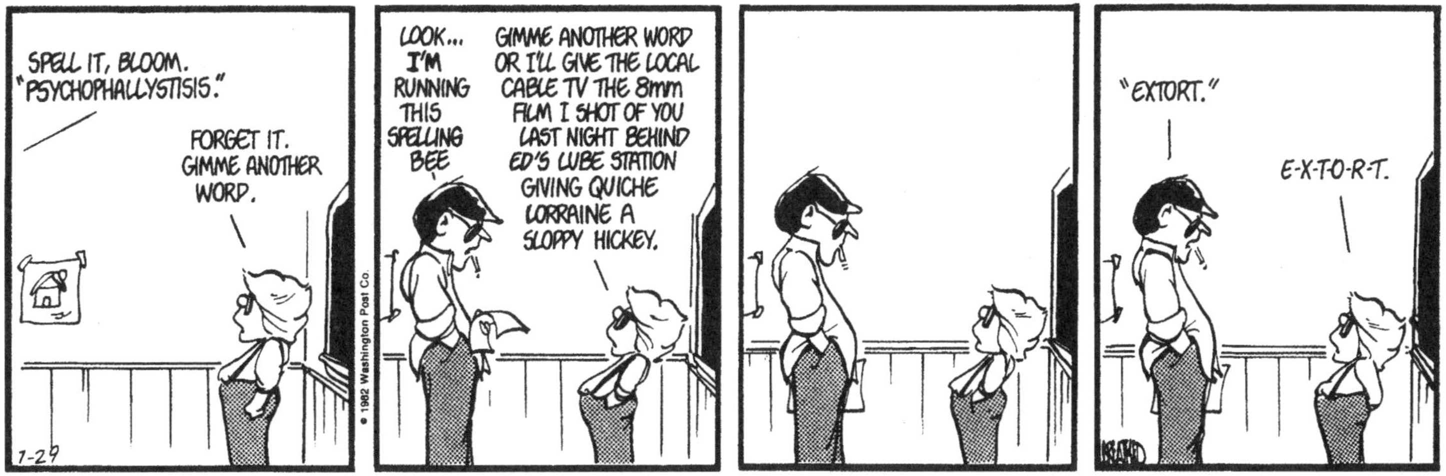
SPELL IT, BLOOM. "PSYCHOPHALLYSTISIS."
FORGET IT. GIMME ANOTHER WORD.
7-29
© 1982 Washington Post Co.
LOOK... I'M RUNNING THIS SPELLING BEE
GIMME ANOTHER WORD OR I'LL GIVE THE LOCAL CABLE TV THE 8mm FILM I SHOT OF YOU LAST NIGHT BEHIND ED'S LUBE STATION GIVING QUICHE LORRAINE A SLOPPY HICKEY.
"EXTORT."
E-X-T-O-R-T.

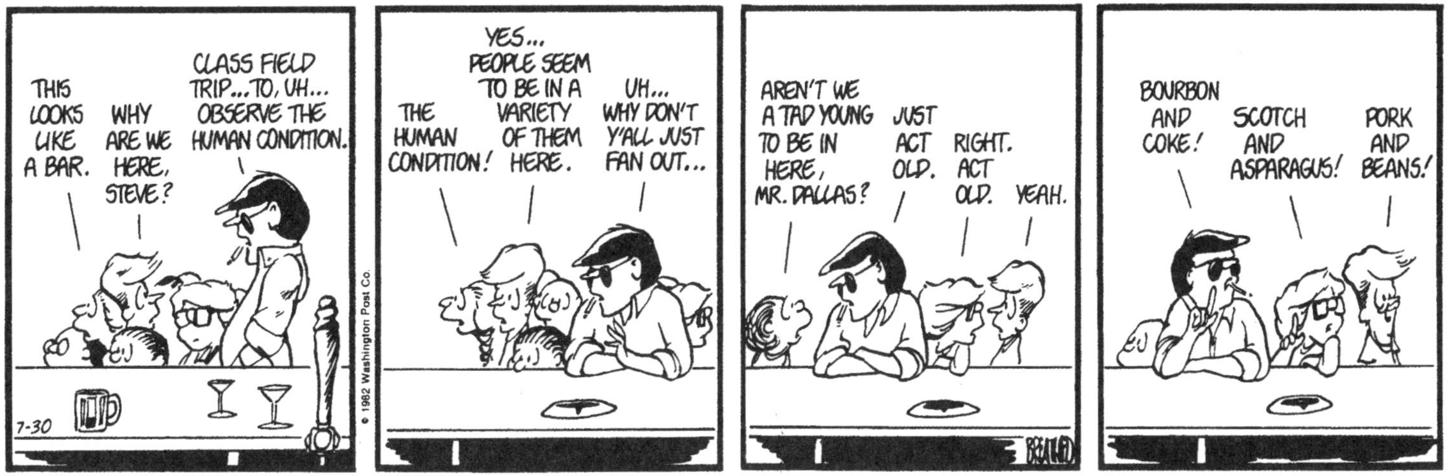
THIS LOOKS LIKE A BAR.
WHY ARE WE HERE, STEVE?
CLASS FIELD TRIP...TO, UH... OBSERVE THE HUMAN CONDITION.
7-30
© 1982 Washington Post Co.
THE HUMAN CONDITION!
YES... PEOPLE SEEM TO BE IN A VARIETY OF THEM HERE.
UH... WHY DON'T Y'ALL JUST FAN OUT...
AREN'T WE A TAD YOUNG TO BE IN HERE, MR. DALLAS?
JUST ACT OLD.
RIGHT. ACT OLD.
YEAH.
BOURBON AND COKE!
SCOTCH AND ASPARAGUS!
PORK AND BEANS!

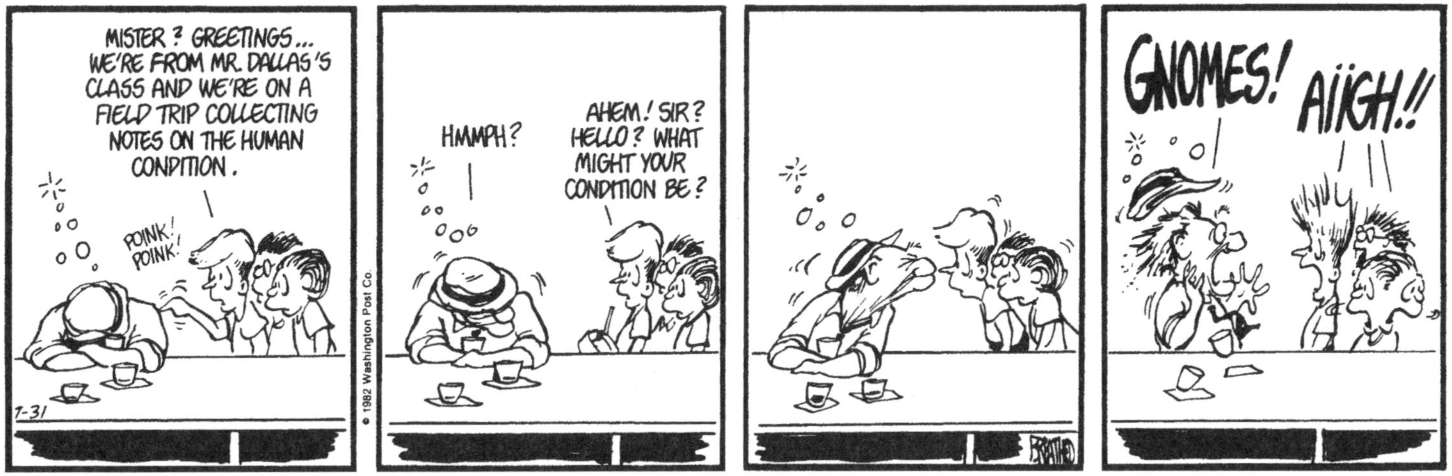
MISTER? GREETINGS... WE'RE FROM MR. DALLAS'S CLASS AND WE'RE ON A FIELD TRIP COLLECTING NOTES ON THE HUMAN CONDITION.
POINK! POINK!
7-31
© 1982 Washington Post Co.
HMMPH?
AHEM! SIR? HELLO? WHAT MIGHT YOUR CONDITION BE?
GNOMES!
AIIGH!!

K

🌐 KIDS ONLY

ADULT PARTICIPATION CAN LEAD TO HEADACHES, HEAVY BODY HAIR AND GENERAL LEWD BEHAVIOR.

AS USUAL... THIS SPECIAL IS SPONSORED BY ED'S GAS AND LUBE STATION.

The Second **UNCLE OPUS FUN PAGE**

FOR MINORS <u>ONLY</u>.

MORE PENGUIN FACTS:

PENGUINS ARE POLITICAL MODERATES... BUT THEY DRAW THE LINE AT WOMEN'S RIGHTS (FOR THEM) AND TV SHOWS STARRING "CHARO" (AGAINST THEM). THEY WILL TRY ANYTHING ONCE, BUT ALTHOUGH GENERALLY HEDONISTS, THEY FIND THE USE OF RECREATIONAL DRUGS TACKY, IF NOT PLAIN UNHEALTHY. THEY DO, HOWEVER, ADVOCATE **PENGUIN LUST**, WHICH IS, OF COURSE, HEALTHY FOR EVERYBODY.

Field Tips #42

CAN YOU FIND THE DIFFERENCES BETWEEN A GALAPAGOS PENGUIN AND RICHARD SIMMONS?

Y-R-U FAT?

8-1

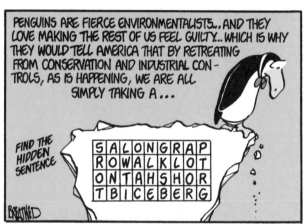

PENGUINS ARE FIERCE ENVIRONMENTALISTS... AND THEY LOVE MAKING THE REST OF US FEEL GUILTY... WHICH IS WHY THEY WOULD TELL AMERICA THAT BY RETREATING FROM CONSERVATION AND INDUSTRIAL CONTROLS, AS IS HAPPENING, WE ARE ALL SIMPLY TAKING A...

FIND THE HIDDEN SENTENCE

S	A	L	O	N	G	R	A	P
R	O	W	A	L	K	L	O	T
O	N	T	A	H	S	H	O	R
T	B	I	C	E	B	E	R	G

BREATHED

COLOR TIME

COLOR THE PENGUIN, THE PUFFIN AND THE PETERSON... AS IN ROGER TORY, LAST OF THE GREAT NATURALIST/ARTISTS.

WHAT'S THIS?

A PETERSON?

EXCLUSIVE! **NAME DAVE'S REPLACEMENT**

RUMOR HAS IT THAT NBC-TV WILL BE CANCELING "LATE NIGHT WITH DAVID LETTERMAN" SOMETIME SOON. MAYBE AT ANY MOMENT. WHICH OF THE FOLLOWING NEW SHOWS IS TO BE THE REPLACEMENT?

☐ "MARLIN PERKINS SINGS"
☐ "THE AMY CARTER/PIA ZADORA SHOW"
☐ "LATE NIGHT WITH UNCLE OPUS"
☐ "YOGA WITH BILL MOYERS"

?

WINNERS OF THE OPUS T-SHIRT CONTEST:

☆ NAOMI SCHWINGHAMER, VINCENTOWN, N.J. AGE 8
☆ ROBBIE BEDFORD, N. OLMSTED, OHIO. AGE 6
☆ MS. GAIL LEVINE, LAUDERDALE LAKE, FL. TWENTYISH

OPUS THANKS EVERYBODY FOR THEIR ENTRIES AND COMMENTS... EXCEPT FOR MARTI MARTIN IN LOS ANGELES, WHOSE UNCHASTE SUGGESTIONS EARNED HER A USED "GARFIELD" SHIRT.

Roger Tory Peterson, arguably the most influential naturalist and environmentalist of the 20th century.
Marlin Perkins was a zoologist and host of the long-running TV program, *Mutual of Omaha's Wild Kingdom*.

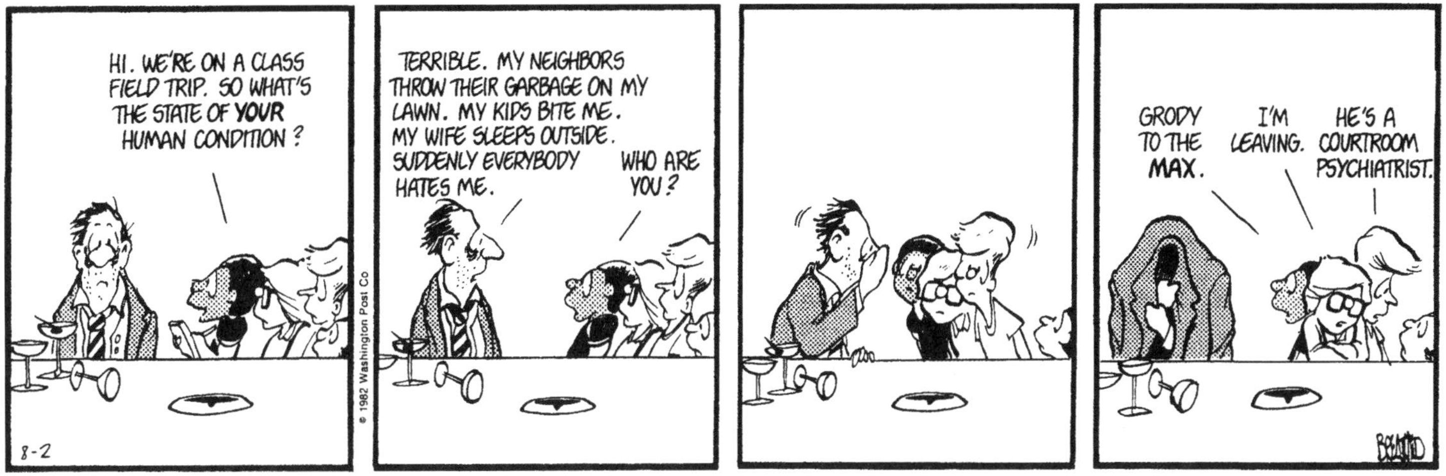
HI. WE'RE ON A CLASS FIELD TRIP. SO WHAT'S THE STATE OF **YOUR** HUMAN CONDITION?
8-2
© 1982 Washington Post Co
TERRIBLE. MY NEIGHBORS THROW THEIR GARBAGE ON MY LAWN. MY KIDS BITE ME. MY WIFE SLEEPS OUTSIDE. SUDDENLY EVERYBODY HATES ME.
WHO ARE YOU?
GRODY TO THE **MAX**.
I'M LEAVING.
HE'S A COURTROOM PSYCHIATRIST.

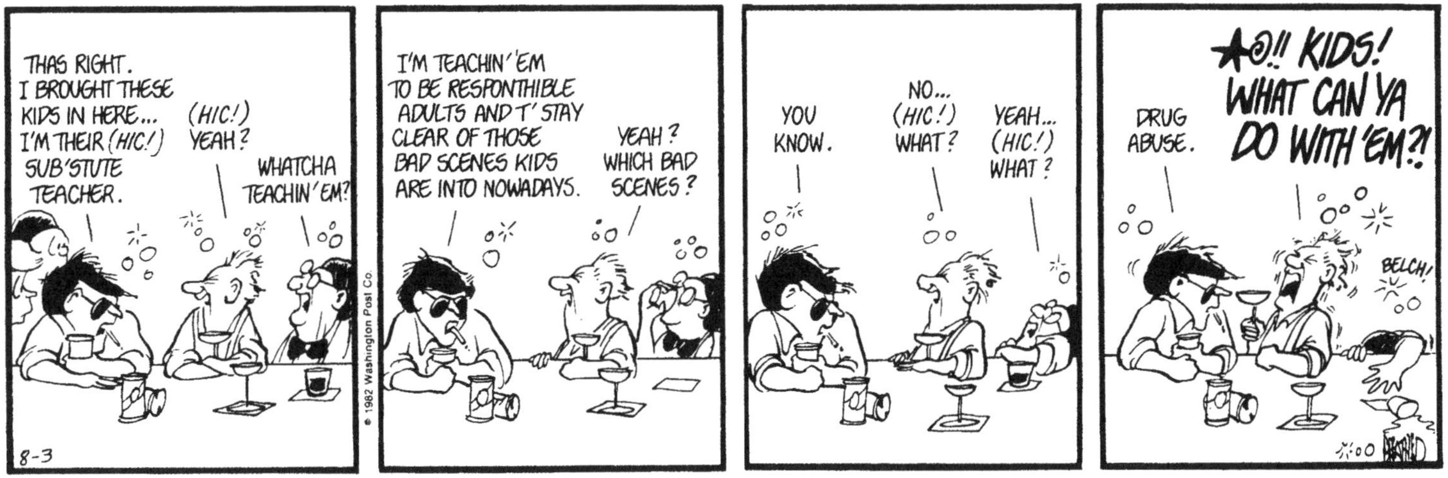
THAS RIGHT. I BROUGHT THESE KIDS IN HERE... I'M THEIR (HIC!) SUB'STUTE TEACHER.
(HIC!) YEAH?
WHATCHA TEACHIN' 'EM?
8-3
© 1982 Washington Post Co.
I'M TEACHIN' 'EM TO BE RESPONTHIBLE ADULTS AND T' STAY CLEAR OF THOSE BAD SCENES KIDS ARE INTO NOWADAYS.
YEAH? WHICH BAD SCENES?
YOU KNOW.
NO... (HIC!) WHAT?
YEAH... (HIC!) WHAT?
DRUG ABUSE.
*@!! KIDS! WHAT CAN YA DO WITH 'EM?!
BELCH!

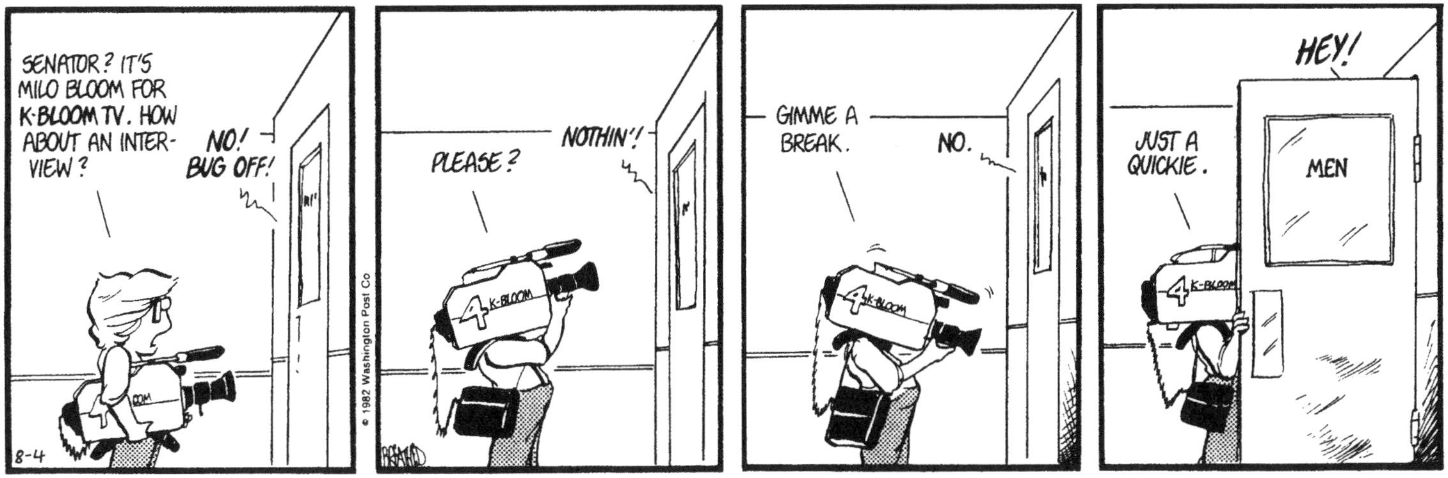
SENATOR? IT'S MILO BLOOM FOR **K-BLOOM TV**. HOW ABOUT AN INTER-VIEW?
NO! BUG OFF!
8-4
© 1982 Washington Post Co
PLEASE?
NOTHIN'!
GIMME A BREAK.
NO.
JUST A QUICKIE.
HEY!
MEN

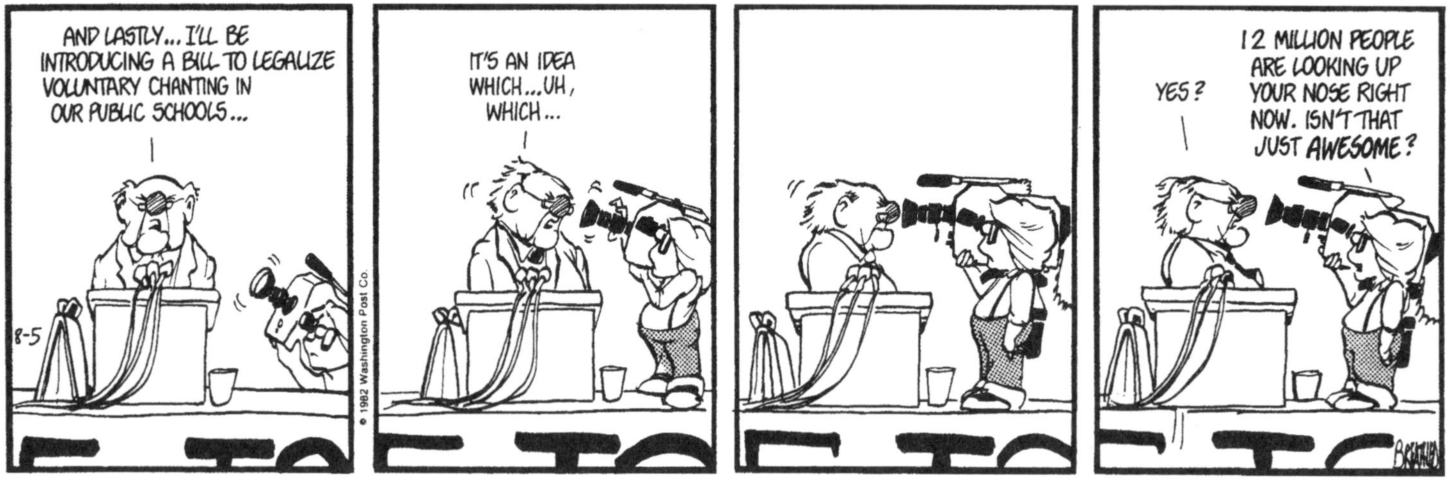
AND LASTLY... I'LL BE INTRODUCING A BILL TO LEGALIZE VOLUNTARY CHANTING IN OUR PUBLIC SCHOOLS...
8-5
© 1982 Washington Post Co.
IT'S AN IDEA WHICH...UH, WHICH...
YES?
12 MILLION PEOPLE ARE LOOKING UP YOUR NOSE RIGHT NOW. ISN'T THAT JUST AWESOME?

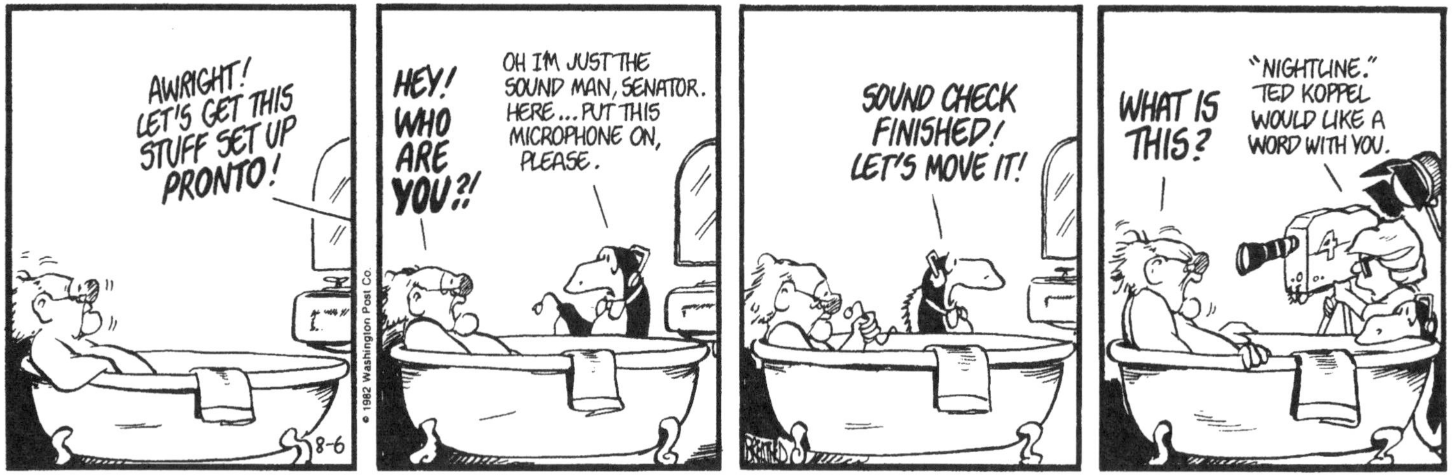
AWRIGHT! LET'S GET THIS STUFF SET UP PRONTO!
8-6
© 1982 Washington Post Co.
HEY! WHO ARE YOU?!
OH I'M JUST THE SOUND MAN, SENATOR. HERE... PUT THIS MICROPHONE ON, PLEASE.
SOUND CHECK FINISHED! LET'S MOVE IT!
WHAT IS THIS?
"NIGHTLINE." TED KOPPEL WOULD LIKE A WORD WITH YOU.

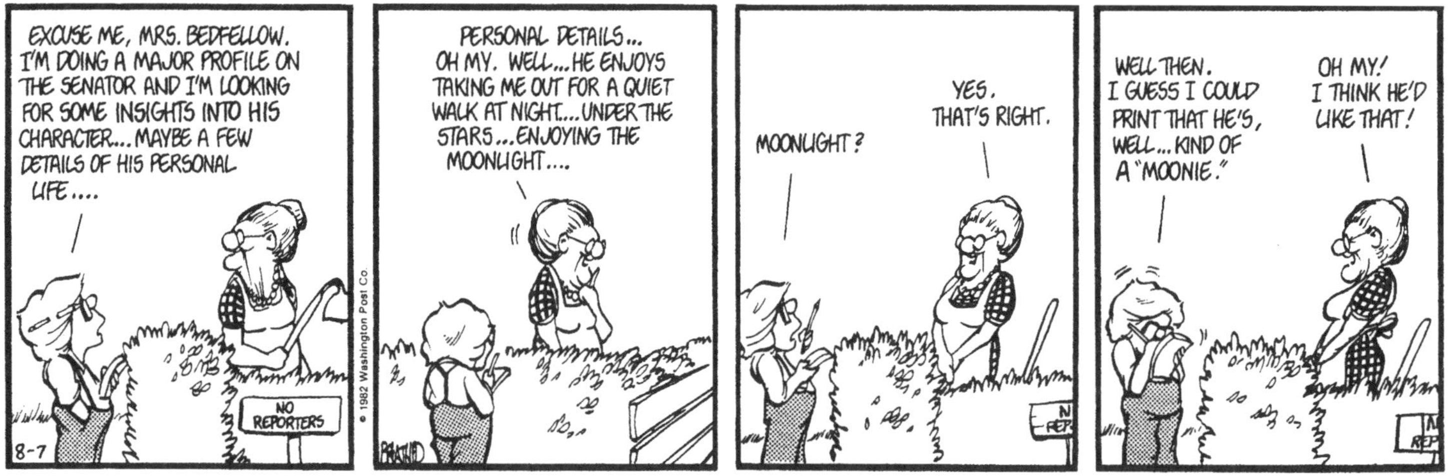
EXCUSE ME, MRS. BEDFELLOW. I'M DOING A MAJOR PROFILE ON THE SENATOR AND I'M LOOKING FOR SOME INSIGHTS INTO HIS CHARACTER... MAYBE A FEW DETAILS OF HIS PERSONAL LIFE....
NO REPORTERS
8-7
© 1982 Washington Post Co.
PERSONAL DETAILS... OH MY. WELL... HE ENJOYS TAKING ME OUT FOR A QUIET WALK AT NIGHT.... UNDER THE STARS... ENJOYING THE MOONLIGHT....
MOONLIGHT?
YES. THAT'S RIGHT.
WELL THEN. I GUESS I COULD PRINT THAT HE'S, WELL... KIND OF A "MOONIE."
OH MY! I THINK HE'D LIKE THAT!

The term "Moonies" refers to members of the Unification Church, which was founded in the 1950s by Korean religious leader and fervent anti-communist Sun Myung Moon.

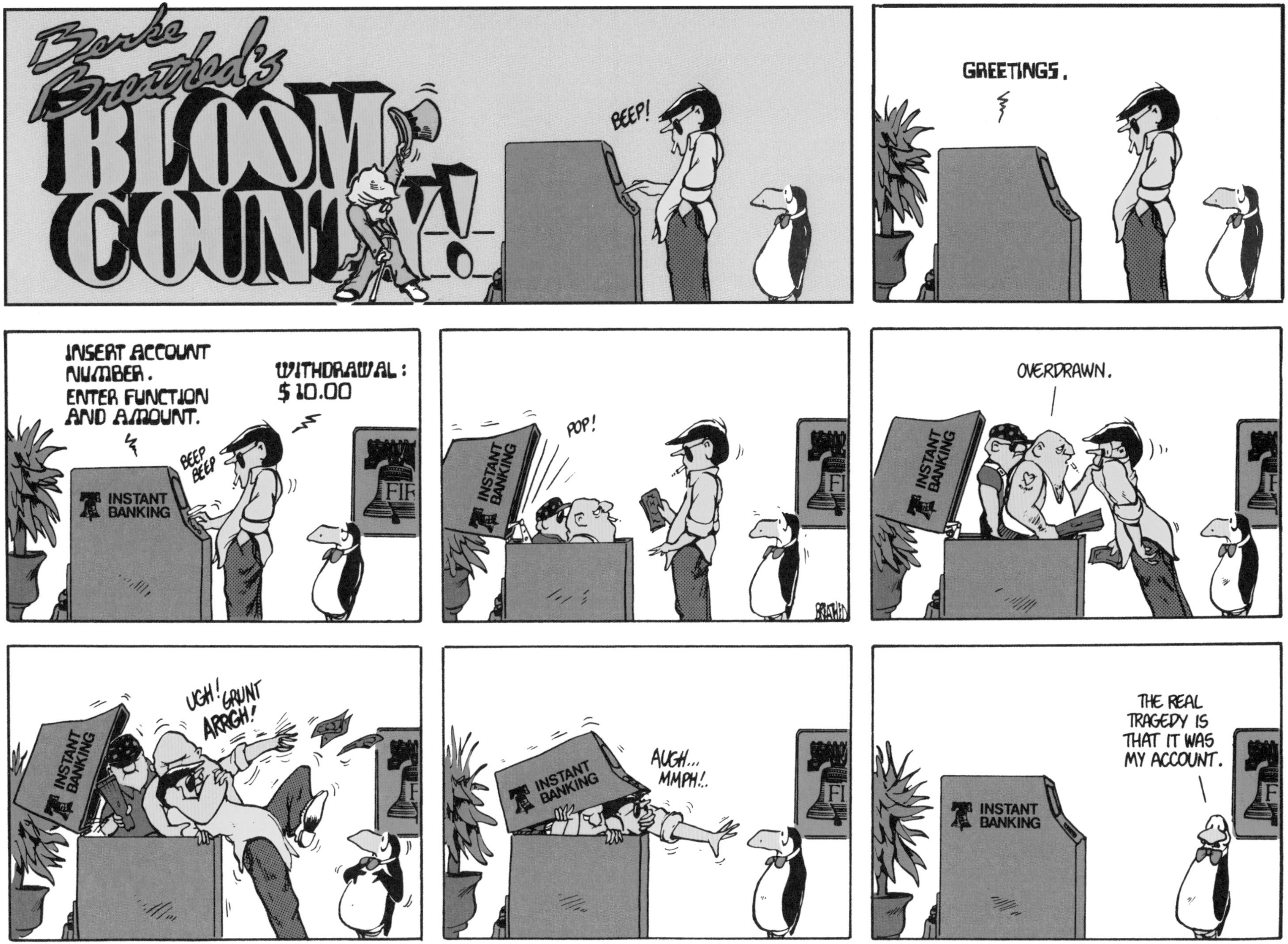
Berke Breathed's
BLOOM COUNTY!
BEEP!
GREETINGS.
INSERT ACCOUNT NUMBER.
ENTER FUNCTION AND AMOUNT.
BEEP BEEP
WITHDRAWAL: $10.00
INSTANT BANKING
POP!
OVERDRAWN.
UGH! GRUNT ARRGH!
AUGH... MMPH!.
THE REAL TRAGEDY IS THAT IT WAS MY ACCOUNT.

Frank Reynolds was a longtime anchor for ABC News.

George Will is a conservative, Pulitzer Prize-winning journalist and former editor of *The National Review*.

William F. Buckley, known as the dean of American conservatives, was an actor and political commentator, founded *The National Review*, and served as host of the long-running public affairs television program, *Firing Line*.

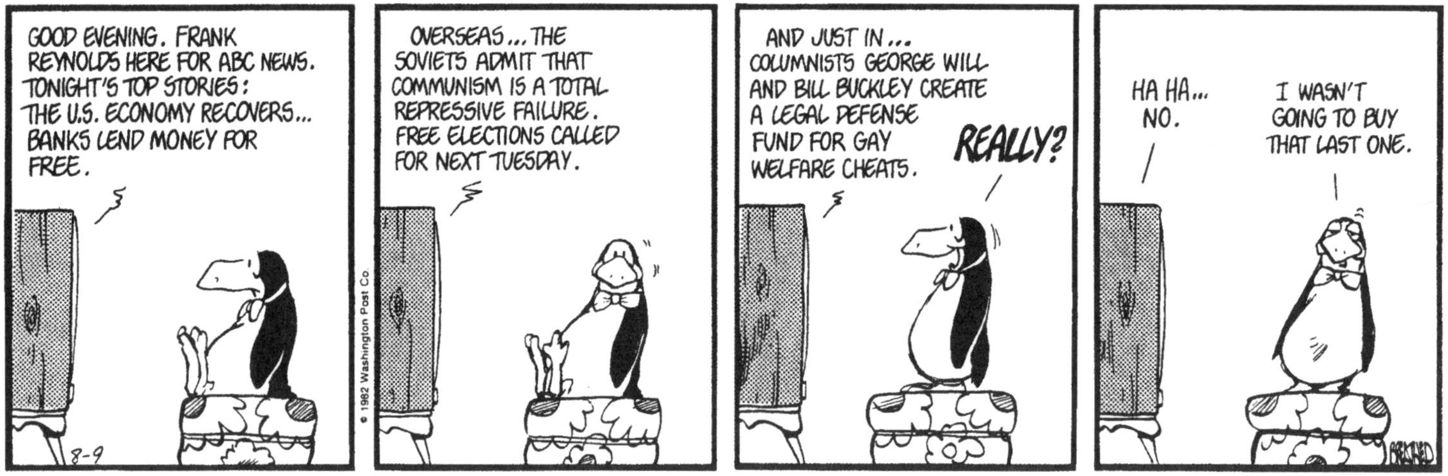
GOOD EVENING. FRANK REYNOLDS HERE FOR ABC NEWS. TONIGHT'S TOP STORIES: THE U.S. ECONOMY RECOVERS... BANKS LEND MONEY FOR FREE.
8-9
OVERSEAS... THE SOVIETS ADMIT THAT COMMUNISM IS A TOTAL REPRESSIVE FAILURE. FREE ELECTIONS CALLED FOR NEXT TUESDAY.
© 1982 Washington Post Co.
AND JUST IN... COLUMNISTS GEORGE WILL AND BILL BUCKLEY CREATE A LEGAL DEFENSE FUND FOR GAY WELFARE CHEATS.
REALLY?
HA HA... NO.
I WASN'T GOING TO BUY THAT LAST ONE.

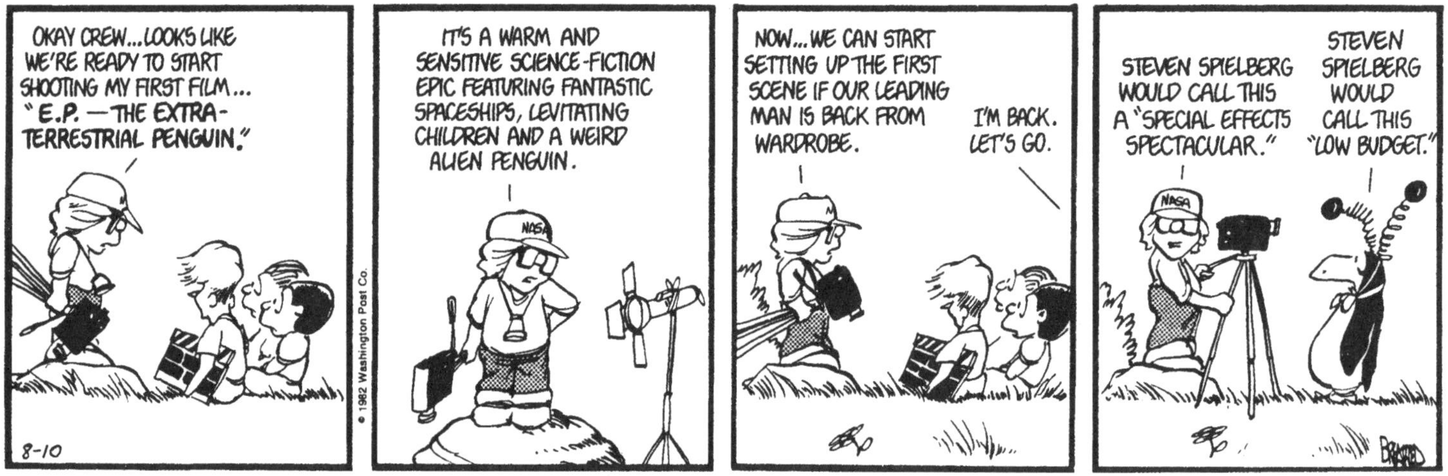
OKAY CREW... LOOKS LIKE WE'RE READY TO START SHOOTING MY FIRST FILM... "E.P. — THE EXTRA-TERRESTRIAL PENGUIN."
8-10
IT'S A WARM AND SENSITIVE SCIENCE-FICTION EPIC FEATURING FANTASTIC SPACESHIPS, LEVITATING CHILDREN AND A WEIRD ALIEN PENGUIN.
© 1982 Washington Post Co.
NOW... WE CAN START SETTING UP THE FIRST SCENE IF OUR LEADING MAN IS BACK FROM WARDROBE.
I'M BACK. LET'S GO.
STEVEN SPIELBERG WOULD CALL THIS A "SPECIAL EFFECTS SPECTACULAR."
STEVEN SPIELBERG WOULD CALL THIS "LOW BUDGET."

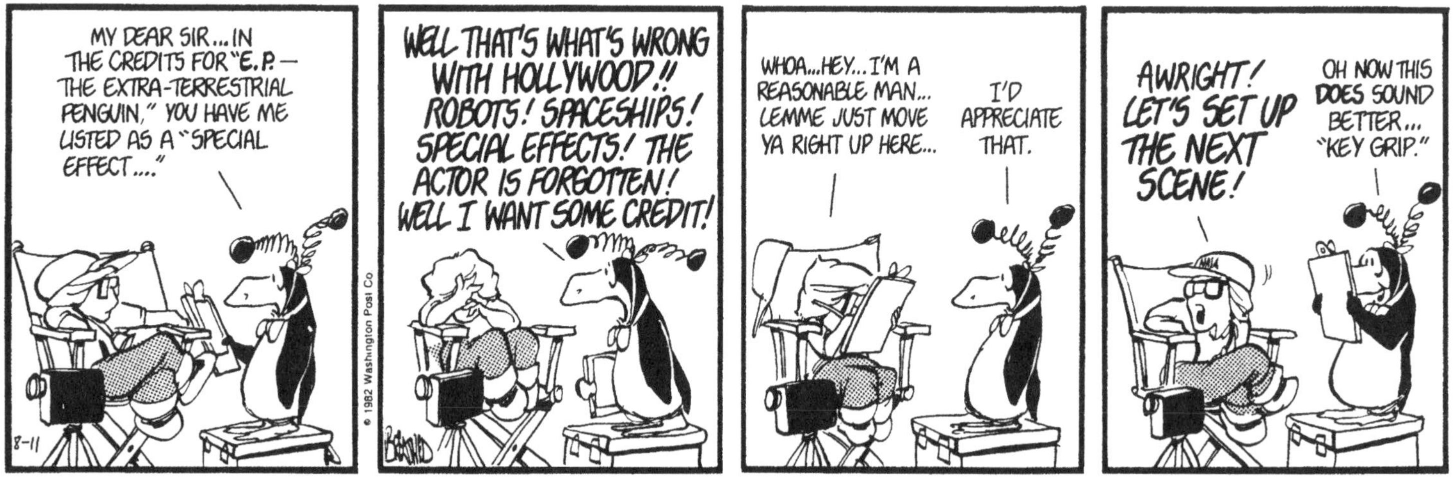
MY DEAR SIR... IN THE CREDITS FOR "E.P. — THE EXTRA-TERRESTRIAL PENGUIN," YOU HAVE ME LISTED AS A "SPECIAL EFFECT...."
8-11
WELL THAT'S WHAT'S WRONG WITH HOLLYWOOD!! ROBOTS! SPACESHIPS! SPECIAL EFFECTS! THE ACTOR IS FORGOTTEN! WELL I WANT SOME CREDIT!
© 1982 Washington Post Co.
WHOA... HEY... I'M A REASONABLE MAN... LEMME JUST MOVE YA RIGHT UP HERE...
I'D APPRECIATE THAT.
AWRIGHT! LET'S SET UP THE NEXT SCENE!
OH NOW THIS DOES SOUND BETTER... "KEY GRIP."

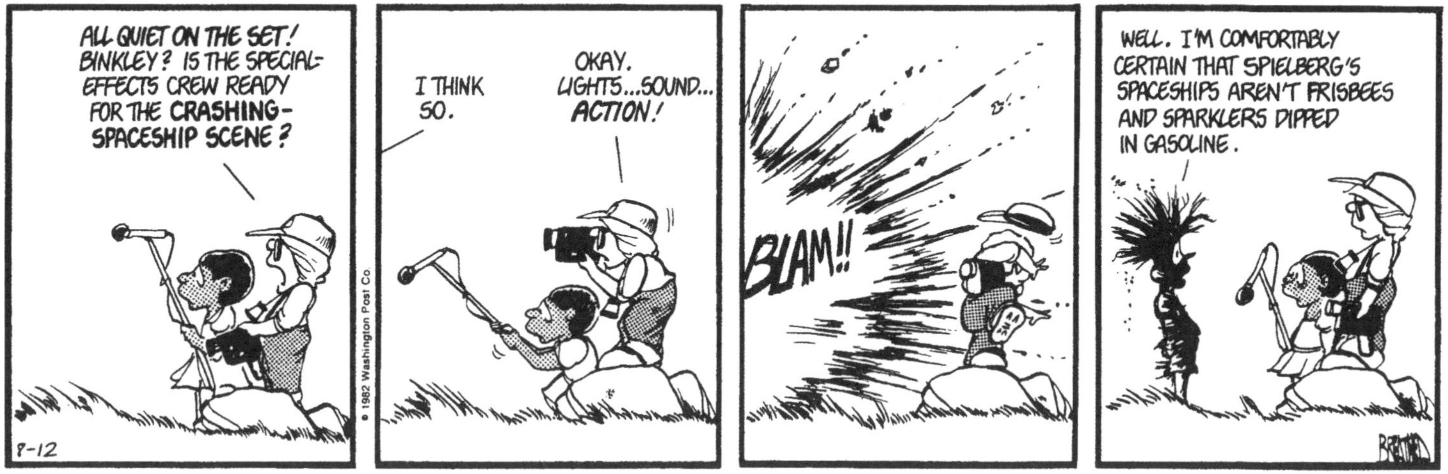
ALL QUIET ON THE SET! BINKLEY? IS THE SPECIAL-EFFECTS CREW READY FOR THE **CRASHING-SPACESHIP SCENE**?
8-12
© 1982 Washington Post Co.
I THINK SO.
OKAY. LIGHTS...SOUND... **ACTION**!
BLAM!!
WELL. I'M COMFORTABLY CERTAIN THAT SPIELBERG'S SPACESHIPS AREN'T FRISBEES AND SPARKLERS DIPPED IN GASOLINE.
BREATHED

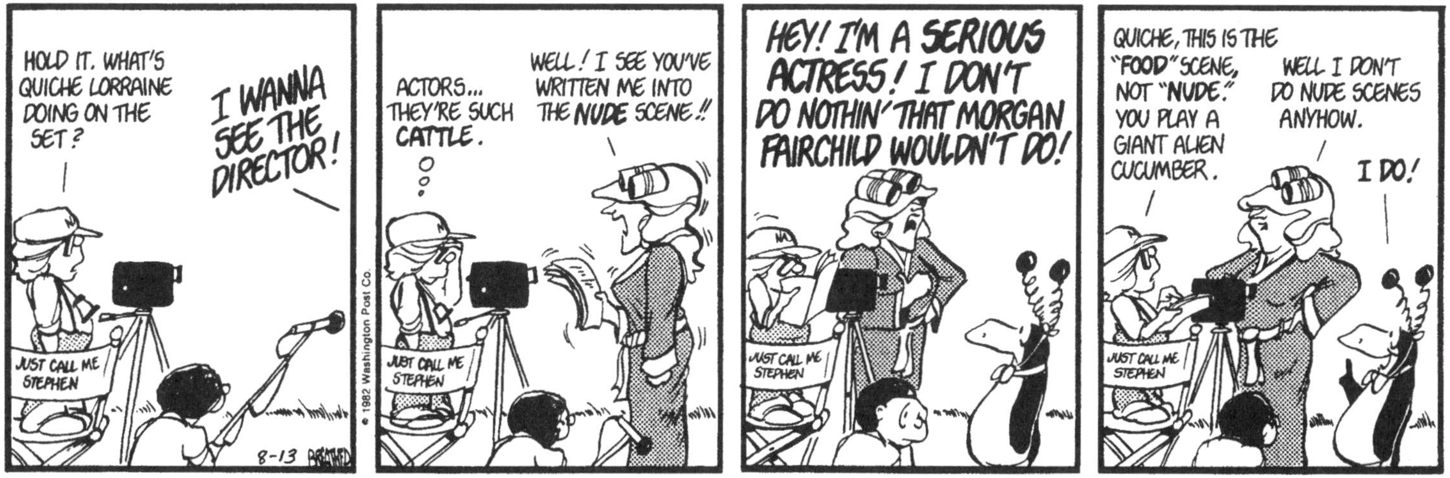
HOLD IT. WHAT'S QUICHE LORRAINE DOING ON THE SET?
I WANNA SEE THE DIRECTOR!
JUST CALL ME STEPHEN
8-13 BREATHED
© 1982 Washington Post Co.
ACTORS... THEY'RE SUCH **CATTLE**.
WELL! I SEE YOU'VE WRITTEN ME INTO THE **NUDE** SCENE!!
JUST CALL ME STEPHEN
HEY! I'M A **SERIOUS ACTRESS**! I DON'T DO NOTHIN' THAT MORGAN FAIRCHILD WOULDN'T DO!
JUST CALL ME STEPHEN
QUICHE, THIS IS THE "**FOOD**" SCENE, NOT "**NUDE**." YOU PLAY A GIANT ALIEN CUCUMBER.
WELL I DON'T DO NUDE SCENES ANYHOW.
I DO!
JUST CALL ME STEPHEN

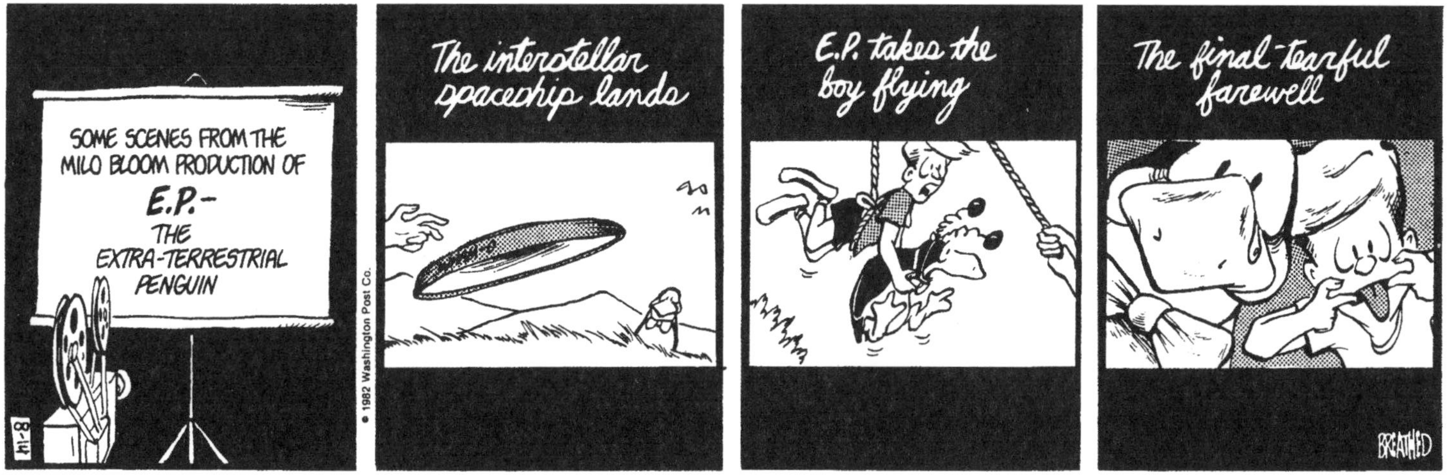
SOME SCENES FROM THE MILO BLOOM PRODUCTION OF
E.P.– THE EXTRA-TERRESTRIAL PENGUIN
8-14
© 1982 Washington Post Co.
The interstellar spaceship lands
E.P. takes the boy flying
The final tearful farewell
BREATHED

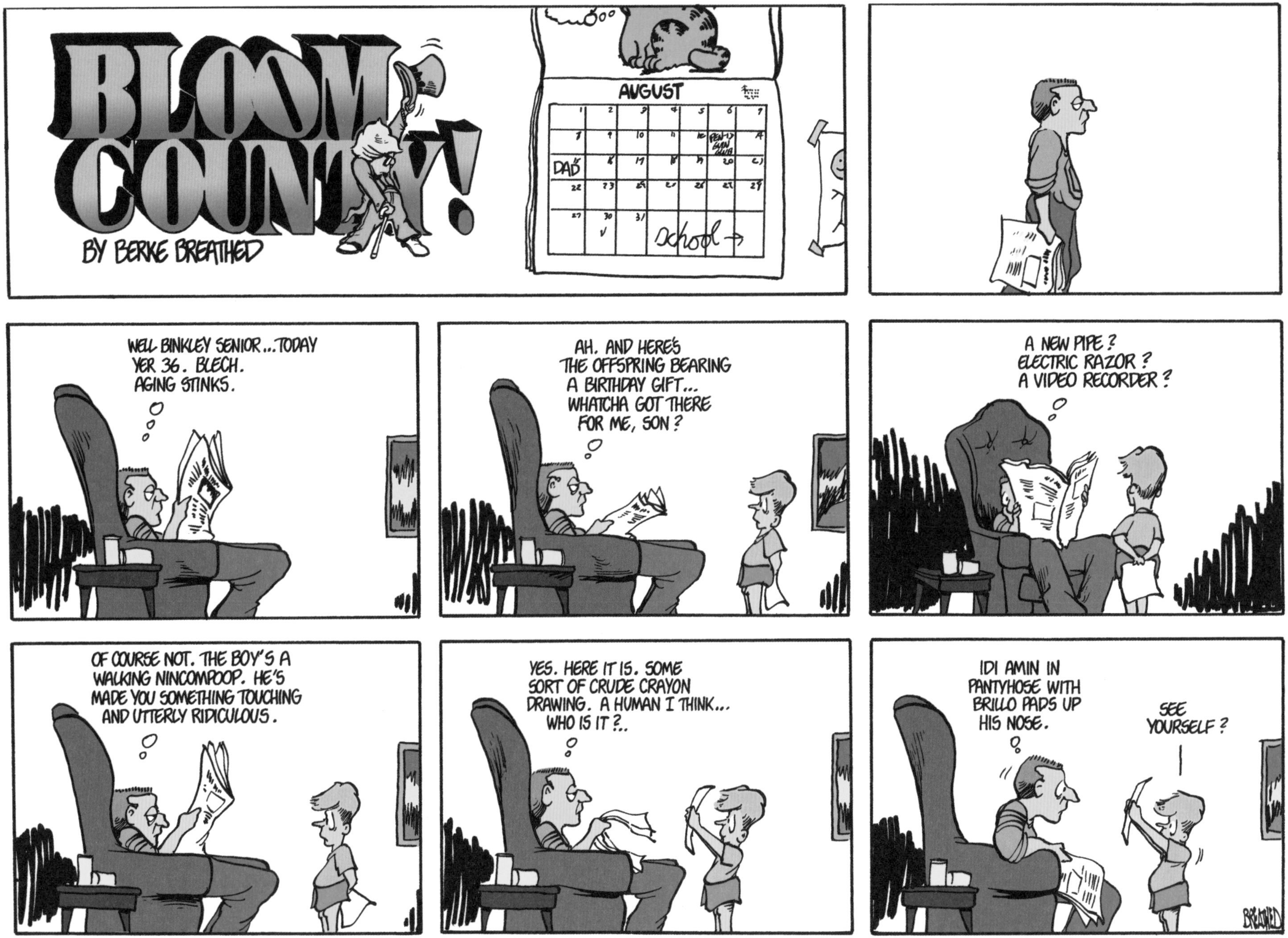
BLOOM COUNTY!
BY BERKE BREATHED
AUGUST
DAD
school
WELL BINKLEY SENIOR... TODAY YER 36. BLECH. AGING STINKS.
AH. AND HERE'S THE OFFSPRING BEARING A BIRTHDAY GIFT... WHATCHA GOT THERE FOR ME, SON?
A NEW PIPE? ELECTRIC RAZOR? A VIDEO RECORDER?
OF COURSE NOT. THE BOY'S A WALKING NINCOMPOOP. HE'S MADE YOU SOMETHING TOUCHING AND UTTERLY RIDICULOUS.
YES. HERE IT IS. SOME SORT OF CRUDE CRAYON DRAWING. A HUMAN I THINK... WHO IS IT?..
IDI AMIN IN PANTYHOSE WITH BRILLO PADS UP HIS NOSE.
SEE YOURSELF?
BREATHED

Idi Amin seized power in 1971 and, until his eventual exile in 1979, ruled as president of the African nation of Uganda. His brutal regime has been accused of numerous heinous human-rights violations.

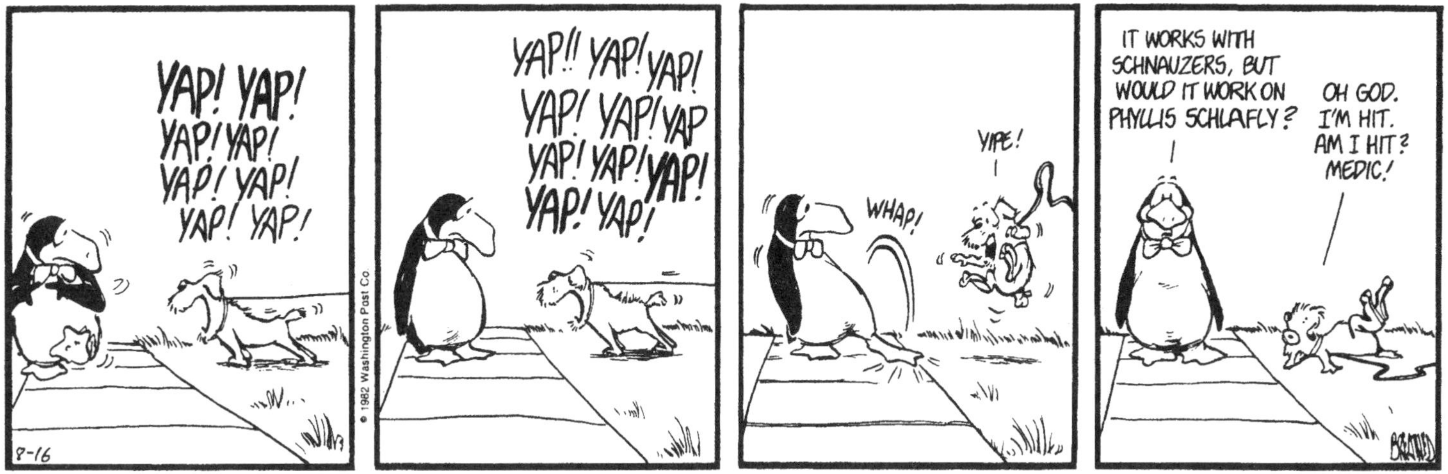

YAP! YAP! YAP! YAP! YAP! YAP! YAP! YAP!
8-16
© 1982 Washington Post Co
YAP!! YAP! YAP! YAP! YAP! YAP YAP! YAP! YAP! YAP! YAP!
WHAP!
YIPE!
IT WORKS WITH SCHNAUZERS, BUT WOULD IT WORK ON PHYLLIS SCHLAFLY?
OH GOD. I'M HIT. AM I HIT? MEDIC!
BREATHED

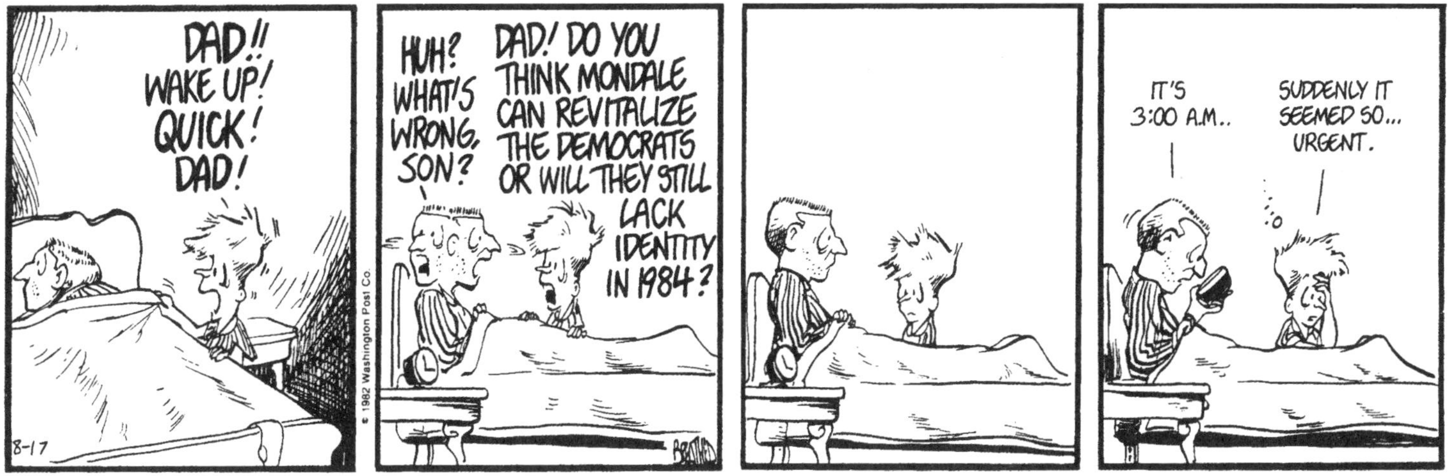

DAD!! WAKE UP! QUICK! DAD!
8-17
© 1982 Washington Post Co
HUH? WHAT'S WRONG, SON?
DAD! DO YOU THINK MONDALE CAN REVITALIZE THE DEMOCRATS OR WILL THEY STILL LACK IDENTITY IN 1984?
BREATHED
IT'S 3:00 A.M..
SUDDENLY IT SEEMED SO... URGENT.

Minnesota Senator Walter Mondale was the Vice President under Jimmy Carter and later went on to be the Democratic Party's candidate in 1984 for President of the United States.

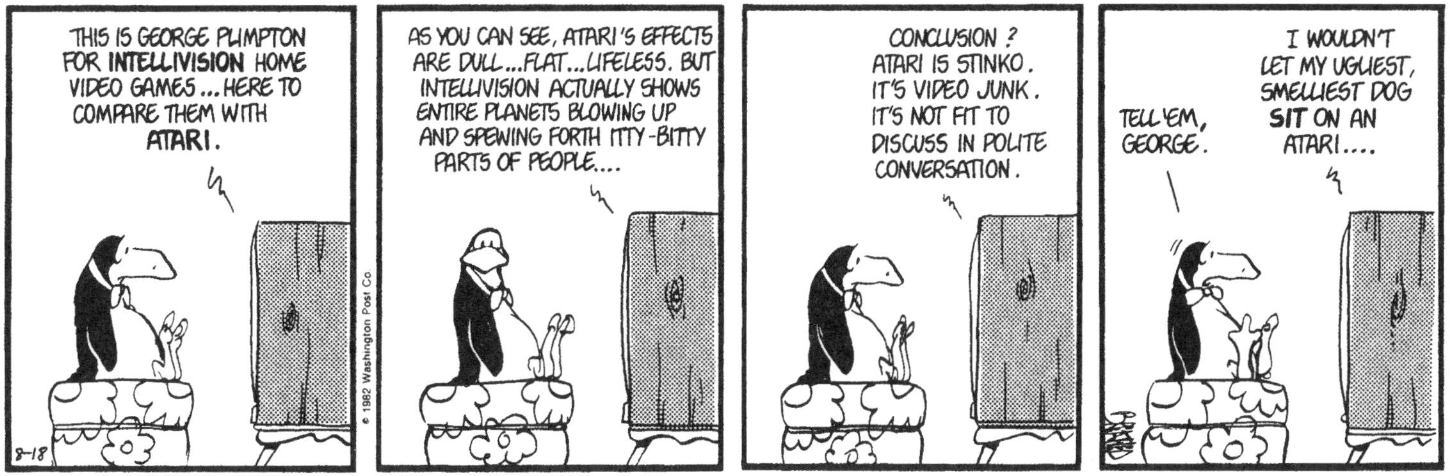

THIS IS GEORGE PLIMPTON FOR **INTELLIVISION** HOME VIDEO GAMES... HERE TO COMPARE THEM WITH **ATARI**.
8-18
© 1982 Washington Post Co
AS YOU CAN SEE, ATARI'S EFFECTS ARE DULL...FLAT...LIFELESS. BUT INTELLIVISION ACTUALLY SHOWS ENTIRE PLANETS BLOWING UP AND SPEWING FORTH ITTY-BITTY PARTS OF PEOPLE....
CONCLUSION? ATARI IS STINKO. IT'S VIDEO JUNK. IT'S NOT FIT TO DISCUSS IN POLITE CONVERSATION.
TELL 'EM, GEORGE.
I WOULDN'T LET MY UGLIEST, SMELLIEST DOG **SIT** ON AN ATARI....

George Plimpton was a writer, particularly well thought of for his sports pieces, an occasional character actor, and the founding editor of *The Paris Review*.

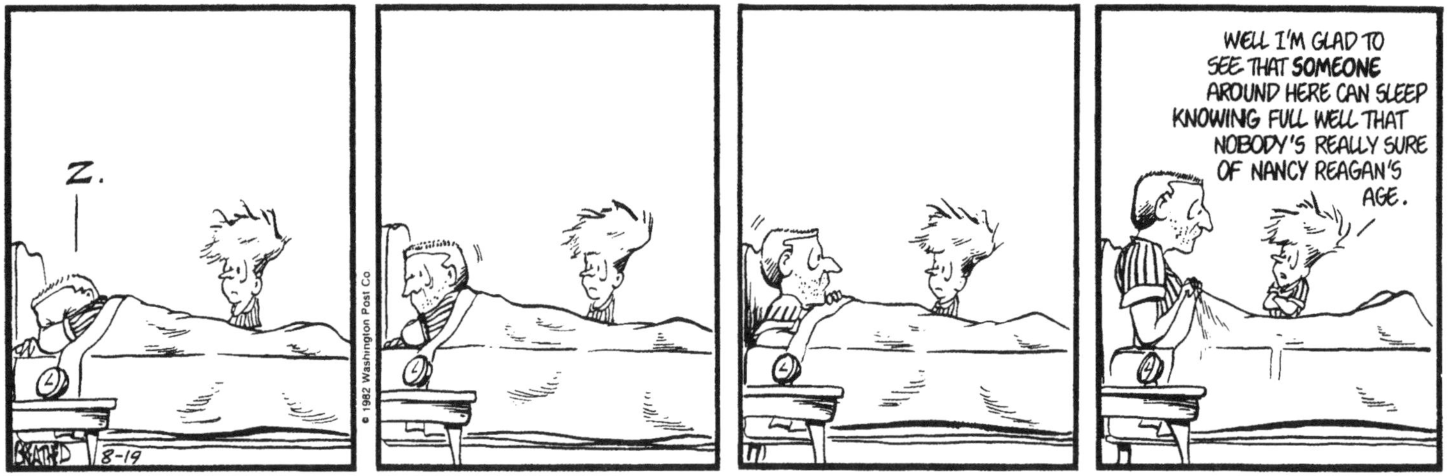
Z.
© 1982 Washington Post Co.
WELL I'M GLAD TO SEE THAT **SOMEONE** AROUND HERE CAN SLEEP KNOWING FULL WELL THAT NOBODY'S REALLY SURE OF NANCY REAGAN'S AGE.
8-19

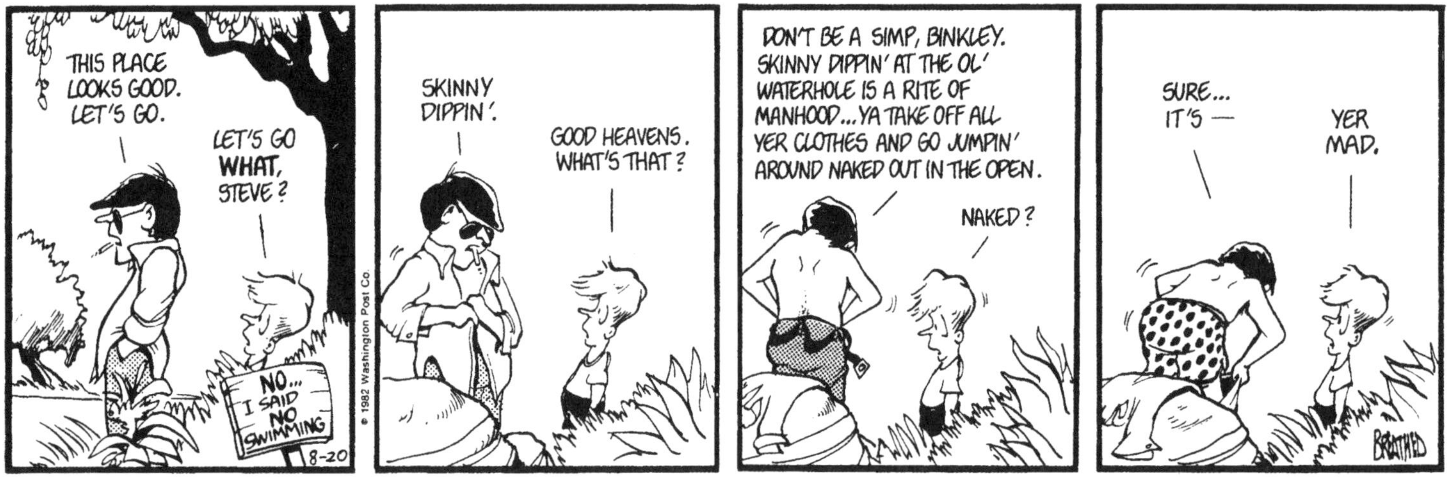
THIS PLACE LOOKS GOOD. LET'S GO.
LET'S GO **WHAT,** STEVE?
NO... I SAID NO SWIMMING
8-20
© 1982 Washington Post Co.
SKINNY DIPPIN'.
GOOD HEAVENS. WHAT'S THAT?
DON'T BE A SIMP, BINKLEY. SKINNY DIPPIN' AT THE OL' WATERHOLE IS A RITE OF MANHOOD...YA TAKE OFF ALL YER CLOTHES AND GO JUMPIN' AROUND NAKED OUT IN THE OPEN.
NAKED?
SURE... IT'S —
YER MAD.

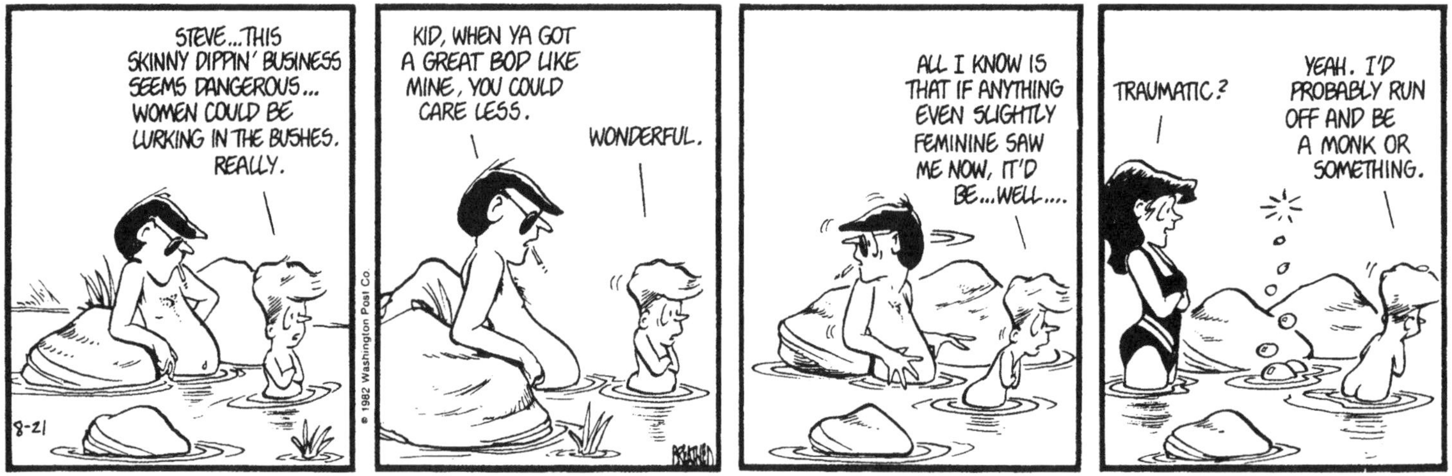
STEVE...THIS SKINNY DIPPIN' BUSINESS SEEMS DANGEROUS... WOMEN COULD BE LURKING IN THE BUSHES. REALLY.
8-21
© 1982 Washington Post Co.
KID, WHEN YA GOT A GREAT BOD LIKE MINE, YOU COULD CARE LESS.
WONDERFUL.
ALL I KNOW IS THAT IF ANYTHING EVEN SLIGHTLY FEMININE SAW ME NOW, IT'D BE...WELL....
TRAUMATIC?
YEAH. I'D PROBABLY RUN OFF AND BE A MONK OR SOMETHING.

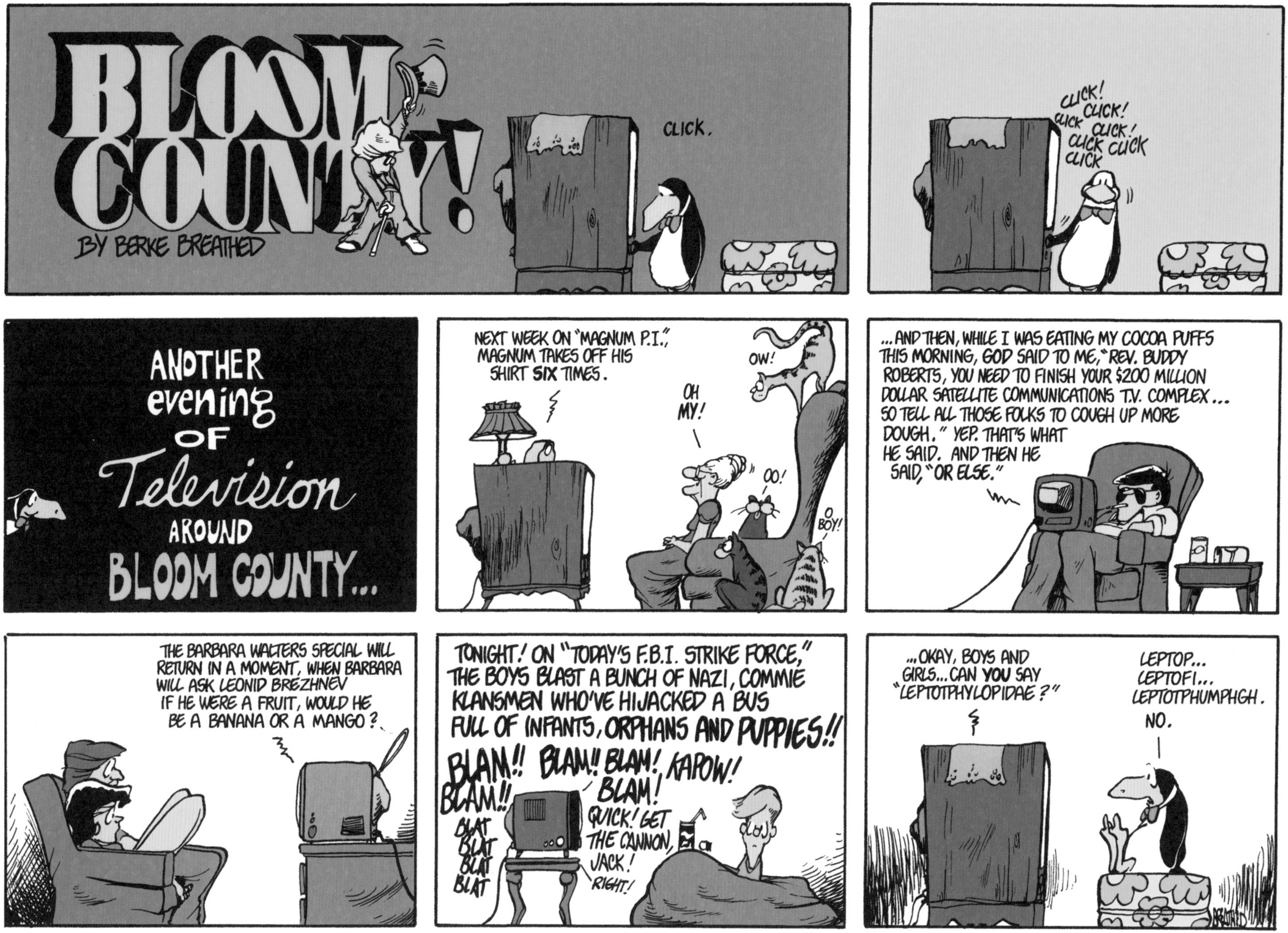
BLOOM COUNTY!
BY BERKE BREATHED
CLICK.
CLICK! CLICK! CLICK CLICK! CLICK CLICK CLICK
ANOTHER evening OF Television AROUND BLOOM COUNTY...
NEXT WEEK ON "MAGNUM P.I.," MAGNUM TAKES OFF HIS SHIRT SIX TIMES.
OW!
OH MY!
OO!
O BOY!
...AND THEN, WHILE I WAS EATING MY COCOA PUFFS THIS MORNING, GOD SAID TO ME, "REV. BUDDY ROBERTS, YOU NEED TO FINISH YOUR $200 MILLION DOLLAR SATELLITE COMMUNICATIONS T.V. COMPLEX... SO TELL ALL THOSE FOLKS TO COUGH UP MORE DOUGH." YEP. THAT'S WHAT HE SAID. AND THEN HE SAID, "OR ELSE."
THE BARBARA WALTERS SPECIAL WILL RETURN IN A MOMENT, WHEN BARBARA WILL ASK LEONID BREZHNEV IF HE WERE A FRUIT, WOULD HE BE A BANANA OR A MANGO?
TONIGHT! ON "TODAY'S F.B.I. STRIKE FORCE," THE BOYS BLAST A BUNCH OF NAZI, COMMIE KLANSMEN WHO'VE HIJACKED A BUS FULL OF INFANTS, ORPHANS AND PUPPIES!!
BLAM!! BLAM!! BLAM!! BLAM! BLAM! KAPOW!
BLAT BLAT BLAT BLAT BLAT
QUICK! GET THE CANNON, JACK!
RIGHT!
...OKAY, BOYS AND GIRLS...CAN YOU SAY "LEPTOTPHYLOPIDAE?"
LEPTOP... LEPTOFI... LEPTOTPHUMPHGH.
NO.

Leonid Brezhnev was the Supreme Soviet, the leader of the USSR, until his death in November, 1982.

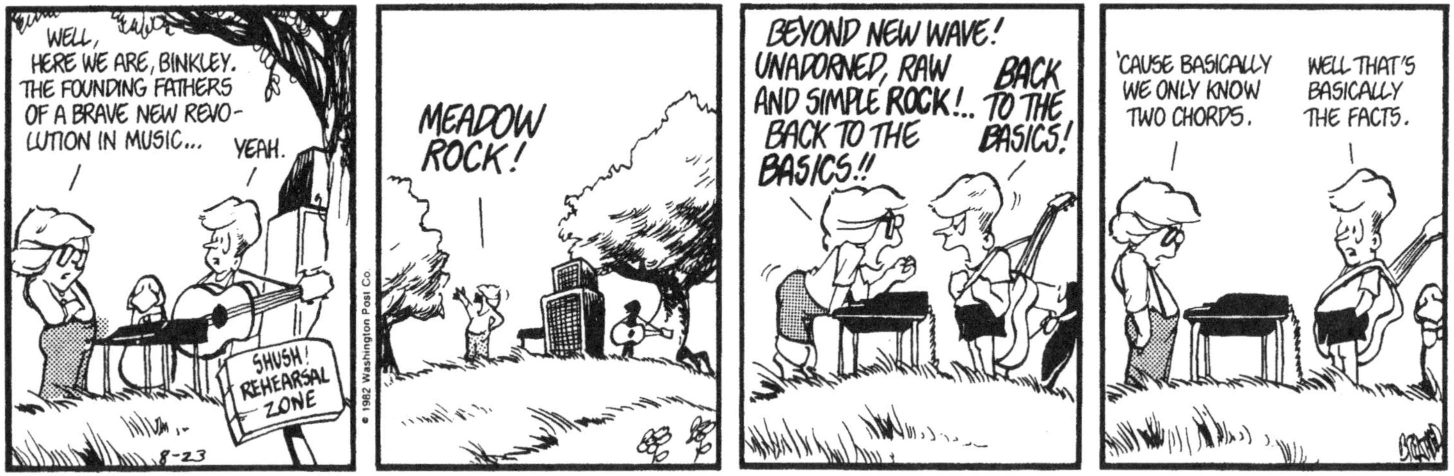
WELL, HERE WE ARE, BINKLEY. THE FOUNDING FATHERS OF A BRAVE NEW REVOLUTION IN MUSIC...
YEAH.
SHUSH! REHEARSAL ZONE
8-23
© 1982 Washington Post Co.
MEADOW ROCK!
BEYOND NEW WAVE! UNADORNED, RAW AND SIMPLE ROCK!.. BACK TO THE BASICS!!
BACK TO THE BASICS!
'CAUSE BASICALLY WE ONLY KNOW TWO CHORDS.
WELL THAT'S BASICALLY THE FACTS.

Conway Twitty was a popular country music performer, with over 40 Number One hits in his career.

Wayne Newton is a Las Vegas-based entertainer who has been a staple there for more than 40 years. He first gained prominence with the song, "Danke Schoen."

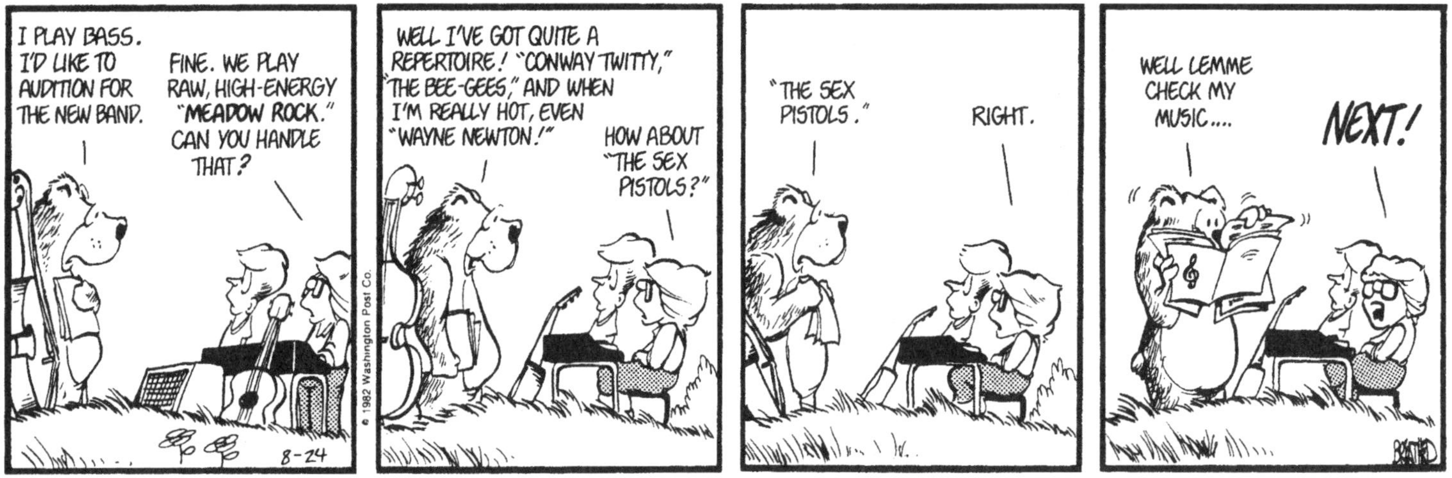
I PLAY BASS. I'D LIKE TO AUDITION FOR THE NEW BAND.
FINE. WE PLAY RAW, HIGH-ENERGY "MEADOW ROCK." CAN YOU HANDLE THAT?
8-24
© 1982 Washington Post Co.
WELL I'VE GOT QUITE A REPERTOIRE! "CONWAY TWITTY," "THE BEE-GEES," AND WHEN I'M REALLY HOT, EVEN "WAYNE NEWTON!"
HOW ABOUT "THE SEX PISTOLS?"
"THE SEX PISTOLS."
RIGHT.
WELL LEMME CHECK MY MUSIC....
NEXT!

Ed Meese served in President Reagan's cabinet, eventually rising to the post of Attorney General.

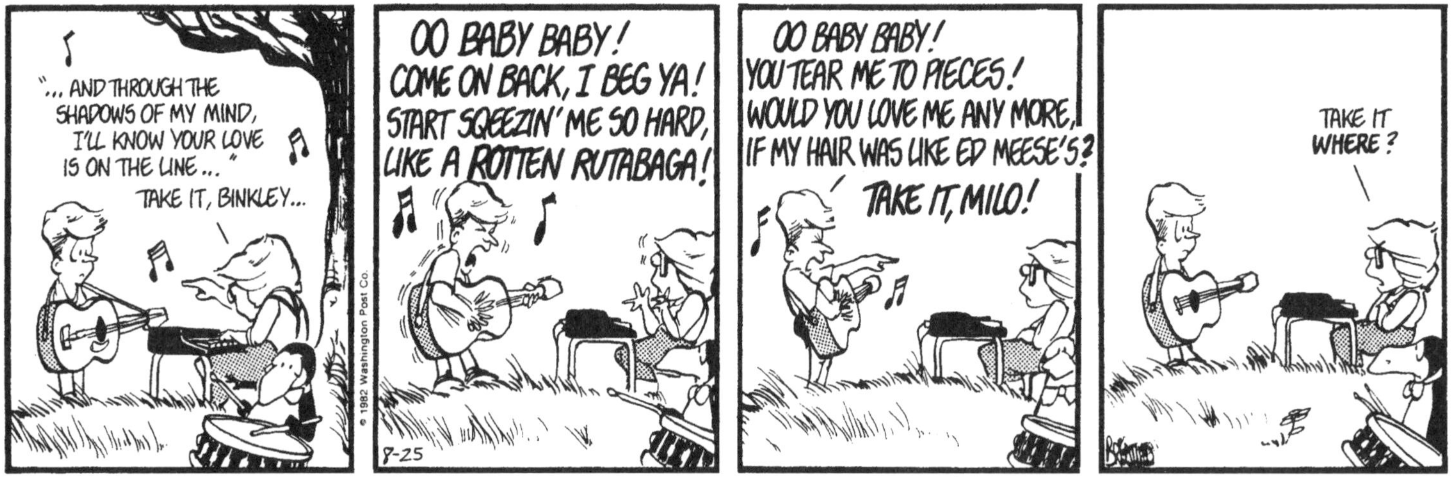
"... AND THROUGH THE SHADOWS OF MY MIND, I'LL KNOW YOUR LOVE IS ON THE LINE..."
TAKE IT, BINKLEY...
© 1982 Washington Post Co.
OO BABY BABY! COME ON BACK, I BEG YA! START SQUEEZIN' ME SO HARD, LIKE A ROTTEN RUTABAGA!
8-25
OO BABY BABY! YOU TEAR ME TO PIECES! WOULD YOU LOVE ME ANY MORE, IF MY HAIR WAS LIKE ED MEESE'S?
TAKE IT, MILO!
TAKE IT WHERE?

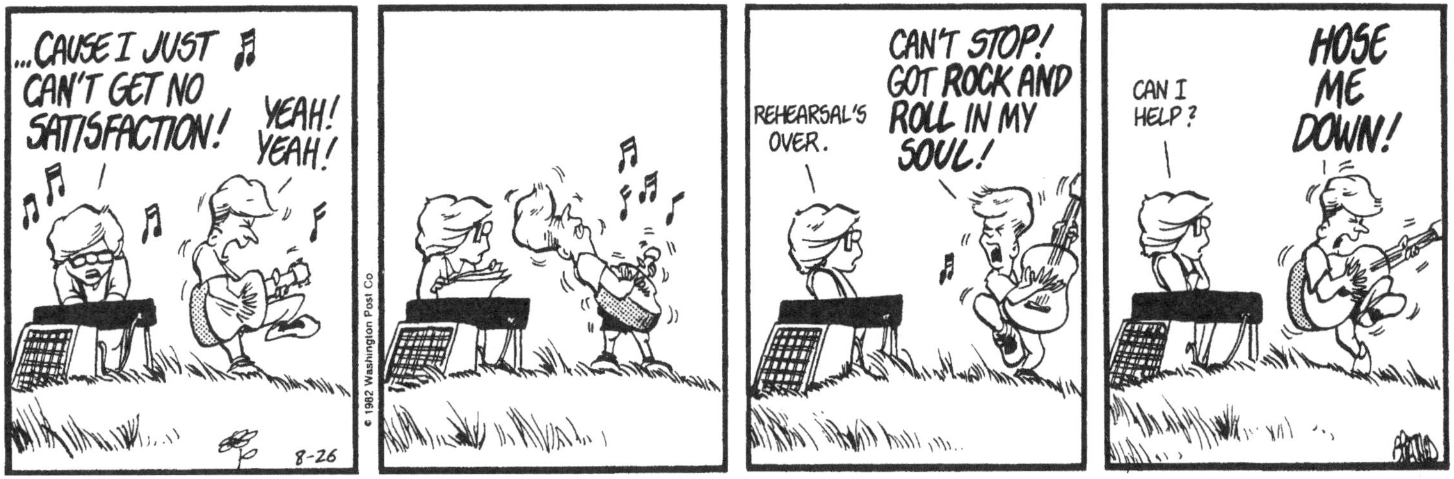
...CAUSE I JUST CAN'T GET NO SATISFACTION!
YEAH! YEAH!
8-26
© 1982 Washington Post Co
REHEARSAL'S OVER.
CAN'T STOP! GOT ROCK AND ROLL IN MY SOUL!
CAN I HELP?
HOSE ME DOWN!

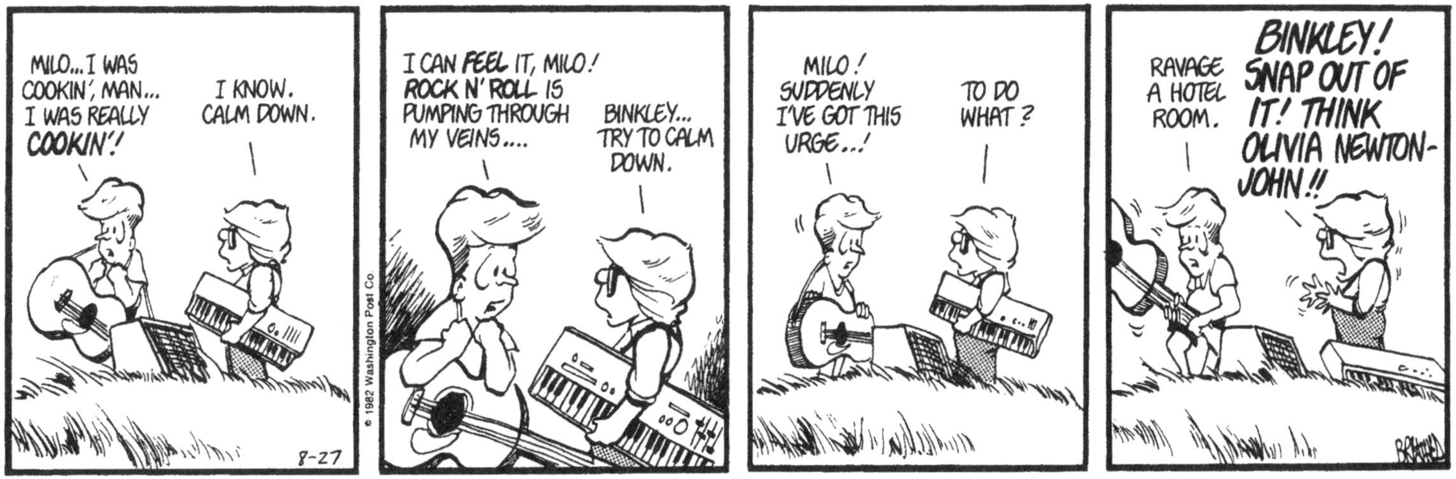
MILO...I WAS COOKIN', MAN... I WAS REALLY COOKIN'!
I KNOW. CALM DOWN.
8-27
© 1982 Washington Post Co
I CAN FEEL IT, MILO! ROCK N' ROLL IS PUMPING THROUGH MY VEINS....
BINKLEY... TRY TO CALM DOWN.
MILO! SUDDENLY I'VE GOT THIS URGE...!
TO DO WHAT?
RAVAGE A HOTEL ROOM.
BINKLEY! SNAP OUT OF IT! THINK OLIVIA NEWTON-JOHN!!

Olivia Newton-John was a pop star in the '70s and '80s, peaking with her 1981 double-platinum album, *Physical*.

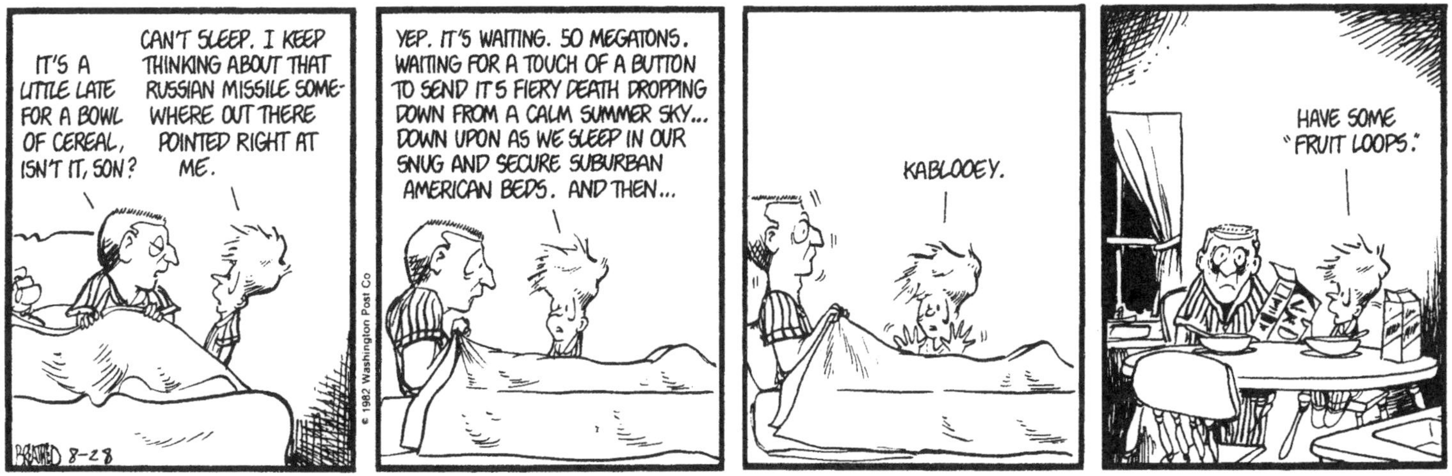
IT'S A LITTLE LATE FOR A BOWL OF CEREAL, ISN'T IT, SON?
CAN'T SLEEP. I KEEP THINKING ABOUT THAT RUSSIAN MISSILE SOMEWHERE OUT THERE POINTED RIGHT AT ME.
8-28
© 1982 Washington Post Co
YEP. IT'S WAITING. 50 MEGATONS. WAITING FOR A TOUCH OF A BUTTON TO SEND IT'S FIERY DEATH DROPPING DOWN FROM A CALM SUMMER SKY... DOWN UPON AS WE SLEEP IN OUR SNUG AND SECURE SUBURBAN AMERICAN BEDS. AND THEN...
KABLOOEY.
HAVE SOME "FRUIT LOOPS."

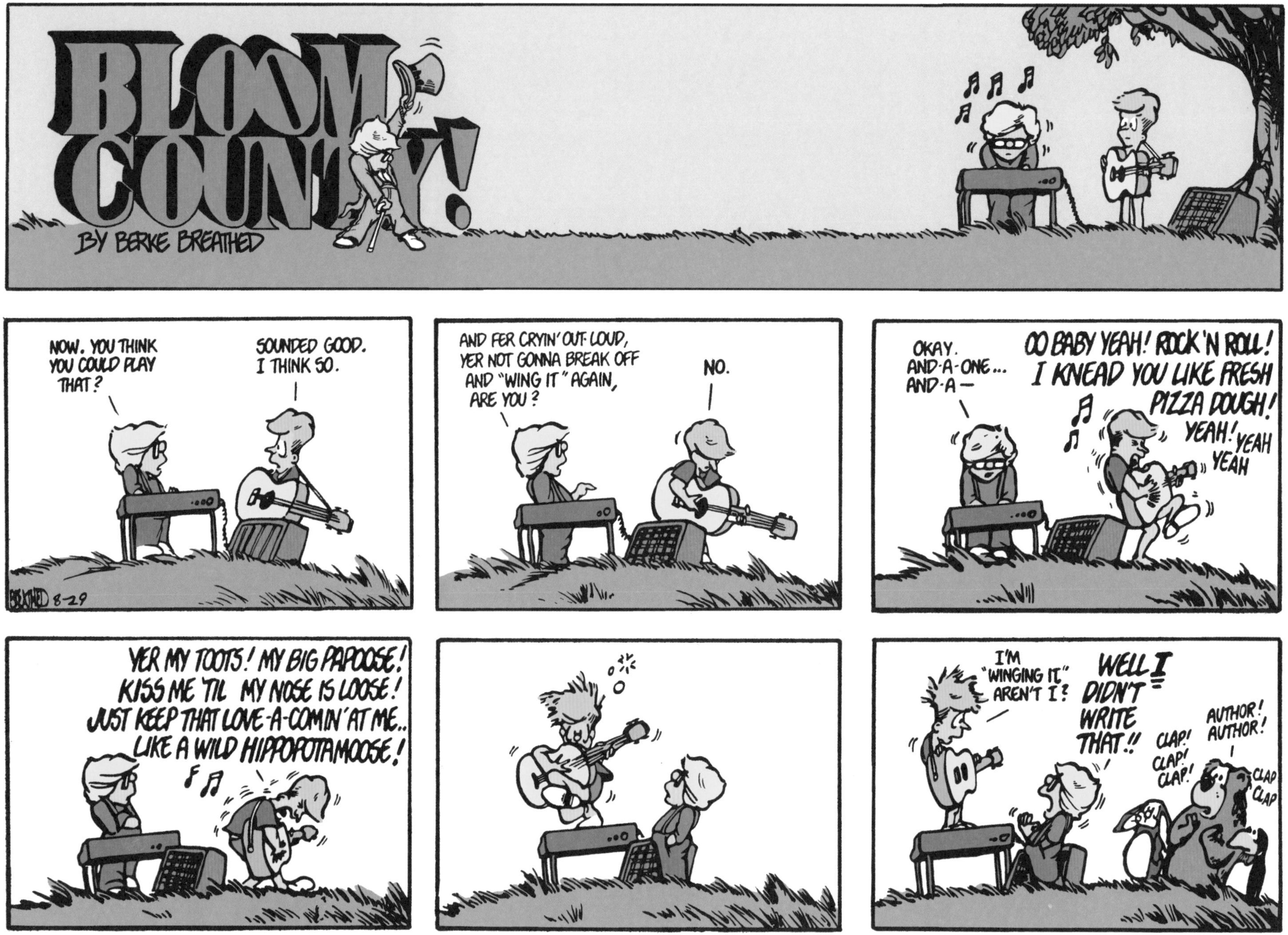
BLOOM COUNTY!
BY BERKE BREATHED
NOW. YOU THINK YOU COULD PLAY THAT?
SOUNDED GOOD. I THINK SO.
BREATHED 8-29
AND FER CRYIN' OUT LOUD, YER NOT GONNA BREAK OFF AND "WING IT" AGAIN, ARE YOU?
NO.
OKAY. AND-A-ONE... AND-A—
OO BABY YEAH! ROCK 'N ROLL! I KNEAD YOU LIKE FRESH PIZZA DOUGH!
YEAH! YEAH YEAH
YER MY TOOTS! MY BIG PAPOOSE! KISS ME 'TIL MY NOSE IS LOOSE! JUST KEEP THAT LOVE-A-COMIN' AT ME.. LIKE A WILD HIPPOPOTAMOOSE!
I'M "WINGING IT," AREN'T I?
WELL I DIDN'T WRITE THAT!!
CLAP! CLAP! CLAP!
AUTHOR! AUTHOR!
CLAP CLAP

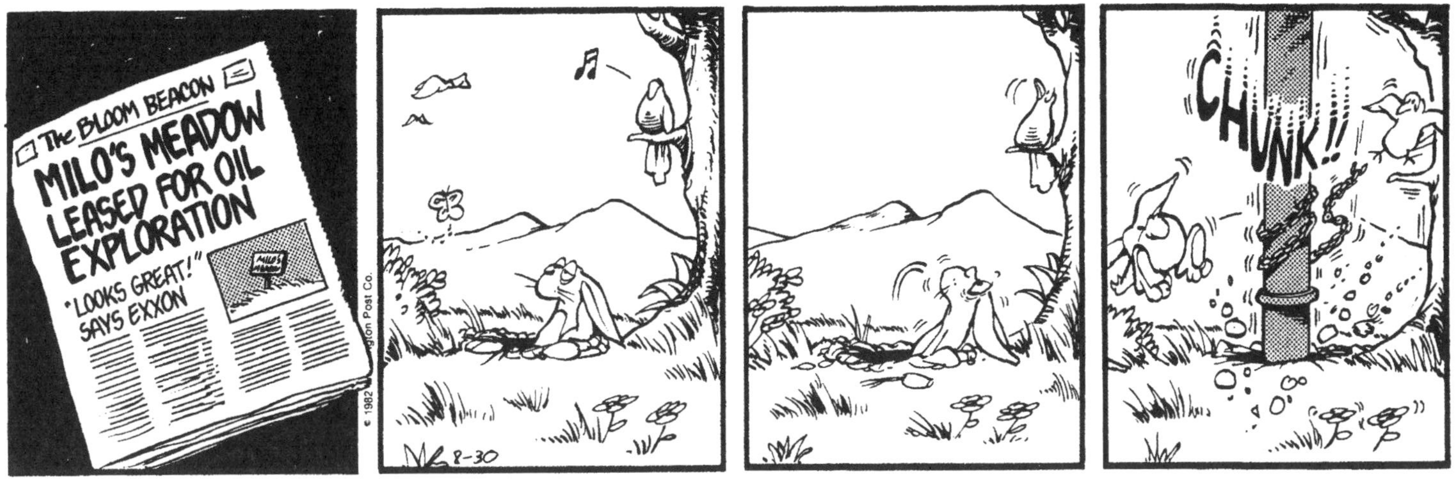
The BLOOM BEACON
MILO'S MEADOW LEASED FOR OIL EXPLORATION
"LOOKS GREAT!" SAYS EXXON
8-30
CHUNK!!

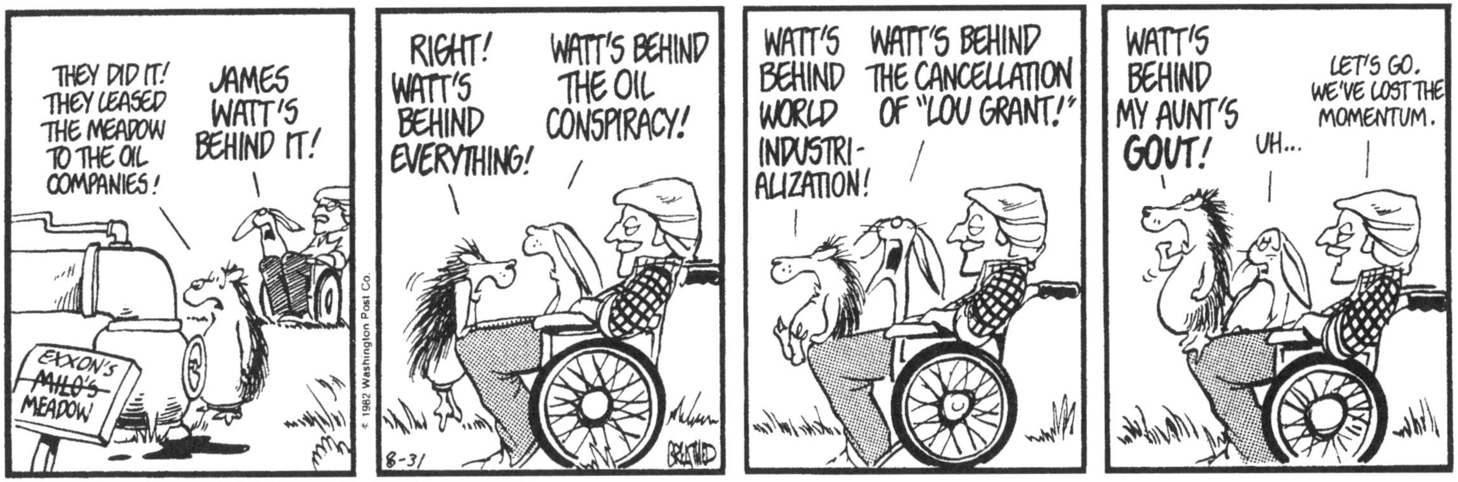
THEY DID IT! THEY LEASED THE MEADOW TO THE OIL COMPANIES!
JAMES WATT'S BEHIND IT!
EXXON'S MILO'S MEADOW
© 1982 Washington Post Co.
RIGHT! WATT'S BEHIND EVERYTHING!
WATT'S BEHIND THE OIL CONSPIRACY!
8-31
WATT'S BEHIND WORLD INDUSTRIALIZATION!
WATT'S BEHIND THE CANCELLATION OF "LOU GRANT!"
WATT'S BEHIND MY AUNT'S GOUT!
UH...
LET'S GO. WE'VE LOST THE MOMENTUM.

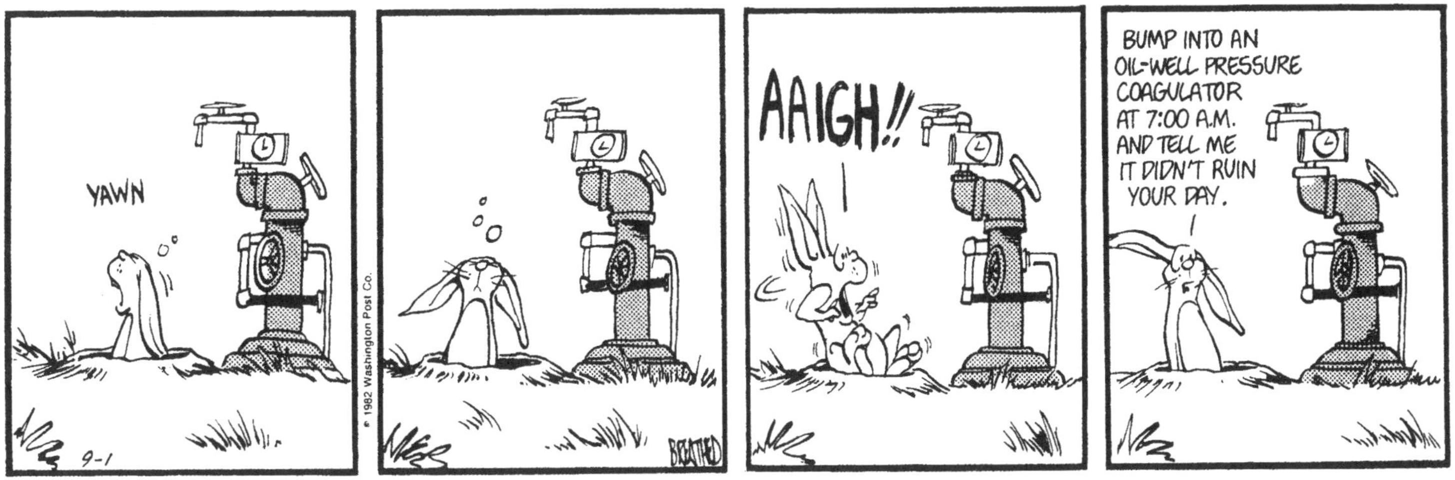
YAWN
9-1
© 1982 Washington Post Co.
AAIGH!!
BUMP INTO AN OIL-WELL PRESSURE COAGULATOR AT 7:00 A.M. AND TELL ME IT DIDN'T RUIN YOUR DAY.

August 30-
September 1, 1982

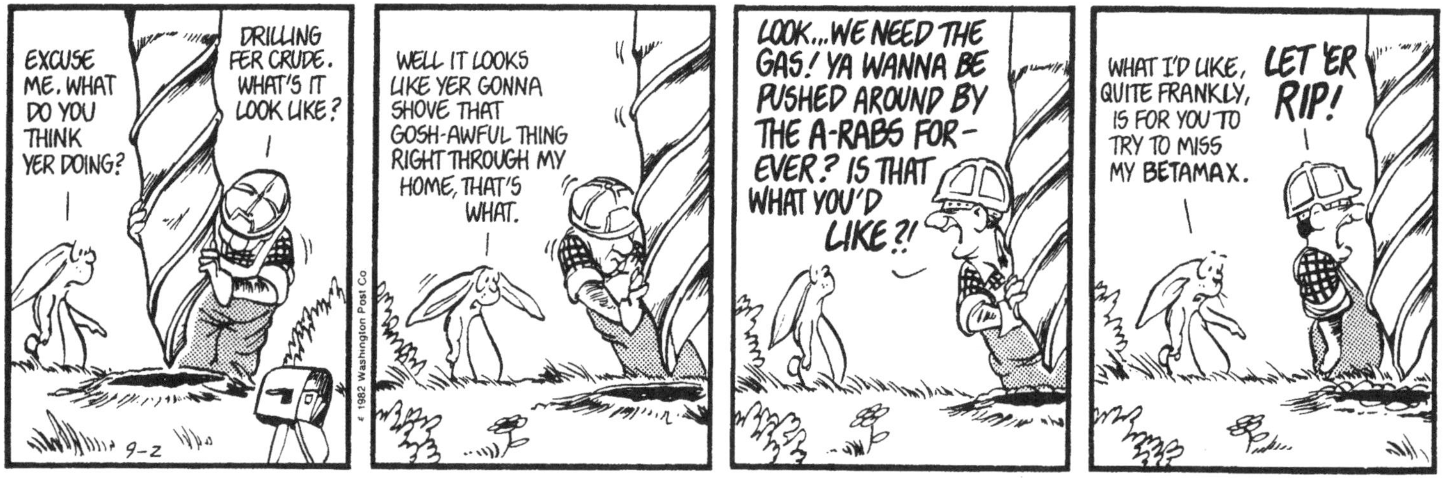
EXCUSE ME. WHAT DO YOU THINK YER DOING?
DRILLING FER CRUDE. WHAT'S IT LOOK LIKE?
9-2
© 1982 Washington Post Co.
WELL IT LOOKS LIKE YER GONNA SHOVE THAT GOSH-AWFUL THING RIGHT THROUGH MY HOME, THAT'S WHAT.
LOOK...WE NEED THE GAS! YA WANNA BE PUSHED AROUND BY THE A-RABS FOREVER? IS THAT WHAT YOU'D LIKE?!
WHAT I'D LIKE, QUITE FRANKLY, IS FOR YOU TO TRY TO MISS MY BETAMAX.
LET 'ER RIP!

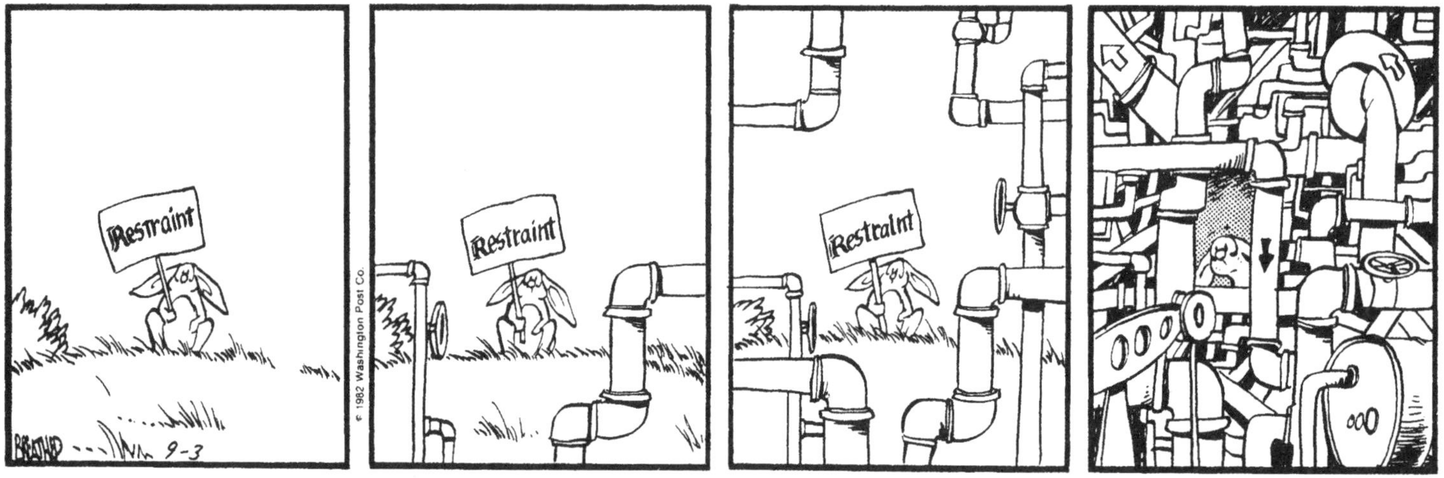
Restraint
BREATHED
9-3
© 1982 Washington Post Co.
Restraint
Restraint

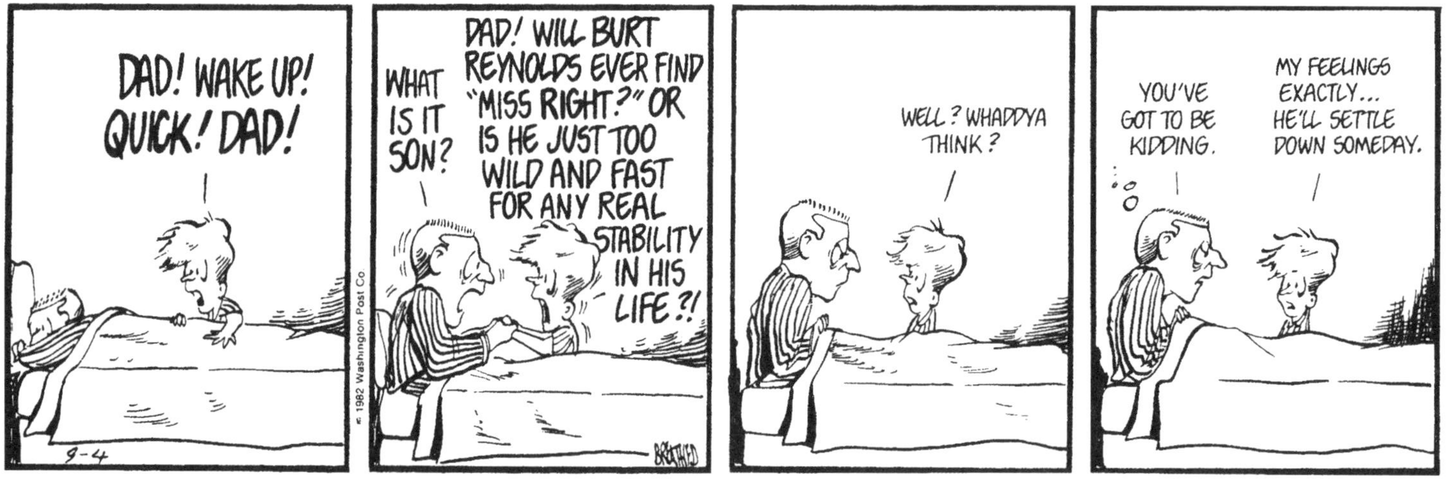
DAD! WAKE UP! QUICK! DAD!
9-4
© 1982 Washington Post Co.
WHAT IS IT SON?
DAD! WILL BURT REYNOLDS EVER FIND "MISS RIGHT?" OR IS HE JUST TOO WILD AND FAST FOR ANY REAL STABILITY IN HIS LIFE?!
BREATHED
WELL? WHADDYA THINK?
YOU'VE GOT TO BE KIDDING.
MY FEELINGS EXACTLY... HE'LL SETTLE DOWN SOMEDAY.

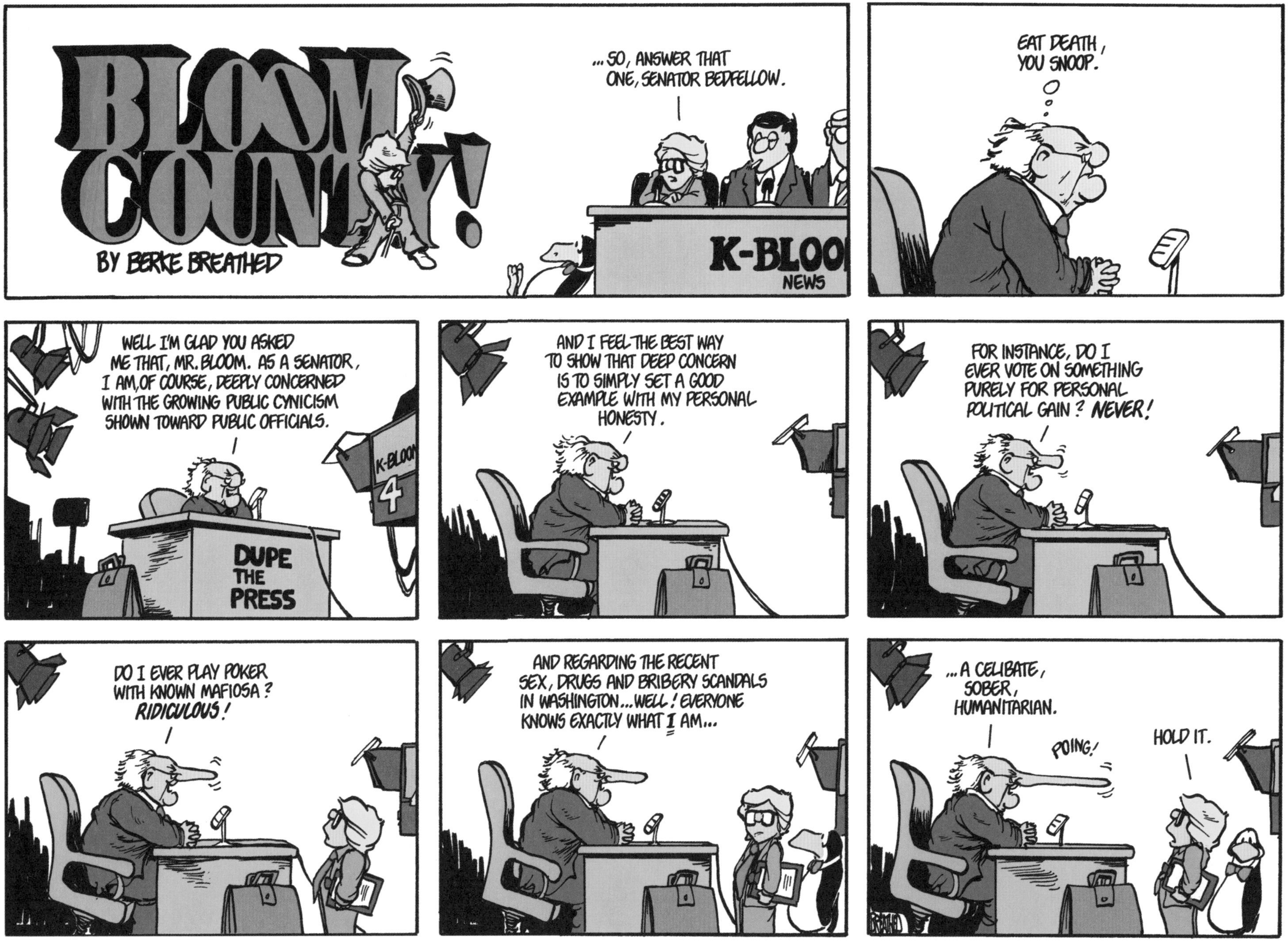
BLOOM COUNTY!
BY BERKE BREATHED
...SO, ANSWER THAT ONE, SENATOR BEDFELLOW.
K-BLOOM NEWS
EAT DEATH, YOU SNOOP.
WELL I'M GLAD YOU ASKED ME THAT, MR. BLOOM. AS A SENATOR, I AM, OF COURSE, DEEPLY CONCERNED WITH THE GROWING PUBLIC CYNICISM SHOWN TOWARD PUBLIC OFFICIALS.
K-BLOOM 4
DUPE THE PRESS
AND I FEEL THE BEST WAY TO SHOW THAT DEEP CONCERN IS TO SIMPLY SET A GOOD EXAMPLE WITH MY PERSONAL HONESTY.
FOR INSTANCE, DO I EVER VOTE ON SOMETHING PURELY FOR PERSONAL POLITICAL GAIN? NEVER!
DO I EVER PLAY POKER WITH KNOWN MAFIOSA? RIDICULOUS!
AND REGARDING THE RECENT SEX, DRUGS AND BRIBERY SCANDALS IN WASHINGTON...WELL! EVERYONE KNOWS EXACTLY WHAT I AM...
...A CELIBATE, SOBER, HUMANITARIAN.
POING!
HOLD IT.

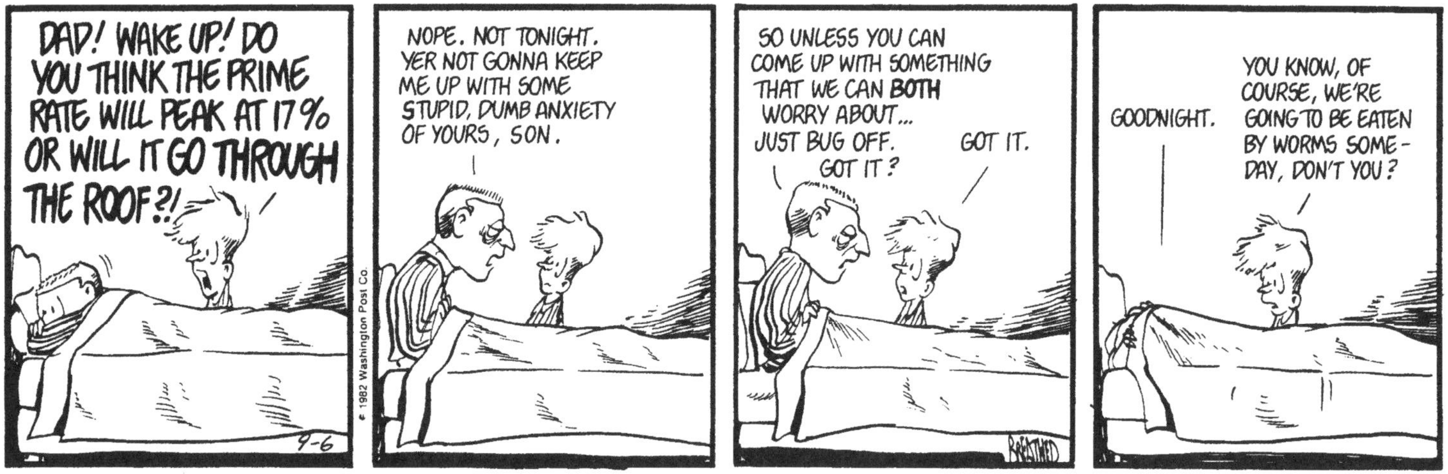
DAD! WAKE UP! DO YOU THINK THE PRIME RATE WILL PEAK AT 17% OR WILL IT GO THROUGH THE ROOF?!
9-6
© 1982 Washington Post Co.
NOPE. NOT TONIGHT. YER NOT GONNA KEEP ME UP WITH SOME STUPID, DUMB ANXIETY OF YOURS, SON.
SO UNLESS YOU CAN COME UP WITH SOMETHING THAT WE CAN BOTH WORRY ABOUT... JUST BUG OFF. GOT IT?
GOT IT.
GOODNIGHT.
YOU KNOW, OF COURSE, WE'RE GOING TO BE EATEN BY WORMS SOMEDAY, DON'T YOU?

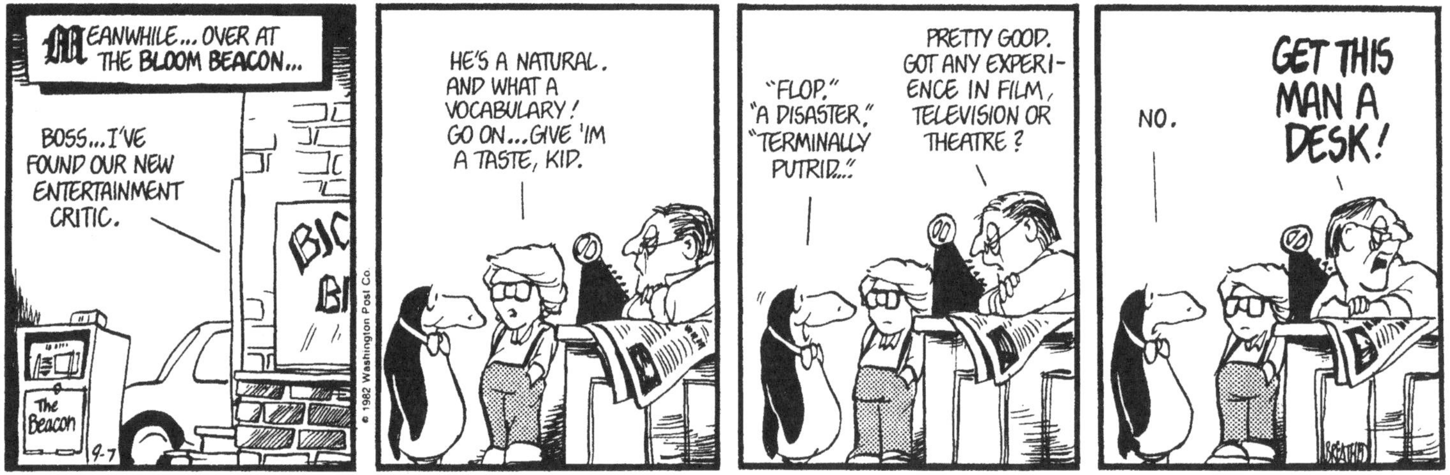
MEANWHILE... OVER AT THE BLOOM BEACON...
BOSS... I'VE FOUND OUR NEW ENTERTAINMENT CRITIC.
The Beacon
9-7
© 1982 Washington Post Co.
HE'S A NATURAL. AND WHAT A VOCABULARY! GO ON... GIVE 'IM A TASTE, KID.
"FLOP." "A DISASTER." "TERMINALLY PUTRID..."
PRETTY GOOD. GOT ANY EXPERIENCE IN FILM, TELEVISION OR THEATRE?
NO.
GET THIS MAN A DESK!

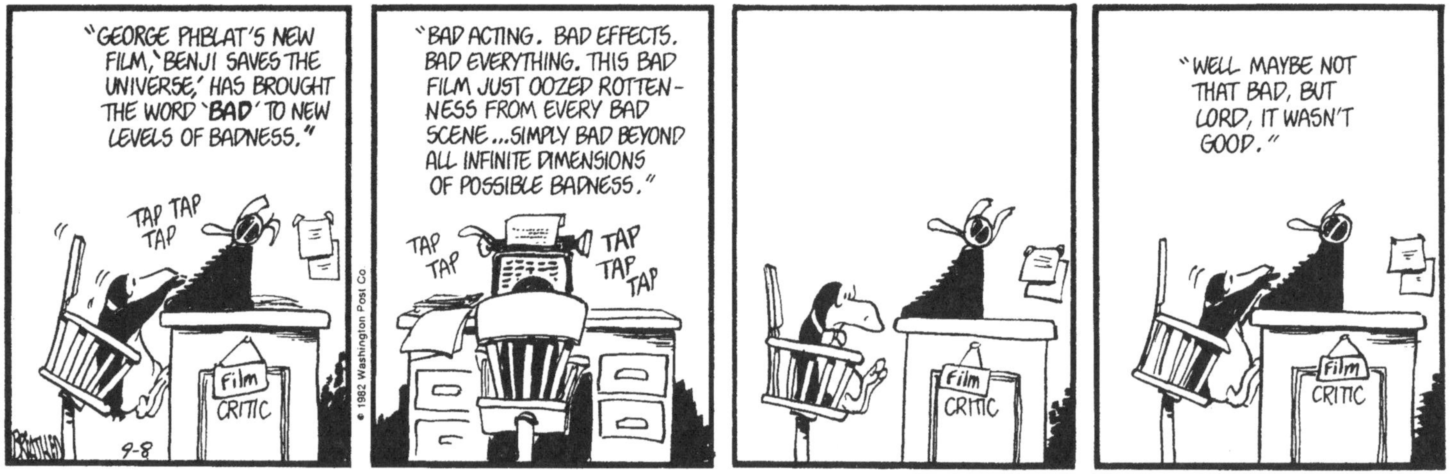
"GEORGE PHBLAT'S NEW FILM, 'BENJI SAVES THE UNIVERSE,' HAS BROUGHT THE WORD 'BAD' TO NEW LEVELS OF BADNESS."
TAP TAP TAP
Film CRITIC
9-8
© 1982 Washington Post Co.
"BAD ACTING. BAD EFFECTS. BAD EVERYTHING. THIS BAD FILM JUST OOZED ROTTENNESS FROM EVERY BAD SCENE ...SIMPLY BAD BEYOND ALL INFINITE DIMENSIONS OF POSSIBLE BADNESS."
TAP TAP
TAP TAP TAP
Film CRITIC
"WELL MAYBE NOT THAT BAD, BUT LORD, IT WASN'T GOOD."
Film CRITIC

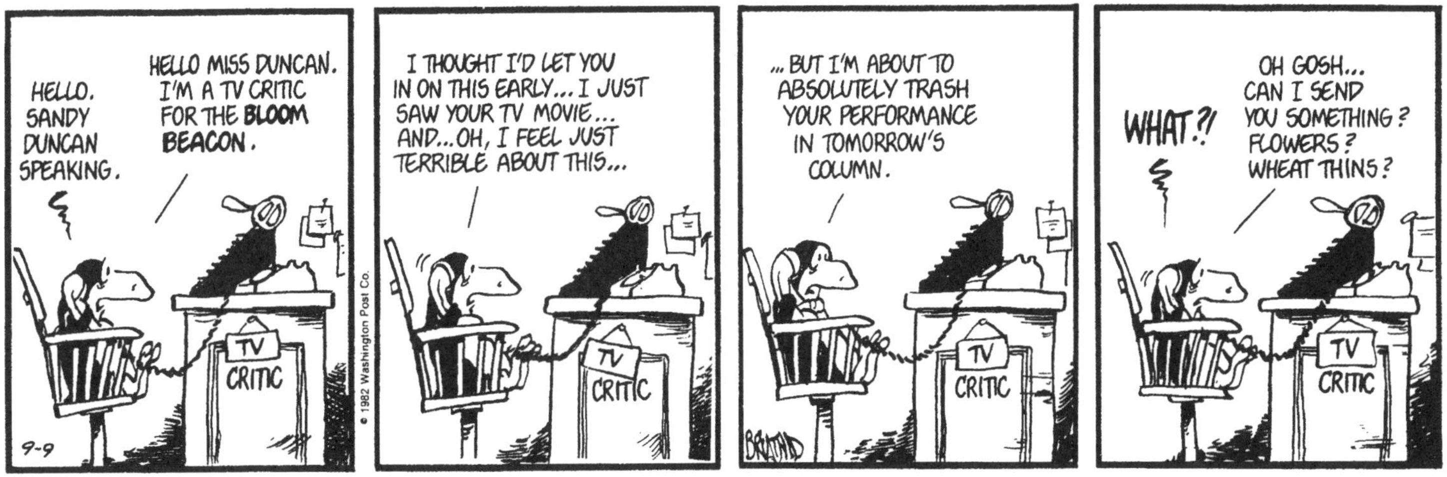
HELLO. SANDY DUNCAN SPEAKING.
HELLO MISS DUNCAN. I'M A TV CRITIC FOR THE **BLOOM BEACON**.
9-9
TV CRITIC
© 1982 Washington Post Co.
I THOUGHT I'D LET YOU IN ON THIS EARLY... I JUST SAW YOUR TV MOVIE... AND...OH, I FEEL JUST TERRIBLE ABOUT THIS...
...BUT I'M ABOUT TO ABSOLUTELY TRASH YOUR PERFORMANCE IN TOMORROW'S COLUMN.
BREATHED
WHAT?!
OH GOSH... CAN I SEND YOU SOMETHING? FLOWERS? WHEAT THINS?

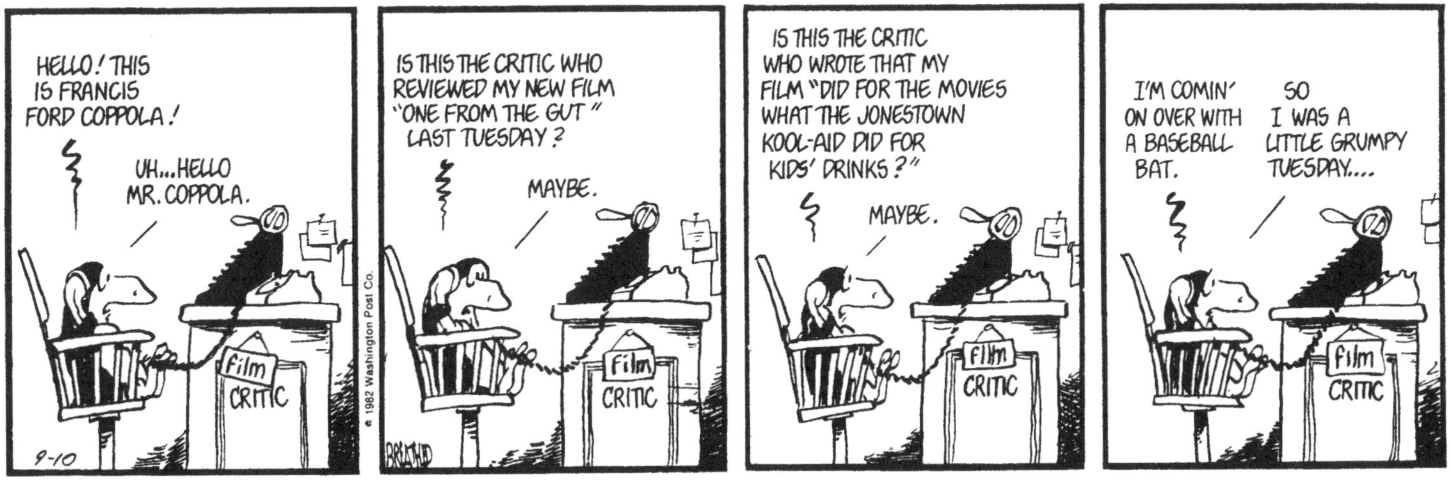
HELLO! THIS IS FRANCIS FORD COPPOLA!
UH...HELLO MR. COPPOLA.
film CRITIC
9-10
© 1982 Washington Post Co.
IS THIS THE CRITIC WHO REVIEWED MY NEW FILM "ONE FROM THE GUT" LAST TUESDAY?
MAYBE.
BREATHED
IS THIS THE CRITIC WHO WROTE THAT MY FILM "DID FOR THE MOVIES WHAT THE JONESTOWN KOOL-AID DID FOR KIDS' DRINKS?"
MAYBE.
I'M COMIN' ON OVER WITH A BASEBALL BAT.
SO I WAS A LITTLE GRUMPY TUESDAY....

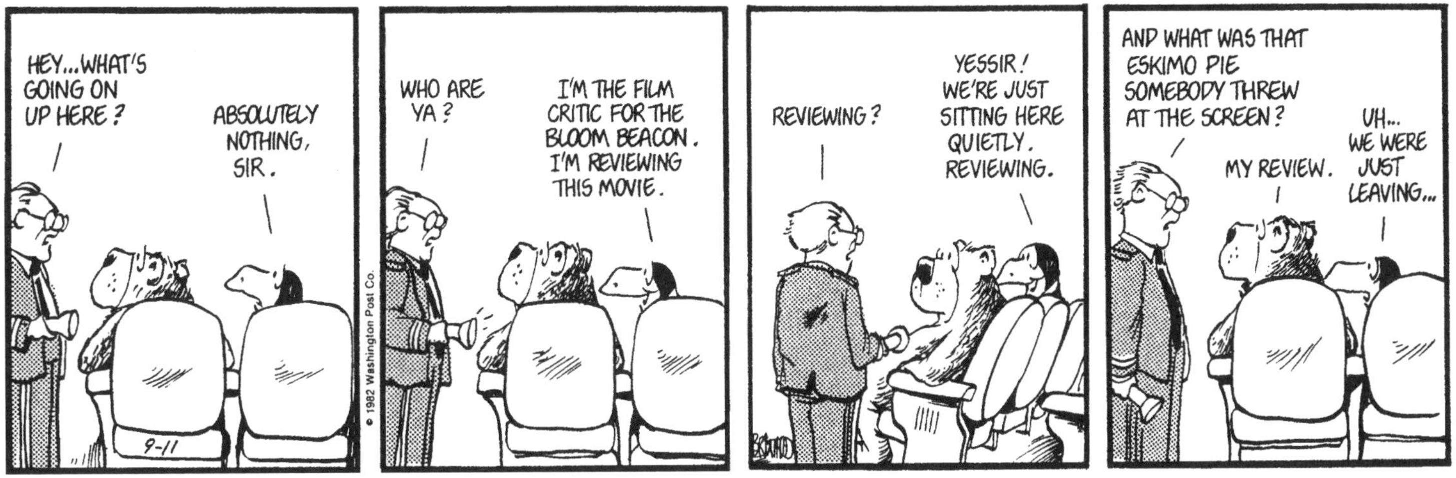
HEY...WHAT'S GOING ON UP HERE?
ABSOLUTELY NOTHING, SIR.
9-11
© 1982 Washington Post Co.
WHO ARE YA?
I'M THE FILM CRITIC FOR THE BLOOM BEACON. I'M REVIEWING THIS MOVIE.
REVIEWING?
YESSIR! WE'RE JUST SITTING HERE QUIETLY. REVIEWING.
BREATHED
AND WHAT WAS THAT ESKIMO PIE SOMEBODY THREW AT THE SCREEN?
MY REVIEW.
UH... WE WERE JUST LEAVING...

Sandy Duncan is a screen and stage actress and singer, most prominently known for her starring role in the Broadway production of *Peter Pan*.

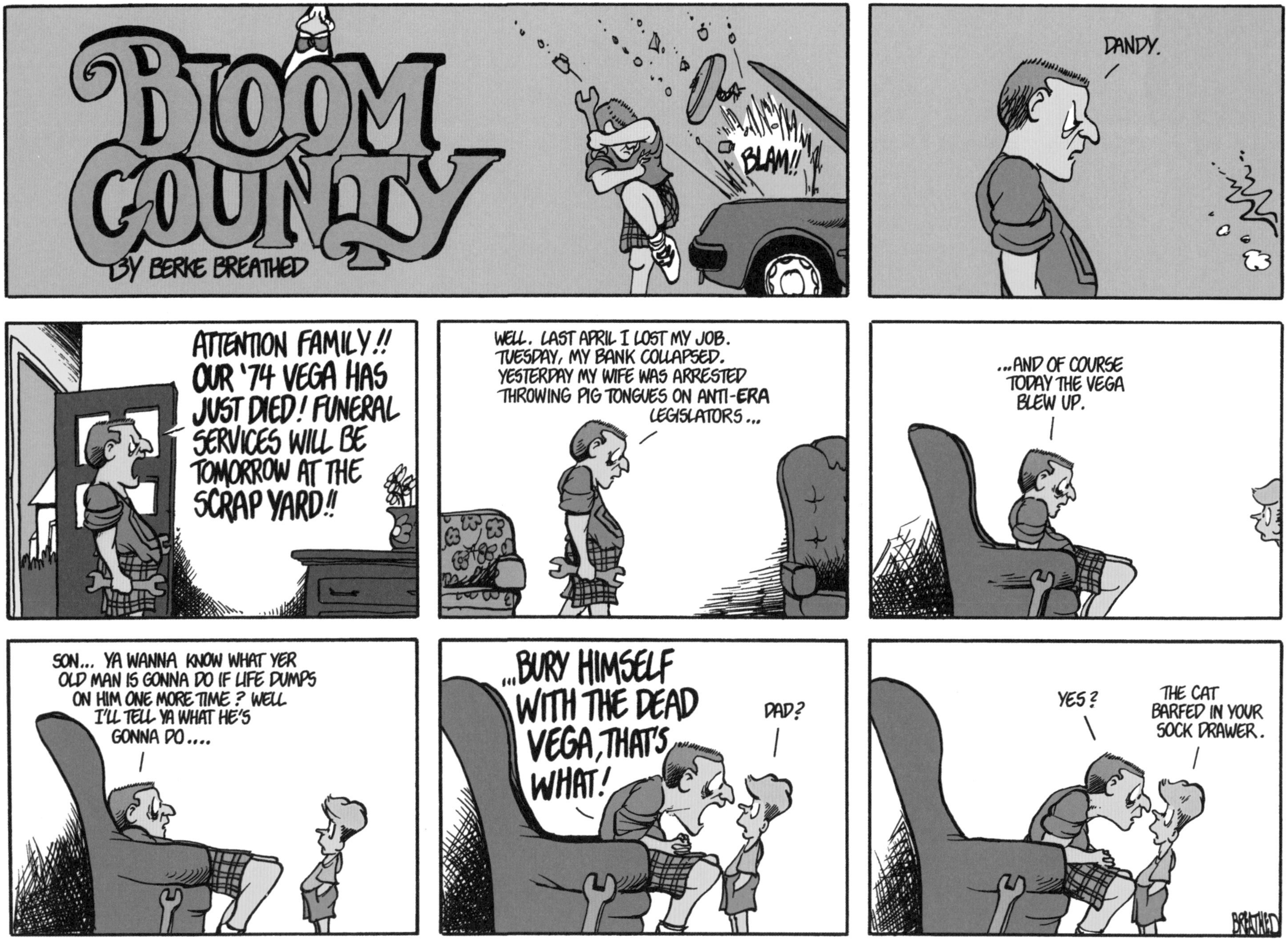
BLOOM COUNTY
BY BERKE BREATHED
BLAM!!
DANDY.
ATTENTION FAMILY!! OUR '74 VEGA HAS JUST DIED! FUNERAL SERVICES WILL BE TOMORROW AT THE SCRAP YARD!!
WELL. LAST APRIL I LOST MY JOB. TUESDAY, MY BANK COLLAPSED. YESTERDAY MY WIFE WAS ARRESTED THROWING PIG TONGUES ON ANTI-ERA LEGISLATORS...
...AND OF COURSE TODAY THE VEGA BLEW UP.
SON... YA WANNA KNOW WHAT YER OLD MAN IS GONNA DO IF LIFE DUMPS ON HIM ONE MORE TIME? WELL I'LL TELL YA WHAT HE'S GONNA DO....
...BURY HIMSELF WITH THE DEAD VEGA, THAT'S WHAT!
DAD?
YES?
THE CAT BARFED IN YOUR SOCK DRAWER.
BREATHED

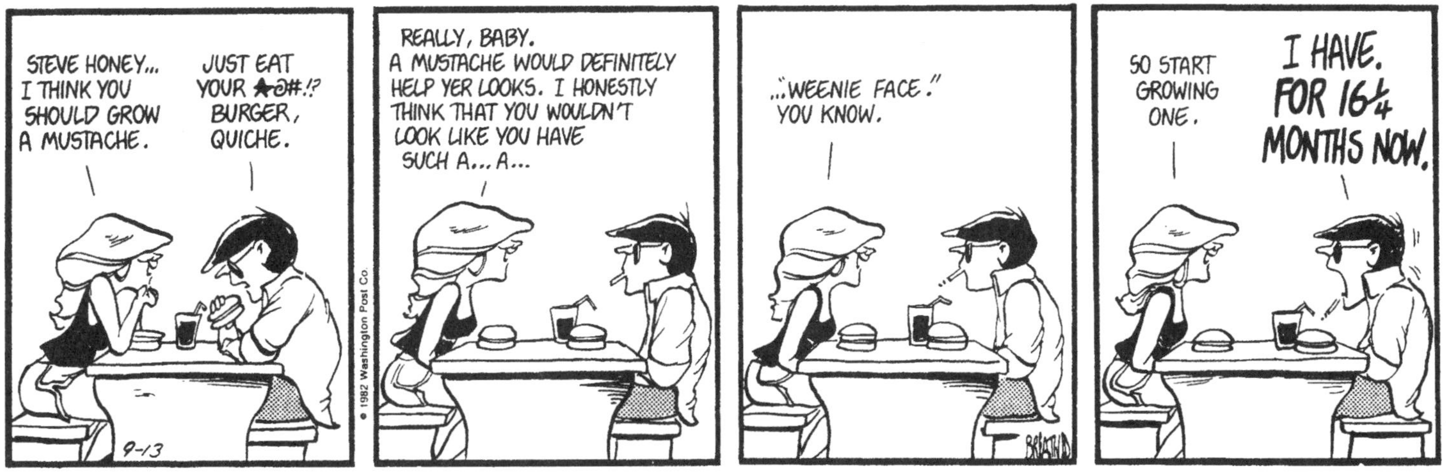
STEVE HONEY... I THINK YOU SHOULD GROW A MUSTACHE.
JUST EAT YOUR ★@#!? BURGER, QUICHE.
9-13
© 1982 Washington Post Co.
REALLY, BABY. A MUSTACHE WOULD DEFINITELY HELP YER LOOKS. I HONESTLY THINK THAT YOU WOULDN'T LOOK LIKE YOU HAVE SUCH A... A...
..."WEENIE FACE." YOU KNOW.
SO START GROWING ONE.
I HAVE. FOR 16¼ MONTHS NOW.

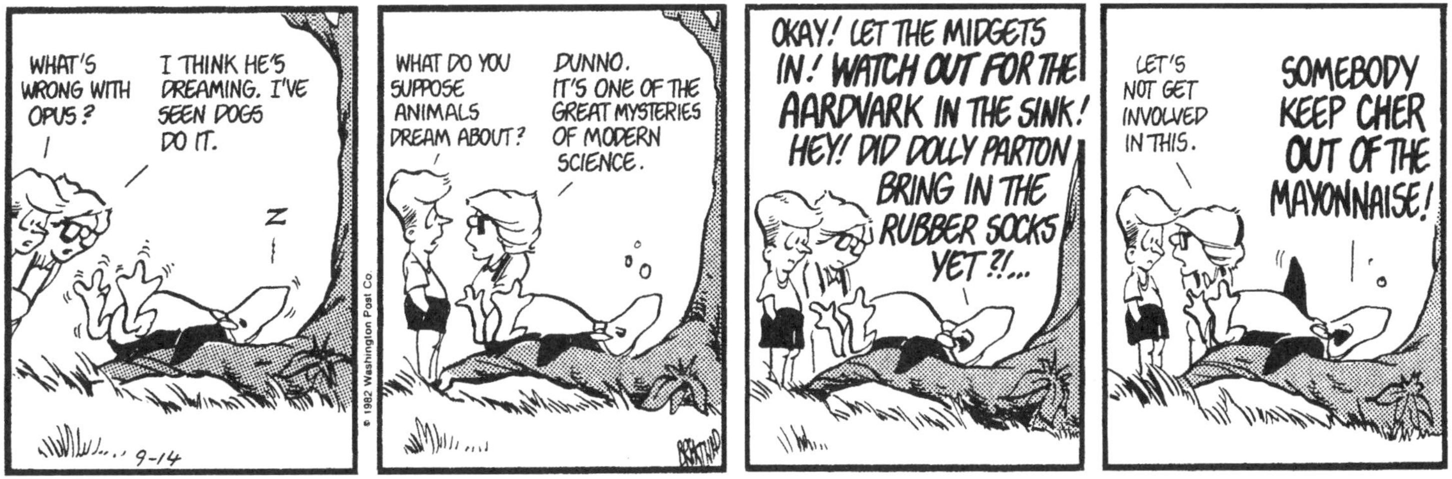
WHAT'S WRONG WITH OPUS?
I THINK HE'S DREAMING. I'VE SEEN DOGS DO IT.
Z
9-14
© 1982 Washington Post Co.
WHAT DO YOU SUPPOSE ANIMALS DREAM ABOUT?
DUNNO. IT'S ONE OF THE GREAT MYSTERIES OF MODERN SCIENCE.
OKAY! LET THE MIDGETS IN! WATCH OUT FOR THE AARDVARK IN THE SINK! HEY! DID DOLLY PARTON BRING IN THE RUBBER SOCKS YET?!...
LET'S NOT GET INVOLVED IN THIS.
SOMEBODY KEEP CHER OUT OF THE MAYONNAISE!

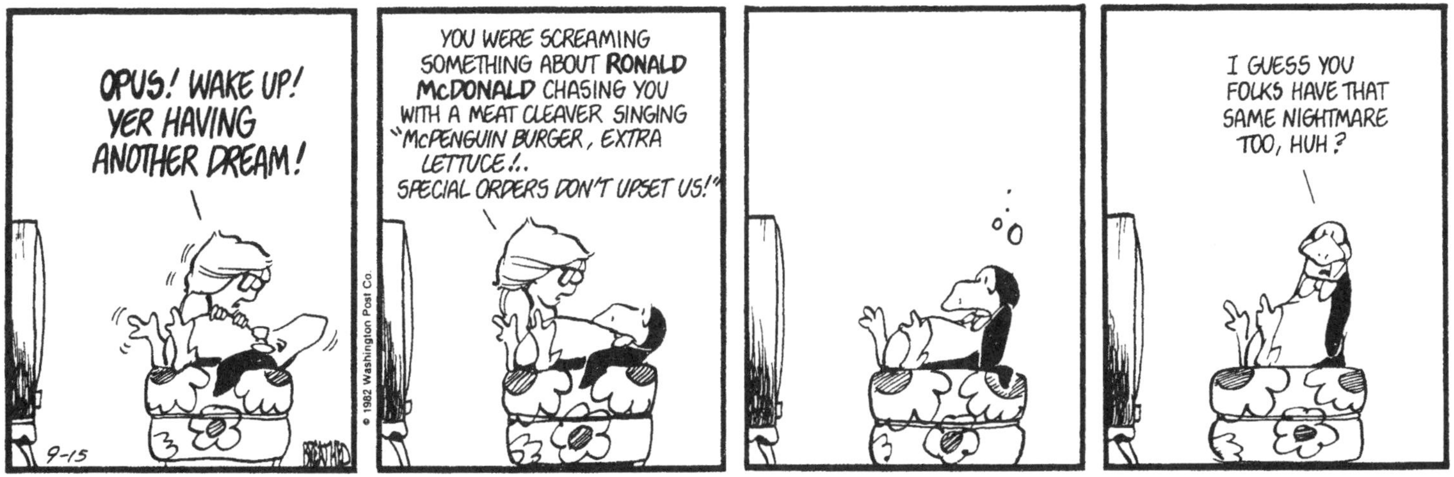
OPUS! WAKE UP! YER HAVING ANOTHER DREAM!
9-15
© 1982 Washington Post Co.
YOU WERE SCREAMING SOMETHING ABOUT RONALD McDONALD CHASING YOU WITH A MEAT CLEAVER SINGING "McPENGUIN BURGER, EXTRA LETTUCE!.. SPECIAL ORDERS DON'T UPSET US!"
I GUESS YOU FOLKS HAVE THAT SAME NIGHTMARE TOO, HUH?

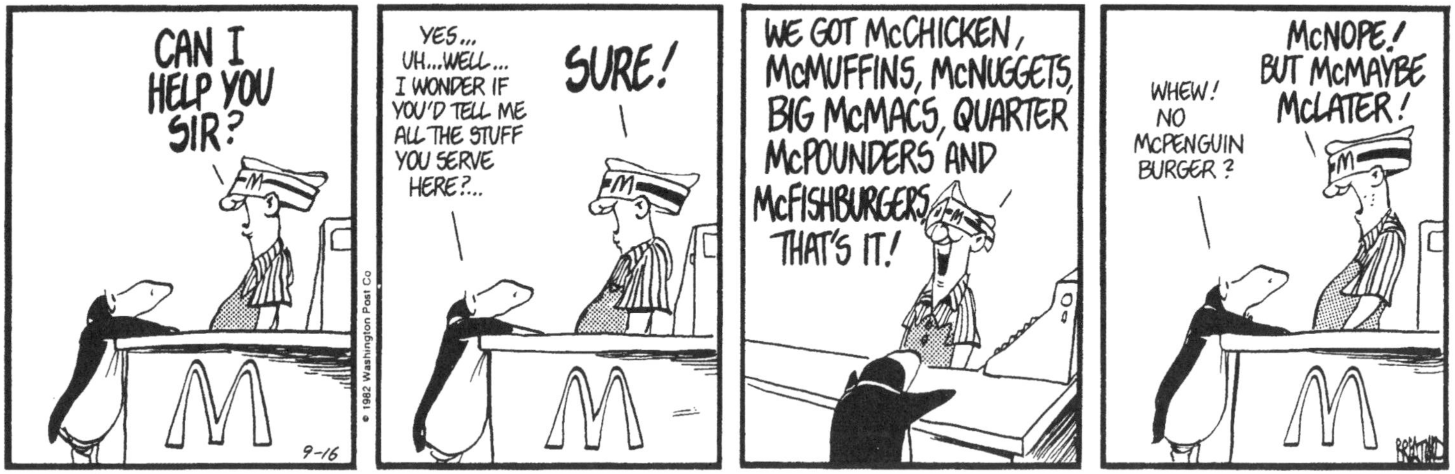
CAN I HELP YOU SIR?
YES... UH...WELL... I WONDER IF YOU'D TELL ME ALL THE STUFF YOU SERVE HERE?...
SURE!
WE GOT McCHICKEN, McMUFFINS, McNUGGETS, BIG McMACS, QUARTER McPOUNDERS AND McFISHBURGERS. THAT'S IT!
WHEW! NO McPENGUIN BURGER?
McNOPE! BUT McMAYBE McLATER!
9-16
© 1982 Washington Post Co.

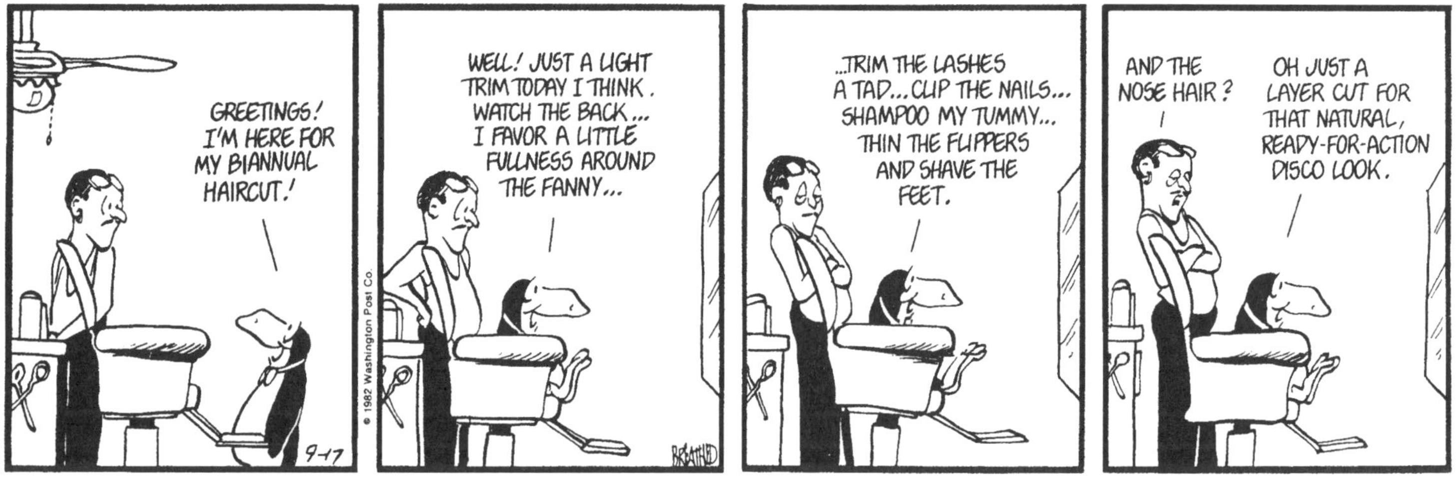
GREETINGS! I'M HERE FOR MY BIANNUAL HAIRCUT!
WELL! JUST A LIGHT TRIM TODAY I THINK. WATCH THE BACK... I FAVOR A LITTLE FULLNESS AROUND THE FANNY...
...TRIM THE LASHES A TAD... CLIP THE NAILS... SHAMPOO MY TUMMY... THIN THE FLIPPERS AND SHAVE THE FEET.
AND THE NOSE HAIR?
OH JUST A LAYER CUT FOR THAT NATURAL, READY-FOR-ACTION DISCO LOOK.
9-17
© 1982 Washington Post Co.

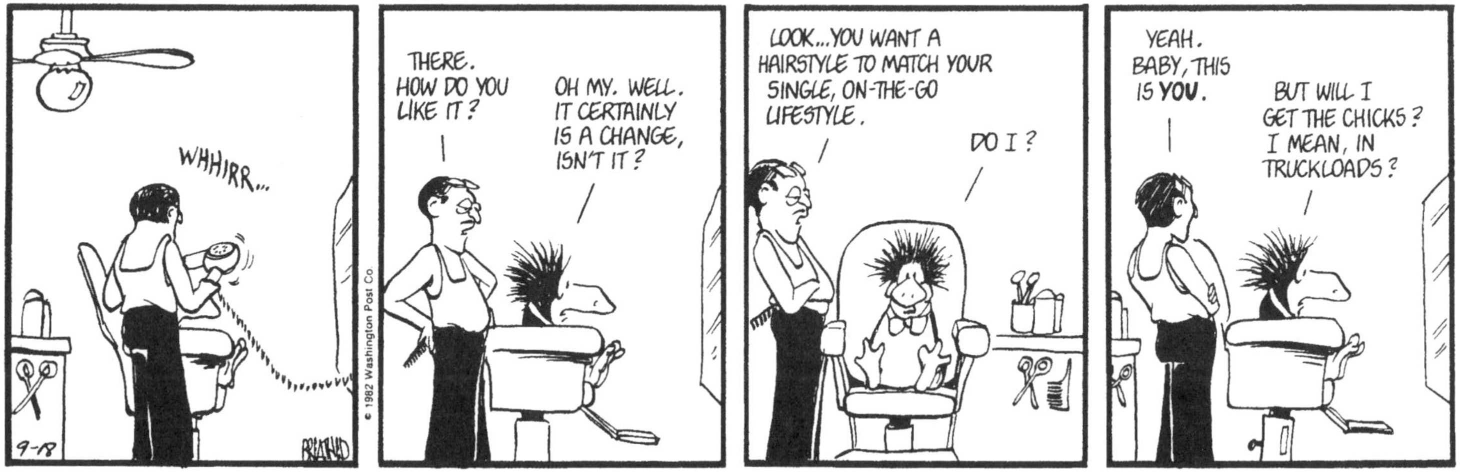
WHHIRR...
9-18
THERE. HOW DO YOU LIKE IT?
OH MY. WELL. IT CERTAINLY IS A CHANGE, ISN'T IT?
LOOK...YOU WANT A HAIRSTYLE TO MATCH YOUR SINGLE, ON-THE-GO LIFESTYLE.
DO I?
YEAH. BABY, THIS IS **YOU**.
BUT WILL I GET THE CHICKS? I MEAN, IN TRUCKLOADS?
© 1982 Washington Post Co.

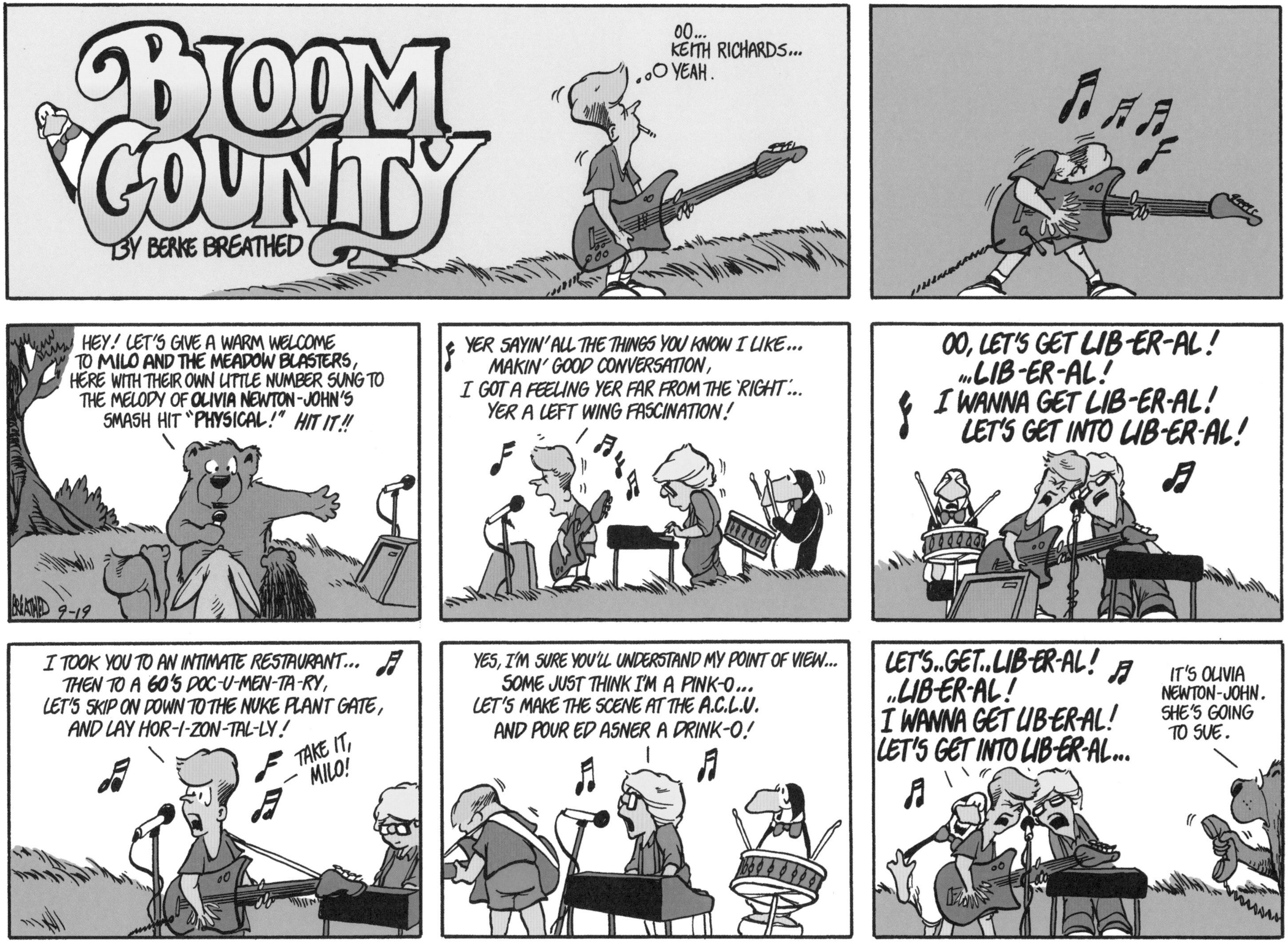
BLOOM COUNTY
BY BERKE BREATHED
OO... KEITH RICHARDS... YEAH.
HEY! LET'S GIVE A WARM WELCOME TO MILO AND THE MEADOW BLASTERS, HERE WITH THEIR OWN LITTLE NUMBER SUNG TO THE MELODY OF OLIVIA NEWTON-JOHN'S SMASH HIT "PHYSICAL!" HIT IT!!
BREATHED 9-19
YER SAYIN' ALL THE THINGS YOU KNOW I LIKE... MAKIN' GOOD CONVERSATION, I GOT A FEELING YER FAR FROM THE 'RIGHT'... YER A LEFT WING FASCINATION!
OO, LET'S GET LIB-ER-AL! ...LIB-ER-AL! I WANNA GET LIB-ER-AL! LET'S GET INTO LIB-ER-AL!
I TOOK YOU TO AN INTIMATE RESTAURANT... THEN TO A 60'S DOC-U-MEN-TA-RY, LET'S SKIP ON DOWN TO THE NUKE PLANT GATE, AND LAY HOR-I-ZON-TAL-LY!
TAKE IT, MILO!
YES, I'M SURE YOU'LL UNDERSTAND MY POINT OF VIEW... SOME JUST THINK I'M A PINK-O... LET'S MAKE THE SCENE AT THE A.C.L.U. AND POUR ED ASNER A DRINK-O!
LET'S..GET..LIB-ER-AL! ..LIB-ER-AL! I WANNA GET LIB-ER-AL! LET'S GET INTO LIB-ER-AL...
IT'S OLIVIA NEWTON-JOHN. SHE'S GOING TO SUE.

Ed Asner, noted actor and former President of the Screen Actor's Guild, gained prominence for his portrayal of Lou Grant, the crusty, big-hearted newsman, on *The Mary Tyler Moore Show*.

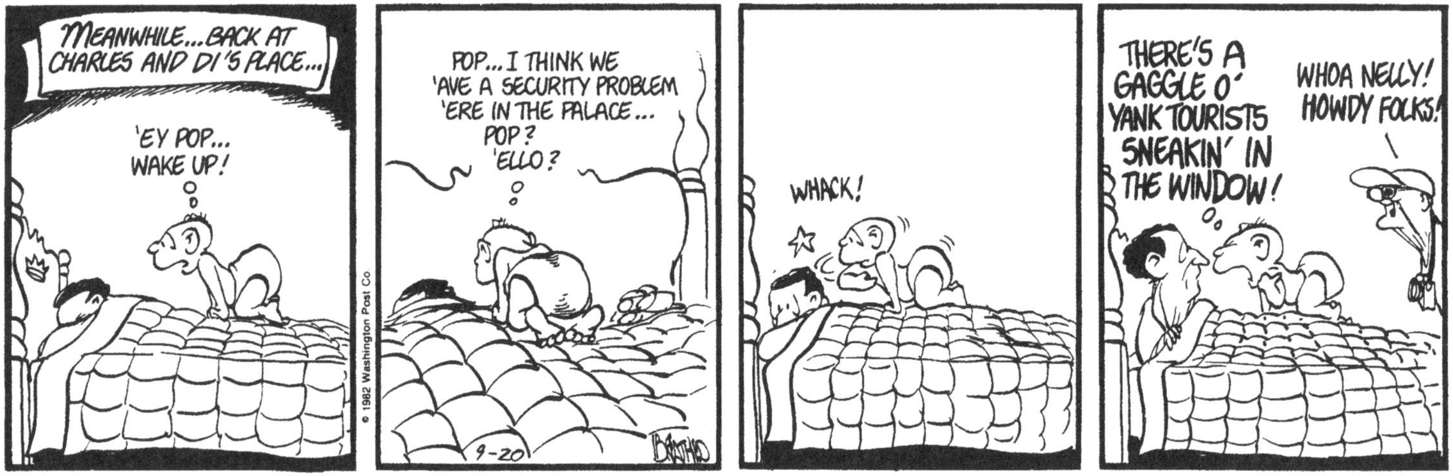
MEANWHILE... BACK AT CHARLES AND DI'S PLACE...
'EY POP... WAKE UP!
© 1982 Washington Post Co.
POP... I THINK WE 'AVE A SECURITY PROBLEM 'ERE IN THE PALACE... POP? 'ELLO?
9-20
WHACK!
THERE'S A GAGGLE O' YANK TOURISTS SNEAKIN' IN THE WINDOW!
WHOA NELLY! HOWDY FOLKS!

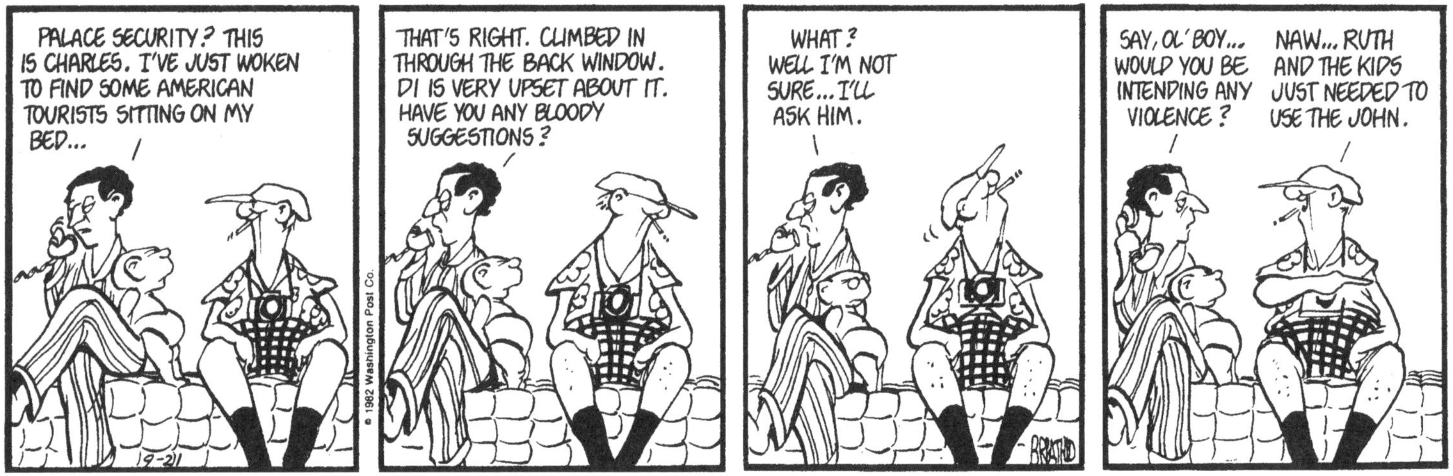
PALACE SECURITY? THIS IS CHARLES. I'VE JUST WOKEN TO FIND SOME AMERICAN TOURISTS SITTING ON MY BED...
9-21
© 1982 Washington Post Co.
THAT'S RIGHT. CLIMBED IN THROUGH THE BACK WINDOW. DI IS VERY UPSET ABOUT IT. HAVE YOU ANY BLOODY SUGGESTIONS?
WHAT? WELL I'M NOT SURE... I'LL ASK HIM.
SAY, OL' BOY... WOULD YOU BE INTENDING ANY VIOLENCE?
NAW... RUTH AND THE KIDS JUST NEEDED TO USE THE JOHN.

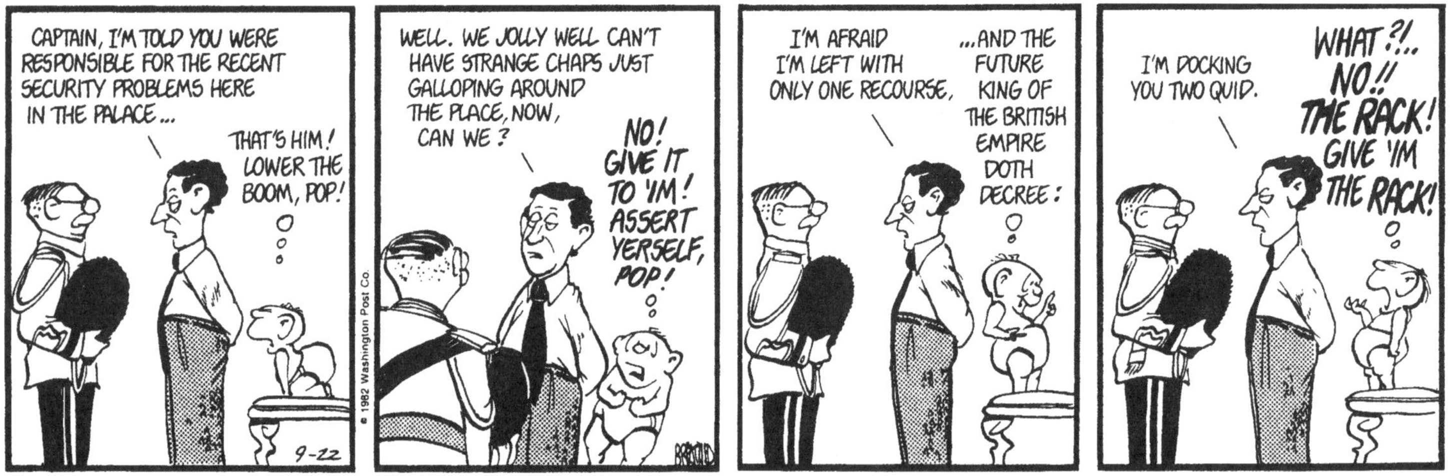
CAPTAIN, I'M TOLD YOU WERE RESPONSIBLE FOR THE RECENT SECURITY PROBLEMS HERE IN THE PALACE...
THAT'S HIM! LOWER THE BOOM, POP!
9-22
© 1982 Washington Post Co.
WELL. WE JOLLY WELL CAN'T HAVE STRANGE CHAPS JUST GALLOPING AROUND THE PLACE, NOW, CAN WE?
NO! GIVE IT TO 'IM! ASSERT YERSELF, POP!
I'M AFRAID I'M LEFT WITH ONLY ONE RECOURSE,
...AND THE FUTURE KING OF THE BRITISH EMPIRE DOTH DECREE:
I'M DOCKING YOU TWO QUID.
WHAT?!.. NO!! THE RACK! GIVE 'IM THE RACK!

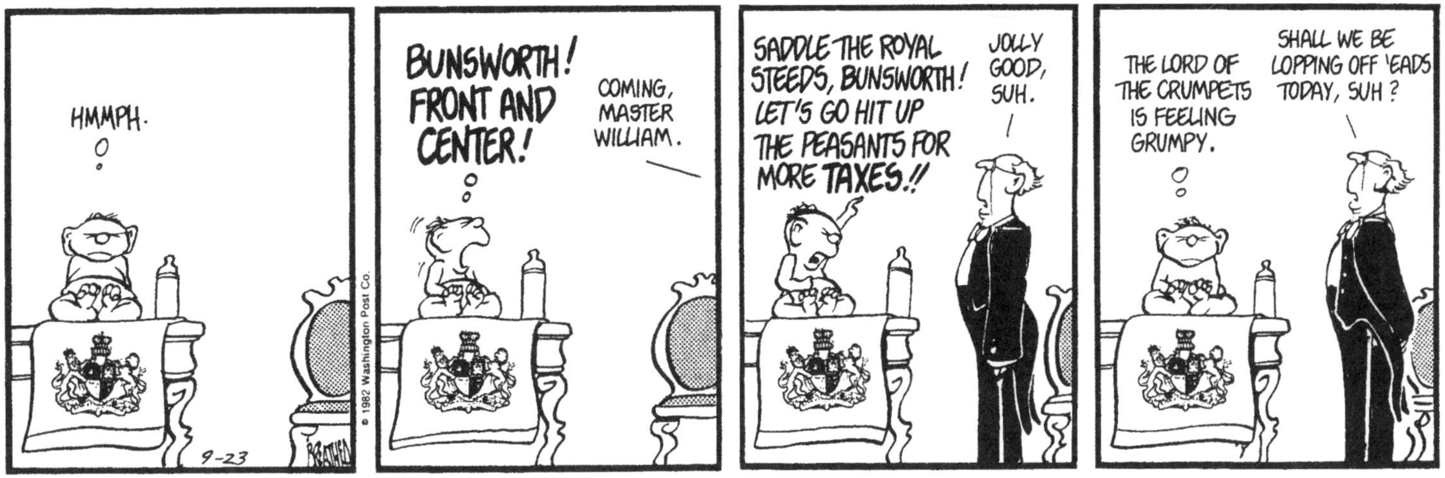
HMMPH.
BUNSWORTH! FRONT AND CENTER!
COMING, MASTER WILLIAM.
SADDLE THE ROYAL STEEDS, BUNSWORTH! LET'S GO HIT UP THE PEASANTS FOR MORE TAXES.!!
JOLLY GOOD, SUH.
THE LORD OF THE CRUMPETS IS FEELING GRUMPY.
SHALL WE BE LOPPING OFF 'EADS TODAY, SUH?
9-23
© 1982 Washington Post Co.

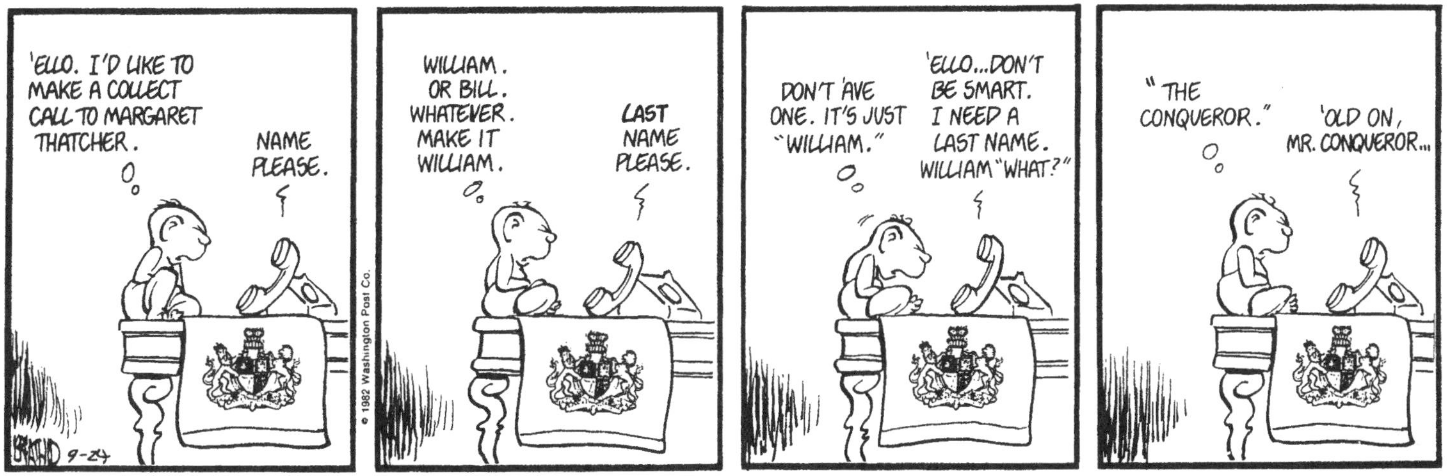
'ELLO. I'D LIKE TO MAKE A COLLECT CALL TO MARGARET THATCHER.
NAME PLEASE.
WILLIAM. OR BILL. WHATEVER. MAKE IT WILLIAM.
LAST NAME PLEASE.
DON'T 'AVE ONE. IT'S JUST "WILLIAM."
'ELLO...DON'T BE SMART. I NEED A LAST NAME. WILLIAM "WHAT?"
"THE CONQUEROR."
'OLD ON, MR. CONQUEROR...
9-24
© 1982 Washington Post Co.

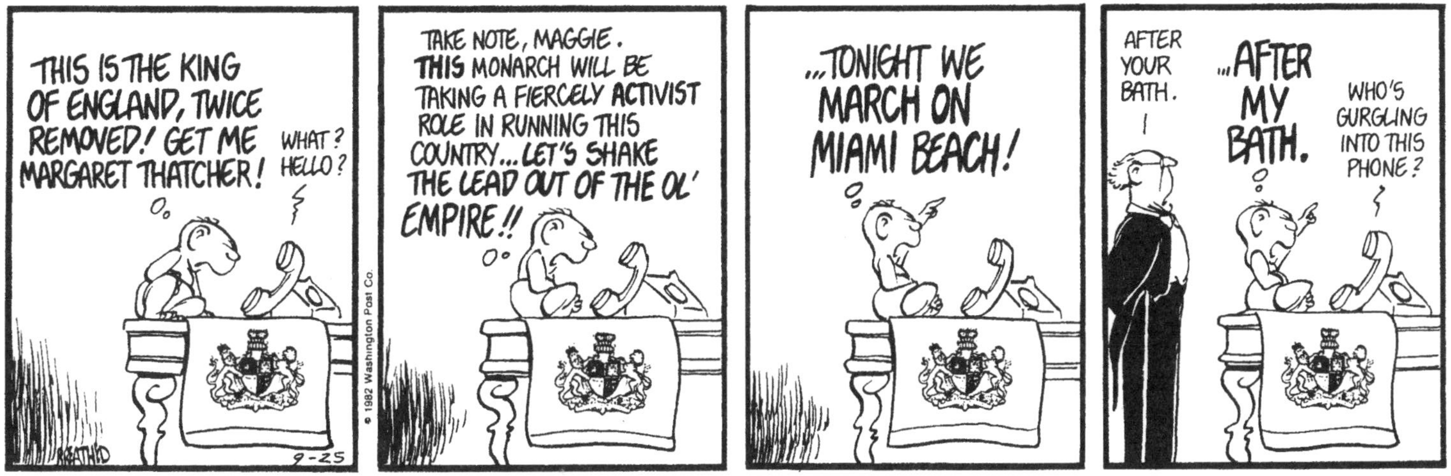
THIS IS THE KING OF ENGLAND, TWICE REMOVED! GET ME MARGARET THATCHER!
WHAT? HELLO?
TAKE NOTE, MAGGIE. THIS MONARCH WILL BE TAKING A FIERCELY ACTIVIST ROLE IN RUNNING THIS COUNTRY...LET'S SHAKE THE LEAD OUT OF THE OL' EMPIRE!!
...TONIGHT WE MARCH ON MIAMI BEACH!
AFTER YOUR BATH.
...AFTER MY BATH.
WHO'S GURGLING INTO THIS PHONE?
9-25
© 1982 Washington Post Co.

Margaret Thatcher, leader of the British Conservative Party and known as the "Iron Lady," served as that country's Prime Minister from 1979 to 1990.

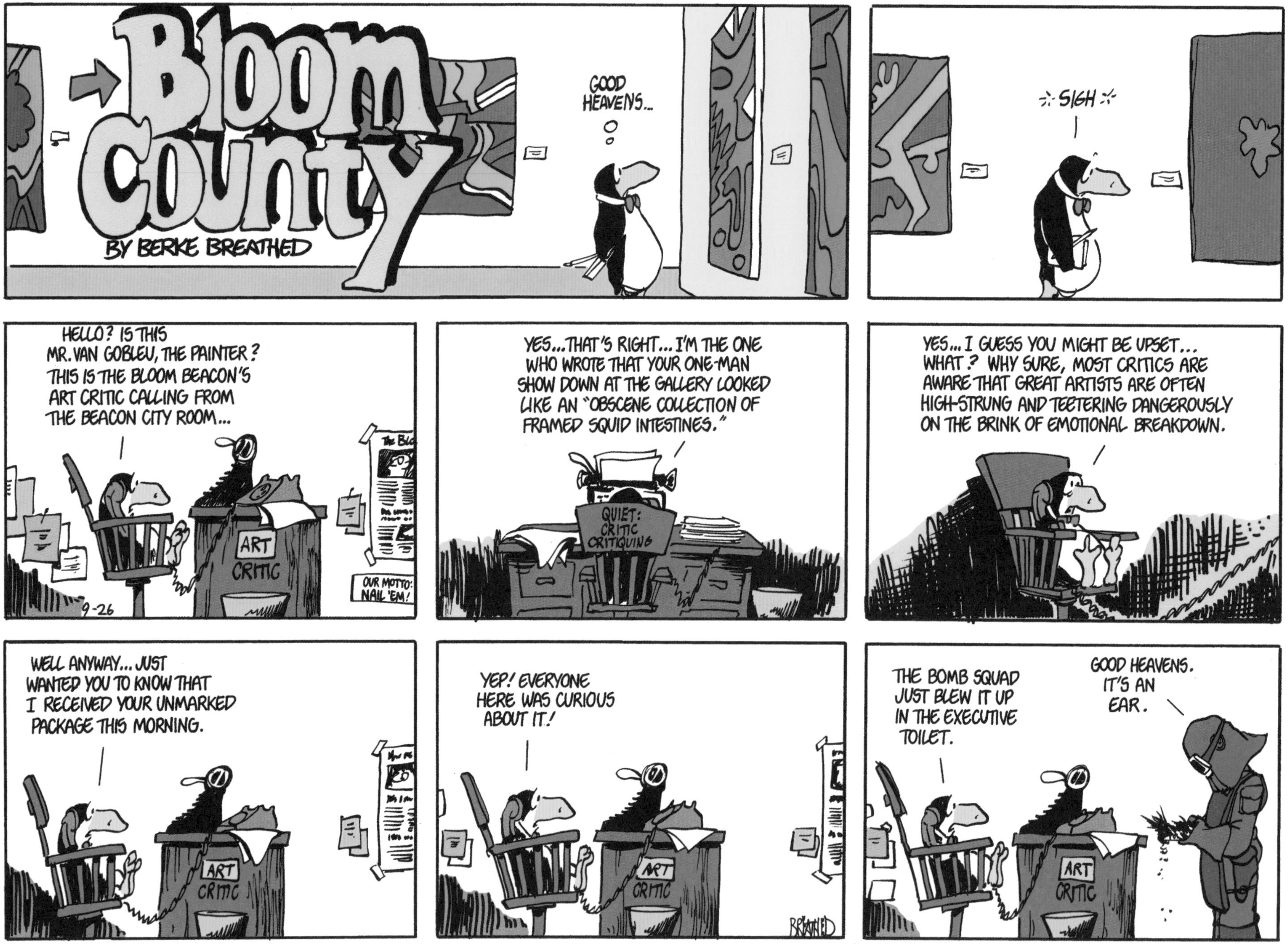

BLOOM COUNTY
BY BERKE BREATHED
GOOD HEAVENS...
SIGH
HELLO? IS THIS MR. VAN GOBLEU, THE PAINTER? THIS IS THE BLOOM BEACON'S ART CRITIC CALLING FROM THE BEACON CITY ROOM...
ART CRITIC
OUR MOTTO: NAIL 'EM!
9-26
YES...THAT'S RIGHT...I'M THE ONE WHO WROTE THAT YOUR ONE-MAN SHOW DOWN AT THE GALLERY LOOKED LIKE AN "OBSCENE COLLECTION OF FRAMED SQUID INTESTINES."
QUIET: CRITIC CRITIQUING
YES... I GUESS YOU MIGHT BE UPSET... WHAT? WHY SURE, MOST CRITICS ARE AWARE THAT GREAT ARTISTS ARE OFTEN HIGH-STRUNG AND TEETERING DANGEROUSLY ON THE BRINK OF EMOTIONAL BREAKDOWN.
WELL ANYWAY... JUST WANTED YOU TO KNOW THAT I RECEIVED YOUR UNMARKED PACKAGE THIS MORNING.
YEP! EVERYONE HERE WAS CURIOUS ABOUT IT!
BREATHED
THE BOMB SQUAD JUST BLEW IT UP IN THE EXECUTIVE TOILET.
GOOD HEAVENS. IT'S AN EAR.

 September 26, 1982

BLOOM COUNTY
THE COMPLETE LIBRARY
VOLUME TWO: 1982-1984
BERKELEY BREATHED

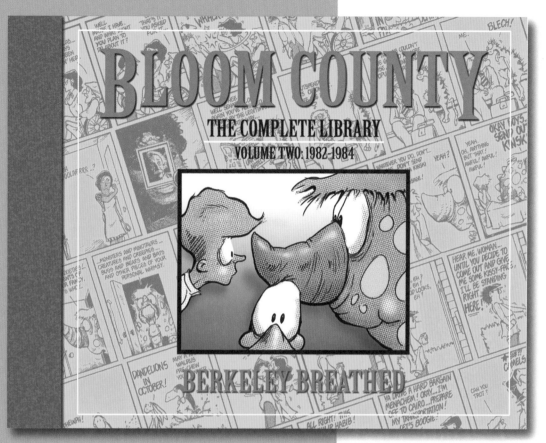

IN OUR NEXT VOLUME

Volume Two of *Bloom County: The Complete Library* continues right where Volume One leaves off, with Berkeley Breathed's endearing, enchanting, and occasionally infuriating inhabitants of Bloom County treating us to their madcap adventures, cynical observations, and optimistic innocence—sometimes all at once!

PENTHOUSE
MADONNA NUDE YET AGAIN
ZE MEADOW MORALS SQUAD

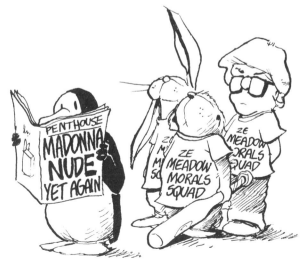

The Great American Comics

THE COMPLETE
DICK TRACY
THE MASTER DETECTIVE MEETS
THE MOLE
BB EYES
VOLUME SEVEN
1941-42
DAILIES & SUNDAYS

THE COMPLETE
DICK TRACY
THE GREAT DETECTIVE BATTLES
PRUNEFACE
LAFFY
VOLUME EIGHT
1942-44
DAILIES & SUNDAYS

SCORCHY SMITH
AND THE ART OF
NOEL SICKLES

THE COMPLETE
TERRY
AND THE PIRATES
MILTON CANIFF

THE COMPLETE
TERRY
AND THE PIRATES
MILTON CANIFF

THE COMPLETE
TERRY
AND THE PIRATES
MILTON CANIFF

Harold Gray's
Little Orphan Annie
ARF!
VOLUME ONE
WILL TOMORROW EVER COME?
THE COMPLETE DAILY COMICS
1924–27
MORE THAN 1,000 COMICS FEATURING AMERICA'S SPUNKIEST KID!

Harold Gray's
Little Orphan Annie
ARF!
VOLUME TWO
THE DARKEST HOUR IS JUST BEFORE DAWN
DAILY AND SUNDAY COMICS
1927–29
SEVEN COMPLETE STORIES FEATURING AMERICA'S SPUNKIEST KID!

Harold Gray's
Little Orphan Annie
VOLUME THREE
AND A BLIND MAN SHALL LEAD THEM
DAILY AND SUNDAY COMICS
1929–31
"Daddy" Warbucks and America's Spunkiest Kid Take on the World!

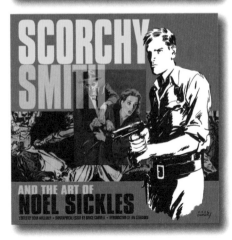

DICK TRACY

BY CHESTER GOULD

The first and hardest-hitting crime series in the history of comics stars the lone square-jawed hero who holds the line against a horde of macabre villains bent on murder and mayhem.

TERRY AND THE PIRATES

BY MILTON CANIFF

The greatest adventure comic strip of all, featuring Terry, Pat, Connie, and Big Stoop, an array of unforgettable brigands, and a host of strong, alluring, and mesmerizing women.

LITTLE ORPHAN ANNIE

BY HAROLD GRAY

The incredible trials and tribulations of the kid with a heart of gold and a quick left hook.

SCORCHY SMITH AND THE ART OF NOEL SICKLES

The complete *Scorchy Smith*, plus a profusely illustrated biography, with more than 200 pieces of his extensive book, magazine, and advertising work.

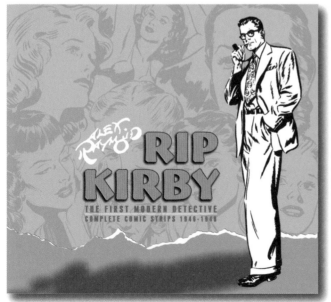

THE FAMILY CIRCUS
BY BIL KEANE

Drawing inspiration from his own family's antics, Bil Keane brings the charming adventures of Billy, Dolly, Jeffy & PJ to life in this iconic American strip.

KING AROO
BY JACK KENT

A long-neglected classic, lauded by critics in the pantheon of great strips such as *Krazy Kat* and *Pogo*. This 60th anniversary edition of Jack Kent's brilliantly conceived world is full of clever puns, visual humor, and good old slapstick.

BRINGING UP FATHER
BY GEORGE MCMANUS

A deluxe, color treatment for the most famous and beloved story from this Art Deco classic comedy. Maggie and Jiggs embark on a cross-country tour in *From Sea to Shining Sea*.

RIP KIRBY
BY ALEX RAYMOND

A modernist classic lushly drawn by the master artist Alex Raymond. Rip Kirby was the first hip and cool detective in newspaper comics.

Berkeley Breathed

is the Pulitzer Prize-winning creator of *Bloom County*. He was born in Southern California and raised in Texas. As a University of Texas student he created what would be the precursor to *Bloom County* for *The Daily Texan*, *The Academia Waltz*. Two small collections of *Waltz* were self-published by Breathed and generated enough profits to comfortably pay his tuition. They remain much sought-after collectibles to this day.

Breathed's initial success brought him to the attention of *The Washington Post*, and an offer to create a nationally syndicated newspaper strip. On December 8, 1980, *Bloom County* launched in twelve papers, a number that would eventually rise to a peak of 1,200 with a combined readership of over 75 million people. Licensing, especially of Opus, would transition *Bloom County* from cult favorite to a phenomenon, one poised to enter the American zeitgeist. *Loose Tails*, the first *Bloom County* collection, began with a printing of 10,000. It went on to sell over one million copies.

On August 6, 1989, Breathed ended *Bloom County*. Later that year he would begin *Outland*, a Sunday-only newspaper strip that featured several *Bloom County* regulars, including Opus. It ran for six years. A final Sunday strip, the self-titled *Opus*, was published from 2003 until late 2008. Breathed is also an acclaimed children's book author and his first novel, *Flawed Dogs: The Shocking Raid on Westminster*, was recently released.

He lives in California with his wife and two children, and is an avid outdoorsman and supporter of animal-rights causes and wildlife conservation issues.